I wrote this for Tara

THE GREYSTONE EQUATION
By
Brian Weidner

October – 2018/Mankato Mn.

"Teri?" A woman in nursing scrubs interrupted the four sisters who were drinking coffee at a table in the Medical Institute's cafeteria in Mankato.

She looked up to the voice; switched on an automatic smile - seconds later......there was recognition.

"Susana?....no.....I wondered where you went when you left St. Thomas Hospital." She was surprised, "Mankato Institute?.....Big medicine..... I'm impressed." Teresa got up and gave her a hug.

"Who are you with?" The woman in scrubs looked at the other three women.

Teresa made the introductions: "This is Susana Vieux; I went to UW with her in the nursing program." She turned back: "These are my sisters: Nicole from Arizona, Killeen – my fraternal twin, and Dixie – the family artist."

"Any R.N.'s?" Susana wondered.

" 'Fraid not."

"I can only stay a minute." She put her travel cup down and took a seat with the four Whitelaw sisters. Susana checked, "The last time I saw you - you just had had your second.......a boy? Right?"

"Yup, Van the Man." she replied. "You had two - any more?"

"One less husband."

"Divorce?"

"What else - give you the story when we have more time."

"You remember my younger twin, Killeen? Her and Dixie were at our graduation?"

Susana stared at the two for just a little bit: "Yes...." There was a slow nod. "That's right she is your twin......Good thing I met you two early that day. I don't remember much after we went to Bennett's Bar. Teri, you're the older right?"

"Eighteen minutes, but I'd have done better with the guys if I had Kill's looks." she replied.

"Looks to Kill for?" Dixie ran her fingers through her blue hair and shook it out.

"You're pushing it." Her voice pitched higher. "......I'm still looking for Mr. Right." Killeen warned.

"In all the wrong places." Nicole sang.

"Hanging out with you guys – for a few nights is what I need. Who has the time though?" Susana changed lanes: "Say Teri, what was your area of concentration?"

"Psychiatry."

"Right....." Susana nodded. "Yeah......Psyche.......Still at St.Thomas the Apostle?"

Teresa raised her fist to the ceiling. Susana was a half-second behind her: "BELIEVE!" They chanted the mantra of the hospital where both began their nursing careers. The Whitelaw sisters chuckled at their mini-reunion.

"What's your classification here?" Teresa reached for the paper coffee cup.

"Pulmonary mostly; usually related to cardio or oncology."

"So you're with the Institute?"

"Uh-huh. They want me to get more training and education. I don't know, maybe next year. The worm turns; you guys aren't here looking for careers......"

"We're here on business – our Dad." Dixie announced and brought them back to reality. "He was referred by the G.I. doctor at St. Thomas. I brought him here yesterday."

"What's his diagnosis?"

The three girls deferred to their sister with the medical background to speak in the secret medical language to her colleague.

"He's got liver disease: Hepatitis C and cirrhosis." Teresa said.

"Alcohol and Drug abuse?"

"He's been clean for 35 - 38 years. None of us have ever seen him screwed up."

"He deserves more time." Dixie couldn't meet Susana's eyes as she played with her coffee.

"How long has he had the hepatitis?

"Almost 40 years." Nicole said.

Susana scanned around the table and focused on Nicole, "You're not the same as these three."

"Same Dad - different Mom." She nodded.

"Dark Nicky." Killeen modified.

Nicole was proud to be a Whitelaw; but at the same time, it set her apart from Dixie and the twins.

"What's on your agenda for today?" Susana asked.

"Consultation with the surgeon in about an hour." Teresa took a breath. "Since we've started down this road, there's been very little to raise our hopes. I'm not optimistic about today's meeting, but we'll see what he's got. He went through a transplant evaluation in LaCrosse. I think a transplant gives him the best chance to pull through."

"Liver transplant.....the magic has got to be there from a number of perspectives." She looked at the clock on the wall, "Teri, I gotta run - call me if you need me." She whipped out her phone, "Give me your number. Who'd you say the surgeon is?"

"We were referred to Dr. Singh........Bachan Singh."

"I've heard stories of him bringing people back from the jaws of death a number of times. Straight shooter.....was involved with a lot of clinical trials for this new class of anti-virals."

"Before you leave." Dixie called to Susana as she started to walk away. "Is there a decent motel around here? The place I'm at........well......it's not too good. People carrying on at all hours."

"Try the 'Hayride Heaven' Motel. The owners keep it clean and turn away the riff-raff." She waved and hurried to get to her morning's first patient.

"One more thing………..How is this place with non-traditional medicine; I've got a connection with some things and people – mostly dietary stuff we are thinking of trying." Dixie said.

Susana chuckled and shook her head, "You're in the wrong place if you're thinking of that screwball stuff. Gotta go……Teri, you got my number."

NOTHING CHANGED IN THE NEXT FOUR DAYS EXCEPT Ryan's liver's enzyme numbers skyrocketed. His legs continued to retain fluid and his urine output was hardly registering in the collection bag. His skin tone was ashen, but getting more yellow by the day.

Dixie and Teresa had set up a consultation with Dr. Singh earlier in the day. It was their father's fourth day under Dr. Singh's care. Nicky and Killeen had to get some clean clothes and went to the laundromat, sent some messages, and made a few calls. Nicky called her husband Rick and gave him Ryan Whitelaw's situation, while Killeen talked to her supervisor at the Post Office.

Teresa walked in Singh's office, and saw Dixie sitting with nothing but a suede leather vest for a top, striped bell bottoms, moccasins, the blue hair, and a pair of fashion sunglasses It lightened the mood for Teresa…..but not for long. The sisters had detailed questions for the surgeon. Both had a pen and paper taking notes for their sisters at the laundromat. Singh's assessment and prognosis, had caught the two flatfooted. He was short on optimism. Teresa was mentally preparing herself; she knew it was possible their father might be drawing to a dead straight.

Dixie would not be put into the negativity box, she thought there was something 'out there' to keep him above the grass. In Dixie's mind; getting out of the hospital was essential to his survival.

Later on, three sisters went to Ryan's room in the I.C.U., but Teresa had to go the non-denominational chapel to pray and seek divine guidance.

Dixie set his cranberry juice on the mobile table with the long arm. She looked at Nicky and Killeen: "Dr. Singh said the cardiologist put Pops back on one of the heart meds..... he said he might be a little more responsive.....more cognitive."

Fifteen minutes elapsed; Ryan was grinning at Dixie.

"Can I get you anything Papa?" she said.

"What's that?" his eyes went to a 3'x2'x2½" Fed Ex box. His voice was unstable.

"Something to brighten up your day."

"Something you bought?"

"No….something I painted for you. If they won't let me hang it in here, I'll buy a fuckin easel at Goodwill and you can look at it like that."

"Atta girl." He struggled to speak.

"Pa, all's I got is a picture of the kids for you. Gee, you make it tough Dixie." Nicky grinned at the artist.

Ryan looked at the photograph and softly said: "Hey…my snowbird buddies: Cody, Cheyenne, and Derrick."

Nicky and Killeen could tell he was almost spent; short and long term. The three pulled up chairs; one each side

"Where's Teresa?" His voice weakened.

"Should be here any time now."

He motioned for Killeen to come near so he could speak directly into her ear: "Shoe box - in Ray's small duffle bag......"

Dixie thought he was talking nonsense, "Old Man, you've got to keep fighting."

"He wants the shoe box that's in Uncle Ray's army duffle." Killeen said.

Ryan nodded and exhaled.

"What about the box Papa?" Killeen again put her ear a half-inch from his mouth.

"Ash.....dust from outer space.....strange forces.......incredible power." He was spent.

"Papa, what do you want?......Pa....." she spoke louder. "C'mon Pops.....you've got to keep fighting." The three kept pelting him with words of encouragement, but the toxicity in his body had traveled to his brain, only allowing the grey matter to function on an intermittent basis. Every time he came to, he was amazed he had regained consciousness.

When Teresa showed up five minutes later, she met them in the visitors' gathering area. They told her Ryan had conked out. Still, she looked in his room before she returned to the waiting area.

"If it's okay with you guys - I made arrangements with hospice care and Medicare to bring Dad back to my house. We've got the space. I think he'll want to be with the kids with the time he has remaining."

"Only if you let us try some non-traditional medicine while he's there. I mean if Mankato's turns him loose, they're raising the white flag. Am I right?" Dixie said.

"I don't know - perhaps. I thought I was doing everybody a favor - that's all."

"No, you're right Teri." Nicole said.

Killeen looked across to the adjacent sofa at Nicky: "That's down the road. I've got to believe we're not there yet. There's a bunch of his stuff behind the seat of his truck over my place.

Nicole took a deep breath, she wished she had a cigarette: "If we bring the old man to Teresa's, I can tell Rick to bring up the kids to say good-bye to Gramps. Time is evaporating. If he's just coming up for a funeral – I'll have him ask Lucinda to take the kids for a couple of days. This is worse than a diamondback bite."

"She lives two doors down?" Teresa said.

"I'll owe her big."

"You're just going to have to pick a date for them to come up, and whatever happens - happens." Killeen said.

Dixie turned to Teresa, "You just missed him. He had a few moments of clarity, he could barely talk - but he did talk."

4

"Dammit." she hissed. "Do you know what he said?"

"He asked where you were."

"Dammit! Anything else?"

"Talked 'bout those olive jars and yellow plastic pharma bottles in the one of the shoe boxes and a mason's bag and another army duffle and the small duffle bag we gave him." Killeen detailed.

"Huh?.......you're talking about the army duffle that used to be Uncle Ray's.....the one Pa had Killeen drive back to LaCrosse to get?" She whipped her head towards his room: "The duffle bag is in that small closet with a few other things. You know he's got a pistol in the duffle." Dixie chuckled and raised her left brow. Three sisters grinned.

"You get that pistol out of here." Teresa said.

"Don't get all worked up, I brought it back to the motel two days ago." Nicole said.

"Did you go through the contents?"

"Just a quick run through.....Killeen was there. There was the shoe box with the jars and containers, a bunch of papers - mostly legal stuff, the two big envelopes with rock & roll stuff and $10,000 in each.

Teresa compressed her lips, "So you went through his stuff?"

"It was just a quick run through: a lot of things concerning our family and his family. We weren't fishing for anything; we were just looking for something that he seems to think is important, and it has something to do with the jars and bottles. We weren't snooping." The three nodded in agreement.

Teresa thought for a moment as she watched Nicole; "This bag is my domain. I am the Power of Attorney for Dad's affairs as long as he is alive." Dixie has the Power of Attorney only for medical matters. This is my turf. She continued to stare for another 15 seconds. It suddenly struck her that she did the same thing to Dixie by setting up the hospice care for Ryan. Now she was sure her father's health was affecting her reasoning ability. Since Ryan had come up from Arizona for treatment of the hepatitis C virus; it was another helping of worry for her full plate. "Mother Mary, help me deal with these things."

"Let's go back to his room; he might come to."

"While Pops is asleep, we've got time to explore the contents and determine if anything is relevant to the time he has remaining." Teresa said. She opened Ray's small duffle bag: "And these." She briefly displayed two yellow pharmacy containers and two slender olive jars without removing them from his duffle.

"You know what?" Killeen began, "The Old Man told me about these jars when we were still in LaCrosse 10 days ago. I wasn't paying much attention; he was talking about all this wild shit. You know how he gets. It might be important.....he keeps talking about their contents. It's also very possible - he's going mad or hallucinating."

"I know I'm ready for the laughing house." Teresa's cynicism etched the premature facial lines.

The four sisters started picking through Ryan's things in the duffle bag, unaware what they were looking for. Half-way through her pile, Dixie said: "Listen to this -

5

'equations for the application of interstellar, solar, and planetary magnetism in organic and non-organic systems." It was all in mathematical language. The equation was 15 legal sized pages, with calculations and formulas on both sides in miniature print. Every available space of blank paper was used. In the middle of page three was the name: Joey Tarts; page seven: Kenny Crawford; page nine: Eric Shaw; page 14: Ronnie Zanzibar; page 15: Cocaine Wayne.

"Joey Tarts must be related to Papa's friend Vinny?" Dixie tried to triangulate power with her hands to her head. "I know him and his kids. We used to visit them when the old man took us out east to visit Grandpa Hal."

"That was a long time ago." The quartet visioned away from the I.C.U. for just a minute.

Nicole tried to see if the Fed Ex box was open.

"They were brothers." Nicky said. "Joey died five or six years ago. These are the guys Papa called the 'Fifth Dimension', 'The High Five' 'The Quixotic Quintet'. He said each one of the crew knew a specific piece of the equation, but only Ray had figured out the quantum and magnetic mechanics of the applied and abstract calculus formula. Vinny Tarts told me just before my mom exiled me to live out here, that Joey and the others were gaining magnetic reality. With or without Uncle Ray, individually or collectively - normal life as they saw it.....and which we take for granted....had eluded them."

"Twins...." Dixie asked, "Either of you hear Papa talk about this stuff before?"

Before they replied, Ryan sounded off; like someone with an ice pick stuck his liver. They watched him. He squeezed his eyes tight and grimaced. They could only imagine what he was going through. Teresa walked over to the meter-pump dispensing the Demoral.

"Turn it up." Nicky said. Killeen jerked her thumb up as well.

"Can't.....I don't have any entry barcode to anything in the Mankato system. I'll ask his nurse to increase the dosage. Hopefully, Singh left instructions to give him more medication if Dad's pain continues to rise."

"He's asleep anyway." Then there was silence. The groaning tapered; they couldn't help feeling this was the beginning of the end. They returned to examining the contents of the bag and box. Killeen scrutinized a piece of paper taped to the last sheet of Ray's equation. "Listen," she said, "Atom Harpur - Kitt Peak Observatory, Route 386, west of Tucson. If he is not available - contact Ryan or Willis Whitelaw.....they may be able to assist. May, 1975.

"Call Uncle Billy." Dixie said.

Nicky handed her the phone.

"Nicole - Is your Dad still with us?" Billy asked.

"This is Dixie, Uncle Bill. We're all here with Dad. We got you on speaker mode."

"What's Ryan's status?"

"Right now, we're most likely going into hospice care in a day or two. We don't have a definitive word either way about the

6

transplant. A liver may not even be available. Dad's Doctor said there were not many things in his favor on his transplant. It's a big question mark."

Willis took a moment to answer. "Ain't this a bitch. I've got to stand up......hang on......... Is this cast in stone....I mean is there anything to hope on?"

"We don't know. There's nothing from the Doctors or pharmaceutical people other than the transplant. Maybe there is something you know which might be of assistance. "We're going through his stuff in Uncle Ray's old army duffle bag....the small one. The one Dad always travels with. It's got these small canisters - jars in a small shoe box. They're filled with this ash-powder like substance; gray-tan-silvery in color. They're labeled Ray or Ryan............... +positive or -negative; any ideas?"

"I thought he might still have that stuff. That was a long time ago. The last contact I had with that shit was when Ray was in that wreck." Billy said. "What's your Dad going to do with it?"

"Are you asking me who he's going to will it to?"

"No....whatsamatter with you? How the fuck is he going to use the shit to get out of this mess?"

"Huh?" She looked at the others from side to side: "Is that possible? We were hoping you might know something." Dixie said.

"I was just a kid back then; 8th or 9th grade. Vinny Tarts was there - he might be able to give you some guidance. Could be that cosmic ash lost its jams after all this time. On the other hand, it might have the longevity of radioactive fallout." The women could hear Billy thinking over the microwaves. "Do you know if Loki is still alive; you might try looking that cat up; in case you can't get a hold of Tarts. Both of them knew more about that stuff in them jars than I ever did."

"Who's Loki? " Teresa asked.

"Joe Ferguson."

Nicole nodded, ".......Yeah.......Loki."

"What about those Fifth Dimension guys? Can any of them help us?" Nicky said.

"The last I heard they all cashed out. Vinny's brother, Joey Tarts, was the last one alive." Killeen squinted.

Dixie got a little closer to the phone, "He's asked for it twice. If it's something that has a healing effect or properties, or is going to send him directly to St. Peter - we need to know it right now. He's in real critical condition. Trying something is better than doing nothing. Ryan's out of time Bill, there are no other options at this point. This cosmic ash......I think we got to roll the dice and hope we don't throw a seven. No hospital or doctor's going to give us a blind eye if we try to use this cosmic agent in their facility. We don't know what we're trying to do, and we can't let anyone know about our plan to use this highly speculative material as a healing agent. So, how do we use it anyway?"

"That's the $64,000 question." he said.

"Okay." Teri said. "Game on. We decide to use the ash in the jars. What do we do with it? How do we use it? Do we rub it on? Does he drink it? Do we put it in a bag in some mixture and intravenously

7

let it run into his blood network? .....For all we know, using it as a suppository might be the right thing - if there is a right thing. Do you know any method or combination we might try with this interstellar material?" She paced like a tiger in a cage.

"I tell you this from first-hand experience: Ray knew how to exploit the cosmic magnetic ash in conjunction with earth's magnetic harmonics in such a way that must have harnessed outer space and planetary polemic fields and could tap star energies. Forty years ago, your Uncle Ray triggered the space ash to effect movement with large objects - and free them from their present magnetic and gravitational configurations. What seems likely from my way of thinking: he wants to meet up with the people he knew in some void between earth and the heavens...........if he's decided he's at the end of the line. It's also possible he has some other strategy I'm unaware of, in which case; I doubt if my mumbo-jumbo is of any benefit to you girls out there."

"No.........he's got to regain consciousness, and give us some direction on how to proceed." Dixie took a deep breath.

"Sally and me will be praying for Ryan and you all. We'll be out there to visit him if he ends up in hospice. Hopefully, he'll be conscious. He's always been a scrapper. At this point, sounds like Ryan's the only one that can save Ryan. The rest are gone. It was just Ray and him who found the fireball, he knew enough about the whole equation to get the comet's ash to work in concert with this magnetic pole reversal. Come down to it, Ryan's the only one left....except for Vince and Loki. All the core guys - the 'High Five' crew, they're all gone.....riding the Milky Way. I can't even remember where I left my smokes. Basically, I'm a veg; I don't think Loki or Vince is in any better shape. You said he asked for the ash twice already, I'm sure he knows it's his only alternative. Don't waste precious time, get started on using that ash in whatever format he tells you or however you decide is best.

"We tried getting in touch with Vinny.....no luck. It couldn't hurt to try a call to Loki while we wait for Dad to come to....."

"No...no...no...., you gotta force the movement. YOU girls cannot watch and wait for him to turn the corner. Now get with it. Hospice?.......c'mon - all that means is you're throwing in the towel. Listen - as soon as they run out of options and set up hospice for Ryan – you get the ball rolling on the polarity ash and do whatever the old man tells you.

The sisters traded glances. Right or wrong, they were ready to do something. "Thanks Uncle Bill, we'll call with any news: good or bad."

OCTOBER 10th 2018, Mankato

THE WHITELAW DAUGHTERS MAINTAINED THEIR VIGIL. At 4:17 p.m. Ryan Whitelaw stirred, wailing. He opened his eyes. They didn't know what to expect and their faces said as much. It appeared he was having convulsions. He choked trying to get some words out. The partial denture on the bottom rolled in his mouth. Nicole had to remove it and insert it properly on his gum. Still, he had difficulty speaking; mostly because he felt like shit and had no energy.

"Sssssstttttt." He motioned with his eyes and a slight head jerk for her to come near. His speech was indecipherable, she had to get real close to understand him.   "My legs......show me." Teresa pulled down the sheet. His calves were as big as his thighs. Ryan nodded, and shut his eyes tight. He thought death was under the bed, in the bathroom, just outside the door, maybe on the other side of the privacy curtain. Scythes and hourglasses adorned the ceiling, walls, and all the flat surfaces. "NO." he said. It was going to have to be wrested from him. He knew he'd have to rally. It was more than a whisper; perhaps a raspy scratch: "Mmmmmix all of it in a cup wwwawwith distill wawawaater, and mmmymy silver .....to....to....to dradrink."

"Huh?" Teresa froze. She squeezed her eyes tight for a few seconds. It was difficult to focus or concentrate, the facial twitches bit like flies.

Her sisters were counting on her to be the one to put their father's cosmic medication plan into action. She was an R.N. at St. Thomas Hospital in the psychiatric section in LaCrosse. What were they expecting? She told them she didn't think she was qualified to interpret or modify their father's situation or the treatment Dr. Singh had prescribed. It didn't prevent any of them from asking for a professional opinion of her. It was a fait accompli move; the Old Man had run out of track.

Teri had to compose herself before she began to put her father's plan into motion. "Nicky, stand guard outside the door. If some hospital personnel want entry - tell them they'll have to wait until we're done with our religious service."

"I can do that."

"Dixie....." Teresa directed, "Get a gallon of distilled water from the CVS pharmacy across the street on the corner."

Dixie was gone. Teresa looked at their father for some response, he looked a hundred years old now.

"Teri.....what are we doing?" Killeen was in the dark.

"You've got to find that bottle of colloidal silver." she said.

"It can't be back in LaCrosse....."

"No way, he's got a bottle of the stuff here somewhere in his travel bag. Not the small army duffle; the Boilermakers travel bag with his razor, denture stuff, rosary, wallet, vitamins, drugs........that shit. That's where his silver would be. It's probably in this storage closet."

"Hey Ol' Man, we don't have time to screw around here - you bring that silver with you?" Killeen asked.

He nodded.

"Is it in that Boilermaker union bag?"

An exhausted nod.

In a small closet, a large plastic bag was on a shelf. It said: Mankato Institute - personal belongings. Killeen grabbed the boilermaker carrier bag and rifled through it.

9

"Here it is, sonofabitch. We got lucky this time: colloidal silver/500 ppm. This is it, right Pops?"

"Do something." Killeen urged.

The twins looked at Ryan, "You want to drink this magnetic slurppy don't you?" Teresa gave him the stink eye and rested her chin on her collarbone.

A slight grin formed on the left side of his mouth and he gave a weak nod.

"Tell us what to do Papa."

His voice was a raspy whisper: "Ash with my name......" He had to pause. "Wrap..."

She moved her ear next to his mouth.

"Wrap ash with my name in pppaaaaaper tatatowel, and get ash wet."

She looked at him, "The cinder ash in the containers?"

A roll of the hand gave the 'thumbs up'.

"Then what?"

Ryan's right hand rested just below his heart.

"The left lobe of your liver." Teresa turned to Killeen as the latter placed the bottle of silver on the long-armed table. Her eyes got wide and took a deep breath; the scene took on the tone of a slow motion hallucinogenic mushroom trip.

"Pppapppppaaaput it here, where mm-mmm-mmmy hand is." His eyes were half-shut.

"Papa." Killeen's brow bore down looking at the two 24 oz. cups. "These are big cups Ol' Man." She divided Uncle Ray's outer space magnetic ash between the two cups and showed her father what it looked like.

He tried to take a deep breath; his head moved slowly from side to side. "Too thick." He coughed at the sight.   Teri had to put her ear close to his mouth again. "Tree cups....use tree."

Nicky opened the door slowly for Dixie. The other two were busier than worker bees.

"What took you so long? We're trying to get going here before one of the nurses show up."

"I had to have a cigarette......I can't deal with all this pressure. Give me a break."

"You got it?......the distilled water?"

"Yeah."

"Give it to Killeen." She handed the gallon jug to the younger twin.

"It's fuckin infant water - you idiot." Killeen shook her head with a sour smile. "You should work for the P.O."

"The guy said it was the same thing. The only difference is they stick a picture of a baby on the label so they can charge more." Dixie said.

"Sssssssttttt."

Teresa's ear again went to his mouth, "Let me taste it."

"Pour a good sip in a small cup and let Dad try it." Kill said. They waited.

He motioned OK with his hand.

"Toldja." Dixie laughed. The three daughters were glad to be doing anything besides being on death watch.

Three 24 oz. cups were lined up. Killeen now divided Ray's negative magnetic ash between the three cups. She showed him the potion. "What's next?"

"Wa-Wa-water."

Teresa began stirring the distilled water and ash in the first cup. Softly she said to Dixie, "This ash isn't blending too well; Killeen overheard. "How much of that silver are we using? The bottle says half a teaspoon a day."

"Sssssstttt."

"Overruled." Killeen's head leaned in to get Ryan's directions: "Tree teaspoons per cup." He whispered.

"Wow - that's six times the dose on the bottle. Is that how much you want Old Man?.........You sure Papa?"

His rugged, tired old face said: "Bring it on."

"We're all going to be charged with mercy murder."

Teresa's face flushed in disbelief. "We're going to feed Papa this cosmic cocktail - this doesn't even qualify as a shot in the dark. We're not dealing with a drug or substance that has any F.D.A. certification on anything. It's probably from outer space."

"And that's why we're doing it, all the earth shit is for shit." Dixie held her hands out – palms up.

"Okay Miss Smartypants, they don't even recognize the silver as having any medical value. In all likelihood, the only thing I'm counting on is losing my R.N. license for playing doctor with voodoo medicines.

"We'll all get charged for impersonating Dr. Jack Kevorkian." Killeen turned to Ryan, "Papa, you want to go though with this?"

Another thumbs up.

"Let's just do it……..we've got to try to save him." Dixie couldn't stand still.

"I'm with youse 110%…….I know if we sit on our hands, we will surely lose him. This I know." Teresa started mixing the magic potion.

Killeen called to Dixie, "Ask Nicky if she's with us with this space formula for Dad."

The eldest stuck her head inside the door. "It's this recipe or the transplant. Pops seems to favor the outer space slurppy over the transplant and surgery."

By some instinct Teri kind of knew he wanted to go with this magnetic field therapy. The mixologists had equalized the ash and the distilled water amongst the three cups; adding the silver she completed the formula. The first completed cup was whipped into a frenzy. Killeen told Teresa the colloidal silver had broken down the chunks. "Papa, you've got almost a gallon of go-go juice here. Do you want it all?"

With his index and middle finger he motioned for her to bring him a 24 ouncer.

"Dixie, tell Nicks to come back in." Teresa said.

"Is that stuff that Dad's supposed to drink glowing?" Nicole wondered what was going on in there while she guarded the room's entrance.

"I believe it is, I hadn't noticed while we were churning it. Draw the curtains and turn off the lights." The glow from the three cups was dim at best, but there was no doubt they were self-illuminating. The unforeseen, was occurring. "Screw it, we're going with it." They were stepping into the unknown.

Teresa directed the team: "Dixie, you and Killeen get Pops in a position that will allow him drink this concoction so he doesn't drown. He might be able to draw the formula through a straw. Don't let the magic potion cake up, keep stirring it to maintain consistency. Nicky, we'll leave the door open, but we'll draw the privacy curtain. You'll have to keep a watch on the other two cups of the potion - give them a mixing every so often. I don't think this stuff can spoil, but we better not give it a chance to get started."

The clock marked off the minutes as the whirlwind surrounded Teresa, she was in the thick of it now.

"This is our last resort" - The power of Attorney for Ryan's Medical matters never thought what they were about to do was thinkable - much less doable. The responsibility was more than Dixie could bear by herself. If she had to......she would........Alea jacta est.

All eyes were on her. This time she was the one: "Papa, this is what you want......what you want to do?"

His voice struggled, "Gaagaagot no cha-cha-choice."

"Let's do it." Nicole made eye contact with her father and sisters.

Following the first few sips, Teri took a deep breath; getting this slurry down his throat was going to take a while. The women took turns holding a smaller cup to his mouth. The big styrofoam cup was too clumsy. Two-thirds of the way through the first monster cup, Ryan was exhausted. They tried a couple of different methods; they had the most success using a 10 oz. cup. After getting 30 ounces in Ryan, he either passed out or fell asleep. Killeen, Nicole, and Dixie were all stirring formula as they watched Teresa. She read the monitors; with her hands she followed a heat path tracing his G.I. system which the comet potion probably had caused. She was frightened and unsure.

"For the record - I don't know what I am doing. I'm only doing what Papa instructed me to do. The rest is intuition, experience, and guesswork." she said.

"It's more than any of us know."

"Lay him back down." Teresa drew an oblong circle with a black magic marker on his abdomen, just below his heart. Ryan's positively charged fireball ash had the consistency of wet sand after they wrapped and dosed it with several tablespoons of the water. "We should tape this to his skin and try to keep it in place."

Teresa mooched some surgical tape from the nurses' station. She came back with the tape and Ryan's nurse in tow: ".....as soon as the patient or his representative signs for him, we'll bring him down off the I.C.U. floor."

Teri hadn't seen this nurse before, she checked his vitals and the monitors; she listened to his heart, lungs, and stomach. Her stethoscope wandered to over to his liver and intestine.

"What's this?" She pointed to the wrapped fireball ash.

Nicole spoke up right away, "I got it from a medicine woman of the Chiqricahua Band of the Apache nation. She said it would help."

Teresa called Dixie over to the I.C.U. nurse: "This is Dad's medical representative."

She looked up from her stethoscope placement, "Sounds like a war going on in his G.I. system." The nurse watched the wall as she listened to his heart and lungs. "Cardio and pulmonary sound good."

Dixie asked: "Dad can sign for himself for hospice assignment?

"It's the best way to avoid legal problems and family squabbles. It keeps everything clean." A moment slipped by.

"Has he regained consciousness?"
Teresa jumped right in: "Not really.....when will you check on him next?"

"Shift changes at 8 o'clock, I'll be back about 7." The ICU nurse said before she left.

Teresa checked her watch: 5:30 pm. She calculated how much time they had to get some more slop in Ryan. "Killeen - extend that surgical tape the long way over the wrapped ash. Make sure it's sticking to his skin in both directions - positive charged ash inside the oblong circle."

"Right."

"6:30". Nicole bent down to retrieve a fallen tablespoon from the floor. Something was off...............the urine collection bag? It was nearly empty last night, now there was almost an inch of piss. 'This is strange.' There was no purpose for the staff to change the bag. "Teri, can you look at the Ol' Man's chart and check his piss output?"

"I don't have a barcode to scan that would let me in. I can only read his chart when they bring it up; and if they want to be pricks about it - only Dixie's supposed to be able to look."

Killeen yelled in her father's ear: "Hey Papa, the house is on fire.....wake up!"

He had difficulty exhaling. His eyes got big, and quickly retreated to halves.

"Papa......Papa......PAPA !......C'mon wake up. C'mon, drink this." Killeen pinched his nose.

"Come on Pop. Dixie - raise up the bed."

She played with the control unit.

He was awake, only because his eyes were open.

"Here Pops, drink this." Killeen gave the remaining silver/gray mud mixture a vigorous stir. Every three minutes he managed a small swallow.

The night was one hour into the shift's turnover before the night nurse checked in; she said she'd return in a little bit.

As soon as she left, the Whitelaw women had Ryan finish the 2nd - 24 ounce dose of the cosmic cocktail; then he passed out. He had only been asleep for 10 minutes when the nurse reentered. His vitals were recorded and compared with the previous shift. She read Dr. Singh's instructions about entering hospice care tomorrow or the next day, either way - he'd be leaving the I.C.U. by tomorrow. Pain management and comfort would supplant the curative and healing activities. Singh or Dr. Judd could sign-off with Social Security tomorrow for the request for hospice care. As far as the staff was concerned, this was a done deal.

The night shift nurse entered the amount of urine in the collection bag. She too did a double-take; she noticed the anomaly that Nicole had; now - there was more than when the last entry was logged in, and there was more than when Nicole had looked at the urine collection bag.

This nurse had dealt almost exclusively with gastro/intestinal cases. She had seen her share of liver cancer, disease, hepatitis, cirrhosis, and failure. This Whitelaw customer was well into the advanced stages of cirrhosis to the extent that his liver was unable to break down his blood's components into what was usable and what was waste. She thought of it as having a pond full of beaver dams in his liver: the water could enter his liver, but very little flowed out. This guy was drowning inside-out. His bodily waste would soon poison him. The nurse squinted as she tried to get a good reading of the collection bag hanging from the framework of the bed about knee-high. To most visitors, it was hidden from view. She squatted down on one knee to get a true reading: there now was 170 ml more in the bag since the last time it was checked. This was going the right way, but it was counter-intuitive to the function of a liver succumbing to scarring. It didn't make sense; cirrhosis is a one-way street. A sample was extracted from the collection bag and sent to the lab for analyzing. The increase in urine output was a positive sign, but she wasn't getting too involved with this case. These hepatitis C carriers were getting a lot of liver transplants. Sometimes they worked - sometimes they didn't. She pulled the sheet up from his feet, they all looked at his bloated calves. The night nurse looked at Teresa and rolled her eyes. "Start praying."

"We have been."

Only about 12 ounces of the 72 oz. of the cosmic culture gravy remained. Teresa and her trio had their father finish the contents of the last cup as soon as the nurse left. By midnight, the nurse had to empty the soy sauce colored urine from the bulging bag, and again at 3:30 am. Ryan had become a pissing machine. Word had gotten around the I.C.U. floor that a miracle was taking place in Room 11E. A number of doubting Thomas' watched as the urine bag filled. The room reeked. Dixie could see her father's swollen legs were shrinking. Teresa had to tell the head nurse on the floor that "Enough was enough - No more sightseers-"

Nevertheless, Ryan was the buzz of the I.C.U., and the news of his improvement would spread rapidly once the shifts changed in a few hours. His nurse speculated on his urine and blood chemistry. It was challenging not to use the word "improvement" in her e-mail to Singh's office. She used restraint and referred to the patient's 'unexpected return to a more normal output of urine production'.

Because the report of his condition gravitated toward the positive, the nurse saw no immediate need to send an e-mail to Dr. Singh's device about the development.

By 5 am, Whitelaw's G.I. System and kidneys were processing solids, liquids, and drugs that were two weeks old. He began having severe internal pains in the area Teresa had outlined for the location of his exterior intergalactic ash pad.

Ryan's daughters had been with him through the night; occasionally spelling off in a chair or down the hall in the visitors' area. Their hopes had been rising with every ounce of piss entering the bag. Now they could see improvement in his legs; their hopes were running strong until their father's moaning intensified.

The night nurse called for the resident doctor who was on duty at 6:00 am. Also, a text message was sent to Dr. Judd's phone telling him what to expect when he arrived. To his daughters, he sounded like he was being subjected to electro-shock torture. A Mankato staff G.I. Physician had increased the pain meds, which tempered the spike pain levels until Singh or Judd arrived. The nurse hoped they would see Ryan before her shift turned over, she didn't want to have to talk to either one from 'The Viking Lounge'.

They received word Dr. Judd would see Ryan around 8 a.m. It was only an hour and a half away. Teresa removed the positive charged ash from the area she had outlined in marker.

"Put it back Teri." Nicky said. "Whatever progress was made, was the result of what Pops and Uncle Billy told us to do." The eldest daughter assured the others - "These guys will focus on the science or the person selling the science. They're not going to know any more about the how's and why's of the magnetically charged ash than we do. Anyway, they don't have time to go on a wild goose chase about a recovery that can't be explained."

Two staff assistants wheeled Ryan down to radiology for some more imaging. The on-duty G.I. physician wanted some pictures for the doctors when either got on the floor. The radiologist's order was to Cat-Scan the area believed to be the axis of his pain; followed by an MRI of the abdomen. Dixie took the walk with Ryan. Prior to going into the machine, she removed the wet paper toweled ash.

"What's that?" the technician asked.

"His good luck charm......his brother's ashes."

"HooooooKaaaaaaay......we'll be doing a Cat-Scan and then you'll be wheeled down the hall for the MRI."

Dixie came back from radiology, helping the assistants negotiate the wheeled bed through the doorway into 11E. Ryan was in and out of consciousness. When they plugged his IV back into the dope bag he started recalling his life in random episodes. If there was a chronological context to this replay it didn't come right away. With all this toxicity on the move within his circulatory system and brain, some things rushed to the surface; while others lurked in the dark corners and recesses of his mind.

15

CHAPTER 2

i

    "Raaaaaaaymond............Raymond and Ryan --- NOW!" Jane was almost yelling in the kitchen of the 4 room apartment. Our lunch was ready, and she returned to fixing hors d'oeuvers, cookies, eggnog, and other Christmas treats I wasn't familiar with.

    Ray surveyed the kitchen table, "Where's our milk?"

    The word "milk" had me searching for something to wash down the slow peanut butter and jelly sandwich.

    "If you boys can hang on and let me get these Christmas cookies out of the oven before they burn - I'll get your milk" she said.

    The kitchen was half food and half Xmas decoration stuff: lights, ornaments, pine cones, big candles, and wrapping paper. One of Jane's students even gave her a plastic menorah, but it had electric candles.....for safety. From the hallway into the kitchen, hanging from the top of the door jamb was a piece of holly and a twig of mistletoe.......Dad had been in charge of that. We had two Christmas wreaths that year; he put the cheap one on the inside of the bathroom door. We got the nice one from my grandparents who lived upstate; Hal hung it on our front door. The kitchen looked ready to burst. It would be the first Christmas I had any recollection of.

    Ray looked around, "Mom - why don't they have Christmas all the time?"

    All I could do was arch my brows.

    "Christmas wouldn't work in the summer. It wouldn't feel right. There wouldn't be any snow either." she said.

    Ray shot back, "Donnie and Dennis say there's never any snow at their grandma's house. They said they went swimming on Christmas Day."

    "Well their grandmother lives in Florida. Some people leave Florida in the summer because it's too hot. Ask Donnie if they ever visited their grandmother during the summer."

    Ray and Jane continued their conversation. Donnie and Dennis were a lot like us: Donnie was a year older than Ray, and Dennis and me were born in 1954. Their names began with the same consonant - both were two syllables. They sounded like names that would bond the brothers.

Hearing our names in repetition: Raymond and Ryan - ....Raymond and Ryan.....When someone called either name, I automatically responded; it didn't matter to me which one of us was actually summoned. This team concept was one of my earliest memories. We may as well have been joined at the hip. Ray's entry into kindergarten was difficult for me - there wasn't anything to do. He was in the a.m. session. Jane and me waited for him when he got out at noon. Jane didn't have dancing classes on Monday, so that was okay. Tuesday thru Friday, Jane took us over to whoever was providing child care for us, which seemed to change an awful lot.

    "Why can't I go to school? The only ones who aren't in school are babies. I want to be smart - like Ray." Right from the get-

16

go, I knew Ray was smarter than me. Some of it was due to age, but he was simply more intelligent, and as time went on, it became an inescapable fact. I learned more from him than from Hal and Jane, the schools, books, and TV combined. He had no peer in his ability to transfer knowledge. When it came from Ray: it was gospel.

"Here's your milk." Jane announced wearing a reindeer/sled pin just above her left breast. Already, I was comparing other kids' mothers with mine. Physically, she was a knockout, but she also had the personality to go with the looks. How could we be so lucky?

Ray registered discontent with the cup of milk, "Mom..........there's some of that stuff in mine." Jane fished out a glob of cream from the top of his cup with her pinky, and in one swift motion it disappeared in her mouth. The habits of wartime rationing and the depression era of doing without, would stay with her until she passed away.

Also with her until the end, was her physical beauty. She had thick auburn hair; it hung past her shoulders and down her back. She stood about 5'8", with an hour glass figure. Her face was an all-dayer, and if you didn't like that - she had a topside rack that garnished wolf calls, whistles, and set off so many car horns........we thought there was a wedding motorcade every time we went shopping. Initial interactions with Jane varied - the men expected a nit-wit and the women were cautious. Her good looks were equaled by her intelligence, wit, and business savvy. Most normal people immediately liked everything about her. She had 'style', and if you wanted some or at least wanted to know what it was; you only had to watch Jane Marlowe, and you could see 'style' in motion.

Whatever she had, I know I didn't have it. Ray was the only one in the family who did besides Jane. Hal coveted it and her. Jane tried to impart it to my sister with limited results. My youngest brother Willis and me, were better off than Hal because it didn't drive us nuts; but through the years, I could only listen to the Jane Marlowe worshippers on an intermittent basis. I didn't hate or envy them, I just didn't understand them; and that was okay. Still, it never really shut off the search for an explanation.

It didn't bug me, but I'd think about how everybody liked Jane and that seemed to make her world go round and complete. From the first day I watched her teaching kids, (97% girls) at her studio - they all loved her. The girls, teens, and women shuffled in and out of the studio. Jane and her assistant, Judy Conolly, had the students going through their numbers and routines. For the hour of instruction, there was nothing but smiles on her students. Then the next time it was the same thing.......and the next time......and the next time. With a pair of tap shoes, and a month of Jane's lessons – a person could kiss the blues good-bye. Really good dancers could pretend they were dancing the blues; but inside, it was all smiles and sunshine. All of her students wanted to emulate 'Miss Jane'. She had the brains, beauty, and talent to be much more than what she was.

Occasionally, Jane needed me to do some painting or odd-job at the studio when I was in high school. I watched the Jane Marlowe dynamism and it really hit me between the eyes. For many girls, taking dancing lessons with 'Miss Jane' was their highlight of the week. My mother was some sort of unrestricted avatar. Whatever it was, my mother had 'it' in addition to her 'style' and 'charisma'.

In the 1950's, Jane was an aberration: she was a dance instructor who owned her own studio, a free-lance choreographer, and a mom. That was quite a plateful back then. Tons of talent, business savvy, and oodles of sex appeal. She knew enough about human nature; she didn't have to run the table. Content where she landed, spontaneous dance steps would appear anywhere, but mostly at home. Her students were magically transported to the world of "Miss Jane"; and they all wanted to be her, and wear Leotards and tights all day long; in her studio - it was possible.

JANE ALWAYS SEEMED TO MOVING INTO OR OUT OF A different studio location every other year. These places were low rent dives where there was scant residential activity. Most of her neighbors were non-profit enterprises, after-hours clubs, art studios and the like. Jane kept a sharp eye out if there was a piano in a studio. Most of the pianos were out-of-tune uprights that would be moved just the one time. With a couple of the uprights, it was difficult to determine the piano's primary function: was it a musical instrument or an ashtray? So many cigarettes had been laid flat on the end keys, you had to wonder.

"No Jane, you're going to have to get somebody up here and tune this thing." one of her piano players would give her the news.

She had a good musical ear, but some of the students did not. A piano player de jour was indispensable in Jane's early years because the state of the art of the record players was inadequate: the sound was poor, Jane had to stand next to the phonograph and replay bits of a song until the students got the steps right. The arm of the record player was raised off the record and Jane would tell the girls how to dance to the music, and she would lower it and they'd try it again. She went through as many needles as a junkie. With a piano player she could make a lot more progress with the dance numbers. With the introduction of the new speakers, amps, turntables and cassettes tapes – it made the piano player only a part-time requirement.

Her dance students were drawn from all over Yonkers. It was a business decision to have a central location and it allowed her students to take one bus to get to their dance lessons. One of her longer tenancies was in tenement on the 4th floor in the central business district of Yonkers known as "Getty Square". Her studio was located there for five years. The area was rugged - even back then. It had the upright piano, and it needed tuning every year.

It was hard to say what the building's function was when it was built; its wooden frame creaked like a whaling ship. The architect, if the 4 story had one, had laid out the stairs in a straight line from the street entrance to the back wall of the building's 3rd floor. There was just a tiny landing for the second floor renters: a dentist on the one side, and a mail- order business across the hall. More stairs daunted the dancers from the 2nd to the 3rd floor. From the 3rd to the 4th floor, it was more of a conventional stairway layout with the traditional switchback design. The pitch of these stairways rivaled that of the grandstands at Shea Stadium. They were steep for adults, but the students had to climb them one at a time considering they had to grasp the handrail and lug their tap shoes and their outfits in some kind of glorified round carry tote.

The shorter girls had a hard time climbing the stairs making sure they didn't misstep. It was a long way to the bottom. We never heard of anybody falling down a flight of stairs except some drunk. Everyone knew, if someone took a spill - they were going to the hospital or to the morgue. I never got around to asking Jane about how the pianos got up the stairs into the studios that had more than one floor. As time went on, I was confident Hal didn't have much to do with moving them. The piano up on the 4th floor is most likely still there with blocks, tackle, and pulleys in some cubby hole waiting for the day when it might be used to bring it back down - if the building hadn't succumbed to the wrecking ball first.

Many of the girls' parents were willing to put up with the studios' shortcomings, but they wouldn't put up with the street tuffs harassing the girls. Jane knew it was time to move.

Whenever she moved into a new studio, a landlord watched Jane with her array of full length posing mirrors, 12 ft. lengths of handrail used for stretching, cork boards of 8"x10" glossies with movie and Broadway stars, (Debbie Reynolds, Peter Gennaro, June Taylor, Donald O'Connor) current and former students, past recitals, and this year's instructors.

Landlords were warned a piano was coming, but they viewed Jane's monster record player and speaker as the real potential trouble. The landlords were hesitant Jane's studio might be too loud for the other tenants to handle.

"My piano players are only here after 5 o'clock on weeknights, so I need to play records between 2 and 5 p.m. I know how to locate studs to hang the mirrors and handrails. Before I leave, I will patch and paint." She had her moving routine down.

Still, not many of the landlords were thrilled with the dance studio as their tenant, but that was under revision when they saw Jane and her assistants in the Leotards and tights. The dreamscape they provided, erased most of the initial reservations the landlords may have had. It was a game; and they kept hitting on Jane. After 2 years in one spot, the landlords knew she wasn't a player and they wouldn't renew her lease.

ii

Christmas rolled in - right on schedule: December 25, 1958. Ray and me got Hal to place the manger scene on top of the television set. Jane gave us some strips of evergreen forming our outer perimeter. Ray was the set designer of our nativity spectacle. Jesus, Mary, and Joseph and the gang were all there; they were carved out of wood. Mixed with the barnyard animals, were Ray's 'Lost World' plastic

19

dinosaurs. Joining the shepherds, 3 kings, and 3 angels were about a dozen Texicans straight from the Alamo, a good half-dozen paratroopers and Nazi Werhmacht right from Normandy Beach joining us for the celebration. He
taped a loose Tommy gun to a dashboard Christ we had liberated from our station wagon, to protect the baby Jesus. Saint Joe was there with a bazooka glued to one hand and his trusty axe in the other, and the Blessed Virgin had a canteen looped on her praying hands to hand out water in the desert diorama. Hal and Jane really came through with the record "Little Drummer Boy" which was perfect as Ray had a Civil War drummer boy keeping the beat in his union blue uniform. On four corners of the scene, the infant Christ was protected by 12 pound cannons.

Hal said it would be rough sledding for King Herrod and his crew if he was thinking about mixing it up. Everyone who visited our house that Christmas thought it was real swell. It was mostly Ray's vision bringing the Christmas concept to reality. He'd tell me which soldier, dinosaur, or object of warfare he needed and I'd dig around in the toy box until I found it or an acceptable substitute.

iii

'Marlowe' was a stage name she came up with. Jane's maiden name had been Hicock, and she didn't think it was right for her dance studio. My uncle Bill had heard enough of being called 'Wild Bill'. Jane loved telling people 'Marlowe' was a stage name. Later on, I realized the name bugged Hal because it emphasized she was an independent business woman.

The studio's schedule had to dovetail with the kids' normal education schedule. She also had to make adjustments for religious and ethnic considerations. In 1959 or 60, a group of Hungarians who had fled their native country during the anti-Soviet uprising of 1956, asked Jane if she could teach their children traditional Hungarian dances.

Jane recalled having gone through a similar request with the Irish - a couple of years earlier. That had not gone so well. The Micks could tap dance well enough, but from the waist up - there was nothing - no swing - no rhythm. To Jane, it looked awkward....contrived. The Irish elders wanted that stoic look, but Jane wanted to give them 42nd Street. Just before the recital, neither Jane nor the Irish elders were satisfied with their performance after the dress rehearsal. It was mutually decided they would not perform at the recital. Approximately 25% of the Irish class returned in the fall to register as regular students.

If Jane was going to give this ethnic dancing another try, it had to be without Hal's knowledge. He had been pretty rough on her about the Irish class, and it ended up being a tug of war on a number of levels.

"You went way beyond your area of expertise... "Stick with what you know." Hal said.

"Those kids were fine - it was the ones that just got off the boat who caused the problems."

"Tell me Janey - who's the dance instructor when you teach the kids the regular stuff?"

"Listen Mr. Know It All.......I gave them a class time for their lesson that was convenient for me and us. That Irish class fit perfectly between an afternoon class and an evening class on Wednesdays. Nothing ventured - nothing gained. That's how I look at it."

Hal didn't know much about dancing, he knew numbers, accounting, profit/loss. His strong suit was on the business side of the ledger. Jane didn't need him to do her books; she could balance her own checkbook as well as her phony set of business books. It just took her longer.

Every year when tax time arrived, the fireworks started between the two. It wasn't until later on when I learned the only thing my mother knew about their joint return was where Hal told her to sign. After Jane had passed away, my sister told me Jane had never seen one of Hal's check stubs, or a completed tax return, but he could account for every nickel she earned or spent with her business endeavors. Hal just lived to bust Jane with an inaccuracy on her tax statement. Doing anything financial with Hal?............you'd better have your ducks in a row.

The Irish dancers ended up being a "ghost class". This meant the class never went on the books. Jane wasn't caught up in any ethical or moral dilemma over the failure to report. She knew she was the one who had earned the money. If she took on the Hungarians, she knew it was going to be entered in the phony books as a 'ghost class'. It had to be - if she was going to squirrel away any spending money for the summer.

A SCHEME HAD BEEN COOKED UP THAT CHRISTMAS with a girlfriend who had 3 kids. They had made plans to rent out side by side bungalows for a week in Wildwood N.J. "I just got to forget about the winter.....every now and then" she told Alice, who was Jane's accomplice in this summer get away plan.

Hal and Jane were getting ready to attend a holiday party at her friend's house on Bronx River Rd. When it felt right, she'd ask Hal about the week in Wildwood for the coming summer. If he was lubricated enough; a vacation on the summer sands of south Jersey might get the green light from Hal. It would ease the next two months of cruel winter.

Mom had been down this road before, and she knew she had to get Hal to agree before he got into the hard liquor at the party. Replying to her flirtatious vacation invite, he had thrown in a few conditions before he'd agree: "First, get me a Manhattan." The drink she returned with was a 'double'...... it was damn near a 'mickey'. Hal took a sip and did a double-take, "Holy Fuck woman!......."

"We were going to talk about the trip to Wildwood?" She wanted to get this deal done before they went to the party, and the alcohol would grease the wheel.

"Yeah, so you want me to take a week of vacation.......in what......August?" He was still trying to focus in from the potent drink.

"That's what we said - that's when Alice has the house rented.....the 3rd week of August."

Hal stood up and tried to focus, "Alright, here's the deal: I'm still saving up money to buy a house; so you've got to come up with the money to bankroll this vacation - all of it - and that includes a brake job for the car.....before the vacation." he said.

"No problem." she answered as she rolled her cigarette in one of the ashtray's grooves.

He continued with his demands: "And I don't want you looking like some grandma or immigrant just getting off the boat. Before August, I want to you to model 3 bathing suits; I'll choose 2 for you to take. He looked into her eyes, stirred his cocktail: "Start dressing like you're single down there. You're a beautiful woman.....make me want you."

Caught off-guard by Hal's gambit, Jane looked at his drink. It was only 1/4 finished; something had unleashed his sexual interest. What did he want to hear?......she didn't know what to say. "If you don't get screwed up during the day - we can play 'Ride the elevator all night'." Neither was smiling, the animals were on the prowl.

"Alright."

"Alright then." Jane said. She had no idea what she just agreed to. What she was sure of was: she would be teaching Hungarian ethnic dance to people who needed to see a piece of their motherland. Jane may also have acquiesced to be a sex slave on the family vacation. "God, just let me lie in the sand, sun, and surf." Jane really wanted the vacation now, not in 7 months. A mirage of the Jersey Shore would have to suffice.

LIKE THE IRISH, THE HUNGARIANS' CLASSES WERE compressed into a half-year. The similarity between the two cultures and their dance expression was that they were not American. Making the rounds amongst her colleagues, Jane investigated all she could concerning Hungarian dance wear, instrumentation, routines, steps, and dance interpretation.

The class was of equal proportion: half male and half female. There were 24 students taking instruction; it would be a money maker for Jane, she hoped Hal had been wrong about being in over her head as far as taking on another ethnic dance class she was unfamiliar with. There were many challenges: the boys and girls danced as partners. Jane's school rarely had boys taking lessons, except for me and Ray; we had been bribed, then coerced into dance lessons and performing at Jane's recitals; in return she bought us used two wheelers.

When the Hungarian boys showed-up; they were eager to dance with their partners. Their enthusiasm took me and Ray by surprise. A couple would hold one another and high step while locking their arms about their partner's back in a wrist grab as the free hand went up into the air to aid their balance.

The different dance segments always started off slow and deliberate, but by the midpoint of the dance, the tempo and complexity of the routine would explode into the finish.
The liaison for the Hungarians was a 55 year old bricklayer named, Zolton Pavels.

"Jane.....meez Jane - I know vat I vant to zee in dis dance, but I not know how to tell you. Zo, you make it up in your head vat dee moosic say to you and make up your dance. Zen vee vill zee vair vee har? Yes?"

"Mr. Pavels, this is exactly the type of situation I wanted to avoid."

"Pleeze...pleeze.......you try, you zee. It vill be good. My people - dey need dis. The children...dey must know who dey are. If, does not verk out - vell vee try."

Jane looked deeply into Zolton's face. He must have made promises that he was not sure he could deliver on. Silence descended between the two. Both were in a jam: Jane needed this 'ghost class' and Pavels needed to show his countrymen that they would not get swept up in an American cultural tsunami.

"I bring you 5 Hungarian dance records....How long do vee have stage in you recital?"

"At most.......12 or 13 minutes." Jane answered.

"O.K. - vee can perform 2 dance number. Vhat I most must have is you to get more records for me." He pulled out 2 of the 5 for Jane. "Den vee have more seelection." Pavels' hand went up, "But also Meez Jane, I vill be here for dee classes. I can say vhat is correct or no good. The musicians - I provide for recital night. The costumes....dance clothes is make by our women in our style."

"Zolton...." Jane began to explain, "Your musicians must play with the dancers at least two times before the night of the recital."

"Don't vorry, dey the best – Mikels, why he play for dee New York Philharmonic - he plenty good alright, you betcha." he smiled.

"How many pieces?" Jane asked.

"Let's see now: accordion, clarinet, percussion, violin, and Tomas play whatever we need."

"Okay Mr. Pavels.......You got yourself a dance instructor." Jane offered her hand to seal the deal.

His ice-blue eyes met hers; "Just one thing........you do not make us look like Russian. Do not insult us."

"You can watch the classes as we develop the performance for the recital. If there is something amiss... ...not right, I will rework it, and just let me know when it is what you want."

"As long as vee understand one another."

"After the first 3 classes, we should have an idea what direction we are going with the dance numbers. I'll pick out the people who will perform solos and duets and those who will be better out of the spotlight."

23

"No....no.....no...dees is not to be pageant - vee vant to put our best foot forward - yes?" Zolton agreed.

They both laughed.

"Sometimes a boy or a girl simply has 2 left feet; we can hide them in the back or along the sides, but in the end, if a kid can't perform the steps with precision.....it makes the routine looks sloppy, the kids' confidence is broken, and the parents feel like they've been swindled." she explained.

"Again, I must agree, but it leaves me vit dee dirty verk to inform Elvira's mother dat her daughter vill not be in dee front line. Vell Meez Jane....vhen dey zee recital - all vill be A-O.K."

"The first class will be in the last week of January."

Pavels was out the door, and Jane wondered what she had gotten herself into.

iv

World War II and the Korea War and had sucked the last drop of ambition from many Americans. A night of listening to the radio or watching T.V. was as much as some could handle, they had had their share of uniformed servicemen showing up at the door. The country just wanted to forget, and start to enjoy life.......if such a thing was possible.

My parents knew about hard times; besides WW II and Korea, both endured the economic Depression as kids. They did without for fifteen years, some had it bad; some had it worse. The Great Depression was something most people didn't understand. Hard times were inescapable during the wars; but with the Depression - it was hard figuring out who was to blame. Jane said that the war had gotten the country out of the Depression, and that was good; but it didn't outweigh the number of who people died during WW II. She thought, 'we might have been better off just being poor.'

Jane and Hal must have been brainstorming some night. They figured with sacrifice, hard work, and raising us kids right...... the American way; they might pull away from the rest of the herd. Our family might raise it's standing economically, socially, and intellectually among other criteria.

Whether by design or chance, the Whitelaw's were taking an alternate route to the promised land. It meant instead of spending time with a full-time mom.......Ray and me would be watched by strange women and teenage girls, during our first two years of school. When Jane was between a rock and a hard place, she'd have to bring us to her dance studio. She always did her best to keep us with the sitters we said we liked, but there was very little regularity or continuity with our daycare. The teenage girls always had some connection with Jane's dancing school. They might have been students at some point or sister's or cousins of them. Some were just friends of current students.

24

As another year's dance recital drew near, the concern for quality child care got lost in the recital rush.

The 4 weeks which preceded Jane's recital in 1958, I was taken over to a former student's apartment. Her name was Bridgette Daley: all-day Irish - freckles and skin the color of homogenized milk. She was pregnant and her husband was somewhere in the Pacific with the navy. Bridgette lived in a basement apartment near Yonkers Raceway. My first day there, her dog knocked me over and I pissed my shorts because I was afraid he was going to attack me.

"Why you little dink....." she hissed with her hands on her hips. "Your mother promised that you were house-broken."

"It was an accident." I sure wish Ray had been around to get me out of this mess.

"If you weren't Jane's brat, I'd paddle your butt right now! ....Alright......you want to be a baby? Then I'll treat you like one. Get those piss-pants off right now....your drawers too. Come on, hurry it up...Baby..."

"I'm not a baby."

"Get them off....Now I've got to wash 'em in the sink."

I was motionless. She came over and pushed me down on my back and tugged off my shorts and jockeys over my sneakers. I was confused and excited as a 4 year old
could be.

"So you want to be a dirty-dirty little boy. Just wait until I tell your mother about that." She pointed right at it. "Going tinkles in your knickers and now you're sporting a stiffy.

"For a little boy, you've gotten yourself in some big trouble."

"I'm sorry." I kept my eyes fixed on the floor.
Bridgette smiled and teased: "I'm sorry too that your Pinocchio came out, because now I've got to tell Miss Jane about her little boy. And then she'll have to tell all her girlfriends, and they'll laugh at you every time they see you." She spoke in a puppy dog voice.

Bridgette tied me up to a radiator pipe with only my shirt and sneakers on and that made me cry, for about 15 minutes, then it morphed into a whimper. An hour or so
elapsed before she untied me, and threw my clothes at my feet. "Put them on. Your mother will be here soon.

When Jane drove up, she noticed that my shorts were on backwards. Bridgette helped me get in the car. Jane's face was concerned and she brought the babysitter's eyes to my backwards shorts with a short directional head sweep: "Did he have an accident?"

"A little one." Bridgette waved it off. "He'll do better tomorrow.....you know...a new sitter, the dog was excited, a new place - he'll be fine.......Right Ryan?" She looked back to Jane, "He really was well behaved; we played some games and I read the story of Pinnochio to him."

"I think he'll be alright - he's only had one or two accidents in the past year."

25

Bridgette spoke to Jane as she ruffed up my hair, "I'm looking forward to tomorrow." she spoke softly to Jane: "I washed and dried his shorts and jockeys."

"Thanks so much Bridgette, some of the sitters I've had would have sent him home wet."

For the rest of the week she had me running around bare assed as soon as Jane left. Bridgette kept warning me not to have another accident: "You gotta go?......you gotta go?" Finally I did, and I missed the toilet and pissed her bathroom rug. I was corrected by her, and Bridgette monitored my use of the toilet. When she didn't like the way I was discharging my urine, she'd pinch my flow off, and align things where she thought the stream would enter the bowl. If she was on the phone, she'd have me pee in the backyard with the dog.

It seemed it went on like that for the entire time I was in her care. About once a week, she'd put me in this baby's playpen and tie me up in there if she was going to be away from me more that a few minutes. She was either outside talking to some guys in a car or talking on the phone. It was like a jail to me. The only time I had clothes on was when Jane dropped me off and picked me up. After the first few days, I had gotten used being without shorts, pants, or underwear. Every three days or so, Bridgette would bring over some preteen girls to watch me while she ran across the street to get a pack of smokes.

The girls giggled and whispered, "Why's he tied up in a playpen?"

Another asked, "How come he doesn't have his pants on?"

"He's just a little boy.....he wets his pants."

They laughed and I got mad, but by the time Jane showed up, Bridgette and the girls had given me some crumb cake and Turkish Taffy, and the humiliation faded until the next day. Jane handed Bridgette her money for the week,   "Bridgette, I won't be needing you after the recital next week. Friday will be the last day."

"I really needed the money with the baby coming: Johnny's money from the Navy doesn't go too far. He's hoping to get stationed at Subic Bay in the Philippines where it's a lot cheaper to live."

"When are you due......November?"

"Early November.......Tell all the kids I said 'Hi and have a great recital'." Bridgette smiled.

Jane let out the clutch and waved 'Bye.' "Bridgette was alright - huh Ryan?"

I looked away from Jane, "I guess I liked when we'd read that Pinnochio story."

v

The way Saturdays went down needed explanation; I'm still miffed about what occurred and why. Usually Hal would drop off Jane at her studio at 9am and pick her up at 5 pm. From there, it was a short drive to Grandpa Helmut's and Nana Anne's apartment at 68

26

Warburton Ave.; just east of Otis Elevator where Hal worked. We were brought to our grandparents - neither Ray or me knew why. There was no explanation. It continued until Nana decided she didn't want to put up with taking care of my sister who cried a lot as an infant.

Nana told Ray they had lived at the Jewish Community Center during The Depression; it was near Otis. Helmut was the custodian there before the war. My grandfather's command of English was never very good, and many of the Jewish immigrants' spoke German and Yiddish. Helmut was a good fit for the custodian job; he knew enough about building maintenance to get a job there. The Orthodox Jews also used my grandfather and father because they were gentiles. They would handle the 'go to' or do the odd jobs Jews couldn't do on the Sabbath or High Holy Days. Ray told me the guys at St. Mary's school used to razz Hal because his family worked for the Jewish people. He said Hal didn't mind working at the J.C.C. because he always got to use the gym and pool; he just didn't like the continual crap he used to get from the guys at school.

When he was old enough to work, he started at Otis Elevator as a summertime seasonal worker after his freshman year at Manhattan High School – a parochial school in the Bronx. When the Japs attacked Pearl Harbor, Hal got a letter from Otis asking Manhattan High to adjust his school schedule so he could go to class in the morning and work afternoons and Saturdays at the plant. At first he was just a gofer - a messenger boy who rode a bike from one end of the plant to the other delivering drawings, communiqués, small parts and tools. A year into the war, some woman got his messenger job, and Hal was sent to the foundry. Otis had him working every legal hour the labor laws would allow.

In early 1943, he talked Helmut and Anne into letting him enlist in the Navy. Like so many other American boys, he signed up for the duration of the war. Grandpa Helmut advised Hal to go into the submarine service. It worked out for Hal, but it was a pretty dangerous for those guys in general. His discharge came in 46', Hal went back to Otis, and worked as an elevator constructor for a couple of years. Other veterans at Otis were climbing the corporate ladder using their G.I. benefits to enroll in colleges that offered accounting, engineering, and international business courses.   Driving all over metro N.Y.C. servicing and building elevators and escalators for Otis wasn't what Hal saw himself doing for the rest of his life. Joining the suits had to be easier and he enrolled at Manhattan College and got a Bachelor's of Science with a electrical engineering major and a business minor thanks to the G.I. bill. The Otis manufacturing facility and corporate offices were a 5 min. walk from my grandparents' apartment; it was another 4 minutes to New York Central's Hudson Line R.R. tracks; two more minutes and you could cool your feet in the Hudson River. The neighborhood was in transition - going in the wrong direction. Unless Otis was running two shifts, the area got pretty sketchy after dark.

Nana and Grandpa lived on the second floor of the Warburton apartment. There was small talk with Nana and Grandpa when Hal dropped us off, but he was always gone for the day. Ray and me headed for the spare bedroom where we had a small box of extra toys we brought from home. Time always seemed to stand still when we were at their apartment. When you played too long on the carpet, its color would come out on the knees of your pants, the toes of your sneakers, and the heels of your hands. About the only thing we enjoyed eating was chocolate chip cookies and a glass of milk. They never had jelly....always preserves with the pits. A pie would be on the kitchen table and it would always be rhubarb. Our grandparents lived on coffee and an occasional piece of toast. Sometimes, I was there alone - without Ray; then it was like a prison sentence.

This set of grandparents liked Ray a lot more than me. I think it had to do with that first-born jazz. Conversely, my mother's side seemed to favor me. Our grandmother Edna, who we called Mom-Mom, and her 2nd husband Mack lived upstate, so we saw them a lot less than Hal's parents. Mom-Mom and Mack were aces, they had a
daughter, Allison, who was 2 1/2 years older than Ray. Woods, cow pasture, dirt roads, our second hand bikes, tree houses, homemade bows and arrows: all that was required was imagination. Sometimes, Jane's brother Bill would come up with his family from the Bronx - it was like a big jamboree.

All the grown-ups would have a wild time on Friday and Saturday. They'd be carrying on, cutting up while they were pouring a patio slab or framing an addition on another
shack, and drinking beer as stuff got built. When they'd run out of brew, we all piled into Mack's truck to make the beer run to the general store. Mack, Uncle Bill, and Hal were up
front and all us kids rode on the Ford's tailgate: Allison, me, cousin Billy, and Ray.

Mack would call to us in the back, "Comin' up to a big dip - Hang on!" All us kids would lock arms. Allison always locked my arm real tight and made sure whoever was on
my other arm that it was as tight as hers. Ally knew all the dips because she lived up there.

"Here it comes!" she screeched, as we experienced the roller coaster effect of the accelerated drop.

It was always better when Jane's brother Bill came up with Aunt Frances and Cousin Billy. He was the same age as Ray; the two of them were like a brain trust. Whatever either one set their mind to accomplish, they could achieve. They were dialed into something that made them smart.

A trail of empties sailed overhead and danced on the tar-sealed dirt road until we pulled into Mack's wide driveway.

HAL HAD BEEN AN ONLY CHILD. LITTLE GERTIE WAS the only cousin Hal had that we knew of. Grandpa Helmut, had 11 brothers and sisters. Nana had one brother and sister. From all those relatives - there were only two first cousins: Hal and Gertie on the Whitelaw side. On Hal's mother's side, he was the only offspring. Hal's parents' apartment was a most lonely place. When Ray wasn't there, I was biting my nails most of the day.

The disparities of the two sets of grandparents could not be more striking. With the experience of parenthood, it is obvious that the eldest might receive preferential considerations over younger siblings. It is simply easier to communicate with the one that is more intellectually developed.

This was the case as far as Ray and me were concerned. Every year his brain power seemed to increase exponentially, compared to mine. Hal and Jane had instructed Ray until about the 3rd grade, after that he never asked for anything other than money or permission. By the time I reached the fourth or fifth grade, I threw in the towel; his superior intellect made me look even dumber than I might have been. I wasn't fool enough to envy or be jealous of him. In turn, he tutored me in schoolwork as well as life. The difference this made, allowed me to pass for being smart or at least sly.

Early on, many people inquired whether we were twins from the time I started walking until Ray started going through the change of adolescence. Jane had dressed us as twins. The twins disguise worked even though Ray was older than me. Ray wasn't short - I was tall - and we stayed in step at roughly the same height until his puberty phase kicked in. Our eyes were blue (his could hypnotize a charging tiger). My brown hair was slightly lighter than his, and our facial features and construction were cast from the same mold. Our physical traits said: 'DUPLICATES'. When it was my turn to let the genetic code do its thing; the transformation from boy to man - it would leave us only brothers.

Not only were the physical similarities cast aside, but also the meta-physical. He had something else going on - it was more than brain power. Ray saw it all; but he always brought me along, he never left me out or behind.

THIS TWINS BUSINESS INTRIGUED BOTH OF US UNTIL spuberty made the subject academic. Somehow, someway - good old Dad might validate the code or give us an explanation to satisfy our curiosities. We were tired of strangers asking the question.

"Hey Dad, are we twins? We asked over and over.

"Well without getting into the mechanics of it....." He already had me confused, so I'd just defer to Ray's interpretation of Hal's answer. ".........Hey, we don't want to give away all of Mr. Stork's trade secrets." he laughed over to Jane.

"In a manner of speaking - yes you are twins....but not in the conventional sense."

Watching Ray concentrate on Hal's answer, I could see he really was interested in his explanation how we had come to look so much alike.

"Now you guys know that one twin is always older than the other – both are never born at exactly the same moment. The big difference with you guys is that instead of being born 18 minutes

29

apart.....you are more like 18 months apart. Twins through and through." Hal's chin went up and nodded.

Like so much of the other crap you hear as a kid, this was just some more to log in our memory banks. Hal was an enigma to all four of us kids and to Jane as well - most likely. The more time we spent with Hal, the more we began to see there was no master plan up his sleeve, we were just a bunch of random kids that came along. I didn't take him at face value, but compared him to other kids' fathers - maybe he was just a goof like me. Ray withheld his evaluation until we were older.

I asked Ray, "Why do we have to spend Saturday's and some weekends with Nana and Grandpa?"

Hal was on salary for Otis Elevator; once in a while he had to work a Saturday, but not too often. He'd usually collect us from his parents around 4 pm., and we'd drive over to one of three of his watering holes before we would pick up Jane from her Dance studio. Ray and me would be shown over to a table or a booth with a couple of 7-ups. He'd also give us some dimes from his bar change to play shuffle bowl, an arcade baseball game, a pinball machine, or the juke box. He'd return to the bar dishing out or listening to some bullcrap. Occasionally, a sweet smelling barfly would sit with us and ask: "Don't you boys have a mommy.?"

Ray didn't answer, but I had to: "She's at work. She's a dancing school teacher."

The barfly looked over towards Hal to see if he was looking at her. "Hal, am I seeing double? These two brats of yours......they twins?" Hal waved her off and went back to his drink and the guys at the bar.

Our parents knew a lot of people. There was a continual parade of strangers and new acquaintances. They all gave Ray and me the once over; then they looked at Hal and Jane, then back to me and Ray.

I asked Ray about these visual interrogations: "Why do these people always look at us?"

"I think, they think they know us."

"Do they?" I took a sip of soda.

"Nah."

It wasn't bad when another kid stared; because you could give it right back to him. What I didn't like was that probing gaze from the adults. Being so young I didn't know what they were up to, but it felt weird. It made me scared. Every time we moved it started the process all over again. One of the major advantages of being mistaken as twins was that guys who wanted to initiate us into the new neighborhood knew they'd have to scrap with both of us. Ray explained: "People will always be checking us out; even when we're apart."

It made me think about how difficult it must have been for Hal being an only child. Once in a while, we'd catch him talking to the T.V. or radio. Ray would motion with his finger over his lips: "Shsssssh." And we'd listen.

Years later, Ray and me talked about Hal's proclivity to talk to himself. It may have been in part due to his being an only child that made him so oblique. He was a "mystery man." the more we dug to discover the nature of the mystery, the more opaque the reasons for his actions became. I never caught up with deciphering Hal's principles and goals. He was an enigma to the whole family. My brother cautioned against investigating stuff that was better off being left alone. Sometimes we could understand the motives for the verbal and physical abuse that he occasionally doled out. The time he caught me mixing bleach with ammonia to create a chemical reaction in the kitchen sink had earned me a number of welts from his leather strap. The punishment seemed about right.

Much of the verbal abuse was alcohol inspired, and we all got our share of his nonsense. Things did change when Ray was a sophomore and I was a freshman. We were too big, fast, and smart to take his crap. He started leaving us alone and concentrated his assaults on Jane, Cathy, and Willis. Ray thought the Vietnam conflict had spooked Hal, to the point he may have begun to believe we both would be drafted and on our way there in a few short years. Every week, the networks and the newspapers reported the box scores of the killed, wounded, and missing of the U.S., ARVN, NVA, & the Viet Cong. Those numbers really disturbed Hal, and just as LBJ sent more combatants to S.E. Asia, Dad sent more whiskey to his liver. The draft was coming with no end in sight; but that was still four or five years away for Ray.

Other school mates had these amazing dads who were always happy, and their sons seemed to have inherited the trait. These fathers took on most of the coaching chores for school athletics and the boys clubs.

Ray came home after baseball practice and beamed: "Billy Peel taught me how to throw a curve."

Hal overheard Ray's claim and came out of his den, "Okay Bob Gibson, let's see your curveball.

We went down to Henry Hudson Park. "Ryan, you're catching." He got behind me like an umpire. Ray wound up and turned it over. It must have broke about a foot and landed right in my glove.

"You gotta be kidding me boy." Hal said, "You're gonna screw up your elbow if you throw it like that."

I doubted that Hal had ever thrown a curveball himself; and here he was trying to bullshit us in the mechanics of pitching. We listened to him, but everything he had Ray try never came close to that first pitch Ray hurled. It'd have been bad if Hal volunteered to coach a sport. The guys on the team knew when a coach didn't have the command of the sport or the respect of the team. Still, Ray and me wanted our teammates to see our old man coach a bunch of ball players to prove we weren't a couple of jerk-offs descending from a line of idiots with the same last name.

A vibe ran through the coaches that had been in WW II and Korea: this civilian life wasn't that urgent or critical. Kids playing baseball? Who cared who won the game? Just be grateful that you had food to eat, clean water, and weren't living in a gulag, or a bombed-out basement.

Hal had been assigned to fight the Japs in the Pacific theatre of WW II. Hal's allegiance to America wasn't in doubt; still, the government thought: "Why take chances?" The government had felt reassured with him fighting Tojo - just in case. He signed up for the Submarine Service, as Grandpa Helmut had advised. The 3 subs he had been assigned to had torpedoed 12 freighters and tankers, a light cruiser, and 3 destroyer escorts. They also sent 10 or so ships into dry dock to be repaired. Once in a while, Hal's photos came out when there was a get together over our house. Mack, Uncle Bill, and Hal had all served in the Navy. Jane's blood father, Bill Hicock, also served in the Pacific, but we rarely saw him.

Ray and me went through these photo albums. It seemed he went through a lot of schooling to be a submariner. There were graduation pictures of him with 45 other recruits from Dartmouth College, Groton Conn., and the San Diego Naval Base. There were also photos of him in Honolulu, Darwin Australia, the Philippines, and Japan. Many of these photos should have been censored. He was an excellent photographer; with the right connections he might have gotten an assignment with the O.S.S. (the forerunner of the C.I.A.).

He seldom discussed his combat experiences; the exception being when he was amongst veteran family members. There were a few photos that he had had enlarged. They were the shots of the crews of the subs he had served on, with the conning towers as the back drops. On each of the conning towers were painted the flags of their kills. The flags of the Japanese Imperial Navy with rays from their rising sun had a deep satisfaction for all Navy sailors knowing they had killed those who wanted to kill them.

Early, before Hal woke up, Ray and me went through his Navy albums cover to cover, when they had been left out. The older we got the less we saw of them. The pages were made of some kind of black felt, and he had captions in white ink. There were pictures of ship mates, him in whites and blues, rows of submarines, various ships in tow to be repaired in dry dock, native peoples etc. One of the ships in tow was a heavy cruiser; it had been in an engagement. The photograph had been enlarged. Besides the holes made in the turret guns, bridge, and stacks; when the Japs ran out of bombs, they resorted to their Kamikaze tactics. We just kept staring at the ship wondering how it stayed afloat and knowing many had died in the battle.

When Ray was 12 and I was 11, it suddenly hit me: my grandparents gave Hal permission to enlist at the age of 17. He was their only child. The possibility that he would not return was multiplied when he chose to serve below the

sea. Not even the airmen on daylight bombing runs over Germany had a higher mortality rate than the submariners. Hal was aware of the statistics, but was confident he could
deal with the depth charges, strafing by the Japanese air force, and the intense periods of activity: chasing and being chased by enemy ships and aircraft. He was an electrician's mate.

We'd bug him ad nauseam about WW II. He'd tell us to ask Mack or Uncle Bill, or the grandfather who we didn't see much. In the rare instance when Hal did reply, he'd acknowledge that he had been in action. Perhaps there was more information to be had; I pointed to a fellow seaman he was in a photo with and inquire: "Hey Dad, what about this guy?"

"Yeah, that was Shorty." He made a tight lipped wince. "Yeah, Shorty didn't make it back. He got sent over to
another sub, and the Jappers sunk 'em. He was a good guy."

"But you made it back Dad." we smiled.

He looked through us with a faint grin and returned the albums to the closet.

vii

Sundays were the only time our family of four were together; even then me and Ray were sent out to play, or if it was cold and/or wet we'd get sent to the movies. Sometimes, a whole gang of us from the building walked down Yonkers Ave. to the Kimball theatre. The Kimball marquee was within eyeshot of our apartment building; it was pretty easy for Hal or Jane to walk us there and have the afternoon for themselves.

Winter and rainy Sundays would send us to the movies. It became routine; they even had us going on our own after six or seven times. Jane gave Ray a dime to call her from the lobby to let her know we had made it. In the beginning, Ray had to have the usher dial for us, but in a few weeks Ray stood on the booth's seat and made his own call.

Too often they'd send us to something dumb like "Peyton Place", but the second feature was usually a western, sci-fi, or war movie.

"How was that 'Peyton Place' guys?" Hal asked.

Ray looked away, "If a movie isn't any good, why do we have to stay and watch it? That movie was a dud."

"How was the second feature?" Jane asked.

"Real swell – "The Blob." Ray answered. "There wasn't any action in that "Peyton Place" movie.

" A real dud Dad" I chimed..

Hal tilted his head, "You're kidding?"

"No battle scenes – a bunch of girls crying, judges, and kissing."

Jane chuckled and Hal put on a perplexed look: "Hmmm."

The Sunday movies continued as long as the weather was bad. We saw 'The Alamo' twice. Everybody from the apartment was

33

there, grown-ups too. We got yelled at by the Super for reenacting its battle scenes in the apartment house lobby and causing a ruckus. Kevin Kutmuller's father said the kids didn't have anywhere to play cause of the cold. The Super shot back that he should buy his kids some warmer clothes.

When it did finally get warm we must have played "Alamo" 20 or more times until we played it out, especially the final assault. We had to switch to some other movie. "Prince Valiant" was a 2nd feature flick. It was a real good movie for us; all you needed was a stick and a garbage can lid. I kept thinking about Janet Leigh in that duchess outfit. Now that was a pair of missile tits. There were plenty of Jap movies too: Godzilla, Mothra, Gidrah. The best films were the World War II flicks. A lot of the time, Ray and me thought the bad movie was the good one.

One Sunday, they sent us to see "Gone With The Wind".
"What's playing with it Dad?" Ray asked.
"It's so good, it doesn't need a second feature. You remember "Ben-Hur"?.......same deal.......and you guys liked "Ben-Hur".......remember the chariot race"?
"Yeah.....that was keen." His face replayed the scene.
"A lot of people think that "Gone With The Wind" is the greatest movie of all time – even better than "Ben-Hur".
We got down to the Kimball straightaway and checked out the movie's posters and still photos in the cases in front of the theatre. There were a lot of women – not a good sign. There were some Civil War soldiers, but the best indicator of all – there was this town square full of dead Johnny Rebs. They had to have a gigantic battle showing how these Rebs got killed. Hal had said there was plenty of action mostly towards the end of the film, and that's where the Bluebellies finally win with General Sherman taking Atlanta.
In we went, things started off pretty good with a Confederate Bugs Bunny and a Union Daffy Duck going at it. The way they wound us up with the cartoon, we were sure the movie was going to be a real barnburner.
Four hours later we came home as defeated as those rebels in the city square.
"That movie was horrible." Ray exhaled. He was as beat as Ashley coming home to Tara.
"Terrible." I echoed.
"Just a bunch of dead rebels laying in the road....a couple of canons, and a big fire – Horrible." Ray was lost as he gazed out the window.
"Didn't they say it was the best movie ever made?" Hal looked to Mom for endorsement.
"I loved it."
"The Alamo" was much.....much better. Davey Crockett, Jim Bowie." Ray was disappointed his father would think "Gone With The Wind" was a good movie.

"It's a movie for girls." Ray shook his head, and gave it a thumbs down just like Caesar at the Coliseum in 'Demetrious and The Gladiators.'

"How 'bout it Sammy – you liked it?" he asked.

Every once in a while Hal gave me the moniker "Sammy/Sammy Bones. I have no idea what its origin was, but I believe it to have been his way of cajoling me, or trying to be nice.

I was having none of it though, I fell into lockstep with Ray. I folded my arms and shook my head: "Terrible."

Hal returned to his original premise, this time with a raised brow, "They said, 'The best ever'…"

We stood shoulder to shoulder shaking our heads in unison refuting any further defense of this dud of a movie. Jane's eyes were watering as she sneaked a laugh and quickly turned away.

Hal offered the bewildered look: "Hmmmm."

AT THE AGE OF FIVE THERE IS A LOT OF GUESSING going on. All one can do is be a pain in the ass and ask questions as fast as a 30 cal. machine gun. I didn't know how to read or write; so books, magazines, and newspapers were useless unless they had pictures. Ninety-eight percent of the knowledge I acquired was visual, auditory, and through experience. I did a lot of people watching. I watched them on their stoops, at the bus stop, in their cars, and just getting on with life. It wasn't a revelation, but a lot of these people were doing a lot of kissing and necking.

Most veterans were lucky and returned from WW II and Korea to their sex-starved, love-starved, companion starved women. Both had gone without, and were ready to be complete again………..and resume where they had left off.

Much of America was making up and making out for lost time; time that had been stolen by the evil wars. When Kennedy got elected, the victory celebration for WW II and Korea was at its zenith, and the clock was soon to strike midnight on Bourbon Street and the party would be over.

When Jane and Hal were happy, we were reassured that everything was alright and we could be happy as well. It made us unaware; we were going with the flow. It was a positive force.

The Whitelaw's came off as normal to most people we came into contact with. Like so many others, Hal and Jane were falling for that Madison Ave. rat race crap. The submarine service had taught Hal to turn it on when the klaxons sounded, and waste was a sin. At the time, Jane thought she was ahead of the curve with Hal as her life partner.

While we lived at 2 Vernon Place, Jane was still flirting with Hal. She could do it simply with the clothes she'd choose, her hairstyle, fragrances, or the way she'd use her make-up or any combination of a woman's attractions. Jane and her girlfriends knew they only had to dress a certain way to get a reaction from their men. It was a different matter if Jane was preoccupied; the last thing she wanted was his amorous attention.

Once, he slapped her ass when she was bent over as she checked the pork chops in the oven. Mom had put on a pair of tight pink Capri slacks that day, and the optics of her pink bum overcame Hal's civility..........."WHACK" ! A pork chop hit the ceiling. The contact between his hand and her ass had put out a shockwave. Ray ran into the kitchen to investigate; I was already laughing. Jane stood, turned, and rubbed her stinging butt. She let loose a venomous verbal barrage and she had me convinced she was fluent in some foreign language. The Ol' Man stood there laughing as well, looking like he had done something really neat.

"You Fuckin' Asshole"!!!

I didn't know what she said, but I knew it was devil talk. I was sure glad I didn't get smacked like that cause it would have launched me into the next room.

Later on when things had calmed down, Ray and me went outside to play in the back lot. "Ray?" I said.

"Yeah?"

"How come Mom smiles when he spanks her on the hiney?"

"I think he spanked her too hard this time." He nodded up and down. "She was mad.....real mad."

"I think so too. But it was funny."

"Ryan.....she was so angry she was cursing Dad." Ray let out with a 'Holy Mackerel' whistle.

"That's cursing?"

"Just don't tell anybody."

The scene replayed in my mind, "Wow Mom cursed Dad."

"No......Mom cursed out Dad. She's not a witch you dumbbell."

I guess it was a matter of degree; Dad could give Mom's bum a slap and she'd smile and call him "Honey"; a big whack on Mom's butt – that would get you cursed.

THE NEXT SUNDAY STINKER CAME IN EARLY MAY WITH thunderstorms predicted throughout the day. We were summarily sent to the Kimball double matinee: an Elizabeth Taylor extravaganza-spectacular *"Butterfield 8" and "Cat On a Hot Tin Roof"*.

Ray had this one scoped out earlier in the week, and knew we'd be better off playing with my Fort Apache set, or even spending the day at Nana and Grandpa's. Anything was better than sitting through another love melodrama. He asked, "Hey Dad – what's this movie about?"

"Not too sure.......How 'bout it Janie?" Hal looked over his Sunday paper.

"Liz Taylor's in it." she reported as if that was her seal of approval.

"Who's she?" Ray smelled rat. When a woman gets top billing....I read Ray's face, and saw his antennae circling.

It was Jane's turn to carry the ball and sell these Liz Taylor movies to us. "Remember that movie on TV about the girl jockey that won the big race. Mickey Rooney was in it."

His face soured....."Her?"

Hal sensed the impending trouble with Ray. He reported the movie times anyway: 'Butterfield 8' – 12:30. 'Hot Tin Roof' – 2:30" Hal looked over the casts, "Hey you know who else is in it?"

"Santa Claus." My brother took a deep breath for both of us.

Hal didn't miss a beat, "No.........even better."

"Who could beat Santa?' I wondered.

Ray kept shooting his six-shooter at the imaginary bandits as they rode by, "How about the Easter
Bunny?"

"No better!" Hal flashed his gold tooth.

"Elvis Presley." Ray emphasized the last syllable.

"You guys aren't going to believe this.........Laurence Harvey...ha-hah."

"He's so good, so suave." Jane said. "I didn't know he was in it. I wouldn't mind seeing the movie myself."

"You'll see 'Butterfield 8' soon enough." Hal assured her.

"If Mr. Seagrams shows up again, I bet I only see Butterfield '4'." She grinned.

"I'm pretty sure Mr. Seagrams doesn't show up until the boys come back from the show."

She turned to us, "You guys don't want to miss the coming attractions." Jane handed us our baseball hats and movie money.

Hal called to Ray as we were almost out the door; and dropped two quarters into his hands.

Two quarters? I knew something wasn't right, and so did Ray. This 'Butterfield 8' must be a dud for Hal to give us fifty cents for treats. Ray figured we'd be going to this movie one way or another. As kids we really had no say in the matter.
Still, Ray had to let Hal know where he stood: "I don't want to see another horse movie.......especially with that girl.

"Yeah - no races." I frowned.

"You boys don't want to miss the cartoons." Jane said from our hallway."

Still at the doorway Hal said, "It's not a movie about a horse race."

"But it's not a war movie." Ray squinted.

"Remember the Alamo?"

No way this movie could touch 'The Alamo'. It had to have some tie-in. They just wouldn't outright lie to us?

"Do you recall that Col. Will Travis?" Hal asked.

Simultaneously: "Yeah?"

"Well in this 'Butterfield 8' he doesn't die.

Ray did not want to go to the Kimball, but I had enough arguing between Ray and Hal. The dialogue continued: "No cowboys, no Indians, no Romans, pirates, knights, Japs, Krauts, or Johnny Rebs.......who are the bad guys? What kind of movie is this Dad?"

The candy was the grease to get us on our way, but he still had to get us inside the Kimball Theatre.

"I'm sure you guys heard of the "rackets?""

"Like when me and Ray are jumping on the beds?"

"No...no...no..."The Rackets" – criminals......gangsters."

There was no response.

"You know........'Elliott Ness' – 'The Untouchables'. Hal rolled his eyes in frustration.

"You never let us watch that show Dad."

"But you know what it's about - Cops and robbers; being a criminal for a living....that's what she does. The girl who rode the horse; she's a crook."

"An under the covers crook." Jane called over Hal's shoulder.

"That's what she is." Hal laughed, "An undercover crook....a spy you might say."

"So the woman's a spy now?" Ray raised his brow and scratched his head.

"You gotta see the movie......" Hal doubled down: "It'll knock your socks off boys." Down the stairs we went.

After an hour of torture, Ray had enough.

"I'm leaving."

"Why?"

"We're out of Good & Plenty, and this movie stinks."

"It's okay....I like it." I said.

"Ryan, I'd rather watch Rocky and Bullwinkle, see you home."

He was talking to himself before he entered the lobby and probably the whole way to our apartment.

Ray returned to the theatre about 20 minutes later, 'Butterfield 8' was almost over. "Dad's supposed to come down and get us. He slumped into the seat next to me. A public service announcement came on about getting to an air raid shelter if the Russians launched some missiles at us.

"What happened Ray?"

"I went upstairs and rang the bell. Mom answered.....in her nightgown. She looked at me all alone and asked where you were. I told her that you were still down here. Then she went kind of wild and let me have it: "You never...never..... NEVER leave your brother!"

"You know your way home Ryan, I didn't think Mom would yell at me so bad. She was really worked up, I don't think she realized that I could almost see through her night gown." Ray was thinking about what he saw.

"Huh? She was wearing what?" I blinked at least three times. "Woooooowah. Was she wearing pajamas?"

"No, but it's what women wear to bed."

I looked at my brother – confused. "Grown-ups don't take naps."

A Woody Woodpecker cartoon came on and we watched that. Then we suffered through the second feature. Liz Taylor looked better in 'Butterfield 8'. The other movie just dragged on and on. Hal never did show up.

We rang the doorbell and marched in. I saw a whispy nightgown and a short see-thru nightie on the trail to their bedroom. They were in bed smoking away. Each had a drink on their night tables, their backs rested against the headboard, a chenille bedspread covered them. Jane was smiling and asked about the movie.

"You boys go to your room, I'm going to change." Jane said.

A couple of minutes later, Hal visited us, "Really – man to man, how were the movies guys?"

"Ryan liked her. Ffffft." Ray scoffed.

Maybe Ray didn't care for Liz Taylor, but I was mesmerized by her facial perfection and her big milkers. I wanted to kiss her and squeeze them.

"That Elizabeth Taylor is all grown up now, and she wasn't any gangster in the movie. She was always in bed, or at a bar, or on the phone. I never thought I'd say it, but even that 'Gone With The Wind' was better." Ray shrugged.

"Well that's because 'Gone With The Wind' is without a doubt the greatest movie ever made. Hal crossed his arms and rested them on his chest.

Mom walked in and looked over towards Hal.

"I think the kid liked 'Butterfield 8'. He smiled.

"She was pretty." I said.

"She was pretty dumb........like the movie." Ray went into the bathroom and locked the door. He didn't speak to Hal for the whole week.

CHAPTER 3

"Remember when Uncle Jack would break out his guitar or accordion at picnics or parties?" Ray said.

"Yeah, we'd all sing along."

You could listen to that stuff up until you were around in …..the 5th grade?" Now you're a 9th grader and his stuff doesn't sound so good." Ray said.

"Why is that?"

"Advancement in sound, taste, the evolution of music - all contribute. Used to be, the only people who knew how to play a guitar had one, but everybody has a record player these days." Ray explained. "Stacks of records increased the variety of music, and it sounds better than when Uncle Jack plays and sings."

He was right: The Dee-Jay might get drunk, but the Victrola didn't. Jane and Hal knew high fidelity sound was here to stay, but they didn't think rock and roll was.

World War II and The Depression had irrevocably shaped the way Hal and Jane reacted to daily life; both events were part of their psyche. In an insidious manner, technological leaps forward would play a greater role in their lives than the man-made events such as war and economic upheaval. More than temporal and generational, these occurrences of technological leaps forward were actually incremental shifts in dimension and magnetic revision. Ignored, unnoticed, dismissed, by the preceding generation; realization comes only to a small minority with a price. Perhaps that movie 'Gone With The Wind' wasn't as dumb as I thought. The movie said: "That Was Then – This Is Now – ADAPT!" It was a tough nut for me to crack, but I believe I got a piece of what Ray was trying to impart to me.

Nevertheless, our parents felt the war and the depression had stolen their youth…their teenage years. Following the war, Jane went back to her roots – dancing. With dance, she could try to retrieve that positive vibe. Broadway musicals, dreams of being a "Radio City Rockette", and The Jane Marlowe Dance Studio helped keep her aspirations intact. At parties with friends, she'd breakout with a soft shoe number as the music played: a High Ball in one hand and a cigarette in the other, dancing to the music. Her face registered: FUN !

Hal could only slow dance with Jane; cheek to cheek stuff. She wanted to fast dance with him, but he had caught some shrapnel in his right leg when his submarine's 5 in. deck gun sank a Jap freighter and some of the topside crew had gotten hit with the debris.

After three tries to get Hal to learn a couple of mixed duo routines with her; something that looked sharp…..professional, something to set the dance floor ablaze; she threw in the towel. It wasn't there – he didn't have "it". There still was metal hardware and a stainless rod in his leg, not to mention that his right leg would forever be an inch-and-a-half shorter than his left. Hal gave Jane his best effort to be her Fred Astaire, but it always looked like she was dancing with a guy with a bum leg.

By the time Ray and me came on the scene, the discord had already taken root and reinforced Hal's conviction about this dancing business being a diabolical plan to corrupt Jane and the marriage. Anything associated with entertainment would light his fuse. There always were a lot of people involved with her school, shows, musicals; they were predominately attended by women; but there was a fair amount of guys interested, and they were all attracted to Jane - both straight and gay. It was the pursuit of her art where the jealousy and envy took seed. For her - it was a gift. For him – it was poison.

ii

Our mother was a very good dancer. She was an exceptional tap dancer. Ray and me could see what it did for girls who took lessons; but we also realized what it did for Jane, aside from providing the family with extra income every week. Jane's interest was contagious. When it came to dancing lessons – she could make them all feel like they were headed for stardom. She had every student and potential student buying into her dreams and fantasies. The newspapers and electronic media were filled with stories about Sputniks, satellites, manned spacecraft, Atlas/Mercury rockets, and associated space travel, but the only Rockettes that interested Jane Marlowe were 'The Radio City Rockettes'.

Dottie (Rusty) Holland had been a lifelong friend. The two had attended Gorton High School and had 'taken' tap dance lessons together as well. They both dreamed about breaking into show business in N.Y.C., and if they could make the right connections – perhaps they'd get into the line at Radio City and high kick the world into ecstasy.

When Jane entered the dream world of dance…..she really let go with her ambitions and desires, she'd look at me and Ray like we should have been sisters or maybe she saw us as girls. She was 'out there' sometimes. Even though Jane never was a 'Rockette', Dottie had made it. Jane would tell us how great it was to be a 'Rockette': "They traveled all over, made a lot of money doing something they loved, lived lives of luxury and fame and met rich men."

"One of these Christmas' or Easters, we'll go to the pageants at Radio City; and after the show – we'll go backstage and you can meet Dottie and The Rockettes."

"Who's Dottie?" Ray asked.

"She's my best friend. She's a Rockette."

"Why aren't you a Rockette Mom?"

"Because I had you fellas." she said.

"Don't Dottie got any kids." I asked.

"Ahhh……not yet."

Radio City……Radio City…….Radio City…….Radio City……I couldn't make the connection. What was the attraction? I'd look at the radio on the kitchen counter; then glance to the television in the living room. Even a television that required continual antenna adjustment to produce a clear picture was cooler than a radio. Radio would just barely hang on until Rock and Roll became a driving force of the Baby Boomer generation. The Boomers reignited radio's appeal with the FM band wave - which carried a stereophonic signal from the station to the dashboard.

iii

Jane took us to the 'Rockette's' Christmas show that year. We met Dottie Holland; with all their make-up and costumes, they all looked the same to us. She came up from Manhattan that summer on the train and got off at Glenwood station to visit her parents and Jane. When Dottie came over, Jane began to debrief her on 'show business'.

"Dottie, it would be a shot in the arm if you and me could put a number together for my next recital. To have a real live 'Rockette' doing a tap routine with the person who owns the studio......well, that's just telling every student and parent: "it can happen." Jane dreamed aloud.

"Plus, you always were a better dancer than me." Dottie admitted. She stared off, "Bankable star talent."

"Hometown gal helped by show biz buddy." They laughed.

Dottie had tried to make Jane's previous two recitals. She wanted to help her friend out. We listened as they gabbed back and forth in the kitchen. I think Ray absorbed much of what they were saying; I only got the obvious stuff. Dottie was almost crying, she felt like she had abandoned Jane by chasing the bright lights. "It's that 'show biz" bug that I can't get rid of."

Jane worshipped the ground Dottie walked on; I didn't understand her dissatisfaction or her inadequate feelings. Dottie returned Jane's envy, thinking Jane was the luckier of the two: "If we only could trade places – just long enough to be sure." Dottie said.

"That we are where we belong?......I think about that sometimes." Jane said.

"I love being a 'Rockette', a professional dancer, and the notoriety. I look at your life and compare the situations. Maybe I've got to get with it if I'm going to have a family." She gazed out the window.

Jane offered her a cigarette, "Be careful what you wish for Rusty........the kids, the studio, Hal -........sometimes I don't know what day it is."

"I've been down the city for three years now, sometimes I feel like I'm getting crushed." She took a Newport from Jane's pack and used it as a pointer before she lit up and went down her list on the imaginary chalkboard. "I love my profession, the glamour, and the opportunities to branch out; but I never thought I'd have to come back to good old Yonkers to catch my breath." It was a moment of reflection for both. "Janie, you know how close Yonkers is to mid-

42

town – 16….17 miles, but it's so backwoods compared to the city -
"It's not even quaint."

"You're right – not much happening here." Jane nodded.

Rusty was about to strike a match, but walked to the screened
window. We watched her scan up and down
the street. She began talking with her back to us, her words were just
loud enough to hear: "Visiting Yonkers is like watching a summer of
television reruns."

Jane raised her voice, she knew she'd have to compete with
the noise from the street, "I don't think about those things too much. I
don't have much time for myself."

Each to her thoughts of the old Dutch city on the Hudson.
The haze and high clouds filtered the sun, the air was stagnant. A fair
amount of ozone was present, and breathing imparted sensations of
panic and entrapment.

The leaves were motionless, Jane asked, "When are you
going back?"

"We've got rehearsal on Monday."

"What about tomorrow?" Mom asked.

Dottie tilted her head and put her top teeth into her bottom lip
in thought. "I told my parents I would take them to lunch, but I can do
that on Saturday. Have you got something in mind?"

"Switch your mom and dad to Saturday, and we'll go to the
beach tomorrow. We'll head out right after the morning rush
hour………just one thing." She hesitated.

Dottie rolled her eyes, then squeezed them tight, "Let's have
it."

"We've got to bring the boys."

"Your boys?" she smiled. "I thought we might have to drag
Hal with us. The kids?............no problem. No Hal………no problem."
They both laughed.

"What beach do you want to go to?"

"Let's go to Long Island." An adventurous smile grew across
the Dottie's face.

"Jones Beach?"

"How 'bout it guys…….you want to go to the beach with
Aunt Dottie?"

Ray and me were all smiles: "Sure."

"Hear anything about the weather?"

"A repeat of today." Jane fanned her face.

"Friday at Jones Beach……..the waves, sand, ocean breeze,
no weekend crowds…….just what I need."

"Me too; even with the boys. Escape for the day."

"Pick you up at 9 o'clock sharp." Dot said; her cigarette
underlining the imaginary get away time.

"You're driving – I'll bring everything else: sandwiches,
snacks, drinks, beach blanket, and towels. Give me a ring if you think
of anything else."

"How about a cooler of lemonade and a thermos of liquid fun
for you and me."

"Can't wait." Jane giggled.

43

Ray helped Mom and Dottie load the car, I wanted to help but mostly got in the way. Dottie had doubled parked her father's '56 Plymouth Belvedere. The dancers were running around the car like a couple of coolies. There wasn't an ounce of fat on either of them. Leather laces tied into four eyelets securing Jane's ankle high sandals. The sole and heel of Dottie's sandals were made of the same piece of cork; the top of her sandal revealed all her toes and a medallion of the French flag with an anchor was sewn into the flat part of the leather. Jane's shorts were soft yellow cotton, with a pleated front and a permanent white macramé belt. Dottie's shorts were white, cuffed, and the waist was cinched by a two inch wide navy-blue belt. There were four inches of elastic fabric centered in the back; the belt was mostly ornamental.

The beach ensemble fashion show continued: A perfectly pressed navy blue seer-sucker blouse with collar and tan buttons looked swell on Dottie. Mom had a tight sleeveless V-neck that was lime green with a royal blue rope protecting the 'V', shoulders, and bottom of her pullover. Their jewelry made their beach statement complete: cloisonné red hoops adorned Rusty's ears, two rings and an expensive looking watch. On her other wrist, she wore a one-inch-wide hammered silver bracelet.

Mom had her engagement and wedding rings, a pair of triangle earrings, (which she later found were made of platinum), and a thin leather banded Timex watch. They knew how to pick and wear sun glasses – they looked like movie stars.

Not many cars were air conditioned in 1959; everyone drove with all the windows down. Dottie wore this Puerta Vallarta hat to keep her hair from getting all tangled up. Jane used this kerchief thing which wrapped around her head, then took two turns around the back of her neck and tied it. She told Dottie she got the idea from Audrey Hepburn in some fashion magazine. Dottie and Jane were blessed with tons of hair. It was the reason her close friends would call her "Rusty". They were more than ready for the Jones Beach. Except for Ray and me, they could have walked from the beach in Monaco to the casino in Monte Carlo.

The '56 Plymouth was yellow. A strip of horizontal chrome divided door panels. The top half was white to the tail section of the car, along with its roof which also was white. The paint job looked sharp. The doors, trunk, hood, and bumpers were trimmed with chrome accenting from Plymouth. It had enough, but it wasn't a Chrysler. The interior was a light gray and the seats were beige. It was one of the first automatic transmission cars I remembered. Mom always made it a point to tell the driver, "Oh I see you have an automatic." She didn't like that clutch; she thought it made a woman look like a truck driver or a farm girl. She also was sold on power steering. These two automotive advances could make city driving a whole lot easier and safer she'd tell us, especially with me and Ray fighting in the back seat.

No one looked at the car when Dottie and Jane were in the front seat motoring around in the Belvedere. On our way to Long

Island, they smiled at us and each other. They sang along with the radio's dual speakers: one in the front – the other in the back. When Dottie drove the Plymouth, Oldsmobile surrendered any claim to having "rocket powered" cars. This 301, V-8 was "Rockette" powered under the hood and behind the wheel.

Ray and me got in the 2-door. What a difference between this and Hal's 1955 2-door Bel Air station wagon. Doing two hours in the Chevy was an endurance test for all the riders, but it had to be worse for the driver, especially in the metro area.

Dottie Holland was pretty busy looking in the mirrors. The Plymouth was so smooth, it gave Jane and Dot time to talk about other things; the ride to Jones Beach was a minor inconvenience.

Jane did a double-take at her friend as they drove south on the Hutchinson River Parkway through the Bronx. "Hey Girl", she lowered her sunglasses to the end of her nose and looked over them."

"Hey yourself." She had a great big smile.

"Let's see Rusty.........come on – turn towards me." Jane said with her radar activated.

Ray and me watched Jane, but she wasn't talking to us.

"What's with this new lipstick?..........A special play?.....or a request from a new guy?"

Jane almost put her face between the steering wheel and Dottie.

"Jaaaaane……..!" she laughed.

Mom went back to her co-pilot seat, "What color is that? C'mon Russ, let me see. You didn't have that on when we left."

"I put it on when you were looking for change at the toll."

"Look at me so I can see your mouth." The words came slowly as she decided. "That really looks good." she said.

"Vamp………not tramp?" she gripped the wheel.

"Double-vamp." Jane's seal of approval meant this make-up was ready for after dark activities. It was different than what most women wore.

Since WWII, or even before, lipstick style had been that loud 'stop sign red' crap. Alfred Hitchcock's female leads had a style apart from other Hollywood directors. It slowly took hold on the east coast, or maybe it came from the fashion houses on the continent. With hair similar in shade to Myrna Loy or Gloria Grahame, Rusty couldn't use what a blonde, brunette, or a vibrant redhead would apply on her lips. She knew the heavy red lipstick made her look like a barfly - eight years older than she was. What she had on that day was a pale pink shade that had a gloss to it.

"Where can I get it?" Jane asked.

"It's in my handbag – in a plastic screw tube without any labels." She went through Rusty's handbag like a customs agent. "I was doing a walk-on for a television soap; the make-up artist put it on. We both knew it was the right lipstick. Try it Jane, our hair color's close…….I think it will work for you."

The three of us examined the tube of pale pink gloss. Jane's eyes got wide and she smiled. "It's so……so……avant- garde?" She tilted her head.

45

"That hard red doesn't work for me, but on stage - we have to wear it. In the 10ᵗʰ row, they wouldn't know you had a mouth if you didn't have the red. This is softer............ more natural, the color takes the contrast off my teeth."

Jane rifled through her purse for a personal sized pack of tissues to remove the standard red lipstick. She watched in her compact mirror as she applied Rusty's shade. The compact mirror being too small, mom stuck her head out the window and got the view she wanted from the door's larger side view mirror. "Oh yeah." She turned and sat perpendicular to Dot.

Dottie Holland signaled into the gator lane and gave Jane her opinion: "Janie, you bring the corners of your eyes out...... and I don't know how you'll be able to fight them off."

"Our hair color is close, but you're so much fairer than me." Jane said.

Rusty took one more good look at mom, "This lipstick will work fine during the day, but just one shade darker at night." Dottie sped back into the hammer lane.

She asked over the bench seat: "How do you guys like Mommy's new lipstick?"

"Keen." Ray marveled.

"Neat-o. Keen-o." I echoed.

iv

It had been a beautiful day at the beach for all of us. Dottie had rubbed baby oil all over Ray and me to get a better tan and so our skin wouldn't dry out. At that point, I thought getting the oil rub from Dottie was the highpoint of my day at the beach.

"It was almost 3 o'clock. If we're going to beat rush hour we've got to leave now." Jane said.

Waaaaaaaaaaaaaaa!!!!! An air horn blast from a semi-tractor trailer trying to merge onto the Clearview from the Long Island Expressway nearly made Rusty's parents' Plymouth the meat in the 18 wheeler sandwich as another semi squeezed us from the opposite side. The two truckers saw the Dottie and Mom and made a duet of their thunderous air horns; they laughed as Dottie's head ratcheted from side to side of the Belvedere. We were trying to get to the Throggs Neck Bridge which would take us from Queens to the Bronx. The trucker threw her a courtesy bird. Dottie let off the gas.

"That dirty motherfucker's laughing!........He scared the piss out of me." Rusty tried to get her heart to slow down as she reduced the car's speed.

"Hate to see what rush hour's like........Dottie watch the cursing - huh?" Jane took a deep diesel saturated breath.
"It wasn't like this when we drove down, now it's like the Indy 500." Jane was nervous.

"The sonofabitch behind me is right on my bumper..." She watched him in her rear view mirror for just a second.

It was high speed insanity, all four lanes were 10 m.p.h. over the limit, and cars were darting in and out. A dude on a Harley was passing traffic on the shoulder. It went on like that for three or four minutes; then a field of red brake lights appeared ahead in an instant. Rusty 'locked em up' as the Belvedere's rear end tried to come around. Ray and me were tossed around like the last two pills in a prescription bottle.

The ass end of the car fishtailed out of lane. She had managed to escape an impact and screeched her parents' car to a stop a foot short of the car in front of the Plymouth.

Surrounded by vehicles, most of whom experienced similar difficulties in bringing their cars to a stop, Jane unlocked her stiff arms from the dashboard.

"What the................." Jane slumped in the seat.

"Damn it.........damn." Dottie's hands dropped from the steering wheel. Her sunglasses were askew, but they had managed to stay on and hid her terror.

"You guys alright? Let me see you." Jane was worried. There was no thought, she was operating on instinct alone.

"I smashed my head on top of your seat. Ray replied. There's a piece of steel on top. It's in the seat....the steel is."

Jane examined Ray's noggin. "How about you little guy?"

"Did we have an accident?"

"That fuckin' Chevy almost wrecked us." Her eyes squinted "revenge".

"Dottie!" Mom raised her voice. "Watch the language – Please......"

There weren't any seat belts back then. Me or Ray could have gotten launched right out the window in a minor impact or a quick evasive maneuver. Dottie looked at me in the rear view mirror. I was next to Ray.

"Ryan, don't you like me any more?"

"Sure – I like you." I said.

"Well get behind me when I'm driving where I can keep my eye on you." she said.

I went right behind her right ear. "You mean like this?"

"That'll be fine Honey when traffic starts moving again."

The dancers were baffled by the traffic jam. "I know we left early enough to beat rush hour."

"You leave Jones by three and you're in the Bronx by 3:45." Jane backed her up. "Frickin' parking lot."

WAVES OF HEAT ROSE FROM THE CARS, TRUCKS, AND pavement. There was no breeze to speak of, but I could still smell Rusty through the carbon monoxide, diesel fumes, and the Long Island Sound. Great hair smell. Standing on the floor of the back seat, I got closer to her hair. The strength of her body odor juggled my senses. Behind her ear, I saw two runs of sweat when they broke the hairline; there was a perspiration ring under her armpit as well. She was too good-looking to be sweating I thought. Everyone was rubber necking ahead to see if the traffic was moving as we crept slowly forward. The southbound lanes were empty. My eyes swept over to Dottie's boobs. The sun flooded the front of the car. It was strong enough and at the right angle; it sent a wall of light and heat into the front seat and put Jane and Dottie into some science fiction menopause-like phase. Dottie put her thumb in between two buttons and pumped her blouse in and out to exchange some stale hot air for fresh hot air.

It was almost torrid, and Rusty undid one of the top buttons, and pumped her shirt again as she peered out into the stationary traffic. I saw the left one – nipple and all. It was hot, but that sight stopped me cold. In that instant, I knew why they always had been concealed. Something as kool as that, probably had the power to suspend reality.

If she caught me trying to 'sneak a peek' and complained to Mom, I know I'd end up like St. Joan......burned like a steak. It might even get back to Hal that I was a "Peeping Tom". I'd have to tell Ray about Dottie when we got home, this was just too fantastic.

Crossing my arms on the top of the front seat, I laid my head in them and watched and breathed in my mother's best friend.

"Ryan...Hon... Why don't you sit back with your brother so Dottie can drive?"

I didn't move.

"Ryan..." Mom raised her voice which faded on the second syllable.

"Who knows how long we'll be stuck here." Rusty wiped her brow and looked at me: "You're not bothering me are you Kid-oh?"

Half asleep I replied, "I'm protecting you".

The cars and trucks that shut down their engines, restarted them only to move a few feet forward. The blue and gray exhaust fumes had put us all in some kind of stupor. The sun, ozone, dehydration, and loss of energy from getting bounced around by the ocean's waves left us listless. I was mad at myself because I could not sustain the heightened hypnotic state that Dottie's exposed breast had put me in. My eyes were barely open and drool ran from my mouth.

V

I saw the red lights of the medical apparatus next to the bed. I lifted my head from the pillow for just two seconds and fell back into the pillow. One record finished and was replaced in its slot in the juke box and the next selection was laid on the 45 r.p.m. turntable.

The story resumed at a different point of time. We were teenagers – early teens. Following a couple of relocations within the city of Yonkers, Hal had bought a house in North Yonkers just before J.F.K.'s assassination. Five years later, Bobby Kennedy had gotten gunned down as well.

Unlike the other places we had lived, there was not much residential housing in this neighborhood. The substantial amount of woodland acreage was all privately owned: St. John's Hospital, a small catholic women's college, a private country club and the old Croton aqueduct used to bring drinking water to N.Y.C. were all within a half-mile radius of 21 Odell Ave., our address. These landmarks were up the hill except for the New York Central's Greystone Station; it was down the hill and hugged the shoreline of the Hudson River. There were two six story apartment houses and perhaps 30 – 35 private houses. For that amount of dwellings – there seemed to be a paucity of kids. This area of Yonkers had more woods than I had ever seen, except up at Mom-Mom's and Mack's place upstate.

During the 7th, 8th, and 9th grades, I carried golf clubs with Ray at the Hudson River Country Club until it closed. My brother wasn't on the caddy master's 'shit list' so he had a fair chance in getting out and making a 'loop'. Five times a week he'd wait to get out, and maybe catch a loop twice. The first year I tried caddying was an eye opener for me, I was a caddy of last resort. To emphasize my lack of rank, they would only let me carry one bag. Ray said we all got to pay our dues.

Club code stated 'Caddies had to be at least 14 years old'. Ray started at 12 and I started at 11. I wouldn't be 12 until September. The last year of operation, I was carrying doubles: two bags for 18 holes. The rate at the time was $5/a bag for a 18 hole loop. The best thing about caddying at H.R.C.C. was its proximity to our house. We lived near the bottom of O'Dell Ave, the golf course was at the top of the half-mile switchback hill.

My brother always got out ahead of me; he was better built and more knowledgeable about golf than I was. In 1967, Ray graduated from All Souls Grade School. That summer, many of the guys in Ray's grade started drinking beer and wine to get ready for high school. In my circumstance, it meant I'd start drinking a year ahead of my grade because I always followed Ray's lead.

Sometimes after supper, we'd walk up to the North End and buy a couple of six-packs or two bottles of Bali-Hai. Drinking didn't start for me until after I graduated eighth grade. We might run into some other guys and drink up there or bring it back, and go drinking down the commuter rail station: Greystone. The four tracks were about 60 feet off the east bank of the Hudson.

At first, we'd always bring our fishing gear with us – in case the bulls showed up. The fishing gear only lasted one summer. By the end of the summer we knew all the ins and outs of the station area. If worse came to worse, half the guys took off north and the other half took off south; the cops never could out run us.

A light breeze was trying to push north. The summer day had been a real scorcher, it was hazy and humid to boot. We couldn't wait for the sun to go down; Greystone station was a good place to get screwed up. The wine could only help us forget about the heat of the day. Both of us had twisted paper bags around the bottles of the Bali-Hai quarts. Ray had an additional pint bottle in his back pocket to split just in case.

"Put the pint in the river's sand - it'll stay cooler." I said.

The burial mound was located between the southbound platform and the river's edge. We cracked open the quarts of wine standing on the small, low mound. We toasted with the wine: "Firewater -" I smiled.

"For the Fireball." Ray responded. We each sacrificed the necks of our wine, and poured it on the mound.

Ray wondered: "Joo catch any breeze on the back nine?"

"14ᵗʰ was dead calm – felt like a sauna….Had to be the same when you went through" I took a pull.

"Pretty much. Supposed to be the same tomorrow."

"Too hot to drink beer…..it don't stay cold in this heat. All's it does is give you a headache and make you sweat."

"That's why Rheingold come out with them 'Chug-a-mug' bottles. You can down one three times as fast as a regular bottle, and you can actually get drunk: they stay cold because they're not always in you're hand." he said.

I looked at one of our chug-a-mug empties on the ground and took a sip of Bali-Hai, "The only thing Rheingold messed up was making them big mouth bottles with only ten ounces of beer. ….shoulda made 'em twelves." I said.

"You sure can knock off a six-pack awful quick" he laughed.

"Who'd you have today?" I asked.

"You remember before Cathy was born…..we went to Jones Beach with Mom and her friend Dottie? There was that monster traffic jam…and them two guys…I think they had a Mercury….and beer?" He waited for me to remember.

I squinted and slowly nodded as that day eight years earlier was freed from its shackles in bits and pieces.

What was important to Ray was that we had all maintained our conspiracy of silence and let Jane do all the talking with Hal. He zeroed in on me: "You remember Dottie?" he asked nodding his head.

"Yeah….Dorothy Holland….Rusty…Mom's friend." Her visage flashed as I sawed my bottom lip with the tips of my fingers. "You can't forget a vixen like that. She held all the cards: Beauty, talent, personality. Haven't heard that name in a long time."

"Two years ago, Mom told me that Dottie and this part-time actor were living in Southern California." Ray took a drink.

A tug pulled four barges up the Hudson, "So what?"

"Guess who was in our foursome today Ry?"

"Obviously it was Dottie. What the deuce was she doing at Hudson River?"

We each took a pull.

"How'd she look?" I asked.

"Real good – as good as Mom. When we got home from the golf course, I asked Jane what ever happened to Dottie. She looked around made sure no one else could hear: "She's making dirty movies in L.A. and is a topless dancer in Las Vegas."

"Wow…." I raised my brow. "She didn't know who you were or anything?"

Ray shook his head from side to side, – "Naa, I didn't have Dottie...Loki was on her bag. I had the two guys; Loki had the women. They were the guests of Mike Shea – the lawyer. From their banter, they all started out in Yonkers. I only interacted with the women on the tees and the greens."

"Shea picked up the tab for all four rounds. He's about an eight handicap, the guests were just actors...you can't expect much." Ray shrugged.

"I wonder why she didn't call Mom up, or just to let her know she was in town. You didn't tell Mom that you saw her? They used to be good friends....some weird crap."

"Hooray for Hollywood!" he sang. "Nah, I didn't tell her I saw her."

"Ray, how'd she look?"

"I already told you....doomcuff."

"That ain't telling me nothin'." I waited.

Maybe Ray was making it up or it came to him, "She seemed like she really wasn't all there – you know - preoccupied."

"Not for nothin' but she knows we live right down the street. She sends Jane a Christmas card every year. She knows the address."

I could tell Ray was in deep water with his thoughts: he had his head tilted, squinted, and stroked his jawbone with the outside of his four fingers. "Let's go over to the platform, too many black flies."

He sat on a bench, and I leaned against the handrail. "You know, something's off with that Dottie."

"I know what's right about her." – I smiled.

"Yeah, I know.......her Rockette tits. C'mon Ry, get off it." It was still tough for the both of us to drop the sexual image once it had been brought up.

"Give it a break man. Everything has a sexual connotation with you." Ray pulled down the paper bag to see how much he had left.

"Those are the only missiles that count."

"Only at certain times." he said.

"If I got a hang-up on Rusty's bumpers, then you're equally goo-goo-gaa-gaa on the missile when it crashed from the heavens."

"You know that wasn't a missile."

"Rocket?"

"That wasn't a rocket."

"Asteroid?"

"Too big."

"A chunk of space junk?"

"You seen the piece it spit out....not man-made."

"Comet?"

"Either that or some fireball variant."

"Meteor?"

"It was cooked and fragmented......and the remnant landed on the other side of the tracks"

"Meteorite."

"What's Rusty Holland got to do with the fireball, or the cast-off piece we buried I asked.

"Maybe nothing……..chance occurrence?………doubtful." He slugged some wine down. "There is a cause and effect for everything. Likewise there are positive and negative forces constantly pushing and pulling for domination. There is good and evil…..light and darkness. There is truth and lies."

"And there are freshmen and there are sophomores." I smiled, happy to be going into my freshmen year. I might even pick up the kind of smarts and knowledge Ray exhibited.

He rolled his eyes and shook his head back and forth and lit a cigarette. "Why do some of these space objects make it to earth; while other explode; and some do a little bit of both?"

"Gotta be what they're made of?" We both pondered the variations. "Metals sparkle on entry, rock gets hot like volcanism and explode after entering the atmosphere……… Say - what about that meteor crater in Arizona? I wonder how big that fireball was and what that was made of." I was on a roll.

"The science books all say most objects crashing into the earth aren't big dimensionally, but it's their density and speed with the power to create big holes like the one in the desert 50,000 years ago. When the conditions are right, some of these extra-terrestrial intruders may work in concert with other forces and variables to do the unforeseen and unpredictable."

Ray was on a much larger roll, I kept listening, he hadn't overwhelmed me yet. One thing was for certain: Loki had light duty carrying the ladies' bags in comparison to Ray. Shea and the other guy had two monsta bags; that was the kind of physics I understood.

It had been more than two years since the comet had streaked across the sky and up the Hudson. Ray had been consumed with the phenomenon. Music, girls, school work (except as it related to math and the sciences) went by the wayside. He had what I called 'FIREBALL FEVER'. The intensity of his interest would come and go; but it was always there as an existential part of his being. I figured he'd lose interest at some point, he didn't………he couldn't. In fact it went the other way. Sometimes, he'd give me a full blown lecture about this astrophysics junk. I had to listen until he was done. The stuff was building inside his head; he was using me as his sounding board. There wasn't much choice, I had to listen – I owed him that much. When the diatribes went over 25 minutes I'd tell him I had to take a whizz or something; there wasn't a lot of the long winded stuff, but there was on this night.

That summer the books started to appear: calculus, physics, applied calculus, Newton, Einstein, Kepler, astrophysics, astronomy, chemistry etc. This night down the river he gave me a piece of what he had stored up over the last year of studying.

"Ryan, what I'm talking about is……." He searched the sky and came back. "Man may be able to mutate the events along the continuum…….but not time itself. The transformation of events can only be warped so much before math and science lose their integrity."

"Do you mean like – mankind is saying: one plus one equals four?" I was confused.

"On this planet.......yes." He took a break for some wine but never missed a beat. He ditched the paper bag. "What have I got here?" He displayed the wine as if he was trying to sell it.

"A bottle of Bali-Hai."

"Which is?"

"A buck and a quarter."

"No.....not how much it costs.......what is it?"

I laughed, "A bottle of wine." I shrugged.

"See how you are conditioned? It is NOT fruit of the vine."

"Well it ain't beer neither."

"It is fruit juice with the alcohol pumped into the blend. It is $1+1=3$."

That I understood. "What about 'Ripple'?"

"Same deal."

"Huhh..." I scoffed. I had a difficult time with the simple stuff and tried to look interested with the rest.

Ray pushed on: "If we stay within certain perimeters, and don't get greedy.....or forget our humanity; then timeline events can be retrieved and reset as original timeline truths.

"Was it random the caddy master put Loki on Dottie's bag?" I said.

Ray took out another cigarette. "Are you asking me why she didn't contact Jane? That I cannot answer. Most likely, she thinks she's too good for Yonkers, or she's afraid Mom's got wind of her doing blue movies and topless dancing in Vegas."

"I'd like to catch that show." I pulled a Marlboro from his pack.

"Why is it that two best friends lose touch with each other but still send Christmas cards?"

"Some kind of game we don't understand cause we're not dumb adults. Dottie probably owes Mom money; hell - Mike Reno owes me five bucks, and I don't see him around now either. That crap happens everyday." I leaned up against the handrail and lit up.

"When that fireball entered the earth's atmosphere – whatever distance it traveled, it arrived with a payload of energy which could and did distort time. Although we saw it, it might not be here.....or its energy is here, but not its accumulated ability to alter time. You know one of these days we're going to have to go back into the mound and take a look at it." He nodded towards it.

"That was a lot of work burying it."

"Consider this: If the cohesive properties of time have not been irreversibly tampered with through a synthetic incident then people, places, and events may have been radicalized and thrown out of whack. It'd be like seeing the flash of a 4th of July bomb before the explosion is felt or heard. There is a sound barrier, a light barrier, but I believe there is a time barrier as well, and this cosmic rolling stone has travelled very far and very fast and it may have brought the continuum, to a state of flux.........instability if you like."

"There's a light coming from the north." I said.

"Train." We both watched. Ray was getting close to the bottom of his bottle.

"Eight car commuter express – second track closest to the river - combo/drive."

The train was almost at the north end of the station's platforms. We faced the incoming express; I opened my cut-off dungaree shirt, and Ray tossed his tee shirt to a platform bench. We waited for the train to pass and collect the trailing breeze. Our arms were outstretched as if the rapture had come, hoping for the maximum cooling effect. When there was no more, we watched the red lights fade to the south.

"Any wine left?"

"Just the pint in the river." I said.

"Get it, we'll kill it on the way home."

When I pulled the Bali-Hai from the sand, I took a long look at the mound and thought about the buried piece of cast-off comet. It was now plain to me he had devoted much more time thinking about the 'Cosmic Intruder' than I had since it landed two years earlier.

We climbed the stairs from Harriman Ave. to the small park dedicated to Henry Hudson. Ray wasn't satisfied with his speculation and I couldn't get to first base with most of what he said, but it was a starting point for my brother...........the genius.

The tentacles of a variable time line was a captivating concept – difficult to ignore and impossible to prove. A force which expended a great mass of energy might have caused the big accident on the Clearview Expressway eight years earlier, Ray theorized. The comet we had seen two and-a-half years earlier might have had some influence on the horrific accident we had been a part of, if in only a vicarious way. He was building a case for this very occurrence, which led him into other directions unknown to me.

Was it just an accident that involved 23 cars and trucks in mid-afternoon with clear skies and dry pavement? Possibilities of mechanical failure, drunk drivers, and inexperienced operators were listed as the probable causes, but a week later the police and the news people were unable to determine the reason for the pile-up. Two weeks later the story faded to the next to last page of the second section of the Herald Tribune, and then......nothing.

This inanimate visitor hurdling through space ignited my brother's drive to unlock the enigmatic question of humanity's function in a universe which seems to be influenced and guided by some design; the vastness of the universe by its size, concealing life and defying scrutiny.

The fireball, in conjunction with the forces of electro-magnetic memory, magnetic creeping, pulses, fields, and friction, would be where his study led him. The alteration of the continuum was just a bunch of science fiction until then. Now, it was at least worth wasting time to entertain such a concept he thought. It was a distraction for Ray, but it was intriguing enough to occasionally revisit because of the fantastic possibilities.

We knocked off the remainder of the pint at the small park. It was before 11 pm, and we had to go caddying the next day. Both of us were feeling the wine, and not wanting to go home until Hal and Jane

54

had gone to bed. Ray was still hot on the trail of gathering the errant pieces from this intergalactic puzzle. He announced to his audience of one: "Time and reality will forever have a new benchmark."

When the state gave us the standardized I.Q. test, they notified Jane and Hal that I had been classified as having superior recall abilities. The fact was: I couldn't remember what I had done today other than going caddying.

Ray, on the other hand, had everything memorized like a movie he had seen 17 times. Although some things remained cast in stone: My days were in a state of mismanagement whenever I saw Rusty in my dreams. She was the focal point of my memory the day we returned from Jones Beach.

"You remember that day we came back from the beach with Dottie and Mom.......the day of the big accident?" I asked.

He went over to a clearing where the trees didn't block his view of the Palisades, he was about ten feet away. I stayed on the park bench. "It's not so much what I recall about that day; the day was but one component of a system. After the comet blazed up the river, day by day, bits and pieces of the empty spaces began to fill in." he said.

"One of the properties of time is the ability to alter its rate of passage. Second, when organic life and inanimate objects share a common plane, dimension, or proximity, they don't necessarily experience time in a contiguous manner. Third, a temporal distortion or warp necessitates an extraordinary amount of energy be expended to facilitate such an event, and may very well involve the introduction of some kind of 'Black Arts.'" He nodded his head and I nodded right back.

vi

After five minutes of sitting and sweating behind the wheel on the Clearview Expressway, Rusty had had enough and shut off the Plymouth's engine. The dancers looked at one another.

"I didn't tell Hal we were going to the beach. I thought we'd be home before him...........I'm drenched." Mom said.

I didn't know how Ray felt, but I thought my head was the size of a pumpkin. The four northbound lanes were now a parking lot.

Dottie bolted from the car: waves of heat made her appearance alien-like. There were exhaust fumes, smoke, and enough mean faces to go around.

Jane hopped out of the car and yelled, "Dottie....Dottie.... where ya goin?"

"See if one of these all-star truckers with a C.B. radio can tell us what's going on."

We could see her about eight car-lengths ahead, standing on the running board of the passenger side of a Texaco tanker talking to the semi-driver.

She returned in slow motion. "Big accident: a bus with passengers from Idlewild Airport had a tire blowout and wrecked across the freeway and there's about a 20 car pile-up into the bus; a big fire…a number of fatalities. They're waiting for the emergency vehicles. The driver said the cops had pulled a number of people from burning cars."

"How bad?" Jane asked.

"I didn't want to get any closer. You can see the smoke from here."

"Mom, can we go see it?" It looked like a scene from the movies.

Mom and Rusty told me to: "Shut up."

"Wow….we'll be here until the victims are on the way to the hospital and the fires are out." Jane thought aloud.

"There's no way to get off this freeway, and get over to the Whitestone Bridge." Dot exhaled and peeked at the sweat under her right armpit.

Jane looked 360 degrees: cars and trucks were everywhere. The Clearview had been shut down in both directions; the southbound lanes were now empty except for the emergency units to assist people involved in the pile-up. They were in a four, sometimes five lane parking lot. A car on the left of us was inching up – getting even with us.

"Where do those clowns think they're going?" Jane asked. Dottie had her door open and sat sideways with her feet on the pavement and her back to Mom.

"Just a couple of troublemakers…….wolves."

"I don't see no wolfs." I told Ray.

"Shut-up."

The dancers chuckled behind their sunglasses. "Oh, they're wolves alright Ryan."

They didn't waste a minute and went straight to work, "Hey Sis……yeah you." The greaser slapped the side of the passenger's door. "Hey Sis…….."

"Our day's complete." Jane moaned.

"Yeah……whaddayawant?" Rusty went real heavy on the Bronx.

He had his head and shoulders through the door's window now. The shotgun rider called out, "What's the deal? hear anything?"

She looked away from him: "Radio said there was a minor fender bender on the Clearview……they should have the cars towed away pretty soon.

Besides the intermittent lane division stripes, there may have been seven or eight feet of separation between our car and theirs.

The greaser stroked his fingers through his DA. "Do you think anybody got hurt?"

"Take a wild guess Sherlock." It was too hot and they were too close to her door to ignore them.

"Maybe somebody cashed in their chips up there." His pointer finger swept across his neck. Jane saw the guy behind the wheel laughing and shaking his head.

Dottie now had one leg in and the other out of the car and tried to focus on the radio and scan the airwaves for news of the accident. It was the only way to drown out the chit-chat from the lane invaders. The dude hanging through the passenger's window was determined and kept at it.

"Hey, I ain't trying to put a move on you gals........I see you're a couple of mothers with the kids. We respect that." The two guys had a hard time not busting out.

Dottie closed her eyes and took a breath, "Janie, we got any screwdriver left?"

"It'll be as warm as the roadway pavement."

"Something's better than nothing." Dottie wiped some sweat from her brow and found an easy listening radio station.

Jane went to the trunk and got the warm vodka/orange juice mix. The driver from the other car got out and said to Jane over the roof of his car: "She's not the mom, you're the mom."

She ignored him.

"Come on......don't be Mrs. Freeze, or is it Miss Freeze.?"

The co-pilot spoke loud enough and directly at Dottie: "Neither of 'em got an engagement or wedding ring. They don't look like the type of girls who would do it out of wedlock. C'mon gals, what's the big mystery?"

"Just who the hell do you think you're talking to?" Dottie ripped.

"We're just trying to have a little fun as long as we're stuck in this impromptu parking lot."

"I don't like that kind of fun and we don't think it is very funny." Dot said.

'We apologize...........no really......We didn't mean any disrespect." the driver said over the roof of his Mercury.

"Maybe we should call Dad." I said.

Mom drank the screwdriver right from the cooler and told me to shut up. I was getting scared.

"My name's Tino, my buddy's name is Tide." They waited for the girls to introduce themselves.

Jane got flustered when Dottie turned towards them, but she knew nothing was going to happen on the freeway, as far as she was concerned. She held the cooler half-way between her lap and her mouth. Just knowing she could attract some guy who wasn't involved in the business was an ego boost if nothing else.

"Calling planet Jane-O. Calling planet Jane-O, or is it Momma Freeze?" The Rockette was urging a splashdown back on Planet Earth.

She warned Dottie under her breath: "Don't take this too far – the boys are in the backseat."

Dottie looked at Janie annoyed: "Whatcha think is going to happen?"

"The unexpected."

Again, Tide called over the top of the Mercury, "Seriously, we don't mess around with married women..... too complicated." He shook his head.

Gradually it was getting quieter as more motorists shut down their engines to prevent overheating. It kept the car's interior a little cooler, and the radio didn't have to compete with the engine to be heard.

The two guys now leaned against the side of the car facing the Plymouth's driver side. Tino said, "I think we got sisters here. The one's got the brats, and lil' sis is behind the wheel."

Tide winked at Tino, "Good call."

"Alright Mr. Know-it-Alls, the kids are our nephews, and we took them to the beach for the day........just so you're up on our family activities." Jane got out of the car and stood across from the guys. Dottie did the same.

Jane went to her power. She turned and looked into Dottie's side-view mirror to adjust her look. She could have squatted and looked into the mirror with a level perspective, instead she stayed straight-legged, giving the T&T boys a wide view of her butt and legs. Still looking into the side-view, she combed her hair with the fingers of her right hand. Standing up straight combing and arching her back, Jane shook her head back and forth so her hair would take the gravity. It didn't fall right and she attributed it to the salt air and humidity. She put her sunglasses back on.

It took the guys a minute to come off the visual ride with Jane. "So are you gals like 'mothers in training'?" Tino mumbled like he had rocks in his mouth.

Jane's blaze green top kept riding up on her. She pulled it back down onto her shoulders and whipped her hair back and forth, "We're professional dancers."

Neither of the guys had a response for Jane.

Rusty looked to Tide, "Tell your friend, he's the one that needs the training." She flat out asked Tino: "What kind of jerk are you?" All four laughed.

"We're the kind that might be found at the Starlight Lounge at the east end of Idlewild Airport."

Tide gave 'the look' to Jane, "Where you from?"

"Riverdale in the Bronx."

"Anything going on up there?"

"More traffic jams." Jane smirked.

"Tide - Hey Ride the Tide." He called to his buddy who was only four feet away. "The dancers live in an upscale section of the Bronx."

"Yeah, I heard.....but that's impossible. The entire borough is under siege. The girls got the va va va voom and all, but I ain't driving up to no Riverdale. What kind of dancers are they anyway?"

Ray waved out the window to get Mom's attention, "Can we come out on the hi-way with you guys?"

"Please." I backed my brother's request.

"No, it's way too dangerous. This is a freeway junior, and when the traffic starts back up – it'll be worse than the Charge of the Light Brigade." Tino said.

"You can come up front where the windows are all the way down." Jane said.

"I got a bottle of coke they can share." Tide looked at Mom.

The word 'Coke' got our immediate attention. Jane asked if they had another.

"Nah, just the one is all we got left."

"The boys are plenty hot."

"What's your friend's name?" he said opening a repurposed milkbox and got the 16 oz. soda.

"We didn't say." Mom said.

He opened the Coke with his fold-out opener and was handing the sweating bottle to Ray when Jane intercepted it and downed the neck's contents. Ray shook his head.

Jane took a couple of steps over to the Mercury, "Say, what's your name......Clyde?"

"No – Tide.....the name's Tide; it's got nothing to do with the detergent. Just a nickname - got it when I was 11 or 12. We'd hit the beach everyday and go surfing. The name kinda stuck, not much to it other than that."

'Am I mistaken, or did I see some beer on ice in the milkbox?" Jane pointed at the square kooler.

"What's your name?" Tide said.

"Jane......just plain Jane – was that beer on ice in the milk cooler?"

"Rusty....?" Jane was stopped cold. Rusty was trading spit with Tino right in front of me and Ray and he had his arms around her. "Dottieeee – you're giving the youngsters quite a show."

Tide called over, "Hey sis, you want a cold one?"

Mom went right over to his Mercury, "You're going to need a cup, we can't be drinking this stuff from the bottle. All's we got are quarts." Tide's head did a 360 degree look around.

"Hey Dottie's friend," Tino barked. "Is she really a 'Radio City Rockette'?"

"Most guys find that out before they know her name."

"Awww cut it out Janie." They laughed, and might have seen Rusty blush if her face hadn't gotten so much sun at the beach.

They filled four mismatched cups with beer. Tide's 1955 Mercury Monterey was a two door also. With the milkbox of beer on the front floor, the unplanned party was under way. Dottie slammed her first one down in three chugs. Jane wasn't far behind. The dancers hadn't had anything to eat except some fruit and Cheezit crackers. It was cold and it tasted good. Dottie danced a cup back over to Tino who enjoyed the gesture.

"Find something on the radio." Mom said.

"Gotcha." Dottie put her beer in Tino's free hand, "Hide it in the shade and I'll find something we can dance to."

She lunged into the front seat, she had Ray and me backed up against the shotgun door. She was acting wild, I guess that was being drunk or lightheaded. We saw right down her blouse. "Hi guys......... having fun?" She smiled as she worked the radio's tuning dial lying on her side.

Tino put the brew in the shade of the car, and he jumped right on top of her. Ray was laughing; I was bewildered and a little scared. Her left elbow came flying back. "Get offa me you jerk. Tino caught the elbow in the temple

"Dammit Tino.......Down boy...down!" Except for Tino, everybody, even Dottie, was rolling. He tumbled out of the Plymouth. Dazed, he picked up their two beers from the shade of the car.

"Rusty – what'd you do to poor Tino?" Jane was smiling.

"Rusty?" Tide wondered, "I thought it was Dottie."

"Her hair." Jane twirled her hair and nodded to her friend as she continued to roll the radio dial to find some dance music.

"She's Rusty alright."

Rusty was wedged in between the big diameter steering wheel and seat thanks to Tino's pile-on attack. Ray and me were keeping our eyes on Dottie's boobs. We wanted to jump on her like Tino had.

The WNEW-AM dee-jay announced: "When we come back after the break and the weather, an instrumental by Al Caiola."

"Get me out......get me out now you dumb creep." She squealed. Tino started dragging her out by her feet. Her tits started coming out the top of her blouse and I dropped the coke. Ray was lightning quick retrieving the bottle..........but only a third of the Coke remained.

Between the two cars, she was already back on her feet, getting the other three ready for this song that was going to come on. Dot instructed Tino with a Parliament in one hand and a cup of beer in the other. She wanted to show her stuff to Jane by giving him a quick dance tutorial. "Okay.....okay....get ready. You two partner up, and do what Janie tells you Troy." Dottie instructed. "Now Tino – you'll get a chance to redeem yourself."

The D.J. came back and intro'd the tune.

"It's kind of a cha-cha number." Dottie flashed her eyes. "Mirror our moves and steps. Expect some dips, spins, tight runs in place, but don't run or go fast. There'll be some back to back moves, over the tops, rope aways, and a couple of pull backs. Listen for the beat changes and dance to the rhythm – not the melody for this number."

The tune started, three minutes and it was over. The dance partners held on to one another until the start of the next song. The next selection was undanceable, so the four refreshed with more beer. Neither Tide or Jane said a word to each other. Tino gave Rusty another short passionate kiss.

She peeked around her partner's head, "Jane, I think these guys have potential.

"Say Jane, weren't you good enough to be a 'Rockette'?" Tide asked.

"Those two rascals in Dot's car..........

"Yeah, I kinda figured." They toasted their plastic cups and emptied them. "I didn't want to drive up to Riverdale anyway."

"Yonkers," Jane said. "I wish the traffic started moving right now."

The beer was charging through the girls' empty stomachs and short circuiting their brain function. "Where'd you learn to cut a rug?" she asked Tide.

"Tino's a drummer, and I play the accordion, in a five piece band; mostly country and western stuff. To go dancing, you got to listen to the bottom and the rhythm or else it's not there. It looks lopsided." He reached into the milkbox, opened another quart, and filled their cups.

"Being a dancer, I know that's true. 'Specially if you're a tap dancer, like Rusty and me. So many guys.......and gals show up at my studio trying to learn just enough to get them through a part in a musical, a benefit, or any function that will tell their partner they don't have two left feet."

Jane rambled, "Sometimes I have to talk with the father of the bride and convince him the most important money he will spend at his daughter's reception are these dance lessons. Mind you, I didn't say the most money, I said the most important money. I make the fathers come in three nights before the reception, I charge $25/hr. and I tell them they've got to make all three lessons. The daughter usually brings her dad and tells me to "Do something with him."

"The guests will forget about the wedding, the rubber steak, the cheap liquor, and the parking spot three blocks away. What the wedding guests won't forget is when father and daughter walk in arm and arm and they're the center of their worlds, and the band starts in with a rock number like 'Don't Be Cruel' and they follow it with 'Pocketful of Rainbows' and finish with Elvis Presley's 'Angel'; their friends and relatives jaws hit the floor.

"This past June, a former student brought in her Dad, Archie. He picked the music and we rehearsed a song a night. Archie was a good 40+ lbs. overweight but with the right shoes, moves, flair, and a great big smile that said 'CONFIDENCE' - father and daughter set the dance floor on fire. The two dazzled like the revolving ballroom orb." Jane shook her head with a smile. "Archie came in the studio the following Tuesday and gave me an extra $50. He said he could die tomorrow because he was so happy."

"Wow."

"Paying for a reception is expensive enough. Let some other tanglefoot embarrass his daughter. If Dad goes home feeling like the reception was a waste of money or all he could do was get drunk - that is a waste. When the eyes of the reception is on the two of them, making the proper dance statement simply puts the guests in a state of awe. It ends up being the best money spent because it is that image the guests take home with them.............before they get tipsy." She lit another Parliament.

"I'll drink to that. Jane you're one smooth operator." Tide said.

We watched Tino and Rusty dance and make out. Much of the beer left their bodies as sweat. We had been parked for over two hours. The emergency vehicles were still chasing back and forth on the southbound side. Even Ray and me had seen enough of them.

There wasn't any beer or fun left, there was nothing but a long ride back to Yonkers, which hadn't even begun. Everybody had to piss despite all the sweating we did. Mom and Dot took Ray and me to a stand of shrubs and bushes about 20 yards off the shoulder. They had us facing the road as they let out some used Rheingold. There were other people doing the same thing, but not that Tide. He had the hood up on his '55 Monterey. That didn't look good. Mom and Dot tried to see ahead from where they were, and they let us walk over to the Plymouth.

Tide had his hands on the raised hood, just looking at his engine. Some guy looked like he was jawboning with him out of boredom. We stood against Dottie's car.

"See ya got a radiator leak."

Water was dripping pretty good at the bottom of the car. Ray told me the fluid was defying gravity, "The stuff should be going to that sewer." He pointed to the grate in the median.

"Tide smiled, "Hey Pops, you know anything about radiators?"

"Don't know a thing about cars." he put his hands in his pockets.

"Me neither" he stepped back away from the car's grill, shook off, and put his piss hose back in his blue jeans and slammed the hood down and said thanks for helpin' out.

Ray gave me the rundown on that disgusting event the next day. Disgusting as it was – I remember it and used it in a traffic jam on the Major Deegan Expressway when I got older. Ray reminded me that we pee in the woods up at Mom-Mom's all the time. It was okay to pee in public as long as nobody was looking.

Ray woke me when we got back to Yonkers.

"I guess that Tide guy was okay."

"Sure."

CHAPTER 4

i

Late August, Tucson

"What's up Nicks? Did the Old Man leave yet?" Dixie asked.

"Been trying to reach you, when I couldn't – I called the twins, and see if they knew where you were....you been out of town?" Nicole was hanging up the kids' clothes on the line. With the strong sun and the desert breeze they would dry in a half-hour.

"We were up in the White Mountains. Camping in an area where the service isn't any good."

"Anyway, callin' to tell you he's on his way to Wisconsin and I tried to talk him out of this trip. He doesn't look good, and he probably feels worse than he looks."

"Of course he's driving by himself." Dixie said.

"Yeah. Got a bad feeling 'bout this trip; Thought you should have your antennae up..........in case something goes wrong with him or to him during the journey."

"I know better than to ask why you let him leave."

"I went over to his place a couple of days ago and he was gone. You're Power of Attorney for Medical - talk him into seeing his G.I. doctor as soon as he shows up. His neighbor said his skin was gray. I tried to get him to see his Doctor at the U.of A. Medical Center.

"No...he'll want to see Doctor Baranpour up here.

"I've tried to call Dad 5 or 6 times when he went out to Yuma in the spring, he not only turned his flip phone off – he pulled the SIM card out so there's no messages of any kind when he turns it back on." Nicky said.

"They're up there in that cyber world waiting to attack. When he turns it back on.......those caring thoughts will be waiting for him."

"Isn't that comforting? Bunch of fake phones, for fake people, in a fake world."

"Let's stay on point Nicks...... Do you want to call emergency people and have them issue a 'Silver Alert'?"

"No, he's sick, he's frightened, and he's anxious for that new drug that the doctors, hospitals, his daughters, and every news outlet says is here but nobody can get it.
He usually makes it from Tucson to LaCrosse in three days, if he's been out on the road for six days and we haven't heard anything – then we've got to start worrying."

"The last three or four years he's been stopping at hospitals and clinics as he traveled. He hoped they would take him in an experimental drug program, but they kept telling him his liver wasn't bad enough. Now, it seems his liver may be past that point; perhaps it is too far gone." Nicky said.

"As soon as he shows up, I'm driving him to St.Thomas Hospital and seeing Dr. Hadji." Dixie said.

"Agreed."

LAYING IN THE FRONT SEAT OF HIS PICK-UP, RYAN
FELT as if he was in the spin cycle of the wash run. "Lord, please
come and take me." Dying in a Wal Mart parking lot in Las Cruces
wasn't the way or the place he thought he'd cash out, but he knew this
was never his decision.

The last five years had been filled with doctors, drug
manufacturers, the FDA, and people telling him that 'they' were close
to finding a cure for Hepatitis C virus. It had gotten to the point where
Ryan stopped believing and hoping.

Sometimes he felt he deserved to carry this liver destroyer
bug inside his body. For the last 40 years this virus had been steadily at
work turning his liver into a piece of rock. Along with other junkies -
he had tried that interfereon/ribavirin junk. He had been lucky; his
body couldn't tolerate it, and his G.I. physician took him off it after 6
weeks. Ryan was 42 weeks short of the recommended course.

For some people it worked and they got rid of the virus. For
others; it eradicated the virus, but the drugs left them with a
compromised immune system, which in turn left them almost
defenseless against some cancers, infection, and other diseases. For the
rest, it was just a waste of time and money.

Ryan's Gastro-Intestinal specialists in Arizona and
Wisconsin were performing ultra-sound tests on an annual basis. Every
year there was less viable liver to do the work of a normal organ.

This annual trek to escape the monsoon season in the
Sonoran desert was different. His daughters bombarded him with news
articles about a series of new anti-viral drugs originally designed to
eliminate the AIDS virus, but with some tweaking, these drugs worked
amazingly well in getting rid of the Hep-C virus. These drugs were
already in use in other regions of the world, and had a success rate of
better than 96%.

Prior to the discovery of these anti-virals, people with an
active Hep-C virus usually only survived 30 years. Ryan's concern and
interest heightened when he was closing in on carrying the virus for 40
years. Two more of the guys he used to shoot dope with had passed
away a year earlier. Most of the others were already dead.

Ryan regularly visited his eldest daughter's family when he
stayed in a rented trailer in Tucson. Even though her father would not
reveal his entire health situation with her, Nicole knew by the way he
spoke and what he said – his time was winding down. All he could talk
about was the virus and he was becoming desperate to do something
about it.

Every mountain the truck climbed, he thought about driving
off a sharp turn and ending what was turning into a nightmare. Just
when he thought the truck would drive itself off the road, he'd see St.
Theresa, or St. Anthony, or an angel, or the Blessed Virgin, and he'd
get back in lane. He was afraid to live and afraid to die. He was still
Catholic, a lapsed or bad one, but he knew it wasn't his life but God's;
and it was the seer of the universe who would call the shots. Ryan
couldn't do it.

Mid-September, LaCrosse, Wi.

They both were asleep; she was cold from the air conditioning, but more tired than cold. Teresa crashed in a chair as her father rested in the hospital bed. Ryan hadn't been awake much in the past few days. The family, his doctor, and the staff knew if he didn't rally and eliminate the fluids accumulating in his body and settling in his legs; his outlook was bleak. Ryan Whitelaw began his eighth day at St.Thomas the Apostle in LaCrosse Wi. His medical chart had all the pros wondering which way the chips would fall.

At 6:00 a.m., healthcare workers with their specific responsibilities shuffled in and out of I.C.U. room 107. Readings were entered into a laptop computer which rested on a cart with wheels. Wires, tubes, plugs, sensors, cables were attached to Ryan and fed into the laptop. They made him look like a spider. Some of these conduits went directly to the computer, some made a relay connection to devices making analytical decisions before sending them to the laptop.

Most critical to the staff, was the amount of urine going into the collection bag. This reading was taken not by any machine or device, but by eyeballing lines on the waste bag and writing the amount of fluid waste on a daily report twice a day. Three of the four nurses and assistants pulled down his sheet and light blanket to observe his swollen legs. After a brief look, a critical observation was focused on the lower right side of his bed where the out-of-view urine collection bag hung. The staff compared the two readings, and recorded the net difference. Optimism was sparse in room 107.

Blasting through the red tape of insurance, government, and an unestablished price for the miracle antiviral drug, Dr. Hadji Baranpour had somehow gotten the approval for Ryan to receive the new drug which millions of hep-C carriers were waiting for. Dixie said no matter what the cost was, they would roll the dice to have a chance at saving their father. What bothered Baranpour and the daughters was they had to deal more with the drug manufacturer and the insurance providers than the medical people. Dixie knew they were only at the beginning of the financial quagmire. For now she was grateful Ryan's doctor would go to bat for her father.

Killeen kicked the bottom leg of the chair.

Dread instantly gripped her older twin sister.

"How's he doing?" Killeen asked. A reoccurring beep from a monitor indicated a fluid being pumped into him. "If it was dark, all they'd be missing is the Christmas tree." Killeen shook her head. "I understand the blood pressure, pulse rate, and oxygen level; not much goes beyond that for me.......I just deliver the mail."

"Parking should have been a breeze this early." Teresa preferred small talk as Killeen stroked their father's sparse silver hair. "Talk to Dixie?"

"Yeah, but not about moving Pa to Mankato."

65

"What do you think?" Teresa drank some of her father's apple juice.

" 'Bout the Institute?" Her gaze remained on her father.

"Uh-huh." Teresa said.

"I have to know a lot more: Doctors, facility, his condition. No one's mentioned the possibility of a transplant, but I'm sure Baranpour will run it by us if it's an option. Killen said. "Listening to him the other day, it sounded like he sees the liver's scarring as Papa's biggest hurdle to overcome. It's hard making a decision on a facility when I don't know very much about the virus or the accompanying cirrhosis. I read some more on the internet; that cirrhosis is enough to make me stop drinking. I'm not much help to any of you …… or Papa. I feel so useless." She paused and took the apple juice from her sister, "At least you're a Registered Nurse. I'm the last person who should have any input on the way to proceed." She looked down at her father.

"Killeen, I'm a psychiatric nurse……….I may as well be a Postal worker like you." the older twin replied. "I'm only slightly more knowledgeable than the three of you. Dixie's feeling a lot of stress, but knowing we're there to help her make competent decisions……….it lets her sleep."

"Really wish Mom was alive. I'm sure the old man had his reasons assigning Dixie as his Power of Attorney for Medical Affairs."

"I'm kind of glad Mom wasn't here for this, she had seen enough friends and relatives go. Remember…… there were like three…..four deaths in a row: Her Dad, her best friend Joyce, and then her business partner Deb. All in less than 18 months." She said.

"Don't forget Aunt Sharon."

"It's odd we've only heard from one of Mom's brothers. I know Dixie texted them about the old man."

"Seven of them; only one asked how Pops was doing?" Killeen lowered her brow. "I know it wasn't Matthew, Mark, or Luke."

"And I know it wasn't Paul, George, or Ringo." Teresa said.

"It's the bridge, John, the fourth uncle. You know he sends my kids Christmas money……….Nicky's too, and they're not even blood to him. Grandma and Grandpa were kind of out there; they name the first four boys after the evangelists, and the second four after the Beatles. Somebody talked them into something." The twins laughed.

"Think about it - after Mom passed away, they kind of forgot us except for Uncle John." Killeen said.

"It was a real ordeal for mom, the incidence of death averaged out to one every six months, and then Mom two years later." The two shivered in their chairs.

There was a caustic smile on Teri's face as she stared at Ryan: "At least we can spread the burden around amongst the four of us. Dixie doesn't have to shoulder all the weight unless she wants to."

"How's his legs?"

"'Fraid to look." Teresa grabbed the sheet, squeezed her eyes tight, and pulled the sheet up from the side.

"I'd say about the same as last night." Killeen said.

Teresa slowly opened her eyes. She looked at the bloated calves. "Yeah.....about the same." Teresa went over to the laptop and put her St.Thomas I.D. in front of the scanner.

"Shit. Baranpour was already here this morning. He must have visited while I was sleeping. Something like this makes me want to bring Pop over to Mankato Institute like right now.....He couldn't even make some noise to wake me." She logged out and folded her arms.

"Modern medicine LaCrosse style." Killeen watched Teri mouthing an 'F' bomb on Baranpour.

"I've got to get a cup of coffee – maybe he'll stay asleep until we get back. Want to go?"

"I just got here Teri.....but you could bring a cup back with you? He might come to."

"Black?"

"No sugar." She answered in password manner.

TERESA RETURNED ABOUT 20 MINUTES LATER, SHE SAT
across from her sister on the other side of the bed. His eyes were half-open. Coffees sat on the window's ledge. She looked over to Killeen who tilted her head and raised her brow. Teresa forced a smile at her sister; she shuddered and tried to take a deep breath. "Papa......."

He opened his eyes. A tear ran down her cheek and she looked over to her twin who was also welling up. She turned back to their father. "Oh Papa...."

"Get my teef – in da drawer." He said.

"They're afraid you'll swallow them." Teresa's voice wavered.

Ryan struggled; he asked for a pen, motioning with his left hand.

Teresa handed a post-it pad and a pen to him. Ryan scribbled and handed the pad back to her. She read it to Killeen: "Dixie ?......Nicky ?"

"Dixie will be here late this morning or afternoon. Nicole and two of her kids will be staying with Dixie; they're lining up a flight."

He pointed to Killeen. "Teresa's stays at my place with me here in LaCrosse when she's burnt out." She said.

Ryan was beginning to fade.

Teresa called: "Ol' Man.........Hey........ Ol' Man..." She had come directly from the psychiatric section of the facility to his bedside after her shift ended at midnight. He was confused because she was still in her nurse's scrubs. His eyes rolled up and his hands pushed down on his diseased liver. The two could see he was pushing down pretty hard until he shut his eyes tight from the pain. It took him a good three minutes to make it back.

Ryan tried to talk; but only whispered with his eyes closed, "Am I dying? ....Get me some ice."

Killeen went to the machine in the hall off the nurses' station.

"They can do a transplant," Teresa said, "Right now, your liver is cancer free. Problem is...they've only started to look for a match. You've got too much scarring. They've started that new anti viral drug to get rid of the Hepatitis C. It won't stop new cirrhosis from developing, but it should slow it down. If we catch a break, it may permit the good liver tissue an opportunity to regenerate. Your liver has been subjected to an awful lot of damage from the virus over these many years. Dr. Baranpour didn't seem too optimistic about the viability of your liver, or finding a donor so late. You wanted it straight Pops. That's all we know right now."

"You were a pretty good dice shooter at the crap table Ol' Man; I think you got some luck left." Killeen managed a smile.

Ryan winced, "That was only wawawhen I had the Gold Dust Twins on each aaarmmm."

They all forced a smile.

"You want to do any praying now?" Killeen squeezed his hand.

"I gagaga...gotta get ow..ow..outta here." Each word seemed to take an eternity.

"Say Dad, - in case the worst comes – Are you ready? Are you right with God?"

Again he pointed to the mini dresser. "Top drawer." He mouthed.

"What am I looking for?" she looked at his mouth to read his lips.

His hands tried to mimic a square. The words came out, "A paper."

"Huh?" Killeen held up two small post-its and he pointed to one. "Read it."

The younger read it to the older twin: "Is there an after life ------ To this age old question there is but one of two possibilities:

(A) You get one more night of sleep

or

(B) What follows the surrender of our life force is beyond comprehension. But it surely has something to do with God."

The twins mulled it over. Teresa said, "Knowing you, I'd say you're shooting for 'B' Papa."

Ryan tried his best to talk, "Yeah, 'A' is for Hitler and Stalin."

The daughters felt somewhat hopeful. It demonstrated his willingness to fight.

A nurse and an attendant came in, "We're going to take Dad to do some imaging in radiology."

"Any idea when he's returning?"

"Minimum.......90 minutes."

Teresa turned to Killeen; "That's at least two hours." She said out of earshot of the two who wheeled Ryan away. The twins walked him to the elevator each holding his hands and kissed his forehead before he was pushed on. He looked above the elevator's control board: Otis.

iii

Reality and inescapable consciousness, or the perception that he was conscious was a problem since Ryan was informed that it was the bottom of the ninth. A continuous barrage of medical news did a major number on his sanity. The nature of his disease prohibited the use of some drugs because they would accelerate further damage to his liver, but there were drugs his liver could tolerate. A few altered his consciousness, and released him from the prison of non-stop thought.

He had to deal with the fact he had been an ignorant conspirator in his own slow-motion assassination by shooting the virus laden tragic magic into his arm. In the early 1990's the medical field had developed a reliable test to identify carriers of the virus. Either by fate or chance, his wife had passed away in 1990. Because he was alcohol and drug free since 1984 Ryan was able to be both father and mother to his daughters without the burden of getting rid of some chemical dependency baggage; he had to be sober if he was going to be both.

Before he got clean, the get-high chemicals and alcohol had stepped-up the Hepatitis-C virus's ability to turn viable liver tissue into scar tissue. He was able to stay clean, and it had slowed the virus down; but no matter how drug and alcohol free he stayed --- the Hep C was getting more virulent and multiplying, and there was no way to kill it.

The medical quandary and the incessant guilt became intolerable as more associates with whom he injected heroin with - fell victim to any number of the maladies of a junkie. The slow-motion poisoning had reached the tipping point as the toxins in his body could not be broken down and eliminated as waste. His polluted blood racked his brain and made cognitive recognition and normal thought patterns sporadic. The sicker he became; the easier it was for his brain to transfer his thoughts and consciousness to an alternate time or reality. Perhaps he was asleep, in a semi-coma, or a coma; in any case he was grateful to escape the here and now, but his abdominal pain was intense and would shock him from the unconscious state at will.

As the elevator descended, he began to drift in and out; recalling his life again in random episodes. Some things amassed together in a chronological line, while other events were presented as wild as a dealer turning cards in a casino.

69

CHAPTER 5

i

Ray was attending P.S.14 all day in 1959; I had just started Kindergarten. I suspected Mom and Ray were wise to the lowdown about this school business. There was nothing bad to say about Kindergarten. For 1st grade, Ray had to take crayons, two pencils, a pencil case with this big 'Pink Pearl' eraser, and sneakers for gym class. Jane gave me this mat, the kind a dog sleeps on, for kindergarten. That was where we learned how to take a power nap, only they had some other five dollar name for it.

My attitude was all wrong Ray said a day before the first day of school. "Listen Ryan.......this is important: Even if you get scared with all the strange kids......DON'T CRY." He eyeballed me real hard. He saw it wasn't sinking in, "Hey you numbskull, this isn't like you and Mom walking me to school."

"What do you mean?"

"There's going to be all these strange kids there and you might not know any of them......just make sure you don't cry."

This wasn't making much sense. "Okay." In my mind, the only reason a guy would cry would be from getting clobbered by someone in a fight or mauled by a dog.

"Look....if you cry on the first day – everyone will think you're a sissy or a baby......not ready for school. Then they call Mom and she's got to come and calm you down, and sometimes they even got to take you home." Now, another look at Ray's face, and it all sunk in.

"Okay Ray."

"Good. Don't worry Ryan, there will be somebody crying for their mama......make sure it isn't you. Just play like we do at home – only you do it with kids you don't know. I'll look for you when school lets out." Ray grinned.

I was put in the afternoon session for Kindergarten. Jane and me did double walking duty: first we'd walk Ray to class, then Mom and me would walk at noon. P.S.14 was about 3/8ths of a mile from our apartment house.

The school was predominantly Jewish, teachers included. Everybody thought me and Ray were Jewish too. When Jane showed up with us at school they had her labeled as a shiksa cause she was so good looking and we were question marks because we never attended temple. We observed the High Holy days of Rosh Hashanah and Yom Kippur, Hannukah, and Passover. Hal drew the line when we brought home dreidels, paper monorahs, and the star of David to top off our Christmas tree with. We learned and sang Jewish songs. We got along.

School let out all at once. At times it was difficult to find Ray, and then we had to find the daycare person who babysat us that week or month. We got bounced around quite a bit; it was bad for Jane – it was hard on us, except for Mondays. We were taller than most of the kids our age, but amongst the rest of the students we qualified as

70

"schrimps". Five minutes of unsuccessful searching for my brother, I started getting a little scared.

Today, parents would never let a first grader be in charge of a kindergarten kid – even if the two were brothers. Now, Hal and Jane would be charged with felony child neglect and the both of us would be sent to live with relatives or a foster home. Even back then, the possibility of being abducted and found in the cellar or car's trunk of some weirdo was real.

ii

The kids who lived in our apartment house didn't attend public school except for Linda Magnano. She was a year younger than me and took dance lessons from our mom

Dennis and Donnie Lowe lived right across the hall. They attended a Lutheran School. Buddy and Susan Howard lived 2 floors down. Their parents bought into that Montesorri education stuff. At first, Jane thought they were Catholic, and attended St. Montesorri. One of the mother's at dancing school informed Jane that it wasn't Catholic, but basically a school for rich atheists. Randy and Kevin Kutmueller went to St. Mary's Catholic school, they lived on the bottom floor. Ann Marie Miselli was the super's daughter: second floor – she went to an all-girls Catholic school.

The layout of our apartment building was U-shaped, with a courtyard in the expanse. There was a clothesline pulley system to dry tenant laundry. On Saturdays, the area above the courtyard looked like a three-masted ship with all the sheets on the lines.

Jane wasn't on the same laundry cycle as most of the women because she worked full time. Her days off were Sunday and Monday. We would do our wash in the mornings, before she went to work. If it was too cold she'd have to take it to the Laundromat or Chen's Chinese Laundry to wash and dry our clothes. There was one bachelor in the building. He'd always brought his clothes to Chen's. Once in a while he'd pay one of us kids to get his clothes for him and give us 15 cents.

Whatever measuring stick was used, Jane logged more hours worked on average than any other woman who resided at 2 Vernon Place. Mondays were Jane's real day off: no Hal, no studio, Ray was going to school all day, and I was only with her until noon. In the middle of the school year they were supposed to switch afternoon Kindergarten with morning's so the kids could get the feel of both sessions. Jane tried to explain her work situation with the vice principal so she could keep me going afternoons, but Jane ended up having to grease her 20 bucks to let her keep me on p.m. Kindergarten. Jane bitched to Hal, and he said that it was just a part of doing business in N.Y. Being alone with Jane that year was pretty special; I didn't know it at the time.

Sometimes Jane seemed to be more of a big sister than a mom. It was possible I got what she gave everybody. She had that

71

charisma stuff; it drew everyone in to discover what the attraction was. Although he never expressed it well, Hal was totally in love with her. There was a problem though; others loved Jane too, and Hal had to compete with them. It was inevitable: Hal's affection turned into a compulsion to possess. There was no way out. The passage of time would become the jury of their marriage and assess the degree of wreckage.

Turning heads was only a portion of her appeal. In some respects Jane's physical endowments were a curse: her magnetism emitted surges of power and desire from those near her. It was critical when trying to understand the Jane Marlowe mystique – if such a thing could survive scrutiny. It was well beyond Hal.....Her aura and attractiveness began with her generosity. She had a heart bigger than Dallas. Whatever else anyone saw was gravy.

She could be mischievous, mysterious, imaginative, and a flirt. A risk taker, her essence was on display every time she put her tap shoes on. We never knew anyone quite like her.

The women in our apartment would wash their personal items during the week. They hung them to dry as early as possible, and get them off the line quickly before the men returned from work.

Watching this laundry being pulleyed to the opposite side of the building was like watching a model train layout in a switching yard. Bras, panties, girdles, bloomers, garter belts, stockings, squeaking to get to the other side. I knew whose clotheslines belonged to who. Buddy Howard's mom needed a big bra and wide panties. Dennis and Donnie lived directly across from us. Their mother's name was Lee. Lee Lowe; her name sounded Chinese. Hal would do an impression of an Oriental person when he was a little drunk.

He'd ask me or Ray: "Hey Yankee boy – who leeve over dat apartment?" Then he would answer his own question – "Oh dat...... Lee Lowe leeve dare. Dat Lee Lowe house." Hal would answer himself once more and buck his teeth as much as possible. "Oh dat Lee Lowe." His head nodded in recognition.

Lee was a knockout, always had the right outfit on. If a five year old could spot value on the street – it wasn't a guess – this lady had "the look". Lee wore tight tops, big red dot earrings that looked great with her jet black hair and pale white skin. She knew how to dress. Bra: 3 hooks. Back then, me and Ray didn't know much about women's bra sizes other than to count the hooks on them when they were on the clothesline. Her boobs were similar to Jane's.

Bianca Magnano lived directly below us. She always sang along with the radio, especially with Bobby Rydell crooning his version of "Volare". To view her at a slight angle, my head barely broke the exterior plane of our living room windows. Bianca was like a miniature version of Sophia Loren or Gina Lollobrigida. She wore low-cut necks and sleeveless tops; it was like looking at a tidal wave of cleavage. Someone could have thrown all these ladies' undergarments in a big pile and I'd have been able to match them up in five minutes. Bianca – four sets of hooks with big pointy cups.

An older lady lived next door to the Magnanos, she lived alone. Jane and Hal and even Ray and me ran errands for her now and then. We knew there was something wrong with her....something delivered from the 'Straight Jacket School' or 'Twilight Zone'. We weren't afraid of her, but we weren't laughing either. "Keep an eye on her." Ray told me. I thought she had been in some kind of a car wreck or something.

Hal and this lady downstairs would drink beer on the stoop out front. Some nights, Lee Lowe's husband, Dan, made it a threesome. For the most part they'd just listened to her. Dan and Hal had been at the front in World War II. Both had been in combat. Hal's Submarine Service in the Pacific and Dan Lowe's action over Europe in the Army Air Corp was most likely the reason why she talked to them. Fourteen years after the war ended, this woman was still unable to move on.

Jane and I came back from walking Ray to school. Jane had some shopping to do before my afternoon session. We took the Chevy wagon and went grocery shopping at the big A & P. Jane had to get our laundry; we stopped at Chen's Chinese laundry to pick up Hal's shirts for his jacket and tie management look.

Twan Chen owned and operated the Chinese laundry right up the street on Yonkers Ave. Twan and his wife had a girl and a boy: Marilyn was in Ray's class and her brother Ronnie was in my class. Everybody liked the Chen's because Twan had signed up for military service in WWII. Twan had received three military commendations: one from the Army Air Corps, another from the Navy and the last from the Chiang Kai Shek government. He hung them on the wall of his laundry. They said his knowledge of the Chinese language was invaluable to the allied war effort in the Far East.

A big smile greeted Jane when we walked in. "Hiya Miss Jane; Got Mr. Whitelaw shirt right here – Put on bill....or pay now?"

"Got to put it on the bill Twan."

"Nobody got money this month....wonder why?" He scrunched his brow.

"You know......a lot of kids at the dance studio asked me if I could carry them to next month too." Mom shrugged her shoulders and arched her eyebrows.

"Miss Jane.....Miss Jane.....before you leave........How my Chinese girlfriend?" Twan smiled.

"Who do you mean?" Jane smiled and crunched down her left brow.

"What you mean - who I mean? He nodded up and down, "You know who I mean."

Jane strung him along, "Lee?"

"Miss Jane she live right across from you; You know.....you know who I mean." He smiled as he squinted.

Jane looked at the clock on the wall. "Oh........you're talking about Lee Lowe."

"Yes ...yes ... yes....who you think I mean? American woman that make Asian man crazy. Yes, Lee Lowe – Lee Lowe – Lee Lowe. American lady with Chinese name. Black hair thick, body of movie star, face of geisha, think like American. U.S. land of plenty......except plenty of Lee Lowe."

iv

We carried groceries and the laundry wrapped in brown paper bound by two one inch strips of paper up the stairs. Mom said there might be time for a grilled cheese sandwich before we walked to the p.m. kindergarten class. Half-way up the first staircase with me following, she stopped: something was wrong. There was some kind of distress above us.

"You wait here."

I picked up the laundry package and climbed the rest of the staircase behind Jane. I went to the end of the floor's landing which accessed the next set of stairs and apartments on the 2nd floor.

A voice weakly called for help. Jane called back, "Mildred." Louder now: "Mildred!" Jane hurried to the older woman. "Do you understand me?" She gave my mother a blank stare into a void.

More forceful: "Mildred, do you hear me....do you hear me? Do you?"

The empty stare scared Jane and she waved her hand in front of her face to get her eyes to focus. Jane looked squarely at her, "Let me get my son settled, and I'll be right back." She hollered up and down the stair shaft: "Hello, hello – can somebody help us?" I was on the other end of the floor's landing.

"Ryan - get up to our apartment – now."

There was urgency in her tone, and I responded, but the closer I got to Mildred the slower my movements became until I was immobilized directly in front of her. She sat on one of the stairs, her back was against the wall of the stair case and our eyes locked for just an instant. Mildred wasn't there, her skin was gray and ashen. I was unable to break free. Jane had unlocked the apartment, came back down, grabbed my arm with the laundry package, and dragged me up to our apartment. We had to squeeze by; Mildred had slumped down... without form.

At the time, I didn't know what was occurring, but years later I kind of felt that she was in some stage of transmutation. Mildred looked at me, but I doubt she saw me. I was positive she didn't recognize or know me.

Mom and me reached our door, "Stay put. I have got to help this woman." She rushed back to Mildred. A woman in one of the bottom apartments called up to Jane.

"Who do you want me to call?" The tenant strained her voice.

74

"It's Mildred." Mom hollered.

"Should I call an ambulance?"

"I think the police will get here faster ."

Watching down the stair shaft, I saw Jane's hand on the rail and the other lady's hand all the way at the bottom of the stairs. We waited about five minutes before the police showed up. I heard Mom talking with the cops: giving them information about Mildred.

"Her name is Mildred Laughlin, she lives alone, I don't know if she's got any relatives. Doesn't drive, and she's been kind of a recluse. My husband and Dan Lowe who lives across the hall from us, talk with her now and then."

I heard the cops say that if they can't come up with any next of kin they'd be back and talk with Jane and the lady downstairs.

The cop's partner said he didn't think they should wait for an ambulance. "We'll take her over to Cross County Hospital right now." The bigger cop carried Mildred like a bride down the two flights of stairs. We followed them down to their squad car as they put her in the back seat with the one officer riding next to her as they drove away.

"C'mon Ryan....you're going to be late." We went upstairs and locked the door and hurried out of the building and double-timed it to school.

"What's wrong with her Ma?"

"You know her."

"Yeah, Ray and me run to the deli for her, but I didn't know who she was just now. She gave me the creeps."

"C'mon we're super late – they may have closed the gate. Hey.....that rhymes." Jane smiled. She started singing "We're late....we're late......they're gonna close the gate. We're late.....we're late.......we gotta get in the gate." The next thing I knew – we were skipping.

We had come to a four-way corner, and a mail truck made us stop. I looked up at Jane, "But there is something wrong with that lady downstairs."

Jane started blinking like there was something in her eyes, and stared off into the clouds, "Mildred can't get past some of the problems in her brain."

"But that was the lady downstairs right?"

"Well it was, and it wasn't. Physically it was, but upstairs," (Jane pointed to her brain) "Un-uh. She's got an awful lot on her plate.......she can't get her brain to pay attention. The 'here and now' for her is 'there and then'." We could see P.S.14 through the trees that lined Crescent Pl.

"You know your dad was in the war?" We kept walking.

"Ray said he didn't fight the Krauts – he fought against the Nips.....in the submarines. We saw the pictures."

Jane focused, "Mildred's husband and two sons also fought in the war. Her sons were like you and Ray, only they were about the same age as your dad."

With a gleam in my eyes I asked, "Do you think Ray and me will be able to go to war?" It didn't look so bad in the movies.

The thought of her sons going to fight in some war was frightening: The image of us in uniform, fighting the Red Chinese in some ditch in Asia unnerved her. She jerked my hand forward. "War is not an adventure you twerp.....a lot of people die.........for what?"

"Huh?" 'Why'd she call me that?'

We were almost inside the gate, we were only a little late. One or two other stragglers were amongst us. Jane knelt on one knee so she could talk to me: "Ryan, that's what happened to that lady – Mildred. She lost her husband and both her sons in the war."

"Can't they find them?" My brows came together in thought.

"Listen to me, her husband and her sons were killed...and she's been all alone...they're all dead. You get it? They're dead. And that's why she's having such a tough time dealing with life."

"A Puerto Rican's horn blasted out the first few notes of "La Cucaracha" as Jane was finishing up with me.

She was really pissed off at the driver. Her response was immediate: her two middle fingers were raised in anger at the disrespect. The driver sped away giving her another blast from a distance.

A woman crossed the street and walked towards us and pointed to the car driving away and complained: "It never used to be this bad – they don't care if you've got a baby in each arm; no respect.......no decency. I'm glad you gave him the finger." The woman's chin went up in defiance. "Screw him."

Jane was aware of the time, she'd have to see the vice-principal to get a late pass for me. We waited in a short line outside her office. There was a need for her to finish her story about Mildred to me. "Ryan, what mother is saying is: War causes tremendous feelings of loss, heartache, you get depressed.......you know....you feel bad all the time, and you don't know if you will ever see your loved ones again. It is a vast misplacement of energy. Mildred is a shadow trying to live in a world that she is no longer in touch with. Her life energy was consumed through death and loss."

The vice principal peeked outside her office and handed Jane her late pass and asked the next mother and student into her office.

"I'll talk to you about it when you get home."

"Talk about what?" I said.

She rolled her eyes.

"What about lunch?"

"No lunch."

v

Once Ray started first grade, we played musical chairs with the babysitters Jane had lined up. One week, Ray and me went through three sitters in four days. Jane had to have been going nuts, but on the outside we never saw it. When it came to childcare, it was similar to being a laid-off worker looking for a job. Ray handled all my negotiating, he knew the standards I required. It was ridiculous, we (Ray) was bargaining with a woman behind a card table desk with a

76

roll of singles in her hand, wearing Leotards, checking off names in the class and whether they were paid up.

"Hey Mom, that new babysitter isn't working out."

"How's that?"

"Ray got shot by a B-B gun." I said.

"Dja get hurt?"

"Got shot in the hand."

"Show me." There was a purple blotch. "Does it hurt?"

"I dunno."

"Go over to the exercise mat and do a cartwheel."

We watched him do one. It looked marginal.

Jane said, "You got all these girls watching and that's the best one you can do?"

He did two more, they looked pretty good to me.

"That's more like it, only you've got to straighten your legs more." Mom said. He looked put upon.

Jane looked at the line in front of her. Toni Teller waited with her four daughters to pay for the month's classes.

"Say Toni, you looking to make some side money?"

"Only if it's off the books."

"You're going through divorce now aren't you?"

"That sonofabitch..........my brother is my lawyer and he said my husband won't be able to afford a scooter to get to work. We're going to take him to the cleaners for cheating on me."

"This is what I'll do. You'll only have to pay me for two of your four, but I'll mark that you've paid for all four when you turn it in to his lawyer for reimbursement." Jane grinned.

"And what do I have to do?"

"Babysit Ray and Ryan for two or three weeks, until I get a full-time sitter."

"Is that them?" She pointed to us doing flips and cartwheels on the mats. "Call them over."

This Mrs. Teller was checking us out to make sure there weren't any mental problems which might make this assignment untenable. A few questions were made, then she called her girls over and had them give us the once over. The next day we were in the Teller apartment playing with the Teller girls.

Toni had her daughters taking every musical, dance, voice, and enrichment course to run up the child support bill on her husband. The girls' musical instruments were always on the floor. They had to sort their dancing stuff every week at class. Mrs. Teller had talked Jane into putting them in the same class disregarding their skill levels. It didn't matter - all four had two left feet and no rhythm. There was a five year age spread amongst the Teller girls. They all wanted to be actresses or singers. Sometimes Toni put us in a Checker cab both ways to attend these performing art courses. We took taxis when Toni was getting her hair or nails done. While we were there, we only went to two 'enrichment' classes a week - at most. When the girls had dance lessons with Jane, they wore their tights and Leotards as soon as they got home from school. When Hal or Jane picked us up they were still wearing their dancing stuff. At least once a week, Toni called up Hal or Jane to ask if we could stay until 8 p.m.; "The kids are having so much fun." Hal'd give the green light to any activity that got rid of us.

Toni fed us with her kids; it was always take out food, mostly Chinese and Italian. I wasn't too keen on the Chinese, but I would eat all the rice stuff and egg rolls. After a little while, I actually learned to like most of the stuff everyone else ate.

We were stuck in their apartment the rest of the time. Monica, the oldest, would assign the roles we would play in her various productions of some movie, play, or T.V. show we all knew. After the fifth production, it became more or less a variation on a theme. It was like playing 'The Alamo' or 'Captain Blood' without the blood and gore. Sometimes we played 'The Mouseketeer Club' or a inverted version of 'Snow White' where me and the Teller girls were the Dwarves, Ray was the handsome prince, and Monica was Snow White. Sometimes she made me be the Evil Witch. Monica would shuffle the deck, and we'd all change roles. One thing you could count on: Monica was the lead girl and Ray was her paramour.

When we played school, it always ended up as some bastardization of 'Snow White'. 'Peter Pan' became 'Snow White'. We got Monica to do 'Creature From the Black Lagoon' on a Leotard day..........it was true to form: 'Snow White'. She was 11, Linda was 9, Sarah 7, Deborah was 6. The play acting was boring and monotonous, but there was always the payoff at the end of every performance: The sisters would hold Ray down, and mostly Monica covered his face with kisses, but as time went on she made him pucker –up and then they would kiss. If I helped hold down Ray, the girls would let me kiss them. We were there with the sisters for six weeks. Something that good; it had to end.

WE HAD SOME GOOD SITTERS AND OTHERS NOT SO good. From our perspective we'd never run into any like Toni Teller again. Toni was on one end of the spectrum and Bridgette Daley was on the other. Hal figured he may have let it go too far when Ray started asking for Moo Gai Pan for supper and I asked for Fettucini Alfredo.

There was something about Russian and Jewish immigrants and refugees; they had this daycare industry down to a science. When they erred, they erred on the side of over booking too many kids – volume was the only way to make money. The business model had girls supervising at about a 4:1 ratio. We'd end up getting bumped because we weren't the prime ethnicity or religion, and they had to take care of their own first.

Jane hit the jackpot when a Russian woman showed up at her studio to enroll her two daughters. Lillian Stanslov had gotten out of the Soviet Union with her parents between the two world wars. She worked for the League of Nations prior to World War II as a translator. When Germany declared war on Great Britain, she was scooped up by the State and War Departments. When she went to work for the government she carried a Level 1 security clearance prior to Hitler's invasion of the Soviet Union. Lilli was as fluent in Ukrainian as she was in Russian. With her clearance, the F.B.I. and the forerunner of the C.I.A., the O.S.S., followed her closely to make sure she wasn't a double agent. She was only 16 when she started, but she was well beyond her years in the theatre of international diplomacy and intrigue.

Lilli got married right after World War II, and had her first daughter three years later - the 2nd daughter followed a year after the first.

Jane and Lilli cut a deal: Babysitting for dance lessons – even-steven. When sister Cathy and Brother Bill came along, Jane ended up paying 'Aunt Lil' for some of the sitting because her girls only used up two dance lessons a week and she had to get compensated for the inequity.

After Lilli's first child, she really cut back on the translating work. She was 24 years old and half her life was spent listening to people talk.

Following the Battle of Kursk 1943, the allies were already dividing up Europe; but the war was not won by any stretch of the imagination. Lilli wondered what would lead these men to such conclusions. Japan's surrender wasn't anywhere on the horizon either, except for those who knew about the atom bomb. Although she had the security clearance, she could not see the future as these men in Moscow, Washington, and London could. Translating for the War Dept. she officially worked for the O.S.S. and was in Army drab for the duration of the war. Lilli spent very little time in N.Y., none in Yonkers during the war, and only half her time in the states. Most of her time she lived in London, but made frequent trips to the Soviet Union after Stalingrad held.

The KGB always knew where she was, and they were always trying to obtain information and secrets from her. The foreign agents kept hitting on her to divulge information about a 'secret weapon' perhaps a 'powerful bomb'. "The only thing I know about any of this is coming from you people" she'd tell them.

"Vee vatch who you translate for. You commins into contact vith scientists too much."

"I flunked chemistry and dropped out of physics. You've got the wrong girl commissar."

She thought she could see the end of her Army career with the fall of Berlin. She was wrong. She was stationed in Berlin a month after Germany's surrender. It was day after day of dealing with the Russians on the confiscation of German industry, resources, electricity, technology, agriculture, and transport. She also had to translate for the British and Americans in the military tribunals for the crimes committed by the allied soldiers after the war. It was rumored that Gen. Georgi Zuhkov had wined and dined her while she was stationed in Berlin, as his troops were looting, pillaging, and raping the defeated Germans in the border areas of the other allied sectors.

She attended diplomatic functions as a translator, and there was sufficient reason the Russian Field Marshall always wanted Lilli at any important bi-lingual function; in some instances his own translators had been working for the KGB, and he couldn't trust what they said in regard to the unresolved questions of eastern Europe. A number of times the KGB (Soviet Army's diplomatic/intelligence branch) translation corps, misrepresented Gen. Zuhkov's positions, intentions, and actions. At a delegation banquet, Lilli informed Zuhkov of this breach as they danced. He was forever grateful, and sent her flowers for the next ten years in recognition of the occasion. It was never verified she had been alone with Gen. Zuhkov. The rumor was out there and the O.S.S. and the KGB had her under surveillance for the next year.

After the atomic bomb was dropped on Hiroshima and Nagasaki, the Soviets declared war on Japan. Stalin had a million soldiers massed on the Manchurian border ready to invade. Stalin tried to convince the allies that it was his Soviet troops who had tipped the scales in Japan to sue for peace rather than the American atomics. The Russian generals were there - on the U.S.S. Missouri to sign the surrender papers along with the allies who actually fought the Japanese Empire. They were there to get a share of territory, war reparations, technology, and whatever else was in their neck of the woods which ended up being the Japanese portion (the southern half) of Sakhalin Island.

In the summer of 1946, Gen. Georgi Zuhkov was recalled and sent to be the military commander of Kiev. Lillian Stanslav had orders for Osaka, to translate with the Soviet consulate as negotiations concerning Sakhalin Island and the U.S. military government of Japan needed further clarification and direction as to the resolution and future government of the former Japanese territory. A year later, Lilli had had enough, and went to work for the State Dept. and came back home and translated primarily for the United Nations under the State Dept.'s supervision. Her paychecks came from the State Dept. and not the U.N.

Lilli made many lasting relationships with officials over the years, and knew which assignments she could not turn down. She knew better than to end the job completely. Through the years, whether she was taking care of Ray and me, or all four of us kids, we didn't know why Aunt Lil had to be somewhere else and we had to go to a substitute sitter: more musical chairs.

When Ray and me hit the 6th and 5th grades, we were given a key to the house, and our daycare days were over. Aunt Lil was still there minding Cathy and Brother Bill. She was in charge of us while we were in the house, but we spent more and more time on the baseball diamond, football field, and running track. When we were at 21 and Aunt Lil was there, Ray and her would carry on: talking about Hungary, Cuba missile crisis, the KGB, the politburo, PRAVDA, Krushchev, TASS, Stalin, and a series of minor coups from 1953 through Krushchev's removal from power. The two would talk about Russia whenever there was time.

Aunt Lil had this great big Packard Clipper, and was paid extra by Jane because she could pick-up and drop-off. Before Cathy and Billy were born, sometimes we'd go to her house, and other times we'd be at 21. Once she went to the store in the morning and forgot to put the meat in the freezer. We were hustled in the T-34 and she put the afterburners on. The Yonkers P.D. pulled Lillian over and the flatfoot started to give Aunt Lil the business:

"License and registration." The cop pointed at her, "Who do you think you are.....speeding with these kids?"

She went through her wallet and had Ray going through the glove compartment, it could have been mistaken for a dresser drawer. "Is this it?" Ray asked.

"It's got the American eagle on it. Keep looking." Lilli handed him her driver's license.

"Listen Sis," he said looking down at her. "This is a.....a....let's see that registration."

She hopped her butt over to the middle of the bench seat; and started going through the glove box. "Here it is" she said handing it to him.

He examined the two documents, "What kind of dog and pony show you got here. You think I was born yesterday? I can see you're trying to say the War Dept. owns the car. There ain't no such department any more so that's one strike. Whooya trying to get over on with this drivers license? The O.S.S. has been out of business for years. What were you a secretary to Bill Donovan? I want to see a license that wasn't made in a shed next to a printing press........C'mon lady, we're going downtown."

We followed the cop to Y.P.D. Headquarters to sort the mess out. The watch captain kept making calls that went up the ladder. The cop who brought us in thought Aunt Lil might have been some kind of foreign agent. The captain looked over to his patrol officer, "We got to tread lightly on this diplomatic stuff."

Senator Jacob Javits' office spoke for the State and Defense Departments. The United Nations vouched for Lilli Stanslov's possession of a State Dept. owned vehicle: one 1955 Packard Clipper/NYS diplomat plates #1080. The Pentagon had issued credentials, a level one security clearance, as well as the International Diplomatic Drivers license. Both were valid, with no expiration. Aunt Lil called from the station house to let Jane know we would be late.

After the incident, Hal could never talk enough about world events and what the latest international scoop was. Lil told him that she was just one of many interpreters in the pool who got called every so often.

As far as I know, Ray was the only person in our small circle who was aware she had the national security clearance. I think she divulged this information to Ray during the last year she sat for my younger sister and brother. She had taken a real shine to Ray and it was reciprocated. He told me about her access to state secrets in 1974.

Most people were treating me like Aunt Lil did: a sidekick, and it wasn't only for the reason I was younger than Ray. It was starting to sink in; I just wasn't that smart. This was confirmed when we brought our report cards home and showed them to her. "Ryan, your grades are not as good as your brother's. You are going to have to work harder."

As Ray and me only needed supervision one day a week because Lil had us for the other three days, we were treated like aliens for the one day appearances. The sitters got so mixed up, they didn't know what our scheduled day was. For about a month, we took the no.7 bus from in front of the apartment to Getty Square and went up to Jane's studio and spent the remainder of the afternoon watching Jane's students practice their tap dance. That was the best we could hope for when Aunt Lil had to go to N.Y.C. and translate. It was hard finding your footing when all these situations were so brief. Aunt Lil was so good to all four of us, it made a bad daycare engagement seem twice as bad.

"It's right across the street where Dottie Holland, Mom, and Uncle Billy went to high school." My brother didn't look up from his comic book. "Didn't she tell you?"

"Who?"

"Mom."

"About What?"

"We're supposed to be moving to the other side of Yonkers." Ray said.

"Nobody told me nothing. I'm happy right here."

"I think were moving around October." He tilted his head: uncertain.

Ray was under powered after a bout with tonsillitis, but he was getting better.

We were moving to the upper unit of a duplex Hal's aunt and uncle owned. They lived in the lower. There was also a unit in the basement, but it hadn't been used since the Korean War ended.

Aunt Gert was one of Grandpa Helmut's sisters. The first time Ray or me saw them was when we pulled up with the furniture. I was eight and Ray was nine; Little Cathy was almost two. The new place might have been ten miles from 2 Vernon Place. Aunt Gert was all Whitelaw. Either she knew a lot of the Whitelaw saga or made it up. She was the one who told us our real last name was Weisslexx. It was anglicized by immigration in Brooklyn at the turn of the century. Hal's side of the family had come over just before World War I.

Gert was strange. She hid in closets when there was thunder or lightning. Blessed with the aim of a Amazon hunter, she could hit any human, animal, or bird inside of 50 feet with a pea shooter. Ray and me thought she probably would have been pretty good with a blow-gun as well. We thought it looked like fun, so Ray and me got a box of them peas and a couple of shooters, to see what we could do.

Uncle Bob had a red face and white hair; the only thing Gert and him did together did was go to church and watch T.V. He liked to drink and shoot off fireworks on all the big holidays, even the confederate ones. He taught us all about fireworks, even the big stuff. When it came to shooting the stuff off - he'd only let us light up firecrackers, smoke bombs, and sparklers. On Memorial Day, Jefferson Davis' birthday, and The Fourth of July, he'd put the heavy-duty pyrotechnics in a paper bag and we'd take it over to Gorton High's football field to kind of get the feel for the stuff and the level of quality. He had about three of everything. He got them from his trucker friend who came up from South Carolina every year, and spread them out in the dirt at the 50 yard line.

"Okay guys you know what any of this stuff is?"

We were only familiar with firecrackers and sparklers.

"Okay, I'll learn you something: this group here is ash cans, cherry bombs, and M-80's which is just about the same as an ash can.

These will take your fingers and part of your hand off." He pointed to the next bunch. Ray and me could see straightaway these were trouble.

"These are my favorite: these are the blockbusters, they're equal to a quarter stick of dynamite.......each. I'm going to set one off. Don't hold your ears; I want you to get the idea of what they're capable of. If an M-80 can take a piece of your hand off you can be sure that a blockbuster will take off your arm and maybe more. Never light these things and throw them. Put them on something that doesn't move, light 'em and run!" He started laughing.

The rest of the stuff were smoke bombs, skyrockets, Roman candles, bottle rockets, aerial bombs, and a matt of 2-1/2" firecrackers. Occasionally, he made his own bombs, but they were too unpredictable. We'd take the experimental stuff down the river and shoot them off with mixed results. Uncle Bob always had a beer going. He married Aunt Gertrude before he enlisted in the Army for the duration of the war. He was a demolition engineer in the service and a hard rock blaster after the war.

We never knew how many brothers and sisters Grandpa had until we moved to 260 Park Ave. When they had a gathering of more than three Whitelaw generations, I was the one that wanted to hide in closets. They were like a clan of prophet troglodytes. Maybe it was genetic overload. Their conversation seemed to be in code. When it became heated, it was mostly in German.

Grandpa Helmut, and his siblings were all pretty keen on Ray. They figured he would be the link of all that is Weisslexx in the succeeding generations to come. As far as this side of the family envisioned, Ray and me weren't close to being twins – no matter what the street said. To them, it wasn't there.

To the Whitelaw's it was cut and dried: I was a Hicock. My mothers DNA ruled my blood. I didn't see it that way; I felt I was a McKay. It was who I wanted to be.......who I identified with. I hardly knew Jane's blood father. It always felt right when I told people Mack McKay was my grandfather on Jane's side. They lived up in Dutchess county, and it was out of sight – out of mind; not as accessible to dislike. There was not much choice for me about Mack being my grandfather. We only had a few photos of Jane's father, and none of us kids with him. Mack was in all our pictures and home movies. He played with us, joked around, and taught us stuff we'd never learn back in Yonkers. For Ray and me - Mack was the real deal.

ii

Jane and Hal had been telling friends, relatives, and neighbors that we had outgrown the apartment on Vernon Pl. with the arrival of my sister in December of 1960. According to Ray, the birth of a girl for Jane meant she would most likely back off with the dancing stuff she made us do. Hal and Jane had both thought the family had been maxed out. Cathy was always on the right side of Hal, more than anything else he just loved looking at her knowing she was true Whitelaw and had qualified as another tax deduction for the year .

Being uprooted from the only home we ever knew was a big chunk to swallow: No more Dennis and Donnie, Randy and Kevin Kutmueller, Ronnie and Marilynn Chen, no more Lee Lowe, Bianca Magnano, No Kimball movie theatre. All gone.......just Ray and me. Linda Magnano still took lessons from Jane, and we'd see her at the dance school's recitals, but from a distance. Jane said she turned into a whiz kid later on and got a full ride at M.I.T.

Hal informed us we would be going to Catholic school, another adventure into another world. His only first cousin, 'Little Gertie', had four kids going to All Souls' Grade School; she said it would work out great for Ray and me because it was so close to the duplex. It was close alright, about a quarter of a mile away. 'Lil Gertie thought it was a good neighborhood and the area would be great for the two boys: "Lennon Park is right next to you, school and church right around the corner, The 'Chippewa Boys' club is on Lake Ave."

"The only problem might be with Aunt Gert, but maybe not." There was hesitation in Little Gertie's assessment.

Jane dealt with a lot of people in the course of her business; she was determined to avoid any kind of spat with Aunt Gert.

"She's one nosey old hag." Hal, Jane, and Ray had said at different times. Most of Aunt Gert's snipes were directed at Jane. Hal and Ray could do no wrong. Mom was too smart for Aunt Gert; her people skills allowed her to keep peace in the duplex by turning on the charm with Uncle Bob. As long as Jane kept things kool with Bob, he would stymie Aunt Gert's power plays. All of a sudden, Hal didn't seem as smart to Ray and me.

All the Whitelaws disliked Jane. It wasn't overt; they didn't like what she did and how she looked. It was real Teutonic stuff. I never understood it; I just knew it wasn't me. Later on Ray had thought it through: "It's ridiculous. Life's too short for that crap." Still, they looked to him to carry on and be what they were. There was something to be said for the family's drive not to change.

A couple of weeks after Hurricane Donna hit the N.Y.C. metropolitan region in September, we got the official word to pull up stakes: P.S.14.......gone. It was the end of everything we learned Jewish, and the intensive start of being Catholic. 260 Park Ave. let us know we were in a different world every day. A fight would erupt for the smallest provocation, and because we were the new guys – we never belonged. I felt that way until the day they gave me my eighth grade diploma.

The kids in my grade in the other class would rough me up, and the guys in my class certainly beat me up. The kids in Ray's grade came after me too, "That's the one.......that's his brother......Get him too." I was laying on the ground after they knocked me down, and some girl comes over and starts kicking me, "And that's for my brother, cause my mother won't let him work you over." Kim McCarthy spat on me.

It was four against two, and Ray and me were taking our lumps again after school. One Monday, Jane met us after school with Cathy in the carriage. Ray and me were clearly losing in an orderly retreat that was pretty close to a full rout when Jane came to the rescue. She brought the four assailants to the principal's office for some justice and relief from the attacks. Ray and me waited outside with Cathy. Jane came out of the office like she had visited an alien planet.

"Thanks for saving us Mom." Ray said. Our clothes were all in disarray, and I had a bloodied nose. We took our time walking back to our new residence.

"Mom, what's wrong with these people? They're always mad, they always want to fight." Ray said.

"I don't have any friends…..none at school…..none in the neighborhood." I shook my head.

Jane pushed Cathy's carriage and complained: "You know what that dumb penguin said to me in the office?.....She asks me, "What did I expect?", 'You're trying to transfer your kids from public to Catholic school.' The dumnunskull smirked at me like I only had half a brain."

"Your father and I have gotten you boys started off on the wrong foot." was what the vice-principal said. Jane scanned the neighborhood, "What is she - some kind of retard?"

"What are we going to do Mom?" I asked.

"We've got to find a way around this insanity." Mom shook her head.

No matter how we tried to accommodate these bullies, 90% of the altercations were resolved the old fashion way: skin on skin.

It was mob mentality, all the guys knew who we were: "They live right across from Gorton - on Park Ave." It was a big drawback. For the first two months, they chased us home every day.

Calls of "chicken……CHICKEN!" Squawks and laughter rang through my head to the point I couldn't do my homework or get to sleep.

I will always……always…..owe Ray. He stood up for me verbally and physically - right or wrong. We were always outnumbered. In the rare instance it was two against two……we'd be duking it out with a couple of the biggest guys on the playground.

By about Halloween, Ray had figured out the scheme: Lilli Stanslov was gone for whatever reason. When me and Ray went up to the second floor flat we always had to keep the door open so aunt Gert could monitor us. Sometimes we would get our gloves and ball to play catch; but most of the time we'd go down to the ball field and get 'chosen in' a game of hardball, stickball, or football. Even then they took advantage of us; they tried to make us steady outfielders, which meant we weren't allowed to bat.

Lennon Park had a lot of action: the teenagers were drinking, smoking cigarettes, necking, and sniffing glue. We didn't know what pot was back then. Our main activity was playing baseball and football. We'd get chased around Lennon park by the older guys; only the slow and dumb got caught and that wasn't us.

Every chance we got we'd play baseball. Baseball was a big deal when it was tied in with Little League. There was Pee Wee (six & seven years), Farm teams (eight through twelve years), and Little League (eleven through fourteen years), but age code enforcement was pretty sketchy; when it was abused, usually it was by older guys trying to play with less experienced players. The coaches showed up from their day jobs with a ham & cheese sub and a 16 oz. can of beer. They would try to transform a melting pot of hyper active boys into some kind of fine-tuned machine and call it a 'team'.

Fathers brought their sons over to the Chippewa Boys' Club to sign up for the summer schedule and play organized ball. It was across the street from Lennon Park where the two ball fields were. The assembly of the teams, division of talent, and having someone on the inside was part of the baseball magic occurring on an annual basis.

A TEAM'S MAKE-UP WAS A REAL SLICE OF AMERICANA: Micks, Goombas, Pollocks, Bohunks, Spades, (Every year a group of ballplayers were cut by the black boys' club, The Astros. The black boys who failed to qualify in the Astro's Boys Club found their way up to Lennon Park. Most got on a team, but a few were cut for reasons other than a lack of talent). * Of all the ironies, none compares to the logic that lumped the Jews and Krauts together as one ethnic unit.

The Puerto Ricans had problems of their own due to a number of counterfeit birth certificates. It turned into a scandal that was picked up by the newspaper, and it almost got the Chippewas suspended from league play. Many of the Puerto Ricans were actually Dominicans and Cubans using someone else's documents for identity and age misrepresentation. Some of these guys were two or three years older than what their proof said. For most, they used their baptismal certificate for a secondary cross check. Soon there were too many ten and eleven year old baptismal certificates on brand new paper all coming from the same parish. One of the officials of the Chippewa's Boys' Club went down to St. Joseph's rectory and asked to see Fr. Tomas Vasquez.

"Father Vasquez......Pat Baldwyn, with the Chippewas Boys' Club up the hill."

"Yes, what can I do for you?"

Approximately 11 Baptism certificates were placed on the counter of the rectory, "These ended up at the Boys' club to support the verification of these boys' ages. They have St. Joseph's seal – What I want to know: Is this your signature on these certificates?"

The priest looked through the pile. "I've only been at St. Joe's for three years. These certificates of Baptism ....the most recent one supposedly took place eight years ago, I was only ordained ten years ago. No requests for document replacement for any of these boys has been brought to the rectory, and most important – "he held up one of articles in question: "This is not my signature."

"Thank you Father, it was what I needed to know. We can't have 14 year olds playing against 10 year olds."

"Yes, I see your point, but the baseball keeps these boys occupied and out of trouble, isn't there some way that we can find some kind of a 'solution'?"

"Not from my end, but they stole from you. Right now, the Boys club hasn't been injured."

"Mr. Baldwyn, do you not think that baseball helps a boy or a young man on many levels?"

"I have three daughters and no sons, but the game is one of the best ways to bring out the good in all boys. It teaches them how to think, reason, act as a unit, sacrifice, how to take criticism, how to be generous, and so much more. If I didn't believe in its positive effect on them……. Let's just say, I'm not in this for me."

"Mr. Baldwyn……I played Babe Ruth ball."

"So you know what I'm talking about."

"Very well." Fr. Tomas smiled…….

"But I also know when I'm being thrown a slider. What's up your sleeve?"

"You can refuse to roster the boys who are not from St. Joe's, that leaves you with eight boys with dubious credentials. Can we not find a way for these boys to stay out of trouble and play baseball for the summer?"

"You're asking me to look the other way Father? What we got here is a conspiracy."

"Yes, every once in a while it feels so good to do the wrong thing for the right reason – does it not?" the priest grinned.

"This will be for this season only, the over aged boys will be divided amongst the eight teams: four for the little League and four for the farm teams. Just so we're not looking like a bunch of fools who had the wool pulled over our eyes, there has to be some punishment to dole out as a deterrent – so the word gets around that using someone else's birth and Baptismal certificates as proof of age won't be tolerated in the future."

"Your Boys' club cannot be involved with any punishment. Should this conspiracy reach the light of day, and it surely will, let us hope it is well down the road. It would be bad for the boys, the Boys' club, not to mention St. Joe's."

"Do you have anything in mind for their penance?"

Fr. Tomas smiled again, "We have a one acre reflection area that has gone wild. I believe there are seven statues of saints and the Blessed Virgin back there. We can only see and pray to our Lady at present. The sisters and our pastor, Father Michael, would appreciate it….if there were some boys who might donate their labor to reclaim the acre."

"I think the names are in that pile." Pat Baldwyn nodded over to the pile of phony baptismal certificates.

The two men shook hands.

Occasionally these coaches and managers would still be short of players, even with the colored and Latino ringers. Motorized recruiting drives cruised all around as they went into the press gang mode. It was a spectacle. Two pick-up trucks with five or six boys each looking like they were on their way to the guillotine.......but misery loved company. They would call out to anyone who was of Little League or Farm team age.

"Heeeeeey Jimmmmeeeeeee."

Jimmy's head ratcheted up, "Wuh?"

"We're gonna get some Italian ices and ice cream – get in." The oldest boy in the bed of the truck had set the bait.

Sometimes the potential draftee couldn't be bribed onto the truck, and the coach riding shotgun had to walk over to the kid and his folks and make a personal appeal. The coach left the paper bagged 16 oz. of beer on the pickup's seat. The coach came back to the truck and asked through the open window: "Hey what's the father's first name?"

"Dave. His old man's name is Dave."

Coach climbed a few steps and made small talk with Jimmy on the porch. Jimmy's dad came out of the house with a half finished beer.

The coach extended his hand, "Whadaya say Dave?"

"Angelo." The two shook hands.

"We need Jimmy to play for us this year.......we'll waive the uniform, the insurance, sign-up fees. All you gotta do is buy him a cap."

"Wait just a cotton pickin minute Angelo, I went to all his games last summer – you only started him once. He ain't no outfielder." Dave took a sip.

"No bullshit - if he makes the pitching rotation he starts, but he can't be layin down on me when he's not scheduled to pitch."

He went over to the porch rail and looked the other direction.

Angelo had to close the deal, "Look, playin' ball a kid stays out of trouble and works off all that excess energy that gets him in trouble."

Jimmy could see his old man's wheels turning, "I ain't playin' no Little League ball." Jimmy whined.

"Hey Shogun, you ain't tellin' me what you're going to do......you got it backwards kid. I'll knock you into the middle of next week." Dave killed his beer.

Angelo had a small grin on the side of his mouth - away from Dave. It was the same scenario 10 times every spring.

Dave didn't like it when the kid tried to pull rank and call the shots. "Here's the lowdown Mr. Smartypants: Either you play ball, or you'll be pushing a mower for your uncle Mark at the cemetery for free. You ain't no playboy, and you ain't hanging out smoking Kools, and chasin' 'nem ponytails all summer."

"Debbie........get me a beer. An, I want an answer right now. You gonna be Don Drysdale or uncle Mark's slave and get real good with a push lawn mower?"

Jimmy hopped off the porch and ran over to the pick-up truck. "They got any of them tri-color ice bomb pops?"

"Angelo got in the truck and grabbed his beer. "Another satisfied customer." The two coaches smiled.

In the 50's and early '60s, the cops, teachers, and clergy all relied on parental reinforcement to maintain discipline. It was critical to keep the system running smooth or had that perception. Corruption was insidious, once it took hold, it was very difficult to get rid of.

iv

The location of Aunt Gert's duplex was about four or five miles north of Getty Square, where Jane's studio had been. Ray had figured out the bus routes. I was right behind him doing my 'follow the leader' act. Yonkers Transit operated most of the bus routes in Yonkers. The no. 2 bus had a stop right in front of her house, probably to accommodate the students attending Gorton High. If they were making a commotion, out came Gert's pea shooter, and she'd disperse a throng with a couple of well placed shots. Once in a while she'd put a bunch in her mouth and blow them out like a machine gun. She didn't do the machine gun too often because she had spit her upper denture out a couple of times.

Jane, Ray, and me watched a duel between Gert and this high school kid. The student had previously gotten the business from Aunt Gert, only this time he was ready; he picked up Uncle Bob's galvanized top of our garbage can, and deflected her rapid fire peas, brought out his pea shooter and peas from his book bag and returned fire making her window sound like it was going through a hail storm. Back and forth it went. "Jane said, I'm embarrassed to live here." and continued to change Cathy's diaper.

About half-a-mile towards the river, Liberty coaches ran an independent bus line on North Broadway. The route started at the Yonkers commuter rail station next to Otis Elevator, and went north through Yonkers, Hastings, and Dobbs Ferry. Both lines got us where we wanted to go most of the time. If we missed a Yonkers Transit bus, we'd run a few blocks west and try to catch a Liberty.

All Souls' Grade School and High School were slightly more that a quarter mile from Gorton High. Both sat on top of a hill that was long, steep, and high. All Souls' church steeple was visible from many parts of the city. The hill was all rock. Many building contractors didn't want anything to do with placing foundations or slabs up there. There wasn't any easy money for a builder on that hill until he got out of the ground. The cost of land in the metro area eventually moved the rocks, boulders, granite formations, and development finally came.

Hal claimed the people were actually living on a butte and didn't know it because there were so many trees and houses covering it. The top of the mesa was five miles long and two miles wide.

Somehow the crazy Dutch made it habitable. The people who lived up there knew a car's parking brake was almost useless and leaving the transmission in gear was unreliable as well. It was best to do both and keep a 4"x4" chunk of wood in the car to chock a wheel. There were 10" pieces of 4x4's in the curb or on the small patch of dirt between the sidewalk and the curb made of slate. You'd find them all over. People would carouse around for a night, block their wheel and run over the 4x4 when they left the bar. The block of wood was cheaper than having the guy adjust your brakes.

Lake Ave. was the only place that had stores, near us. There were two drug stores, one grocery, two delis both made sandwiches to go, a horrible pizza joint called the 'Hoagy Hut', a Post Office, the Chippewas B.C., a laundromat, a couple of candy stores and two liquor stores. There were also two bars: 'The Emerald Isle' and 'Hanratty's.'

It was all two and three story buildings with apartments above the storefronts; nothing was newer than 50 years old. It was a hub of activity, kids, teens, gangs – something was always going on. There was a funeral home too; their parking lot always seemed full.

The people were about 90 – 95% white: all ethnicities, but mostly Irish and Italian. It was overwhelmingly Catholic. This cluster of humanity fit in the middle and lower middle class strata with ease. It could only go downhill. For most, living near Lake Ave., Gorton High, and All Souls' church and school were good enough. Their grandparents had put down roots here, they made it through the wars and The Depression, what was the point of leaving? A solid job connection with a major employer, or a Civil Service career led many to believe Lake Ave. = ea$y $treet. Hal saw it approaching; he knew the neighborhood was slipping into decay. Disrespect of law, the elderly, women, and escalating crime; the blackboard jungle crap continued to encroach on the hill's mores. Hal would talk about it, but not overly so. Like the coming attractions at the movies – he knew the feature film was only minutes away.

During our brief two year tenancy at Aunt Gert's, the onslaught never let up. The physical stuff may have been winding down; mentally - life was a continual struggle for Ray and me. Jane knew it was rough sledding for us; I don't think Hal gave it much thought.

EITHER WAY, THE AREA WAS ON THE MOVE, AND THE path of least resistance was Lake Ave.'s most probable route. The electricity was there, guys and gals from all over North Yonkers were making it into some kind of conduit to be noticed and score whatever they were trying to find. They thought they could find it up there. Gangs were looking to rumble, common street fights, cars burnin' rubber and peelin' out. The girls were in on it as well: big make-up, big hair, skin-tight clothes, leather, studs. Legal age to drink was 18, which meant 16 and sometimes 14. Back then everybody smoked, it was the thing to do. Grocery stores never I.D.'d anybody, especially if you were buying a can of beans and a loaf of bread: "C'mon Mr. Malone, it's for my mom."

91

"Okay for this time, but next time you bring me a note from your Ma."

"You know she don't know how to write." Frankie looked at the grocer like he was the stupid one for not rememberin'.

"Have your sister write the note next time."

"Sure thing."

The liquor stores were a little stricter, they only I.D.'d the girls. If you were white and buying liquor from a colored liquor store owner, you never got carded. The opposite was true for the blacks buying from whitey. The white and black store owners always told the cops, "I got a business to run, that's you cops' job to make sure they ain't drinkin' illegally. Officer - I'm pleading the fifth." The owner would smile as he bagged a fifth of Canadian Club, and handed it to the smiling bluecoat.

"Just tighten it up....." and went back to his squad car.

There were card and dice games in Lennon park as soon as the warm weather came. The crack of the bats could be heard as the teams began to limber up for the 6 o'clock game. If a ballplayer was runnin' a hot streak, the ballgame was going to have to wait, and that would really piss off the manager. The Chippewas tried to get the cops to enforce the no gambling ordinance, but it was too petty to bother with. The Boys' club had to do their own enforcing, which had guys squealing on each other, and led to a lot of 'bean balls' during the games.

The motorized stuff had our heads spinning and jaws dropping. Them Hot Rodders, Greasers, and Bikers were kool. They brought the TV's concept of our strata of society to a level of realism. We had to watch them from a distance because they'd always chase us away. The big Hot Rod club were the "Hilltoppers"; 'Stayin on Top' was the motto on their colors. There was plenty of drag racing back then...... right on busy Lake Ave. Mostly, they raced to Park Ave., but sometimes they'd block off traffic on Park so they had a longer run to the next big street, Palisade Ave. These guys were so kool; the way they smoked, drank, and the way they dealt with the chicks - even the coppers wanted to hang out with 'em.

There was this one dude, Dave 'The Rave' Trent, he would challenge all the bulls that cruised Lake. Word got around pretty fast - Trent would drag race any Yonkers cop who had a fast enough set of wheels. He said he'd race them straight up for registrations. Nothing came of it as far as we heard.

These hot rodders and motorcyclists were magnets for young girls who just got into high school, and Trent really pushed it. He took out the bench seat in his 1960 Chevy Impala and put in front buckets. The bluecoats from the north precinct knew all the Hilltoppers by sight, they didn't like the bitch calls about the burn-outs, but they weren't criminals. With some things they looked the other way - once in a while they'd write them up. It was different with Trent, they loved to shoot the shit with him, and when they were on the corner with his crew, he always had the cops in stitches laughing. Ray said Trent was on some sort of 'good will' mission and introduced his flavor of the

92

day to the cops. The current one was this girl he dated since it got warm: Wanda Marz. She was 14 but looked 16 because of her big rack. Ray heard she was going to Gorton High but we didn't really know how old she was.

'Dave the Rave' already graduated Saunders Trade and Technical H.S. which was just south of Getty Square. This drag racing was a big deal, the word be out: "TRENT'S RACING TONIGHT".

It was the third week of July......plenty hot. And this club with four cars had come up from McLean Ave. looking for action. They had dropped the flag on three races already, but it was tough trying to keep Lake Ave. clear of traffic so the guys could race.

I remembered the smell as Trent was burnin' in his tires at the dead end of Lake Ave. by the laundromat. He was making lots of smoke and noise - causing a ruckus. The driver from McLean had hand painted lettering on his car: "Mangini......The Magician". He was about 40 feet in front of Lennon Park doing the same, inching towards the starting line. Trent had the hammer down as he came out of the dead end, getting all bent out of shape and passed the white crossing stripes at the intersection of Lake and Morningside. He burnt out in reverse to get his Chevy behind the starting line. He had gone too far again in the other direction and it looked like he had his front wheels off the pavement. Trent watched the flagman as he brought both drivers forward to the line.

The McLean Dodge and Trent's Chevy were revving their engines, waiting for the flag to drop. Before the flag dropped, the crowd is in a state of full confusion – the Dodge peels out and heads south on Morningside Ave. abandoning the duel. Dave got out of the Impala and stood in the middle of the intersection and asked the large crowd: "What the fuck?.....I can't leave you guys standing here." he called out. He summoned Wanda to come over. The two get in the car. Smoke's pouring out from both exhaust pipes, and rubber's burnin from the rear tires. The crowd on both sides of the street were waiting for the Dave Trent show. Right at the intersection of Lake and Morningside he does two tight 360 degree doughnuts, and the crowd goes wild. People are agog, coughin', laughin', pointing, and they got their hands on their knees trying to stay upright. They're all smoking and drinking. He whips the Chevy into a racing line position as the car's recoil leaves it out of square with the crosswalk/starting line. Everyone is cheering and fist pumping from Dave's impromptu deviation from the usual drag race.

Ray and me were there; sometimes I am still there.

The smoke had subsided enough to see Trent and his little girlfriend Wanda Marz. Those who could see through the dense smoke saw Trent laughing. He had the Chevy's wheels buried all the way to the left and floored it jamming the brakes: more smoke, gas, rubber, exhaust, and thunder. The double and triple takes went through the crowd on the street. The sight I saw didn't make sense to me: Wanda straddled Dave Trent in his seat with her back almost up against the steering wheel. Her small head fit under his chin like a fiddle. In typical Trent style, he had Wanda sucking her thumb. Years later, I thought, 'What a sick ticket and laughed.' At the time we didn't know what to make of it.

He revved the '60 Impala   again and let the clutch out in short burst to get the street worked up again; then he let enough out to do a lazy 180. We could see he wasn't happy with it. He got back into it: smoke, rubber, exhaust, and thunder. The Chevy came to rest on the opposite crosswalk line. Now the crowd returned the Trent thunder. The excitement was at a pitch. His car was now facing the Dead end.

A member of the 'Hilltoppers' ran out of the 'Emerald Isle' with a shot of whisky for Trent. Wanda was motionless, her superslim body melting into Dave's. He wrangled his neck and threw down the shot. She kept her eyes shut, and Dave kept her sucking her thumb. Three 55+ year old ladies were on the sidewalk across from the Emerald. They were thoroughly disgusted at the outrageous display. More back-ups, burn outs, and smell of the hi-test rich exhaust followed. The thunder made me and Ray put our fingers in our ears.

Now Dave had the front end off the ground; rear tires squealing like pigs to the slaughter. The Impala came to rest half-way from where all the summer night hi-jinx had started. A cop had parked his prowl car right up to the crosswalk line which barricaded traffic from entering Lake from Morningside. The flatfoot left his flashers blinking, but kept his 'Pull over Beacon' off, and double-timed it to the Emerald Isle. He ducked inside for an 'emergency double' and came out with a big grin.

A kid in the 5th grade showed up, camera in hand. "Hey mister, can I take your picture?"

Dave kept revving the 327, "How much film you got?"

"Almost a whole roll." The kid was shaking a little bit.

"Get up on the roof of that plumber's van and shoot the roll, first: take two shots of me and Wanda right now. Her eyes were half-closed in the first, but wide open for the second. "Get up there and shoot the rest." He smiled.

The only thing Trent was concerned about was the tachometer gauge. He had to be careful not to redline it. Too many R.P.M.'s and he'd cook the top end of the engine. More smoke, hi-test exhaust, (probably some additives as well), tires spinning, and thunder from the engine.......we all were expecting at least another 180 rotational. It was another 180, but this wasn't like the others; this one was so compact that the driver's side wheels lifted off the ground from the G-force.

Next Dave did a couple of short burn-outs in reverse and jammed on the brakes and the front end got just a little airborne with the rear bumper hitting the pavement. He peeled out to where the car had first started. We all cheered him on, hoping for more. Trent revved it up, the tach was real close to redlining and he popped the clutch; Wanda's back compressed against the steering wheel leaving it's imprint on her the next morning. The air from her lungs caused her to cough out her thumb. With one hand she grabbed the back of the bucket seat, and was back sucking her thumb with the other.

Dave drove down to the dead end. Everybody wondered what Trent was going to do; one of the older guys said he had to get out of the small dead end facing the right way. Un-uh; Dave had the hammer down with the rear end coming out of the dead end first. The Chevy sounded like the tranny or the rear end was going to let loose with the reverse gear winding out. They said later on they were surprised it didn't throw some teeth. The four barrel carburetor was wide open and he was doing 45 m.p.h. before he was even with the Emerald Isle. The wheels were cut hard to the right, Dave's eyes were wide and he tried to recover from the oversteer. Maybe he got into the turn later than he thought, or perhaps the steering wasn't as crisp as he thought. It was a wide sweep of the car in reverse gear. The Chevy looked to be almost out of control. There was panic on both sides of the street and both sides could envision it crashing into them; some were running for their lives, but the Impala was still between the curbs. We saw the rear wheels stop spinning, but the car had so much momentum, additional force was needed. He tossed Wanda in the shotgun seat, worked the clutch and gearbox – threw it into 2nd gear and let the clutch out reversing the car's direction and did a 180 in the opposite direction.

Drinks, beers, hats, newspapers, and hot dogs all ran for cover. One drunk remained stoic, standing next to the curb, throughout the finale. Later he would recount the evening's events to the cops, reporters, and hot rod enthusiasts throughout Yonkers and the North Bronx: "Yup, the Chevy missed the parked cars and us in front of the Isle by millimeters I'm tellin' ya."

That shot of whisky may have relaxed Trent too much; it might have reduced his cat-like reflexes and his falcon vision. What he lost on the front end, he made up for in his recovery. His final move was the 'coup de grace' parking the Chevy side-ways in front of the Bar, about 17 degrees out of parallel with the curb. Everybody on the street mobbed him. The 'THRUSH' dual exhausts still thundered, and Dave the Rave realized him and Wanda would have to get out of the car. They all wanted to see the stunt driver in person. He threw his boots in the back seat, and she did the same with her flip-flops. He began looking for the kid with the camera. Dave saw the plumber's van.

"How many you got left?" He called with his cupped hands.

The kid held up three fingers.

"Don't shoot any more until I give you the word."

The kid gave him the 'thumbs up'.

The crowd circled the Impala, "Listen the kid's got three pictures left." He told us. "We might need more light. I need two cars shining their hi-beams at the back of the car, and two more doing the same on the front...." Dave's eyes darted back and forth, "Before the cops get here."

"Hey Dynamite." A patrolman called.

Dave squinted at the bull.

"The cops are here." He tapped his billy-club in the palm of his other hand. "I can hi-beam with the prowl car and I got the side spotlight.......for your close-up."

Everybody laughed. The cop was okay.

Dave and Wanda stood barefoot on the trunk of the car. His arms went into the air, and his hands became six-guns in victory. She wrapped her arms around him and rested her head in the narrow part of his waist. The next shot was similar; this time he blew imaginary smoke away from the pistol's barrel. The last photo had Trent solitary, crossing his arms with a pair of sunglasses and a self-satisfied grin.

The crowd had been much larger than those who made it in the three photos, the kid taking the pictures did the best with what he had. After that night, I didn't see the camera guy until I saw him again when I went to Gorton High. He was two years older than me. I can't remember seeing him without a camera looped around his neck.

The close-up of the car with Dave and Wanda in it came out pretty clear. About half of the action shots came out, Ray said the guy should have used a higher speed film, and that was the reason some came back blurry. The last three photos on the roll - with the two of them on the trunk lid, and the last one with Dave by himself, standing on the roof of the car with the sunglasses was best of all. About 30 or so people had surrounded the car in the last three shots. There was a little too much light, but all the faces were recognizable. Anybody who had a drink or beer in their hand had it raised in tribute to the show Dave Trent had just performed.

The cop who had helped out, told Trent the 'Heat' was on the way and he'd better make tracks. Trent pulled out from in front of the Isle, and found the nearest telephone pole and eased his front bumper against it, and used it for a dead-man to put a wall of carbon monoxide laden exhaust, smoke, the taste and smell of rubber, and a deafening roar of thunder down Lake Ave. for his curtain call.

Ray and me smiled, awe-struck. You had to see it to believe it.

There was almost an entire page in the sports section which hit the Statesman about a week later. Story: Art Devore. Photography: Jack Devore. There we were on one knee in front of the driver's door. The right side of Ray's face got washed out by the headlights, but his left side was intact - you knew it was him. His shadow gave my face just the right amount of light. We told everybody Dave Trent was our uncle to juice it up.

After a solid 45 seconds on the telephone pole, Dave knew it was time to put the '60 Impala under wraps in the garage for the next week. There was a rumor he was getting around on a Vespa motor scooter wearing a helmet and dark green goggles for the next ten days.

A couple of men were talking nearby, "Who was that chick with Trent?........his sister?"

"Some guy in the Emerald said it was his girlfriend."
"Huh?"
"Yeah, he said it was his girlfriend."
"What was that 'thumb sucking' all about?"
He took a sip of his beer, "Maybe she's a retard?"
"I dunno, she looked pretty good, but a little too young."
"That's what everybody was saying."

We went home full of excitement. Ray said not to tell Mom or Dad about the drag racing. After our prayers and we lay in our beds, I asked him why that girl was dating a guy much older than her. "I think I act more grown up than her, I never even sucked my thumb.....Why does he let her do that ......in public. Man, that's weird." I looked into the darkness.

"Yeah, but it was still a real good time." He muffled a laugh into his pillow.

v

The coach had his fungo bat working, and we were practicing catching pop-flys and doubling up the base runners with our Farm team, "The Jets". Officially, I was too young to play Farm team baseball, but my talent was adequate. The Chippewas looked the other way because they were short on bodies, and I looked like Ray who was old enough, so they let me play.

It was late Spring and daylight savings time was already six weeks old. The sun had just gone down behind the palisades on the west side - the Jersey side of the Hudson. The moon had begun to rise in the east. Our view from Lake Ave. was mostly unobstructed, and this big yellow ball was in direct line with the street. I never remembered seeing a moon this size or color; not in another dimension, in a reincarnated life, or in a parallel universe – nothing. There was a heavy current of disbelief as the moon rose. It kept getting larger and clearer, therefore it must be getting closer Ray reasoned. We could see its craters and mountains with the unaided eye. In a matter of minutes, a complete Lunar profile would be displayed.

The four teams practicing in Lennon Park were immobilized, and slowly we all drifted into the street to get a better look of this monsta moon. In three or four minutes, the orb would completely fill the east end of Lake Ave. It appeared that it was getting closer instead of rising.

Ray was in a trance. A low pitched buzz filled the street and gained in volume until the moon's circumference extended beyond the buildings' exteriors on both sides. This ominous pale creamsicle's orange glow filled the sky. His eyes got wide, "This may go into some phase of supernova, if such a thing is possible for a satellite."

Everyone was fixated at the spectacle, I asked Ray while looking at the moon, "Which is moving the earth or the moon?"

"Don't know." his face awash in moonglow.

The moon continued to wax, brother Ray turned and observed the western sky. He turned back and watched the people watch this big orange pumpkin. Some of them were trembling, others were transfixed in place. The patrons of Hanratty's and The Emerald Isle emptied into the street and gaped at the phenomenon.

My teeth began to chatter; I was sure something apocalyptic was going to follow because this was no movie. Had we stayed in

97

public school my panic would not have been as intense, but with a year of Catholic education; it compounded my anxiety and paranoia.

"Ryan.......Ryan." Ray shook my shoulders from behind.

Astonished, I asked him while continuing to watch, "Are we going to die?"

"Ahhhhh.....I think it's just a big.....Big moon phase......... maybe." His eyes darted back and forth.

"I saw some people kneeling down praying. Should we start praying too?" I clenched my fists.

"We should get back home – we can say some Hail Mary's on the way."

A quick glance at the moon, "We better run - just in case." I felt safer in my P.F. Flyers burning rubber like Davey Trent as I raced home.

The shoe store had been out of P.F. Flyers in Ray's size so Jane had to buy him a pair of Keds. The Flyers had tied in with Disney with this "Spin and Marty" show with their official decoder ring, but someone had already pinched the ring from the shoebox. All I got was a P.F. Flyers rubber label on the heel.

Ray's Keds had a round emblem on the ankle bone of his high tops; their mascot clown held a bunch of balloons that was glued to the ankle bone. How did Ray ever expect to win any race wearing circus sneakers?

We got to Aunt Gert's duplex in record time, urgently calling, "Dad....Dad....Ray huffed, as I stood there. He was out of breath. "Dad, the moon........look at the moon!"

I had to be sure he got the right one so I pointed and echoed Ray, "Dad, look at the moon. It's gonna s'plode." He looked at us from the window as we pointed. He came out of the house and down the stairs.

"Pretty darn big." he commented. "It'll shrink soon enough."

Ray and me were sure Hal was wrong. Ray reasoned: "It's big now, but it was a whole lot bigger ten minutes ago."

The Old Man took a slug of beer and gave us a piece of his experience: "When we could get topside out in the western Pacific......."

"We watched his face replaying the large Pacific moon he was remembering almost 20 years earlier. "That moon was beyond comparison. Hal's gaze returned to this one as it continued to rise and shrink. This one is pretty big and throwing out the most light I've seen in quite a while."

Our faces were illuminated with the pale orange glow. "When you guys do your military service, you'll go to distant lands and you'll see things you can't imagine right now."

vi

From my earliest memories, Judy Conolly had been part of the Jane Marlowe landscape. Judy's father used to drink at the Pac-

Coy Club where Jane had her first studio, in the social room on the other side of the bar. Judy's father used to bring Judy to the bar just like Hal brought us to the bar. He'd watch Judy watch the girls tap dancing. Weekly dance instruction for Judy which gave him a bona fide reason to go to the Club every Saturday afternoon. Jane's month to month occupancy at the Pac-Coy Club only lasted another year. There were too many girls showing up for dance class unaccompanied by an adult and they'd walked through the front door of the bar. The owner told Jane that her dance studio had grown too much and she simply had to find another place.

Judy was about nine or ten years younger than Jane. As the years melted away the age differential meant less and less. Dottie Holland had been with Jane when she first opened up the studio, but she was always taking off for tryouts and auditions downtown. After one year, Dottie walked away from her half-interest in the dancing school – leaving it all to Jane. For the most part, Dottie disappeared from the radar screen for a few years - chasing her show business dream, and Judy took her place. I guess I could have done some investigative work and got to the bottom of the story after I married Karen Cahill. I had too much going on in my own life to answer questions like: "How'd that happen?"

Jane and Judy were good friends; every bit as much as Jane and Dottie had been. Judy had wanted a family and Dottie didn't know what she wanted.

Judy got married around '61 or '62; Jane got knocked up, and Judy was in lock step and got pregnant too. They both had boys in the summer of 1963: Willis and William. Judy and Mack were my sister's godparents. Every year we saw more and more of Judy around. The two shared more with each other than they did with their husbands.

Their friendship had evolved into a bond. Judy could run the Dance Studio when Jane wasn't available. She taught Ray and me how to tap dance in a duet in two recitals. It was a clear case of extortion on Hal and Jane's part in '60 and '61. Hal said he was introducing us to the world of the barter system.

"How else can we get our two wheeler bikes without dancing for them?" Ray asked.

"You can't." Hal said.

Ray slapped his forehead with the heel of his hand in disgust.

We learned our dance routine on Saturday afternoons at Mom's studio. There were one or two classes going on as we were on the side getting taught by Judy. Occasionally, she'd dish us off to some junior high girls as she smoked and did the books. They would always make a fuss over us, especially if we performed a complicated combination that was advanced for six and eight year old kids. Two or three of the girls took the piano bench and set it up in the corner and pushed the upright about three feet from the corner walls with just enough space to go behind it in seclusion.

Ray and me took turns being called to go behind the piano to get our reward for dancing so well. The reward usually ended up being getting kissed on the lips, or getting our faces washed in a budding pair of boobs. Unless we wore dungarees to dance class – the more experienced and older girls were quick to point out to the others there was a boner alert in the studio.

We didn't enjoy the teasing - I don't think; but there was something about getting your face mashed in a set of boobs. The smell, softness, the little jiggle. We all smiled and the jr. high girls put their finger over their lips and we nodded. I kept thinking of Darlene and Annette of the 'Mouseketeers".

Two weeks of dance lessons and Jane knew something was going on when we stopped our belly-aching about going for our Saturday lessons. She confronted us in the car with Hal driving home.

This was a perfect opportunity to be the younger brother, and I deferred to Ray to provide the explanation. As innocent as a new born lamb he said, "They kept kissing and hugging us. They said it was our reward and encouraged us to keep up the good work."

"Who's teaching you besides Judy?" Jane said.

"Diane, Mary Ellen, and Cheryl."

At next week's lesson, with Judy by her side, Jane corralled the three novice instructors, and told them they ought to have known better than to tease a couple of kids. "That's it with this nonsense, I don't need people thinking I'm raising a couple of wolves and letting them loose here in my studio."

"Yes Miss Marlowe."

"So knock it off."

Judy didn't have the dancing skills that Dottie had. She was content to hitch her star to Janie's wagon. Judy was a better instructor than she was a dancer, but she was a solid journeymen dancer that looked good in a pair of Leotards;
her students admired that. Jane needed that confidant who knew the angles and how to work them. The fact that she didn't hesitate when asked to run two sets of books gave Jane the green light and gave them both the degree of financial independence from their husbands they wanted. Too often they had seen women in situations making them prisoners in a loveless marriage with no way out. Jane had seen it first hand with her mother and father. 'That'll never happen to me', she promised herself.

Cathy was almost three years old when we started moving from Aunt Gert's to 21 O'Dell Ave. in September 1963. There was some kind of legal screw up with the people who were selling the house to Hal. They couldn't leave 21, until the people they were buying from moved out of the place they were supposed to buy. We had to put our stuff in storage for a month or two. Sounded like one big clusterfuck to Ray and me. We had lived at 260 Park for 2 years, it had seemed like four. Summer was drawing to a close. The Dodgers took the Yankees four straight in the Series in October.

The last week of the summer of '63, we went up with Judy to her parent's bungalow on Sherwood Island in Connecticut. Ray was disappointed there were no waves to ride. Long Island kept the Sound calm, protected from the Atlantic. The salt water was dirtier as it got closer to the shore. There was too much garbage; and the sewage was only half treated. It was similar to swimming in the Hudson with double the salt content. The beach was half broken shells, half pebbles, half sand, and cigarette butts, bottle tops, broken glass and the flies were riding horseflies. After lunch we asked Jane and Judy to blow up a couple of inflatable rafts. We needed them just to lay on the beach. The thin towels we had brought provided no cushioning.

At the Judy's parents' beach house, the two dancers were smoking Judy's Salems and drinking coffee and listening for Cathy napping on the screened porch. Each had blown up about ¼ of the two rafts. Ray and me were waiting on them. The women were hard at work, but not much air was getting into the rafts. They got about half-way through before they burst out laughing at each other, and handed the task to Ray and me.

"Oh that's sad." Jane wiped a tear from the corner of her eye. High clouds, smog, and ozone – the bane of many a smoker. Both had been dedicated smokers since high school. We had them inflatables blown up in no time, much to the relief of the women.

We took one swim in the water and then lay on the rafts: drifting. We were in the sun for over four hours. I had gotten a real bad sunburn, but Ray was in big trouble as two blisters had already begun to form near his heart. Jane took him to the hospital the next day and he had to stay overnight and then he got an infection in the blister area, and spent three more days at St. John's Riverside. It took him almost three months to heal up. I felt real bad for him. He wasn't even interested in the World Series, I didn't know if he was going to make it. I guess I had been crying in class in fourth grade and Miss Arnold had the class say a whole rosary for him during school. She asked me if I was okay, and I thanked her for helping out.

Jane was at the point where everything that could be done was done to facilitate the move - other than the actual move itself. She was getting overwhelmed: there was the move, the new school year for Ray and me, the new year at the dance studio, fixing up the house, praying that Aunt Lil was available to provide daycare for us kids. Ray was still having health problems related to the 3rd degree sunburn and the subsequent infections which kept returning.

It took a long time for Ray to recover from that afternoon in Connecticut. He couldn't do anything without getting wiped out. When we finally did move to 21 O'Dell, he was unable to help. 21 O'Dell was 2 miles away from All Souls, Ray couldn't run or walk very far. We had to take the bus to and from All Souls'. There was only so much I could do hanging around the house; I thought for sure he'd want to go exploring all around the area with all the woods. Instead, he mostly would help Jane with the house stuff, read, or we'd make these different track layouts for the H-O racing cars.

I couldn't be sure, but it seemed Ray might be getting his strength back by mid-November, slow though it was. They told us at school President Kennedy had gotten shot. They suspended class for the rest of the day which wasn't much of a break as we were on E.S.T. School let out at 2:00 pm. Ray jumped me as I was leaving the school building.

"Can you believe it? They shot the President!" he said.

"Is he alive?"

Ray inhaled and exhaled trying to absorb the magnitude of the event. "That's all I heard. All the nun's were crying.....They said to go home and pray for him."

"Miss Arnold was crying too." I added.

The whole school was empty in ten minutes except for the first and second graders. They had to get word to their families about picking up their kids an hour early.

Ray took off half-running and half walking. Any cars that passed we'd yell: "They shot the President......They shot Kennedy." We had only lived in the house at 21 O'Dell for two months. The two mile trek back home was rather bizarre due to the lack of traffic and pedestrians. We ran down the middle of the side streets and the middle of the oncoming lanes of the main streets. We got blasted by a few horns. A bunch of people were down the North End in front of the news and stationary store. Everybody wanted to buy the EXTRA Edition of any newspaper with coverage of the assassination attempt, but they hadn't come up yet. We hustled down Roberts Lane to the old Croton Aqueduct, we followed it for another mile when it intersected with O'Dell Ave. which ran within eyeshot of our house. The roof of our house could be seen from the aqueduct.

I stayed behind Ray for a while......just to see if he was struggling with the distance. Since we had been let out early, I was amazed at his replenished stamina. We had to make our way through some washed out gullies before we picked up the Aqueduct, once he was on it he began to sprint north. His acceleration caught me off guard. He was putting distance between us. Catching up to him was not as easy as I expected. When I did catch him, I looked over and laughed and put on the after-burners. To my disbelief, he came even with me, and now he started pulling away from me.

"No way!" I yelled and redoubled my effort.

Ray could see me overtaking him with the wild look of an animal being pursued; he dropped his gymbag and ran all out, his arms working with the motion of his body. Again he was putting distance between us. I was so mad I'd had to jettison my bookbag too, to have any chance: "NO FAIR!" I yelled. No choice; dropping the bookbag, I gave it all I had. In about 30 yards I had caught him. For the next 100 yards it was all out – neither of us could get the advantage. My foot hit a protruding stone and I fell into some high soft grass......totally spent. It took Ray another ten yards to come to a stop. He trotted back to where I lay, and fell down beside me. Our chests were heaving.

"What a race." He said.

"Cheater."

We both laughed.

"I'm awful glad you got it back......your strength."

"It felt good to run hard."

I pulled a stalk of grass from its bunch and chewed: "Why would they shoot Kennedy.......everybody liked him?"

"There'll be more stuff on the radio and TV; maybe he just got winged. You know he made it through WWII in one of them PT boats, and then he survived on one of those islands that have cannibals. Kennedy's too young to die."

"Hope you're right." I said.

"You got any homework?"

"Nah."

"Sister Adolphus gave us a 250 word composition to write about what President Kennedy means to us."

I thought about the shooting, "Ray just tell her you were too broke up to write a thing."

I thought it was funny because I didn't think he was dead. Ray managed a weak laugh, I knew he really liked Kennedy – we all did. The assassination attempt had him concerned for reasons I didn't connect with. It was even worse when the papers ran a special 2nd edition confirming he was dead. On Monday morning Ray turned in his assignment; he had written 250 times – "President Kennedy got shot."

CHAPTER 7

Ray took over the paper route from Mark Aronson. Mark was two years older and lived up at the northernmost point of the number 2 bus. It was a development named 'Tudor Woods' and it was about a 5/8^{ths} of a mile north of the 'North End'; it was one large oblong circle, with the traffic running counter-clockwise on the one-way street. Condos, co-ops, and apartments were inside and around the road. For whatever reason, the road was named DeHaven Drive.

When Mark was breaking Ray in to do the route, Ray asked, "Why do they call where you live 'Tudor Woods'?

Mark laughed, "Why didn't they name De Haven Drive – "Anne Boleyn's Block"? Mark and Ray laughed some more; I rolled another newspaper to throw on a porch.

Mark was old enough to make more money somewhere else, somewhere closer to where he lived. Walking up and down O'Dell must have been a factor when he decided to turn the route over to Ray.

Aronson went to Emerson Jr. High. The junior highs: grades 7 through 9, were never a stand - alone educational facility in Yonkers; they were either attached to a grade school or a high school. There were a lot of raging hormones and awkwardness in the junior highs. Girls…..like Wanda Marz were occasionally getting written up by the Junior High Vice Principal for hanging out in Gorton Sr. High. She was interested in older guys - particularly if they had a set of wheels to slither around with them in a car. She must have felt old enough when she hooked up with Dave the Rave, but she didn't make a move on him until she was a freshman.

Guys were lucky; they could release their pent-up angst and confusion with sports. At All Souls', we only had a grade school (1 thru 8) and high school (9 thru 12). It didn't make a difference – hormones came when they came - no matter how the educational system wanted to compartmentalize them.

The boy to man transition had occurred in the later half of Mark's 8th grade. To Ray and me, he seemed like a high school dude rather than going into his last year of jr. high. He made the mile walk each way to deliver the *Herald Statesman*. Included somewhere in those two miles was the inspirational and invigorating climb and descent of the 6% grade of O'Dell Ave. It was the only street that connected North Broadway and Warburton Ave. this far north in Yonkers. Broadway and Warburton ran parallel to each other and parallel with the Hudson River.

These two thoroughfares were also bus line streets. They're only a block apart when they left downtown Yonkers, but traveling north to the Hastings border, they spread apart approximately ¾ of a mile. Warburton ran a mostly level route, while Broadway climbed with the lay of the land, on top of the Ridge, or mesa as Hal called it.

At the top of O'Dell, Broadway was about 300 ft. higher than Warburton. With its road course features of hairpin turns, two switchbacks, no shoulders to speak of and the 6% grade.......wintertime challenged the best of drivers. O'Dell Ave. was a connector street and an important link between the two roads.

Two non-profit organizations owned the woods and overgrown gardens on either side of O'Dell Ave. Elizabeth Seton College on the east side owned acres of pine and evergreens, ornamental stonework, paths made of slate, and pergolas with stone benches beneath - had it not been for the sounds of vehicles outside the college's wall, a person may have thought they were in Middle Earth.

The west side of the street looked down on the Old Croton Aqueduct. There was a pretty good drop over the guardrail in two spots of about 20 feet. This is where people would dump their junk in the middle of the night. It was a real dump: plaster and lathe, tires, old washing machines, 55 gal. drums (most were rotted through), rusty iron frames for something, dirt, concrete, slag from foundries, bottles, cans. A small stream ran from the college underneath the street and became an underground stream and fed into the Aqueduct. In the two areas where the drop from the street was the greatest, they built up a pile of dirt to run their wheelbarrow over the 2 ½ ft. guardrail and launched a whole mess of asbestos floor tile.

When it snowed, O'Dell was undriveable for many rookie motorists. It was great – we'd watch cars coming down the hill sideways; they'd take out 3 or 4 cars trying to come up the hill. Sometimes they would crash into Elizabeth Seton College's 7ft. granite wall on the east side of the road or wreck into the guardrail on the west side. The west side had that serious 20ft. drop when they blasted through the guardrail - usually landing in a sea of old tires and junk. Cars were better off eating the college wall.

New Yorkers, being class "A" road warriors, never missed an opportunity to ride the bumper of the car in front of them. Rear wheel drive, bald tires, and monsta hills gave the Yonkers' motorist the superior skills a driver from the Bronx could only dream of. Bad road conditions on O'Dell had us hiding behind maple trees to avoid impacts. They provided great protection, we never saw one get knocked over by a car or a truck. Most of the time Ray and me walked past these drivers cruising at a 3 m.p.h. as their engines turned 3500-4000 r.p.m. We got to wave to a lot of pretty women.

Jane had a difficult time driving a manual transmission; that's what our '55 Chevy wagon had. She might have even had trouble driving a manual in Kansas. Operating a car with a clutch was going to give her a nervous breakdown. Mom would go through a couple of Kools trying to crest N. Broadway on a bad weather day. She thought God had answered her prayers when Hal announced he had bought a new car.

"'Nother Chevy wagon." he beamed.

Our old '55 Bel Air Wagon had done its duty: Big whisky dent in the right front quarter had its headlight looking for japs, nazis, and commies in the trees. The front bumper showed a new version of Chubby Checker's "Twist". The clutch disc had been worn down to metal and was chewing up the flywheel......thanks to Jane's driving skills. Ray and me were busy changing out half-sheets of 3/8$^{ths"}$ plywood under a hard chargin' 6 cyl. power plant that leaked more oil than a V-twin Harley. Hal sold it to 'Lil Gertie's husband for $45. He kept it running for another 4 years.

The Old Man brought home the new Impala station wagon – with room for nine passengers. It was Pea green with just a little metal flake to the paint.

"Say Hal, doesn't General Motors usually throw an 8 cyl. in the station wagons?" the next door neighbor said.

"Yeah.......could of had one a week ago, but I had them order a 250 cu. in. 6cyl. for me." He nodded up and down, "Plenty of power, but I'll really save on the fuel mileage with the manual transmission and the six." He smiled, drink in hand.

Some more neighbors came down the driveway to check out the new Chevy. It was odd that Jane hadn't come down yet. All us kids were playing in the car. Hal was drinking and smoking telling all the other Dads what a deal he got. "The seat belts come standard." He puffed.

Mom walked out from the basement, and said 'Hi' to everyone. George from across the street asked, "So Jane, what do ya think?"

She walked it from bumper to bumper, staying on the passenger's side. "Nice color." She then looked in the front seat and down at the floor of the driver. Her head whipped out and said "HEY YOU-" to Hal who was still jawbonin'. "Why's this car got three pedals? YOU SAID" she pointed across the roof, "YOU SAID" – Her lips were trembling and her eyes went to slits. "You said........we would get an automatic." She held her stare on him and crossed her arms.

Hal finished his whisky, "The clutch grabs real low.......it's damn near an automatic. It drives like one anyhow. I figured we got a new house; we should have a new set of wheels." He nodded as his chin went up.

"This thing got seat belts?"

"Enough for the whole gang." He waved his welcome hand in front of us.

"Well buckle up Hal, I'm going to buy my own car; it might not have seat belts but it's going to have an automatic transmission.........I'm done driving a damn truck." She lit a smoke and stomped off.

Word got around about what a heel the Old Man was. All the women stopped over when Hal was at work to give her support. Jane didn't want or need support, she wanted an automatic.

Ray slept on a cot in my room and Hal slept in Ray's room for two weeks. The only thing that got him back in the saddle was Christmas. It was only 11 days away.

Even though there was a sidewalk on the college's side of the street, the only ones who used it were people who did not walk O'Dell too often. The sidewalk was heaving, pitching, and out of level at every joint. A personal injury lawyer's brother-in-law must have been the contractor for the job.

Mark, our paperboy, never used the sidewalk or that side of the road for that matter. A week of using the sidewalk was enough to wise most people up. Mark no sooner came down past our house than it seemed he was heading back up O'Dell. Ray estimated Mark could do his route in about 35 minutes.

Friday was collection night for the week; he'd deliver and try to collect from whoever was home in the afternoon. A lot of people didn't get home from work until after six, which meant ringing doorbells on Friday night for paperboys. A weekly subscription for the Herald Statesman was $.70/week. Like most, Hal and Jane gave us three quarters to give to Mark when he came collecting and told him "Keep the nickel." There weren't any big tips except at Christmas; they were just delivering a newspaper.

The Statesman gave their paperboys this canvas bag to carry the papers and to keep them dry. A four inch wide band was slung over the shoulder and supported the bag. When the new paperboy bags were issued, they had a new blaze orange, reflective safety strip sewn into the band. The Statesman charged the paperboys $2.50 for the bag, @.25/week. Mandatory. Aronson and Tony, who had the other paper route on Warburton going north, started calling it the "*Sterile Hatesman*".

The weather was rotten on a Friday night. Mark rang the doorbell.

Ray opened the front door, "Hey Mark."

"Paperboy - Mom." I called into the kitchen

"Bring him into the hallway."

"Just a minute." Hal shouted from his small den.

He can't yell at Mark? What the heck? I thought.

"How much do you make a week delivering papers?" Ray asked as we waited for Hal.

"Depends on how many people I got to deliver to." He replied.

"On average."

Mark's head tilted, the higher eye squinted, "If everybody pays.........maybe $7.50"

Ray's wheels were turning.

Hal walked over into the foyer, and we stood to one side. "You're running a little late." Hal said

"I try to get them delivered by 4:30."

"The other day, I saw you waiting for your papers in the sleet and rain."

"If your paper was unreadable, you only have to pay me sixty cents this week. Some of papers turned to paper mache' that day."

"Yeah, it went right in the garbage." Hal laughed. What impressed me was your dedication......says a lot about your character......your resolve. Your name is Mark?"

"Mark Aronson."

"You're not related to Benny Aronson?" Hal's eyes lit as a past connection energized a positive memory.

"I've got an Uncle Benny."

"Is your father Max the Axe?"

"Haven't heard that one in quite a while." Mark smiled.

Hal shook his head laughing, "Me and your Uncle Benny played basketball together at the Jewish Community Center. Your Dad Max is 3 years older than me........now he was as good as they come. He had them colored boys running in circles – a pure ball handler and shooter. Me and Benny: he was fast and I was tall. Between the two of us, you had a good basketball player. Bottom line.........I'd say we were a little better than okay."

Smiles all around.

"Does Benny got any boys?"

"Nah - all girls - three of 'em."

"Hey Mark, tell your Dad, and uncle - that Harrold Weisslexx was asking for them." Hal said.

"Weisslexx?" Mark said.

"Immigration anglicized our true family name. My father Helmut was one of the last from the old country and then they left our name alone. It was my father's brothers that made him get an American name."

"Right." He started to turn away.

"Hey, ...you want your collection money?"

The paperboy raised his eyebrows and shook his head at getting side tracked.

Hal handed him a buck......."Keep it."

Mark Aronson got a dollar every week until he quit at the end of the school year.

iii

One afternoon, Ray and me were shooting baskets in the driveway. He called out to the street as Mark climbed O'Dell after finishing his route.

"Mark......hey Mark.....hold up." Ray waved and we chased him down. "Hey - Tony's got the other paper route – right?"

"Yeah, the one that runs up to Hastings."

"Well - me and him were talking, and he said he was going to be quitting in a couple of weeks. What do you think about me taking over his route?"

Mark's face was confused, "Tony said he was going to quit come summer like me, but now he's going to quit in April? Hmmm....that's when Little League really starts – April. Guys try to do both every year and it never works out. The paper tells the carriers before they take the job - they can't do both. I've seen the paper hire guys who told them they were going to play hardball and the Statesman still gave them a route because they were in such a jam for help."

"Well what do you think about me taking over his route?" Ray said.

"It's got the two 8 story apartments, but it's also got a bunch of private houses that are out of the way." Mark reviewed Tony's route in his mind, then said: "Lotta dogs, and they don't give us the spray like the give the mailmen, and it's got the Dekker house right on the Hastings/Yonkers line......I know I did his route for two weeks last summer when their family went to Canada.

"Hmmm." Ray's mind seemed to be changing by external forces.

Mark switched gears and offered some advice: "If you do get a paper route – never sub for anybody. It isn't worth it."

"How's that?"

"When I subbed for Tony, he left me his book with all the people and their addresses on his route. Just having his route book wasn't enough; I should have done the route with him first. Big mistake. Took me 2 weeks just to figure out the short cuts. I got the customers names in the apartments, but a lot of them didn't have names on their doors. Then you've got to go down to the lobby and do the detective work matching names to apartment numbers and letters – plus, his book wasn't current with the starts and quits." Mark shook his head.

"Wow."

"Ain't as easy as it looks." Mark went on, "I could do his private houses faster than the one apartment, and that included the ones you had to climb 75 steps just to reach a point where you could throw the paper 25 feet to the porch. The old apartment wasn't too bad but the new one…1100 Warburton…..that was bad news. And collection night …….what a joke! A couple of little dogs come running out of 3G at 1100 and attacked me: bit my ankle and shred my pants. Four people said they didn't get a paper twice one week. The circulation department shorted me twice, so I had to wait for the truck to deliver the shorted ones. Twice they sent me 4 extra papers. Ray listen, nobody wants yesterdays news."

"But Mark, you make it look so easy." I said.

"It'll take your brother two weeks just to learn the route. I got home so late the first night I subbed, my mother thought I had gotten mugged or something."

"But if I knew the route like Tony………I'd be okay?" Ray said.

"Those aren't the Herald Statesman's newspapers, they're yours. You're a middle man. Those papers sit on the corner overnight because you didn't deliver them……..you just bought yourself 72 papers for $3.60

"I thought all you did was deliver them…..for the company." Enlightenment was hitting Ray.

"One of their all star coordinators, Ron Bloch, had us in the delivery truck telling us how good we had it: "You guys make all this money and we teach you how to be responsible businessmen. You guys should be paying us.""

It didn't sound like Mark bought into the logic of Ron Bloch.

"Once you get the route down, the starts and the stops, and the collection system; then it's like second nature. Tony makes more money than I do cause he's got that 2nd apartment; I'm done quicker, but Tony lives down here. And..................I've got to walk the hill. O'Dell Ave. is fucked." He spat on its pavement, Ray did the same.

"I'm too young to get a route, but I walk this stupid hill too." and added my phlegm to the asphalt.

Mark and Ray laughed.

The word "fuck" wasn't thrown around too much back then. When some guy broke out with it, that person pushed the reality of a situation commanding immediate attention.

"Ray and me have been walking this hill for almost 2½ years."

"Our dad calls it a slow motion escalator."

The three of us laughed at how the hill beat us up every day.

"You know - "Aronson thought aloud, "I'm quitting at the end of this school year. You could take over my route Ray.....unless you can't wait. The paper can't get anybody down here to take it. All I got to do is tell Bloch I've got a replacement all lined up, and the route would be yours."

"That'd be great, I'm sure I can get permission from my parents."

"You're 12 years old? - Right?"

"Turned 12 in March."

"You'll have to get your working papers."

"What's working papers?" I was miffed.

Mark ignored me and answered my question looking at Ray: "The office is right next door to the Jewish Community Center.......same place you'll get your social security card. They make sure you're not a retard and that you can hear."

"Why's that?" I said.

"They both gave me the "Shut Up." stare.

"Just for your general knowledge.......'Mr. Gotta Know' - it's because we cross the streets a lot and you've got to be able to hear traffic coming. I almost got run over a couple of times." Mark nodded.

iv

When Ray made his commitment to take over the route, Mark showed him the ropes his last three days on the job. Dropping papers at the front or the back of houses, never leaving newspapers where the weather could get at them; common sense stuff mostly. Things like starts, terminations, and collecting was a pain in the neck.

Ray had a bad habit of not notifying the supervisor or the circulation department of changes in his paper count. Sometimes we had two or three extra papers at the house, and sometimes we didn't have a paper because Ray was short on the route. I knew if I ever got a paper route - when a client moved........I'd make sure their subscription got cancelled with the circulation department.

It didn't make a lick of sense that Ray could lose money on the paper route and not have it bother him. He didn't miss any sleep over the mismanagement of his business. When he was old enough to caddie, he jumped to that job, and the casual nature of the work suited him just right.

In the summer of 1965, Ray took over for Mark. Hal was glad to see the entrepreneurial side of his eldest son developing on a number of levels; one of them being his resolve to hold down a steady summer job, which allowed Hal to use Ray's commitment to the paper route as his excuse to stay home when Mom brought up the possibility of going to some destination for summer vacation. He'd tell Jane to take the car and Cathy, Willis, and me up to Grandma Edna's (Mom-Mom's) for getaways. Mostly, it translated into day trips to pools, beaches, amusement parks, and picnics; a lot of work on her end and not much relaxation. She never did follow through with buying a car with an automatic transmission, but she was determined that day would come. For now, she still had to get permission to use the car.

ONE OF THE DAY TRIPS WE TOOK WAS TO THE World's Fair. The location was adjacent to the Mets new home, 'Shea Stadium' and LaGuardia Airport. Hal never allowed Jane to take the family car anywhere in the 5 boroughs of New York, except to see Uncle Bill, who lived near Fordham Road in the Bronx. Driving in the city was like being a drone in a bee hive after mating. Jane's lack of proficiency with a standard transmission made her frightened of N.Y.C. traffic as well.

Jane had talked her brother Bill, who was a Port Authority cop, to drive us to the World's Fair. The five of us squeezed into his Chevy Corvair. There were no seat belts, baby or child restraint devices, no air bags, no whiplash head rests, just a car that got us where we were going. If there were any hiccups along the way, Uncle Bill could flash the tin.

Uncle Bill had just gotten off the graveyard shift and caught a couple of hours of sleep when he picked us up at 21. When he dropped us off in Queens, he looked half asleep.

"You're alright then Jane?" he mumbled as we got out of the car.

"Yeah Bill, I just had to get out of the house, Hal's vacation doesn't start for a couple of weeks."

"How are you getting back to Yonkers?"

"Yonkers Transit has been running buses since April through the end of October. We'll catch one going back around 5 o'clock.

Hal's going to pick us up down Getty Square where the bus lets us off. I'll call him from down there."

Mom wrestled Billy's stroller from the trunk of the Corvair which was in the front of the car. The Corvair was Detroit's answer to the Volkswagen Beetle. We thanked Uncle Bill for the ride and waved good-bye. He was too tired to do anything more than nod at us.

We got down there around 11:30. I didn't know a thing about this "World's Fair", but Ray had been there last year with the altar boys and he ended up being our tour guide. Lines of people were waiting to see the popular exhibits; they extended past the points of it being worth the wait. Ray's enthusiasm could not be diminished as he described certain landmark exhibits he recalled from last year. The only fair I had been to was the annual Dutchess County Fair. One year they had the Bonnie and Clyde car there. Mostly, they had the usual stuff: rides, greasy food, 4-H club animals, freak show, and a demolition derby at night. I didn't know what to expect with a world's fair: I thought it'd be more of the stuff Duchess County had - at 3x the price. My brother was the catalyst behind this day trip. Jane was unaware Ray had been selling her on the World's Fair even before school let out. He was the one who put it in her brain. Ray must have been consumed with this Fair, in an act of overkill, he kept on selling it to Uncle Bill as we drove. Ray kept on barking and Uncle Bill turned up the radio.

Making little headway with the adults in the front seat, he directed his excitement to Cathy, Willis, and me in the back seat. He made many of the exhibits sound like episodes of the "Outer Limits" with a happy ending.

This excursion was Jane's responsibility; it had trouble written all over it – even I could sense that. Mom's mind was made up. When Jane put her mind to something, she didn't need Hal or any man to screw up her plans. She had enough of Hal's caution, advice, rants, and votes of no confidence. When she wanted to do something that was customarily beyond the scope of most women back then – she took the bull by the horns and did it. Ray's smooth steady pressure had Jane bamboozled as well.

v

The newspapers, television, and radio had pumped up the '64-'65 World's Fair into a big deal. It was mostly an advertisement for corporate America: "Look At Us". Some of the corporations spent lavishly on exhibitions, displays, artwork, and amusements that would only stand for two years. Many of the engineering and technological concepts they proposed and predicted somehow had come to fruition somewhere in the future.

Ford, IBM, GE, GM, and the aerospace industry were all making bold statements as well as other nations in the free world.

There were also companies like NCR whose exhibitions amounted to bringing in a bunch of cash registers that didn't work. Ray and me played check-out for about six minutes and left. Even the Oscar Meyer Weinermobile made an appearance. Some countries had expositions about the things they wanted the world to know about them. There were amusement park rides, but the carnival stuff was kept on the fringes, and there weren't many considering the overall size of the Fair. We went on an amphibian attraction that had sea/land cars that ran on a mini road course before we drove into the water of Sheepshead Bay. They let Ray drive because I was too young. There also was a sky-bucket ride that traveled 30 feet above the fairgrounds from one end to the other. Schaefer and Rheingold Beer had a presence there. Schaefer sold more beer because they had a larger asphalt beer garden, but Rheingold had 10 buxom babes vying for the title "Miss Rheingold – 1965".

We had lunch on an aluminum picnic table with a family from Indonesia. The father worked at the consulate in Manhattan. We were pretty close to the stainless steel "Unisphere"; a depiction of the land masses of the earth attached to ribs of longitude and latitude. The father showed us where his country was. The stainless rendition escaped being scrapped after the Fair's two-year run. It still stands today.

Jane knew Ray and me were itching to go off on our own. "Okay…..meet us right here at this table at 5 o'clock." She called as we ran off.

Same old New York: too many people, too many lines, and everything cost too much. In 1965, Jane let us do our own exploring at this huge fair at the age of 10 and 12. In a few years, there were very few activities a 10 and 12 year old would be doing without some kind of adult guidance.

Most of the big and medium sized exhibits were free after you paid the Fair's admission fee. The carnie stuff, souvenirs, food, and beer is what most people spent their money on. All Souls' took the altar boys down to the fair in 64'. Ray said he had gotten free peanuts from the State of Georgia exposition. We walked the length of the fair grounds to get some. They had run out when we got there. They gave us a roadmap of the state instead.

The Vatican even had an exhibit. They had their Swiss Guards in their Bozo uniforms with the conquistador helmets and spears, at the entrance and exit of the building. Michelangelo's marble sculpture "Pieta" was on display behind bullet proof glass. Fairgoers were only given a specific amount of time to view the statue of the crucified Christ being held by Mother Mary. They put everyone on a slow moving walkway – the kind you see in the airports. The small hall was pitch black except for the light illuminating the sculpture. They had painted silhouettes of shoe soles of where the spectators were supposed to stand. If everybody followed the plan, the people in all the rows would have unobstructed views. Anything involving a crowd in N.Y. ends up being a free-for-all. The Vatican's attempt to bring religion and art to Queens had limited success. When Ray and me went through, some 'gabbagool' put his girlfriend on his shoulders and there was almost a fist fight.

"The Pieta" was about 20-30 feet away from the nearest moving walkway. Michelangelo's marble masterpiece was separated from the art worshippers by a complete wall of 25 mm bulletproof glass. A lot of good it did; approximately 25 years after the fair, a megalomaniac thought it was a Pinata and not the "Pieta" and worked it over with a ball peen hammer.

vi

We hadn't seen Jane all afternoon. We got back to the 'Unisphere' on time, and Jane was sitting at the aluminum picnic table almost in tears with some black guy hitting on her. He was telling Jane how beautiful she was, when he noticed us listening to him.

"Ooooohh, Uh Huh.......Ah Huh….. Alright......deese yo' boys - Okay….Okay….." The man looked at us and back at Jane, Cathy, and brother Billy. "Well I see you been pretty busy." He said, "You take care now." and walked away.

Jane stood up, pulled Cathy by the hand, and pushed the cheap stroller with brother Bill; both were crying. Mom snapped at us: "If we don't get to the parking lot…..right now – we are going to miss the bus back to Yonkers!"

"Hey Mom, we went to this building and they had all these cash registers." My face dazzled from all the buttons we got to punch, even though none of them could add or had a roll of paper in them.

"It was the NCR pavilion." Ray smiled.

She grabbed us by our ear lobes and yanked hard, "Listen you nit-wits, if we miss that bus, the next one doesn't leave until 7:30……just stop the crap until we get on the bus."

"You mean we're leaving?" I raised my brows.

Jane kicked me in the butt, "That's for being a numbskull."

The kids were crying, Ray was trying not to laugh, Mom was sweating, and I was rubbing my butt. It would have been a waste of time to ask why Ray didn't get any.

Like a mini tornado, we arrived at the bus yard. The Yonkers Transit bus was beyond standing room only, and people were still trying to get on. Mom had Billy with one arm and she tried to collapse the folding stroller. Cathy and me were concerned. Jane appeared to be in the early stage of a meltdown. She tried to get the stroller to start to fold before she unbuckled Billy. Two more minutes she wrestled with it, using her foot to hold down the stroller - she pulled up on it to get it to 'break'. Three or four times Mom jerked it…….nothing. Brother Bill's face looked like he was riding a mechanical bull. She knew she needed two hands to fold up the stroller, and Billy was tossed like a football to a surprised Ray.

"This cheap piece of shit." She wrangled with it some more. Besides the people on the bus, a small group of on -lookers watched the wrestling match.

Ray asked Mom if he could help. The action stopped.

114

"You know what I want you to do?"

"What?" I could see he was confused as much as I was.

"SHUT UP!" she screamed.

Cathy and Billy resumed crying.

"Mr. Know it all – Take your sister on the bus and Raymond you take Billy. Jane fished through her handbag and handed me the fare, "Pay the driver."

Once again, she tried to fold the stroller.

A lady with an accent called from the buses window, "Missy, I tink we're leaving. The driver says we're full."

Jane had put a gash in her hand on her last attempt. She winced and watched the blood dripping from the webbing of skin between her thumb and forefinger. "Sonofabitch!" She spun around whipping her hand.

Jane picked up the budget stroller by the handles and tomahawked it four or five times on the pavement. The wheels were all bent and busted, the tubular scissor frame as well. Mom tried to put her Roman sandals through the fabric seat three or four times just to release some more frustration, but the seat held. It was junk, she made sure of that. She ripped her handbag off the asphalt, and pulled one of those hair things out, and put that Auburn hair into a pony tail. Before she got on, she straightened her blouse and shorts, and lit a cigarette.

The driver asked her on the first step: "Hey lady – You'll feel better if I run it over.......why dontcha put it under the tire?"

"You know what?" she pointed at him, "You're right." The bent up stroller would be a pancake with the tire's first revolution. The driver held his line and flattened the stroller with his front and rear tires. Everybody was happy........for a little while.

vii

Although the bus had left the fair grounds, it was in fact an epilogue to the day's exhibits. This one might have been titled "Dante's Meltdown" sponsored by Yonkers Transit and the NYC gridlock system. At least no one was riding on the roof of the bus; although it probably had as many passengers as might be seen on a bus in Bombay. It also was close to being a can of tainted Daniel Boone beef stew ready to explode – but it didn't. Everyone was dripping sweat; the old ladies were unable to fan themselves because their arms were caked in position from the overcrowding. There was no air conditioning on buses back then.

There were a lot more rugrats too; at least 14 on the bus and every one of them crying. Brother Bill was part of the choir. The wailing was non-stop from Queens to Yonkers.

"Bil-leeeee......thut up." Cathy yelled. She had lost her Bugs Bunny teeth a couple of months earlier.

Cathy and me held hands, my free hand latched onto the hand grab of the 2nd row seat. None of the passengers could see past the person they were next to in any direction. A lady yelled, "Sophie….Sophie!" Everyone around her told her to shut her yap or get off the bus – which she couldn't do anyway. The heat, sweat, and grime were bad enough, but it was the stench that defied classification. I'm sure some of these bastards will remember the stench when they reach the gates of hell.

As the bus driver rolled up to a traffic light, his experi- ence told him we would be stationary for two or three red/green rotations. He directed the passengers at the doors to get out, and he exited as well. He stood outside the front of the bus looking at his reflection in the big windshield.

"The first five of you mugs under 30 – out of the bus. C'mon! Hurry up!" he yelled.

He pulled a comb from the front pocket of his shirt, and he ran it through his black olive oil hair. When he got the look he wanted, with his hands shaping as he combed, he pointed to two strapping young bucks with his comb. One looked Puerto Rican, the other was Paisan.

"Here's the deal: it's too damn hot in that fuckin' bus. We gotta ride wit the doors open so the people don't die like dem jews in 'nem camps."

No response.

The driver got real serious, "Listen, either these old people will die of heat stroke or suffocation, if you two don't cowboy up and give us a hand. Or….how bout' dis – you two one-way mutherfuckas can start your walk back to Yonkers right now. How bout' dat?"

Their faces were blank. The clock was ticking.

"All you gotta do is hold back the people and yourselves from falling out when I make a left turn."

"So it's like we become a human door kinda." The goomba said blowing on his St. Anthony medal around his neck.

"Yeah, comprende'." Chico nodded.

"Youse do the job and I'll buy a couple of rounds at Dock's when we get to Getty Square. You're old enough to drink right?"

"Hell yeah."

The driver told everybody to get back on the bus. He got back in his driver seat and yelled, "Everybody shut up! Now listen up: I deputized the two guys at the doors. They're the boss of them. Do what they say, or I stop the bus. We're gonna be riding with the doors open until we make our first stop." The way he handled the driving, he was being real deliberate with those left turns.

Cheers and smiles followed but not for long - the traffic continued at a snails pace. At least they knew the driver had done what he could to improve the situation.

I thought the driver and the deputies were kool. I wish I had been old enough instead of just holding onto Cathy.

viii

116

It was twilight when we made our first and only stop at the junction of McClean and Central Aves. About 30 people got off. At the stop, the men had bolted from the bus and took relief in the nearest doorways of closed businesses or between parked cars. Many let it happen on the sheet metal and tires of the bus. Two teenaged girls took a squat. Hard to say how the rest of the women held on. For sure a couple of people pissed in the bus; there was too much liquid on the floor and it reeked. Rheingold and Schaefer were selling pitchers for a buck.......it had to be expected. Ten people got back on the bus, but it was still SRO. The ride from McClean to Getty Square was better; we weren't mashed up against one another. The 2 hr. rush hour was over; the last leg to Getty Square would take 20 minutes. With ten minutes to go, two year old brother Bill was caught unprepared when a pressurized burst of watery crap gushed out of both legs of his shorts. Ray had held him in his arms since we got on. Everyone pushed away from my brothers. Ray had started the change from kid to a teen and busted out with the last high pitched scream he ever let: "Mom.....Mom.....Billy did a
doodee on me!"

Brother Bill had managed to hang on to that undercooked, ptomaine infused, mutant hand-tossed pizza since the fair. As it worked out, we were only four miles from our destination. There was a subsequent bowel explosion that didn't rival the first. Ray straight armed Bill under his armpits trying to avoid any additional mess.

After that, no one spoke. When we arrived at Getty Square - no one bothered running from the bus. The riders exited the bus like they were walking to Bataan. The Whitelaw brothers stood frozen.

The driver came over to Jane, "Hey lady, don't worry about the mess – the guys in the yard will give this thing the fire hose tonight."

"Thank God, I was worried how I was going to clean up this mess."

"You know when a kid has an accident.......it's an accident. What really gets us wild is when the drunks and the junkies pull crap like that. Throwing them off the bus ain't enough punishment. Hey lady, you know, they got a hose on the side over at TOM-TOM'S hot dog stand. No taxi's gonna let you in his cab smelling like dat.....Good luck." The driver left the bus and locked the doors.

She thought this was the longest day she had in quite a while. 'The little guy just started wearing underwear three weeks ago.'

Cathy chim-chymed from outside the bus's rear door as she looked at our brothers, "Billy got cockie all over Ray-Ray."

"What are we going to do Mom?" I didn't want any part of the clean up.

The door deputies chased down the driver. "Hey what about our beer?"

"You want beer after that?" He aimed the hitchhike symbol towards the bus.

Their faces turned sour as they looked at Ray and Billy standing covered with crap.

The driver took a deep breath, "I gotta go back in and get the coin changer and fare bag and lock up again.

"C'mon, we'll have a couple of shots over at Dock's."

"Each." The Paisan said.

"Where's Dock's?" the Latin frowned.

"You know.....The Dockside Bar."

The three started talking and looking towards Dock's neon and flashing lights.

"Man, that bus was packed, how many people you think were on it?" The Paisan wrung out the bandana tied around his head.

"There were 63 riders on that bus." He smiled sideways.

"No way............you mean 163."

"I'm tellin' youse – 63. That's what the capacity says right above the destination scroll box.....63."

"Yes, but we were way over capacity." The deputies shook their heads.

"But guys, that would be illegal and unsafe. Hmmmm – I can't let Yonkers Transit know that I can't follow the rules. The only way they'll find out is if I turn in all this extra fare money," holding up his coin changer and fare bag. "So I guess I"ll have to rat hole the extra fares or buy a new Holley 4 barrel carb for my Dynamic 88.......rust-free from New Mexeeeco." The three laughed and headed for Dock's.

ix

"Ryan."

I walked over to Jane.

"Do you have a dime?" she said. I fished through my pockets. "I want you to call Dad and tell him we're by Tom-Tom's down the Square. I called him from the fair and told him to meet us at 7:30 but we are really late."

Jane walked Ray and Billy over to the hot dog stand. She went to the side door and explained the situation to an employee back there placing a couple of dollars in the guy's palm. She marched Ray and Willis up the narrow alley. The pot washer kept them going until he ran out of hose, and he let 'em have it. They had taken all their clothes off except their drawers, and laid them on the pavement – close to a grated drain. He hosed them and the clothes off. Willis started crying as soon as the cold water hit. Next, the TOM-TOM guy told them to take off their underwear and put them on the grate. Billy's got shot down the drain by the pressure, but he was able to get Ray's washed out. It took about five minutes to get their clothes hose-washed. Jane, Cathy, and me stood with our backs to them to give them cover. Most of the pedestrians had crossed the street to avoid the water running from the alley. Ray wrung their shirts and shorts, and only put on their shorts. Both of them had chattering teeth and I felt cold just looking at them.

"Dad didn't answer at the house." I shrugged at Jane.

"Shshshould wa-wa-we take a ba-ba-bus?" Ray shivered.

118

"Maybe a taxi?" I said.

"I'm hungry." Cathy said.

"NO FOOD." Mom shouted.

Another half-hour, 2 more phone calls, and we were complaining: "Why'd we ever go to the World's Fair in the first place?" There was a ton of strain in her face.

Around 9:45 our big Chevy wagon with the little engine made a turn and rolled up in front of TOM-TOM'S. It was like the cavalry coming to the rescue in some cowboy and Indian movie. Hal had a big alcohol smile and a bagged quart of beer between his legs: "Where ya's been?" He flashed the one gold tooth he had.

"Where the hell were you?" Jane was in no mood for his shit.

"Gary's."

Ray and me knew where 'Gary's' was; it was the only bar one street east of TOM-TOM'S. He brought us there on Saturday afternoons while we waited for Jane to finish up with her last class on Saturdays. Gary's looked out on a gigantic parking lot that was called "Chicken Island". The gangster Dutch Schultz, operated an illegal brewery at the site, and had a four inch pipe running to his barreling and bottling building over by city hall.

"You were at 'Gary's' all this time?" her hands went to her hips and her eyes beaded down at him.

"Been there about an hour." He smirked.

She knew he had a buzz going. We all filed in the car. Billy fell asleep as soon as he hit the back seat. Cathy and me climbed over the back seat to the back-back seat which faced the cars behind us. Ray lifted Billy's head, snuck his leg underneath and shut the door.

"What the hell smells like cow dung?"

"The kid had an accident." Mom said.

"I thought the boys had him trained?" He grabbed a pack of smokes off the dashboard.

Jane went for the beer, and just before it made it to her lips, he let out the clutch. Beer spilled down her chin and neck. She didn't bother to bark at him; she took two long chugs and slammed it back between his legs.

"Want to play games?"

"Don't need it Hal." She grabbed the cigarettes, lit one and inhaled deeply.

We would be home in 15 minutes, but they kept at it. It was his turn to take a pull on the quart. She grabbed it before he could put it back between his legs.

"Must have been a dandy of a day."

"We had a good time. The kids had fun."

"I didn't think they had livestock at a World's Fair, them boys stink."

"Well, now you know." She downed some more beer. "The bus ride was the worst......a sardine can - all those people. I thought we were going to suffocate."

"Where's the stroller?"

There was one more drag left and she tossed the butt out the window. "Got stolen."

119

"Early on or late in the day?"

"Bout' an hour before we left."

"Told you not to go."

"The thing was a piece of junk."

"Told you not to go."

"Don't need it Hal."

"Told ya."

"Yeah.Yeah.Yeah......well we went and had fun." Now he was ruining the escape the beer and cigarette gave her. She lit another.

"You all look like you went to World War III and not the World's Fair."

She looked at us kids, she saw that I was the only one awake. "You're a fuckin' jerk."

I was shocked worse than when she called him an asshole when he smacked her butt back at 2 Vernon Pl.

"And I don't need your bullshit." She gazed at the glow at the end of her cigarette.

"You left the house a mess."

"Just get us home ---- so I can start cleaning."

It was 10:10. They stopped talking for the remainder of the ride.

He cranked the parking brake. She barked out the orders before we got out of the car.

"I've got to give Billy a quick bath. Raymond, you take a quick shower as soon as I'm done with your brother. Ryan and Cathy, brush your teeth and straight to bed."

It was about 11:35 when Jane laid down and 11:36 when Hal got on top of her.

X

When Ray and me finally had gotten to bed, he may have been lying down for three minutes before he called across to me:

"Ryan.........Ryan.......you awake?"

My mind wandered, trying to digest the day. We never made it to IBM, Ford, General Motors, GE - we missed them all. The cash registers, Travelers Insurance, the sea/cars, the sky buckets, State of Georgia, and "The Pieta": we probably didn't get our money's worth. I wasn't sure what I missed, still - I was sure most of the exhibits I saw couldn't have been seen at the Duchess County Fair.

"Ryan." His volume had brought me back from the future fantasy world that I left six hours ago.

"Wha...." I rolled toward him.

"Help me do my papers, I forgot all about them."

He was up putting his clothes on, "Huh?' I said.

"Yeah, you got to help me with the paper route." He whispered.

"You're nuts, besides Mom and Dad won't let you out this time of night."

"We'll sneak out. Hal's already in bed. When Mom comes upstairs, we'll go out and do them."

"What are you gonna give me?"

"Think of something we'll settle up later on."

"You owe me." I said getting dressed.

"You got it." Things were getting more expensive as we got older, and getting a blank check from Ray was something tough to come by.

We got down to the drop-off spot for the newspapers at the corner of O'Dell and Warburton Aves. There were Ray's two bundles of papers.

"Thank God it's Thursday."

"Why's that?" I was plenty tired.

"Wednesdays and Fridays always got a lot of advertisements……..doubles the size of the paper. Sonofabitch……..one of the bundles has been busted open."

"Somebody steal them?"

"Nah ---- probably a few people got tired of waiting and just took their paper."

"How do we know who took them?"

"We don't."

"How many do you think are missing?"

The human computer side of Ray engaged, "I get 73 papers…Count how many I got in the bundle that isn't open."

"37."

"This bundle should've had at least 36. I have to count this busted bundle to see how many papers they took." The wind started to pick up and made things more challenging.

"I got 37." I said.

"There's 26….27 here."

An incandescent streetlight above us lit Ray's face. He looked at me with one eye squinting: "Go down to the boiler room in the apartment and put together about ten papers. Make sure they got a front page, got least three sections. Leave them on the third floor across from the elevator." He had a smirk on his face. "And don't make any noise."

"I get it." I returned his smirk with a wink.

If I hadn't been so worn out, it might have been fun: nobody around, dead of night, and we were acting like a couple of inmates busting outta the joint. I felt like there should've been a girl involved in this scheme. Ray did the apartment in record time. The minute he decided to use boiler room newspapers, he knew which subscribers were going to get them.

He caught up with me doing the single family homes. I told him I didn't get the house down by Greystone Station on Harriman Ave.

"Gimme a paper, I got to give them one."

"Let it go."

"No way. She always answers the door, hardly wears any clothes; she always' got a drink in her hand. Plus – she smells like that

'Jungle Gardenia' perfume. You know – sexy. And.......he's a big tipper."

"What's he do?" I asked.

"Who knows what any of them people do who get on the train and go downtown. He doesn't work a real job like Mack does." He switched gears, "What's left?"

"The single families on Hawley Terrace and O'Dell."

"You just do 45 and I'll see you home." he said.

45 O'Dell was another long distance delivery. Ray could deliver the 11 residences on O'Dell before I came back from dropping the one paper off at the mail box at 45. The residences of 15 Harriman and 45 O'dell were the furthest distances apart on the route, it was like the people that lived in each house were opposites in just about everything: The residence at 45 was owned by Elizabeth Seton College and was at the bottom of their campus. The caretaker for the buildings and grounds lived there. It must have been some kind of a large estate before it was bought by the college. The caretaker's four acre compound had nine foot walls on three sides, a long paved driveway, a large 12 room brown limestone home, servants' quarters, stables, and a meditation grotto. The college's administration building, gymnasium, and classrooms were up the hill across from the Hudson River Country Club.

Some order of nuns who were from Belgium taught there at Seton. Many of their order got Liberal Arts degrees from the college. The nuns lived in the servants' quarters above the stables. The stables had been converted to a garage/maintenance facility. Two Flemish brothers and their families shared the brown limestone. This place was off limits to the public. Ray had to set up an appointment just to collect on Fridays. A young novice nun would meet him at the gate to pay him.

The caretaker compound was about 20 yards east of the Croton Aqueduct, running parallel with it. It was creepy at night, always had that bad vibe for me. I put the paper in the big farmer's mailbox they had attached with copper bands and bolts on the wrought iron gates and ran home. It was 12:40 am.

Back in our room Ray whispered, "Hey Ry."

I was too tired to answer.

One hundred students were divided into two classes: 6-1 and 6-2. Peter McGrath transferred in and Jack Swinnburne moved away in the late winter–early spring. The latter ended up being a lawyer and then an athletic director for a major Midwestern university. It lent credence to my belief that success did not flourish in Yonkers. To have any measure of achievement, all roads led to some place else. Both Peter and Jack had been altar boys, and neither had what it took to be in the clique. I had gotten along with both.

Perhaps by chance, All Souls' grade school administration had paired the lay teachers with each other: they taught the 4th and 6th grades, while the nuns taught the rest of the grades. An old battle axe, Mrs. Foley, taught 6-1, and a young black-haired French Canadian, Miss Boudreaux had 6-2. Ray had Mrs. Foley last year and I was assigned to her class for the 6th grade the following year.

There was a different feel to everything in the 6th grade, nothing that I could identify, but it was more than the advancing puberty. Either the cosmos was sending out signals on a seldom used wavelength and my analog brain was bombarded by digital information, or it was this sperm retention syndrome that all the guys knew was coming and talking about. My birthday was on the last day of summer – in less than a month and I would be 12, neither child nor adolescent. Acts of arson, vandalism, petty theft, studying females in catalogues and detective magazines, started filling my free time. There were a bunch of new distractions, they couldn't be ignored.

A good thing about 21 O'Dell was – it was so different than Vernon Pl. or Park Ave. Ray and me relied on each other more than ever. Our situation at school hadn't changed that much, but the fact was: the sphere of influence ended every day as soon as All Souls was out of sight. We'd try to throw the ball around Henry Hudson Park, but the narrow pie-shaped park was just too small, and to make it even smaller, the city had put a sidewalk through the wide end, and lined it with three benches and four trees from Warburton Ave. to the stairs which led to Harriman Ave. From the Warburton curb to the Harriman curb, the park was 35 yds. wide. The park sloped about 6 ½ ft. from Warburton to the top of the park's stairs. The stairs delivered a commuter or fisherman to Harriman Ave.'s street level - 45 ft. lower than the park.

We started our smoking careers down the park. Ray and me took our first puffs there with some high school guys. We tried variations of baseball: running bases, calling balls and strikes, stickball. Any activity which had you running or taking your eyes off where you were running - that was not good: the dogs ruled the park. There were land mines everywhere except on the sidewalk. One spring the city put up a "CURB YOUR DOG" sign. All the time in Yonkers, I never saw a dog take a crap in the curb. Ray said not to blame the dog – they didn't know how to read. So the only thing the park was good for was smokin' and later on when we had cars Loki showed up with a set of horseshoes, they worked out pretty good. Still, we had to clean up the dog turds before we could start.

One Saturday, before Hal came back from the store; I nicked two Tareyton's from his pack in his den. I thought I earned them because he left me minding Cathy and Billy without telling me, while he went up to the liquor store to get ready for the weekend. Jane was into her 2nd week of the new Dancing school year and Ray had to serve mass for a funeral. Hal didn't tell me I was "on duty". When he got back, I went down the park and lit up. I was hoping one of the few neighborhood kids might be around but it was dead. Some guy walking his dog told me smoking would stunt my growth. I told him I was trying to quit. He got the last laugh when his Boxer took a dump in the grass.

There was a guy with an attaché case waiting for the bus where the park's walk and Warburton's sidewalk intersect. I was neither in the park nor at the bus stop. The bus picked up the guy and the driver called, "C'mon........LET'S GO."

Making sure he wasn't yelling at someone else, I tried to look like I was going to Getty Square. Henry Hudson Park began to disappear behind us. At the coin box, I fished around for the fare. I knew I only had $.40 – ten cents light for the round trip.

"Hey......The fare's a quarter."

"I'm workin on it."

The bus had already traveled 2 miles and other people had boarded.

"You got the fare or not?"

An older lady inquired, "Where are you going?"

"I'm going to the library, the Trevor Park branch doesn't have the books I need for my school project." The lady gave me a quarter and I dropped it in the fare box. The coin dinged as it passed through the hoppers.

"And, I hope you find the information you're looking for." She smiled and the driver rolled his eyes at the con job.

She got off at the Square, I had to stay on for the next stop to make her feel good. Doubling back to the Square, I went to a couple of department stores, and a novelty shop. It was pointless to go to the Music Man or Normandie music and look at records, I was broke. Going up to her studio and asking Jane for a dollar would only lead to more questions and I'd get tangled up in some bullcrap I made up.

'What a waste.......maybe Ray was back home from the funeral mass. Nothing was happening here.' On the way to the bus stop, I stopped into George's Sports Shop on main street. They wanted $14.50 for a Rawlings catcher's mitt. There was a bow and arrow set on sale - $11.00. I started casing the place. There should have been at least three salesmen there, but there were only two. I had walked past a display when I first entered the store. It said: "Clearance * MUST GO! *" There was a copy of a new Westchester County ordinance outlawing compound slingshots or what we called "wrist rockets". It had a metal frame that wrapped around the wrist and forearm and it gave the shooter a lot more accuracy and a ball bearing or a marble went three times as fast as a home made slingshot. The one salesman

124

was helping a high school kid with a sneaker purchase; the other was showing a teenage girl a tennis racket. There were three left in front of the display; I glanced at the guy doing the sneakers, grabbed the box and walked out with it on the opposite side of the salesmen. Half-way down the block near Dock's Bar, I looked back once: nothing. As soon as I turned the corner on to Warburton, it was off to the races. Two miles later - I caught my breath.

A white boy running all out in the colored neighborhood with silver/gray plastic window box would bring eyeballs from every direction. I had to get a bag or get off Warburton. I took a connector street between Warburton and N. Broadway. The old Croton Aqueduct could be picked up on Lamartine Ave. It was a long walk to O'Dell, but it would take me off the radar screen if the bulls were after me. The aqueduct disappears underground through downtown then it ended up some where on its way to N.Y.C. Our cousin Billy said it ran somewhere down by Fordham Road, but it might have been a different aqueduct down by their house. This one was underground as well.

The bluecoats seldom cruised the Aqueduct, but they would chase people who used it for escape or to hide. With a hot wrist rocket in my possession, it provided the best route to remain undetected.

Ray and me alternated buying bags of marbles, ball bearings, and nuts for ½ inch bolts. The nuts didn't work too good because the hole made the nut slow down and not fly true, but they were cheap. We got damn good. Ray had made his own slingshot, it was pretty good for homemade, but the wrist rocket.......that was the ticket. The wrist rocket had the speed and accuracy to hit a rat at 50 ft. They would have sent me to reform school for all the havoc and destruction I was causing. It wasn't all vandalism though. The city might have taken into account the civic service we performed at the city dump.

Vinny Tartaglione would call us up whenever he got some B-B's for his air rifle. The county had outlawed their sale and possession as well: first the air rifles, then the B-B's. Vinny could only get B-B's when some relative was going upstate or to N.J.

"Ryan, you and Ray wanna go dumpin'?" Vince would ask.

"Sure......I got a bag of nuts."

Every now and then, the cops warned Vinny about his illegal air rifle. "We catch you anywhere away from the dump, and we're going to confiscate it."

Ray, Vinny, and me would pick out a high mound that overlooked the pit area and scan for rats below. The three of us let 'em have it – especially them big breeder rats. We could clobber a dozen of them before they would get smart and hide in the small mounds of garbage. We'd take a break and look for playboy magazines amidst the piles. It was hard to find a good one that was intact. After ten minutes of garbage picking, we returned to the hunt. There were never any breeders following the initial blitz. The big ones didn't get that way by being dumb.

ii

"Your father is coming out of the anesthesia. Dr. Baranpour is consulting with the cardiologist. He will be along shortly to see you all: – but he needs to see the medical representative first so he is complying with the HIPPA protocol. He can tell you what he did and how the surgery went. It is up to you if you want to share this information with your sisters." The nurse said to Dixie.

Ryan and Kate's three daughters were becoming numb to a non-stop barrage of medical people, facilities, insurance forms, mailed denials of coverage for certain drugs, procedures, (doctors who were out of plan), devices, and taking turns visiting Ryan.

Even though Nicole had returned to Arizona, the four wanted to feel they were making the right decisions concerning their father's diseased liver. The weight was squarely coming down on Dixie. She knew Ryan had chosen her to be his legal representative in health matters because he knew she could pull the pin if and when the time came. The sisters were in agreement about a liver transplant. Dr. Baranpour had only mentioned it as a possibility, but they weren't at that point.......yet. A transplant opened another Pandora's box of medical testing for the recipient and finding a matching donor.

The 41 year old Dr. Hadji Baranpour was a well regarded physician and surgeon. He had interned at the Milwaukee College of Medicine. With the large number of alcoholics in Wisconsin, there never was going to be a shortage of patients with liver disease, usually cirrhosis and cancer.

When he finished his residency, the wave of viral hepatitis in all its variations, types, and genus was a major concern to the CDC. Bits and pieces of research information about this Hepatitis-C was growing – along with the amount of patients who seemed to have it. The primary method of transmission was routinely identified as being intravenous drug use. The disease was mostly being spread within the subculture of the drug world.

There was a huge learning curve with this disease. Baranpour was dealing with it: Hepatitis C was a stubborn customer - tough to get rid of. Following two years of prescribing Interferon/Ribavirin with only an eradication rate of 40%, he stopped prescribing it to his patients. There were too many problems.........too many side effects; still, some patients had gotten clean. He kept listening, networking, reading. In the last three years, Big Pharma knew they were getting close to a cure. There were so many variables: dosage, duration, side effects. At first, every prescription was a custom fit: what variation of Hepatitis C did the person have? There were four types, and there was also one that was none of the above. The same with the genus. What was the viral load? How much cirrhosis was present? More than once, Dr. Baranpour thought he could limit his practice to viral liver disease exclusively.

It was through the seminars, clinicals, lectures, Pharma companies, and conferences about the disease where Baranpour met

Dr. Bachan Singh of the Mankato Institute. Baranpour was intrigued when Singh spoke of tests and research on the livers of people who died of cirrhosis caused by alcoholism and those caused by the Hepatitis-C virus. Singh reported the two were very similar, but not identical. "Nevertheless, both will destroy the organ."

Hadji Baranpour was leaning towards referring Ryan to the Mankato Institute and Dr. Singh for a possible liver transplant. He wasn't there yet, but things had to start breaking one way or the other. At Mankato, Ryan would be in a first class facility with a top-shelf surgery team if his liver was going into failure. Baranpour could be reasonably confident in a transplant's success if Ryan didn't have any other health issues, problems with the donor's organ, or post operative complications.

Teri had done some research as well: When Ryan first showed up looking for treatment, he asked Teresa to recommend somebody. Three years ago, she handed Baranpour's card to her father. Ryan got the same old song and dance from Hadji: "They're getting close." Baranpour was the best G.I. doctor in LaCrosse." and urged him to "hang tight".

Now, Baranpour assured Teresa: "Bachan Singh is the best transplant surgeon in the upper Midwest." She felt this wave, she knew it was bringing her to Makato. "Lord, let the Old Man live his life with his original equipment." she prayed.

Ryan was a good patient. Being sober wasn't a problem for him, though he tried to avoid wakes and funerals. He had given up drinking and drugs 30 years ago. He had gotten violently sick when he drank the few times he tried - he couldn't get drunk and he couldn't get sober. Being clean and sober only kept the virus from a more advanced rate of scarring. Like rust, the virus never slept and the latest CT and MRI scans indicated more scarring.

He wanted to bring the viral load of Ryan's blood down - to undetectable numbers with the new drugs. Baranpour's objective was twofold: he wanted to stabilize the viable liver he had remaining, and hoped there would be some regeneration in those areas where the cirrhosis was not as concentrated.

Ryan's legs, particularly the calves, had been swollen even before he left Arizona. They were collecting fluid and ammonia. It made the drive to LaCrosse excruciatingly painful. He had to pull over every 3rd rest area or every hundred miles and elevate his legs. Since he was admitted to St. Thomas, his urine was cloudy and there wasn't much of it. By the second week of Abbvie's anti-viral combination drug therapy: Vikeira-pak/ribavirin, the doctor could see minor improvement in urine output and clarity. The fact that Ryan had never decompensated was one of the reasons Baranpour had hope, not so much to be cured; but to get out of St. Thomas alive.

Dixie had a tentative look on her face when he walked into the gathering area after her father's endoscopy.

He followed protocol, and only wanted to confer with Ryan's designated representative for health matters. "Miss Dixie." He tried to call her away from her 2 sisters.

"Dr. Hadji, whatever you want to tell me – you say to all of us. In fact, it is better that I don't have to be the relayer, because I am not likely to know what you're talking about....perhaps worse......I might forget what you said. With my sisters beside me, it'll be better for us and Dad. It's bad enough I have to try and explain this to Nicky over the phone."

"As you wish." He motioned for them to sit on a sofa.

They sat facing him from different angles on two sofas.

"I am pleased Ryan exhibited alertness and was talking two days ago. That is positive." Baranpour went through the procedure that was performed a couple of hours earlier. He examined the throat, esophagus, stomach, and the top of the small intestine. As he withdrew the fiber optic camera, he stopped in the esophagus. A micro banding tool was snaked into place and one at a time he applied it to the three bulging varices. Once the bands were in place, he anticipated the blood starved varices would fall off in roughly two months.

"This procedure.....is the one you were explaining to me and Nicky when she was here." Teresa said.

"You are the R.N.? It took me a moment to recognize you without your Psyche scrubs on." He refocused. "What I did today was minor surgery; the banding was the only thing of note." He gave them a weak smile.

"What's next?" Killeen scrunched her brow.

Even though Dixie had the authority, Teresa knew her father as well as she knew her sisters. If and when his health began to fail, she knew she was going to be the center of gravity, the prime advisor, the translator for the others. Despite her intention to be invested with only a quarter of the responsibility of Ryan, when they wheeled him into the doors of the hospital, de facto: she had 50% of the action. Like an old car jack, it kept ratcheting up her involvement. It required a Gastro-Intestinal crash course of the G.I. staff, internet study, and talking with nurses familiar with Ryan's type of case. All this background work took time away from her husband and her family.

Teri's experience and knowledge would bring Dixie, Killeen, and Nicole to somewhere close to her knowledge of G. I. medicine; giving them a degree of fluency in Ryan's treatment.

Three years earlier, Teresa had been confident and relieved hearing other health care workers evaluate Baranpour: "He's the best in the LaCrosse area."

Just hearing that catch-all endorsement was no longer going to be good enough in light of Ryan's continued liver deterioration.

Ryan had plenty of associates who got caught up in the world of drugs; for some, a liver transplant was their only option. Most of the transplanted livers were a success, but there were rejections as well, and sometimes the new liver was cooked by a recipient who resumed using alcohol and drugs. Transplantation could be a scary endeavor.

BACK IN ROOM 107, RYAN WAS COHERENT BUT STILL under the effects of anesthesia. Teresa told Dixie and Killeen it was doubtful their father would remember their visit.

A big fear rushed him as he tried to sit up. The sedation had thrown his equilibrium out of balance and he was unable to figure out how gravity worked.

"Easy Pops........easy." She grabbed hold of him and tried to smile and then looked at Dixie, her eyes showed concern.

"You're alright Papa......the doctor had to do some minor surgery. He'll explain it the next time he stops in – probably tomorrow." Dixie tried to give a friendly grin. Her eyes were full.

Ryan wasn't sure if what he was experiencing was reality, a dream, or a hallucination. He'd try to sustain a conversation with his daughters in either case.

His voice was soft from the tubes the doctor had used to examine the upper part of his G.I. system. He looked around, "Where's Nicky?"

Teresa replied, "You remember.......she went back to Tucson with her kids. She'll be back. She's coming alone once her and Rick get someone to stay with the kids. He's out of personal days and vacation."

"Tell her to call Aunt Lil, she might be available." A minute of confusion: "Tell her I want to see her before she goes." He looked wildly about the room.

"Well he's on a ride", Killeen said.

Dixie gave her father a double-take, a low whistle, and shook her head.

"That reminds me – we've got to call her to bring her up to speed on everything. How bout it Dixie, you want to give Nicks a call?"

"Why don't you handle it, I'm still mad at her for hitting me."

"Huh........When?" Killeen said.

"When I was 12, I told Pops that she brought that Matt Stuart over when he was working up in Wausau."

"No boys over when I'm out of town......them's the rules." Dixie tried to imitate her father.

The three laughed.

"Long day Ol' Man?" Dixie smiled.

He kept his eyes closed as he answered, "Hard to say........I was swept.......swept back to the beginning."

"TERESA, HOW IS HE?" NICOLE ASKED FROM ARIZONA.

"Still out there from the anesthesia."

"Sounds like Dr. Hadji's putting everything on this anti-viral drug that was just approved. I don't know if this is going to come together for Pops." Nicole said.

"He's got other shit going on besides the virus." Teresa read from a small post-it sheet Dixie had given her. "It's that cirrhosis - that's the gum in the works. Hell, the drug they're using has a 96% kill rate, but that damn virus has been turning his liver into rock for 40 years. He's lucky he's had that long. Three things have to happen: his liver has to be clean of the virus, regeneration of the liver has to occur,

129

and areas which have just begun to scar or have minor scarring need to be reversed."

"Is that possible?" Nicky coughed.

"No." Dixie scoffed.

"It's not being advertized on the drug packaging." She said.

"You knew about the surgery today?" Teresa checked.

"Killeen called."

"When are you coming up?"

"Looks like a couple of days. I called Dr. Hadji yesterday. He wouldn't give me information. If I'm going to be in on Dad's decisions I've got to be there with you guys - I've got to get up there." There was an extended silence.

"Listen, if things start going south, Dixie will need all of us; been a lot of nail biting already. Baranpour thinks the viral load numbers will give us a window as to what the next move will be. We know a transplant is an option….. maybe our only option. This waiting is going to drive me nuts." Nicky said.

"Nicole"

"What?"

"We need you."

"I'm trying."

iii

"What do you mean swept back to the beginning?"

"My life…….when I was a kid…..with Ray; then through the years: teens, adult, Karen and Nicole, your mom, you girls, work, on the road, never having a home, the drugs…..all the shit. It streamed through my consciousness, sub-consciousness, or comas…..or something; select a track and push 'play'."

"Lord, I know I wasn't in heaven." he softly said from memory. "I found myself at a central point in an alternate dimension, from which many terrazzo-like paved roads flared out like spokes from a hub. In between the terrazzo were clear sections of translucency that let me look below where I stood. A comet, satellite, and perhaps a mini-star orbited above. Some distance away, a large clear cylinder/tunnel ran off beneath me; I couldn't see its beginning or end. The circling celestial bodies above burned bright with varying colors and emitted a gray ash and minute aggregate which had a magnetic charge and only landed in specific locations. As I got closer to the translucent circular tunnel, there were lights arranged in helix patterns of all colors. It had to have been a representation of a genetic code that cork screwed for the length that could be seen."

Peering at Killeen and Dixie, he couldn't be sure he had spoke. Even if he had, he wasn't sure they comprehended what he said.

The sisters looked vacantly at one another. Killeen tilted her head to her right shoulder and squinted with her left eye, "Papa, what are you talking about?"

Dixie was waiting for the punchline from his mind excursion, "Hey Ol' Man – they give you anesthesia, LSD, or some other hallucinogenic?"

To Ryan he had clarity of thought, observation, and imagination when he was sedated, something he didn't have when he was awake. He tried to unravel this dichotomy with his daughters. "This life I have lived is in this replay mode when they knock me out, or when I am being poisoned by my liver because it can't neutralize the toxins. Why are these images so vivid, more so than a dream? Some things have been injected into areas of my brain that have been dormant for years. I see them as a full screen image; they come - they go. All that I have seen comes from the past or variations of my past. There is nothing of the future." It was at that moment the three discerned the lack of future images might indicate a cessation of earthly life. He had to get out of this place and drive his truck off the mountain road.

"Papa...Papa.........you still with us?"

"For now. Are we at UA-Tucson?" he frowned.

"No, LaCrosse. Remember..........summers in LaCrosse..... Winters in Tucson." Dixie reminded him.

"Yeah.....yeah......that's right. I don't mess with that winter crap, and I get to see Nicole, the kids, and Rick. Say, where are Teresa and Nicky?"

Killeen rolled her eyes, "Nicky's still in Tucson, she'll be coming up soon. Teri's by the window talking to her on the phone."

"Right.....Right." His burst of energy was gone and he started to fade.

When Teresa came back, she told everyone the nursing assistant was coming to change the bedding, gown, empty his urine bag, and bring him something to drink.

The aide waited for the girls to leave,

"Need anything else Papa?" Dixie called.

A quick wave good-bye sent the sisters off. None of them wanted to be around when he was getting changed. Teri took a quick look at Ryan's calves: the swelling may have gotten worse.

They walked toward the waiting area. Before they got there, Teresa informed her sisters she had to get home. "I'll be here tomorrow after work –around 6:30." She left.

"Let's get a drink, Ryan'll be conked out for the rest of the night, and I'm done." The two sisters went to Dixie's flat, ate some leftovers and walked to a nearby gin mill.

iv

This compulsion to start fires and commit acts of vandalism was getting out of hand. Hal had caught me setting a fire in the empty lot on the north side of our house. A week later, he caught me starting one in the garage. He worked me over with the leather strap. I thought he was a real Simon Legree, at the time. I had a few welts on my back, but that wasn't what got me to give up the matches.

131

"Hey Ryan, what kind of retard are you? Why are you trying to burn down our house?" Ray's look made me feel ashamed.

"I dunno....... You were delivering papers, nobody was around........there was nothing to do." I shrugged my shoulders.

"So you start fires to amuse yourself? You're fucked in the head - you jackass."

He hardly ever cursed at me. Letting Hal down was bad enough, but when Ray called me out for doing stupid shit, it sunk in – in a compound way. They all gave me that "You're a degenerate look." - everybody except Cathy and Willis, who were too young to know what was going on. It took about 2 weeks for Hal, Jane, and Ray to start forgiving and forgetting it happened.

When we started the new school year, I could see some more changes in Ray. They weren't only physical, they were intellectual as well. Our interests and activities were diverging. September revealed a social shift occurring in his life. Up to the 6th grade, he had been motivated by sports, organized and unorganized. The sports had consumed much of our free time. His cadre' of friends now included guys and a few girls who were the 'brains' of the grade. 'What was that all about?' I wondered. It was going to be interesting to see where his grades went when the first report cards were handed out. Phone calls came from people who had made the High Honor Roll. Ray could pull an occasional Honor Roll report card. I achieved Honorable mention twice, but I think it was a matter of the teachers shuffling the deck. We were still on the track, basketball, and baseball teams. Baseball was still with the boys' club. I could see his interest would flow and ebb at varying times.

My interaction with intellectually advanced kids only occurred when I was unable to get a hold of Ray. It was always the same; find one of the High Honors girls in my class and see if they'd help me with math. There was only one good lookin High Honors girl: Julie West. It was damn near impossible to get help from her, she had the guys take a number. I know she liked me, but that wasn't enough to get a confirmed tutorial. Thank God for Ray; I'd have flunked out into public school if he hadn't helped me. I may have taken advantage of the situation; but he had to help me – I was blood.

We had to serve the 9:00 Saturday morning mass with two other altar boys who were in the 7th grade with my brother. After mass, the three of them were laughing and chumming it up. I wasn't in on it.

The two other altar boys, I knew by sight: Tommy Priano and Bobby Pappas. Tommy had two younger brothers and Pappas had an older sister in the high school. I knew Tommy and Bobby from the altar boys, plus you always knew the students who were older than you. Not too much attention was paid to the students who were a grade behind.

After mass, they were going down Getty Square to see a couple of coin collecting shops. They'd trade $10 notes for a roll of quarters. They had quarter collections and were looking for ones the mints had not produced a lot of; I didn't know which years they were looking for – kind of a waste of time I thought. We'd stop at the record store, and the army-navy surplus store. They asked Ray if he wanted to go. He didn't hesitate, "Yeah." And then he asked if it was okay if he brought me along.

"Sure, we'll make a few stops that'll wise him up." The two laughed and looked over to Ray, and he started laughing too. They all turned to me. I had no choice but to join in.

We caught the no.2 bus going south; we'd pass Aunt Gert's house on the other side of the street. I took a quick look at the duplex. It had been a weird two years at 260 Park Ave.

Bobby Pappas had two sacks filled with coins: one was U.S. half dollars, the other contained foreign coins. He'd give the money changers a buck and he'd trade them for a different sacks. Priano and Pappas were working some con with the coins. The other sack had nothing but these Hong Kong dollars. Pappas' father was involved in the commodities and exchange markets in Manhattan. Priano and Pappas had a regular routine down Getty Square, Ray and me could see that. We followed them.

We stopped at 'New Fortune' – a Chinese take-out joint. Tommy had some fried Rangoon, Bobby had cold sesame noodles, Ray got some shrimp fried rice, I didn't have much money so I got an egg roll. "Tommy said, egg rolls are bullshit – try this. Pappas and Ray gave me a taste of theirs. Then I remembered I had had cold sesame noodles at Monica Teller's house. I looked at that dumb egg roll and ate it anyway. It wasn't like Jane or Hal telling you to eat something. This food was different and exciting, it became a ritual whenever I went to Getty Square. I was confused about the 'cold sesame noodles' because they were hot and spicy.

We followed Tommy and Bobby up and across the street. They went into a newsstand/novelty store; there were nude playing cards in the storefront's window. Ray and me were fixated on the topless queens. We marched up a slight incline into the store. The novelty items were in the front of the store, and what Ray and me thought was a newsstand was in the back.

"Hey Tommy......buy me a deck of them naked playing cards." I whispered.

"They cost $2.49 – you got that?"

"I got two bucks.......Ray, loan me the fifty cents."

The store sold stink bombs, cigarette loads, cheap handcuffs, and switchblades. I knew I'd be back to this store when I had more money – it sold all the stuff a guy wanted.

Bobby and Ray went to the back of the store, and we followed them after I bought the cards. They had a magazine rack with a bunch of paperback books, racing forms for Yonkers Raceway, Monmouth Park, and Aqueduct and whatever track was open in the metro area. A sign on top of the rack read: NO MINORS. Tommy led us right over there.

Ray turned Tommy around away from the guy in the elevated counter. "It says no minors."

"So?"

"Well?......."

"I not a miner, I'm a student." Tommy wiseguyed.

"Semantics." Ray started going through the rack with the other two altar boys and picked out a cop magazine. On the cover was a detective with a badge on his belt and snub nosed .38 in hand, a lusty redhead with tattered clothes and exposed boobs except for her nipples. The body of her would be defiler lay face down in the gutter.

There were a couple of old bald guys working the rack on the adjacent wall. They didn't hang around too long, it looked like they put their hour in and would be back tomorrow.

Pappas had gone back up front talking to the guy up there. He was interested in a starter's pistol they had, and he was trying to talk him down. He didn't get anywhere with the negotiations and worked his way back to the paperbacks and the magazines. Tommy nodded to the closet on the right. The smut purveyor in the elevated counter was watching more for the bulls, perverts, and shoplifters than he was for rookie masturbators like us. Bobby opened the closet door and Tommy pushed Ray and me in. It was as dark as the Dark Room on the Magic Carpet ride at Playland in Rye, N.Y. We heard a coin drop in a machine. A small framed motion picture started to roll. First, it was a couple of dogs running around, the one was chasing the other. Then, this lady picked up the dog that was getting chased, petted it and talked to it. The only sound was the projector ticking away. I reckoned the lady was saying something like, "Poor Fifi." Bobby dropped another coin. This guy with a big grin scolds the chaser dog saying "No...no...no...with his index finger in the pooch's face. Looked like it was something better than a mutt, but it could have been a miniature pony for all I knew about dogs. One thing for sure, that dog's tongue was nearly touching the ground and his tail was wagging. Next, the lady starts dancing – no steps – just stupid freestyle junk. It was just a way to throw off a piece of her clothing. It cost Bobby two more coins. At last there is nothing remaining but her bra and panties. The camera pans down and she starts climbing out of her panties, before they get to the money shot they bring in the camera and they give you a close-up of her face. Coin. Dancing and swiveling, the panties are tossed off. Coin. The film continues, the peroxide blonde keeps the bra on and elbow squeezes her tits, cupping them, shaking them, wiggling them. For whatever, Fifi has been perched on a barstool since the third coin, and is all charged up with nowhere to go. Coin. Now Blondie puts her finger in Fifi's face and the dog calms down. The dog is picked up and now Blondie has a dancing partner held tight to her boobs. Coin. The camera pulls back and she's naked except for the bra. The speed of the film slows and closes in as Fifi removes one of the bra straps, and Blondie pantomimes shock and surprise. The dog continues and reveals one of her breast's nipple and all.

Tommy quietly cheers: "Alright!"

Again she scolds the dog, and it licks her nipple apologetically. Blondie is too overcome by Fifi's lick of repentance. She kisses the dog and holds Fifi's face next to hers, blows a kiss to her devoted audience, smiles and the projector stops.

"Holy shit, that was groovy." Tommy laughed.

Ray and me wondered what we had just seen. Even if I had seen the complete peep show, I could only see the projector in between

134

the three 7th graders every now and then. I got the overall impact, I wasn't sure it was that groovy.

We left the novelty shop, and I got my deck of cards from Tommy. Ray wanted to look at records, so we went over to the 'Music Man'. Everyone got a 45; I had to borrow some more money from Ray. Looked like I was going to know his paper route pretty well if I couldn't get my spending under control.

"Hey Bobby, how much did you put in that machine?" I wondered as we waited for the No.2 to go back up the hill.

"Costs around $4.00 a movie."

"Isn't that kind of expensive for a fifteen minute movie?" Ray chuckled.

"Not really. I'm filling these machines with Hong Kong dollars." Priano and Pappas grinned from ear to ear.

"Lemme see one of them." I asked.

Pulling a quarter out of my pocket, I matched a George Washington with the Hong Kong slug. A perfect match as far as I could tell.

"They won't work in every machine; the Coke and Pepsi machines don't like them." Bobby said.

"My Old Man works on the foreign exchange market in the city. He pays about 8½ cents for a Hong Kong dollar. It won't be long before they start minting them just a little bigger or smaller. They're showing up in too many machines. They aren't considered slugs, but they may as well have be." Bobby felt the increasing heat of the racket going bust.

Waiting for the bus, I opened the deck of nude playing cards. Tommy and Bobby made me give them some to look at. I gave Ray a quarter of the deck as well. We put the cards in our pockets, and paid our fares to go back to North Yonkers.

The bus was about half-full. We took the seats that faced each other over the rear wheels. There was a colored couple in that long last row. He had his arm around her. There were older women sitting in the seats close to the back door.

We stayed focused on my deck of cards. The cards were making their way around: "Lookit the pair on this one."

"This one's a goddess…..I wonder how old she is?"

"Wow…………she's got a set of missile tits. Holy shit."

"Hey Bobby let me see." I said.

He gave the card a toss and it ended up in a lady's shopping bag. Quickly, I reached over her and snatched the jack of hearts.

"Sorry." I said, and hoped she hadn't seen the topless woman.

The three of them had done a 180 degree move and were looking out the bus' window. I'd be taking the heat if the lady had seen the card. Enough time had elapsed, and we went back to the naked deck of cards as if nothing happened.

"Hey, let me see that jack of hearts again." Tommy called.

I offered it across the aisle. Tommy concentrated on her image. "I'll bet her parents are proud of her." The card made the revolution once again amongst us.

Ray said it best: "She should have been on the ace of hearts."

"Ray." Bobby squealed and laughed, "Check it out......'The Joker.' He tossed the card, this time it landed on the seat next to another lady; this time the woman had a good look at the joker card, looked at us and marched right up front to have a word with the driver. She pointed at us from the front.

"It was those four degenerates back there.........THEM."

The bus driver came back, confiscated my cards, and threw us off his bus. We were about a ½ mile from All Souls. Tommy and Bobby didn't have far to go. The Whitelaw brothers were looking at 2½ miles ahead of us.

"By the way....." I began, "Looking at them magazines and that poodle licking the lady's tit........What is that?......like a mortal sin?"

The three 7th graders laughed.

"Where'd you get that from?" Tommy grinned.

"Who said it was a sin?......if there was any sin; which I doubt, it was the dog's. The poodle was the one who licked her nipple." Bobby smiled.

We all looked to Ray. "The fact that they try to hide the sexy stuff in the back of the store means it's wasn't on the level --- we could've walked out." He said.

"The only reason they got that stuff in the back is so it doesn't offend the women who come in to buy a pack of smokes or breath mints. It's really okay for guys." Bobby tried to get us to agree with him.

Priano backed Bobby up: "There's nothing wrong looking at a naked girl. Hell my folks took us to the Museum of Modern Art and The Metropolitan Museum of Art. There were statues, paintings, and photographs of naked women every time you turned a corner."

"Yeah, and what about all the naked artwork that the Pope owns? I wouldn't say they're promoting sex, but they're naked alright." Ray said.

"And they call them 'masterpieces', I'll tell you what a masterpiece is: it's that doggie show in the closet." Tommy was cracking up.

This was a discussion worth pursuing, Ray got the ball rolling for the short walk: "There is surely something to be said by putting a high money value on nudity; all of a sudden it's no longer perceived to be dirty or pornographic." Ray imitated some high class art dealer: "It becomes a reflection of humanity's beauty and desire to procreate. As we are not curators of museum grade art – are we doomed to gratify our carnal and artistic needs with mass produced magazines, playing cards," (he looked directly at me) "and small gauge celluloid films?" We all busted a gut.

"Yes....." Pappas endorsed Ray's reasoning. "We're not rich, but we deserve the same as the patrician class. We should not be denied a poor man's art."

"But is it a sin?" I repeated.

"They would have us believe we transgressed, but if it is not a sin for the wealthy because they can call what they view 'art'; how

136

then is it a sin for the commoner? Where we may have sinned was in the payment of the coin that did not have the value of the price of entertainment rendered." Ray turned on the Shakespeare.

Tommy laughed, "We may have been a little light in our compensation."

Bobby made his ruling: "We pinched a couple of bucks from a business that was pushing smut.........a venial sin.......at most."

Tommy cackled, "Say an act of contrition before you go to Communion."

V

A few days after the New York City blackout of 1965, Mrs. Foley had the class doing work in our English workbooks in the afternoon. A few students were having difficulty with the exercise distinguishing the different types of sentences: simple, compound, complex, and compound/complex. There were about 20 sentences on the page in groups of 5. The class would do a set of 5 and go over them. We were to write to the left of the sentence in the space provided: S, C, CX, or CC to signify the type of sentence it was. It took me about 2 minutes to do the five sentences. I was way ahead of everyone else, so I started making these exaggerated letters to kill time.

Four or five students were having problems with the exercise, and Mrs. Foley was annoyed with the slower students. She threw a blackboard eraser at me from the front of the room when she caught me talking to Samantha McAvoy. "What's the problem over there Whitelaw?"

"No problem – I'm done with that set of sentences."

"Not likely." She hobbled over as quickly as she could with her arthritic hip. "All five are probably incorrect."

"No, they're right."

She picked up the workbook and started going over my answers and came upon the exaggerated S's and rolled the workbook into a tube and began clubbing me with it. She dropped it and was yanking my hair with one hand and used her closed fist on my face with the other. I could have took her out right then and there but I didn't want to get expelled.

Mrs. Foley drilled me with a clenched fist and by the back of my neck she smashed my head into the top of the desk. She tried to pull me out of my seat by my hair but she tore a bunch out. When the hair pulling didn't work, she dug her hands into my throat and neck, and by the third yank she got me out of my desk and bulldogged me into the nearest blackboard arthritic hip and all. Two headshots into the slate, she rammed the side of my head into the classroom door. I grabbed hold of the doorjamb with blood running from my head and neck.

"Clean yourself up and report to the principal's office, you're getting suspended." Foley was trembling - visibly unnerved.

Shaking and confused from the blows to the head, I staggered down to the basement where the boys' washroom was. Johnny Juliano had just finished taking a whiz and looked shocked: "Ryan......what the hell happened to you? Did you fall down the stairs.......I didn't hear anything."

"John.....................I can't talk." I tried to whisper.

"You look bad man. I'll get some paper towels. You're bleeding man, your neck is all gouged up and you got some hair missing. Your head's bleeding on top too. Were you in a dogfight?" his eyes didn't know where to look.

"Foley beat me up." I forced another answer. I thought I was going into convulsions.

Johnny compressed a wad of paper towels on my neck and head. "It wasn't just Foley; did a priest clobber you? You're a mess Ryan."

My body continued its spasms as my back slid down the lavatory's wall onto the tile floor and I cradled my head with my hands. Johnny looked down at me and went out the door.

It may have been five minutes later when he returned with Tim Hurley the custodian from the boiler room where his workshop was.

"Well what the deuce.....?" he scratched his head. "Who beat you up?" He turned to Johnny Juliano, you know anything about this?"

"Ryan's in 6-1, I'm in 6-2, I was taking a leak and just leaving, and Ryan shows up like this."

"Okay. Okay now. Let's take a look at you. Ah, what is it Ryan or Brian?"

"It's Ryan, Mr. Hurley – Ryan Whitelaw." Johnny said.

He lifted me up, but I had a hard time staying upright.

"Come on, we'll go over to the nurse's office and we'll clean you up over there. Hurley turned to Johnny, "You better get back to class..........Listen, were you with this guy when this happened?"

"Hey Mr. Hurley, I'm in 6-2, it's like I said: he walked in when I was walking out." Johnny did what he was told.

In the nurse's office, Hurley had me sitting in the examination chair. He used his flashlight to look me over. Hurley was a good guy, about 55, cleaned up a lot of messes us kids had made. He maintained the school, the church, and the grounds. I wasn't sure if he worked the high school. They may have had a separate guy for that building.....maybe not.

"You're in 6-1, right?"

I nodded.

"Yeah......" He put some gauze under the warm water and began to clean up my neck and the gash on my noggin. "Looks like she tried to strangle you."

I shook my head, and raised my chin with a scowl and tried to show him how she grabbed my throat.

"Evelyn Foley – she's a dandy, kid. I thought she was too old to paste anybody this bad. She likes to pick on the bigger guys in her classes. Some kind of hangup or something. Mmmmm, where she dug her thumb in your throat - it's still bleeding. That bitch really had a death grip on you. You're missing a big clump of hair too. You'll end up bald like me if you continue to mix it up with anymore of these all stars." His hands lightly searched my skull. "You got a fair-sized knot on the left side of your head too. What'd she do - use your tie like a hangman's noose to pull you out from your desk?"

"Just her hands." I croaked.

Hurley said, "We'll have to make a dressing for the gouges that are still bleeding."

Five minutes later, Mr. Hurley pulled away the gauze, and took a look: "The one on top has kind of stopped, the gouges on your neck are slowing down some........except that big one – probably where she dug in her thumb. Listen Brian, I'm going to have to get Sister Celeste to take a look at you, this is kind of big medicine. Be right back."

The only reason the school had a nurse come in was to assist a doctor for checking for hernias, and to give eye and hearing tests. The doctor came in to check for whooping cough once. The rest of the time when the nurse showed up, it was only for the girls. The nurse's office was basically unused. Catholic schools didn't have money for a full-time nurse like public schools.

The Principal walked in with Mr. Hurley. Sister Celeste got over the shock of my appearance fairly quickly. "Thank you Mr. Hurley, I will be handling this matter."

He gave me a soft punch to the shoulder – you'll be okay Brian."

After he left, the Principal inquired what I did to cause Mrs. Foley to inflict such a beating.

She moved her ear next to my mouth, I whispered I didn't know.

"Let me know if your voice hasn't improved by tomorrow. Now - you don't have to answer me verbally; just nod your head yes or no. Did you curse at Mrs. Foley or anyone?"

I shook my head.

"Were you acting inappropriately with any of the girls?"
Negative shake.

Sr. Celeste was starting to have doubts about being able to resolve this matter. "Were you beaten up on school grounds by one person or a group of boys?"

Negative nod.

"Did Mrs. Foley do this to you?"
Positive nod.

"Was she the only one?"
Positive nod.

"Do you know what caused her to correct you so severely?"
I asked for a pen and paper with hand motions.

"Just whisper in my ear as before."

"Look in my English workbook." I turned away from her veil and choked a little, then resumed; "I made two giant S's because I was bored." I tried standing and wobbled a bit, but I made it over to the sink and got a paper cup filling it up half-way.

The Principal said to wait here. She'd return soon.

She was just a little older than Jane. It was difficult to say what she really looked like with all the garb the nuns wore. In some bizarre way, even though I was hurting pretty bad, I liked being close to her and whispering where I guessed her ear might be located beneath her headdress. She smelled okay too.

SISTER CELESTE SHOWED UP AT MRS. FOLEY'S classroom, and then they went into the hallway. Their voices echoed throughout the building, even into the basement where I was. Evelyn Foley jumped the Principal: "Well?"

"We are attending young Whitelaw." She said.

A confused look descended upon the veteran grade school instructor. "Call up his mother and have her attend to him. Perhaps while she's playing Clara Barton to her renegade son, she can teach him some respect, obedience, and discipline to begin with. Nothing like his brother… nothing. He's trouble and he's going to get in trouble. Nothing like his brother."

"Evelyn, you beat the kid up for Pete's sake…….he's a mess." She clenched her fists at the waist.

"Suspend this troublemaker for the day tomorrow, and he can rest up over the weekend and we'll forget about it Monday morning. Tell the parents you're investigating an incident which took place today in my class, but he should return to school as scheduled on Monday. It'll all be fine; the inmates may be running the show in the public schools, we can't let that happen here."

The Principal rolled her eyes and clenched her fists even tighter. "ENOUGH." She hissed. She entered the classroom without Foley and asked: "Where's Whitelaw"s desk?"

Samantha McAvoy answered, "Right here."

Mrs. Foley was aghast watching from the hallway.

Sr. Celeste picked up the workbook from the floor next to a few drops of blood.

The lay teacher waited for her outside the classroom: "Just look at the willful defacement of his workbook."

"Shut-up. All Souls will be lucky if we don't get sued."

"You worry too much – they should have straightened him out at home…….now he's our problem?"

"You keep your hands off him for the rest of the school year…..and this year has got a long way to go."

The teacher smiled returning to her class. Sr. Celeste walked down the stairs. Outside the nurse's office she examined the workbook: a half-page of blood and two exaggerated S's like he said. "For the love of God Evelyn."

I was studying my image in the mirror when she walked in.

She began, "Ryan, it might be for the best if you stayed home from school tomorrow and let things calm down. You are not being punished in any way, and there are some personnel problems that I have to resolve."

"Yes, sister." My voice was useless.

"How would you feel if I switched you to Miss Boudreaux"s class?"

A bunch of red flags popped up right away. First, everybody in 6-2 had been complaining about the heavy homework load she assigned nightly. Second, the majority of the clique was over there. Third, I really liked Valerie Moore and Samantha McAvoy, and I sat next to McAvoy. I thought about it; getting beat up was better than dealing with the extra homework. If there was a next time, I'd drop her. "I think I'll be alright in Mrs. Foley's class – I won't mess up the workbooks no more." I whispered.

"Think about it this weekend, and see me Monday morning before going to class, and let me know if you feel differently. Come up with me to the office; I'll explain the incident to your parents, and why you are to stay home tomorrow with a written explanation. You are to tell them to call me or stop by and see me if my note is unclear or needs further clarification."

RAY WAS DELIVERING PAPERS WHEN HE FIRST SAW me. "So you did get beat up. Mike Chizek said you did.

I held back and didn't answer.

"Come on Ryan......I'll finish my papers, and we'll go kick his ass. Was it somebody from All Souls?......from Lake Ave.?"

I nodded, "All Souls."

"Eighth grader?"

Another "no." this time my eyes faded shut. I kicked some imaginary dirt.

"C'mon, we'll go back up there now, or we'll get him tomorrow after school." He was plenty hot.

"We can't wup him 'cause the person that beat me up is that old witch........Mrs. Foley." My voice and pride struggled.

"Huh?"

"She beat me up, for what I don't know."

"Holy crap.......she beat you up?" He gave me a good inspection.

"Don't think I'll be able to lay my head on the pillow." I tilted my head back so Ray could see my neck.

"Holy shit! She's not a witch, she's a damn vampire. What did you do Hombre?"

"She said I marked up the English workbook."

"Were you drawing pictures of naked women?"

"Bad scene. Principal was there too." I choked.

"Celeste didn't hit you though – did she?"

"Uh-uh. Took my side mostly, but not in front of Foley." I had to stop talking, but I showed Ray the knot on my head and then mimicked how she bulldogged me....."right into the blackboard and door. The Prinzpul said I could switch to Boudreaux's class if I want."

"No, that's a bad move Ryan, on the volume of the homework alone. The kids in 6-2 last year said there was so much homework, there was no time for anything else. Who's decision is it?"

"Mine." My voice was running dry.

"Ride it out cowboy.......there'll be someone else in the barrel next week." he folded a paper. "And lay low tomorrow – try to be the invisible man."

"Right."

When I woke the next morning, I was still dizzy. Once I got walking up the hill with Ray, it got better with every step, although I didn't look any better. In fact I appeared worse as the big hits into the doors, desk, and blackboard started turning black, blue, and purple. I was off my game for sure, I ended up using paper towels to sop up a lot of my urine from the floor since my aim was no good.

Neither Hal or Jane had gotten a good look at me that night or the next morning. Ray covered for me. When Jane and Hal saw me on the weekend I explained, "I got the bumps and bruises from playing tackle football." Back in the '60s the only guys who played with equipment were high schools and Boy's clubs. The Chippewas didn't have a football program because it cost too much. Sometimes a guy came home from a pick-up game of football in bad shape, and sometimes you came home beat up because you got in a fight. Coming home and trying to explain why the teacher worked you over; it was better to tell Jane I got jumped by some guys at school. She still believed they had it in for me.

Laying the dime on Foley would end up being more trouble that it was worth. I decided not to give Sister Celeste's note to Hal and Jane, and ride the year out and hope for the best.

Close to the top of O'Dell, I told Ray I was "tapped out", I hadn't told Ray that I had been excused from class for the day. I had a plan, and it had to work out because I had no place to go. Ray left me at the bus stop at St. John's Hospital. Four bucks in my pocket and I had my bus fare. I caught the Liberty bus down to Getty Square.

vi

After goofing off all morning, and too many people wanting to know why I wasn't in school, I had enough and was going to catch the no.1 bus which would leave me at the bottom of O'Dell. It was noon anyway, Jane would be at the studio, and I'd be all alone until Ray got home. Everything would be kool as long as I resisted the temptation to start a fire.

Right across the street from the No.1 bus stop, the RKO theatre got my attention with its chasing marquee lights: "Major Dundee" 12:30, 4:00, 7:00, 10:00 - 2nd feature on weekends.

That was it, I dodged the traffic and looked at the 8x10 stills out front – nothing but action. This was a Civil War movie; not like that hugging and kissing "Gone With The Wind" bullcrap. It had a great cast for action: Charlton Heston, James Coburn (soon to be America's James Bond – Derek Flint), Richard (The Mick) Harris, Jim Hutton, Ben Johnson, Warren Oates, Brock Peters, and Slim Pickens.

There were a few more, but I didn't know their names. When I showed up for school on Monday, all the guys wanted to know if I had seen a doctor or went to the hospital after Foley assaulted me. Instead of answering, I went right into my review of "Major Dundee". I probably told 20 - 6th graders, and 10 - 7th graders of the movie's story line.

A few of my classmates kept eyeing the bald area, and the bump up on the side of my forehead which had made my eye black and blue. During recess a couple of the guys wanted to look at my neck. I had turned up the collar of my white shirt on the side where Foley had done most of her damage. Most likely my enthusiasm for the movie had won them over, and I had them looking at my eyes and not the dings and the dents.

Leaving the movie theatre, I kind of likened myself to having been under Dundee's command, earning my battle scars in an earlier skirmish. As my eyes adjusted from the dark of the movie house to daylight, I saw the rear end of my no.1 bus going north. Another wouldn't come for 15 minutes. Instead of standing at the bus stop like a mannequin, I walked north on the Warburton route and kept watching for a bus behind me. Almost through downtown and out of Getty Square, I could see the Yonkers train station from Warburton Ave, it was about ¼ mile at the bottom of this big parking lot called Larkin Plaza. About 95% of the Plaza was metered parking, the remaining real estate was a small park dedicated to one of the early Dutch settlers, but we all knew it as "Hooker Park". There were 8 benches around the park's perimeter, and there were two big trees dividing the park into thirds. Their canopies almost shaded the entire park. A granite headstone was erected in the middle and was easy to miss on a sunny day in the summer.

The police were driving in and out of the rows of parked cars; they were in pursuit of somebody. I walked and watched from the south side of the plaza, looking for the guy who the cops were chasing. It looked like a game of cat and mouse. I stopped even with the Post Office, one of the workers left the loading docks and came over. "Hey kid, see anything?"

"Cops lookin' for someone." I needed a cough drop, my throat was killing me.

"Been a lot of shit going on down here lately." We continued to watch the bluecoats.

"Hey Mister, zat train go to Greystone?" I said softly.

"You'll have to ask one of the clerks in the ticket cage for a schedule. The bus is cheaper. Last week, a couple of working girls rolled a drunk from the 'Tyrone House' in that little park right there." He pointed across the street. "The action should be slacking off when it gets colder."

"I'm going up to Greystone Station."

"The bus is cheaper." he repeated as I walked away. "Don't make a fuss – Ride the bus." he grinned.

A set of four railroad tracks ran the bridge overpass at the Yonkers' Station to allow access to Alexander St. to the west side of the tracks where the city jail, Yonkers Canoe Club, a sewage pump station, and the naval reserve were. There also was an abandoned two story ferry facility that used to take people across the Hudson to Alpine, N.J. at the bottom of the Palisades where they would fish, picnic, and get drunk.

The clock in the station read: 3:12. A pair of sirens and a paddy wagon made the scene at 'Hooker Park'. I went outside to see the action; it was hard to watch with Foley's shellacking yesterday, the bluecoats were smashing heads with their nightsticks.

At the Yonkers Station, there were ladies' and men's bathrooms, a newsstand, two ticket windows, but only one had a clerk, and a bunch of hardwood benches. The station was dimly lit and smelled of piss, tobacco, and brake shoes. It was an enlargement of the Greystone station. Yonkers didn't have a pot-bellied stove and was always in operation.

The clerk in the cage at Yonkers station had the whole get-up on: white shirt and tie, R.R. blue uniform (with his jacket hanging on one of the hooks behind him), vest w/R.R. watch and chain, a sweat stained visor with the translucent green brim.

"Destination?" He didn't look up and was marking something on a sheet with a New York Central logo on the letterhead.

"Greystone?"

The clerk looked at me – Dollar ten. Don't take the next train – that's an express. The next local leaves at 3:30, arrives Greystone-ahhhh…..3:42. He read his timetable.

I spoke to a passenger who waited on the platform, he said the way it worked was: the locals make all the stops and the express trains only make the important ones. A dollar-ten was a lot of bread for the same basic ride you got from the no.1 bus, plus you had to walk a good quarter mile from the train station, to our house. The bus left you at O'Dell and Warburton, which might have been a 120 yard walk – for 25 cents.

Most of the grown-ups I had to deal with on that quasi-hooky day had given me a free pass. Sure, I'd cook up a line or story to make it easier for them to let me slide or get rid of me. Making trouble or calling attention to myself was the last thing I wanted to do. Wearing the All Souls blazer didn't help at all. It wasn't my way with words, personality, or demeanor; but my appearance could only invoke sympathy as it made them want to avoid eye contact. Nobody was going to call a truant officer, they felt bad enough for me. They all turned away pretty quick. I could hear them thinking as I walked away, 'Boy, that kid lost a chunk of hair.'

'So this is what goes on in the real world while we're at school'.

vii

Three commuter train lines ran out of Grand Central Terminal to the north: The New Haven ran to the east, The Harlem line ran through the center of Westchester County, and the Hudson line ran the eastern shore of the Hudson River up to Albany. The New York Central owned the Harlem and Hudson lines outright. They were in some kind of partnership on the New Haven Line.

One major difference between the commuter and the subways trains in N.Y.C. was in the manner of the collection of the fare. To ride the subway, a token was purchased and dropped in the turnstile to enter the platform. Payment of one fare gave the rider access to four boroughs......quite a bargain. Aunt Frances always took us on the subway because Uncle Bill never taught her to drive. There wasn't any room for street parking where they lived. In the Bronx, owning two cars wasn't a convenience - it was a hardship.

Commuter train riders paid by the distance they traveled. The person who rode the train everyday would buy a monthly pass at a discount, otherwise a ticket could be purchased at the larger stations or on the train when the conductor came through the car collecting fares. As I got older, I could see that this conductor system invited theft and corruption. With any long term theft scheme, the key to being successful was not to get greedy, and stay out of all conspiracies.

Jane would take Ray and me on the Harlem line to Grand Central Terminal when we lived on Vernon Pl. on the other side of Yonkers. We'd walk from Grand Central to Radio City to watch Dottie Holland and 'The Rockettes' dance and perform. Mom would point out Dottie to us, but they all looked the same. There had to be 30 of them in a line. They all looked the same backstage with their faces full of make-up.

Riding the subway was reality. It made the rider confront the city: good and bad neighborhoods, good and bad behavior, beautiful and not so beautiful people, and all of the variations filling the city. Take a long look and enjoy......or ignore. It was replayed throughout the day --- everyday.

Ray and me laughed on our first ride on the subway when the pervasive smell of piss hit our senses. If all a passenger smelled was the electric motors and the brakes, it was a good ride. When the subway's doors closed, you could count on being accosted by the pungent smell of urine, cigarette or marijuana smoke, alcohol, and the electric motors. Hot and humid days tested the riders' resolve to get to their destinations. Even though the subways weren't air conditioned when we were kids, it was light years ahead of the buses, at least they could move the air through the cars by going fast. The buses had to deal with the street traffic, and no air moving at all.

The upper strata of society who rode the commuter trains were able to enjoy amenities such as a toilet and a tiny sink in every car (The older commuter cars dropped the metal toilet's contents right to the tracks below). When we were in high school, the Penn R.R. bought out the New York Central and slowly retired these older passenger cars with the bomb-door toilet. On Fridays, they had a bar cart tended by two bartenders selling cocktails airline style so the commuters could get in the 'weekend mood' before they got in the car with the wife and kids.

THE LOCAL PULLED INTO YONKERS STATION AND I
boarded. The four cars weren't even half-full. The train passed the city
jail, Otis' storage yard, and Proctor Paint. I had bought the ticket from
the guy in the cage and I waited for one of the assistant conductors to
catch up with me and punch my ticket. I was looking for a way to scam
their system. Just before the next station Glenwood, the asst. conductor
came in our car and was punching the tickets of the people who just
got on. There was a whole lot of information given out in the receipts
and seat stubs: how many people were sitting there, where they
boarded, where they were getting off, day-week-month, peak or off-
peak. The conductors all had their suitcases filled with these different
colored seat tickets, cash receipts, daily cash, and change bag. By the
time the train reached Greystone, I decided that it was too complicated
to figure out a scam right now.

The conductor took my ticket right after Glenwood and
informed me Greystone was next. "Who are you with?" He gave me
the once over.

"No one."

"Kind of young to be on a train by yourself."

"No different than riding the Jerome Ave. subway."

"'Spose not. Greystone." He called through the car.

From Glenwood station, the passengers could see Greystone
about three miles to the north because of the sharp curve a quarter mile
ahead.

The conductor pulled up the hinged ¼" steel checker plate
which denied passenger access to the use the train's stairway and
fastened it vertically against the wall of the stairwell with 2" flat bar
used as a hold back. The conductor let four of us off, signaled ahead to
the guy looking out the engineer's window. He climbed back up the
stairs, rotating the flatbar position from 12 o'clock to 3 and lay the
checkerplate back into its floor position.

With the Pennsylvania R.R.'s deeper pockets, it was
financially able to initiate long overdue upgrades to the track, purchase
new cars and engines, make bridge and physical structure
rehabilitations, as well as instituting uniformity of all station platforms
to match the elevation of the floors of the commuter trains.

Differences in elevation between the trains' floor and the
elevation of the stations' platforms had created all sorts of problems
since passenger rail service began. The necessity for the passengers to
use the train's stairs, to get on and off the train, the accumulation of ice
and snow in the stairwell, the general laziness of the train crew to only
use one stairway when at least two should have been used. It had
commuters stacking up much like the line to disembark from a jet;
causing accidents in the stair well because some guys wanted to jump
the last two steps to get out, not to mention how hard it was for the old
folks. The stairs were steep; and the commuter car's handrail was
nothing but a piece of chain. The railroad installed treads with grating,
but quickly got rid of them as women's fashion shoes with spiked
heels got caught in them. They tried steps with pans, but they collected
snow and ice. Senior citizens looked like they were climbing a ship's

ladder when they boarded the train. The sharks at the law offices were circling their prey. A sizeable number of personal injury law firms dedicated their practice exclusively to the railroads.

By 1970 in New York, all a plaintiff had to show the judge was their lawsuit wasn't frivolous or fraudulent in these railroad cases and they'd win their case. They didn't have to prove negligence. Submit the hospital and doctor bills along with a 'lost time' claim, and they would be reimbursed. A compensation award was baked right in before any testimony was given.

The corruption took hold with the assignment of cases involved with a railroad having tracks in more than one state, and the lawsuit had to be filed in federal court because of the Interstate Commerce laws. After the plaintiff got their settlement in Federal court; they still could sue later on in the state court. Word traveled quickly about the initial awards and perpetual monthly checks following these judgments. It was a bonanza for those on the inside of the game. The number of personal injury cases was staggering after only a few years. The Interstate Commerce Commission had introduced legislation to grant it the authority to establish a court whose scope was limited to personal injury incurred while involved in some manner with the railroads.

This was something right in the Mafia's area of expertise: they owned the judges, commissioners, lawyers on both sides, the investigators, and medical experts. They were all sleeping in the same bed. It was tailor made for organized crime. Through this little court, which got bigger every year, the Mafia had achieved legitimacy, doled out justice, played Robin Hood with the railroads' money, and never stood for election. For a number of years, the mob ran the whole game. It spread the wealth around.....in the early years. It also provided high profile employment to its members in the justice system. This included connections to the unions and other spheres of the transportation and building trades.

Greed and power ultimately did in the personal injury/railroads court. One of the pre-arranged settlements went sour, somebody wasn't greased, an investigator turned states' evidence and the next thing you read was about this corrupt court which "fixed personal injury" verdicts in return for kickbacks. It was like a Ponzi scheme, but it ran out of money. Plaintiffs kept wanting bigger and bigger injury awards, and everybody wanted to work for the injury court. When the Don's had to put money in, it started to collapse under its own weight. There were boards of inquiry, F.B.I. investigations, jail sentences, restitution money. After a year-and-a-half, organized crime was out and they were replaced with hardened bureaucrats. There never was any thought to the dismantling of the Railroads Personal Injury Court once the bureaucracy flushed out the mob.

I CLIMBED THE CONCRETE STAIRS FROM HARRIMAN Ave. to Henry Hudson Park/Warburton Ave. It was another switchback design, and most likely belonged to the city. Our house on O'Dell was about a furlong from the park. If we cut through a small wooded patch behind our house - it was less.

Ray waved to me as I walked up and he walked down O'Dell. His look said: 'he knew something was up.'

"Don't bullshit me – I'm the guy that's got to back up your bullcrap alibi. Give it to me straight."

Taking a deep breath, I showed him Sister Celeste's note for Jane and Hal.

Handing it back - he acknowledged I really hadn't played 'hooky', but I might expect trouble if it came to light I had concealed a note intended for our parents. He said, "We left for school together, but you weren't at school – so what did you do?"

"Like we did with Priano and Pappas, but the guy at the newsstand store chased me away. And then I saw this cool movie: "Major Dundee." On the way home, I was just shy of Nana's apartment, and I seen some cops down by the train station with their lights flashin'. The coppers chased me over to the Post Office side of Larkin Plaza. There was blood all over. They even had this one woman, she only had these skin-tight pants and a bra on, but she had a leather coat and that covered her up mostly. She was drunk too. They Billy-clubbed two or three guys in 'hooker park'. It should be in the paper tomorrow – happened right in front of the Herald Statesman building.

"Wow. Then what?"

"Then, I took the train from Yonkers to Greystone…..and here I am. How's my face and head look? I'm still beat up? I couldn't tell by looking at my reflection in a store window – I needed a mirror."

"Ryan……it's only been a day."

"I dunno, all these people gave me at least a double-take."

"You know – I don't ever remember Foley going ballistic like that, not even with Puggy Ring." Ray stopped and gave it some thought: "Your beating took me by surprise at first, but the more I looked at her today – the more I realized she's a genuine nut-job."

I squinted my eyes to slits: "I'm going to get her back."

"What are you going to do?"

Don't know where or when or how, but I'm going to even it up. Write it down.

viii

Sam McAvoy and Val Moore received Saint Valentines' day cards from me. They were the first and only ones I ever gave out. Jack Swinnburne had moved to Indiana the first week of March. People were still talking about the big blackout back in November. Just before St. Patrick's Day, Mrs. Foley started once again with her attacks; this time she limited them to verbal tirades. She was offended when I sat at my desk with my ankle on my knee. "You're not at a tavern Whitelaw. Get both your feet under your desk."

A week later she caught me sitting barroom style again: "Whitelaw – what's does the school's uniform code require for socks?"

"That they should be worn at all times." Most of the class laughed or chuckled.

"Well Mr. Comedian, the uniform code calls for white or black socks, and just what are the color of your socks?"

"Red."

"Red......yes.......they are red." She said with a politician's sweep of her hand. "Red sock Ryan. I want you to write 300 times: The boys' uniform code is white or black socks - by tomorrow. Now go down to Sr. Celeste's office and show her your non-compliant socks."

"What are you here for Ryan?" Sr. Celeste said.

"To show you my socks."

"This is Mrs. Foley's directive? What's wrong with your socks?"

"Wrong color."

"Are we going to get through this school year without another physical incident?"

"Ask her, she holding all the cards."

"I think you're smart enough not to let her win Ryan. There isn't much school left - a few months, let's just get through to the last day of school without further drama."

I felt like Foley had won; I wished Hal had pulled up stakes and moved us to Indiana with Swinnburne.

"Go back to class."

TRACK AND FIELD HAD JUST STARTED AND NONE TOO soon for me. We didn't have to try out for the team because we had made the cross country team last fall. I fell into the groove with the 2.25 mile - cross country format.

Spring track and field were different. I could run the mile, but going around the track oval, was too monotonous. Still, that was what spring time track was: running the oval, dashes/sprints, pole vault, discus, hurdles, high jump, long jump, triple jump, the mile, javelin. In grade school, it was mostly the track; it was cheaper. Once we got into high school we could see how the field aspect took real dedication, technique, and coaching. Grade school field events amounted to the hurdles, long jump, and the triple jump.

The length of the cross country course was two and a quarter miles in grade school. There were hills, trails, woods, obstacles: fallen trees, creeks, and streams. I felt free running cross country, but not so much on a cinder or asphalt track. Track and field became boring in a short time. The clock challenged you; running track took a great deal of concentration and determination to do well. For me, cross country was freedom and I found it easier to excel. Both required endurance.

ix

Major league baseball had its opening day eleven days earlier. For April, it seemed warm. Leaves were already sprouting on the Maple trees. We had slept late, probably because we left the

149

window open. Fresh air in the room may have deepened our slumber. Neither of us had heard Jane and Hal get up. He had already gone to work.

We were about ten minutes late, trying to get out of the house. Ray told me to put the hustle on as he started downstairs. 'Damn these socks!' I thought. My clean pair of reds stared me in the face.......along with a black and a white that looked like a couple of unwanted orphans in the top drawer. Wearing a mismatched pair was sure to incur the wrath of the old battle-axe if she looked at my ankles. It was beyond disobedience; it would be defiance. I sucked it up and rifled through the hamper and put on a stinky black sock.

Ray was almost out the door, "C'mon, we're late."

I wiped the math and science books from my desk into my gym bag, and rushed downstairs.

"Ryan..........Ray forgot his lunch." Jane said as she handed it to me and kissed me good-bye. I tossed our lunches into my gym bag and was out the door. He had to be past 45 O'Dell already I thought.

The sun blazed on our front door. I couldn't see until I got to the sidewalk and scanned up the street. Ray should have been half-way up the hill by now, but instead he was in the middle of the street in between 30 and 45 O'Dell gathering up all these papers and magazines. He had created a minor traffic jam in both directions. He put his thumb and middle finger together in the front of his mouth and gave me a loud whistle, and waved me to come over.

"Start picking this stuff up." He was in a panic; his arms were full and he unloaded it to me. There was still quite a bit of the garbage in the street, curbs, and on the sidewalk. The scattering was mostly caused by the wind wakes from the traffic.

"Put half in your gym bag and half in mine."

"Yeah Ray." I dashed back to the slate sidewalk, dodging cars, blasting horns, drivers screaming obscenities and giving us the finger. There was something going on, he wasn't just picking up garbage. He had given me that look, "Don't ask questions.........just do it."

It was a ball of confusion for me, but my brother knew what he was doing – he must have. The anti-littering campaign by the Indian on TV must have really given him a guilt trip. I opened the mouth of my gym bag and stuffed the magazines and paperbacks in them. One of the magazines fell to the sidewalk with the pages opened.

I can't say what occurred to alter time; or cancelled the passage of time. Either may have happened. I was intensely studying two nearly naked women fondling each others' breasts. "Holy Fuck......" this was no detective magazine or dog and pony show. I could feel love rising from the page as waves of distortion altered my vision. My eye closest to Ray raised up. Perhaps he was playing some kind of practical joke on me. April Fools was 14 days ago. We snapped up the girlie magazines and paperbacks faster than a couple of armored truck guards chasing a bag of fifty's that had found freedom.

"Pick that shit up, we got to go NOW."

His yelling brought me back to the here and now, but again I got jammed tight where I was: this car came down the street passed me and stopped at Ray's gym bag which couldn't have been more than 20 ft. away, and the passenger got out and grabbed it.

"Them guys in the Pontiac just swiped your gym bag." I yelled as the two-way traffic continued throughout our clean-up.

"The hell with it – let's get the rest of this smut and take it to the woods. We'll look at it after school." The street was clean enough, just some printed advertisements for more porn. "We got all the paperbacks and magazines except the ones the guys in the Pontiac made off with. Fuckin' jags." I said.

We stashed the stuff beneath the overhang on O'Dell where you had to climb down a rock wall from the street. He stayed above and dropped my gym bag to me, and about 18 magazines.

"See any good spots? You know just for today until we get back after school."

"There's an air conditioner. We dig a hole underneath and put the air conditioner on top of them?" I said.

"Yeah....Yeah.....but hurry it up."

The damned thing weighed a ton, and when I rolled it, all this fluid started leaking out. "Got all this liquid shit in it."

"Nah, that isn't going to work." He kept looking from above. "Right here, nearer me." He pointed, "What's that white thing – push away the leaves. What is it?"

"It's the top of a washing machine." I lifted the loading door. "Looks dry."

"Yeah, that's what we want. Make sure the stuff fits and cover it with leaves."

I took the top of the washer and relocated it over a depression. Some wood was used to isolate it from the soil. Maybe there were 20 magazines, and about the same number of paperbacks. We would have had double that if them crooks didn't rip us off. I had to put the paperbacks in a dry area at the bottom of the wall and cover them with leaves. I wasn't too interested in the books anyway. I launched my gym bag back up to Ray, and made my way to where there wasn't much of a climb to the guard rail.

"C'mon, we are so late." he laughed.

We trotted up the rest of O'Dell to where it meets North Broadway. He looked at his watch, "We got to keep going." We began trotting again, at least Broadway wasn't as steep.

"We'll have to take the first bus we see – Liberty or a no. 2 bus."

We ended up at Tudor Woods and Palisade and waited for the no. 2 bus.

"Hey Ray, ain't no high schoolers from Gorton or All Souls at the bus stops. We must have just missed one." I said.

"Yeah. If we don't see one in five minutes we'll have to start walking again."

We had only been at that bus stop for 2 or 3 minutes, and a bus came around the curve.

"Ray you forgot your lunch, Mom gave it to me, it's in my gym bag."

"At least them thieves didn't get that. A month-and-a-half left in the school year and I'm missing my English, Math and my notebooks. I need the notebooks." He shook his head.

I reached in my pocket for bus fare as Ray got his lunch from my gym bag. "What the fffuuuuu-----? No.......you're kidding me. Why didn't you stash this crap on the hill with the rest?"

A wiseguy smile ran my face, "I'm going to show it to the guys........they've never seen anything like this before." I said.

"Most sailors never seen crap like this – you can't bring this shit to school. Are you out of your mind?"

"It'll be alright, I won't get caught."

"No, I won't let you get caught cause you're going to chuck it down the sewer."

"You're crazy." I said.

"Yeah Ryan, I'm the one who's crazy. I'm the retard trying to bring a smut magazine to school. You'll get sent down if they find this shit. What's wrong with you?"

The two of us stood there face to face. The bus driver looked around the two high school girls as they hastily paid their fares. You two comin'?"

We were too possessed with the stare down; the bus left.

"Listen jackass, either take it back down O'Dell, or ditch it somewhere, or chuck it."

"Get bent." I waved him off.

"Hey doomkuff, they're not even human beings. You're brain's twisted."

"Don't tell me what's what – I didn't buy the magazine, I found it............we found it. How's this, I won't show them to anybody, and I'll take them home at the end of the school day. I won't show anybody anything, before during or after."

"Uh-uh. That thing doesn't go to school." And he reached for the gym bag and I pushed him away.

"What's not getting through? – you go to All Souls, you're an altar boy, and amongst the books you bring to school is a copy of, he looked at the magazine's cover, is a copy of "Rauncho Rancho", they'd kick you out of public school for bringing that to school."

"I'm telling you, I'm not going to get pinched."

"That's right, cause I won't let you." he again reached for the gym bag.

This time I pushed him back and we went at it. Not many of my punches connected. We were about the same height, but he had 15 pounds on me.....all muscle. One of his punches laid me out on my back in the dirt between the sidewalk and the street. He grabbed my gym bag, had his foot on my stomach, and began clubbing me with the athletic bag. I was seeing stars but I was too old to start crying. Blocking the punches and the kicks, and the bag blows as best I could, I lay on the bus stop's bare ground until he got tired.

Lying there motionless he said, "Toldja." He went into the gym bag and dropped the magazine through the storm sewer's grating. Ray walked away on Palisade Ave. towards the North End. A couple of people who passed asked me if I was alright. When they left, I went

152

over to the storm sewer at the corner. There it was, about a foot beneath the grate on the catch shelf of the sewer. Laying in the gutter, I extended my arm in the mouth of the sewer and tried to reach around and grab it off the catch shelf. One slip and it would fall way down into the slop. I couldn't reach it with my thumb and forefinger. No sticks or wood around, I ended up using my index and middle finger like a pair of chop sticks.

My middle went under while my pointer finger squeezed the magazine. Gingerly, the smut was extricated from its subterranean jail. I threw it by my other books in the dirt. I hoped I didn't run into anybody I knew, with the magazine laying there. I had to get going.

This section was predominantly Jewish. An older lady had witnessed the fist fight from her first-floor kitchen window between Ray and me. She knew by our school uniform we attended parochial school. She wiped the blood from my face with a wet handkerchief.

"You go to dee Catolish school, and this boy who leavens you here......he beat you up. Who is deesh boy.......What ist heees name? You are O.K.?" She asked giving me the once over. "Vee clean up deesh mess. Who vas that boy?"

"He's my brother."

"Vat? Vat you say.........deeesh boy ist your broodah? Oy vey ---- Deesh your broodah – no, I don't tink so. Vee get you stuff, and you can gettens clean in my house." The woman reached down to put my books back in the gym bag.

"Hey you, deesh ist yours?" Holding up a magazine with only two words in its 40 pages: 'Rauncho Rancho', I watched the woman's face jettison to an unbelievable world where human and animal worlds attempted to produce some miscreant life form. I walked over with two textbooks and put them in the gym bag. She was revolted.

"Deesh ist you book.........Is deesh vat they teachens you at dis Catolish school? You broodah should ha beat you up more good. Jes, I mean it. Vat deesh vorld cummins to?" She looked at me with an icy stare and gave out a righteous laugh: "You not Catolish". She tossed the beastiality pictoral in the gutter, spit on it, and walked away.

As soon as she turned away and walked back to her apartment, I wiped her spit off the magazine with my sleeve and put it in the bottom of the gym bag with my other books and started trotting towards the End. When I reached the North End, I checked out my reflection in Salon de Ric's Glamour Parlor window: another shiner, a bloody nose, fat lip, dried blood all over, and a tie which looked like it had been used to hang deerkill. With all the blood on my shirt, I might have passed as a Guernsey cow.

The Jewish lady's disgust and reaming out made me accept the fact that the 'Rauncho Rancho' mag would be dynamite if anyone found out about it. I felt as bad as I looked. Five or ten minutes late wouldn't matter now. If I could make it by the end of recess – 10:15, that was good enough, so I continued up Palisade Ave. The winding diesel of a climbing bus was starting to come up Palisade Ave. I thought I had time to spell off, and sat on the low wall in front of the Methodist Church. Why was everybody so pissed off at this

153

magazine? It was best to take a quick look and know what I had gotten myself into.

No one could dream this stuff up. I never heard of such activity. Wait a minute, I had. Somewhere I heard about these shepherds that would screw their sheep when they were without female companionship for weeks or months at a time. Maybe it was bullcrap. The photos were real enough: mostly animals doing each other – no interspecies stuff, except a jackass banging a horse. Equines, canines, and bovines filled the pages. I flipped through until I saw a human woman.

The final eight pages was of a pretty farm woman with a medium-sized Border Collie. The first photo was of the two of them in profile looking at one another. They might have been smiling. It was the type of picture a dog owner might have on their desk or coffee table. The photos in the next pages, wouldn't be seen in any book case, mantel, or next to a phone. These were the kind of situational pics that a nutjob kept in a strongbox in his cellar. The dog probably wouldn't have cared if the F.B.I. seized these pictures.

Each page was broken up into 2, 3, and 4 individual shots. It was most likely a personal defect of mine, in my genetic code, but I recall there was a water bowl with the dog's name: 'Lucky'. It was professionally painted on the side. That dog had the right name. Thinking..........'I suppose the dog's name and the magazine's title made a grand total of three words. There was no name who printed it, no address, no copyright......not even a page to tell the deviant where to send money to buy more.' "Hey Ray, now I get it." I said aloud.

The 'Rauncho Rancho' was concealed in the middle of my science workbook. I sat there lost, when the bus pulled up: "Kid.......hey kid......this isn't a bus stop." the driver called from behind the wheel.

"No shit Sherlock." I said under my breath. The gym bag started taking on function and feel of a James Bond attaché case.

"Why aren't you at the bus stop?"

Is this guy a truant officer, I had to come up with something: "I had to finish my homework."

"Well come on then, you're already late." he fired back. "Who jumped you? Sit over there he motioned with his head to the seat that faced him.

"They took my bus and lunch money too." I rubbed my jaw.

"Don't worry about the bus fare, I just wish I rolled up when they were working you over – how many of them were there?" He had the front door open, it was already getting warm.

"There were only two." I didn't want to lay it on too thick.

"Were they bigger or older?" He made a stop to pick up. "You know watcha do when you're outnumbered kid?" He was becoming animated and driving aggressively. "You run to the nearest car and rip the antenna off and put your back against a wall or a car and start whipping that thing head high"

The bus driver blasted his horn at the car ahead of him. "C'mon ya dipstick while we got the light." He laid on the horn some more. He pulled out from behind the car and passed on the left. The traffic coming from the opposite direction locked up their brakes, giving way to the bus making the left turn. "That's the way we do it." He laughed and waved to the motorist frozen in the intersection. I could see my stop down the road straight ahead.

"You'll be O.K. cruiser." He shouted through the people who were trying to get on.

I gave him a nod and a wave. With every step, All Souls got closer. What was my explanation for being late and for my classmates? How do I deal with Ray except to tell him he was right? I had to come up with some b.s. for being late and getting beat up.

x

The Jewish lady couldn't wipe off all the blood and dirt on my face, so I was a dead give away for an interrogation by the administration. I had been thinking about trying to blend into class after recess, but my appearance was too conspicuous to try. Vinny Tartaglione had pulled it off last fall, but the next guy who tried got rung up and was sent to Sister Celeste's and she gave him a week of detentions. Mrs. Foley always knew where I was, no way she didn't know I wasn't in class before recess. Looking like I had been in a rumble, I didn't think there'd be a big fuss about something that occurred off school grounds.

The school clock read: 9:50, recess was at 10:00. I was an hour and five minutes tardy. Kathy D'Costa was in the office with her mother about some problem with the gym teacher playing dodgeball --- "too rough" her Mom whined. Sister Alexa, a real young nun, was substituting for the year - mostly 7th grade. We had her a couple of times when Mrs. Foley didn't show up. Sister Alexa was looking for Mr. Hurley to help her get the classroom's windows open. The last time they were open was in early November.

Sister Alexa turned from the counter in the office and crashed into me. "Well, what happened to you?" The office secretary directed her attention to Kathy D. and her mother.

"You." Sister Alexa pointed at my chest – let's go outside."

"What's your name and whose class are you in?"

"Ryan Whitelaw, and I'm in Mrs. Foley's class."

She gave me the full visual once over. "You were involved in some disciplinary matter that went to the Principal earlier this year. You're in Mrs. Foley's.......so what's going on today mister? More of the same?"

"I was scrappin' with two guys from school 16. I'll catch up with them." I squinted my eyes and nodded my head. There was never any intention of getting Ray involved, this whole mess was of my doing except for the recovery of the dirty books. I looked too beat up for this woman to have anything but pity for me.

"The school will have to have an explanation that assesses responsibility for the fact that you didn't receive these injuries on school time or property." Sister Alexa said.

She was real young, good looking for a nun, but with that habit, you could only see her face. I thought she sounded like some kind of lawyer. Sr. Celeste must have told the faculty about a student receiving corporal punishment that was in excess of the nature of the infraction. All these teachers knew who I was.

I told her it was no big thing, I'd catch up with them mugs when it was one on one.

"You're still going to have to see the Principal. Let's see you." Sr. Alexa put my chin in the palm of her hand and rolled my face so the light caught the shiner on my left eye. "You've also got a fat lip, a couple of scratches, and you had a bloody nose. Any body blows or contusions?"

"Just where they kicked me when I was on the ground; there's a couple of black and blues I absorbed. I've gotten worse playing football."

"Where's the most severe body blow?"

"Probably my left hip. I don't know what it looks like but it hurts the most."

"There's no nurse here – we'll take a look at it in the boys' bathroom. The nun made sure the bathroom was empty and she blocked the entry door with a trash barrel full of paper towels. "Just pull your pants down to your knees and show me the bruise."

I had to pull my boxer shorts down on the one side to reveal my left hip. I focused on the zipper of my gym bag. It was still closed. I looked down at my bare hip. 'A pretty good kick Ray' - I thought. She got a little closer so I pulled up my shirt.

"Anything else?" she said.

"No, I don't think so."

"You're going to have a colorful bruise there. Wash up the best you can, you'll just be a mess the remainder of the day. You go see the Principal when you get cleaned up."

"Yes Sister."

The image in the mirror wasn't too impressive. My hair still hadn't come back where Foley had yanked it out back in November. I looked in the mirror at the bald patch on my head; I couldn't wait for the summer when I could get a buzz cut to even it out. At least Ray wasn't no hair pullin' sissy when he fought. Someone else was in the Principal's office, I couldn't see who it was because of the way the furniture was situated, though the door was wide open. I waited on a padded bench in the administration office.

A science test was coming up, the gym bag was next to me on the floor and I thought it'd be a smart use of time to review for it. Most of the material I was familiar with, but I'd have to go over the periodic table of elements with Ray, I was sure he'd forgive and forget about this morning; anyway, he still owed me for helping him with his paper route and not just the night we got back from the World's Fair. I wasn't sure what an element's atomic weight meant and how it was assigned. I put the science book away and looked over the counter, and into Sister Celeste's office.

With my new black eye, I'd get a lot of attention at lunchtime. It might be good or bad. I wasn't like Ray, I couldn't do a

180 and turn a negative into a positive. It was a part of his DNA.......second nature to him.

Sister Alexa came out from the Principal's office. I couldn't figure out why she was down the administration office for so long. Sr. Alexa must have been having a bull session with her mentor and burnt up her recess. She left the office with a folder in her hand.

"Whiteside, Sr. Celeste will see you now." she said.

I took a deep breath trying to imagine how the principal was going to deal with me. All she could discipline me for was for being tardy, and Ray's tune-up pretty much explained that. Everything happened off school property; I couldn't see how she could make much of the whole thing. I felt pretty good, but the second I sat down across from Sister Celeste - I knew my gym bag with the "Rauncho Rancho' lay on the floor outside next to the cushioned bench. Being in her office seemed like an eternity because she took two phone calls. It might have only been eight minutes before I was sent to class with a tardy slip. The gym bag's zipper had been left open when I had been looking at the science book. I rushed into the bathroom and dumped the contents on the tile. My arm swept the contents into a five foot arc: The Human/Mammal hybrid fun magazine had vanished!

xi

September, LaCrosse

Killeen had fallen asleep watching her semi-comatose father. She wished she could meet him wherever he was - out there in the heavens or expanse of space; it wasn't happening here in room 107. She sunk into her dream world from the past: it was a few years after she had graduated from UW-LaCrosse. All the sisters had gotten together. Nicole and her new husband Rick were at one of the family barbecues. He asked Ryan why he didn't drink. They got an answer they weren't expecting:

"You see, I got this virus.....Hepatitis C from being a dope shooter back in New York, and it's destroying my liver. Some people only live 30 years before the virus kills 'em. I'm at 30 years right now. On borrowed time you might say."

The dream was mostly a nightmare, and it woke Killeen up. Ryan was propped up, but not quite sitting. He was awake watching the younger twin with as much smile as he had.

"Hey Ol' Man," Sleepy eyed she asked, "How many years you been carrying that Hep C?"

"Just about 40 - "Had this monsta inside of me for over two thirds of my life."

"You are one tough vaquero Pop."

Ryan struggled to clear his throat and motioned for the cup with the straw. He drank a little cranberry juice from the styro-cup.

"Killeen." It was almost a whisper. "My foot locker in your house.......inside it.....a mini-duffle. Two jars and two plastic
157

pharmacy containers inside it. I don't know, I think the olive jars are full. The yellow prescription bottles......maybe half." He took a sip of juice and continued: "Find them.......they're labeled something like 'Ray' – 'mine' – 'pos.' – 'neg.' We may need the ash inside them. Keep an eye on everything in Uncle Ray's duffle......keep it nearby --- I'll tell you what to do with it when it's time."

"Sounds like some dark arts or black magic." She tried to laugh.

"It might be my last roll at the table. Be certain I am conscious again, because you won't know what to do."

"Pop's, are you hallucinating?"

"What day is it?"

"Wednesday."

"No.......probably not."

The disappearance of the magazine had to remain
unmentioned until Ray decided to bring it up or until some bad news
came from school connecting me to it. At first, I was on pins and
needles, but after a week of anxiety, the missing 'Rauncho Rancho'
began to fade. Looking at the glass half-full; we still had all those other
skin magazines in our library of flesh below O'Dell Ave...........and
the paperbacks in reserve.

I was more interested in the stuff we found on the hill than he
was. He'd go through them and mostly laugh and move on to the next,
but the dominant comment coming out from the both of us was
"WOW." The dirty magazines had me captivated.

"Ray, how we going to keep this stuff dry?" I said.

"Take a couple of 'em home and hide them real good. If
Cathy or brother Bill stumble upon them, that would be the worst. He's
young and she's a girl; we got to make sure they never find the stuff."

"Yeah but – it isn't like we bought the junk."

"Ry, that argument isn't going to save your butt. Just by
attending All Souls; you're kind of responsible to know right from
wrong. Say – where did that nasty magazine end up?"

"I got rid of it. I was getting this feeling that it was a big sin."
I looked at him for a reply.

"Now this is where your 'I didn't buy the stuff fits in'. You
didn't make the stuff......You didn't purchase it......You're merely an
innocent bystander, curious in the mores of modern life. A venial sin
as Tommy Priano would rule." Ray reached for another magazine from
the pile.

Maybe for Ray that logic worked, but he was only casually
looking at the action photos of the naked parade. That wasn't my style,
I was studying it – intensely. I listened to the traffic above us on
O'Dell climbing and descending. Nobody walked the hill except us.
"And besides - How can it be a sample of the moe-rays of modern life?
Hell that guy was standing on a milk stool packing Elsie with
unpasteurized, and the milkmaid was doing something naughty with
Rin-Tin-Tin.........I don't even remember what she was doing. That's
not modern life --- that's caveman territory."

"Just think how far mankind has come; and how much we're
turning back the clock studying this filth." Ray grinned. "The church
says if you have sex – that's original sin, and if you have sex outside of
marriage that's a sin too. But wait a minute.......what about – 'be
fruitful and multiply?' Someone has to tell me how and why you
would get sent to hell for being a spectator. I know where you're
coming from Ryan...... It isn't easy thinking you can just throw the
smut down the sewer. Temptation has a big say in the matter."

"That's why I'm gonna bring up a big plastic bag and wrap
them in it. I'll decide what's junk and what's the good stuff."

Ray gave me the eye roll.

The abandoned Croton Aqueduct, Elizabeth Seton College, Untermyer Park, The Hudson River Country Club, and St. John's Riverside Hospital grounds were able to remain undeveloped because of their non-profit tax status, religious affiliation, or were owned by some governmental agency. Ninety percent of this acreage had remained woodlands.

The Croton Aqueduct had carried water to the Bronx and N.Y.C. for over a hundred years. The Croton Dam was approximately 25 miles north of where we lived. Hal told us the aqueduct was abandoned before WWII when N.Y.C. had changed the delivery of the dam's water to an alternate underground tunnel and used a concrete pipeline to minimize biologic, industrial, and unknown contaminants. Now the Croton Dam's water ran on the other side of Yonkers, more central in lower Westchester county before it reached the Bronx. The vestiges of the aqueduct were scattered in towns, villages, and cities in southwestern Westchester. Because it was an underground aqueduct, most people didn't know it existed. Mention "aqueduct" and many people are thinking of the ones the Romans built. The only time the emperors ran the water above ground was to span rivers and gorges.

The Croton aqueduct was now an abandoned dirt road with an overgrowth of trees, grass, and brush guarding the two tire trail. Many of the aqueduct's limestone structures remained standing in Yonkers, Hastings and Dobbs Ferry. The most prominent of these were the 14 ft. high aerators, made out of large block; circular and telescoping in design. At first, Ray and me thought they were ornamentation and/or location devices: leftover from an estate's landscape expression. We rode at least ten miles of the aqueduct with our bikes, travelling north and south in our second summer at 21. Ray had a J.C. Higgins speedometer/odometer from Sears on his bike. He figured there was a limestone marker every mile.

Hal might have the answer why they built these limestone markers, they had to be more than an architectural feature Ray reasoned.

"Dad, what's that short stone tower on the aqueduct for?"
"Behind the Kennedy house?"
"Yeah, them." I said.
"They go about one every mile." Ray added.
"Yeah…Yeah….Hold on, let me find something." He came from his den with three snapshots. A short limestone tower and Hal were the subjects of the photos. "You mean these objects?" He grinned.

"That's not the one behind Kennedy's house. Ray held the photo in his hand, "This one is shorter."
"Or………….or am I taller?"
Ray raised his eyebrows. "Can I see those pictures again?" He wanted to ask Hal to stand next to a tape measure so he had a reference, and take Hal up to the short cylindrical stone pillar that was

visible from our house, but he knew better. "This stone pillar is not the one up the street."

"What do you want to be a flatfoot like your uncle and Judy's husband? No, it's not the same as the one up here. This one is near Lamartine Ave. You've got good recall, and analytical and computation skills --- why would you want to be a cop?"

"Who said anything about being a cop?" He gave Hal a crazy expression.

I broke in before they started arguing. "Well – what are they for?"

"They're photo stops."

We deadpanned and looked at each other and shook our heads, "Aw - get out."

"They're photo stops - I'm telling ya's. They're places where people take pictures", he chuckled.

"Dad..............they didn't have instamatic cameras when they built the aqueduct." Ray's sarcasm was oozing.

Hal and Ray's verbal sparing left me in the dust when Hal went and got his pictures. My brother however was ready for more.

"How old were you in this photo?"

"About 17. Grandma and grandpa had just given me written permission to join the Navy."

"Who took the shot?"

"Grandma or Grandpa I'm sure."

"It wasn't either of them." Ray said. "Look at this photographer's shadow on the ground......too thin to be Nana, and the long hair and dress rules out all the guys."

Brother Ray's powers of deduction were impressive for someone in the 7th grade.

"Give me those pictures Wisenheimer. You got copper written all over your face."

I had held one of the pictures, "But Dad, what the deuce are those things for?"

"O.K. Ray of sunshine.......you've got all the answers – what are those stone towers?"

"I wasn't around when they were handing out directions on how the system worked."

Resuming his rightful position of knowledge and authority we could see the big mystery was coming to a resolution. "They're aerators for an underground aqueduct system. Gases build up in the tunnel, and the fumes and vapor has to have a way to be vented."

I could see Ray's mind at work. "So these block towers are similar to a chimney."

"That's the long and short of it." he said. The top row of limestone brick conceals the vent and shaft to the tunnel."

"Who took the picture?"

"I didn't know your mother back then, so it doesn't matter."

It sounded like Hal was getting sore about the girl who took the picture. We let it drop.

Ray and me thought it was more than just random chance that brought us to the same conduit where Hal had spent time on as a teenager. He warned us to stay alert and be wary of everything going on the aqueduct. There was a hypnotic lull brought on by the woods, the underground water, and overgrowth; you just knew to have your antennae out, especially at night. The height of the trees and overgrowth had obscured Manhattan's skyscrapers. The tranquility, solitude, and sanctuary of this area was a facade; lose that perspective and Jack the Ripper might tap your shoulder and try to bum a smoke. As the years passed, more and more incidents with the location: "The Old Croton Aqueduct" made the 'Street Beat' section of the Herald Statesman.

The aqueduct ran pretty straight; too straight for Ray and me. We didn't see people often, when we did, we'd go into the woods to avoid them, especially if they were carrying something. There's was an underlying vibe; something concerning the flow of the water that used to run under the trail. It was something which couldn't be measured by our senses. Somehow, it was at work and it defied identification. At times, it gave me the creeps.

"This force – it may be benevolent, but I wouldn't put money on it……..something's going on." Ray turned and gave my eyes a prolonged mesmerizing probe. "You feel it? Know what I mean?"

"Yeah, I know."

"You don't know." He laughed.

"I know." I shrugged my shoulders and laughed too.

MOST OF THESE EXPLORATIONS WE MADE TOGETHER. As we got older, we would do our own thing. We were growing apart - we were on good terms, but it wasn't the same. Initially, we were cautious of the area surrounding O'Dell, Hawley, Warburton, and Harriman Aves.

Approximately a mile south of the aqueduct aerator, was a two story limestone building. It had two large doors which could be opened together and allow something as large as a wagon or a truck to enter and perform some kind of routine maintenance. The second floor had a window on each side. Like everything that was a part of the Croton aqueduct; it was abandoned. The building had been sealed off from the outside with $5/8^{ths}$ plywood, 2x6's, and barbed wire. There was another limestone building four miles to the north. It was a similar design, but half the size.

We scouted around checking out the building's exterior. Ray started probing weak points for places of entry. I watched him push the plywood with his hands, shoulders, and kick the bottom of the sheets.

"Well have to bring a length of pipe and something to pry with when we come back."

Near where we had stashed the dirty magazines, was a 4"x4" piece of hardwood and a length of angle iron. We used the hardwood as a battering ram. Three stiff charges knocked one side of a plywood sheet into the building. Inside, there wasn't any floor or roof. There was a junk pile in the expanse of the cavity below the building into the aqueduct itself. They appeared to have been wrought iron rafter beams, the second floor's support iron, along with iron gears, wheels and rods which might have engaged the operation of the gates, weirs, and

162

pumps. "This has got to be a control station of some sort and regulating the rate and volume of water." We could see a lateral offshoot from the aqueduct's primary flow main. There also was a gate which would be raised or lowered allowing water to discharge to a concrete lateral down to Warburton Ave. and probably to the Hudson."

"That's what I was thinking." I tried to look serious.

Ray looked at the dormant machinery: chains, levers, pulleys, gears and such. The operation of the support station materialized in his head: "Sure, that's how it worked: the workers would only show up here once in a while. The same crew most likely attended three of these stations in a day.....and not everyday."

An old iron ladder was anchored into the concrete shaft which descended into a trickle of water and flowed towards Getty Square. There had once been a big water works near downtown up until WWII.

I looked at Ray. "We can't go down there."

"Un-uh, no flashlight, no rope, you know there's going to be rats down there.......rabies. Bunch of rusty iron and nails."

"Lockjaw city." I stuck out my lower jaw.

"Probably dead animals.........maybe even a skeleton."

I took a hard look. "Come back some other time?"

"These tunnels and shafts ....I don't like them." He looked around to see if someone was observing us. "Let's get outta here."

iii

There was one track meet left to go in the school year. Ray had placed in the 880 yard run in his age group in every race but had failed to win any races. I had placed three times in the 1500 meter, but that was the best I did. Our final practice was on Thursday after classes. The coaches had a pizza party after the practice and gave us our winged foot school letters. Dusk was coming. The early June evening was damn near perfect when we started home.

"Guess what?"

"What?"

"Finally paid back Mrs. Foley today."

"What did you do - glue her text books shut?"

"Put a thumb tack on her seat. Ray, she jumped a country mile, her eyes got wide and she circled her desk twice and left the classroom. She came back and focused on me and Samantha McAvoy. Foley's been on Sam's case because she's been hiking up her uniform's jumper. Foley don't know who tacked her chair. I think she's losing it. I'd like to get her one more time before school let's out."

"Maybe she'll flunk you for spite." he said. "Just concentrate on your grades, and get out of the 6th grade."

"You're right – just get away from her."

"How you feeling about the mile on Saturday?"

"My times are getting better, Eddie Gibson is our best. We'll be on varsity next year, he's only getting better. In the dual meets - I do okay, but the meet on Saturday is an open meet. All the Catholic and public schools will be there."

We made our way home through the North End, Ray pointed with his track shoes, "Let's take the aqueduct." We started down Robert's Lane. He stood still for a few seconds like he was trying to hear something.

"What's up?" I looked about. "You listening for something?" I yawned.

"No......I thought I felt something." It passed. "You know the public schools never win any dual meets."

I laughed. "Some of them can't get enough interest to field a team. Last year Longfellow Jr. High showed up with five guys – that was it. If they had two more mediocre runners they would have won the meet."

"Yeah they were fast, those two black guys – the Burton brothers, they're going somewhere on scholarship.....too much talent. Then they had that Columbian kid for the distance races; him and Gibson were first and second in the 1500 meter and the 3000 meter. The Columbo won the 1500 and Eddie came back and won the 3000." Ray's memory of the meet had him wondering if All Souls was as good as we thought.

Robert's Lane came to a dead end and we had to make our way through some concrete and brush debris to get through to the aqueduct.

"One thing's for sure Ray, we're going to have to have our best times to beat St. Joe's. They own all the long distance races and they always place in the sprints. The open meet might work to our advantage ....you never know. Just wish they had a cross country event."

"Baseball starts soon."

We continued walking north, the sun was almost gone but there was still some light left as we passed what we started calling 'Limestone Control' since we had busted in a year earlier. Water works personnel had once again sealed off the building.

We walked about a half mile north and passed the old caretaker's quarters of the Untermyer estate; it had been torched before WWII.

A loud rumble came from the south, the volume steadily increasing. We turned 180 degrees and looked towards the sound. The upper limbs of the trees began to bend. We still couldn't see anything.

Ray took off and ran like a cop was chasing him, "C'mon!" I didn't know where he was going except it was north. The rumble got larger and louder. The air was shaking ....maybe the ground as well. Any moment the source would be within sight. A thin trail veered off the dirt road to the right, leading to a small outcrop of stone, 20 feet above the aqueduct. Ray was already up there and could see over the tops of most of the trees on the down slope which eventually ended at Warburton Ave.

Again Ray began to scan to the south; there had to be something to see. The George Washington Bridge to the south and the Tappan Zee Bridge to the north; our location on this mound was about equidistant between the two.

Standing there.......waiting.............waiting; then a blast of pressurized air almost laid us out.

"Whatcha see?" We sprung back up to see the visual component of this phenomenon. I swung my head back and forth and side to side like I was watching a 360 degree ping-pong match.

"Whatever it is...........it's moving awful fast. The ground is shaking." Ray kept looking towards the center of the sound.

"Don't know about the ground, but I am."

"It's not thunder." Ray said.

"A jet?"

Ray was almost yelling. "Getting real loud now."

"Sound's like it's right over the river." I may have screamed. We were only about a mile from the east bank, but maybe a good 500 feet higher than the water.

"Lights are coming!" His eyes bulged out and his chest expanded. He had no sooner made his observation and the fireball had passed us.

Glowing chunks of the object peeled away or were ejected as it sped north at a fantastic rate of speed. Protecting our ears from the sonic boom we thought was imminent, we watched the light show.

"Breaking up.................it's breaking up!"

Nodding in unison, we watched and listened as the extraterrestrial object or top secret weapon zoomed out of sight; behind it trailed an unknown quantity of projectile debris, a thick plume of smoke, cinders and pulverized ash, along with an odor that Ray and me were confident did not originate on this planet.

"St. Mary save us........is this the end of the world?" My teeth began to chatter.

Amazement and disbelief froze his face, somehow he managed to ask: "What was that?"

"This was way beyond that super moon on Lake Ave. I think we should might probably pray." I was rattled.

"Yeah, just to be on the safe side." We dropped to our knees. Ray called, "Three Hail Marys." He led with the first part of the prayer and I answered with the rejoin. We prayed hard and with conviction.

I got to my feet and asked: "What's with all them colors?"

My pupils began to react to the absence of light, but there was radiation in Ray's face.

"I doubt there's names for all the colors we saw from the UFO." Ray shooed away something in front of his face

I tried to reassemble the event, even though it had just occurred. It was next to impossible to recall what I had witnessed, and now Ray throws in the UFO bullcrap to put the icing on this spectacle. "What the Fuck was that?" I put it to him. When he offered an answer, I was ready for something I wouldn't possibly comprehend.

"Did you see that big piece break off where the river widens near the Tappan Zee?" His brow registered doubt.

165

"It hit the water......I'm pretty sure. Something went real bright up there, and then nothing. Maybe that piece skipped like a stone on the water – then nothing. Must have sank." I tilted my head.

In a sweeping motion, Ray's left arm swung south and his index finger indicated the direction from where the fireball made its appearance. He spoke with some kind of crazy authority: "There was debris either breaking free or ejected from the space object as it shot up the river canyon. Did you see it?" He pointed to the locations where the small remnants of the space intruder had entered the river or possibly the shore. Next, his arm came back towards where we first saw the object: "You can still see smoke trails." Now, his arm swung to the north.

"Look at that one smoke trail, I swear something landed down by Greystone Station.' I said.

"Yeah, I thought I saw something break off and land near the shore. You smell that?" He folded his arms reviewing the images of that last minute or so.

I nodded, "I smell it. Maybe it was a satellite that couldn't maintain orbit?"

"It has a metallic odor........that doesn't necessarily mean it was man-made."

"Yeah.....I suppose."

"How high was it when it flew over the river? It was certainly higher than the Palisades."

"I don't think it was a whole bunch higher, that's what struck me - its speed and altitude and the air it pushed ahead of itself."

"Shhhhh," He pointed to his ear.

"I hear it too." I raised my head, but had to look down as something was falling from the sky. "It ain't raining?"

He pointed with his index finger straight up and listened. Something was landing on the oak trees' leaves above and behind us. Ray held his palms out to collect what fell from the sky. I did the same. Soon our hands were filled with a gray and tan ash. There was so much - it began to overflow our hands.

"Man-made or galactic debris?"

"We just might bring this to the science department over to Gorton. They've got a better science department than All Souls."

I cast the ash in my left hand in front of us in a wide arc. Ray started to say something, but it was unintelligible. I was in an overload state; I believed I caused a temporal rift in the time continuum by opening a portal with these space cinders. They were suspended in a specific pattern which defied gravity; emitting varying illuminating intensities and colors.

Our collective consciousness left our bodies and we observed ourselves standing with arms extended and the palms of our hands collecting the ash and cinders. Ray said he was looking down at us, while I was looking upward. The laws of time must have been suspended; whether it was for us or the planet – I couldn't fathom a guess. All was in total suspension. We watched our corporal entities in a different dimension or in a matter/anti-matter complexion. The duration of this temporal oddity may have depended on the individual

166

it affected. To me, I thought I was standing there a couple of hours, but Ray swore it was over in less than a minute. He told me that the ash was still falling from the burning comet as proof of our quick return from the brief transfer from our time and space.

"Holy Fuckin' Shit!" I gasped.

"Wha….. wha…..what was that?" Ray stuttered. "Fill your pockets with the stuff that fell from the sky." He ordered.

We collected what we could. There didn't seem to be too much falling now. We recovered a little bit more from the oak leaves, and some from a flat beer carton that was last year's garbage. Our pockets were full; we funneled some in our track shoes. We had at least the same amount which first rained into our hands. Ray felt the power and potential of this material that had arrived from somewhere thousands of light years or alternative universes away. He may have somehow known this residue had in some way caused or was a factor in what occurred a few minutes earlier. It was some pretty good speculation on his part I thought. Two differing experiences had transpired. After the brief moment of shared consciousness, we knew things irrevocably would never be the same.

We started back down the trail and picked up the aqueduct where the two rejoined.

"You think Hal saw it?"

"The entire metro area saw it."

"Maybe Hal's got an explanation?"

"This wasn't no shooting star." I shook my head. "Ray, I've never seen or heard anything like this."

He began jogging and I stayed with him. I huffed along. O'Dell was about half-mile away. He slowed and came to a stop by a tree.

"What's up?"

"See if there's any cinders on the top side of this tree's leaves." he said.

"Huh?"

"Ash on the leaves on the south side of this tree." He repeated and pulled some smaller branches low enough for me to collect any ash. The amount wasn't very much at all.

I called over to Ray, "This isn't an ash – it's an elm." I gave him a sour look.

"No you doomkuff – ash from the comet." I hoped Ray thought I was playing stupid.

We checked another tree on O'Dell near 21. There was more dust on top of our TV set. Perhaps it was random or the wind; maybe there was some kind of magnetic field depositing the cinderash in certain locations and not others. At this point neither of us could hazard a possible explanation.

It was an unusual entrance for Ray and me on this school night. The older we got the less we called on Hal. Ray was already at the point where he was avoiding him; I wasn't very far behind. If it didn't concern money, Hal and Ray just didn't interact. Ray thought

167

what we had just witnessed was bizarre enough to run it past the Old Man and get his viewpoint of the fireball's pentration - despite past ill feelings between the two of them.

It was near 9 o'clock. Ray asked, "You know what Dad? – we saw a comet just a little while ago on our way home from track practice......have you ever seen one?.........you know like one of those UFO's they talk about?

He went over to his mixing counter, "You mean a shooting star."

"No, more like a comet or meteor. Maybe a UFO."

"You two birds stand at attention." he ordered. "Let me smell your breath."

Ray exhaled first. "Now you." The test was over. He looked back at Ray: "What the hell are you jabbering about?"

"We saw something streaking across the sky. It was loud, bright, and cast away debris and particulate matter. There was a smoke trail and smelled extraterrestrial. Ryan an -----"

"You don't even know what the word means." He challenged.

"Not of this world."

He clamped down on his lips, "Like I was trying to say: Ryan and I believe it may have been from outer space, perhaps a comet. It could have been a spaceship from NASA or a Soviet spacecraft that burned up upon reentering the atmosphere."

"Comet?" Hal shook his head from side to side, "Very unlikely. The guys that look into deep space with those big telescopes and radio telescopes would have seen it six months ago. It would have been all over the news. Did it have a tail? Comets always have a tail."

"Yeah, it left a smoke trail." I said nodding my head.

Hal and Ray looked at each other and adjusted their vision and tried to digest my remark. It took a few seconds.

"If you were outside about 45 minutes ago -" He looked at me for a time verification.

"Or a couple of days ago." I didn't know what time quadrant I was in - due to the fireball's ash dispersal. It had temporarily robbed me of my bearings as it related to a possible temporal distortion. I tried to go with the flow, and was not being very successful.

"Get over here you, let me smell your breath again." Hal gave me another whiff. "What did you do to this kid?" He asked Ray.

Hal mixed himself a double. I guess he wanted to get as screwed up as he thought we were.

"Dad, you couldn't have missed it........it came right up the river, it sounded like a squadron of B-52's. The fireball smelled like the Milky Way......great big smoke trail......shooting particles of light, stone, and metal probably doing mach 4 or 5 travelling north." Ray said as Hal looked out the kitchen window.

"Our sense of smell is totally useless in outer space....... Smelled like the Milky Way...............you better stick to eating '3 Musketeers." He looked to the heavens, shook his head, and took a long drink.

"There's no way we were the only ones who witnessed it." I said.

Hal told me to get my transistor radio and meet him on the street. Hal had come out of his den with a pair of binoculars. Ray was already outside.

"Alright knuckleheads, give me the radio. He tuned up and down the AM band as we listened: Yankee game, Met pre-game from St. Louis, Cousin Brucie on W-A-Beatle-C, Imus WMCA, Screwball Alan Burke and troublemaker Joe Payne on WOR. We listened intently for 7 or 8 minutes; no comets, no shooting stars, meteors, sputniks, Telstar satellites, super secret developmental aircraft, no UFO invasion, but Hal managed to find "ol' reliable"......Reverend Ike on the revival station.

I pointed to the sky over the Hudson, "You can still see a faint trail smoke."

Ray looked above, "Dad, you can see the faint trail from the fireball we saw." The three of us stood on the side walk searching the sky for something more substantial. Hal was scanning the sky over the river with his binoculars.

"Just some smoke and not much of that." Hal said.

We looked at one another and concurred. South of our house, we heard a distant boom. The super sleuth Hal scoffed a laugh. He believed he had an explanation for our mumbo-jumbo mystery. He asked, "What's today's date?"

"June second." I guessed.

"What's going on in about a month?"

"Fourth of July?" Ray answered.

"You guys witnessed some kind of big sky rocket or aerial bomb. Don't let your imaginations get carried away." He waved us off.

"No way........no way. This thing wasn't any pyrotechnic device." Ray was adamant, and I was right behind him with my chin up and head nods.

"If I hear you retards shooting off fireworks before the Fourth – no baseball for a week." Hal squinted and sniffed, "What the hell stinks?"

We had school the next day, and I followed Ray up the stairs, and mentioned, "That was our proof: the smoke, the smell, the cinders."

"Nah – it really isn't proof; besides, he doesn't want to hear our story. We're too young to know what we're talking about. His gig is drinking, smoking, and playing power trips on Mom." He inhaled and shook his head in capitulation, but turned at the top of the stairs. He had an after-thought about the fireball: someone else must have witnessed the phenomenon as we had. "We got to start asking around; there's got to be something in the papers tomorrow." Ray wasn't going to be talked out of what we had just experienced.

"Hey Bro.....I was there."

The next day we listened to the radio. We asked everybody at school; the North End and the neighborhood. We were glued to the news on the TV; and read the newspapers. The Daily News, The

169

Herald Tribune, and the Journal American, none of them had anything on the spectacle last night.

"You guys can take them home for forty cents." Herb, one of the owner's of the North End newsstand cracked.

"Sorry Herb........ Say did anybody hear or say anything about a meteor entering the atmosphere last night?" Ray asked.

"You're the first one that's said anything about it. Everybody's too busy having sex to go stargazing." He laughed.

There should have been something on the radio we thought; even that wing-nut out in L.A., Art Bell, never had a guest report this sighting/incident on his taped show – and he was the King of the extraterrestrial rumor mill.

Three days after the fact, a 2 paragraph blurb appeared on page 12 of the Journal American: "A TWA 707 jet had made a 'blue ice discharge' earlier in the week and put a hole in the roof of a home in Plattsburgh N.Y. The same jet was also blamed for making a mess in the bed of a pick-up truck in Peekskill.

iv

Jane's boxes of recital costumes were jammed throughout the first floor of the house. She had situated small paths around the monsta boxes of the nearly 20 dance classes. With the fireball's priority, we had forgotten about Jane's annual Dance School recital. We knew it was only a few days away, it had to be next Saturday. Dress rehearsal would be on Thursday. Our weekend was shot; we would be press-ganged into set-up and breakdown.

The nucleus of the Jane Marlowe Dance School was Jane, her lieutenant Judy, and Rich her piano player and arranger. They were going over the program, music, awards, and the costumes that were promised, but had not yet arrived. There was a problem with the costumes every year. Jane could order them in December and they still would be late.

The cosmic intruder had me and Ray all screwed up as far as the calculation of time was concerned. We had to get our fireworks for the Fourth and Little League had just started. In addition to helping Jane with the dance recital, final exams were coming, and I had to knuckle down and make sure that wicked witch Foley didn't flunk me. Sometimes I didn't know what day it was. Ray had never been a scatterbrain as far as I remembered, but he didn't have his game together either. He attributed his sketchy brain function to the distortional waves left over from the path of the comet.

On Monday of recital week, we had served a mass that involved the Greek Orthodox rite. Ray and me and two other Roman rite altar boys served the mass. We got home and were all pumped up about the ritual. We tried to walk into the kitchen. The costume boxes were everywhere and the sound of sewing machines going non-stop. Five mothers/seamstresses had volunteered to help out Jane, and were fabricating costumes for the Honey-bee number. Even Mom-Mom had come down from Straatsville to join the fun.

"You boys showed up just in time. Take these boxes to the garage and bring up all the boxes that say "ALLEY CATS.""

The first floor was a cornfield maze of confusion. She had us set a couple of monsta boxes in the dining room. Jane wanted a firm commitment: "I can count on both of you to help me out this week......right?"

"The only thing I got going is caddying. I'd only be missing Saturday during the day, other than that..........I am at your service Mother." Ray poured it on for the women who came to sew.

"Ryan?"

"Yeah – whatever Ray said." It was obvious to her my enthusiasm wasn't equal to his.

"Where's Dad?" Ray looked around, he might have been buried by some costumes.

"I think he's on the porch with the portable TV."

Hal's voice bellowed through the dining room window from the porch on top of the garage: "How the hell can I watch my program with those sewing machines blasting away faster than a punch press in the fab shop and you women gossiping?"

Silence descended; Hal and Mom started going at it and Grandma Edna took a vodka break to flip Hal the double bird. "Atta girl Edna." The other sewers cheered.

"I saw that Edna......"

"Look my way again, and you'll see it again." She laughed looking at the other women.

The women all stopped their machines and stopped talking and were drinking and smoking waiting for Hal's next pleasantry.

The war of words ended when Hal figured he'd quit while he was ahead and not give the women a chance to gang up on him.

We had three or four more boxes to bring up. The garage door was open. We started carrying completed costumes down to the garage. Before we brought some more upstairs, we saw the real reason the verbal jousting between Mom and Dad had ceased. Linda Conroy from next door had come out and was weeding a patch of flowers bordering our two properties. She might have come out to listen to Hal and Jane go at it.

We had just made another full circuit, and were back down the cellar. Ray grabbed hold of my T-shirt, "You know the Ol' Man's watching Linda."

"Watching her got to be better than watching TV." I said.

Linda and her husband Mitch had four kids in five years; she was seven years younger than him. Their kids were the same age as Cathy and Billy, and they all played together. They had a nicer house than us because Mitch had made some home improvements. Hal never did anything to 21 except to keep things running.

Linda would wear them low-cut tops. From the porch Hal had a better view than Lee Harvey Oswald. She knew what she was doing. She'd get on her hands and knees and weed with one hand and support her upper body with the other. The Old Man'd get all charged

171

up, and if he wasn't smashed he'd tried to work out his fantasies on Jane.

The day after the Conroy's moved in, it only took Linda one day to pick up a bad vibe from Hal. After Mitch told Linda about our new car with the clutch, she had nothing but venom for him. She knew how much Jane disliked the standard transmission in the old Bel Air. From Linda's perspective, Jane had endured enough abuse from Hal to deny her bedroom services and give him a good taste of sexual tension. Linda would help, support, or counsel Jane any way she could. She thought raising Hal's sexual anxieties was just what the asshole needed.

During the summer, Jane and Linda occasionally visited each other on weekday mornings in their relaxed summer wear. Either of them would bring over a pot of coffee and smoke on her porch or on our porch on top of the garage. Once in a while they might even do some yard work, but not too often. Linda never initiated conversation concerning Jane's relationship with Hal, but once Jane opened Pandora's box and told Linda of some of the stuff about Hal or their marriage – it was fair game.

Linda handed Jane a lawyer's card more than once. "Just leave this card laying around where you know he'll see it. This gal will stick it to him."

"Sheila Carlucci – DIVORCE LAWYER – A woman attorney?" Jane was surprised.

"She'll take him to the cleaners. He'll have to move back in with his parents." Linda's eyelids became slits as she mashed her lips together and nodded, "We'll fix him."

Sometimes they'd talk over the property line fence. The sight had traffic on O'Dell slowing down so the guys could get a good eyeful. Horns were honking – wolves were whistling – guys were oogling – and the asphalt Romeos were hanging out the car windows and banging on the sides of the door panels. One day Mom and Linda were having a blast – show time. Perhaps they planned it..........maybe they didn't, It was innocent and fun................back then.

They both had great shapes: great legs, big melons, Linda's hair was dark brown with a couple of streaks of copper. No dye as far as I knew. Jane still had her voluminous auburn hair, but she had to go to the bottle to keep her color fresh. I was surprised her hair didn't lose all its pigmentation - just from the manual transmission. Best of all, they had two beautiful faces. I would have been whistling too. Still, it made me mad when guys gave them the business. Some of it was really brazen. They didn't have an ounce of suave; it was raw.......animal. It was best not to play with fire..........but it was a different time. Although each had a brood of brats, it was reassuring they still had their game working, and that was all Linda and Jane wanted to know.

V

My brother stayed on the paper route into the second week of January. He gave the paperboy coordinator his two week notice during the week between Christmas and New Years. He had had enough of the route, especially with the heart of winter upon us. From my point of view – Ray wasn't a hustler: he let accounts go into arrears; he wasn't into looking for new subscribers. His view of what his job entailed differed quite a bit with the Herald Statesman's original job description. They wanted new customers? They should hire someone to knock on doors and find some people who wanted the rag. "My job is to deliver the paper. I'm not a salesman."

It wasn't like the Statesman was giving the paperboys anything more than minimum wage for the job; at the time, it was a buck and-a-half an hour. Not for nothing, but Ray wouldn't even ask the new tenants he'd see moving into the apartment at 1 Hawley Terrace if they wanted the paper. It was like throwing away money. I mean you're on the floor anyway – you may as well toss another paper as long as you're there. I figured there was a 10% annual turnover at the apartment house. Money didn't motivate Ray most of the time. He was smiling the first nasty day after he quit. He knew he wasn't the guy who'd be slipping and sliding up and down stairs and hills, carrying those ice encrusted, wet newspapers.

He did have a twinge of conscience when he had asked me to sub for him; in a way, I think it bothered him. At first, I'd do them whenever he asked. Over a couple of months his number of requests increased. Soon, I realized he just didn't want to deliver papers. It was for no other reason than a lack of will or interest. I didn't mind doing the route if he had something legitimate to do, but sitting down Hudson Park or Greystone just to smoke Parliaments and watch the secretaries detrain while I did his route? It was obvious he was taking advantage of me; that wasn't going to fly. He was getting Hal and Jane off his back about loafing because he had a job – but I was doing the work.

"Ryan.....doing anything?"

"Reading."

"Reading what?"

"The Fellowship."

"You're still on that?"

"Kind of hard to finish it when I'm delivering your papers all the time."

"I was going to ask you if you could do them today?"

"C'mon Ray.......it's Wednesday."

"C'mon Ry......just this once – just for today."

"You're pulling my leg - right?"

"What?.......I got to do your papers because I'm dumb and I need your help in math? That's bullshit man – fuckin' bullshit. Just quit, then we'll both be back on planet earth. I'll do the papers today, but it'll cost you four math homeworks."

"Deal."

The paperboy coordinator knew me on sight because I had subbed for Ray so many times. Ronnie Bloch would tell me: "Go down and get your working papers, I got a route right now that's opening up in a week."

"I'm not walking a country mile to deliver papers - if it ain't Ray's or the Warburton route – I'm not interested."

When Ray finished up in January, a week later Bloch knocked on the door to see if I was interested in the route. It was 14 degrees and the wind was howlin'. I didn't want to burn the bridge, and told him Jane wouldn't let me because my grades were down. The coordinator had to deliver Ray's route for two weeks, before he found a replacement.

Before I could consider taking this paper route, I had to let the subscribers forget Ray's performance. They saw me delivering the papers enough to link me to every paper they didn't get. No, I had to give them time to forget Ray and me.

Bloch did find a replacement for Ray, and the first thing he told Bloch was the date he was quitting at the end of the summer. The new paperboy, Leon, made my brother's job performance seem spectacular. The bundles were thrown from the Statesman's truck on the corner of O'Dell and Warburton. On bad weather days, Leon didn't deliver; he might take one bundle and do the apartment house. The second bundle lay in the mud - getting drenched by the rain. The people in the private houses might get a delivery five out of six days a week – at most. Every day we didn't get the paper, Hal had it marked on the calendar: 'no paper'. The Campagna boys were all pissed off - now they had to walk down Hawley to Warburton and get the three papers for his grandmother and the other two houses on the compound. Kids were making forts out of the bundles of newspapers. Ray thought Leon was actually getting paid by the N.Y. Times to destroy the Statesman's home delivery.

By mid-March it was basically a self-service paper delivery without the box. Hal usally sent either of us down to get our paper. "And don't forget to get one for Mrs. Hillman."

Once Leon had a particularly bad week – 4 out of 5 days --- no paper. He made it in on Friday – collection day. Hal was amused.

The doorbell rang, "I'll get it...I'll get it." Hal got up from his desk.

"This is going to be good." Ray winked at me.

We listened to Hal dealing with Leon. We thought he was going to read him the riot act. "How much?"

"Seventy cents."

Hal gave him the usual three quarters.

He asked Hal if he cared to by a chocolate bar so he could get points for some program he was involved with, which was gracefully declined.

Hal came back in. "I thought you were going to complain that we didn't get the paper all week except for the one we got tonight?" Ray scratched his temple.

"Anybody that does that bad of a job and doesn't apologize or at least have a legitimate excuse for not doing his job could care less about anything a customer has to say. Didn't say thank you, didn't acknowledge the tip. The boy is clueless. The kid's got to run for office.........natural born dumacrat." Hal cancelled his subscription by phone, he knew it was a waste of time trying to do it through Leon.

In May, Ronnie Bloch and his boss came calling at our house looking for Ray or me. Ronnie's boss was almost in tears because Leon gave him 2 weeks notice he was dragging up at the beginning of June instead at the end of summer. Ronnie Bloch was quitting as well.

Ray looked at the two guys; "I'm no Einstein, but the Statesman is better off without Leon. The guy was costing you readers."

A person who bought the Herald Statesman had a vested interest in the City of Yonkers, the recent arrivals from the Bronx and other parts of the greater metro area were still going to read the other papers; Yonkers meant nothing to them. The Statesman had to niche out their core readership: let the big boys handle the national stuff. The Statesman had to concentrate on the "street beat", high school sports, a city government which seemed to be like a chicken running around with its head cut off, the classifieds, obituaries, and the boys who made the ultimate sacrifice in Vietnam.

It had to be tough medicine writing those obituaries; the senior staff writers did a good job. Around 1969, the paper began injecting more and more of a political slant in their coverage of the fallen airmen, marines, sailors, and soldiers. As Ray and me got older, our parents and grandparents looked at us a little more intently. They were hoping the war would be over before our birth dates went into the fish bowl.

vi

Turning down the paperboy job had nothing to do with the manual labor or the paltry wage. The main reason was Ray didn't push me into it. He had done a good enough job in the first three months when he had the route; then school started back up and he started to lose interest. The business end started sliding and the requests for me subbing came more and more often.

Later on, I kind of figured out most of the requests were legit, but not all were. Some of it had to do with the comet. Much of the time he took off was to talk to the staff at the Trevor Park Planetarium and the Physics department teachers at Gorton High. Just from these two, Ray was advancing his knowledge about the comet, which it was not, but it might have been a meteorite he had come to find out. As long as he was doing this science stuff, things I wasn't close to understanding, I could do his newspapers.

The Statesman would call every other week. They had some 30 year old guy doing the route now, and he looked thrilled about his new job. He swore up and down to Hal - if he resumed his subscription, barring a pressmen's strike, his paper would be on the porch daily.

It was obvious they couldn't get anybody for the route after five weeks. A young woman was outside 21 talking to Ray while I was

175

shooting baskets. Back and forth they had been talking for ten-fifteen minutes. I kept checking them out. Must be one of Jane's associates I thought.

Tommy Capps had called to give us a heads up that they were biting down the river. The last day of school was June 27th not even a week away, and that same woman showed up again at the front door. "Is Ray here?"

"Ray." I yelled. "Somebody at the door for ya."

He came downstairs with a glass of milk in hand. "I'm going fishin'" I said. I went down the cellar and started getting my fishing grip together. I started shooting baskets as I waited for him. I dribbled the ball and watched the two of them again in the front of the house. The last time she showed up, I should have asked him who she was. This was taking too long, he could jawbone with her all he wanted. I grabbed my tackle box and started down the hill.

"Ryan – wait up." he called.

He said good-bye to her and she drove away.

We got down to the river and starting getting our rigs together. "Who were you talking to?" I cast out about 30 feet.

"Some wheel from the Statesman. Are they biting?"

"Tommy Capps and that sawed off Frankie Flynn caught a big striper, two middle sized ones and an eel. Put your seat belt on...... Tommy got a shark - he told me on the phone."

"A wha?"

"He said he caught a shark. A big bad shark."

"Bullshit." Ray smiled.

"A big bad honkin' shark." My head nodded up and down.

"A shark? That's boss." He was trying to read my face.

"Is it up at his grandmother's house?" The Campagna's lived at the very end of Hawley Terr. in a well maintained compound with three residences.

"Nah...I shook my head.......but they both confirmed it was a shark."

"Frankie got those Coke bottle glasses." Ray's face was now one of doubt. "It's a maybe as best. I know we're not going up to their house - so it's obvious whatever he hooked got away."

"They're like both in the fifth grade; Tommy's like Louis and John: straight shooters. They just might have had one on the hook. At first Tommy thought it was a sturgeon, but they're more rare in the river than a shark, which you never see." I said. "He said it put up a helluva fight, they finally got it near the shore rocks, and that's when they watched it wriggle off the hook cause Tommy couldn't keep tension on the line. Flynn said he smacked it with a stick, but the shark had a lot of fight left and it swam away."

"That would've made the front page of the sports section. What was he using?"

"Hell, that would have made the front page of the Daily News." I came back. "He was using the eel they caught earlier. They sliced it lengthwise to get the blood scent in the water.

Ray was baited up and prayed for the shark as he cast. "You know if either of us got that sonofabitch, they'd be calling one of us:

'Shark' for the rest of our lives. That'd be kool. Even if I caught the lunker you'd still catch the 'Shark Junior' handle. You just don't want it to devolve into 'Junior.' That's one you want to lose. Glad they didn't name me Hal.........I don't like either of those names." Ray lit a Kent.

"How long do I wait before you tell me what that lady wanted?"

It was easier for Ray to lower the boom on me while we were fishing --- he didn't have to look at me head-on. We watched the barges and boats and we were far enough apart so our lines wouldn't cross. "Well – I got you a job." He started reeling in to make some noise.

I shut one eye, and looked at him with the other, "Ya did?"

"It won't be that bad..........you know the route. I got the lady to throw in a few sign-on bonuses: No charge for the carrier's bag with the day-glo safety strip, a coin changer, you wear on your belt, and a hand warmer for the winter." Ray checked his bait.

"So you signed me up for the paper route." This was rubbing me the wrong way and it wasn't Ray's style. "What else you got up your sleeve?"

He knew he pulled a fast one; he was edgy with the deal he had brokered. "Look, I'll give it to you straight -- she gave me this am-fm radio. You can play it down here on batteries, or you can plug it in and listen to it at home."

"Well who's radio is it?" I saw my line tug and I yanked it quick to set the hook. Nothing.

"Huh?" he said.

I knew it was his. A fuckin' coin changer, a hand warmer, and a bag. "Thanks Brother." Ray knew I was mad. "You'll sub for me like I did for you.......right?"

"Absolutely.......and you get to listen to the radio and take it fishing."

"Somehow this has that 30 pieces of silver ring to it."

I stood and stewed on the bank, we didn't talk. I watched the Palisades and the river. I wanted to talk to The Campagna brothers and Frankie about the shark story. If there was no shark; at least Tommy could make the story come to life. I could already see Frankie Flynn with his coke bottle glasses smiling and nodding.

"Yeah – I'll take the route but only after Fourth of July weekend."

"That's the deal I set up with her. She wasn't too keen on it, but I told her it was the only way you could take the job. I said we were both committed to go our grandfather's birthday celebration on the Fourth."

"That's about the only thing I'm getting out of this railroad deal."

"Heck Ryan, I'll be missing the biggest caddying weekend for the entire summer. I'm taking one for the team too."

I gave him a "Do you think I was born yesterday look."

It was always a good time going up to Mom-Mom's and Mack's. Going up for the Fourth was doubly good because Edna wouldn't let him do any work unless it was related to his birthday bash. She'd warn us not to go snooping in the little house where she hoarded all her yard sale stuff. We found a pile of nude magazines in there and she caught us looking at them. We wondered where they came from. She'd tell us not to look at them, but she really didn't care, she was just happy we were stimulated by the naked female images.

"And no beer for them boys......" Mack shook his head and pointed to his chest in innocence.

Hal had worked hard making himself 'Persona non grata' at the McKay home and family functions. When times were better, Mom-Mom and Mack had heard the Armstrong's 9 acre apple orchard was for sale, it wasn't even a half-mile away. Everybody started leaning on Hal to buy the property, which he didn't want to do because it meant work. He gave in; built a shack and a garage. They had planned to add a small house later on. There was some big blow out one weekend a couple of years later between Hal and Mack and Mom-Mom. Hal didn't come up very much after that. Every time the Old Man came up, it was like everybody was walking on eggs – except him, he was usually drunk and didn't give a shit. Hal didn't like anybody from Jane's family, he thought they were dumb and he was brilliant because he wore a tie to work.

Mom-Mom wasn't too sharp with religion, but she'd tell us kids: "As ye sew – so shall ye reap. Your father can dish it out, but he can't take it. He may have gone to college, but he's got a lot of learning to do."

The property up in Straatsville was more or less a curse for Hal. He got mean with Jane, he was done with beer, and he would only drink whiskey. It was Hal's way of telling Mack he didn't want to drink with him.

When he had to go up to the orchard to attend to the roof, grass, and varmints trying to get into the house; he'd return as soon as the small repair or project was completed. Either he came back to Yonkers that day - if everything went right, or got smashed for the 36 hours he was up there. Sometimes he wouldn't even stop over Mom-Mom's to say "Hi." Many people would tell us Jane should divorce the Old Man. He was one lonely dude by the time I got the paper route.

"YOU KNOW RAY, I REALLY WAS NEVER AGAINST THE paper route." I told him the next day as we tried to get that shark if he was still around.

What drew me to taking the delivery job was the complete access to be all over the neighborhood and in the apartment house without question or restriction. Even when I didn't have any papers with me; I could be collecting or soliciting new clients. Once the super had it in for me 'cause somebody stole his Crescent wrench; he blamed me for it and banned me from the building. I called the Statesman and they sent the cop to straighten the doomcuff out. The way I saw it, they needed a newspaper more than stopping their leaky faucets. I had a

178

line of crap for the entire paper route, whether they got the Statesman or not.

What made the Ryan Whitelaw act work so well was the bald patch on my head – some of it had filled in, but people knew straight away there was some defect going on with this guy. He was too young to go bald genetically. With long hair really coming into style for guys, I had garnished a lot of sympathy from all sorts of people. I didn't know what I could do about it. I decided to get the buzz cut to minimize the missing hair before we went up to the country for the Fourth. People also bought into me walking around carrying a dozen papers without the bag. The bag was bullshit.

I could strike up a conversation just by pointing to the front page. I would be 13 in September, but I looked 2 years older. With the new buzz-cut, some young woman thought I was in the service. The image they saw was favorable; they weren't overly hesitant about having a conversation with me. I didn't want to talk to any guys about stupid crap. If I was going to throw the bull with dudes, it was going to be with the ones I knew. The older guy who had the route just before I took it over had got Hal to resume his subscription as well as the others which Leon lost. I should have gotten more subscriptions than I did. Still, I was pimping for a marginal newspaper.

Knocking on doors and ringing doorbells in the apartment was awkward at first, but the adage was true: the first one is the most difficult. Now I understood why Ray wasn't into the route very much, it was this salesman nonsense. Pushing the Statesman door to door cold....... with no leads; that was tough money, unless it was with a congenial woman. By the end of October, the only time I'd knock on a strange door to sell a subscription - was if they had just moved in. The paper would run these contests for the paper boys, and if you got a certain number of new starts, they'd reward you. I told Ray they'd give me a 'Wristrocket' if I got three new starts before Thanksgiving. Even Ray was ready to help me work the route for those three news-starved households to get the high tech slingshot. He found the Statesman's rewards program a little too much to digest. Here they were giving away an item like the 'Wristrocket' when they had editorialized against the very thing by name. They said it was as dangerous as BB and zip guns.

Ray took his home made slingshot and I brought the wristrocket I boosted when we went up the country for the Fourth. We figured we'd mostly be shooting off fireworks, but there was no point in leaving them in Yonkers.

Mack's 4th of July/birthday bashes were always fun – at every age. This was one year he had his core group of ironworker buddies out of Local 417 come over, he also invited four ironworker boomers (men who were out of town/on the road) to the birthday bash. Two played guitar and one played harmonica. The fourth played bass, but he couldn't travel with his bass guitar and an amp; so he played rhythm guitar when the others wanted to take a break. The local ironworkers and the boomers were all a bunch of cut-ups.

There was a half-barrel of Schaefer, a Victrola, a poker game, horseshoes, people were dancing, Mack did all the barbecuing, and we were told to shoot off the fireworks on the tar sealed road. There wasn't another house in sight.

Allison, Ray, and me were swiping half-finished beers off the tables. Allison said we could have more - once it got dark, but just a little right now is all we should have. The party started getting loud around five. The guys would shake the keg every time they went and drew a pitcher.

We watched two ironworkers load up my wrist rocket and launch an ash can into the sky. There was a flash of light and a powerful Boom. Folks in the house came running out smiling. They fired off a baker's dozen that way. It was a two man operation; one of them had the wristrocket, and his accomplice only had to light the fuse. Because the fuse was in the center of the bomb, they had to be real slick with the operation.

Two of the ironworker boomers thought they had enough expertise to wristrocket a blockbuster into orbit: "BOOM!"

Everyone got low and covered their heads. The two pyrotechnic overachievers took a bow and toasted Mack's birthday and the Revolution. Mom-Mom was in stitches because her friend from the other side of the woods had pissed her pants. It wasn't even sundown yet and they were just getting started.

Mack told everyone we were going to shoot the rest of the artillery off at night, firecrackers and bottle rockets were okay for now. The wristrocket got tossed on a picnic table. The three piece combo had resumed playing and everyone was watching them and doing that cuddle-up dancing stuff. Mack reached for a beer with one hand, and my deluxe hi-power slingshot with the other. He walked to the back of his property.

"Ryan." he called.

I trotted over like I was running out a ground ball. "Yeah Mack."

"That's a real swell slingshot, but these guys don't need to lose any fingers or hands. We'll just set the big stuff off the regular way tonight. Don't you and your brother try shooting anything off that way – it's an accident waiting to happen. So listen, you take this slingshot and hide it up a tree and you get it tomorrow morning."

"Sure thing Mack."

Mom-Mom hit the jackpot when she hooked up with Mack. Allison, their only child, was my aunt and only four years older than me. Ray and me figured Mom-Mom had Jane when she was 16 years old, uncle Bill at 19, and had Allison at 40. Allison sure got the better end of the stick with Mack being her Dad than what Jane and Uncle Bill had. We saw quite a bit of Mack as we grew up, but we hardly ever saw our blood grandfather except at Christmas. Jane's blood-father liked Ray, but he thought I was a goof-off.

Mack let us shoot his .22 rifle, showed us how to set a snare, use a level, square, change a tire, skin a rabbit. We thought it should have been the other way around; the blood grandfather doing all the

teaching and the step-grandfather doing the ignoring. Mack was
teaching us stuff we didn't know we were learning.

vii

Soon, when we came back from Mom-Mom's, something
wild took place – almost as weird as seeing that fireball last month, but
this was bad – powerful bad. Eight days earlier I had started the route.
Things were going pretty smooth, I even picked up a new account and
I didn't have to ask him. It would have been better if the rewards
program had begun, because this new start didn't count for nothing.

On July 14, 1966 that bloodthirsty, jackass/junkie – Richard
Speck, went over to an apartment of 9 student nurses and whacked 8 of
them in Chicago. Prior to Speck's rampage, when I rang the doorbell
most people answered their doors; some opened their door, some
opened it with the security chain in place. A fair number of women
talked through the door to find out what your business was or who you
were. Some of the apartment dwellers just opened the door; you could
look right into their apartment. A collection of humanity emerged,
which I would have not have seen if I didn't take the paper route.
Although it was just a snapshot; the paper route gave me a brief
glimpse into their world. There were WASPS, lapsed Catholics, Jews,
atheists, Democrats, Republicans, commies, socialists, anarchists,
nihilists, and a left over Trotskyite who favored Marshal Tito of
Yugoslavia. There were a few blacks, Cubans, Puerto Ricans in our
neighborhood. They seemed to be professional people. A lawyer from
Tobago who specialized in personal injury, was always leaving his
business cards in the seam of every mailbox.

A Yonkers cop lived in apartment 3-D. He was black, he
wasn't there very much. He was in my subscriber book, and never paid
regular. He might pay one week out of the month. The book and the
circulation office said he was a weekly collection. After twelve weeks
of chasing this jerk for my money, I cancelled him.

That didn't work out too good for me - after I gave him
notice he was cancelled, there always was a paper missing off the 3rd
floor four or five times a week. Instead of listening to six or seven
people on the floor complain when they didn't get their paper during
the week, it was easier to restart the cop and eat the loss. Another new
subscription and again the paper wasn't running a rewards
scheme.....'I'll never get that other wristrocket' I thought. Paying for
that flatfoot's paper three out of four weeks sucked.

There were around 80 units in the apartment at 1 Hawley
Terrace. There weren't many kids. It seemed like there were more kids
in the apartment house at 2 Vernon Pl. with only 1/3 of the units. The
apartment manager was most likely discouraging prospective tenants
with kids from renting. Swinging couples, single women, divorced
people, and a handful of 'young' retirees' made up the tenancy at 1
Hawley. The lack of kids in the neighborhood must have been due to
the nearest school being about a mile away, and that was the Catholic

181

grade school down The North End. Nobody from the Greystone area went there.

It was a wake-up call; the first collection night after the Speck murders. Some of the people would open their door only an inch, see it was the paperboy. "Be right back." The door closed and would reopen with the security chain in place. Their hands would extend through beyond the door jamb past the door but not very much. The money was exchanged and change made: the transaction was swift. They couldn't get that door locked fast enough.

"Ding Dong."

"Who is it?"

"It's not Richard Speck." I tried the humor approach; only a couple of people were amused. Somebody complained to the super. I had to try something else.

I had to ring their doorbells and call out before they had a chance to answer: "Paperboy...........Collecting." It helped.

Although these gruesome murders occurred 1000 miles away, the way the residents were terrified, Speck's murders may as well have taken place in Yonkers just down the street. Everyone was scared and suspicious – especially the women. It was a self imposed lockdown, even after they caught the killer. The paranoia continued as it got re-circulated and recharged by the media throughout the summer. It wasn't enough to scare the people with the likes of Speck, the media had to bring back Albert DeSalvo, (The Boston Strangler) for an 'in-depth' comparison in the newspapers, magazines, and TV. Now the women could see there was a world of killers in America.

I pressed another doorbell. "Want do you want?" came through the door.

"Paperboy....Collection."

Nothing at first, "Go away...my husband didn't leave me any money." Panic came through the door.

Straight-arming the wall I thought: 'Damn lady – you aren't even married....it's only $.70 cents'

"Go away. Come back tomorrow."

"Tomorrow?" I raised my eyebrows.

"Tomorrow.....Go away."

Collection was a real chore for the remainder of the summer. I collected for Ray at least a dozen times when he had the route; it was never like this. It was all because of those shitheads Speck and DeSalvo.

"Who is it?" A female voice replied to the door's chime.

"Paperboy......collection."

"Be right there."

The door was unlocked, the deadbolt rolled back, and the door chain remained engaged. A three inch slice of air between the hallway and the door permitted two quarters and two dimes which had been taped together to be tossed into the hall. I heard the locks secure the door once again as I chased my money. "Damn near ridiculous."

"Ding-Dong....Ding-Dong."

The apartment's door opened wide. The first thing I noticed was a snub nose .38 hanging in a shoulder holster from the top of the closet door. Next, I saw a small menorah on the bookcase. I gave him the once over as he probably was doing the same to me. He had sandy curly hair, well built, clean cut; he looked like he was all speed.

A big exhale, 'What a relief.'

"Whaddya want." he said.

"I'm the new paperboy. I missed you last week." I said.

"Yeah, I had nights. Danny Kryesler, I'm the new gold shield." He shook my hand that got lost in his. "What's your name?"

"Ryan......Ryan Whitelaw."

"You a mick?"

"Some Irish in me."

"Put the Irish in the girls." We laughed. "Seems like half the force is Irish. Hey you know what a gold shield is?"

"It means you're a detective. My uncle Bill is one."

"Zee with the Yonkers Department?"

"Port Authority."

That's a good outfit.......next stop – F.B.I."

"My other uncle is a Westchester County cop. He's a sergeant. I think he's going for lieutenant next. He says it's all politics."

"The county is all political. It's kind of a shame."

He went to a dish on the coffee table and fished out three quarters. When he handed the coins to me, I noticed the black pupil of his right eye was asymmetrical, some of it extended into the iris. It gave his face an outer space alien appearance. I thought he was kool.

"Ryan – don't even try pretending you're fumbling around in your pockets for the nickel , I used to have a route on DeHaven Drive. I know how it works." He had me laughing with him.

"It isn't the nickel – the customer just want to see the act you go through searching for it."

As long as I had the paper route, Danny treated me right. It reached the point where after I rang the bell and yelled "Paperboy." He'd answer, "Door's open. Get your money from the table." He was at the sink doing the dishes.

"I've got to get this place regulation. I got this overactive 'shiksa' coming over tonight. I'm trying to impress her."

"What the deuce is a schika?"

"Shiksa. It's Hebrew........no......it's probably Yiddish." He looked at the ceiling. "Anyway, it's a gentile girl who goes out with Jewish guys."

Nearly a month had passed since the Speck murders. Danny asked me if things had been loosening up now that Speck was back on page eight.

"It's better than it was - not like it had been - but it's getting better."

Danny laughed, "The chicks are just now sneaking a peek in the elevator. Hey Ryan – your hair's coming back in."

"Yeah but not in the big bald spot." I soured my face as I took my money from his dish.

183

"Don't worry it'll come back, just going to take time. You learning anything from this Speck shit?"

"Sells papers, but it's made collection night a pain in the butt."

"Take a buck – see you next week", he winked.

viii

There was not much summer left. Labor Day was on the 5th that year, we got a few extra days off. This was the first summer where I couldn't pinpoint every activity. It was the first of many blurs: baseball with the Chippewas, altar boy duty, the paper route, way too much time looking at the dirty magazines in the dump between O'Dell and the aqueduct. Summer recess didn't drag for the first time; it felt like it lasted a month.

Dusk was coming sooner; July's heat and humidity lingered into August. It had been five weeks since the Speck murders, another steamy Friday night collecting for the newspaper. Not many houses had central air conditioning, if people did have air conditioning - it was most likely from a window unit.

I was working my way up to the end of Hawley Terr. where Tommy Capps and his brothers and sisters lived. It used to be a large estate. It was similar to the one at 45 O'Dell. The two were probably the only dwellings in this area for quite a number of years. Unlike 45 O'Dell, there were no exterior walls or fences around the compound. The big house where the Campagna's lived was up front; the caretaker's house and the stable's house were off to the side and behind the main house. The three formed a triangle. They were all made of stone like 45. The big house had a cupola and a spire on top. Cobblestone, slate, and flagstone surrounded all three, except for the back of the stable.

According to Louis, every so often someone in the family wanted to go to court to break up the property. The lawyers would come in and go back into the annals of the convoluted mess. Setting up the living quarters arrangement must have been a lawyer's dream or nightmare. Variance and easement language must have filled 10 pages alone for just one of the properties.

Louis and John had to introduce me to the grandmother; and then the residents of the two other dwellings. With her approval I had access to the compound. There was complete privacy for each of the residences because of the layout of the trees, shrubs, hedges, stone ornaments, and rotation of the houses in relation to the other two.

The only thing I could say for sure was Louis' grandmother was running everything that had to do with the land, the buildings, and the people who were living there. They all knew each other, and they were related more through marriage than blood, but it was the blood that bound them. It was tenuous at best, but they made it work. I don't believe this triumvirate got along very well; I never saw any two of the three women together at any one time.

184

I asked Ray what his take on the Campagna compound was. He said it was so screwed up the Campagna kids weren't sure themselves. He called it an 'enigma.'

ABOUT THE FIFTH OR SIXTH TIME I COLLECTED FROM them, I was catching on with the way they wanted things done: they sort of had a round robin system where one of the three paid for the week for all three subscriptions.

The young woman who lived in the caretaker's residence had two kids. The kids had to have been the blood connection. She didn't look anything like a Campagna, she was no Paisan. It had been hot and humid all day. It was the caretaker's week to pay. Sundown was still an hour-and-half away.

I walked up three steps to the landing outside the side entrance. I was just about to knock, and swallowed my two sticks of Juicy Fruit instead. Immobilized, I peered through the screen door, I silently observed the younger woman who lived there and a woman who was about 10 years her senior. The two women were smoking and drinking. The older one chased her whisky with a beer, the younger one was drinking beer from the bottle. They were only wearing their bras. The dining room table blocked my view of what they might be wearing below their navels.

"Holy shit.........holy fuckin' shit." I barely whispered. My heart was racing along with my breathing. This wasn't any movie or skin magazine, I had to straight arm against the outside of the house. I didn't want to, but I had to get down to business. Twice I tried to ring the bell, my eyes kept me from pushing it.

Knocking was no good, it would startle the two. My hand blindly found the bell button. Glued, I had to watch the two in their underwear and not reveal my presence. They were laughing, smoking, and drinking. Unless they were really blasted, I couldn't believe they didn't know I was only 15 feet away. I had to ring that bell.

First though, I had to get a good look at their milkers......... then their faces – the young one was pretty, the other was pretty good looking too, but clearly older. I was showing through my dungarees. "Holy motherfucking shit." How could this get any better? My finger was still on the doorbell button, and I still hadn't pressed it.

For another five minutes I observed the two women, concentrating on their boobs. Although the side door was mostly secluded, someone might come and make an incident of the voyeur aspect of my prolonged surveillance through the screened door. I pressed the button. It ended up being a buzzer. They were slightly startled. "They're here --- they're here."

The older one smiled and walked over to me. She turned back to the younger woman. "It's about time." She looked at me. There was confusion. "Karla, it's not the guys. There's only one of them – I think he's selling something."

The younger one walked over trying to see through the screen door. My face was in the shadow. She pushed open the screen door. She I.D.'d me and the hand with her cigarette came up and covered her cleavage. "Just the paperboy."

Karla rolled her eyes at her friend for making her investigate the intruder at the door. She went back to the dining room table and searched her handbag for my money.

The older lady made no attempt to hide herself from me. "Did you say paperboy or papertoy? Or did you say paper-man?"

"Connie......do not start.......just don't." Karla continued the search for the collection money.

Connie was looking at me and our eyes met – just for three seconds. "Which is it handsome?"

"CONNIE!" Came from the table.

Karla had put some money on the table and watched: I was panting. There was sweat over my upper lip, in the middle of my chest, under my arms. There was plenty of ozone in the air, and the scantily clad women had delivered me into a near state of panic. Connie acknowledged my sexual charged dungarees and laughed.

Connie turned to Karla at the table, I shot a quick look at the black-hair woman's panties. I looked where I figured the action would be: I couldn't see anything – just some hair escaping the confines of the elastic on the legs.

The weekly money was placed on the table, black-haired Connie walked over to the table and motioned with her head for me to follow. I stood just inside the door. She had a cigarette in her mouth, grabbed a beer with one hand and my collection money with the other. Her ass was a little wide, but I thought it was real kool.

Karla cautioned her again. She mashed her lips and squinted her eyes.

"Karla, you father had me when I was 14 years old. Nobody stopped him."

Connie took a long drag and put it on the edge of the table; money in one hand and beer in the other. She looked down at her boobs, poured some beer between them, then shook and jiggled them for me. She turned her butt my way and rocked that thing better than some of the girls on 'Soul Train.' The beer and money went back on the table, and again she nodded to come over to the table. Bending over, her hand slapped one of her ass cheeks and looked at me through her spread legs and peeled, "Paperguy.........start collecting."

I didn't know what to do. In a trance I stuttered: "It's $2.10 for the three houses."

"You want this?" Connie picked up the money and the cigarette from the table.

I guess it was some kind of ransom being exacted, and I was sure I wanted whatever she was going to give me.

"I sure do." I panted.

Connie went out of view of the side door into a small pantry. Karla wondered what her friend was going to try. "Come on paperguy, you want to kiss me don't you?"

I turned the corner of the small division wall, and Connie pulled me to her and stuck her long tongue in my mouth and swabbed my tonsils. Exploring our mouths our tongues met. It was my first French kiss. Her tongue and mouth sucked my tongue all the way out as the kiss ended. She could see me through my jeans and gave it a tug.

Karla was the voyeur now, "Connie - come on......the guys are coming."

"Now, you've got to do something for me and I'll give you the money."

"I don't want to get in trouble; I just got this job six weeks ago."

"I swear Connie........if you wake up the kids."

She replied, "No – we got to know if we've got a paper – boy – guy – toy – or man. Now that I've kissed you.......you've got to kiss me back."

"No problem – just tell me what to do."

"It's hot, and I've been sweating all day – I want you to kiss my ass." Connie smiled wide. Karla looked embarrassed.

Going down this road had caution and stop signs on both sides. The only sign Connie wanted me to obey said 'Yield'.

"How does that work?"

"You kiss my butt like you kiss your teachers' butt. Only... this will be for real. You're old enough to like it, and I know I'll love it." Connie teased.

"To tell you the truth, this is a 'first' for me." My brow arched and I took a quick breath. I looked over to Karla for some kind of guidance.

"Don't worry – you'll love it." Karla exhaled some smoke.

"We'll, I really don't want to lose your three subscriptions."

Up and down, Connie gave me a once over. You're like in the 8th grade or going into the 9th – right?"

"Yeah, I'm 15."

"Nice."

"The guys will be here real soon. Whatever you're up to – make it quick Connie."

The cigarette in Connie's mouth glowed orange; she looked at me over her shoulder: "Pull down my panties and kiss my ass for starters." She had her hands on the wall with her legs spread wide.

Before I followed her directions, my face questioned both women.

Karla chugged the beer in her glass. "Just do what she wants – and then we're throwing you out. Hold on to that wall Connie." Karla laughed.

I looked all around to make sure this wasn't some kind of set up. There were some fine black hairs at the top of her ass crack. Her smell of the stifling day was quite strong. Another fast look from side to side, and I pulled down her underwear.

"Pull them all the way down and take them off so I can spread my legs – hurry." Connie said.

Whatever I had between my legs was all wood. "Ah......now what?"

"Spread my cheeks and kiss me where I stink.....with your tongue."

This attraction must have come from the fireball. I was pretty scared. This might be something an alien would get a charge out of. Sure enough though, something as weird as this had to be a sin. It might have helped to have gotten Ray's slant on this mess. The women were waiting on me, and I guess I wanted to be the paperguy. "You're not going to tell anyone?"

"The only way some one finds out is if you tell them. It's our secret." Her leg was twitching.......""Now hurry."

I looked over to Karla, she took the bottle from her mouth. "Our secret." She echoed with a smile.

"Pour some beer down the crack. Don't make a mess." Connie directed. "You know you want it."

"I really don't know." I took in a deep breath – 'Man, I can never let anyone know about this humiliation.' I thought.

"Kneel down and get to work or we can cancel the three subscriptions." Karla said and swiped the rest of Connie's whiskey.

I took another deep breath and spread her ass cheeks, "Hey… you want me to do the front too?" I smiled.

"If we've got time. Just do the back for now."

I spread her ass wide with her arms braced up against the wall, I planted a big wet French kiss on her sweaty stink star. Connie was going through gyrations and Karla was laughing.

"Twirl it…..twirl it…..twirl your tongue." She gasped. It went on for two or three minutes. She started heaving and groaning. I had managed to get my tongue to the bottom of her box. I thought it was more interesting - at least it smelled better. She liked that back door stuff, that I was sure of.

They paid me and told me to leave. I'd see that Karla every 3rd week. The late summer sex session – It seemed to have been a one shot deal. It was all business with her from that point on until I quit the paper route. I never saw Connie again.

ix

The summer was almost history; the paper route was never hard except in the snow, wind, and rain. There were things about the job, I didn't see when I subbed for Ray. Most of the time I floated through people's yards and the apartment house unnoticed, except when I chose to interact with them. Maybe that nutjob Richard Speck had been a paperboy and was able to get the drop on those nurses. Somehow he had gained their trust to commit such a heinous crime.

Making the rounds of the route, I didn't intentionally stare into windows. As the days got shorter, they turned their lights on earlier. Sometimes it was difficult not making a prolonged study. I told this stuff to Father Darius in the confessional. He ruled, if I was tripping over stuff, then I was looking too long. I confessed about the incident at the end of Hawley Terr. with those two women. From past experiences, I thought Father Darius would give me a break about Karla and Connie. "I mean come on Father, I sort of walked in on it. It wasn't a date – I was just collecting."

No.........to Darius this was big medicine. He was trying to see who was confessing this one-way ticket to hell. There was a real possibility he'd withhold my absolution. I might have been sorry when I walked into the confessional, but he kept wanting every little detail about the episode. Karla and Connie had said to forget the entire affair: "Like it never happened." I ended up making a quick dash out of the confessional and ran out of the church. I'd have to dump this confession in another parish.

My thoughts regurgitated the late afternoon with Karla and Connie. Seeing Karla every so often when I did the route, it was hard not to think of my introduction into the world of flesh. Even though I swore to myself and the women, I would never tell anyone about that day.

Coming clean with Ray about that late summer evening was only going to upset him. Sooner or later, I'd have to run this by him, but I'd tone it down and tell him I only caught Karla and Connie in their bras and panties. There was no way I was going to reveal to him I had to kiss her dirty spot; this act of pornography had to stay classified. Long term guilt and shame were destined to haunt me as long as I was Catholic. If the church wasn't going to give me absolution – Ray would.

Except for jackass Speck making everyone paranoid, and the incident at the end of Hawley, the paper route was about what I expected. Ray's caddying adventure at Hudson River C.C. hadn't worked out the way he thought. It started out pretty good in the spring, but taking off for Fourth of July weekend didn't help his standing in the caddy yard one bit. The caddymaster, Sy Simmons, was a firm believer in payback, and Ray sat around the yard way more than he figured. I got a little taste of guilt about this also. He had cut the deal for me with the Statesman, and part of that was being able to go up to Mack's party upstate. It worked out for me but not Ray.

The weather was supposed to be hit and miss showers throughout the day. Right after Ray left for the golf course, a pretty good thunderstorm let loose. There might be some temporary water on the south side of the course. Those six holes were as flat as a football field. The gnats and mosquitoes were partial to it as well.

The papers had come up around 3:30. I waved to him as he was coming down O'Dell. The guilt I had from the Connie and Karla episode didn't hang around too long and that surprised me.

"Were you at the golf course all day?"

"Pretty much, there was more lightning and thunder than there was rain."

"Did you get out?" I sorted the papers.

"The rain let up enough and stopped by 8:30. The caddy yard was almost deserted, when 14 golfers decide to show up with their spikes on ready for a round. Sy gave me a twosome." Ray played it kool.

"DOUBLES?........Wow." That was ten bucks I thought. "How hard was it?"

"Hell, I'd have been glad to just get out with a single bag, and Sy gives me doubles. It was a lot of work chasing these two duffers: raking their traps, watching their shots, holding the pin for them. $10.00 for the two, and they hit me with a $5.00 tip."

"That's more than I'll make in two weeks........sonabitch."

There was more: "There'd be some clouds breaking up, and it'd piss for five or ten minutes, and then the sun would come back out. By 11:30 we finished the 18 holes, I started eating my lunch, and figured I'd come home. Right on time, the sun comes back out with a bunch of liquored up players looking to play. Ry, you would have gotten out today.....with doubles........if I only could have called you."

"There were only four caddies in the yard at noon: an underage kid, a drunk (sleeping off last night), a moonlighting fireman, and Black Joe – who'd rather caddy than go home and fight with his wife. Like it or not, Sy pressed us back into service. If we didn't take a loop - he told us not to come back for the rest of the year. I already had enough of that, and there isn't much summer left. I felt bad for the winos. Each of us had a foursome and they gave the golfers a cart, because Sy was unable to supply the caddies." Ray mimicked a caddy chasing a golfer around trying to hand him a putter.

"Going down the river?" I said.

"Give me Evan's and Day's paper." he said.

I'd still have good old 45 O'Dell to do.

"You're not doing anything after the papers are you?....

.......Meet me down the station on the northbound side... north of the platform by that little swamp." He was carrying a medium sized paper bag in the one hand.

"Should I bring down any fishing gear or the wristrocket?"

"No.....none of that. Wanna show you something. I think I found the cast away from the Fireball."

I checked back home on my way back from 45. At first I thought he had uncovered a new stash of skin books. "A piece of the comet?.....wow." I didn't think there was going to be a part 2 to this cosmic interloper's story.

The old passenger platform was only two and–a-half feet above the rail bed of ballast rocks. There were a bunch of cat-o-nine tails and reeds at the north end of the platform; it was impossible to tell if the swamp was wet or dry. A black plume of smoke rose where he said I'd find him. We never hung out on the station side; what was going on?

Gnats and mosquitoes were in abundance as I walked towards the mini-swamp. Ray was eradicating them with carburetor cleaner, spray paint, and some other pressurized spray cans of stuff. Before Ray began treating the small swamp with the stuff he brought, it smelled like a cesspool. Despite the morning rain, the water in the swamp only amounted to a puddle here and there. He had thrown down pieces of scrap wood which had been left for someone else to dispose of properly. We used them to walk on the swamp's soft mud.

When there was standing water in the swamp's pool, the top water drained into a 10 in. diameter concrete pipe which ran under the rail tracks and fed into the river. Some junk and debris had blocked the swamp water from entering the pipe. We cleared it away to allow the water we couldn't see to drain.

There were possum, muskrat, and raccoon tracks all around. He sprayed all the insect eggs and larvae with the improvised flame-thrower. I still didn't know what he was up to, but I always liked playing with fire, and he had a good one started.

A commuter local from Grand Central was letting off passengers; next stop: Hastings, four miles north. When the train was almost out of sight, Ray tossed the paper bag and pressurized can into the fire. He yanked me by the Tee-shirt and yelled, "TAKE COVER!"

About 15 yards away from the mini-swamp we were partially protected by a fallen tree. An explosion, a fireball, and more black smoke were followed by a concussive movement of air.

"What the hey?" I looked at him with a laugh.

"That can was almost empty." he scratched his head.

"What was in the can?"

"Cheez whiz."

"Gee whiz."

We sat on the trunk of the fallen tree. He asked, "You got that dust and ash from the comet?"

"Yeah – it's still in the closet, I got it hid. You got some right?"

Failing to reply, he walked over to the fire kicking the remnants of it towards the mouth of the pipe. There was just a little swamp water flowing in from the hit and miss thunderstorm, the summer drought absorbed much of the fallen rain. Ray used a discarded chunk of galvanized sign post to splash water on the rest of the stuff that was burning.

We repositioned the scraps of plywood in the swamp to walk around the area where he believed he last saw the comet fragment.

"Well it has to be buried, there isn't anything around here from outer space. This is where it was." He pointed. "The first time, it was right on top of the swamp muck. The next sighting....same spot only deeper, two feet down. I came down yesterday – it had vanished." He looked up at me with one eye from a catcher's squat.

"What did it look like?"

"We'll have to dig." He was surveying what he saw and compared it with his memory. The tip of his right foot was placed where he thought dead center might be. He drew crosshairs and said, "Dig."

He was immersed in thought. After digging a foot down, I tossed the piece of sign post where there was dry dirt. "This thing isn't any good to dig with." I put my hands on my hips: "It's just two pieces of angle iron bolted back to back."

"Next time we'll bring a shovel." Ray said.

"That old lady in the gingerbread house....Mrs. Sachs, she's got a shovel on the side of her shed. It's got the short handle. We could borrow it for the digging we got to do. We'll bring it back when we're done."

"Tell you what – go get it now, then stop up 21 and get some of that cinderash from the closet; one from me and the other from you. Put each in a container – not a baggie and not made of metal."

I never gave it a thought to question Ray in any of this cosmic voyager business. Some of the scientific stuff he'd rattle off to me I did understand. If he went over it slowly enough times – I would get some of it. He wanted me to know and talk to him at his level. I was ready to label the thing a UFO – that sent out probes or transmitting devices with messages. He probably knew it was from outer space from the first.

Returning with the ash containers and the short handled spade, I saw what had to be the spewed out projectile from 'The Fireball'. It was sitting in some dried mud in the small muddy pond. Except for its bottom, it was fully exposed.

There was a hole in the swamp muck and the galvanized sign-post lying next to it. "That figures." I threw the shovel down.

Ray said he hadn't moved it, just dug around the cast-off piece of comet. "The characteristics of the swamp's mud changed when it came into contact with the orb, it doesn't retain heat. Rather, it is a conductor of it. I think we move this visitor across the tracks by the river." he said.

"Why's that?"

He crossed his arms, and brought his right hand to his chin: "I don't know......we can go fishing and keep an eye on it. Besides, look at us; do you want to play in this muck every time we think we have a notion as to the origin of this projectile or how we can use this thing?"

"Is this object something that was part of the fireball, or are you guessing?"

"It can sink just as easily on the other side of the tracks as it can here. To me, it seems like it should be over there." He pointed towards the riverside.

It was my first look at this thing: It was spherical – about the size of a basketball - but lacking roundness. Its shape was half a rugby and half basketball. There was duality in its nature and appearance. The one half looked like a piece of anthracite coal: small angular protrusions dominated the side. The other half displayed a hemisphere of a multi-colored obsidian embedded with shiny metallic flakes. I peered up to Ray, "I've never seen a rock like this........You think this was ejected from the meteor?"

"Pour a little bit of that ash in small pile on the angular side where there's a flat spot. I'm going to add some water and make a paste of it."

"How much?"

"'Bout a good teaspoon." Ray began to stir the ash and swamp water. In slow motion the ash was attracted by the smooth obsidian side. "Whose ash is this yours or mine?"

"Mine."

Something was going on; I was trying to understand the basics of his experimentation. He was trying to prove a magnetic orientation of the cast-off. Ray wanted to be fairly confident in his designation of positively and negatively charged materials. Back and forth we experimented with the charged ash matter. He knew about magnetism; I did not. I was just grateful to know more about its properties and forces than the day before.

"This little chunk of the universe needs a lot more study. It's going across the tracks, where we don't have to deal with the skeeters, gnats, and mud." He looked at me straight-on, but he got busy shooing away a new batch of mosquitoes and small black flies. "We don't want to use any more of the space dust, I believe it to be some type of catalyst to engage its magnetic energies. It may also have something to do with the time continuum." he said.

"Did you say you picked this thing up out of the muck?"

"I dug around it. I tried picking it up; I couldn't free it from the suction. I couldn't move it. Maybe both of us can carry it." Ray said

"Maybe not."

"We'll find something to carry it in or on."

"Just leave it here; it's not hurting anything." I waved it down.

"No way – something else is taking place in it or through it. How is it still warm three months after its arrival?"

"Duh?.........you just cooked the damn thing." I laughed.

"Not two and-a-half feet below the top of the mud. Why is the mud only drying on the smooth side?" he probed.

"If it's too heavy it's too heavy. We'll have to leave it."

The extraterrestrial visitor had a hold of my brother; "Let's see if we can roll it into a barrel or a bucket and we'll use the sign post to two-man it across the tracks."

We found a bent-up, rusty milk crate; its structural integrity was questionable. Ray was struggling just trying to move it close to the milk crate where the edge of the mud turned to dry dirt. Because the orb wasn't truly round, it didn't want to roll. He thrust the galvanized sign post in the mud underneath, and tried prying it up. "Ryan dig underneath the orb so we can see the bottom. If we can get this sign post underneath, we might be able to roll it out of here.

"BE CAREFUL. You don't want your hands crushed."

"Ray - my hands are away." It should have tipped one way or the other from gravity. Take away the sign post." I said.

"Huh?"

"Just take it away, it's all clear."

He removed the fulcrum. "Ray..........it's levitating. Come have a look." I wiped the sweat from my brow, as he got down to my vantage point and looked amazed.

"It's defying the laws of gravity.........Why?" he asked himself as his brow compressed together.

We were sure some unknown force was at work. I reached down to feel its temperature with my hand. I looked at Ray, "Wasn't it hot?" My hand got closer, but there didn't seem to be any radiant heat.

His eyes revealed deep thought, and he repeated his warning to be careful. At first, I swiped it with my index and middle finger.

193

Each successive pass was longer than the last until I put my palm on top of it. I gave him a faint smile: "No, it's kool to the touch."

"Huh?" He put the top of his hand on the side of the projectile. "It's hotter than it was before."

"Bullshit." I countered. I felt it again, but my hand was off-center, and my hand pushed the space rock with ease. The movement caught us off-guard.

"How did it move? Did you roll it?" He looked sharply at the irregular orb.

"I must have." I stood up with it resting in my hands. It was no heavier than a watermelon. We were dumbfounded.

"Give it here." Ray said with his palms ready to receive it. The weight of it was too much and it immediately fell back into the swamp's dried mud.

"Too heavy for me......Ryan. You pick it up."

"You're giving me the business.......you just want to get me to carry this cosmic piece of magic to the riverside by myself."

"I don't know what the deal is with this thing; it seems to have its own science which governs it........harder than diamonds.......denser than gold."

"It is part of that comet we saw – sure thing." I nodded. "Let's get this thing across."

"Ray – we ain't going to walk this thing over the pedestrian bridge?" I looked at him.

"Why would we walk the length of the platform, climb 50+ steps, cross the bridge, go down the other 50 steps, and walk the length of the southbound platform? We can go right here. Thirty yards..........straight shot. He shook his head when I had come up with the long route.

All OF THE FOUR TRACKS HAD A RAISED 3RD RAIL; each was insulated and encased by lengths of wood cut into the shape of a channel, they were soaked in creosote like the rail ties. Protective wood insulation was banded covering the power rail like a sandwich. The 3rd rail was an actual piece of metallic rail and carried the current to propel the electric trains on the Hudson Line. This 3rd rail ran outside the two rails which carried the wheels of the trains. None of the railroads who owned the track had ever installed any gates, fences, or signage to restrict access to the tracks or warn the public about the amount of voltage the 3rd rail carried.

Hal always told Ray and me to step over all 3rd rails. It was a pain in the butt. The four 3rd rails running through Greystone station were built about 18" off the bed of #5 ballast stone. The electrified portion of the Hudson Line ran from Grand Central Terminal to Croton-Harmon Station - everything north of Croton was diesel powered. Once in a while the insulation's banding fell off and the rail was exposed; the power rail looked like it was either iron, steel, or copper – I didn't know which. The only time the 3rd rail was exposed was at the splices, and the raw rail could be seen. Either the railroad paid a lot of money for copper rail or paid a lot for electricity as iron and steel are not very good conductors.

194

The railroad devised a control system to only energize the power rail just ahead of the train, and shut it off just behind it. The engineer and train may have had the capability to perform this function, but Ray thought it was done in the same central control facility where the track switching and control lights were operated from.

The last of the peak trains were making their runs, and the off-peaks began heading to the Bronx and Manhattan on the southbound side. It wasn't a big deal crossing the tracks as long as you paid attention.

I'd have to lug this errant space traveler to the other side. There wasn't much point in debating the matter whether Ray could carry it or not. We had to get to cracking, and get this thing riverside. He grabbed the spade and the sign-less sign post. We waited for a local to leave and start heading for Hastings. The northbound picked up speed and faded into a wall of heat generated mirage waves. All clear. I had just crossed the first set of tracks and dropped the mini-meteorite from an instantaneous increase in its weight.

"Peter and Paul.......now what?" Ray dropped the shovel and sign post on the southbound platform.

All at once it had gotten heavier than a wheelbarrow of Mack's concrete. "We're gonna need Superman or the eighth grade strongman – Shooey to lift this thing." We stood on the ties between the rails just looking at it.

"Maybe there's kryptonite in it Superman." Ray chuckled.

"Why don't you roll it onto your surfboard Silver Surfer and get it over there?"

Ray took the challenge: he tried lifting it, then he tried kicking it into a low spot between the two northbound tracks. There seemed to be enough of a pitch to make gravity work for us in this situation. He kicked the sphere with the heel of his converse sneakers. There was no movement, he may as well have kicked a concrete pillar at city hall. "Son-of-gun that hurt.........dammit." He winced – I laughed.

Ray placed his hands on his hips, "I don't think we can leave it here. Its very nature brings attention upon itself by its shape and magnetism. It so unearthly – it demands further investigation."

"I 'spose.....if the guys come by on that flatcar with the crane......it'll be gone." I bent down and tried to move it.......... again, without success.

Although there were at least two hours of sun left, a bright light from the north had gotten Ray's attention. It had to be a train – at least a mile and a half away from Greystone. It had to be running on either of the interior tracks – most likely an express commuter or a freight train. Whatever it was, it was travelling at a good clip. In less than a minute it would be at the station.

Straining my eyes, the waves of visual distortion from the sun, heat, speed, and the bouncing of the train at every rail splice made it impossible for us to know what type of train and the track it was travelling on.

"Ray called over to me, "Anything coming from the south?"

"Nothin." I replied.

"It's an electric commuter: two headlights burning. They've energized the 3rd rail already. Let's go back to the northbound platform in case there's any stray arcs or voltage. Something was wrong with the train coming south. It had a definite lean towards us, and the cosmic intruder. There was a noticeable reduction in speed also.

Watching it come south, I knew something was radically wrong and screamed: IT'S GONNA DE-RAIL! The steel wheels' flanges dug into the rails making a deafening noise. We could see the engineer's face; panic and horror had taken control of him and his train. The 7-car express was decelerating, but the list of the train had me believing it would roll off the tracks. It was hard to think as all the wheels were screeching and squealing. The train had enough momentum to wreck right into us. I got down on my knees, prayed, and was ready to witness my demise.

The express had come even with the comet remnant. It had slowed to about four m.p.h. The engineer and the conductor were immobilized by fear once the train started the exaggerated tilt. The train's crew watched smoke billowing from the left side as the wheels were being scorched by the friction of its flanges digging into the rails. As each car passed the comet, the electric motor of each commuter car cried in agony. The shadow of the train revealed the intergalactic visitor to be pulsing with power and a warning beacon.

The express commuter almost came to a full stop. As the fourth car passed the orb, it slowly accelerated and the roll became less and less severe.

The distortional waves returned when the seventh car passed under the pedestrian bridge and continued until it made the bend went out of sight towards Glenwood Station, the station to the south.

We stood motionless on the northbound platform gaping at the intergalactic castoff. For me it was pointless to speculate what we had just witnessed. Ray was going to give me the real version of what we saw, but I was going to get my two cents in before I got overruled or corrected with his intuition or logic. I started out with my usual mumbo-jumbo nonsense. He listened, but knew right away it was just regurgitated television science fiction crap.

He said, "Didn't it seem like the engineer had the brakes engaged but the accelerator wide open? I thought there was going to be a meltdown rather than a de-railing."

Approximately three or four minutes after the express went out of sight, we went over to the cosmic visitor to attempt once again to get it to the strip of shore running parallel with the southbound platform and the river. Just as before, his eyes beaded down on one beam of light - this time coming from the south. Again it was on one of the interior tracks. This train would not be stopping at Greystone either.

The giant headlight in the middle of the first car only meant one thing: a diesel locomotive.........it might be pulling cars with passengers and sleeping compartments as we saw in the Alfred

Hitchcock movie – "North By Northwest". I think they called the train 'The Empire Builder'. It also might be just a freight train.

Ray said, "We got to get out of here now! This thing is going to wreck and wreck big. "If it's a freight train it'll have four locomotives pulling at least 80 cars."

We ran from the platform and headed up Harriman Ave.. On the stairs of Henry Hudson Park, the diesel engines were getting louder. With that chunk of space laying in the track bed, Ray thought we'd see the freight train getting out of control when it got even with the park's stairway. It was only 30 seconds south of the station now. How it was going to wreck and in which direction its momentum would take it, were the only two questions left to be answered.

The Armenian club was directly across the street from the park's stairs. We seldom saw people in the club; once in a while a band would rehearse there because they could turn up their amplifiers. The only residence nearby was the swingers shack belonging to Evans and Day. When the freight wrecked, the Armenian Club made of concrete block and its adjacent impromptu junkyard, would be squeezed in a vise of tanker cars, coal hopper cars, freight cars, four locomotives and the retaining wall of the park which held Warburton Ave. in place.

To be safe, we climbed to the third landing to observe the impending wreck. Ray was sweating: "I hope we don't kill anybody."

I was panic-stricken with the probability both engineer and conductor were as good as gone. I made the sign of the cross and began to pray for them. Ten seconds elapsed; the four diesel locomotives sped past us.......then past the cosmic orb, its pistons pounding northward. We sat on the steps as our panic and the rest of the train passed.

"Well - that don't make a lick of sense." I scratched my empty patch of scalp.

"Why should it? We're most likely dealing with a force from a distant universe. It's also possible it has no recognition of the scientific paradigm which this world operates by. It is from a very distant place, its laws of science may be the same, or totally incompatible with ours. The only consistency would be that its laws of science be based on truth and fact. I'm just taking a guess."

"Yeah, Hal says every time you hear the words: feel … believe…should….seems….ought…..etc. – you better prick your ears up and listen to what follows, because it is not based in fact or logic."

"Let's see if we can get that thing off the tracks." he said.

Ray gave lifting it another try with the same result as he had at the swamp, "Your turn superstar."

With little effort, I picked it up from the track bed. We weren't shocked but we were bewildered with its behavior. It was active; it was responding to whatever we were doing to it.

"Look." Ray pointed to the track the commuter express had travelled on. I paused for a brief moment. There was junk strewn all along its path into the station.

""We've got to get this sphere off the tracks and find a place for it."

The cast-off got warm again - just on the one side. Like feeling for fever, I took its temperature with my hand. Ray picked up the spade and the sign post steel and we looked for a place to hide the irregular orb. There was a dried up gully half-way between the river and southbound platform. He dug a shaft into the heel of an embankment; angling two feet down and three feet over with a shaftway.

The gully was about three to four feet deep. Every time I saw it, it had always been dry. The space traveler was brought off the top of the embankment. With my arms over my head I carried it to the hole Ray had dug, and prepared to leave it in its new temporary home - a bed of mostly clean sand.

"What do you think? It's just as far away from the tracks as it was in the swamp. I don't think it will disturb the trains." Ray said.

"Looks good to me."

We watched it in its new environs. The metallic flake sparkled in the tunnel's darkness. I hadn't felt it pulse, but a hum was present.

"Was it warm?"

"Just the coal looking side......maybe a little warmer than before the trains came."

"Getting late........filler up. Mom must be wondering where we are."

Making our way up to 21, I asked, "What are we going to do with that chunk of comet?"

"It's got this outer space force which we know nothing about. What we've seen it do today........only leads to more questions. What causes it to levitate? Why are you able lift it? Did it cause the express to almost de-rail? The thing's got more questions than a Quija Board. I think we're best off leaving it undisturbed for a while until we understand its nature and/or power more fully. That thing is big medicine..... for some of us."

"It has no classification; to figure out what it is......we need an astrophysicist, a chemist, a mathematician, a geologist, an astrologer and that's just the beginning. "He sat on the platform looking at the Palisades across the river.

"How's it change its temperature at will and alter the energy output of things in its general area? Listen.....a train......" I said.

Ray smiled as we watched one come into and out of the station: "That one ran true blue and straight through."

"The thing's an orphan and doesn't even have a name."

"We'll call it what it is: 'The Ejected Remnant.'"

Ray pitched me this line about paperboys being more than paperboys – we had a responsibility to the community, the neighborhood, and especially the veterans and senior citizens. Mark Aronson had handed this code off to Ray. He thought it was the right way to go: "If we're lucky, we'll all be old some day, and we'll be needing some young people to give us a hand."

The knucklehead between Ray and me couldn't even deliver his papers, so watching out for the old timers didn't even come on his radar screen. This community service was even for folks who didn't get the newspaper. Although there was a point where some tasks were beyond the skill level of a 12 or 14 year old. It was kind of an obligation of employment my brother reasoned via Mark: "You'll see things you never would have by staying on the sidewalk. There will be opportunities as well. Some people will take advantage of you because they know you're helping them, without looking to be paid."

"I hope some paper carrier is helping out our Nana if she needed a hand. You're pretty sharp Ray." I said.

It kind of made me proud to be part of this tradition - it didn't come down from corporate; we did it on our own. It was still summer when he told me about this "paperboy duty".

It took a while for me to catch on; at first I had a problem lending a hand to the people who didn't get the 'Statesman': "I know it's an obligation to help out senior citizens, women who aren't married and have kids, cripples, veterans.......but it's kind of hard when they don't get the paper. I mean one hand washes the other." I said.

"I know what you're saying, but when you do something good it comes back to you – you'll see." Ray answered.

I didn't do a thing for anybody yet, but six weeks into my paperboy career, the spontaneous ass worship with Connie might have come under the label 'Community Doodee'. I was sure it did. I found it difficult to resolve who had helped who that evening. If something good happened down the road for no reason, I guess I had done her a good turn. If this was the type of payback I could expect, I was going to help the old timers, the disabled, single moms and the rest, every chance I got.

WHEN IT CAME TO DOING STUFF IN THE APARTMENT building, Ray said to do the old timers chores without question; they're on fixed incomes and they're plain old worn out.

The single moms? a little more discretion might be the best way to proceed. The criteria he used deciding whether or not to help out a single mom was how good looking she or her daughters were. "If you walk into their apartment, and you think you walked into a kennel.......best off telling her to give the super a call."

The things the seniors in private houses asked for most, was to shovel snow from the front door to the sidewalk, bring their garbage cans to the curbside, try to coax a cat out of a tree; and once Mrs. Dominczyck asked me to knock off a raccoon who had taken up residence in her attic. I used the wristrocket on that job. I threw the dead coon out the attic window, she said she didn't want me taking it through her house. Mrs. Dominczyck had been so scared she gave me five dollars. I told her 'no' three times. I ended up leaving with the money. I thought she was going to have a heart attacker.

JUST BEFORE THANKSGIVING IN '66, RAY GOT CALLED across the street - down a couple of houses. He planned on quitting the route after New Years. Mrs. Hillman's street number was 16 O'Dell. Ray had switched out her storm and screen windows earlier in the Spring when he first took over for Mark Aronson.

Her husband, Mr. Bradley Hillman, had been in ill health the first day we met him. He passed away two years later in mid-summer 1965. When it was warm, he'd spend the day in his wheelchair in the sun on the porch. She put the phone outside on a small table along with a portable radio. Mark and Ray hand delivered his newspaper whenever he was out there. A rotation of vets from the V.F.W. were looking after him, and wheeled him in and out. Neither of us knew how or if he slept upstairs. We got called over a few times when the rain blew onto the porch and we had to bring him inside.

People in wheelchairs were really screwed back then: No ramps, no handicap parking, no motorized wheelchairs, no public transportation with handicap access. Mr.Hillman liked Hal: first - because he was a vet with combat duty, second -
he worked for Otis Elevator, and engineered hoisting devices and machinery which greatly assisted the disabled in getting around multi-story buildings and hospitals. There was a big write-up in the paper about Mr. Hillman when he died.

Mrs. Hillman had asked me and Ray to change out the storm windows before winter set in. The wind charged down the Hudson River with a fresh batch of Canadian air. I was glad I had put my gloves on; keeping them warm was the main reason, but they also protected my hands from splinters. The wind made handling the storm windows a real chore. Ray would hand one out, and I had to keep it close to the house to keep the wind from catching it and losing one. He gave me step by step instructions to remove the screens and hook the storms on the trim hardware. I had no doubt I would have had the sash and the sills all dinged up if I was on the inside of the house.

We carried the storm windows from the basement, and put numbers 1 and 2 in her room, and 3 and 4 in his room. We removed all 4 screens at the same time and stood them against the wall in her husband's room. It was a stroke of luck we were able to use the porch's roof as a work platform. Working from a ladder in the wind......I'd have lost one for sure.

The windows on the north side of the house were protected by the house next to hers. They were changed out in a half-hour. Mr. Hillman's room faced the street and was catching all the wind.

200

"She hasn't touched a thing in here since he passed away." Ray said looking around the extra bedroom which also served as a mini-arsenal.

He closed the door behind us to prevent the outside air from penetrating into the warmer rooms. We started snooping around. There was a small cache of arms and ordnance in his room and closet. This guy was ready for the Russians, Chi-comms or any civil insurrection. Although he was confined to his wheelchair, Bradley Hillman was on guard against anyone who wanted to tear apart the country he valiantly defended in WWII.

From the dress uniform in the closet, it was obvious he had been in the thick of things in the war. He was a hero: 114th Army Airborne, the Silver Star, Bronze Star, two Purple Hearts, Battalion and Regimental citations, and a battlefield commission. He was discharged with the rank of Captain. Bradley Hillman had enlisted right after Pearl Harbor and made P.F.C. out of boot camp. He received an individual citation noting a significant contribution in the advancement of field radio for the allied forces.

After the war, he was retained by the Defense Department. In combination with British Intelligence, this collaborative research in this sphere of communications and intelligence revolutionized airborne radar technology and gave our side an advantage in aerial combat.

There was a framed newspaper article hanging from a hook; his brother had been shot down over Belgium. In the corner of the brother's framed article was an obituary clipping in the corner.......the Hillman's also had lost a six year old son to viral meningitis.

Although Mr. Hillman had fought in the Pacific, most of his war momentos was Nazi stuff: 2 Walther pistols, a Luger, a high power scoped rifle for sniping, a damaged field radio – he restored himself, 2 kinds of Hitler flags, and a Waffen SS helmet.

The Jap stuff didn't amount to much: An Imperial Army rising sun flag with a bunch of Japanese script on it, and a seppuku belt dagger. Perhaps he traded all his Jap stuff. Hal told us those Jap samurai swords commanded a big price when they were getting discharged.

The real treasure we found was his stuff from the U.S. Army. Every once in a while, you'd go over to a friend's house and you'd see their father's souvenirs from the war. Mr. Hillman had enough here to arm Sgt. Fury and his Howling Commandos. He had a B.A.R. rifle, (2) M-1 .30 cal. carbines, (2) colt .45 pistols, a 7 round .25 semi-auto pistol, (2) fragmentation and 1 concussion grenade, ammo boxes, which we figured were full because they weighed a ton. He had: Insignias, I.D.'s, Special Clearance I.D.'s, ribbons, patches, badges and on and on. We checked out a wooden box on the closet's floor. There were about 15 knives and bayonets; these were from all over – only two were army issue: a belt knife and a boot knife from the Army Airborne.

Our Dad had a J.C. Higgins 12 ga. Shotgun and a .22 rim fire Hornet rifle. He had enough of armed combat. He liked the verbal conflicts with Jane because he always won. The one souvenir Hal had was a Nazi belt knife, like the one Mr. Hillman had. A Hitler sign was sunk into the handle. "Someone probably mass produced them here and sold them to the returning servicemen as they got off the ships." Brad Hillman said.

His wheelchair was in the bedroom next to a dresser. On his night table was an 8"x10" photo of both of them; on the bottom it said: 'Marian and Brad'. I moved his wheelchair out of the way so we could have easier access to the porch's roof through the window. An object in one of the chair's side pockets caught my attention. It was a knife......a push-button knife – but not a switchblade. This thing reeked of death. It was the tool of a commando.

Barely over a whisper: "Ray.......Ray.......look." I handed it to him.

Ritually, he examined it with a keen eye. The blade was locked in the handle. "It must have been important to him. Of all the military stuff he's got, this is what he keeps next to him. I'm going to push the release latch."

The blade shot out with precision and force. He looked at the bottom of the blade where it met the handle. There was a hallmark, a date: 1939, and the word Turku. He brought the knife into the closet and pushed the point of the blade on top of an ammo box. Using his weight, he managed to reset the blade into the handle's spring mechanism. This time, he had the handle against the wall of the closet and released the blade. The entire blade length entered the lathe and plaster without any recoil.

He looked my way, "If I could have just one thing in this room, it would be this knife......this stiletto. It is something from the pages of Ian Fleming, M.I.- 6, James Bond. This is a tool from the world of assassination and spies. What a fine piece of workmanship. Here." He tossed it to me. It was everything Ray said and more. It wasn't just a mechanical knife, it was a machine by its nature. The one shortcoming may have been in the difficulty in resetting the blade. With practice and just a touch of high grade lubricant, I was sure proficiency could be achieved. Along with the knife's operational advantages, it still required the elements of surprise and sleuth to be the ultimate killing weapon in the field of espionage in an offensive posture. Coming from behind an opponent, grabbing him by the throat and pressing the loaded knife against the ear's canal or temple; the blade sent its victims to Hades. I looked at it in my hand, the only monster I wanted to kill was that no good, rotten Richard Speck, and throw that other creep in with him......The Boston Strangler.

We brought the screen windows down to the basement, and carried the last two storm windows up. He passed them to me, one at a time. When we got to the last one, Ray said he had to get Hal's extension ladder so I could get off the roof when I had the last storm secured. He said through the house windows: "I can't do all the thinking; it might be good experience for you to try it every now and then." He quick drew the switchblade from his pocket, pointed it at me and released the blade mechanism and nodded with a grin.

He just didn't want to get Hal's wooden extension ladder was more like it I thought. We switched out three sides of her second floor. The backside of the house facing the aqueduct didn't have to be done because the storm windows stayed in place year round; the screens needed to be replaced, and she never got around to it.

The neighborhood residents had spotted us on Mrs. Hillman's roof. They asked Hal and Jane if we could do theirs. As much as they wanted the screens storms switched out, some were more interested in getting their windows washed before it was too cold. Jane told them: "Widows and veterans only.........and nothing above the second floor." One lady down the street was losing her marbles. She asked Ray to do her windows; trouble was she had these modern aluminum storm/screen combo windows which the contractor installed when they re-sided her house. If she could open her house windows by herself, she could open and shut her storms. The first time, Ray showed her how to do it, but she kept calling Ray until he went to Purdue. He took her ten bucks just to make her happy.

With all the exposure and word of mouth, the people on O'Dell and Hawley were always asking us to cut grass or trim trees and hedges. They were happy to see energetic teenagers. Wearing the All Souls blazer to and from school didn't seem to bother them much anymore. Even the Jewish people started hiring us. I wasn't looking for that level of visibility. To blend into the mundane, and at some point to become unseen was my goal. I wanted to be there, but leave only a wisp of an uncertain memory of my presence. The passage of time would determine if I had been successful or not.

ii

There was a limit to this blending into the background and dissolving into the landscape. It was not invisibility; it didn't help either when some people thought I was "getting to be a handsome young man" – except where Foley had ripped out my hair. Jane's friends and some of her students had told her: "He'd be a looker if his hair would fill in that bald area. He looks pretty good from the one side." There were a bunch of reasons why people liked me, I can't remember one of them. Danny Kryesler, the detective, said he saw something of himself in me. The guys down the North End liked me because I was Ray's brother. It was hard work burying my identity.

The 'Statesman's' carry bag helped, the school blazer helped. Wearing a baseball hat and a watchman's cap for a year helped. I wanted the anonymity, but I wanted that hair back Mrs.Foley had ripped from my skull. Hal and Jane said it would come back. At the age of 13 I had a comb-over.........I was sticking with the G.I. buzz cuts.......when there was warm weather.

Lynn Van Metter lived on the corner of O'Dell and Hawley. From the street to her house was 74 steps. I don't know who had it the worst: the milkman, the mailman, or me. Lynn and her sister had returned with their mother from vacation in New Jersey. They left a couple of days after the Speck murders. Ray and Lynn were the same age, I had known her from doing his paper route. She went to public school – R.W. Emerson. With her, I wanted to be as visible as possible. She had a younger sister – too young for anything other than to ask her if Lynn was home.

I always had a big smile for her, and she always had one for me. We started talking about rock and roll, we couldn't talk about school. There were a few kids we mutually knew; most of them went to Emerson and Gorton Jr. Highs. They were mostly guys who made it their business to be feared and respected by everyone, I knew them from The North End and the golf course; none of them lived around Greystone. She knew them from school. I wasn't getting into any more fights...........and I wasn't gonna scrap with any badass over a girl.

She told me she really liked the bad boys of rock and roll – The Rolling Stones. When I got home one afternoon after the papers, I asked Ray what the Stones' hits were. All I knew them for was that one hit "Satisfaction." He rattled off some so I'd have some material to work with.

"You must be talking to Lynn.........you never were keen on the 'Rolling Stones' before or is it someone else?"

"Lynn, I guess."

"Yeah......well, I thought she liked me, and ....she did like me, but only to a certain point. Good luck hombre."

"Hmmm." I scrunched my brow.

How could I be high profile with Lynn, or Tommy Capps' sisters or anyone new to the neighborhood and still be doing my disappearing act: Impossible.

With the paper route, I knew I had a leg up on everyone else about the composition and workings of our small enclave.
The bulls didn't even have a round number of the residents living down here. They showed up for 30 minutes every two days, mostly deadheading between Evan's and Day's house and the Armenian Club on Harriman. A car break-in, domestic call, or a traffic accident; they were the typical reasons for having the bluecoats visit the Greystone area. Yonkers cops didn't have jurisdiction on the railroad facilities or properties.

The mailman and the milkman substituted route men more often than the N.Y. Knicks. They were lucky if they knew which side of O'Dell they were working. There were no bars, no churches, no food joints, no gas stations, no stores, no schools; the closest commercial activity was in the North End.

The only thing the neighborhood had was Greystone Station, an ejected cosmic remnant, two paper routes, and the Hudson River.

The end of one school year and the start of the new one had me wondering where the summer went. Ray had been caddying all summer up at Hudson River C.C. Now he was coasting along in the eighth grade. I was lost in the passage of time. I needed him to help me sort out my imbalance. At first I thought this puberty crap had hi-jacked my brain. I may have stepped into a prism, an alternate reality --- but not all the way. Life's rules were not as I knew them; but they hadn't been cancelled or suspended either. Biology class says every cell in our bodies is replaced every seven years. I knew it didn't happen all at once, but it felt like something was on its way to becoming something else. There was little doubt this was a milestone in my life - it had to mean I would be getting smarter. Ray was always with me, but three worlds ahead. Maybe this move into adolescence could advance me at least one world closer. Some of the stuff he talked about was plain 'off the wall'.

iii

This change of life continued to baffle me. Ray was done with it, and I was well into it as I started 7th grade; life and the universe had reached the point of acceleration. It was biological; most people saw puberty to be function of physiology. When I considered Ray, it was only a part of the body undergoing the change into sexual maturity. For him it was more of a mental leap into a futuristic world of unsolved problems and equations. For me, a post-puberty Ray, was an undefined image, some kind of Avatar. His accelerated life was beyond my intellect. In the 7th grade I thought I might catch up; but now that I was in the 7th grade - I knew there was no way......no fuckin' way.

A significant amount of energy had to be expended during the day to get to sleep some nights.
"You're a long distance runner..........run four miles every other day and you'll be sleeping like Rip Van Winkle. Maybe by Christmastime you might be through this puberty business." He said. He looked at me sideways: "You having any of those milky discharges?"
"We just started school Ray." I shook my head. "I know all about the sex stuff from the magazines."
"Yeah......yeah - that's right."
"You can tell a guy that jizz is going to come out of his rod, but he really can't relate to it - never having experienced it. If you look at a magazine or a movie, it takes it to another level." I thought I knew what I was talking about.
"Well, did you have a wet dream yet or not?"
I gave him this "guilty as charged" face and looked a 180. "Not quite. I was about to bust my nut twice and woke up at the last second. The first time I was screwing a banister in a library."
Ray laughed pretty hard. It was ridiculous and funny simultaneously. "What about the next time?"
I instantly felt like I had just been inducted into some kind of organization or club. I wasn't inhibited at what was taking place in my body. I could joke about this stuff now instead of carrying some kind of guilt trip.
"I was riding this race horse....at the Preakness, and all these ladies got these expensive dresses and hats on and have drinks in their hands. I'm real anxious because I got this fast horse. Two of these women look like Jane's friends' and they tell me they got a big surprise for me if I win the race. I am ALL charged up. The bell rings

and the starting gate opens and we're off....... We're going around the first turn and I'm getting into the rhythm. I got my arms around the horse's neck and I'm screwing the horse or the saddle somehow. It was tied in with the horse's gallop. I never saw the finish line – never made it......woke up. The dream came around 3:45 a.m.; it wouldn't go down. I'd tried to piss to get it down - so I could get some sleep, but it wouldn't piss. It wanted to cum. I can't take a cold shower – with the pipes banging it'll wake everybody up. Pffff." I scoffed and Ray laughed.

"You should have taken that Honeymoon hardon and stroked it off. That's the only way you can get them boners to go down and get your mind free. One way or another that stuff's going to come out. If you don't whack that thing off ...... "

"What?"

"You'll be walking around with a rocket in your pocket and all you can think about is girls and women. When they see how bad you want it - it becomes an anti-magnet, and it repels the very thing you're trying to get."

"Ah fuck you man."

Ray talked and laughed at the same time he was so amused: "Yeah, God threw us a real knuckleball which nobody can hit when he laid this sex number on the human race. It's bad enough on its own, then the church has got to stick their nose in the business and make everything ten times worse than what it already was. It's retarded." Ray smiled at the irony.

I was just plain worried. "Never thought about it like that." His viewpoint didn't sit well with me.

"Now take a little advice from your big brother: what you do is become friends with a girl. You got to be friends with them first, and then get her to whack you off........as a friend. They don't want to get pregnant and they won't give you a blow-job, like they will in public school, but they just might give you a hand job, especially if her friends are older than her. She'll want to know about this sex stuff, so she can be as smart as them. If you're getting laid in high school and you break it off – it's a mess."

"Just teach them how to give you a tug job and you won't be dreaming about horses and banisters anymore." He laughed.

Most of the guys at All Souls had the traditional relationship with their fathers; not like what Ray and me had with Hal. The thought of getting the facts of life and talking sex with him would have been awkward and probably a waste of time. He wasn't smooth at all. I found out later on Jane had asked her brother when he was going to give cousin Billy 'the talk' and would it be possible to give it to Ray also. They said they got most of the information from health class when they were in the 7th grade.

Cousin Billy and Ray had this bull session with Uncle Bill about how they told you in health class you had to protect yourself against social disease. Billy and Ray wondered why the Catholic schools were teaching 'safe sex' when according to Church doctrine having any sex outside of the sacrament of matrimony was verboten.

Cousin Billy and Ray told Uncle Bill the church couldn't have it both ways without looking hypocritical.

"Listen you two know-it-alls.........you just keep yourselves protected."

WHEN THE 1966-67 SCHOOL YEAR STARTED IT WAS fait accompli my age of innocence was gone; Connie had seen to that. When something leaves, something fills the void; it may be filled by the complete opposite of what had been there. The continuum doesn't care what events fill its log books, but I cared and I didn't want Connie and Karla on my rap sheet when I got the call by St. Peter for my day of reckoning.

If I was seen not receiving communion too many times when I served mass, somebody would want to know what I had done. I decided to ask for absolution at St. Matthew's in Hastings; nobody knew me there. I already tried to give this 'Connie confession' to Father Darius at All Souls; and he came flying out of the confessional to see the viper who was the author of this degenerate sexual handiwork. There was a good chance I had committed a 'mortal sin'. I'd have to check it out with Tommy Priano, also, I'd have to get him to promise not to tell Ray.

The 7th grade had hardly started, and my head was already spinning mostly due to sex or the lack of it.

iv

My confusion with the new school year was nothing compared to the meltdown Hal was having over the All Souls uniform crisis. He was all worked up because Ray needed a new blazer. We were close in size, but we were too rough on our clothes. The only thing he handed down to me were the All Souls blazers. The one he wore last year didn't fit me too well. The sports coat was a tired piece of wool blend with sleeves. The sleeves were short to boot. Hal said it fit me fine, but the jacket was everywhere I wasn't.

Jane gave Hal a wild look, "Would you wear something that fit like this to Otis?"

"No, it'll be fine. We can squeeze another year out of it and then he'll have Ray's for next year."

"Don't worry Ryan, you should fit right in the Rag-a-muffin parade in October." Jane said.

"We're a little chipper there Jansey." He went to the kitchen to pour himself a long one.

The All Souls school uniforms were a continual flashpoint between Hal and Jane. She detested them; they had no style. Both boys and girls looked like they just got off the boat from Donegal. Jane's middle name was style and fashion; the boys' uniform was neither.

The boys' uniform was: Green Blazer w/All Souls emblem on front pocket, white shirt w/green tie, cuffed gray slacks or trousers (they were as thin as Kleenex tissue), no sneakers to be worn during class. The administration didn't take into account all of the roughhouse games we played during recess and after lunch: variations of King of the hill, kill the man w/the ball, strap, Johnny ride a pony aka: Buck-Buck.

These schoolyard games, probably long forgotten, were guaranteed to keep a kid from gaining weight. Perhaps the games were too rough. Most feel today is much better by putting a phone in the hands of a kid to play video games, watch porn, get all charged up and go back to class ready for English composition. Back at All Souls, when the temperature was above 45 degrees, we got two sessions of outdoor recess a day. A guy could blow out a pair of those cheap school-boy pants every month.

My brother was a genius; he came up with the idea of wearing dungarees with the green blazer. That move got us sent home with a warning: Blue jeans are not part of the uniform code. Hal and Jane were in a panic.

Hal called upstairs, "Hey you two – put your gray school pants on and bring your blazers down here."

Ray went down the steps with a blown-out ass which was off the seam. I was three steps behind him with my good pair of - five inch/highwater gray slacks.

Hal looked over to Mom who rolled her eyes. He looked back to Ray: "You got another pair, go put them on Elvis and come back down; you too 'Sammy Bones'." I don't know why Hal used the 'Sammy Bones' moniker, he hadn't called me that in quite a while.

He asked her, "What the hell is going on here?"

She shrugged her shoulders and looked like she bit into a lemon.

"Hey Dad, I got these black chinos I could make do with them for next few days. Ask Mom: black goes with everything......... just a thought."

Again we lined up in front of the old man: Ray's second pair of gray trousers must have been used to wipe up some 80 weight gear oil, and they had a big air vent in each knee. I didn't even go through the charade of putting mine on; they were nothing more than a network of polyester balls clinging to a shiny mesh network which somehow retained the frame of an adolescent. Hal held them up to a 25 watt light bulb; the result was similar to looking at a solar flare.

"No....no......No.......Why didn't you tell your mother you needed new uniform trousers....This can't be happening - .....can't be." Hal was almost in tears. Though none of us cracked a smile, the three of us were having a hoot.

Ray saw an opening, "We just throw 'em in the hamper Dad, we don't know how to sew."

Hal was becoming desperate, "What about Princess' blouses and jumpers ? She's set for the year – isn't that right Mother?"

"Princess?" There was another one Hal pulled from the treasure box. A three year hiatus for that gem.

Jane looked doubtful, "We'll have to hope Cathy doesn't grow too much; I had to buy a jumper that barely fits her. It was the

208

last one on the rack. Basically, she'll need a spare in January." Mom laid it on the line.

"OOOooooooh NOOOOoooooo – no…..no…..no! Don't you even comprehend basic economics? It's all about economics – from Wall Street to the kitchen table. You got to make ends meet; you've got to make do – like we did."

"During the war." Jane, Ray, and me completed his thought in vocal unison.

He poured himself another Rye whiskey and club soda. "Now where's young Bill?"

"In bed – asleep. I can wake him up if this is going to be important." She said.

Jane was looking over some of her class rosters for her coming year. The lists went to the side of her leg: "Listen – I buy all the clothes anyway. Why are you getting worked up so much?"

"That ------- is not the point! THAT…….is not the point!" He raised his voice, he was almost shouting.

"Well, they all can go to public school and we won't have to worry about uniforms any longer." Mom said.

"And no education and no discipline."

"I went to public school." Jane reminded him.

"And look at the results." He smiled, and was happy to have bested her in front of us. Just a little more whiskey and the tables may have turned. Her eyes went to slits and cast beams of payback at him.

The air was thick with something, I didn't know what else was going on between the parents, but it was a safe bet I was getting more sex with the museum banister than he was with Jane, at least on this night.

"How do I dress them for tomorrow?" She laid it at Hal's feet. There was no response. She pressed on, "Everything is closed by now, and I wouldn't buy anything from that Stan's Style Towne uniform store. Everything they have is overpriced, on back order, and Father Mahoney and the parish is probably getting a kick back to direct the school's business there."

Dad looked at Jane and smiled, "Don't you do something similar at recital time?" Hal nodded and raised his brow.

"Don't go there mister."

"Sell the kids a costume for a night's performance." He scoffed.

Jane was full of venom, "Let's stay on the subject…..and remember: My school makes it possible for us to keep 'Tobacco Road' only a place you've heard about."

Silence. I had a difficult time believing this was all coming out in front of us. They were stirring the pot, and bringing up stuff from the bottom. It was another revealing moment. It testified to some of the challenges many families faced. What was the object to the game of raising a family if it was like this? There had never been extravagance or excess in the Whitelaw household, and Hal was intent on sticking to his economic plan.

We went to school with the excuse note Hal had given Ray to give the office. He explained we were financially strapped, and already

209

had three children in the grade school. He ruled out going to school wearing dungarees, but he asked for temporary relief to substitute Black chino pants (which were nothing but black dungarees) until the weekend when we could go shopping for dress code pants.

Nothing came back from the school's echelon, and after three weeks of black chinos, Jane had found time to take us shopping. Hal said before we left: "No tissue paper pants and no Stan's Style Towne." Before we left, the old man asked, "How are those chinos working out guys?"

Jane beat us to the punch. "They're as rugged as Levi's dungarees, and cost half as much as the crap at Stan's Style Towne."

"That's the ticket then, we'll get the boys 2 pr. each of those black dunga........I mean chinos." Hal cuffed his hand over his mouth to conceal his smile. The parents were relieved they had been able to put one over on the uniform code. By October, ¾'s of the boys in the 7th and 8th grades were wearing black slacks of some variation. Nobody liked those gray cuffed old man pants - nobody wore cuffs anymore. Ray asked Hal what was the point of cuffed pants?

"It was the style back in the day; maybe they had a purpose, ask Grandpa Helmut.......maybe he knows."

Ray told me to wear any color sox as long as they're not white. "White sox are for sports.........period."

V

The first day back to school after summer vacation, we started out in our 6th grade classroom with that old battle axe Mrs. Foley.

She called the roll. "Stand up when you hear your name." She rattled off our last names. I couldn't believe she was back for another year. This was the division of the class; half would go to 7-1 and those students who remained sitting would go to 7-2. Samantha McAvoy was standing and Val Jones was sitting. Everybody got passed from 5th grade on up. The dumbbells would be passed through for the remainder of their educational careers. The teachers tried to threaten you with getting left back, but everyone knew it was all talk. If a student didn't get expelled, they were just pushed into the next grade.

"Tricolli, Twomey, Van Der Velt, Waldron, and here's a gift...........barstool Whitelaw.....I'm surprised they didn't send you back to 5th grade." The class laughed at Foley's cut.

"Okay people, go upstairs to 7-1 with Sister Alexa. The rest of you will go to 7-2 with Sister Acquila. Ray had Acquila last year. I remember he said she had lost her marbles. We heard she'd talk to the blackboard, the books, the pencils - asking the Lord why the children were unable to learn. Ray had his doubts she would make the year. A class roster of 44 students was a challenge for any instructor. The 8th graders had the new 7th graders all wised up about Sr. Acquila, and they had her on the run from the first day.

Sister Alexa however was on the other end of the spectrum. This nun was fresh – right out of the box. She showed up in the second half of last year on a substitute basis. I thought she looked like someone's older sister. Kenny Crawford asked her if she was a real teacher or a real nun, because if she wasn't either – she should be wearing a gray habit like they make the newbie cops wear...... a beginners uniform.

Sr. Alexa's eyes beaded down at his slur, she grabbed one of the long chalkboard cleaning erasers and walked lightly behind the seated Crawford.

"What's your name?" she asked.

"Kenny Crawford."

"Well Mister Crawford, just what are you insinuating?"

"I'm not saying nothin'......I'm just saying if you're a rookie – you should dress like one."

"SMACK." ----- right in the back of Kenny's head with the chalkboard cleaner. That big eraser didn't hurt, but it got you full of chalk. We all laughed, Sister Alexa did too, and then she told us to shut up. Crawford was onto something that first day back. Sister Alexa had this quarter inch wide piece of black band across the bottom of her starched white habit. The habit cut her forehead in half.

One of the girls said the ribbon must have some significance; nothing a penguin wore was for adornment or flair. It was difficult to imagine what these nuns looked like in street clothes. It was an odds-on bet - none of them got voted the Homecoming Queen in high school; it may have been why they chose to enter the convent. In street clothes, it was impossible to say what they might have looked like, but in the penguin outfit, all the public really got back then was the face and the outline of the body. Alexa was the youngest nun I had ever seen, and by default - the prettiest. She was about the same height as I was, but she might have been a shade taller when the height of her war bonnet was taken into consideration. Sister Alexa was slight in build.

She belonged to the order of Sisters of the Sorrows. They were the template model you'd picture in your mind when someone would talk about nuns. They had been assigned to All Souls parish from the beginning when the Parish decided to have parochial education. You could see the sisters' face and hands, but not their ears, so the face was everything. Sister Alexa was the best looking teacher in grades five through eight. It wasn't close. Either something wasn't going to work out for her, or something wasn't going to work out for the school: she thought young and acted the same way. A school like All Souls wanted team players, not boat rockers. In just a little bit of time, the order would bake out any egotistical notions which involved vanity, social issues, woman priests and other 'groovy' notions. After the long year with that hatchet face Foley, this Sister had my vote. She kind of had a big nose with big pores, but her youth overrode the flaw. From my desk, she looked like the best house in a bad neighborhood.

She was not short on confidence; she even thought she'd be able to change the convent, school, antiquated attitudes about civil rights, hunger, women's role in the church, and help end that damned war in Vietnam.

211

Most of the nuns were old enough to be her grandmother. Despite her desire to change the world for the betterment of all, the old guard didn't have the time or patience to listen to this beatnik dressed up as one of them mouth off about changing the world. The Pastor put Sister Alexa in charge of the altar boys to shut her up and keep her occupied. As 1967 approached, Alexa was resigned to the reality the only things she was going to change were within the four walls of her classroom and her underwear. "What is wrong with these people? We're supposed to be in this together." She said aloud to no one in particular in the classroom.

There was plenty of steam in her engine, but she had no way to apply it to advance her vision and achieve her goals. It was a personal purgatory and morphed into an incarceration in the city of Yonkers. More and more her thoughts turned to Newton Iowa where she grew up. A job on the assembly line at Maytag with her friends didn't sound so bad lately.

vi

I started up the first few steps to Lynn Van Metter's house when I heard my name: "Ryan.........Hey Ryan –" She came running down Hawley Terrace – probably from Lisa Campagna's house at the dead end.

I got down on street level with her; she climbed up to the second step. We were face to face. Neither of us had instructed the other to adjust elevation. Her face captured what was left of the sun.

"What's up?" I smiled.

"I'll take the paper up for you."

"THAT, will definitely be appreciated."

"You decide what you're going to be for Halloween?"

My confused face met her inquiry, "Halloween? I guess I thought last year was it." I scratched my bald acreage with the paper.

"And not go this year? Your brother went last year – the same age as you are now."

I started laughing, "Ray went Trick or Treating last year.........with a can of shaving cream, a bar of soap, and some rotten eggs. He went with Ronnie Pharmer – remember?"

"Pharmer is such a jerk", she said.

"C'mon Ryan, a couple of my friends from school are going – and they're eighth graders like me." She puppy dogged.

I took a deep breath. "I gotta think this over."

"Ryyyyyan......we'll have a good time....you'll see."

"It's different for girls, they can get away with that kind of stuff. Trick or Treating like Ray and Ronnie did last year – that wouldn't be a problem, but actually costuming up?"

"It'll be wild, and I told my friends at school you were taking me."

I hadn't had a lot of interaction with Lynn, her forwardness had caught me unprepared. Last winter both Ray and me got

212

Valentine cards from her. We always said "Hi", but the only thing we really had to talk about was music.
When Ray had the route, he had the opportunity to get things going with her. He said the physical attraction was there.

I waited to watch their sparks fly and see how this boyfriend/girlfriend stuff worked. It didn't happen. He said he didn't know why. At first he thought it was because he went to All Souls, but he was only guessing.

Now it was my turn at the plate; I did not want to be called out looking. I could make my move talking to her about the Rolling Stones, but I'd need more than Keith and Mick to get to first base.

Every chance I had, I shot her 'THE LOOK' .....seldom with a smile. Shoulder length brown hair, light brown eyes, a nice set of bumpers; what attracted me most was her smile and her teeth. She had this Dracula smile. The bottom eye teeth were prominent in relation to the others. The two upper teeth guarding the buggs bunny ones, were longer and pointed as well. They were set outside of the otherwise straight run of teeth. When she gave me a big smile, I was mesmerized and could think of nothing but surrendering my neck and whatever else she might want to take. Both Ray and me sensed Lynn was self-conscious about her grill. She told us individually she was going to get braces to bring her canine teeth to line up with the others. Ray called her 'Draculynn'. As far as I was concerned, her smile was her calling card; I had a hard time looking at her other features when all I could think of was getting the blood sucked from my neck.

"Is this some kind of date or something?" I asked.

"No.......not some kind of date, but it might end up being something." She made her eyes wide. "We're going 'Trick or Treating'............together. It'll be fun." She gave me the teeth.

That was it.

"Say Lynn, I'll go with you, but let's not tell anybody, I don't want word all over the hill that I'm still 'Trick or Treating'."

"Nobody down here goes to All Souls – just your brother." she said.

I squinted my left eye down thinking. He was the only one who could bring this news up the hill or even spread it around school. I didn't give it too much thought, he wasn't into spreading dirt around. He might not even find out I was going to do Halloween with Van Metter. Ray already had his turn with Lynn, if anything he'd build me up instead of trying to take my place. When Lynn knew he had given up the chase, they just became friends. If he wasn't friends with her, he would never have seen 'The Draculynn' smile again. Also, if he stayed pissed off because she didn't want him for a boyfriend, it would mean he'd have to avoid her. Losing her smile out of pride, ego, or spite – that was plain dumb.

"Her smile will last 20 years in your memory banks, and if she likes you for a boyfriend, add another 10." My brother was right about that, those fangs are still non-stop.

"Ryan, what about your costume?" She smiled.

"I hadn't even considered doing any Halloween stuff. Maybe I can get an idea from yours – what are you going as?"

213

"I'm not going 'as' anything; I'm going to 'be' a butler. It's a stupid costume, but the costume is not being a butler – it's - I'm dressing up as the incorrect sex. It's pretty wild!.....I'd say." A crazy look came over her face. "Why don't you go......as a girl?" Her eyes got big and dared me. Something was going on that I knew very little about.

"We'd both be taking chances." She could feel my reticence. There was a lot of down side to this date now, and there had to be more than walking around collecting candy. Somewhere it had to lead to making out like Connie and me did, or maybe just feeling her up. There was no upside to walking around in a female persona. Too big a risk of Hal and Ray finding out and calling me sissy or worse:

'Your father says you look better as a girl than you do as a boy, and your brother wants to fix you up with one of his friends.......'

I took a long look at Lynn: "I don't know – Trick or Treat - I can do. I don't know about being a girl." I shook my head.

"Your Mom owns a dancing school – she should have all sorts of costumes. She's must have wigs and stuff to complete our combo costume – to make it real?"

"She's got an attic full of that stuff from shows and recitals."

"I've got a real neat idea: if you could get a French maid thing together – that would be perfect. I'm the British butler and you'd be the French maid. I'll glue some cups to a tray and you bring a feather duster.......please? Ryan?......We'll have such fun." She gave me the teeth.

"No promises Lynn – I'll come up with something."

She was overwhelmed with excitement, she got jittery and her eyes flashed: "My parents are going to a party and my sister is doing Halloween with the Gunther sisters.....Meet me right here before dusk.........before the black cats come out." She howled like a cat and her hands clawed at the sky. Slowly her head turned towards me and peered through my eyes and straight to my heart – her Draculynn smile upset my equilibrium. I looked at her ready to kiss her before she left. I closed my eyes and tried to embrace her. When there was nothing there, I saw her scurrying up her steps with the newspaper.

"Shit." Running up to the next house on my route, I strained my eyes to focus, but I kept envisioning Lynn with a witches hat, stirring a cauldron of 'Love Potion #9'. Running as I delivered the papers, I ran out of oxygen; just couldn't catch my breath. More and more air filled my lungs. I threw a paper on Mrs. Sachs' porch, went through the backyard and up the short steep hill leading to the aqueduct with 15 papers in my hand. I crossed the trail on top and dashed into the woods. Many of the leaves had fallen; there wasn't much cover. A quick 360 degree scan, I unbuckled my belt, undid the waist button, and zipped down. It had already found its way through my boxer's fly. The papers fell into the fallen leaves and I started waving it all about trying to get rid of the loaded spring. That boner was stiff for the next 15 minutes as I tried to calm down. Though I had my eyes open, all I saw was Lynn's face.......smiling. "Sonofabitch !

214

This fuckin' thing won't back down." I got to get these papers done –
dammit. I complained to the fallen leaves.

I knew the basics from the skin magazines still hidden under
the washing machine top. Ray would tell me whatever I needed to
know. What was this clear stuff coming out? It wasn't piss or jizz.
Maybe when the unit got all bent up, this clear stuff squeezes out. I put
the unit straight up towards my belly button and used my boxer's
waistband to restrain it in a way where I could get the rest of these
papers delivered.

I took the aqueduct to O'Dell and did 45, and then delivered
the rest of the route backward.

THAT EVENING AND THE NEXT DAY AT SCHOOL, I
couldn't escape her. Yesterday's episode at the end of Hawley Terrace
with Lynn Van Metter were hammering me with some devastating
images. Lynn was no woman like Connie or Karla. It wasn't likely I'd
see the Connie again, and Karla never spoke to me except about
newspaper business - if at all. Some Fridays there was only an
envelope with "Paperboy" written on it - clothes pinned to the
mailbox. What was with this Hawley Terrace ? How could it change so
much in such a short time?

It was dark when I got home. I went right up to the attic and
began going through Jane's monsta boxes of costumes. I didn't know
what I was looking at or for; what was the front or back, what
stretched and what didn't. I'd have to come clean with Jane and get her
advice after I finished my papers tomorrow.

That night, Ray and me lay in our beds. I was lying on my
side thinking of Lynn with my back towards him. "You awake?"

"Of course." He never slept and I could never stay
awake.

"Watcha think of Lynn?" I asked.

"She's pretty sharp I guess. She helped with some math
problems on ratios last year." He said.

"She asked me to go Trick or Treating with her……..told her
I'd go. Ray - you don't need Lynn to help you with math – you've
always been a whiz in it."

"I wasn't having any math problems; I just wanted to try and
get something going with her……to see if there was any electricity."

"Well, she's got me boxed; I'm hung up on her."

"It's easy to get hooked by her. We were only together a
couple of afternoons and we met in the apartment's garage. She didn't
want to come over our house and she didn't invite me up to hers, so we
went down Greystone in the overpass. I brought my math workbook
for show, but we started talking about music. I told you how it played
out for me."

"Who did you say your favorite band was?" I couldn't
remember who he said.

"Who is the antithesis of the Rolling Stones?" he asked.

"Who's the what of who?"

"What band is the opposite of the Stones……you know…
the anti-Stones?"

"Got to be the Beach Boys – they're the best." I said.

"Not to Lynn........Just tell her you like the Rolling Stones. That's your best bet if you really like her."

"But you like her.......I mean she's good lookin'.......right?"

"Do you want to be her steady boyfriend............you're too young for that..........I'm too young for that. If you just want to sneak her over to our house when no one's home, or her house.....that's probably the best move you can make."

"I don't know anything about this girl stuff, but it's always got me thinking, and with Lynn with those fangs and those crazy eyes.............I don't want to screw it up."

"Take her to a dance up at Emerson."

"She doesn't walk to school; I doubt she's going to walk to any dance with me."

"You can make out with her on the way home. Say... aren't you a little past this trick or treat business?"

"Yeah, but so's she. As long as Draculynn is my candy collecting partner, you can make fun all you want. At least I'm not going with Ronnie Pharmer like somebody I know last year." I laughed.

"That was a miscalculation. What's Lynn going as?"

"A waiter or a butler.....something like that."

"The costume is the male persona.....not the occupation."

"Right."

"And you?"

"Ahhh......thinking about going as a Beatle – Mom's got those wigs, drumsticks, and phony rings.....go as Ringo.....can't go wrong?"

"That'll be okay: black turtleneck, black sportcoat. John, Paul, and George are better looking than you anyway." I laughed and tossed my pillow at him."

CLASS WAS UNEVENTFUL ON HALLOWEEN; THERE wasn't any need for me to be wasting my time up there after school. The guys in my class were committing themselves to minor acts of vandalism to celebrate the eve of All Saints Day. I bragged I was going to shoot out some street lights with my wristrocket to make the mood dark and spooky. Anything I said I did in the Greystone neighborhood was unverifiable. None of my classmates were talking about getting costumed up to fill a bag with candy, which is probably what they ended up doing.

Halloween fell on a Tuesday in 1967, so Catholic schools had Wednesday off. It was just the most odd day to have off. It really screwed up Jane and her day care for Cathy and Brother Bill. I think she ended up paying Ray to babysit for the day. She just didn't want anybody to use the stove – NO COOKING! All Cathy and Billy ate was Halloween candy. We were supposed to go to church for All Saints day, but Jane let it slide.

While he was in charge of the house, Ray was already thinking about this holiday, and all holidays in general. He thought the government, Christians, and Jews should eliminate Wednesdays from

216

being holidays. If a religion or the government had a holiday to observe or acknowledge; by law - all holidays would be celebrated on Thursday, Friday, Monday, or Tuesday. This way people got either a three or four day weekend. I was well aware the golfing season was over, but from Ray's perspective, which applied the golfing slant: long weekends translated into more loops.

He wasn't stopping there; he came up with this brilliant observation about 'Leap Year'.

"Just who was the genius who figured out we needed another day of winter?"

The calendars had been nicking us every year; the seasons and the calendars were getting out of sync to the tune of one day every four years. "Somehow the church gets control of the science of time and makes the necessary adjustment to add the day every fourth year." He asks me: "Why did this poppin pope decide we needed another bloody day of winter?"

Cathy and Brother Bill ignored Ray and continued watching 'Space Ghost'. The argument came to me......."Ryan, don't you think we'd all love to have 31 days in June once every four years?"

"I'm sure when Brother Bill celebrates his birthday on June 30th and he is of drinking age, he will appreciate having every fourth birthday followed by a day with no date."

"I'm doing it for you Willis." Ray said. He kept watching 'Space Ghost' and waved acknowledgement. "Don't you think everybody would enjoy June 31 or September 31 ?........ Better still, let the world call a big time out – a 24 hour time out, somewhere in the summertime. A day with no date, no work, no school; the only people permitted to work would be the ones to save life, limb, or property. The money hungry maniacs will just have to take the day off."

"Makes sense to me." Still, something wasn't squaring up with the matter, "Why'd they stick it in February in the first place?"

"Aaaaay, the pope said Easter wasn't working out the way he wanted, he had to have Easter spot on. It would have worked out if he could have waited a year.....un-uh. It's added up to nearly 125 extra days of winter – if anyone is interested since the Church screwed with the calendar."

"That's bullshit man...... fuckin' bullshit!" The kids turned around to see what caused the cursing.

Lynn never said anything about church or religion; I don't think it meant anything to her. She knew I was Catholic and left it at that.

School let out. I had to get home as fast as I could and to get the papers delivered. I'd try to get this costume business resolved. It had been driving me nuts all day. Lynn was going to be a Maitre`d or a butler......and she wants me to be a French maid? Shooting out street lights with the slingshot had a lot more John Wayne appeal. There was some face saving with Lynn dressing as a guy, but I had sensed she really wanted to do this tandem costume. If I was to show up as a pirate or a hobo: my usual, I may as well meet her wearing Beach Boy white chinos and a candy stripe shirt, a big wave of hair, (which I no longer had thanks to Mrs. Foley), and carrying a surfboard. It looked like I was going against the grain.

As I hurried home, I knew I needed Jane's help. I had to explain to her about Lynn's costume and how it was going to be a combo-costume deal. I had to come clean and ask her if she had any French maid outfits. She lifted a risqué number from one of the shows she choreographed; it had a line of women in maid's outfits and she put it in her recital a couple of years ago. Odds were favorable I could remain undetected for the three or so hours of 'trick or treating'.

I took all the short cuts home and walked like someone was chasing me. It might have been a record. Everyone was home except for Hal; Otis was not interested in Halloween hi-jinx, he got home at his regular time.

"Why are you here so early Mom?"

"Where were you?"

"Took the short cuts."

"I probably would have seen you if you took the regular way home. I got Ray and Cathy from school and Judy's bringing Billy and her two boys over to go trick or treating with us.

"Huh?"

"My last two classes are private lessons, and they both cancelled."

"I still have to do my paper route. Lynn Van Metter and me are going 'trick or treating'. I need a wild costume – probably something from the attic. Is there something you can think of?"

Some kids were about collecting candy already. I did the paper route in record time. The private houses slowed me up a bit, but I turned on the afterburners to get started on my costume.

The sun was setting fast by Oct. 31st; 45 O'Dell got the last one.......as usual. Our house was a beehive of activity; Ray put on a Lone Ranger mask – the rest were street clothes. Later I saw him down Hudson Park with Ronnie Pharmer smoking Viceroy's and shaking down kids for their candy.

Jane had Cathy made up as a miniature Geisha Girl: kimono, slippers, and a jet-black wig. Brother Bill was as bad as a four year old Frankenstein could be. Judy had brought her two boys over because her neighborhood was too rough. I was hoping they wouldn't see me in whatever costume I ended up in.

It was almost dark a little after 5 p.m.; daylights saving time ended three days earlier. Judy had to get her two boys costumed up.

"Mom, you don't have anything in the attic that might work for me tonight?"

"You got to give me some kind of idea. She goes to Emerson Jr. High?"

"Yeah..Yeah...Yeah....and lives down the street from Tommy Capps...on Hawley. Lynn Van Metter – she going as a butler."

"Have I met her?"

"Mom, it really is getting late."

"You know it's just about all girls' stuff in the attic. You don't want to go as a female, but it might get you out the door the quickest."

"Got anything like a French maid?"

My inquiry had caught Jane by surprise and her face registered mild shock: "I had those outfits a couple of years ago – but they were for the adult class. Their husbands and boyfriends made them take those costumes home." She chuckled.

"You see Mom, she's the butler – and I'm the maid. I got to do this in like 15 minutes.

"I can put something together, but it's going to take time; plus I've got to do your face and hair."

"No, that's not going to work. What else do we have?" I was desperate.

"We've got Indian Princesses, Honey Bees w/antennae, sailor girls, and Kit Cats."

"I'm already late." I said.

"Welcome to the Kit Cat Club Ryan."

This Kit Cat deal wouldn't have the stigma of an outrageous French maid outfit. I'd just have to spin some b.s. and tell Lynn I couldn't find one. The cat costume wasn't a French maid, but she might be able to accept it and not be disappointed. This black cat might even conjure up images of Friday the 13th, broken mirrors, $50 bills, and hats on a bed. With Lynn I could be a docile companion for a butler, nudging my body against hers looking to be petted. If any guys came along and exposed my disguise, I would turn into a ferocious black panther. I didn't want to turn into a killer cat unless I was unmasked, but a Kit Cat costume was definitely not a French maid's. I didn't think the line of being a sissy had been crossed.

Jane had me sit on a stool as she applied the make-up and did the fake hair. She had this thick braid of hair on a band which fit around my head and was crowned with a skullcap with ears. The body of the cat outfit was where it got sketchy. It was all black tights: the top had long sleeves, bangles on the wrists, a silver bangled triangle on the chest, and it had this three snap crotch which brought the front and the back together. The bottom of the Leotard had feet, and from the butt they had sewn or glued a three foot cattail.

"What about shoes?" she said.

"I was going to wear my low black cons."

"Do they have white laces - ?"

"Huh?"

"Nothing………..Put the Leotard bottoms on without your boxers, then put the cat's cap with the ears on. The Leotard top is a little tricky, you shouldn't have an undershirt on. Get your sneakers on we'll see how it looks."

I ran upstairs thinking: Doesn't matter how it looks – it's going to be good enough. I searched the closet for my sneakers. One of the pharma bottles had been hidden in the
left sneaker, and I had upset it. Some of the ash escaped from the yellow pharma container because I hadn't screwed the top down tight

219

enough. Before I melted onto the floor I do remember the ash particles being displayed in a specific pattern.

When I regained continuity with this dimension, I still held a sneaker in one hand and the remaining ash in the plastic container. How long I was in the closet would have been a guess at best. My timetable and that of reality were not in sync. A few years down the road I made the determination I had entered the same kind of Salvador Dali pole reversed reality where I had been earlier when we first encountered the comet. Time, as I knew it, had ceased to exist and had accelerated where I thought days had passed.

I looked at the objects in my hands, and looked at the alarm clock on Ray's desk. "What a Halloween......" I said, and tried to focus.

CHAPTER 11
i

"Ryan…..Ryan….Hurry up – you're going to be late."
Jane came back from the kitchen with my Kodak instamatic camera.
She probably used it more than I did.
"Okay…" I shouted downstairs.
Nothing was for certain. I blinked my eyes and knocked
above my ear with the heel of my palm. I looked down; I had one low-
black converse sneaker on, the other was in the mix of the other shoes
and sneakers. Some of the comet's ash had spilled out; some was on
the tongue and some was still within the sneaker with the pharma
bottle. The hell with this Halloween crap; I had to take inventory of the
ash I thought I had: the ash in the sneaker, the dungarees, and the
yellow plastic jar was poured out on my desk. Tapping the sneaker's
heel on the top of the desk, the amount of ash I retrieved made me feel
a little better. I kept a cigar box filled with junk in one of my desk
drawers, and dumped its contents out and pushed the junk as deep into
the drawer as possible. The cigar box would be the cosmic dust's new
temporary home. Better containers had to be somewhere in the house.
Ray said the stuff was too valuable to store the way I had. What I had
witnessed with the trains last summer, I should have been handling it
like Plutonium 231. The amount of cinderash in the cigar box had me a
little worried; I shook my head - aware I had lost some since the night
of the fireball's entry. Getting this stuff inventoried and securely stored
would be job one tomorrow.
        Before I left our room I looked in the dressing mirror: I saw a
female Kit Cat. The alarm clock read: 5:31. I had been in that other
world in our closet for close to 2 days by my calculation, and I did not
recognize the image in the mirror.
        "The call came up the stairs again: "RYAN…….we're going
to be leaving soon."
        "This Kit Cat is all bunched up." I said aloud as I wriggled
around trying to get it to look right.
        A quick look in the mirror, 'Damn, Jane's given me this Kit
Cat get-up, but I look more like a girl than I do a cat'. I went
downstairs and waited for someone to say something.
        Mom took a picture of Ray, Brother Bill, and me on the
staircase. She told Ray she wasn't going to waste any more film on
him in his Lone Ranger mask. Cathy, the little Geisha, in her Kimono
got three pictures. Billy and me got two pictures, but only one came
out.
        The streetlights had been turned on, but there was still a little
light left. We were all anxious to go. Before Ray left, he said I looked
ridiculous. After his pronouncement, everyone had a good laugh on
me: Judy and Cathy, Brother Bill and Judy's boys. Jane wasn't
satisfied; before she let me out the door, she had me stand in the
kitchen where there was some decent lighting. She had me walk
around the room twice.

"Your tail isn't right. Stay right here."

"Mom.....I'm late." I gave the reply a whine.

"It's almost there. You need this short elastic pleated skirt, or put your jock-strap on. The coup de grace was Jane's taped on falsies.

"Why do I need to be a girl cat?" I looked at them under my Leotard; every guy was going to notice this rack.

"That's show bizz." She laughed.

"Yeah – that's show bizz and I just crossed the line."

"What's that mean?"

Judy and her boys couldn't wait any longer and they said they would be working our side of O'Dell and they'd meet them on the way back up. Billy was cracking up.

"Meeeooooow?" I said trying to emphasize the feline over female.

The skirt started at the waist, but was short enough to keep the tail in full view. Thank God I wasn't anywhere near All Souls; the guys would make me take gym class with the girls. I wouldn't have worn this costume up there.

"Do a spin." She smiled, "You look great. Bring an extra bag – I think you'll fill two bags up for sure." She gave me a black cloak for warmth. "Leave the front open and you'll get more candy." She said.

The sooner I got into the stream of Trick or Treaters the better I would feel. 'What the hey I thought – it's just one goofy night.' If the family and Judy and her kids had been where I had just come from, they wouldn't be making such a big deal about Halloween. I looked away from Hal as he passed me on our front walk. The disguise worked.

My eyes scanned up and down the hill on both sides of the street. My plastic pumpkin was empty except for the rubber rat inside. My other hand held my tail tight for security as I ventured down O'Dell. If I saw someone I knew, the cat would scurry across the street. The costume had blackmail written all over it.

In some manner, the Kit Cat provided the same anonymity as being the paperboy. The clothes, hair, make-up, and accessories often matter a great deal to the people on the street. Walking through life in costume; the level of invisibility received - never equaled the amount of effort invested, but it was a real blast being the voyeur with the all-access pass. It was learning about life with a kink to it. I don't know where it came from, but I heard it first from Danny Kryesler: "Cheap thrills are the best thrills, and they're the only ones you'll remember." He had to be speaking from experience.

From Mrs. Hillman's side of the street, I spied the Halloweeners. Hal always hated this night, and left the lights off and never answered the doorbell. Quickly, I went back to our side of the street and made my way to Hawley. In the mix, I was officially a celebrant along with the witches, ghosts, princesses, robots, Batmans, and a few Boy Wonders - no butlers yet. I went to the Conroy's door. There were three 4th or 5th graders ahead of me and I fell right in line behind them. Mitch had been manning the action. It had gotten so busy, he had made up a shaker of some cocktail, and sat on the porch to hand out the candy. I stuck out my pumpkin, he never even looked at me. He just dropped the candy in. At least I had a 3 Musketeer and a Nestle chocolate bar to eat while I waited for Lynn at the bottom of her steps.

The steps provided some more anonymity: seated on the Van Metter steps, my height became a non-feature. A handful of 8th and 9th graders from Emerson had already given me the once over – twice. Nobody was going up Lynn's steps for a Crunch bar or a junior packet of M&M's. Her parents had left 2 plastic pumpkins at the bottom – one on each side. A note was taped to each: "HONOR SYSTEM – only two treats per ghost". Hard to say where her parents were from. That honor system crap worked as long as you were out of sight of a Manhattan Skyscraper. Tommy Capps said the Van Metter pumpkins had been picked clean 5 minutes after it had gotten dark.

Cathy and Brother Bill said every year they passed Lynn's house, the pumpkins were always empty. Same note.......same empty orange pumpkins. Ray and me didn't think Lynn was dumb like her parents; in fact we thought the opposite. Nobody was going to climb those stairs to see if there was more candy at the top – especially the parents with little kids. There were no lights to illuminate the way. None of the house lights were lit either. It was a two story house with an attic and a cellar. Dark brown cedar shake shingles were used for the siding. The neighborhood called it the "House on Haunted Hill". Even Draculynn referred to it as "Dark Shadows" after the TV show.

Safety in numbers gave me the courage to get off my butt to beg for candy at the private homes where I could keep my eye at the bottom of the Van Metter steps. I followed a throng of unescorted kids, held my tail and presented my quarter-filled pumpkin for donations. Distraught, I returned to Lynn's house and sat down and jumped up from the steps: "Whoooooooaaaa!" I sat on a bottlecap.

A small group of three and four year olds walked by with two adults. "Yeow.... Mister, do you know what time it is?"

"It's 7:45.......only an hour and a quarter left." He said.

I put my paws under my chin, "Meow." I replied. 'Ahhh shit.' I jittered. 'Stood up on my first date'.......probably never have another chance with her again. What'd I do wrong?' I looked up Hawley and then over to O'Dell. Nothing. I couldn't do any real candy collecting for fear of being exposed in the Kit Cat uniform, but more importantly – I'd be sure to miss Lynn. There was no alternative but to climb the steps and try ringing her doorbell. Taking a peak in the windows was probably useless; the house was dark........I rang the bell one more time and started walking back down the steps to the street. This Halloween crap ended up being a waste of time and reality.

There were a couple dozen stairs to the street when this guy in a leather motorcycle jacket charged right past me and knocked me into some scrub grass. I didn't get a good look at him, but he wasn't anything close to being a butler. When I got back on the concrete stairs, it became clear he was most likely the reason Lynn had stood me up. With Cat-like speed I overtook this guy at the porch. The two of us were bent over with our stiff-arms on our knees. We faced each other down. I hadn't a clue who this guy was. The darkness didn't help and it was impossible to discern if this guy was in some kind of costume. There was a prolonged silence which I broke: "You pushed me off the stairs ya jerk - Who are you?"

"Hey I live........." Confusion. "................Ryan?"

"Huh?" Recognition was slowly coalescing; "Are you Lynn's brother or something?"

The motorcycle guy started laughing.

"Lynn......that's you isn't it – you're Lynn Van Metter." It was too dark to see her facial features. I recognized the voice.

"Ryan.......are you a cat?"

"Yeah my Mom talked me into it, and then she did the make-up."

"Let's go inside, I'm freezing out here."

"Hey – I'm the one with the skirt."

ii

"One of the disadvantages of female attire." The greaser took the cat by the hand to the rear entry of the house.

"Even with this cat vision, I can't see a thing."

"No one's home. My sister's with Amy and Susie Gunther. When they finish, they're going over to their house and go through their treats. She's supposed to call around 9:30, and I have to go get her. My Mom and Dad are at a party, they'll be back late."

She turned the lights on down the cellar and led the way. "Come on." She gave it the all-star Draculynn smile.

The two entered a spare bedroom/playroom. It was cluttered with books, games, a few dolls, and a mannequin. A matched series of mirrors stood in an incomplete semi-circle. It revealed perhaps a 270 degree view of a person. On the interior face of the room's entry door was another full length mirror which allowed the person to see themselves from behind.

"Be right back."

"Ryan asked: "Are you changing out of costume?"

"Do you want me to?" The greaser put on a sexy face.

"I don't know – I want what you want", the cat said.

"Then I won't."

"Yeow." Followed by some purrrring. The cat clawed an imaginary post.

"Be still, and I'll bring you down a bowl of milk." The resident biker grinned.

The cat looked at the reflection in the mirror, its mother had made an amazing transformation, although the feline didn't see the need for the falsies she had taped on at the last moment. Studying its own reflection, the cat was overcome by what it saw.

"Damn !...........that is one crazy lookin' cat."

Lynn in leather came down the steps with a can of beer in each hand. "Here 'Midnight'.......sssspspsssppss." she handed the cat the beer, catching him by surprise.

"What did you call me?" the cat's head tilted to the side.

"Midnight seems right. You really play the role well."

The cat got its first good look at the biker in the light: black T-shirt, shiny black faux-leather pants, and a real leather motorcycle jacket. She tossed the Marlon Brando motorcycle cap with brim onto a cushioned wicker chair. Her hair was all slicked back with wave set and bobby pinned up into a DA; the wave on top patted down for the greaser effect.

The mirrored area was filled with light. They stood face to face, and back to back, then side by side. They alternated, trying more variations, both in profile in the same direction; next they did an – about face. The two were getting all charged up just looking at one another. Their desire was at the border. The cat attacked, grabbing the human by the hips, Lynn's arms went over Ryan's shoulders and his tongue went in her mouth. The kiss lasted all of two minutes.

Midnight was panting and whispered, "I've got to use the bathroom."

"The door next to the laundry sinks.............Are you going to squat and pee, or will you use the kitty litter box?" She gave the cat a teasing smile.

The feline leaned back against the door; purring and squeezing its eyes tight. Midnight pulled down the short red skirt - just above its knees. He reached under to the three snaps of the Leotard's crotch and undid them. It sprang out wildly and waved like a castaway on a desert island. Looking down at that boner, the cat knew the thing would have to go back undercover. It might be possible to cup a handful of water from the toilet's tank and cool it off so it wouldn't be so prominent. The cat's dislike of water had to be considered, but after a moment's thought - the option was discarded. The cat's physical expression of desire wasn't giving up, and was vented to run out the left side of the Leotard with the elastic of the leg's opening's digging into it. The red skirt barely hid it. The cat hoped for the best exiting the toilet.

"You certainly went all out with your costume. Was it for me?" The biker drew closer to the cat. "I must apologize for being late. I didn't get this leather jacket until after six o'clock."

"This is my last 'Trick or Treat'........I figured I'd go all out."

"Really Ryan, I had no idea it was you until I heard your voice. Your mom must have helped with the great costume – and look ....you've sprouted a beautiful pair of tits." She reached to his chest and fondled the feline's falsies. "Nice – come over to the dressing mirrors." The biker led Midnight by the hand.

Once again, the greaser led the cat into various poses. They faced one another and kissed again. The cat purred into her ears; first one then the other. They were picking up steam. Greaser was fumbling around trying to access the ad hoc boobs. In a matter of seconds, she knew she was dealing with a "onesie". As the cat sucked on the lobe of

225

her ear, she looked down and saw Midnight's protruding unit. "This cat is ready." The biker's eyes sparkled. The cat watched the images in the mirrors.

The biker jacket was flung over to the day bed against the wall. A pack of Kool's had been rolled into the left sleeve. The greaser's melons were larger than the Kinky cat's fake ones..... once she removed the back brace she wore to restrain them. The cat placed its paw on her back, and the other up the biker's Tee shirt and felt up her breasts with its claws retracted. Fondling each in turn, it dialed in the greasers nipples. Lynn moaned, and Midnight breathed hard as they kissed. The wild one stared at the cellar's unfinished ceiling, "Oooooooh." And stuck her tongue in the cat's human ear and gently bit into the lobe. They began to make out; he made the move and pulled the greaser's Tee-shirt over her head and threw it on the day bed with the leather biker jacket. Now the cat pulled all of its Tomcat equipment through the left leg of the Leotard onesie. The young woman stood there naked except for the faux leather pants.

This midnite rider knew her feline companion was monkeying around with its costume; however she was startled with the cat's showmanship of its equipment. With its unit ready, Midnight was trying to stroke the biker's crotch over the fake leather. The Biker pushed the cat away, looking at her Halloween partner; "Well, it certainly is proud. What should we do?"

"We should make it go down. A real big bad greaser would know that."

"Oh, I know a lot." She stepped back to get a good look at the cat's front tail, she got a hold of it, looked at him and smiled. The Biker marched the black cat around like she was pulling a red wagon. The cat was positioned opposite the center mirror. She knelt and silently studied his front tail and looked up at Kinky Cat. Again they laughed. Greaser pushed the head down for a couple of seconds and let it spring back up.

"Sonofabitch....." The cat shook its head accepting the fact his unit was on automatic pilot. The Midnite rider concurred and continued playing springboard with the cat's sex toy – holding it down and letting it spring back at least a dozen times.

"Stay there." She got up and opened one of the beers she brought down. The beer was sipped and she continued to play springboard with the Tomcat aspect. It was fighting back not to stay down. "Let me know when it starts feeling really good to you." she said.

"It's starting to feel..... real....real good to me."

The girl greaser looked up at the cat. He was in trouble. He was close. She got up and the two were face to face in lockature.......transfixed. It was time to do something. She put her hand on the back of his head and forced his face into hers. Snaking her tongue as far as possible into his mouth, her hand began working back and forth – almost as rapidly as Midnight's breathing. This cat had to get out of her killer kiss. He wasn't getting enough air. She leaned her head back to look at him; his eyes were shut.

"Krazy Cat." She summoned.

226

Ryan looked at her and she showed him the Draculynn fangs. Midnight's kinky cat eyes went to full exposure and he was devastated. The Draculynn teeth went to the meat of his neck, she didn't sink them in, but started working on giving him a hickey which had more suction than a deep space 'Black Hole'. He held her ass cheeks tight; and the speed of her stroking increased.

Though he had an experience this summer, this was so far removed from the Karla and Connie show; it made this Halloween seem other worldly. She used her hand on the back of his head to let him know the hickey was her mark on him. There was a real temptation to four fang his neck, but it was too early.

Ryan was losing it.

She was shining up his cane real good; saliva oozed from her mouth and the Cat's neck. Twenty seconds later she directed his dick to the side as the goo shot all over. She kept stroking the cat and she had her hand in her pants getting herself off. Kinky Cat meoooowed to the ceiling. He thought the orgasm was as bizarre as the cinderash abduction earlier this evening.

"Fuckin' 'A'...... What the deuce was that? That was the best thing that ever happened to me."

"You were a virgin."

"Didn't I do it right?" The cat scowled.

"A big blast like that and all that love potion that shot out......I had a good time too." The biker smiled.

"Anything you want me to do to or for you – I'll do it. I'll do anything you want I'll even lick your......." The cat almost went somewhere it hadn't planned.

The feline asked, "Is the first...........Am I the first one you've been with outside the underwear?"

"You mean are you the first female cat I've seen with an anatomy that belies the essence of being female?" She played it straight, but they both ended up laughing.

"Are you asking me if this is the first dick I've seen?...........No it isn't. I must have given my cousin three hand jobs a week when we were on the Jersey shore this summer."

The cat looked downhearted, "I don't have any girl cousins." It said.

"This was your first orgasm Ryan?"

"Meow.....Meow." The cat licked its front paws.

The midnite rider went to the make-up table, and brushed her hair and put it in a pony tail. She now looked like a young woman with no top. Midnight made his way over to shirtless Lynn and began flicking her nipples as it would lap up a saucer of milk. Kinky Cat thought this kind of fun might land an altar boy a place in between Nero and Caligula shoveling coal. Kinky Cat would have to worry about that later.

"Let's do it again." The Cat was still quite randy and its equipment for making little kittens: at the ready.

"First, I've got to have a cigarette and another beer and we'll have to clean-up your first blast." She laughed as she looked at the floor: "Bad Cat.....BAD."

227

They shared the cigarette, but she drank the beer. It was just enough to make her take a chance. "I'll do you, but you've got to do me first."

"Sure anything – just tell me what you want."

"Halloween's over. Take your cat cap off." She led him by his front tail to the edge of the bed. Lynn pulled her leather pants down to her knees, her feet were on the floor and she laid back. "Lick my kunt." she said.

'It can't get any better' Ryan thought, as he followed Lynn's directions. She was going nuts teasing herself with his face and tongue. When it became unbearable she mashed his face and tongue into her box. First moans and squeaks, then the pleasure sounded as if Ryan had been whipping her with his tongue into an orgasmic frenzy. Lynn screamed for 13 seconds as she climaxed. Ryan was envious of her auto ecstasy overload. He didn't even know what he did. They lay in bed.

"Get me a cigarette."

She saw he was ready again. "Your next performance is going into some Kleenex. Go over to the vanity and get the bottle of Jergens lotion – we'll get the nasty stuff out of you in short order." She looked over to him, "You let me know when you're going to shoot. You make a mess on me and we're through."

He didn't know if she was serious.

She got out of bed smoking the Kool and lubed up the already stiff Ryan; she knelt using both her hands watching the show in the mirrors. "Let me know" she warned.

"Yeah...yeah....I will....I will."

Lynn didn't need to be warned, she stood up beside him and worked him with one hand and got the Kleenex ready with the other. It was over in less than four minutes.

When they came out of the post-orgasmic haze, they tidied up. "Ryan......remember – Listen to me – Ryan...not a word to anyone about tonight; not even Ray."

ii

Friday after Halloween, Ray asked to borrow ten dollars. After I had collected for the paper route, I'd only had enough to take Lynn to the movies on Saturday. It went back and forth - finally, I told him to ask Jane. His face soured and said the well was dry. He knew I had rat-holed some money.

"You know I'll pay you back – I always do. I'm tapped out right now, and the job opportunities are non-existent at the moment. The guy in charge of dining at the Hudson River C.C. said he might......might......need another bus-boy for the New Year's Eve bash, but it depends on how many tables they fill. I might get a job selling Christmas trees at that garage over in Homefield on Saw Mill River Rd. A whole bunch of maybes, and it isn't even Thanksgiving. C'mon champ." He patted me on the back and forced a smile.

"Shoulda took the money from Mrs. Hillman when we did her windows."

"Don't be stupid." Ray said.

"Didn't you get five bucks for altar-boying a wedding last week? What happened to that?"

"Ha……" he scoffed. "This scoop should be in the Statesman." His eyes stared off, looking for payback. "Know what I found out? You know we get five dollars for weddings and nothing for serving a funeral – right?"

"And nothing for any other masses – so? It's always been that way." I said.

"So Franny Caruso's uncle owns River Rest Funeral Home."

"So?"

"So Franny sees the bill for the funeral of that big shot politician who everybody was crying for." Ray said.

"Tonsils O'Toole."

"Yeah…..always hanging out at the Emerald."

"The guy ran the Yonkers D.P.W. from the bar."

"So?" I was waiting for the punch line.

"Franny sneaks out a copy of the itemized funeral bill: Coffin-$500, Body Prep-$400, Hearse-$100, Limos(2) $200 (2 car discount), Funeral director-$200, Pallbearers- to be provided by the North Yonkers Democratic Party/Club. There was also the Honor Guard, burial plot, cards for the wake etc. Next, it was All Souls turn at the trough: Priest-$50, organist-$40, cantor-$40, church-$100, altar boys (4)-$40, and a few more incidentals and add-ons." Ray asked, "Did you ever get paid for a funeral?"

"I was happy just to get out of class."

"The church charges them for the four altar boys but we never see the money. Someone's getting the money, and it isn't the altar boys. If I had all the dough for all the funerals I served, I wouldn't be asking for a loan right now. I'm just trying to take Bev Hennes to see "A Man For All Seasons" at Brandt's."

"I know you're smarter than me, but even I can see the church has been pinching the altar boys' funeral pay all this time. The altar boys have always been taken advantage of. You serve mass 'cause you want to get to heaven."

"C'mon Ry, help your brother out."

I knew I was obliged, but he could have kept the paper route.

"The word's out anyway, you're going to have to pony-up for me to forget about Your Halloween get up."

"Blackmailin' your own brother……that's chicken shit Ray and you know it. How'd you find out?"

"Louis Capps."

"Who told him?"

"Frankie Flynn. He said you were dressed up as a girl cat with ears, red beret, knockers, and swinging your tail as you walked down O'Dell. You didn't have all the female stuff on when I left the house. You were just a cat when I left." he laughed.

"I'll pound that four eyed jag."

Ray was still laughing.

"That date was worth dressing like a girl, and it was her call anyway. You would have done the same to be with that Vixen."

"Did she give you the fangs?"

"Yeah." Now it wasn't so funny........now Ray wanted to trade places.

I pulled the collar down and revealed the monster hickey. "Wow." was all he could say as he took a close look at the purple welt. She left four faint fang marks as well. "I always liked her." A short pause, "What else did you guys do?"

I couldn't betray Lynn, but with that all-star hickey on the side of my neck, I had to have a plausible explanation. "We kissed.....French kiss style, and she let me feel her up....and then......."

"Yeah....yeah.....go on what happened?" Ray looked to and fro as if a replay was somewhere around the corner. His eyes got intense and he started nodding up and down. He motioned with his hand to give him the goods.

"Like I said, she was sucking on my neck like a lamprey eel; her vampire fangs put me in a spell. It felt so good. I didn't think she was ever going to let me loose. It wasn't love, but it was an act of love." I looked at Ray and hoped he was buying it. He stared off – recreating my session with Van Metter. He wasn't interested in my non-physical appreciation for her. This was a departure from his customary thoughts and feelings for the opposite sex. The animal was coming out; it was a side I had never seen. Returning from his interpretation of Lynn and my eventful Halloween he said, "That is boss.......did she show you her monkey? Did she let you play with it?"

"Huh?" I wasn't sure what he was talking about.

"Her kunt........the thing you stick it in to go spooey. The thing in the skin magazines – her pussy."

"No, I dressed up as the cat, and she dressed up like a Harley rider." I wasn't playing dumb anymore; I was dumb.

"Did she show you her tits, or did she just let you play with them over her costume?"

"She let me lift up her shirt." I gave Ray a bewildered look.

"Did she show you the gash between her legs?" He tried again.

This interrogation had to end. I'd most likely get tangled up in some lie. "Damn Ray, I already told you we didn't do anything down there. 'Sides – all I know is what I seen in the skin books. I tried to put her hand on my salami, but she didn't want anything to do with it. It was the first time I seen a real live pair of milkers.....c'mon, it was my first date and all."

"I know.....I know; but you've got to stick with her..... she's got those Vampire fangs."

"With the Lamprey suction. I hope I dream about her tonight." I grinned thinking of my next hand-job.

He looked at me with one eye closed, "She let you suck on them?"

"I wanted to suck on her like she sucked on me." I said as I went into the back of a Lafayette speaker and got him ten dollars so he'd could go to the movies before I cracked.... and told him she had wacked me off twice that night.

230

I WAS STILL UP WHEN RAY GOT BACK FROM THE MOVIE; "How was it?"

"No matter how many times they keep trying to tell that story with Henry VIII, it always ends up with Anne Boleyn's head on a pike on the Tower's gate; only this time Sir Thomas More beat her to the block a year earlier.

From Anne Boleyn to Lynn Van Metter, Ray must have felt there was some existential cosmic thread between the two. Boleyn had bewitched Henry, and Lynn had a magnetic force dragging or pulling both of us. It was something neither of us wanted to be free of.......not yet.

I was walking on thin ice talking with my brother about Lynn. It was inevitable; I would tell him she had busted my 'cherry'. I tried to send the discussion off on a tangent.

"Before we went 'Trick or Treating', while I was getting the kat costume together; that world appeared.......that Alpha Centauri stuff – that world that didn't have explanation." Ray sat Indian style on his bed and listened.

I gazed straight ahead: "I was trying to find my low black cons in the closet and I disturbed my dungarees with the Fireball's ash. Some of it was floating in the air – not a lot. The dust wasn't random, there were patterns. It tagged along as I left the closet. Although my pair of cons were under my arm, but I still searched under the bed to find them. An image in the mirror waited for me to 'catch up.' It seemed as though time was barely moving. Though the Kat in Jane's dressing mirror didn't move, it was difficult to superimpose my likeness in the correct posture and dimensional depth; I felt like it took 10 hours for my two images to become one."

"If I didn't owe you ten bucks, I'd say you had been on one of those LSD trips. Mirror, mirror, on the wall........" He wobbled his head and crossed his eyes.

"C'mon Ray."

After a few minutes, he was deep in thought, he was back at the river – at Greystone Station. I could see Lynn was gone. Ray stared through the walls down towards where we buried the comet. "Do you think this 'cosmic intruder' is bad..........evil in nature?"

"Neutral – more or less. Some things were different." I said. "Can't be sure about anything, I think I came into contact with dust or ash when I was getting my low-cons. Maybe it activated a residual magnetic inter-phase making the magic world reoccur. It was enlightening and wild. I'm not sure of anything, but with the other meteor dust in the sneakers, when I waved them in a sweeping motion over my jeans; ripples of displacement started to control my senses."

"Waves of pulsed energy gave me the sensation of being shot through a rifled bore, until I found myself at centerpoint, a translucent tunnel, and orbiting celestial bodies – giving off shots of energy and light. There was so much to absorb, I didn't have the presence of mind to be scared. It was beyond my intellect to interpret the event on any level. It seemed to last for an undetermined length of time, I can't be sure."   "Coming back, it was through the same rotation as the initial departure……..not reversed. Back in Kat clothes, I got off the floor and faced the mirror."

"How long were you not here?" Ray tried to analyze the occurrence.

Adjusting my vision two or three times hoping to make my reply more rational: "It's going to sound like nonsense, but in earth time it felt like five minutes. In the land of enchantment it played every bit of two days."

He looked perplexed, but he still was enthralled with Lynn. "How'd she smell?"

"She was wearing something, it attracted me alright." I said.

Ray compressed his lips, and his head went from side to side. "Everyday this Fireball becomes more and more of an obsession. It should be fading, instead its grip on me increases. I don't want to be thinking about the comet; I want to be thinking about Lynn and Bev Hennes."

"Maybe the main chunk of the comet and the castoff are dissimilar in substance."

Ray latched on to something…….."No…no…..You're right – I was thinking along those same lines. It's acquired other properties and capabilities in its travels through the cosmos. Its origins may have been in a parallel universe or it may have been a piece of a star which survived a supernova event, picking up gravities as it travelled through space."

I nodded in agreement to keep him theorizing.

He started massaging his temples, "I think I'm getting a little weirded out about this comet. Been doing some investigating - asking around……and mostly reading anything vaguely connected with the object's ride through space. By chance or design – it ends up penetrating our atmosphere. The trains, your abduction by some star engergies, your transportation to some prism world where you question the reality of all you see there, and the cosmic traveler's ability to alter its mass as well as the mass of all within its effective reach, and other phenomenon we've experienced…………. something is occurring beyond traditional science. We've got cause to believe it has its own laws of physics governed by nothing we understand, and would lead a person to reason these events are incongruent with what we currently trust as being science and how this planet has operated for 5 billion years; thus creating a paradox." He nodded his head, encouraging my agreement.

I responded with a smile of an escaped prisoner. "Will I have to wait until Christmas to get my ten bucks back?"

Ray's investigation and analysis was worth the ten dollars maybe twenty, when I considered I wouldn't have to waste my time with this outer space stuff. I could waste my time with Lynn, and find new ways to amuse ourselves.

Things started going south with Lynn between Thanksgiving and Christmas. Whatever her reason was, she wasn't letting me in on the secret. They got worse by Christmas and New Year's. Saint Valentine's Day was a waste of time. She took fewer and fewer of my phone calls, and some guy from Gorton was giving her rides home in his '65 VW Beetle. Her activities rarely involved me. There hadn't been any foolin' around since the Christmas holidays.

Ray was in debt to me in early March – $60; by St. Patrick's Day – it was up to $70. A few years later, I figured out I was paying him for head shrink services. It kind of hurt when he confirmed what I knew was coming. He said, "The writing's on the wall Chico."

Saint Patrick's Day is on the 17th of March, and Ray's birthday is on the 18th. The Irish social clubs have in conjunction with the Catholic church - a gigantic Parade marching north on 5th Ave. in Manhattan. It is one big drunken debauchery. As St.Patrick was the patron saint of the Diocese, all the Catholic schools were given the day off. I started going to the parade in the 10th grade. It was pretty much a ten hour Mardi Gras where everybody got so drunk, it was an ordeal just to get back to Yonkers.

Ray was keen on this Irish holiday, he'd tell everybody he was Irish and all that nonsense, because his birthday was the next day; I guess it was okay for him. The day always had a bad vibe for me.

WHILE THE GIRLS WERE HAVING GYM CLASS, THE BOYS had health with our Phys. Ed. instructor, Father Joe Danaher. Sister Alexa would do lesson preparation in the mimeograph room. The girl's gym instructor was Miss Days. She was an older black lady who had a lot of life. People would run into her all over North Yonkers. One year she even showed up at one of Jane's dance recitals.

Hal had been Jane's M.C. for all of her recitals as far as I remember. Jane had asked Ray to take over if the Old Man couldn't tone down his drinking. Hal brought his little gym bag: he had two packs of Tareytons, a bottle of club soda, and a quart of rye whiskey. He would mix his whiskey sodas backstage in front of everybody. When Jane asked him to recognize Miss Days in between numbers, he said....... ...."It's not on the program." Miss Days had to hang around until Hal got a little looser. Everybody clapped when she stood up, even though Hal made Jane and Miss Days wait through two numbers.

She talked like "Mom's Mabley". Ray said she needed to get a new set of dentures.

Father Joe was the youngest priest they had at All Souls; he was low man on the totem pole and he drew all the junk assignments. It included being the Phys. Ed. and Health instructor for the 7th and 8th grade boys. For my money, he was a better teacher than he was for saying mass or giving sermons. Pope Paul threw him a bone when the church did away with the Latin Mass. The Latin, and yelling at people from the pulpit wasn't Fr. Joe's strong suit.

The girls had been getting the heavy duty Health instruction when class resumed after Christmas vacation; we were still playing dodgeball. They segregated the sexes: boys and girls no longer shared the gym. When they were in the gym we were in the classroom and visa versa. Fr. Joe would show up and Sr. Alexa would leave. He'd ask if anybody had any knee or ankle injuries. I think he felt I was getting beat up at home because of something administration wrote in my file. He always said to let him know if something bad was going on outside of school.

One of the things that concerned him the most was with guys lifting heavy stuff the right way - using leg power instead of our backs. After ten minutes of Father Joe's health stuff, we had 50 minutes of bull session: Who was a better quarterback _ Joe Namath or Fran Tarkenton? What's wrong with the Knicks, the Rangers, The Yankees, the Mets?" We thought it was pretty cool wasting 50 minutes talking sports.

The first week of March the class instruction started going in a different direction: "You guys know a change is coming – and you guys aren't going to be boys anymore. You're going to be young men."

"Father, I'm already there. Do I have to listen? I mean what's done is done." Frankie Falcone laughed.

"Alright....alright. Whatever state of development you're at - this is all stuff you can use to stay healthy; so listen up." he said. "You guys who have older brothers and sisters – you can see the changes in their bodies. These hormones go wild. Their voices change, facial hair, as well as hair in other places."

"Hey Father Joe do you think Ryan will get some hair to grow on his head where Mrs. Foley ripped it out last year?" 'Fast Eddie' Mason called out.

"Father Terrence said that was just a rumor." Father Joe answered.

"That was no rumor, I was there Father." Kenny Crawford testified.

"That was a year ago; maybe the change will restore it huh Ryan?"

"That's one change I'm looking forward to." I spoke down into the top of my desk.

"I think most of you guys know what I'm talking about. You guys with older brothers raise your hand." Fr. Joe counted. "The ones who raised their hands talk to the guys that didn't, and get the straight dope from them – but get it from them when you take recess. I saw this one boy grow four inches from 7th to 8th grade. Just try to take it in stride.....be kool.....don't flip out and act like a jerk."

He moved on. He wanted a hand count of how many of us played organized sports. A bunch of hands went up, and he tried using his 'sermon on the mount' skills: "If you nimrods are going to play sports – you've got to play protected. Any activity where they have

you wearing shorts – you've got to keep your manhood stuff……
you've got to keep it indoors."

"What's that mean Fr. Joe?"

"That means wearing an athletic supporter, and if you're
playing football, or if you're a catcher on the baseball team; you've got
to wear a cup. You take a fastball in the cookies – you'll wish you had
put the cup on. Protect yourselves boys…….don't let them get you in
the cookies."

The priest was on a roll, "Starting in April and for the rest of
your Phys. Ed. careers, you'll be taking showers after gym class. With
all the running and activity – you guys will be stinking and sweating.
They're going to give you an extra 15 minutes to get cleaned up. Bring
a towel and a bar of soap, the first week of April – any questions?"

Vinny Tartaglione stood up and asked: "What about the girls
– do they have to take showers?"

"Miss Days' has the girls, and it isn't anybody's business but
theirs. You guys got it? – the first week of April."

TWO WEEKS SLIPPED BY, THERE WERE RUMORS
ABOUT some 8th graders who had gone down to the parade. It caused
a pretty big dust up because some parents wanted to know how the
school could have let their kids get so wasted. The principal informed
the parents those 8th graders who had gone down the city for the
parade, had attended the parade of their own volition, and were not
under All Souls' supervision. Furthermore, it was a school holiday.

If they had just gotten drunk, it would have been forgotten,
but Denise Price was babbling drunk when they returned from the
parade and she got picked up by the bluecoats on Lake Ave. for
underage drinking and carrying a baggie of pot.

Ten students from the 8th grade were implicated as the ones
who went down for the St. Patrick's Day Parade. It became big
medicine for All Souls when it made the 'Street Beat' of the
Statesman. They reported an All Souls student was picked up for
"public intoxication and possession of marijuana." Denise was sent
down and had to finished 8th grade at Gorton Junior High. The other
nine, were placed on some type of probation which guaranteed
expulsion if there were any misconduct issues before graduation. Ray
was one of the nine.

It wasn't until the end of March when things at school cooled
off. He told me later on they all had been smoking pot, and Denise was
left holding the bag.

"What was that like?" I asked as we lay there in the dark.

"I don't even know if I got high, we were already pretty
drunk. Stupid Denise."

"Can't wait for the warm weather, Yankees and Mets will be
coming back from Florida soon. Hey Ray –What's the deal with Phys.
Ed.? What's this taking a shower business all about?"

"Didn't Father Joe explain it? The puberty change….being a
teenager…..all that biology crap. You're not asking me about the birds
and the bees bullcrap are you? You've studied those skin magazines so

much they're falling apart. In fact you should be an expert. Hell, you even know you can put it in her mouth or up her butt........if that's what she wants."

"I'm not talking about that stuff. I'm talking about the showers – you know taking a shower with a bunch of other guys. Something's off about that whole deal. Why are all these showers open? Everybody sees everybody – what's that all about?"

"I don't know – save money – probably."

I looked up at the ceiling, "You know I wouldn't think twice about being naked in front of a girl, but I'm not interested in seeing any naked guy in a shower – and I don't want him watching me. That's queer shit."

"They'll give you a hard time if you don't shower with the guys."

"For what? Who?" I scrunched my eyebrows.

"It's just the way it is at all the schools when you reach the 7th grade on. Don't make a federal case out of it. A couple of years ago they worked over this Tony Worley when he wouldn't shower up. The gym coach back then gave the rest of the guys the green light. They tossed a big towel over his head and took his drawers off and ran the cold water. He was two years ahead of me. That's the story." Ray remembered.

My brow stayed locked in disbelief. "Cause he wouldn't get naked?"

"Yeah that, plus Loki and Jimmy Blanko said he had it coming for bringing the spotlight down on everybody. They turned the cold tap wide open, and they pulled his towel away. Word worked its way around, if he had any less equipment he could have showered with the girls. I don't know; maybe the guy had a legitimate reason not to take a shower. You know what Ryan.....you see all these articles in the paper about people smoking in bed and burning down the house......."

"Yeah?"

"Well, now I know why."

"How's that?"

"Well, I'm not tired, and I'd like to have a cigarette right now."

"It still doesn't make sense to me." I shot back.

"It's just some Greek or Roman tradition: Roman baths, gymnasiums, communal shithouses, natatoriums. There's Roman influences everywhere you look." He said. "And you know what they say?"

"Yeah...........et tu Brute."

"No ya Doomkuff – When in Rome – Do as the Romans do." Ray smirked in the dark.

"Just because I'm in a gymnasium, it doesn't mean I'm in Rome."

"Don't worry about it. As long as you're not a boy anymore – no one will give you the business."

"I know I don't have to worry about that, I passed Lynn's "man test". She said I was a certified man, but had the brain of a kid.............whatever that meant."

236

A silence followed, I thought one of us was about to give in to the sandman. Ray caught a thought just before he fell asleep. "Yeah Romeo..... what's going on with you and the Vampress? I saw her the other day and she asked me if you still had the paper route."

"That dumb cluck gave me the shaft. I haven't been with her since Valentine's day. Didn't get anything off her then; it's over. When her father answers the phone – he tells me she ain't home."

I'm still attracted to her, but it's all one-way. She's with that guy with the Volkswagen.

"You got to stay in the game." Ray said.

"If she didn't have those Vamp-fangs, I would have said, "Good riddance."

Danny Kryesler had finally gotten off six straight weeks of nights. At least I could collect from him in the afternoons on Saturdays. He asked me how it was going with Lynn. We didn't have much interaction when he worked 4 to 12, now I had time to catch-up. I gave him my version of heartbreak city.

"Ryan, sounds like she's calling a new pitcher in from the bullpen. You're going up against a guy with a set of wheels in the winter, and this guy's got three years on you. Until that car is gone, you're better off trying to hook up with one of your classmates. You can't make somebody want you." the detective said.

I knew it was true, Ray almost said the exact same thing. One thing I was positive about: I really....really....really dug this girl who busted my cherry. Early on, I thought she felt the same about me.

"Hey Ryan, think you'll feel better about the break-up if you talk about it?" Kryesler said.

"Nah."

"Well tell me anyway. I'll give you some pointers so you won't screw up like you did with what's her name?"

"Straight truth" - She said she was going to polish my middle leg like a piece of furniture. She used that Jergens lotion. I'll never forget that smell. Lynn made it squirt twice on Halloween night. I tried to help her get off, but I needed instructions from her. I did the best job I could, but I was guessing half the time. Maybe she stroked it out of me like – ten times from Halloween to New Years."

I looked at some 'Swank' magazine he had on his coffee table while he was doing his dishes. He was probably going to bang another shiksa tonight, I thought. Danny was fuckin' kool; he must have gotten a lot of women just by having that wild assymetrical pupil in his right eye.

"Listen Ryan this is what we do. We'll get rid of that punk-ass hippie, and well see if she comes back to you." Danny started ironing a couple of shirts.

"How are you going to do that?" I looked over this nude model, Carol Doda, in the skin magazine.

"I still got my traffic/parking violation book. Every time I see a beige Beetle parked on Hawley, I'll write him up for parking too far away from the curb."

237

"There is no curb on her side of Hawley Terrace." I said.
"That's what makes the parking violation indefensible.....he's gotta pay. "

I rubbed my hands together about the prospect of Danny running the Flower Child out of the neighborhood.

A couple of days later we were down Greystone Station's overpass. It wasn't warm, but it blocked the wind. Ray asked me what I had lined up for summer besides the Paper route.

"What do you mean?"

You think you'll make it on delivering papers?"

"No.....I'll have to go caddying with you.....just tell me when they need caddies?"

"April's coming, you'll want to get your face seen up there. When they play that Masters down in Augusta; the following weekend - the club members will have the fever." He took a drag off his Marlboro."

"You give me the word and I'll be there."

"You won't have to worry about taking Drack out on a date. Just another way to save some money." Ray said.

"It's over between us, but I'm not over her. Kinda hurts real bad."

"Hey Groover.........get over her. What did you think was going to happen? You were going to catch hand jobs with the Vampress all summer?

"No – but she seemed to like giving them to me – sometimes more than I did. Ray, I really like getting them handjobs......I don't know which of us thought we were getting over on the other."

"That's not reality brother. You can't expect a tugjob three times a day for the 60 days of summer."

"Yeah but if she really liked me......maybe she would do it."

"You'd be dragging them golf bags and dragging the paperboy bag, and you'd go out at night and Lynn would be ready with the weiner schleider for your night love session. Plus you got to keep her happy and do her." There was a brief pause. "Say.......what did happen with you two on New Years Day?"

I was occupied carving a heart with Lynn's and my initials into one of the plywood windows. I had to back date the heart with a phony in case she came down here and happened to see it when she was reading some of the other graffiti. She'd see the date, laugh, and say something like: 'Dream on'.

"Aaaaay, I had to mail something for Hal; I saw her crossing Hawley going into the apartment house. I chased her with a line of bull saying how much I wanted to wish her a Happy New Year. I was going to give her a New Years kiss and try and stick my tongue down her throat, and it ended up being a quick lip smacker. I tried to be kool, but I wasn't. I asked her if her parents were home." I kept carving with my pocket knife.

"Yeah." Ray said. "Go for the 'Trick or Treat' replay." He walked down to the southeast corner of the pedestrian bridge. A pencil

238

came from his pocket and he started sketching something. "What happened?"

"No replay." I scoffed at his endorsement. "Draculynn said her parents were home and she was supposed to be over Vicki Montgomery's apartment. They were mad at her because she drank too much bubbly on New Years Eve."

"You should have brought her to 21."

"I tried – she said she was on lockdown."

"Well, did you get anything?"

"I got her to go down the laundry room in the apartment. I used some guilt trip lines on her 'bout not having the backbone to tell me it was over when she wasn't interested in me anymore."

"It wasn't like the Beach Boys, I wasn't picking up any 'Good Vibrations'. Can't we start the year off being boyfriend/girlfriend again?" She didn't answer me, instead we start making out, and I start feeling her up."

"Journeyman move." He was sketching some kind portrait of Draculynn with those teeth being displayed in full Vampire rapture............"Not too close." he titled it.

I didn't say anything about the uncompleted drawing since I couldn't draw anything near as good as what he was doing. "The only reason she hooked up with me on New Years day was because it was better than hanging out with Vicki, or being at home with her parents. It was an easy choice for her. It wasn't much of a choice for me, I wanted her."

Ray interrupted, "Any vampire action.?"

"She was pretty stingy with the suction. She latched on one or twice and gave me four bite marks. It was bullshit......here it is winter and she could have turned me into a bat and I could've worn a turtleneck until April and all I could get was a couple of nibbles. That was when I knew I was there just for the ride. Whenever I'd tell her the Dracula teeth were her best feature, she'd never buy into the compliment."

"She thinks they're a defect." he said. "Tell you what vaquero – she isn't getting away this time." Ray continued to draw.

"The Vamp Look" is the best thing she's got going. Maybe she thought I was making fun of her. She didn't want to hear anymore about her grill so we went back to making out."

"Did she actually say this stuff or is this some garbage you've imagined?"

"Real deal Neil - anyway the elevator comes down to the garage level. Nobody's doing laundry. They are all just coming and going to their cars. I'm ready to try something with her - out of sight, behind the double-decker dryers. We heard footsteps coming towards the laundry room. She pulls me into that tiny toilet before we can be seen and locks the door. I was hoping whoever came in was only getting a quart of milk from the machine. We listened and two washers started sloshing water. Lynn gave the intruder the finger with both hands. There barely was enough space in the ½ toilet to stand up and piss – in case you're down there with some babe thinking about doing something."

239

"I've been down there 20 times - at least; so what happened?"

"She sat on the can with the lid down, and I stood facing her. We were trying to figure something out – how we're going to do our usual thing. I think she wanted to, but the lack of space gave us a challenge.......we had to get creative. Lynn takes my pants down to my knees, lifts the lid, stood behind me, and reached around worked my unit with one hand and squeezing an ass cheek with the other."

"Holy shit.......she should have been my girl." Ray had to suspend his drawing.

"Get bent. Anyway, I'm all rock and roll ready, and she makes it squirt in about a minute. She directed the jazz into the toilet. I'm panting like a dog and howling like a wolf; she falls into the door, and I'm doing push-ups against the back wall."

"Unlocking the door; she fell out of the shitter. I'm left there in a daze with my meat hanging out. Sitting on top of a washer is Danny Kryesler, the cop."

Lynn's already in the elevator and gone.

"Kryesler?" Ray asks as he starts doing some filling-in with his pencil.

"Yeah......Danny. The comedian asks me if she's Jewish? He's laughing a ton. Then he says: 'And clean up that mess ya dipshit' – and laughed some more." I carved away on the 'L.V.M. heart.'

"Best cop on the force." Ray bulldogged his chin and nodded.

"Yeah." I said. "The jack of hearts."

"Don't look back Ryan, she wanted it as much as you." The detective said the next time I collected from him.

"There was no next time for me and Lynn – only her image on a Key Lime Green plywood window on the New York Central overpass bridge.

CHAPTER 12

i

Introibo ad altari Dei -
Ad Deum qui laetificat juventutem meam.

This was going to be the last three months Ray and me would
be serving mass together and answering the priest's prayers.   All
Souls parish continued saying Mass in Latin on the even hours, and
English on the odd ones. When the congregation got over the novelty
of hearing mass in the native tongue; attendance went up for the Latin
mass and down for the English. The simple fact for the lopsided
attendance was the Latin mass was shorter. The English mass required
a degree of theatrics to instill a feeling of mysticism from the priests.
They couldn't mumbo – jumbo the canon of the mass facing the
congregation with the microphones picking up their words.

All the Latin we learned to be altar boys was obsolete. Many
of the traditions of the mass were gone, or abbreviated: no more
kneeling when receiving Communion, 24 hr. fast - reduced to three
hours and eventually done away with altogether, no more patents to
catch an errant host, no more bells to wake up church goers for the
consecration. Observances such as first Friday adoration,
neighborhood processions, May crowning of Mother Mary all seemed
to lose value.

"The Protestants should feel right at home with the Catholic
mass said in English now." Hal complained when the mass ran long. I
had seen a lot of changes the four years I was a knight of the altar.
'How could these traditions have been so important one day and cast
aside so easily the next?' It made me think it must have been a bunch
of b.s. all along. Ray believed the mass was the centerpiece of our
faith, and we received some transfer of grace and perhaps knowledge
when we stood in front of God.

I understood the thesis, but I believed too hard in the old
ways and liturgy: "The rest of ya's can go to hell --- I ain't." Perhaps I
was speaking a bit prematurely.

At the same time, my faith in this revolutionized church was
something not to be trusted; it was easier not to take it seriously.
Throughout high school, Ray and me cast our lot with the growing
number of absentee or lapsed Catholics.

My older brother was geared to science and math, and his
belief in God was heavily influenced by what he was drinking and who
he was reading. My faith in the church flowed and ebbed, but not in
the basic tenants of Christ's teachings. My faith remained steadfast for
two core beliefs: First, my fear of going to hell far outweighed any
motivation I could dream up to make me question God's existence.
Second, I knew man could be evil; I knew the world God had created
could be made to reflect the design of man. We only had to look to
some their standard bearers throughout time: Hitler, Stalin, Mao, Tojo,

Jack the Ripper, Caligula, Speck, and DeSalvo. There is and was an endless parade of evil motivating this sordid crew, and they're always looking for new recruits. If it is possible for an anti-Christ and his boss to exist; the converse must be equally true.

Science and reason dictate - if there is evil, then the opposite force must also exist: good. The fact the world has been able to carry on – creating societies for the good and advancement of mankind provides sufficient evidence both forces exist. There is matter and there is anti-matter somewhere in the universes; should the two forces come into contact with each other: total annihilation. There are also forces of magnetism which seem to mimic the constant tug of war between matter and anti-matter on a much smaller scale. I accepted the light and the dark: the good and evil, what I found difficult to understand was the concept..........'without humanity, there could be no good or evil.'

Unlike Ray, my motivation to believe in the existence of God in a religious context was out of fear – nothing else. To deny God's existence was an incredibly stupid bet. There was nothing to be gained if the bettor was right. The wager was all downside. If a person bet on the existence of God – you might be on the winning side. Wagering on the non-existence of the prime force of the universe, the bettor aligns oneself with the Dark one – if one exists. If either exists: so does the other. Should one exist and not the other, you have another paradox, and a new scientific standard which is beyond our comprehension and becomes our new reality.

It was only after getting spoon-fed by Ray with these theories, I was able to realize everything I did was out of fear: I couldn't help it – the church had gotten in there first. He had seen my paranoia for what it was not – a reaction not for Christ but against the evil one. At times I'd lay awake at night asking the almighty why I was even here; I thought I was mostly happy before I was born. My questions and answers were unsatisfactory.

ii

Just before the showers started for the boys, Father Joe had been relieved by this priest, Father Bertram, for health class instruction. Hard to say where they dig these guys up. Bertram had been appointed Asst. Pastor three years prior. Father Terrence Mahoney had been the pastor for seven years. I asked Mack McKay how these people end up in careers such as: education and religion. He knew the question bothered me. He spat out a tooth pick, he said it was because they couldn't do anything else, nothing in the real world anyway.

Father Bertram walked in and Sister Alexa walked out. He had this sick smile; it didn't mean: "I'm happy." He wore this cassock around the parish with so much gold braid, we thought he was some kind of French Admiral when he first showed up. Everybody knew straight away he was some kind of wheel for the church. They were in

242

love with the idea they were Jesuits, and were considered to be the brains of the Roman Catholic religion – not for my money.

He scanned the hallway and closed the classroom door; The smile grew and went from ear to ear. He was small in stature and about 40 years old. Vinny Tarts, Kenny Crawford, Joe Conte, and me could have laid him out with a couple of combination punches. With the smaller guys in the class, it would have been interesting. We all knew who he was because the 8th graders had tipped us off. Bertram was always talking sex to the male students. He wrote his name on the chalkboard. All the altar boys knew him from serving mass. If nothing else – at least he could say a quick mass.

We pretty much knew we weren't going to get much in the way of health instruction because there weren't any books. He was going to wing it for the next ten weeks.

"Soap and Towel on Thursday for Phys. Ed." he wrote on the board. "Have you all got this? You will be taking a shower after gym class next week." He wrapped his knuckles on the blackboard for effect. Bertram started right in with the reason he was conducting Health class and Father Joe was not.

"I am here to help you creatures to understand about life. Do any of you know how life comes about?" He looked across the room throwing the question out to the class.

We all were wised up enough to have known none of us were going to be able to answer the loaded question to his satisfaction, I was sure somebody was going to take the bait; it just wasn't going to be me. There was no response for almost a minute.

Bertram realized he was going to have to prime the pump, "Come now.....just in general terms."

Crawford raised his hand.

"Yes creature."

I didn't know what his deal was.......why was he calling us 'creature'?

"In general?" Crawfish was being careful.

"Yes how does it come about; the origin of life?"

"It comes about every month in the mailbox." He kept a straight face and looked at us for approval. We all were smiling, laughing, looking away or covering our mouths.

"I'm not talking about 'Life' magazine. Sit down you idiot. I will re-phrase: Does anyone know how a baby comes into this world?"

"Father, I believe God set it up with the story of Adam and Eve." someone said.

"Anyone hear of anything a little more recent.?"

Another hand went up. "What is your name creature?"

"John O'Connell."

"Yes, John." Fr. Bertram said.

"The answer is on all these Tee shirts and jerseys everyone is wearing."

"And what do they say?"

"They have the number '69' printed on them."

"Without getting into the gutter or being vulgar - can you tell the class how this number is related to the creation of life?" Bertram smiled.

"Yeah."

"Let's try - 'Yes Father.' The priest raised his voice, and corrected O'Connell.

"I mean, yes Father."

"Explain your theory."

All eyes were on John O'Connell. We knew this was going to be good. He started by swishing and dipping as he spoke: "The '6' is the man and the '9' is the woman."

"Yes?"

"Well they are interlocked and kissing each other on their pee-pee's." John started laughing and then the rest of us burst out as well.

A crazed look on Fr. Bertram's face had him immobilized behind the lectern, until he flipped out from all of us laughing. He knocked the wooden lectern on its side and sent all of Sr. Alexa's papers flying as he bee lined to where John stood and delivered a roundhouse right to his head. John fell to the floor like a sack of potatoes. This level of ferocity had us all gape-mouthed. I rubbed the bald area of my head unconsciously.

I turned away from John and looked at the smartest guy in the class, Mike Penske. I watched the mauling through Mike's facial expressions: he cringed his eyes, woooed his mouth, and did a triple take. O'Connell must have been getting creamed. I didn't turn back until the noise died down; O'Connell lay on the floor in a fetal position.

The priest rolled down the sleeves of his Jesuit robe and returned to the front of the classroom. "Pick that thing up." he told two boys in the front row. While they stood the lectern upright, he cast a hateful stare at the boy on the floor. I felt the same as the rest.........'What the fuck?'

Fr. Bertram moved to the side of the lectern, eyeballing the rest of us as he searched and squinted with hate behind his rimless spectacles. His fists were still clenched and his lips trembled. He lashed out a venomous tirade and finished promising: "You'll get sent down for this....."

John O'Connell tried to get up, but after a couple of attempts he just lay there.

"Quit your Oscar performance and take your seat you little faker."

"I'm not faking." The clump of clothes stirred.

Once again the lectern went over and shook the floor. Like Batman, the priest bee-lined back to Johnny and dished out a second helping. He left the classroom with John O'Connell laying there.

We got O'Connell up. Blood was coming from his ear; his left eye had started to swell shut after Bertram gave him his boot. Sister Alexa returned before the girls got back, she tried to contain her disgust. "John.......John......are you going to be able to get home at the end of the day?"

"My brother will help me."

Craig O'Connell was in Ray's class. There were five O'Connell boys, John was number 4. Their mother was about as pretty as Jane. The O'Connell family should have had a daughter. They lived in the big apartment at 35 Pine St. Their father worked for the city of Yonkers, his oldest son was on the payroll for whatever Mr. O'Connell was in charge of. He got paid for February 29 and 30th. It wasn't a leap year. It made the Statesman when the city closed the books for the fiscal year.

At lunch, I asked an 8th grader, "Hey Pete, what does the number '69' mean?"

He looked at me like I was playing dumb. "Whaaa?"

"I can't figure out why O'Connell got worked over by Bertram so bad – "

"You ain't as smart as Ray……..are you Ryan?………You can't be talking that sex shit to a priest and think they ain't gonna give you the second sorrowful mystery. They don't like being reminded they took a vow to only beat their meat." Pete jerked his fist and laughed.

"Well what the deuce does the '69' mean?"

He broke into a big shit eatin' grin: "6 inches – 9 months." Joe Bourke was in 7-2, he said Johnny had crossed the line when he went on with the oral sex enrichment. "Them priests and brothers don't like it; they think it's real evil stuff. Vinny Zumpano shook his head, we heard Bertram really tuned O'Connell up."

"Yeah, he's going to have a tough time getting home. He's in the classroom trying to recover…..His brother Craig is supposed to help him home." I said.

When school let out, I saw John hobbling with Craig's help. He was just trying to have a few laughs.

THE NEXT WEEK, FATHER JOE LED US DOWN THE stairs to the locker room and showers; "Find yourself a locker and put your stuff in it and get changed. You guys got your soap and towels. And watch out for the hot water – be prepared to turn it back quick. Take your shower, get dressed, and you all meet upstairs in the gym. When everybody's up there – you all go back together…….as a unit. No early birds/no stragglers – you got it? Tommy Gorski, you're in charge."

"Hey Father……….That Nancy Jericho doesn't need the health class, she just needs the daily shower……she stinks." Tommy said.

"That's enough Tom. Everybody get changed, we're going to do some time trials for the track team."

We put on our gym shorts and sweats. Most of us wore off-label sneakers. Converse's Chuck Taylor all-star sneakers were good for one thing: basketball. Nobody I knew had two pairs of sneakers - unless they were the youngest kid in a big family. Vinny Tarts sported a pair of loafer sneakers; I think he got them at 'John's Bargain Store'. Everybody kept giving him the business about his 'Mr. Boardwalk' sneakers. The guy knew fashion and how to dodge work. Vince was a big time Paisan, but looked like a Dutch immigrant. He could play both sides as the situation warranted.

At the time trials, Vinny turned on the afterburners right out of the starting blocks. All the guys wearing cons were toast. He was a blur in the 100 yard dash, and even faster in the 220. Steven St. Pierre ran track with Ray and me last year, and Vinny left him in the dust. That was amazing as St. Pierre really ran well against the black dudes. Tarts had it - running sprints.....his specialty. I beat most of the guys in our class. I couldn't beat Vince, St. Pierre, or Crawford; and only on a good day I could beat Ray. The mile - and up were my strong races. In spring track, Eddie Gibson came in 1st, Brian Walsh 2nd, and I came in 3rd.

Vinny didn't compete in the circuit races, he wasn't interested in the format: "I already been there.......what's the point?" Another reason Vinny wouldn't run any race over 220 yards was borrowed from his older brother Joe: "Every Goomba knows most cops won't chase a juvenile delinquent past 220 yards."

I had never been in class with Vinny since we enrolled at All Souls; if I was in 3-2, he was in 3-1. It was that way throughout grade school until they assigned us to Sister Alexa's class in the 7th grade.

It was a mystery when all this new found speed had come upon Vinny. When the cops were chasing us down the city dump, his speed was only average. I had to take into consideration he had to run carrying his air rifle, but still.......

After Father Joe gave the dash times to the track coach, Vinny avoided him like a hippie avoided soap. "I'll run a mile to see Marie Timateo, but I ain't running just to get a ribbon."

In the 7th grade Vinny finally gave in, but not to track – he signed up for basketball in the fall and baseball in the spring. It kind of was the glue which cemented our friendship. We were the tallest in our grade, and with 'Slick Dick Sheldon' we formed the back line of our Varsity team. Our team was good, but we only had one good backcourt man, and it seemed we were always playing catch up. The league had ten teams - we came in 3rd place. Vinny was there for every game sporting his 'Boardwalk Loafers' from the discount store. Vinny's motivation: girls and rock and roll.

The descent into the locker room/showers was filled with trepidation; no one knew what to expect. Out of nowhere Kenny Crawford came charging down the stairs almost naked screaming like a jungle boy and was in the shower like a flash. I wish I had been as uninhibited. It was show and tell time. We barely got into the locker room and Claude Sinclair had already changed and made a weak general announcement: "Ah, I didn't get too sweated up." And he started up the stairs.

A chorus of "Yeah" and "me too" ran through the dungeon. A future attorney, Mike Penske, threw a curve at the rest of us, "Anybody got any spray deodorant........ Man, I smell like I played 4 quarters."

George Hardin said: "How 'bout we just wash from the waist up. Nobody will know and our towels will be wet."

Stick your head under the shower and schlick back your hair." Came from a row of lockers over.

The conspiracy had taken form, but approval from Tom Gorski was not forth coming. Also a problem; the guys who's plumbing didn't work at home – mostly émigrés from the soviet bloc countries. They looked forward to taking a shower at school – what could be better?"

"How 'bout it Tom?"

"I guess it's okay for you guys, but I've got to at least run through the shower, Fr. Joe left me in charge. 6 out of 22 – that's pretty fair compliance I guess."

THE GIRLS HAD BEEN TAKING SHOWERS SINCE THE beginning of March, and they had kept it secret for a whole month. I didn't believe it. Most of us knew the layout of the girls' shower room. The floor plan was the mirror image of the boys'; the only differences were the dressing partitions and curtains installed for when they were naked outside of the shower. The boys locker room was divided into 3rds, with a bench in the middle of each row. Armed with only a towel, it was where most guys changed from gym shorts to having their underwear on in a flash. The showers themselves were communal. There were also hot air dryers with swivel heads so the girls could blow dry their hair.

When I was on detention, I was directed to scrub the shower floors, walls, and fixtures. I saw the much discussed, but seldom seen 'mysterious Kotex machine'. Twenty-five cents for one blood stopping sanitary napkin.

Ray and me were in the driveway just shooting baskets and throwing the bull.

"Ray, I know you never return to being a kid once you made the change"......I said putting the basketball between my knees and making the quotation marks with my hands. I resumed taking shots.

"It's a one-way street; you can take that to the bank. The only thing that'll be screwing you up without fail will be your preoccupation with chasing girls or doing things to attract them."

"That's not what I had in mind, but it seems to be the way it's working out." I laughed.

"Look at the number Lynn pulled on you – at least you can say you had some fun with her. Loki's a year older than me and he say's 'You spend all this time and money on them and all you get is a thank you.' You break-up with them anyway.........why waste your time?"

"When I had to serve detention for throwing wetted down paper towels onto the ceiling – I saw something odd."

"Wait a minute.......What did you get detention for?" He stopped dribbling.

"Me and Botch......"

"Buongurri?"

"Yeah, Butterballs." I confirmed as Ray took a shot.

"We were wetting up paper towels in the basement lavatory

247

across from the boiler room, and throwing them against the walls and the ceiling. Mr. Hurley caught us and laughed. He reached in his pocket and said he was going to flip a coin and the loser was going to the Principal's office. He looked at me and said: "Call it in the air."

I called Tails. It came up 'heads'. Joe Botch waved and went back to class.

Mr. Hurley said the jobs he did with his arms over his head were really starting to take its toll on his shoulders.

"Hurley's been there a long time. He knows where the ghosts are in those buildings." Ray got the rebound.

"He told me his hands were even falling asleep at night...... said he gotta get up in the middle of the night and smack his arms into the door jambs to get them to wake up.
Hurley tried to laugh it off. Then he asked me, to let him see my neck scars."

I wrenched my neck to show Ray how I exposed my neck to the custodian. "Hurley said they should have shit-canned Mrs. Foley years ago."

I took a deep shot from the grass. It was all net.

"Nice one." Ray said, and stood with the ball under his arm to stop the shooting. "So what happened?"

"Mr. Hurley says he's got a good job for my detention - if Sister Celeste will give him the green light."

"Yeah.....what's that?"

"He says, 'You've got to get the girls' shower cleaned up, and you got to give it the works: shower floor, toilets, sinks, locker room. The fixtures got to shine, and you gotta clean all the crud collecting around the drains.' With the girls' long hair and all - it doesn't take much to back up the drains." I said.

"I guess." he replied.

"About a week after the paper towel incident, Sister Celeste and Hurley scheduled when the detention would be served. It ended up being a Saturday job. He gave me a couple of scrub brushes for the shower and a couple of smaller ones for the sinks and fixtures. The tile's grout wasn't recessed, so it was easy to clean. Three hours in the shower/ locker room job, I thought I was done. Hurley was somewhere in the building, that was good enough to turn the water on and making sure all the drains were sending the water through. There were eight shower heads and four big drains. The sinks and toilets were on the opposite side of the locker room. I watched the water run down the drains in the shower." We continued the shoot around.

"Something was odd Ray: One of the drains' for two of the shower heads - drained in the reverse direction in relation to the others."

"Say what?"

I tried to reach for the basketball but Ray was interested and didn't need a ball bouncing to distract him.

"The water went down the opposite way than it was supposed to."

"IMPOSSIBLE."

"Possible.......I seen it. In fact, I turned all the showers off except one of the two. The head on the right drained down normally. Next, I stuffed a rag over the drain and let the water rise high enough to make it over to the next drain over. Normal again. I repeated with the left showerhead. And, I'm telling you the truth --- the water went down the drain clockwise."

"That's the wrong way."

"It's one of the first experiments we did in science class to prove pole magnetism." I said.

"You sure?"

"Yup."

"Well G'day mate." Ray put some spin on the ball and hit the backboard 18" wide of the rim. With the traction of the spinning basketball hitting the backboard it went through the hoop.

"What the.......?" His shot had me thinking on a couple of levels. "Ray, I wouldn't have even noticed it, but I remember those scientists from NASA on TV explaining how they were going to use the moon's gravity to slingshot the Apollo Spacecraft and return it to earth. They also had an astrophysicist explaining how they could use gravity as a way to propel or slow down the craft's speed. He went on talking about Sir Isaac Newton, gravity in general, and referenced planets and moons where there is gravity, will also have magnetic poles. He used this example to explain why water drains counterclockwise in the northern hemisphere and clockwise in the southern. Is that correct?"

He took the basketball and made it spin using his pointer finger and transferred the rotating ball to the pointer of his other hand. The ball went back between his arm and his body. "There is some anomaly taking place. It's not the force of the water making it drain incorrectly --- You prevented the water from draining. Also, it is not the composition of the water, as the same supply feeds all the pipes. Keep alert for more of these unusual occurrences going against the grain. If it is a one time event – the question becomes: Why?"

"Should we ask Hal for an opinion?" I said.

"Other than the fact he could verify the rotation of water in the southern hemisphere, I don't think he could add much to your discovery. One more thing...........and I don't know what it has to do with anything, or perhaps I am writing more because of the increased workload at school --- my signature is changing into something which is foreign in nature to me."

"You still spell your name the same and you're not using your middle name are you?" My hand felt for hair in the bald area.

"I'll show you later."

iii

September, LaCrosse/Arizona

Richmond Sand looked at his utilitarian flip-phone. The name and number of the caller came up: Dixie Whitelaw. "Hey Dix...... you can't reach Nicole -"

"Been trying all morning Rick – nothing. The call keeps going to voice mail, and her mailbox is full. Is everything okay out there?"

"I'm in Las Cruces right now. We're in the yard swapping cars, then I'm off to El Paso, more dropping off and picking up. After that we stop at Willcox to pick-up some agricultural hopper cars.......mostly beans. They'll let me off in Tucson and pick up a fresh crew before it leaves for Yuma and San Diego before it comes back to Tucson in 22, maybe 25 hours." Rick said.

"Was she going out for the day?"

The noise from the train yard made both sides of the conversation nearly inaudible.

"Wouldn't be surprised if she took the kids to the mountains. They may have even gone for the weekend. It's been pretty hot down here. The cell tower connections are pretty sketchy in the mountains, even worse when the wind is up."

"Yeah – I know." Dixie said.

"What about your Dad?"

"That's what I'm calling about."

"Getting' worse?"

She could see his face cringe through the phone's radio waves.

"Listen Dixie, I don't have to know anything – it's you girls' business. Ryan and me always got along..........He was always right with me." Richmond said.

"You know you're family Rick......."

Silence......

"Something's come up – Even though our phones are linked with "What's App" for family messaging, if one of us is out of network – that person is stymied. Dr. Baranpour called, I think he's going to lay a heavy number on us. I've got to write down what he says so I am accurate when I do connect with Nicky."

"Were you able to get a hold of the twins?"

"Yeah. He also wants us to write out our questions for him no matter how trivial they may seem to us."

There was a lot of radio squawk on Rick's Motorola in the background, he was almost yelling into his mobile phone: "The latest medical report Nicky gave me was about his improvement as a result of the introduction of the new anti-viral medicine. She said the Old Man was even talking to you guys. Obviously, things have regressed. You all don't need me or Peter right now other than to take care of our kids. You'll let me know if the situation warrants me to come up there."

"Exactly; I'm so relieved Nicky and Teresa didn't marry a couple of Bozos. With this liver business - time is important but not critical right now. I sense Baranpour is uncomfortable about something; I think it has to do with a liver transplant. I know in my heart he wants to get the ball rolling. We'll find out soon enough."

There was a blast from an air horn in the freight yard. "Your train leaving?" she asked.

250

"'Nother locomotive 4-pack in search of some freight cars and tankers."

"If I can't get a hold of her, please tell her it's pretty likely she'll have to come back up. She's a great help figuring things out." Dixie shuddered.

"That's why I married her." He looked inside his hard hat at a cheap gas station watch he had glued to the side of his helmet after cutting off the wrist band. "I'll keep trying to make contact with her, but more likely she'll get one of your text messages or voice mails first. Union Pacific sends me out on theses runs, and I may as well be in Omaha. Nicole is pretty much the boss when I'm not there; pretty much the boss when I am there. She don't hang around and she don't hang on – she's a good woman."

Dixie picked it up.......""She's a good sister."

"Just enough stress to keep us all on the edge our seats."

"Thanks Rick. Hey, I'm coming down your way with the Ol' Man once he's on the mend. You, Nicks, and me can drink some mescal watching him get better. Love ya bro'."

Dixie left the waiting area for Dr. Hadji Baranpour and left a message with his office. She was going down to radiology. A nurse or tech was with Ryan. She hadn't seen this one before.

"Can I help you?"

"I believe that's my father on the gurney in the radiology room."

"You should be wearing a hospital I.D. issued on the main floor at the front security area."

"I'm his daughter. I am the Power of Attorney for his health." Dixie got a little short with her.

"You still should be wearing a visitor's 'stick-on I.D."

She looked down the hall, "I can go back upstairs if it will help."

"We've had a lot of people walking through who have no business here. The administration is tightening the security in response to the increase in theft from the hospital and personal property from patients. They're walking off with office equipment, furniture, drugs, even toilet paper. Cars have been stolen from the parking structure, strong arm robbery, sexual assault, and an abduction." The employee turned towards Ryan – Dixie read her badge: Debra LaValley/ULTR SND TECH.

"I'm sorry, it has been a long day. Dr. Baranpour ordered the ultra sound for my father."

She wasn't sure, she thought the patient on the gurney was Ryan. When Dixie hadn't seen him for two hours or more she checked his wristband to be sure it was him. Every time she looked at him his appearance seemed to have modified in some respect.

"Do you know if Dr. Baranpour is still here?" Dixie asked.

The tech scrolled through the list of Doctors on site, "Hmmmm.......Yes, he's still here. You'll have to call him – he could be anywhere."

"If I can't reach him by phone, could you page him over the hospital's system?" Dixie put on the soft sell.

The ultra sound tech looked put out, "I'm not supposed to put out a 3rd party page.........only in an emergency."

Dixie's concern and inability to do anything had her in knots.

"We are waiting down here for the radiologist's report. I assume Baranpour and the radiologist are conferring right now as to the extent of his liver's damage. He may ask for a MRI of the abdomen or a C-T scan of his upper abdomen..... or he may be going back up to his room." Debra said.

"How was he this morning?"

"When he was brought down he was conscious enough to respond to my directions. With the MRI, we need the patient to take deep breaths and hold it at different levels of pressure in order to image varying aspects of the organ and the spleen so we get a good mapping of the scarring that has taken place. I thought the imaging went well, but it's what the radiologist sees that will determine if further testing is indicated."

"Can I talk to him?"

"He went to sleep right after the test. He's still in the image room. You can look in on him."

"Thank you." She walked in softly. Ryan lay motionless; Dixie turned on the recessed ceiling lights for only a second.....they were too bright and she shut them off and stood next to him. She kissed his forehead and put her hand on top of his. A moment passed; before she peeled back the sheet and light blanket. The swelling in his legs had increased, particularly the calves. With the small light above the sink providing the only light, it was hard to see the contents of his urine collection bag.

Dixie came out and asked the technician for her small flashlight: cloudy. It was enough for her and she began making calls to her sisters. She left a message on Teresa's phone, but Killeen answered. They only had a few words, and Dixie had to put her on hold when she saw Baranpour was calling.

"Jyess Ms. Whitelaw, I will meet you in the visitor's area outside of the G.I. section of the floor. Right now I'm am ordering a two more tests for your father."

"Yes, I'll be there. Any ideas of the time to meet up?"

"Not for at least an hour."

Again she said she would be there. She ended the call and picked back up with Killeen: "We'll meet at St. Thomas after 7pm?" Dixie continued spewing forth logistical medical information. "I haven't spoken to Nicole since yesterday, mid-afternoon. I should have the information we need to make some decisions about Papa after the meeting with the doctor in a little while. Here he comes now. I didn't expect him this soon." 'It's never good to see a doctor early she silently thought.' "Gotta run......love you." she said.

"Okay, love you too." The younger twin replied.

Baranpour met her on the fourth floor, his hand gently embraced her upper arm, and walked with Dixie to a window wall looking out onto the Mississippi River. They stood silently, a tear rolled down her cheek. The Doctor couldn't see that side of her face. She wiped it away. He tried to direct her back to the portion of the waiting area where there was furniture.

"No tell me here." she said.

"As you vish. You are the one to make the decisions for Ryan."

She nodded.

"And your Christian first name is......." He waited for a reply.

"Dixie – is really just a nickname."

"And what is the name on the legal document?......the P of A?"

"Dixie."

"So okay then Ms. Dixie."

"Just Dixie will be fine."

"So....." He began to read from his notes: "We are still on the Vikiera-pak therapy, and there has been significant reduction in the viral load of the Hepatitis C virus......very good. A reduction from 1,500,000 ppm to 500 ppm. I believe we will get down to zero levels in 2 to 3 weeks. This is encouraging, but it does not necessarily indicate he is virus free. Only when he has been at zero levels for a year will we be able to say the virus has been eradicated from his body, and at that point we will know we have slowed the cirrhosis for the present. This Hepatitis C virus is virulent and is very good at hiding in diseased areas of the liver, it is why we retest annually for the next few years. We are not out of the woods on this front yet." A brief silence followed. "Any questions so far?" The doctor was trying to be upbeat.

Dixie was cautious while absorbing Baranpour's assessment. "I think I have understood most of what you said, but there is something else you're holding back from me isn't there?"

"This is more critical to Ryan's recovery. He has significant liver damage. His liver is shrinking and turning into rock. It is unable to properly process a sustainable diet. The cirrhosis does not permit the proper breakdown of solids, liquids, and medicines he requires to stay alive. The platelet count is down, white blood cell count – down. The amount of ammonia is rising, and it is poisoning him. It is positive that he has not decompensated or has significant fluid retention yet, but his bile is murky, and this indicates the liver and kidney are barely keeping up. 'Tis hard to get an accurate profile with blood work alone. Still, there may be enough healthy liver left for him to recover."

"Miss Whitelaw - We must be ready to pursue the transplant option, if things as they say: 'go south on us.' Blood work....suitable donor, availability; There is a real possibility we will not find a liver for your father, and he may run out of time and options."

"Doctor, I started to hope so much........we all did and still do."

"I recommend University at Madison or the Mankato Institute to be the medical facilities I would go for the transplant operation. He is walking a tightrope now, I need your decision as soon as possible so we can begin testing."

253

"Do you have a relationship with either medical facility, and if you do which one do you recommend?" She watched his face.

"I have referred patients to both. I do have a relationship with Dr. Bachan Singh over in Makato. We have worked together previously. He has a high rate of successful liver transplants, he is most competent and has a remarkable skill to determine whether a candidate for transplant has the ability to survive the surgery and have the transplanted organ function normally in the recipient."

"You will have our decision once I have spoken to all of my sisters."

"Transplantation has made many advancements; it is not the 'crapshoot' dat it once was." Baranpour smiled, "And we still have Vikiera-pak w/the Ribaviran to stop the virus from inflicting more damage......at least your father has a weapon to fight with."

"Thank you Doctor." She said as he left.

Dixie fell back into a chair in the waiting area of the Gastro-Intestinal section of the floor. Her head spun trying to remember everything she had heard today. She took out her smart phone and began making notes on today's conference with Dr. Hadji Baranpour. Her jittery hands typed too many mistakes onto her screen; she switched to pen and paper. She'd transfer the hand written notes back to her phone from the closest gin mill.

1. Call sisters for conference call with Nicks 2nite.
2. Get input on transplant for Pop.
3. Discuss his case – make sure they're aware of how bad of shape his liver is in.
4. A transplant may be his only way to stay alive –
5. When should Nicky come back up?

Her 'WhatsApp' was engaged, she hoped to include her sister in Arizona with all her communiqués to the other two.

Dixie slumped back into the sofa and started reading about the liver and liver transplants while she texted and responded. Good texts from Nicky and Killeen. It was a relief getting Nicky back in the loop. The latter wanted to know when they'd meet up at St. Thomas.

'Thanks for the extra duty Papa.' She thought as she continued to read, but started fading and crashed out.

Two small kids woke her up, she looked at the phone: she had been asleep for over an hour. The text message app was pressed; still nothing from Teresa. That woman is just so busy --- 10 hour days, taking 4 credits of advanced study, the kids, the house, and whatever else came up, and now this. In her mind, Dixie watched her older sister balancing spinning plates on wooden dowels.......it didn't look like fun. Ryan had kept after her and Killeen to start their families.
254

"It's not that easy Papa." Dixie told him more than once.

RYAN HAD HUNG AROUND THE GADSEN
PURCHASE
until the monsoon season started. When it was too hot in Arizona, he
worked his way up to Wisconsin to see the three girls and Teresa's
kids. A few times he'd drive to the east coast to check in on brother
Willis, Loki, and Vinny Tarts. The drive to LaCrosse was long enough,
it was another 1000 miles to N.Y./N.J. He hadn't made the trek
recently, but he had to fly out there to go to wakes and funerals.
        He would play round-robin with the girls in LaCrosse for 2
or 3 months; never wanting to overstay his welcome. Each of the
Wisconsin three wanted to get as much time with Ryan as possible.
        The last four years, he kind of favored staying with Killeen.
A teacher lived in the upper flat and Killeen lived in the lower. The
teacher was never there in the summers, and Ryan was able to use his
parking space until school started. The grandkids were a big draw for
Ryan, so days were spent with Teresa and Peter, and nights were with
Dixie and/or Killeen.
        Ryan was a creature of habit and he'd begin and end his
visits at Killeen's flat. He traveled light and she had that extra room
and parking space. Dixie moved too often, and Teresa's husband
always seemed to be involved with a summer remodeling project
around the house. It was a true blessing being able to get out of
Arizona for the monsoon season, and to see his family. What irritated
him the most was hearing from retired Boilermakers and Ironworkers
about recent deaths, diseases, divorces and incarcerations. It was
inescapable. All it took was a three month job, and 2 or 3 names were
added to his address book. The more contacts he had made, the more
he'd hear: "Hey Whiteshoes; did you hear about so and so?" None of
these guys ever told him one of their co-workers had won the lottery. It
was always: "Go to Jail – Go directly to Jail – Do not Pass Go – Do
Not Collect $200.
        Recently, he felt the tug of his daughters: individually and
collectively – they all wanted a piece of him. Perhaps they intuitively
sensed his life force ebbing. It also may have been his ability to read
people and interpret events which could affect them if he wasn't
around. He didn't know.

A NURSE'S AIDE HAD BROUGHT RYAN FROM
RADIOLOGY back into room 107. Dixie, Teresa, and Killeen had
assembled there. They would make a call to Nicole and have her on
speaker mode.
        "Sorry I'm late." Teresa said. "I've been in overdrive all day.
Neither Killeen in her postal shorts and blouse, or Dixie paid any
attention to the tardy arrival.
        Dixie brought the twins up to speed on their father's current
condition. She added, "Baranpour advised if we 'green light' the
transplant route; he'll transfer Pops to the Mankato Institute sometime

tomorrow. He'll be getting the best care there as they search for a suitable donor match. They'll want to get him to Mankato tomorrow. Time is critical"

"What about the risks?" Killeen asked.

"Well have to ask Baranpour, but right now I'm led to believe – either it is successful or it is not. The question becomes academic if a suitable match cannot be found."

"I thought I read on the Internet, they could take part of a human liver and transplant it.........you know - maybe one of us could be a donor?" Killeen said.

"Yeah, I saw that too, but it's almost exclusively done for children.....not adults. Sometimes it is used as a bridge for a child waiting to find a suitable donor." Dixie said. Isn't that right Teresa?"

She put her phone down and looked up, "Huh?.......I'm sorry. Emma starts school in a couple of days – she can't find her lunch box. I'm sorry, what were you saying?"

"Just why they don't perform partial liver transplants..." Dixie said.

"Yes, they do them, but from an adult to a child – and it would most likely be from a mother or father to their child. I never heard of it going the other route. Transplantation between two adults is too risky – if they use a live donor......there is the possibility neither patient or donor will survive.

Dixie looked over to Killeen, "You're P of A and successor Trustee. When we get Nicks on the phone we'll try to get a consensus on the transplant. When was the last time you went over his Trust agreement and/or his Will with him ?"

Teresa's and Killeen's heads popped up, The elder twin's eyebrows scrunched together: "Are things this serious? I thought this Vikiera-pak was some kind of wonder drug?"

"You really are a psyche nurse – aren't you?" Dixie said.

"That's what I've been trying to impress upon you guys; and with your hair dyed blue.......... that speaks volumes too." Teri explained.

Killeen almost lost her coffee. Some levity was overdue.

"Well here's your scoop Mrs. R.N.: The Vikiera-pak with ribaviran is killing the Hep C virus, but it's never been sold as being able to reverse cirrhosis; this scarring will kill him before the virus does."

"I know that." Teri rolled her eyes shaking her head from side to side.

"Check this out – two days ago they drew blood for his viral load count and it's almost non-detectable."

The twins' faces were amazed. "Wasn't his viral count like 1.4 million?" Killeen grabbed her travel mug; it was empty. "That's great."

"It doesn't mean much, it's the cirrhosis that's gonna do him in, and they don't have a drug to reverse that. Dixie said.

"And that's why he needs a transplant." Teresa directed Dixie's comment to Killeen.

"I haven't spoken to the Ol' Man about the will or his Trust for two or three years. She hadn't thought there would be such a rapid decline. I'll be going over these documents ......with you guys and his attorney when Nicky comes back up, if I have to." Killeen went over to the machine and got a hot cup of coffee, "Another adventure," she said filling her cup.

Neither answered; but walked with her to the self-serve coffee. The viral load numbers had taken Teresa and Killeen by surprise; with news like that, the younger sister could upstage them all she wanted.

There was little doubt Dixie was running the show; they were confident she was taking care of their father. She did the things and asked the questions that might extend Ryan's life - if he was lucky.

Teresa whispered to Killeen, "She's making all the moves I would have made if I was the P of A for Pop's health." The twins were relieved in that respect.

The previous night, Dixie sat watching her father in the hospital bed, she spoke to him: "You knew I had the time for you and to do this job. You know all of us in our own special way.......our strengths and our weaknesses. You're pretty smart Ol' Man." She smiled as another tear rolled down her cheek.

'How did he know?' Dixie wondered.

Dixie was the daughter who could see the big picture: the artist. Killeen - generous and loving to a fault. Teresa – where the role of 'Motherhood' had no bounds and Nicole – the realist.

The call to Tucson was made. Her half-sister picked up right away, "Dixie, what's the latest? Hold on, I've got to make sure the kids are occupied and aren't getting into anything. I've got Derrick with me, Cody and Cheyenne are in the back imagineering. I can watch them from the back porch. Please say there's some ray of hope."

"We're all here with Papa, back in his room. He's not conscious right now, he had some tests today. I got you on the speaker mode so we all can talk."

"Hey guys."

"How's Rick and the kids?" Teresa said.

"They're all getting ready for me to come back up and see grandpa."

"How 'bout yours?" Nicks inquired.

"Start school pretty soon. Emma's in third grade and Van the man will start first grade."

"As soon as we got back from Wisconsin ten days ago – Cody and Cheyenne started the next day........crazy schedule. Okay Dixie – how's the old man?'

Dixie began reading from her list: Pops is semi-conscious or in a semi-coma, I really don't know the difference or if there is one. His liver is starting to fail.........too much scarring from all those years carrying the Hep-C virus. Baranpour recommends transferring him to either UW-Madison or the Mankato Institute.

Teresa looked at Dixie's phone, "They're about the same distance from LaCrosse in opposite directions.

"Proximity doesn't matter at this point. The facility that has performed the most procedures is the deciding criteria." Nicky said.

"I believe that would be Mankato." Teresa replied.

"If I was aware of the choices and was in need of a transplant; it would be one of my top considerations. How do you all see it?"

The Wisconsin Whitelaws concurred.

Dixie said, "We better check his insurance for something like this. Maybe it doesn't make any difference, but if it's got to be done......we just do it and hope he has coverage for it."

"If you want Dixie, I'll call the Boilermakers Health and Welfare Fund tomorrow. There's going to be enough surprises coming down the road." Teri said.

"Remember around 10 days ago, the conversation he had with us?" Killeen tried to conjure up the memory. "Nicky, you and Teresa were there. He said he didn't want to get a liver before someone younger than him."

"It's commendable Dad thinks that way Killeen, but I seriously doubt any transplant program operates within those parameters.......then again.....maybe they do." Teri said.

"We'll ask Dr. Hadji." Killeen said.

Nicky's voice had an edge, "I'll let you all know right now, I am not leaving this up to Papa, this is our decision. I'd tell Baranpour - dad's delirious and incapable of making this decision for himself. And I don't like saying this-this way, but if I was P of A for health, I'd go full ahead and have the transplant or whatever they could do to keep him alive. We don't want to know any of the particulars of the donor or the age of the next person on the recipient list. We have enough to deal with, and debating ethical questions serves no purpose here."

Dixie was silent. She knew Nicole's remarks were directed more towards her than the twins; she also knew she was right. "If we decide to move him, they'll want to move him right away; the doctor has to know A.S.A.P. if it's Madison or Mankato so Hadji can bring in the new team on Pop's case. We don't know any of the surgeons available."

"Once we have some names, I can call over to Mankato or Madison and make an inquiry concerning Doctor so and so. I'll also do an internet search, but a physician doesn't end up in either facility by being mediocre." Teri advised.

"The final decision will be mine, but I want you guys' input about the course we are on. I think we are pretty much on the same page; it will be a lot easier for me if we are in agreement, so I'll ask you for a non-binding vote on the things I am not sure of. Ryan had his reasons for assigning different responsibilities to us. We've never had major confrontations amongst the four of us except when I was a heavy into drugs. I know I have the greatest responsibility because it deals with actions I take affecting his life and keeping him alive. I cannot do it alone."

"Baranpour told me this afternoon of a highly recommended colleague at Mankato; a very good doctor and a superior surgeon and who has performed many liver transplants."

258

"Did you get a name?' Teresa asked.

"I have it written down somewhere, Baranpour said he was a Sihk."

"Then his last name is Singh." Killeen said. "It seems we are placing all of our trust and hope in Dr. Baranpour's connections."

"What else do we have?" The voice came over the cell phone.

Dixie started her poll: "Killeen?"

"Mankato."

"Teresa?"

"Mankato."

"Nicky?"

"Mankato. Just know we are all behind whatever you choose."

The gravity of Ryan's situation descended on the four sisters. "I'm not going to make this a drawn out decision. I will tell Dr. Baranpour we have chosen Mankato. There's not much to go on other than our trust in him and his good judgment and the reputation of the Mankato Institute. Just because someone needs a liver doesn't necessarily dictate they will receive one. I am sure Baranpour will go through the details of the Mankato transplant program for us. It is very possible no suitable match will be found, and that would be our worst outcome. If Dad is ready for surgery, there's not much else we can do. After the hospital does all it's pre-op work; there's a possibility they'll send him back with me or Killeen to wait for a liver……..I think he's too sick to leave the hospital. My God, this is getting tough. When I can, I will seek your input on the major decisions."

"I doubt they'll send him home…..he too sick." Teri wondered if they were looking at the same patient.

The twins had never seen this side of the youngest sister. She was the artist – the free spirit. This take charge woman was never part of her exterior. She felt confident with her handling of the situation; she was confident Ryan had made the correct selection putting her in control of his health matters.

"Do you need me up there, is anything imminent?" Nicky said.

"You will have to come, might be for the best if you prepared Rick and the kids for your departure. Get done what you can so it's not such a jolt on him and the kids."

"Time frame?"

"So much depends on whether he catches a match. Boy wouldn't it be great if the liver was divisible and they could use one of ours like they do with a kidney transplant?"

"It'd solve a lot of problems." Teresa gave a nervous smile.

"Before I sign off I'd like to pray and call for Jesus to come upon us, guide us, and heal Papa – You guys can handle that….." Nicole said.

"I'm the least religious of us, but you must believe I'm ready to pray." Dixie squeezed her eyes shut.

The four were on their knees as Nicole led them in prayer for another 15 minutes.

259

We were into our 3rd week of taking showers. Before we returned to class; word got around we were skipping our showers. It pissed the girls off, and they made a stink about it to Sister Alexa. This week, she was going to find out what was going on and ask Father Joe if in fact we were skipping our showers.

She left the mimeograph room when gym class was finishing up to speak with Father Joe. Four guys saw her in the gym and they were all dressed for class sitting in the bleachers. They watched her go outside and looked around the asphalt area where we had the time trials. The only other place Father Joe could be would be downstairs in the locker room.

She continued searching the gym. I could see the bottom of her habit from the locker room and showers in the basement. I didn't think anything of it until I realized some guys were already in the gym waiting for the rest of us so we could all go up together.

Later on I found out she was quizzing the guys in the gym why their hair was completely dry. She put the squeeze on Little Johnny O'Connell, "Where's Father Joseph?" She had her sleeves rolled up.

"Oh he went back to the monastery after gym class."

"Did you take your shower O'Connell?" She turned to the others, "Why are you boys up here already? What's going on here."

One of the four explained they were all on the injured list, so they didn't take gym.

"That's a bunch of crap boys, you all were playing football during recess. What's going on here?"

Around six boys emerged from the locker room and walked into the gym, unaware of Sr. Alexa's presence. She walked over to the boys and grabbed them behind the ears, and felt their hair at the back of their necks. She took a whiff of her hands: "No soap......no water.....all sweat. All of you – back downstairs........you too O'Connell."

"But Sister ----"

"Shut up you little skater."

She marched them all downstairs. I could see her half in the boys' locker room and half in the stairwell. It was a little strange; however nobody was naked. The soviet block guys had been in and out of the shower already. Alexa never turned and peered at us. Her eyesight was cast upon our mascot painted on the wall - some guy in a coonskin hat with the caption "Pioneer Power". With her cupped hands she called through the locker room: "All of you will take your shower right now. You've been instructed what to do. Be back in class in 20 minutes. She climbed the stairs back up to the gym.

"Now what?" a lost voice called.

O'Connell was in the next row over and I asked him what she was doing in the gym..

"Oh I think somebody ratted us out about how we were skipping the shower. She said she was looking for Fr. Joe, but I think she was just snoopin' around." Johnny said as he started to undress.

Chubba Nikos, one of our immigrants from Hungary always took a shower from the first day. He didn't look none the worse for it. "Not a big deal in the old country. I am happy to take the shower. They have community showers in Hungary – whole family can go. The boys and men go on one side and the girls and women go on the other side. Just like they got at Tibbett's pool.

Out of the blue, he starts getting naked again which caught me by surprise because he already took a shower. Chubba's the first one back in the showers; then two more, then five. Next thing, there's guys in front of all eight shower heads. Clouds of steam began to pour out into the locker room.

We all laughed at Chubba, he was cursing because his towel was already wet from taking a shower when he was supposed to. "Sonabitch!"

With the clouds of steam and streaming water, we let our past insecurities flow down the drain. On the other end of the shower, somebody was singing that Elvis tune: 'Love me tender- love me sweet'......and this rube from our end sings the rejoinder: "Come on baby......beat my meat."

It was all behind us now. Everyone was singing, laughing, dancing, hootin' and hollerin'. Our hips were gyrating to and fro, and side to side; shaking our skinny asses to the songs inside our heads. We had broken through some kind of psychological barrier. Guys were dancing Tarzan style on top of the benches, beating on the lockers for that deep jungle effect.

Dennis O'Leary and me were rinsing the soap out of our hair; something was going on through the steam at the other end. We walked over to a whimpering sound. Dennis looked at me, I could see three or four other boys, and shrugged my shoulders. O'Leary motioned with his finger on his lips to shush; we inched over. The power clique was up to something. They had run everything from the day Jane brought us to All Souls. They weren't giving up their control now: they had the poster boy of what most people would recognize as the embodiment of the phrase – 'he looked Irish' and had him backed into the shower. We saw him trapped in the corner.

Smart Alec and Phil Vittorio laughed, "Look at dat."

"Fuckin' Jimmy Desmond got a boner," Dave Roselli teased.

"Yeah......What's that mean Jimmy when you get a hardon for the guys?"

"It just happened fellas – I can't control it."

"Bullshit Desmond, you're a fuckin' queer."

Back and forth it went: "You are....I ain't.....You are.....I ain't......You are......."

Dennis and me gave a nervous laugh. No good would come of this. "Let's get changed."

They used to have this popcorn product at the grocery store; they pushed it with a good commercial. They called it Jiffy-Pop Popcorn. It came in an aluminum pie dish with an aluminum wire hanger to form the handle. The popcorn was covered with expandable aluminum foil. It'd grow into a volleyball sized orb filled with the popcorn. The metal dish, cover, and handle were pressed into one unit at their factories to stay in place.

To cook the popcorn (adult supervision recommended), the aluminum fry pan was held about three to four inches above the stove's burner. The commercial showed it being cooked over a campfire, but the manufacturer preferred an electric stove's burner. It had been on the market for about a year or so when stories hit the newsprint and airwaves about kitchen fires, popcorn exploding through the foil, and kids misusing the product in various ways. Still, it sold fairly well due to the commercial and a catchy jingle. Families would gather at the stove after dinner, or before a ballgame or prize fight, and watch a flat pie pan grow into that aluminum ball of popcorn. The kernels could be heard exploding inside the growing ball, and the chanting would begin: Pop – Pop – Jiffy Pop!"

Hal thought the Jiffy Pop was really neat. He loved making it when he was stewed. He told Ray and me: the jiffy pop process was similar to a modern nuclear reactor only in miniature. He said the kernels were the uranium rods and the expandable foil top was the containment dome producing a controlled nuclear reaction. Ray knew what Hal was talking about, but I was lost......as usual when it came to the technological junk. I liked making it more than I did eating it.

The big clique boss, Vic Renko, came into the shower, summoned by his crew who had Jimmy Desmond prisoner.

"Vic.....Check this out." Phil Vittorio called.

"The boy's got a hardon.......a boner." They laughed.

Vic was disgusted and oozing contempt. His voice came through the fog, "What is wrong with you Jimmy ---- You pop a rod in our shower? What's wrong with you?"

I didn't want any part of this crap and neither did O'Leary, I rinsed off with some cold water again, as this Jimmy Desmond business had me a wondering if these showers were really necessary as we went to our lockers.

These guys took Jimmy's towel, and he had to exit the shower with his hands covering up his excitement.

Smart Alec announced to the locker room, "Jimmy Desmond got a boner in the shower."

Another tuff chimed in, "How 'bout 'dat......Jimmy popped a rod."

Terror flushed Jimmy's face red.

"Pop a rod for the guy's Jimmy? You ought to know better than that."

Popped a rod.......Popped a rod. The words came together from the commercial: "Pop....Pop.....Jimmy Pop. The words ring-rhymed together, and were repeated over and over. The chanting got louder. Wet towels began snapping Jimmy's butt and boner. They were pouring it on. Desmond went into a fetal position in the corner for protection.

"ALRIGHT." Big Vic bullied, "Piss on him........Give Jimmy a nice golden shower." Vic laughed, so they all laughed.

Jimmy whimpered in the corner of the locker room. Vinny Tarts, totally naked, put his forefinger knuckle into Vic's chest and pushed him into the lockers: "That's enough Renko." Next Vinny looked over to Jimmy, "Take a shower Jimmy and use Roselli's towel to dry off."

We knew Dave Roselli wouldn't put up a fight if Vic wouldn't back him up. They did what they were told for once. Vinny was taller and bigger than those other jags. What gave him the authority to call the shots was his speed on the track. Everyone all respected that.

Jimmy Desmond took another shower, the last two guys were finishing up as well. The 7th grade rite of passage had not yet been fully ritualized. The drumming on top of the lockers began. Soon, we were all dancing, chanting, and singing: "Pop....Pop....Jimmy Pop........Pop....Pop.....Jimmy Pop."

Cole Westen, Mark Mueller, Dennis O'Leary, and me were using the first row of lockers closest to the stairwell. The 18 other guys were using the two other - less exposed rows. Our row was relieved we didn't have to see anymore of Desmond.

The middle row of guys were doing their version of 'The Gauntlet'. Most of us were still naked. They had a crazy beat going. Dennis the Menace and me were dancing on our bench like a couple of spearchuckers. Cole and Mark kept banging and singing: "The Belgian – Belgian Congo!....The Belgian – Belgian Congo!" Our hips went from side to side, and to and fro, and we reached for the ceiling. I made every move Jane and Judy had ever taught me. The entire class did this freeze step. Crazy John Pomeroy froze a couple of times standing on one leg, his other leg up to the sky as he grasped his heel with his hand: His tool box out there for everybody to check out. Kenny Crawford and Fast Eddie Mason were on the floor laughing hard.

The four of us in the first aisle were dancing on top of the locker room bench. Cole and Mark had their drawers on at least, but O.B. and me were celebrating our nakedness. My hands were clapping the beat above my head; an apparition came through the fog of the steam........It was Sister Alexa. The first thing she sees is me, about eye level with the one-eyed serpent and a couple of large eggs. She gets a good eyeful. Cole and Mark hid in the lockers and Dennis was facing towards the second and 3rd rows. She looked at me for a good 30 seconds, and it started getting excited. Word that something was going on had reached the other two rows and the locker room got progressively more quiet except for Desmond's puppy dog cries.

The nun walked over to the center row so she could see most of the guys. She used as much voice power as she had from her small frame: "FREEZE.......EVERYBODY FREEZE !" Even the fog in the locker room stopped moving.

"I have never seen a more depraved bunch of sick individuals carrying on like a pack of wild animals." Alexa emphasized every word. Somebody in the middle row tried to cover up, and another tried to turn to the side.

263

"I told you perverts to FREEZE! --- I'm going to get Father Mahoney to deal with you devil worshipers." She reduced the opening of her eyelids to about an eighth of an inch slits probably from her revulsion. "And, I'm not seeing anything I haven't seen before. I have five brothers, so don't think any of this is new to me."

"Desmond, get off the floor."

"Sister….. those boys they……." Jimmy wanted justice.

"Shut up Desmond." Her hands went back on her hips. She returned to our row.

'Dammit. I said when I looked down. It had Pinnochioed a curve right over to her, it really was on automatic pilot and looked right at Sister Alexa and beckoned her. O'Leary was the only other witness.

"You two get down." She watched as I took the big step off the maple plank. The bouncing movement, her voice, and my inescapable attraction to this quasi-dominatrix had intensified a weird attraction to her. The movement of my body relayed the springboard effect to my unit. I stole a glance at Denny: Flaccid and passive.

'What the fuck? Anyway, she ain't supposed to be down here in the first place. How the fuck is this possible? What's she going to do - send a note home to Hal? Hey your son's got a boner for me? Inwardly I laughed, and I almost broke into a physical smile.'

"Are you amused or just excited Mr. Whitelaw – Do you think this is some kind of joke?" She lowered her volume when she spoke.

"No, I don't." In my mind, I was cursing Cole and Mark for having enough sense to squeeze into the lockers.

She moved closer to me. "Something's stimulating your sick…..sick mind." Sister Alexa stared at the antithesis of one of her intended vows.

The steam's fog was still thick; one of the showers spurted more hot water by the last guy who didn't turn off the hot water. The nun seemed to float through the locker room. She stood at the end of the center row.

"Everyone get dressed and wait down here until Father Mahoney comes." With so many boys having been in the buff, she knew she'd have some explaining to do if she tried to manage this incident on her own. Up the stairs she hurried off.

"Is she gone?"

I recognized Crawford's voice.

He stood up on the change bench in his black chino's and cupped his hands around his mouth, "Hey Cleo!" It had taken almost the entire school year, but Crawford came up with a handle for her, and it stuck. Tarts and me never did find out the meaning from Kenny. We'd ask him once every two weeks and he'd make this vee with his fingers and stick his tongue between them kind of lapping at it. I knew he was doing an oral thing from the porno magazines. Vinny would ask him again to explain, and Crawford would bust a gut laughing like he was on drugs.

Later on I asked Tarts what Crawford meant and he said, "That's Kenny." and laughed.

I was used to Ray explaining the unexplainable, but this shit was from the world of Crawford, and he was off the wall.

Unable to get any of the priests to come over to the grade school to discipline the boys in her class, The office secretary advised Sister Alexa she should resolve this matter on her own if possible, or with the Vice Principal's assistance if necessary; Sister Celeste was at a conference in the Bronx for the day.

"Who is the Vice Principal?" Alexa's brow squeezed together.

"Sister Acquila." The secretary replied.

"Sister................?" Alexa took a deep breath and laughed. The young nun knew getting Acquila involved could only make the situation worse.

The boys were dressed; the flesh show a half-hour earlier seemed to have quelled, and disappeared in the fog. The Jimmy Desmond episode never saw the light of day except amongst our class. Poor Jimmy was a nervous wreck for the remainder of the school year.

Sister Alexa appeared once again at the bottom of the steps, barely in the locker room. She was brusque, "Not a word from any of you – go straight to the classroom. We marched single file past Sister Alexa. I was almost past her; she grabbed me by the ear and pulled me out of line. "You wait here." After the rest had passed us, she pushed me back into line at the very end.

Something was holding up the line, and she quickly climbed the stairs on the left. At the top step, Desmond was having a meltdown and he had to pick up his soap, comb, and washcloth he had dropped. "Hurry up Desmond." She said standing over him.

There were some more mumbles and whimpers as he tried to catch up with the line. When I reached the top step, she wound up and slapped me on the back of my head.
I was propelled forward and fell onto the gymnasium floor. "What'd I do?" I reeled back with my left fist. I was dumbfounded and rattled.

"Detention after school Whitelaw."

The letter 'F' was formed on my lips as I went by her. I thought she was okay until this health and gym class crap started. 'Thanks a lot Desmond' I thought as I made my way up to class. The way rumor travels, I was sure Ray would ask me at lunch what went happened at gym class. Either way, I'd have to get his advice about this debacle, and find out if I had any options.

v

The next day, Sister Celeste had been brought up to speed about yesterday's incident. Sister Alexa had reported Jimmy Desmond had been the victim of verbal taunts, some undetermined hazing, and there was an incident of willful disrespect to a teacher.

Again I stood in Sister Celeste's office with Sister Alexa in attendance. The Principal said: "Ryan Whitelaw, you've been in this office too many times with these issues. Is there some explanation? You have some misconceptions about what constitutes respect to the teachers, other students, and to the school in general. Sister Alexa feels you are in need of some detention time to think about your conduct."

The Principal made sure our eyes met as she spoke; "I'm not sure detention has made enough of an impression to improve your conduct. I am more inclined to have your parents come in to see if they can exert some leverage at home which might improve your conduct at school."

The Principal turned to Sister Alexa, "How are Whitelaw's grades?"

"Somewhat better than average."

"Altar Boy?"

"Yes."

"Sports?"

"Track......basketball."

Sister Celeste turned back to me, "You've got all this going on but you're determined to make a career of goofing off." She wrote something in my file and turned to Sister Alexa, "What's causing this behavior?" The Principal was tired of the affair.

"I believe Ryan wants to be Mr. Big Shot."

"He's not a ringleader."

"No. The boys who degraded Jimmy Desmond, they're the ringleaders." Sister Alexa said.

Sister Celeste resumed: "A lone wolf.....?"

"Yes that would be more to the characterization." she said.

"Whitelaw, you're excused." She waited for me to leave.

"We're smarter than them – at least we better be. Menial work as punishment.......it starts becoming ineffective at this age – reinforces rebellion. We don't want to do the work of his parents either. This will be a good learning experience in disciplining your students. Let's see how you handle this. Bring your boys to the gym at 2:00 o'clock and have them sitting in the bleachers. I'll talk to them alone; it will be brief."

The call to the principal's office had me miffed. Nothing was mentioned of Sister Alexa's 'walk in' on the undressed class in the locker room - never made the light of day. I don't even know if it made it past Sister Alexa. It might have been buried by everyone who had power or knew what had happened.

Sister Celeste addressed the boys' from both 7th grade classes in the gym. We were warned for our disgraceful, licentious, and cruel conduct. Her rant only lasted six to eight minutes; she sternly cautioned us: any further hi-jinx in the showers and locker room would have both the innocent and the guilty parties being sent down with no hearing. "It is in the interest of all to maintain order and decorum."

The administration couldn't have been too seriously concerned: Jimmy Desmond gets towel whipped, humiliated, and pissed on. There were skinny asses shining all about the locker room gyrating to the jungle beat and dancing and jumping like Watusi warriors. I wasn't doing anything different than anyone else, and I pull detention.......the only one.

266

Our class was lining up for the dismissal bell. One of the other mile runners was near the end of the line. I asked Eddie Gibson: "Hey Eddie, how come no one else got detention .....we were all naked?"

"Awww.......she must have got shy when you flexed your love muscle for her." He laughed.

My face contorted. "You saw that?"

"Nah, O'Leary told me."

"Now the whole class knows and soon the 8th graders will know too." I shook my head.

Eddie tried to put a positive spin on it, "At least it was for the best lookin' nun they got."

"There goes track and baseball. This is a set-up Eddie, you know it's pure b.s."

"Looks that way to me – maybe you'll only have to do a week. What can she do to you? Make you write 500 times – 'I promise never to get a stiffy when a nun enters the boys' locker room'? It's absurd. See you tomorrow Whitebrokelaw."

The classroom was now empty. I went back to my desk and started on my home work. Sister Alexa was down in the mimeographing room making hand outs for tomorrow, I didn't know when she would be back. I'd be an hour late with paper delivery. If there was anything else coming down on me, they would have already let me know.

The only thing close to this incident was when Vinny's older brother, Joey, got caught boosting a quarter keg of beer. The keg never got tapped at the jubilee celebration for some priest. On Monday morning, Joey Tarts got pinched by the coppers with three Gorton Jr. High girls and Mitch Stokes who dropped out of Saunders Trade and Technical High School in the 10th grade. The keg of Rheingold was wearing an All Souls sweatshirt. Joey was three years older than Vinny. He finished his High School education at Gorton High, where he wanted to go anyway. Joey was pretty smart when it came to school, but he wasn't the best criminal around. He was too interested in getting high.

Sister Alexa showed up around 3:30. "Come up here and do your homework – sit at McAvoy's desk."

She had her head down looking for typos on the material she had just copied. The silence was protracted. She looked up from her desk and looked at me until I looked back at my homework.

Alexa finally spoke keeping her eyes on her desk, "You know why you are here?"

"Not really."

"No -- You DO know why you are here." she insisted.

"If I am here, then so should every other guy in that locker room."

The teacher again gave me this weird stare, "They didn't do what you did."

Disbelief rushed me; I closed my eyes and shook my head. "I haven't a clue as to what you're talking about Sister."

267

"You know so well what I am talking about – your sin towards me." she said.

"Sin?......You smacked me in the back of the head – I didn't do a thing."

"You may not have had the sin of willfulness, but your body......your body followed the true desires that pollute your thoughts which were manifest in the response your body displayed."

"Hey sis, I don't have a clue of what you're talking about."

"It is Sister – Sister Alexa. Where do you get off ---?"

"Okay....okay. I apologize. I misspoke............Sister."

Alexa reduced her eyes to horizontal slits: "I am here with someone who's made carnal advances towards me." This time it was her face registering disbelief.

"What's that mean?" I said.

"It means you wanted to gratify your sexual appetite through me, with me, or in conspiracy involving me. Do you deny you have such desires?.......The truth is you cannot deny you have such passionate feelings.....as I have witnessed your body in a state of complete sexual stimulation and excitement. Don't even try to deny your lust Whitelaw. Just think on this: Lusting for me is more than desiring a woman, because it is directed towards a woman who has sworn herself to the Lord. You have committed sin......perhaps mortal to your soul."

I couldn't see far enough ahead to know what she wanted: an admission of guilt, a valiant defense, a complete emotional breakdown. This incident had to stay within the walls of All Souls, I didn't want Hal or Jane coming up here to deal with this. One thing the young nun was right about – this was bad.

"Sister, I don't know what all the fuss is about."

"You are going to sit there and tell me I didn't see what I know I saw." She shook her head and laughed.

It was almost 4 o'clock. "Alright Whitelaw – I'll give you some time to think this over. You be here at 8 am on Saturday morning. Look at the servers schedule and call the altar boy serving the 6 a.m. mass, and tell him you were instructed by the coordinator to serve Friday and Saturday for him. Who's serving that mass now?"

I read the schedule: "Gerry Poole."

"I should have never given him that early mass, sometimes he can't make the 9 o'clock mass on Sundays." She thought aloud.

If word got out I flashed her the bone, I would be expelled for certain. Some cop or prosecutor would want to throw me into reform school and label me as being a compulsive exhibitionist. There was one possibility: because the thought of the act was behind the pail, it might just be dismissed as one big misunderstanding because of my age, her stature as a nun, and the damage to the reputation of the All Souls parish. As I sat there, something was 'off' about this matter – it wasn't adding up.

Sister Celeste should have been in the middle of the mess; I had only been confronted with the fact I was there when the Jimmy Desmond incident had occurred, and that I was some kind of "Lone Wolf" who the two nuns didn't want to see go 'bad'. I watched her watch me – I knew right then she never said anything up the ladder about my sexually charged display. Dennis O'Leary had been the only witness, and he had his butt facing Sister Alexa in the fog. Guys like Eddie Gibson only got the story second-hand from Denny-O, and maybe Cole Westen and Mark Mueller who had been hiding in the lockers. This was between Sister Alexa, O'Leary, and me. To everyone but the three of us it was just 'hearsay'. Still I had no options except to say "yes" to her and get out of the 7th grade as fast as I could. There were about 2-1/2 months left to the school year.

MY MIND RACED ALL THE WAY HOME WITH THE EVENTS of the last two days. Nobody was at 21 O'Dell, but Ray's school stuff was on the first landing of the stairs. He was somewhere in the neighborhood, and I had to get going on the paper route. At 5:30; I only had the rest of O'Dell to do.

Daylight Saving Time did a number on me for some reason; I knew we had lost an hour, but it seemed we gained it instead. It had been about a year since Ray and me had witnessed the comet doing mach 4 up the Hudson River like a laser. Just because the government says we've lost or gained an hour - have we truly lost or gained it? Is it reality or convenience? The measurement of time is scientific; the keeping of it was merely a point of view.

Three papers remained to be delivered; I saw the green Chevy station wagon coming down O'Dell; Hal was driving with Cathy and Willis in the back seat – no Jane. He spotted me at 45 O'Dell. I knew it made him happy…..when a guy was working, he didn't have time to get in trouble…… standard or daylight saving time. I entered the house through the garage. Hal was ranting in the kitchen, so I hung out in the cellar until he got some whiskey in him. It had been calm for about three minutes, he was boiling a hunk of kielbasa and retired to his cubby-hole den as he waited for the Polish sausage to cook. He caught me going upstairs to our room.

"Where's your brother?"

"Watchin' TV." I knew he wanted to know where Ray was, so I told him where Willis was.

"The genius……..where's the genius?"

"You're talking to him." I figured I'd give Hal a little bit more.

"On your best report card - you're average at best."

"His stuff is here – he's around." I'd already had enough interplay with him.

He took a long pull on his Tareyton, "Yet once again Ryan, I can count on you for the obvious. A point of information for you and Werner Von Braun: Until the Dance instructor finishes and get's a ride from her partner in crime – Judy, dinner will be 'Everyman for himself'. I've fixed up the junior set with some Cap'n Crunch, but I have to inform you they've finished it off. There's only enough Kielbasa for me.

"Hey Dad, I'm going to scout around for Ray."

"You might want to stick around, she might be bringing home some doughnuts.

I went to the laundry room at the apartment. Some knockout hippie lady who didn't get the paper was folding clothes. I dropped 35 cents into the machine and got a quart of choclate milk for the quick walk to Greystone. As I left the apartment on Hawley Terrace, I shot a quick glance at Lynn's house 'Dark Shadows'.............nothing.

THE DELLWOOD DAIRY MADE SOME SUPER CHOCOLATE milk.........better than Yoo-Hoo, and it was made right here in Yonkers. To Ray and me Dellwood Chocolate milk was the best – hands down. Jane's blood father had worked for Sheffield dairy after WWII. They were bought out by Sealtest - the big metro dairy. Jane was always keen to have her dad's company milk in the fridge when he'd make his Christmas visitation. Last Christmas when I thought I was going out with Lynn Van Metter; Ray explained why Mom-Mom and Jane's father had to visit at different times.

Mack had a different play on the Dairy business. In Straatsville, he lived near the source of the milk which was sent to the metro area to be processed into homogenized milk and other dairy products. For straight white milk, we liked the milk we got up there best.

Mack, Ray, and me would go across the gravel road onto Mack's brother's property. His brother, Chubb, had about 13 acres of pasture land. This dairy farmer, Cookingham, paid Chubb to let his dairy cows graze on his property. Chubb was an ironworker like Mack, and renting out his land to farmers was just a sideline.

First Chubb moved out of Yonkers with his family. Two years later Mack and Mom-mom, built their shack about 1/4 of a mile away on the other side of the road. No indoor bathroom in the early years. Mom-Mom was ready to spend the rest of her life using an outhouse just to get out of Yonkers.

Usually before dusk, the three of us would cross onto Cubb's property. Ray carried the milking stool, I carried the galvanized pail with a tall-boy of beer, and Mack carried another pail, and drank the half-quart in his hand. We had to spread the barbed wires to get in and out of the pasture. Dairy farmers were still running herds of Guernseys and Jerseys back then. Once the Holsteins started making inroads into the production of milk, the milk companies found it cheaper to herd Holsteins. Gradually we saw less and less Guernseys and Jerseys. The two breeds were all about milk quality, while Holsteins was a production cow. Mack didn't have to ask any Dutchess county dairy farmer about the difference – you could taste the difference.

Sometimes Mack had to tie a cow to a split rail fence, when the cow didn't want to get milked, but the cows were generally happy to get rid of a load. I thought they were a lot like us guys.

A three gallon pail was filled up four inches from the rim. One was from a Holstein and the other was from a red and white Guernsey. There really was a lot of difference between the two breeds. The Guernsey output sometimes was about six inches from the pail's rim. Ray and me thought it was a real panic when Mack would shoot

270

cow milk in our faces. When we finished the milking, we'd have to hand the pail over or through the barbed wire. We always spilt some getting back to the road. The one time Mom-Mom set up a blind taste-test; she poured out two cups for Allison, Ray, and me, and we were supposed to figure out which of the two were better.

Everything was going fine until I ran into this one cup Mom-Mom had poured for me. I took a gulp from the cup and sprayed the milk from my mouth into the grass: "ONIONS!" I choked. I swiveled off the bench onto all fours. Everybody laughed.

Mack looked across the road to Chubb's pasture. It wouldn't be long and the cows would trek to the old barn and get milked by one of the Cookingham girls. Hurry up boys, we'll get a different cow – one that didn't feed in the onions.

Ray reasoned the move to Holsteins was all about money, but he wouldn't be surprised if Dellwood Dairy was still using Guernseys to make their Chocolate milk. Mack said, "Next to beer, it was the best drink a person could have." The dairy up by Mack was still making their milk 1/5 Guernsey; 4/5ths Holstein. It didn't sound like much, but just about every other dairy was going 100% Black & Whites. The Red & Whites were being used for cheese, buttermilk, half & half, and ice cream at the better stores and restaurants.

By the time Ray and me were in the 8th and 9th grades, Cookingham had passed away, and his kids didn't want to go dairy farming so Ma Cookingham sold out and they trucked her Black & Whites west towards Rochester and the Red and Whites went to Vermont. Mom-Mom and Mack had to buy their milk at the Grand Union with the rest.

vi

I made my way down the steps of Henry Hudson Park, spilling some of the chocolate milk as I descended. Chances were 50-50 Ray would be down the river or the train station. The last two days had me in a quagmire; I had to run this nightmare by him. It was highly probable he had heard something of the 7th grade locker room incident. I scanned the station area and beyond without sighting him, even from the top of the pedestrian bridge I couldn't see him. The swinging door of the covered overpass had been hooked open; probably by a commuter. The breeze off the river did what it could to push the tepid smell of alcohol and urine out the other end. There were no intakes or exhaust vents in the overpass. When its doors were closed, it'd fill up with any smoke fairly quickly. If and when they finished the station's improvements – the New York Central might install a few vents in enclosed overpass. Many of commuters would brave the elements rather than wait it out in "the gas chamber".

Soon after I graduated high school, the Penn Central installed sheets of Plexiglas to replace the sheets of graffiti-strewn plywood, but only at the four corners. This let the commuters see the oncoming trains and get to the platforms in time. There still remained a lot of room for the graffiti artists to express their inner feelings, should they find the inspiration. Every so often a true artist would draw a caricature of the female form. Most were junk, but this one drawing was ahead of the others. It was of a vixen kneeling on a bed with a pair of Dominatrix boots. Off to her left in gothic lettering he had written: "Paulette". She was wearing this zippered leather thing; the hips were cut really high, almost to her beltline and sleeveless. It had an upturned collar. The piece was unzipped just below her navel, revealing one of her breasts. Paulette's hair fell over one eye and had a curl at her shoulders. This guy had it just right.......at least I thought he did.......she was beautiful. The artist signed his name:

"Headshot Harry"
Cobbeskill
C – Block/'64-67'

       The Penn Central's anti-graffiti squad made the rounds at least once a year........give or take. They'd give the overpass a new coat of paint and a fresh smell. With Ray's 'Draculynn' on one end and Harry's 'Paulette' on the other, it was a good bet some of these guys didn't know whether they were coming or going.
       These drawings were so good, the graffiti crew taped paper over them and then painted the paper. They knew art when they saw it.
       The majority   of the graffiti was the usual stupid shit you see; perhaps that was why Lynn and Paulette looked so devastating.

       THOUGH THERE WAS A COOL BREEZE FLOWING, I wasn't going to drink the pint remaining in the chocolate milk's paper container. There was a small platform at each end of the pedestrian bridge. The bridge's roof cantilevered over the small platforms, but it really was part of the stairs and not the bridge. There were expansion joints between the two structural components to compensate for their movement. Outside the enclosed portion on the west side of the overpass, there was a mostly unobstructed view of Greystone Station, the Palisades, oncoming trains, and the river.
       About 100 yards away – somebody was near where we had a lot of business. It had to be a guy; girls just didn't wander around a train station unless they were looking for trouble. He was in that narrow strip between the southbound platform and the shore of the river. It had to be Ray. He waved when he saw me. When I got up to him, I handed him what was left of the chocolate milk through the handrail. There may have been six ounces left. He took a sip.
       "Kill it." I said stepping through the handrail and jumping three feet to the ground. "Whatcha' doing?"
       He motioned with his head over to the fishing pole wedged in a big piece of driftwood. "Was going to throw a line in.......couldn't find any worms in the usual spots. Didn't bring down the tackle box."
       I laughed at him, "Nothing's running yet – it's too early."
272

"AAAAaaayyy, it was something to do; besides – I didn't want to be around when Hal got home from work." Silence.

"So what's this business with you and Sister Alexa......you two going steady? You having a session of show and tell detentions?" Now it was my brother doing the laughing.

"Long.........long story; it keeps getting longer. And......." I've got to serve one on Saturday." I kicked some dirt.

"You're not that close then?"

"Give it a break Ray. How come this crap never happens to you?"

"Cause I'm not dumb enough to go messing around with no penguin."

I shook my head wondering if there was a way out.

"You know why I'm down here?"

"Other than the phony reason you're trying to avoid Hal? You're too close to it. It's right here." I answered.

"Feel the sand over there." He watched me lay my hands palms down on the surface about 15 feet away. "Now feel right here."

I repeated the temperature check --- WOW. It's not hot, but there's got to be a 20 degree difference in the short distance."

Ray looked across the river at the Palisades: "Remember when you told me about the way the water drained in the girls' shower......and I told you my signature had undergone some type of metamorphosis – not of my own volition?"

I nodded.

"Something's going on, and this thing we put in this hole has something to do with it." He said.

I tried to go with his flow of unusual occurrences, "And that's why Sister Alexa has got me on the hook with this outer space relationship. It couldn't take place anywhere else or in any other context."

"That's got to be the dumbest shit I ever heard." Ray froze me with a look channeled from some parallel dimension. "Are you in love with your teacher? Listen Romeo.......I'm not talking about you and your infatuation with Alexa."

He had hit an open nerve and it agitated me. "You know what's really dumb – is you being afraid of your own handwriting."

"Is it? You think so? I first saw it occur when I was writing Beatles lyrics in the overpass. I was writing the words to "She Loves You". I get through the first two verses and chorus and it starts turning into a mathematical equation. It ended up being two lines........the length of the bridge."

"What does that mean?" I was amazed.

"Not a clue, but I know the advanced Algebra is correct. I don't know its purpose or what it's related to. I think it looks kool with Lynn and Paulette guarding it."

"Or are they merely adorning it?"

"About a half-hour ago, I replicated your water experiment right here."

A silver plastic pail lay in the sand. Ray had punched a 7/16ths inch hole in the center of its bottom. He hade made certain

273

there were no burrs to impede or alter the water's natural drainage pattern.

"Ryan, I'll submerge the pail in the river;" compressing his index finger against the drainage hole at the bottom, "We'll pour the rest of the chocolate milk in for coloration to verify the rotation of the drainage once the river water starts to come out uniformly."

The experiment started, "Pour just a little bit of the chocolate milk to confirm the rotation of the contents." he directed.

"Same deal as in the girls' shower, but you can see the water's action a lot easier using the pail." I said.

"Tie me kangaroo down sport..........tie me kangaroo down." Ray sang the Aussie song to indicate the water was draining the opposite way for the northern hemisphere. He worked his thumb and forefinger on the bridge of his nose. "There is some alien power at work, this anomaly is more pronounced the closer we get to the cosmic intruder. I'll have to start doing some intense reading and asking around. Thought I had some answers before about the train and the projectile's levitation, but now I've begun to wonder if the water's rotation is even related to the 'cosmic intruder'."

"Have you found out anything?"

"THERE WAS THIS DUDE, EDGAR CAYCE, WHO DIED not too long after WWII. He was a future seer and a real religious man. You ever hear about something called 'Remote Viewing'?"

I didn't respond. " -Remote viewing- allows a person to observe others and events, interpret them, and effect outcomes without physically being there. Cayce, mostly provided healing solutions and strategies for very ill people after doctors, tests, and medicines were found to be ineffective. Occasionally, this Cayce would give readings and/or make predictions which dealt with natural or geo-political events. These readings had the scientists stumped because he was right a good percentage of the time. He foresaw floods, earthquakes, Hitler, Stalin, FDR coming .....their ascension to power. The deaths of FDR and JFK were predicted with amazing accuracy. The great tank battle at Kursk also was foretold."

"Wow...." I was mesmerized. "How'd he do it? Some kind of 'Black Arts' --- 'Black Magic' stuff?"

"Don't you listen? I told you Cayce was a deeply religious man. He'd lay down in the afternoon with his secretary taking notes as he spoke. In a trance-like/self hypnotic state, he was usually fed questions about patients who were unable to find cures for their ailments. The books say he had a really good cure rate considering he was dealing with patients who had been written off by conventional doctors."

"Never heard of the guy."

"It's always the wild stuff that makes the news." Ray said. "Listen, before he died, he predicted the earth's magnetic polarity would begin to reverse. From what I've read, he was unable to be specific when this might occur, other than he felt it was near. Also, he was unable to pinpoint what effects could be expected, or when it might conclude. We've got solid evidence the magnetic reversal may have already started. Some egg heads feel it's going to be easy as flipping a switch with a few minor inconveniences. It may take a millennia to go through a magnetic reversal, but it could as just as easily take a hundred."

"So what? The water goes down backwards." I rolled my eyes.

"It's just not the water Doomkuff........Remember those trains we thought were going to wreck?"

"Yeah........yeah." It hit me: "The diesel locomotive ran normal, but the electric commuter train powered by the 3rd rail – that one had all the drama..........But Ray, who's to say it was caused by a pole reversal and not by the comet?"

"Or a combination of the two?" ......Working in some kind of symbiotic magnetic field from the universe and earth gravities?" He took a drag off a cigarette.

Ray recalled a recent class outing: "When we had the trip down to the Hayden Planetarium, there were a bunch of brainiacs from all over N.Y./N.J. We asked these astronomers and physicists about all sorts of stuff, but mostly about the stuff in the night sky. I asked if they had heard about a sighting last June of a fireball from space that made it through our atmosphere. A few of these space watchers said they had heard sporadic reports, but nothing definitive or noteworthy."

"These experts commented the sun had been producing abnormally strong magnetic, solar, and radiation storms recently. One of the students from Bronx High School of Science asked whether these storms might alter or interfere with our way of life on earth. One astro-physicist said it was certainly plausible."

"Ryan, there was this one whiz-kid babe – She was beautiful in her skirt and blazer. She theorized: the more dependent the world became on the information that was received from orbiting satellites, the greater the probability these bits of information would become magnetically charged and its information corrupted."

"Now, I'm postulating – but if the earth has already begun its pole reversal, it might be accelerating into its new alignment as these storm particles, -magnetic and otherwise- attach themselves in some matter to the waves of information we send up to the satellites and draw down from these orbiting vessels circling the globe. The earth's atmosphere is supposed to prevent the penetration of the harmful stuff. I am afraid we have done much more than bounce phone calls off these Sputniks. These magnetically charged space particles may have attached themselves to our data and crashed through the atmosphere and is peppering the earth's skin."

"Are they harmful?" I asked.

"I don't want to think about it..........The earth is being bombarded by stronger than usual magnetic pulses not only by the sun, but also from deep space. These magnetic fields are having some effect on the planet and life as we know it. Who knows – maybe we'll all start having hair as thick Elvis, or if you put jug of polluted water on the porch, and it catches two or three hours of radio-magnetization; it becomes as clean as rainwater."

"Nah......things were good when the Indians had this land. Whitey screws around and delivers a supercharged edition of pole reversal.............I don't know......we'll have to pray and hope for the best. Maybe we'll get lucky, and nothing will happen." Ray's index finger horizontally sawed his lips.

vii

Yonkers Transit and Liberty Coaches weren't very reliable when it came to sticking to their early schedules on the weekends. Saturday was the last day I had to serve Jerry Poole's 6:00 a.m. mass. I thought I might be able to serve mass, do my detention with Sister Alexa, and maybe make our track meet down the War Memorial sports field - everybody knew the place as 'The Glen'. Not knowing how long Sister Alexa or maybe Mr. Hurley might put me to work, I felt I'd be watching the clock all morning. Track meets started around 11:00 am. Instead of messing around with the buses, I thought I could control the clock better if I took my three speed bike.

For some reason, whenever I rode the bike, I ended up behind schedule, and Saturday morning was no different. I knew I'd be cutting it close as soon as I left 21. I ditched the bike behind some of the hedges at All Souls Church, and charged up the steps to the sacristy. Hanging up my windbreaker, Sister Alexa was carrying some priest's vestments to be put away.

Father Sigmund was almost ready – he had yet to put on the chausable and stood in meditation.

"Hurry-up Whitelaw." She scowled.

I buttoned the cassock, skipping to every fourth button or so. Everyone who had anything to do with the 6:00 am mass were half-asleep, except for the priest. The priest saying mass had to be on the ball; most of them were. This Father Sigmund was an asset to the parish; he taught Greek, Latin, and the classics at City College of New York in Manhattan. Everyone said what a wizard he was. I grabbed a surplice off the rack and slipped it over my head and waited a few feet behind the priest.

It was best to be selective when dressing in altar boy garb. Mostly, we wore the black cassock. On Sundays and Holy days we dressed in the color the liturgy required: purple at Lent, white at weddings and anything to do with St. Mary, red for the Christmas holidays, and green for St. Patty's day and the Pentecost season. All the colored cassocks were wool, but the everyday black ones came in wool and cotton. In the summer, a rookie altar boy would be in a full sweat by the time the gospel was being read if he had chosen wool.

All Souls' heating and cooling technology in the church amounted to a little more than lighting 6 candles in the winter, and only two in the summer. There was no air conditioning – and the heat coming off the radiators went 40 feet straight up to the ceiling glorifying God.

The best thing about having a church too hot or too cold was one of comfort - most of the priests were willing to give the congregation the short version of their sermon. About a year ago, we had a substitute or a visiting priest say Sunday mass; it was awful hot and the church was like an oven. It was one of the best sermons I had ever heard: "It's way hotter than this in hell…..remember that." he said. That was it.

All the men and some of the women wanted to know when this priest would be returning. Someone must have felt they had gotten shortchanged and wrote a letter to the bishop about this priest. Word came back, he had gotten reprimanded.

Father Sigmund and me left Sister Alexa who organized the vestments that had just been washed, restocking wine and hosts, and making up the altar boy schedule for the summer. I rang the bells to wake everyone up as we left the sacristy with the priest following. We went to the foot of the altar. The Church was switching over to the all English mass on the first Sunday in August.

The 6:00 am mass was still all in Latin, and as the only altar boy serving this mass, my Latin had to be good. An altar boy trying to mumble though the responses and prayers might find himself writing the responses every day after school for a week. The only English those attendees heard were the Epistle, Gospel, and sermon; the other 95% was said in Latin.

Back then, the priest didn't even face the people in the church; the mass was between God and the priest. The attendees were merely spectators. These weekday masses had no music, a very short sermon, and if a priest could machine gun the Latin off pretty quick, and took care of business, he could wrap up the mass in 20-25 minutes. Only one altar boy was necessary, and the usual number of people for a 6:00 am mass numbered about 20 in a church with a 1200 seat capacity.

Sister Alexa could not be around the altar floor during mass because she was a woman. Before the mass started she had been getting the altar ready for the weekend masses: sweeping, vacuuming, arranging leftover funeral flowers, filling the cruets with water and wine, changing out the altar linen, and newly washed hand linen for the washing of the priest's hands. The youngest nun in the convent, Alexa was assigned every task requiring physical strength and mental toughness. She also had to put up with a lot of crap from those nuns who thought they had already paid their dues, thinking these menial tasks were beneath them. It didn't take long to figure out who she had to take shit from and who she could hand it out to.

The mass had ended; Father Sigmund and I marched back into the sacristy. Throughout the mass, I could see Sister Alexa off to the side, working in the wings as the mass progressed. She had seen me almost fall face first when I came down the four steps of the altar. The server's cassock had been improperly buttoned to save time and left the right side longer than the left. This was much worse than walking around with one's shoes untied.

Alexa was clearly upset with the distraction I caused during the mass. She directed me to the servers' change area. I hung my

277

surplice up and stood in the black cassock and looked at the mismatched button pattern below my waist. Sister Alexa pushed me into the corner, and I almost fell backwards.

"What's going on?" I was bracing myself for more of the Catholic school 1–2 combination punch.

She made sure the sacristy was empty. The next mass would be in 40 minutes. "Can't you even get your cassock buttoned properly?" She raised her voice and starting undoing the errant buttons from the floor up to my waist. The mismatched buttons and holes were clearly in front of my pants' fly. For sure she was more than fumbling around as my hands were raised as if I was told to "Stick 'em up". Confusion ruled. I didn't think I had amorous feelings for the nun, but with her jostling me around - I could only think of my immediate physical attraction to her, and the memory of the surprise visit to the boy's locker room on Wednesday.

She was a nun, and this was dangerous territory. Even if she made a move……an unsolicited advance; we were still in one of the most sacred parts of the church. Under no circumstances could I make any move other than to get out of the sacristy and away from Sister Alexa.

SHE WAS NOTHING LIKE LYNN VAN METTER. RED FLAGS were everywhere, being waved by devils with pitchforks. 'So you're moving in on God's harem?' I thought. Another one of life's propositions with unlimited downside, it was truly infinite and final. I asked Ray later on when we were in high school, why God gives us this insatiable sex drive, and the Catholic Church tells you to ignore it. Ridiculous. I wasn't sure she had even messed around with me after mass. Perhaps she didn't know a thing about sex. That couldn't be the case – she talked a big game about seeing her brothers naked and all.

I learned more about sex from books and magazines than I did from Lynn or Connie. I could only do what I was told. The straight fact about Sister Alexa was I was afraid of her. The idea was absurd and exciting at the same time.

There also was the mystery of the nuns' habits. What lay beneath all those layers of black muslin, the starched white head dress and accompanying head wrap and collar, plus the highly recognizable veil; all devices of a throwback period to hide the female form. A couple of times I caught her going up the stairs to the 7th and 8th grade classrooms using the inside lane of the stairway. The girls knew we were looking up to see underneath a girl's jumper or up a teacher's skirt or dress. You had to be quick about it; I tried to check out Sister Alexa earlier in the school year. There was nothing there but black stockings and her black habit, I don't think I could see anything past her ankles. It was a 'Peeping Tom' situation, and if the women caught you hanging around the stairs, they'd call your parents in because they knew what you were doing. With the Penguins, there just wasn't that much to see. Still, Sister Alexa had a pretty face for a nun. With the head wrap though, you couldn't even see her ears. To see what she looked like - a guy had to use his imagination. There just wasn't much to work with. She was the best nun in the convent on a number of levels and everyone knew it.

A female student had made an outlandish suggestion to Sister Alexa: she suggested Father Joe and her should get married as they were the youngest and best looking couple All Souls' parish had. She reminded the student that they had vowed to be celibate and they weren't Protestants. When she walked over to the window and looked out, I wondered if she smiled at the compliment or regretted she had gotten into the sisterhood. I thought she had enough on the ball to make it in the real world.

"HOW COULD YOU MISS SO MANY BUTTONS ON YOUR cassock?" She scrunched her brows together.

"We don't have the best lighting in here.........come on Sister – give me a break."

Alexa scanned the sacristy. We were alone, but we knew anyone involved with the 7:15 mass might walk in anytime.

"Whitelaw, I'm serious......just who do you think you are?"

"You haven't forgotten detention today?" She said. "I could extend it."

"What'd I do?"

Another no-win proposition; it sounded like the Saturday was ruined. I was trying to hold my words. 'What was with these people?' I looked down at the floor; psychologically and sexually confused.

"Didn't do anything else than what the rest were doing." I said softly.

Sister Alexa scoffed and said, "Still stuck on that.....my version of what took place is very different young man. I'll see you at 8 o'clock in our classroom."

There was time to go to Busy Bakers and get a buttered roll and a pint carton of milk on Voss Ave. - just off of Lake Ave. I found two quarters, two dimes, two nickels, and three pennies in my pockets to pay for breakfast. One of the dimes was silver; I took it out of circulation - the coin went into the small fifth pocket of my dungarees.

The treasury department and the public started snatching up all the silver coins ever since 1965. Treasury took all of the silver coins and silver bank notes out of circulation and replaced them with cheap nickel-copper-nickel sandwich coins. The only thing backing up the new money was the United States good faith – whatever that meant.

The government said they were melting down the silver coins into bars and stockpiling it at Fort Knox and other U.S. mints and depositories. Every year there were fewer and fewer silver coins and silver backed paper notes in circulation. All the people who grew up using silver remembered that unmistakable ring the coins made when they hit the counter, the floor, or when it was stacked like casino chips. Silver dollars and halves made a music all their own. When paper currency said: Payable on demand in Silver, you knew the money wasn't some idea of future payment, it said: solvency – immediate and verified. No middleman needed to clear funds.

It was 8:00 a.m., Ryan watched Sister Alexa through the reinforced glass of 7-1's door. He didn't think she heard him in the hall and observed her in profile. A strange sympathy clouded his brain. He entered the classroom. She didn't look up. "Sit where I put you Wednesday and get going on your homework."

"Finished it."

"Well – try concentrating on why you are here and no one else is."

Ryan sat daydreaming for the next 35 minutes........ wondering how much of his Saturday he'd have left when she cut him loose. She got up a couple of times and left the room. The 3rd time she questioned him: "Well then – why do you think you are here and no one else is? Surely, you aren't thinking I am picking on you?"

"I lose no matter how I answer." Ryan's eyes beaded down on her.

"It is my recollection you were the one carrying on in an outrageous manner in the locker room."

He looked away.

She raised her voice: "I am talking to you mister."

Ryan turned and they riveted their stare on each other.

"Please don't deny you were sexually aroused."

"What are you talking about?"

"We've been through this."

"Alright Sister – you've got your mind made up.........You tell me what happened.

Her eyes baited him. "I know what I saw."

"So do I, but my version can't possibly be the same as yours."

"You were the first boy I saw when I entered the locker room. You were standing on a bench waving it."

"Sister, I saw you gaping at me for a good 10 seconds; then you turned to Dennis O'Leary, and then back at me for another look which lasted longer than you would care to admit to."

The intensity of their eye contact increased and Alexa raised the tone and volume of her voice. "I assure you, I didn't stare at anything.........least of all you. If anything – you were staring at me; after I was dealing with an out of control pack of wild animals in the other two rows, I came back over to deal with your row and you. And you young man - were in a state of full excitement."

Ryan winced, looked away, and scoffed at her.

"You think not? Well either you like boys or you found me attractive – which is it?"

"I tell you this: I don't find boys sexually attractive, and if I did have a rod on – it was by mistake and not over you." He wondered if there was a way out of this mess.

"If.........if it is true, and you are not stimulated by boys, then am I expected to believe the sexual part of your anatomy became enlarged for no apparent reason? Please restrain your imagination Mr. Whitelaw."

"Sister – when you're a guy they just happen." He rubbed his eyes with the binocular fists of his hands.

"This - I do not believe. Furthermore, I suspect you have a crush on your teacher." Again she used her pencil for emphasis.

"You? Gimme a break." He laughed aloud.

"Yes, and it is very dangerous for so many reasons."

"Holy Crow." Ryan smiled, but the smile began to fade when he felt it growing.

"You claimed you weren't excited by me the other day, but your body displayed one of the primary responses associated with desire and lust."

"I don't even know what you're talking about Sister. I don't love you or want to be your boyfriend."

"Go into the cloak room and turn the light on." She followed behind him. Alexa closed the door behind him. The clock read: ten to nine. She went out into the hall and listened. There were no sounds coming from within the school. She stood in the hallway for another two minutes.........nothing. The classroom door was locked from the inside. With one hand she pushed the door against its jamb and threw the door's bolt into the latch hardware locking it.
Her hand grasped the cloakroom door handle, she stood there with her eyes shut for 20 seconds. Alexa closed the door behind her as Ryan stood there.

"You are going to pull down your pants, and if you are not excited – then I am in error and detention is cancelled, but if you are aroused – you are going to be sorry you don't have any self control. You will have lied about your desire for me and your passionate feelings for a nun whom you wish to tempt. Are you not concerned for your soul Whitelaw?"

He pulled his dungarees down below his knees, space eyed.

"Take your shoes and pants off."

Quickly, she stepped into the classroom and opened the door and again listened: nothing. Sister Alexa locked the door and went into the top drawer of her desk and grabbed an 18x2 inch wooden ruler and closed the door behind her.

Alexa was close in height and weight to Ryan. They again faced one another. He didn't know what to expect next; he knew it was going sideways. How weird could it get? How physical? Maybe he was in Connie territory. Ryan was confident he could take her if she started with any roughhouse stuff.......unless she slit his throat like Speck or the Strangler.

"No more games.....the truth."

"Huh?" he stood before her immobile.

The nun reached in and pulled it out......erect as a steel column. "Those shorts will be coming off." She said.

Ryan looked down. 'What a time to get the boner of the year.' he thought.

Sister Alexa waited for about 15 seconds. "Alright then." She knelt down in front of him and pulled down the boxers from his hips.

281

She yanked them three times before Ryan's stiffy made it over the waistband. "No.......you don't like me one bit do you Whitelaw?" The nun gave it a few gentle taps with the ruler and smiled at its resiliency and laughed in contempt.

Halloween night with Lynn raced through his mind; perhaps she wasn't as good looking, but this was starting to happen on a different platform.

"Have you no shame Ryan?"

There was no reply.

"Step out of your underwear."

He was naked except for his Tee shirt. Alexa rotated him 180 degrees using his handle; then turned him in the opposite direction to give him a complete inspection. She played with him a bit, and absorbed the feel, sight, and smell. She looked at the object in her hand: "Nice." The nun finally looked up into his eyes: "I knew you liked me, you do....don't you?"

"I'm sure I do." he replied.

"But you did lie about it. You know you will have to be disciplined."

He was concerned. She brought back a short stool from the corner and sat with her back against the cloak room's wall. Alexa wielded the wooden ruler.

"I'm a little old to be given a spanking." Ryan said.

"I don't think so. Let me ask you: do you think there should be no punishment? Come here." She grabbed the back of Ryan's neck and laid him over her legs, and locked him in place by scissoring his body and placing her right leg behind his neck forcing his head down. His butt was fully exposed with just the right arc to use the ruler. She bit her lower lip with her upper teeth and started to turn his ass into the color of Bazooka Bubble Gum. The two were breathing hard. Sister Alexa applied some more ruler and would stop to inspect the coloration of his ass. "Stand up." It wasn't what the teacher wanted. "Face the other direction."

He rubbed the cheek she had just been working on. "Never mind that." She said, reaching for his stiff handle and forced him face-down exposing the opposite cheek across her lap. "Just a little more."

He peered under her thigh: he could see her undergarments, but couldn't see anything else. Alexa's female scent was sending Ryan into orbit. He didn't think his unit would go limp until next week at the earliest.

Again, he followed her instructions, and her leg locked his head down. Ryan didn't think this was too new to his teacher. He didn't have time to think as the ruler began to be applied to the other cheek; she now had his ass looking like a stop sign. Sister Alexa kept working the two inch wide rule until she had his butt looking the way that made her feel good and in command. It was possible she might have been a little cruel.

Again, she ordered him to stand. Rotating him with his hardon, Alexa had almost had him facing away from her. She ran her flat hands in a downward direction on his cheeks.

"Your bum is on fire." She smiled, finding Ryan's condition to be slightly humorous.

"No thanks to you."

She generously gave him a wink with her left eye: "I'll get your mind off that flaming butt of yours." The nun took another deep breath after another look. "Oh my." She grinned. While sitting on the stool, she slowly spun Ryan 360 degrees by his hips so everything could be appreciated. The inspection and exploration was intense and satisfying her needs. Holding on to him, she paused to look up at his face and smile which was returned by him. No words were exchanged. They were breathing hard. "Just a little more." Alexa said as she fooled around with his stuff. She shuddered; a generous exhale left her lungs.

"Ryan.........We must never – ever tell anyone about today."

He was well aware how fast this might end by saying something dumb. "My brother says people who can keep their mouths shut never have problems."

"I would take his advice. You'll promise to never say anything about this.......us?"

"You know I do – I promise." Ryan wasn't too keen on the spanking stuff, but if she made it squirt.......he could endure all the spanking she wanted to hand out.

"Alright then, we'll continue." Sister Alexa began.

She was busy fondling all of Ryan's equipment to the point where he was getting close. The Sister spun him around and locked him in the spanking position once more with her leg over the top of his neck. He started to complain.

"Shut up."

Alexa played his ass cheeks like she had a bow and was playing a cello. Back and forth the bow sawed until she judged his butt needed a tune-up to maintain color. He didn't complain. Through his legs, Alexa fished his dick out the back to get at him. Stroking him with one hand, and shining his cheeks with the other, she was pretty sure he wouldn't last long. "Ryan, is this your first time?" she whispered.

"No......one other." he said.

"I wanted your cherry. Who is she? I'll make sure she doesn't get out of 7th grade."

He didn't know if she was serious, "She doesn't go to our school."

"You must let me know before it starts coming out – I don't want your mess on my habit."

"Okay." He said with blood rushing to both heads. He thought the spanking might be over. Alexa's hand used a gentle stroke. There was some rustling going on. He caught glimpses of her other hand fumbling underneath her long black habit. He deduced she was bringing herself off. As with Lynn, it was a semi-educated guess. According to the porno magazines, Ryan knew his prick was supposed to be in the girls' box. Neither Alexa nor Lynn made any attempt to have Ryan in them. He was just happy to be invited to a party and do whatever he was told. If a girl or a woman taught him how to get them off, he'd be more than compliant to their needs.

Alexa knew what she needed; her sighing, moaning, and rhythmic rustles left no doubt she was near her climax.

"Sister, I know I'm close."

"Okay.......yes. Stand up and try to maintain just a little – I've got to catch up. He watched; her one hand raised her long skirt and the other one disappeared down her underwear. She focused on his eyes, her body convulsing. Her hand left him, and she worked on herself. "Jerk yourself off Ryan, let me see you ejaculate." Alexa was too far gone, and she broke the bank before he did. She rested her back against the wall, her hand still in her underwear.

Ryan focused on her, he thought she might have ridden in on the comet. 'Man, she hit a home run.' he thought. Relieved, he was amazed: "You made it – I could tell."

"It's so much more intense when you are with someone. I thought you might have gone down, but I must be impressed that your interest is so keen......you've stayed up nicely. I guess I wasn't boring you." She smiled.

"No way."

"Let's just see how bored you aren't." The nun got behind him. Before she reached around she withdrew a handkerchief from her sleeve. She forced her body hard into his back and her right hand went back to work – stroking her star pupil as her other hand waited for the liquid climax.

The fact Alexa seemed to know quite a bit about the ways of sex captivated Whitelaw. He wanted to impress her but he didn't know how to do it. Going with her at her speed was probably going to be the way if he wanted to stay in the game. It was so exciting being so close to the edge of insanity - at the orgasmic precipice; Whitelaw felt he was riding the crest of a 60 footer on the North Shore.

"Let me know Ryan." She whispered and bit his ear lobe.

She watched his face and his love unit as she worked it over. Being in complete control was fascinating to her, but his hips began to automatically pump and his movements were out of control and a few drops hit the floor. Her snot rag fell from her sleeve onto the floor and took both her hands and started pumping from his side.

"I'm losing it Sister." His eyes bulged watching the spectacle.

"Give me the dirty load." She urged as she stroked him off. "Just give it to me." The nun's eyes were riveted as the stuff pumped out.

Alexa's aim had been fair, most of it hit the floor's wood She gave him the soiled handkerchief from the floor. Ryan grabbed it and fell forward into the corner where some winter coats had been abandoned in a random pile.

"Stay there." She said, and returned with enough paper towels to sop up the monsta load.

"Ryan, did you not know you started squirting love fluid prior to your actual orgasm?

Her student pleaded ignorance.

284

She grinned, "I'll have to keep my eye on you and that." She nodded using her pointer finger indicating the thing she just played with.

"Wish I could have made it last longer."

When it comes to sex and lust, a participant always wants to believe the time can be manipulated to extend or slow down those moments we define as 'ecstasy.' She alluded to a topic where these stolen minutes of physical pleasure were not without price: "Ryan, we will have to go to confession today."

"No kidding, that was a sin for sure."

"Even though the priest is bound through ordination never to reveal what he has heard in the confessional, do not confess this sin at our church. Go to any of the neighboring churches and confess; anywhere but here."

"Don't worry – I've had to go out of town plenty with the stuff I've had to confess to." He said.

"And no mention of being with a nun.........and don't let the priest see your face – just look at the floor."

"Sounds good." He looked into the classroom and read the clock on the wall. "Am I off detention now?"

"Why do you ask?"

"You know I'm on the track team. We have a meet at the Glen at 11 am. If I left now – I could make it."

The nun looked at him, the eyes frowned down, "Never will I understand the male gender. Yes, go to the track meet, but that means no more adventures for today. Run around the track with the other boys – that's your decision."

"You mean there's more?"

"Of course stupid, but you'll have to help me get some work done."

"That was the best thing that ever happened to me. I'd like to serve the full detention." he paled at the thought.

It lasted until one o'clock. When he left Ryan felt like he had run a full marathon.

Before they parted he said, "I feel like I should kiss you."

Alexa's eyes grew large, "Remember what I told you...... You can never say anything about today or anything we do in the future. You can never make an outward display we know one another in this special way." They shared a long passionate kiss.

"I understand.........I promise." Ryan nodded.

ix

This thing with Sister Alexa was a big deal on so many levels. Analyzing it on the basis of age alone, it seemed more and more plausible she might not be playing with all 52 cards. Back in the 1960's, it was a toss-up whether she would have gotten arrested for corrupting a minor. The judicial system would have made her take a hike and go somewhere else at the minimum and it would have been covered up and put to bed with no one being the wiser. It would be a totally different story had the rolls been inverted: a priest having sexual relations with an underage girl. Getting caught with that rap, a priest might end up in Sing Sing or worse.

Without photographic evidence or the testimony of an eye witness, all me and Sister Alexa had to do was play dumb and never say a word. They could have shoved bamboo shoots under my fingernails like the Japs or the Krauts using electric shock torture to extract info from the members of the underground; they'd never find out about us through me.

If we were found out by someone at All Souls because of our own carelessness, it might be worse than if the cops handled the case. I knew I would be expelled and she'd be off to a cloistered convent. We had to be careful.

The way bigger picture was - there was a good possibility of going to hell if the powers of the confessional couldn't absolve me from my sin. The way I understood the sacrament of penance: it obliges the sinner to be truly penitent for one's sins before they wipe the slate clean. My problem was: I wasn't sorry....not really. I wanted more, and I always felt my time with Sister Alexa was one of the best experiences I ever had.

She taught me about possessiveness, envy, and jealousy. In late May, just before Memorial Day weekend, I had been talking to Samantha McAvoy during recess out on the asphalt. She was always friendly and was one of the few girls I didn't have to be someone else with. She probably had some left over sympathy for me when Mrs. Foley worked me over last year. There weren't any head games with her. Although there wasn't anything going on between us, I always hoped there might be; there always was an undercurrent with her - I wished it had risen to the surface.

Samantha was pretty good on the piano, she played by ear, and could play better than the kids who had taken lessons. She knew music, and knew rock and roll; and had a lot on the ball. We talked mainly about records, bands, gossip, and TV. Sam told me about this Beach Boy record "Pet Sounds". It really moved her. I liked "Pet Sounds" because Ray told me to, but it took me a while to reconcile this revolutionary departure from their earlier material. Conversely, as soon as the album was released, Sam felt this record was the bands' ultimate statement. According to her, Brian Wilson was a genius amongst journeymen. With her musical background, I felt inferior. I wished Hal or Jane had made me take some kind of musical instrument lessons.

Ray had shown musical interest and talent when we were goofing off at Jane's studios. He talked about a lot of musical stuff with Samantha and the two would fool around on the piano in the music room. They combined talents when they played "Heart and Soul". I wish I had had Ray's musical ear. The two were sold on Brian Wilson.

The other 7th graders who were into the music craze were loyalists to the British sound: Beatles, The Who, Stones, Zombies, Cream, Bee Gees, etc. They all lay ruin to the American music scene.

286

Sam, Ray and me liked the Beatles; we just felt the Beach Boys had been getting shortchanged with radio air play, television, and print media. Metro N.Y.'s top radio station, WABC, had gone so far as to tweak its call letters to W-A-Beatle-C. "The first time I heard their Dee-Jays drop that one on us I almost puked." Sam said.

Across the blacktop, I saw Sister Alexa talking to one of the lay teachers who was also on lunchtime monitor duty. I saw her watching Sam and me. The bell rang and we returned to class about five minutes later.

7-1's class was ready to start our afternoon session; Sister Alexa called me out of class from just outside the doorway to see her in the hall. Tarts asked me, "What's up?" on my way out. I shrugged my shoulders with my back to him. I didn't remember doing anything to warrant a reprimand.

"Shut the door behind you." She moved the business from the view of the class. "What's going on with you and McAvoy?

"Nothing." I turned my palms up.

"You spent the entire lunch recess laughing and talking with her." She rolled up her sleeves to her elbows.

"So?"

"So........So, what were you talking about? Going out and doing things with her when I can't?"

"Sister......" I began.

"And don't call me sister."

"Alexa......?" I tried.

"And don't call me that either."

"Okay – What do you want me to call you?"

"What do you call McAvoy?" Her hands went on her hips.

"Samantha."

"Well – I have a name too."

"You can call me Nicole or Niki when we're alone." She withdrew a hanky from a pocket in her habit and daubed her eyes and wiped her nose. I recognized the pattern; it was the one she had in the cloak room. "What were you talking to her about?"

"Just music mostly: Beach Boys.......Beatles.......and this new band – The Doors."

"Anything else?"

I shook my head; chin up.

"Ryan.".........She waited for eye contact..........."Don't mess up a good thing."

"No way." I shook my head again.

I went back to my seat and Fast Eddie Mason gives me the "what happened?" look.

I mouthed, "Later." to him. I had all afternoon to think up some bullcrap for him before the class was dismissed.

Sister Alexa had a piece of chalk in her right hand and the math workbook in the other as she copied some problems on the blackboard. As she wrote, she turned her head slightly so the class could hear. "Mr. Whitelaw......Detention this Saturday morning for sassing me back and disrespect."

Eddie Gibson bumped his forehead with the heel of his hand, "Jesus, Mary, and Joseph." He took a deep breath.

"But Sister – " Eddie called out, "We need Ryan for the track meet at Tibbetts."

"That's enough Gibson, or you will miss the meet as well."

I only made one track meet in June. The school year was almost over. The eighth graders were full of themselves. Many were going on to All Souls High School. The families too poor to swing the tuition were headed for Gorton. Ray's schedule was completely booked: parties, girls, caddying, and going places I never heard of with people I never met.

I WAS KEEN TO KNOW WHAT THE SUMMER ALTAR BOY schedule looked like. While most of the altar boys were switching their masses around and trying to get out of their commitments, I was trying to increase my mass load to be with Niki. The more I was up at church, the more I would have to run into her. She was going to be my main source of excitement for the summer.

There wasn't any way I'd have as much excitement as Ray. The paper route was unpredictable, but mostly boring. Ray brought me up to Hudson River Country Club to caddy for the July 4th weekend. Lynn Van Metter disappeared the day after public school let out. For me, having a great summer in 1967 depended on a penguin. In two months, I'd be a hot shot 8th grader at All Souls.

The day before the last day of school, the altar boy schedule for summer vacation was posted. Compared to the others, the number of masses I was assigned to serve was considered 'heavy'; most the guys in my grade were glad they weren't me. Vinny Tarts wasn't even an altar boy and he smelled a rat. Kenny Crawford suggested greasing Sister Alexa to reduce my mass load. I played it straight, and made it look like I was taking one for the team. No one knew it was for the Niki/Ryan team.

Secretly I thought: 'She really wants me.' It made me feel so good. I was high just thinking about Niki and the summer.

The last day of school was Wednesday, the 28th. Ray graduated the previous weekend. He got a bunch of money from relatives and friends of Hal and Jane's. The take for my graduation was about 30% less than what Ray took in. Somehow it was always that way: Baptism, Communion, Confirmation, and now Graduation, they were all short when compared with what Ray hauled in.

Sometimes I thought it wasn't fair; most of the time I didn't care which way it worked out. Ray was first born, so he had it coming by birthright. Cathy was the only girl, so she got treated like royalty. Willis was the youngest and they didn't want to leave him short. I knew what was happening – I knew the way it worked; I had to take it in stride. There was no point in trying to blame any of them. What disturbed me was they all had position and I was nothing. Getting to hang around with Ray was my pay-off, and now that seemed to be waning.

SINCE THE NEW GYMNASIUM HAD BEEN BUILT,
ONLY the overflow activities of the parish were held down the church
hall, but they did have sports events down there for fifth grade and
younger. Eight of the church's basement columns were part of the
basketball court. You could also hit the ceiling taking a shot if you
arced it enough. The church hall was old, but it wasn't dirty. It had
been kept in good enough condition; Masses would be held there for
Christmas, Easter, and when there was an overflow in the church.

Sister Alexa had gone away on retreat over the 4th of July
weekend, and extended into a 7 day hiatus from the parish. Before she
left, we rendezvoused twice in the church hall. The first time by
accident: I was getting a box of votive candles for St. Patrick's
devotion display when Niki came out of an unlit hallway with a box of
Hymnals. We both thought the other had left. The candles and the
Hymnals made it up to the church a two hours later.

Summer vacation was in progress and the grade school was
empty. The church hall was perfect for what we were doing. There
were many alcoves, foyers, hallways, electrical rooms, boiler rooms,
and a ladies and a men's room. Any space not needed to say and
observe mass might become a storage area for church and school
materials. In winter it was always cold down there, but in summer, it
seemed to be air conditioned. There was a single person stairway from
the sacristy to the backstage of what used to be a performance stage.
The stage curtains were still the originals, and still hanging.

The Saturday following the Fourth was the 8th of July. I had
been assigned with three other servers for the 9 am mass. It was the
last mass for the day – no funerals, no weddings. Confessions would
be heard at 3 o'clock. Sister Alexa had just returned from retreat and
was working in the sacristy when I arrived for mass. I never knew
where she would be on the parish grounds: school, church, convent.
She seemed to know whenever I was at All Souls. If I was exuding a
vibe - she was receptive to it. It was unexpected seeing her just before
the 9 o'clock mass. We made eye contact and exchanged smiles. I
can't remember the priest's name or the altar boys who I served the
mass with.

During one of the parts of the mass when we had to kneel, I
was closest to the room storing all the extra stuff needed for mass. It
was hidden from sight from the people attending the mass. Basically, it
was a candle shake-out room. The important masses got the big
candles and more of them; they were replaced as necessary. Nuns were
frequently in the sacristy if there was a Holy day to celebrate, if they
didn't have other pressing duties. Being in one of those side rooms was
like watching a Broadway show from the wings. Alexa was as far
away from the altar as the small room would permit. She was
confident she'd be hidden from view from everyone but me.

As the priest was muttering away in Latin, I stole a few
glances at her and she enjoyed the attention. I tried another glance a
couple of minutes later and I was immobilized and contemplated an
image most likely sent to me via the chunk of comet on the shore of
the Hudson. Nicole was in the candle room with this great big grin that
said to me: "I'm insane!" She's got her hands on the 3 inch diameter,

cream colored, 2 foot long candle, and she's stroking this thing like it ain't no sin. I shook my head, tried to focus the image, and raised my brow.............."IMPOSSIBLE." I whispered to myself.

Next, she pointed to her watch and indicated the number "10" by holding up all of her fingers, she then signaled down to the church hall.

My thumb and forefinger made the OK circle.

Niki replied by putting the candle on the side of her face; she seemed to be in a state of rapture. I was ready to quit the mass right there and tackle her, instead I flashed 10 fingers at her and she gave me two thumbs up.

The priest blessed us: "*Benedicamus Domino*" and we replied, "*Deo Gratias.*" In 15 minutes the church was empty.

I stood and listened for the sound of Niki's whereabouts. I went down to the church hall. The only light down there came through the glass brick windows set about 2 feet above grade. There were four on each side of the church basement. There were operational ceiling lights, but they would only attract unwanted attention. I cleaned an area as best I could; it was off to the side of the stage. Fifteen minutes later, Niki came flying down the very steep and rarely used iron spiral steps. How one entered this stairway from the sacristy was unknown to me. In fact I had only known about it through my fun nun. It must have had something to do with breaking into heaven or crashing into hell. She was the only person I knew who utilized this exclusive passageway, and like it or not we were serving the Dark Lord. Sister Alexa made me feel real good, but I knew I didn't like having one foot in hell. The sex acts didn't bother me so much, it was who I was doing it with. She wasn't mine she was God's. What a roll of the dice. As God knows all, he must have known it was the sex, and it had nothing to do with the theft of one of his devoted servants. For that, I was truly sorry.

With a paper bag in each hand, she somehow made it down the spiral steps without falling or losing either paper bag - plus, she had all that nun clothing on.

The ladder's last two steps had been removed to prevent use. Sister Niki tossed the two bags to me one at a time, and leaped from the 3rd step. She crash landed, and her bum made a loud thud. Her rolling and laughing had me laughing as well. Her index finger was vertically pressed against her lips. I tried to be quiet, but her war bonnet was cockeyed and it made me grab hold of the old curtain and laugh into it. It took a minute, but we regained our composure. We listened for any sound of someone who might be investigating Niki's crash.

"Wow........that was close." I said.

"Nobody's here you dunce." She hiccupped.

We each carried a paper bag, and I took her by the hand and led her to a small change room. A musty, faded curtain substituted for a door.

Following her performance in the candle room during mass, I had no idea what to expect. She was about to speak when I covered her mouth with mine trying to stick my tongue down her throat. We kissed for three or four minutes.

I gave her the once over, "When did you start drinking?" I raised my brow.

She busted a gut trying to hold it in. Grabbing a handful of habit she laughed into the black muslin. Niki's fit lasted longer than our three dimensional kiss.

I wrapped my arms around myself: I had caught her laughing fit by contagion. For another four minutes, we didn't look at one another for fear of bursting out._

Why my favorite nun of all time was consumed with riotous levity – I could only guess and asked her later. What I found humorous was being able to pull off a major league sex scam. Nicole and me were in a world where the rules are suspended every now and then, and we took a lot of chances. She was as reckless as I was. The difference in our age, the sex, the compulsion to risk...........it was all part of the thrill. I couldn't explain it, I could only do it.

In the back of my mind, I saw Saint Peter writing in figures on the withdrawal side of his Pearly Gates ledger next to our names. I wasn't given one break for being underage. Down the road – this bill would have to be settled up.

Niki laughed out loud.

I put my pointer finger over my lips with the one hand, and wound up my fist with the other, and silently warned her as I shook my head.

She muffled a laugh, "I ga.....ga.......gotsa.....sa......some some.......wine.....ahahaahhhahhhaahhaha!

"Shhhhhh." I laughed.

Niki peeled back the paper bag. She was doubled over, and almost lost her war bonnet; and it sat cocked again to the one side of her head.

"Say Sis; Take the headdress off so I can see you. I raised my brow smiling.

She nodded up and down as she continued howling and handed me the bottle she was drinking: "Why don't you grow some hair?" she countered.

I took a good pull, "This tastes like the wine we got at church." I gave her a serious look.

"I didn't get it from the liquor store - Blaaaah- hahahahahah! Take a long one, you've got to catch up."

"Won't they miss the wine at tomorrow's masses?" I took a sip.

"Who do you think restocks the refrigerator?"

"You?"

"There's four or five cases on the rectory side of the sacristy in the wooden cabinet by the statue of St. Ignatius. There's a small padlock on it. The priests, brothers and you altar boys drink more than one bottle out of every three. A nip, a slug, a chug, - it all adds up. That weirdo, Fr. Bertram, blames you altar boys for the pilfering, but I know it's 95% the priests and the brothers. They never lock the cabinet."

"When the priests' cleaning lady had a stroke – Father Mahoney talked our Reverend Mother into having one of the Sisters' come over here and cover for her until they found a replacement. Sister Eugenie got the assignment. She found 14 empty vodka bottles under Fr. Gilbert's bed. It's no surprise he never makes any sense; he's either drunk or hungover........Pass me the opened bottle."

"Father Gil?.......a lush.......wow..."

"Yup, good old Gil; and don't think he didn't put his grubby mitts on my ass at Father Mahoney's jubilee celebration."

"Had I'd seen that move, I'da knocked his block off."

"That kind of loyalty deserves a kiss." She had her tongue in my mouth, took a sip of wine and started giving me a hickey. It felt great. As she worked on my neck, something disturbed her and she broke off. "Let's go into the hallway, there's a storage room back there, and we won't have to worry about talking or whispering." She said.

We went into this room of boxes and boxes of stuff – mostly old Latin hymnals All Souls no longer used. "Set the boxes up so we can use them. I've got to pee." She hurried off.

The water to the bathrooms was shut off. Sister Alexa ran over to the convent. She returned with a couple of peanut butter and jelly sandwiches in a paper bag. "Let's have that wine." She took a drink, "I can't have you getting shit-faced drinking on an empty stomach. I can see you're already feeling the wine."

"Niki, you get more irresistible with every drink." I started in on one of the sandwiches.

"Shut up." She adjusted the posture of her headdress and veil.

I wanted to get the physical thing going, but something was going on with her. Alexa needed the wine and was getting a glow. She knew she was pitching to an almost 8th grader. I thought this was the beginning of a conversation about how I had to do more than get stroked off by her. She didn't have to talk me into anything.........I had been with Connie. I loved taking directions from women.

Sister Alexa never came out and said I wasn't fulfilling her sexual needs. She never even told me what they were. I tried to let her know I'd do anything she wanted me to try. The wine couldn't break through the barrier which prevented her from maximizing me as the partner to send her into orbit. Much later on, I told Ray about the affair. He attributed her inability as having some kind of hang-up, and being a nun didn't help.

Her sexual needs, and her accompanying anxiety and frustration brought on by our age differences complicated our unconventional relationship. I thought if we had more time together we might be able to overcome them. Later on I could see we could never overcome the age thing or the habit; there was only 'now'. I'd be lost trying to grasp her psychological problems. A bottle of wine and a hot blooded sex slave nearby should have been able to provide a calming effect for the young nun, it sure worked for me.

292

"No kidding Ryan, I feel like a damn prisoner, except when we're together. When I'm with you – I am telling them: "You can't control me.""

"The wine will set you free, and the sex is free from me as well."

"That's not what I'm talking about you ditz."

"The sex?"

"You, the wine," Hiccup. "the sex......they are all just....."

"Sins?"

"Shut up......of course they're sins. Sins of the flesh, sin of excess, desire, lust, envy, domination, jealousy. They are more my sins than yours because I took advantage of you."

"Hey Niki, I'm the one catching the outtasight handjobs." I tried to assume my share of the guilt. She wasn't going to talk me into feeling bad about anything we had done. I regretted what we did was a sin, but not the act of committing it. "Hey Alexa – "

"I have a name."

"How are we going to open this other bottle?"

She tossed over a corkscrew from a pocket she had in her habit. Out of the same pocket came a pack of Kools and a book of matches. Niki lit one up as I was trying to get the cork out of the bottle. Suddenly, the cork let go and I crashed into the back of some boxes. "Want one?" she extended the pack to me and laughed.

I sour-pussed the Kools, but took one anyway. "Where'd they send you over the Fourth?"

"That's what pushed me over the edge. I had to go on this Retreat with a bunch of nuns of our order. I didn't know many of them.....a nun convention – more or less. A 55 year old Sister ran the Retreat. There were 60 and 70 year old nuns there too. There were also some of us young ones, but they skewed old school. It was difficult communicating with most of them...........Pass the bottle."
Niki took a big gulp of wine and a long pull off her Kool. "This is not what I thought it was going to be. I'm on an altogether different wavelength." Another slow sip; "Real different......like I'm a paranoid schizophrenic - type of different." Zeroing in on me, "Do you think I'm having a nervous breakdown?"

Another sip, "Because I do." She giggled, flicking the Kool. "Perhaps I have a multiple identity crisis currently in progress. What do you see Whitelaw?"

"I know I'm better with you than without you. I don't want you to leave."

"No, you wouldn't." Nicole passed the bottle back. "Here take another drink; Look at it from my point of view."

"I think I'm getting blasted." I said.

"You've got to straighten up a little before you leave. You know what will happen if we're found out..........Bad news for us both. Another half-hour here for sure; How long will it take you to get home?"

"A half-hour."

"Half-hour? You'll be okay. "Just don't screw things up."

Here I was, being sent home. Three hours earlier at mass it was rockets red glare......bombs bursting in air. Those other penguins must have disillusioned Niki to the point where she had lost her foundations. Trying to rebuild her self esteem would be futile; hell, I didn't even know what it was.

"That paper bag." she pointed. "That's for you when you go." We smoked two more Kools. It went back and forth. It was easier carrying on with me than the nuns at the Retreat or the convent. Once again our age differential had become irrelevant, and the temporal continuum melted away.

Sister Alexa, even though she was drunk, was back and Nicole had vanished. Before I served my next mass two weeks later – they both were gone; forever as far as I knew.

x

The wheel turned; the people at All Souls going in one direction, and Vinny Tarts, Ray, Reno, Fast Eddie, Kirk and me going in another. Somehow baseball was the way out of Catholic school, and those last three months with Sister Alexa also told me I had a lot of soul searching to do if I wanted to continue with All Souls. It was just tough being under the Catholic school oppressive regime: the system, the faculty, the religion, the clique. Ray explained to me it wasn't going to be all that frightening not to have God on our side – if such a thing was possible. The way we looked at it: God was there for everybody – not just the Catholics.

It was this 3rd option – baseball – It was the bridge we were looking for - until we could quit or graduate from All Soul's. Baseball gave us a crew to be part of.

Going it alone like Ray, you had to be sharp. Me.......I knew I needed a back-up because Ray wasn't always there. The seeds of our crew germinated within the Chippewa Boys Club baseball program. We were divided by age. Ray and me were on our last year on the farm team – one division below Little League ball. How they decided who was going on which team is probably the same today as it was back then; if your Dad's the manager – you know you're going to be in the starting line-up.

There weren't enough players to complete the rosters for the farm teams. The farm team clubs couldn't use the Little League press gang technique to fill their needs. The farm teams got what they got: Little Leaguers who didn't make the cut, cast-offs, malcontents, and there were five or six who showed up with mandatory participation documents from Juvenile Court. Most of us were playing in the hope of getting called up to play Little League in the course of the season. The farm teams were required to put a division of four teams together and each had to have a minimum of a 15 man roster. This way a manager felt pretty good if only 12 boys showed up for the game. This summer though, three teams had the 15 man requirement, but no fourth team.

They needed the fourth team so we could play two games on weeknights, and one on Saturdays. Word came from Chippewa Club officials for each of the three teams to donate three players each to the new fourth team – The Jets.

The four teams congregated around the four bases for the new team to see who we were getting. The manager's son, Kevin Walsh, Ray, and me were the original nucleus of the Jets, the rest of the guys were cast-offs, scrubs, wise guys, romeos, and stumble bums. Mr. Walsh had argued with the Chippewa people that he should be able to at least pick one of the three donated players. They told him – nothing doing. I had seen Vinny before all this fourth team business got started. He said he was playing for the Topps. I had hoped they'd send him over to the Jets, but they kept him a Topp.

Most of the guys were from Gorton Jr. High, P.S. 9, P.S. 25, and four of us from All Souls.

"Alright you mugs……….huddle up." Mr. Walsh called us over to a splinter infested bleacher."

Michael Wray announced, "Hey Walsh – this is baseball. You ain't even got the right sport." Mikey Wray looked like Alfred E. Newman of Mad Magazine so we thought everything he said was funny.

Marty Peterson was cast-off the same team as Wray and was just as pissed. The two thought they had just said good-bye to a first place season. Marty caught, and had a rifle down to second, plus he could hit. Mikey Wray said the Topps coach got rid of Marty cause he was making moves on his daughter.

Mikey didn't even try to hide his dislike of us when Marty asked him who Ray and me were. "I played with Whitelaw before, and that's his kid brother."

"They any good?"

"Hah? They're fuckin' altar boys."

"What's an altar boy?" Marty asked.

"You go fuck yourself Michael Wray." Ray pointed at his face.

"Enough!" Walsh said. "If I call for a huddle, a pow-wow, or a convention – you guys get your butts over here……on the double. Get it straight right now – the only time you walk, is when you get walked by the pitcher…….and even then you run to first base." He turned to Wray and drove his 2nd knuckle of his pointer finger into his chest. "And from now on – it's Mr. Walsh or Coach."

"You're hurtin' me." Mikey wailed.

"Alright guys." Walsh smiled at Mikey and took his finger out of his chest. "Some of you guys were with the Chips, some – the Topps, and some were Comets. That's history….now we're Jets – all JETS. The other teams think were a bunch of…… retreads…… throwaways……a bunch of junkers who can't play. You know what guys? I think we're going to surprise a lot of people. Some of your baseball skills aren't that good right now – but that doesn't mean we can't learn and improve during the season. If we all work hard, and achieve some individual improvement during the season - I think you guys will surprise not only the other bums, but yourselves as well."

"The other teams are looking down on us right now; but I promise youse.........we will not end up in the cellar. And, when the last game comes around, we'll make believers of a lot of people who said we was the scraps everybody else threw away."

Playing for the Jets worked out perfect for me; it occupied the vacuum Sister Alexa had left in my daily thoughts. Mr. Walsh put in some overtime with us the first two weeks; just teaching us how to field, become better hitters, and the intangibles of the game. Over and over we drilled; he never hit a ball without giving a situation: "man on second – one out."

Then it was up to us to make the correct play in reply to wherever he hit the ball, whether it was a pop fly or a grounder.

"We might not have the hitting of the other teams but we'll make up for it by playing smart baseball." Walsh knew our Achilles Heel was hitting or lack of it. Like he said, we'd have to make up for it with our fielding and pitching. We lost our first two games – they were blow outs. The first weeknight game came and we beat the Comets. It shocked both us and the Comets.

The extra practice started to pay off, but it wasn't the only reason things started coming our way. We were lucky; somebody always came through in the clutch. Our ace, George Holter would throw a shut-out when we couldn't buy a hit. They'd smash a hi-hopper over the 3rd baseman's head and brother Ray on a dead run from left field threw the runner out at first because the batter thought he had a hit and coasted into first. Mikey Wray and my brother got along after the spectacular play he made.

Danny Wray played short, and I played second base. We had our double-play running like a 289 Mustang. Michael Wray played first base because he was left handed, and Marty Peterson caught. Walsh rotated our defense around depending on the situations and the absenteeism.

Things kept breaking the Jets way. We had two starting pitchers: Holter and Walsh's kid – Kevin. The rest of the team were the relief pitchers when Holter or Walsh got knocked out of the box. When the manager had to pull either starter, the pitching assignment became chaotic. Our first go-to-guy was Marty Peterson, and my brother had to catch. Marty had one pitch – heat. It was what he used to throw out runners trying to steal second. When the batters for the other teams saw Marty for the second time - they were ready for him.

The Wray bros. took their turns with limited success, Ray and me too. When the bullpen got involved in the game, we only won half the time. When Holter or Walsh were off - we usually got creamed. If somebody just walked by and glanced at the scoreboard, they must have wondered where the football game was with scores reading: 31 to 6, or 28 to 3. We needed a long reliever and/or a 3rd starter. Two weeks into the season things started getting away from what Mr. Walsh had in mind, we were 2-4.

Our answer arrived in a Gary Busey lookalike at the age of 14. He went to Christ The King, and should have played ball with the Colts Boys Club down Napeara Park, near Homefield section of North Yonkers. His father had gotten the business from the Colts' last year when his son sat on the bench the entire season waiting for a chance to play. That wasn't going to happen in his last year of eligibility.

The Topps, Chips, and the Comets all had one more kid on their rosters than the Jets. Walsh was promised another player, but he was sick of waiting. While we were getting pasted, Joe Ferguson and his father went across to the Chippewa Club and got his kid signed up. By the 3rd inning, the Topps had already batted around. The bases were loaded with only one out. Our pitcher was smiling and glassy-eyed and four runs had crossed the plate. Walsh called for time, and looks over to the new guy and his old man.

"Walsh asked, "How's it feel to be a Jet? Just put the shirt on for now – it's showtime kid. You got a glove?"

He held up his black Voit, Orlando Cepeda, model.

"What's your name?"

"Joe Ferguson." His father replied.

"What do you play?"

"Anywhere but the bench." Joe said.

"Can you pitch?"

"Some."

"Put your hat on kid and get loose. I'm making a pitching change." Walsh said.

The infielders circled around Holter, I couldn't hear them talking but I could see Joe's pop was digging that his son was going straight to work.

Walsh and Joe walked out to the mound. "This is our new pitcher – George you can't find home plate."

"You're tellin' me." Holter was relieved to be relieved.

The manager asked George, "You can go to right field, I'll have Kevin sit down. You're a better hitter than him."

"Not today I ain't." Holter laughed.

"What's up George?"

"I drank the rest of my mom's cough medicine. She just got a new bottle from the druggist.......I didn't think she'd miss it."

The manager rolled his eyes and took the ball from George and handed it to Joe. "Take some more warm-up pitches with Marty." He asked Joe: "There's an infield grounder – where's the play?"

"The play's at home."

"Remember....they only have one out so let's try to double them up and get out of the inning. There's a play at any base, we've got to get at least one." The infielders still circled Walsh.

We all looked at one another, not knowing what to expect from the new guy, but Holter was all screwed up. "It's four to nothing, we can't let them bring any of the guys across the plate. The manager talked strategy with us while Marty warmed up Ferguson.

"Batter Up!"

Walsh went over to the mound, "So what is it Joe?; or do you got a nickname?"

He gave a chuckle, "Some call me Loki."

"Loki?" Walsh gave him a wild look.

"I'll explain it later."

"Lookit Loki, just get the ball over the plate....Throw strikes.

Walsh leaned against the batting cage fence with his chin resting on his forearms as the count was one and one. "Put some stuff on it Loki." He yelled to the mound.

The count went to two and one on Vinny Tarts who was batting for the Topps. Both teams knew this new guy had to throw strikes or he'd walk in a run. Vinny looked like Paul Bunyon with that overhand chop swing he used.

The count was two and two, and Loki threw one low and away. If it wasn't a strike, it wasn't a strike by much. Vince wasn't able to use his Paul Bunyon chop and he had to reach out to make contact. He sent a line drive bullet to Bat Maaterson at 3rd. He jumped for all he was worth; the velocity of the ball pushed his arm back ten inches before his feet hit the infield. The runner who had been on 3rd was half-way to home. Maaterson took five steps over to the bag and doubled-up the runner – ending the inning. The Jets were four runs down; it could have been worse. Loki and Bat would be major heroes if we could start getting some wood on the ball......... and we did. We beat the Topps that day when Loki showed up.

Mr. Walsh bought us sodas after the game. We were all aglow with the victory as it seemed to come out of thin air. "What's with the nickname Ferguson – what's this Loki stuff all about? What's it mean?"

Joe chuckled again, "Loki's kind of a Norse god – but he's a trouble maker."

"How'd they come up with that?"

"I'm hooked on Marvel comics, I read most of the Thor stuff; Loki's always mixing it up and makes a mess of things for Thor and Odin. I'm kind of partial to Loki – he goes against the grain." Joe said.

"Wonderful." Walsh took a deep breath and walked away.

Baseball was the bonding agent and the access to a different strata of life. In just a few games it could be determined if you had physical stamina and judgmental skills, or if you could be rattled by the spectators or other players. It showed if you could stay kool under pressure. We didn't know what it was: grit, tenacity, determination. You knew it when you saw it – and you wanted a piece of it. The game revealed so much about a person in such a short period of time.......you knew who had "it" and who didn't.

It was like someone had flicked the switch, we were playing stickball, football, basketball with all the guys in baseball; and when Vinny Tarts was around, he'd take us down to a park on Vineyard Ave. which me and Ray never knew existed and played bocce ball with old goombas. The park was only a quarter mile down the hill from where Lake Ave. dead ended.

Ray and Loki, Holter, and me thought it'd have been really kool if Bobby Herrick and Vinny Tartaglione had been on the Jets with us. Something wanted me to make this more meaningful – tighter. I didn't know why. The six of us were only a year apart in age, except for Loki. He was two years older than me and Vince. The next few years, we wove a braid of life experiences through a brotherhood. None of us knew what was occurring – except for maybe Ray. It seemed so right – but not organic. He honed in on something a little later. He was confident the bonding might be attributed to the disturbance of the 'Cosmic Intruder' and magnetic realignment. From the way I saw things, it was possible, but it was equally possible to have been a random event.

xi

A quartet of altar boys: Kenny Crawford, Tony Newman, Tommy Gorski, and me served the 8 o'clock mass on the Feast of the Assumption on August 15th. It had been three weeks since the Saturday in the church hall with Sister Alexa. My hope was dwindling, but it was more or less fait accompli - she was no longer at All Souls. There was an active rumor started by the Reverend Mother pushing the notion Sister Alexa would return for the start of school in September. The cover story was she had returned to Iowa to attend to her ailing father.

In her absence, the altar boys took over her duties in the meantime: we got the altar ready for mass, set fresh cruets of water and wine on the servers table, clean linen and dish for the priest to wash his hands; when there was a funeral or high mass – we made sure there was charcoal and incense; plus there were the candles.

When there were four altar boys, we could get these chores done fairly quickly. There was time to spare and we congregated in our area of the sacristy.

Tommy Gorski said, "Joo hear………..'bout Sister Alexa taking a powder? She's gone."

"Huh?" My face contorted. "Sonabitch."

Kenny Crawford wedged in, "Yeah." He looked straight ahead without expression: "Fuckin' Cleo drug up. She hooked up with some peacenik – She's gonna change the world."

"Sonofabitch – With some guy?" I asked Kenny.

"Beads, flowers, Nehru jacket, Volkswagen Beetle…….a real peace-nik." Tony Newman added.

"He had long hair…….like Sonny Bono."

"Looked like he just got off the set of 'Laugh-In'." Gorski gave a half-laugh.

"And the Beat Goes On." I said.

"Crawford followed, "Yeah, The Beat Goes On." Kenny and me snapped our fingers.

299

Newman mentioned, "Looks like you're off detention."
"I was off – the last day of school you nobblehead."
"La di-dah di di........."
"La di-dah di dah......" Kenny answered.
"She wasn't teaching eighth grade anyway." I said.
"Showtime." Gorski said.
That summer was the last any of us would serve a mass said in Latin.

I DATED A JEWISH GIRL, ANNE HOFNER, WHEN I WAS in high school. Her Mom was upset with her because I was a goy. Not only was I a goy; I was a goy with a Teutonic background. Anne tried to pass me off as being Irish. One of Anne's girlfriends spilled the beans about me being German to her mother and after that she no longer had the 'Welcome' mat out. But, her father and me got along really well. He was pretty sharp, he saw the big picture and I think it was from being in WWII.

Her father knew I was Catholic and had been an altar boy. It really bothered him when the Church threw 2000 years of tradition and tossed it in the waste bin. "Your law, manuscripts, art, official language – the language which binds your church to its religion throughout the world...........GONE! Ryan, how can this be?" I agreed with Mr. Hofner. To make him feel better, I told him I had just passed my Regents exam in Latin. He was overcome and somewhat in a panic.

"Ryan.......now Ryan, promise me you will take all four years of Latin. Please – you do it for your God, your religion, the rule of law, the foundation of society, and you do it for you." There was fear in his face: "I'm afraid to ask: Just how many students are taking Latin in your class?"

"There's Paul Coker and me."

"Only two students in Latin III? What about I, II, and IV?"

"Sad to say, Jason and the Argonauts, Caesar, Aeneas, Cicero, Virgil and the rest must be feeling rather isolated; we are the last two in the city of Yonkers studying the language. Unless one of your yeshivas are still teaching it – Paul and me are the last. I believe all the Catholic high schools have discontinued the dead language." I reported.

"Oy vey." Mr. Hofner looked down and put his hands on the sides of his head. Anne's dad knew what tradition meant – the continuation of what you are, every bit as important as the blood running through one's veins. Morris Hofner most likely knew the entire scenario of the switch from Latin to English.

Catholics are always confessing - whether it's in the confessional, in the news, or on the street. "Catholics simply cannot shut up and they cannot stop telling other people how to live their lives – it's part of our DNA." I said.

I couldn't divulge my sordid past with the Catholic Church to Morris; losing Latin was bad enough – *"Quid faciendum."*

BEFORE THE DIE WAS CAST, WE SERVED THE
8'0CLOCK mass with Father Allen. The Latin mass suited him
perfectly; he might have been the most spiritual man I would ever
know. His sermons were short and to the point. He was very, very soft-
spoken, he couldn't get close enough to the microphones for most of
the congregation at his masses.

In 1942, he had joined the Army Air Corps, he was only a
teenager. The B-24 Liberator was his plane, and he trained as a
bombardier. Half of the crew died when they got shot down over a
refinery in Romania. He spent a year and-a-half in a POW camp in
Hungary. After the prison camp and the war, his health was never the
same. The bombing of civilian populations caused nightmares and
daylight stress throughout his life.

We all kind of knew Father Allen's war story, but Ray had
talked to him at length. The two hit on a common denominator; it
made communication effortless, and he gave Ray the inside scoop.

After his separation from the service, First lieutenant Allen
Erdman became a rummy riding the rails from coast to coast and
border to border. In 1953, he woke up in a mental hospital in the alky
wing in Poughkeepsie, N.Y. In 1960 he took his vows of obedience,
poverty, and love in the Capuchin order of Saint Francis. He was a
listener, not a preacher. "If everyone's a preacher; who is there to
listen?" he said.

Soft-spoken, deliberate, and frail; because Father Allen spoke
so sparingly – when he did speak, it was from the heart and hit his
mark. The German and Romanian Nazis guards tortured the airmen
from his bomber group, and when they still didn't talk, they tried
freezing and starving them to death. Father Allen was a shadow of a
man, but he found true peace in the Capuchin order.

After a couple of years of altar boying, you got to know the
priests – the way they wanted things to go during the mass. Either you
did things their way or you'd get yelled at. If you got caught pulling
some horseplay, you could figure on catching one on the side of the
head. Many of these pranks and misunderstandings were rooted with
the wine and anything to do with it. Father David just about always
used all the wine in the cruet. He always had us using the larger sized
cruets for his masses. I never saw him loose.

With Father Allen, all he wanted was a half-a-shot glass of
wine for his chalice. Ray said Allen might even be happier with half-a-
thimble. The older altar boys said the early morning bracer put the
priests a better frame of mind for the day ahead, but that was a bunch
of bull crap.

An unknown person, most likely an altar boy, slipped Father
Bertram an alternate wine selection for a Sunday mass. After the priest
poured this wine into the chalice for the offertory, he detected a fruity
fragrance. He looked around: where were the flowers? He knew he
smelled them. Stray perfume from a woman sitting up front? The wine
looked right, and Bertram continued with the service. He consecrated
the bread and wine into the body and blood of our savior. Bertram
raised the chalice at communion to drink the blood of Christ. The
closer his nose got to the chalice.......there was no doubt - this was the

source of the putrid aroma. Bertram knew he was the object of a prank. We knew it was street wine as well and we knew Smart Alec was the protagonist of this mischief. Father Bertram stayed on the case all year without any luck. I didn't like Smart Alec, but he evened the score a little for Johnny O'Connell.

Father Bertram and Father Allen were very different: Bertram was a Jesuit and Allen was a Capuchin. Bertram disliked Fr. Allen on that account alone. Father Allen had been loaned out to All Souls, but he never got recalled to His order as I remember – though it had always been the plan he would return when his services were no longer needed by the Jesuit parish. The one was matter and the other anti-matter in a screwed-up way. I began to see the world divided into two spheres: one good – the other bad.

The four of us: Crawford, Gorski, Tony Newman, and me had a specific set of tasks to perform during the mass. You knew the things you had to do by the number you were assigned on the schedule. Newman and me brought a cruet of water and one of wine over to the side of the altar, where the priest usually poured the wine in the chalice with just a dash of water at the offertory. With Fr. Allen, the ratios were reversed. As a recovering rummy a half a teaspoon was even too much. The little bit of wine was so diluted he could handle it.

After communion, the priest came over to the side of the altar again; Tony Newman brought over a cruet in each hand. It was the priest's responsibility to consume all of the communion crumbs from his golden saucer plate and on his finger tips. He'd wipe the communion crumbs from the saucer into the chalice and had the altar boy pour wine and water over his fingers and using the chalice as a finger bowl, the priest then drank it all and repeated the procedure with just water.

All the altar boys knew Fr. Allen, and to go real light on the wine. It was Newman's job to pour the wine after communion; he turned to us and gave us this look: "Watch this." The priest brought over the chalice with the crumbs and tiny fragments of communion wafer in the cup. Newman begins to pour the cruet's wine into the cup. Fr. Allen tries to shut him off, Tony looks at us and is laughing and empties the cruet's contents. Fr. Allen's eyes are almost out of his head and he was in a state of panic. That jackass Newman is busting a gut. Crawford, Gorski, and me were in a panic for the alcoholic priest. It was Christ in the chalice suspended in the wine, this had to be consumed. This was not good.

The priest brought the chalice to the center of the altar in front of the tabernacle; no one in the pews could see what was going on because we had our backs to them as did Father Allen. Back then we prayed to God, and they weren't interested in communicating with the congregation – unless they told them there was going to be a second collection; that was always in English.

Father Allen looked at the half-full cup on the altar in front of him, and spread his arms and braced himself. For two minutes he went through these minor convulsions and rested his chin on his chest to compose himself. He looked over his shoulder, it was Medusa's stare he fixed on Tony. Father Allen's look tried to turn Newman into stone. He had to compose himself; again – he confronted the cup – and once more he had to look away. Fr. Allen's hands laid flat on the linen covered altar, he closed his eyes with his head bowed down in prayer. The three of us reckoned this situation was every bit as bad as when the B-24 bomber was going down in flames........maybe worse.

Not a moment was wasted, Crawford went to the backside of the altar. A hemi ring beam supported by four marble columns formed a semi-circle 25 feet above the altar with half a dome on top of the beam. Suspended by brass chain, an 8 foot Crucifix seemed to float above the tabernacle. Two long velvet drapes were hung from the hemi ring beam isolating the altar and focusing the attention of the congregation on the priest, tabernacle, and crucifix. Hidden from view from everyone, Kenny climbed the step ladder the sisters used for fastening decorations from the backside of the altar. There was a thin slit between the two green velvet drapes directly behind the tabernacle. Father Allen was still in deep contemplation. Like a cat burglar, Crawford's hand withdrew the chalice which contained the essence of Jesus Christ, and chugged the contents of wine and remaining communion wafer crumbs and particles; replacing the chalice in front of the priest in about 11 seconds. Gorski and me were the only ones who knew what had happened. That imbecile Tony was silently laughing kneeling with his rump resting on his heels.

From behind, it looked like Fr. Allen was getting squirrelly. He looked up and back down – grasped the chalice and upended the contents. Except for the two drops Crawford had left, the priest was basically drinking air. He had prepared himself to get violently sick from a case of alcoholic poisoning.

We had heard his version of this miracle second hand from Father Joe. Father Allen swore Saintly intercession had taken place, but he had been quite prepared to die. Later on, Gorski and me started calling Crawford: "Santo Kenny". The name didn't stick – Kenny was doing a lot of questionable stuff on the street.

The four of us knelt in a row at the foot of the altar; I bent over and whispered so Newman could hear me: "You're a fuckin' jerk."

Tony laughed again. The mass was almost over. He stood up first for the final blessing and stood on my cassock making me fall to the tiled floor. Kenny and Tom Gorski were laughing as I struggled to get up. I swore to myself I was going to ring his chimes when we got out on the street. Newman was in his own world, he didn't want to be where he was so he was going to screw with everyone. Meanwhile, Father Allen stopped at the meditation altar as we marched into the sacristy.

In the altar boy change area, I was taking off my surplice and cassock and I pointed to him. "I'm calling you out as soon as we hit the street. I was ready to rip the damn buttons off I was so mad.

Newman starts laughing and does a half-squat with chicken wing arms fluttering and he makes like his head's pecking: "Ooooooooh.........I'm scared."

"On the street shithead."

303

"I'm waiting for you dickbreath." Newman replied as he went out the door down the steps to the street.

It took me a minute to hang my altar boy stuff up; we went out into the street ----- no Tony. With all the chicken imitation he was doing no wonder he chickened out on me.

We stood there and looked up and down the street.

"That's something about Cleo calling it quits." Crawford said.

"One of the nuns that can't hear should have left instead."

"Huh?" I cupped my ear. The three of us laughed. "Alexa was okay." I couldn't say anything to give our affair away even though she was probably gone for good.

"I wonder who the 7th graders are going to get next month?" Gorski said.

"We'll find out in 20 days or so." I said. See you guys around.

I got back to 21 after mass, I rushed down to the cellar and the bag Niki' had given me was still being squeezed by the rack over the rear tire . When I had put my bike in the garage, all I had seen in the bag was some peanut butter and jelly sandwiches. I had thrown the bag in the pile.

In the bag was the three week old, moldy peanut butter and jelly sandwiches in wax paper, a greeting card which said good-bye, and three pornographic magazines, one of them was the 'Rauncho Rancho' I thought I had lost over a year ago. The other two must have belonged to Sister Alexa 'Twisted Teens', and 'Blow Job City.' Same deal as Rauncho Rancho except they were 100% humanoid content, all photographs, not a word in either publication. I found them just in time; the ones Ray and me originally found were in bad shape from being kept outside. No Nicole, no Lynn, no Connie – I had to take care of myself and these skin magazines would help me prevent the jizz build up from making me act like a guy with a real character flaw. There were only a couple of weeks left of summer. I'd look at the magazines Cleo gave me and spread my seed in secluded spots in the woods, not far from the top of the washer where we first hid the magazines. Ray didn't seem interested in the porn; I never saw him there when I knew it was time to study. Every time I looked at them I thought of her.

CHAPTER 13

i

Ray started 10th grade at All Souls, but half-way through he had enough of the Christian Brothers education, and decided to switch to Gorton H.S. for his Junior and Senior years. Ray and Hal cooked up another plan; I would attend Emerson Jr. High for my freshman year. The following year, both of us would be going to Gorton H.S. It was right up Hal's alley; we were removed from his tuition burden, and he would only have Cathy and Willis to pay for at All Souls.

For the Old Man, it was a real push-pull question: "look at the education they gave your mother at Gorton – an open and shut case of outright fraud. Believe me boy, it's only gotten worse at the fun house which masquerades as a school." The more I thought about it - unburdening the family budget of two monthly tuition payments - had swung the argument. The almighty dollar weighed heavily in many decisions made in the Whitelaw household.

What I had a hard time coming to grips with was how Hal and Ray cut this deal and never consulted me. The one controlled the finances, the other had the smarts. There was no choice for me to make. It was the type of decisive action I was looking for with Lynn and Niki: take the bull by the horn and "tell me what I've got to do to trip your trigger baby."

Had Ray put the proposition to me saying he was going to Gorton next year and why don't I go to Emerson Junior High and I'll meet you in Gorton for your sophomore year – at least it would have saved me some dignity. He knew he could talk me into anything, but I wanted to be consulted. I wanted to be asked. Hal, Jane, and Ray knew there was no point of going through the charade; and I was informed: "You're going to Emerson next year."

I only had to do a year at junior high school – 1968/69. I had been top dog in 8th grade at All Souls grade school, and now a year later top dog again at R.W. Emerson. At All Souls, I knew the lay of the land and the pecking order of the students. In public school: "Here's your desk, here's your locker...........see you in June – have a good time." The only choice the administration gave me was for my choice of language. There was Spanish, French, and Latin. There were about 10 students taking Latin I at Emerson; one of them was Anne Hofner, but we didn't go out until we went to Gorton and she had dropped Latin and started taking French.

We had to share a classroom with construction workers who used the extra room to store their tools and equipment. The workers were there the entire year.

It was similar to P.S.14 when we lived at 2 Vernon Place. The student body was primarily Jewish. Most of the students had a hard time with the sizeable bald area off center on my head. I had gotten used to it and everybody in my grade at All Souls knew what the score was. This was a new school and I had to explain that I got beat up by a teacher at least twice a day. It was fair to say most students and teachers thought I was delusional or full of shit or both.

305

The girls who believed me - felt sympathy for me, but there weren't many. After discovering I had gone to All Souls, a lot of them thought I had gotten what I deserved. I got along with the Jewish guys for the most part, my stock really went up with them when they found out I knew Danny Kryesler and I was over his house when I had the paper route. He was admired by just about all those Jewish guys. They really liked when I'd call him the "Israeli Steve McQueen".

Both Ray and me thought there was a chance Lynn Van Metter might have chosen Gorton. She went to Gorton for the 10th grade while I was in Emerson and Ray was still at All Souls H.S. When we switched over to Gorton we had heard she had enrolled in a private Fine Arts School in Riverdale in the Bronx. Kirk Lis and Kenny Crawford both got into Saunders Trade and Technical school for their 10th grade studies. It was where I should have gone to high school. Looking back, I wonder how Hal and Ray could have missed that.

When the girls finished junior high, the only specialty school Yonkers offered to them was Commerce H.S. The girls got beat when it was stacked against Saunders. The curriculum they offered was geared to office work, beautician licensing, commercial art, culinary skills, bookkeeping, and accounting. Mike Reno went there to capitalize on the 7:1 chick to dude ratio. Mike Reno: what a character. The forces of magnetism imperceptibly drew our crew together.

Ray sensed this dynamic. There was some of that sociological bonding taking place; he felt strange magnetic fields come and go.

Emerson was only a quarter mile away from the 13th green at Hudson River C.C. I started caddying with Ray in the summer of '68. Casual - part-time - as needed - was the basis of carrying golf clubs at nearly all country clubs using caddies. For Ray and me, it wasn't such a big deal when we didn't catch a loop. We were pretty used to being broke. No loops meant we'd end up down the North End or by the river and hang out. When the merchants had had enough, they'd call the bulls to chase us over to Kinsley Park. It was one street east of Palisade Ave. With the caddy yard, the North End, and Lake Ave. came the gambling, the chicks, the fights, beer, petty crime, and vandalism.

A lot of 8th and 9th graders were changing schools in the fall. These schools were full of baby-boomers; and they had to get their higher education some place. The Yonkers school system might have gone belly-up had there not been Catholic schools. There was All Souls, Christ the King, St. Josephs, St. Casmir's, St. Bartholomew's, St. Anthony's, St. Peter's, and St. Mary's; Those were the ones I knew about. I knew girls who went to Our Lady of Victory, All Souls, Blessed Sacrament, Tolentine, Immaculate Heart of Mary, and Spellman High Schools. The girls from All Souls Grade School who ended up at Gorton, were either High I.Q. material, or wanted to go steady with any guy with a set of wheels who could appreciate a Halloween face full of lipstick, eye make-up, foundation, and zit hider.

A month of Emerson under my belt, I didn't quite know what to make of it. There were no more: uniforms, corporal

306

punishment, serving mass, candy drives for some cause every month. It really.......really would have been wild if former Sister Alexa showed up teaching as a real person, I knew it would never happen.

Hanging around at the golf course and the North End, I recognized some of the faces at school, but Ray was the only person I could trust. As time went on, my 'Lone Wolf' persona was taking hold at Emerson. I started to get a lot more self-conscious about the chunk of hair I was missing. At first, I didn't give it much consideration; I still thought it was going to grow back. As time went on, I went against the trend and I'd get a buzz cut after Labor Day. With only a sixteenth of an inch of hair, the bald area wasn't so noticeable. The guys were okay with me on account of Danny Kryesler. It was somewhat different with the girls. I couldn't say for sure, but I think they viewed me as a whack-job who was Gung-Ho, G.I. Joe, desperate to sign up for military service.

The summer of '68 I grew three inches. The three inches translated into me looking two years older than I was. It scared most of the girls. It was becoming a task trying to figure what my role was and where I fit in. It sure was different than All Souls had been. Ray could see I was basically lost. I knew he felt responsible, but what were we to do? He was in the play-it-safe world of All Souls and I was out there on the frontier.

I was having no success with breaking through with the girls at Emerson. I kept the three skin magazines from Cleo with the others below O'Dell Ave. They were just about done. A lot of seed was sewn in half-dump/half woods between O'Dell and the aqueduct. Those magazines Sister Alexa had given me were pretty kool, I wasted a lot of time with them.

Schools and Protestant churches held dances. I got shut out by every girl I asked to dance until Easter when they thought my hair had covered up the bare spot enough; I got two girls to dance with me. They were big girls, but we were happy just to feel kind of wanted and 'normal'.

Searching for a pack to run with, and not finding one - kind of left me out there. It wasn't new to me – after all we were mostly by ourselves down in the Greystone territory anyway. The socialized group thing didn't matter. They knew us as 'River Rats'. When I saw three feet of new equation had been added to the problem on the plywood in the overpass, I knew Ray had once again gotten busy. It was all about the Fireball, the other stuff didn't matter. I knew Ray's theorem was dynamite, but I still didn't know what it meant and he couldn't explain it to me yet.

Ray was busy interpreting its power, purpose, potential, and perhaps being able to control it in some way. Keeping it secret.....made us reclusive to a certain degree. I didn't know enough about it; still - I was the one the dust had sent to the surreal dream world. He was the theoretician and I must have been the test pilot. He'd come back from Greystone:

"You got your ash stowed away safe.......tight....tight seal?"

"Yeah Ray." I was tired of being asked.

"We can't lose any." He looked at me for a reply.

"I know it's important Ray – don't worry, everything's kool."

"Yeah, I just got a lot on my mind. I've got to find some math wizards or astrophysicists who can lead me in the right direction." He watched me. "You know who could have helped us........ that Mr. Hillman. He knew a lot about radio stuff: how the waves travel, can they be woven into a light beam. Does their electromagnetic force attract or repel similar radio waves, and can they be amplified to produce a radio beam?"

"Just tell me what you want me to do Ray. If we weren't brothers, there would be no reason for me to be your associate. I'm sure it's the blood chemistry binding us – has to be."

ii

This freshman year at Emerson Junior High was a mystery to me. I don't believe I was alone trying to figure out where I fit in. There was a sizeable amount of transferees who like me were only going to be there for the one year. Most of the other students who left All Souls after graduating eighth grade were going to Gorton Junior High. There were a few people I knew on sight from the North End.

One or two guys I knew from caddying. Nothing felt right like the vibe I had with the Jets and Niki last summer. Neither lasted long enough. I just started making a nuisance of myself with the chicks. I hoped they saw something in me I didn't know was there. As an equal opportunity 'lone wolf' - I didn't care about religion, race, or ethnic background, but it would be better if a girl was devoid of moral character. Anne Hofner was the only girl I got close to dating that school year; I'm sure it was because she had been taking Latin I. Ten of us were in Latin I: seven girls, Paul Coker, Joe Stellin, and me. Anne liked me because she could only see my good side, I think. I helped her with her vocabulary and translations. The next year at Gorton High, only Coker, Joe Stellin, and me continued with Latin II from Emerson, there were some new faces to make up a class of nine.

It had gotten so bad at Emerson, I couldn't even make it with the girl who was putting out for everybody - Ruthie Rosen. I was all set to use the "Cover up that Bald spot with Spray-on Hair". Ray saw it on my desk and threw it in the garbage.

"What are you doing? The shit cost $3.99." I gave him a wild look.

"Ryan......don't make a fool of yourself – crap like this never works."

"Well.........I just got to get something going with the chicks."

"It'll happen, grow you hair long and let it fall over the bald area, besides the school year is almost over. You can get a buzz cut soon enough."

"C'mon Ray – I ain't no hippy. I like it short, if I get into a scrap - they ain't got nothing to pull out."

"Yeah – I know.....I know."

"Straight truth Ray – I was down the river fishin' – well I started out fishing and I got distracted by this Wall Street Journal weekend magazine which ended up in the high grass and scrub bushes. So they got them high dollar models all sporting fancy clothes and jewelry and they start looking good to me. This older guy and his grandson had been fishing and were walking by and the old guy caught me workin' it over."

"He calls me a sick bastard and a degenerate, then he says for me to wait here cause he's going to call the bluecoats. I grabbed my pole and put the afterburners on." I shook my head and took a breath.

Ray was laughing and said I was a dumb fuck.

"It wasn't even a skin magazine......I don't why he was all wound up."

Ray laughed, "Hey you can't be whipping it out everytime you think you're alone."

"I know that..........I know that."

Over the weekend, we bumped into George Holter down the End; he told me the crabs were running down the river.

"Ray and me ain't even got our crab nets out of the cellar yet."

"Well get 'em out, me and my brother-in-law Phil caught over a dozen Saturday night. Pretty good sized ones too." George nodded.

"Dija go down the marina?"

"Uh-huh."

"We'll have to go north of Greystone where that derelict barge is." Ray looked at me.

"Yeah, it's the only place that ain't shallow at low tide."

"Go over by the yacht club. What can they do chase you off?" Holter said.

"Who covers the river – the Yonkers cops or the railroad cops?"

"Depends on who the calls come into I guess." Holter squinted and scratching his head.

Ray looked to me, "Better off crabbin' from the barge, George is right....all's they can do is chase us off."

"George, you wanna come?" I said.

"I ain't walking from Lake Ave. with a couple of crab nets......what are you nuts?" He laughed.

There isn't any caddying on Mondays at any of the private courses. Greenskeeper's crews use Mondays to get the courses back into shape after a heavy weekend. Caddies were allowed to play a round of golf, but some of the holes were under too much maintenance, so you had to skip them. Ray could send the ball for a ride off the tee, my game was better off if I stuck with miniature golf.

We took a six-pack of our beer and our crab nets and tried to find a spot that was at least 8 feet deep. At low tide, you might have to walk 15 feet into the river before the 16 inch high crab net was fully underwater. We saved all the chicken parts from Saturday night's barbecue for our bait. The water surrounding the derelict barge was deep enough, but it was stagnant for some reason; we thought there might have been a sand bar just beyond where we could see. Plus, there was no shade. We had finished our six pack of Schaefer tall boys, and our rotten chicken looked like it hadn't been touched.

"How they running?" a guy from the riverbank called.

"They ain't." Ray replied.

"You two guys looking to earn some money?"

"Doin' what?"

"Scraping and painting that silver bridge." The guy pointed to the bridge the yacht club leased. Later on we learned the club lease agreement said they were responsible for maintaining the bridge.

The bridge was 3/8^{ths} of a mile north of Greystone Station. It was owned by Penn Central and it carried 8 signal lights – one for each track in each direction.

"How much?" Ray quizzed the guy. He looked over to me: "Ryan get our nets together – let's go see what this guy wants."

We got off the barge and walked over to the boatman.

"What do you want us to do, and how much are you paying?" Ray asked.

"You guys start right now and I'll pay you ten bucks apiece until 6 o'clock." You'll be scraping and wire brushing the whole bridge from end to end; top and bottom." The Boatman said.

"There's a lot more than a days work there."

"I know that."

I was ready to seal the deal.

"When's this thing supposed to be done?" Ray's left eye started blinking.

"Friday – 6 o'clock."

"Here's our deal: $10 each for today cause were getting a late start. $15 each for every day we work until completion. And…..we get a case of beer everyday at the end of work."

"Huh?"

"A case." I thought my echo would help.

The Boatman glanced at the bridge's peeling paint. We knew he was in a jam when he looked away squeezing his eyes tight. "Yeah – awright. But you only get the beer after 6 o'clock." He pointed to Ray and then he pointed to me….and he ain't no 18."

"That's got nothing to do with the job, except if he was 18, he'd be asking for more money." Ray said.

"And beer." I smiled.

"Deal?" Ray held out his hand waiting for the Boatman to shake on it.

"Deal. Follow me up to the boat club; we got a large toolbox there with a couple of pails with scrapers and wire brushes. Got some broom sticks with three inch hose clamps to use so you can make extensions on the scrapers, wire brushes, and paint brushes."

When it was knock-off time, the boatman took a walk across the bridge and came down the stairs. Ray and me were in the kool river water where the boats docked. We had to get all them paint specks and chips off. We knew we'd be wearing long sleeves and no cut-offs tomorrow. This was a dirty job.

"We don't have half of the bridge scraped, and none of the underside. We'll be pressing to get this done by Friday." He looked at the bridge and took a deep breath. "Let's go get your beer – and he still ain't no 18."

I couldn't let the underage reminder slide by, "Hey Boatman, listen: we don't take no checks – Strictly cash - there ain't no oweseys."

Ray butted in, "We get paid every night in cash and beer."

He looked like we kind of got into him, "Hey I don't have a problem with that – that was the deal we made."

We carried our nets across the bridge and got in his car. Ray said. "Let's go get that case."

We got the case at the A&P in Hastings. Ray had the Boatman drop us off at the corner of O'Dell and Warburton. By Wednesday, the caddie master and the other guys knew we were AWOL from the country club. Nobody missed us; Ray had been staying in touch with Loki. He said it was slower than molasses and asked Ray if the Boatman needed any help.

I heard Ray on the phone: "Loki – We'll see you up the North End tonight. It's a good news/bad news type of thing."

"How's that?" Loki wanted the info right now.

"Meet you up the End." Ray said. "Around 7:30 - 8:00.

We saw Loki sitting on the three foot wall with a six pack. He didn't see us so we went over to Palisades Foods and got a six pack each.

"The yacht club doesn't need any more help......it's pretty much a two man gig." Ray shrugged.

"That's the bad news right?" Loki said.

Ray sensed Loki's trepidation - like he should have cut a deal to include him. "Here's the good news – we're gonna have a big beer blast down there – Friday night."

Loki was unsure, "At your house?"

"No you Doomcuff – down the river.......Greystone."

"Yeah?"

"We already got the two cases of brew in the cellar fridge,- we'll have five by Friday night........but I was thinking....we've got to get some jams. Somebody with a good sound system in their car and they got to have good music too – none of that "In A Gadda Da Vida" bullshit. Maybe see if you can get some babes to come down for the bash. Drinking with guys all the time is getting old."

"I ain't prejudice and I ain't particular." I said.

"Why don't any of these chicks have wheels. Hell I'd be delighted to get hijacked by a bunch of Hot Roddin' babes." he said.

Ray brought Loki back to the here and now. "Without the chicks – it'll be just another night of drinking and shootin' the shit. Any reefer around? – that's shit's like katnip to a kat."

"It's the up and coming thing – everybody's got the word out, but 'slike nothin's around.

"You're our man on the outside Loke – we're counting on you. This is the priority order: #1 Babes, #2 Reef, #3 Jams. And try not to spread the word to any shitheads."

"What about Jimmy Blanko, the girls love him and he's got wheels?......." Loki said. "Don't you got some weed Ray?"

"'Bout half a nickel, but that won't go far." He shrugged.

"Ray....Ray...." I brainstormed and turned to Loki: track down Mike Reno – if it's free - he'll be there. He's got that lemon-lime Nova with the vinyl roof. He's always got a couple of girls riding with him."

"Yeah.....A.M. Mike." Loki snickered. "He's always selling pot; not much of it is any good."

"We'll call you around suppertime – Friday."

RAY AND ME WERE TAKEN BY SURPRISE BY BOATMAN; we thought he'd try to stiff us for the money or the beer or both. It was a dangerous job, and half of the time we spent on the exterior of the open-air pedestrian overpass. The most dangerous and difficult part of the job was scraping and painting the underside of the bridge. Boatman gave us six caution cones to block off our work areas on the first day when he told us how we'd have to remove two – 2"x12"x16' floor planks that were bolted to some iron cross members every so often to get access to bridge's bottom. It was a bear of a job. We had to make sure the floor planks were back in place at the end of the day so nobody could fall through to the tracks.

The pedestrian/signal bridge had: a 12" I-beam in each corner, there was Tee iron on top and bottom forming the overpass into box, and there were diagonals all over the place to keep the box rigid. The channels, angles, gusset plates, tee iron and junior beams were held together by ¾" rivets. It took us two whole days to finish work on the bottom chord. Ray thought we might be cutting our completion estimate kind of close, so we started working from 6 a.m. to 7 p.m. for the rest of the week. Boatman stopped by everyday to check our progress, deliver paint, rollers, brushes, and pay us in cash and beer.

We started cleaning up around 4 o'clock on Friday. It was hazy, hot, and humid and dead calm. The structural components were painted the same color that we scraped off: silver. The boss man had us paint the handrail a kind of royal blue. He told us not to mess with any of the signals, Penn Central maintained them.

"We'll just throw these clothes away. They're history-" Ray said. We faced south towards the station: "There's where the fireball is Ryan."

"I knew it was there the whole time we were painting and scraping........didn't you?.......Why was that?" I didn't let him answer.

"Hey Ray...." I called.

He rotated his head just enough, he caught me out of the corner of his eye.

"This was a dangerous job." I half-laughed. "I almost rolled off one of the planks trying to scrape one of the bottom cross-members."

"We didn't do as good a job on the bottom as we did on the top and the sides." His eyes were lost again on the 'Cosmic Intruder'

The train engineers must have thought it was snowing – we sent so many paint chips to the tracks." I laughed.

"But if you look up at the underside from the ground......it looks as good as the rest." Ray said.

"What about the clean-up?"

"What clean-up? Fuckin' trains' wake will spread the silver lead paint all the way up to Hastings and down to Glenwood Station." He laughed. Although, we had to use some turpentine to clean up some spills on the 2"x12"x16's planks; we were able to flip over several of them and call it good.

"You got any paint left in the gallon pail?" I checked.

"'Bout half. What are you going to do?"

"Gonna give a freight train a silver shower - if one comes along." I smiled. Ray rolled his eyes.

As we waited for a freight, we hand lined all the stuff we used for the job back down to the ground. It sure came in handy learning them knots from Mack, hoisting and lowering the tools and equipment with boat rope saved us a lot of time. It was only a short walk from the bottom of the stairs to the yacht club's large tool box and paint cabinet. No one else really used the bridge except their members. It would prove to be a good escape alternative when the cops were chasing us out of the station.

There were no freighters – just commuter trains bringing workers from Manhattan back home. Ray didn't want to get stiffed on our last day. He sent me back to 21 to clean up and get changed while he waited around in case the Boatman showed up. Around 6 o'clock he arrived, I had already returned with two quarts of Dellwood chocolate milk for the both of us. He walked the job over with Ray; he checked the tool box and the paint cabinet.

"I already got your beer in the car. Here's your pay." Boatman handed us $20 each. "A little extra for doing a good job."

We thanked him and followed him up to his car. He made Ray sit on some newspaper because he didn't want his interior getting messed up. Next to Ray, there was a case of sweating Chug-a-mugs. He dropped us off at the usual spot and said, "See ya's around". I don't think I ever ran into Boatman again......maybe Ray did.

I carried the case up O'Dell, even though I was on "E". At some stores, either of us could pass for being legal; Ray threw his painting shirt on top of the case to lessen the chance some Bible thumper might try calling the bulls on us.

"So what's the plan?" I grinned.

"Boatman was right.......we did do a good job. Doing the underside........that was a bitch."

"If these Rheingolds' were ice cold – I'd have one right now.

313

"Painting's easy. It's the prep work – that's the hard part. We were a mess after we finished on Monday. Hal and Jane would have read us the riot act if we put them clothes in the washer and left millions of paint particles behind. That stuff might have even clogged the drain."

I put the beer in the fridge and Ray tossed his painting clothes in the garbage can. "You know that stuff that came off our clothes in the river?"

"Yeah?"

"It was like a cloud, and then it turned shiny. You know iridescent?"

"Yeah." He nodded. "Kind of like spraying carburetor cleaner in the water."

I shook my head, "Can't be good for you."

"As you Latin scholars say: *"Alea jacta est."*

A bad feeling jarred the conversation. Ray tried to reason it: "Even when you think you're on the ball doing good ....something's always nearby to bring you down."

I kept the fridge door open and kept looking at the five cases of beer, that sight was enough to make anybody feel good. "Man...... that first one is gonna taste good – might not even taste it." I kept looking at the cans and bottles in front of me, like I was talking to them.

"Hey you knucklehead – that's Mack's line. Make up your own."

"Well, I'm using it, and he'd be the first to give us the copyright to it - if he'd seen the good job we did on the bridge."

"Hey kool your jets 'lil brother, the party's not til 8 o'clock."

"Why'd you put these Schlitz tall boys on the side – they're ours too?

"You'll want some beer after caddying tomorrow." Ray said.

"Caddying.......tomorrow? Hearing that was like watching that iridescent crap float off of my skin. "Ray you're kidding me right?"

"Ryan, we got to make an appearance tomorrow, or we'll spend the next two weekends on the bench.........Those beers do look good." He nodded before he closed the fridge door and went upstairs and took a shower.

Brother Bill called down from the kitchen, "Suppertime Ryan."

Cathy and Billy had grilled cheese, the rest of us had breaded flounder, French fries, and cold slaw. Hal really liked this meal, but he had to razz Jane anyway. He'd start talking to Ray and me like she wasn't there, then he'd start talking about Mom in the 3rd person. Ray and me didn't like it when he tried to make it look like we were his cheering section.

"Let's say Grace as we have an all-star Lenten meal before us. And.....And......I will lead us in prayer: Bless us O Lord, and these thy gifts which we are about to receive from thy bounty through Christ Our Lord. Amen. And P.S. Heavenly Father; Please instruct the converted Protestant that Lent ended last April, and a God damn T-bone would be appreciated next Friday."

Jane took her plate from the breakfast nook and ate standing up in the kitchen.

THE FRIDAY NIGHT BEER BASH WAS A HALF-BAKED idea at best. After supper, Ray sent me back down to Greystone and had me bring a case of beer with me. He went up to the North End to meet Loki and see if he made any progress on his assignment list. The beer was cold when I pulled the case from the cellar fridge, but the cans were sweating plenty by the time I reached the tracks. The station was deserted – just commuters coming and going. I crossed the tracks and ended up by the buried Comet remnant.....I knew I would. The cans of Budweiser were held in six-pack formation with the new keepers made of plastic around the cans' necks, which littered the streets and waterways replacing the cardboard packaging. The plastic came along after the pop tops showed up. The river's shoreline water was supposed to keep the beer cooler than being out in the air, but the water's temperature was around 68 degrees. 68 degree beer wasn't a party – it would be a disaster. A Styrofoam kooler and ice would remedy that, if anybody showed up.

This was the final summer of the 1920's version of Greystone Station. The Penn Central had put up a large sign in front of the station saying improvements and upgrades were coming, but the signage now was over two years old. Somebody had spray painted "bullshit" on the announcement. A lot of commuters were caught off-guard when the improvements started in the winter/spring of 1970. They installed overhead electrical radiant heat in the overpass. The incandescent lighting, the rusty light poles, and fixtures were replaced with mercury vapor and fluorescent lights, aluminum poles, and a new 480 volts electrical service. The new lighting removed any trace of Film Noir the station had, and zoomed it into 2001: A Space Odyssey. The original station house remained the same; except for a pay phone upgrade, and additional radiant electrical heaters to replace the original pot belly stove.

The old station platforms still required commuters to climb the trains' five steps to reach the floor of the commuter cars. Penn Central must have had a bellyful of lawsuits with those low platforms and they'd be dollars ahead by avoiding the rigged railroad court. Both the north and southbound platforms had yet to be demo'd. It was going to happen sooner than later. There were huge cracks in the concrete; a kid could put a foot through a few of the holes. There were epoxy patches on top of concrete patches, and the rusty rebar was exposed. There was spalling and flaking everywhere. The benches on the platforms had been anchored at one time and numbered six to a side; now neither statement was accurate. For now, the railroad wasn't laying out any more money for maintenance knowing the upgrade was coming. I ripped a Bud from a ring before I put the other 23 in the warm river water. At some point the river would be kooler than the air

315

could keep them. My brother and Loki had to know we would need ice.

Many of the commuters from Manhattan were already home. It was past six o'clock, the schedule had switched over to 'off-peak'. I gazed into the Hudson, then the Palisades, and to my watch. It was just a little behind me. Three years had elapsed since it penetrated our atmosphere and was ceremoniously placed between the railroad tracks and the river, and very much "the elephant in the room." Ray said.

He had been investigating and theorizing about this cast-off piece of the cosmos: an outer space intruder of unknown origin and composition. I took a long drink and looked at the label. "That's number one." I chugged the rest of the can to catch a buzz. I did the same with the second can.

I started feeling the alcohol. What made me feel good was how Ray and me really clicked. It had to have been the teamwork. We hadn't communicated on that level for a long time; it had been close to telepathy at times. The more we didn't talk - the more there was an electron flow of dialogue. By instinct we knew the moves to take. A 16 and a 14 year old performed this dangerous job with no safety precautions or equipment. How one of us didn't land on the track bed below made me laugh. 'Love playing with fire', I thought.

That Fireball........something was going on there. It was like seeing a hot babe in class – you were always watching her. I wondered if it had gender.

Whenever we'd go down Greystone after we painted the yacht club bridge something was different. Functionally, things were better, but the station was losing it's soul......its class. I wanted to dig out the "Cosmic Intruder" and find out more about it, or if it had changed in any way.

"Do you want to get whisked away to that mini-universe with the stars, mirrors, pinwheel floor and corkscrew subway? The next trip there........might be a one-wayer." Ray arched his brow.

He scared me enough to buy into his way of thinking. It might be wise to let the infinite universe know I was on their team and wavelength, albeit glued to a blue ball by its gravity. To show my respect to this errant fireball, I poured the remainder of my Budweiser over the ground where we had buried it. If the forces of this "Stardust Drifter" were benign, it might pay off somewhere in the future.

Sitting Indian style on the yellowed commuter southbound platform, I was on my 3rd beer and watched the sun sink below the Palisades. If Ray and Loki didn't show up by 9:30, I'd stash the remainder underneath some brush, and go caddying tomorrow. There was no point of hauling it back to 21 unless I had a car. The most beer I had drunk at one time was eight cans. I didn't want any more than three if I was by myself. All I had to do was look at Hal to know getting plowed by yourself was a drag.

DURING THE DAY AT THE GOLF COURSE, RAY AND LOKI were putting together the plan for another attempt to throw this party down the river. Loki said he'd be able to borrow his father's car for the preliminary stuff.

"We'll bring the beer over to the boat club and keep it kool over there. It's better off over there in case the cops show up uninvited." Ray nodded at us.

"The boat club? I didn't see any kooler over there Ray." I said.

"The one on the dock.....the crank device that swiveled. You'll see it when you bring the beer over there after supper. Boatman said we could use it; "Just don't fall in - the marina was dredged three years ago. It's around 15 feet deep. Loki's getting his father's car tonight for about ?"

We looked to Ferguson. "I can only get it for maybe an hour. I might be able to stretch it."

"We'll load the beer in the trunk and drive down the river. We'll have to carry it over to the yacht club. Loki, you can drop me and Ryan off down the North End, and bring the car back. We'll wait for you down there."

"Check." Loki said.

Ray and me both caught a loop, and it was probably because we didn't need the money. Loki needed a loop in the worst way and lady luck intervened. He got out the first time all week. We were all on a high when we left the country club.

Loki pulled into the train station's parking lot with over four cases of beer. We crossed the tracks and carried six – six packs each: a case of Schaefer Tall boys, 21 cans of Bud, a case of Chug-a-Mugs, a case of Miller malt liquor, and about 12 renegade cans of Colt 45; it had been waiting in the fridge on emergency status. We had to tote them north another eighth mile to the boat club's dock.

It was all loaded into this cage apparatus. The cage was raised and lowered by this hand crank hoist with a 3 foot long boom coming off a 7' mast. When the crane was swung over the water the beer was lowered. They had this gear on the hoist drum and it allowed us to 'hold' the load at a specific height so we could turn the crane and land the load right on the deck. Boatman gave us permission to use it, but he told Ray this usage was just a one time thing. We didn't want to hang around up there anyway – it was too far away from the girls and the music. For this party, it would save us a lot of bullshit with koolers and ice.

We had to pinch a milk crate from the club they had laying around to carry the beer back to the station. The cans and bottles packaged in cardboard had disintegrated. The beer was as cold as being in the cellar fridge, but it couldn't stay cold for long after we cranked it up from the depths of the yacht club's dock.

Before Joe started the car Ray asked, "How's the priority list going?"

"NG."

"Huh?"

"We'll have to make a quick cruise......see who's around. I only got 20 minutes of drive time before I got to take the car back." Loki said.

My hand began scratching the barren area on my head, "What do you got - a junior license?" I laughed.

Loki thought I was burnin' on him: "Yeah, but with my Drivers Ed. endorsement card – I can drive at night. My old man just doesn't loan me the car unless it's for a date."

"This is a joke - right Joe?" I asked.

"C'mon, let's just try to find some babes. Make the circle: Lake, Morsemere, and back down the End. Then drop me and Ryan off down the End. We'll try to get something cooking while you're walking back down." Ray said.

Right off the bat, we saw Reno in the parking lot next to the Emerald. He knew all these chicks mostly because he went to Commerce High whose student body was like 75% female. Ray and me had attended All Souls with Mike Reno, but we could only take him in doses.....the same as most people. The guy always had something going on: peddling hot car radios, ran card games, he'd steal tires and rims by order, sold untaxed smokes and pot, etc. He was in Ray's class in the eighth grade but somehow he lost a year, and now he was in my grade. He had some bullshit line he flunked a year at Commerce just because he had to service so many of the girls.

Loki pulled into a space putting Ray and Mike right next to each other. Loki and me let Ray handle the diplomacy.

"Free beer?" Reno took a drag, raised his eyebrows; "What's the catch?"

"We need you to round up some female talent, and bring them to the beer blast."

"Yeah – I'll see who's on the street. I'll get the girls for the party......that's not the hard part..........at least for me." he smiled at us. "Where you having this party?"

"Greystone."

"Why the train station?........what's down there.....isn't the North End good enough anymore?"

"Something different.........less cops. Any reefer around?" Ray said.

"What are you looking for nickels, ounces, quarters......?"

"Just a nickel – if it's good I'll buy a dime."

"The only guy who got anything I know of is Chooch, you know – Ronny Crestwood, but his counts aren't the best. He knows it's dry out there." Mike said.

"The chicks don't want to drink beer cause then they got to find a place to piss, and they don't like that."

It was time for me to give Reno some shit, "Why don't you carry some T-P in your trunk?"

He looked a little behind Ray, "Hey 'Lil Whitecastle – I didn't see you in the back." He got out of the Lemon-lime Nova and walked to his trunk. "I want to show you something." He opened the trunk of the Nova and held up six rolls of toilet paper. "You see.....I know how to treat women. I got what they need."

The four of us were cracking up.

"Hey man, you gotta give 'em what they want." Reno stiff armed over Ray's door.

"Listen Mike, we need chicks, reefer and tunes. I got about half a nickel, but we can't smoke it out in front of everybody - there won't be enough to get everybody high."

"Ray, you might have to roll me a couple of jays for bait in case I don't score with Chooch."

"Listen, this is what we'll do: Loki's got to bring his Dad's car back. We'll meet you down the end. Mike - me and Ryan will go with you and we'll be looking for other people we know to go to the beer bash. You'll have to drop me off at my house to get my stash, and we'll drop off my brother down Greystone so they see him and know that is where the party is."

Ray and me got in Reno's car. Ray called Loki through Mike, "We'll see you down the end."

Loki nodded.

"Fuck......hey you two lawyers – can you help me out with some gas money........a buck each?

Immediately I looked at his gas gauge. It was on 'E'.

"It's all downhill to Oil City, and you can stop at Orchard Street and see if Crestwood is around after you get gas." Ray said.

"Un-uh, the weed gauge is what gets checked first in this car." Reno smiled.

He was good for one eye roll every four minutes.

Ray rode shotgun and shouted to the stoop, we knew the Carr brothers from the golf course. "Hey Roger.........Chooch around?"

"Should be back in a little bit. Everybody's looking for him. He might be up Morsemere." Carr yelled back.

"Roger......just tell him me and Reno are looking for him." The Carr brothers knew what it was about.

Even Reno pitched in for his own gas. $3.00 bought 9 gallons of go-go juice.

"Reno - let's try Morsemere – it's on the way to the End." I said. I knew Tarts hung out down there; he always had a way with the chicks.

The Morsemere neighborhood was a delicatessen, Ralphs Pizza joint; mostly a take-out place, a Gulf gas station, and a strip park down the street. The guys who hung out there were basically overflows from Lake Ave. and the North End.

Kenny Crawford's '66 VW bug was in front of the Pizza joint. We parked right behind him. We all got out. Mike asked Vinny if Chooch had been around.

Everybody with Crawford shook their heads from side to side. "Bobby Herrick asked, "You looking for weed?"

"You're fuckin' brilliant Bob." Mike scoffed.

Holter came out of the deli with a quart of beer. "Hey! The Whitehouse is here – What are you guys up to?"

"That's why we stopped. We're throwing a party down the river."

"The Marina?" Vince guessed.

"No. We're giving Greystone a tryout."

"Interesting. You guys got a kegger?" Crawford raised his brow.

319

"Nah – just about five cases. A real duke's mixture of industrial brew. We got it in this depth charge beer cooler cage at the yacht club. It's gonna be good and cold. No imported crap." I squeezed in.

"Any reef around?" Reno took a drag off a Camel.

"The only reason you're looking for Chooch is you heard about the hash he's got." Tarts said.

Barb was sitting on Kenny's bumper and she giraffed her head over when she heard 'hash'.

"So what's the big deal? He's selling and I'm buying. It's called free enterprise." Mike replied.

We saw the new sign over the Pizzeria: 'Progressive Pizza'. It used to be Napoli Pizza. Ray asked, "You tasting any progress in your slice brother?.................. "Hey Vince, what gives? What happened to Ralph.......did he sell out?"

"Ralph's still here......same pizza. A new name came with the divorce." He laughed.

Ray told Holter, "That divorce crap can reverse the magnetic poles of your world."

Vinny laughed, "The guy's got a Lincoln, and sleeps in the back of the pizzeria."

"Hey Ryan, how much?" Kenny said.

"Nothing for you guys; it cost Ray and me plenty.

"Any reason you guys are throwing a party?"

"No reason.......the start of summer? Will that work for you?" Ray smirked. "We got to stop down the end and get Loki."

"Loki?" Crawford repeated.

"Joe Ferguson. He played for the Jets with us a couple of summers ago. Kind of a mystic." Holter said.

"I still think he was jazzin' up the ball on us." Bobby Herrick said.

"The ump said otherwise." Ray pretended he was the umpire and rung up Herrick on strikes with his right hand: "Steeeerike!"

While we were chewing the fat over that championship season, I seen Reno working on that girl Barb.

I asked Kenny if Barb was going out with anybody. Holter answered, "She's just hangin' with us - she rides around with Reno......sells pot for him........goes to Gorton. I think she missed a grade or got left back or something."

I watched her get in the back seat of Reno's Nova with the dark green vinyl roof. "Ray.....come on, let's go find Chooch. Mike said."

"Now what?" I asked Ray.

"Ryan - Catch a ride with Crawford. It'll probably be better if you stop down the End too. You might run into some girls who want to drink some beer."

"They're going to end up being Irish/Catholic." I predicted.

Ray looked at his watch; "It's going on 7:30, we're running out of options. Reno and Crawfish got the wheels.....they're calling the shots."

320

"I got to get a pack of smokes down the end."

"Ray......C'mon..." Reno called from behind the wheel.

"HEY RENO – BARB'S WITH US!" Crawford shouted.

Mike Reno laughed and waved. Mike never liked having a guy riding shotgun, it was bad for his image, but this was business.

Loki got bored waiting for Reno; he ordered a slice of Palisade pizza down the North End and washed it down with a bagged tall-boy. He was killing time with Cocaine Wayne when we pulled in the public lot across from Barca's supermarket. Three guys in the back seat of the '66 Bug was pretty tight; I was glad to get out and get a pack of Marlboro's. The next thing I see is Loki and Cocaine Wayne getting in Reno's back seat with Barb.

Crawford turned to Tarts: "What's Reno doing with Wayne?"

I met Wayne a couple of summers ago when we played Little League ball with the Colts Boys club. He had given me the spikes sliding into second. It cleared the benches when they saw the blood coming from my ankle. We had a scrap down the End the next time I ran into him. A beat cop broke it up, and later on Wayne and me patched things up in the fall when All Souls played Christ the King in basketball.

All I really knew about him was he had gotten into the world of magic powder and needles. Brother Ray knew more about him than I did. If there was an empty stoop down the north end, Wayne would cop a bag and occupy it.

iii

As soon as Crawfish pulled into the small lot in Greystone; Holter and me went to get a case of brew from the depth charge beer cooler cage. We figured Reno and Ray would be right behind us. Reno must have taken a quick run back over to Orchard St. checking if Chooch had returned. If they hooked up with some babes, Reno would have to run a taxi service to bring them down to the train station. I remembered Ray still had to get his hold-out nickel of pot from home too. 'Holy fuck', it was getting complex just to throw a party. Three happy faces looked at the beer. With all the chug-a-mugs opening, it sounded like automatic gunfire. Bobby Herrick asked, "You got the beer kooler stashed around here Whitestone?"

Holter answered and tried to explain the boat club's beer kooler. "Bobby, you go with Whitewater when we get the next case, you'll see what they got rigged up."

Reno showed up about 20 minutes later and added five more merrymakers to the thirsty list. I suppose we couldn't count Cocaine Wayne and Barbara as being foot soldiers; though she could probably out drink him. Crawford had his eight track cranking. I didn't know the band. Ronnie Zanzibar had installed the VW's sound system for

Kenny with four speakers: one in the front and back, and one in each door. It was true stereo, but not quadraphonic which hadn't come out yet. The speakers were Jensens and they were on an 'A' or 'B' switch. Kenny could only have two speakers on at a time. He was pulling 25 watts per channel for a total 50 watts of eardrum degrade when it was maxed out. Everyone knew when Crawford was coming down the street during the summer months.

"Mike Reno," Ray called, "You wanna take a ride to Glenwood and see if your harem is around. I got a five gallon bucket at the house and we'll get some ice at the supermarket down Glenwood and we'll fill up the bucket with ice and throw in the beer down here?"

"I thought you had a kooler up at the yacht club?" Bobby Herrick was confused.

"The river will keep it cold while it's in the river. We should have the ice and five gal. to keep it cold once we pull it from the depths." I said.

"Yeah – right." Bobby shook his head up and down.

Reno talked Vinny into going on the talent search for some off-duty girls and a big bag of ice. Ray and Loki were dropped off at 21 to get the 5 gal. bucket and a couple of joints for female enticement. Mike was leaning pretty hard on womanslayer 'Valentino Vince' to go with him.

"C'mon Cinzo." Reno said, " – all the hippy girls love you. They know I only want sex from them. I don't have the rap you and Holter can lay down. "What can I offer? A car and occasional reef? Chooch is probably up Lake Ave. right now. We'll score some hash and go down to Glenwood and see if the Warburton girls are around." Reno kept the hammer down on Vince.

He finally gave in. They took off with Ray and Loki in the back seat. Vinny knew from his brother Joe - you could plow a lot more pussy with hash than you could with reefer. It was mostly because the pot back then was basically ditch weed. The stuff looked and smelled first class, but smoked like the sweepings off a tobacco shed floor. Not much of a high - just a king sized headache.

Ray gave Reno a couple of 'bait' joints they got at 21. Ray and Loki were only gone for about 15 minutes before they came walking back down. They had some fresh beers, and both were animated - talking wild shit. They heard Crawford's jams and they started hand clapping and doing the slide. They were stoned high.

Barb came around the corner of the station house pulling up her cut-off shorts. She had short dark brown hair. I think it had been a different color, but she had this look that really worked on me; and she didn't talk like other chicks – a real wise ass. It made me listen to her. She didn't have big eyes - her lids worked so you hardly ever saw the entire iris of both eyes. I had seen Barb around Lake Ave., she may have lived near P.S. 9.

George Holter, Bobby Herrick, Kenny, Barb Wells, and Mike Reno were all a year older than Vince and me, but we were all in the same grade. They all copped to absenteeism rather than admitting they had been overwhelmed by the grade level or workload. I couldn't recall seeing her down the North End, the farthest north she went on foot was probably Morsemere.

The first case of beer was gone; Loki was complaining the party needed a refill from the boat club.

"Barb, you want to take a walk to get another case?" I tried.

"You got a cigarette?"

I coaxed a couple from the Marlboro softpak. We both took one.

"You friends with Crawford?" she said.

"Kenny, Vinny, Reno, and me went to All Souls in grade school. Ray and me are brothers. I know all the guys here either from school or baseball. I don't know you, I've seen you up on Lake Ave. What's your last name?"

"Wells. And yours is......?"

"Whitelaw. The guys are always fucking with my last name. Not too many people use my first name.......once in a while."

"You got any Colt in the beer locker up the tracks?"

"Yeah, I think there's a six or two. How many you want?"

"Two will do."

"You got to watch out for that malt liquor........it's stronger than beer."

"That's why I like it; you don't need as much to get where you're going." Barb took a long pull off the cowboy.

"Be right back." I said.

Everybody except Ray was bitchin' at me for taking so long. I knew it was more razz than anything else. Barb had taken center stage sitting on Kenny's back bumper. There were only the five of us guys there. We took our turns talking with her. You can tell when the gals have had enough of you. Barb was different – she didn't hold it against you. She'd give you another chance to get kool with her.

Some stupid shit came on the tape. Loki reached into the Bug and turned it down some. Kenny said it was okay......he owned up to the garbage. He explained you had get through the 3rd track to get to the smokin' songs on the 4th track.

"Know what? I don't think Reno and Vinny are coming back at all." Robbie Herrick said.

Cocaine Wayne's head immediately popped up. Wayne was getting awful squirrely. Holter said he was probably coming down from whatever he had in his veins. He only had one beer as far as I could tell, and he might not have even finished that.

"Loki, did Whitetop ever tell you the story of him and Reno on the recess grounds at All Souls?" Crawford asked.

"What happened?"

"The two of them were going at it, and Ryan was taking it to Mike. But you know he's a good year older than Whitelaw; they're rollin' around on the blacktop and Mike gets him in a headlock. With his free hand he pulls out a ring of keys and starts drilling the big key into his temple." Everybody starts laughing.

"Huh?" Barb Wells was rubbing her temple.

"I think it was Tarts or Joe Butterballs who ran over and got Ray. On the run, Ray could see his brother in Reno's headlock, but not the key he was trying to screw into Ryan's head. Ray didn't give Mike any warning and he came out with this roundhouse karate chop to Reno's neck under his chin. It put him on all fours choking, wheezing, and searching for air. Word got around faster than a Richard Petty lap at Bristol: "Big Whitelaw knows karate'."

Brother Ray heard Kenny's version of the fight. He knew there wasn't too much embellishment; but at the time, he knew he didn't want to get branded as a martial arts expert. It would have been tantamount to being labeled as the "fastest gun in town" – somebody was always making you prove yourself. Ray had gotten me out of another jam; in this case: a chokehold.

On the way home that day, I asked Ray where he picked up that jujitsu stuff. He denied any knowledge of the martial arts. The reason he went into the Bruce Li stance and followed through with the karate' chop was because he thought he'd never get a fist in between Mike double chin and barrel chest.

Mike Reno was just one of those guys it was hard to stay mad at. A small riot surrounded him wherever he went. He was an operator. A lot of chicks dug his bullshit: the attention, the grass, his wheels; but guys knew he was all flim-flam and scam. When Reno and Tarts left the station, we knew it was even odds they would return with some babes or reefer. Reno never took the long view of anything; it was always the here and now.

If you were a dude – you went to Gorton High, Saunders Trade & Tech H.S. Maybe if your folks had money, they'd send you to All Souls H.S. If you were Mike Reno – you went to Commerce H.S. His family had a painting and wall papering business. Commerce had a few home improvement courses and Mike thought he had a leg up on their curriculum. Most of his reasoning and decisions were based on hedonistic outcomes; he had the logic to back it up. "I'm attending Commerce H.S.; they teach us how the law of supply and demand is in play every day. To further my value and exclusivity: I got the Nova."

At times, it was just a bit too much.

Cocaine Wayne went to the Boat club with me to get another case - the party wasn't slowing down; because it hadn't got off the ground. It was dark, but still early. There didn't seem to be a part two to the night.

Carrying the second case back, we took the overpass instead of going across the tracks. Wayne looked at the bookend babes: Draculynn and Paulette. The advanced algebraic equation Ray had started a year earlier, expanded vertically and horizontally. The beer was getting heavy and I left Wayne in the overpass. He was probably studying the two hand drawn images by Ray and 'Headshot Harry'. After I killed another beer, he was still in the overpass. He couldn't be studying the portraits; he must have been immobilized trying to decode the mathematical formula.

Holter and Crawfish weren't finished burning on the absentee Reno. They pleaded their case to Loki so he'd get on the anti-Mike wagon, but he didn't care enough about Reno.

Herrick picked up the cause: "I asked him why he goes to a girls' high school."

"This ought to be good." Holter said.

"Reno says they were short on teachers."

"So what?"

"Holter started to chuckle, "Mike claims he went to Commerce to teach."

"What.......How to paint a dining room?" I had to light up.

"Teach? Teach what?" Ray asked. Now, Loki's interest was piqued.

"Sex education......after school and on weekends." Holter scratched his head laughing, "And then he gives you the Mike Reno grin – you can't help but laugh with the motherfucker. He ain't a guy you love to hate...........he's a guy you hate to love!" Holter grinned shaking his head.

Barb Wells had had enough. "I'll give it to you straight from a girl's point of view – He don't know a thing about sex: he don't know what turns a girl on, he don't know how to French kiss, or do anything except have us push his crummy pot for him. All he ever did is slobber all over my face and dry hump me in the back seat."

"What about riding around with him looking for Chooch or Ricky Shaw to buy reefer?" Ray said. "Wasn't he cutting you in on the action?"

"Big Dealer – Mike Reno.......buy quarters and sell nickels." she took a long drink of Colt 45.

"He's looking for Chooch to buy some hash right now........" Crawfish said. "Wells - you know you and him would have smoked a bunch and ended up in his back seat if you went for a ride with him instead of Vince. Then he'd tell the rest of us he couldn't find Choocher.....who you kidding?" Kenny laughed smoothing his chin.

"That's different.......he can be nice sometimes." she laughed.

Crawford rifled through the Bug's small trunk. "There it is." He handed her a half roll of TP and held up an 8 track tape: "I been lookin' for this since we went upstate."

It was a homemade tape; Rexall had made for him. The sound system in the '66 Bug was pretty powerful. The store bought tapes played better than the homemade ones, but Kenny just had some horrible music. The Z-man had set Kenny up with this equalizer/booster after he complained the 50 watts didn't push the Jensens to the limits. The boosted tape deck now had the wattage to crank out the jams. The music Kenny Crawfish favored was worse when he cranked up the volume. A guy had to be in full-blown party mode to find the hidden groove Catdaddy said was there. In the end, there was no way to turn a crummy composition into a good song with more amplification; and other times the volume destroyed the music.

There were other drawbacks: some of Rex's homemade tapes were so distorted they were unintelligible because they were recorded with a cheap unit. Rex's recordings got progressively better as time and technology went on. At the Greystone blast, Crawford had his front and rear speakers on the Bug's rooftop. Both had boxes with long speaker wire. The parking area was plenty loud. Sometimes the equalizer helped to minimize the distortion. Studio Doors played great, bootleg Cream was hard to get through. The speakers could digest all the bass he fed them. The VW's stationary rear windows at times could vibrate with the equalizer slide bar and the bass dial wide open. This was cutting edge stuff back then.

Kenny wanted the 'rep' of being a travelling radio station, but he was only mildly interested in the music. When it came to dancing – that white boy was in a class by himself. That was how he hooked-up with all these girls. They didn't care if he looked like Frankenstein doing the Hitler goose step. They were thrilled they had found a white guy who wasn't self-conscious about getting on the dance floor.

What wasn't classic – was Kenny's tape collection. When you were going to be cruising around with Crawfish, you'd better bring a tape of your own, otherwise you were at his mercy. He had a box of tapes in the boot in the back: Marty Robbins, Buck Owens, Vanilla Fudge, Steppenwolf, Wilson Pickett, Otis Redding, Iron Butterfly with the infamous "IN A GADDA DA VIDA". After you made it through the soul music, you were forced to turn on the FM radio. You never could count on Crawfish's musical tastes – except if it involved 'Tommy James and the Shondells'. The ultimate arbiter was how high he was or wasn't. The music didn't have to be blasting for Kenny because he wasn't listening to it most of the time anyway, but he played it loud just to get people's attention. For him and to a certain extent us; the music was mostly a soundtrack to our movie. Most of the time, the volume was at a level which allowed us to shoot the shit whether we were just tooling around or parked somewhere smoking a jay.

Like a bolt of lightning Crawford locked his brakes up. The braking wasn't uniform and the Bug tried to pull into the other lane. Beer and wine escaped from the cans and bottles.

"What the fuck Kenny?"

We wondered if Crawford had a heart attack or aneurysm or something. I looked at his hands as the clapped in time with the O'Jay's song: 'I love Music'. He brought the car to a stop, and he turned the music up, and started boogalooing right there in the middle of the road. If we were high or drunk enough, we got out and started shakin' it down right there with him. I'm sure some passing motorists thought we were making a commercial or something.

"Hey!" Vince cautioned: "You fuckin imbecile - we got reefer on us. Use your fuckin' brains.........let's get outta' here before the coppers show up."

Crawford paid Tarts no mind and kept right on booga-looing, and laughing right in Vinny's face."

Catdaddy would catch a guitar riff, a major drum beat, a kick-ass vocal, or a real fat bass line......the equalizer toggle was engaged and the world on the other side of the windshield became irrelevant. The steering wheel became an instrument. He sang, he clapped, drummed, and snapped his fingers and hardly looked at the road. I even saw him pull this move when he was all alone. Something was wrong with that boy. We all knew it, but at the same time we envied his wild sense of freedom.

After the way I saw Crawford use a car, I knew I had to get a set of wheels. Kenny never flunked a grade; his parents must have started him late. Everybody was older than me. In a month I'd be 15, still a year away from getting my driver's license. Getting a car? I'd have to save a lot of bread to pull that off. How did these guys in high school swing a set of wheels? Realistically, I was looking at my senior year before I could get on the road. Ray could have had his license last March if he wanted. Crawford was in the same grade as me and Tarts, but he had to have been Ray's age because he already had his driver's License. He was one kool kat, but he sure wasn't any brainiac.......Still, Kenny was slick enough to get his license and own a car.

iv

A car barreled loud and fast down Harriman Ave. It had to have been travelling north on Warburton. The car veered left off Warburton onto Harriman at the 'Y' configuration; Harriman leading to the train station and Warburton heading into Hastings. A guy could do 60 m.p.h. on Warburton; aim the car a little bit towards the River and coast the last $3/8^{ths}$ mile into the commuter station. What was this midnite rider up to? The engine was shut the down and the lights had been turned off. The vehicle was bouncing in and out of pot holes; we could hear its suspension disagreeing.

A narrow construction road led out of the station into the swampy area where Ray and me had found the Fireball remnant; the road was still viable. WOOOOSH! An incandescent streetlight revealed a dark primer gray sedan doing 30 m.p.h. into the dried bog.

Holter said with a Chug-a-Mug in hand: "Don't think that was Vinny and Reno."

Barb ejected the eight track tape.

"Should we check it out?" Herrick stood gape-mouthed.

I could see Ray's concern; he was looking across the tracks at the Cosmic Intruder's burial mound.

He said, "I didn't hear any crashing or cries for help – just a bunch of reeds getting mowed down." He turned, "Those parking barricades against the wall – C'mon we'll use them to block the construction road..........those traffic cones too - make it look like that car never came down here."

We could hear sirens getting closer. They were coming from the same direction as the primer gray four-door had. The chase cars raced north on Warburton as we watched the underside of the maple leaves in Henry Hudson park turn red from the flashing lights three times in close succession.

"That's for this gray car." She took a drink and motioned with her head where the car might be.

Kenny grinned on the one side of his mouth and his eyebrows went up. "Wells, why don't you break out some of the marahoona you got?"

I didn't think she was kool; I knew she was kool. She didn't do that handbag trip like the rest of the girls did. She took a folded sandwich baggie from her back pocket and got some rolling papers from the side pocket in the driver's door. She handed one to Crawford and she smoked the other half-way down with two strong hits before she passed it off, even Cocaine Wayne got high our style.

Not much was said as I did my share of choking and gagging as we entered the next level of 'high'. Holter went through Crawford' case of tapes.......again. He put something back on. I think it was some bubble-gum rock. Holter would play that shit just to piss everybody off.

I cupped my eyes and looked where I thought the mystery car might be. If a fire didn't start or nobody walked out of the swamp, we'd have to investigate......but it was still too soon.

Robbie Herrick started walking towards the construction road.

"Hey Herrick, you don't want to be walkin' in on those people yet. They might be getting off to get rid of evidence, they might be murdering somebody, dividing up some robbery loot – don't go over there man." Cocaine Wayne called.

"Yeah – better not," We all echoed.

"Holy fuck.......I'm fuckin' wasted." I put my hands in my face.

"Toldja my shit is good." Barb nodded.

"I didn't think I was this high until Big Whiteflag got me digging my head." Loki inhaled at his reassessment.

She took a seat on the bumper and looked at Holter and Crawfish and smiled, "If I get any of that hash from Mike or Chooch – you guys won't be able to do anything but one thing."

"What's that?" Holter smiled.

"You guys aren't so smart. Be like Whiteflag – go with the flow. What are they playin' on the radio?" she crunched her eyes and shook her head.

"Look." Wayne pointed.

Emerging from the dry swamp were four figures: one towered over the other three and the Cat-o-nine tails. Each was toting a bottle of something. As they came closer, we noticed this far off stare – like they had been awake for three days.

Loki spoke just loud enough for us to hear: "Druids – they must be the Druids.

"Druid?........What's a Druid?" George Holter laughed. "Hahahahaha..... They ain't no Druids. They're The Huns from Lake Ave.

The four continued their advance toward us. George I.D.'d them as they came closer: "Connors McKool, Davis Quinn, Eddie Van Trex, and 'Ranger Rick' Lynch – that's them...... that's The Huns." My confused mind saw four guys who been on a three week cattle drive, or were roadies for a carnival.

Holter and Herrick were the only ones who knew The Huns. They all had some variation of facial hair to go along with their long locks. They looked vaguely familiar; I remember seeing the tall guy around. The crew had been out of high school for a year or two. They graduated from 'street high school'. McKool was the tall dude, the driver of the '61 Bel Air. His name always came up as being a sharp drag racer. McKool and Dave Trent had gone to the line a number of times. After Trent's car got out of shape and wrecked dragging with McKool on Lake Ave., the two decided they had gone beyond racing on the street. When they raced now - they brought the action up to the Hillview Reservoir just north of McClean Ave. The last I heard, the number of wins was about even. McKool was supposed to have been the better all-around wheel man. I didn't know what that meant, but I used it to describe him.

Whoever labeled these guys 'The Huns' had hit the nail on the head. They were my concept of what a Hun would look like. Who would know better than me except for Paul Coker as we read about them in Rome's histories as the Empire struggled to keep them in the Teutonic regions. The length of their hair on their heads and faces grew from neglect rather than any style statement. McKool's blond hair was as straight as a Chinaman's, Quinn had that thick Skid Row hair; the only guys who get blessed with that type of mane are the ones who don't care about it. Van Trex could have been a rock star if he knew a guitar like he knew transmissions and rear-end differentials. Ranger Rick was Frank Zappa's double. The latter two were destined to see those locks on the floor of boot camp either at Fort Dix or Fort Drum.

The Greystone lot started to feel like some episode of 'The Outer Limits' with a 'Gunsmoke' showdown. Ray watched them coming; out the side of his mouth he said he had seen their car before in the middle of a rumble down Homefield Bowling Alley.

They walked closer. This Connors McKool towered over Holter; he towered over everybody and I was 6'1". He had a good 6 inches on me.

"Que pasa vaqueros?" Holter laughed. He turned and looked at us: "I'm fuckin' blasted."

"Cops been around?" McKool squinted. The other Huns faced us in a line.

"No cops. We could tell from their sirens and lights they went north on Warburton towards Hastings with the 'hot pursuit' bullshit." Crawford answered.

"They'll be down here, just make like we're having a Saturday night get together. You guys dummy up…..we'll do all the talking." McKool outlined his plan.

I was wondering why the bulls were chasing The Huns. It wasn't likely they were being pursued for open intoxicants. Maybe it was just a speeding rap they wanted to nail them on; or perhaps something a little more exotic. Holter said when they weren't wrenching on cars - they were working on destination: Valhalla.

Ranger Rick soured, "Why are you guys torturing the tape deck with that music?" Quinn's face looked like he bit into a lemon.

Crawford spoke up, "It's Tommy James."

Connors told Davis: "Go get some of our stuff."

"Run over to our car Sis, and get three of our tapes." Davis said.

"Don't know where your wheels are." Barb replied.

"I'll go find it – I know this place." I said.

I felt bad for Kenny. Tommy James was his all-time fave. He might have taken it personal; he said he had just bought two Tommy James tapes. He really liked "Mony Mony" and "Hanky Panky" 45's because he could dance to them, and Kenny loved to dance. I didn't know what to say about his musical tastes after Tommy James.

Vinny Tarts swore Crawford knew 55% of the jukeboxes in Yonkers packing T.J.'s tunes as well as some of the bars which ran along the Bronx/Yonkers line. If we got in the car when Kenny was on one of his dancing runs – we knew we'd be shuffling in some bar.

"Holter, mind if we ramp up the playlist?" Ranger Rick laughed.

"No…no…go ahead – Okay Kenny?" Holter asked Kenny. "It's his ride." Holter said to Rick.

McKool ejected the tape, looked at us, and then to Barbara. "You the only Chick?"

"Yeah."

"Reno and Tarts are supposed to bring a couple of girls down." Herrick said.

"Fuck Reno." McKool turned back to Barb, "I've seen you before…….we picked you and your friend up. You were hitchhiking."

"That was us – me and Jill."

"Mmmm…..I remember." He pointed at her with the 8 track.

"We were freezing."

"You got a name?"

"Barbara…………Wells."

I watched peripherally. Tonight she was captured by The Huns, she owed them for the ride on a cold night with her friend. Unless Mike Reno and Vinny arrived with the Warburton/Glenwood girls; this was going to be just another night with the guys shooting the shit.

Davis called Crawdad over, "This is what you're looking for."

330

The other Huns told us to "Check it out." One was another homemade compilation: 'Mothers of Invention', 'Doors', 'Creedence Clearwater Revival', Paul Butterfield, Otis Redding. They had a Wes Montgomery tape, and the first 'Blood Sweat and Tears tape. We stuck with the compilation tape, the other stuff was too advanced for us. Crawford finally found out how good his stereo sounded when he heard tapes which had been recorded correctly.

I had been with Crawford since grade school, I knew he'd be sticking with Tommy James and the Shondells; at least he was willing to try new stuff.

Ranger Rick and McKool were drinking their fortified wine: 'Thunderbird', Davis worked a bottle of what he called 'groove wine', and Trex nipped on a half-pint of 'Early Times' and helped himself to a Chug-a-Mug.

Then seven of us watched the Hun show. Ranger Rick parked his butt on a station house window sill; two and-a half feet off the surrounding slate walk. His back was against the substitute stran board window and spread his heels: "Hey Barb, any beer left?"

I looked over there, 'Why doesn't he drink his own wine?' I turned back to Ray. At least we were able to reach a state of confusion with Barb's pot.

He grabbed her as she gave him a beer, spun her around and wrapped his arms about her thin frame. Rick put his face against her ear and squeezed the air out of her. What a move – I thought. She cut one and everybody laughed. I was watching this over the top of the Bug as he brushed her gas off his lap. Now they were making out. I'll bet all of us were thinking: 'Where the fuck was Reno and Vinny?'

The couple carried on with their amorous activities. I heard McKool talking about the war. We all were interested, but only to a point. It was another gorilla in the room. It was going to impact us one way or another: Either you, your brother, or someone you knew got drafted and did a tour there. A few people knew someone who died there. Not many of us knew someone who ran away to Canada to let some poor white, black, or some fruit picker's kid take a mortar round so the runaway could grow up to be a college professor telling everybody how brave he was because he ran away.

Davis was ready to count the guys he knew who cashed out over there........"Ahhh fuckit – they're gone."

Holter and Bobby Herrick knew Eddie Van Trex's older brother who had signed up at the end of 1965. Jesse Van came back all screwed up.

"Say when did Jesse disappear?" Herrick's face was looking for an answer, his older sister used to go out with Jesse...... We all left it hanging. No one answered. No good would come of chasing his ghost.

"McKool – what's you're draft classification?" Loki was trying to find out how this draft thing worked.

"We're all '1-H'." Eddie Trex said.

"What's that mean?" I said.

"It means, eligible for service - pending you pass the physical. Some guys know they're getting drafted - they sign up before

331

they get Uncle Sam's invitation. This way they can join the Navy, Air Force, or Coast Guard where it's not as hot." Van Trex said taking a pull of his whiskey. "Sometimes you still end up in Nam."

"The only thing to do is to party down and wait." McKool took a breath. "Don't do no good to go to college, they eliminated those deferments.

They drafted Ronny 'Chooch' Crestwood and Ronnie Zanzibar when they were 19 and a couple of months." Kenny Crawford said.

Crestwood had been an MP and Z-Man was and still is an electronic wizard, he was working at the Yonkers Police Department after he got discharged. Ronny Chooch was an MP when the Tet Offensive hit Saigon. He said it was real hot for a week. He seldom gave out any details; you just kind of knew it left some big psychological scars.

Holter almost had the can of Colt to his mouth: "My old man was pissed off when Z-Man got drafted. He needed him to do some electrical work on his cab. He had to take it to some idiot who screwed it up even worse."

Chooch and Zanzibar came back with a few problems. They were part of the Orchard St. crew where Kenny had begun his career, after he got out of All Souls.

THE HUNS HAD ONLY BEEN DOWN GREYSTONE FOR 45 minutes before the bulls made their appearance. They were in their commando attack mode: three squad cars came down Harriman Ave. with their engines shut down and their lights off; the same way The Huns had - except they coasted down the hill at about 5 m.p.h. Three cars – six cops. They spread out in the parking area. Five of them walked closer. They looked at the old construction road, but they weren't too interested in it. One of them was sent to look down the road anyway. They saw us all near the station and made their move towards us.

Quinn said, "Keep kool……..keep partying…….stay kool.

"Alright Romeo – get your hands off the girl." A cop who came from the riverside of the station directed Ranger Rick. He looked up and down at the rest of us: "C'mon you fuckheads - Get your hands up or on top of the car. Let's see some I.D. – one at a time. First you Lurch."

Only The Huns, Loki, and Crawfish had real I.D. like Drivers Licenses, and Draft Cards. Brother Ray showed them a library card, Holter gave them his Gorton High athletic booster card. I told the cop I piggybacked on Ray's library privileges. Cocaine Wayne showed the business card of his probation officer from the juvenile delinquent dept. of Social Services. Barb got a pass; one of the cops felt her up saying he was looking for drugs.

The patrol officer emerged from the construction road which dead ended just before the dry swamp behind the 14 story apartment building.

"Anything?" the ranking cop said.

"Mosquitoes and gnats. Didn't see anything." he reported.

"You guys see any cars down here in the last hour.......
specifically: a gray 4 door sedan?" he asked.

Davis' eyes met McKool's; they were going to get out of
this. One of the cops took the wine and Eddie's almost empty bottle of
whiskey and pitched them horseshoe style onto the tracks.

Four disappointed faces responded to the broken bottles.

"Party's over......if we come back – you better be gone." the
bottle pitcher said. They raced up Harriman with the bubble-gum lights
on their roofs aglow.

It was only 10:00 o'clock. We knew we had to hang around
for Reno and Tarts. Ranger Rick was already back smooching with
Wells, it was evident he had unfinished business with her.

Ray asked McKool what their next move was going to be.

"We'll hang out here a while; I think the Y.P.D. is lying in
the weeds. We can't leave yet – not in the Valkyrie Express." McKool
said.

"Listen, I'd rather go to the crowbar motel than get my
wheels impounded. I'm goin to park my car up on Warburton." Kenny
said.

"I'll go with you." Wayne said. He was in bad shape, he was
all herky-jerky. We were surprised the cops didn't give him the 3rd
degree.

Crawford and Wayne drove off, and we followed The Huns
to the riverside southbound platform. I was starting to feel I had a
better time last night by my self. Mostly, we just listened to The Huns
talk music, Vietnam, cars, and women.

On the southbound side we'd be able to see anybody who
came down the station. Strategically, it was a good move. We carried
the remaining beer back across the tracks from the station's parking lot
to the platform on the riverside.....screw the overpass. Everybody
followed the migration except Ray. He waited at the station for
Crawford and Wayne as he nursed a Tall-Boy; the two showed up ten
minutes later.

The Huns were still lathered up about the bluecoats smashing
their wine and whiskey. They helped themselves to our beer in the
milk crate. I carried so much beer, the only thing to make the situation
worse would have been toting around a quarter barrel.

ii

Barb told Rick, "Won't do no good to stew over it."

"Fuckin' cops........Hey sis.......you got any weed?" they
leaned against the handrail.

"Yeah.......I hid it in the wheel well of Kenny's VW, I got it
before he parked his Bug up the hill."

"Well, don't hide it.........divide it." he laughed.

She rolled what remained in the baggie, fired up, took a hit,
and passed it to Rick. The smell of pot took a ride on a light breeze to
the station side.

333

Crawford and Wayne came back and were talking with Ray. They asked him to hang around a little bit after they caught a whiff of reefer from across the tracks. They hoped there would be some left as they climbed the stairs to the overpass. Wayne talked to himself as he followed them.

It had been obvious to everybody but the cops: Cocaine Wayne was going into the cold sweats. It surprised us when he took a couple of hits off the reef just before The Huns came out of the swamp. He was shaking – we knew he was coming down. It wasn't a major thing once the cops had left. I didn't like looking at him hugging himself. Wayne knew he had to get out of Greystone.

"Kenny, you gotta drop me off up the End. I think I miscalculated where I was." He shivered.

"Wayne - we just got back down here. I'll drop you off in a little bit."

The pedestrian bridge was dimly lit with three - hundred watt bulbs; one on each end and one in the middle. Wayne and Kenny walked, looking at Ray's equation on the plywood sheets facing south. Kenny slowed - first reading the left side of the calculus formula. Cocaine Wayne watched the equation as he walked past center and stopped when his interest in the graffiti began to captivate him. They were trying to decipher the montage of art, names, messages, but were drawn to focus on the astrophysical statement. Ray stood in between the two but slightly behind them and watched as their faces left the here and now. Illumination was cast on their faces by no discernable source of light. He couldn't say one way or the other; he thought they were transfixed and infused with what they understood of the mathematical theorem. Ray had begun work two years earlier, but recently had expanded his scope to include some serious concepts he found difficult to digest. Of late, each new installment became more rational and self-evident with each new revelation he committed to the plywood windows.

Wayne squinted, "I know what this part means.......I mean - I got a piece of it." He continued, "Me, Joey Tarts, and Erik Shaw got off down here about a month ago. Joey said it was a modern day hieroglyphics using mathematical notation. He interpreted it as saying we are outcasts..... outsiders.... miscreants who never dial into the mainstream. We are doomed to exist on the outskirts of that which can't be explained. Wayne said.

"All this stuff might make more sense if I just shot a speedball. He pointed to a three foot long section: and I kind of understand that. It has to do with electro/magnetic stuff......right here – right now. If I go back up to the End; it'll fade fast....I'll lose it".

"Being doomed, I've always felt it like it was my karma. Getting wasted seems to help." Crawford said from the other end of the overpass.

Ray used his cigarette as a pointer. "This is the most recent segment, it may indicate why we react to life in the way we do."

Cocaine Wayne and Kenny attempted to study it. Their faces were illuminated by a pale blue light – but brighter than the overpass lights. The intensity of brightness of their faces corresponded with the degree of comprehension they absorbed. The alcohol, marijuana, and heroin's effects - suspended.

"Do they have fireworks up there?" Davis tried to adjust his vision to the mini-light show occurring on the pedestrian bridge.

"Should I drive him back up the End?" Crawford whispered to Ray.

I walked up the stairs from the southbound side to the overpass to see what was going on with the three of them. None of them knew I was there.

"Wayne's got a lot of shit going on." Ray grinned at Crawfish. "Can't say with any conviction, but I think he has a case of pole reversal more than a chemical deficiency." A level of intensity came upon him as there was some kind of satisfaction in Crawford's and Wayne's ability to decipher parts of the equation; "This pole reversal has extra punch from magnetic forces well beyond our solar system; it has been underway for a while. The degree of intensity will determine if it can alter our lives…..people like us have an overwhelming necessity to respond to this alternate wavelength. We can't live like the rest of humanity." He told Kenny and Wayne using his hitchhiking thumb indicating the others on the southbound platform.

"How long can something like this last?" Kenny said.

"I feel neutralized up here……peaceful." Wayne was barely audible.

Ray took a sip and a drag from the cigarette, "It will last until the poles are no longer in reversal……transition. Scientists believe the last time it happened it took over 700 years to reach stability. Modern machines and organic life on a molecular level might alter their magnetic paths, order, and properties during this pole reversal. The earth's magnetism in concert with the sun's electro-magnetic storms may even cause our orbit to be disturbed. Something's underway….I feel it…..I know it."

"I know what you're saying is real, but I don't know if it's real for us." Wayne let go with a scary laugh.

Kenny studied the equation which had taken on an Einstein like length "It's incomplete isn't it? Why do I know that? It should look as indecipherable to me as Arabic or Chinese."

"I can't predict the future – we can only know the pole reversal is underway and it will cause unforeseen events in our lives whether they are small or large in scope as the universe strives for its proper order."

Wayne speculated: "From what I can make of this formula, I'd think the outcomes of the magnetic realignment have just as much chance of being beneficial as causing harm.

Ray and the two members of the 'fifth dimension' as Ray called them, forced a nervous laugh; the illumination was gone.

They weren't trying to keep this classified; I don't believe they knew I was up there.

THE HUNS WERE RUNNING DRY AND WOULD BE
OUT of our beer pretty soon. They were going on about music,
keeping a set of wheels in trim so it had the power and handling to
elude or overtake what they saw as trouble. They expounded on the
complexity of women. Barb Wells' put up with that stuff for a few
minutes and decided it wasn't worth holding in any piss and she went
in the bushes between the platform and the river. Had I been their age,
I would have called "Bullfuckinshit" three or four times, but with my
lack of worldly experience it was best just to sit, drink, and listen.

Good bullshit always made a good time, serious jive could
start a fight real quick. Ray warned me to refrain from acting on
bullshit as it could potentially bite you in the ass. I took out this
Christina Martina, (who's last name was really Martino) but Martina
sounded like sexy fun so it was what we all called her. We were
drinking down the End, and on the sworn testimony of Joe Lamar and
Roy Justice: "Christina will go all the way on the first date if you get
her stoned." I took her down the city to see "A Clockwork Orange"
and nothing. She wouldn't even make out in the movie theatre and we
were blasted. It was all bullshit.....bad bullshit. The only other
possibility was that it was me.......I did have that hole in my hair....so
maybe.....

Vietnam was the topic which wouldn't go away, and nobody
had anything funny to say about it. It had The Huns rattled. The four
Huns used to number six and they cruised around with the two sets of
wheels. 'Clean Donnie Wyck' died when NVA mortar fire hit the 4th
Division ammo dump in the battle of Dak To in the Central Highlands.
Donnie's sister got his hopped up F-85 Oldsmobile. Davis said it was
tough watching Donnie's sister with her two kids driving the
Oldsmobile around.

Eddie's brother Jesse had enlisted and done his year there.
He had signed up for three years in the fall of '65. I never knew Jesse
or Donnie, but I saw him driving the F-85 when he was home on leave
one time on Lake Ave. When Jesse Van Trex got discharged, The
Huns knew he was off; even his brother Eddie didn't know how to
communicate with him.......after 7 months in the states he
disappeared. His family received one postcard from Puerto Rico; and
that was it.

We were close enough to the Orchard St. gang, to know
about Chooch and Z-man and the baggage they came back with. They
were nowhere near the situation Jesse Van Trex dealt with: Jesse was
chasing demons. Ronnie Zanzibar, and Ronny 'Chooch' Crestwood
were running from them.

This Vietnam stuff had me thinking about the year I would
have.....maybe a year-and-a-half before I got drafted. I started doing
everybody's calculations: Loki – 2 years, everybody else – 3 years,
and for once it paid off being the runt of the litter – I had 4 years
before I was 19.......draft age. How could this war go on for another 4
years? Easy.....United States' involvement in Vietnam started the year
I was born, 15 years earlier. In 1961, there were approximately 400
hundred 'special forces' personnel as well as 100 advisors in Vietnam.
A year later, troop levels exceed 11 thousand and casualties number

over 110 killed or wounded. No one could predict the number of troops Johnson or Nixon would send there, or for how long.

"Hey White-A-Matic........What the fuck, go get that last case of beer."
"Who ya think's been haulin' it since the party started? I ain't no St. Pauli girl." A quick glance at Barb; Ranger Rick didn't have his greasy mits on her, "How 'bout it Barb – give me a hand?"
"She stays here." the Ranger pulled rank.
"I'll give you a hand man." Bobby Herrick walked up to the boat club dock with me.
When we came back, she had her legs wrapped around his waist............making out again.

10:45 – No Reno.......No Vinny. The Huns weren't waiting for them, but they thought enough time had elapsed and they were itching to move on.
"Ryan, are you going caddying tomorrow?" Loki nodded.
I didn't want to deal with it, and told him to ask Brother Ray.
"Crawfish.........we owe you one. We'll catch up with you guys for covering for us." McKool winked with a thumbs up.
They walked away with a beer can in each hand, except for Rick who held hands with Barb. She took off with a can of Budweiser, and he had taken the last Rheingold Chug-a-Mug.
Cocaine Wayne tried to hitch a ride with The Huns. He was in tough shape, his body needed a fix. McKool told him: "You wait for Mike Reno." Wayne looked bad enough to hurl the two beers he had drank; Connors didn't want the junkie to mess up the Valkyrie Express. Wayne was so disoriented, he had forgotten Kenny's car was parked on O'Dell. He marched back and forth on the southbound with his arms wrapped around his torso. Under the overhang where there was a rack of train schedules, he pulled one out and tried to read it with his shaking hand. His hands were shaking so bad he was unable to read the departures for the southbound trains. Under a station light he tried to read the list using his index finger. "Ray.....Ray Whitelaw......Ray! Read this fucking thing will ya?"
"One train left, it'll leave here at 11:10." Ray said as the schedule floated to the trackbed.
Holter laughed, "Wayne-O.......You going to Harlem?"
Kenny watched Ray, then back to Wayne. Kenny had the itch. He was considering taking Wayne down to South Yonkers. He knew he might not come back the same if he went down there with him.
"Harlem Wayne?" Holter laughed.
"Ludlow.....I'll make my way over to Lawrence Street." He said not looking at George.
Crawford was almost as edgy as Wayne. He knew he was coming up to the plate soon, but not tonight. He hadn't gotten his wings yet. Soon he would hook-up with somebody going downtown. Kenny knew it was through the calming effect of the drugs that allowed him to hang around for a while. As he observed Wayne he

recognized and felt the entrapment he exhibited. Ray was searching for the access door to a different path where they could possibly side-step the chemical solution.

"Crawford.......Hey...........Kenny........come out of it - Hey Groover ...." George tried to reel him back in. "You think Reno's coming back?"

We looked at Kenny. "Not a chance – maybe the bulls corralled him........or maybe he ran into Chooch's hash."

Across the station, Barb moved the horse barricade and the caution cones from the construction road; the primer Gray Bel Air emerged from the swamp. The Hunmobile's wheels were spraying gravel looking for traction. McKool had his hands full of wheel with the Chevy in reverse. He broke out into the empty parking area, cut the front wheels all the way and stood on the gas. They left a trail of blue-gray exhaust as they sped up Harriman Ave.

The Hunmobile rode like a dragster: The front bumper was about six inches off the ground. Davis used to jerk McKools chain: "Fuckin' Bel Air don't need a fuel pump; you got all the gas you need – gravity fed." he wise-guyed.

"Let's just raise the ass end three more inches Quinn."

"What doya want? More attention from the bluecoats?" his lieutenant asked.

McKool mashed his lips, smiled, and shook his head; he knew Quinn was right.

Herrick scrunched one eye shut, "Now Wells is gone. We all goof on her, but at least it was better than watching you shitheads."

I couldn't argue with him.

A train was coming from the north, I looked at my watch – it had to be Cocaine Wayne's 11:10. The headlights were flickering as it approached. The four electric commuter cars were having propulsion difficulties as it limped into Greystone. The passenger trains only came to a complete stop if a passenger was getting off or people were on the platform waiting to get on – in most instances.

Crawfish raised his arm as if he was hailing a taxi, but he had no intention of getting on. He was trying to help Wayne get down to Ludlow station. The train was screwed up; it was bucking as it slowed trying to stop for Crawford, Wayne was busy hugging his body. He had to rally if he was going to make this train.

The conductor looked down at us and told 2/5ths of the fifth dimension to "Stand Clear. If we can't stop, we can't pick you up." The train was going maybe 3 m.p.h. Wayne had this wild look. Ray and me got this magnetic vibe he was going to do something. Wayne kept up with the train's last car. He took one step up into the stairwell of the last car and grabbed the chain handrail. Though the train was going slow when he grasped the handrail, it jerked him into the train's wall and he smacked his noggin. He was stuck there for his ride to Ludlow as the piece of checkerplate floor was latched above him.

"What a fuckin nobblehead." Crawford shook his head, "He could've gotten all mangled up."

"There was a fair chance he might be eating number 6 ballast stone and railroad ties." Loki looked amazed.
Wayne had been able to stow away in the tiny two-and-a-half stair at the end of the train car. Barb's pot may have made it look more difficult than the feat actually was.

"To think that idiot was reading calculus equations only 20 minutes ago......." Ray took a deep breath and shook his head and considered Wayne's desperation.

"Any idea why the train came into the station like a bucking bronco?" Kenny scratched his head.

"Can't say...... me and Ryan saw one react similiarly one other time; but it was 10 times more erratic."

"Magnetic reversal?"

"Possible."

Kenny rubbed his eye sockets and worked them back and forth. "Ryan, we're gonna take a couple of roadies...... okay? We're outta here." he said.

"Go head."

"Shoulda been a blowout tonight. All that beer, Barb's pot......but no babes, no hash, bulls show up. Even The Huns with their protection, music, and bullshit couldn't't salvage this night. And that one-way motherfucka Mike Reno let us down. Kenny, let's go up to Lake Ave., maybe there's some night left up there." Holter kicked some gravel.

"What's the point?" Herrick asked.

They walked up the Henry Hudson Park stairs to get Crawford's VW on Warburton.

Ray and me gravitated to the fireball burial mound, we sat in the sand on top. Loki followed after he let out some used beer. We were about midpoint between the George Washington Bridge and the Tappan Zee. The slinky GWB and the rigid cantilever Tappan Zee spans and towers were outlined with sodium vapor lights giving off a greenish hue. Ray recalled the 'Intergalactic Traveler' had been comprised of rock and metal and the mothership had cast off a chunk of itself – barely missing the Tappan Zee bridge. Ray would ask boatman – the next time he saw him – if he would take us up river on a wild hunch the larger ejected piece which dazzled with so much light might be found.

"The Edgar Cayce prediction might be coalescing." Ray massaged the bridge of his nose.

"Because of the train?" Loki popped another beer.

"Just on the face of it - these occurrences could be random, but if we view the events and calculations together - we can extrapolate a pattern: a force seems to be directing the movements from a design. Ray said.

"Is this design contained in the equation in the overpass?" I looked at a barge coming down the river.

"There are early stages of where it might be going." Ray said, I handed him a beer.

He gave Loki a thumbnail sketch of what we believed we knew through three years of observation, research, and analytical astrophysics modeling; the latter of which I had nothing to do with. Loki was highly skeptical; he believed it to be pure science fiction. I was sticking with Ray and tried to back up everything he said. All I could actually attest to were the comet, the disruption of electrical power on the train line, and the water going backwards down the drain.

Ray bummed a cigarette from Loki. He was thinking about the equation; while Loki was dreading the specter of caddying tomorrow, and I was still hoping Reno would show up with some girls.

"Was tonight some kind of heavy acid trip?" Loki laughed.

"A bad trip." I hiccupped.

Ray modified, "For now…..just a trip…..just a trip." He looked at a sky of stars: "The earth's magnetic poles are reversing. Ryan and I have scientific as well as empirical evidence. The latter having direct correlation with the scientific. We've come to the conclusion the sun's magnetic storms are bombarding the earth with positive and negative magnetic charges using the radio transmissions of meteorological and communication satellites, sputniks, space platforms with guided missiles, spacelabs, space stations, cosmic penetrations by space flotsam and jetsam, and interstellar fragments which have sent charged signals to this Earth."

We attempted to muscle through the beer and pot in our search for understanding as the genius continued: "The defensive rocketry of the U.S., the Soviet Union, and China has also contributed to the penetrations through the atmosphere of the sun's magnetic bombardment, and we sense these magnetic infiltrations have accelerated the pole reversal which is evidently underway and causing strange events and phenomenon to increase in living organisms, as well as mechanical devices, static and dynamic solids, liquids, gases, and plasmas. The ability to modify what we accept as 'The Natural Order' may result from being disturbed from their usual paths or events, now routed in an alternate pattern."

Loki checked his beer and turned to me, and said to Ray – "Well, that's just about everything on earth."

I was as dumbfounded as he was, but if Ray was going to accept the Nobel Prize for Physics…….I hoped to be riding his coattails on a good will tour of academic institutions around the globe. I raised my Schaefer Tall Boy, only a detective can get to the core of that insanity and offered a toast: "Mazel tov!" Cans and bottle collided.

Loki shook his head, "Run this shit by me at the caddy shack tomorrow. I've got a good hike in front of me…….How do you guys do it day in and day out?"

"It's automatic now – we started out taking the bus at first, but it took too long. We made better time walking it, so we just stuck with it."

Loki was eyeing up the station's pay phone; he was tempted to call Caesar's taxi or his father for a ride. Going into his senior year of high school – calling your old man for a ride because you were drunk or lazy or both……it wasn't exactly the position you wanted your father to see. He was figuring it out: "5700 yards yesterday, maybe the same tonight, and another 5700 yards tomorrow. Man, I'm going to be burnt out after caddying. How do you guys do it?" There wasn't any way he could call his father and save face unless he had a broken ankle.

The night was over. The three of us climbed the stairs from Harriman to Warburton Aves. In four minutes we were at 21 O'Dell. We gave our last beers to Loki for his journey. Once he made the North End, he had 5/8ths of a mile to go.

iii

Some of the caddies at Hudson River who attended college had already returned for the Fall semester. The number of Sy Simmons' ace caddies were cut in half; having to choose from P.T.S.S. vets, winos, high school drop-outs, moonlighting civil service workers, and guys from high school like Loki, Ray, and me.

Labor Day weekend '69 was upon us, again the caddy master was short on man power. Everybody carried two bags except the underage kids. Hudson River's membership was heavy with people in all levels of government, Simmons had to make an attempt to follow the labor laws when it came to the minimum age to carry clubs. He wouldn't force a kid to carry doubles, but if the kid was big enough – he could shame him into at least toting two ladies' bags.

The big buzz was still the Woodstock concert in upstate N.Y. two weeks earlier. A lot of people went. They came back acting like they were movie or rock stars. The best we could do was go to the movie, a bunch of us went down the city to see it when it first came out. We smoked so much pot on the subway - I got a sore throat and barely got high. I got a bigger buzz off the wine we snuck in. The movie was better than nothing.

The week going into Labor Day was real laid back; there was a lot of horseplay, pranks, smoking some 'happy hay', and gambling at the golf course. The caddies who showed up were looking to make those last few bucks before school started.

They had poker and black jack going by 8 o'clock; black Joe was running a dice game. I knew how to play the card games, only the older guys knew how to shoot dice. Black Joe showed Ray, me and a few others the basics of craps. By 11 o'clock, the ranks of the caddies had thinned to the point there was only one game of poker going.

Six days in front of Labor Day, this guy from the North End, Joe Lamar, who had a terrific head of orange hair; made another holiday appearance (1 of 3 per summer). Joe was there for one reason: to play cards. He won $20 on Tuesday and $25 on Wednesday. That was a lot of scratch back then considering a loop carrying doubles only paid $10.

What was amazing was the amount of experience Joe had playing cards; he knew all the games, and handled the cards like a magician. He was the same age as Ray, and went to Gorton I think, though I rarely saw him there. Here was another good odds-on bet: it

341

was highly probable he didn't get his diploma. Gambling action was all that interested Joe and the life that went with it. Later on, there were rumors he had taken a few math courses down City University on Games of Chance, Odds and Odds Making, and Gambling – all unsubstantiated. Joe paid for his gambling education one way or the other.

At Hudson River there was a junction of one green and two tees; the holes shot off in different directions. Ray was a foursome ahead of me. Usually there was just enough time to bum a smoke from another caddy. This one caddie 'Graham Cracker Jack', who was a professional bum by trade, came over also to see if any of us had an extra smoke.

Jack lit up and asked, "Hear 'bout Lamar?"

"Is he still runnin' hot?" I said.

"He turned down Simmons when he gave him a couple of bags."

"Huh?" Ray didn't know if he caught it quite right. "He what?"

"Joe turned down a loop." Graham Cracker Jack had a quick laugh and wiped his mouth with his bare forearm.

"What the ha hah ha ha. What the fuck?" I was losing it.

"Jack," Ray said with a king size chuckle – "You sure you got it right?"

"Yeah I'm sure Ray, I'm on the loop Lamar was supposed to have." Jack laughed with his mouth closed cause he didn't have any teeth.

My brother looked at me, "How can you deny the pa....pa ....pa.....pole reversal?" he was doubled over.

"Sy took the deck of cards, ripped three of them up to ruin the deck and threw the rest in the trash barrel. He gave the three other card players enforced loops and told Joe he was looped off for the rest of the year." The three us couldn't stop howling, and it annoyed the members.

"And that ain't all -" Graham Cracker added, "Joe tells Sy to go back to the pro shop before he wraps a 3 iron around him like a straight jacket."

"Sy screams, 'I'm calling the cops – you're trespassing.' Then Joe says: 'Hey Simmons...........make a request call for Uncle Tommy Lamar - he's working days this week.'

"Joe had it all covered." the wino smiled as he walked over to the 2nd Tee.

What drove Sy nuts was he couldn't discipline or cause financial harm to Joe. He couldn't even be considered as a part-time caddy. The only thing the caddy master had the power to do was threaten the other caddies playing poker with Joe. He tried to loop-off the card players, but the caddies backed up Joe Lamar with a job action, and Sy had no one to carry clubs. He was in an untenable situation; many of the caddies were all related by blood, neighborhood, school, co-workers, bar patronage. When Sy messed with one – he messed with us all. There was a point where the older guys wouldn't

342

back you up on ridiculous shit. When you pulled a stupid stunt – you made your own bed. From his viewpoint, Sy had a legitimate bitch; when Joe dealt cards - he removed 4 or 5 guys from the pool of available caddies.

Word spread pretty fast down the End; not so much about the labor discord at the country club as the high stakes poker games. Guys from different neighborhoods were showing up not to caddy, but to throw dice and play cards. In the end all this gambling was working out to Simmons' advantage, the wannabe card sharks were getting wiped out at the poker table; they had to make some money by carrying clubs.

The Caddy master put out these two walk-on caddies who wanted to get paid by the hole. By the 7th hole they told these lady golfers they were draggin' up and they wanted their money. The women were dumbfounded, and told the two walk-ons what they were trying to pull would get them terminated.

"Listen Sis, you owe us $3.90 apiece."

"We'll pay you at the 9th hole." One of the foursome offered.

"Get your purses out ladies. We don't have any written contract. We're calling it a day and you owe us for seven holes of toting your bags.........that comes out to......"

"$3.90 each." His partner came through with the math.

"This is highly irregular." one of the women complained.

"You want regular? Get a written contract. You want casual........this is what you get."

The foursome was rather upset, and their predicament was causing a problem. Golfer traffic began backing up and coming to a standstill. Like it or not, it seemed the caddies would have to be paid off straightaway. "How much is it?" one woman asked.

"Ah....$3.90 each."

"Come on girls – let's pay these extortionists off before we bring our grievances to Mr. Simmons.

The other caddy was dissatisfied when the lady golfers paid him. He counted the money, "Hey c'mon ladies....you're not going to stiff us for our tip?"

Indignant as all get out, "Were you raised in a cathouse? You're not getting any tip." She looked away.

"You asked for it sis." He turned his back on the women and pissed on the golf bags he had carried.

The other two ladies immediately handed their caddy $5.00 for seven holes. "Please don't urinate on our bags."

"That's more like it Honey."

We never saw those characters again, The caddy master and the club President yelled at us the next day, but it was half hearted; They knew it wasn't the regular group of caddies who were responsible.

One of the Vietnam vets told us the one guy was a bouncer at a strip joint on Saw Mill River Rd., and his partner was an unemployed hod carrier.

343

Every so often, these moonlighters would show up and they clearly did not belong there. Some could handle running up and down the hills, the three-plus mile course, the club required proper etiquette, even if their knowledge of the game was nonexistent. They were ill-suited on many levels.

In my first year carrying doubles, this dandy shows up on Fourth of July weekend. First thing he does is announce to the caddy yard he's some hot shot professor down at NYU in the Bronx. The only caddies listening to him are like 12 or 13 years old.

"Why aren't you playing golf instead of trying to carry clubs?" Jimmy Blanko was bewildered.

He talked to Blanko for a couple of minutes. The professor became animated and out of his back pocket came a translated copy of Chairman Mao's "Little Red Book" which he held high in the air. "These fat cats are taking advantage of your work, and the least they should do is pay you fairly. $10/a day is a disgrace.

Kevin Doucette had gotten back from Nam early in '68, and asked this man if he had ever been in the service.

"No."

"What have you done or what did you do besides teach?"

"It's my profession.....I've always been involved in education."

The Deuce looked from side to side, "Jags like you usually end up being officers. Can't keep your head down in the jungle. If it wasn't for the enlisted men and the NCO's - guys like you usually end up in a black plastic bag. And you know what – you ain't going to last too long here. We don't need an idiot like you telling us how to live our lives. Go find material for your dissertation, or the Great American Novel somewhere else."

"You don't seem to understand....."

A left uppercut came out of nowhere. Down the professor went, blood streaming from a split nose. Deuce had knocked him out cold. Simmons had one of the caddies take him out in a golf cart over to North Broadway and sat him up against the stonewall of the small women's Catholic College across the street.

Loki came over to Blanko, "What was that all about?"

"Some guy with a college degree thought he was Che Guevera. He said he was a full professor or something."

"A professor? You're kidding..." Loki said.

"Yeah, I think he said he graduated Magna Cum Rowdy" Blanko hinted a smirk.

"Fuck you Jimmy." Loki scoffed.

AFTER SOME OF HALS BURNT HOT DOGS, RAY AND ME went up the North End for the night. There wasn't much light left by 8 o'clock, but it was still plenty warm. A North End regular, Sal Del Bene, came over by Ray and me in Barca
Bros. parking lot.

"Hey Law firm.....you guys caddy at Hudson River." he stated. "Zhat true dat Joe Lamar won a bundle on Tuesday and Wednesday at the caddy shack?"

344

"Won over $20 on Tuesday; don't know what he pulled down today. What did you hear Ray?" I said.

"Over 30 today, and that was with the caddymaster suspending the game for a couple of hours when he tried to loop-off Joe, but he'll be back tomorrow. No way that's going to stick."

Sal's eyes bulged, "Holy fuck." He laughed. "Well how much he win?" Sal's hands went palms up.

"Heard 30 plus today – something like that.......I dunno." he repeated.

"He wins so big – he doesn't have to caddy – just plays poker." I said.

"Can anybody go caddy there?"

Ray looked annoyed, "For the love of fuck Benny, you can see the golf course from your apartment building. Do you want to caddy or play cards? You can play cards or shoot dice as soon as there's an open seat or Black Joe's got an opening. If you want to carry clubs --- Simmons, the caddy master, won't put you out until the yard's empty."

"The hell wit caddyin'; I'm a better poker player than Lamar." Benny took a drag and stiff-armed a lean against a light post.

"You can't shuffle or deal half as good as Joe – I've played with you Benny." Ray said.

"Be there tomorrow.....we'll see if dem sharks are swimmin'. What time you want me to show up?"

"Stay home......save your dough. Joe Lamar's running too hot for you." I lit a Camel.

"Seven-thirty.......eight." Ray nodded and I wrinkled my forehead.

We watched Reno's lime-green Nova make a hard left across the oncoming traffic into the public parking lot. Mike had made a number of improvements to the car's appearance. I could tell he had worked on the car: stiffer leaf springs raised the rear end, headlight – half covers, gave it that Nazi staff car look, mag rims for the rear wheels, (He said he didn't have the bread to do all four), fuzzy mirror dice, and a beer tap handle for a shift knob. No tape deck, but he did get an FM converter. A "Love Power" rikki tiki stiki ornamented the trunk lid. Reno knew all about love.

He screeched to a stop when Del Bene whistled from Barca's lot. We all walked over to see what was up with 'Mr. Love Power.'

Benny was all charged up: "Mike, you hear 'bout da action at the caddy shack at da golf course? Lamar, Loki, Jimmy Blanko, and some other card sharks are playing for some big pots."

Ray and me burst out laughing: "Loki lost his ass. He didn't even make up on the course what he lost playing cards."

"That's because Loki's a junker.....he plays junk hands." Mike scoffed. "What are you lawyers doing?" you playing cards?" he turned down his radio.

"Nope, just carrying clubs." I said.

"Reno, whadya want?" Ray tried to digest the car's new appeal.

"I want in on the game up there."

"Listen, I'll get you a seat at the table, but Lamar's got the table stakes pretty high." Ray crossed his arms on his chest. "And it's going to cost you a couple of six packs......right now....and they're going to be Tall Boys Mike."

"Huh? That's four bucks. C'mon Ray, that's pretty steep." The buy-in was holding up Reno's decision.

"That's what Benny just paid." I said.

"That's the buy in price Mike." Del Bene nodded.

"You say you're a hustler Mike; we'll see if you can go toe to toe with Lamar."

"Any day junior partner......any day." Reno had the itch.

"What time they start dealing?"

"Around eight."

"How much money is over there?"

"Plenty, everybody's been getting out all week." Ray said.

Del Bene and Reno's eyes were as green as the Chevy Nova with greed. Reno handed Ray $4.00. We went over to Barca's as soon as they left. It was hard to believe neither one showed up for any of the Labor Day weekend action. Joe Lamar kept on winning and never carried a golf bag.

Loki figured he only cleared $6.00/day after the shellacking he took gambling. He tried them all: Poker, Craps, Blackjack, he was even pitching quarters with the single bag kids. He threw a deck of cards a day from Friday through Labor Day. Lamar went into his paper lunch bag and pulled out a sealed deck each time someone threw a deck. Some guys thought Joe was pulling a fast one.....no 17 year old kid was walking into a card game with sealed replacement decks. None of the players thought he was dealing off the bottom, but they didn't like Joe bringing sealed decks. Something was off about that move; all it said to me was: "I mean business."

Lamar showed up at the caddy shack with two cups of coffee and the Wall Street Journal. By the time he was reading the stock quotes, the guys were begging him to start dealing.   Reno in the same league as Lamar?......no way.

iv

The summer vacation was down to a couple of days, hours, and minutes. Another new learning institution awaited Ray and me. It was difficult to put the summer in perspective, perhaps because we had had nothing to stack it up against. Being exposed to the news all the time because we had been paperboys, the events weren't as shocking to us as they were to most of our peers. Some weren't shocked or surprised at all; they just didn't care about the bigger world.

It was the pace of these events; they put us in a quantum quandary. Moon landing, moon rocks, Woodstock, Manson Murders, body counts in Vietnam, more pot, more rock, more Bugs and Toyotas, Panthers and weathermen, and the Zodiac Killer. If the poles weren't reversing, something else was causing us to act like a bunch of lunatics.

I already believed the magnetic realignment was catching up and destined to be involved with a collision between the two forces: Human/organic and cosmic/infinity magnetic. This aspect of pole reversal lagged behind the human dimension. It was the expected upheaval of the natural catastrophic events which Ray explained should coincide with human exploitation and the ability to vie for dominance of the inner workings over the planet.

The number of floods, earthquakes, volcanic eruptions, twisters, and drought were no greater or less than usual. I was stymied by this. The wrath of God or the universe was building inside the collective human intellect..........such a thought was too large for me to deal with.

It was just another one of those enigmatic questions I'd lay on Ray, whose answer was so complex I'd tell him: Just forget it man, I'll ask you some other time.

ALTHOUGH WE HADN'T BEEN IN THE SAME SCHOOL FOR two years, it played much longer than that. We were apart in this one aspect of life, but we had gotten closer in others. There also was the 'Cosmic Intruder', and it defied categorization. I felt my time at All Souls was light years away in the rear view mirror. Gorton High School was loose. Intellectually, Ray had already been there once he graduated from All Souls Grade School, he just wasn't there physically.   It was due to the comet, it sent him on a quest to understand the nature of the relationship between the cosmic and the organic......if there was one.

We had crossed some kind of dimensional line or phase, and it thrust us into manhood. When it was just him and me; our dialogue wasn't limited to being verbal. It was difficult for me to describe. Ray knew what was going on, he'd explain it to me but most of the scientific and psychological stuff was way over my head. By and by, I thought Ray was using me to hear his ideas aloud. Perhaps he talked to himself, but I never witnessed it.

I didn't know what was wrong with me other than my bald patch of scalp. Trying to fit in at Emerson just never happened; it was somewhat less challenging at Gorton. With Ray there, most of the guys from the Jets, and Vinny, Fast Eddie Mason, and Reno from All Souls; walking the halls wasn't a solitary proposition. The girls in his chemistry and trig classes sometimes made a fuss when Ray was walking in the opposite direction.

"Hey – it's Mr. Scientific Congeniality!" they teased.

I walked past two of Ray's fan club and observed them. How does he do it? I shook my head and went into English. Except for Chippewa baseball nearly all of my social connections were via Ray, these were social contacts I would have never made on my own.

His circle ran the gamut at Gorton: he fit right in with the brainyacs. He made the rounds with the greasers, Latins, Jews, the blacks, the hippies, the few Asians; he got along with most everyone.

347

He could have been student body president. There were also the Irish and Italians down the North End, the caddies from Hudson River, the leftover friends from All Souls. Many of these high school students were old enough to get their driver's license, and new kids were showing up from all parts of Yonkers.

Raymond was charismatic - I was not. Many of his associates who interacted with me thought I might be a malleable version of Brother Ray. They were disappointed as they got less than what they anticipated. It didn't take long to realize I was no Ray Whitelaw. Girls seemed to tolerate my personality shortcomings somewhat better. What the romantic arts didn't require was brain output. Most of the time I could come up with a line of bullshit, and if I could bring the conversation to rock and roll; I'd had a chance to be the boyfriend. It didn't hurt to follow Ray's advice about growing my hair long enough to cover the bare spot. A few of the girls turned me down because of the defect. Like the girls at Emerson, many of the Gorton girls didn't buy story my sixth grade teacher had ripped it out.

When it came to girls, Ray didn't need a line of bull – he was good looking, intelligent, had a ton of humor and a quick wit. He had all that going for him before they even knew him. Some of the more eager girls made a move for me in an attempt to get to Ray. Many times they were assigned to Ray's Triple A team.......also known as the Ryan team.

"Go see Ryan, he doesn't have a date for the Homecoming dance. The girls we were attracted to were from totally different ends of the spectrum. My brother's female interests were sophisticated, engaging, ...mysterious. They saw through me right away, and it would usually end things. Occasionally they tolerated my pawing and they'd reciprocate after an hour of reefer and alcohol, but it was a lot of effort. All I really wanted was to hook-up with low morals or sexually deviant girls.

Following the 'Homecoming Dance' on Saturday, Jimmy Martin called our house and ran this wild rumor by me. He said he had been at the dance and Ray had gotten up on stage when the band was taking a break. He commandeered a microphone which he brought over to an upright piano and pounded out and sang three songs: "Nadine", "Great Balls of Fire", and "Skip Softly My Moonbeams"

As Ray performed, Holter, 'Bad Brad' Guzzutti, and me were down Lennon Park drinking 'Pagan Pink' Ripple and smoking some reef. We never made it to the dance. I hung up with Jimmy wishing I had caught Ray's musical debut.

I saw Jane in the breakfast nook, "You hear anything about Ray performing up at the dance last night?"

"Oh......he's been working with Gary Cairns. He taught Ray the songs in three weeks. The one rock tune Ray wanted to do.....'Skip Softly' took longer; Gary had to play the record over and over because there was no sheet music." she said.

Two weeks of notoriety was Ray's limit. Soon after, he consistently denied ever being at the Homecoming. There was a performer's streak in him, and now I found he could play instruments well enough to perform in public. When people asked me what I played, I simply responded, "We're trying to put a band together."

On a Friday afternoon between Thanksgiving and Christmas, I saw Ray in a booth at 'Copies' Tap'. It was a 'beer only' joint because it was too close to Christ the King church to get a liquor license. It was around 3:00 pm. Perhaps Sally and Ray had cut out of class at noon. It would be dark soon.

There were a couple of old timers at the bar, and Kaye was on the other side pushing beer. Ray and a group of junkies had a pitcher at their table. If there were enough of true North Enders in the bar, they would tell the 'inter- dimensional junkies and dopers to 'hit the bricks'. When there were two or more addicts conGreggating - the group was tagged as a bunch of junkies. Cocaine Wayne, Sally Englund, Esther Shaw, and her brother Erik had a pitcher of beer at their table for show – they were waiting to make a drug connection; but they were still high from when they last got off.

Except for Cocaine Wayne, I knew the rest through Gorton and Ray. All the girls were hooked on the junk, Cocaine Wayne as well. I had only known Rikshaw since the start of the tenth grade. He was in my Latin II class – highly intelligent, but I kept seeing him with the wrong people more and more; he might have been just a weekend blaster. Rikshaw reeked of kool.

The barmaid Kaye gave me the 'stink eye' trying to place my face. You couldn't act like you didn't belong, otherwise they'd tell you to 'hit the bricks'.

I looked over to Ray, "How long you guys been in here?"

"'Bout a half-hour. Wind picked up; we had to get out of the cold."

"Anything going on?" I raised my brow. The junkies were nursing the pitcher of Schaefer. I thought they were going to offer me a glass. Instead, I had to get a glass from Kaye. When I returned, I asked Ray with a nod: "What's up?"

He nodded over to Sally. He had been seeing her since around Halloween. He gave me a wink and he bulldogged his chin, like he 'did her' earlier in the afternoon. Except for Ray and me and maybe Rikshaw, the other three were strung out, all of them were of the specter world. They came out of their mothers backwards, upside down, inside out; laughing when they should have been crying for air. Their circuitry flowed in the wrong direction. Wayne-O and the three girls weren't any part-time players who were "just chippin", they were genuine escape artists; determined to find a way out, but they didn't want to sacrifice their lives in the process.

Rikshaw pushed a glass over to me. Streetwise and book smart; he was always on the go, I thought he was too smart to get hooked on smack.

Erik's father was a Caucasian and his mother was Chinese from Macau. His sister, Esther, was a year older than Erik; she was a hit and miss junkie who had a big ego and tons of attitude. The two had all Asian features – the only thing they got from their father was his pale Irish skin. Rikshaw was almost as smart as Ray. He pushed the pitcher over to me.

"Thanks." And I caught a look from him......he was high.

They were all high on the dooge.......except Ray. None of them were nodding, but that warm glow made the blood path through their bodies. The owner, Kurtis Copie, wasn't putting up with any drug activity in his place. His barmaids Fran and Kaye didn't care as long as they took their business outside, and didn't cause a scene when they came back in.

"Beep.....beebeebeebeep.....Beep.....beebeebee......Beep." Now the horn blasts came in threes. The next time the driver outside the bar laid on his horn: "Beeeeeeeeeeeeeeep."

"Hey you." Kaye shouted.

My head tilted and I pointed at my face .

"Yeah you......Go out there and tell that knucklehead to knock it off."

I shuffled out to see what the guy wanted. I had seen the car around, and had even seen it on O'Dell. It was Chevrolet's answer to the Volkswagen Beetle: the Corvair. It was a '63 or '64; red body....white convertible top.

"Is you brother in there?" the driver raised his voice over the loud radio. "Ask him if he wants to go see Procol Harum down the Fillmore next weekend."

The guy had two years on me, but I wasn't any messenger service, "You go in and ask him." I looked at him like he was nuts.

"Come on.......the battery's weak – it might not start back up."

"Just don't shut it off."

"Leave it running?....... This isn't Scarsdale."

"It ain't the Bronx neither." I put my hands in my pockets – I gave in. "Hang on – I'll get him." 'Fuckin' knob' - I thought on my way back in the bar. "Ray, guy in the Corvair wants to talk to you."

"Who is it?" he peered over Sally's head.

"You guys are too much. How many people you know with a Corvair besides Uncle Bill?" I shook my head.

"It's John Dunbar. He bought it off of Billy O'Brien." Cocaine Wayne I.D.'d car and driver.

"Said it was something about a band playing down the Fillmore." I said.

He hopped out of the booth.

An index finger directed me to where Ray had been sitting. Sally Englund asked, Where have you been hiding Ryan? You know I'm only going out with Ray to get to you."

She stole a kiss with me and forced her tongue into my mouth. It happened so quick – I wasn't sure it happened. I looked through the large bar window. Ray had gotten in the Corvair with Dunbar.

Rikshaw threw a quarter in the jukebox and played "You Can't Always Get What You Want", "Fortunate Son", and "Revival". Copie had a great jukebox. I was positive Copie would have seen a lot more of Kenny Crawford, if the mafia guy loaded the 45 single of "Hanky Panky" in the Seeburg.

Only the patrons of the beer joint can testify to this, and not many would make book it actually occurred. The jukebox had a 45 r.p.m. record with a pressing of two different artists. It was most likely a demo for radio stations, or the pressing was a mistake, or perhaps a special promotion of some sort by the record company. The 'A' side was Otis Redding's recording of his song "Respect"; the one Aretha Franklin made tons of money on. On the 'B' side was a single of a new group – 'The Allman Brothers Band w/Steve McQueen, playing an original tune "Revival" – four months prior to the release of their second album.

Breaking a single before an album's release was pretty common, but putting it on the 'B' side of another artist was something rather unusual. In fact it was never done, so it must have been a mistake pressing. Redding and The Allman's came out of Atlantic, but the latter were signed to their rock division ATCO. It was another reason the pressing should have never taken place. The oddest thing though had to be the issue with Steve McQueen. It had to be some session cat with the same name; no way was it the actor. It couldn't have been. The band had a new sound, and it kept me coming back to Copies'. We tried to find out more about them; it wasn't until the next summer when the word about them started getting around.

Through the big front window, I watched Ray kiss Sally goodbye. He had a couple of text and note books in a grocery bag; he didn't want Kaye to see he was taking high school courses.

"What's the deal hanging out with the junkies?" I asked Ray when we left the bar and started for home. The sun was low, without much warmth.

Loki had stopped in one time and put his books on the bar and ordered a beer after school. It was slow and the other barmaid started looking at his books. The two started arguing whether his books were college level or not.

"Don't matter Fran, I'm 18. You got to serve me" he said.

She pointed to the sign above the bar, 'We reserve the right to refuse service to anyone.' "Let's see a draft card Gayblade." she blew some smoke in his direction. From that day until the bar shut down, she I.D.'d Loki. If you wanted to drink in Copies' - you stayed on Fran and Kaye's good side.

Ray pumped a cigarette from his pack: "I don't know why – I've got a direct link with these drug phantoms. I believe I know their world or the dimension holding them prisoner. Some are junkies – some ....are something else besides being addicts."

"How's that?"

"Look at them; but before you take a hard look at them – I must differentiate between an addict who wants to get high, and a specter who has no choice but get high, or else they will go mad. He pivoted, "Let's get a pint of T-bird from Harmonie liquor. We'll drink it down the river when we get home."

351

This was news to me, I thought one size fits all when it came to intravenous drug users. In Ray's oblique world, this was not the case. We dropped his books off and walked down to Greystone. In the overpass, Ray cracked the T-bird, took a sip, and went to work. With one of those big black graphite pencils they give you in kindergarten – he began to write:

$$\text{EQUATION } 17$$

$$w(z) = w_0 \sqrt{1 + \left[\frac{z}{z_R}\right]^2}$$

z DENOTES THE PARALLEL DISTANCE BETWEEN THE HORIZONTAL DISTANCE (DIRECTIONAL MATRIX) AND THE FOCAL POINTS OF THE TWO MAGNETIC POLES IN TRANSITORY REVERSAL (THE POSITION OF THE CENTER OF THE MASS OF PLANET.

$w(z)$ DENOTES THE FOCAL POINT/POSITION OF ENTRY OF SOLAR MAGNETIC CHARGE WITH $w = D/2$ BEING VARIABLE DURING SPECIFIC PHASE PULSING – ALLOWING MORE CHARGE TO BE INTRODUCED AT IRREGULAR INTERVALS. REPRESENTED AS:

$z_R = (\pi w_0^2 / \lambda M^2)$ (SOLAR MAGNETIC TRANSFER TO PARTICLES FOR RE-ENTRY TO EARTH)

$$\text{EQUATION } 18$$

BY SUBSTITUTING z_R INTO PREVIOUS EQUATION; z CAN BE WRITTEN AS:

$$z = \frac{\pi}{\lambda M^2} \sqrt{w(z)^2 w_0^2 - w_0^4}$$

Although pole reversal has been initiated w/o forces beyond the earth's atmosphere and gravity - introduction of magnetic force directed by a planetary focal point created by positive and negative energies, will accelerate pole reversal.

The pencil kept going. Occasionally, Ray stepped back and looked at his computations; unconsciously reaching for the Thunderbird which I placed in his waiting hand. He studied his equation: "Ryan, how much of the original dust do you have?"

"Maybe......like six, maybe eight ounces – I'm guessing. Then I got some from when I went into the parallel dimension or where- ever I was. It wasn't a lot. I couldn't say if it was the same as the original material."

"I've got close to that.....maybe seven." He began thinking aloud, "I believe it takes more of this cosmic ash to effect me than you. Our blood types are different – you're positive, I'm negative. I see this as one of the factors as to why you were able to lift the space remnant and I could barely move it. I wish there was a way to devise a timetable to make events more predictable. When the magnetic poles

352

reach the point of complete balance, there has to be a catalyst that brings them past the tipping point"............Ray went back to work.

"..........Therefore, inter-solar and/or galactic forces entering planetary atmospheres during periods of magnetic disruption may affect any man-made device(s), also magnetically charged organisms." He scoffed a laugh, "As well as altering the orbit of a planet. The more the man-made development – the greater the chance of possible disruption."

Ray used the pencil as a pointer for my benefit I suppose: "Light and the rate of magnetic and radio particles bombarding the planet can only enter in ultra precise access attraction points through the atmosphere........that is based on the earth's magnetic flux and the penetration threshold. The entry position access point can be symbolized by AP/d-solar gravitational force (power)/diameter of ultra prism corridor from space through atmosphere into the planetary core:

$$\frac{P}{d} = \frac{\sigma L_i}{A I} \sqrt{\frac{\pi m V}{K T_s}} + \frac{2\sqrt{2\pi}(T_v - T_m)\lambda_i}{\bar{A}_I \, exp\left[\frac{P_{l_c} \, lvd}{4\lambda_I}\right]}$$

$$+ \frac{2\sqrt{2\pi}(T_M - T_0)\lambda_i}{\bar{A}_s \, exp\left[\frac{P_s C_s \, vd}{4\lambda_s}\right]}$$

(REF. 31)

"There."

"There what?" These two pieces of the equation were the culmination of two years of work. The mathematical problem was 45 feet in length and varied from one to three feet in height.

"This may give us insight to the comet's force on earth, but also how and probably why it is contributing and advancing the rate of magnetic pole realignment. We got to safeguard all the fireball ash and dust - in particular, the original material. I suspect the only way it can lose potency is by dissemination."

"Ray, I ain't got a fuckin' clue of what you're talking about. You got a mathematical equation here that rivals Teller, Newton, and Einstein; it runs the length of the crossover - 2 ½ feet high. You say it's about magnetism, atmospheric holes, pole inversion, and a bunch of other stuff I don't understand."

The formula was running out of space. If Ray was going to add more he'd have to get something to stand on.

"Give me the hootch." He pointed to the 'Cosmic Intruder'.. ....we might have to have a peek at it this summer. The ash has undergone a transmutation that the cast-off has not. It's been a while, it may be time." he said.

"How do you know all this stuff?"

"I know these things because first – I feel them, then I have studied and applied this knowledge to this/these event(s). I am no

Einstein, but I am able to grasp many things you cannot. One is: Not all of humanity responds the same way to magnetic fields. You know this is true. Look at Sally, Joey Tarts, Wayne-O, Rikshaw, Crawford, and Z-man; they're all on the edge. Reality is an everyday challenge. Their thought patterns, and the manner in which they use information is accelerated and irrational. It's as if their protons, electrons, and neutrons are travelling clockwise around their nuclei in our bodies – the opposite of yours. They function in a mode that is in a constant war with the universal laws of science and those of magnetism. Over a short period of time, our thought and observatory capabilities will have started to overload with the magnetic inversion."

There were two cigarettes left in the pack, and he offered me one, "Once pole reversal is complete, the outcome of humanity and other organisms would be speculative. Machines would certainly be rendered useless. The possibilities would be frightening and fantastic at the same time. The deeper we analyze and imagine this future existence, if there is to be one – you see the paradox of such a world and it disqualifies itself. Then there is the time continuum......the corridor in which this pole reversal must be played out. My calculations lead me to believe this current one cannot take longer than the last because of all the introduced magnetism from outer space. Ice cores from Antarctica reveal the last one to occur was almost 700,000 B.P. The actual reversal might only take a lifetime, but getting through the realignment from start to finish might take 4000 to 7000 years. Edgar Cayce didn't record what stage he felt the earth was in this planetary phenomenon."

"I may be wide afield, but it sounds like these shadow junkies are trapped in a parallel dimension."

"And what about me?" I leaned against the north side girder.

His stare was far off – probably in Antarctica.

"Huh?......no......you're normal."

"What's that mean.......you want to be a junkie? C'mon Ray."

A scowl, "You think they want to shoot dope? The reason they get high is to escape......the speed, and the path of the protons, neutrons, and electrons run wild, but always in the opposite directions of most people on this planet. If the phantasm people smoke, snort, ingest, or inject a substance it allows them to slow these atomic particles down and they can, for as long as the particular substance is in their bloodstream come close to being what we call normal. Not enough drugs – they're caged animals; too much they're nodding out or waking up in the morgue dead."

"You mentioned Kenny......Crawford. He's no heroin user."

Ray killed the rest of the Thunderbird, "I looked at him – he's one of us. I know he's got to get out of himself. He's not going to be able to dodge this bullet. Crawfish knows he's trapped in this prism with the rest of us; the reality we experience can only be equalized or put on hold through mind altering substances or extreme acts of passion, love, hate, or valor. It is a disruption of the operation of the body and mind. What we might term as the: metaphysical."

"Dude.........you're losing me." I shook my head.

354

"Listen, The monkey on the back of the specter people are not the drugs, it's the conforming functionality of life. This is where the addiction or at least drug usage becomes a gateway to freedom from - not an escape to. The paradox is the outward appearance of the reverse polarity people. We believe they are in slow motion – static – catatonic; while what is really occurring in their brains and metabolic systems is the exact opposite.

I followed Ray down to the southbound platform and went over the guardrail to the buried meteorite. As we thought……. the ground was warm.

It was difficult for me to digest this grandiose account of magnetic pole reversal as it related to a crew of dope shooters in North Yonkers. We started for home. The old incandescent street lamp lit the corners of Warburton and O'Dell. There were two bundles there waiting to be delivered.

"Hmmm." I stopped walking. Ray pulled up as well.

"You're saying – these rummies, pot heads, dopers, pill poppers and the rest exist in their negatively charged world….Damn Ray: Hal is an alky so he ain't right neither. There's a zillion of them - they're in the majority It doesn't make sense." I said.

He slapped the back of my head as we started back up O'Dell Ave. "Listen Doomkuff…….not everybody who's getting high, drunk, or stoned is wired backward like the fifth dimension. It's only a very small number of people, but I can spot them like a naked chick in a crowd."

"You might be able to make that call, but to me a junkie's a junkie – they're all the same."

"Hey fucknuckle - Look at Cocaine Wayne, Joey Tarts, Rikshaw, Sally, Z-man, and Crawford; they're no different than a tiger in a cage. They feel and live trapped."

"I'll give you that. They aren't like 'Mixer Don' or Hi-lo Heller. Those two make shooting dope look like fun, or that it's not that big a deal." I said.

We reached our front step and sat on the cold brick stoop. Those guys are just having a recreational high. The fifth dimension and me are on a mission. Destination: Tranquility Base. Purpose: Get Home." He looked spent, "Ry, go get us a beer and a couple of Kools from Jane.

I came back out and lit up. Ray smoked like Robert Mitchum, all I could do was cough on those stupid menthols. I had to wash it down with some beer. I walked over to the fence line and flicked it into the woods. "How does Mom smoke these things?"

He laughed, "And Mom-Mom too."

"Going out tonight?"

"Sally." he nodded. "What about you?"

"Told Vinny Tarts I'd meet him down Morsemere. We might go to the basketball game – sneak in a bottle of Bali Hai - try to sit next to some lonely girls. Bad Brad might show up.

I never looked at a junkie the same.

V

February 1970. The Penn Central had begun their commuter station upgrade projects a few months earlier. The improvement we liked the most was the installation of over-head radiant electric heaters in the overpass. There was a significant amount of heat loss because of the temporary plywood and Plexiglas band aids they used to enclose the bridge. Even with the new heaters it didn't get much above 55 degrees at night, but it didn't get much below that either. If the sun was out - it raised the temperature pretty nice. It was a lot better than drinking on the street or in a park. The big drawback - it wasn't near any deli or liquor store. Alcohol, girls, drugs, and music had to be brought there. If there was a party of more than six people, it could get complicated. Cops were a problem when drugs were being utilized.

When guys were partying down Greystone it usually meant plan 'A' didn't work out. At this point in time, not many guys down the End, or Lake Ave. knew about the new radiant heaters. The Orchard Street crew didn't come down the Hudson too much at all. I knew if we could just keep the word from getting out, we'd have a place to party until the weather turned in April. We just had to keep it hushed up.

Ray, Brother Bill, and me were watching Errol Flynn doing his thing in the 'Charge of the Light Brigade'. It had started at noon. Flynn was always one of our favorites. It was a harmless way to spend a winter afternoon. Hal was in his den crunching numbers for Otis who had the contract for the elevators for both of the World Trade Center towers. He already had his whiskey mug going, but he was still pissed off because we were home. Even though he never said anything, we felt his irritation because we were in his living room, watching his TV, and watching our program. In this stage of life, nothing made Hal happy except a mug of whiskey soda.

It was Sunday; Jane had the day off. She walked into the living room: "You guys want some P.B.&J. sandwiches?"

There was a chorus of "Thanks Mom."

"What are you guys watching?" She answered her question: "That's an Errol Flynn movie. All my girlfriends and I just loved how dashing he was."

"Was? What happened?" I said.

"He drank away his looks........then he drank himself to death." She projected her voice into the den.

On her way into the kitchen, Hal shouted from the den: "I don't want a sandwich Jane, thanks for asking." Mom had lit the fuse. Hal yelled from the den, "No lunch for you two birds until you clean up the garage."

My lips rolled on each other and I squinted down hard. Jeffrey Vickers just escaped the massacre at Lohara with Olivia deHaviland. Ray laughed.

"How about this Dad – We'll vacuum the car and do the windows if you give us the money for the Windex?" Ray offered.

Hal had made a "command decision" and traded in the '64 Chevy wagon and bought a new car – a 1969 Chrysler Newport with a 318 cu. in. eight cylinder with an automatic transmission. Jane was in highway heaven for a little while. It had dual speakers: one in the front and one in the back. There wasn't any stereo action on the AM radio. Hal was pretty keen on keeping his new set of wheels clean. With Otis getting the contract for the WTC, Hal had to drive down to lower Manhattan at least twice a month with other engineers, accountants, and Otis reps. As the project got more involved, sometimes he was down there every week. I'm sure they razzed him about driving downtown in the Chevy wagon with a manual transmission in stop and go traffic, and no air conditioning. The pea-green metallic flake '64 wagon was history. It had had only 62,000 miles on it.

"Here's a couple of bucks, get one of those Christmas tree air fresheners too. I want more space in that garage so I can get the Newport in easier." he said.

With the garage door closed, there were only 4 inches of space between it and the rear bumper. The garage would have been more suitable for a Dodge Dart, Plymouth Valiant, Ford Falcon, or a Chevy Nova. The Newport was a battleship.

According to Hal's college transcript, he had majored in electrical engineering, but he did his share of mechanical engineering as well. Because of the enormity of the project – Otis management kicked the old man over into accounting. Engineers were plentiful and Otis could hire one right out of the box for less than what Hal earned. Accounting and scheduling on the WTC had Hal burning the midnight oil in his den with his slide rule and problems for the IBM mainframe. Two packs of empty Tareytons were in the trash bin every day, and extra whiskey washed down the smoke on Friday and Saturday nights. Somehow he managed to keep his intake at a pint/night during the week. With all the hours he was logging on the project, it could have gone either way, but Ray and me got the feeling he was determined to be on this project from beginning to end.

The papers on his desk read like an alternate universe of some crazy world. It was the world of adults…..business.

"Accounting" the heading on the printed sheet said. There were subheadings of: labor/shop - labor/field – cost overruns – back charges- back charges incurred (OTIS) – miscellaneous. When the towers came out of the ground, Hal was going nuts because Otis had all the escalators feeding from the subway lines into the bottom of the WTC. Once things hit a predictable schedule, Hal got somewhat of a break. In the beginning of the project, Hal and a vice-president were at the jobsite every week to give and get answers to and from the General Contractor, the sub-contractors, Otis' superintendent, and general foreman. They had to coordinate with the other trades, resolve labor issues as they arose, and explain to the field office why certain parts were not on the jobsite. It was a nail biter for him. We never really talked about his job with him; we probably should have.

Ray got his driver's license back in Oct. We drove up to the North End, and got the Windex, the car air freshener with a cinnamon scent (which Hal threw away after two days, because he said he wanted the pine scent – he never specified a flavor) and two – six packs of Colt 45 Tall-Boys. Ray popped a can and got in the passenger's seat and told me to drive back, but to also "Cruise the Loop."

"Cruise the Loop?" I looked at him as I got behind the wheel.

"Go up to Lake Ave., down Voss Ave. go past Morsemere and we'll end up back down here.

"You got it." I peeled out from the End's public lot and drove up Palisade Ave. My only city driving up to that day was to take the Chevy out of the driveway and park it on the street.

"Want a beer?" Ray smiled handing me one.

On Lake Ave. I spotted Jimmy Martin, Bushrod, and Holter. They were loading a case of beer in his mother's car. Ray hung out the passenger window in the cold as I pulled along side. It took Jimmy Martin a few moments to recognize us in the strange car.

"Hey – it's the lawyers.....who's wheels?" he smiled.

"The old man's."

Holter called from Jimmy's car, "We're going down Greystone – meet us there."

"What's going on?"

"Ranger Rick.....got drafted.......goin' away party." The Bushman said. "I'm bringing down some moonshine from back home, from the mountains of Virginny."

"Any babes?" I popped open the can.

"A cast of thousands......cha...cha...cha..." Martin cackled.

"Reno'll probably show."

"That humphead is most likely already down there.....you know he'll at least show up with some chicks."

"The party down the river last summer, turned out to be a bust because of him." Ray said.

"Don't remind me." Holter shook his head. "You guys got any boo?"

"We're looking pretty lean in that department. See - what we can come up with." Ray said.

"Fuck – this winter won't give up. You know The Huns are down there already. They're on a mission."

"Sure, it's their man. They'll be looking for replacements. Eddie Van Trex got drafted right after Christmas. Ranger Rick said he wanted a party on account they let Eddie leave without one. McKool and Davis said they didn't have any money for a hall or a bar, so they're having it down the train station.

"Somebody got a way into the station house?" Ray said.

Bushrod replied, "McKool's using the overpass for the party."

"He must have done some reconnaissance.....the electricians just wired those heaters up there recently."

The Huns get around." Jimmy Martin raised his brow and nodded. "Hey Big Ray – don't forget the weed."

"If I got it – you got it."

We were going to miss the climatic charge, we'd have to catch Flynn in another movie. This party was coming together – not like our summer bash. I drove down to Morsemere Ave. Crawford, the Tartaglione brothers, Rexall, and Danny Stax were in front of Progressive Pizza; it had just opened at 1 o'clock. Joey was high – Kenny Crawford might have been. The rest were stoned. Ray and me gave them the lowdown about Ranger Rick's going away cocktail party. They were all charged up for the party and the Bushman's moonshine.

I was disappointed, again we had failed to get a female in the car – we hadn't even seen one who we could invite roaming the streets. I cruised the North End again for any female activity and/or more well wishers.

"RYAN !"

I jammed on the brakes. "What the fuck?" My chin ate some steering wheel and Ray crashed his arms into the dashboard. "Whadja see – a Ben Franklin blowin' across the street?"

"Nobody's behind us; back up and take a right up Douglas Ave."

A mop of blonde hair was bouncing up the street. We looked at each other at the simultaneous recognition: "Loki." we smiled. The deli made a scramble on a bun with cheese, and he had a quart of Dellwood chocolate milk in his gloved hand. I inched the Newport along with his bounce up Douglas. Ray had rolled his window down waiting for him to look over towards us. He was focused on his scramble and getting home. Ray thought we had waited long enough and yelled: "Hands up motherfucker."

Loki, visibly shaken, managed not to drop anything. He looked at us through his hair: it looked like it had been combed with a pack of firecrackers. "I knew somebody was shadowing me. I didn't know it was the 'Bluelaw' brothers."

"Doing anything?" Ray smiled.

"Fightin' a killer hangover. My cousin Linda got married yesterday. Reception was in the Bronx."

"Save that hangover for class tomorrow." I said.

"Ahhh....I dunno.....I think I'm still drunk...I think."

Ray raised his brow: "I got about a half a nickel of reef – it'll override the hangover." He pulled up the doorlock pin and Loki got in, his scramble on a soft roll bounced off the door and hit the floor.

Loki held the remaining Kaiser roll halves: "You know if you guys weren't here, I'd wipe off the egg's bad side and put it back together and eat it." He studied the side of the egg that hit the car's floor. To our amazement, it was thoroughly examined by Loki and reloaded.

"ZZZingggg." He launched it frisbee-style, missing my face by millimeters onto the windshield of a parked car.

"You're coming with us.....big party down Greystone Station." Ray had his arm across the bench of the front seat.

"I may as well, my other option is to go back to bed for the rest of the day. Drive me back down the End, I'll get a meatball sub and a six of Colt."

Ray and me had to switch seats in case Hal saw his Chrysler pull in with me driving. We generated an incomplete for the garage and the car. There would be a chewing out when Hal realized we hadn't done any of the work we said we were going to do. Ray said it was a case of 'Play now'/'Pay later'.

We left Hal's car at the bottom of the driveway. The beer was still in grocery bags so it was hard to say what we were up to. Our six-packs had shrunk to 5 packs, and Loki had trouble getting started on his 12 ouncer. Monday morning was going to be a dandy for all three of us. There were a lot of cars down Greystone for a Sunday – too many. This had bust written all over it. 90% of the vehicles were there for Ranger Rick's send-off party. We could hear music and see smoke coming out of the two new cupolas in the overpass' roof. Three impromptu benches had been assembled with two – five gallon buckets on each end of an 8 foot 2" x 12" plank spanning the buckets. Most of us were standing to start. There might have been 25 – 30 people there already. The Huns even had a guy from Dobbs Ferry cooking chicken, burgers, Polish sausage, and a big pot of gumbo just outside the swinging doors of the bridge. Davis Quinn had boosted all the food from the A&P on the other end of O'Dell Ave. and the Saw Mill River Parkway. He used to go out with this one checkout girl who was still sweet on him and rung up a hundred dollars of food for $6.35.

The top flanges of the bridge's two girders made a great bar rest for the drinks, beer, plates of food, and homemade ashtrays. The makeshift benches were okay, but barstools would have been perfect. The more we told Rick what a great guy he was, the worse he felt. I was still mad at the Ranger from last summer when he hogged all of Barb Wells' attention.

The few commuters who braved to walk the gauntlet of the bridge party found us quite amiable, I don't think they minded us at all and might have looked at us as their start of their afternoon in the city. There were a few double-takes when they figured out the smell wasn't all food and tobacco, and they visually swept the overpass until they saw who was smoking the herb. Nobody said anything.

Around 4 o'clock, the Vietnam vets from the North End showed up: Tommy Thompson, Jimmy DiSantini, Joe Griffin, Chris Hardesty, and Ronny 'Chooch' Crestwood from Orchard St. Devil Dogs Billy Van Nahl and Danny Stax, and the swabby – Denny Lewellyn rounded out the veterans present. The sailor wore his ship blues and pea coat. He had enough style to top it off with one of those Jackie Stewart driving hats, leaving the dumb sailors' cap home. Jimmy Di, Chooch, Stax, and Ronny Zanzibar (who had to work on Sunday) were the only ones who actually knew Ranger Rick, but when all these vets got back – they were all brothers.

Rick Lynch didn't think he was capable of passing the physical. He knew he had a bad back at the age of 19, it was mostly from bending over the front fender of cars and bumpers to work on the carburetors of the hot rods. His diet wasn't the best: coffee, alcohol, illicit drugs, and cigarettes. Rick said he would have enlisted with Eddie Van Trex on that 'Buddy System Program' where they stuck you in the same regiment as your buddy for the duration of the enlistment, and now the two Huns were lone wolves most likely heading off to Vietnam. The vets were pretty low key, they knew too well it was a roll of the dice for anyone going into the military with a war going on.

Connors McKool let out with one of them loud whistles where you use your thumb and third finger to get everyone's attention:

"Well......everyone knows why we're here. We're sending off another one of our own to Uncle Sam. It's common knowledge 'The Huns' have done more than our duty for our country: Donnie Wyck died over there; Jesse Van Trex, Eddie's brother – one of the founding members of 'The Huns' returned........only to disappear nine months later. Brother Eddie is currently at Fort Dix for basic training, and now our best carburetor rebuilder/mechanic answers our country's call."

"I call on you brothers and friends – raise your heads and drinks and salute our Hun brothers and pray........

At that moment a family of commuters entered the pedestrian bridge and froze just inside the swing doors as McKool had just started the ritual. He peered down to the east end of the bridge:

"Step forward strangers as we send our brother off to war. Display the steel of Odin."

They pulled two broadswords from their scabbards; both hands were required to wield them. Davis Quinn and a temporary - Honorary Hun, Jim Nymchek, made the steel blades ring loud. The commuters were aghast. Bare-handed, McKool made an obtuse angle of the blades above the head of the sitting Ranger Rick Lynch. He withdrew a bandana from a rear pocket with his free hand and wrapped the blades with it to get a tighter grip on them with his right hand, and raised his left in a hailing manner to invoke the spiritual forefathers and gods, then pulled from his suede leather vest, an old piece of paper and unfolded it with his teeth:

"All powerful Thor and his mother Jord, we ask you to intercede with the father Odin. Protect our brother member: 'Ranger Rick' Lynch. Give him a steady hand, a sharp eye, and protection through the strength of The Huns. Give him the senses of the Wolf and the right of retribution to slay themthat seek to slay him."

"Return him to our crew to enjoy the delights of our woman-folk -To drink the powerful fire of our wine – "The Thunderbird" and smoke the fantasy herb that relives all panic, agitation, pain, and paranoia. Let him enjoy the vibes of The Doors, Otis Redding, CCR Santana, and The Mothers of Invention." May Rick come back to experience the speed of a Hi-performance 429 c.i. Ford Galaxie."

"But more than any of these, return Rick because The Huns – Lake Ave. chapter need his wisdom – humor – and car boosting skills."

Let Odin's will be done! ALL KNEEL! ......Raise your cups for Rick and Eddie's return."

McKool took both swords with his oversized hands, and rested the blades on end of Lynch's shoulders. He invoked the Norse god's name in a wolf-cry style: "Ooooooooooooooo-Oooohdinnnnnnnnnnnnnnn....."

Quinn turned to us, his chin went down with his eyes and he nodded. We stood back up. I watched the dumbstruck commuters. They had no choice but to keep in sync with the 'Commitment to war Rite.' The cups of alcohol were raised as we all howled with McKool and Quinn: "Ooooooooooooooooh-Dinnnnnnnnnnnnnnnnn!"

Chants of "Thor powered Ranger Rick." "Odin." Wolf yips and cries flooded the overpass. The family of four commuters were starting to choke on the second-hand smoke as they made their way to the other side to get to the southbound platform.

Loki was kind of jittery, and told all who knew him to use his Christian name 'Joe' for the duration of the going away party. Loki being the name of the Norse god of troublemaking and mischief, he felt his nickname had no place in this send-off party, and no good would come of it if he started throwing it around. Very few of the well wishers knew anything about Norse mythology. It was for the best to forget the nickname for the duration.

It was just a matter of time before the bluecoats made an appearance. McKool asked Rexall to stow the broadswords in the trunk of his car. McKool didn't want the hors d'oeuvre stickers getting confiscated. The North Command Patrol all knew the '61 Bel Air – AKA – The Hunmobile....AKA 'The Valkyrie Express'. They routinely requested McKool to open the trunk four or five times a year as a matter of public safety.

Rexall showed up, he was same age as Loki; he had gone to public school while Loki had gone to all Catholic schools. Rex's link to us was through Crawford, Danny Stax, and Kirk Lis. The four of them went to Saunders Trade & Tech. Saunders was closer than Gorton for Rex to attend, but he ended hanging around Morsemere with us. He had a '63 Buick Special. It was a good car until he wrecked it.

The calls started: "Speech......Speech.......Speech! and they continued until the overpass was filled with the request.

Ranger Rick asked for a moment with his raised right hand and extended index finger as he took a hit of reefer. Betsy Risko reached into her bra and brought out a small sterling silver cylinder. She arranged two monster rails on her compact mirror. She gave Lynch a silver straw and the lines disappeared.

Slightly above a whisper I told Ray, "Hey man, that's cocaine."

His brow went up in amazement: "I thought it was Ajax cleanser."

A quick nip from old reliable 'Jim Beam' and Rick was as speech ready as he would ever be.

"Gonna make this short – To our allies from the North End and the veterans from up there –" (a loud cheer from the North Enders who had the most people there), and the new crew recently formed down on Morsemere Ave. and Rubeo Park area......the girls gave them the name: 'The Rogues'......."

A cheer went up from our loose collection of thrill seekers: George Holter, Danny Stax, the Busch Bros., Kenny Crawford, Jimmy Martin, 'Fast Eddie' Mason, 'Bad Brad' Guzzutti, Vinny Tarts, Rexall, and me raised our fists and cheered. Somehow our gang had gotten status, identity, and respect thanks to Ranger Rick and The Huns.

"Finally – but never last, our closest cousins: my other family, my first crew, my protection, and always my allegiance to our closest allies – the Orchard Street crew as well as the Lake Avenue Lakers and the High Street guys, who always answered our requests for aid. Rick lost his balance a little bit as he raised his fist and yelled: "To The Huns!......To The Huns!.......To The Huns!" The chant went up and all around. "Brotherhood forever.......Brotherhood forever!" I heard McKool chant with the rest of us, but I could also detect the loss of his Brother Huns: Donnie Wyck and Jesse Van Trex. I was sure him and Quinn had confronted the possibility that neither Eddie or Rick might not return.

Backslaps, handshakes, a few photos followed. Rexall plugged the 8-track boom box back in. The Bon Voyage party now took on the feel of a victory celebration. Things started picking up. Some guys broke out the good stuff.....the girls too. We outnumbered them by 4:1. I watched Crawdad and when he wasn't up dancing right away, I studied him. Barbara Wells tried to get him to dance – nothing doin'. When he turned her down.......I knew what he was doing. Kenny and Joey Tarts were high, but Kenny was good and high. Joey was hooked-up, but he was already thinking two highs ahead; "Livin' the nightmare.........Chasin' the dream." he'd say.

Now it was starting to make sense - all that jazz Ray said about these compulsive junk people. I had to remember to ask him: which of us is going to have to adapt to the magnetic pole reversal.......him or me? He said, "When it starts getting real weird on a number of levels, you'll know it's time to react. Until then, we'll just have to watch the traffic from the window."

Loki and Ray were quizzing Jimmy Di Santini and Tommy Thompson about boot camp, getting drafted, the war and what their next move should be. The vets counseled not to go to college and "stay away from long term commitments like marriage and/or having a kid because you might not be coming back. However you work it - just plan on being fucked up in the head for a while – especially if you're in the thick of the shit."

"Sign up for the trades before you go. The union will give you credit for your service when you come back." Billy Van Nahl said. "And sign up for the Civil Service jobs before you go in: Cops, Fireman, Post Office - those jobs take a long time to clear a list, but you get extra points for your military service" Jimmy Di took a drag from his cigarette.

Kathy Cruz and Passion Penny led Rick down to a van in the parking area. The two girls slid the side door shut.

Our conversation turned to the miracle season when the Jets won the farm team championship. Reno had brought Kathy and Penny, and wandered over by us. He was looking for conversation a little less esoteric. Looking at him, I thought he had some catching up to do.

"Hey Reno, go check out the Bushman, he's got that Virginia moonshine........before it's all gone." I nodded over to Robin Bush.

"Nah.....a few beers and some smoke, I don't want to make it a career down here." he replied.

"Ranger Rick's got to report down the Draft Board tomorrow." Holter shot back.

People drifted in and out, back and forth. They moved away from the boom box when they didn't like the music and toward it when they heard what they liked. Wells and Tarts were right across from the music smoking it up and of course Reno made his way over to get in on the peace pipe or to mix it up with Barb, maybe both.

Joey Tarts, Kenny, and Jay Swanson from the end were leaning up against the south girder. Each was looking at a different phase of the magnetic pole reversal equation. Next to Ray, we observed them as they absorbed a portion of it, the same as Cocaine Wayne and Kenny had done last summer. Swanson didn't see a thing except pale green plywood covered with graffiti. It was obvious Joey and Kenny understood what they were reading; although they didn't have the scope Ray had. Neither of the mis-wired duo enjoyed getting high, but they only gained this insight after reading Ray's formula. The principles of magnetic fields, and their compounding by solar and cosmic storms with these magnetic waves, would not only flip the gravities of the poles but also organic and inorganic materials in and on the planet.

These 'Phantasm' or 'Shadow' junkies were different than the everyday "get me high" junkie. They were never in the moment, never could enjoy the moment. They were always somewhere else – a place where they didn't want to be. They were always fading – always coming down, but at the same moment concerned about being in neither dimension and being unable to find equilibrium or tranquility. Pushing the plunger forward.......and drawing it back. The escape had escaped. It was gone – running through their circulatory system and in an instant advancing their minds in time into a temporary no-mans land parallel dimension. The respite was finite and it was time to repeat.

The question Ray needed to formulate a model for was: what to do once the pole reversal had stabilized and the specter junkies' physiology had 'dialed in' to the new magnetic order – would those of the old alignment go completely mad? Would they merely change

364

places in physiology and watch the other side start to squirm and suffer as they had?

Should humanity make it through the reversal, would the shadow people become the placid ones, and the part of humanity which could not; would they assume the role of wanderers and nomads doomed to a life of insanity? A life without purpose - other than attempting to escape themselves. There would always be a winner and loser; a positive and a negative; good and evil. Infinity goes in both directions or does it or can it? If infinity has a starting point, surely it is with God.

Ray knew what chemical evasion was about, but how did these ghost junkies escape their fates prior to the use of mind numbing or psychedelic substances? Was suicide the only way out? Ray had compounded his personal situation; he thought there might be a way other than the drug alternative to avoid this assigned universe he found himself part of. He knew he wasn't meant to be here. My brother knew the drugs wouldn't give him what he was searching for; but he couldn't say if he could hang on to his sanity and stay straight. It was a question yet to have an answer.

MORRISON HOTEL HAD THE PLACE ROCKIN'. AN HOUR of daylight remained. A few guys left and a few got louder, things were at a good pace. There was a west breeze off the river. The tenants of the lower three or four floors of the 14 story apartment didn't hear our noise with their windows shut. A few more commuters were going to Manhattan for social activities. We knew they wanted to wait in the heated overpass for their train; but they passed through and waited in the cold on the southbound platform. Sometimes New Yorkers were pretty astute.

Passion Penny and Kathy Cruz climbed the overpass stairs. They came by us: "Got any Ripple?" Kathy said.

"No Ripple." Rexall laughed. The two walked over to Wells and Betsy Risko.

"What do you guys got to drink?" Kathy said.

"I got a pint of Southern Comfort that's half gone." Betsy said, "......if that'll help.

"I'll chase it with beer." Kathy eyes rolled.

"Does he need us?" Barbara Wells head nodded to the van.

"I don't think a couple of faggots could satisfy the Ranger." Penny choked.

"Hi-Ho Silver!" They giggled, Betsy had to turn away when she knew we were watching and listening to their report.

"He's a warrior." They tagged off to the fresher troops.

We watched the two vixens descend the stairs and go into the van. "Almost pays to get drafted." I was mesmerized. "Who got the girls?" I nodded over to Betsy and Barb.

Ray glanced at Loki and me, we all turned and looked to Rexall.

He smiled, "McKool asked me to get a couple of girls for Rick's party. He said he needed them just for him – he didn't need

365

pros......no strippers or dancers. I gave the job to Reno – he promised them an oooo-zeee."

"Each?" Loki's eyes bugged out.

"What are you crazy?.........To split." Rex said.

"Shoulda known Reno was going to have an iron in the fire." I said. "How about this Ray?......Maybe we give him – some of the comet dust to keep on his person - to repel the bullets. It's got the strength to alter motion of some objects?"

Loki called down the other end of the overpass, "Hey Reno." and waved him to come over.

A cigarette dangled out the side of Reno's mouth, "Let me finish." He continued counting money out in some transaction with Jimmy Martinique, Sue Herr, Wacky Nancy, and Beth the Mess.

WE HUDDLED AROUND AS WE WAITED FOR RENO TO finish his business.

"Think it'll deflect a bullet?" Joey Tarts asked Ray who was concentrating on the equation. He turned his focus from the plywood to Ray.

"It nearly derailed the one train." Ray said.

We walked from one end of the bridge to the other, taking it all in, keeping an eye on the van. Loki went down the tracks and let out some used Colt 45; Rexall switched out tapes and put on 'Disraeli Gears'.

"Hey Kenny – " Crawford was on a slow burn. "You extracting any of the time/space, astrophysical, speed, magnetic force material?" Ray tried to get Kenny's eyelids to open further.

"You guys know I shouldn't be able to interpret any of the stuff."

Catdaddy's overall demeanor indicated there wasn't much junk-high remaining. Had he not been so intent on the equation, he might have realized he was out of feel-good fuel.

"This one section has to do with the sun's magnetic bombardment of the earth, and when the moon is positioned thus: (he used a can on the girder for the sun, and held two cans to model the earth and moon) the earth and moon will retrieve magnetic waves which are stronger and of longer and longer duration. Am I right?" Crawford looked to Ray. I looked to Joey, and the three of us stared at Ray.

"Yeah, that's it.........Kenny, let me know if you come across anything indicating when this might occur.........you too Tarts." he said. "It's important to know – this pole reversal is a planetary initiated occurrence. I'm surprised you were able to read it."

Crawford and Big Tarts were blown away to have been able to decipher what they saw as hieroglyphics. The two were going to leave soon; Crawfish rubbed his nose with his flat hand, and started dancing. He'd step with one foot and drag the other shake his butt and clap.

Jay Swanson from the End took a look at the puzzle on the green plywood to see if he could see what Joey Tarts and Crawford had seen. There were no spark in Jay's eyes, they were glazed. He copped with Cocaine Wayne a lot. Joey Tarts asked Swanson if the equation on the wall made any sense to him.

"Just bits and pieces." Jay replied.

According to Ray, Jay was like the vast majority of junkies: He was there to get high. He only had a fragment of understanding of his position in this four or five dimensional cosmos.

"Jay, any clue as to what all that shit means?" Ray pointed to the formula.

"Nah…..ain't got time for that noise." he said. "You know I dig them two dolls on each end. I know where they're comin' from." he laughed.

What I couldn't grasp was how Ray seemed to have the whole thing in his head. My speculation was it had to have been connected to his witnessing the meteor's entry into the atmosphere, the ash/dust particulate matter, and the subsequent outer body experience which left him immobile and staring, as he hovered 15 feet over me. Perhaps the most significant factor altering the tether to an earthly reality, was the continuing contact with the 'Cosmic Intruder'.

Swanson wrinkled his forehead and took a drink of beer, "I don't much give a fuck, but that's a lot of shit on the wall, and nobody goes to that length to do something like that unless it means something."

Joey Tarts was along side Jay, "That's Big Whitelaw's mathematical masturbation. Listen up and you might learn something. -- It means magnetic charges from the sun and outer space can be carried by the radio waves of satellites, sputniks, communication and weather satellites, missile platforms, and whatever else they got orbiting the planet. The sun's magnetic bombardment is an opportunistic event of this solar system and maybe others. The equation says our descendents won't have to endure what we have gone through." Joey Tarts said.

"Yeah. – Yeah. Whitelaw knows it all." Swanson's dope dazed eyes traveled to the focus of cognitive reasoning where an image of a montage of events, astrophysics, and humanity had him in a state of suspended animation for two minutes. The picture faded: "That doesn't change anything………they're way into the future and we're here. In fact, that's some of the dumbest shit I ever heard Joe."

Tarts turned to Ray: "Is there an escape hatch for us -right now?"

"All this –" Ray's arm swept the length of the pedestrian bridge pointing to the computations on the plywood, must have some relativity to our present state. It is quite unlikely this is all a product of some kind of predestination." My brother placed his beer on the girder and started massaging his temples

Their fuel gauges were at different levels – the three were below an 1/8th tank. Crawford could still get clean with minimal withdrawal. Joey Tarts and Swanson would have to get high soon; when the two left I knew Joey left with a new outlook. Maybe it was hope……if anyone could give it a label besides Joey it had to be Ray.

The music kept blasting. Ray went over to the Bushrod to see what that 'white lightning' was all about. Although I hadn't been there

367

to see his solo performance at the school, I thought with all of this Equation stuff on the board in front of us, it must have been similar to that night. I watched him take a shot of the Virginia elixir. Jimmy Martini and Buddy Busch encouraged Ray to try another, but he "woooooed" a smile, waved, shook his head from side to side and drifted over to the Vietnam vets.

Denny Lewellyn was with his sister Sue. He had this '58 Biscayne which was a bucket of bolts on wheels. When he got his discharge, he ran out his unemployment and somehow got a job at Otis cleaning castings for minimum wage - $1.50/hr. Denny was okay, he would buy beer or wine for the younger kids and drink with them at Kinsley Park when there was nothing else to do.

Most of the vets didn't talk about Nam to us younger cats, they kept their experiences to their circle. If they knew a kid had gotten his draft notice they'd open up and tell him what to watch out for. I'd always stay near them vets when they were talking about the war; trying to get some idea of what they went through. Jimmy DiSantini and Joe Griffin were much looser than usual about Nam at Rick's party – still that wasn't much. Denny however talked a blue streak about it, he would go on about his tour, until even a guy like me figured him out. It was easy to determine who saw combat and who only heard about it. Billy Van Nahl said, "Dammit Denny – you never left the fuckin' boat."

Denny shot back: "Well what the fuck? It was a goddamn munitions ship – we all could have blown to smithereens. Now that was one helluva perilous situation. They had MIGS and them Sanpans floating around us."

"The N.V. Air Force were never near you Denny." Van Nahl said.

While Jimmy DiSantini and Joe Griffin were in country, their younger brothers Frankie and Tony would tell us about their brothers' close calls, the atrocities on both sides, and they always mentioned "Not everyone walked away." What seemed to have the most impact on Ray were the extraordinary incidents of bravery and heroism; the self-sacrifice, the ability to adapt, the can-do attitude. Hearing even a little bit of these veterans stories 1st hand, gave him a break from his anti-matter universe. He speculated he might affect a transformational leap from where he was to where the vets were. These guys had been pushed into another dimension and would never see life as most of us did. He also was aware he could come back as screwed up as Kevin Doucette from the golf course. The big risk about going to Nam was physical and psychological, and if you came back, there was a good chance it'd be with plenty of baggage.

Not many people were talking about the impaired vet or non-verifiable humanoids who ran backwards. They had no standing.......they didn't count to most of society. Who was to say who was worse off? Not many cared about the damaged vet, and no one knew about anti-magnetic junkies.

DiSantini and Griffin had come back looking none the worse. They may have evaded the psychiatric trauma for the present, but seeing a buddy getting blown to kingdom come was destined to come back visiting them somewhere in the future. This business with the vets and Nam stayed with Ray. I thought he gave it way too much think time.

THE PLUG ON THE BOOM BOX WAS PULLED. JIMMY Martin announced: "The bluecoats are here.....open the doors, and hide the shit."

It was one of those instances where everyone figures someone else is going to clean up the evidence. We had been in that overpass for quite a while, and cars had been coming and going all afternoon to the beer store, getting new players, and a restock of exotic substances.

Martin could smell a cop a mile away, "Railroad coppers." He called out.

With a situation like this, the only thing they could bust you for was for possession of illicit drugs. It wasn't illegal to drink on railroad property – people stepped off the train carrying cocktails they had purchased from the carman. They couldn't pop you for trespassing because we were waiting for a train. Through the haze of the alcohol and reefer, I couldn't see these cops busting anyone holding less than an ounce – it wasn't worth the paper work.

They got out of their squad car, and double-timed it up the steps. Normally, a few guys would have made a break for it, but most of us were too screwed up and we relied in the 'safety in numbers' axiom.

"Alright....." The older cop boomed his voice so he could be heard on both ends of the bridge. "Up against the wall.....Face the wall. Throw all the hardware on the concrete."

I threw my K-55 down with the rest; there were around 20 blades on the floor, three straight razors, and two brass knuckles. The cops confiscated the razors and knuckles.

"Youse over by the river side – what's this all about?" the older cop bellowed. "Turn around.......all of ya's."

"Hey Alvin...." Joe Griffin said softly to the tall younger cop.

"You know this guy?" The older cop asked.

"Yeah." His partner said. "Hey Joe......Jimmy...... Billy....... .....Swabby.....Swabby Denny." The young cop grinned and shook his head. He looked over to the older cop, "Phil....I know these guys, we got drafted around the same time. We all served in Nam. Billy tried to get me to sign up in the Marines before I got called up."

Phil went over to Billy Van Nahl, "You a Leatherneck?"

He rolled up his sleeve revealing a bicep tattoo of a bulldog wearing a drill instructors hat and the monogram: U.S.M.C.

"If you're dirty – I got to bust ya – but if it's just blowin' off some steam with a few beers.......we're not going to make a federal case out of anything. I always take our duty for the Corps into consideration." Phil said. The two marines shook hands.

Billy said, "I know you guys are on the job, but would you have a beer with us?"

As the senior cop, it was Phil's decision. "Just a quick one." He looked over to Alvin, "We'll file this one under 'Community Relations." The bulls smiled. "But I got to call it in first."

Alvin smiled and winked at the guys he knew. This was great I thought: Drinking with police protection.

Phil called in on his walkie-talkie: Dispatch south, this is Bravo Two–Nine. Responded to disturbance at Greystone. Teenagers disturbing commuters. Teenagers took off as we entered the parking area. Pursuit negative."

"Bravo Two-Nine.....return to patrol."

"Roger that South. Bravo Two-Nine.....out."

"What's the party for?" Alvin got ready for a load of bullshit.

"One of our compadres reports to the draft board tomorrow." Phil gave McKool the once over, "'Bout time for a haircut."

"Was waiting for my draft notice.......figured it'd be cheaper if Uncle Sam did it."

"Where's the poor bastard that's goin' in?"

"Passed out in the van."

"Do I know him?" Alvin asked.

"Probably to see.....he's from Lake Ave. Rick Lynch?"

The younger cop gave his head a quick negative shake.

"Let's toast that he returns.....God, Mother, and Apple pie." Again the cans and bottles were raised high: "May the angels watch over him and keep him safe." Jimmy's D's eyes crested.

"Not too late guys – and looking at you mugs – I'd say this going away party is just about done. If the Yonkers P.D. comes down, they'll bust somebody for something." Phil said.

"We'll take care of it boss." McKool nodded.

Ray and me read it in the Herald Statesman: "Hudson River Country Club to close – No plans for the immediate future." They waited until the last week of March before making the final decision. No more caddying. Summer work was always scarce.

St. Andrews was the nearest private golf club employing caddies. It was 10 miles away from 21 O'Dell. There was no transportation there. It was more work getting there, than it was doing a loop. We sat in the caddy yard and shack for the months of April and May. The guys who went to college had been caddying for almost five weeks and we were still in school. The long school year put us behind the eight ball. Being at St. Andrews on every weekend day, which amounted to approximately 20 days, we had only gotten out twice; we were batting .100. The rate at St. Andrews was $6.00/bag for 18 holes. It worked out to $1.20 a day. Even I could figure out I was better off fishing down the Hudson.

Getting up there was a real nut. Ray had his driver's license, but no car. Jane would drop us off up there every now and then, but it wasn't working out. It ended up being a patchwork of walking and hitchhiking: two hours to get to St. Andrews, at least 6 hrs. of waiting around and looping, then two hours back home. Half the time, you might catch a ride with a caddie who had a car and get picked up and dropped off at a certain point so you didn't have to walk and hitch from and to Yonkers.

The Caddy Master's name was John Marcus. The school year ended on June 29th. On June 30th we showed up ready to carry some golf bags. After not getting loops for five days straight, he called Ray and me to the side and gave us the lowdown: "Listen, I know you guys are good caddies, but I've got too many caddies already. I can only use you guys on the Fourth of July weekend" He gave Ray a slip of paper; it had other dates when he probably could use us. It amounted to 10 days for the summer – weather permitting. He also gave us the names of the other courses and their caddie masters we might give a try. That wasn't going to cut it.

Despite John Marcus' advice, Ray invested in a used bike and peddled to St. Andrews six days a week. Marcus hadn't lied. Ray read a novel every two days, and read 'Ulysses' in five days. He borrowed a copy of 'Finnegan's Wake' from one of his brainyac friends', but I don't think he read it. Later on, I know he read 'Gravity's Rainbow', so maybe he did read 'Finnegan's Wake'.

I was hardcoring it down Morsemere Ave. and Rubeo Park. Only a few of the newly formed 'Rogues' had summertime work: Jimmy Martini got a job up at the GM assembly plant in Tarrytown through his father. Vinny Tarts worked in the produce section at Associated Grocers with his father. Crawford got a job for an electrical contractor through his step-father who had an Irish last name. Rexall had just graduated from Saunders and went into the Carpenters Apprenticeship after the fourth of July. His father told him where to sign up. The Business Agent saw Rex was over 6 feet tall, and he figured he'd hang a lot of drywall.

For the rest of us, we were resigned to the reality we would have to 'make do' with spotty work opportunities, dates in the woods, and street partying. If a special night was coming up – we'd have to save up for it. The working Rogues brought the action to the JFK Memorial Marina. We were divided up that summer into the 'haves' and the 'have nots'. No one could blame them for not hanging out with us. The haves could carry one or two of us but not half the crew. The line had to be drawn somewhere. The 'have nots' understood. Every now and then we'd all unite if something special came up or we needed the manpower to make a statement. Everybody got together on Friday and Saturday nights. The guys that didn't work always ran out of money by midnight. It was just the way the summer went.

Buddy Busch and his brother Robin (Bushrod), Bad Brad Guzzutti, Holter, "Fast Eddie" Mason, Danny Stax, Robbie Herrick and me were on the street corner for almost the entire summer. Our work prospects were nil, our pockets were empty, and the summer had just barely begun. We were so tired of being broke we had our resident artist George Holter make up a big sign:

DAY LABORERS: cut grass –
trim trees and hedges – movers –
painting/scraping etc.

MUST PAY MINIMUM WAGE

We moved our sign back and forth between Lake Ave. and the North End. The sign was usually put at the entrance or exit of the parking lots where people could haggle with us, and give us the scope of work they wanted done. The first thing we told them was they had to provide all the tools and equipment if the job required it.

It was already 23rd of July before we got our first bite. A lady came out of Cassidy's pub down the End around 12:30pm and tells George and Buddy to get in her car she's got work for them. She lived in the apartments along DeHaven Dr. She looked around 40 something. I gave her a real good once over. I didn't buy her line that she had work related to home improvements. Our two guys were all smiles as the three drove out of the lot.

When we met up with them the next day, the two swore up and down she had them snaking a hair ball from her tub.

People who stopped by were impressed with our ambition. The old timers would tell us of their hard times during the Great Depression. We had no luck turning these brief encounters into work. We'd stash our sign in the parking lots overnight. We needed a minimum of two days of exposure to have any effect. I was the first guy down the End the next morning; someone had tossed our sign into the street and it was full of tire marks, dirt, smudge, and oil stained

372

when I peeled it from the asphalt. It was so dirty, I hadn't seen it at first. Buddy and Guzzutti brought me over to watch it get run over. Without our sign, we had nothing. We made a couple of replacement signs on cardboard, but they were too small. A passerby couldn't read it unless they were a couple of feet away.

"Ain't this a bitch......" Brad wrung the sweat from his bandana.

"It ain't happening." Fast Eddie chimed.

"Fuckin' July's just about spent." I rubbed my buzz cut which already had grown a good 3/8ths of an inch of hair.

Across the street a couple of girls came out of Barca's grocery store, and walked over to their car. The sun was in their eyes. They could see us as human beings, but they didn't know who we were until the 'ladykiller' Holter called to them as they stood with the car doors open to let the hot air escape.

"Hey Meris.......Sarah." he gave them the big smile.

The girls used their free hands as sun visors and focused in on us: "Hiya George, Buddy -".....A bigger smile, "Hiiiiya Ryan. What are you guys up to?"

The elder Busch brother, Robin, stepped forward, "Trying to find work."

"This is Buddy's brother Robin, 'Fast Eddie', and 'Bad Brad'." I looked over to the girls: "This is Meris Klein and Sarah Nussbaum."

"Howdy ladies," Bushrod gave them a little Dixie.

"You guys are looking for work?"

"Yeah, no luck for just about the whole month." Buddy wiped his forehead with the short sleeve of his tee shirt. "Hear of anything?"

"Just babysitting." Sarah said.

Man – she looked good. I and grabbed her grocery bag and Holter took Meris's. They opened the car's trunk. Sarah had a pair of monsta hoop orange earrings that contrasted with her jet black hair. Her eye make-up was so good I thought she was going to a Broadway opening night. She looked like a Harley-Davidson accessory; made me wish I had my motorcycle license.

Meris asked, "Ryan, is it true Ray got 1450 on his SAT's?"

"Yeah, something like that."

"Wow.......I didn't know he had scored so well." Her eyes marveled and she took a quick inhale of ozone saturated air.

There was no doubt these two were going to college. They went to Gorton, but they were in the academic program - the road to college. They took the same curriculum as Ray: chemistry, biology, physics, intermediate/integrated algebra, trig, calculus. All the disciplines needed for the upper strata of society. Being Ray's brother, and taking the academic curriculum, many assumed I was intellectually on par with Ray. Anyone who did a little bit of digging saw I was a year behind in math and was just keeping my head above water in the sciences.

My poor showing in math was primarily due to an instructor who couldn't master the English language. He was unable to direct you to the pencil sharpener much less convey an abstract geometric concept. His hiring had been a quota requirement. Marginal grades in the sciences were of my own ineptitude, and I barely passed chemistry and biology. I flunked trig I my senior year, and substituted industrial arts for physics. When it came time to take the SAT's, I barely cracked the 1000 threshold on the combined math and verbal.

Following my brother in the academic curriculum, I came to the realization failure was again a possibility. Failing too many courses, the administration would call the parent(s) in, and tell them in a nice way: "The kid's not college material. We recommend he switch to a course of general study."

Still, I pulled off a pretty good scam with the Latin language: Quoting and translating Cicero, Pliny (Elder and Younger), Ovid, The Caesars, The Aeneid, The Wars: (Punic, Gallic, and Civil), Jason and the Argonauts etc. Translating legal, corporate, union crests, as well as courthouse inscriptions and monetary notes from various countries awed many of my peers. I could read and write the 'dead' language most had given up on. By 1971, Gorton was the only high school in Yonkers, teaching Latin. Teachers and administration knew me as the Whitelaw taking Latin.

MERIS PAUSED JUST BEFORE GETTING IN THE CAR, SHE turned to me - one on one - and asked: "You and Ray doing anything tonight?"

"Can't speak for Ray, but I'm free and I think everyone here is available......You got a moving job you need some muscle for?" I said.

"Nothing like that. Something good – on Long Island..... probably an overnighter." Meris smiled.

"Huh?"

"It's in Stony Brook – Long Island. My cousin attends the university. There's a concert tonight. We'll meet you and Ray right here at 5 sharp. How about it? Think your brother can make it?"

"I'll bring him if I can.....he might not even be home at 5 o'clock. Knowing it's you, I'm sure he'll go for the overnight in Long Island."

"She moved even closer to me; if Ray doesn't show up...... then you're my date. If he does, then you're with Sarah. Put the hard sell on your brother, then you'll be with Sarah, which is where you want to be anyway."

"That's not true at all." I checked my look in the reflection of the car's window.

"Well then, if Ray can't make it, I'm sure things will still be interesting. We'd rather have you and Ray with us, but I know George, he was in my homeroom – see if he might want to go. It'll be fun." she said.

Meris was the same age as Ray; she was good looking, but not as stunning as Sarah Nussbaum. Her appeal was difficult to categorize. Perhaps her willingness to go with my brother or me, and be blunt with the either/or option caught me off guard. Later on, I thought it put me in the same box as Ray. This was rarely the case.

374

Meris and Sarah got in the car and waved as they drove off to Tudor Woods.

Holter was anxious to get the lowdown. It was 2:36. Job quest was over for the day. Bad Brad was pissed off the girls were partial to George and not him. Holter came over by me to find out what was going on with Meris and Sarah.

"So Whiteout......what's going on?"

"It all depends on Ray."

"How's that?"

"Sometimes Ray doesn't get back from caddying until after 5 o'clock, he might not even be home by the time we're supposed to leave. Meris's calling the shots – she's got the wheels. You're the utility man......the pinch hitter. We're going to Long Island" I explained.

"Huh?"

"If Ray wants to go – he's with Meris's and I'm with Sarah Nussbaum. But if Ray isn't around or doesn't want to go or the overnight deal is a problem for him – then you go with Sarah instead."

Holter gleamed, "Sarah Nussbaum?......I'll pay Ray to take a powder." He thought about the scenario, "What's in Long Island?"

"Her cousin's taking a summer session at Stony Brook, and there's a rock concert tonight."

"Anybody we know?"

"I don't think she mentioned who the band was."

George thought about things, "How much money you bringing. A two day adventure? I know I'm gonna have to borrow some. My old man don't want to know me anymore."

"All's I got left is ten bucks from caddying on the fourth of July weekend.....it's not going to improve our position if we start mooching off them as soon as we get on the road." I said.

"Not likely. Do they expect us to pay for their tickets, them concerts ain't free."

"Holter – if Ray shows up, you ain't going to be able to go........so you can loan me ten bucks. I'll pay you back. I got to get some trim and get out of Yonkers."

If Ray came with me tonight, I knew he'd be running the show. If George was the stand-in anything could happen. I didn't care either way, but with Ray – things might get too cerebral.

Relief and gratitude swept him: "I'm just glad to have something to do tonight besides hang out on the corner."

Holter double-timed it for a quarter mile to catch up with the other Rogues who were on their way back to Lake Ave. via Morsemere.

"Do me a favor Ray?" Holter called to the sky.

HOLTER WAS WAITING IN THE NORTH END'S PARKING lot where I left him a couple of hours earlier. He had spruced up a bit: His dungaree jacket and jeans were clean and he had a tie-dye shirt on. Cleaning up for Sarah was just a smart move.

375

Squeezing his eyes tight, a smile ran across his face when he opened them and didn't see my brother with me. "No Ray?"

"Un-uh."

"Yes!" Holter shook his fist in the air.

"I left him a note. He might show up in the next 15 minutes - but I think you got the gig Tex."

"I'm going over to Harmonie Liquor – want anything?"

I reached into my pocket and gave him $1.25: "Get me a fifth of Wild Irish."

Meris turned into the lot while George was shopping. She looked at me from the driver's seat, "Where's your brother?"

"No Ray.........he didn't get home yet. Where's Sarah?" I looked around.

"When her father figured out we were going on an overnight visit to a college, he put his foot down and told her he didn't think it was a good idea and he didn't like the way our trip appeared out of thin air."

"No Sarah?"

Meris closed her eyes and shook her head. I was disappointed but couldn't show it.

"No Raymond.............. Hmmm.......Where's George?" She scanned the lot.

"He's getting some wine at the liquor store."

"We should get going." Her eyes drilled mine. "You want to ride in the front.......with me?" her smile commanded an affirmative response; maybe it was just a suggestion.

"Definitely."

Meris heard what she wanted to hear.

"I hope Ray doesn't mind." I asked out the window.

She looked at her watch.

"How many tickets did you get?"

"I told my cousin to get four."

"There's only three of us. I guess you called around to your other friends to see if they were interested. We might be able to find a fourth if we drive around." I said. "But listen.......we don't need no more guys. We got to find a girl for George."

"What's wrong with another guy?" She grinned.

"That's okay for you but we lost Sarah, so we lost twofold."

Holter got in the car and Meris asked, "Whatja get?"

"Ahhh - fifth of Bali Hai, a pint of Zombie, and a fifth of Wild Irish." Holter laughed. "We're ready for a weekend during the week."

Meris looked concerned, "That's not for the ride to Stony Brook?"

"Nah...." he laughed. "We'll get a couple of sixes for the ride."

I looked over to her, "We won't get drunk until the concert." I had to back Holter up. "Bad news George: Sarah got benched by her old man."

He looked at Meris, "Meris?" he said.

"Stay kool Georgie-boy, you'll hook-up with someone at the college."

He cracked open the Zombie trying to take the edge off, "I was really counting on Sarah."

"Can we get a fourth?" I asked Meris.

She looked at the dashboard clock, "We should be leaving right now."

"If you don't want to have to eat the ticket......go down Morsemere and we'll see if anybody's around."

As we got closer to Progressive Pizza and the deli, I could see some activity out front. Vinny Tarts was wolfing down a slice. "Not likely we'll find a replacement at the last minute. Meris, you know Vince – besides there'll be more of us to adore you."

"He was in my typing class last year, but you guys ask him if he wants to go." she said.

Meris pulled over across the street from Progressive. She gave me the look and whispered in my ear, "Ryan, you're my date tonight, I don't care how it works out for George and Vinny." She waved her tongue in and out for me to see.

"I'm ready to rock in more ways than one." I smiled at her. I wasn't sure, but I think she was telling me not to get wasted. The way I reckoned, if there was no romance – then I would get wasted.

Vinny walked around her car and put his forearms on my door and looked in. What's up?" before we could reply he sent a big smile over to Meris: "What are you doing with these two rough cuts?" he laughed.

"Get bent Tarts." Holter laughed as well. "Hey Cinzano – we're going on an overnighter on Long Island and stayin' with Meris' cousin."

"Oceanside or Sound?"

"Sound." she answered.

"The Sound's bullshit." Vince ruled.

"We ain't going swimming – Meris's taking us to a rock concert at the university. Might sleep on the beach. Wanna go?" I said.

"Who's the band?" Vinny asked, but Holter and me were still in the dark.

Meris replied, "My cousin Rachael saw these guys two weeks ago.........The Allman Brothers? She told me we didn't want to miss this show – said they're the real deal."

Raconteur Vince deadpanned: "Never heard of them."

Holter called from the back seat, "Is it another night in Yonkers, or are you going to see the world?"

"Be right back – got to get a few things from home."

She called, "Bring a beach blanket."

"Bingo." George laughed. His mind was still planning: "Whitewash, with Tarts tagging along we better get a couple of sixes from the deli."

"I'm on my last $10.00 from caddying on the fourth of July weekend.

"I bought the wine."

"The hell you did – I gave you a buck and a quarter for the Wild Irish – what are you having an anti-flashback?"

"I got the car." she chirped.

It didn't sound like I was going to get any help with the beer purchase, I hurried to the deli. Vinny came out from his parents' basement the same time I came out of the deli with the beer.

He had the beach blanket over his shoulder, "You with her?"

"Yeah - via my brother Ray."

"That's what big brothers are for." he smiled.

"Sounds like Meris's cousin will be available for you or George. Meris said her cousin wasn't going out with anybody. Sarah Nussbaum was supposed to come with us, but her dad cancelled her ticket."

"Mmmmm.........Sarah....." he saw her in his mind and nearly got clobbered by one of Caesar's taxicabs as we crossed Morsemere.

I handed a ginger ale to Meris. "That's for tomorrow morning. Crack one of those Bali Hai's open." She bolted from the car and came out of Progressive Pizza with a Sicilian slice in one hand and a bunch of napkins in the other. Ralph never spared the olive oil when he made his pizzas. Next thing, George gets out of the car and headed for Ralph's.

"George – get me a slice too." I called to him as I put the beer on the floor of the front seat.

The three of us leaned against the car opting for beer to wash down the pizza.

"Tried drinking on an empty stomach." Meris's closed her eyes and shook her head.

We got on the Hutchinson River Parkway. It went past the old "Freedom Land" amusement park. Developers razed it and built Co-Op City, a massive apartment community where the 'Son of Sam' had once lived.

Despite all the napkins she took from Progressive, Meris had two runs of olive oil shining on the backside of her forearm. She washed down her last piece of crust with some wine, and took a long pull when we were over the Throggs Neck Bridge. The traffic coming from Manhattan was heavy as usual. I was unfamiliar with the Long Island Sound side of the island. We took the Long Island Expressway for just a little bit, and then exited onto the Northern Parkway. None of us guys knew Long Island except to go to Jones or Gilgo Beaches on the Oceanside. Vinny was right, the Sound was bullshit: pollution and no waves. It only looked good at night. Connecticut was on the other side, where Ray and me got those real bad sunburns in the 3rd and 4th grades.

"How far Meris?" Vinny Tarts said.

"Not even a half-hour."

Holter looked at her eyes and forehead in her rear view mirror, "What's the band that's playing?"

"The Allman Brothers.........A-L-L-M-A-N Brothers Brothers Band." Meris spelled out their name.

"It's not an acoustic act is it?" Vinny checked.

378

"Can't be the same band in the jukebox at Copies Tap.....If it is man, they got this killer single. The name sounds real familiar."

"Rachael says they're all plugged in - 6 guys.....Hot Rockers." Her head bobbed up and down to an imaginary beat in her head. "They played there two weeks ago."

I gave her a miffed look, "And they're playing there again so soon?"

Cinzano picked up the train of thought, "Are they some kind of regional or local band?"

"I'm pretty sure it's a real band."

"Hard Rock?"

"Rock Hard." Meris smiled at me.

The smell of salt water was everywhere now. We knew we were getting close to the university.

"Wha?" Meris turned around instead of searching the mirror and looked at Vinny. He was puffing away on a thin joint. Holter and me were laughing, but she was annoyed. "This is my mother's car. I can't have this thing smelling like the Fillmore."

Diplomacy was always in vogue with Tarts, and he passed the joint directly to her. She took a monsta hit off it. There was only a little bit left by the time it came around, I don't think Holter got anything more than rolling paper.

"Gimme some Bali Hai, that stuff is really harsh." She waited for the traffic light to change.

"Thai stick from brother Joe." Vinny grinned.

"Thai stick?"

"Thai stick. he confirmed.

Meris laughed taking a pull of wine: "Bali-Hai Thai.... stick."

She was just a kool chick, way ahead of me. We passed a sign: Stony Brook – 4. That was good; I didn't get much of the stick, but I was getting hyper. I opened a beer and drank half the can. Meris was really.....really starting to look good. I wanted to get out of the car.

I guess summer sessions at colleges weren't heavily attended – parking was a breeze. We met her cousin Rachael at the vacant dorm where she lived. She showed Meris the room she'd be staying in, and told us guys we'd have to rough it in the common area on a sofa. 'How can it get any better we thought?' Rachael looked at her watch and told us the concert was open seating and the sooner we got to the hall the better.

Our hostess was emphatic, "I saw this band two weeks ago – I don't know if their music can be explained. By the third song I'll know if it was my imagination or they really are as good as I thought."

We left the rest of the beer in the mini-refrigerator at the dorm. Holter and me carried the two bags of cheap wine. The four of us had killed about a pint and half of Bali on the drive down. Meris and her cousin didn't want anything to do with the super strength varnish: Zombie. George went to work transferring the fifth of Bali Hai into the empty pint bottles. He topped them off with the Wild

Irish. He held out the Wild Irish Rose. Rachael grabbed it and took a long one and handed it to me.

"Oh my God, that is rank." She laughed.

As we got near, we could see people were walking in with koolers and bags. We figured they weren't bringing in lunches and cokes. This is going to be a blast we all thought.

The concert was held in the student union cafeteria. There were even tables there. It cost $2.50 – general admission. The Student Activities Committee had hired student hippies to work the entrance – no muscle. All the hippies wanted was your ticket. We could have walked in with a team of huskies pulling a sled with a whiskey still – nobody would have noticed or cared. It was different back then.......better. A place to flop, cheap music, girls with no bras, get all screwed up.......college looked like a real gas.

Brother Joe's Thai stick had me daydreaming as we walked in..........'I could dig this higher learning jazz. I already knew how to get stoned and I could fluff them with the Latin crap.' All the while during my mind excursion - me and Meris had been holding hands. I was taking short choppy breaths. The opening band was still playing their set: mostly blues stuff – they weren't too good. There were bleachers on each side of the low-rise stage. The hall seemed about half-full. She hugged me tight, "That pot........Wow.....I am too high." Meris's eyes got real big. She didn't smile.

"I didn't get a big hit of that reefer, but what I got....... Wooooooo........." I looked at her through the THC – "Meris, now I really see your beauty."

Holter, Vince, and her cousin watched us kiss. She looked at the others and back at me and hugged me tight: "Ryan....... remember......you're with me tonight."

The opening band was still playing; they needed more rehearsal time. Although no one called for one, they played an encore anyway. Vinny's suave ways were making gains with Rachael. As long as women were around, George felt he was in the game – so he didn't need my sympathy. These two Valentino's were the best ladykillers the Rogues had. Maybe.....maybe I was in the middle of the pack. I'd been beating myself up since the sixth grade because I had that.........it couldn't even be called a spot – it was a bald area. Almost sixteen years old and I'm working a comb-over. It looked like I had half a Mohawk working..........what the fuck hey –

Meris wised up Rachael about Vinny's age. She was almost three years older than him. I thought it'd be a tough one to negotiate if Rachael thought she was babysitting and not on a date with someone who had the potential to be her equal. Vinny's M.O. was to be brother Joe for the evening; I had seen it work before.

Even as the girls waited to use the Ladies' room; George worked the line with jokes, good looks, and would offer to take a girl into the men's room and guard the stall while she did her thing. I thought we had gone to Stony Brook to see a band, but it seemed like a Saturday night in Jersey.

The five of us were toasted and it felt great. The hall emptied out after the opening band finally gave up. We were still in the union milling about and were thinking of going back to Rachaels's dorm to regroup. Cinzo asked: "How do we get back in?"

"Just show your ticket stub." she said.

It's was a beautiful night. "They should have had the music outside." I said.

"Rachael, where's the water......you know.......the Sound." George asked.

"It's a couple of miles that way – to the north. But don't go - you DON'T want to miss the Brothers." She said aware he was on 'cloud 9' working on 10.

I hadn't gotten a good look at Rachael until the campus lights had come on. Meris had bragged Ray had scored 1450 on his S.A.T.'s.

"Impressive." She turned to Tarts and asked him what he got.

"About the same." he smiled.

The cousins burst out laughing. Rachael asked George about his test scores.

"I'll take them college boards if and when I get back from Nam." He didn't smile and took a drink of Zombie.

The specter of Vietnam threw a wet blanket on everything. Vince maintained his focus and pulled another joint from a hard pack of smokes.

"Watch out Raich......it's strong weed."

"Don't mind me if I start whirling when the band starts getting into it." She said.

Holy shit I thought, 'I'm pretty high already.' I had to wait and see how hard Meris inhaled the joint. The end of the joint glowed bright orange when Rachael passed it to Meris, and my date hit it just as hard as her cousin. I didn't want to punk out in front of the girls and hit it as hard as they did. Holter was squatting catchers style; joint in one hand the paper bag wrapped Wild Irish in the other; he scanned for the bulls or security on a foot patrol: nothing. I was getting paranoid and grabbed her hand.

Rachael suggested we get back so we wouldn't be forced into the bleachers again. It was good to be moving, Vince and Rachael were just ahead of us.

"Hey Cinzano, was that Thai stick again?" I said.

"He turned around with a grin: "Brother Joe."

"Brother Joe?"

He nodded, smiled even more, put his arm around Rachael's waist: "Brother Joe."

We were almost in the student union. "Holter asked me: "How'd we get here?"

"We drove you idiot."

"No....no....we were out there in the grass and now we're here. Like time a mini-time warp; I don't get it." He scratched his head.

"One of two things Quasar: Either it was an actual magnetic time displacement or.........or the Thai stick wasn't Thai stick.......it was pot laced with angel dust or dunked in hash oil. Or, I don't know." I said.

He squinted, tilted his head, sawed up his jaw with the outside of his fingers – "I think it was some kind of additive, but I like it. ah-hahahahahaha. I hope they got a good light show." he laughed.

Inside I became real aware. I was apprehensive, but not paranoid any longer. We all were ready. I was hoping Rachael didn't build this band up too much. The band walked on and started doing a little tuning for the first number. The one guitarist motioned to a gal on the side of the five foot high stage.

She went over to the center of the stage. Obviously she was a student and talked about how the student activity fees made the Stony Brook Concert Series possible: "We had such a tremendous response to this band's initial appearance two weeks ago, when the performing artists committee found out they were in the metro area again. We took a chance and called their booking manager and they were available – and........Well - here they are. Word must have spread because we sold a lot more tickets for tonight's show. The committee thanks you for your support." The bassist played a few notes.

"Okay......okay. Their second Stony Brook appearance.... from Macon, Georgia: The Allman Brothers Band....."

They started off good enough with three blues numbers. The bandleader said they were on ATCO records, and they were going to play some new stuff from their second album. The band played this one song and I could see this guy on keyboards doing the singing. It was the same voice as the one who sang the blues numbers. I was all mixed up. This keyboard player was white w/blond hair, but he sang like a soul brother. They had two drummers, and one of them was black, so I figured he must be doing the singing. The confusion had to have come from the Thai stick. Finally, I asked between tunes, "Who the fuck is singing?"

Vinny's brow raised, "The white guy.........I think."

"Don't sound like no white boy to me."

Meris told me to "Shut up, I'm trying to listen to the song."

Next the band did two long tunes; the one had a little bit of vocals with extended instrumental breaks being its core. The other was a straight instrumental. These two tunes were 15 – 20 minutes in length. They did this one killer tune where the two guitars were playing this call and answer thing on the fade out that lasted four or five minutes and abruptly ended. It left us unable to move. It kept getting better and better, I thought the entire student union was on their feet: dancing, bumping, shaking, handclapping, and grooving to the beat. These guys weren't from Georgia – they came in on that Fireball from the other side of the Milky Way. Except for Rachael, none of us had ever heard anything this unique. In between songs, I huddled up with George and Vinny: "We gotta tell the rest of the Rogues about this band. Wherever they play in the metro area – we've got to catch them."

"This is major league shit." Holter chopped down with his hand.

I was hoping the positive vibes were from the band's music and not Brother Joe's jazzed-up Thai stick. It seemed like the people there were pretty much on the same wavelength. I sure hoped this was real, cause it was really good.

At the start of the concert, there were probably 1000 people in attendance, but half-way through there weren't as many, and the band had yet to play their 'killer' tunes. I explained my concerns to Tarts and asked him what the deal was?

His head tilted as he thought about it: "I dunno, half of them dig it, half are screwed up, and half don't know what music is and they're here because it's a groovy happening, or some shit like that."

The bandleader made a couple of quick strums on his Les Paul and went up to his mike: "Say – lookee here, time kind of got away from us.......and well.....they shut down the town at 11 oooh clock so we only got time for one more. Ain't going to be no encore, so don't go carrying on and making us feel bad." There were a few more key checks by the band. "Uh…we don't play this one too much – with the countdown on – it should work out. He counted off quick: "one..two…three….four......"

The two guitars started with a big rhythm line and a contagious up tempo lead guitar solo with the other guitar playing a harmony lead slightly underneath. These two guys stood next to one another going up and down on the necks of their Gibsons. This thing these two were doing musically was unusual: doubling up on guitar lines. Mostly they did it on the longer tunes, but whenever they did it, your focus intensified as you watched how they were making this original sound.

The people who hung around to the end got their money's worth, the fans were going wild. Some were even dancing on the tables. The keyboard guy sang the few lyrics there were: "People can you feel it – Love is everywhere." It was a great song to end with as it ran fast until it hit a dead stop. The band members were introduced by the bandleader, they waved and walked off.

"What a show!....." Meris was transfixed. She was still absorbing whatever particles of energy were left in the hall.

"They are my band, and don't you guys ever forget who turned you on to them." Rachael beamed.

Meris and me held hands as we started for the dorm. Rachael and Vince were right behind us.

George came up along side.

"No love connection?" Meris said.

A stargazed smile flushed his face, "I connected with the jams. It's still early – they got bars around here. I may get lucky yet. Nothing's going to beat what we just saw in there." His thumb hitchhiked back towards the student union.

Rachael pointed to a main road just over a berm made of sand and long grass. There's a couple of floodlights over the sign: "Stoney End. It's the campus bar that's off-campus."

"I'm going over – anybody want to go?"

Vince and me looked to our dates, what they wanted - they didn't sell at the bar.

"Cinzo, before I make this run – you got any more of that reef from your brother?"

We sat on a concrete slab bench near a group of long needle pine trees; the last Thai stick was drawn from the Marlboro box. The five of us each got an adult hit. Tarts, Holter, and me killed the last of the red liquid they put in bottles and sold as wine. George stood up, "That band - unfuckinbelievable."

"Smokin'."

"Toldja."

"Got to see them again."

"Man, I'm fuckin blasted." The four laughed at my admission.

Holter took off for the Stoney End, and we walked back to Rachael's dorm. I heard him wail off in the distance: "Sarrrahhhhh."

Rachael and Vinny went into her room and closed the door. We were the only ones in the Hall; we could do whatever we wanted without interruption – and we did. Meris stood in the commons room on a low sofa. When I came over, our faces were at about the same height. There must have been at least a foot difference between us in real life. She was a couple of inches taller than me now. I grabbed the cheeks of her bell bottom dungarees to steady her and kissed her as my tongue explored her mouth. Meris was on the same wavelength, and the traces of humanity evolved into raw animal passion. Licking the back of her ear where it goes into her skull, I undid the buttons of her peasant blouse blind. It had some red, turquoise, orange, and blue embroidery on the collar, pockets, sleeves, and wrists. She had worn a black tank-top in lieu of a bra. The short-sleeved blouse was tossed on a chair. I started feeling up her tits. It wasn't good enough, I worked her arm through the tanks top's arm hole and left the rest of it on like a bandolier. She held onto my shoulders as I went right to work on her exposed breast.

"Suck it harder......suck it hard.....I'll tell you if you're hurting me."

What I needed was someone to bark out orders, I was blitzed. I had the desire, but with Meris directing the action, I knew things would go a lot smoother. Besides – too many things were going on with this force of cosmic energy I was feeling. She got out of the bandolier tank top and tossed it on the chair. I wanted her to walk around with her jeans on and bare breasted just to see how everything looked, but I remembered she was calling the shots. I couldn't just tell her to take a walk around the common room for my visual gratification, but that didn't mean I didn't want the show.

I undid her waist button and unzipped her fly. I examined her tits in the dim light. They were devastating, I was hoping she'd let me tit fuck them. I also knew because I wanted them so bad and do it again and again with her, I knew this would probably be the last time I'd have them in front of me. I just knew it. Working on just her tits, I had Meris squeaking and moaning. She tried to push her pants down and she lost her balance and crashed into an end table made of wicker. She wasn't as high as me, although she was high enough, and her body turned into rubber when she crashed. The side of her body took the impact as she tried to stick the landing. 'Save them fucking tits honey -' my thoughts panicked. We tried to withhold our laughter. They were the sexiest boobs I had ever seen, and it included the ones I saw in the Playboy magazines.

We expected to see Rachael because of the racket we made, but she must have been super-occupied with Cinzano. The end table was going to be permanently out of level until it went into the junk pile. Meris threw her tank top back on and grabbed her cotton blouse.

"Grab a couple of beers." she whispered. I followed her out the door. We got Vinny's beach blanket from the trunk of the car, and made our way to the group of pines where we had been earlier. With the trees and darkness it was as secluded as we were going to find outdoors on campus. We lay down and resumed our carnal activities. She looked like a Lee Grant/Jill St. John hybrid - a professional woman with her bobbed hairstyle.

It was hard not to wonder if she liked me, or was this a way to get to Ray.

She was trying to pull my dungarees off while I was certain I had not paid enough attention to her headlights and bulbs.

She huffed, "Stand up."

I got up slow.

"Come on." she urged.

Meris undid the waist button and unzipped my fly. She was on her knees and had one hand down my boxers and the other hand through them. She found it easy enough, but it was as stiff as a new length of compressor hose. My jeans and boxers were like a combination lock and the flys didn't line up. They were almost by my hip before she got it started through. There was a big smile on her face and I was going to pieces watching her looking at me. Meris finally got it through, "Oh yeah." She looked up at me and gave me the smile of a siren.

If Brother Joe's Thai stick had been laced with anything, it musta been an aphrodisiac......our desire was off the scales. She gave me a full visual inspection and cleared her throat and took a sip of beer. She moaned as she did all sorts of things with her tongue and mouth. Every 30 seconds or so she took it out just to look at it. She no longer looked at my eyes and face. When she took it from her mouth again I stopped her: "Meris, I'm not making you do this."

A raspy voice replied: "Shut up."

How could this get any better? I knew it couldn't, it could only end somewhere down the road, most likely sooner than later. I had to let that thought go and get back in the moment – the state of total hedonistic ecstasy. Later on, I wasted too much time figuring out if she got off more looking at me or I did watching her look at me. She played with it, she'd push it down to watch it spring back up. This was three chicks in a row with the same moves.......what was this with these girls? Something must have been stamped on my forehead: "NO ENTRY". She didn't laugh or giggle – she just watched. I just watched. This episode was more than I could deal with. I washed my face with my hands like Crawfish had done, probably for the same reason - to bring myself back into my body.

For some reason, time had slowed. Whenever something enjoyable occurs it's over before you know it, and when the inverse happens time drags on and on. It's just the way it is. I couldn't have lasted more than seven minutes before it squirted in her mouth. About half-way through, she quick stood up and spun me and shot the rest of the jazz in the pine needles. The stuff in her mouth went into the pine needles as well. I curled up into a ball on the blanket. Meris washed her mouth out with some beer and crawled on top of me. "You're going to take care of me...."

"Name that tune Meris." I smiled.

"Are you going to be ready?"

"I'm ready now."

She looked down, "No you're not."

"Help me get ready?" I said.

"Love to."

"Do you want me to do to you what you did for me?"

She washed her mouth out again, then took a drink. "I think I want you inside me. Lick me down there first." Meris only took one leg out of her dungarees and panties. The smell of woman was real strong and I was excited again. She was wet and I tried to remember what I did with Lynn to bring her off. If there was a 'reset' button located somewhere in my brain or on my body she knew where it was.

Again she exhaled; shudders of deep moans from within. She was pinching her nipples; and she mashed my face into her 'Y'. It was a good bet I wasn't on my best game with my work down there, but when I dialed up the muffled cries of pre-orgasmic rapture, I knew I could bring it home. She knew what she was doing – at the time I was guessing.

"Ryan.... That's enough.....I want it in me. Get up" She looked at it and gave it a several quick jerks to judge its readiness. She shook it and shook it. It got stiffer and longer. As she played around, she helped me along, doing what she did earlier. It was nice and stiff.....ready for her to 'cowgirl up', but she kept on playing with me. Her hand went to work on her equipment, the other was jerking me while I was in her mouth. "Suck on my nipples."

I knelt down and did what she asked. "Pull the other one with your thumb and pointer finger. Suck it.......harder.......ooooooh...... mix it up......harder......suck it ...... come on.......come on.......shit......SHIT......suck them." She was at the brink of orgasm. I didn't know how long it went on, she got so wild and out of control I was afraid someone might think a girl was getting molested or raped. She pushed me away as she lay down and had me lie beside her with my stuff even with her face. It went back in her mouth and her other hand went back to work. Her eyes were closed concentrating on her desire to do me.

The primal drive was strong; maybe she did want me inside her; the urgency wasn't as important as it was before when her fireworks exploded. The way she controlled me, it was way more than sexual. She thrill-killed me. I was the object of her fascination, amusement, passion, hunger, and desire. I knew very little in the formation and sustaining of getting it on with a girl/woman, but it was common knowledge the guy was supposed to take the lead in all things especially in the romantic department. I had it upside down; I didn't

386

care, she was doing me better than I could have. Something in this deal with Meris had me thinking it had something to do with the comet. I'd have to get a ruling from Ray – it was too heavy for me. This night would never diminish in my memory banks – one of a kind.

Following a few minutes of afterglow she asked: Don't you ever jerk yourself off........I like giving blowjobs, but Ryan – your volume is ridiculous. "Give me another beer." We both laughed, I didn't know what to say.

"Straight truth Meris........it was all you. It was my attraction to you that made the goo."

"Give me a kiss and let's get back to the dorm."

THE MORNING'S LIGHT CAME BEAMING THROUGH THE dorm's window. I lay on a couch across from her. I was either hungover or in a fog or both. 'Man – I'd like to jump her bones this morning.' If we were quiet, we might get away with it and I could be inside her where she wanted it last night......kind of finish the job – be the man.

I watched her sleep. She was beautiful; it was a shame to wake her. I thought there was enough room to lay next to her; my hand went between her panties and the cheek of her ass, shining it up like a crystal ball.

"OH NO YOU DON'T!"

There was no mistaking her rejection, and she probably woke the others up.

'Well fuck me runnin'' I thought. I shook my head, mad at myself for not knowing a caveman move never turns a woman on. I backed off and sat on the arm of the sofa. She rolled on her side letting me look at her bum. A toilet flushed across the dorm. There was some traffic driving around the campus, mostly maintenance and delivery trucks.

Later that day she was short with me and told me she was in the "red zone". I wondered why she couldn't just tell me instead of yelling at me; it made me feel like I had accosted her or something.

Holter and me walked out into the real world – off campus, got a tray of coffee, and two cups for the walk back. "The chicks got to have that coffee.....hey whatja do to Meris?" he laughed. "You fuckin' woke me up."

"Aaaayh, I don't know......tried to get something going, but it went the wrong way. Last night was such a good time, I naturally assumed I was 'In Like Flynn'.

"Listen to me Whiteline – there's a solid core of women that don't want nothin' to do with 'bedroom boogie' in the morning." He tried to sip the hot coffee. "If this coffee was any hotter it'd be vapor."

My watch said we made it back to Yonkers in good time, but it was one long ride; hungover and nothing to look forward to. Meris was agitated about something. The radio blasted so nobody could talk or sleep. Just to piss her off I was going to whisper in her ear: "I love you." If I laid that on her - things had to go one way or the other, but I kept my mouth shut. There was still hope we would go out again sometime.

She hid behind her sunglasses all the way back – only looking at me for toll money.

The three amigos were dumped off at Morsemere, with just a "See ya fellas", and a wave as she sped away. Sam's deli was open, but Progressive wasn't. Vinny sat on the step, and Holter and me leaned against a parked car. Vinny's rock and roll hair hung down as he looked over to me. "Okay Whitesands, what did you do to Meris to give us the ice queen treatment?"

"Fuck if I know......last night I'm the man and this morning......I ain't. How'd you guys do?"

Vince reported Rachael took him to school, and he was a better man for it. Next, George said he got a girl to leave with him, but when she asked him where they were going, and he said back to the dorm. She replied: "I don't date students."

I gave them the rundown on my sordid mess: "Everything got screwed up once the sun came up. Last night though." A great big grin came upon my face. "Them Allman Brothers......they were smokin." I shut one eye and looked at Vince, "You know I heard that one song they played – the last one that had everybody going nuts. You remember..... 'People can you feel it......love is everywhere'... that one. It's in Copie's jukebox, I play it everytime I go in there. Rikshaw played it by mistake when I heard it the first time."

"Must have been another band or they were doing a cover." He put a batch of hair behind his ear.

"Maybe." Holter said.

"I'm pretty sure it's the Brothers...and it's an original tune cause Steve McQueen played on the record as a special guest. It's hard reading the label going around at 45 r.p.m."   A car was barreling down Frederic St. from the Lake Ave. direction. It looked like Meris' mother's car. She locked up the brakes and the car skidded, the front tires screeched. She let off the pedal and the rear end straightened out. She was pretty smart. Her attitude had a complete makeover.

"Ryan......." She whipped her head for me to come over.

"What did you forget?"

"Do me a favor – Let me know which science and math classes he's taking this fall. You tell me, and you'll be glad you did. And what happened last night........never happened."

"Impossible." My face went sour like I ate a lime. "Already told Cinzano and Holter."

Meris's eyes met mine: Tell Vinny and George to get a real serious case of amnesia."

"Can't speak for them, but if I tell them it never happened – they'll erase it."

She reached for the neck of my shirt and pulled my face into the car and stuck her tongue into my mouth. We kissed for at least a minute. Her left hand went into my front pocket and she fooled around just long enough for the bulge to be noticed. She smiled and drove towards the End.

Once more I leaned against the parked car in front of the pizza shop with George and Vinny on the step.

"What a fuckin night." I wondered what our next rendezvous would be like.

Except for the brief getaway to Long Island, the summer of 1970 seemed to drag on. The lack of work affected Ray and me. Ray was still slugging it out at St. Andrews, peddling his way back and forth. He had little to show for it other than the stack of books in our closet and under his bed. I speculated if my meteor dust would transform me into some kind of wizard like Ray, it might give me the thirst to read at least one of these masterworks. It was obvious he was losing interest in literature. Early August the college texts on mathematics, chemistry, geology, calculus, astrophysics, the cosmos, gravities/magnetism and works by Einstein, Newton, Kepler, various other science giants replaced Dostoyevsky, Joyce, Kerouac, O'Neill, Fitzgerald, Faulkner, Garcia, Crews, John Gardner, and Pynchon. The only books I read that summer were 'My Secret Life' and 'The Bad Girls', the latter being 66% still pictures. Both of them were discarded on O'Dell Ave. near where we had stashed the others. It was like a porn delivery service.

St. Andrew's club championships for golf and tennis for men and women were held on back to back weekends which bridged the months of July and August. It about 10 days after the overnighter with Meris. The date was one of the days on the list John Marcus gave Ray when he first said he didn't think he'd be needing us. The Championships were the only opportunity for me to make some money between the Fourth and Labor Day weekends. I caddied for this one lady who was supposed to be pretty good, and another lady who had a hard time keeping it in the fairway. By the 15th hole, their day was over.....too many double and triple bogies. My hope of getting another loop was pretty bleak.

Marcus had enough common sense to give Ray two men. His situation was just about the complete reversal of mine: his guys could drive the ball, and their short games were adequate. They were going to make the cut in the 'A' flight. My two ladies got erased from the tournament on the first day: $12.00 – no tip. Ray had bags all four days. By the last day he had amassed $76. I had gone up to the golf course the following weekend just in case there were any 'leftover' loops – there weren't. He got paid off around 3:30, I knew he felt bad for me being almost shut out of making any real money. The recent excursion had left my wallet on 'E'.

He was still watching out for me, and he was always in that communist frame of mind: "What's mine is yours". Ray was concerned with my psychological state. In the caddy yard as we were just about to head home, he looked at me, "Hey I got these tickets for

the Schaefer Music Festival in Central Park on Wednesday night;
Sally, Loki, Sue Herr and me. Loki might not be able to make it – he's
got to help his father switch out their water heater. His dad's going to
do the plumbing, Loki's just the muscle to bring the new one down and
the old one out. Even if he is able to go – we should be able to score a
single ticket outside. No assigned seating: once you're in you'll be
with us."
 "Who's the headline?"
 "Delaney and Bonnie."
 "Who's the first band?"
 "Seals and Crofts." Ray said.
 The two bands starting to get airplay on the FM dial, but
majority of broadening fan base was from concerts, record sales, and
word of mouth; similar to the Allman Brothers path.
 "Yeah, I'll go if Loki can't make it."
 "You might even get lucky with Sue Herr.

iii

 The days of hunting rats at the city incinerator and playing
school basketball had brought me and Vinny Tartaglione together. We
were good friends, and guided by the special relationship with our
older brothers. We were cognizant of a weird dynamic taking place
amongst the four of us. We had the possibility of conspiracy every
time we assembled. We'd plan heists, start rock bands, political
takeovers, take down drug lords. They were manic, and Vinny and me
could be talked into anything. There was a dynamic going on I was
unable to define, but it was obvious to Vinny and me it was due to our
older brothers.
 Joey had three years on his brother Vinny, Ray was a year-
and-a-half older than me. It was different for us: they had this 'wild
card' vibe, they were spellbound in their magnetic pole reversed world.
Conventional reality didn't have the force to make them deal with the
everyday. They fed us their interpretation of the "Big Picture". I
bought Rays bullcrap hook, line, and sinker. For Vince it was more of
a 'leap of faith' with brother Joe being a full-time junkman. It was
harder for him to buy into the Joey school of career guidance.
 Joey and Ray had this weird relationship which seemed to be
guided by some basic scientific principles: likes repel/opposites attract.
I believe they intentionally avoided one another, but if they ran into
each other by chance – that was fine. They went through all this
bullshit as if they were communicating in a language which wasn't
voice based. When they got together, they'd go into all this nonsense.
Ray was charting the stars in the cosmos and Joey was building the
warp drive and spacecraft to get them there.
 Fate or destiny or some unknown sequence of events had
wired their electro/mechanical thought process to function in a newly
configured magnetic world - yet to be fully engaged. They weren't
friends, but there was continuity between them, something more of a
business relationship. Of course, there was nothing between them

when Joey was on the nod or trying to get the materials to get there. With Vinny and me, our friendship was based on loyalty, a recklessness of life, going against the grain, and our common past. To a certain extent; it was emotional. Joey and Ray's thing was predicated on raw data and the application of the same.

After the comet blazed up the Hudson, it may have affected the 5th dimension junkies but not in any overt manner at the time. It was more as if the seed had been planted, and come what may. The ghost junkies belonged to a future realigned magnetic inverted world long dormant. The pole inversion made them progressively self-aware of their place on this earth and in this universe, though it ill-suited them. They had to wait; the world they knew was in the process of transmutation. Thus, they'd rid themselves of the reality Vince and I knew – primarily through chemical deadening. Joe speculated that intense or extreme emotion might actually do an "internal job" and get better results; none of the 5th dimension went down that road – especially Joe. Later on, Ray likened their experience to being on 'death row' with innocent men who had run out of stays and appeals.

It was pointless trying to grasp the "why" without the intellectual capacity to convert the Greystone Bridge Equation into some digestive logic for the unpolarized person. We had to accept the interpretations from Ray and the 5th dimension at their word. We had no 'Rosetta Stone' – just a bloodline. It said Vince and me were part of it all in a twisted way. What we couldn't square up was guys like Kenny Crawford automatically comprehending different sections of the equation. Sometimes it was hell just watching Cocaine Wayne, Rickshaw, and Ronnie Zanzibar searching for the emergency exit to reach the passageway to the other side of the magnetic divide.

iv

It was looking as if the night in Stony Brook was going to be the high water mark for the summer. I took my brother up on his offer to go down to the Schaefer Music Festival, with or without a ticket. Loki called Ray and said they got the water heater in, but now his old man had a line on a used set of wheels and he wanted him to check them out; he'd need them to commute to college in the fall. Loki would let him know if he could make the concert.

We met down the End, Ray had handled all the logistics. It didn't sound like Loki was going to go. Sally Englund was hanging around with Ray more and more. We spotted her in the shotgun seat of a '65 Plymouth Fury in the parking lot.

I turned to Ray, "Who's that driving?"

"That's Sue Herr........one of Sally's friends." he replied.

"Yeah, she was at Ranger Rick's party."

Sally got out of the car, and gave Ray a bear hug and a big kiss. I turned away. I took Sally's spot up front, and the love birds hopped in the back. "Is that it?" Ray said.

"Joey Tarts is coming with us." She motioned with her head over to the parking lot's phone booth.

"I'm going to get a quart of port at Harmonie." I buzzed out. When I got back, Joey was sitting in the shotgun seat.

Alright I thought, Ray said I might connect with Sue. Maybe I was just a tag along out of sympathy because Ray felt bad I hadn't made much money during the club tournament. Still, I felt like a fifth wheel.

Sue looked at me in the back seat, "Hey let me see your bald spot......your brother says you're missing some hair."

"Sue! you're cruel." Sally said.

We were sitting caddy-corner from each other so I had to turn almost 180 degrees and push the comb-over out of the way. "Happy?"

"Ughhh."

"That's enough Sue." Ray said.

Sue Herr was the same age as Ray and Sally, but she had wheels, so she was light years ahead of everybody else in the Fury. I was going give her some shit about her name.... came close, but I let it slide. With a name like that – once you met her, you knew her for good or ill. She was better than average to look at. Her hair was straight and brown; she had it up in the back with some kind of leather piece and a quarter inch dowel holding it in place. When she let it down it was pretty long.

"We got to stop on Lawrence St. on the way down. Somebody owes me money down there. It'll be just a couple of minutes." Big Tarts directed Sue.

Ray looked at me.

Sally was the aggressor and had Ray in the corner behind Sue. They were carrying on, and I don't think either was high on anything. Still, I didn't like the way this adventure was starting off. There seemed to be an abundance of 'otherside' energy.

Joey had Sue double-park: "Be right back."

We had our doubts. Tarts Sr. had little regard for punctuality, or time for that matter. He bolted from the car into an old run-down apartment, and returned just as quickly. He called to me from the sidewalk: "Hey 'Lil Ray."

That 'Lil Ray' crap pissed me off, he knew me for at least eight years.

"Let me ride in the back with Sally and your brother."

"He had the seniority, and when my mind started working again I figured it was where I wanted to be anyway – next to Sue, even though she gave me the business about my missing hair.

She smiled, "Hi stranger."

"Sue, pull alongside Van Cortland Park.....as close as you can get to the 242nd St. subway." Ray said.

"Ray – one more quick stop." Joey scratched his nose. "We got time."

I didn't know if Joey was telling or asking Ray. He had Sue drive into a small parking lot on the west side of Broadway. The building's signage said it had been an architectural /engineering firm. It appeared it had been vacant for a while. In the rear of the building there was a loading dock and a 30 ft. section of overhang protecting deliveries. The Bronx was crowded, eyes were always watching. Joey had enough savvy not to use the same place twice.

"Circle around the lot, his eyes darted back and forth. "Don't park under the overhang. Park in the back.......where them overgrown trees are."

Ray told me to get out of the Plymouth, and watch for the bulls or anybody. I wondered what was going on. Nothing was out of the ordinary except us. As soon as I got out, Joey and Sally were assembling their works and bags of smack. Now, I knew why Joey had Sue make the stop on Lawrence St. The throng was mesmerized – anticipating blasting off and going into orbit. I shook my head........Ray wasn't going to shoot up? Was he? I would have to prevent that. I had to look up to Ray – hitting up some dooge - I wouldn't be able to trust anything he told me, if he was one of the people he railed against. I circled back to the car and   leaned against the front passenger fender; watching the lot, and the busy people in the car. There was a lot of yelling in the car, except for Ray who had his eyes closed grinning. Joey and the two girls were going to get off, Ray wasn't, he moved up to the front seat.

Watching for cops and dog walkers was impossible; the activity in the Fury was as captivating as viewing my first 16mm reel hardcore porn – I couldn't look away. The girls each had a set of works in their ditty bags. Sue gave Ray a spoon and a lighter. Joey gave Ray three bags of smack.

"Ray, take the shit – divide it in half. Sue gets a half a bag. Sally gets a whole bag and I get the rest.....bag-and-a-half. Up their left sleeves went and the makeshift tourniquet was pulled tight. It choked off the circulation.

"Blastin' out of orbit." Ray said.

My eyes strained to absorb the spectacle inside the car: three anti-matter magneto people, and one chick who was just getting high. My brother sported these lightly shaded wire rim glasses – half for dimming – half for fashion. I watched him instead of the others. It was the same transmuted person I had seen writing formula, stopping electric powered commuter trains, and undergoing a life changing event when a fireball streamed north raining ashes on us. Now, it was also someone who was transfixed and absorbed by the task at hand..........the mad scientist he had become. Months ago he had concluded the smack had a weird aphrodisiac component to it – but for women only. A dude would be so high he couldn't get it up, keep it up, or get it to shoot. Sally loved the junk more than Ray, but she loved him because of his incredible staying power. Years later, he told me she had him fuck her for four hours one night. She had ten orgasms to his one. After their first marathon session he had to keep a tube of lube nearby. Their first long distance episode had given his love muscle a case of road rash. That summer Ray lost over ten pounds and Sally's ass found it. He really loved banging that girl.

She liked being the boss......in command. She knew what she wanted and how to get it. Her family had money, and she was talking this shit about going to Brown University like her older sister when she graduated next June. Bottom line for Ray; he didn't think she could do more with her life other than what she was currently doing: she knew how to get high and get fucked.

A small bottle of water, a small diameter rubber vacuum hose, a spoon, a lighter, two rigs (the spare was in Sally's purse, she tried to always have a spare in case she had to get high with someone she didn't like and might carry some disease.) and three bags of transportation powder. Ray cooked up the shit. Joey watched the ingredients breakdown into a watery milk solution. "That's good." His eyes went wide and he loaded the syringe through the cotton filter. Sally had boosted the rig from her doctor's office. It was new sharp. The needle went vertical and he gave the syringe several knocks and pushed the plunger to expel the air. Joey gave the hypo to Sally and made a fist. She flicked the vein a couple of times, and slid it in. The blood backed into the plastic vial. He released the rubber hose, and operated the rig like a veteran.

He booted it in and out a couple of times as he looked at his arm and up to the car's ceiling. Next, Ray cooked up Sue's portion, she was all fidgety as she glanced at me, then back to Joe.

"You're on Sue." he said. She used the same cotton, and drew up the feel good formula into the rig. She held the loaded syringe in her bite, as she worked on getting her vein to rise a little more. It was good enough.

"Do me Dr. Ray." She smiled never looking at him.

Almost parallel to her forearm, Ray injected her mainline like an expert. Then Sue took over and pushed the plunger slow but steady until all the dope disappeared in her arm. Her face went flush and there were beads of sweat on her forehead and upper lip.

"Gimme it.........Come on." Sally was sick of waiting.

"Ray – give me the port on the floor." I called. He handed me the bottle out the window. I needed a charge to watch the three ring circus.

Ray emptied the rest of the dope in the spoon. A twist off bottle cap was used for a cleaning pool for Sue's rig. Joey continued to boot what was left in his syringe trying to maximize the amount of rushes he could extract from the smack. Sue's chin was on her chest and she started nodding. Ray filled the hypo with water and cleaned it by gushing the water onto the asphalt. He did it twice unaware it was a waste of time. Still, the act made most junkies feel like they weren't injecting someone else's diseases into their bodies.

Sally and Ray prepared the rest of the dooge. He gave her the spike and he put the small wad of cotton back in the spoon. She was ready to draw it up and Joey kicked the front bench seat.

"Hey you fuckin retard!" Ray just barely saved Sally's hit.

He never heard Ray or anyone else. "Fuck that no good Layton – Fuckin bullshit! Same beat shit as he had last time. What do I got to do to get a true bag......Fuckin Bullshit man......fuckin bullshit."

Sally never heard Joey – even though he was right next to her. She had Sue's works primed and loaded. "Ray.....do me." He up ended the rig and flicked it for air. It was all formula. Ray reached over the back seat, and shot Sally up. Joey was looking out the window

biting his thumbnail, "Fuckin bullshit man......fuckin bullshit."
Layton had let him down.....again.

I got back in the shotgun seat, and Sally released the vacuum
hose, two small boots, she took a breath and then sent the motherlode
in and emptied the syringe with a smooth push of the plunger. Her
head rolled back then forward, then snapped back. "Oh Fuck." she
whispered and her head slumped down.

"Push her over......you drive Ryan." Joey ordered. Ray and
me were only a couple of miles away from the 'L'. These three were a
solar system away. About ¾ of the port remained. We didn't have any
reefer so it was going to be a liquid concert.

From this vacant lot, to the short drive back to Van Cortland
Park/242nd St. subway, I realized I could have landed in some heavy
duty trouble with the law if we had gotten caught. The dope was now
in their bodies, but they still had their works in their possession. It was
a stone's throw away legally. Joey must have gotten a bag that had
been stepped on because Sue and Sally had full blown cases of
nodding out. Seeing them, Joey was in total meltdown.

"There's a space." Ray pointed to the other side of the street.

I was ready to make a U-turn and Joey instructs me to keep
driving south on Broadway.

Ray looked over to Joey Tarts: "What's up?"

"I know where there is a beer distributor – we'll get a case."

The next thing I know he's got me in the south Bronx down
by the stadium and we're headed for Manhattan via the Willis Ave.
Bridge. Now we're in Spanish Harlem: "Just go down here.....take a
left one more street over.....aaaay – this ain't it.....go up that one-way
just a little ways."

"Turn the radio on." Sue slurred.

"It is on - you retard." Harlem didn't scare me. The Shadow
people did - with their drug injection equipment, and barking orders as
if I was a taxi driver.

"Babe – you love me?" Sally put her head on Ray's shoulder.

That was it. I had enough as Ray stroked her hair. Two
blocks west I could see the IRT elevated trestle at 125th St. I brought
the Fury curbside and got out, "Come on Ray."

He played tug-of-war with Sally; she was content to nod in
the car with Sue. Ray finally dragged her out, and we pulled her to the
subway, and dragged her up the 'L' steps grasping her belt on each
side. Both of us were out of breath when we reached the turnstiles.

"You got any of that port left brother?" Ray hoped.

"Sonabitch.....it's in the car. There was less than a pint left.
Fuckit." I hissed.

"We'll find a liquor store down there." We dropped the
subway tokens in the turnstile, and climbed a few more steps with
Sally in tow to the downtown side of the platform. An Ike Turner lookalike approached us and asked if we were looking for some dynamite
weed or anything else.

"Whatcha got?"

"Some ELLLL...SSSS....DEEE. Good trips – pretty colors."
he smiled.

"What's it like?" Ray said.

"The opposite of that." Ike motioned with his head to Sally slumped on the bench.

I had to get a bottle of something for the concert, Ray drank half the port, and so far this was a groove-less excursion since we left. Acid? Heard a lot of stories about the stuff; some good.....some not so good. Once again I'd have to rely on Ray on the way to proceed.

He asked the soul brother, "What's this version like sunshine or window pain?"

"It all the same. The hippies just mix it up when they sell it: different color tabs, put a smile face on 'em. Give it different names: window pain, orange sunshine, blue barrels, micro dot, blotter acid. Sell better when you call it something stupid. Couple of white boys manafacture it over at Columbia. Only thing that matter is the size of the droplet they lay on the tab or paper – that's all. This shit's real – not that jive ass shit they sell down the village or Central Park to them weekend hippies.

"How much?"

"Seven for two." He looked over towards Sally. "This ride will bring her back from wherever she is. Then you don't haff to carry her ass around. Even NYC cops don't go for that.... Gimme nine – I'll give you three hits."

A train was coming. Ray pulled ten dollars from his front pocket. Ike pulled a yellow pharmacy bottle came from a vest pocket. He steadied himself against a steel column as he counted out three. It looked like he had a hundred in the plastic bottle.

"What's the dosage for this shit?" Ray handed him the money.

"I don't mess with that electric shit – I'm like Con Edison ......I just sell it."

We wondered what we had gotten into. "Come on Witchcraft." Ray said, as we helped her onto the subway car. We soon descended under Manhattan. He tore off a small piece of an abandoned Daily News and folded up the three tabs of acid in it.

"You ever take a trip?" I looked at him.

"I did some mescaline with Loki and John Dunbar. We went down the Fillmore to see Freddie King."

"LSD is man-made.......different shit." I said.

"Yeah, that's one thing, another is I might have bought St. Joseph aspirin for children."

I almost had to shout to be heard over the noise of the subway: "Full tab? Half? ¾'s?"

"Columbus Circle is the next stop, We'll decide when we get above ground......I can't think or hear down here. Sally was only slightly more ambulatory as we made our ascent; still, we were out of breath. We rested on a granite planter in front of an office building. Music from the Wollman Skating Rink in Central Park could be faintly heard - there must have been a slight east breeze and the music bounced off the buildings.

"Ray I got to go to the liquor store and get some wine."

"Don't need wine – we got acid." Sally was leaning against him.

"Still got to wash it down with something......and maybe you did buy children's aspirin."

"Just hurry up."

I came back about ten minutes later with a paper bag in my hand and they were making out. 'What the fuck?' I looked at these two, and motioned: "What's up?"

His hand replied with an open palm. I interrupted Sally's insatiable desire for Ray whenever she was junked up.

"I had to get this thing going in the right direction: "Let's Pahhhhteeee." Like I was a jerk from Boston with a great big smile.

"Whadja get?" He reached into the bag and pulled out one of those mini-bottles of champagne they give you at the hotels......not even a pint. He looked at the three bottles.

"You're kidding.....?" He shook his head and rolled his eyes.

"This ain't Yonkers Ray – they don't sell street wine up here – not 'til you get around 42nd St. - that's about a half mile."

"Champagne?............Champagne?........You better hope the acid ain't beat."

"It was the only thing I could afford – it was on sale....a buck a bottle, one for each of us."

"Bon Voyage," He twisted off the cap from the bottle and took a sip: "For the love of fuck Ryan........it's turpentine." He got the tabs of acid out and washed his down, and handed me one.

"I'm with you squadron leader.......I tried a sip of the bubbly, "Ain't so bad." I was thinking and praying to St. Joseph: I hoped this was his aspirin and not that mind bending acid shit. There were tons of stories about kids flipping out.

"The acid wasn't bad – it was more the rookies weren't ready to take a psychedelic trip." Vinny Tarts said more than once.

I looked over to Ray: "We got tickets for the late show...... right?"

He nodded back at me as her head slipped off his shoulder once again. We knew the walk over to the skating rink in Central Park could only be beneficial for Sally, but we had to get her going in that direction. The initial rush where a minute is a lifetime was left in Sue Herr's car. The only thing the dope was doing now was keeping her in a stupor. We had to get her moving. I wanted Ray to give her the remaining tab of electricity, but it wasn't Ray's style - too much risk. Ray knew she needed to walk and get her blood flowing through the liver to metabolize and detoxify the smack in her bloodstream. How could Sue and her get so blasted and Joey Tarts seemed as crisp as a new $2.00 bill?

Ray was a proponent of the theory you could walk yourself sober, he and Loki had done it countless number of times entertaining all sorts of chemicals in their brains, but mostly reefer and alcohol as they walked to and from anywhere in a seven mile radius. They liked going down to Greenwich village, drink at 'McSorely's' or Malachy Mc Court's 'Hell's Bells' and walk up to midtown and either catch a

the subway to 242nd St. or the Penn Central at Grand Central Station
back to Yonkers.

WE WEREN'T THE ONLY ONES IN THE FAMILY TO
USE Manhattan as a playground. My sister Cathy related the story of
Jane getting blitzed with a couple of her friends while she went to see
the musical "42ndSt." Cathy was playing the lead on Broadway in the
1980's. They went for drinks after the show, Jane got roaring because
she was so proud, and when it was time to go home, they went to
Grand Central to take the train back to Greystone. The entrance on the
north side of G.C.T. goes through the Pan Am building, and there are
stairs and escalators to access the terminal's main floor approximately
two or three floors below. In between the escalators, is a stainless steel
sliding pond. Usually there is some architectural safety feature which
defeats any thought of taking a ride down. This safety device is similar
to a stainless steel round disc attached to the stainless sheet metal at
three strategic elevations negating any attempt of going for a ride. At
the bottom of the escalators is a nice hard floor of terrazzo.

There were no such obstacles or safety devices fixed to the
stainless slide at that time.

My sister, and Jane's two friends, Judy and Lydia, were
going down the escalator as Jane flew by them screaming: "MY
DAUGHTER'S ON BROADWAY!" doing near 30 m.p.h. The people
at the terminal's floor parted like the Red Sea when they saw this out
of control mop of auburn hair wildly waving her arms coming at them.
She took flight when she ran out of sheet metal, and crashed beneath a
closed ticket counter some 40 yards away.

The blue coats were going to write her up for something;
they had her in their holding cage until she used Uncle Bill's name
(who had his gold shield by that time). They were going to throw her
in jail for the stupid antic. My sister and Jane's friends assured the
cops they would get her back to Yonkers safely.

IF I HAD MY WAY, SALLY WOULD TAKE THE 3RD
HIT, AND she'd be on the Hudson line going north. It was Ray's
decision; we grabbed hold of her and encouraged her to try to walk,
but we mostly wore out the toes of her shoes dragging her towards the
music. If this had been Yonkers, there wouldn't have been any way to
drag her sorry ass around with all the hills. She was lucky N.Y.C. was
flat. By the time we made it to the park entrance, I was positive he
should have force fed her the acid.

"I'll hold her up.......put my sunglasses on her. Her eyes are
bad." He was sweating and so was I. Security gave us the once over –
twice. Ray put a concerned face on, "She's have having a tough time
with the heat. We get her a seat.......she'll be alright. Riding the
subway didn't help."

"Get her a cold beer when you get in – that should help." the
security guy said.

Just before we sat down – her legs started working. Ray held
her hand and they walked the last 20 feet. The psychedelics still hadn't
kicked in yet. The smell of pot and patchouli filled the rink. Sally

agreed to do half a hit if we would get her a beer or soda. We found her a seat in the bleachers about 8 rows up. It was still pretty hot, but there was an occasional breeze from the east.

When a corporate entity underwrote or gave sponsorship to something like a musical event; in this case The Schaefer Music Festival in Central Park, it was generally understood aside from certain negotiated costs and expenditures, the brewer would sell their product at a nominal profit to the concert goers. A patron could actually get drunk and not end up in the poorhouse – similar to the way they operated at the World's Fair. The drawback at the Wollman skating rink was access to the concessions between acts. They would only let you buy four beers in a pressed cardboard 'party tray' at a time. In 1970 that meant: four-14 oz. beers for $4.00. General admission: $2.50. They had concerts 3 or four nights a week, with early and late shows from June through Labor Day weekend. What a deal......in New York City!

We passed a beer up to Sally, she got about 11 oz. by the time it reached her. She was glazed. A dollar bill was folded into a square with a half a tab of fun inside. Ray used sign language to place it on her tongue and wash it down. He asked a girl to pass it up to the girl who got the beer. Sally tried to stand up and reach over, but she fell back; her butt was guided back down by a couple of well wishers. I thought she was going to lose the acid, but she didn't. I saw it on her tongue before she washed it down. Maybe things were starting to go our way. She waved to Ray, he gave her a thumbs up, and called: "Atta girl. We'll get you after the first band." She gave him an okay with her the thumb and forefinger. The house music stopped, and the stage got as dark as the sunset allowed.

Some executive director of something said she was proud "To welcome T.A. Records recording artists – Seals and Crofts." Half-way through their set Ray asked for another bottle of turpentine. "It's been over an hour........I don't think we got acid from that guy. You feeling anything?" he asked.

"Just from the Cham-pain........not the window pain." I didn't want Ray to know how relieved I was we had gotten beat and he had probably bought aspirin. Drinking, smoking reefer or hash – that was good enough for me. We kept on the move in the rink and watched and listened. The security people would chase you to the back of the rink if people started collecting in the aisle, they said it was a safety issue. We went from one side to the other, from the front to the back aimlessly. Checking on Sally two or three times; elbows on knees – fists supporting her chin. She smiled with her eyes closed in that position for the duration of the set.

The vast majority of the crowd were teenagers and younger adults. In between bands, they rushed to the bathrooms and to the concession stands. Ray had to climb the bleachers and get Sally, they had turned the house music up and she didn't hear us calling her.

"Ryan and me got to piss, you come with us. Get on line to buy some beer. We'll be done before they serve you." I looked at her, she looked like she was in the next century. "Ray, why don't I wait with Penny Robinson here – then we'll switch off when you get back.?"

"Listen Sweetheart, lean up against this fence right here and don't go anywhere until me and Ryan come back to get you. Okay?"

"Put her on the concession line for beer – what's the difference?" I raised my brow.

"Nah, leaning against the fence is a challenge for her right now."

When we returned beer-less, I took the sunglasses off and put them in her handbag. Delaney and Bonnie were tuning up, and a radio dee-jay made the introduction. The husband and wife duo entered the stage from different sides of the drummer's riser, and went to their respective microphones. The band and the duo had a lot of energy and everybody was on their feet for the first number. Three songs into their set, Delaney said it was great to be back in N.Y. He then introduced his special guest on lead and slide guitar: Duane Allman. "Duane's band has been around N.Y. playing up a storm."

Duane jumped in: "Maybe some of you caught us out on Long Island a couple of weeks ago."

Delaney came back: "If y'all get a chance catch 'em…..The Allman Brothers are on fire!" Delaney Bramlett made a big deal of Duane all night long.

I thought they were having sound problems; echo was coming from all directions. As we stood in the back of the rink, I could see the band playing instruments and singing, but what I was experiencing was like viewing a film where the audio and visual are not synchronized. I looked over at Ray and he was doing the Sally routine: eyes closed and groovin' to the music. Sally Englund was having something of a religious experience or close to it I thought. Not much of this was making sense.

The crowd's noise was overwhelming at the conclusion of the song. "Ray"…… I yelled, "What's going on?" Sally and Ray started laughing. Delaney and Bonnie went into their FM – hit tune: 'Soul Shake' "Dooooooooo…do do do …..do do do ….do…do…do… do.do.doo – intro. Bonnie was wearing purple velvet bell bottoms and matching top. She wasn't pretty, but she sure was sexy.

I hadn't been on the concert circuit long, but this was the most confused event I had been exposed to. Large bubbles filled with smoke danced in the air above the rink. A man wearing a business suit and Nixon mask walked the division aisles with his arms in the air waving the 'V' for victory. The mask's nose was exaggerated and on closer examination it I believe it was a dick. A scantily dressed Mrs. Uncle Sam would suck on it and 'Tricky Dick Nixon' would take a bow.

When the band finished "Soul Shake" they followed immediately with "Living on the Open Road", the rink seemed to explode with energy. I had to talk with Ray when the song finished; I wanted to keep the benign confusion going but something wasn't right. There was no use trying to understand the flow – hysteria seemed to be in charge. A glance over toward Sally: her eyes transformed from glazed to a starlight bright. I rapidly shook my head from side to side,

"Wooooooo". I blew out in disbelief. Grabbing a hold of my brother's arm: "Ray – This is real close to the world I went to on the other side those two times when I fucked with the ashes of the comet. But I'm not there......I'm here in Central Park.......am I not?"

"Be kool Ryan......be kool. I didn't want to send you off on a bummer – a bad trip. We got off on that acid." he smiled. "You're on a psychedelic trip, but you're doing good man.....you're doing good."

"Huh?"

"I don't know why there was such a delayed reaction for it to kick in." Ray may have thought about the reason.

"You mean we're trippin'?" It was obvious to me my respiration and blood pressure began to rise, and I started getting hyper. He handed me $4.00 and told me to get a quad tray of beer. The alcohol wasn't going to have any power to override any of the LSD's powerful effects, but Ray wanted me to think it might.

When I returned from my private trip, Delaney was talking about this guy who had an apartment on Central Park south and how kool it would be if he was listening in to the music and came down and jammed with them and Duane – it would rock the rink. Being as high as we were, we thought it might be Eric Clapton because they had written some songs together and he had played with Delaney and Bonnie on a couple of tours recently. It didn't happen.

The guy they brought in to jam with them was this jazz cat: Herbie Mann. One of the guys working the spotlights focused his beam on an apartment window and the essence of Herbie Mann was supposedly transported on the beam delivering him to the stage, only he strutted in from stage left carrying his flute. Even I wasn't screwed up enough to buy that bullshit. Nothing like a flute to put the brakes on a smokin' rock and roll show. It was 10:30 and Herbie's soloing away on that song 'Push-Push' for around ten minutes. Half of the crowd headed for the gates. We stayed until it was over, but I don't know what for.

We rode the train up to Greystone. As the local pulled away, Sally and Ray walked down the platform and towards the station: "You coming?" he said.

"Little bit." I replied.

"Right." He knew what I was up to.

I crossed at track level, and found the buried meteorite waiting. The ground was warm as usual. To be this alert and wide awake wasn't what I wanted. On my back I slithered and dug into the sand; there were weeds and tufts of grass all around me as I watched the night sky. I was still tripping, but hadn't hallucinated since we got on the train, the peak was long over but I was still high. I know I had zoned out, but hadn't fallen asleep. The Tappan Zee and the George Washington were still lit, they hadn't vaporized in some post-psychedelic trip. The acid wasn't what I had expected, it wasn't bad, but now I fully understood how people could do stupid shit while under the drug's influence.

Ray had fallen asleep in the cellar. "Ryan." He whispered as I entered in the darkness.

"Yeah ?"

"Sally's in my bed......I'm going to the golf course in a little while. Walk her up to the North End, but make sure Hal has already left for work...."

"Right. How do you feel?" I spoke low.

"Depleted........not with it. When the sun comes up it'll be worse. How 'bout you?"

"Aaaaay – half and half I guess. Don't worry, I'll get her up there."

v

There were four universities Ray applied to in the fall. Hal told him he could only afford state college tuition; anywhere else meant loans, grants, work study, a scholarship or any combination. I went back to Latin III with Cicero and the orations, and the cross country team. Early winter, the teachers went on strike and walked the picket line. In the Spring of '71 the black students went on strike also, not many people including most of the black kids, knew what the strike was about. Bathrooms were vandalized, fires were set in vacant lockers, false fire alarms were pulled, and there was chaos in many of the classes as the malcontents aired their grievances deviating from the intended course study.

What was the bitch about? We'd ask some of the brothers the $64 question and they either wouldn't say or didn't know. Everybody had an individual gripe, or a bitch about a particular teacher. The same could be said for all the groups within the walls of Gorton H.S. The black students running the strike all wanted to be the next H. Rap Brown or Stokely Carmichael. It was a fairly chaotic spring.

The Superintendent of Schools cancelled classes for a number of days because of fights, fires, and sit-ins. The showdown came when a Brazilian immigrant, Tomas Grecas. - a top prospect for athletic scholarship because he could toss a discus and a javelin - had already missed two head-on track and field meets because of the school closings. No class – no sports was the athletic code. The track and field team was now looking at forfeiting the city wide meet because of the mess.

The Phys. Ed. Department Chairman asked the Principal to open the school and direct all students to the auditorium for an assembly and they would "clear the air". If something backfired, and the students' safety was put in jeopardy, the responsibility would fall squarely on the Principal and the Phys. Ed. Dept.

Coaches Fuentes, Jackson, and Del Vecchio were on stage at the mike explaining the situation. Unless these boys were allowed to participate in the city-wide meet, they would have little chance to be evaluated by the college scouts.

"Awww fuck them." One of the troublemakers shouted. The small group intent on keeping the school closed had gathered just in front of the stage to get to the mike and say their piece. Their spokesmen were Freddie Niles and Dante' Hooks, with their gang of eight all around them. Hooks bulldogged his way to the mike. He was

402

talking about hypothetical situations that didn't exist and read from the Socialist Workers' Party newspapers. He soon got drowned out in a sea of boos and cat calls.

Niles on the other hand was trying to incite a physical altercation right there in the assembly. "I……..me ….
….Freddie Niles am shutting down this Jim Crow Gorton High School right motherfuckin' now! Y'all get the fuck out!" There was silence – nobody moved. "An……and….. I got my boys here to back me up." He crossed his arms on his chest and looked side to side, "Now that's that."

It was damn near theatre of the absurd. There was a spontaneous burst of laughter: first, from the track team and then the student body joined them.

Niles yelled into the microphone on the podium: "Fuck you coach, and all you stupid honkie ass track team." More laughter.

Coach Jackson went over to the podium and Niles stood to the side. He looked over at Freddie. "I am black, and 50% of the track team is black. As of today, you have missed 54 days of school. What's not right, is…….you cheated Freddie Niles out of an education and maybe his diploma.

He grabbed the free mike, "They ain't shit. I run faster than Roscoe Clark in the motherfuckin hunrid. You runnin' track for one reason -" he said as he looked at the members of the track team: "For you onliest wannabe cracker selfs. Now you bess listen good: I, me, Freddie Niles will burn down this no good motherfuckin' Gorton High if we don't get our grievances addressed. An all you Phys. Ed. motherfuckers can kiss my black ass – with shit in it."

Again, everyone laughed at his tirade. The track team formed a semi-circle around the malcontents from both sides of the stage. The Brazilian, Tomas Grecas approached Niles and took the microphone and gave it to Coach Jackson. Now you could hear a pin drop. Tomas went to the microphone at the podium; looked at the troublemakers, the track team and coaches, and finally the assembly. With his Portuguese accent he said: "For the record……I play for the honor and pride of the Gorton Wolves – not for myself. The fact that I excel at javelin and discus are the result of hard work, practice, and dedication." He turned from the podium and went back and stood with the team.

The student body got up from their seats and cheered as the malcontents held their noses, gave a thumbs down, and waved them off. Grecas went back to the podium to even louder cheers: "P.S. Freddie – I am sure a match race between you and Roscoe can be scheduled when you feel you are ready. I know Roscoe has trained hard for the city meet, so if you are ready right now, let's go out to the track."

As Tomas stepped away, Freddie tried to sucker punch him. The Brazilian was lightning fast and caught his fist with his hand and started squeezing. He fell to his knees screeching in pain. "And we all go back to class…….right Niles?" Tomas increased his crushing power on Freddie's crumbled hand, "Right Niles?"

403

"Yeah....Yeah.....Yeah." he cried. "Let me go you fuckin' gorilla."

"Say it to the student body Niles......Tell them your issues have been resolved, and we all can go back to class. And you will help to end the fires, false alarms, and other nonsense that has been going on......Say it." Tomas raised his voice. We knew he was all done being polite and gave him the mike.

"Y'all heard Tomas – School back in session......to the cheers of the assembly. Freddie Niles' small cadre of 8 (5 blacks, 2 white communists, and one dumb teacher) looked at the floor in shame and defeat. They were all suspended, Freddie was arrested for threatening to burn down the school, and the stupid teacher was fired. The commotion was over.

Tomas Grecas ended up at Princeton University and later became an assistant U.S. Attorney for the southern district of New York.

vi

The date was January 23 1971. I was playing bumper pool, with Joe Griffin's younger brother, Tony, in Copies', down the End. It was a Saturday around 4:00, Tony looked kool in some battle fatigues his brother had gotten from an ARVN conscript.

"C'mon Tony, sell me the shirt..." I shot and missed.

He laughed, "We'll be able to get our own soon enough."

Bad Brad Guzzutti's older brother and Frankie McPhearson were at the bar. Fran was tending bar.

Tony and me were just hanging out, killing time. Maybe somebody would have a car or reefer or both. The third week of January, you could almost say the daylight was getting stronger and longer. It was still too cold to try and stay out and drink a six pack. The weather forced you into somebody's car, house, or Copies.

It was 50 cents for a tap beer of Schaefer. I was too poor to get drunk there but had enough money to get warmed up. Copies back room was pretty small; he stuck a bumper pool table back there and made it even smaller. A couple of guys walked in and didn't order anything, and walked in the back when they saw us shooting pool.

"Hey Little Whitesox..."

I kept on my shot aiming my cue stick, "What?" I struck the cue ball and a red ball went down the hole.

"Where's your brother?"

"With silly Sally." I still didn't look at the guy and lined up my next shot.

"Zee got anyding going tanite?"

I knew it was Sal Del Bene, "Think he's going with Rikshaw and one of the O'Rourke's tonight......don't know what they got going." I missed and looked up. 'Half-court Pete' was with Sal. We called him 'Half-court' not because he drank Tall Boys which was what everyone who just met him thought. He got the handle from

404

sinking a shot against All Souls from half-court with no time left and gave Christ the King the upset victory.

"You and Ray went and seen Delaney and Bonnie last year." Benny said.

We put our cue sticks on end, "Yeah down Central Park."

"One of 'em die?" Tony took a sip of beer.

"Nah – Nah.....Why are you such a downer Griff?" Benny continued, "They're playing tanite. We got some tickets. A couple of guys were going ta bring dates......but the girls don't like Bonnie. Long story short – me and Pete got four extra tickets. Starts at 8:00."

"I'll call up and see if Ray is home." I pushed a dime across the bar. GR-6-5707. Fran dialed and handed me the receiver. The three of them were talking about Delaney and Bonnie while I was on the phone. "He ain't there." And I handed the phone back to her.

Sal asked, "Tony – you or Ryan want to go?"

"How much?"

"$4.50 each."

"That's why you can't unload them." I said.

"Tell me about it."

"They playing at the Fillmore?"

"No...no Fillmore." Benny knew staying away from lower Manhattan was a plus.

"They're playing at the Capitol." Pete rushed.

"Jersey's even worse."

"No – the Capitol Theatre in Port Chester." Benny said.

"That ain't far at all." Tony said. He turned to me, "You saw them last summer......any good?"

"Can't really say – I was all screwed up." I closed my eyes tight - wishing to forget the acid. "The band before them was pretty good."

Pete looked down at the bumper pool table; "You guys want to go? You'd be helping me out big time. I got to get rid of these tickets."

I didn't hang out with Tony too much, being with him in Copies was just a chance thing.

Tony told Pete Half-court, "I'll go, but I got no way to get there."

"I got the Impala, if you and Whiteslime go, you can ride with us."

Just because these guys were always a year or two older- I was always taking a ribbing from them and it usually came out on my last name. I even had to take it from guys I could whup with one hand, I just had to ignore it. "Pete, you know who else is on the bill?"

"I dunno, some band I never heard of brothers band."

"Chambers Brothers?" Tony offered.

"Nah....not them." Pete said as his face let us know he had heard the name, he just couldn't remember it.

Goofy Benny laughed, "The Smothers Brothers?"

Tony rolled his eyes and lit the cigarette he had behind his ear.

405

I winced my right eye and tilted my noggin......"The Allman Brothers?"

"Yeah....Yeah...that's it. I think they're the second band." Half-court said.

"Fuck yeah!.....Best band I ever seen. Vinny Tarts, George Holter and me seen them on Long Island last summer. This girl from Gorton took us - over the top. Smokin'. Them guys know their instruments, they can play." I gleamed.

Calling on short notice, I could only get a hold of Tarts. I called up Meris to see if she would be my date, but she wasn't home. Two other guys who we knew walked into Copies and got wrangled in by my testimony that this band was unlike any they had ever seen. "They are the real deal Neil."

Vinny had to break his standing date with his steady girlfriend. We picked him up in front of Progressive Pizza. He told us he had asked Stacey if she wanted to go. She didn't like it when we came back from Stony Brook with all this talk about the band we discovered. She didn't think he would break their date to go rock and rolling with me. Stacey was wrong. Vinny was in the doghouse for about a month.

The Port Chester Capitol was small; the acoustics were fantastic. It was essentially a mini-Fillmore with a lot more intimacy. So many of the old theatres weren't suited for live music; the sound would be bouncing off the plaster walls and ceiling. The acoustics were even worse for rock and roll.

Half-court's big '68 Impala parked within sight of the Capitol. There was even a liquor store a half a block away from the entrance. The Marine - Billy Van Nahl, Vince, and me made a bee line to the store. Billy got a half-pint of Jim Beam, Vince got a pint of Night Train, I got a pint of Wild Irish and we'd split a pint of port.....we didn't want to get drunk. It was winter and with all the coats and sweatshirts we had on, it was no problem sneaking in some hooch. Once again nobody had any pot.....another liquid concert. I found out when they were changing bands' equipment, Pete, Benny, and Tony had smoked some hash before they picked me up down the End. Nice guys.

The house was about ¾ full, and we had first row – balcony seats. I never had better seats for any concert or event than that night. The house m.c. made the introduction. As the band was not the headline act they didn't waste any time and got down to business to give us a sample of their sound. The layout of their set list was well conceived; blues to rock to jazz all tightly woven around a concept reclaiming ownership and the origin of this art form.....back where it all began. I was starting to figure it out; Cinzano and me had Meris to thank.

The Allmans were tight -in sync - sharp. Bandleader Duane limited his comments to announcing the name of the tune and composer. When a number required a change in tuning, it was done quickly; Duane would count off with the beat of the first bar of the tune. I had not recalled their musicianship being this formidable. They were well beyond journeyman. The guys from the North End were caught off-guard by their performance as well. A large portion of the audience was dumbfounded when they realized the majority of their set were instrumentals, except for the blues numbers.

Sal Del Bene, Vinny, and me were up rockin', reelin' and shakin' to one of their up tempo numbers, but we were the only ones. Most of the audience were stupified. One specific tune blew the roof off the building. It was an instrumental and defined the word "band" through its performance: the integration of the instrumentation, the breaks, the solos, the jams, there was a seamless flow, the guitar interplay between Duane Allman and Dicky Betts, the melody and harmony lines.................perfection. This 16 minute tour de force titled "In Memory of Elizabeth Reed" came to an abrupt finality; the crowd was shell shocked. The band was all smiles and waves. Duane looked up at Sal, Vinny, and me and pointed with his pic in hand: "Ahhh......they're getting it up there." He laughed and smiled.

When the Allman Brothers finished their set, we brought them back for two encores: one long song, and the second encore was a quick five minute number.

Delaney and Bonnie had Duane play two songs with them, but it didn't seem to increase the audience's interest. For me and Vinny Tarts, what we saw and heard could never be topped that night. It was a gift from the almighty on so many levels.

RAY HAD BEEN ON THE FILLMORE EAST'S MAILING LIST, and he left it on my desk in our room. Immediately I looked at the dates for the upcoming acts: March 11, 12, & 13. The Elvin Bishop Group, Johnny Winter, and extra added attraction: The Allman Brothers Band was the line-up. No matter what the flyer said, The Brothers got top billing.

The original three Rogues from the Stony Brook concert went to work on being there for one of the six shows. Holter was working on getting some hash or Thai stick. Vince was going to work out the logistics of how we were going to get down and back from the Fillmore. I was going to get the tickets and make sure we wouldn't get sold out. I was obligated to see if Meris could make the show with us. She was sitting in the cafeteria with Sarah Klein. They looked great – as usual, even for just going to school. Sarah had the edge, but I was learning to choose attitude and character over beauty.

I sat next to Sarah and across from Meris, "Hey you gals interested in catching the Allmans at the Fillmore: March 11, 12, or 13th ?" Can youse make it?"

"Don't say that Ryan........damn it.....Sarah and me are committed to go to Binghamton to look at the University on the 12th and 13th. Is Ray going?"

"Doubtful. He kind of likes the Grateful Dead --- that west coast stuff.

"Can't make it Ryan. They'll be in town this summer for sure. They'll be back at the Fillmore or down at the Schaefer Music Festival."

"Haven't you heard – Graham's closing the Fillmore in June."

"There's too much money involved, he can't walk away." Sarah said putting a forkful of mashed potatoes in her mouth.

"Just had to ask…..you are the one who turned me on…..to them." We smiled. Silence. I lightly pounded the table: "Got to run."

"Ryan….." she called.

I came back and whispered in her ear, "All you have to do is snap your fingers."

Word was getting around about the Allmans, pretty soon it was going to be a hard ticket to come by. The Music man record shop was a ticket outlet in Yonkers for the Fillmore: they only had single seats left in the orchestra, and a few doubles in the second balcony. I could deal with a single seat situation, I was into the band that much, I wasn't sure I'd be able to sell it to the others, and the recent experience I had seen with Half-court Pete trying to get rid of his tickets made me kind of skittish.

We had off for Lincoln's Birthday, I decided to go down to the Fillmore box office and see if I could get four seats in a row. It was a raw windy day. I took the No. 1 bus to the 242nd St. subway and it was a straight shot to Washington Station.

At the box office, I stood in line as it ran out the door. After a good half-hour in the wind and the cold: "Looking for 4 in a row for any Allman Brothers shows."

He never looked up and placed 4 tickets and an envelope on the cage's counter. "Twenty-two." He gave me back three dollars. I looked at the Fillmore's marquee as I left: Fleetwood Mac and Van Morrison. As I had come this far, I knew I had to check out 42nd St. to make sure it was still there. The street walkers, skin movies, porno shops, and peep shows were doing their usual brisk business in the middle of the day. Although the tickets had wiped me out, I took the Penn Central back to Greystone. The concert was less than a month away. $5.50 was a lot of scratch back then, I had to get a job or something. I was damn near tapped out.

Tarts had talked Rexall into driving down and he got the fourth ticket, I wish it had been Meris. Holter could only come up with some boo, nothing special, but it had us in the right frame of mind. Vinny and me were just hoping we weren't expecting too much. Rex and me sneaked in two pints of wine, Holter brought in a pint of vodka, and Vinny brought in a pint of mescal……ole'. We had orchestra seats for the early show on the 12th. The seats were so far left we could only see the band in profile and from the waist up because they had house speakers blocking the view. The seats were on the aisle, and it was easy to get to the can, but our view was poor compared to Port Chester or Stony Brook.

George and Rex were frozen in their seats, there was so much to absorb. Rexall found it incredulous: how could a guy like Duane be only 24 years old and have the musical vision, intensity, command of his instrument, and leadership he displayed. He was in awe – we all were. The band had the energy to transport the listener to another dimension. Their focus, unity, improvisational skills had

408

heretofore been the domain of the jazz artists; Coltrane, Parker, Montgomery, Tyner, Mingus, Monk, and the like.

None of us drank a drop until Elvin Bishop took the stage. When it was over, we all had leftover alcohol to consume on the ride back to Yonkers. The way Rex was driving, we knew he wasn't drunk, and we were confident his brain was recalling the concert: "Still blows me away.......they were so good...so professional. In a couple of years, who knows where they'll be musically?"

"They're already out of this world." Holter sipped some Smirnoff.

"Nobody's close." he said, "Maybe Santana – they're the only ones brave enough to play instrumentals.

"Whitelaw – give me a taste of the T-bird, this vodka's killing me. What about the Dead?" George smiled at the Thunderbird's flavor.

"This is our band.....no one's close." Rex announced.

It gave me a real good vibe to know others heard what I heard, feel what I felt, see what I saw. Something special was added knowing Meris and her cousin were on the same wavelength with the sound. Girls who went to see the Brothers, did it because of their sound and not out of some infatuation or idolatry of the band members; the music meant something to them on a personal basis. It hit me and never left.

In May, Ray got a letter from Purdue University informing him he was awarded a partial scholarship. They waived his tuition for one semester and a year of on-campus room and board. It was the only grant he got from the four colleges he applied to. Hal framed the letter and hung it in his den. I knew he was proud of his eldest son. At the same time it was my wake-up call to get on the ball and make a statement of my own: athletically, artistically, or academically. My hope rested with a chunk of meteor buried between Greystone Station and the Hudson River, I recognized the absurdity, but hope can discount reality.

AFTER LAST SUMMER'S MISERABLE PERFORMANCE securing work, I was keen to find something regular. Crawfish told me about a country club on the west side of Scarsdale. He had caddied at Sunset Ridge Country Club after we graduated from All Souls grade school. It was further away than St. Andrews, but they had an old school bus to bring caddies from Yonkers to Scarsdale. I felt out of place; most of the caddies taking the bus seemed to be younger than me.

All around me, people were getting jobs and buying cars. Caddying was no big money maker, but it was better than last year, and I had to start banking money like Loki had. He had saved up for two years and he was in a position to buy a car on his own without his father kicking in half.

The caddy bus' pick-up points were pretty close to one another; they were adjacent to the Saw Mill River: Lake Ave. (at the bottom), Lockwood Ave. (at the bottom) and the Homefield section. After a couple of weeks, the bus driver knew you by sight. He started picking me up at the city dump/incinerator, saving me from walking down to Lake Ave. Pick-up time was 7:00 sharp. If you missed the bus, you were S.O.L. Sunset Ridge's bus service was a one-way deal - you were on your own to get back to Yonkers. The country club only ran the bus on weekends or any day they expected a lot of golfers.

Caddying was an easy job, except if you were over 45 years old; then it started getting tough. Watching Ed Detore do the course carrying two golf bags -- that was scary. He was a veteran of the Korean War, and he was still riding the caddie bus and mooching a ride back to Yonkers after he made his loop. But Ed was a kool guy; he had completely different view of life than most of us. I didn't want to end up like Ed Detore, unmarried and childless, but I sure dug his tranquility.

As long as a golfer could keep the ball in the fairway, caddying wasn't half-bad. With some golfers, you had to give them a lesson as they tortured the golf course.

"Hey, I can help you off the tee, in the fairway, give you the distances, and read the greens, but I can't help you in the traps or your short game." I admitted my limitations.

Most of Sunset Ridge's members were satisfied with playing bogie golf. Lady golfers never asked for golf instructions if she was playing with her husband or was on a date. It was a completely different dynamic when the more randy ladies went out as a foursome. The caddy yard knew who these ladies were and we all wanted to carry their clubs; making a loop with them was anything but routine.

Around eight of these women had found the 'new morality' of the swinging '60s much to their liking and they brought it into the 70's as their looks began to fade; they used sexuality and aggression to fill in the blanks where previously their physical beauty had been the attraction. To me and most of the other caddies; we thought they were still good looking, but these women members must have seen a different person in the mourning mirror. They were afraid to rely on the hand they had been dealt, some only drew one card, most took two, one took four from the plastic surgeon. We thought the boob jobs worked out the best. Nose jobs, facial tightening, 'wash away the gray', and neck reduction mostly helped to hold back 'Father Time'.

There were three or four ladies who were completely outrageous in the flagrant passes they made towards their caddies. More than one of the women complained about the lack of bedroom performance of their husbands.

We were on the fourth tee; "Ginger – you know your caddy can do more than carry your clubs......if you want." Pamela Spearl said.

"He might have to – that cheating bum of mine can't take care of me and her." Ginger replied.

"Anyone we know?"

"Some shiksa lawyer – she does work for the firm occasionally."

"Divorce him; I thought Andrew was smarter than to get caught. Take him to court." Pam advised.

"You know I've really been thinking about it, but I'd have to give up my membership here."

Pamela informed the other two women: "That's the club's by-laws......Ginger's membership came through Andrew's."

"That's too much of a price because now I enjoy your company more than his......and two can play that game right?" She turned and looked at the other caddy......"What's your name again?"

"Huh?" he stammered, "Ah.....Rich." he smiled.

One of my ladies interjected, "You don't mind if we call you Dick." Sondra giggled.

Digesting this conversation would go better if I had had some pot and a pair of sunglasses. I'd ask around the yard when we stopped after the 10th hole to get a drink. The golf course was screwed up because golfers got to the clubhouse after playing 10 holes instead of the usual 9.

"Ryan.....Ryan........you're not just caddying for Claudia – get over here.........Now. Why can't I get the ball to go straight? How's my stance?" She smiled with her perfect teeth gleaming. It was warm; she had a low-cut 'hot pink' sleeveless top on. "Ryan how is my stance?" She squeezed her boobs to the point where I had to wonder how they stayed inside her top. Sondra looked down at her cleavage, "Now how does that look?"

"Oh Sondra, just put his face in them." Claudia laughed.

"Not until he checks out my form from the rear....are you watching Ryan? I'm going to take a couple of practice swings." She brought her butt out just a little bit to get that extra power. "What do you think caddy?"

The other two watched and Claudia had her hand over her mouth she was laughing so hard.

"Well how's my stance dammit?" Her arms went out and her palms went up.

Without hesitation I answered: "I think you could win the U.S. Open looking like that."

"Let's just give it a good whack."

Ginger called, "Sondra – you do that – give him a good whack." The women were laughing and Rich and me were red faced - not from the sun.

The dean of the lady foursome, the 50 year old Pamela looked at the ball she was playing: "Boy......I mean .....caddy........I mean Dick......that's right isn't it? Dick?" We all laughed even Rich.

Pamela gave him this big vamp smile, "Could you – Would you - please wash our balls in the washer unit?"

The ball washer stood just between the waist and the shoulders of most golfers on every tee. It was a manual device with soap solution in its reservoir and small broom bristles inside, which cleaned the golf ball of mud and dirt. Through a series of thrusts of the handle which held the golf balls; they received a thorough cleaning. To me, it looked like simulated masturbation. If you could contort your face, it really added to the effect, and this eclectic foursome appreciated the extra effort.

"Now......Dick........I want my ball clean, really work that thing." Ginger smiled.

He did what I thought was an adequate job, and he was going to put the towel to it and she stopped him.

"You put my ball back in that washer and clean that dirty, dirty ball." She handed it back to Rich.

I thought it looked as clean as the one I gave back to Pam Spearl. Rich put it back in the washer and started thrusting the handle that holds the ball between the stationary brushes.

It still ain't good enough for Ginger, she's got Richy pumping that handle in the cleaning unit like a pro in a cat-house. I was grateful to be off to the side. All four golfers watched Rich simulate some kind of weird act of self-gratification. The four golfers were in some kind of state of suspended hysteria. He handed her the ball after he dried it off. Ginger ran the ball on her cheek.

"This thing's ready for a hole in one." It took her a minute to compose herself.

"Enough girl talk......Claudia it's your honor." She smashed a drive right down the middle of the fairway.

"Nice shot." I said as she handed me her driver.

The farther we caddied away from 21 O'Dell, the more time we wasted getting to and from a golf course. The caddies with wheels had it made. Although we saw the Hudson River Country Club every time we were at the junction of North Broadway and O'Dell, there only memories left.......the 18 holes reverted back to nature.

ii

Hal and Ray had made the trip to West Lafayette, Indiana to scope out Purdue University in May. They drove out there in the Chrysler Newport. This was a big....big trip for any of the Whitelaw family. The furthest any of us had gone was to Cape May in New Jersey, Niagara Falls, and Hal took me up to Boston when his uncle Henry died. Hal had been on the other side of the world with the Navy, but he never went anywhere more than 300 miles away from home after he got his discharge.

Indiana? I thought. Otis had their big manufacturing plant there. Hadn't Jack Swinburne moved there in the sixth grade? We might have moved to Indiana if Jane could have made a break with her dance school, and her side of the family. May was the month her recital had to start coming together. It was always scheduled in one of the first two weekends of June. Mom was going nuts without a car, but Hal pulled rank when he made a 'command decision' and he and Ray drove off to Hoosierland for a week and left us without transportation. The nearest food store was up the North End.

Jane asked him, "What are we supposed to do?"

"Better start calling in some favors." Hal said.

If it wasn't for Judy Conolly, Jane's assistant, we might have been eating the food hidden in the dark corners of the closet.

Jane did make a call. It was to Caesar's Taxi. After three days without a car, we hopped in the cab and got left off on Tuckahoe Rd. in front of 'TNT Dynamite Used Cars'. She asked me to go with her to the car lot; she was wise about used car salesman and how they took advantage of women who were looking for cars on their own. A woman with two young kids walking into a used car lot was pretty much in the same predicament as an 18 year old hippie walking into the shower of the state pen for the first time. TNT was somewhat different; two of her students' mothers had gotten cars at TNT: the one was still running good, the other had been stolen.

"Ryan, do you know anything about cars?" Jane said.

"I can kick the tires with the best of them." I laughed.

"I can't make a mistake here." Her upper teeth squeezed her lower lip.

"Kenny Crawford told me to look on the ground under the engine for oil. A couple of drops is okay. Then you're supposed to run it on the Thruway whip the steering from side to side to make sure the front end is tight. You take it back to the lot and park it where it's dry and you look again for oil. Don't buy a car that leaks as much oil as a Harley. I think he said to go down a big hill and make sure the brakes

are okay. You know… go down Roberts Ave. and make sure it stops."
I told her what I knew.

The four of us walked into the fenced lot; half was used cars, the other half was a junkyard. They had a medium sized mutt tied up to the door handle of a Rambler; he was barking away at us. Herbert Van Leer, the owner, was a tail chaser. When he spotted our Mom, he was out of his paper laden office pretty quick.

Before he got to us, she looked at me: "Ryan……NO third pedal."

"Huh?"

"No damn clutch……..automatics." she said.

"Right Mom."

Herbert threw his cigarette away as he approached Jane.

I'd have to tell Jane when we were alone not to buy a car with over a hundred thousand miles on the odometer. Crawfish said the only thing that was reliable with that kind of mileage was a Volkswagen and a Ford pick-up truck. You had to make sure the floors, and bed of the truck weren't rusted through. Both of those weren't options for Jane: she didn't need or want a truck and the VW's were nearly all stick shifts. She was apprehensive; it was a real big move for her. It was the first instance I recall where she treated me like an adult. I had some knowledge of cars and she needed that. I didn't want to let her down.

With Cathy and Brother Bill in tow, we walked around the small lot. Herbert had 20 or so cars. Five or six were real beaters…… ready for a teenager to drive away, but most looked to be road worthy.

"What about this one?" I opened the door to a Mercury Comet. It was clean inside and out and had good rubber.

Herbert smiled, "Take it for a test drive: Go up the Thruway and take it back down the Saw Mill Parkway." He came back with the keys. I had the popped the engine hood and checked the oil, coolant, power steering reservoir, and the battery.

"We changed the oil and filter." He handed the keys to Jane. It started right up. "Don't be afraid to get on it girlie, the brakes are good and the front brakes are brand new. It's got a 289 Mustang engine, good mileage for an eight cylinder – plenty of power too. You watch…..your husband will want to drive it more than you. Seat belts front and back."

She drove off the lot towards the I-87 Thruway. "Check out the speedometer Mom." I said.

Jane tried to absorb all the things the Comet was telling her. They overwhelmed her: "Rides nice at 60 m.p.h."

"Mom – how many miles are on the car?"

Her eyes darted back and forth, "Ah……Five, three, oh, one, two. Is that good?"

"Depends on how much he wants for the car?…….Say, what were you and Herb talking about just before we left the lot.?"

"He thought you were my brother."

"Huh? – Impossible." Disbelief. "Nobody's that dumb. The guy's hitting on you."

"I'm no dummy when it comes to that, but if you were a girl, you'd know how to turn it into an advantage."

The final choice was narrowed down to the gray Mercury Comet or a white crème puff '67 Ford Galaxie with Red interior. She was leaning towards the Galaxie but the caveat was threatening Hal's ego with his big Chrysler. In the end, she chose the mid-size Comet. She needed transportation more than she needed a reoccurring debate about the extravagance of having 2 battleships in the driveway. Jane agreed to buy the Mercury for $861.25 which included tax, title, and tags.

"And Honey.......it'll be easier parking the Comet than that long Galaxie. When you come down to it - a Galaxie is just another name for space, but the Comet takes you to your destination through space. Van Leer, the wheeler dealer, smiled from Jane to me with his mouth open displaying his gold crowned teeth. They did the paperwork in his small concrete block office.

"What the hell was that all about?" I asked my younger brother and sister who shrugged their shoulders.

They completed the paperwork and she paid for the car in cash. "I need the car right now." Jane said.

"Nothing to worry about – you've got a 90 day – bumper to bumper warrantee on it........except for accidents; that would be through your insurance. Keep the Dealer plates on it Sugar, until I get the permanents from the DMV. It'll take a couple of days."

We drove away in Jane's new ride, "What do you think Ryan?"

"53 thousand.......I didn't see any oil on the asphalt while you were in the office with Mr. TNT. No problem passing cars or stopping."

"I like the way it shifts.....firm.....crisp. The Chrysler's transmission feels like mush."

"Watch out this car doesn't end up in West Lafayette – "

"Ray wouldn't do that to me." she said.

"No, but Hal would."

"Mmmm." I watched her grappling with the possibility.

Hal saw the name on the Mercury's title: Jane Marlowe Dance Studio. The battle Royal was on for the entire summer.

The Comet really helped Ray and me out. It was a boon Jane had summers off. She was happy to loan the car to Ray when we needed it for work, or when he went on a date with Sally. Sometimes, Ray would caddy at Sunset Ridge or I'd go over to St. Andrews when either was going to have a busy weekend. We didn't get the use of the Comet whenever we asked, but we got it enough to make us real appreciative, especially when we thought about how tough things had been the previous summer.

iii

The day was coming, he knew it, I knew it. Ray had graduated and skipped the ceremony. The ceremony meant something to Jane; it didn't mean a thing to Hal. What was important was what it meant to Ray. Apparently not too much, but we did celebrate. We were down the North End, sitting on Barca's supermarket three course block wall. The Chug-a-mugs went down faster than a gallon of gas going through a Tri-Power Pontiac GTO. I mentioned something about graduation and he stared straight ahead. I mean way ahead.....maybe behind. He was looking somewhere other than the North End.

"Well, that was a waste of four years." We laughed, but I could feel his observation dripping with cynicism.

Loki showed up with a six pack of them red cans - Tall Boys of Miller Malt Liquor.

"Kind of favoring that malt liquor gig – huh Loki?"

"Don't say beer – Say Bull!" he repeated the TV commercial.

"But you ain't drinking Schlitz Malt Liquor Loki." I called him on it.

"No........although I did go into the Greek's to buy the Bull; they didn't have any cold; ended up with Miller Malt – same shit when you come down to it. The way I see it.... I went in to buy Bull, so I can use their commercial because it's the thought that counts."

"Logic.......direct from the Norse gods." Ray said.

I called to Loki across Ray, "Give me a sip of that shit." They waited for my opinion. "Might be better than the Bull – can it kick like Colt?" I took out a Marlboro.

"I had it before – it does the job, especially in the 16 oz. format. Let's toast the graduate." We raised our cans and did our best to coax a clink from our aluminum and glass.

"I'm starting to get a complex; Ray says high school was a waste of four years." I said.

Loki Ferguson laughed looking over to Ray, "Not if you're a teacher." Another slosh of malt: "I needed a teacher for math. No way I was going to pass the regents exam without help."

"Same here Joe." I said.

"That skin-nye-ver Mike Reno bragged he hasn't taken any math courses during his entire high school career so far." Ray reported.

Something was going on with his high school record. First, he's in Ray's grade, next he's in my grade because he flunked too many courses. He comes to Gorton - he didn't graduate did he? I'm missing something.

"Nah. They put his name on the graduation program, got the monkey suit and hat, he's even in the yearbook as a graduating senior. Sally said he was at the ceremony.....went up on the stage. Under penalty of perjury I swear one of two....no three things will happen with Reno. He goes to summer school to get his diploma, he does more time with you at Gorton – gets his diploma, or he drops out.......Mike Reno – a high school drop out." Ray laughed.

"Huh?" Loki quick-looked to Ray.

"Yeah, he kept telling the guidance counselors at Commerce High he was going to fulfill his math requirement in his junior and senior years so he could really concentrate on the subject. Commerce said okay, and he transferred to Gorton to finish high school."

"Then what?" I asked.

Ray lights one up, "Then he works the Mike Reno magic he's known for. The registrar in Gorton's office wants to know why there's no math credits on his transcript. He tells the registrar he took the classes they assigned him, and he said he didn't know nothing about nothing'. The registrar says Mike's got to make it up. Reno says: 'No problem......I need my math for the family business.'

Ray chugs half a mug: "The guidance counselor's got Reno doubled up on math for the next two years. He probably spent more time in the guidance counselors offices than he did in the classroom. Come September, he's attending classes he wasn't assigned to and missing the ones he was." Ray said, "He was in my gym class, Ryan's typing class, and Sally's home economics class and got the three credits. None of the administration had a handle on what he was up to.

"I think he greased the guidance counselor."

"Glickstein.......?" Ray scrunched his brow.

"Nah....the new one, the proxide blonde – Daisy Goudenov."

We shook our heads and laughed. People do a number on our last name, but everybody just ripped her name apart.

Loki was trying to restrain himself, "He does have parents........I assume"

"According to his cousin - "Fast Eddie Mason, his brother Dave raised Mike and his little brother Gino. The parents live in Vegas now." I shrugged at Ray and Loki.

"He'd have Wells or Betsy Risko do his math workbook. Now, I got this straight from Reno and this is how he plans on graduating next year: He's already got his brother Dave and his on again/off again partner contractor, Jay Randell, to write up this super letter to the Principal about how the painting company needed Mike because he was the only guy who could squeeze behind the girders of this bridge their company was painting. They had to sandblast the ends before they painted them......and only the great Mike Reno had that expertise. Next, he had to mix this super futuristic two-part rust inhibitor/epoxy/paint before applying two layers of clear coat for the first three feet of the ends of the girders. After that, they gave it a couple of coats of girder green.

The N.Y.S. DOT awarded the stripping and painting on this old historic bridge in Tarrytown to Reno Painting contractors not because it was the low bid, but because of their extensive knowledge in the field of restoration and preservation of significant historic structures as it pertains to the "Old Sleepy Hollow Bridge".

"The DOT actually sent Mike to a weekend seminar to a certification course on the preparation, use, and proper handling and storage of these sealants." Ray threw his cigarette into the gutter.

"Reno?.......unfuckinbelieveable." Loki tilted and looked at Ray.

"The guy could sell a Ford to the President of GM."

Dave Reno, Jay Randell, and Mike had the DOT guy, who was the engineer in charge of the project, sign off on Mike's certification and gave him a letter stating he was a definite asset to the historic project."

"How'd this Randell Painting fit in this deal?" Loki wiped his mouth with his forearm.

"He was the guarantor – the bankroll for Reno painting. The state needed a business entity to sue that was bonded in case there was an accident or Reno failed to fulfill their contract." Ray explained.

Jo-Lo Ferguson popped another Miller Malt, "How'd you come into this front page news?"

"He got it through me, and I got it from his cousin." I said.

"Fast Eddie Mason?"

"Yeah......"Fast Eddie".

"Well – who did the actual work.........not Reno?" Loki chuckled.

"Fuck no.......It was Big Brother Dave. He's the estimator, accountant, the bidder, and the painter for the outfit. Mike and Gino, all they can do is use rollers and six inch wide brushes. They're splashers. That's what Eddie calls 'em. Davey does all the trim. When he was in Nam, he painted the emblems and specialty stuff on the choppers and jets. Mike kept some pictures of Davey's work in his glove box while he was in Vietnam. He's a true artist." I heresay-ed.

"He was in Nam?" Loki raised his brow.

"Used to paint Dragsters and Funny Cars when he first got back. He did the artwork on Dave Trent's pick-up truck." I said.

"What happened that he had to go back to the family business?" Ray puffed away.

"Fast Eddie said as soon as Dave got his discharge, the parents started making their move to Las Vegas and left Dave the painting business and the responsibility of raising Mike and Gino." I said.

"Holy fuck." Ray shook his head. "No wonder Mike's as screwed up as he is. I didn't know that."

We sat on Barca's parking lot wall for a few minutes kind of speechless.

Ray looked over to Loki, "You get your draft notice yet?"

Loki took a long drag off a Parliament, "Yeah, but I'm a dual national. My Mom's from Ireland. I'm classified 4-C. She was working in Holland and my father swept Bonnie off her feet when he was stationed there. She brought me down to the Irish Consulate and registered me as an Irish citizen. The luck of the Irish, I guess."

"I'm less than a year away from 19, I can't bring myself to go to Canada, even though the war is a bunch of crap. It isn't like fighting Hitler and Tojo, they were attacking us. I'll deal with it when I'm told to report for military service." Ray said.

"Same for me.......Say Jo-Lo: were you any relation to Tojo?" Ray and me laughed, and Loki told me to get fucked.

"You know Joe, you might end up drinking with young Brother Bill by the time the war ends." Ray stomped on an empty can of Miller Malt.

It was almost funny.

"Ray, how's Purdue looking for next fall?"

"I'm signed up......I need some serious scratch when I go to Indiana. My bank account is looking real lean." he said.

418

"You going caddying or you got something else lined up?"

"Caddying, but it'll be different this summer; our Mom got a car and we can use it when she isn't. We just can't take it out for nighttime recreation."

The Big night down Central Park is coming........July 21st ......Allman Brothers at the Schaefer Music Festival. You ever catch them Joe?" I said.

"Nah." His eyes scrunched together, but he mentioned they were making some big noise on the music scene.

"They got a 4 ticket limit on individual sales. I got to get them before they sell out." It was less than a month away.

"You can sit outside and hear the music pretty good. There's only a few spots where you can actually see the bands from outside the rink." Loki said.

"You can see them from that Big Rock outside, but it's always full, specially if it's a hot act." Ray said.

"The Rogues are going – en Force – That's our band." I pointed with my cigarette.

Ray turned to Loki: "We should check them out too." My brother looked back to me: "I'll go with you, we'll each buy 4 tickets. There's a lot of interest. No caddying on Mondays – we'll go down then. Loki, if you go – that'll be 12 tickets total. There isn't going to be any problem getting rid of them. Their music's getting a lot of play; the radio stations can even get away with playing their 15 minute tunes."

"There's going to be a big turnout from all of North Yonkers." I was getting rather animated.

"I could take Sally."

"Kind of a budget date." Loki mused. "Maybe I'll call up Lori Silver or Linda Datlow."

"You got anything special goin' on this summer?" Ray asked.

JoLo let out a belly belch, "Going over to the cop shop and get my hack license."

Doubt and skepticism came over Ray's face, "Hey Joe, neither Main or Valentine taxis are air conditioned, and only a few of Caesar's are." Sounds like some hot summer fun. Hi – Lo Heller says the action's pretty slow in the summer."

"Wait a minute Mr. Fergmeister – How old you gotta be to get your hack license?" I asked.

"I think it's 18. How old is Heller?" Loki said.

"Same as you." Ray replied.

"Well, I'm going down and getting mine."

"Doesn't Holter's old man own a medallion cab?" Ray said.

"You can bet your ass that cab is air conditioned." Another Chug-a-mug was history. "George knows the minimum age to get a hack license. And I think it's why George doesn't get his drivers license; he doesn't want his old man bugging him to drive his cab. Maybe the minimum age to get a hack license was reset by the Taxi commission when they lowered the age to vote."

419

Joe 'Loki' Ferguson was not worried about the age requirement. "I'm going to start driving a hack this year or next year. The license is good for a year. I'll drive weekends during school." He tipped some more Miller malt. "Didn't Jackie Hart drive his old man's taxi?' What was the name on the cab.........?"

"It was something goofy." Ray laughed. "Something like Hart-On Taxi."

"I'm older than Jackie Hart and he had a hack license." Loki said.

"Yeah he was in my class at All Souls, him and Kirk Lis. They both must have graduated from Saunders this week too.

"Just because Jackie was driving his old man's cab didn't mean he had a valid hack license. I remember him driving the taxi when he was a junior." I fired up a smoke.

"Either way, I'm getting a hack license the first chance I get."

"Why not do both if you're that fuckin' hungry?"

"Go fuck yourself Ryan." Loki said. We all laughed.

"Better off caddying." Ray said.

"Where?"

"You're probably better off at Sunset with Ryan......more loops there."

"Anybody there from Hudson River?" Loki said.

"You know I haven't seen one caddie from Hudson River at Sunset." The observation puzzled me. "Ray – what's going on at St. Andrews?" I killed another Rheingold.

"Too many caddies. It's slightly better for me because I sat on the bench almost the entire summer last year. You're better off up at Sunset with Ryan: more golfers mean more loops."

"It's $7.00/a bag now – but here's the rub at Sunset: Them skinflints just won't tip you the buck to make it $15/a round of golf......they just won't." I bitched.

The $7.00 had the caddies all worked up. There was no way you were going to get that dollar out of those members because the method of payment was a computer punch card which allowed the caddy to be paid for ten holes (the course had a front 10 and a back eight) to make the 18 hole loop. They had us boxed.

The only time I saw cash flashed was when the club rented out the course to an outside organization for a one day outing. Two bags – 18 holes - $20.00. Those outings only came twice a summer.

"So it's going to be Purdue......Big Ten.....Big expectations." Loki raised his eyebrows.

"Give it a break Joe. I just got to go somewhere away from here." Ray said.

I stood up and arched my back; "Getting' outta Dodge." I drawled.

"See Ryan, that's why you're still a lone wolf – you got that dumb-ass cornball mentality." The future Boilermaker said.

I laughed when I had gotten a rise out of him. The three of us knew the summer would be just a quick memory. The Fourth of July was about ten days ahead, but the feeling the summer was fading was

420

somehow very real. The next 60 days would vanish if we waited to be swept up by the continuum's juggernaut. I sure wish we had that June 31st Ray had talked about.

iv

It was just a few days after Ray graduated, Bad Brad Guzzutti and me went down to Central park to catch 'The Band'. Ray and Loki were supposed to come with us, and we would kill two birds with one stone. Once we decided we were going to go to the concert, why make an extra trip to just get tickets for the Allmans? We went straight over to the Music Festival's box office. Both The Band and the Allman Brothers early and late shows were sold out. Although the Allmans' appearance was three weeks away, their shows had been sold out two weeks earlier. Brad and me would have to be the bearers of the bad news to the other guys. We'd have to listen to the music outside the rink. The sound was really good considering it was an outdoor venue ....Visually - the most someone could expect was a glimpse of the band between the branches of the trees.

Guzzuti was having a fit; he had heard us talk about the Brothers so often and with such enthusiasm, he just wanted a piece of the experience, and just having the audio version wasn't going to make it. I was hoping we could find somebody selling tickets the night of the show. If there was one guy that 'needed' to get in – it was him.

We knew they'd be back in the metro region before the summer was over, and we'd have to make that concert. For now, just hearing them outside the rink would have to be good enough. The band from Macon Ga. had the vibe and the intensity to send the music through the fence unimpeded. The Wollman Skating Rink was the one venue where being outside the fence wasn't a "game ender" – this was the best place to hear a concert outside the confines. On the other side of the rink, a person got caught up in the side show of hippies, street people, bra-less women, teenagers from Jersey, Long Island, Westchester, and the ubiquitous smell of reefer, chestnuts, and patchouli. The side show outside the rink was inconsequential and ignored when good bands played.

We knew the Allmans would be back in the metro area, but nothing had been posted. It wasn't until September 19th. As serendipity would have it – that show took place at Stony Brook once again. The band had to take a hiatus from touring in August. Three or four of them went into rehab to clean up. The caliber of music, record company executive pressures, the road: it all takes a toll. Duane's counterpart told some guy doing an interview about the business, "We travel from coast to coast: On the Super Slab the tolls are paid in lives, wives, and sighs."

THE SECOND OF JULY KICKED OFF THE JULY 4TH weekend in 1971; it was a Friday. Sunday was the actual Fourth of July; the official day off was Monday, so there was the possibility of scoring three - maybe four days - of barnbusting caddying......
weather permitting. If a guy was fortunate, he might pick up two loops

421

on two of those days. By July 5th, the golf course would mirror its caddies: burnt out and worn thin. Loki made a temporary decision to caddy at least for the holiday weekend. The money was there. He said he was thinking about not showing up on Sunday, but his conscience got the better of him, and he knew it was his patriotic duty to make sure the rich folks enjoyed Independence Day.

"You ain't even American.......Patriotic duty - my ass." I cut him when no one was around.

He laughed, "Law says I'm a citizen – 100%. Irish Government says I'm a citizen too. It means I'm a 200% man.......a true schizophrenic!"

"I'll give you that much citizen."

"Get bent Ryan. I knew as soon as I said I was only half-American – it'd come back at me." He sipped some hot coffee from the Greek.

Showing up on the Fourth was a smart move, otherwise the caddymaster would have had Loki sitting on the bench for a week – loopless. We all had seen the punitive measures before.

"Joe, you might luck out and get the Pam Spearl foursome......that'll make the loop fly by. You'll have so much fun you'll forget they're rich and you ain't." I said.

"Mmmm. The caddymaster only gives us young guys that loop when there aren't any greyhounds left in the yard."

We cashed our computer punch cards in, the caddymaster, John Murdock, didn't look up as he counted out our money. "Get a good night's rest – big weekend. I don't need hungover caddies."

"Right John." We agreed.

We had the ten mile return to Yonkers in front of us; at the least the first leg of the two-lane country road was down hill. We were almost off the grounds, this occasional caddie, Joe Edwards, was sitting on the trunk of his car where the help has to park, and calls us as we headed for the gate. We knew him, he was a character and was laid off from his regular job as a crane operator. He had this big Manitowoc sticker on the trunk lid of his Dodge Polara. It was supposed to go on a 4100w crane he was operating on his last job, but he put it on his car instead.

"Loki.......Whitecloud.......comeer."

We walked over to see what he had. In N.Y. it could be anything......and that meant anything. As long as you knew the guy or seen him around – it was worth a look. The weekend just started, and I'm spending money I should be saving. Joe Lamar, the card shark, may as well show up tomorrow too, so I don't have to go home with any money. This kind of shit always got the better of me; I knew I was always better off in the long run to walk by.

There had been some wild stuff in them trunks..... especially if the guy was going through divorce. It was typical to see moonshine, hot liquor, leather clothes, stereos, untaxed cigarettes, stag movies, guns, peyote buttons and pot, counterfeit $20's, (the guy called 'em nightimers because they only worked in the dark), fake I.D.'s & passports, quarter slugs for coin operated machines; Vinny Tarts and

422

me had even seen a tied-up girl who only had a bikini bottom on. The idiots selling her were real criminals. This wasn't fun or funny. "That's somebody's sister," Tarts said to me.

"More trouble than just a little bit there." I replied.

If it could be imagined, it could be in a trunk in metro N.Y.C. We were on either side of Edwards' trunk. Loki's jaw dropped and my smile went from ear to ear. There had to be over 50 boxes of Blockbusters in the trunk of his Dodge. Each box had three dozen in them. It came out to 1800 units.

"They're not ash cans." Loki froze at the sight.

"Duh."

"They ain't M-80"s." I was trying to identify some possibilities.

"Where da fuck you from.......an M-80 is a ash can. You two got shit for brains. They're blockbusters – you guys interested or not.....I gotta move this shit quick." Edwards said.

I didn't hesitate, "Yeah we're interested."

"Where's your car?"

"Got a ride up this morning, we were hoping to catch a ride back to Yonkers with somebody." Loki said.

"Get in." he slammed the trunk.

"That's a lot of ordnance." Loki gulped as we pulled out of the lot. About two miles down the road, we stopped on a shoulder enlargement; it ran into a small transformer yard guarded by a fence. Eight foot concrete walls isolated each transformer within the fence. Electrical transmission towers ran north and south of the small yard. Joe Edwards parked out of sight of the road behind the walls.

We got out and opened the trunk's lid. Loki pointed, "THAT – is a lot of firecrackers." Each time we looked, it seemed like there were more boxes in the trunk.

"Already moved a whole trunkload in the past two days. I gotta get rid of this shit today and tomorrow. Tell you what - $25/box......3 dozen to a box. Youse gotta buy a minimum of four boxes. You buy one box – the price is $35. You sell them for a buck apiece if you got time to piece them out. You can buy ten boxes, but the price is never lower than $25/box. I'm not going any lower than 25/box."

The numbers started tumbling through our heads. "Joe, set one off so we know what were dealing with." I said.

He reached into a box with a black "X" magic markered on top.

"Wait a minute........let me pick out the blockbuster."

"You fuckin' mugs don't trust me?"

"I don't trust nothing that comes out of a trunk these days Joe." All three of us had a nervous laugh.

"Go head. Pick one out from any box."

They were three times the size of a M-80. The crane operator lit one up, made sure the fuse was going and threw it in the air as far as he could. There was a gigantic explosion; even in the daylight we saw a bright flash of light and a billow of smoke. Loki and me looked at each other and started laughing. Edwards' eyes were gleaming: "They kind of sell themselves. I'm telling you though - these fuckers are bombs......take your arm off in a heartbeat. You gotta respect 'em."

"Ya think? Holy Fuck........How many boxes can you front us?" I started taking out a cigarette and Joe shook his head. "Yeah, I was getting a little wound up." And put it back in the pack. "Well, how many boxes can you front us?"

"Can't do that Whiteshade – too close to the Fourth, unless you make a bigger volume buy: pay me for four boxes, and I'll front you two additional boxes."

"Total of six….." I said.

"A total of six……….same deal for you Loki."

Loki shot back, "I can't move this artillery, not that fast."

"Okay Whitehouse, what do you want to do – buy 'em one at a time like the Spades on the corner buy cigarettes – or – or do you want the pack?"

I knew he was working me, probably like somebody was working him. "I ain't got the clock to sell them like that."

Right in front of us Edwards says to me: "Nobody got a gun to your head Loki………..Whitebang - you sell 'em to your people tonight, and then you sell 'em to the caddies tomorrow and just keep going til' the 4th is over. Ain't no revelation……..you ain't gonna sell anything on the sixth. You got that extra day to sell 'em on Monday cause that's the day off. Come Tuesday, if the old timers start having cardiac arrests the headbreakers will charge you with possession and trafficking. If you guys are in - you got three nights to move this shit……..Whitebirch?"

"Yeah."

"How 'bout it Loki? You in?"

He took a deep breath, hmmmm'd and hawed, and kicked some gravel and said, "Okay."

"Meet you guys down the North End at 6 o'clock."

"Hold on Joe…….no good……too busy. You go down Morsemere Ave. There's a blacktopped park just down the street from the gas station and the pizza place. That'll be just right." I said.

"Huh?"

"Right around the corner from the Gulf station and the deli; the park's half woods – half blacktop. We'll be by the basketball court at six."

"Joe……this stuff got a federal pricetag?"

"Not unless you get caught."

The crane operator got serious, "You're fuckin' with a quarter stick of dynamite. If we get pinched, it's gonna be the same as if we were pushing drugs. We're going up against the ATF. Hey Whitecrime…..you ain't 18 yet?"

"No."

"Loki – let the kid do the sellin'."

"I 'spose." he said.

"Drop us off at Saw Mill River Rd."

We watched the tumblers align across his eyes.

"I got business down the Bronx – youse want a ride to O'Dell……Lockwood?" our new business partner offered.

He let us off at the O'Dell exit. 21 was about two miles west. Edwards looked at his watch: "Better meet around 7 at that park, I'm runnin' late already." The Dodge Polara peeled away and got back on the Parkway.

I used Loki's Christian name to impart the gravity of this transaction: "Joe can you do $100 by 7 pm?"

"Ryan......I don't know if I can do this – I can't sell fireworks to students and hippies. Fuck, half these hippies want to burn down the government. They don't want to shoot off fireworks to celebrate it."

"That's right; their trip is burning flags and smoking pot.........daydreaming.......Can you at least loan me a hundred and get your dad's car so I can get the shit back to my house?"

"Yeah.....give me a call around six."

"You got the money?" I looked at him trying to figure out where I stood with his flimsy commitment.

"Yeah, I got money."

I noticed the heat and the humidity. I was perspiring more than I had been when I was carrying golf clubs. "Loki... listen man --- I think I can move this shit. I know they ain't sparklers, and this is illegal everywhere."

Loki's hands went in his back pockets, they're a big deal if we get caught with them.......and for what? – a couple of hundred bucks in profit? The return is not worth the risk."

"Is it a fully automatic machine gun?"

"No."

"Is it moonshine, untaxed cigarettes, or counterfeit money?"

"No."

"It's the lowest thing on ATF's to do list. They only chase this nickel and dime crap when people misuse the stuff.....We're just trying to help the citizens celebrate the heroes of the Revolution. If you want to get in on this, it'd be better for me. Otherwise, I'll owe you a hundred and have to come up with the other two hundred for Joe Edwards. I still need wheels to push the shit. I can't operate out of Hal's house. Call me when you made your decision, I've got to start moving it the minute I buy it."

"Right." Loki said.

It was getting more real than I had expected. I started walking up the backside of O'Dell past some houses, Emerson Jr. High, and the Hudson River Golf Course – which was into its second year of neglect. It had retained the country club appearance from the street. Those of us who knew it, immediately recognized the back to nature movement.

The paperback novel turned into a make-do fly swatter as Ray was trying to read. Nobody was home, both cars were gone.

"Did you.....? Bang...Bang....Bang." Some firecrackers were set off down the street. "Did you guys get out?"

"Yeah."

"Loki too?"

"We both got out twice. Murdoch gave us computer punch cards as soon as he saw us coming in off our first loop. Our foursome started off the back eight. It was so busy, I thought they had a tournament going."

"You going out tonight?" Ray said.

"You want to come out with me and Loki?"

"Sally's been behaving; only because the supply on the street's drying up. That's the word from Rikshaw and Ronnie Zanzibar. The day Hal and me left for Purdue, she O.D.'d. Ran into some potent smack. Sue Herr and Cocaine Wayne left her at St. John's emergency entrance. She stayed clean for about three weeks.

Is it any better with her when she's straight?"

"Yeah – in some ways; when she's high......there aren't any surprises."

"Got any cash around? – large?". I kind of looked away.

"For what?"

"Loki and me are going into business."

"Drugs?"

"No drugs."

"How much?" He shooed another fly off, maybe it was the same one.

"A hundred.....maybe two."

"For two hundred - you tell me what I'm bank rolling."

I smiled knowing how stupid it was going to sound: "Fireworks."

Ray's face melted sour and he shook his head, "You're a fuckin' retard. Be real man. Why is Loki going in on this?"

"It's a sure thing Ray, you want in on the action?" I lit a smoke.

He gave me an incredulous look. "You are going to be a senior in September? Really? You and Ferguson are going to sell bottle rockets down the end. I think......no.....I know Loki is dumber than you."

I looked Ray straight in the eye and raised my brow just a bit: "This ain't kid's stuff. These are the biggest bombs you ever heard."

"Tell you what brother – I'll loan you the deuce. I'll need the money back before I leave for school.....Deal?"

"You got it." I nodded. "What do you got going on?"

"Dunbar and me are going with our dates to a liquid barbecue/Fourth of July party in Dobbs Ferry."

"You're taking Sally?"

"Yeah, she better not be shattered, I'll tell Dunbar not to let her in the car if she's got them tombstone eyes..."

"She back on it?"

"I toldja it's dried up. There's a little bit around, but the shortage has got her pretty straight. She's just getting warm once or twice a week, doin' something pharmaceutical. But if she's using that spike, that'll be bad all over again."

"Think Dunbar can drop me off down Morsemere?"

"What happened with Ferguson?" Ray said.

"I just talked to him when I got out of the shower. Said he was backing out of the deal. It's a no-go."

"No-go-Joe?" Ray said.

"It's no go Joe, and no dough."

"Maybe his year of higher learning is starting to take hold."

We left 21 and I got in the back seat of Dunbar's car.

"You're not going with us kid." Dunbar turned to Ray who had got in the front seat, "What's going on?"

"We can drop him off down Morsemere before we pick up Sally?"

"What's next?" He looked like he was really going out of his way and forced some used air out the side of his mouth; "Yeah… Yeah…why not?"

"Thanks John." Ray said.

'Get fucked John.' I thought.

We pulled up to the Rubeo Park and I gave Dunbar the obligatory "Thanks John." He didn't acknowledge it and sped off as soon as I got out of the two door Pontiac. I didn't have to imagine his reaction if I asked him to take the equivalent of 108 sticks of dynamite from the park to 21 O'Dell.

Rubeo Park was a block away from the Pizzeria and the deli. We had to split our time up between the two places. Too much of any group of guys hanging out got to be a pain in the ass for businesses and nearby residents. During the day, the locals would complain to Vinny: "tell your friends to keep the noise and music down after 11 pm. Once we started getting cars - we could bring our mirth and merriment to other neighborhoods.

When Dunbar and Ray dropped me off, I was the only one down the park; I was early for the connection with Joe Edwards. I decided whoever showed up first with transportation – he would be my new business partner. 7:15, No Joe Edwards……No Rogues. I looked at my bankroll and counted it out. $200 from Ray, $100 of my secret stash money, and $18 just to have in my pocket. At 7:20 Vinny Tarts came walking towards me, his hair was still wet from taking a shower. He offered me a half-smoked joint with an extended arm.

"No thanks, I got to be smooth. I'm meeting this dude from the golf course down here to conduct some business."

"Private business? I can go up to Ralph's and get a slice." he said. "It's got to be reefer." He took the last hit and discarded the roach.

"No – hang around Vin, it might work out."

About five minutes later, the laid off Edwards rolled up. He didn't say a word and opened the trunk of the Dodge. Joe had gotten rid of a sizeable amount of inventory since he dropped me off this afternoon. "Been a change in plans……I can only do a dozen boxes." he said.

"$300? Right?" I reached for a cigarette and then remembered the product I was dealing with.

Smokin' Joe gave me a wink – "You'll want more tomorrow……… Listen Whitewalls, I'm gonna give you a half of a demonstration box for your clients."

427

"Thanks Joe" and handed over a hundred dollar bill, two fifty's, and ten ten's.

"Tomorrow you'll be sold out. Your cost ends up about 70 cents each. You ain't gonna have time for single unit sales – not until your last two boxes; that's when you sell "em for a buck apiece. Remember……..Don't get fuckin' greedy. The more people you bring in – the more likely you'll have cop problems. I don't have any problems selling 'em 2/$3.00. This guy with you? You don't look like Loki."

"Aaaaay…….he took a powder on me." I said.

"Keep the circle small and the quicker you can sell, the more money you'll make and the less chance the bulls will get you on a possession or trafficking rap."

"Got any larger boxes or grocery bags?" I said.

"Come on Slick…….you gotta start thinking ahead. You ain't……thinking about walking around with this shit? Tell me you got someone with a set of wheels lined up. Come on Ace…..come on. This ain't big time crime, but you can do big time time for this stuff. Get on the ball……QUICK! I'm late already." he looked at his watch.

"Who makes this stuff – where's it come from?" Vince asked.

"Just sell the fuckin' shit." The Joe waved and sped off.

12 boxes of 36 blockbusters each was stacked behind a park trash barrel against the park's retaining wall.

Tarts shook his head and laughed, "Whatchoo get yourself into? Who's supposed to be buying this arsenal?"

"Nobody yet…..kind of doing it on speculation" Waves of nervous energy ran through my body.

"You're fuckin' nuts."

I forced a laugh and Tarts looked at one from the sample box: "Way bigger than an M-80." He weighed it in his hand.

Rexall's '65 LeMans made a wide turn at the corner. I thought about him. It seemed everybody but Joe Edwards and me had a skeptical view of the unfamiliar contraband – why would Rex be any different?

The Pontiac coasted to a stop. Vinny watched Rex as he got out. "I think you're looking at our new partner….. Partner." Vinny smiled.

"Huh?" I was confused.

The Rollodex in my mind ran through the file: Bushman/no car, Jimmy Martin/his hand would be in the cookie jar as soon as I brought him in. 'Fast Eddie' Mason/bloodline to Reno…..no way. Holter, Bad Brad, Robbie Herrick – no wheels. That left Crawfish with his '66 Bug and Danny Stax with his .327 cu.in. Chevy II.

I was partial to Kenny Crawford; the problem was you might not see him until 11 or 12 at night. I had to get rollin' on selling these bombs. Where's Danny Stax been? I asked Vince.

"What about Danny?" Rexall's eyes darted around and he knew we were in some type of conspiracy. Fuckin' guy was suspicious…..it was Rex's nature. Of course, we must have looked like we were up to something. He started nosing around. He walked over to the 4 ½ ft. high concrete retaining wall and looked behind the trash barrel, and looked inside the demonstration box. Rex took one out and held it up: "This your shit Whitepages?"

"Yeah, Cinzano and me got some business going." I answered.

He saw the other 12 boxes. Looks like you guys are doing a lot of business. He took one from the sample box, "Firecrackers.......big ones." A faint smile came across his face and vanished; I could see his wheels turning. A brief silence was broken by a distant explosion. "I hope these things are louder than that." he chuckled. "You two arsonists get pinched with this shit.......this shit's federal. What are they?"

"Blockbusters – quarter stick of dynamite." I dimmed my eyes to slightly more than slits.

"How you gonna move it – you don't have any way to transport it."

"Vinny and me are going to move it you'll see." Vinny smiled as I had just made him a partner.

"Tarts spoke up, "We were thinking about Kenny or Danny Stax."

Crawfish is camping with Kirk up in the Catskills, and Stax's car got that Sammy Davis headlight; a good reason for the bluecoats to pull you over." Rex said.

"Why you want to get in on the action?"

He smiled, "I dunno......tell me more."

"I fronted all the money - equal risk......youse pay me $100 each, or we each buy four boxes. It's $25/box for Rex and me, and $30 for you Vince of which Rex gets $10 for transport, and I get $10 because I took all the risk and put the deal together." I said.

"Hey Quasar – we got to set off one of them blockbusters." Rex said and he reached in the car and pushed in the cigarette lighter.

"WOAH.....WOah.....woah.....Not down here you retard."

"You fuckin' nuts Rex?" Vinny's eyes bulged.

"You in or not?" I looked as pissed as Vinny, and he didn't know a thing about the product either.

"I ain't in - until I know how loud these things are."

"I'm telling ya Rex we'll sell out before 10 o'clock." I bulldogged my chin and nodded.

The trunk was opened and he started moving a junkyard of crap – just enough so the blockbusters wouldn't get crushed. As he was situating the ordnance Rex said, "Where should we do this?"

"Go to Lake Ave. first, we'll get some wine. Then we'll give you a demonstration down the River." I said.

"Greystone or the Marina?"

"The Marina – I don't want to disturb my neighborhood." I laughed.

Just as Harriman Ave. was the access road to Greystone Station from Warburton; Kennedy Memorial Dr. was the spur to The Kennedy Marina from Warburton Ave. The city had built a bridge for car traffic to go over the railroad tracks and made it easy for fishermen, picnickers, partiers, and romantic couples to do their thing with the river as their backdrop. The Marina could barely be seen from the Greystone overpass. A distance of about three miles separated the two.

The Marina was built on the cheap. It was about two football fields long but wasn't very wide. It might have been 60 yards from the water to the railroad tracks. Corrugated sheet piling was driven into the river on three sides which formed a cofferdam/retention barrier. The water was pumped out and Yonkers' garbage was used for fill. The top six feet was compacted dirt, gravel, hard pack limestone, and good ol' #6 stone was used as the icing on the cake so everyone could break an ankle. The #6 and ruts also prevented speeding and drag racing.

We looked around, Rexall drove to the south end where a small channel divided the marina from the old Phelps Dodge plant. The nearest fishermen were about 50 yards north. People were already shooting off fireworks. It was ideal for that: there was no residential housing around; all the rocketry was aimed out into the Hudson.

Drinking Pagan Pink Ripple was like drinking carbonated Kool-Aid. The alcohol content was about 11 or 12%. The quart was gone in three major gulps. The sun hadn't gone down below the Palisades, and there were no cops in sight. It was 'all clear'; a perfect time for product demonstration. We parked and got one from the trunk. I had a blockbuster in my hand. "Do it." I said. Cinzo made contact between the cigarette lighter and the wick.

If the bomb was laid on the ground, half of the explosive's sound would be absorbed by whatever it rested on; I had to wing it as far and as high as I could. I was trying to showcase the blockbuster as a amusement device rather than its destructive capabilities. I was getting jittery as I calculated the burn rate of the fuse, the burn-off rate had picked up speed as the fuse burned down. I threw it over to the old copper wire's deserted powerhouse. BIG FUCKIN' "BOOM!" There was a major echoing explosion as it still ascended. Pigeons flew in all directions. The fusing of these bombs were unpredictable, I wish I had gotten rid of it sooner.

Everyone down the marina looked in our direction. "Let's get out of here." Vinny wiped his mouth of the Pineapple wine he was drinking.

A soul brother and his girl waved to us as the Le Mans climbed the ramp up to the bridge. "Hey….." he called to Rex. He stopped and turned down the 8-track.

Rex fucked around with the brother and his phony face of amazement: "Did you hear that?"

"What was that?" the brother said.

Rex's brow came together, his eyes got big, and he smiled: "Fuckin' loud." he wooooed.

Vince called through the back seat's half-window, "Some guys were on the Phelps Dodge property."

"My eardrums are still ringing……later soul man." Rex put it in drive, and we drove back up to Lake Ave.

"Holy shit." Vinny laughed.

"Sounded like a grenade…….did you feel the concussion? – Partner?" We clinked our wine bottles and the partnership was formed.

430

Our first stop was the Hun's garage. We drove past and saw they were there; we doubled back to Lake Ave. to get four quarts of Colt 45. McKool and Quinn didn't like visitors; it kept them away from their repairs and restoring cars they were trying to sell. Periodically, they'd work on other cars, but not without a referral. We had gotten chased off before. A couple of times they'd tell us to leave the beer in the fridge before we left. They had rank over us, there wasn't much we could say or do.

They had a car on jackstands; their legs stuck out from under the Chevelle. An uncooperative drive shaft had the two Huns cursing as they wrestled with it trying to convince the splines of the tranny and the drive shaft to line up.They had already replaced the transmission with one from Saw Mill Auto Wreckers.

"McKool.......Davis." Vince looked underneath the Chevy.

"You match-marked the driveshaft and the rear end?" McKool asked his partner.

"Sure did."

"Too much fuckin' grease. One of youse get me a can of that Brake-kleen so I can find the match mark."

A hand reached out from underneath the car and Vinny put it in McKool's hand. "Roll it to about five o'clock."

"How's zat?" Quinn answered.

"Push it in a touch.......raise it up a touch. Push it in a little more." The driveshaft slid right in. "Most girls aren't that easy." The two Huns laughed. "Who it is? Whatdya want?"

"The Rogues.......brought you some ice cold Colt." we said.

Quinn told Conners, "Just got to bolt and torque the universal joint connections and Christine's ride will be ready. "Let's see how cold that Colt is. The two came from under the Chevy with greasy hands and arms; rust-flakes peppered their faces. "What do you cats want?" Conners McKool said.

"Maybe some business the Huns might be interested in." Rexall grinned.

"Straight or shady?"

"Darkside."

"Drugs?" he said.

"No."

"Keep talking."

I pulled out a blockbuster from the sample box. Davis recognized it straight away. McKool rolled his eyes and shook his head, "Don't need no firecrackers."

Quinn immediately spoke up: "That thing's a quarter stick of dynamite.....it'll blow up a car and set it on fire. Use two, and you'll get the money box from a pay phone. They'll take apart any coin operated machine with two charges. You just got to know where to place the second charge after the first blows it open. Sometimes – you don't need the second.....the coinbox will just lift out."

Tarts smiled at McKool, "Now you can look at a payphone like it's your personal neighborhood bank. You'll never be overdrawn again, and……..it's open 24 hours a day. That's what they mean when they say: convenient hours."

"You got a problem with another crew – toss three of these in their clubhouse and you've just evicted them." Rex put on the salesman's pitch.

Quinn got serious; ""You can also maim or even kill an innocent bystander……..collateral damage shit."

That possibility had caught us off-guard, I had only thought of the injury to oneself in handling the explosives.

He resumed with the details of a pay phone cracking job using the blockbusters. "It's a two man job: one's the blaster/mechanic, the other is the lookout/muscle. You need 3 blockbusters – one's a spare - just in case. You need a sleever bar or a crowbar, a three lb. smash (hammer). Depending on the last time Ma Bell emptied the coinbox – you can expect a $40 haul on a moderately visited pay phone. The phone company keeps track of how many calls are made each month – they know when it's time to empty them."

McKool turned to Rex, the latter was 6'3" he didn't get a chance to look up very much when he talked to people. McKool was 6'7". Vince and me were 6'1", we were taller than Quinn, but people who had tangled with Quinn had equated the experience with taking on a wolverine. "How much?" McKool asked.

" Three dozen to a box…….give you four boxes for $125. That's a 144 units that'll sell on the street for a buck apiece." I said.

He countered: "$115."

"Come on……I know I'm younger and everything, but we got to make some scratch too." I played up another angle which was true enough: "McKool…..no one else is getting this deal. We came to the Huns first out of respect and for the career guidance you gave us in the past. We're showing our appreciation."

"$117 – Final." Davis said.

"$118." I countered.

"Done." McKool's hand slammed on the roof of the car. "But you guys got to finish bolting up the Chevelle's drive shaft universal joint to the rear end. Me and Davis got to finish with the stick shift and the console. I hate these Muncie shifters. Had a Hurst shifter on the workbench for almost a year – I was tired of looking at it so I sold it to Shooey. A stock Chevy shifter would have been easier to install.

Three creepers were under the Chevelle. Vince called over to Davis, "Tell me what to do."

"Clamp the two flanges together so you can see daylight in the four holes and take the two driftpins on the creeper……"

"Wait a minute, what the deuce is a driftpin?"

"Them long slender punches that come to a point on one end, and line up the holes with them at three and nine o'clock. You should be able to make the bolts at six and twelve. If you can't figure out the rest - get a job with Mikey Reno." Quinn shouted from underneath, "Hey Rex."

"Yeah?"

"Why don't you wait in the truck."

432

"I'm busy reading this issue of 'Naughty Neighbors' that's on the workbench." he laughed, "Besides; somebody has to push this job."

"What are you too good to be a wrench?" Quinn talked as he worked.

"Too smart." He replied as he placed the four boxes of shellshock on the workbench.

"How tight?" Vinny asked.

"That u-joint is turning the rear wheels with occasional burn-outs. That's a lot of torque even for a GM car. Get 'em as tight as you can with that 3/8ths socket wrench.....but not breaker bar tight." he said.

"You got to keep them blockbusters dry – no moisture." I said.

"Right." McKool agreed.

"Like you said, they got a shelf life......any more around? Who's dealing them?" Davis said.

"We're the only ones around here with them. Tell you the truth – none of us ever seen them before."

"I ran into them about five years ago in quantity. Since then the most we'd come across would be like ten here and there." he said.

"Any word on Eddie Van or Ranger Rick?" Vinny asked.

Davis Quinn squinted, "No news is good news."

"McKool...." Rex called, "We got to move this shit.....we got to go."

"When they get the driveshaft bolted Rex." Conners said. Where's the next stop Rex?"

"Orchard Street. I think we'll be able to move some down there." Vinny said.

All the bolts were made and torqued. Me and Vince came out from under the Chevelle.

"Seems like they only got money for one thing down there; and you guys don't sell it." McKool said.

"Hadn't counted on that."

"Nothing lasts, it's always changing.....got to stay sharp." he said.

"Don't feed them with the payphone shit – one of 'em gets pinched, and it'll come right back on youse." McKool said.

"And don't take too many phones down in the same area.....next thing you know – you'll be thinking every van near a pay phone is taking your picture." Davis added.

McKool looked at the three of us: "Don't be greedy ...... don't be in a rush. Don't work with junkies and don't become one. They have a real knack for making bad moves. Other than that......" Connors raised a quart of Colt.....

We raised our remaining wine, "To the Huns!"

We starting walking out and I heard McKool tell Quinn, "Make sure the Rogues job is a 100%."

I smiled and looked at McKool and shook my head. I knew he was teaching me something.

WE GOT IN REXALL'S CAR, "HOW'D YOU THINK OF THE Huns?" he said.

I chuckled, "I saw the garage lit up."

"Chance?"

"Or fate.........dumb luck......who's to say?"

"We got eight boxes left – where to?"

Vince said from the back seat: "Go over to the Legion Hall, they got the bar and they always want to smell gunpowder, not so much for the smell but for the memories it brings up. I know what that smell does to 'Blackie', (Vinny and Joey's Dad).

The good thing about these veterans, they knew how to handle this grade of fireworks. The bad thing was they only bought one box.

We hit the North End, Lake, Lockwood, Nepeara Park....... Anywhere people conGreggated. Around midnight, we heard a trail of bombs from the circuit of sales we had made. It made us smile knowing we were the catalyst. We had sold ten boxes of blockbusters.

"Rex, it's late for me; we ain't going to sell any more tonight. Drop me off down the end, I got to go caddying tomorrow."

Somehow Rex found it somewhere in his magnanimous heart to drive down to Warburton. I couldn't believe he was giving me a ride to my front door. It seldom happened. As we went north, the Harriman/Warburton 'Y' approached. We steered left and went down to Greystone's parking area.

"Now what?" I said.

"Shut up queer bait.......we're doin' a phone."

"Come on Rex – some other night."

"Just to see if Quinn is right about crackin' one."

"For the love of fuck man......some other night."

"Vinny?" Rex was looking for a majority

"Let's just do it quick, we're here anyway – maybe we don't even want to sell anymore. Sounds like an easy way to make money. We sell out of munitions – no more easy money."

"I should be able to get more from the dude......the fuck had a trunk full of the shit."

Rex's curiosity could not be quenched: "The first one goes in the coin return slot. That'll obliterate the bottom corner from the back frame plate. Then we got to bend the side up by hand and expose the coin box. The second blockbuster goes between the coin box and the frame/backplate. No. 2 is supposed to blow off the face of the phone so the coin box securing bolt is history and the coinbox should pull right out." Rex recalled in detail.

It was late; I was half-drunk, smoked up, and tired, but there was some compulsive thrill about taking apart a pay phone with explosives and it overrode our fatigue. With the station's recent improvements, the phone company installed a payphone on both north and south bound platforms. Both had a 3-sided aluminum shroud to protect the caller and phone from the weather.

He opened the trunk. We took out what we felt we needed for the job: 5 blockbusters (2 for each phone, and 1 in case of a misfire), a

434

crowbar, a tire iron, a 48 oz. ball peen hammer, and a pair of work gloves. The car was turned about and left running with the trunk open. Rex watched me and Cinzo at work, and kept his eyes peeled for unexpected visitors watching from the overpass.

"Do it." Rexall cupped his hands to project his voice.

We started on the riverside platform, despite Quinn's advice we decided to go with one man per side, for the detonations. Vinny started off on the riverside with me as Rex played chicky from above. We got everything ready for the southbound and the northbound. We loaded both phones with the explosives. The first charge was placed in the coin return as deep as it would go with just a little bit of the fuse showing. We lit it and laughed and ran behind one of the overhang's columns..............."BIG FUCKIN' BOOM!" Pieces of plastic and metal shot out in all directions. The metal on the coin return side peeled up and out like Davis said; I used the crowbar to open enough space between the frame plate and the moneybox so Vinny could fit the second blockbuster in vertically. He left the tire iron and the leather-palmed gloves with me and he ran across the four tracks getting ready for the northbound phone. He had exploded his first charge before I had my coinbox free, bits of metal and plastic came whizzing by. Like Vince, I crossed over the tracks instead of using the overpass with the tools and the first coinbox. I used the crowbar as a prybar and separated the remainder of the phone from the frame plate as he placed his second charge.

"Here it comes!" he warned, and I dropped everything got underneath the elevated platform. I pushed my fingers into my ear canals: "BOOM!" The same result.

Rex saw a few lights come on in the 14 story apartment; only two guys came out and stood on their balconies to try to see what all the commotion was.

We tossed the tools into Rex's trunk, "Whitelaw, take the moneyboxes to your house." They dropped me off, and sped up O'Dell Ave. "Call you tomorrow." Rex was anxious to get up the hill.

THE COINBOXES AND THE HALF BOX OF SAMPLE blockbusters were hidden in the coal bin in the cellar. I tried to go upstairs with as little noise as possible. Ray's voice floated through the bedroom's darkness. "Caddying tomorrow?"

"Meeting Loki.....we're going to catch the caddy bus by the city incinerator." I whispered.

"Mom said I could take the Comet."

"I've got to get my license." I said.

"You won't be 16 for another two months."

"I still want and need one."

"The DMV doesn't issue them on a need basis."

Saturday morning arrived almost as soon as I put my head on the pillow.

"Ray, give me a lift to Loki's house. We're gonna walk down to catch the caddy bus."

"Told you last night, I can drive you guys all the way today. Call him up – tell him we'll be there in 15 minutes." he said.

Hal's voice blasted through his bedroom door, "Hey you two birds – keep it down; you're not the only ones living here." We weren't down the stairs when we heard someone set off a pack of firecrackers. We were thinking along the same wavelength: righteous justice.

I went down to the coal bin to take a closer look at the coin boxes. Both were ruptured and deformed by the blasts. I came up from the cellar. He was having peanut butter on a couple of Ritz crackers. I looked in the breadbox to make a sandwich......no bread. The door to the downstairs cubby-hole toilet was closed. Sonofabitch......Hal was up. We had to get out of the house before he was finished and laid into us.

"Got your lunch?" Ray said in the breakfast nook.

I held up a partial roll of Ritz crackers, and we eased our way out the front door. "We gotta stop at the Greeks and get a couple of scrambles on roll for me and Loki." I said.

"Make it three and three coffees." We took off in the Comet and got our order from the Greek.

"$4.50."

Last night came right back at me; it looked like we could sell more blockbusters tonight. Rex and me made about $140 each and Vinny got his reduced rate of the pie just for being there. He'd have to get a full 1/3rd on the pay phones cause he really was part of that whole deal. I know some people throw a lot of money in them phones; still, it was hard to estimate our haul. We had four or five dozen blockbusters left in Rex's trunk, maybe we'd sell them or keep them. Most of our take last night came through selling them 2 for $3. Tonight had the possibility of being a real bonanza.

"Hey Nick, I got a can of Coke too." I said.

"Five dollars."

I hopped in the car and tried to get some cash out of my front pocket. I should have taken it out in the deli. Two hundred was handed over to Ray as we drove to get Loki.

"What happened?" he said.

"The stuff really sold."

"Wow....What da?"

"Cinzano, Rex, and me are already in the black."

"With fireworks? How you figure?" he made a unibrow in disbelief.

"Say wait a minute.....I might need that two hundred back if Joe Edwards has more product he wants to get rid of."

Ray beeped the horn in front of Loki's house. I didn't think I'd get my money back this quick." He handed the two hundred back to me, "You owe me two hundred......again."

"Right. Hey Ray, don't say anything to him about the fireworks. He had his chance to get in and he didn't."

I gave him his egg on a poppy seed bun, and his coffee. He may have woken up a bit with the sight of food. The damn coffee was too hot so I had the coke with my scramble. Ray only drank his coffee, he'd eat his egg on bun when he got to St. Andrews.

We pulled into the entrance of the country club. At the far end of the lot I saw Joe Edwards.

"Drive over by that guy with the open trunk. Edwards puts his face in the car, How 'bout it Whitebank – you got anything left?"

"Sold out......gotta reload. Whatcha got?" I smiled.

"Motherfucker." He lit a Camel, sucked deep and let the smoke fill his lungs. He finally let the smoke go; the tar and nicotine was traded for frustration and disappointment. "I was hoping to buy back some product if you hadn't sold out.

"Wha? I wanted to buy more for tonight." I said. "You got anything?"

"Nobody wants the little shit after they've heard the big stuff." Edwards said. "All's I got left are a couple of apples."

"Lemme see." They looked like a couple of Christmas tree ornaments, " What the fuck Joe?"

"You want them......20 bucks a piece.

I didn't say anything.

"Give me 30 bucks for two."

I handed him three 10 dollar bills."

"Take'em – I got to get going." Edwards said.

"You're not caddying?"

"Going to Jersey for the rest of the weekend."

Loki chuckled, "Any room?"

"Murdoch needs you here captain."

"Ray could you open the trunk?" I said.

Joe brought over the two remaining apples, he looked in the trunk and saw some of Jane's costumes in there: he asked, "You dressing up for the Fourth?" he laughed.

"Funny." I said.

"Be careful with them." He turned to Ray: "Park the car - in the shade."

This isn't like nitro – I don't have to worry about any bumps.........do I?" Ray asked.

"Just make sure they stay in the same place. Heat is the thing you want to avoid." Then Joe nodded and got Brother Ray to nod in agreement.

That was the last time we saw the crane operator at Sunset Ridge.

Once again the two hundred was back in Ray's hands. I'd see him after caddying. What the hell was I going to do with those two apples. I'd have to ask around, maybe someone had run into them before. Unless they had bits of metal inside, they would essentially be a bigger version of a blockbuster........a concussion grenade. There was a shelf life to these blockbusters and apples. One of the real bad things was when they failed to explode. There were too many stories out there about people losing body parts because they were trying to get the stuff to go off. Fuses would decay and in a short amount of time fail to ignite the gunpowder in one way or another.

The explosive materials and their inability to ignite in certain cases made me think of my relationship with Ray. Hanging out with people who were older than me, they saw in just a short amount of time – something was not quite right with me. I had this desire for equality. I looked the part, but I didn't act the part. With this ordnance, I became the 'contact' for the 'stuff', and almost overnight people knew who I was. It didn't do a thing as far as making me more desirable to girls, but the guys now found me to be a perfect bookend to my older brother: Ray was the genius and Ryan was the unpredictable daredevil. Our close associates knew who we really were – they knew Ray was the real deal. I didn't know what they thought of me, and I didn't want to know.

vi

Another double-loop day: 36 holes for me and Loki. Sunset Ridge was having its annual Fourth of July tournaments, followed by a dinner-dance later that evening. The party rental company had put up a large tent on Friday afternoon adjacent to the clubhouse. The party atmosphere had everybody laughing, joking, smiling.....flirting and the everyday had turned into something I hadn't seen very much of at these country clubs: 40, 50, 60, and 70 year old people cutting loose and having a good time. It kind of made the specter of 8 hours of looping not as bad. Most of the time, these people were just plain old pissed off at life. They weren't like Edna and Mack out in the country, who didn't see a helluva lot of people and seemed happier for it.

July 3rd didn't start off the way I wanted either – no blockbusters – . There was a major logjam getting off the first tee. The caddymaster gave Black Tommy Withers and me the foursome ahead of Loki and Kevin Kresso. It didn't take but 4 minutes of observation to see something was screwed up with the foursome Murdoch had given Kresso and Loki. The caddies knew who the good golfers were. However, when there was a big Fourth of July celebration there were tons of guests showing up and playing. It was a crapshoot from the caddy point of view. Loki and Kresso came over by Tommy and me and asked, "You know these guys Murdoch gave us?"

"Shit.....y'all look the same to me." Tommy laughed.

"Freitag's the member, he'll shoot high 80's – low 90's. He'll have a couple of bad holes and it'll screw up his score. He's okay." I answered.

Kresso said, "The two older guys are brothers, them 30 year old guys are their sons.....cousins I guess. They're all Freitag."

"I think they all had the champagne breakfast." Loki rolled his eyes.

"Who you got?" I said.

"I got the old guys." Kresso replied.

"Just look at that foursome.......is there any hope?" Loki wondered aloud.

They didn't appear a bit out of the ordinary, but they're out there I thought. The one son was running in place at the rear of the tee. The other was doing a Buddhist chant and doing yoga exercises to limber up. I guessed they had drawn the attention they wanted.

"En Garde!" The two cousins started to sword fight with their drivers as they waited to be announced on the tee.

At first, the other golfers found their antics amusing, but not the golfers who were trying to tee off. They were an immense distraction, and they called for Murdoch who doubled as the day's official starter, to reel in these two tap dancers.

"Freitag – four......on the tee if you please. Murdoch had no option but to get this four-man carnival on the golf course and away from the clubhouse and 1st tee. Withers' and my golfers were pissed off they had been jumped and would have to play behind this Broadway musical-comedy. Though the Freitags were on the tee, they were a long way from teeing off, and they were going at each other like cats.

"I thought the honor was settled at breakfast." Donald, the Sunset member, said.

"Oh no it wasn't, not by a long shot." his son, Jackie, laughed.

"Then what was settled?" Bobbie, his cousin said, hand on his hip.

"We settled who was paying for breakfast." Jackie said.

Bobbie's father, Roger, tried to untangle the champagne, "Well.....whose honor is it?"

Jackie said, "It's certainly NOT my honor – I left that at "The Ball Game" last night.....and I don't care who knows it." He cooed, and whipped his chin up to the sky and posing a few seconds for all to admire.

Up to that point, Kresso and Loki's heads followed the banter as they watched the ping pong match, but Jackie's lastest admission left the caddies frozen looking at one another.

"Glad they ain't our loop." Withers shook his head.

"Your golfing outfit is loud enough; I don't think anyone on the tee is interested in your personal life." Don told his son.

"Daddy – please.......please can I tell everybody?" Jackie gave out with his screwball laugh.

"Now Jackie, you know Daddy's been in enough trouble last year with the review committee." He went over to his golf bag and retrieved a brown pharmacy bottle. A quick cough to justify the use, and Don downed half the bottle. He gave the bottle to his caddy to put back in the golf bag's compartment. "I must be coming down with something." Don cleared his throat into his fist.

"Did you say you went to the Mets game last night?" Jackie asked his cousin.

"No!......I said I went to the 'Ball Game' on Christopher St., and believe me cousin – that establishment is NOT for switch

439

hitters......or boys who want to be bench warmers. They are brutes!"
Jackie squealed.

"Last call – Freitag – 4! On the tee immediately! Come on
guys, let's play some golf now." Murdoch pleaded.

"Be right with you Mister Caddymaster." Bobbie smiled. He
ran over to Loki who had his bag standing on the ground. "We've got
to freeze this day in time........with........a photograph. And if we all
smile, you too Mr. Caddymaster, this frozen day in time will cool off
this afternoon's heat." He continued to fumble through his golf bag
like it was his purse.

"No pictures, people are waiting to play golf." he said.

He finally dug out his small instamatic Kodak. Loki was
getting embarrassed, and it was one of the few times he wished for the
apathy of a hangover. There was no way this foursome could have any
semblance of a golf game, the caddies thought.

Murdoch was real close to sending the Freitag 4 back to the
clubhouse or at least make them start off the backside of the golf
course. Don slipped Murdoch a twenty, and Loki snapped three
pictures as fast as he could advance the film: Brothers Don and Roger
were behind cousins Jackie and Bobbie on one knee in front, with
Murdoch and Kevin Kresso on each side. Their professional sized bags
stood like sawed off columns guarding the entourage.

Murdoch set the order off the tee to eliminate any further
argument about who had the honor. Roger shanked his drive and
everybody laughed. The next two dubbed theirs fifteen feet into the
rough. Jackie at least got his drive airborne, but sliced it so bad it went
out of bounds into the parking lot. The young men got down on both
knees begging John to let them take a 'mulligan', but he would hear
none of it - they had wasted so much time already.

The caddymaster walked back to the starters box, "Lord
Love a Duck". He looked around and down at his obsolete schedule:
"Blau 4 on the tee....Feel free to hit into the Freitag experiment." This
garnered cheers, laughter, applause, and eased the tension of the
Fourth of July golfers. Next year, Murdoch recommended the shotgun
format for Independence Day to the golf committee.

We watched the Freitags as they marched up the long par 5
in zig-zag formation. They hadn't reached the green and we saw Loki
and Kresso, both were sitting on the base of a golf bag as the golfers
argued with one another. They were throwing clubs, and Bobbie
launched a sand trap rake at his father, Roger. They pointed at one
another like a couple of politicians, stomped their feet, crossed their
arms, and turned their backs on one another. We had already teed off,
but were dead in the water as we waited for Loki and company to get
all four balls on the green. They were nearly screaming at each other,
we picked up a lot of what they were saying.

Our foursome were dumbstruck as we all watched the drama
in front of us. Three balls were on the green and one was on the fringe,
so they argued whose shot it was: the ball furthest away or the ball on
the fringe. While the two brothers argued the rule, Jackie and Bobbie
went into their golfbags and pulled out some clothes. They went
behind the green in a thicket of bushes and changed, and came out

440

wearing hot pink, lavender elephant bell bottoms, blaze lime and white slacks and tops; and if they weren't wearing women's beach hats and oversized Jackie-O sunglasses – then my aunt's - my uncle.

Those two goofs were dressed for Churchill Downs or Mardi Gras. Murdoch had his binoculars out now, saying to no one in particular: "Got a good idea how George Pickett felt when his troops assaulted Seminary Ridge." He looked down at his watch.

Word had gotten back to Murdoch by golfers who had reached the 10th hole – the Freitag foursome had the front ten holes in a state of pandemonium. Assistant Caddy master Pete was instructed by Murdoch to take a golf cart and track down the renegade foursome. Pete told Roger, the non-member brother to pick up their pace, or they would be cited for slack play and ordered to let the next five groups of players behind them play through.

Roger advised his brother and the two sons of the warning, and reached into his pocket and took a pill from a pharmacy bottle, and put the medication into the small compartment at the top of the bag. Donald and the boys went to their bags as well. Don gave the obligatory cough, and downed the rest of the cough elixir. The boys sniffed a hit of Rush (butyl-nitrate) and popped a couple of dexedrine capsules each.

I'd see Kresso and Loki at just about every tee or green and get the play by play after or before every hole. It was pandemonium.

Loki asked, "Kevin, what pills did Roger pop?"

He started laughing, "Fuckin' guy did a 5 mg. of Xanax. He's gonna be in the land of Oz real soon. I'm gonna have to carry the corpse on the back 8."

"You got any reefer?" Loki asked Kevin, Tommy, and me.

"You want one of Roger's zombie pills?" Kresso laughed.

The Freitag cousins had to wait for the uppers to take effect, so they had Loki and Kresso play the next two holes for them. Don would tee off and if it stayed in the fairway he'd keep playing the hole otherwise he picked up his ball and told Roger to put him down for an 'X' for the hole. Roger thought he was really accomplishing something by walking the holes while playing in another galaxy.

Our golfers were stupefied, and Mr. Blau asked me: "Why are those caddies playing golf?"

I didn't have an answer that would help Loki and Kresso's situation. Tommy Withers stepped forward: "A few of the more progressive clubs in the area have instituted the Revolution #9 rule."

"Revolution 9 rule…….what the devil is that?"

"It's where the caddies declare the Revolution #9 Rule to be in effect in honor of Independence Day and the caddies get to be the players and the players have to tote the bags for five holes. It really seems to be catching on."

I figured out where Withers was going with this bit of insanity, "You know Mr. Blau, I always thought the revolution rule would be more appropriate for the Labor Day holiday, but we're not unionized, so perhaps it isn't the right holiday."

"How come I've never heard of this Revolution #9 rule?" the member said as we watched one Freitag and the caddies putt on the eighth green.

"Nevertheless," Tommy said, "It's obvious Mr. Freitag's brother must belong to one of the more progressive country clubs that have chosen to invoke the #9 rule. I've heard it's quite an event in France on Bastille Day. There, the caddies are the true celebrities on July 14th. Just let us know if you want us to take over for a couple of holes." Tommy walked away trying to contain his laughter.

Blau asked, "Is this guy for real?"

I nodded, "It's for real, I believe it was why they shut down Hudson River C.C."

"My God....."

With only 3 guys playing, and Kresso and Loki hitting the greens in regulation, the foursome was able to catch up to the foursome in front of them and erase a four hole deficit.

"Oh......super shot Loki.......Where did it go?"

He turned around and squinted with a half-smile, "You're the caddy now – you're supposed to be watching the ball."

"Hey Buster, I'm katty, but I'm no caddy until I start lugging that bag around, and don't wait for that to happen. I do like your swing Lokey......are you a swinger Lowkeee?"

Kresso could hear Jackie and Loki's chit-chat. He was bent over laughing into the professional sized bag of clubs. The 10th hole brought another innovation to the game of golf: 'Polo Pony Golf – without the pony. At the end of the 10th hole, we were back at the clubhouse. The cousins made Don rent a cart for the back eight. All four liquored up: Bobbie ordered a "Big Banana Daiquiri", and Jackie had a grasshopper. Their fathers went with a Manhattan, and a double vodka martini.....two each.

We caught up with Loki and Kresso and they gave us the highlights of their romp in the woods so far.

"To quote B.B. King: 'The thrill is gone'...........We just got to get some pot." Loki said.

"C'mon Loki, it ain't that bad, take one of Roger's calm-down pills." Kresso prescribed. "They're getting a cart, it's gonna get better. Take a pill, you'll feel better." He laughed. Tommy and me found it contagious.

Don made Roger drive the cart, Tommy Withers and me watched as Roger made a hard left on the fairway which threw Don and their golf bags from the cart. Kresso came over and put him back in the cart and cinched brothers down tight with their seat belts.

"Slow it down Roger.....slow it down." Kresso said with his hands in prayer. The foursome headed down towards the 11th green. With the senior citizens golf bags back in the cart, Loki and Kresso gave the cousins some real personalized service. It wasn't complete and undivided attention because Roger thought he was operating a Sherman tank running over shrubs, driving through sand traps, parking on tees and greens. Don was at the point where the Jackie-O sunglasses didn't help very much and drooled from the 12th through the 18th holes.

Kresso had some rough sledding with Jackie; he purposely hit his ball into the woods. He inhaled some of that "Rush" stuff, and made a pass at him. Kresso grabbed him by the neck and smiled, "Listen Jackie – you're signing an extra 10 holes for me and Loki on our checks for all this crap."

"Whateverrrr........say don't you and what's his name want to have any fun?" He rummaged through the big side pocket of the bag , put his beach hat over the woods golf clubs and whipped up his head with a wig of Jill St. John hair .... "Interested?"

"What planet are you from?" Kevin asked straight faced.

"C'mon you daytime hustler......take a walk on the wild side."

"Jackie, let's just finish the fuckin' round – I swear to God." he said.

"No 'Light my fire'?"

"Play golf Jackie.....play golf."

"Oh alright – but now I'm disappointed." The wig went back in the golf bag.

A par 3 and a par 5 remained. Roger decided to cruise around the course on a public relations tour, trying to undo the ill-will the Freitag's delinquent course etiquette had incurred. Roger waved and doffed his hat to which he received thumbed noses, extended middle fingers, clenched fists, and shouts of promised revenge. Don hung on to the metal post of the canopy with one hand and waved with the other. He reported: "Another bird Roger."

He responded, "We played are bess, and dis is how we're treated. Fug 'em."

Roger tried to drive over to our foursome, but Mr. Blau warned, "DO NOT COME ANY CLOSER FREITAG. I'll see you in front of the membership committee."

The 17th hole was a beautiful par 3, surrounded by tall trees. The elevated green was protected by a small pond in front and sand traps on all four sides. The boys decided to have the caddies play the par 3 with them. Bobbie pulled a 7 iron from the bag.

"You got enough club?" Loki asked.

"I need loft – I don't want that ball running the green into the back trap. He teed it up and swung at it." "Fuck!" I could hear Bobbie yell from the 17th tee. He had topped the ball. Another was teed up and he put the 7 back in the bag and took out the 6 iron. He took a couple of practice swings....
"There it is – that's the speed." He continued coaching himself: "Slow it down, let the club do the work."

"Whack." Bobbie put the golfball dead center on the green 10 feet away from the pin. "Your turn."

"Mind if I use the six?" Kresso said.

"Whack." Eight eyes followed the ball. "Comin' in hot." Loki said.

"Down…..bite……down….." Kresso's face winced. It had hit slightly right of center a foot away from the pin and rolled into the back trap.

"You're up Loki." Jackie said.

He teed up as far left as possible. He looked at Bobbie's and Jackie's six irons and chose the shorter of the two. "Whack." The ball had landed pin high, but it had too much backspin and it ended up on the front fringe around 7 o'clock.

Jackie stood behind his ball with his seven iron – lining up his shot. The golf club grip rested in his crotch. He held out his hands – palms up. They were shaking enough to have thought he had Parkinson's disease; Loki attributed it to the speed. He addressed the ball and stepped away and took two more practice swings and got ready to hit. Jackie stood motionless like a coiled spring and: "Whack." It stopped six feet from the hole. Looking at Loki and Kresso he said, "Wow…..that little faggot can really hit the ball." Jackie and Bobbie laughed at the caddies.

Kresso and Loki were pretty much awestruck. "Great shot Mr. Freitag.

He made birdie, and Bobbie made a par because he didn't count his first shot.

The 18th was a long par 5 that doglegged to the left. Only the big hitters could take it over the trees and save a stroke. Jackie had rescinded their playing privileges when neither caddy could make par on the 17th.

Bobbie played the hole as a par 5 not wanting to get hung up in the trees. Jackie tagged one and was 150 yards ahead of his cousin. It was another birdie for Jackie and a legitimate par for Bobbie.

"If you guys can smack the ball around like those last two holes, why don't you have some fun and play for real?" Kresso said.

"You mean like traditional golfers?"

" Yeah, I suppose." Kresso said.

"It's very difficult to be the persona they want us to be." Bobbie opened the trunk of the car and the caddies loaded the three bags. Jackie signed the pay cards. Both caddies were paid for three rounds of golf. Kresso thought it was worth it; Loki wasn't so sure.

TOMMY WITHERS AND ME BROUGHT OUR PLAYERS' BAGS to the rack in front of the pro shop. Loki had been sitting on a piece of slate near the golf cart barn. He looked my way and continued eating.

"Your guys had the course all screwed up – what was going on?" I couldn't help but laugh.

"Guys? You saw them first hand, you already know the story……you're just razzin' me. Them guys were genuine gay-blades." Loki squeezed his eyelids shut.

"Hey gimme a cigarette." I scratched my bald patch.

"Yeah dirt road Romeos, pill poppers, and cross dressers to boot." He finally started laughing trying to keep the last bite in his mouth. "One of the Dads got loaded on cough syrup, fuckin' brother was on tranquilizers. The weird thing was the cousins could play

444

scratch golf like somebody had flicked a switch. They just didn't give a fuck for nothing. The one told me the family was filthy rich and living off of Grandad's trust fund."

"Ready for another loop?" I said.

"Not really."

"Still a lot of bags out there."

"I'm still going to require more money for college. The first year blew a gigantic hole in my wallet."

"Beats being in a hot cab all night. You ain't going to get held up here." I said."

"'Spose."

Something had Loki going in a circle, we walked over to the soda machine. "Ryan look, I got all of these prerequisite math credits. I've got enough in two semesters to make it a minor. Thought I might get a job in a lab for a pharma company with a couple of chemistry courses – you know. Doesn't CIBA-Geigy make pills or tonics?"

"I still got my senior year to do – I thought driving a taxi for Main or Caesar's sounded pretty good."

"Fuck….Ray knows more about astro-physics, calculus, integrated algebra, trigonometry, than I will after four years at Pace University. What's the use? Could those last two holes the younger Freitag's played be some kind of sham or are they related to the pole reversal. Are they like Ray, Joey Tarts, Sally and the rest?" There was genuine concern and confusion in his movements. "Be right back."

He returned from the pole barn. The building was right around the corner from the caddy yard. Golf carts were housed in it at night; most were electric. There were four or five lawn mowers, a couple of cars. Loki had a plastic jug with a spout of motor oil in his hand.

"Ryan, comeer." I walked in the barn, he was by the utility sink. "Put the stopper in the drain." He turned the tap on and put six inches of water in the basin. Looking at the water, he handed me the plastic bottle of motor oil. Loki turned off the water and we waited until the water became placid.

"Pour it in….that's enough." he said. "You can differentiate the two liquids?"

"Yeah, the oil's floating – looks normal – where you going with this Loki?"

"Pull the plug."

We watched, there was no movement of the water or oil. We observed the experiment for a few minutes.

"Gravity should have drawn the fluids down the drain."

"Drain could be clogged."

"Which way does water drain?"

"Clockwise in the Northern hemisphere…..pole reversal will make it drain counter-clockwise." I said.

"But right now it is doing nothing. Neither. No magnetic influence. The drain's not clogged, I had the water running down the drain just before I called you. Get a scorecard pencil and mark the level of the fluid right now, and we'll come back and check it in a little bit." he said.

445

He went back to his slate seat and resumed eating his sandwich: "How can your brother be so cocksure of pole reversal?"

"Joe, I've been confused and unsure of every decision I've made – including which side to part my hair since we saw that fireball that night in '66. Ray reminded me of the blackout in the fall of '65. How far away was the comet when the electrical grid went down? Could these events be independent of each other, or are they interconnected in some way? The wizard says it's up for speculation. I say it's doubtful.

We sat, our thoughts trying to grab a piece of something with substance. He was looking at his PB&J sandwich. I thought Loki was expecting it to jump from his hand and run down the 11th fairway, instead his intensity increased. "What is it........some kind of 'Black Magic'.........'Dark Arts'......'Cosmic Mumbo-Jumbo?"

"It's about rotation – the positive becoming the negative and visa-versa; a surplus and a deficit of attraction and repulsion. As long as there has been a universe this rotation has been taking place. It never was a big deal until man and his machines came on the scene."

I waited for a question, but none came so I continued with Ray's theorem albeit second hand: "Ray contends organic life, because it operates on an electro-mechanical basis, is going to be affected as anything else on this planet. The collisions and atmospheric penetrations will increase and the human species is unknowingly accelerating pole reversal. If mankind is to survive this pole reversal, it will be through the magnetic adaptation of the outcasts, phantasm nomads, and shadow people who end up being the tunnel dwellers. 'Cellar dwellers' is what Ray calls them. They are the ones genetically wired to run optimally under a counter paradigm magnetic world." Again, I waited for a response from Loki. None........"That's how he explained it to me, or at least what I got out of it. There is a good chance I got it all wrong."

"It sounds better when you hear it – instead of looking at it on a railbridge overpass with your brother pointing to the equation and dissecting it with a pint of Thunderbird in hand. Say Ryan, what are we going to do when he goes to Indiana?"

"I got a whole bunch of exciting options: I'm going to get brains, looks, charisma, character, and maybe......maybe some integrity. One thing's for sure, I won't be able to live off being Ray's brother." I lit a cigarette.

Trouble was approaching: Asst. Caddymaster Pete had four computer cards in his hand.

"Loki, take Barbara Marx, and Mrs. Entin. Ryan, - Easton and Mrs. Froelich. They're on the tee, and why are you guys trying to hide from me?" he said.

We were exhausted after our 36th hole for the day. Murdoch cashed our computer cards right away. We almost forgot about the water/oil in the barn sink. It was empty. We refilled the basin with the same mixture and waited for calm on the fluids. I pulled the stoppers chain: normal clockwise drainage.

"Now what?" he said.

"Let's get out of here." We got a couple of cold drinks from the machine and caught a ride to Ardsley with Steve Olson; his brother Artie had gotten looped off for spitting on John Murdoch's windshield. "One more day." Steve said.

It took us 45 minutes to hitch a ride to Yonkers. Loki said he was going down the end and try to score one of Reno's low-count nickel bags. "I'll be ready for tomorrow.....18 holes and that's it, and I'm going to get high for lunch tomorrow.

We ended up getting a ride to the End. No Reno to be seen. The place was pretty deserted. I had to choose between 21 and Morsemere. I was out of steam. If I went home there was a good chance I wouldn't make it back out. "See you tomorrow Loke." I waved.

"You're going the wrong way." he called.

"Pole reversal."

Fireworks were going off everywhere. Pizza, a qt. of Colt and my share of the remaining blockbusters were beckoning. The corner and Rubeo were deserted, and everything was closed. I fell asleep on the step of Progressive Pizza.

"Honk......Honk......Honk.Honk."

I came to. Bad Brad Guzzutti was laughing at me from the wheel of his mother's car. His latest girlfriend smiled from the shotgun seat.

"Hey......Rip Van Winkle." he called.

My head felt as big as a watermelon, "Anybody around?"

"Rex and Danny Stax drove down to Belmar this morning."

"Who went with them?"

"The Bushman, Fast Eddie, and Jimmy Martinique went with Rex. Tarts, Barbara Wells, and Holter went with Stax." Brad said.

"Fuck," I exhaled. "Brad.....gimme a ride home?"

"Slide in next to Cheryl. Cheryl, this is my goombadacicci – Whitewine."

She looked at me. "That's not your name."

"No....not really, and it's a long story for another time." I said. "Barb Wells went with them?"

"Yeah – wait 'til Reno finds out." Brad said.

vii

Vinny and me knew we had to spread the word to all the Rogues: They had to witness the phenomenal music of the Allman Brothers Band. It was something they had to experience. Their music was at the core of who we were. We borrowed their concept of Brotherhood and took it to heart. They had struck a common chord with us in a way which was indefinable.

We were all keyed up for Wednesday, July 21, 1971 for the band's appearance at the Schaefer Music Festival. It was the largest gathering of Rogues there ever would be: Full blooded (dues paying....if we had had dues), potential Rogues, happy to be a Rogue for a night Rogue, Rogue Bitch, and 'on loan to the Rogues' – Rogue. Billy Van Nahl's allegiance was to the marines, but he had caught the fever back in January with Vinny and me at the Capitol. We were glad he came down with us. It was the music, and he just blended in. He said it helped him forget about Nam.

The Busch brothers Robin and Buddy also brought their just turned 13 year old brother George, who everybody called 'Presto'. According to Robin and Buddy, no one but their mother knew where he had come from. He showed up for breakfast one morning when they lived in the hills of Virginia and never missed a meal since. They yo-yoed back and forth between N.Y. and Virginia until Robin and Buddy joined the marines.

It was one of the last trips for Crawford's '66 Bug. The guys with the wheels decided to drive to the 242nd St. subway and find a space along side Van Cortland Park, and catch the subway to Columbus Circle. The VW was heaving pretty bad, no one had much confidence it could do a round trip that night.

Tarts and me had been talking up the Brothers to everyone. Ray and Loki were willing to see what all our yaking was about and perhaps shut me up. About 25 of us piled into the IRT subway. At the other end of the subway car I spotted Barbara Wells; again, no Mike Reno. The same girls who gave Ranger Rick his send off were with her. Like the Fillmore, I had called Meris Klein on Saturday through Tuesday; there was no answer. She must have been on vacation with her family.

Soon the subway car was filled by an impromptu party with clouds of smoke and all varieties of alcohol. It started taking on that 'feel', it was infectious. Those of us who knew the band were like evangelists spreading the gospel. "Just wish we had tickets." I kept apologizing. The one saving factor was the sound. Usually the sound made it over the 20 foot tennis screens; the music outside the rink was better than some college gymnasiums where colleges tried to stage rock shows. It was generally acknowledged where the large granite formations were, was about as good a place as could be had for free. Listening to the concerts from 'The Rock', a person could almost hear the same quality of sound as you could from inside the rink unless the wind was howling. The viewing never got better than fair. The big drawback was the lack of space; it could only accommodate 50 fans at most.

In 1971, the gypsy beer, wine, and mixed drink purveyors were allowed to do their thing without police interference as long as they didn't bark stadium style. Vinny and me made the journeyman move going with T-bird quarts.

Entering the park with a bag of beer was a liability; without a cooler there was no way to keep it cold and every jag down there was trying to mooch a can off you. It was totally different if you were drinking wine. No strangers would ask for a sip of wine, and that was double-true when they saw the mighty Thunderbird label. With some high grade pot, a concert goer could almost get ripped if things fell the right way.

The acoustic band, 'Cowboy' were about half-way through their set when we got there. The Allman Brothers had just released their seminal 'Tour de Force' live album: "Live at Fillmore East". FM radio was giving it a ton of airplay. Our crew from the subway was trying to find the best spot as we walked around. The early show had produced an unusually high turnout outside the rink; by the time we got there, the park was mobbed. We knew we'd all have to fend for ourselves when it came to finding a good spot to listen – so the search was on. Very soon we realized it was like 'little Yonkers' down there. Besides us, we ran into people from Lake Ave, Orchard St., and the North End. I recognized rockers from other neighborhoods: Park Hill, Lockwood Ave., Homefield; there were even some black dudes from Gorton and Puerto Ricans from the Hollow that I knew from track and cross country meets.

It was hard to get a sound reading from the acoustic Cowboy. A good spot to listen to them would be not be the same for the Brothers. We ambled on the one lane asphalt road from eastside back to the granite rock side. Vinny stopped when we came to the rock and pointed:

"Look."

Rexall and me were pretty buzzed; atop of the large granite formation towered Conners McKool standing close to the edge. He was with his Hun contingent: Quinn, Jimmy Deep Freeze, Dr. Kildare, and Demo Derby Dan. We were transfixed until one of the bluecoats told us to "keep it moving."

I was high enough - I thought I was in Rio de Janerio looking at Christ the Redeemer statue on the mountain overlooking the city.

We passed beneath them, and the cry went forward: To the Huns.....To the Huns......To the Huns!" McKool and Quinn stood side by side folded arms on their chests; grinned and nodded and accepted the homage. There were people there who I was sure didn't have a clue who the Huns were or where they came from, but took up the chant as well. I guess when they thought it was enough – McKool swept his arm once, with his palm down and the chanting ceased.

If I knew what a psychological boost was – I thought this would qualify as one: the Huns validated our choice of rock artists whose sound gave our crew definition and meaning. I had been pretty sure none of the Rogues had let the Huns know about the Brothers' Central Park engagement. They had taught us a lot about music. Seeing them, I felt we had paid down some of our debt. Connors passed his Thunderbird to Quinn.

Rex and Vinny were a few steps ahead, I looked up towards 'The Rock'; I had never seen it so full. There wasn't any point of going up there. No matter how much we wanted to get the entire Allman Brothers experience, we were only going to get a piece of it. Holter and Vinny suggested we buy some street acid, and we'd see the show one way or the other. It was too much of a risk, with the wrong batch of acid, we might miss the whole show and be a veg. I told them I'd play the hand I had.

Jimmy Martin, was a Rogue from our inception. If there was such a thing as a 'Renegade Rogue' – then Jimmy was it. Crawford

449

was a renegade as a course of nature; he was wired not to work in the conventional configuration of the current polemic systems. With Jimmy Martini, it was all a conscious choice; in league with the Busch bros., they were a three man wrecking machine. They were the muscle when things got sketchy. The trio went right up to the rock and staked their claim. They left 'Little Presto' with Sue Herr, Betsy Risko, and Denise the Piece. The girls weren't thrilled.

There was a lot of backslapping, toasting, sharing smoke at the musical event of the summer. I hadn't seen Barbara Wells since we got off the subway. The realization she was some kind of chimera was starting to take hold. Feeling that, I still couldn't help keeping my eye out for her.

Ray and Loki had come down with Jimmy Blanko and John Dunbar. We were talking with them arguing Dead vs. Allmans when Sally Englund and her friends showed up.

"I thought you gals were going to stand us up." Ray said.

She was higher than Ray......much higher. Later on he told me she had smoked a bag of smack with Wacky Nancy and Beth the Mess. The latter giving Loki a big open mouth kiss. A few days later he told me they had a history to justify the sumptuous greeting.

The acoustic act had finished and Tarts and me could feel the electricity building. "Ryan – Loki and me are going to hang with Sally and her mates. You want to come with us?" Ray used his eyes and directed his head towards Nancy. She looked pretty hot, but she was older and I thought smarter than me. "That 'Wacky' handle was a misnomer that had somehow stuck. I didn't think she would make out with a kid in public, so I begged off.

I told Ray, "We got to catch up with some of our crew, we'll catch you later." I smiled at all the girls and waved. "Pay attention to the music. The Brothers are gonna smoke it up to-night."

It was getting loud just from the number of people. When I jawboned with Ray, I had lost Vinny, Rex, and Holter. The P.A. played some boilerplate warnings and advisories. Showtime was getting close. The sound people went back to running the loop of the Schaefer theme:

Schaefer is the beer to have when you're having more than one. The most rewarding flavor in this man's world for people who are having fun – Schaefer is the one beer to have - when you're having more than one!

Frantic to find any Rogues, as sound checks and drum rolls could be heard, I walked around and tested a number of spots where the sound was good. It would probably all change once the band started. I had given up on trying to peek between any minute gaps in the tennis screens or through the leaves of the trees. The 'rock' was covered in humanity. I was watching a couple of Latino guys trying to throw a can of beer to their amigo 25 feet up an oak tree.

"Hey Chico......."I yelled. "Can you see the stage from where you are?"

"Yeah."

"How good?"

"Real pretty good"

"The whole stage?"

"Just about."

"Can I come up?"

"Fuckin' tough climb Hombre, but I make it – you probably can too."

"I'll be back."

"Hey dude, bring me a beer or something."

"It'll be a little bit."

I looked at the mid sized oak, there weren't any branches for the first 18 feet. It would be shinnying and bear hugging the tree's trunk for most of the climb. I'd have to think about this move.

"BOOM!" Seconds later another "BOOM!" followed. Two monsta explosions rocked the people on the 'rock'.

"What the fuck?" Holter's face went blank.

"Where'd you come from?" I said. Rex and Vinny were standing right next to me.

"I know what that was." Rex was straightfaced.

"It was right on top of the 'rock'......sounded like a buster." Vinny put his finger in ear and worked it around.

"For sure. The Huns ain't dumb. They wouldn't set them things off down here."

"Yeah, but Martini would." Rexall scoffed with a slight grin.

"Fuckin' idiots."

The coppers started clearing the area on and around 'The 'Rock'. Nicky 'Bingo' Butoni, Danny Stax, and Fast Eddie Mason came down. There was a lot of commotion. They started walking away from us and we called to them. Vince used his whistle with his thumb and middle finger and blew. We waved them over.

"What happened up there?" Rex said.

"Way too crowded."

Stax said, "I stood up and started talking to Jimmy Deep Freeze and Quinn. Then I was going to sit back down and some shithead was sitting where I had been."

"Standing Room Only - Stupido." Rexall shook his head.

"These hippies on the 'rock' – they're here all the time. They looked at us like we were the trespassers. You know like.....like they had a deed to it or something." Bingo said.

"Then the 'fuck you' shit started and went back and forth. The number of the parksters grew." Fast Eddie said.

"There were only about 11 of us up there including the Huns, Martini, the Bush brothers, and Bad Brad." Stax used his fingers to count. "11......if that....."

"Nobody wanted to scrap up there – fuck.....it's at least 15 feet to the asphalt below.....Where'd everybody go? We needed manpower up there." Bingo's palms went up, turned and waved us off.

451

"You guys didn't need manpower........you needed brain power." Rex laughed.

"Gimme a fuckin' break Rex." Stax lit up a joint.

Walking towards us, Bad Brad Guzzutti's face read mischief and guilt. To no one specific, he rambled like a mad man drinking at the end of the bar. He bopped in circles with clenched fists: one held the neck of a bottle in a paper bag, the other was a fist ready to lay someone's nose over. "Fuckin' hippies want to mix it up?" he laughed.

We all looked at him and looked at one another. Brad was wound up tighter than a thoroughbred in the starting gate.

"Brad, why'd you let them punks push you around? Somebody get shot up there? Sounded like fuckin' Vietnam." Holter laughed.

I thought Brad was going to take a swing at George. He gave him the 'Your next' ..... look.

Peacemaker Vince was in no mood for this stupid crap. He knew Holter was just winding up Brad for his own amusement. The night was too early for that shit. "Hey Brad, what were those explosions?" Vince gave his question a matter of fact tone.

Like a gorilla in a cage he paced back and forth in front of us. "Somebody forgot to tell the hippies that Woodstock's over. We were there first.......dog eat dog motherfucka."

"You tell 'em Brad."

"Plumb 'em up brother." Rex said smiling.

Vinny looked over to me and rolled his eyes and shrugged his shoulders. The crowd went into an uproar and the Allman Brothers launched into "Statesboro Blues". After the fourth number of the set – there was a technical problem with one of the monitors sending out nothing but feedback; they had to stop until it got fixed.

"So Brad, what happened up there?"

"George......" I pleaded.

"Wha-haha...ha...ha?" he laughed.

Too late the clenched fists returned with a face straight from Halloween. "I'll tell you what happened:" his caged gorilla bop turned into a triumphant strut in our small area. "McKool led Fast Eddie, Bingo, Stax, and the Huns from 'The Rock'. They were catcalling us, you know......'here chickee chickee, fuckin' kunts take a hike, go back to Jersey' – that shit. Buddy, Robin, Jimmy Martin and me – we hang back like we ain't with the other guys. Then somebody tags us for being with the rest. We tell 'em – Take it easy.....Take it easy we're leavin' we're leavin'." Guzzutti's face morphs into a truly spite-filled mask of revenge. "Buddy hands me one of them super ash cans you guys had left over from the Fourth. I bent down with Robin covering for me, I lit it and dropped it in a some gal's purse. I tried to get away as fast as I could – maybe six feet, then "BOOM MOTHERFUCKA!" Brad started to giggle.

"All the shitheads oooooed and ahhhhh'd and looked at the smoke. We did another one to a 24 can plastic kooler." Brad started laughing again: "There were pieces of kooler, spouting beer cans and smoke everywhere. I told 'em – let's see you rock out now ya buncha

452

mommalookas." Brad concluded with a weird laugh from another dimension.

"The man was looking to bust a few people." Bingo Butoni said. "They ended up clearing everybody off and putting some cones and barricades up and taping 'The Rock' off. Then they had some rookie cops stand guard.

We didn't hear anybody had gotten hurt; them blockbusters can propel plastic and aluminum out like a fragmentation grenade.

The Allmans resumed when the sound was fixed. They played a long one about twenty minutes, and three tunes which were each under 7 minutes. It was 10:15 and they were in top form. This house with a starry roof was cookin'. The Allman Brothers improvisational jazz and blues style of rock leant itself to two and three hour sets. It was one of their trademarks, and it was one of the big shortcomings of the Schaefer Music Festival. A band like the Brothers were just getting their juices flowing and it was time to turn out the lights. The problem was the upscale neighborhood, the noise, and the congestion........and maybe the detonation of a couple of blockbusters. The neighborhood association had filed for injunctions and filed lawsuits against the Parks Department, the promoter John Scher, The Schaefer Music Festival, Schaefer Beer, and even the musical artists themselves, because they played past the 11 pm curfew. Every year there was some carry-over legal action going on, and as the summer disappeared we wondered if we had we seen our last concert.

Bandleader Duane Allman was brief with his announcements; often one song led right into the next. For a few they had to tune-up, but it was all business. I heard the familiar opening chords as they were tuning I knew what was coming.

"Vince, I gotta piss so bad I can taste it.....be right back." I went right over to the oak tree that was actually closer to the rink than the 'rock'. Only a pint of T-bird remained. The quart bottle was tight in my back pocket, and I put a loop of my belt around the bottle's neck and started up the oak. Half way up I had my doubts, but I could hear Duane's voice and the faster I got up there the sooner the reward would come.

"Hey man.....you made it!"

I was totally out of breath and I sat on a medium sized branch with nothing but air beneath me.

"Como se llama?"

"Artimo.....Art's okay."

I went up another branch and handed him the T-bird.

"Thunderbird? That's my wine. What's your name?"

"Ryan."

"He toasted me: To the Brothers."

"Damn right."

"Watch out folks cause it's a-comin".

Tuning done, Duane said into the mike: "Elizabeth Reed." As we could only remember the visual of the band from Stony Brook, the Capitol, and the Fillmore shows, it was still difficult to get the image and dynamic of the band to take shape. At least Rex, Cinzano,

453

Holter, and me had seen them before, so we had an insight the others hadn't. The instrumental tune's framework was fairly consistent: Introduction, 1st coda, Dicky's solo, Gregg's organ break transition, Duane's solo, short drum break, 2nd coda and abrupt end. Although Dicky wrote the piece, it was Duane's blazing guitar work making it new and exciting every time they played it. This night however was Dicky's, his solo work was so over the top; after Gregg's organ break - Duane's guitar was speechless. Inside and out, the fans had been delivered into a state of audio ecstasy; at that point. Duane was rarely at a loss for a direction to counter or compliment Dicky's solo. His hand searched the frets of his Les Paul. He must have known he might not be able to surpass Dicky's statement, but he might pull off the impossible and equal it. Duane started and backed off twice trying to find that path and figure where this jazz flavored tune had to go. All the while, the rhythm section was moving ahead knowing Duane would catch up. Dicky and Gregg were putting down some fantastic jazz flavored rhythm pieces for Duane to pick up on. It was some solid up-tempo stuff; they were having fun because they knew their leader could and would deliver the mail.

It took him longer than usual to get the solo's direction nailed down, but it sounded polished from the first note he played. It was free form music and he started to stretch. He stayed within the band's groove. The band's bass player, Berry Oakley, watched intently as Duane must have given him that "stay with me look" which I could only imagine on account of the distance. It started to build – everyone who heard it felt it. The brothers knew it was coming; it was something like an audio organized riot........But not yet, and Duane brought the band almost to a dead quiet, but not quite. A more dramatic moment had never been seen in an O'Neill play. The band knew where they were and holding it back for so long – but not too long......Duane let Bessie Reed loose, a millisecond behind him, Dicky and Berry played 3 and two fat strings in one gigantic note with Duane coming back plucking a 4 string powerchord sending their Marshall amps and speakers redlining and gasping for electricity. From the band's speakers and the rinks P.A. system, a musical force of notes, vibration, and orgasmic melody erupted. The wires delivering the sound from the amps to the speakers defied containment as the music distorted the wires being squeezed through their sound system and exiting the speakers. Wires were smoking, amps were all lit up, speakers were shaking, and a jet engine of music and compressed musical notes and feedback blasted into the rink and beyond.

This sound tsunami was so violent, people grabbed whatever they could to prevent them from being blown over. Art and me put the bear hug on the oak as we felt the tree sway. It was raining concert garbage, but the band and the people kept on rockin'.

Elizabeth Reed was a musical journey that had no equal, and that was particularly true this July night. When the short drum break and final coda had played, the song shut off like someone had pulled the plug. Bandleader Duane had just done the impossible and went to the Mike.......'Dicky Betts's song......Dicky Betts. The latter giving a wave and a quick bow. It was the longest and best version of the song I had been witness to. I said "Adios." to Art, and slid down the tree acquiring a case of road rash on the inside of my arms and legs and belly.

Inside and out, the crowd was in a spontaneous state of melodious rapture. The band kept the hammer down with the 'Mountain Jam', brought the spacecraft back to earth with 'Stormy Monday'.

"Uh.....the clock man says we got time for one more." Duane said.

Duane and Dicky started banging out an up-tempo theme which morphed into the two lead guitars playing in harmony. It was the familiar tune 'Revival' sans Steve McQueen. The band drove the beat hard. I found Vinny, Rex, and Holter where I had left them. The instrumental portion of the song lasted about 3 ½ minutes. I called over to the trio with amazement plastered on our faces:

"It's our song......the one with Meris.....Love is everywhere – people can you feel it?" Inside and out the rink everyone sang with Gregg Allman. Again, the band ended on a dime. Duane said good night and thanked us for a great time.

Holter banged his chest like Mighty Joe Young: "The night that wouldn't end." he howled. We continued to sing 'Revival's refrain as we exited the park.

There was the matter of regrouping and making our way back to Yonkers. I wondered where Ray and Loki were. Crawdad also had been MIA for most of the night. Though the music had ended there was still electricity, a force still all around. It was real; you could feel it. We were on such a musical high, maybe all the T-bird and reefer was catching up. Everybody had a smile of exhaustion as we slowly walked.

Some guy couldn't wait and was off the asphalt taking a wiz near the bottom of 'The Rock'.

"Is that Kenny?" The guy had this blue light around his neck and it illuminated his face. Is this guy some kind of angel or avatar?

"Hey George......Zhat Crawfish pissin'?" I said.

"Yeah – that's Crawdaddy alright."

Vinny yelled, "Hey Catdaddy.....C'mon – join the herd."

"Hey Cinzano..........look around........some people got that same blue light as he does." I said.

He looked around, here and there they had this blue light around their necks and on their heads.....like halos. "Yeah, but not too many." he said.

"I dunno, something's going on with them. They're like the Children of the Damned. Check it out....if they got the light they're like transfixed.....suspended animation."

Vinny handed me his nearly empty bottle, "Don't kill it."

"Maybe some park vendor was selling them." Holter shuffled along.

"Hey I know I saw two people lit up; and they weren't wearing any glow rings, halos, or flashlights.

After Crawford zipped up, I went over to him and pulled his light ring apart and held it in my hand. I stepped away. Kenny retained the illuminating aura.

"Watcha think?" I said.

"I don't know. There's got to be an explanation, I never seen nothing like it." Cinzano said.

"Kenny – you feel okay?" Rex asked.

"How many wishes do we get?" Holter laughed.

We put him in the group and moved along.

Connors McKool didn't have any illuminary assist. At 6'7" he stood on a three foot chunk of granite and towered over us as we continued to walk toward him. His arms were outstretched and we heard him. It sounded like preaching. We got close enough to hear him.

"That.........That's what I mean! Tonight will forever be known as the 'Kamikaze Concert'. Did you feel that Straight-Line musical tornado rocket through the sound system?"

Holter said, "Yeah, McKool's right, I had to put my back against a tree so I wouldn't get blown over."

"Newspapers and Schaefer cups were all airborne." Rex nodded in agreement.

McKool called out: "This music has a special power."

THE NEXT TIME I LOOKED AT CRAWFORD, I WAS exiting his Bug down the End. He didn't have any glow when dropped me off. It must have been difficult to conceptualize the sensory experience of the concert when most of the Rogues had to imagineer the missing visual images of the tight band performance, interspersed with the impassioned soloing, or the two guitars doing that call/reply thing, as well as doubling up on melody and harmony lines. Fast Eddie bought "Live at Fillmore East" the next day, and he didn't even have a record player.

When Crawfish drove off, I thought 'That engine needs some hard core TLC. He had asked Quinn to do some troubleshooting on his VW. Quinn told him he made two mistakes: First, buying a foreign car; Second, thinking they would work on it. The Huns had an ironclad rule: "NO FOREIGN JUNK."

Copies had a few people inside, Ray and his bunch were at a table in the back drinking a pitcher. The small group was animated, and didn't notice me standing right behind Loki. They were going on about the Allmans; I thought it was rather remarkable for Ray and Loki as they were avid Dead and Kinks fans. Sally, Beth the Mess, and Wacky Nancy were sold on the Brothers from Macon.

Loki turned and saw it was me: "Great show."

Nancy's head went from side to side, "You should have hung with us."

"Huh?" I gave Ray a 'what's up?' with my head.

456

His lips mashed down on each other, and took a breath: "Nancy had tickets from her cousin cause he couldn't go. Her uncle works for All Star Beer distributors."

"Don't tell me I could have gotten inside.....why even bother saying that - other than to crush me." I went over to Fran and got an empty glass. I filled it and kept standing.

They were running out of admiration and superlatives for the band. Hearing this stuff from true fans was expected, but hearing it from these Johnny-come-latelys turned my stomach. "Any spare reef – just looking for a quick charge."

"Love that Gregg." Beth said.

"You would." Loki laughed.

Nancy and me came back in. Fran knew what was going on. She wasn't too keen on girls smoking 'that shit', she didn't care what the guys did. She had seen an awful lot in the last five years in that little beer joint. Most of it had to do with drugs and the war. A lot of guys got hooked on smack back in '68 and '69. Word on the street was the dope they were all doing was from the 'French Connection' bust. When the cops checked it out of the evidence cage for trial and brought back baby laxative one of the times it had to make a court appearance.

Billy Van Nahl said the shit was going for $5/a bag, and a junkie could get high twice. It hadn't been cut. "I had to get out of the End before temptation got the better of me. Made it through Nam, but the magic from Marseilles would have gotten the better of me." he admitted.

The junkies were having such a party they painted with rollers in large white letters: "Welcome to Junkies Paradise" on Palisade Ave.

So when somebody came in all screwed up, Copies unwritten rule was 'Pour 'em short and charge 'em extra." The two ceiling fans were spinning hard, but the place was still hot.

I had Fran draw another pitcher of Schaefer, "Ray, just give me the punch by punch rundown of the show.

Loki jumped on it: "When they play in tandem – say Duane is playing lead and the other guitar is playing harmony- the sound becomes much more than two guys playing the same note. That's rookie stuff. This band's got something totally different and revolutionary. Their power is not multiplied but exponential in nature."

"Yeah.......sounds great, but I'm not convinced you two know what you mean. Big deal - Ray plays piano and you play bass that don't mean a helluva lot. Whatja' do with the 6th ticket?" I said as I took one of Loki's Viceroys.

Nancy said she sold it for ten bucks so they could buy beer inside. This was painful listening to them talk. "So did you see McKool after the concert?"

"Un-uh." Loki replied. "Why, did he kick some ass?"

"No – he was giving a lecture after the concert as we snailed along getting out of the park."

"A lecture? The Huns?" Sally's head tilted.

457

"I dunno what you'd call it. How about a bull session in transit?" I said.

The gals continued to smoke, drink, and laugh. However, Ray's interest was piqued when I mentioned McKool's discourse.

"What did he say?" Ray threw a half a beer down.

"I might remember more tomorrow, but he was going on about the show......He called it the Kamikaze Concert."

Loki looked confused and suspicious: "I didn't see any Samurai or Ninjas there."

"Kamikaze.........Kamikaze..........Kamikaze Concert." Ray's wheels were turning. Divine wind –" he nodded with a faint smile. "It's got nothing to do with suicide. They played that barnburner of a tune – the one that brought the house down."

"Lizzy Reed." I said.

"The instrumental." he clarified.

"Nothing like it; it's in there with Coltrane, Parker, Miles, those cats." I said.

"Yeah......'Lizabeth Reed." Ray gazed into the half-lit street. Duane was using that stop and go stuff, and that last ridiculously long pause....and then he lowered the boom, and out came a tsunami of musical sound converted from a miniature electro-magnetic field created by the band and thrust through the sound system by the positive charged musical force which McKool correctly characterized as a "Divine Wind." Ray had seen what McKool had only heard, smelled, and felt. The result was the same, or perhaps McKool had gotten more out of the experience because as far as the concert was concerned he was essentially blind.

I had heard enough of this bullshit, I was just going to catch the band when they came back around. We all knew we had experienced a tornado of sound; it had struck a chord in the people who were open to receiving it. To bring this beyond an existential level was borderline mental illness.

His stare into the street remained undisturbed. "The Kamikaze Concert was absorbed by those in the reversed magnetic phase."

I burst his thought: "Like when we stopped the Penn Central commuter trains?"

Ray tilted his head from side to side, and one eye squinted in thought.......mmmm....yes and no."

Fran called over to us, "Hey listen, you kids leave now so I can close, and I'll give you a six pack of shorties for the walk home."

Loki walked Beth over to the steps of the bank. They sat there and started to get to know each other a little better. Ray and Sally were making out across the street in the entryway of Robbins' Pharmacy. Nancy and me sat on the hood of her car. Nancy was still three years older than me, same as when I saw her earlier this evening down Central Park.

"You wanna make out? Love is in the air," I smiled.

"Drop dead." She took a long drag on her cigarette never really looking at me. She was pretty enough to kiss but not pretty enough to say 'no'."

458

"Come on Nance – "

"Fuck off junior." she raised her voice. "And what's wrong with your hair?"

"Teacher ripped it out, but it's coming back." I'd been hoping since the sixth grade.

We were sitting next to each other on the hood of her car, I stood up and tried to wedge my legs between hers. I was making the move to give her a hug, and she kicked me in the cookies.

"Ugggha.....oooooh." I went down on my knees doubled over. With a horrible voice I called, "Ray....Goin home."

"You better you young pup." She smiled as she took another puff from her smoke.

"Go ahead – I'll catch up." He said.

I limped until I was out of the North End. Ray caught up with me around Untermyer Park.

"Hey muchacho.......What happened back there with Nancy?"

"She didn't have to kick me in the nuts." I said.

Ray laughed and handed me a shorty. We began our descent down O'Dell. Watching for clowns on the hill I said: "You're thinking Duane is from your side of the pole......you are all here, but you belong over there."

"No, we belong here. We just don't fit here. he said.

When we got down to 21 he said, "Go down to the old newspaper drop, meet you there in a minute."

I was under the streetlight, the city still had an incandescent bulb in there. Ray carried a bag with two cold Tall-Boys in it. We started walking down the park steps and down Harriman to the station. Three cars away, a couple was going at it; smoke came out the open windows. It was pot. We walked past in silence.

"Something I heard tonight......something I sensed from him."

"Duane?"

"Yes."

We crossed the tracks and walked up the riverbank instead of the elevated platform. The phone company had only replaced the phone on the northbound, and removed the blown-up phone on the southbound side. I laughed. Though a quarter moon remained, most of the light came as overflow from the station. A tug's lights burned as it pulled three barges up the river.

Some debris was cleared from the top of the site where the intergalactic visitor rested. The ground was warmer than usual. No plant life grew, but there were bare spots all over. We'd replace the debris before we left; there was no reason to invite curiosity.

"They're going to renovate the overpass pretty soon." I said. Crawford, Vinny Tarts, Ronnie Zanzibar and Cocaine Wayne took photographs of the equation – the whole length. The drawings of Lynn and Paula too. Figure they're gonna trash everything down to the concrete and steel – except the electrical they did last year......that's permanent....you think?"

459

"Yeah, it's a good idea......getting it on film." Ray popped open a Tall-Boy. "But I could never lose it up here." His index finger went to his temple; I did write it down in a notebook, just in case. It's not complete you know."

"Ray, I ain't got a fuckin' clue about anything since that comet arrived that night after track practice back in the sixth grade. You tell me and I just take it as gospel."

"Seventh grade.....either way.....two copies are better than one." he said.

"What could happen?"

"A cataclysmic movement of the earth's surface due to magnetic pole reversal, an EMP (Electromagnetic Pulse),........ maybe another comet?" he chuckled.

"And what of Duane?"

"We know nothing about him. Still, he has shown us his lifeforce - his soul, through his music. He must be aware of his duality......existing in two planes or dimensions simultaneously. I would say he has the ability to maintain his sanity without the aid of chemical override unlike the rest of us."

"You mean the specter people?"

"Yes." Ray was getting torn up and his face showed it. "I must believe he is a shadow person and operates from the opposite pole – the same pole as myself and the 5th dimension currently occupy; how is it he is not in a constant battle with chaos? Might he exist in some transitory dimension/state for short periods? If not, ...I am at a complete loss.

His paradigm was being challenged, would it hold up with people like Duane existing? Was the question scientific or sociological? I asked: "Are you saying Duane and others like him are beyond you, and the other ghost Junkies?"

He downed half the can hoping to catch more lubricant. That tune – the competing solos, the delivery, the impact; if he is a specter, a phantom from the new alignment to come.....more of an original being from the new alignment rather than a miscreant doomed to a life trying to escape physical and mental torture.......if that is what he is, then there is hope and perhaps more promise for our longevity and those to come after us."

"This may not be the case, and he may be one of us, and found a way – an escape hatch rather than the obvious relief valve (drugs). If.......if this is the case – the laws of magnetism of the reversed pole world - that is attempting to assert itself; it may explain the brief desertion of electromagnetic sound bearing a more complete density of sound particles, oriented for realignment of the poles." He knit his brow; deep in thought.

Now it was my turn to take a healthy chug on my Tall-Boy: "Speculation?"

"Duane quells insanity through his art and/or intense emotion. It overrides or at least modifies his magnetic imbalance; it must be the very same imbalance the drifter shadow people live with. I tell you this Ryan: even though I think about putting a pistol to my temple every day .... the escape method of Joey, Z-Man,

Cocaine Wayne, Rikshaw the rest is much.....much easier. I've got to find a way like Duane, but that would only have a chance to succeed if he wasn't a life form from the new magnetic alignment, if he was just a phantasm like the rest of us."

"I am being magnetically drawn with the irresistible urge to undo my physiology and escape.............I am not talking about seppuku or a juggernaut, but having the ability to alter the atomic configuration of the nucleus and orbiting paths of sub-atomic particles. Not a form of alchemy, but change the magnetic code and its operation, so we can live as you live. Can the human will, through intense emotion........without chemicals provide this pathway?"

In the dim light I was intent on his facial expressions. "Tell me one thing Ray, and it's got to be the straight truth."

Our eyes locked. "What's that?"

"Did you drop any acid tonight?"

"Fuck You. I wish I had, then I wouldn't have to be obsessed with this jive-ass, bullfuckinshit."

"Those who burn brightest – burn fastest." I said.

He replied, "Do junkies live longer than geniuses? Ask Jimi, Janis, and Jim. They all weren't doing dope, but they were all trying to escape. Ryan – anytime you want to trade places amigo, let me know......I'll take your comet dust and you can have my electro-mechanical body and brain which doesn't work too well in this phase of magnetism." Ray grasped two fists of rough sand and stood in silent prayer. Looking at the stars in the heavens, he released the sand. "C'mon.......getting late."

Throughout the summer, we read in the 'Sterile Hatesman' or heard the word on the street about a rash of car wrecks. These weren't fender benders, they were all out wipe outs, the cars were totaled, there were injuries – some severe .... some critical ..... some guys cashed out. A couple of guys from All Souls H.S. and Mixer Don left planet earth in separate wrecks.

Tony Griffin had been in the car with the mixmaster. Both were ejected from the vehicle. Tony lived, Don didn't.   The police report never determined who was driving. "Negligence of intoxicated operator" the Police report said. Tony wasn't held responsible, one minute he's in the car with Don, the next - he's in the hospital and Don is gone. It was like a mini-time warp. A few years later Tony said they were doing Quaaludes that night.

Danny Reese and Jack Morgan from Lake Ave. – same deal; only they both checked out. It was getting scary, the Quaaludes kept showing up, and the guys kept eating them......and driving.

Nicky Butoni, aka 'Bingo', was the Rogues' premier burglar. He did a number on his Electra 225 while in the grips of the all-purpose feel good drug. It was in the body shop until October. The insurance adjuster told Bingo straight out:

"If the shop can't straighten the frame, I'm gonna have to total it partner."

Bingo being Bingo, he tried to get the body shop to fix unrelated whiskey dents he accumulated in the last two years. Three months in the garage, he had no car all summer and had to ride with his uncle to his house painting jobs. Finally, he greased the insurance guy, which is what the adjuster was looking for from day one, but never would come right out and say it. The repair was called 'good', but it wasn't good. When we rode behind Bingo's Buick, it looked like the car was going in one direction, and the wheels were going in another. He went through two rear tires in two months.   "Fuckin' guys ripped me off." he bitched.

It was an ongoing story and everybody was sick of hearing about Bingo and his car. What was more important was the Rogues were down a car when the weather turned cold. Partying in the deuce and a quarter was like having a clubhouse on wheels.

Around Thanksgiving Nicky had enough. He saw Buddy Busch down the corner. "The car's a piece of junk. I got to get at least blue book on this sideways driving dog of a car."

"What's in it for me?"

"I got to get rid of the motherfucker, or buy stock in Goodyear if I keep it. You wanna get rid of it for me?"

"It's a two man job, I'll get Jimmy Martin to give me a hand. When do you want it gone?"

"Before Thanksgiving, I got to start looking for a new set of wheels right now. What do you need for the job?"

"Any ludes around?" Buddy said.

"Get the fuck outta here." Bingo looked away from Buddy.

"No, I'm serious."

Bingo gave him a double-take......"Yeah, I'll hook you up – you pay Martinique. I'll getcha 30 of them troublemakers."

"Deal. Get all the shit out of the car you need. Where you going for Thanksgiving?"

"I dunno.....probably Pam's parents house."

"That's good. Good alibi. Gimme a spare key."

Thanksgiving night we met up with Jimmy Martin over Rexall's house; he couldn't wait to brag about the arson job they pulled for Nicky:

Thanksgiving Day, Jimmy followed Buddy down to Woodlawn in the Bronx where the Jerome Ave. subway line ends. There's a golf course, woods, a cemetery; it's just about on the Yonkers/Bronx border. There was hardly any traffic – no people. Jimmy said he watched around – nothing. Buddy parked it in the grass. He screwed the body puller into the ignition and popped the switch out of the steering column, a flathead screwdriver was left on the floor. Around six screws and the radio's mounting plate was removed – wires snipped. Jimmy got the radio and body puller and threw them in his car. Buddy popped the hood open and removed the battery.

"That's it." Buddy said.

Jimmy went over to the car lit two blockbusters; he threw one in the front and one in the back. They were already doing a U-turn when they heard the first explosion. They split a bottle of Plum Velvet Supreme and started laughing.

Rexall cruised by with some of those showstoppers. He had about 50 of them in a baggie: $4 apiece. He sold me four for $15. Your body turned to rubber and so did your brain. Music sounded great, you felt great, - everything was great in ¾ speed. It didn't take long to realize Quaalude required a handler; even more than LSD. The capsules had markings like it was pharmaceutical; after a few test runs you knew the voltage varied with every batch. It was unpredictable but it was still a good time. If a guy had the money, he could buy a dozen of them, find out the strength and adjust the dosage for the next time. In the end, it didn't matter because we always drank when we were doing them to get more screwed up.

Sally Englund liked them so much Ray almost got her to kick her junk habit for them, but he had no reliable connection for getting them. They'd be on the street for four or five months, then nothing for the next 6 months. When the rich people's kids started wrapping their cars around trees and crashing into trucks........... then the law came down hard on the ludes, and they dried up for a long time. If them Quaaludes hadn't been the catalyst for so much death and destruction, it might have been crowned "Drug of the Year". Instead we knew it as "The Summer the Quaalude Struck."

BY THE THIRD WEEK OF AUGUST, RAY HAD LEFT FOR Purdue. I called it Hal and Jane's Reconciliation Ride, as they took their eldest and my beacon of light and wisdom to the university. Mother and son were at odds with the old man, but he wasn't giving an inch to improve his relationship with either. The tug of war started as soon as they put the trip together.

The campus violence at Kent State was still fresh in everybody's minds. The three felt trapped in the car and they began talking politics.

"And our son gets killed in Vietnam or here at home." Jane argued as they drove through Ohio. For Ray, neither seemed as bad as riding in the back seat through the Midwest. The parents had somehow turned this three day 'stop and drop' into a 5 day odyssey, detouring on the way back to see Jane's cousin in Niagara Falls. Whatever they were hoping to find up there - it eluded them. They seldom talked except to argue, just like they did at home.

Brother Bill was left with Jane's right hand, Judy, her assistant. She had two boys around Brother Willis' age. Sister Cathy went somewhere with one of Jane's friends and her daughter. I didn't know them too well. When they left for West Lafayette – the party was underway. Meris Klein stayed over the first night. She told me Ray and her never did get together on account of Sally. I wanted her to stay another night; she said we'd have to make it another time.

"Ryan, I'd love to, but I've got to move in the dorm at Binghamton and I've got a million things to do. Come up and visit if you get some wheels. I'll give you the phone number."

Ladykiller Holter showed up the next night with this chica from Ecuador, and a Polish girl who spoke very little English.....wow.

The hits kept coming; the third night went real wild with a couple of All Souls girls gone bad: Reefer Rita and Dominica Viglucci. It was like an All Souls class reunion except I didn't know Reefer Rita. Vinny knew her because he did his Freshman year over there. I knew I had a kinky streak, but Vince tells the girls: "Don't come over without your school uniforms – you can change at Ryan's house. Vinny said they gave him an eye roll to end all eye rolls.

"You are sick Tartaglione." Rita said.

"Hey, it ain't me. It's Whitebread. Says since he's been at Gorton – he's really missed a well dressed girl. He said to ask you nice – so I'm asking." Vince smiled.

When Cinzano gave me the call, I picked them up at Progressive Pizza in Jane's Comet. We bought a small pie, went up to the North End to the liquor store and got quarts of Boone's Farm, Bali Hai, and Night Train. I was sure Rita had brought what she was known for.

It was a night of madness; Vinny was on something other than just the pot and the wine. He told the girls they were to only take off their blazers and panties, everything else stayed on including the ties and knee socks. I thought he was a genius. The girls looked real sexy. Because Vince instigated the orgy, he must have felt obligated to call the shots. I think I made a mess 4 or 5 times, but by morning I was still a virgin.....it didn't mean anything to me.

The Conroys next door, thought I was running an escort service the way I was shuttling girls back and forth. The beer, pizza, and Chinese take outs; they must have thought I had passed my road test. I drove the two the All Souls girls to Dominica's house at 7:00 am; they left in their school outfits. I told Dominica I was re-enlisting back at All Souls...."I'm hooked."

When I got back and Vince had the coffee going and was out on the porch over the garage. Three days into the malaise of debauch, Linda Conroy called up to me from the fence line: "Ryan.....you pull your shades down tonight."

"I asked Vinny, "Was that her?"

"I think your neighbor's talking to you."

"Hi Linda." I waved my cigarette.

"My kids watched that orgy the last two nights – pull them damn shades down." Linda shouted up to us.

"She's hot, and I don't think I mean gorgeous."

Hungover and full of myself, I checked my look out in the reflection of the porch door, there wasn't an ounce of fat on me or Vince. My hair stood up straight everywhere it grew. I tried to pat my hair down so I didn't look like I was a hooked up to a defibrillator all night, and had a three day old stubble. Hungover enough – Stupid stuff started coming out of my mouth. "Hey Linda – C'mon over and get some." I laughed and Vinny wide eyed me like I was nuts.

"Just who the hell do you think you are? I'll have Mitch come over after work and jack your jaw.....who the hell do you think you are? You're just a young punk making a pass at me. Your parents brought you up better than that....at least your mother did......besides –" she smirked, "You're not man enough."

She was wild........bad wild.

"Linda..... I was just asking you over for a cup of coffee. I didn't expect you to get all agro on me." I backed it down – way down.

"You wouldn't be playing this loverboy crap if your friend wasn't here."

I had to unravel this mess, before it got worse. I stood up: "Linda, really – I apologize. I'm sorry you're right. I was way out of line."

"You don't even look over here anymore – that's it we're through. Your mother and Billy are the only ones worth anything in that house." She waved me off......palm down.

"Vinny, let's get out of here.....We left 21 like a couple of cat buglars. When I came home, it was after dark and I parked the car up the street.

Stupid stuff like the 'Linda Conroy Incident' typified where my life would go when Ray wasn't around.......and he hadn't even been gone for three days. I made trouble by the bucketful for myself. Cross country track couldn't come soon enough when school resumed – it helped burn off the excess stupidity which had blossomed like a sunflower.

Labor Day rolled around; most of the Rogues went down to Seaside or Belmar on the Jersey shore. Caddying required you serve the people who actually got to enjoy these holidays. Ray and me must have spent the big three national holidays celebrated during the summer at a golf course for the past four years. It included the summer

465

of no work .....because I got to caddy with Ray at St. Andrews. No one asked us if we wanted to go anywhere on the weekends. If we could go it meant there was inclement weather. It amounted to getting wasted in some bar and spending money we didn't have......Catch-22.

When Jane and Hal returned from Indiana, they weren't talking – so much for the marriage encounter get away. Both were anxious for summer's end. Both were resolute: I couldn't hold a candle to Ray. I felt it, but I knew they were right. For better or worse, it was the last solid weekend of caddying. September was warm enough for the golfers, but tapered off as October approached. Loki now had wheels, I don't know how he got down to Pace University in his freshman year. It was the start of the "people would disappear and magically show up three months later syndrome"; you never knew where they were or when they got back. Now he was driving down there four days a week and still majoring in mathematics. We caddied together during the month of September.

Loki had twisted his ankle when it got hung-up in a bar stool over at Cassidy's. When he pulled up to 21 on Saturday morning, he said he didn't know if he could caddy. I went back into the house and got my stash.

"Listen Ryan, I'll drive you up there, but I don't know about today." He said.

"You listen Joe, I got some Quaaludes." I smiled. "Drink a 16 ouncer and it'll be like floating for the four hour loop."

"Aaaaah, I got to study when I get home....not fall asleep." I knew this had nothing to do with magnetic reversal.

Nine o'clock, Murdoch partners me up with Ed Detore. Loki 'cowboyed up' and hung around and caught a loop, two foursomes behind ours.

Ed was a professional caddy; that didn't count for nothing unless you were on tour, which he never was. Ed was 50...... could pass for 56. He had a lot of miles on him: got drafted, went to Korea and had a hard time getting over it. The bunker his troop slept in took a direct hit from an artillery shell. He had been outside trying to take a crap until his cheeks froze. He hadn't shit for five days and he had to at least try to get things moving . Walking back from the ditch, he immediately recognized the whistling trail of the shell.

"They had been bombing us on and off all night. You get familiar with it, but you never get used to it. I heard this one coming straight away. I got as low as I could and pushed my face into the dirt wall, and said 'Hail Marys' over and over. "Thy womb Jesus" was as far as I got. The concussion blew the bunker and rushed ahead along the trench. I figure I went 20.....22 feet in the air and 30 feet down a slope. I lay there until daylight. A couple of guys were still alive, but not for long. Can't hear out of one ear, plate in my head, got a gimp, and a piece of something passed through my left lung......almost bled to death." Ed wasn't complaining – he was just telling his story. I liked him......everybody did.

He was a proud veteran, he had a small apartment on Lockwood Ave., didn't drive - rode the caddy bus, His teeth were going and he liked to drink boilermakers. The clothes he wore were always clean, no wife, no kids.....had 'a ladyfriend'. That combat stuff, there always seems to be an issue when the boys come home. They never are truly 'free and clear'.

Murdoch gave us some guys who were all retired; they kept the ball in the fairway. It was the right loop for Ed even though his hip was aggravating him.

"Say Ryan –" Detore said as he panicked checking the front pockets of his bowling shirt for his Lucky Straights.

"What's up Eddie?"

"No shit Ryan, I'm almost out of steam." He coughed and spat.

"Ed, they haven't teed off yet."

"Went around twice yesterday." he winced.

"C'mon Ed, you know better." I said.

"We're getting close to the end of the season, I got to put some money away. I get a check from the VA every month but it barely covers my rent."

"You can't get greedy man." I gave him the once over, "You're not going to have a stroke or a coronary?"

"No. No. No." he coughed. "Just running out of zoom, and my hip is clicking like a bazaar wheel."

"Got just what you're looking for.....watch my guys." I said.

When I came hustling back, the first guy still hadn't teed off. "Whatcha got?" he said.

"A fuckin' goof ball.........a pain killer." It was just a quaalude.

His head shook up and down as he grinned, "Yeah. Yeah. Yeah."

"Here Ed." I gave him a capsule. "Get something to wash it down."

"Right.

I bummed a Lucky from him on the third tee. I scoped him out on the other side of the fairway for the second shot. He gave me a great big grin and a thumbs up. If he had had his grill together and boot polish for his hair he could have doubled for Clark Gable. "Feels like I'm floating, and when I do feel the ground, it's like walking on tits." He laughed.

One of Ed's golfer's caught a whiff of something not right as he stepped up and addressed the ball. He took a couple of practice swings and never looked at Detore: "Say Ed, You didn't have an eye opener this morning?"

"No Mr. Bloom. I was at my brother-in-law's retirement dinner last night, a fine affair. 35 years with the Yonkers school system." Mr. Bloom still had not teed off, so Ed continued, "I'll probably carry clubs as long as I can." He took a long drag off his Lucky.

"Well perhaps you'll fall into something less demanding with a small pension."

"Hopefully Mr. Bloom, hopefully." Ed said.

467

OCTOBER 29, 1971: WHILE ATTEMPTING TO AVOID A SLOW TURNING TRUCK, BANDLEADER, DUANE ALLMAN LOST CONTROL OF HIS MOTORCYCLE AFTER MINOR CONTACT AND CAUSING AN ACCIDENT. ALLMAN SUSTAINED SEVERE INTERNAL INJURIES AND DIED SHORTLY AFTER ARRIVING AT MIDDLE GEORGIA HOSPITAL. HE WAS 24, AND IS SURVIVED BY A 2 YEAR OLD DAUGHTER.

ii

There were perhaps 3 or 4 letters from Ray from late August to early November. All were brief, and had to do with the fireball and the cast-off remnant we had buried. He wanted me to do some calculations and experiments with the meteor's ash and debris. I wrote back I would, but only got around to half of the things he asked me to do. Hell, I wasn't even sure if it was his handwriting. The individual letters of the words had become angular: the C's became two lines at right angles, D's the same - from the other direction and so forth. It must have taken him twice or three times as long to scribble this way. Over Thanksgiving when I watched how he used a pen and paper, I discovered the opposite was true.

I thought I'd be receiving the lion's share of the phone calls from him. It was an erroneous assumption. They were mostly to Jane, then Hal, and then to me. Our brief conversations didn't have much to do with who got busted, who wrecked their car, who broke up with who, or the bands who were coming to town. I had written him and told him Copies was rumored to be closing some time next year, and who got drafted.

Loki was watching a 'Dracula' movie with 'Half-Court' at Copies on a Saturday afternoon in late October. It was getting kool. They looked at me, nodded, and they went back to the movie. The commercials started: Loki said Ray had called him out of the blue. "Your brother was toasted man. He was adamant he was going to see the world and he was taking me with him. Ray also said he had put Sally on notice that he wasn't going to take anymore calls from her if they originated from the Alpha Centauri system."

"Hey Copie, how about a beer."

Loki looked at me, "You see her lately?"

"I thought she was supposed to be at Brown University."

Half-court leaned forward and looked at me, "Seen her with Cocaine Wayne and Joey Tarts......bout a week ago."

"So much for that style of higher learning." Loki arched his eyebrows.

"Copie I.D. you?" I asked him.

"Nah, I think he finally got off that."

"What about Fran and Kaye?"

"Kaye just don't like me. I'm sure she'll ask for I.D. the next time she's tending bar." He said.

468

The next mailing I received from Ray came with detailed instructions, sketches, and directives regarding the fireball. I kind of let him down with his first requests, this communiqué seemed somewhat more urgent. He might have viewed me as an employee of 'Raylaw Inc.' while he was at Purdue. The astrophysics department wanted all sorts of info and data. I was making observation, tests, retrieving initial phenomena of the comet's entry into the atmosphere. They wanted monthly temperature readings at the burial site. I went to a shop that sold temperature gauges with varying lengths of sensors. They had a few; they were used for precise temperature readings for differing applications – mostly in the medical and food service industry. I knew I was obligated to help out with this project; I just didn't care enough or had the intelligence to match Ray's interest or involvement.

"GREAT........GREAT NEWS SON." HAL WAS ON THE phone. "Okay.....we'll see you soon." We all gathered around Hal, we really didn't know what to expect. It had been so long since he had smiled, all of us were smiling in anticipation.

"Don't leave us hanging Dad.......did Ray win a slide rule in a raffle?" I had no one to share the wisecrack with.

"You wish you knew what a slide rule was for." his smile remained. "Ray's catching a ride here, and getting one back to school after Thanksgiving break. This is wonderful. Now Mother, let's get a fine turkey this year – no Butterballs."

"Dad, that's just swell." I went to the food closet and put my hand into a box of Cap'n Crunch. One more handful and I could call it a meal.

Tuesday after school, Brother Bill answered the phone. Having him answer was just a way to put the caller on hold until Jane and Hal or Cathy or me could take the call. Jane got at least 90% of the calls in the house.

When I got downstairs to see what the call was about, I could tell it was for Billy, though he was only in the third or fourth grade. I waited a little longer, then I knew the conversation was brother to brother.

"Billy, who's home?"

"Just me and Ryan. You want to talk to him?"

"No way – I can talk to you. Now go get a pencil and paper."

"Okay."

I was tempted to pick up the receiver off the small bookcase where the phone rested in the hallway, and take charge – but I didn't. If Ray thought Billy could handle this; it was good enough for me.

"Ready Willis?"

"Go ahead Ray."

"I'm getting the 4:20 from Grand Central. I'll be down Greystone around 5:15. Bring Ryan with you okay?"

"OK Ray."

I read the message as Billy was writing it. I knew he was coming. I felt kind of strange; I didn't know why.

Billy and me got down to the station about 10 minutes early. It was cloudy, and it made it darker earlier. The street lights were already on. The one at the corner of Warburton and O'Dell had been upgraded to a mercury vapor blue light, not for safety or a traffic issue, but as a crime reduction measure. It was paid for with Federal grant money. The feds reasoning was 'people do bad things in the dark'. The three streetlights on Harriman Ave. were also upgraded. None of the couples who used the street as a Lovers Lane appreciated the switch.

We waited on the northbound platform. I looked at the new pay phones and wondered about the money in their coin boxes. I didn't get my portion of the unsold blockbusters from Rexall for almost a month. When I did get them, the box was light. They were a premium item the day after July 5th.

I had gotten 80% of them back, so I wasn't going to be a Captain Queeg over the missing ordnance. 20 bucks wasn't worth the ill-feelings I'd garner. It came back to me though - I kept the coin boxes. I kept the one that opened easy and gave the other to Vince and Rex to split. Maybe it evened out.....maybe it didn't.

A group of high school students from All Souls were on the southbound platform. I recognized one of the guys, the rest I didn't know. None of the girls were Rita or Dominica, but they seemed to be all juniors and seniors. They had their party going; they were being discreet, they weren't loud. I could smell the pot. New signage had gone up in modern lettering on the old stationhouse and both platforms read: Greystone.

They tried to stop time with a series of photographs. We watched the boys and girls pose and mug for the guy with the camera. They continued, the flash went off at least a dozen times. They posed on three sides of the new signage: two girls on each end and four guys down in front.

This one guy who sat on the cold platform at the end of the sign, pulls out a folded paper, and in the same size and font he had drawn the letter "d" which he held at the end of the station's name for three photos: 'Greystoned'. The real Greystone was about 15 yards from where they stood.

"I'm getting cold." Brother Bill said.

"He'll be here soon." It was more damp than cold, and I wished I was going downtown on the southbound with the All Souls party. "C'mon, let's wait inside the overpass, it'll be warmer. It was the first time I could see the station's facelift, it was almost complete. Utilitarian was the only word I felt. They weren't going to spend any more money for a new station house or renovate it. It might have been worth restoring. Greystone was a facelift gone awry: a bad comb-over.

"It's cold in here too." Willis said.

"C'mon, I think I know where it's warm." I could see the southbound coming from the overpass. We started down the stairs, and were behind the windbreak wall, walking through the dying brush as the southbound took the All Souls students downtown.

"Right here Bill, sit down if you like you'll get warmed up."

"Why is it warm here?" he replied.

"There's an underground steam line; I think it's leaking, so the ground gets warm sometimes."

470

The meteorite had been buried for five years; I thought about it almost everyday. Maybe this was the day when Ray would explain why it came to us......who it was for.....and whether it might help or harm us. The heat of the surrounding sand had me thinking something was yet to occur.

Ray told them junkies.....the real junkies, the science behind the magnetic reversal. They bought into it – all the way. Why not? It let them off the hook for shooting dope. When the euphoria of Ray's exoneration faded, they could only hope the pole reversal would arrive A.S.A.P. They were cognizant it might not take place for a thousand years..... In geologic time, a grain of sand on the beach.

I stared at young Bill. Without Ray, I was a ship without a rudder going in circles. I certainly was the wrong role model for him. There was a strong desire to be headed somewhere..........to be more than I was. The temptation to ask Ray how to wield this cosmic ash bothered me more and more. I thought it might be possible to see the future or turn back time, resurrect the dead, become invisible and grab the genie from the bottle.

"Ryan – here it comes." Billy pointed.

We stood on the tomb of starfire rock and watched the two headlights tooling up the track. We waited for the train to pull away and then we saw him. The both of us yelled out his name simultaneously: "Ray!" and we waved. He held his arm straight over his head and waved back.

"Come on." he smiled and called.

We ran and crossed over the tracks to save time keeping away from the third rail. We triple hugged, I didn't think I had missed him this much. Brother Bill took his small carry-on. I wouldn't let Ray carry the monsta suitcase and it left him only his mid-size carry-all to tote. We climbed the Henry Hudson Park stairs, and switched off at the mid-point. "Ray.....you want to go out with the Rogues tonight?" Billy was already at the top.

"Pretty much all booked up 'til I head back."

"Huh?" my face went sour.

"Where's your ash?" he said. We started up O'Dell.

"Bottom drawer of my desk."

"Where's yours?"

He pulled a green glass pharmacy bottle from an inside pocket of his coat. The small bottle flew into my hand so fast it was like catching a Bob Gibson fastball without a glove. We were walking side by side.

"Holy fuck a duck." My right hand stung. "I thought you said it was degrading.

"Apparently not." he grinned.

We walked into the house, no one else was home.

RAY'S SCHEDULE DIDN'T LEAVE MUCH TIME FOR ME OR anyone else named 'Whitelaw'. He hardly had time for Sally. Thanksgiving came and went without Ray. He gave Jane some ridiculous excuse he would be having turkey dinner with Sally's family, but he would be home around 6:30 for leftovers and an after

471

dinner drink. He was definitely chasing something. I received a phone call from him, he wanted to know when I was going out.

"So you'll be home at 6:30?"

"Yeah…..should be."

When he returned he was keen to do some simple experiments with the original cosmic material we had collected. Four sheets of 14" legal paper were handed to me. There was a bit of calculus and typed instructions and hand drawn diagrams on graph paper; they were taped to the mid-page and dealt with electrical generation, magnetic acceleration, propulsion, and levitation. He was on to something, but with all the variables, data, and the unknown – he was second guessing much of his original overpass equation. The plywood windows had been removed and replaced with……….new plywood windows, painted the same green as the bridge girders. Penn Central had upgraded the overpass minimally: Now there were eight panes of Plexiglas on each end – four per side.

Like a possessed scientist, I listened as he was talking with me in our room, but it felt like my only purpose there was so he couldn't be accused of talking to himself.

"I can extrapolate the approximate size and mass of the mother fireball that landed up near Plattsburgh with the remnant down the river. – I can make approximate calculations on the rate of disintegration and compositions of other pieces which broke off along the way."

He looked up from his legal sheets: "Bring your ash over here." The contents of my jar were poured into an identical green pharmacy bottle marked with an 'X'. In the act of pouring - a hum was noticeable. A tiny bit of ash clung to the bottom. He tapped the jar with his pocket knife, and the rest fell on the desk. The small amount was laid into a thin two inch coke rail.

Ray unscrewed the top of his cylinder – a higher pitched feedback came from his container. It wasn't irritating, but we looked at each other aware this was active material – more so than it had been. As he separated the two specimens, the amplitude lessened.

"Tests I ran last month in the lab were inconclusive…. unreliable. I needed your oppositely charged ash. At first I thought one pole was losing strength as the other increased. I asked one of the physics professors about the possibility of pole neutrality and whether a true balance could be achieved. He went into a long lecture that it was possible, but not for extended periods. One was simply gaining while the other was decreasing. The earth's natural event of periodic pole reversal, coupled by solar/galactic magnetic storms, and cosmic intruders from other universes, with pick-up or attachment to these magnetic storms and man's devices sending them to earth will destabilize all the advances in technology in the last hundred years.

"Is that why this cosmic ash is emitting sound?" I asked.

"I don't know. My speculation is it may be the result of momentum. Magnetic storms will follow the path of least resistance. A modern industrialized world, reliant on positive or negative charged machines and systems, probably will not operate properly – if at all. We know biological life can also be affected because of the

472

composition of cell structure and the components of protons, electrons, and neutrons all carrying a magnetic charge.

" Wow – that's wild." I shook my head.

"If.......it can be proved true." Ray squinted. I got a real strong feeling Duane was aligned with my side. How he managed not to let the negative magnetic field or prevailing pole to dominate him - was due to his total focus and dedication to his music – had to be. His talent and his intensity allowed him to side-step the compulsion to escape."

"But he did escape." I said.

"Perhaps, but only on a certain level, or was it something else?"

"I know he's irreplaceable." I shook my head.

Ray scoffed, "Only saw them the one time: He was the engine with the vision. What are they going to do?" he said.

"That twin lead guitar thing......plus his extraordinary slide work. No one else is that good. He was the linchpin. I sighed.

"Hear any news?'

They had to fulfill a contract appearance earlier in the month. Without Duane, how good could they be?"

"It's a shame. Like Albert King says: born under a bad sign." Ray said.

"Clapton's got his own band, and his link was with Duane not Dicky. Thought about Robbie Krieger from the Doors. Morrison's gone. No Jim – no Doors. Solid player, good writer. If they don't break up, they might be able to tour with a ringer......you know....The Allman Brothers with special guest......maybe someone we never heard of. Whoever it ends up being they got to be compatible with Dicky Betts.

"Ryan, I'm leaving some notes, computations, and looking for some data from the three wise men." Ray said.

"Three wise men?" He had gotten the response he wanted.

"Cocaine Wayne, Rickshaw, Z-man, Crawford, and Joey Tarts."

"Wait a minute, that's five." We laughed some more. "Crawfish's VW threw a rod through the engine case. It had been leaking a little bit of oil all summer and he was sick of checking the oil so he put in double the oil capacity. He went 10 miles on the Cross Westchester Expressway, the engine built up so much pressure she blew. He already bought Betsy Risko's Datsun." I said.

"Crawford may have blown up his Bug, but he knows all this man-made space junk is going to impact and accelerate the reversing of the magnetic poles." Ray said.

"Never said he was dumb. I'm just saying nothing seems to bother him. When Ranger Rick was burning on 'Tommy James and the Shondells' he didn't get out of shape about it. He just rolls with the heavy stuff too."

"Believe me.....he's in knots. He just doesn't exhibit it."

473

When he went back after Thanksgiving, he had been concerned about the propulsion – repulsion, attraction, and deflective properties of the orbiting satellites, space junk, and other devices shot up into space and the signals they transmit back to earth. He didn't like the green bottles for some reason, and I washed out a couple of clear slender old olive jars Hal had in the cellar, we transferred the ash into them. The hum was present, but not as strong. We placed them a specified distance apart on the graph paper so Ray could record any movement. If the ash in the clear olive jars moved, it was imperceptible.

During Christmas break, we performed a series of trials with the comet's ash in conjunction with the winter solstice at full apogee. Equal amounts of ash were removed and put into coke rail rows: parallel – perpendicular – inverse diamond patterns on the graph paper. Both the negative and positive charged specimens had the power to repel and attract, only minimally, unless momentum was introduced, then things began to happen. We ended up in the cold garage, and duplicated what we did in our room, only this time Ray had taped the jars to the spokes of the back wheel of Billy's bike. Patterns of coke lines in various shapes were carefully positioned on top of a card table over the rear wheel. We had turned the bike up-side down and I cranked the pedal's chain and spun the wheel. Both the positive and negative lines came alive and uniformly worked their way in to a spoke pattern copying the spinning jars.

"Ryan.......STOP.......we're gonna lose ash." he yelled.

"What the.....? What was that?"

"I don't know." Ray said, "There's reason to believe inertia, momentum and gravity as well - may be the catalysts to cause pole reversal when working in tandem. I'll have to set this up in a lab at Purdue and recreate this model. I'm going to need this ash of yours."

"Sure.....whatever you need Ray."

I'm not going to take it with me........yet. I'll contact you, and you can send it to me." he said.

"No problem."

"I think the poles are coming to a state of flux/transition. There is some kind of timetable involved, but it has been thrown off kilter because of the extra gathering and acceleration of magnetic fields of space and the delivery of non-intended magnetic forces by all the man-made objects orbiting the earth.

"What kind of time are we talking about?"

"The way we measure time in hours, days, weeks, centuries millennia..........IRRELEVANT. The pole reversal might now be untethered to any measurement of time." Ray shrugged and laughed. "Aw - fuck this." He shook his head and laughed some more.

I thought he might be losing his marbles.

Ray hung around for the first half of January and then went back to Purdue. There were only 5 months left before I graduated from Gorton. I felt like I was the orbiting asteroid; in the belt between Jupiter and Mars doing laps going around and around and around. I was getting more and more detached from reality. I didn't have anything going with any of the girls at school or anywhere. A big void awaited me at graduation. No after school job….no money.

Nixon was winding down the war, and the government was transitioning to the 'all volunteer military services'. By the time election day came, Nixon had beat that sodbuster McGovern to the punch………there were only 25,000 combat troops left in Vietnam. McGovern was a one issue candidate and Nixon out McGoverned him.

Since 1971, most of the troops had been pulled back to the firebases. According to the returning vets who came back in '71 and '72, there was a lot of turmoil amongst the troops there: unwillingness to fight, racial discord, low morale, and the perception we could never win a defensive war.

We looked in the newspaper for the Draft Lottery drawing. Ray's number was in the three hundreds. The Selective Service only drafted the first 14 or so birthdays they drew from the fishbowl.

Huns Ranger Rick and Eddie Van Trex did their two year draft service. Both had abbreviated tours of Nam as a result of Nixon's drawdown. McKool could be a Nixon man now that the Huns would be back at full strength: Four seats – four Huns with room for an occasional babe in the middle……the way it should be.

RAY PHONED HAL AND JANE; HE WASN'T GOING TO BE back for Easter break. "I'm heading into crunch time, if I come back – I'll get hung up with partying with the people back there. I simply don't have the time for that nonsense." Watching the conversation on the phone, I saw miles of concern in Jane's face. His voice was resolute from what I gathered from Jane's side of the conversation.

Panic was in her voice and she started getting short on her breath. "Raymond – we haven't seen you since Christmas …….now……now you get on a flight and be here for Easter. You hear me?" she was plenty worked up.

"Let me talk to Hal." he said.

"I don't want you mother all wound-up." Hal said.

"Dad, here's the deal – I am going to pass all my courses if I come home. No worries there."

"Then do as your mother wishes, and get on a plane." Hal looked over to Jane who listened as father and son continued. He raised his chin and nodded, as he paced with the phone in one hand and the receiver in the other to his ear.

"If I really smash the ball out of the park with my grades this spring…..Dad – are you listening?"

"Yeah, I'm with you boy."

"They'll convert the partial to a full scholarship for the remaining three years……three years Dad."

Hal motioned to me to get him his whiskey-club soda. He turned 90 degrees away from Jane and smiled. I handed him his drink and the smile got even bigger.

Hal emptied the drink in two swallows. His eyes met hers and he smiled. "You don't say……..Hmmmpt. Three years you say?"

On the other end Ray said, "Dad, I could have gone to
Florida with half the student body or come back to Yonkers and party,
but I need these two weeks to get three years. I have to study." Hal
recognized the urgency.

"When's your last day of finals?" Hal said.

Jane grabbed the phone away from Hal: "Raymond – you get
back home – you can do that for me can't you?"

"Mom, just moment with Dad – put him back on please."
Ray said.

"Don't disappoint me Ray."

Hal rolled his eyes at me.

"Mom, I have this opportunity here."

"Ratshit.......it's all going to ratshit." She scowled knowing
where this would end up.

She let go of the receiver; it fell to the floor.

Hal picked it up, "Ray......Ray....you there? Mother will be
alright. And she will be proud of your achievement. She's a little
irrational at the moment." he said.

"Classes resume in 11 days. My last exam is on May
10th - a little more than a month, five weeks at the outside. You'll be
saving on the transportation now and the tuition for the next three
years."

"You know Ray, with that scholarship extension, now we can
think about sending Ryan to vocational/tech school when he graduates,
we've got to give him a shot at advanced learning." Hal smiled at me.

I had to sit down after that last exchange. Once again these
two were staking out my future while Jane planted her head in her
crossed arms against the foyer's wall.

"He's pretty smart Dad." Ray said.

"Yes, but he's got to tone down the party." Hal looked my
way.

"You were young once."

"Raymond, your brother came home one Saturday, and it was
at suppertime. The lad didn't even know he was here. He stood at the
front door monkeying with his key. Finally, I opened the door and he
fell flat on his face trying to put his key in the hardwood floor. Come
on Ray, how pissed up does he have to get? He should learn to drink in
moderation like I do."

Ray had to let Hal's last bit of wisdom go without comment.

Jane and me were getting clobbered from differing aspects of
Hal's attack. First I was getting downgraded by Ray; and catching it
head-on with Hal. Janie was handed one of her worst defeats a mother
could have: overruled by her husband, ignored by her son. Jane and me
took a shellacking.

"And I may as well tell you what I think as long as he's here.
There's no way.....no flippin' way he was only drunk that afternoon.
He was in zombie land with the hippies. Drunk? You can't get that
zoned out on beer." Hal ranted.

"I'll talk to him." Ray replied.

"And that's precisely what mother was trying to do by asking
you to come home for Easter – so you could find out why Ryan is on

this path of self-destruction. He's a high flyer, and the bunch he runs with – they're headed for trouble. They're NMFG period." he said.

Ray heard Jane cry, from the other side of the hall, "Raymond just come home dammit."

Hal looked at his empty mug. I sat on the steps with my elbows on my knees, supporting my head with my hands under my jaw. Hal called, "Willis......young Bill - get over here and say hello to your big brother."

He hopped off the couch and took the hand off from the old man. Hal made a bee-line to the kitchen and poured both bottles simultaneously - like the pros. A handful of new cubes and he jerked the receiver from Billy's hand before Ray could return his greeting. Hal knew it was time to build Jane back up; he couldn't let her walk away from the phone call feeling this bad. Jane had put up with a lot of his bullcrap. The taps on her shoes were getting worn out.

"Mother and I are hoping – praying – wishing......that Ryan does something productive after high school, and now Ray, you've made that possible. I don't know what interests him other than the Latin, and that is a dead language as well as a dead end. What a reversal of fortune. I thought you boys would be off to fight in Vietnam. We all watched your lottery number get pulled. It's all coming up clover now boy. No. 2 son has got to straighten up and fly right though; instead of being a high flyer."

I knew he was eyeballing me, though I never turned towards him.

Hal went on, "Still – it might be beneficial in Ryan's case for him to go down to the recruiting office and sign up."

"Pa-leeez." Jane cried and stormed out.

"Ray, you know what's going on. You know how to get through to him. Right now he's majoring in Chemistry at the college level......if you know what I mean."

I'll see him after exams. We'll go caddying together. I'll get his mind right. He doesn't need the service." Ray said.

"This long distance is costing me a fortune. You reversed the charges." Hal said.

"Yeah. Tell Mom I love her."

"Great talking with you boy, great job with getting the extension. Anything else mother?" he called into the direction she stormed off to."

"Just tell him I love him." her voice rattled.

"That's about it kid; talk to you soon." The receiver was placed back in the phone's cradle.

Jane tried to call the next day, but there was no pick-up. I was relieved her busy season was fast approaching.

iii

Once the country and its teachers started believing the war and the draft were over, there was this big push to send the next generation off to college where the opposing pole magnetic pole would wield its influence.

It had the taste of pole reversal to me; in this application it seemed to affect humanity's duality. Perhaps I was mistaken, and it had nothing to do the magnetic reconfiguration.

The teachers at Gorton thought I was Raymond Whitelaw part II, and I 'must' go to college. I didn't have the grades, but there was a consensus in the teachers' lounges that I just didn't test well; but I was definite college material. My plan was quite different: I planned on getting drafted in '73, and was entitled to take my interim year off between graduation and receiving my Draft Board notification to report.

A lot of students and teachers hounded me about where I was going next year. The only place I knew I was going was to the DMV, and getting a Driver's license and a set of wheels. Fuck the rest of that college jive-ass bullshit.

Without a license and a car, the summer would be a repeat of the last two. With a car.....I could get to work if I found a job. Caddying? - that was the last resort. Holter, Vinny, and me had taken Driver's Ed. in the last half of the school year. We received credit for the course by passing the road test. Also, the insurance companies were required to reduce the liability portion of your insurance by 10% because now you were a card carrying 'safe driver'. Passing the road test was the easy part, finding a set of wheels in my price range was not as easy as I thought.

"You homo's got any wheels lined up?" Rexall laughed.

Blank stares from the three of us. "I was hoping the Huns had something laying around. Vinny said.

"Kirk Lis is selling that '62 Olds.....the one they brought back from California last year."

Like a revelation it hit me......yeah...yeah....that's why I didn't see any of them guys last summer. Who went out there?...... Kirk, Kivel, Frankie, and ....Robbie. "Robbie, you went out to California too – didn't you?" I asked.

"Yeah, I missed you too Whitewash." Herrick said.

"Who's name is on the title?"

"Kirk's. When we bought it we all pitched in, but Kirk bought us out; one guy at a time." Herrick said.

"How much?" Vinny said.

"Think he wants a buck-and-a-half. Rexall answered.

I mashed my lips and started crunching the numbers in my head and nodding. "Robbie - how's it ride?"

"We shoulda had the Olds from the start. The Step-Van wasn't made for the plains, the mountains, or the desert. It was made for delivering Twinkies and coffee cakes. Frankie and Kirk made these bunk beds, and put a couple of vents in the roof. It had a rockin' 8-track.....great sound system. The engine didn't like the open road. No fuckin' power." He shook his head.

"Herrick......what about the car he's selling?" I said.

"It's a four door – had as much room as Bingo's deuce and-a-quarter. Still, we had to go to the drug store and buy that cough medicine with codeine to get to sleep."

"Robbie, I know the Step-Van had more room – I ain't asking you about that you fuckin' retard. How did the motherfucker run? How was the engine, tranny, the heater…. that shit." I shook my head and took a breath.

"Kool your jets Whitehammer. I'm getting to that."

"While we're young Herrick."

"First off, it's like the top shelf model they sold that year. You know – like an Impala or Galaxie. Old's thing was the 88, the 98, and the Starfire." Kirk's got a Starfire. The stock engine was a 394 cu. in. with a four barrel. They swapped out the 394 with a 455 cu. in. Buick Wildcat engine. A retired Air Force guy owned it – the guy's wife said it was too big for her, she had to have something smaller. Loads of power, the top speed in the desert was 75 m.p.h. only because the car needed new rubber all the way around. We weren't close to flooring it. With new tires, that car will do 125 – no problem. We had it up to 100 for about a half a minute but it started getting scary, so Frankie backed off the throttle to 75. Nobody wanted to spend the money for new tires, cause we were all tapped out. We decided to roll the dice; and hope if we did get a flat - it wouldn't be a blowout."

"What else?"

"Heater's fucked, stopped working in the mountains when we needed it most. We bought two bottles of cough medicine: one for the front seat and one for the back to get to sleep. The window behind the driver don't crank, so you got to leave it up. That sucked once we hit the plains. Three days - Amarillo to Yonkers, we slept during the day and drove at night."

Jimmy Martin said: "If I didn't already have a car and had $400 to put into it – fuck…..I'd buy it right now. With that Wildcat powerplant under the lid, you could outrun the state troopers."

"How many miles on it?" I said.

"61 thousand on the car. The mileage on the engine is a question mark. Don't burn no oil. California car – no rust."

"Is it running?"

"Yeah, I seen his brother driving it this week. I know he wants to get rid of it. Offer him a hundred. Drive it all summer with no insurance and the California plates. Do all the legal junk and get it ready for winter when you got the money. Robbie said.

"You can drive outlaw in the country. Too much can go wrong in the city – better have liability insurance." Rex arched his eyebrows.

I was thinking aloud, "It's $550 to get insurance through my father's policy. 150 to get the car some new shoes. That's $700 already."

"Plus title, taxes, registration, plates, inspection and don't forget the C-note for the car." Rex said.

"Fuck me runnin'…….life can't be this fucked up?" I took a breath.

"It gets better.....just wait." Everybody laughed, and Rex shook his head slowly from side to side.

"Those kind of numbers are going to keep me walking." Vinny backed off from his thoughts of buying the 'Starfire.'

"Whitesands, think of all the trim you'll get with that bedroom on wheels. Before you make one improvement – get the pillow and throw a blanket in the trunk. Put it in a plastic bag to keep it nice. Then, you get the tunes. Then you get the tires." Loverboy Holter advised.

"Who the fuck made you an authority? You ain't even got any wheels Holter?" Rex's face said: 'Dumb fuck.'

"My sister Candy told me what it takes to get to third base in a car with a girl. Some reefer, and a quart of Bali Hai makes it a home run." He said.

There weren't any objections.

I had the cash to buy the Oldsmobile, but only about half to get it street legal. No way was Hal going to let me park it at the top of the driveway and work on it while I got the money together to get it on the road. 21's driveway was just too damn small: no turn around area, too short, too narrow. Hal almost had a meltdown the first time Jane pulled into the top of the driveway with the Comet when there were no spaces on the street.

It looked more and more like I'd have to run outlaw style for a while until I could get the scratch together to be legit, insured, and road worthy.

And then ....WHAMO!......it hit me: I could get Kirk's car on the road and escape the weight of the state's compulsory liability insurance law by wiring the olive jar of comet ash to a narrow brace in front of the radiator, behind the Starfire's grill. That would be my insurance policy. It should more or less act like a deflector shield against all front end collisions, and getting rear ended was always a money maker. Front or back I had a funky kind of insurance and would be protected.

One week into May, I had to let Kirk know If I was going to buy it or not. "You gotta give me first shot at buying it........you got time to take a test drive with me like right now?" I said.

"Take it for a week Ryan – then decide. You got your license now."

"A week?.....You sure?" I raised my forehead.

"It's just been sitting in front of my father's house. It's a pain in the ass.......moving it with the alternate side of the street regulations. The neighbors are sick of seeing it sit there too." He handed me the Starfire's keys.

Mrs. Hillman had passed away two years earlier, or her family just moved her and sold the house. I never knew the whole story. A lot of times there would be an open space in front of the Hillman's house. I was pretty sure the house sat vacant for an entire two years. One day I watched as they took three foot lockers, rifles in cases, a mortar or a machine gun tripod was carried uncovered into a van. That Mr. Hillman was ready for anything. His Finnish commando push-button stiletto was still in my possession; I only carried it when I thought something heavy might be coming down, or I was going into an unknown situation and I might need something more than a knife.

The Starfire sat in front of the Hillman residence for a couple of days as I tried to piece together this financial puzzle of getting on the road: I might get Kirk down to a hundred, $700 for liability, another $200 for all the things Rexall had listed, plus $200 for tires. Driving outlaw was a risky proposition. The whole package started to overwhelm me.

Cranking the ignition, the Wildcat's engine immediately fired-up. Straight away, I learned the 455 cu.in. engine performed best using Hi-Test gasoline. It might have been the Buick's power steering pump interfacing with the Starfire's steering box - making it the smoothest power steering I ever encountered. A short quarter turn of the wheel and the front tires turned until it hit the stops to the left or right.

Kirk was a kool guy, him and Ray went to All Souls, and were occasionally in the same class. His brother Shane was in my class every other year, but he never hung around with us. Kirk loaned me the car – just like that. That was Kirk.

"Remember, there's no insurance on it - just a current reg-jo."

"With the after market 'Force Field Protection' installed, I pulled away from the space in front of the Hillman house. With ease it climbed up O'Dell. This is one smooth ride I thought. The Thruway and the Parkway.........had to stay away from them....too many bluecoats. Their only job was to watch for speeders and equipment violations. Out of state tags were particularly lucrative when it came to filling the coffers of the city, county, or state. Until I got a good feel for the ride, and familiar with all the bells and whistles – it'd be best to stay on the streets of Yonkers.

THE THOUGHT OF HAVING TRANSPORTATION WHEN-
ever I wanted wasn't powerful enough to erase my fear of getting in an accident while driving a car with no legal or financial status on the public roadways.

I telephoned Loki to see if he was going looping over the weekend. Like Ray, he was buckling down for his last two finals on Monday. Hopefully, the weather would cooperate, and I could make some money over the weekend for the car. I looked at the parked Starfire as I walked up O'Dell.

Herman the mechanic/driver said the caddy bus was being repaired, so he used Sunset's van to pick up the caddies. He'd have to make a double run to get us all. Herman greeted us with good news: All the private country clubs using caddies in southern Westchester raised the rate up to $8.00/bag. Those cheap ass skinflints just didn't want there to be any tipping. By the time the rate reached $9.00, I hoped to be long gone from the caddy circuit.

When I returned from Sunset Ridge late Sunday afternoon, it seemed like a good time to check out the street characteristics of Kirk's California car. The high performance engine and crisp hydraulic power transfer of the power steering; it was like the Starfire was catapulted from the parking space into traffic. If there was two feet of clearance between the Olds' rear bumper and the car behind, it was a three step maneuver getting into the traffic lane.

Waiting for a traffic light to turn on the steepest hill wasn't a problem as the tranny never gave up an inch. It made me think about Jane and those Chevys with clutches. Turning north on Broadway, I was doing 65 in a 45 m.p.h. speed zone. Heading into Hastings where North Broadway splits into a divided highway, the northbound lanes get a little squirrelly, before it's okay to get back into the throttle where the south and northbound lanes are again one road. So far, everything felt right. The only things I noticed were what Robbie Herrick said. I knew I'd have to get the hammer down and see for myself how bad the car handled at 75 m.p.h.

Directionals, wipers, headlights, tail, brake, parking lights – all operational. I cruised down Warburton back into Yonkers, and drove until I reached one nasty ass hill – Lamartine Ave. It was so steep, the asphalt formed rumple bumps from the summer heat and compromised its bond to the underlayment.

I got into the gas as the Starfire turned up the hill. The 455's claws ate up the incline like a big cat climbing a Ponderosa Pine. I did a U-turn at the top of Lamartine and Broadway and came back down. This steep hill would be good to test for the car's braking, suspension, and rear end. The road caused the Olds to hop-skip and become airborne like Steve McQueen's Mustang in the film 'Bullitt'. The car was ten years old, and didn't have a sports car chassis like the Mustang. I whizzed past the Old Croton Aqueduct Trail. Warburton was coming up real quick; I started worrying. The pitch of the hill made the rear end extremely light; the front wheels were doing 90% of the braking and were smoking. The front bumper was almost into the asphalt. Unless the rear end came down and engaged the road allowing the back wheels to be of use; my only hope was in the cosmic deflector shield, which had been a sketchy idea from the git-go.

The intersection looked busy, I ventured a peek of the immediate future. The Olds had to have been doing 50 m.p.h. with a freight train of momentum. The elevation of the traffic light was dead level with my eye line for a split second. It was red and I was standing on the brake pedal with both feet. I couldn't get it to stop and I couldn't get it to turn. Right on schedule, two kids were in the crosswalk at Lamartine and Warburton on the far side.

What happened in the next four seconds happened. Why it occurred is still a mystery. Maybe it was the olive jar of ash, pole reversal, magnetic intervention, St. Christopher pulling rank on mother nature and science – or perhaps I am Formula 1 driver material. The Starfire's rear end bottomed out as it came off the hill onto level Warburton Ave. It was enough to change the direction of the front wheels of the car and make that 'French Connection' move. I turned it hard left until the steering box ran out of gear, let off the brakes and floored the gas. The car did a 450 degree counter-clockwise turn in the intersection and caused a two car fender-bender. The collision froze the kids in the crosswalk and it was probably the reason they escaped injury.   Smoke and the smell of rubber filled the intersection, and I sped down Warburton towards Getty Square.....doing 35 in a 30, and watching in the rear view mirror for the bulls. All shook up, I took the side streets to Hanratty's on Lake Ave. and got a quick shot of rail whiskey and looked outside at the Starfire. 'What kind of car is this?' I wondered. I parked where I could watch it in case the cops came nosing around looking for a white Olds with Ca. tags.

The heat didn't seem to be on. I wanted to get the car back to O'Dell Ave. just to be safe. Driving on Palisade, I turned towards the river on Arthur St. It came to a 'T' at Warburton; it was the last east-west street connecting Broadway and Warburton until O'Dell Ave. There was nothing but woods for about a mile, and the cars would do 10 – 20 m.p.h. over the limit for the short stretch.

I had to determine if the ash gave me any sort of protection with it's capability to repel objects directly in its path. To perform this experiment was going to take a lot more thought. At first I was tempted to get the hammer down and aim for an oncoming vehicle and see if the two vehicles might bounce off each other. The more I thought about it the more ridiculous the thought became; bad enough I had the encounter at Lamartine and Warburton earlier. The olive jar had been all wired up and there was no interstellar assist occurring earlier – this was just nuts. I parked in front of the Kennedy's house on O'Dell.

iv

A month earlier, Jane had just got under the wire with the April 15th tax deadline. Once again, Hal whipped her into a frenzied state by questioning the amount she was declaring for her business on the books. Last year she carried two "Ghost" classes and a number of unreported cash jobs. Jane had a number of legitimate business expenses: she moved the studio to a new location, car expenses, paying people (like me) to paint and clean, and her printing bill was always exorbitant, and she could never account why it was so high. Accounting was Hal's forte and we all knew it. He'd send her to guys in offices to do her taxes and he go through her returns and call up the tax preparer and ball him out for being incompetent.

From tax crisis to recital hysteria from April through June and throw in some melodrama with Ray-burn from Indiana, Jane was reaching the point of critical mass. At first, I thought she was going to pull it off because of all the dance studio stuff had siphoned off her motherly concern normally directed to her own flesh and blood. It was a valiant attempt, but she ended up at the doctor's office with stress and panic attacks, insomnia, and anxiety pangs.

One week in May, Jane started wearing gloves, because she didn't have any nails left to bite. She told people she had a severe case of poison ivy from upstate. Her doctor started her on 5 megatons of valium. She went through them like grease through a goose. He upped her dosage to a 60 day script of 10 megatons, and a 90 day-er of 5's, prior to the physician even seeing her. It was a minor miracle she survived the 90 day run.

Hal was the liaison between Jane and Ray – until the day after the recital. Ray's grades arrived in the third week of May; she didn't know what half the courses were. She looked up from the grades' report at me: "Something's not right." Jane looked over to Hal, "Something's not right."

'Here it comes.' I sensed.

"Dammit Jane, he calls every weekend. He's 19 years old. When I was 19, I was in the south Pacific fighting Japs.....quit suffocating the guy."

"Cathy and Billy have talked to him more than I have. The next time he calls – I'm talking to him......period."

"Okay little Miss Smartypants........call him up.........call him up now." Hal said.

"Well, he's never there. There's never anyone there to answer the phone." she said.

"You might be calling a pay phone in the dorm. Don't blame Raymondo." I replied.

"Well how is it that your father seems to be talking a blue streak with him whenever I'm not around." Jane left us and went upstairs.

"If this isn't a case of the kettle calling the pot black..... Guess what Suzie Q......you're never here either." he yelled back.

Jane's voice echoed down the stairway, "You don't have to think very hard why that is." She cringed.

Hal scoffed off her last remark.

With Ray's absence, his skills to prevent these flare ups were sorely missed. He could prevent these skirmishes from ever getting started. Whereas, my role was anything but a peacemaker. I was an 'official observer.' I had no intention of getting in the middle of this husband-wife feud. Dealing with them as 'Mom' and 'Dad' was far as I wanted to be involved.

I felt bad for Cathy and Brother Bill; I knew their marriage was 'on the rocks' and deteriorating more each day. It wasn't pleasant living at 21 O'Dell. With the Starfire, I'd have the means to fly the coop if it became intolerable; however, Cathy and Billy were inmates doing time. The volume and acrimony were hitting new heights every month.

In my mind, the purchase of The '62 Olds was a done deal. I'd arrange a time to complete the purchase. What I wasn't too keen on was driving outlaw, but that's the way it had to be until I got enough scratch together to get legal.

The Ray Whitelaw affair of West Lafayette was already a battle royale. It was a round-robin slugfest and being in Indiana, neither could put a glove on Ray. The first wave of deceit began with Ray staying at school to study over spring break. Next Hal concealed the Purdue's award of the full scholarship from Jane. Now, the latest revelation from West Lafayette was Ray had enrolled for the summer session and got a summer job in the admissions Department. He would not be returning to Yonkers until mid-August. The last two items were also withheld from Jane on the basis: "Your mother is already coming apart at the seams – she doesn't need to know this."

Letters, Ray's phone calls – mostly to Loki, Hal's secret communiqués with Ray, as well as Jane's with Ray (she wasn't totally in the dark) all fed me with information I didn't care to know about. From my vantage point, Hal knew the most, did the least, and played the martyr the best. "I have done the most for this family, but have failed to reap any of the fruits. Dammit Ryan……..man to man: I haven't gotten a piece of nookie off your mother since the night before Ray called saying he had to stay at school during Easter vacation."

I slowly shook my head, "That's awful Dad."

"And that's not the half of it." His hands went to his hips as he watched the peeling ceiling paint.

"No Pops – that's all I want to hear."

"Ryan…..now just listen…..we've got to do a little strategic planning of our own. I don't believe Ray has any intention of coming back this summer."

He hadn't really gotten into the bottle yet, but it sounded like some bullcrap. I didn't know what he had up his sleeve.

"In the Navy, we got our orders and followed them. Your brother isn't taking any orders, he's mapping out his own future." In between Jane and the whiskey sodas, Hal was like a Midas; but instead of mounds of gold in a chest, he had information. It gave him some kind of weird thrill being a step ahead of Jane and me. I didn't care so it had no power over me. This wasn't the case with Jane. Hal thought this information restored the leverage over her which he'd lost years ago. If he could deliver Ray back to her, she might love him again. Too much water had passed under the bridge, even I knew that. Things would just have to play themselves out.

When I passed my road test, Hal made a stink about having to pay for another male driver on his policy, but he paid for Ray, so I argued am I any less a son?

"By blood no – by content?…….the answer is yes all day Ryan." Hal laughed.

I admitted my shortcomings to him, which I sensed he enjoyed hearing.   Later on, things would be different.

Jane leaned on him to do for me what he had done for Ray and made him put me on the car insurance policy. It was to his benefit; now he could send me to run the errands he used to have to do. This included picking up bottles of rye whiskey and club soda before the liquor stores closed.

Joe O'Clair owned Harmonie Liqour up the North End. He knew all the guys from the End. He knew I was a wino, but I threw a him a curve when I started buying Hal's brand of rye.

"Hey Whitelaw, there's only one other guy who buys that brand of whiskey, you related to him?"

"Nah….tryin' something different."

Joe raised his eyebrows and put the money in the register.

When I showed up with Kirk's Starfire for the trial week – Hal said it was time to have another man to man.

"Are you going to buy this car from California?" he said.

"Most likely – got to have a car to get a job. Had a couple of guys check it out. Needs rubber all the way around....a few other minor things."

I put his quart of rye on the sink counter where he mixed his drinks; he went right to work fixing a whiskey soda for himself.

"Ryan, I need you to do me this favor – I want you to go out to Indiana and bring your brother back. Not so much for us, but for your mother and her sanity. She's not going to have a moment's peace until she sees him. I've got to get her off my case and stop with the missing person's nonsense. You bring back Ray, and I'll help you with the financial end of your car."

"Whoa......wait a minute Pops – The help's got to be on the front end of this trip. I'm not talking about shocks, ball joints, or tie rods either. I need insurance, plates, tires, oil change and a lube job. And, I'll need liability insurance for six months."

"Wait a minute boy......insuring you as a driver on the Newport and the Comet and putting liability coverage on a third car – that's a major cost differential."

We were having something of a staredown. Maybe it was that man to man b.s., or which of us could hold the longer gaze. I could do it with girl, but this was a challenge. With a guy who was your father, it played beyond weird. There might have been a transmutational dialogue going on as a result of the genetic similarity. I didn't like it. He knew he needed me; I was the link between him and Ray for right now.

"You know I still got school?" I said.

"You are to get him over Memorial Day Weekend. So you miss a day or two of class. This is family business, it'll help your mother get off those stupid pills." he said.

"Six months of insurance right?" I said.

"Right."

"And tires?"

He cut me off – used or retreads – not new."

"They got to be a set; I already got four renegades on the car right now. The left rear.....I got more hair on my head than that tire's got tread."

"Mein Gott, that isn't much." My father thought he was being funny.

"You want to make fun of me, you drive out there and you get him." I squinted down hard at him.

"I didn't know it was that sensitive an issue."

"And a hundred cash to cover: the title, reg-jo, plates, tax, and a few odds and ends."

"Fix it up and get ready to go. By the way, this is your Graduation present." Hal smiled.

"Gee – thanks Dad. By the way......this is your Birthday present." It was on the 25th of May, he was 46 years old.

"Alright then – we're square." He took a long drink: "What are you going to tell Jane why you're not here?"

"Graduation vacation at the Jersey Shore."

"Well, we got that aspect covered. Does she know about the car?"

I put my hand in the box of Capn' Crunch in the pantry cupboard; it was empty. "Not yet, I'll tell her it's Vinny's."

"Good."

THE FOLLOWING TUESDAY, WE CLOSED THE DEAL ON the Starfire. Kirk made it easy for me. He knocked the price down to $130, gave me a Pioneer 8-track tape deck with a mega amp like the OTR truckers used so they could listen to their radio, tapes, and C.B. radios with their windows wide open. Jimmy Martin knew I was getting the Starfire together, he showed up with a pair of big RCA television speakers. I don't think he charged me on account he had pinched a half-dozen of my blockbusters from Rexall's trunk last summer. I think I came out on the short end of the deal; at least I got something back.

The speakers had some muscle, but I had to climb in the trunk to screw them in from underneath to the hat shelf on top of the back seat. The labor was worth more than the RCA's. At least Jimmy made the attempt to make it right. Having a nice set of speakers coming out of the hat shelf was an invitation for someone to break in. I made a good move taking the time to secure and camouflage them by putting a piece of fabric screen and old dish towel over the mouth side protecting them. Kirk's 8-track had the power to drive those RCA's; they handled the highs and lows real smooth......no cracking......no distortion.

I looked for Ronnie Zanzibar down Orchard Street; that heater fan had to get fixed. He was sitting on a stoop and had his own fix going. Z-man wasn't the guy I needed – not right now. McKool and Jimmy Deep Freeze were in the Lake Ave. parking lot. The primer gray Bel Air was waiting for a throw down. They were there to take on all comers.

When I got out of the Starfire, Quinn was standing behind me . "White-lie....Did you buy Kirk's Desert Runner?" he said.

"Yeah."

McKool and Deep Freeze were doing their thing in the back of the lot close to the park's south entrance. Quinn and me walked over to the Hunmobile.

"Smart move with the Olds......it's got that 455 big block, and a 4 barrel.......nice." he said. "Kirk wanted to sell it to us when they first got back from Ca."

"Why didn't you buy it? Anything wrong with it?" I asked.

"No fuckin' room." McKool exhaled."We got the '56 Bel Air project car, the '57 Ford Sunliner, and the Valkyrie Experimental." His hands stayed in his pockets as he motioned with his head, to what I knew as the 'Hunmobile.'

I guessed the '61 Bel Air was now a prototype. A paper bag was wrapped around whatever Quinn was drinking.

McKool motioned to walk back to the Starfire: "C'mon." He looked inside, "Fucker's clean. Can't get over it......only 61 grand – California car....no rust. Wildcat engine, more power and more

487

reliable than the 394 cu.in. Starfire engine GM put in 'em. We should have jumped on it when Kirk showed it to us."

"Not many of these around." Davis added.

"The one thing I can't get to work is the heater's blower."

The three Huns laughed, "It's not the fan – it's the switch." Jimmy Deep Freeze said. "How much time we spend on the Bel Air trying to diagnose why the fan didn't work? Even got one from the bone yard – still didn't work."

"We were ready to get one from Curry Chevrolet, and Shooey shows up looking for a set of mag wheels for Danny Stax's Chevy II. He asks why we're so bent outta shape and we tell him. Shooey says to me and McKool to sit tight." Quinn chuckled.

"I think I came along just in time." Shooey says.

"Half hour later, he's back." Freeze says.

"It's not the fan.......it's the fuckin' switch. GM's all got the same switch. Anything GM makes has the same blower switch." he grinned.

"Huh?" I scrunched my brow down as I listened to their experience.

"General Motors went from an on/off switch to one where the fan's switch is integrated with a low-speed activator. The switches are junk." Shooey told them.

"Quinn what's my move?" I said.

"Go down to Saw Mill Auto Wreckers, pull one. Curry wants $18 for one......probably a five dollar switch at the bone yard." He looked at the tires on the Starfire, "See if they got any good matching rubber as long as you're down there."

"McKool, you want to test drive it?"

"Nah, people see me driving this cruiser, they'll think I'm getting married. Let me know when you're going to unload it – I'll have the money and primer gray on standby." he smiled, a cigarette dangled out the side of his mouth.

"Thanks for the tech tip with the switch." I got in the car, and started backing out of the spot and McKool straight-armed his hands on the roof.

"Hey Whitepaint, you went to school with Shooey-"

"Yeah....he was a year ahead of me."

"Isn't Shooey's real name Drew – Drew Saxon?"

"Yeah."

"How'd he get the nickname?"

"He was in my brother's class; he said he always wore shoes to gym."

I waved to the three Huns and left some rubber as I peeled out of the parking lot.

RONNIE (Z-MAN) ZANZIBAR WAS WITH THE ORCHARD Street crew. He was as good a wrench as any of the Huns or Shooey, but his specialty was electronics. The sprawling motor pool had been his gig in Danang. When he returned from Nam after doing 13 months, (he was one of the few guys we knew who got drafted by the Marines, so his tour was 13 months instead of 12); he came home with a monkey on his back.

Z-man had a good rep for adapting APC's, cars, trucks, jeeps, and salvaging usable parts from three wrecks, and putting two back into service. He produced many hybrid vehicles, the likes of which were a one of kind. It drove other motor pool mechanics crazy. There were tags on trucks and messages in white paintstick in and on armored cars, APC's, jeeps etc. explicitly instructing the user of the vehicles to see Ronnie Zanzibar @ the Danang motor pool for maintenance and service.

Upon completing his tour of duty and discharge, he was hired by the Yonkers P.D. to keep their squad, patrol cars, and motorcycles running with a half-dozen other mechanics. Zanzibar's knowledge to integrate radio systems and frequencies, safety equipment, and after market accessories
came from the service. It was the perfect setting for learning – smoke pot all day working on cars with no clock on the time spent fixing them or the amount of money spent on new parts. Talk shop with the cops and other wrenchers. Ronnie was a mechanical, hydraulic, and electronics wizard.

As a conscript, the Marines tolerated him. The Police Department administration would never tell him he was doing a good job, but his accomplishments and versatility in the garage simply made him the Ace. The Marine officers were always telling him to cut the hair, shave, and no tinted glasses at night. The cops told him the same, but not as often. The cops' main complaint was the music volume in the garage.

Vinny Tarts and me were trying to line up some electricity for a concert. Crawfish directed us to the Z-man without telling us what he had. He gave us a ride from Morsemere to Orchard in his new ride: the Aquamarine Datsun B-210. He bought it from this mini-version of Sophia Loren.......Betsy Risko. She was Italian in everything but her last name. We all thought her mother had gotten a divorce; remarried and gave Betsy the stepfather's last name. We knew she was a goomba, with mob connections. Vince and Kenny gave me a hard time because I still didn't have the Olds squared away yet.

Most of Orchard Street were a few years older than us, they were in the age bracket for the big draft call ups. Bingo, Bush, and Danny Stax were the only ones who had to go down to the draft board. Robin Busch and Danny Stax did their two years in the military. When Robin was inducted his brother Buddy signed up too. Robin went to Germany, and Buddy went to Korea; while Stax went to the Mekong Delta where they repelled the Viet Cong who tried to overrun their firebases.

Kenny was tight with the Orchard St. crew; he knew them better than any of us. His parents used to live down there. Through his brother Joe, Vinny had a good line on the situation down there too. Between the two of them, we always got word when they had Quaaludes or exotic stuff available.

Vince knew straight away they were rolling some heavy dice – at least half – of them. It wasn't Vinny or my business; this is where

Crawfish got his start. It wouldn't shock either of us if he went back there to get his wings.

"What's the word over at Morsemere?" one of the Carr brothers asked when we pulled up.

"Trying to track down some hallucinogenic substances: peyote, mushrooms, acid, mescaline, Chiracahua cocktail …..prefer organic not from the chemist." Vinny said.

"How 'bout it Z-man – can we hook our brothers up?" Carr said.

"What's the occasion?" Zanzibar grinned.

Crawfish motioned his head toward Vince and me: "They're gonna see the Allmans."

"Without Duane….they're playin at the Academy of Music. Won't be the same, that's for sure. That's why we need the electricity…….in case they suck." I inhaled.

"We're just prayin' and hopin' for the best." Vinny left it to fate.

"Only thing around now is shitty weed and expensive coke." Z-man said.

"The search continues." We nodded, waved, and said adios.

Kenny drove us around. It was getting desperate; we were even looking for Mike Reno. We stopped at the liquor store and got some go-go juice and patrolled some more.

"Want to split an 8-ball?" Catdaddy watched the road with a straight face and turned to Vince in the shotgun seat and began cracking up.

"Get the fuck outta' here." Cinzano said.

I took a look at him from the back, "You're fuckin' serious……man you are fuckin' whacked." I said.

Vinny chimed in……"You got some serious head problems – you're a fuckin' nut job."

Kenny tried not to laugh. I knew it wouldn't take much to get him going again. He put on this dumbfounded "Who me?" face, and looked over to Tarts and we all broke up again. That was Kenny.

Vinny pushed his shoulder into the door, "You're a fuckin' retard."

Like a hurt puppy he came back, "If we shot it…..bigger rush……longer high." He broke up again cackling at his latest suggestion." Crawfish was a panic.

"What about Quaaludes, see any of them around?" I said.

"Not since Christmas."

"You two rock and rollers are going to have to go with the Peruvian flake." He kind of laughed I think.

Vinny was pissed, "First of all you Marblehead, we're going to a concert not to an orgy. Second, we want to be high longer than 20 minutes."

"I'm only trying to help." He took a slug of Bali Hai and slowly looked over toward Vinny, I could see he was cracking up – his head was bobbing up and down and he put his hand in front of his face and sprayed it full of wine. He pulled one of his emergency stops in the middle of the street and got out and sprayed some more wine on the double line.

Parked in the street for three minutes, Crawford got back in the Datsun and drank some more wine to get rid of the sour taste. "Hey – no kidding, I got to drop you guys off." We didn't see him for a week.

v

All the DMV and insurance nonsense was buttoned up by the third Friday in May. I still had to get tires, adjust the brakes, and do the heater fan switch. I drove over to TNT Dynamite used cars and see if that screwball Herbert had a matched set of used tires for the Starfire.

"Where the hell did you pick up this bucket of bolts?" he huffed.

"Bought it off you......come on Herb, get with it." I tried to look annoyed.

He scratched his temple with one hand and pushed his hair off his forehead with the other. Walking around the car he asked, "How's it running?" Focusing on the Olds, he sucked his teeth and started flossing them with a matchbook cover.

"Anything wrong with the car? You want to trade it in? Slick, just why the fuck are you here?" Herb asked with a head nod.

"Need some used tires Herb, you told me to come back when I needed 'em. Well, I need them."

He looked at the rubber on the car, their wasn't a pair on the car and the cord was showing through on the one. "I sold you this car with these tires?" I watched as he searched his memory. Out came the Camels, he lit up and scratched his head again.

"There was a blow out and one flat." I said.

"What's the spare look like Slick?"

"Like a slick." I tried to keep a straight face.

"Open the trunk, let's take a look."

"I pulled it out."

He took a look at it and raised his eyebrows – "Just put it on the side. Your right rear is your new spare. You know you got mag rims. I don't know if I got the width for them – I got to look." Herbert whewed.

"How much?" I tried to keep the heat on.

"I don't know if I got four......I know I got 2 and 2; a car don't like that set-up, especially a boat like this one. You put 4 matched tires on this ride – and it'll ride like it just came off the assembly line. Hey Slick, I didn't sell this car to you did I?"

"Nah, I bought that Mercury Comet from you last year, with my sister?" I threw him another one.

"Oooh yeah with that girly girl.......with the two kids...... yeah. Now I remember. How's the Comet running?" he grinned.

"Like a champ."

"How much you pay for the Olds?"

"$200."

"You stole it. How many miles?"

491

"61 grand." I said.

"That's a real deal Neil." he jazzed. "Come back after lunch – I'll let you know if I can help you."

I had study hall and lunch; my next class was trigonometry. Trig was pretty much a lost cause. I know I could have passed if Ray had been around. The entire senior year was not my best effort. I was disappointed in myself. Things were getting away from me.....I didn't like the way it felt.

When I came back, there were four tires on rims, they were off to the side. They were a matched set – the rubber looked pretty good.

Herbert came out of his little office: "Couple of things handsome; you know what a radial tire is?"

"Not really." I said.

"Well – those are radials. That means you'll get better gas smileage, handling, and traction on bad road conditions. What you won't get is a cheaper tire. All four......$150: broke off those Chrysler rims, mounted and balance on your mags. Plus – plus I'll have to fuck around with your spare and bust that down so you'll be riding with four mags and a regular rim for your spare; should really be $160." Herbert said. "Come back around 4 o'clock and you can pick it up."

"Buck-and–a-half...........right?"

"Cash?"

"Big Green." I nodded.

"No checks.......no tax. See how that works?" Herb smiled. "We're both saving money."

"See you at four."

"Right."

Walking out of TNT I hoped these radial tires were as good as Herb said. The name on the sidewall said Cooper tires. At least they were a name brand, not cut outs. Coming down Lamartine that day did a number on the right front. I had no choice, I had to get better tires than came with the car.

I had to kill three hours waiting for the car, when I got there Herbert was waiting for the spare to be balanced.

"Take your car out on the Saw Mill Parkway – you'll see the difference right away."

"Where's the keys?" I said.

"Where's the money?"

He counted the money in front of me puffing on a Camel. I did like he said and took it out on the Saw Mill; there was a big difference in the way the car handled and drove. It was worth the money. Herbert was a character, but he knew cars. The radials ate up that snakey parkway. The Cooper tires looked right on the mag wheels, and that made the mags look right for the Starfire.

Once again, my wallet was on "E".

THE ROGUES ASKED ME WHERE KIRK'S CAR WAS THAT Friday night. "Whatja buy it to keep it parked?" I told Jimmy Martin and Bad Brad - I was still taking care of a few odds and ends before I gave them "The Reveal". It didn't take a whole lot of common sense to figure out alcohol and cars didn't mix well. Cars were for chicks, smokin' reef, and groovin' to the jams. My 18th birthday was more than three months away, and I already had known five or six guys who died in car wrecks.

The weekend before Memorial Day, I took the Starfire up to Sunset Ridge both Saturday and Sunday. There was a dream-like feeling to it, something dimensional as well. I was hoping to run into Loki up there; he had been out of school for a couple of weeks already. No Loki, just the regular guys; it was good seeing everybody after a long hibernation.

The trip to Purdue was right around the corner. It was probably for the best to tell Murdoch I wouldn't be available for next weekend because of a family obligation. The caddy master kept chewing his gum, and face buried on the golfer list for tomorrow. He never looked up at me, it didn't matter I suppose.

"What's your number?"

"444."

I told Ed Detore about it, he said it was the right thing to do - "just common courtesy."

After the loop on Sunday, Hal had me cut the grass, he was pretty well tankard up. Between my solo trip, Jane's annual recital, Otis and the WTC - he was most likely eyeing Jane's valium in the medicine cabinet. He had to be in Manhattan on Monday.

Before I came back from the golf course, the Old Man had been grilling burgers, hot dogs, and some chicken wings. The burgers were the size of Morgan silver dollars, the hot dogs could be mistaken for sausage links. The chicken wings had shrunk to the size of crab legs. Flies and yellow jacket were at work reducing their size even further. Two English muffins were loaded up with high-fat burgers, ketchup, and cheese. You got used to Hal's Sunday cookouts. It was even money he didn't even know I had come and gone.

Two dollars for a six-pack of Schaefer Tall-Boys at Barca Bros. Supermarket. The North End looked like a ghost town. I made the run down to Morsemere/Progressive/the Deli, Rubeo Park, and then Lake Ave. The only guy I saw was Mike Reno parked at the Lake Ave lot. Checking out Reno was better than cruising around by myself and the Tall-Boys. The Lennon Park lot was half-full; Mike's snot green Nova w/dark green vinyl roof stood out amongst the other cars. Kathy Cruz and Penny Paschen (Passion Penny) were smoking cigarettes and leaned up against Reno's car. He was in bad shape. He stood writhing in pain; his hands squeezed the chain-link fence as if he was taking 20 lashes at the whipping post. The girls saw me, but Mike didn't.

Silently, I asked the girls with a head tilt and a nod towards Reno – "What gives?"

Kathy Cruz shook her head from side to side and looked away from me. I caught her laughing.

"Oooooyyyyaaaaahhhmotherfucker!" Mike wailed.

Kathy and Penny snickered.

"My tooth is going to S'plode." He grabbed the fence and began yanking it to and fro.

"Reno......what the......you gonna make it?" I looked at the girls and they turned away from me again. The girls weren't sympathetic to Reno's dental complications. There was a good chance they saw Mike's trauma as some justifiable payback for being a jag.

"Get me something for this tooth abscess......I'm fuckin' dyin!" he cried.

The contingency nurses were beside themselves trying to keep their laughter muffled.

"Whoooozat?" Reno cried over his shoulder.

"Whitelaw."

"You got anything for s'pain?" his hand wanted to touch his cheek, but didn't.

"What's he saying?" I asked the girls.

I finally got a look at him. The abscess was into his right cheek, he was in pain alright.

"You got any goof balls?" Penny smiled.

"Hey Mike – what gives?"

"Aaawwww, fuck you too." He replied and he started punching the fence.

The girls had tied a bandana on his head; it went under his chin and was tied in a knot on the top of his head. Reno must have had Kathy and Penny try to immobilize his jaw.

"Ryan.....you got any beer?" they asked.

"Take one.......and share it." I turned my attention back to Mike, "Okay champ – let's see that tooth – c'mon Mike.....open up."

He put his claws back into the chain link fence, and again started pulling it back and forth. He locked his arms straight and had the fence doing a four foot accordion spread and screamed over and over......."mutterpucker...... mutterpucker." We had to laugh. He was a mid-sized Frankenstein gone bezerko.

"C'mon Reno – open up - let's take a look at that mother. C'mon."

Reno didn't let up for another two minutes, he relaxed his arms and rested on them against the fence. His fists were a mess. He was fighting the pain, but he wasn't winning. Finally, he turned and faced me. I took a breath; the sight was pitiful and comical at the same time. With the white bandana-handkerchief he had grown jack rabbit ears. Cruz and Passion had obviously been paying Mike back.

"God damn Reno........ your right cheek is filled with puss. You got yourself a dandy of an abscess, paisan. Open.....open up, I won't touch you." The girls stopped laughing. "Put your face into the sun, and open as wide as you can so I can get a better view." I went to the car and got what was left of my 16 ounce.

He sat on a pressure treated "8x8" guard rail post. "Okay... alright Mike – wow - I had one of these abscesses, only not this severe."

"Whiteslaw, got any downs?" His eyes were clamped down so tight; he had to be dealing with a full 10 on the pain scale.

"We'll figure something out. The wisdom tooth is coming in and it's impacting the molar in front of it. Then, there's the infection that's gone from your gum to your jaw to your cheek. All that throbbing pain is coming from the infection/puss. You get rid of that – you'll get a lot of relief. The wisdom tooth coming down, that's got to get extracted. Go over to St. John's emergency and have them drain that puss and get it pulled tomorrow." I took a big swallow of beer.

Reno asked again, "Got any jruggs?"

"Not really, not what you're needing. I guess I could swipe 20 megatons of valium from my Mom, then you could chase it with a quart of Colt. You'd probably get some relief with that technology." I said.

"Get it for me, will ya? I'm dyin'." he said.

"What about us Whitespurs?" Cruz gave me that heavy eye action.

"Cruz, this is medical not recreational, you're off your rocker." I answered.

"C'mon Ryan." Penny echoed.

"Whiteroom, you've got to do it – you got to cut ma gum."

"No way Mike. You're out of your fuckin' mind." I saw something close to insanity in his face.....his eyes.

"You do it.....you do it now." His hand spread across his forehead like a visor.

"Get the fuck outta here. No way Mike."

"You do it or I jump in front of a fuckin' train."

"Whitelaw......you've got to." Penny said.

I scoffed, "Yeah I'll do it in a parking lot. Y'all got brain damage."

"You can do it at my house, nobody's home. What do you need?" Cruz asked.

"I don't believe this shit. You think I'm Che Guevera?" and we're in the jungle in Cuba? This has got to be some kind of movie.........Yeah sure.....why not? Cruz, you got an exacto knife, or something to make a fine incision, sterile pads, and hydrogen peroxide?" I joked.

"Yeah, at my house."

"Where's that?"

"35 Pine Street."

"That's where Rikshaw lives."

"Who?" Penny took a drag from a cigarette.

"Eric Shaw, the Chinese guy"

"Yeah, and Messy Beth." she added.

Neither of them had a license. Reno went right to the back seat with Penny, and lay his forehead on top of the front bench seat. "I'm going to stop and get that valium for Reno. Hey Reno I'll give you enough to get you through 'til tomorrow." I said.

"What about us?" Kathy asked again.

"Have another of my beers." I met the trio 20 minutes later at Cruz's parents place. I couldn't believe I was doing this.

"Hey Kathy you got the stuff?"

"It's on the kitchen table." I gave Mike a 10 megaton pill of valium, and had him chug 12 ounces of the Colt 45. I washed my hands and had Penny cut a new razor blade with a pair of scissors into a quarter inch strip. Kathy used a pair of tweezers and sterilized and wiped it with a sterile gauze pad and alcohol. I held the abbreviated blade between my thumb and forefinger: "Don't fuckin' move."

He replied with another moan.

"Penny wash your hands real good with hot water and douse them with some of this alcohol. Take a gauze pad and push his cheek away from the outside of his gum so I can make the incision."

"Reno.....DO NOT MOVE. When she pushes your infected cheek, it is going to hurt: DO NOT FUCKIN' MOVE." I inhaled.

"Just fuckin' do it!" his eyes bulged.

"Alright Penny – push. More....." I watched, Mike cried. "A little more." I told her. Kathy smoked, and had this crazy expression like she enjoyed seeing Reno on the edge. I got back to business. I thought he was going to pass out; the arms of her chair were in a death grip. I sliced the upper gum with a 1/16th incision between the molar and the wisdom tooth. All this clear puss shot out from the opening. "Cruz – take a dish towel on the outside and push his cheek and force the puss out. Kathy, get a bowl so Reno can get rid of the puss inside his mouth.

The cheek swelling was subsiding, but it still flowed from his gum and jaw on its own. I put a couple of fat rolls of gauze between his cheek and gum for absorption.

Five minutes had passed, "How's it feel Mike?"

"Hurt's like hell – but nowhere near like it did in the parking lot this afternoon. Wooooo –" Reno exhaled.

"If all's you're is getting is blood from that puncture, gargle every two hours with the peroxide. Get that useless wisdom tooth pulled tomorrow. And when that all-star oral surgeon asks how you got that cut.....just tell him you don't know. That wisdom tooth of mine – it came down so hard it cracked one of the tri-roots of the molar in front of it. They had to pull them both." I winced, "Can't afford to lose them big ones."

EVERYBODY WHO HAD A CAR KNEW PARKING NEAR Gorton was a headache, and unless I had some business after school, I was better off leaving it on O'Dell Ave. It was a few days before Memorial Day; people at school were acting like the holiday weekend had already started. The drinking age of every state I'd be driving through was 21. I knew I'd be better off taking at least a nickel bag of weed, and maybe getting another baggy at Purdue. They all smoked pot on them campuses, the reefer they had might even be better than the stuff they had around here.

I drove south on Warburton, I coasted to a stop at Glenwood Ave at the red light. Joey Tarts, Cocaine Wayne, and Z-man were loitering in front of a small grocery and a liquor store. The traffic light turned green, and I pulled into the bus stop that extended beyond the corner. Barbara Wells stood in a recessed entrance of the run-down apartment. Trouble couldn't be far from this quartet. There seemed to be so much shadow radiating off these guys, the neighborhood may have thought they were experiencing a partial eclipse.

Reno was back in action, his car was across the street in the lot of a closed-down A&P; maybe he had gotten his wisdom tooth pulled. What was Reno doing with these guys anyway? - he was a lightweight. Most likely, he was trading taxi service for weed or hash. The Z-man gave the Starfire the once over. Zanzibar was kool standing against the brick wall putting it together. Looking over the top of his prescription tinted glasses, he grinned and walked over to my side: "Hey.... Hey.....Whiteflame." he greeted.

Joey and Wayne looked in from the passenger's side: "This cruiser's yours?"

"Bought it a couple of weeks ago from Kirk...........Lis. He brought it back from California last summer. The car's been parked in front of his father's house. He's got that VW camper now. It's been kind of just sitting there; I told him I was looking for a set of wheels." I said.

Z-man looked concerned, "But he did drive it. He didn't just let it sit?"

"Yeah, he said he took it to work once a week when the alternate side parking rule was in effect."

"Just letting a car sit ain't good for a car – three maybe four months.......that's the most." he said.

The three amigos were hanging out for a reason, and it wasn't to talk about my ride. I was a distraction, they were anxious and jittery.

"Anything going on in CEEEE-AAAAAY." Joey had his hands in his pockets.

I shrugged my shoulders and tilted my head.

"What's Ray up to?" Joey scanned up and down Warburton.

"Still at Purdue."

"Still Boilermakin'?"

I laughed, "Yeah, still Boilermakin'. I'm going out to Indiana this weekend to drive him back."

"Memorial Day traffic - not as bad as the Fourth or Labor Day, but it's still a mother." Zanzibar rolled his eyes and walked back to the sidewalk. He looked through the front passenger window: "Happy Motoring." Z-man and Wayne went back to the apartment's brick wall and resumed lookout for their connection.

Joey Tarts leaned against the rear of the car in front of me - waiting for the magic man to show up. Wells came out from the alcove of the building. She was the only reason I was still there. I watched her as she took a few steps to the passenger's window. To the street it must have looked like a drug buy, until Barb rested her arms on top of the Olds and put her face into the window. Her ass was higher than her head and whether she knew it or not I could look right down her shirt. Then she lowered her chest even further to give me a better view down her low-cut top. Barbara kept piling it on: the way she talked to me, what she talked about, the way she looked, her laugh, the wild side, but it was the eye contact. Barb caught me looking down her shirt, I didn't bother to avert my stare, and she didn't try hide.

"Lookin' real good Babs."

"Thought you might like a show."

"Turn right a little......so the sun gets in there."

She obliged, "I'm not too big." She looked down but smiled.

"Don't have to be for me." We smiled at each other.

"Ain't that Reno's car across the street? Where is he?" I made a 270 scan.

"Yeah." she said as her eyes got large. Heard you were doing a little moonlighting - playing surgeon yesterday - .....he was calling you Dr. Whiteknife?" Barb smirked, "What was that all about?"

"The chump wouldn't go to the emergency room, and he wouldn't stop crying – Had no choice – I had to cut him." I chuckled.

"The oral Doctor's giving him the gas, I don't have to be back until later to get him. Whereja get the car?" she looked at the interior.

"Hey Barb, and I just ain't saying this: I think you'd be a great oral Doctor."

"An I'm just not saying this, I mean it – you're a fuckin' jag Whitecar." We laughed. "No, when did you get the car?"

"Hey Wells, you going to let me feel them?"

"Anybody watching?" she said.

"The phantoms of humanity are looking for something else; there's kids down the street. Just a little bit- c'mon."

"Take it out. I wanna see if you really like me."

I couldn't get it out with all the wood; I had to unbuckle, undo the brass button, and unzip for her. She scanned the street – it was still just the guys. Z-man gave an occasional glance over to the car.

"Go ahead." She gave me a far off stare.

I moved over to lessen the reach and put my hand in her shirt and started feeling her tit. She looked down.

"You like me a lot more than Mike.....a lot. Ryan, pull my nipple......a little harder......more."

Her one eye was closed, the other was a slit. I gave it a long hard pull. Her eyes opened and rolled to 12 o'clock and took a deep breath. Her hand went to the other breast, and she started working on it. I tried to watch what she was doing to copy it, but all I could see was her pulling and dialing the nipple. I came to when I heard the bus driver let off the air brakes on the other side of the red light   .

"I got to move for the bus." I looked down and it was still wild. I reached over to the back seat and got an old long tail dungaree shirt to cover up with.

"Go around the block......the bus'll be gone by then."

My legs were shaking, and my middle leg would not go down. Barb was waiting where I left her. I could see the Yonkers Transit bus way down the street getting smaller and smaller.

"Vinny Tarts said you bought a car." Barb said she getting in the front seat.

"Yeah – yeah. Bought it off Kirk Lis. Bobby Herrick went with them last summer to California." I said.

"Yeah......last summer.......yeah." She recalled:"I like Kirk Lis, but I don't like Kock Less." Wells gave me a sly smile.

"You're a fuckin' dumbbell." We laughed. "So what are you doing? Copping with the three musketeers or for them?" I squinted looking at her.

"Just making $10 doing the transportation."

"Reno don't know you're drug running with his wheels?" I said.

She raised her eyebrows and shook her head: "Mike would never run the risk driving these guys around. It's all weed with Reno: You've seen the operation. He drives around and I roll it into joints and do the selling. Reno knows a girl can sell way more pot than a guy."

"Yeah but a chick can get ripped off five times easier than a dude."

"That's where Reno comes in – he's the muscle."

"You want to get high playboy?" Barb cracked a big grin.

I gave her a sour look, "Who you talking to? Are you in with the musketeers with that heart pounding powder...... What are we talking about?" Reality had returned.

"Talking 'bout doing some big time." She nodded over towards Z-man. I'll split a bag with you.....they're waiting for the guy right now."

"Whoa – I ain't messing with no rig.....fuck that." Reality multiplied.

"Whiteride – we'll lace a joint. It'll rock your world.....you'll dig it."

Coming from her it sounded great; I thought of Adam. "I never did it before, I didn't know you could smoke it."

"Refined opium – Reno won't feel like doing anything tonight with that hole in his gum. We should take this trip to the stars and I'll give you a road test." A big vamp/she-devil smile.

"How 'bout a 7 o'clock rendezvous down the corner? I'm taking a trip to Indiana....probably leaving Thursday. Think about riding with me." I gave it to her right between the eyes.

"What's in Indiana?" she said.

"Look at that back seat; it's a damn bed. This ain't no snot green Nova. It's even bigger than Danny Stax's Chevy II Nova.....that's Starfire luxury." I pointed to the back seat.

"You got a pillow and a blanket?" she said.

"Ready for blast off." I wagged it with my left hand to show her how hot I was.

"Memorial Day weekend - Indiana?" She scrunched her eyebrows and puckered her lips to the one side and took a deep breath. "I don't know about Indy, I'll see you Wednesday.

While Wells and me were talking, the musketeers were transacting business with Joey's soul brother connection who I'd never seen before. Zanzibar stepped back and leaned against the brick. The connection brother parked in a delivery zone space, and got out. Joey and the soul brother went into the three story apartment. A few minutes later, the two came out. The supplier drove off, and Joey had

499

to lean against the wall next to Wayne and the Z-man. They looked at Joey and liked what they saw: Stone junkie, a trip to the far reaches of the universe. Cocaine Wayne and Z-man were giddy and itchy.

"Be Kool Wayne-o......be kool." The Z-man said. "Barb." He called, and motioned for Reno's car with an imaginary steering wheel in his hands.

Wells shouted over to Ronnie, "Did you get mine?"

A quick grin and a thumbs up from the Z-man.

Barb got out of the car and looked through the window: "See you Wednesday at seven." She waved and went over to get Reno's car in the vacant parking lot.

I pulled out of the bus stop looking at Joey, he appeared to be absorbed by the wall. 'Wow......that's high.' I thought.

Most likely, Sally heard through the grapevine I was going to Indiana to bring Ray back for summer break. Sunday, she called 21 after supper. Cathy answered the phone and handed it to me; Sally sounded like death warmed over. She said she was 'cleaning up' and would be ready to go on Friday.

"But I'm leaving Thursday and I didn't ask you to go."

Even with five days of 'cold turkey' – her body might be on the mend, but her brain would be no better than 'Sally Putty'. When Ray went back after winter break, she got strung out all over again and remained on the dope train until this latest attempt to get clean. I remember seeing her in a lot of parked cars in the winter on the nod.

"Sally......call me tomorrow." I started rubbing my chin trying to focus.

'That's all I need, she just wants to go on a road trip to clean up.' I looked at the receiver – slowly placing it back in the cradle, and crossed my arms on my chest. Torrents of possibilities streamed by. I wasn't sure if she was wired backward....a through and through specter junkie like the 'High Five' – I thought she might have been. I wrote to Ray and asked him where he stood in their relationship. She had them tombstone eyes – but she had an allure.

I was surprised to get a reply from him; as well as the content: ".....She's not on the run trying to escape this reality – this dimension. Sally's just a one column junkie....like most of them."

It kind of shocked me to see his letter dismiss her so sharply. Her good looks were fleeting. Sometimes a woman's vanity has more power than the powers of addiction. How it would turn out for Sally Englund remained to be seen. The Sally I knew - loved that 'Tragic Magic' but she also wanted to retain her physical luster. She could have one, but not the other. I had known her since the tenth grade in Gorton. I felt bad for her.

I was on the verge of getting involved with my own 'Twilight Siren'. 'Fuck me running'; I thought she was the coolest person I ever met. I sighed thinking about 'Barb Wire' Wells. Having the word out I was using junk, because I was in love with her not only sounded ridiculous, it scared me more than the junk itself. There were going to be a lot of people who got disappointed if they found out I was using the shit. As much as I didn't want Ray to know, I couldn't let Vinny Tarts find out either.

His brother's addiction was difficult for Vinny to deal with - even when Ray explained Joey's reality to the younger Tarts. He didn't want anything to do with substances you could get hung up on. Getting overtaken by a girl, and being unable to break free was nowhere near the same thing. From my viewpoint, Sally and Barb were galaxies apart.

Dope? What the hell was I thinking? The sooner I hooked back up with Ray, the quicker my moral compass would return to true north.......I was resolute: my sanity and ability to reason would be reestablished in West Lafayette.

Driving out there with Barb.......that was what I wanted. Taking Sally Englund with me, was dragging a boat anchor; and no upside to it. So Sally sees Ray out there? – we're coming right back. It was bugging me why she wanted to go with me. She wasn't going to see Ray – she was going to get clean because she'd have no connections to score out there. When I ran into Rikshaw, I asked him how it was going. "Dry as the desert.......we're all waiting for the monsoon."

The only way I was taking Sally was if Ray called and told me to take her. She could tell Ray she's been a good girl, but neither of them would have believed it. Taking Sally......it screws it up for me and Wells, plus there wouldn't be any room for Ray's stuff he'd be taking back.

IT WAS ALREADY 7:15 OUTSIDE OF PROGRESSIVE pizza. Nobody was around and I listened to the 'Layla' tape waiting for Barb. I'd be on the road early tomorrow with or without her, but definitely without Sally. I had a feeling Barb would be going with me. After a while of hanging around – "Sonofabitch......I think I got stood up." I laughed. I drove up to Pete's grocery and got a six of Miller Malt liquor because Pete's was cheaper. When I returned, Wells was leaning against a four foot chain link fence. She had a mini-purse slung over her shoulder.

I did a 180 turn from the gas station to where she stood, "What happened?"

"Couldn't get rid of Reno." She got into the Olds.

"Just tell him to fluff his nuts." We looked at each other and broke into laughter.

We cruised around.....smoking, drinking, talking..... I had to park and get her answer about driving out to Purdue, and run this Sally business by her. Greystone at 8:00 pm would be pretty dead, it'd be a good spot to get organized, and find out if she was coming.

We parked on the access road where the Huns had parked the Hunmobile/'Valkyrie Voyager' that night a couple of summers ago. The swamp reeds and cat-o-nine tails had been left alone despite the Penn Central upgrade. I thought they would have tried to make a parking lot out of it; it probably wasn't their land. I turned toward her.

"How do you feel about going?"

"I feel like goin' in the back seat." She got out and waited for me with a big smile.

I got out and pissed; the Miller Malt liquor exited as Budweiser again. If I only knew a way to bottle the shit......   We went to work in the Starfire's luxury apartment. She knew what she wanted and how she wanted it. I was trying to get past her physical attraction, and see what lay beyond. She was smoking heroin; that much I was pretty sure of, but at least she hadn't been gunning it. I didn't see any tracks. One thing seems to lead to another with the

502

white powder from Marseilles: smoke it, shoot it, mainline it, O.D. with it.......... Somehow I could see myself getting caught up in this nasty element of people and drugs. It shouldn't have had anything to do with my attraction to 'Barb Wire' Wells.

Reno was never involved with the shit. It was unlikely he knew how entangled in the drug she was. He may have just given it a blind eye as long as she did what he wanted.

There were a lot of things to consider: Was I just the next guy after Reno? Barb had worked and put out for him for over a year. Now, the thrill of their relationship was gone...... if there ever was one. In my mind, I had to reconcile their connection as a business matter - with the fringe benefits going to Reno.

The way our shit just seemed to happen down on Warburton; neither of us could say we were high as an excuse for our compulsion to carry on in public. At least down here on the old construction road, we were secluded. We'd find out what was real and what had been imagination. She removed her peasant blouse.....no bra – she didn't need one. They were more nipple than tit. She'd wear one, "just to keep them flat." she said.

Barb pulled me down onto her and we started doing everything except the activity that could make a baby or a doodee baby. We had to kool off after about 40 minutes of getting to know each other. I stretched over to the dashboard and got her one of my Marlboros. I opened a can of malt liquor and passed it to her. "What about......going all the way Barb?"

"I'm not on any birth control pills. We'll just fool around unless you got a rubber." she said.

"Nah, I any got any of that stuff."

"Maybe next time." Barb Wire drew hard on the cigarette. "Hey Ryan, I want to get you high.....get high with you." she gave me a know-it-all smile and dug in her purse. Sure enough – there was a drilling rig and a spoon. I rolled my eyes: 'I got shit for brains.' I thought. The irony was magnetic, immediately my thoughts turned to Ray and Sally. I scoffed a laugh, borrowed her cigarette, and shook my head. Still, I wasn't amazed or shocked. "So you're hitting it up now?"

"C'mon Whitestyle, let's get started. Don't start by going 'Reno' on me."

"Just sayin." I breathed her in. She really looked good to me.

"I'm not like the fifth dimension guys." One of them must have told her about the polar reversed junkies. "I just do it for special times.....like now......with you."

Her face told me the thought of doing skagg had transported her to a distant place as she stared right through my corporeal shell to another place. Wire laughed, "How 'bout it Whiterock?.......You want to get your wings?"

To get out of this mess, I had to give in: "I thought you said we were gonna smoke it in a joint?" This is what the experts must have meant when they said: 'The guy was smoking dope.'

"C'mon – we'll do just a little chippin'."

"Rather just smoke it." I said. The truth was, I didn't want to mess with it at all. I didn't want to be one of them – just using dope to

503

get high, not using it to escape like the fifth dimension. It didn't look like much fun. Wells said it was just refined opium. If this was what it would take to hook up with her, I knew I'd do it. Messing around with the dooge; that was a full-time commitment. Any guy who got lured into the junk game by a woman, would always love the white lady more than the girl who got him into the crazy world of addiction. The smack always took away a dude's manhood: he loved the junk more than getting it on with a chick.

Like so many other idiots, I was one who thought he could play with fire and not get burned.

"Let me do you first." Barb started getting my dungarees off. "Dammit Ryan, lift your ass up so I can pull your pants down. I'll make that thing squirt real fast....I'll do you real good.......damn c'mon.......that dope joint is waiting."

She was no rookie – and told me what she wanted and how to do it. Her sex game was so good, I couldn't figure out why she needed the junk. We had a blast on the old construction road amongst the tall reeds.

There was too much right about her: the way she looked for one. She wasn't labeled pretty, but she was to me in a way - kind of like the way Sister Alexa had been. She had the "right" something going on as far as I was concerned. Barb was kool in a lot of aspects. Smart enough to go down to the Allmans concert in Central Park on her own without Mike Reno. Reno probably told her she couldn't go. I could see her telling Mike to take a running jump for the moon. Wells had that dialectic wavelength, and it let me know her in a unique and personal way. Reno could have never reached that plateau; Barb brought out the barbed wire for Mike - she needed it.

She put the peasant blouse back on. "The third time pays for all." She teased, "Ohhhh.....my friend has wilted, we'll just have to take care of that." Barb shook it back and forth as she watched. "It's coming back.....that's better." Wells mashed her lips and nodded her head in approval ".......nice."

"Do you want to go into orbit or just take a plane ride?" Barb raised her eyebrows. "This is your first?"

"You're not a junkie." I tried to convince myself; she was just an occasional user – had to be.

"Dippin' and dabbin' once in a while."

"Right. Tell you what – I'm not too keen on needles. Load a number up, and we'll walk over to the river."

Barb wet the reefer down with a couple of drops of spit so the smack would stick, and rolled a tight one. "Where we going?"

"Just follow me, we're going by the river." I knew where we were going.

"Hey Groover – you better have a seat lined up after toking on this number, maybe even think about lying down."

I had brought along the remaining beers from the car and we sat atop the cosmic intruder's resting place. Barb fired up the loaded joint and slowly inhaled and passed it to me. "Aaaay......fuck all." I said and brought the smoke into my lungs. Straight away, the effects wrapped around my brain and my upper torso fell like a tree into the

504

pebbly sand. I handed her the laced joint, she took another hit and put it back between my fingers.

Neither of us could speak, I thought I finished the joint but I wasn't sure. Barb laid next to me in the sand amongst the bottles, cans, pop tops, and other garbage. My chest was pounding a bit, the sound of the river could be faintly heard washing to shore.

It was a white, black, and gray movie, waves of energy crashed into my brain. It made sense to be paranoid, but the opposite occurred: fear, tension, anxiety dissolved. My life force.....my soul was whisked away and my thoughts put on 'hold'. Barb had removed her jeans. My consciousness was 2.5 miles above the forms in the sand, I looked down on them with perfect clarity. She was naked from the waist down and mounted my face as if it had been a saddle. I was still ascending – to the edge of the ionosphere. The Barb and Ryan show continued, but it was rather busy up there as debris from deep space and the asteroid belt came whizzing by – bouncing off the atmosphere, being reduced to cinders on re-entry or disintegrating on entry to earth. Space junk was orbiting; waiting to be drawn into the earth's gravity, and be further directed by either of the magnetic poles.

It was incongruous to be under the influence of a depressant, while at the same time feeling free and exuberant. The sex we had in the Starfire, and now what we were doing it the sand......I couldn't be sure it was happening. Perhaps it wasn't; maybe my life had expired. I stopped looking at the earth and turned my focus to deep space. The expanse of the universe was only there for a brief moment, and my consciousness returned to the Hudson River sand over the buried cosmic intruder, with Barbara using my tongue to wash the underside of her carriage.

After she ripped off another orgasm, I tried to sit up, but it was difficult. I felt like I was in the slanted room on the 'Magic Carpet Ride' at Playland.

"Got to make a phone call." I wheezed.

"Who you calling – it's pretty late."

"Got to make a phone call."

"Who you callin'?" she said.

"Sally Englund......you know her."

"Sally?......yeah......yeah...yeah. Your brother's girl friend." Barb mumbled.

I staggered all the way around the platform. I didn't think I'd be able to hop over the hand rail without a mishap. I went up the five steps to the southbound platform and goose-stepped to the year-old pay phone. The coins were dropped: "Yes information?.....ah...uh.....the city of Yonkers....Englund – Amakassin Terrace. Hold on...hold on. Give it to me slow:....GR....8.....1-5.....56. Thank you. Two dimes dropped into the coin return; I re-deposited them and dialed the number.

"Sally?"

"Ryan, I've been waiting for your call." she said.

"What about tomorrow?"

"I'm coming.....I'll be there." I could kind of hear her smile. "What time?"

"Pick you up at 9:00 am sharp. What's your house number? I said.

"16 Amakassin."

"Right. See you tomorrow. Got to go - got a million things to do." I was so zonked, I didn't know if I was talking to Sally or her mother.

Barb made the move over to the southbound overpass stairs. "I've got to sit down." She crashed into its handrail and slid down into the steps. It looked like the place to be.

"Scoot over a little bit." I crashed into her trying to sit.

"Get offa me ya fuckin' knob." She tried to push me over to the other side of the stairs with her eyes half shut.

I was rubbing my nose and face with my flat palms just like Crawfish showed me. "Sorry....sorry..... So where you live?" I slurred.

"11 High St. Just south of P.S. 9."

"Pick you up around 8:30."

"How about 9:30?" she said.

ii

Hal looked in our room, "Got in pretty late.....huh boy?"

"Ugh-a-uh......" I looked up from the pillow and crashed back into it. "New girlfriend."

"You've got to protect yourself lad. I don't plan on being a grandfather yet." He said.

"Got it covered Pops."

"When are you leaving?"

"I'm all packed.....be back Saturday night." I leaned over the edge of the bed to find the glass of water I knew I'd need when I woke up. I downed some as Hal was dishing out more advice. He knew what the water meant.

"And no drinking and driving – you got that?"

No reply.

"Hey knucklehead.....no drinking and driving. I'm talking to you."

"Right – no drinking and driving."

"Your mother and I are counting on you." There was a pause, I thought he wanted me to ask him something. He switched over to the Starfire: "How's the car running?"

"The used tires made a big difference. Handles real smooth." I tried to show some enthusiasm.

"Okay Sammy Bones – see you in a few days."

I heard him go down the stairs. He fired up the Newport and was off to work. 'Sammy Bones'........again? He must have watched some 'Twilight Zone' or 'Outer Limits' episode journeying into the past. I was still screwed up from last night with that stupid heroin joint. My brother and sister were getting ready for school, and Jane was cracking the whip for them to hurry up.

8:30. I had permission to park Jane's car on the street so I could load up yesterday. Ray's advice was to bring any alcohol with

506

me just in case. It was 21 to drink in all the states except for N.Y., La., (18 to drink) and 20 in Hawaii. It was best to be prepared like the Boy Scouts said. I packed a case of Colt 45 tall-boys, a qt. of Gavilan tequila, and a qt. of Canadian Mist in the trunk. We'd be cutting it close especially if we had to share our alcohol with some of Ray's friends. I told Barb and Sally not to bring any drugs. It was too big a risk. State Troopers and County Mounties would stop you without a reason. Next thing you know, Smokey Bear wants to look inside the trunk – just for a look-see. Straight away you know the beer and booze are confiscated because you're underage in their state, but I wasn't going to make this run dry. It seemed the older I got - the more risk choices I had to make; each one having more consequences than the preceding one. Wells didn't have a license, but had driven all over Yonkers for Mike Reno. Sally had one, and she had driven with Ray on dates in her family car.

I borrowed four tapes from Rexall; Vince loaned me five, and I asked Barb and Sally to bring some tapes they liked. With approximately a 1600 mile round trip, you've got to mix up the playlist; even I couldn't digest 'The Allman Brothers' - all the time.

"There's a chance of thunderstorms as you drive west this afternoon." Jane stood looking at her cigarette in the ashtray.

"Good to know – if they get real wild, I'll pull off under a bridge. How was the trip with Hal last summer when you guys drove Ray out?" I looked at her, it was the wrong question.

She took a drag from her Kool and washed the smoke down with some Folgers, "Oh I don't know.....you're old enough to know what's going on. I'd rather have driven alone, or with you and Ray. Neither of us would allow the other to make a solo trip. We'd use the absence of the other as a matter of neglect of parental duty to surface in a future argument when 'pile on' ammunition was needed." She turned away and rested her crossed arms on the kitchen window sill and looked out towards the Palisades.

"Didn't know it was at that point." I crinkled my forehead.

Jane was still looking out the window: "Hal ever talk to you?"

"He tells me to cut the grass, shovel the sidewalk, rake the leaves, take the garbage to the curb – that stuff. We did talk about the Big Band Era; you know....Satin Doll.....String of Pearls.....In the Mood......we were drunk." I threw my palms up.

"No, that's not what I mean."

"When Hal gave me money for the car and the trip – he called it a man to man deal." I didn't know what Jane wanted to hear.

"That's not what I'm talking about. Does he ever talk to you about your conduct, values, right from wrong, mercy, goals in life, what you want to be.....an occupation...career.... Profession? - those kind of things." She still dreamed out the window.

"We kind of get that stuff from Mack. When Mom-Mom hooked up with him our whole family kind of hit the jackpot. Everything we did with Mack was about learning something, I didn't realize it, but I'm pretty sure Ray did." The residual heroin in my system was just starting to leave. My thought process was coming back, but I was in a haze. "Mom, what time is it? I got to get out of here by nine."

"It's already after nine right now." she replied and gave me a hug.

"Gotta go." I walked out to the driveway and she looked at me from the porch.

Jane told me to be careful, "And no drinking and driving, and call me when you get there.......and another thing – don't pick up any hitchhikers – and remember - I love you."

"Love you too Mom." I turned the key and the engine came to life. As I backed out, I waved to her through the windshield and she blew me a kiss. I beeped the horn and waved again. By the time I reached the North End, the morning sun made me aware I had left my sunglasses at 21.

"Dammit." I turned around and went back. Jane's Mercury Comet was already gone and the house was locked. I got my shades and went to my stash in the cellar, and stowed 6 blockbusters in one of Hal's dirty socks on the basement floor. Missing a sock always drove him nuts.

I rang the bell at Sally's front door, knocked, then I called out her name. I walked around the house and tried to look in the windows.... Nobody. From the nearest payphone I called the house. It was only seven numbers to remember, because of the haze – I had to call information again. No answer.

I was late for Barb too. I drove up to High St. There it was: number 11. No bell. All you could see now was the outline of a bell's faceplate where one had been. I knocked on the dirty door three times and Barb opened it. This ended up being one of those dwellings where these women got all these cats, but this house had a kid for every cat I saw.

"What do you want?" a big lady yelled through Barb as she cracked a couple of eggs into a frying pan while trying to burp a two month old on her shoulder.

"Mom – it's one of my friends from school." She stamped her foot.

"This is where you live?" My eyes were dazzled by the insane asylum on the other side of the door's threshold. It was obvious: Barb Wells lived in a four dimensional side show of a carnival. I knew she tell me to "Fuck Off." if I burst out in uncontrollable laughter; and I could say good-bye to all the blow jobs, tug jobs, and pull-out fucks that waited down the road. The more I absorbed - the more pitiful the scene became.

Her mother called over Barb's shoulder, "Ask him if he's hungry......ask him."

"Hey Wire, thanks for the invite, but I just had some waffles......some other time." I may have smiled. "You all ready to go?"

"Haven't asked her yet."

"Huh?"

508

There was so much cat stench, I could barely smell the bacon. Half of the kids were crying, half of the cats were meowing; and that was just for openers. The TV had 'The Gong Show' on, the radio was blasting Don Imus on WMCA. Cups and saucers with cigarette butts were everywhere. Wire's mother had lit one off of another since the door opened. There couldn't have been a clean plate, bowl, cup, pot, pan, or eating utensil in sight. It was magnificent.

Barb stepped outside the house to tell me something she didn't want her mother to hear: "Look in the window in the kitchen........that kid in the booster chair - that three year rug rat is Butchie Junior.......it's a rape baby. I guess he's my half-brother. Butchie raped my mother, and my half-sister Sylvia, and he tried to rape me. The punk put a screw driver in my ear and made me blow him. He warned me I better put my heart into it next time." Barb was shook up. She looked away from me when she was telling me this stuff.

"Gimme a cigarette?" Barb asked. "I overheard Mom talking he's supposed to be up for release pretty soon. I really don't want to be around."

"Who's this guy?" I winced. I didn't need to hear this horror story right now; I couldn't help but wonder what else had gone on in the bedrooms in this house.

Barb said Butchie was the meanest and the most opportunistic of the whack jobs her mother had brought home from nearby gin mills. "Ma said, the next thing she knew this guy was throwing a loaf into her on a Saturday afternoon, and didn't leave until the bulls picked him up on a parole violation three weeks later."

"What the fuck?" I tried to focus my eyes. "He's back in the joint - right?"

"Yeah, he's up in Greenhaven. He always shows up when D.O.C. lets him out. He uses Butchie junior as his entry key to our house. When he's not in jail – he's here. It's a living nightmare until he leaves. Butch clears the fridge of our food – never buys any, is screwed up on something most of the time - but is mostly a drunk, he beats up the younger ones, and tried to rape me, and I know the motherfucker raped Sylvia." she repeated. "The sonofabitch tried to rape me again last summer......kept taunting me about how he was going to bust my butt's cherry.....and have prison sex with me."

"He's still in the joint?" I needed a confirmation.

"As far as I know."

"If he comes back....." I started, "Got something for you. It's about as close to a gun as you can get in personal protection. Hang tight – got to get it from the car. I was taking it with us; in case we got in a jam. I'll leave it with you when we get back."

"Whatcha got Whitespur?"

Wire watched me pull it out from underneath the front seat. "Comeer." I called. It was the Finnish commando knife I had boosted from Mr. Hillman's effects when Ray and me had hung her storm windows. "Hold it tight, push it hard against his body and send the blade home by releasing the spring by pushing the release button forward. Try to put it against his neck and sever his vertebrae. This

509

stiletto will penetrate his skull and shatter bone." It was going to be hard to part with this weapon when we got back, but she needed it more than I did.

"Unless someone kills him in prison.......he'll be back." We walked back to the front door. "A house full of women and children? The guy's a coward......a predator." She took a last drag and tossed it.

"If Butch comes back and either touches you or Slyvia again.......I will kill him." I looked deep into her eyes without blinking and held her in a telepathic stare: "I will kill him." I had never been so resolute about anything. It might be manslaughter or after the fact retribution; either way – if he terrorized these people again, I would dispatch him to meet his maker.

We were at her front door; I didn't know how I'd help her with her traveling bags unless I went inside this annex of the Bronx Zoo. I couldn't appreciate the full scope of the operation of Barb's home. It was a good bet the felines had a better grasp of the situation than the humanoids.

"What's dis guy want?" Marge yelled. "Barbara.....you seen my teef?"

"He wants me to go to Indiana." she raised her voice over the noise of the house. Barb blew a couple of shocks of hair back on top of her forehead. A two year old with a runny nose grabbed hold of her leg. She pushed the door open a little wider.

The more tame cats were hard at work cleaning the floors of food dropped by the kids. Empty tins of cat food were everywhere; the kids had made skyscrapers of the empties in every corner. They became little cities of imagination. The filtered cigarette butts were stood on end and became the inhabitants of the urban centers of tin. In the living room, foyer, and kitchen there were approximately 28 hearts beating. Just about every kid had a shiner, a Hitler mustache made of blood from their nose, or a fat lip. They all had scratches on their arms and hands. The ones who weren't crying seemed to be engaged: fighting, looking for food, or beating a cat with a pot or pan.

Barb's mom still held the infant, and a one year old who was crying was scooped off the floor and slung onto the sofa as she sat down. The two and three year olds had Marge's housecoat open in a flash, and went right to sucking from her tits. She smacked their foreheads until they backed away. The infant and the one year old wasted no time and resumed their feeding. The three year old pushed the one year old off and went right back on his mother's tit. From the couch she explained to me: "That's Butch's boy, and he's got the devil in him. Just look at him go.....I can't get him to back off – he's going to be a bad one; just like his dad." she shook her head and grinned. "Okay.......okay." Marge Wells tried to calm the year old girl down crying from hunger.

There was little doubt Barb was ashamed of her living circumstances. "Ryan," she took a breath of the outside air; "If I go with you, I can't come back."

"Things can't be much worse for you here – not unless Butch returns." I watched Marge fill a short baby bottle with Dellwood milk.

The bottle had some old milk at the bottom. She shook the bottle to get what was at the bottom to blend with the rest; it was uniform enough. The baby grabbed the bottle and started sucking. The entire scene was losing its humor.

"Are all these kids your family?" I asked Barb and raised my one eye not really wanting to know the answer.

"I only have one full-blood brother and he's in reform school. The rest are half brothers and sisters."

"Is he older or younger?"

"Younger.......Mom took in two cousins when her sister went into the joint last year. Right after she got out of jail, they put her in the laughing house in Nyack, when she took up with a 15 year old kid who went to Yonkers High."

"How old is your aunt?"

"21....22.....something like that." Barb replied.

"This is no way to live, not for you, your mom, or any of these kids. I can't base my feelings for you on pity."

"Listen man: Marge calls the shots in this house. This is how she lives. I just need a place to crash and this is it for right now. You think I feel good about this living situation? I've been through it over and over with her. I don't have many options at this point in my life." Wire said.

I pressed my lips together, sharpened my focus and shook my head. Kon-Tiki-like, I told Barb I'd be right back.

With a grocery bag, I returned 15 minutes later with two-half gallons of milk and the giant-sized box of Cap'n Crunch. Barb put the bag on the floor of the kitchen; it was immediately surrounded by cats and kids. Marge Wells went all around the house filling empty Friskee tins with milk.

She poured the remaining milk in a large water bowl for two puppies, filled a glass of milk for herself, and five dirty bottles with nipples. She left the remainder of the Dellwood next to the cereal. It was a free for all. The Cap'n Crunch was ripped out of one of the kids' hands and the cereal flew everywhere. Both species ate as much as they could: off the floor, out of dirty cups and tins, and picked out from between the sofa cushions.

Ma Wells sneaked up behind her eldest child and whipped her around: "Just because dis guy buys food – don't mean you can go joyriding with him cross country. You fine my teef and we'll talk about it."

Barb turned to me: "I can't make it this time."

"I understand."

"You get to school after you change the little ones' diapers." Marge barked out.

On the far side of the house there was a calamitous racket taking place; it had the thunder of a demolition derby and the wailing of a bunch of tom cats tossed into an industrial dryer and the person outside was cranking up the heat. Marge never batted an eye and went back over to the ratty sofa and held little Lucy. From the backroom where all the commotion had been, the biggest cat I had ever seen came strutting into the living room like he owned the joint. The scene had an unreality, the likes of which I hadn't experienced even on a psychedelic trip. This member of the feline family wasn't fat; it was a damned Bobcat: wide flat face, ear and jaw tips, muscular legs, and a short stout tail.

"You're fuckin' kidding me." I said to Barb.

Marge smiled, "Dere's my Chauncey…." She patted the couch. It sprung five feet and landed right next to Marge and gave her a powerful nudge. "OK…..okay – tiger." She smiled at the bobcat and then to me. Marge got up, and left Lucy sitting next to Chauncey. She returned with a chicken thigh and almost a pint of milk.

I pointed to Chauncey, "That ain't no Ka…Ka….Kakaka….. Kitty cat."

Marge smiled on the one side of her mouth, "Chauncey wouldn't hurt a fly." She petted him as the bobcat lapped up the milk.

"How long has Chauncey been here?" I lit a cigarette.

"Three or four years……Chauncey and Butch showed up around the same time I'd say." Barb said.

"Gimme a fuckin' break. I got to leave on this high note." I said. I walked backwards…..away from the porthole to a reality of a different world.

"Call me when you get back." Barb said.

"It's a good thing the phone's on the wall, cause you'd never find it otherwise."

"No drinking and driving." Barb waved a finger of warning with a smile.

I responded using finger language of my own: "Okay." with my thumb and forefinger making a circle. "Comeer." I said.

She stuck her face in the window of the Olds, and we kissed for five minutes. I wished she was coming with me, instead I headed for the Henry Hudson Parkway solo.

iii

Interstate 80 in Pennsylvania was being rebuilt at various stretches throughout the 320 miles of a state which I believed was a piece of Tolkein's 'Mordor'. In between the construction zones, the posted speed limit was 60 m.p.h. In the construction zones, my speed varied, but if I averaged 50 m.p.h. while in the commonwealth of Pennsylvania I was lucky. The way I drove and the way the Starfire handled – man and machine's frustration was obvious. About half-way through I stopped for gas: Hi-test for the wildcat engine and a couple of tall-boys from the kooler in the trunk were paper bagged…..just to take the edge off. The malt liquor didn't work out so good. I hadn't had anything to eat since the day before, and the Colt went right to my head.

Drinking and driving with an expanse of road in front of you – it was the birthright of every American. The way the miles dragged on, I would have been better off smoking some boo. There hadn't been one hitchhiker since I started: no hippy chicks or even bums. It was just one ugly ride through Sauron's evil empire .

512

When I got out of Pennsylvania it was 4:30, I veered off towards Akron and Columbus. Ohio was pretty flat, and it was a lot easier on the car and driver than the hills and small mountains in Pa. Both the Starfire and me were in a better mood. I pulled into a small campground west of Columbus; just to park the car and crash in the back seat. I didn't need the bulls harassing me for parking in a shopping center.

There were still some open campsites left. Most of the campers were here just for the night - like me, on their way to somewhere else for the Memorial Day weekend. The lady at the office put me down this lane where there were only sites on the one side of a one lane gravel road. They faced some cow pasture. There was a young couple in a tent three sites down and me in this one section. The campground owner was making his rounds and asked me when I was leaving.

"Early tomorrow morning. I don't got money for a motel. I'm visiting someone at Purdue tomorrow, just trying to get a good night's rest."

"Well here's the deal – these critters in the tent right over there.....well it's her. She's going to get loud - just want to give you fair warning. I've had to warn them before", he said.

"That I-80 in Pee - Aaayy took a lot out of me today – I'm plenty tired. I shouldn't have any problem staying asleep." I said.

"I just didn't want you to think somebody was getting murdered."

"Thanks for the warning."

I took a walk to the end of the row to have a cigarette and take a look at this wild woman so I wouldn't have to imagineer a face and body. A great face and skinny as a rail; she was bouncing around getting anxious.

"Motherfucker." I exhaled and said as I pulled a pack of Viceroy's out.

About a half-hour after dark, the two had that love machine sounding like a marathon session. I kept the vent windows open. It was impossible for me not to superimpose Barb and me onto the love cries of the couple three slots down. I wished I could do Wells and make her wail and moan like this, perhaps I had the night before down Greystone. The dude was applying satisfaction to his camper-gal like they were handing it out at the county fair. Some women come into heat just like the animals, and this was one who did. Her heat wave sounded insatiable. Somehow their calls of love faded and I fell asleep.

My dreams blended to a scene at 11 High Street with Barb and her home life. It was beyond anything I had witnessed previously. The Rogues, the Huns, Reno.......we all knew her – how was it that I had never heard about it before? It was pitiful.....a disgrace. The stand up thing to do would have been to marry her and get her away from there. Nobody else except Mike Reno, was hot on her the way I was. Reno liked her because she could sell his weed for him, but also we knew he was banging her despite her denials he wasn't. It was a disturbing dream and I woke up.

Maybe I was nuts......she wasn't any Sarah Nussbaum, but I truly thought Barb was Triple 'A' ball and I was only single 'A'.......I hoped. What did she see in me that attracted her? I took a few nips off the Canadian Mist and chased it with some Mountain Dew. The audio sex show still played three sites down as I crashed out again.

THE GUY AT THE GAS STATION SAID WEST LAFAYETTE was a little over 200 miles west. The Starfire got the Hi-test again: 20 gallons @ .34/gal. cost me: $6.80 for fuel. I bought a big Amish apple pie and a quart of milk for breakfast. I had to get my base back; there'd be plenty of drinking with Ray tonight. It had been mid-January since I had seen him, I was looking forward to the reunion. To my reckoning, we really hadn't hooked up since last summer because the Thanksgiving and Christmas visits didn't add up to much time together; everyone else was getting a piece of Ray except me – and I was the one who probably needed him most. I was going through a five month withdrawal, doing all this thinking for myself wasn't what I anticipated and tougher than I expected. This was the opportunity I had been waiting for: to catch up with Ray -- going 16 hours with him head-on. Everybody down the End, Morsemere, Gorton, Lake and Orchard Aves. had more of my nonsense than they cared for. They'd be happy to hear I was under Ray's control once again. Getting some of that 'big brother' career guidance was sorely needed.

It was a little before noon when I rolled onto the Boilermaker campus. The place was deserted: in between spring and summer sessions. Ray was on campus at this Wheeler Hall - two students to a room. I walked in and looked for number 4. This was the place I sent his mail to, but the place was empty. The dormitory was getting ready for a major cleaning. All the furniture in the students' rooms had been moved out to one of the two big common rooms. There it was #4: a name place receptacle still had two names in their slots – #1: M. Rivera and #2: R. Whitlaw. Whitlaw was close enough; as you got older people would mess your name just to screw around with you. The Hall was empty, there weren't any personal effects there. They must have moved him to a different dorm. Everyone directed me to the Registrar's office. They didn't have Ray listed as a registered student for summer classes. Next, I was sent to Administration, and that led to financial aid/work study program within the Bursar's office. None of the office people were able to help me locate Ray, so they sent for the Director of student/work study. She finally showed up with an envelope in her hand.

"I'm looking for Ray Whitelaw."

"Well he was..........in fact he only worked one day with us. He said he had another job to go to. A student of the first echelon. Five minutes into my interview with him, I knew I had the right person to help the Physics Dept. move to a temporary building as the contractors renovate and modernize the permanent Physics facility."

I looked from side to side, "Any forwarding address or where he went to work?"

The Director looked at the name on the envelope. "Are you Ryan Whitelaw?"

"Yes. I'm his ride back to N.Y."

"Hopefully the answers to your questions are within." She said passing the manila envelope to me. "You are Ryan Whitelaw?" she asked again.

"Ryan Whitelaw.....brother. You need some I.D.?"

She checked the information on my license. "I am sure he's left word in the envelope as to his whereabouts. We wish you good luck."

I left the small office and sat on a bench near the Starfire. I opened the envelope with a pocket knife and started reading the handwriting that was alien but legible.

Ryan – Sorry you had to drive all the way out here for nothing. I left school the day after I started a summer job with the University. I cannot reveal to you at present where I am or what I am doing. Things will be much clearer to me by about mid-August. No one – friend or family should know that I have gone AWOL from Purdue. It will serve no purpose, and only invite more inquiries. Might be best if you simply say I am working on a farm in Illinois with a classmate; that's all you've heard. We don't want any missing persons investigations getting started.

For me there is/was a message....a force...a power to redefine and interpret the shadow role of the specter junkies during the random pulsing of the poles. That audio tsunami held us in a state of magnetic ecstasy last summer emanating from Duane's guitar, amps, speakers, and soul. It was a divining rod showing us the way out of this maze. It is, I speculate, the concept that extreme positive human emotion – when put into action might override, but not eliminate despair and entrapment of the phantom people.

Duane was dealing the cards when he cut loose with the top-heavy load of magnetic muscle. He let my heart beat without the fear that it might stop, I could taste and breathe uncharged air; my brain didn't migraine when I had to make critical decisions. It was how I felt when we were young.

There is NO going back – Duane is gone, but he may have left us the map to find the key. This is where I have gone.

Tell Loki, the fifth dimension, and my nether world crew......I'll be back......Ray-gun

P.S. I may need your comet dust in four or five months...You'll get it back.

It was a long ride back to N.Y. I managed to salvage the Sunday and Monday at Sunset Ridge so the Memorial Day Weekend wasn't a total bust.

THE FIRST WEEK BACK WAS BRUTAL; THE INTER-rogation from Jane and Hal was intense and relentless: "Where is your brother?" "You know where he is – tell us." "You're in some sort of conspiracy with him." "You better not be holding out on us boy."
      "Here's the phone number for seasonal work grants, student housing, the registrar's office, and administration.
Knock yourselves out.....they'll tell you what they told me: he ain't there." I raised my voice a little.
      "Ryan, if you're holding out on me, I swear I will cancel your car insurance. I think you're holding back something from us." Hal said with Jane next to him.
      "Wait just a cotton-pickin' minute......how do you think I feel – I drove out there by myself......for nothing! If you two went out there they would have told you the same thing they told me: Ray Whitelaw isn't here." Perhaps if I just told them I saw him and he was shoveling shit at a pig farm they would have backed off.
      By Thursday Hal had backed off considerably; Jane however was riding me into the following week. I couldn't help but wonder if either of them would have shown as much concern if it had been me who did the disappearing act. Jane had to let it go since her studio's recital was only days away. She used every pill the doctor had prescribed the night I returned. Only her assistant Judy knew how close she had come to a total meltdown five days prior to her studio's show.
      Her mental state was obvious to me, and I made an extra effort to do more than move sound equipment, transport folding tables and chairs, fill ice chests, bring soft drinks and keep Hal from over serving himself for the duration of Jane's annual show.
      This was the first revue Jane had where I actually liked hanging around backstage to 'help out'. These older women in their 30's and 40's were the 'Jane Marlowe Seniors' and they started making passes at me. I responded by melting an ice cube down to the size where it would fit in their front cleavage or down the crack of their ass if the costume was cut low enough in either direction.
      My presence at this year's recital reassured Jane. I was able to convince her I was being truthful about the information I received from Purdue. Nothing was going to alleviate her feeling of loss with Ray's disappearance, and this summer would play a lot longer than the ones she had been used to.

VINNY TARTS AND ME CAUGHT THE LATE SHOW
AT THE Academy of Music downtown. The Allman Brothers without
Duane were good, they still had a better live show than most bands,
but after the third song the void was glaring. Like the orchestra seats
we had at the Fillmore, these were almost in foul territory and this time
were on the right side of the band.

Tarts looked for the entrance down the tunnel to the subway,
then back to me: "Maybe we didn't get high enough?"

"The sound was lean and the energy wasn't there." I
shrugged.

"Not good when the rhythm section outnumber the guys
playing the melody and harmony."

"Know what you mean, but who's out there to play lead with
Dicky? Gregg can only cover so much on the keyboards. It's not like
someone's all suited up ready to go in for Duane." I said.

"They need another guitar for their sound; otherwise it's
really lean." The click-clack of the subway's tracks put us in a
hypnotic state of void. We had a difficult time getting off the train at
the last stop, wondering what it was we saw at The Academy of Music.

We waited to catch a bus, the weather was cool, we thought
it would've been warmer, and talked about their performance until we
were blue. Tarts asked, "You going to school today?"

"Wasn't planning on it – now I don't know."

"Everybody knew we were going......we blabbed about it all
last week." He said.

"How 'bout we sell it like this: The people who want to
know how the show was, - we tell them it's coming together....... but
they got some work to do. They took a big hit losing Duane, but they'll
be back."

Cinzano tilted his head back and forth as he thought about it;
his chin went up and he nodded. "That's about the truth as I see it. If
they don't like it - they can go see Joan Baez." We laughed.

Our Graduation was in the last week of June. The teachers
had been bugging me about which college I would be attending. Not
many of my friends were going to college. The war was still going on
in Vietnam, but there were very few combat troops there. Nixon threw
us a slider and pulled all the combat troops back to the fire bases. We
thought we'd have jobs with the military for his second term. They still
had the Lottery. I didn't recall seeing our birthdays posted in the
newspaper. It was possible the Selective Service never released the
lottery numbers for 1954. Perhaps it was true; they would go to an all-
volunteer army.
By the end of 1972, there were only a little more than 25,000 combat
troops left.

I had to hook-up with Loki. He already had two years under
his belt at Pace University. He'd know if I was wasting my time going
to college. The higher education I was attracted to was down in Stony
Brook.

About three or four years earlier; the TV networks put the
weekly casualties on the tube every Friday - a guy couldn't help but

plan on going over to S.E. Asia when he came of age. Somehow I figured I'd have one year to go wild before I'd turn 19 and receive my draft notice. If I didn't get drafted then, I'd talk to Ray and ask him about going to university.

Loki and Jimmy Blanko were sitting on the wall of the North End parking lot; Loki was reading, smoking Marlboros, and drinking beer. He was making his summer statement for all the girls from Tudor woods who came down the End to buy alcohol and groceries: 'I am available, sophisticated, and intelligent!' The fact he was reading 'On the Road' by Kerouac let the passersby know he was also with it. I never heard of the author; maybe that was why people attend college. I bought into those axioms: "Every picture tells a story"; "a picture is worth a thousand words"; and "without a picture – you ain't got nothing." Most likely, it was the reason magazines like 'Blow Job City', 'Twisted Teens', and 'Rauncho Rancho' always outsell the skin novels: 'My Secret Life', 'The Bad Girls', or 'Picked up and Fucked'.

For the North End, 'On the Road' was exactly the right selection. Everyone wanted to be on the road, but nobody left. Loki liked reading the stuff, it was mostly a means to an end.

"Hey Joe." Jimmy Blanko wondered aloud, "Didn't Sean Dolan go down to Mexico and try to duplicate "On the Road" in real life?"

"Seeing Sean dressed in traditional peasant garb, with your explanation....now it makes sense." I said.

"Think he brought back any peyote or mescaline?" Blanko looked at the 12 oz. Miller in his hand.

"Only said 'hi' to him when he walked through a couple of weeks ago. He had some of that Apache cactus wine with him......He called it Tizzwin?......I dunno." Loki recalled.

Blanko changed lanes, "What's going on with your brother – it's like he dropped off the face of the earth. Loki called your house, and your mom started crying. He said Hal picked up the phone and told him to call another time and then: Good-bye." Blanko quick looked at me.

I gave them the story as I knew it, and told them about the letter's contents.

"Sounds like big medicine."

Loki pounded some malt liquor, "What about your next move Starfire? You got anything cookin?"

"Caddying......if nothing else comes through. How 'bout you.....you coming up to Sunset Ridge?" I said.

"Thinking about moving, but I need some scratch first. Might try working two jobs if I can find them. Figure I'll caddy during the day, and drive for Caesar nights." Loki looked like he signed his own death sentence.

"Hey Ferguson, where'd all this ambition come from?" Blanko laughed.

"Gimme a smoke.......how old you got to be to get a hack license?" I asked.

"Used to be 20, now everything's 18." Loki puffed.

"Caddying isn't cutting it......no money in it."

"You got to have connections – otherwise you're stuck in jerk-off jobs." Blanko looked at his can of beer.

"Caddying wouldn't be bad if a guy could catch loops during the week like you can on weekends." Loki stated.

"Nah....it'd still be screwed up – you'd end up having too many caddies." Blanko said: "Kind of like Heller's Catch-22."

"Hey Joe - how do I get my hack license?"

"Got to have a clean record – no felonies. Your driving record's got to be spotless also. Two people who own businesses in the city of Yonkers got to vouch for your character, and the initial license goes for $50.....a renewal costs $25.

"Did you get yours yet?"

"Couldn't find the second business to vouch for me. The thing is; a business can only vouch for one driver. Every business down here has been vouched out. Think of all the guys you've seen behind the wheel of a Main, Caesar's, or a Valentine Taxi?......Joe Lamar, Frankie Fush, Cocaine Wayne, Tony Di, Puggy, Reno, Jo Ping, Billy Van Nahl, and those are off the top of my head. They all used to drive hack. You got anybody that'll vouch for you?"

Blanko pointed with his beer, "Hey sport, what about your mom's dance studio? There's one right there."

"Yeah, it's in her best interest to help me find employment. Who am I going to get for number two?" I rolled my eyes and took a breath.

"Yeah, that's the stickler." Loki smiled, "Ryan....you're lucky.....you used to need 3 vouchers, but the taxi commission revamped that when they lowered the hack license age."

"You ain't mad at me for piggybacking on your idea?"

It's not like you'll be making any real dough – you'll just be manning a job no one else wants; there's no money in the one, and there's no money in the other – plus your life is always in danger driving a cab."

"Cocaine Wayne used to drive for Main, he said it was slow action in the summer." I gave the Parliament filter a toss.

"Didn't he get held up?" Blanko squinted.

"They put a belt around his neck and strangled him. Wayne floored it and wrecked. He got knocked out and they robbed him." Loki said.

"How'd your car run out to Purdue?" Loki motioned to the Starfire.

"That Pennsylvania is fucked; it's a real asset having a machine that can turn the Pee – Aay hills and mountains into Kansas flatland. Like I told you guys – Ray was a no show –just left a letter."

"Now you really need a job - Whitecrime." Jimmy Blanko peeled the bottle's label.

"Can you think of any pay phones which might pay big?" I grinned.

"You're still playing with them ash cans?"

"Blockbusters."

"Whatever......"

519

"You know, people are already asking me if I'll have any blockbusters for the Fourth this year.......... Check this out – some Baddazino wanted me to car bomb his wife back in March. I wasn't even out of high school and the guy wanted me to do a contract hit. Might have been Rexall that put him on to me, maybe it was Crawfish. Fuck that noise – I kill for one reason: self defense."

Loki got an anxious look in his face: "You know Whiteroom......if we start driving, we'll know where the busy payphones are. Every once in a while, we can knock one over."

"It's like them Huns say: Don't get hooked on drugs to the point where you got to blow them up to pay for a habit, and don't get greedy."

"Makes sense."

I asked Loki and Blanko if they wanted to go down to Morsemere.

"Anything going on?"

"I'm seeing Barb Wells, supposed to meet up with her."

"Have fun Sport, we'll catch ya later." Blanko said.

GRADUATION WAS ONLY A FEW DAYS OFF; I WAS mimicking the nonchalance Ray had exhibited a year earlier towards the Commencement ceremony and the Diploma itself. Vinny had a big dust up with the administration about his credit count. They said it would have to be made up in summer school, or he could come back in the fall and make it up.

"What's the big deal? It took me and Robbie Herrick four years to do a three year program." Holter shrugged.

"It's looking like the 5 year plan for me." Herrick shook his head, and spat in the gutter.

"How 'bout it Fast Eddie, you going to get out on schedule?"

Fast Eddie Mason almost had the pint of Gallo Port to his lips when Herrick's question stopped him cold. "I dunno Bobby, it's touch and go....touch and go."

"What do you mean Ed?" Rexall gave him a face.

Fast Eddie took a major chug before he replied, "They're going to the State's Education Board......the regionals. Some commie told my folks I was a hardship case, and the regionals could issue me my diploma."

I was confused, "Are you talking about the Board of Regents?"

"Yeah.....those cats."

I looked over to Vince and watched his face and saw the wheels turning. "Eddie – where's this guy's office?"

"Hey Mason, I don't mean to be burnin' on you, but you're dumber than me – how the fuck do you graduate on time?" Holter chuckled.

"I dunno......you're right Holter......absolutely right." he smiled and shook his head and shrugged. "You got to use the law to graduate nowadays." he smirked and nodded. "Tarts, go see the commie. He's got an office across the street from the Board of Regents in the state office building in White Plains."

"Whitepaper – can you run me up there tomorrow before lunch?.....Fast Eddie.....what's this guy's name?"

"Had his fuckin' card.....I dunno what I did with it. I dunno – it's something like Res.....Restle.....Restov...... no....Rost.......ROSTOV! ......that's it Yuri Rostov. His office is right across the street. He says they got to give me a road test so I can get my drivers license, and the Post Office has to give me a job once I graduate." Eddie snickered.

"Get the fuck outta here.....you're a fuckin' mongrel." Rex shook his head and his eyes bulged. "A job with the P.O.? - for what?"

Fast Eddie's Italian heritage was becoming evident as he used his hands for emphasis even though he had a bottle of wine in one hand and a cigarette in the other. "That's the hardship – that's what I'm trying to tell ya's."

Holter squinted, "Your biggest hardship is that you're Reno's cousin."

Caught mid-span, Eddie Mason turned to Holter and grinned: "That I know."

I laughed; still I was as confused as the rest of The Rogues. "But Ed – what's your hardship?"

"Yuri says I way over performed compared to the other students; the board of education misclassed me."

"Hey Nobblehead....." Rexall put on his lawyer's face, "How the fuck do you get a driver's license, and a P.O. job because you're too dumb to graduate? Square that jive ass bullshit up Ed."

"Yuri says....." Mason started.

"Here we go with the Yuri bullshit. What - is this Rostov a fuckin' member of the Politburo or the bar?" Robbie Herrick quizzed as he took a sip of screwdriver.

"Listen Herrick, I don't know if he's a lawyer. I do know he's a true communista.....a commie......a troublemaker and he's helping me out; be nice if you guys were on my side too."

"Ed, before I waste my time driving brother Vincente` up to White Plains tomorrow, I find it hard to digest that you got the city, state, and feds to work in unison and sign off on this backroom – 10th inning settlement that' gives you the deal of a lifetime." I gave him a skeptical look.

"Amazing isn't it?" he said. "The Marxist Rostov says it's all because we lived in public housing and it had lead paint and radon gas in it. Yuri said it was an unnecessary exposure."

"Kind of refresh my memory Ed......didn't my family live one row north of yours.........fuckin Jimmy Martin's family lived in the Mulford Gardens projects too?" Holter bitched.

"Yeah Ed." Robbie Herrick jumped in, "Our family lived almost at the bottom of Mulford Gardens....almost on Ashburton Ave. Your family didn't even do a year there."

"When Blackie came back from Germany in '47, my mom and him couldn't find any work so they ended up in the projects. They lived down Cotttage Gardens off North Broadway. I was born there and I think I got what Fast Eddie got." Cinzano bitched.

I could see the angle coming.

"Fuckin' Fast Eddie got it bad......look at him." Holter had us all laughing – even Fast Eddie.

"Fuck you George." he smiled.

"Leake and Watts, Mulford and Cottage Gardens, and the other low-rise public housing were built around the same time with the same materials." Rexall said. As a union carpenter, he had the inside information with all the government housing projects.

"Only three days until graduation Tarts. I'm telling ya...... Go see comrade Yuri. You might be on stage with the rest of us." Ed said.

"Go see Stalin – whatdayagotta lose Vince? That Soviet power kicked our butts in Korea and Cooba; and Nam don't look much better. It might work. You and Mason might be walking across the stage with a diploma in your hand with the rest of us." Holter said. "I'll even draw a hammer and sickle on top of the stupid graduation hat..........a little advertising for the commie."

The next day Vinny extracted all the information he could out of Eddie before we drove up to see comrade Yuri. I found a space right in front of the Regents' offices. We crossed the street and walked into Rostov's two-room storefront office. A young potential anarchist banged away at a typewriter. There were posters of all the commie superstars: Mao, Lenin, Ho Chi Minh, Gus Hall, Castro, Che, Trotsky, Tito, and Smokin' Joe Stalin, whose execution numbers made the Nazis look like amateurs.

I was sure the Eastern European refugees who fled Soviet repression in their countries would have loved to lob the two apples Joe Edwards had sold me into this office.

"Where's Yuri?" Vinny said to the young woman who donned a black beret with a red star on the front.

"He's across the street – performing miracles for the proletariat.....as usual."

Vince looked at the clock on the wall which had a poster beneath and read: 'Time for Change!' "When do you expect him back?"

"Around 3:30. Who are you?" she said.

"Uh... Comrade Vinny Tarts. I was referred by a client: Ed Mason. I have a very similar set of circumstances as comrade Ed, but unlike him, I merely am trying to get the high school to release or issue me my diploma. If I only knew that comrade Yuri was here two weeks ago .....helping the people." Vince pounded the card table. "I'm hoping to graduate Friday, so it's pretty urgent."

"Leave your name, address and phone number." she said giving us both one of Yuri's business cards.

We returned to his office around three. The comrade secretary saw us and walked into Yuri's office. "He's on the phone, he'll see you when he's finished."

He came out and sat on the side of a real desk, and offered us a couple of folding chairs to sit on. He had an accent; he had been here a while. His English was good. "So you are friends of Edward Mason?"

"Yeah."

"Things have gone well for him today – we have had a successful negotiation with all the parties, with the exception of the DMV; he will have to take both the written and the road test. I had to cave in on something. Now, what is it that you are seeking?"

"I brought a copy of my high school transcript. The administration says I don't have enough credits to graduate, and that is not true." Vinny said.

Yuri went through his high school record – "Yes, it appears you are one credit short. How is that a concern of the people? Mr. Tartaglione, if you had gone to one of your Phys. Ed. classes in your three years at Gorton High school and passed.....you would have been two credits rich instead of being a credit poor..........Drivers Education? What's this some kind of road safety course?" Rostov continued to read Vinny's transcript.

"Yeah....teaches you to drive safely."

"Is it possible Commrade Tartaglione never paid the $25 fee to take the course, and never had his driver's safety card validated, or showed the instructor his state issued drivers license as proof for course credit?" he looked up from the transcript.

I took a copy of 'The Daily Worker' and slapped the back of Vinny's head. "You dumb fucknuckle."

"Let me know when you have a true injustice." Yuri said.

We thanked our comrade for his time and attention to detail and celebrated with a fifth of Pagan Pink Ripple for the drive back to Yonkers. Anybody else, I would have made their ride unbearable, but me and Tarts went too far back. All we could do was laugh. More than anything else, he didn't want to look like a dumbbell to his girlfriend Stacey, by being a credit short for graduation. What made me laugh the hardest was seeing Vinny hitting up Fast Eddie the next day at lunch for money for the driver's ed. fee. He knew better than to ask me.

Stacey was going to some high end Catholic school for girls in Scarsdale. In the fall, she was going to attend college 20 miles from Yonkers, but she was going to live on campus. Her folks had plenty of dough. Vinny and Stacey Keegan had been going steady for the last two years; the dude was head over heels for that girl.

Commencement was on a Thursday evening at 6:30. Jane asked me about it. I told her I'd only be going if it meant something to her or Hal. She said she didn't go to Ray's, and she'd just as soon skip mine.

"But I've got something for you."

"Yeah?" I thought she was going to throw me a twenty or some graduation money.

"You know my uncle might be looking for some help this summer."

"You mean your father's brother?......Did I ever meet him?"

"You might have – I don't recall if you did or not. Anyway, I asked him if he was putting on any help this summer."

"What's he do run a hot tar roofing company or pour concrete sidewalks?" I wasn't expecting the world on a silver platter.

"Stop being a shithead." Jane hardly ever used that language with me. I returned to treating her like my mother.

"Sorry Mom."

"Harry is the Park Superintendent at Tibbetts Brook Park, the pay is $2.50/hr. Just do whatever job he gives you, but you've got to tell me now because he's got somebody else waiting if you don't take it."

"Yeah Mom, sounds great. Thanks." The more I thought about it, the better I felt about not having to go caddying.

"One other matter Ryan, remember.....it's only a summer position. Do you still want it?"

"It's got to be better than the feast or famine of the caddy rollercoaster."

"That's the way to look at it." She smiled.

I couldn't help but thinking she would have given Ray first crack at this job if he had been around. It didn't make any difference. She told me to be at Tibbetts before 8:00 tomorrow morning. I looked at her, she was still in pieces not knowing where Ray was, I was merely a pinch hitter.

Tibbetts Brook Park was operated by Westchester County, which included a one million gallon swimming pool built during the depression. My first paycheck stub read – Position: Pool Staff/level 1. A more precise job description might have said, 'pool boy'. The swimming pool facilities and administration building were side by side, and were structurally connected. Administration was at a higher elevation and looked down on the massive swimming pool. The lockers, changing facilities and ticket sales were on the main floor. Stairs brought the bathers down from the women and men's lockers to a common corridor leading to the pool which seemed to be as large as a football field.

The county provided two short sleeved shirts w/epaulets, sewn on patches, and a badge with the county seal that read: Attendant. The county provided the females with a forest green skirt, in addition to the shirts with all the bells and whistles. The county couldn't have intended for all the girls to wear mini-skirts, but that was pretty much what happened. The shirt was mandatory, the skirt was optional. The jeans only came out on kool or rainy days. My guess was the county was going for a quasi-law enforcement look. The image was made to deal with kids under 12 who were cutting up. Some of the teenage boys kept messing with the girls; you'd yell at them to 'knock it off', but if they kept causing trouble, you'd have to inform the cop and let him do his thing.

The park bordered on the Bronx to the south; it was a big draw for the people down there especially when the 'dog days of summer' had a chokehold on the metro region. Sometimes the thunderstorms couldn't persuade the concrete, asphalt, and bricks into releasing their heat. The pool and park would teem with people. Fourth of July weekends or successive days of relentless heat and humidity did funny things to folks when they couldn't get out of the barrio, in Yonkers or the Bronx. The ones who were able to get to the parks and pools should have been cooling off.....winding down..... decompressing. Instead, many were lashing out; they arrived agitated, aggressive, opportunistic, and confrontational. Some were victims; others were prey: gang fights over turf and girls, cat fights, gambling, cutting in lines led to more fisticuffs, stolen locker keys and contents of the same. There were shake-downs for patrons' pocket change, jewelry, medallions, and transistor radios. The rate of incidents increased with the heat.

Like the endless minor law infractions; the wrappers, straws, bottle caps, pop tops, aluminum foil and Saran wrap and the ubiquitous cigarette butts and filters never seemed to find the 55 gal. barrels. Sweeping the pool deck and stabbing garbage with a spiked stick anywhere on the grounds was better than working the lockers or the basket cage in the change facility. The long handled drop pan and shortened witches' broom was the easiest way to leave the caged work space of the lockers and the roofless changing room. Some of the guys stayed in the cage all day.....not me.

On those sweltering weekends; it was impossible to swim – there were simply too many people in the pool. All the bathers could do was stand or sit in place and talk. Sometimes the lifeguards couldn't see the pool's bottom except in the deep end which was for diving only. If a kid was drowning on the bottom in shallower water, or an old timer was having a stroke – it might go unnoticed for two or three minutes.

The third weekend in July qualified as a barnburner. It was terrible hot on Wednesday. The humidity rose on Thursday – making it more oppressive. On Friday, Uncle Harry had a stand-down meeting at 9:30 at the east end of the pool's concrete deck in the corner where there was the most shade. The pool had just opened with a skeleton crew on duty. It was mostly moms/w kids and senior citizens going for their morning swim, before it got crowded. The chief lifeguard, Skip, had a team of two monitoring them from the pool's deck. The full 'on duty' life guard crew was: ten guards in the eight foot chairs, and two walking the deck.

About 35 employees attended this meeting. A tight semi-circle was formed three deep. Harry and Sergeant Don Sansone stood side by side. Uncle Harry had brought a bullhorn.

"Ok.....okay." He got started.

The sergeant cut through the thick air, "Alright people - listen up. We don't have much time."

Harry put his hand on the cop's shoulder, "Thanks Don." He focused back on us, looked at the bullhorn, "I don't think I need this. You all can hear me okay? Right?" There were nods. "Alright then, we have many new hires this summer. You guys and gals who worked here before have to teach these rookies the job and their duties; and that means the right way to do it, the way somebody taught you. These aren't difficult jobs, but they require that you pay attention and use good old-fashion common sense."

"Yesterday we had an incident. We could have performed better when we had to get that boy who went off the diving board and went straight to the bottom – like a lead weight. Skip..... the lifeguards' job was the only thing that went right. The pool attendants who were on the deck or in the concession area; in a situation like we had yesterday - your primary duty is crowd control. A couple of you guys were part of the crowd gawking. You are to form and maintain a pathway for the emergency personnel to either bring a downed swimmer to the nurse's station or keep a pathway clear so the paramedics can remove the person directly to their emergency vehicle. And always follow the orders of Sgt. Sansone or any of his officers in these situations."

I shifted my weight to my other leg and folded my arms. As Harry continued, I felt two hands from behind on my belt loop above my hips. Now my face showed the same concern and interest the rest of the crew exhibited – but for a mysterious reason. Peering down on my left side, I saw painted fingernails. That was a relief. As a new hire, I had to maintain my focus on who was speaking, what they were saying, and nod when appropriate.

There was enough space, I lowered my crossed arms to the hands at my sides and placed my hands over hers.
She interlocked our fingers; I wanted to turn and see what I had caught. There was no logical reason for one of the hot looking girls to make this move, I hadn't sent out any signals I was on the hunt. Barb was taking real good care of things, she knew what I needed so I wouldn't go looking for some strange shit. Anywhere guys and girls were working in the same location, the game was on. The hot ones at Tibbetts had guys panting in line. For me, if a girl wasn't a psycho and had an interest in me; nine times out of ten – I would return the attention.

Talking to a female who was a beautiful woman and clearly out of my range - was something I tried to avoid. I didn't do well in those situations. Manufactured answers and head games were ingrained in some female's behavioral responses – absorbed through magazines, moms, sisters, senior polls, TV, books, and movies. The visual media was the worst. I took a lot of ribbing from the guys because I'd walk the halls in Gorton with girls no one else would. I would also go out with them undercover.

Ray gave me his formula two or three years ago: On the physical scale of ten, the girl's got to be at least a three. Anything lower he said - would result in nightmares. Going to the movies was okay because it was dark. "Try to see a movie neither one of you will like, so there's no excuse to do anything but make out......The best date is to go over the girl's house when nobody's home to listen to records." You're already in her bedroom," he smiled, "The rest is up to you and her." He went on, "The best 'first kiss' move is to grab a record album with the small writing on the backside and ask her to help you read the credits because the print's too small. Next thing you know - your face is next to hers and your tongue is exploring her mouth ......Smokin! ....Woooo!" He fanned his face with his hand.

Our fingers played as Sgt. Sansone had been talking......."and if you feel a crime has been committed – get a patrol officer or one of the full-time employees.....A.S.A.P. Until this heat wave breaks, the park and pool is going to be packed, but we will get through it ....."

I heard the words, but all I could think about was the person behind me. I looked down at her feet and legs: sandals with a raised heel - that meant fashion. Her legs almost had a tan. She had to be a provocateur - she pushed the action. Only a good look would reveal if she had siren status. It sure wasn't the way Barb came at me. This one was from the other end of the female spectrum. What could I tell from one leg and foot; all of my information came from her overt move to touch me without any enticement. Any guy would like that, but I couldn't help feeling this would be more trouble than just a little bit. It would really make it easy if she was facially a two. I had been at the pool since the end of June and every girl working there was at least a five or better.

"...........to facilitate the public's use of the park and pool. We are committed to save lives number one." Harry paused and glanced over to Skip who nodded acknowledgement. "To prevent crime, keep the park, pool, comfort stations and picnic areas clean. If people stop coming to our park – it is because we haven't done our job. If the numbers of the visitors decline, the people in White Plains will have this park under a magnifying glass........and nobody wants that. Any questions?" He looked at us. "Alright, let's get to work."

I grasped her hand and spun her before we started back - we were facing one another. I took a long look at her; I knew who she was. I had asked a couple of the guys who knew her from last summer what the lowdown was on her. They said the word was a couple of the workers and one of the cops had tried to go out with her last summer and found her distant.....not worth chasing. This was my first encounter with her, I didn't know what to do. It didn't matter, Barb Wells was where I was at; nevertheless, she had caught me flatfooted. Her name was Karyn – Karyn Cahill. We walked with our pinky's locked. No words were spoken as we broke our tiny connection. We smiled. She went up the women's side........I went up the men's.

"GOING OUT." I CALLED AS I LEFT. THERE WAS NO acknowledgement, not even from Brother Bill, and he would always say something to me. He had to be out with Tommy Campana and Frankie Flynn. Jane's car was gone, but I knew Hal was around somewhere, perhaps in the backyard. It was just as well I missed him; he wasn't in a good mood of late.

I turned the key: the Olds fired up right away. It seemed like every time I drove up O'Dell Ave., I grinned with sweet revenge. Some guys were born litterbugs......they were still tossing their used smut magazines and dirty novels in the leaf strewn dirt where the city should have poured a sidewalk when they had only installed the guardrail. In the interest of the current anti-litter campaign with an American Indian being pelted with garbage at his feet, I was obligated to salvage the pornography and review it when I had some spare time.

My life really changed with the purchase of the Starfire. It was freedom3: anytime, anywhere, any reason. Freedom had a price – work was required to keep the wheels turning. Like everyone else.....once you owned a car, not having one simply cannot be considered. The freedom cruise had to keep rolling. It was my good fortune I had a head start, indirectly due to Ray's refusal to return to Yonkers. Hal and Jane were glad I had a job with her uncle Harry. Although the three of us knew this summer job was short term. Another job had to follow this one, and I had no marketable skills or training in any trade or profession. I thought I was a good fuck but that skill only pays fringe benefits..... The summer would be over before I knew it. I had to start asking around now.

The Fourth of July arrived about ten days after graduation. Harry told me the first day I met him for work, my days off would be during the weekdays.....no weekends off. If I came back next summer, I might get Friday/Saturday or Sunday/Monday off, but no seasonal help got Sat./Sun. off. Fair enough, being told up front.

Everybody and his brother were looking for blockbusters. People were calling the house; Hal and Jane were hoping desperately the voice on the other end was Ray. Hal thought I was dealing drugs. If it wasn't for the fact that Ray could possibly call, I believe Hal was ready to rip the line out of the wall. The only blockbusters I had left were the ones I was using to crack open pay phones. There were less than 50 left in my stash in the cellar, and they were degrading. If I was in a jam for money, I could of gotten $2/apiece for them. Last summer we even made page three of the Herald Statesman: "Fourth of July celebration rocks downtown for third successive night......citizens demand police crackdown on illegal fireworks."

Vinny was down the corner on the Thursday before the Big weekend. I parked at the Gulf station across the street from Progressive Pizza and the deli. I got a slice from Ralph's.

"How's the new job?"

"Still got to work the weekends, but it beats carrying golf clubs......You get a job yet?"

"Still on 16 hrs. a week at Associated Foods. I'll never get out of Blackie's house on that kind of money."

"This gig at Tibbetts is only good 'til Labor Day, then I got to find a real job." I said. "See anybody else around?"

"Crawford, Bad Brad, and the Mason jar were going down the marina. Gotta be kooler by the water. Hey Whitedust, stop by Levine's liquor store on the way down."

I winced shaking my head, "I got to get a tall six of Schaefer. I can't get jammed tonight....work tomorrow, but we'll stop at Levine's too."

"Right on." Cinzo said. "What's the deal with Ray – Joey and Rikshaw were wondering and Englund's all fucked up."

"He's alright.....okay, but he's incommunicado for right now. Truth is, I really don't know where he is."

"That ain't like him."

"No. This is off script." I ran my fingertips on my dried out lips.

We got down the marina and I parked on the north end with the trunk facing the river; the nearest car was 20 yards away. It was early yet. I had the trunk open so we could hear the jams better.

"Any progress on getting a set of wheels? You got to have a ride to get the chippies to look your way."

"I know – I know.....Fuckin' Stacey won't let up about a car. Ronnie Zanzibar said he might have a line on a '60 Impala. One problem though......."

"Which is?"

"He says the car got significant carnage on the passenger side. It's a four-door.....family car. The shotgun door has been crashed locked – won't open."

I shook my head; "Even I know she's not going to like that. She's got some pretty high standards."

"Tell me about it.........Why's she going out with me?" His follow-up laugh was half-hearted. He was depressed; and bought a quart of T-bird. "The Z-man's looking at the damage at the hinge points and the mid-post. Says it's possible a door from the bone yard might work if the frame is still true."

"How's the rocker panel?"

"Said it was straight, and that's why he thought it might be repairable."

"Did you actually see the car?" I said.

"Nah.....If you can't trust Z-man – who can you trust?"

"So what's going on this weekend?"

"Nina Simone down the Schaefer tomorrow night, then nobody until the 7th."

"You're not going to the shore with Rex, Martin, and Bingo?" I lit up a smoke.

"Really Lawwhite.....I am tapped out."

"Did you ask Rex if the Carpenters were taking apprentices?"

"I'm going over to the hall and put my name on the list for the test again."

"I'll go with you, if you can wait 'til next Thursday?" I killed the rest of my beer. "Hey.....Loki is getting his hack license. I can't get mine until I'm 18 in September, but you're already 18."

"I dunno." he mumbled.

"Now don't get upset, but I got to put it out there Tarts: there's going to be four barnbusting days of looping at Sunset this weekend – I know you can catch a ride with Loki."

"Be Real."

"You're just going to spend the Fourth with Stacey?"

He took three swallows of wine, "They own a beach house in Connecticut. Figured I could mooch off her and her family, look at her sisters' tits and get high. Her mom told Stacey: "NO CINZANO'. We're just going to have a Fourth with our family – no boyfriends."

"Must be swell to have that kind of money." I opened another Schaefer.

"You got any of them blockbusters left?"

"None for recreation, they all designated for business purposes." I said.

"How about a little mixing business with pleasure?"

I nodded, "Good timing......the explosions will fit right in with the fireworks over the long weekend. We can't do Greystone, tapped the northbound two months ago. The pay phones got to have activity during business hours, but it's also got to be somewhat secluded."

"What was the most you hit Ma Bell for?"

"Like $65 split three ways: Rex, Jimmy Martin, and me. It was at Adventurer's Inn bus stop. We waited until the #7 bus cleaned out the stop; then we cracked one of the three phone booths there. Martinique wanted to do all three, but there was too much activity around Christmastime. Martin's always been one hungry motherfucker. That three-way split just kills the margin unless you can knock off two or more."

"What about stirring up some babes....there's got to be something left in town?" he said.

"That's your department Cinzano – next to Holter..... you're the ladies man."

"Barbara been asking around about you."

"MOTHERFUCKA!, I seen her riding around with Reno two weeks after I got back from Indy; she told me they were through when I came back from Purdue, and then she's with that jag all over again. Gimme a hit of that T-bird."

"She might be up at Hanratty's, she's turned into a regular barfly since she turned 18. You ready to go skankin?" Vinny laughed.

I crunched my eyebrows: "Is this the way poor grown-ups spend their holidays when they don't have the money to get out of Dodge?"

"Apparently." He took another pull off the T-bird. "You got any weed?"

"How about this.....I call up Meris Klein and Sarah Nussbaum. The last time Meris and me got together was last summer the day before we had that orgy at O'Dell."

"You haven't seen her in a year?"

"She's been going to S.U.N.Y. - Binghamton for the past year. I 'spose I could have gone up and seen her since I got the car but what the fuck, I just got on the road six weeks ago. I seen her around Christmas, but nothing happened – not since last summer." I side armed a railroad rock into the river.

"No action for a year.....I dunno man and calling her up cold." He turned and looked at me with one eye, "You fucked her."

530

"Nah." I shook my head and laughed.

"Get the fuck outta here. You didn't bang her at Stony Brook?" He pushed my shoulder. We both laughed, "What the fuck Slo-poke?"

"She likes me, but she doesn't love me. Someone else is going to get the grand prize.....we're just helping each other out. I don't nag her for it, and that's why I think we're able to go on." I wiped some sweat from my temple.

"So you never got laid yet – "

"Not in the traditional way."

"What the fuck does that mean?"

"I guess I'm a virgin."

"You ain't a virgin......you're a fuckin' retard."

I raised my hand: "Guilty."

"Well - with the wheels, some babe is going to need a ride home from the bar and you'll be there with the Starfire and one thing will lead to another."

"I asked three or four girls to let me in them, but it was always the same shit.....it was like beg – borrow – or steal it from them. Then you had to tell them you loved them, but that was a lie cause what you really loved was 'it'. I don't know what that love stuff is all about. If it's lying to get the pussy – why bother?......but you're in love with Stacey right?"

"Yeah?"

"Did you have to beg or lie to her for it?"

"No, we were just overcome with passion and it just seemed natural." Vince took a deep breath.

"Well, what's natural to me is a babe who likes the edge, and got a good sense of humor. We run into each other now and then, have sex with no commitments and she doesn't have any hang-ups that make her feel like she's sleeping around. We get each other off without the threat of pregnancy, commitment, and we turn it on when we want to."

"That doesn't exist."

"You 'member Monica....Monica Williams from the 11th grade?"

"Yeah – you were going out with her for a month or so. Didn't she go to some Catholic school in the Bronx?" Vince tried to remember her in detail.

"Yeah, I knew her from Latin III, but before she dropped it, I was going over her house after school to help her with it."

"I know where this is going and how it ends. She was kind of chunky – not that good looking."

"And I am?" I lit another Marlboro. "Long story short; Monica boosted this Aubrey Beardsley book of lithographs from the library of naked guys in full heat. We never got to any of Cicero's orations. She wanted the short course on male biology and physiology, and I was more than eager to be the experimental specimen."

"Here comes Crawford.......is Rex behind him?" Vince strained his eyes. "So what happened?"

"In the span of two weeks she ruined my season as a cross-country runner......tell you the details some other time."

"Every once in a while I'd see you two walking the halls, having lunch, or study halls."

"Yeah, neither of us killed it."

Holter and the Z-man walked over with their suitcases from Crawford's Datsun.

Rex started laughing from the driver's seat of his Pontiac, "I know Whiterock ain't going to Jersey......what about you Tarts?" It sounded like a challenge.

"No skins, I'm down to the wire......I got to get some wheels and a job with some hours."

"You queers make me puke." he laughed.

"No money Rex."

"We're not staying at 'The Breakers'. Probably stay at the 'New Irvington' or the 'Surfside'; they're as cheap as it gets."

Holter broke in: "The Surfside got the 'Saigon Room' bar......you know where love connections magically occur." There seemed to be a twinkle in his eye as George pushed the notion of the forlorn mermaid nursing a double martini at closing time.

"C'mon Vince, everybody's going. I'll front you the hotel." Rex nodded.

Holter ran down the roster available for the Fourth's celebration on the Jersey shore: "Bingo, Fast Eddie, Danny Stax, Robbie Herrick, Martinique, Bad Brad, and the Z-man. "How 'bout it Crawfish – You coming?"

"Un-uh. Jersey's been trouble for me." He shook his head. "Their state patrol got it in for me; I owe them money for an unpaid moving violation. They'll send me straight to the crowbar motel."

Holter still called for volunteers. He must have made a big cash haul for his graduation. "How 'bout it Vince? Stacey left you on your own – if she loved you, you'd be going to Connecticut this weekend. You owe her one. C'mon."

"I'll go, but Rex – you, me, and Lawless got to make a call by Yonkers Raceway." Vinny's contingency was sure to involve the phone company.

"You got it brother." Rex grinned.

"Ryan, loan me four blockbusters."

Rex and Vinny followed me to 21, I had two wheels on the sidewalk as I dashed down the cellar to get the ordnance. Four warm tall boys were put in the cellar fridge; I came out with a quart of Colt and a bag of explosives. The trotter track was about 8 miles away. The two paisans followed me to the Saw Mill Parkway to the Cross County, to the N.Y.S. Thruway and exited at Yonkers Ave. The noise from the Thruway would provide some cover from the loud explosions. The Raceway Diner on Yonkers Ave. was the biggest problem – witnesses. Rex parked past the diner and the traffic light and covered his rear license plate with some gutter newspaper in the street.

I was nervous; it was our first job that qualified as a day-light gig. We had knocked over 11 phones during the year. We were mindful of Davis Quinn's warning not to get greedy. This was as close to a theft of necessity as we made to date. The other jobs were pulled because we knew if we didn't get the money before the phone box collectors, it would be gone and it'd be another three months before it was ripe for pickin' again.

Rex pointed to us and gave us the thumbs-up. Two charges were lit at the same time and went off within a second of each other. The explosions blew out the Plexiglas of the two booths. It gave us the clearance to work the two pry bars. The second set of blockbusters went off almost as close as the first. In about three minutes Vinny had his money for his weekend in Belmar. They headed north and I drove west on Yonkers Ave.

HAL, JANE, CATHY AND BROTHER BILL WENT UP TO THE apple orchard in Straatsville. Mack and Mom-Mom's was a shy half mile away. Jane was smart enough to take her Comet and leave earlier than Hal. It was a high voltage situation. When they returned on the Fourth, they were still arguing about Ray's whereabouts. He had been missing for more than a month.

Friday night I just cruised around, being a wise guy – cranking the music, drinking Chug-a-mugs......trying to look kool. The Starfire did all the work. I looked for people in all the familiar hangouts. On a chance, I called up Meris Klein after work. I was mystified when she answered the phone. We talked briefly; she would only be in Yonkers for a little bit. She was going to Rhode Island for the rest of the holiday with her mother and her aunt. "I'll call you when I get back." she promised.

Loki.....same deal.....gone for the weekend. I wondered why he wasn't caddying?

It was Friday, since I was just burning up hi-test, I thought I'd get a jump on Sunday's liquor laws and get Sunday's bottle of wine tonight. It was a smart move which I didn't do too often. Ed O'Clair, had this wine called 'Macrita'; it was supposed to be a tequila or mescal chaser. The stuff was outasight. Sure enough – as soon as you find something you like – they sell out. Ed said he couldn't get anymore. I bought a case of it, and put it in my trunk.

Friday through Tuesday fireworks were going off everywhere. I heard a few blockbuster explosions, but no-where near the numbers that went off last year. Still, there was a lot of the usual stuff.

I had to work the late shift at the park, and I didn't get off until 6 pm. It was a zoo from the moment I showed up. As one with no seniority, I got all the crummy shifts and jobs. The county cops had a command of six temporary-summer cops stationed there and one patrol car. Tibbetts was a free for all - once people were out of sight of the pool and the administration building. There were drugs, gang picnics, underage drinking, bachelor parties, loud music, fireworks, and on Sunday morning the Puerto Ricans and Cubans had set up a small fenced area with wood chips and sawdust and were into their fourth hour of cock fights before Sgt. Sansone broke it up. It wasn't as wild at the pool, but it was an eye opener, and I had an epiphany about crowd control and a cop's job.

533

At quitting time, I was glad to get out of there. All Star Beverage was doing a brisk business. I got a six of Chug-a-mugs, an eight pack of Schaefer shorties, and a big bag of ice. Having the 12 bottles of macrita in the trunk was like an insurance policy. Everybody couldn't have left for the Fourth.   I had to make a stop at 21 to check the answering machine and get a Styrofoam kooler, but the former hadn't been invented yet and latter would be outlawed sometime in the future, deemed to be a pollutant nuisance.

Searching the usual haunts, my last gasp was going to be to take a ride down the marina. It wasn't where I wanted to go; everybody who had fireworks were directed by the bluecoats to shoot them off down there. I'd take a drive through, maybe Crawfish was around, I knew he didn't go to Jersey.

The only action I ran across down there were the Warburton chicks. I made two passes before I decided to try and hang out with them. The three girls were leaning up against this couple's car, who they knew. The Starfire was even with the girls and we acknowledged them. They called out to me as I cruised doing 3 m.p.h.

"Whitedude.....Whitedude......." Kathy Cruz called.

I knew they were there, I had seen the three girls on my first drive through. It was a lot easier joining their throng than inviting myself. I stopped on the marina dirt road.

"Hey Kate......Passion...... Denise 'the Piece' - where you been hiding? I haven't seen you for a while."

"Park the car Whitetime."

The marina was only half full, there was room to park. Mostly bottle rockets and firecracker were being set off – nothing big. It was still too early break out the artillery.

"What are you guys doing? See any of the guys?" I said.

"Nah, we're looking to party." Denise said.

"I don't know if I'm going to hang out here if they start shooting bottle rockets and Roman candles at each other. Some asshole set my hair on fire last year." Passion Penny reminded us.

"Yeah – at least yours grew back." I put my beer on the roof and used my hands to separate my hair and reveal the full extent of my bald patch.

"Who did that to you?" Kathy cringed. "Kenny Crawfish said it was a teacher?"

"Aaaay, I'm sick of the long hair bullshit, think I'm going to get a G.I. cut again.....at least it'll be cooler."

"I don't think you look too bad." Denise kind of gave me a half-smile.

"Fireworks are fun only when you're the one shooting them off." I got another beer from the trunk .

"I just don't want to get blown up." Kate said.

"Any reef around?"

"Got a nickel bag." Denise grinned.

"Tell you what.....Trade you a blockbuster for a couple of joints?"

"What's a blockbuster?" Kate bummed a Salem from her.

"It's a quarter stick of dynamite."

534

"Dynamite?" Penny asked.

"'Bout equal to three M-80's."

"Let's see this blockbuster." Kate said.

I undid my belt and undid the button and began to fumble with the zipper.

"Whoa! hey.....hey Eeeeee! hold it right there Whitelaw." They screeched.

They knew by my smile I was messin' with them.

Penny covered her mouth.

Cruz gave me the look that asked for trouble. "Okay Whitebone.......I'll take a look."

"You mean Wishbone." I grinned.

"What about you Denise – you got the smoke." Penny's eyes said "dare ya."

"Not interested."

"How 'bout it Passion?"

"I'll look for free."

"Penny you know better than that.....ass-grass-or gas... nobody rides free." I quoted.

"Nah......ain't worth it." she said.

"You guys are pretty free gambling with my maryjane." Denise reconsidered.

"Here's the deal: Denise, you give me two jays for one blockbuster. Kate, you got a side bet to check out my real blockbuster for another joint. If you think it's a dud, the look's for free.

Denise's head tilted, "Cruz, you're playing with fire."

"C'mon Denise – let's have some fun." Passion giggled.

"Fire up the one number anyway." I was anxious to get in the right frame of mind for this stupid bet I made. "You guys want a beer?" I brought them to the trunk of the car. We all grabbed a shorty and emptied the eight pack carton. I put a bottle of Macrita in the ice of the five gallon bucket with the six Chug-a-mugs. Denise' reef had power. My eyes made the circuit of the three. It must have been one of those things; some force shuffled the deck, and a different outcome was possible. I would have never hung out with the girls by myself if the Rogues had been around. This was the best game in town and it was a smart move to make the most of it. Fireworks were going off, but most of it was happening towards the middle of the marina. I didn't know Denise too well, but I did know Cruz and Paschen. They were there for Ranger Rick's going away party and when I played dentist on Reno. These girls were a year behind my graduating class. Right now, they all looked good on account of Denise's happy hay, and there was no one to give you a hard time about hanging with them.

"How 'bout our bet Cruiser?" I thought I could win the bet.

"How 'bout it?" she had a beer in one hand, the other was on her hip.

"Denise you want to bet and get some cheap thrills?"

"Hey Whiteperv, I don't want to see your shit. Wells has already given me the lowdown on your equipment. She's been looking for you all week; why don't you go up to Lake and Voss and give her what she needs?"

"She's been riding around with Reno again. I ain't sharing her with him – she's got to make her choice. I'm almost past it anyway." All the fun of the night was extracted when I thought about losing Barb back to Reno.

"Not true!" 'The Piece' countered. "She's got it for you Whiteheart. After you and Barb were together - she's been hot on you. Maybe she rode around with Mike to make some deliveries, but I swear on my probation she never cheated on you."

These sisters of the gash lied better than we did, and it was easier to believe.

"Is she up there Kate?" I was getting real interested now.

"She was earlier, before I came down here. Just take the one joint. I don't want no dynamite or see any man stuff." she replied.

I gave the three amigas the rest of the beer.

THE SUN WAS GETTING LOW – THE CLOUDS REFLECTED the sun's orange hue. Denise's reef was the best I had in a while, but I only had the one joint. I got stuck doing baskets at the pool for Monday and Tuesday for the July Fourth weekend. The patrons changed into their swimming trunks and put their clothes and valuables in the baskets and we kept them behind the cage and gave the patron a brass disc with the corresponding number on their basket. We used the baskets when they ran out of lockers. Everybody had a key or a disc on a rubber elastic they wore on their wrist or ankle. There was a 25 cent deposit on them.

I took one hit just before I went in and another at lunch. The bathhouse was like a sauna, it was loud with all these kids screaming, and it constantly smelled of chlorine. Any job out on the pool deck was better than being in the cage doing baskets. The more I got stoned, the more my thoughts turned to Barb and Karyn.

After the third day of the four day weekend, there was a little sunlight left, it was around 8:00 pm. I drove past Hanratty's Pub three times over the course of an hour. I started looking for a space, and ended up on Voss a little past Busy Bakers. I recognized some people on the street – but no Barb Wire to get hung up on. Three patrons were on the street in front of the bar smoking cigarettes and carrying on. They most likely had gotten started this afternoon. I saw Sue Herr, and a girl Vinny had been dating prior to his Stacey Daze: Dona Del Bello. He was still partial to her and he'd see her on the sly, when Stacey pulled moves like she did this weekend. Dona had 'the look', but Stacey Keegan's family had the bank roll. The third leaf of the clover had his back to me. He had a marine crew cut, some real short cut-off dungarees, a blue tank top, and some kind of hippy beads around the neck. Dona and Sue were already blasted.

Sue asked as she hugged me, "Hey Ray's brother – where is everyone?"

The buzz cut instantly did an about-face. I studied this person; my hug was frozen. There was something very familiar with this person.

"How do you like me now.....still interested?"

'Holy fuck' I was mesmerized......."Barbara?" Definite I.D. She stood behind Sue waiting in line for something more than a hug. Why she made this move, and who she was trying to emulate was a mystery at this point. It was okay with me I guess as long as she was the same inwardly. She jumped on me and wrapped her skinny legs around my waist, and squeezed her face to mine with her arms about my neck and tried to stick her tongue down my throat.

Guys coming back from Nam didn't get this welcome from their wives'. A display of affection for each other on Lake Ave. was okay right now. There weren't many people around. Maybe I really didn't mind it, it occurred so infrequently. There were a good two minutes of street romance before Wire took the barbs out.

"How you doin' Dona?" I smiled with my arm around Barb's neck from behind. She had gone out with Vinny in freshman and sophomore year. I only knew her through Vince. Dona was from Lockwood Ave. and had gone to St. Bart's for grade school. When Stacey busted them up, Dona was going to Commerce High and I just didn't run into her very much when she left Gorton. Dona was a goomba like Tarts. She had that Italian upbringing and knew the lingo from her grandmother. Joey Tarts knew Italian, but Vinny was all-American. He knew a few words and phrases but so did I by growing up around All Souls and the hill. There was something about Dona and Vinny; she understood a lot of things Stacey didn't care about. I knew it had to do with being Italian. It was smooth for the two of them, the olive oil greased the way.

Stacey and Vinny, that was something else. I never knew what the attraction was. They were like vinegar and oil. At times I thought their relationship bizarre.

Dona knew the answer before she asked, "Is he around?" I locked my lips together, and shook my head back and forth.

"Connecticut?"

"Jersey." I replied.

"Vinny didn't go with her." She said.

I started laughing, "She told him to stay home."

"That's not love......that's a bad habit. Ryan, can you give me a ride home?"

"No problem. Barb you coming?"

She put her arm around me as far as it would reach.

Dona resigned to the situation, exhaled: "He said he was going to hang around.....Had the apartment all to myself on Sunday and Monday, my parents went upstate."

The three young women got in the Oldsmobile. We took off and Dona sulked: "I was going to out Stacey – Stacey. All I've been is a pinch hitter to Vinny since she showed up. She's got him doing handstands and back flips for her. I don't like the box he's put me in." The three of us could only listen to Dona about how Vince screwed up.

I sympathized with her. I thought she was better looking than Stacey. "Hang in there, Cinzo is no glutton for self-inflicted punishment. One day he'll realize the guy beating him up with the 2x4 – is the guy in the mirror." I lit a cigarette.

537

"I know he'll get wise; but for me it's the final scene in a three act play." She thanked me and waved to us as we dropped her off.

"Sue – what are you up to?"

"Just drive me back up to Hanratty's, I'm waiting for Cocaine Wayne and Kenny C."

"I was looking for Kenny all weekend."

"He's been running one. Tomorrow he'll have to pay the fiddler." Sue nodded.

I stopped at All Star and got a six-pack of Miller bottles – on sale for $1.75. Barb waited in the Starfire using the rear and side-view mirrors to adjust her new style. Putting the beer in between us, before I got in I said,"Excuse me, I don't believe I have the right car.

She pulled me in, "You asshole."

I offered a beer to Sue; Barb took one and ransacked the glove compartment for a bottle opener. "It's a twist-off top......and don't fuck with my tapes."

"Don't start the Mike Reno crap on me."

I didn't say anything and turned the music up until we let Sue Herr off at the bar.

"Are you still seeing him?" I said driving off.

"He dumped me after the haircut. The day before graduation."

"Did you go to commencement exercises?"

"What the hell is that?"

"Graduation, ya ditz." I shook my head and stopped short over the double line on Saw Mill River Rd. Barb lost her beer and bounced back off the windshield. I studied her as she scrambled for the loose beer. "Do I know you?" I may have been serious and I squinted my good eye to truly see her.

"You Whitesnakin', asshole, jerk off – motherfucker!"

"If you are Barbara Wells please reveal yourself." I said talking to the windshield.

"You are a complete idiot." we laughed some more.

We resumed our ride. "Showdown time.....just give me the short version of the makeover."

"Aaaaay.....we got lice from the cats, I'm pretty sure."

"Lice?" I whistled.

"Knits....whatever. The cats were going nuts scratching. My mother sent me to the store and I got this electric hair clipper and shaved all the kids, mom, and Sylvia did mine.
I tried to shave the cats, but they went bezerko. Mom just kicked them all out. Then we had to deal with that great big bobcat – that fuckin' Chauncey. Ma had to drug him and had the Humane Dept. take him away. They didn't believe it." Barb recalled.

"Whyja shave your eyebrows?"

"I wanted them to come in darker; instead that anti-lice soap burnt them off. I'm not that good with an eyebrow pencil. My hair's starting to come back. It's okay with you – huh?"

"You look like you got off the bus from Area 51. But, you look good to me......I'm serious."

She stayed the night at 21. I closed the shades and we worked on each other. We drove to work the next morning.   "My house key is on the car ring. I'll see you at six. Don't fuck with anything."

"You ain't got nothing."

"Don't go snooping."

"Have a good day at work Hon."

I handed her a five: "Go get yourself a pair of big Jackie-Oh! sunglasses up the End."

She met me with the Starfire at Tibbetts.....on time. "Nice shades." I smiled.

I knew three of the other seasonal workers before I had started work there, they had gone to Gorton or I vicariously knew them through other track teams. When the work day was over around 15 of us went to the employee lot to get our cars. Most of them saw Barb leaning up against the Oldsmobile waiting for me. I reversed positions with her and spread my legs and put her in between them to bring her closer. She had the same clothes from Sunday. We started going at it, I didn't pay any attention to the others in the lot. All a few could do, was stare. I was sure they couldn't figure out if she was a guy, a girl, a kid, or a creature from outer space. There'd be a ton of questions from them tomorrow.

We stopped at the pizza joint down the North End and got a small pie to go. Wire and me waited in the parking lot, again making a visual statement of our desire. Everyone who saw us were gape-mouthed and rubbernecking. I guess we were more of a spectacle than I thought.

"You want any beer?"

"Yeah.....get some Colt." she said.

I went to Barca's for some beer and she waited for the pizza. Barb's hair had grown back an eighth inch since they had the scalping party over at the Wells' house. She was as flat as a sheet of plywood, no eyebrows, but what made them zing us was Barb was wearing high black Cons, and those sneakers were the reason for the word getting around I had been making out with a guy down the North End.

Tony Griffin was stunned when he saw us; he did a U-turn on the south side of the End and quizzed me from his car: "What the fuck........Whitelaw?" He started off laughing a little, "What's the do? Who's your beau?" he smirked.

"Griff......why don't you dig yourself fool?" I looked away. Barb walked up carrying the box.

"I ain't the one making out with a boy." He shook his head.

"Okay Mister know-it-all: this is my girlfriend Barb Wells. So she got a G.I. haircut? You want to make something of it?"

"Did you check things out?"

I turned to Barb, "Tell Tony to go get bent." I said.

"Go fuck yourself Tony."

"You sound like a girl."

"Shoot him the beaver." I was pissed, and I took the box of pizza so she could prove her sex.

Wire yanked her cutoffs to the side with one hand and pulled her tank top up with the other and exposed her smooth boob. "Anything else you need?" she said.

"How 'bout it Griff, you gonna get your bitch to strip for me when I think she's a guy? Or question your manhood?"

"Ryan........hey man I am totally wrong, I am so far out of line.....I feel like shit. Can I make it up to youse. I'm the one who needs the tune-up, I apologize to you both....Really." He kept his eyes on the ground, shaking his head.

"I'm sure other's saw what you thought you saw: a bald guy, high black cons, mini titties. Not a good fashion statement for gals." I said.

"No......I'm flat." she rolled her eyes with a grin.

"You're not the girl who rode around with Mike Reno?" Tony scrunched his brow down trying to make the connection.

"Yeah." She shook her head 'no'.

"Whiteman.....let me buy you guys a six......Heineken?" he offered.

"Faghettaboutdit."

When we got to 21, I asked her as we ate on the porch: "How'd that break-up go down with Reno?"

"As soon as he saw me after the electric clipper - shock treatment he dumped me. It was over anyway." she said. "It was totally over when I started seeing you."

"Yeah, but I saw you riding around with him....."

"That was just business."

"It was over before the haircut then."

"Yeah, and then after I got it cut, Reno didn't want me riding around with him. He said I looked like a Venusian; and I'd be bad for business."

"You're still the same to me." I said. "You know I remember when you wouldn't give me the time of day."   "Times change." She looked at her reflection in the glass of the porch door. Barb vigorously rubbed her noggin.

"At least it's starting to grow back. I looked and felt like I stepped out from another dimension. It's hard to explain."

iv

Unusual activity was occurring with my calendar, I hadn't any idea what was going on. Perhaps graduating high school had something to do with it, approaching adulthood, or taking too many exotic substances. It was just a general feeling, nothing definitive I could point to.

The transition from caddying to working a 40 hr. job made the passage of time accelerate. The car, the girlfriend, and not having Ray around to feed me all the answers forced me to figure things out on my own.

Individual events consumed an unusual amount of time – blocks of it. The summer, and a quarter of the year simply vanished. Some weeks, even the real hot ones, disappeared as fast as a convict's

pack of camels, waiting on death row. Word spread fast about me and
Barb making out in the employee parking lot; they kept razzin me
because we kept going at it for the rest of the summer. One of the full-
time workers would look at us with his binoculars; he was trying to stir
up some shit. Finally, there were other bath house antics and romances
occurring. By the time that bad heat wave hit, Barb's hair was dark
enough to cover her scalp.

When there were only a few cars left in the lot, we would lie
in the front and back seats with our feet sticking out the windows;
music was low enough so we could talk. We'd pass a cigarette over the
bench seat, making plans for my Thursdays and Fridays off.
Sometimes we'd go to the nearest deli and get a couple of quarts of
Schaefer or Colt and go back to the parking lot. It was probably love:
another ingredient to push the clock ahead. She was so kool in my
eyes. We had only been together since Memorial Day, when I first had
gotten the Starfire. I knew having a car was a draw, but maybe it was
the Starfire.

The lot was empty when we left – making our way back to
North Yonkers, Wells and me got a couple of slices from Progressive
and to see if anyone was around. It was too hot for beer, so we drove
up the End for some wine. Harmonie liquors seemed to always have
these low end, cut-out brands of wine. Joe O'Clair had pushed the
Macrita on me earlier and now he was pushing this 'Kon-Tiki' shit. He
said it was some kind of hi-test Bali-Hai. Barb was a Ripple girl; it had
to be Pagan Pink or pear – she didn't like red Ripple. The End was
deserted.

"Try the marina." she directed.
"You got any reef?"
"There might be some down there if we run into somebody."
"No shit......"

We hooked up with Holter and a 28 year old woman from
White Plains he had met at a street festival. She was married, so he
called her 'Married Girl.' Holter's black book was bigger than the
yellow pages. The sun had begun its descent behind the Palisades; the
lovers were getting tuned up. George supplied the corn cob pipe, I'd
make book it was the fornicating wife who had loaded it. He waved us
to come on in the car.

"This is Janet." He automatically passed the pipe back to me
and it went around. How'd these women always seem to have
dynamite pot? All I kept copping was ditch weed.

"I didn't have any papers, good thing George had the pipe."
she said.

Three cars in a row drove down the northside ramp and
inched along towards my car. The first two I recognized, but as the
convoy got closer, I made Vinny Tarts behind the wheel of the third. It
was a '60 Chevy Impala with Stacey riding shotgun. It was an ugly
royal blue. The four of us got out of Janet's car. Vinny sandwiched
Janet's car from the other side and Rexall parked on the outside of me.
Bad Brad got to see the carnage on the passenger's side of the new
beater. This was the unveiling of Vinny's new wheels. Long hair

Vince with Stacey riding shotgun: looked like an updated version of the Beverly Hillbillies and Stacey knew it.

Z-man's report was accurate; one side was crashed out, but Cinzano's side was cream puff. He thought it was a good first car, it had a V-8 and didn't leak much oil. Stacey huffed and bristled at the sight of the 12 year old Chevy. What put her over the top was she had to get in and out of the car from his door. Because the Impala had bench seats and four on the floor, Stacey had to back her big ass out so she could sit in the driver's seat and then get out normally. All of us knew why Vinny went out with her.

"That's all day." Brad sniffed.

"And night." George wiped his lips.

"An overtime." Rexall watched with his elbows on top of his LeMans.

We stood between Janet's and my car and looked at the driver's side of the Chevy.

"Tarts.....how bad is the passenger' side?" She was still working her way out of the front seat.

Bad Brad and his date gave me and Barb a rotten egg look when he looked at the crashed out side. Nobody wanted to go over and tell Vinny his sheet metal had a bad case of schizophrenia.

Stacey didn't give her boyfriend a chance to sell it: "The car's a damned rolling junkyard."

"Does the window roll down Stace?" Brad's date asked.

"Of course." Vinny smiled. The two started having a private discussion. We couldn't hear them. She had her back to us with her arms folded; and her head was in bobble head mode.

It was obvious he was plenty proud of his new ride. Rexall now rested his head on his arms on the top of married girl's roof hiding his amusement and burying his head..

Everyone watched Vince and Stacey. Holter looked straight ahead and leaned into Barb: "Class Warfare 101."

Barb didn't know Stacey except by sight. She looked back at George, "Does she think she's too good to ride in Vinny's car?........I don't get it?"

"No. You got it Wells."

I figured Vince had talked her into coming down the marina and hanging out with us. We rarely saw Stacey except when it was on her turf; Vinny might ride by Morsemere and stop to talk to us while he was driving her father's car.

"Vinny we're going to be late." And they'd be gone a minute later.

The marina, the car, Vinny's friends, a cheating wife, Brad's flavor of the month, and an alien from a galaxy far away........we were all trash as far as she was concerned. The three gals felt her radiating animas when she crawled out of the Impala.

This was the first time I saw her in dungarees. Blue collar threads were beneath her. The other Rogues and me were glad she turned her back on us, we all liked looking at her big ass anyway. She had big tits, a big ass, and a business woman's face. Stacey was nice to

542

me, but it was just a sham. In the first few years, I was sure they were still in love. They ended up getting married.

Barb ambled over to the Chevy's wrecked side. Stacey led Vince away to maintain privacy.

The last thing Stacey wanted to hear came out of Barb's mouth: "It don't look so bad – it's just there's a lot of it. It'll getcha where you wanna go though I bet." she called over.

Vince walked over to Barb and left Stacey to stand there or follow him. Her face was turning to stone. "Ronnie Zanzibar says he can fix the mid post, and he's got a yellow door for it." Ronnie's assurance of a working passenger door had Vince all pumped up.

"Vinny....." Stacey started. Somehow it came out sarcastic and polite at the same time, and she let him have it in front of us. "Who's going to be your girl to accompany you in this 'Grapes of Wrath' dream ride?" She threatened him with an ice cold laugh. "Because when you drop me off – I will have taken my last ride in your demolition derby leftover." She smiled blinking.

Wells went right back at Stacey, "How can you run him down.....he giving you the best he's got." I knew Barb thought Vinny belonged with Dona Del Bello in the first place; we had all been rooting for Dona and Vince.

"Listen you ragamuffin – you keep out of my business. I'm not getting in the gutter with you." Despite what Stacey claimed - her claws were out and she scoffed, "Your only notion of class, is when you go to school."

The cut went over Wire's head. "A couple of months in this car......you won't think about getting in any other way." Barb broke into a grin.

"Ryan, tell your concubine to smoke some more pot - she's having another headache." Stacey said. Just before she went through the drivers door, Stacey had the last word: "Take one last look Vinny.....you too, boys....this is the last time you can watch my sweet ass getting in this car." She climbed in on all fours.

By the time Stacey was seated, Barb realized she had been in a verbal scuffle and had to get a lick in, but didn't know what to say. She knew Stacey looked down on her; it was something she didn't understand. The two young women vicariously knew each other; Vinny and Dona being the common denominator.

All of the Impala's windows were open, and Barb megaphoned her hands and called into the car, "Vinny, Dona says 'Hi' and says to give her a ring."

'What a car.....' It could transport people from one location to another, but it also had the ability to drive the passengers to various emotional places they were unaware of.

It was the first time I had witnessed Vince getting this close to a meltdown. We watched and listened to the verbal sparing as it got louder and louder between the two of them. "It's just a fuckin' car", he told her.

"We're going to have to get you straightened out Mr. Tartaglione. She looked straight ahead with her arms crossed and her face could have been carved out on Mt. Rushmore.

"Don't leave Stacey......don't leave." Barb gave her a schoolyard tease.

Stacey turned toward Barb as Vinny pulled the Chevy away from us, and slowly drove towards the ramp. A tirade of venom, piss, and vinegar was hurled at Wells: "You sexless, Martian, whore, junkie-monkey, BITCH.....I curse you and your bloodline!" From her window she launched a half-full bottle of Mateus wine backhand by its neck and hit Barb in the shin on the bounce.

They were cursing at each other and Vinny stuck his head out the window looking back at Barb, "Hope you're happy with the mess you made ya dumb bitch."

Barb was compressing her shin, and the rest of us couldn't restrain our laughter, the blue Impala climbed the ramp.

"It is true, she is better than us." Janet stuck her elbow in Holter's ribs.

"What are you fuckin' crazy - you don't even know the two faced bitch."

I took a long gulp of the Kon-Tiki wine, it was horrible. "Maybe it's my fault Vince is breaking away." I said.

Barb's eyes bulged out. "Are you nuts? What are you taking about?"

"He wants to marry her." I said.

"Un-uh. She's got him under some kind of spell.....'Black Magic Woman." Barb's eyes beaded down.

"We're not that intuitive Wells." Rex smiled.

"Take them $5 dollars words Rex and get in the car with Stacey." Brad said.

"No....no....Brad, Rex is right. We ain't no brain trust." George agreed.

"Neither am I; but I know a one-way motherfucka when I see one." Barb held her ground.

Holter had enough of the Stacey Keegan's version of 'Peyton Place'. "Heard the Allmans are playing at Gaelic Park.....you know the Manhattan College rugby field. What is it like – 238th St. & Broadway?" He didn't want to dwell on Cinzano's problems – neither did any of us.

VINNY TARTS WAS IN STACEY'S DOGHOUSE FOR four months – maybe more. He seemed happier and I knew he was freer. Wire and me never spotted Vinny and Dona Del together during his 'dog house' period. I thought he was seeing Dona, but it was speculation on my part. What wasn't guesswork was all the one night only performances he was giving at least once a week. There were plenty of barflys around and the word was out Vince and Stacey were history, which wasn't really accurate. He told me they were in some kind of period of separation to see if they still loved each other.

"Are you fuckin' nuts?" I asked Cinzano. "This stinks of Stacey. If you agreed to some kind of deal where you don't see other people while you're separated, you bought into some dumb ass shit."

544

"I agreed to it, but I'm a hot blooded Paisano. I'm gonna do my thing. I just got to be careful. It's Stacey's idea – any way - she's the one who's got to follow through with the abstinence bullshit."

"Fuck, you ain't even married! A woman can go without sex easier than a soul brother can do time; and they can do ten years standing on their heads."

An uneasy feeling racked my brain about where Brother Vince was headed. It was a convoluted mess; this wasn't magnetism or a fuckin' comet – this was raw humanity in all its full blown glory. In my daydreams at work, I saw Stacey and her sisters boiling a kettle of piss, feces, and contaminated blood and dipping Vinny's voodoo figurine in the horrifying cauldron. Cinzano was under her spell even when he was on suspension.

Brother Joe Tarts, Rexall, Brad, and Danny Stax tried to wise Vince up; the only thing I'd tell him was Dona was better looking than Stacey, and it was reason enough to cut her loose. Stacey was a manipulative and controlling woman. At the time, I didn't know what motivated her; what I saw was: she was all about Stacey Keegan. Why she didn't find a sucker who wore a suit and tie and carried a briefcase still baffles me. She'd only interact with us and our girlfriends when there was a wedding, funeral, or some kind of function. Hanging out was verboten.

Vinny should have been a physician or at least driving a hack 'cause she had him on call; whenever she'd cook up some crazy scheme to go out and have 'fun'. Stacey could get Vinny to think all this crazy shit they did together was his idea: go to plays and museums downtown – burn up a couple of hundred on a room at the Plaza Hotel. It made perfect sense: he was the first to run out of blockbusters .....he spent it all on her.

She enrolled in one of them fancy women's colleges which recently started admitting men. I think she went to Sarah Lawrence. It was a college she could have commuted to, but she talked her father into paying for room and board so she could have a well-rounded college experience. In three months she could have learned more at Camp LeJune than four years at Berkeley, Brown, or Sarah Lawrence.

TIBBETTS' POOL STAFF WAS 50-50, GUYS AND GALS. The administration was all male and over 40. Uncle Harry was looking at three or four more years before mandatory retirement. The staff consisted mostly of college students on summer vacation. Many were happy to trade in their books for a summer fling.

I was not immune to the passion kool-aid; there were so many summer romances it was hard to keep track. After the staff stand-down where Karyn made her move on me, we started having lunch together when we worked the same days. Karyn and Barb were so dissimilar; I speculated the latter might be in league with Ray in some way. Wells was more 'out there' than here; but she might have been a chimera, a phantasm, or specter 'lite' of straight polarity if such a thing was possible or even existed. I was entranced by their unique identities.

Cahill had long dark, dark brown hair. She always changed into and out of the county uniform before and after work. Karyn was the total package: a model's face, great legs, missile tits, and an ass that wouldn't quit. Why she was attracted to me was an enigma. Perhaps she was just doing some summertime trolling. "Why" was not a good question for me; I had wasted too much time in my life chasing non-existent answers to questions beginning with the word. We exchanged phone numbers and continued sharing lunch.

Barbara Wells was on the other end of the spectrum, she had tons of character, but many would say she had none. She was generous to a fault, had a great sense of humor, an unpredictable wild streak, and an authenticity seldom seen since my experience with Sister Alexa. To me she was physically beautiful, again this feeling was against the grain. The more I knew about Barb, the more I wanted to peel the onion.

v

She was down the marina with Crawford, Jimmy Martinque, and Danny Stax. The sun was setting a little earlier every evening, it was summer's third act.

A big Daddy-O smile filled her face as she ran over to me. Barb put her mug through my open window.

"Hey Kat-Woman." I gave her a quick smack on her lips. It was the start of my weekend.

"Thinking about you all fuckin' day."

"Leave your hair at this length for me?" I asked. It had a uniform length of about an inch-and-a-quarter.....maybe an inch-and-a-half.

"If that's what you want. It's fine with me – all I got to do is wake – up......do my eyes, and I'm out the door."

"Let it spike." I said.

"What about tomorrow? We doing anything?" she said. She was up to something.

"There's a storm out by Bermuda. Probably be some breakers coming in.....thinking about trying Jones Beach."

"Haven't been to Jersey or Long Island all summer." She hammered me.

"Tell me about it. Not much summer left....2 1/2 weeks? Then what?" I got out of the car.

"Then I'll have you full-time......on my payroll." She smiled.

"What of the future?"

"That's after Labor Day. For now this summer should be ours.....I copped with the guys." Barb motioned her head towards the guys up against Stax's car. "I got us some shit for tonight too." Her eyes said she wanted to explore Ursa Major later on.

She looked hot. "Who you getting high with mostly?" I asked.

"The Rogues, Z-man, ...Denise, Sue Herr,......Sally and Messy Beth if I got to."

"You know Jay Sawnson?"

Wells let a bellow of air leave her lungs, "Yeah, heard about him 2 days ago. Reno and me drove him downtown and the South Bronx a few times." She lit a cigarette.

"You're still chippin'? I don't want to lose you to an overload, or some unexpected potency." I put my arm around her and hugged her tight.

She held out both her arms, "I'm not runnin' it – just drillin' some test wells.........Rikshaw said it was 'French Connection' shit that Jay ran into. Cocaine Wayne got off with him."

My face went sour. "How come whenever anyone O.D.'s – it's the 'French Connection' shit. The bust went down in fucking 1962 and ten years later it's still layin' them out. Fuckin' bullshit man...... it's bullshit." I motioned for her cigarette and took a drag.

"That's what Sally and Wacky Nancy claimed."

"I don't want to see either one of them." I said.

Wayne-O, Z-man, and Crawfish.....they wanted to get high, but escaping this dimension was more critical than blasting off. If Ray ever came back, I'd get a ruling on Barb's status: whether she was polarized or just having a 'good time'.

When Barb and me left the marina, I had some reservations about her plans to rocket into orbit with Swanson's demise being so recent. We drove over to Greystone, had our style of sex in the Starfire, crossed the tracks to the warm spot and got off. She hit it up and I laced a Marlboro. When the rush dissipated we stumbled and lay in some river sand a few feet away. Just beyond the man-made objects orbiting the planet - we drifted in and out of a nod; watching a belt of the nuclear club's telescopes, communication, navigational, ultraviolet, gamma ray detectors, magnetic detectors satellites, and 'defensive' missile platforms.

Sometime on the Long Island beach, the next day, the ocean's waves washed away the smack residue. Wire knew better than me: if last night's escape wasn't paid for the following day, it became an extended voyage. It was all compound interest and would be collected at the next stop.

Cocaine Wayne's advice was always: "Stay on the locals – don't ride the express." We all knew he didn't follow his own counsel.

vi

The final week of August I got a call from Loki, he asked to meet me down the End. This time he was sitting on the low concrete block wall in a bit of shade of the parking lot. The formation of a six-pack outlined a brown paper bag.

"What's going on Trixster?"

He handed me a beer and an envelope: "U.S. Military COURIER/In country: REPUBLIC OF SOUTH VIETNAM." It was addressed to me in care of Joe Ferguson. "I'll read this over by the car." I swallowed hard.

"Yeah." He said.

5th day; U.S. Army; 525th Intel. Brigade; 519 M.I. Bat.; 45th M.I. Co.; C.I.C.V.; South Vietnam.

Ryan:

Just know - somehow I convinced the Army recruiter to send me here before it is over, and I made it a condition of my enlistment. Something about duty and the notion I was skipping out on the guys who died and the ones who served. Remember – my lottery number was like 315. On the face of it – this move goes against logic, current anti-war sentiment, and self preservation.

I had hoped to be stationed at one of the fire bases up north where there might be a way to absolve my feelings that I had avoided my duty,

More critical to this quest are the currents running through me about this concept I've hit upon of: total human emotion override. I believe it to be the antithesis of Albert King's anthem: "Born Under A Bad Sign". Listen to it a few times and you'll understand.

As the magnetic poles are reversing, it is impossible to quantify the speed or the force of realignment. Electro-magnetic pulses will affect guidance systems, machines, and technologies dependent on magnetism; and what is the human body? It is an electro-mechanical organism of interrelated systems controlled by involuntary or intentional movements and actions. The human machine – the shadow people aren't undergoing atom charge reassignment....my atoms are the same as yours. It is the electrons, protons, and neutrons orbiting the nuclei in the opposing directions. Speculation: Must be why the 5th dimension is so screwed up.

Escape or relief through drug infusion; or via Duane Allman's methodology where immersion in being human outweighs and causes the polemical forces to subside – may have the potential to quell the phantom imbalance.

I didn't come here to kill – but I'm not on some kind of suicide death wish either. Maybe…..just maybe – by putting my life on the line with these guys here, I will be able to attain unity with your side; in a way that has some longevity & hope. The Kamikaze concert was the Rosetta Stone.

What may be a problem in proving this theorem is the reality I did not get stationed in a 'hot' location, and there is not much fighting going on now. I am presently assigned to CENSORED @ CENSORED command @ CENSORED near CENSORED about 20 mi. CENSORED of Saigon. Everything I see, read, write, and hear is classified. The only thing I can tell you is my expected return from overseas. The Army said to expect my tour of duty would be the usual year. The ground war for us is basically CENSORED. ENTIRE NEXT SENTENCE HAS BEENCENSORED.

This is some kind of convoluted parallel world where very little makes any sense. Sometimes I think I might be better off being preoccupied with survival than worrying about cosmic and terrestrial pole collapse. Should Vietnam fall, I wonder if it had been influenced by or related to Magnetic pole inversion.

My letter to the family should follow in about two weeks --- please get mom and dad prepared.

Until next time – Ray

I walked back over and gave the letter to Loki. After the first two paragraphs he said, "Wow…" then continued reading. "I don't know what to make of it……I don't understand why he enlisted."

"We know he's trying to find existence without insanity; some kind of jive-ass bullshit pluralistic existentialism." I turned to Loki, "Is such a thing even conceivable? The equation is in his notebooks; he had them with him at the university."

"Only faith can part the seas and move the mountains. The 2% Specter contingent are busy dealing with the earth's current magnetic state of flux through mind-numbing technologies. I doubt he'll find anything of value in Nam which might help him find the end game." Loki cracked another beer.

"I think it's fair to say Ray didn't go out looking for this job."

"No…..true enough."

I held up my beer and toasted his resiliency; "After three months of no word - Now we know he's in Nam, I guess we can increase our worry level. Loki …..we got to keep this under wraps – for my mom's sanity."

"It's going to come to the surface eventually."

"As long as it's after Ray's letter hits the house."

"Right." Loki nodded.

"You been out of town or on vacation?"

"Driving for Caesar --- nights. I'm also working at Supremo Liquors on Thursday, Friday, and Saturdays…..12 to 9." He said.

"How's the money?"

"60-40 split Caesar's way. He pays for the gas…….can't make it on one job. Got to work at the liquor store too or I'll never get out of Yonkers."

"What happened to Pace University?"

"Couldn't keep up the pace." he chuckled. "I'll try college again some other time."

"I got to get my hack license. Once this seasonal job at the park ends, I got nothing." I took a deep breath.

"Get a P.O. Box down the Bronx and go to college for free; Open admissions/Free tuition. When they ask for a physical address – tell 'em your homeless and living in an abandoned building on Gun Hill Rd."

I had a feeling Loki had scoped this thing out and I'd be putting his plan into action. "I dunno…..I had enough of school for a while."

He laughed took a drag and launched the filter, "Come on Whitecaps……that wasn't school – they give you a diploma and you have no work skills?"

"So what's your plan Joe?"

"Heading south. Hitting the road like Kerouac advised."

"Where'd you say?"

"Miami…..Dade county. Nicky Mussio's down there; he says I can stay with him and his wife 'til I get situated. Said they're always looking for hack drivers. Got to get out of Nueva York before the snow flies."

"I don't turn 18 until the 20th of September."

"The action should pick up by then. Summer isn't taxi season. Listen Ryan, get all your hack paperwork complete now so they can issue you a hack license on your birthday. Ends up costing $61.75."

"Vinny's coming with me, figures he'd give driving hack a try. He's been 18 since January."

"Tart's got the right temperament; he'll be okay."

"Thanks for the beer, the tip, and the letter …..I got to roll." I gave him a short double beep as I left the lot.

THE DAY AFTER LABOR DAY WAS THE LAST DAY OF THE season at Tibbetts . A few of my co-workers had returned to college before Labor Day. A few like me just pretended to be going to college after we finished the season. At noon Uncle Harry handed out our final paychecks. The county paid us for the day.

Karyn Cahill said, "I'll walk with you to the parking lot."

"So when do you start at Fordham University?"

"Wednesday." she said. "Should we have a couple – to say good-bye?"

"Sounds good. We didn't get sacked…..that's something to drink to."

"Huh?" Karyn almost stopped and looked at me.

Getting canned wasn't on her radar. I didn't know any of the bars in this part of Yonkers. Maybe I did stop with Crawfish out this way trying to find bars' juke boxes. The second, but more important question was if there were any Tommy James songs on them.

"Ryan, follow me to my house, it'll be more like a date if I drop my car off."

She was fast. "Is this what we're doing - going on a…….."

"You were supposed to ask me out after I grabbed your hips back in July. All's I got were crummy lunches." she pouted.

"Be thrilled we're going out now." I said.

"I am." ………a smile.

When we left her parents place I still didn't know where I was taking her. I wasn't a bar guy, I never had enough money to do it more than twice a month, and then I'd always run out of cash. We drove along Yonkers Ave. I might have stopped with Kenny and Stax at this bar within sight of Yonkers Raceway. From the Central Paradise Lounge, I could see the phone booths across the Thruway. They were wrapped in plywood.

Everything was clean. Lighting was just right; neon signage was scattered about, the rest of the lighting was fluorescent except for the bathrooms – they were incandescent. It made you want to take care of business and get out. You felt like you were in a movie….a real good vibe. There were a half-dozen booths, and another half-dozen hi-stools with hi-cocktail tables: two to a window. One looked out on Central Ave., the other faced the racetrack. There was a great bowling machine just before the hallway to the cans. It also had a long

551

shuffleboard table with the sawdust. Danny Stax found the place when he ran out of gas one night with Crawdaddy. Sure enough, Kenny strikes gold with the juke box: two Tommy James 45's – four songs. It was a little pricey, but when a date walked in – she felt like she could get smashed.......with dignity.

Crawford stayed at the bar and started dancing, while Stax and me walked to get gas. They had just come out with the plastic gallon jugs for milk that year and Bobby had a couple of empties in his trunk, it was a half-mile to the Gulf station to the south. Two gallons – 70 cents.

"Karyn, I got to get a slice of pizza before we go in."

"See you in there."

"Order a drink for me, I'll be along."

Two guys were at the bar's corner, and an old timer was drinking a Social Security beer near the cans. The TV was on with no sound. She was in the darkest booth with two drinks: a tequila sunrise and a Kahlua and coffee on ice for me. "You get the next round."

"I think I better, I won't be ordering any more of these." We laughed.

I leaned to the side to find some quarters, and gave her two. "Play something that interests you. One of the songs should be a Tommy James tune."

Karyn got up, she knew this was some sort of test.

The first record was "Summer Breeze"/Seals & Crofts, "Crystal Blue Persuasion/Tommy James, "Layla" (single version)/Derek & the Dominos, and "Jackie Wilson Said"/Van Morrison.

I looked at my glass; "Interesting drink......who do you know drinks these?"

"No one; I saw a guy order one in a restaurant, you vaguely look like him." She answered.

"You're going to get blitzed drinking on an empty stomach."

"I'll have something to eat with the next round."

"It's recommended."

"So Ryan.....what's your next move?"

"No one uses my first name; if you find it to your taste – you can use it."

"How should I call you?"

"They all just use my last name or butcher it up: White – and invent your ending. Mostly it's a situational thing. I work at Tibbetts so they would call me Whitepark.....shit like that. Spent an entire night two years ago talking about it as we were getting wasted down Greystone station during a party down there. It kind of stuck after that."

"Even her?"

"Yeah."

"If I might ask......" she began.

"If this is going to be about Barb – don't bother. I'm not going to run her down and I'm not explaining to any one why I go out with her or what I see in her." I had immobilized Karyn for a moment.

552

"You are very attractive, intelligent, sophisticated; that is what I see on the exterior. It'd be a disappointment to look deep and see envy, possessiveness, duplicity, and jive-ass bullshit."

I had blindsided her. Karyn stared at her drink as her hands searched for her cigarettes in her handbag. Automatically, she lit one up, and I pulled one from her pack before she put them back in her purse.

She spoke twirling a Parliament in the ashtray: "I feel bad you thought that of me, but since we're already there – do you know how ridiculous you look with her?"

"So I should be with you?" It was getting weird.

"It's obvious isn't it?" Her eyes began to glow in the dim light.

I had to get this off the Barbed Wire. "So like......you're going to be a career girl?"

"Well, I've been thinking....." she looked out into the empty bar.

"Accounting?"

"No – about something to eat."

"A burger......a cheeseburger?"

"No – I'll have a martini......I'll eat the olive." Karyn smiled and so did I.

I brought back her cocktail; I had Miller long neck in my hand. We clinked our drinks before I sat down. "Here's how."

"I gave you my number?" she half-asked.

"Roger that."

"Don't wait too long to call – life moves on and so will I." Her stare cast a spell on me.

vii

Not too long after Loki gave me Ray's letter, I knew I had to come clean with Jane and Hal. Despite Ray's instructions to piecemeal his whereabouts to them, there wasn't any way to make it more palatable to digest. The possibility Ray could be in Vietnam became more remote as troop levels decreased every month. Both thought he had probably gone 'hippie' and was out there 'on the road'. Hal kept calling Purdue's Registrar's office hoping he was enrolled for the fall semester. They had no choice other than to stay medicated with more Xanax, valium, and rye whiskey.

Just before I was going out one evening I dropped the bomb on Jane and Hal; I told them Loki had received a letter from Ray, but not that it was written to me. I told them the post mark was from the U.S Army - country of origin: South Vietnam. I didn't give them a chance to question me.

"According to Joe Ferguson, we can expect a letter any day." They were both in the kitchen when I gave them the news. Jane stopped making dinner, and poured herself a double – neat. Hal had a couple of doubles as well. The two zombies looked straight ahead and never said a word to the other. Neither one said a word to me for the next eight days.

553

A big weight was lifted from my shoulders when his first letter arrived in the 2nd week of September. Again, a good portion of the letter was sanitized by the Army censors. We were relieved he was back in the family line-up.

Our only method of communication was through the mail. It had gotten to be quasi-regular; mostly Ray sent us post cards. At first, he used the typical post cards a tourist might send – all pre-war scenes: sunsets, Buddhist monks and temples, peasants in rice paddies, women wearing 'ao dai's' dress/pants combos. He was keen to avoid mention of any military activity; it would have been censored anyway. Instead, he casually wrote about other soldiers and the Vietnamese people he had contact with. After the traditional post cards had run their course, Ray started sending repurposed six-pack cartons advertising Pabst, Bud, Miller, Schlitz or a Filipino beer on the blank brown inside where he'd write his cryptic messages. Sometimes I didn't think he understood what he wrote. The script was almost undecipherable. It was possible he might be transforming into a higher life form with altered identity traits. I carried the puzzles from Vietnam in my back pocket. Sometimes I found the meaning behind the words....however oblique. He had to have been drunk or stoned when he wrote half of those postcards. Hal and Jane didn't comment after the first three or four.

Jane eventually calmed down after the initial shock of his enlistment. The media continued to report week after week of no U.S. Casualties. Three or four years earlier, U.S. KIA's had numbered 200 – 300 a week. The heaviest fighting occurred at Khe Sahn, Dak To, Hue, Na Trang, Pleiku, A Shau valley, Hamburger Hill, and Saigon during the '68 Tet Offensive. I could only guess what he was doing. The goofy postcards gave his tour there the texture of being illusionary and unreal. When he did send letters, they always came with photos of Vietnamese women with Ray having some laughs and enjoying themselves. After a couple of months, there was always this one girl in his pictures who was quite striking. By the third or fourth letter, it was obvious they were having a relationship.

Hal was afraid Ray would try to bring her home with him. Jane didn't care, as long as he came home in one piece. Besides Loki, only Vinny Tarts and Barb knew Ray was in Nam.

THE SUMMER JOB AT TIBBETTS HAD ENABLED ME TO squirrel away enough money to pay for the next six months of car insurance. Herbert Van Leer over at "TNT Used Cars" had already been vouched; he sent me up the street to a heating oil business which also sold diesel and kerosene. 'Oil Augie' vouched for me on Herb's assurance I was legit. Loki advised me to get down to Caesar's Taxi on the 22nd – a Friday.

"Ask Caesar or whoever's dispatching if they need any drivers. He'll most likely tell you all he's got open are Friday, Saturday, and Sunday nights.....take whatever they offer." he said.

Driving for Caesar was just a patch to be added to my quiltwork of work history. The same was true for Loki and Cinzano. The three of us were searching for career oriented work; we went the civil service route. We filled out applications for the Postal Service, U.S. Marshall's, Yonkers' cops and firemen, Border Patrol, the State Dept. the D.P.W., the railroad, and Con Edison. We'd make out an application and get a pint of T-bird, smoke some pot, or both in the neighborhoods we visited. All the Federal stuff was in lower Manhattan. For some of these jobs, there were preliminary tests; you'd see a line of 3,000 people circling some federal building freezing their butts off waiting to take a test for 50 jobs. More than once we drove down only to spend the morning goofing off on 42nd St. watching the circus.

When we were able to get work somewhere, it was with short weeks and hours, or if it was a 40 hr. gig, it'd last no more than two weeks. Most of it was off the books. Loki had the job at the liquor store; Vinny was still working four hours a day - four days a week, he also picked up spotty work with this black dude from Trinidad doing roofing and a little sheet metal. Vinny said Titus, his boss, was against hiring black Americans. He said: "They never show up and steal from you when they do." Rexall got me a job as a non-union laborer. The company was a front for one of the Luchese Family soldiers: Palomar Projects. They had the contracts to renovate the city's methadone clinics in the Bronx. Every payday Rex and me would drive over to Hunt's Point and visit the working girls. It was five bucks a throw – all volume work. I never got too worried about social disease because I wasn't into banging them.

Loki got more fares once there were a few cold evenings in a row. He was really hustling now, he really wanted to get out of New York.

"NO O.D.-ING IN THE BACK SEAT".... I SAID AS THE meter ran while I was parked.

"No problem sweetheart." she replied. These junkies ran the gamut, from N.Y.U. professors - to the mother of eight down on Lawrence St. There were no social or economic boundaries.

In a way, driving a taxi was similar to caddying; The casual basis gave it that feel of impermanence....no commitment from the driver, or from the cab company to the driver. The major force behind the industry was to keep as many cars rolling on the street as possible.

We'd meet at the Riverdale Diner before we came on the night shift.

"Vinny, how much did you book last night?" Loki said.

"Had to wait two hours for Jose' to fix the throttle on the carb. Only took him 20 minutes to do the actual fix, but there was a car ahead of me with a dead alternator; the replacement had the wrong electrical connection with the prongs instead of the stud terminals. Should have just gone back home."

"First two hours were slow anyway.....you didn't miss nothing." Loki said. "You just can't miss the first weekend of the new month - that's where all the money is."

"We're learnin' Joe." I sucked my teeth.

"Told youse to show up on Friday; it was worth it wasn't it?"

"It's only worth it if you can get on the road." Tarts replied.

"You can't expect everything on a platter. You and Whitewalls are the young bucks – drivers come and go all the time. The longer you drive a chariot for Caesar – you start getting the better shifts, they give you the checker cabs where you got the room to double-up the fares, and dispatch starts throwing you the fares that pay the big money." Loki nodded.

I lit a cigarette from Loki's pack and chuckled: "I told Jose' I wanted a Checker cab last week. So he gives me the one he just finished a front brake job on. I'm into my second call and radio blasts – 'who I got in Caesar 8?.....Caesar 8....Caesar 8.' So I'm laughing, 'It's me Dan......Who the hell are you? Turn that Checker in you idiot and take a Ford. Who's driving #8?'

Dan Rodan, the dispatcher, sounded like he was in meltdown, and I'm busting a gut and so's the fare listening to all this.

"Ryan Whitelaw in #8.....new driver. Don't worry Dan, I know the city." I radioed back. "I started getting hyper with Rodan barking at me 'cause I had a couple of hits of reef."

The three of us were having a good laugh as the image came through.

I talked into the tall sugar jar with the metal spout: "Error Caesar 8 – Mistake – return to garage A.S.A.P." Rodan says.

Loki shook his head smiling, "The only time we get assigned a Checker is when......well never."

"I made $30/a night, the first five times I drove. As the weather got colder, the more money I booked." Vince said.

Caesar had about 20-25 Taxis, eight of which were Checkers. The rest were Ford LTD's. They all had medallions with meters. A driver could sit and wait for a radio call, or roam the streets looking to be hailed. Loki turned me and Vinny on to one of his tricks: He'd walk into an upscale gin mill and call out: "Who called a cab?" It worked best when it was getting near closing; half the time you'd pull out a fare though no one had actually called. Sometimes the bar's patrons would fight over the cab and other times you might be able to double them up and not log either into your daily total.

Caesar Moreno also had four LTD's with Livery plates; if a driver with a hack license got stuck with one of them, he was at the mercy of the dispatcher. By law they couldn't be hailed from the street. Caesar was always looking to buy more medallions from other companies or independents. He'd run the Livery cars in the first week of every month and during the stretch between Thanksgiving and New Years.

The three of us would hang out over at 'Hooker Park' at the bottom of Larkin Plaza, across the street from Yonkers Station. When the action was slow we called it 'Parkin' Plaza'. The rename caught on with all the cabbies. After WWII, the city made it into a huge parking lot with approximately 225 parking meters making money for the city. The Plaza went from the railroad station all the way up to Warburton

556

Ave. It was a collection and drop-off point for the hookers, winos, down and outers, and transients. It was a good place to dead head and watch the show during slow summer nights.

There was a jurisdictional matter coming to a boil, in the sex trade. The real hookers were pissed off; the she-males had moved in on their territory. The guy-girls were getting paid for something they liked to do; whereas for most of the working girls - it was something they had to do. After a bunch of cat fights, the cops resolved the issue giving ¾'s of Hooker Park's sidewalk to the girls and the other ¼ to the guy-girls. Officially, the bluecoats disavowed any knowledge of the arbitration. It was one of the few smart things the Yonkers' P.D. did.

There never seemed to be much taxi action down the train station.

viii

McGovern was running against Nixon in 1972. Everyone knew the ground war was over. The last of the ground troops had left in the summer. Only advisors, intelligence, transition, medical, and support troops remained, and their number decreased every month. We all prayed Ray could stay out of harm's way. The ground war for the United States seemed to be over, but the Air Force and the Navy were the busiest they had been during the conflict. Nixon gave the North the ultimatum: "Come back to the negotiating table or we'll bomb you back into the stone age".

'Tricky Dick' was bringing his campaign for another term to the N.Y. metro area. The Nixon and Governor Nelson Rockefeller motorcade went through Westchester which included Yonkers. They came through Yonkers from the north on Broadway. It was 50 degrees with a breeze.....plenty cold for October. Holter, Bad Brad, Jimmy Martin, and me were in front of Untermyer Park waiting for the procession. We bought some port wine to keep the chill off and get the glow. Broadway hadn't been closed off to traffic yet. Danny Stax was driving north, he spotted us and made an illegal U-turn and parked his Chevy II.

Foot cops were sporadically placed along the route; they guarded the President and Governor and other politicos who followed. Stax had Nixon bumper stickers on the Chevy II, and he was wearing his dress green marine jacket, with his corporal stripes, so the cops gave him a warning ticket for the U-turn.

We all talked about, Nixon, Johnson, and McGovern and figured them all to be shitheads. Martin said they were all a bunch of no-count M.F.'s. Brad was surprised, and said Jimmy should like McGovern because he was Irish like him.

"McGovern ain't Irish – he ain't even Catlick. That crackerjack is just an Orangeman from the North. Fuck them Tommie loving snakes."

"Stax – you're Irish, how say you on McGovern?"

"Anybody hear about Sally Englund?" Danny Stax asked.

We all knew the next thing coming out of his mouth had a 99% chance of being bad news. I took a long drink from the fortified wine and waited for the punch line.

"She didn't find a suitcase full of hundreds." Brad said.

A worried face came over Stax as he looked north for the President's limo. "They found her in a drug house off Jerome Ave. in the Bronx.....a couple of days ago." His eyes darted back and forth; "be in tonight's paper. The Bronx Medical Examiner didn't release the body until today. Whitelaw – where's your brother?"

"Wow." I shook my head rapidly like I was trying to shakeoff a horsefly.

"Unfuckinbelievable." Holter looked at some fallen leaves in the gutter.

Jimmy Martin bit into his lower lip: "Must have been some good dooge."

"She was getting real strung out. I took her down to Lawrence Street and the Bronx to cop." Stax looked out into the nothingness.

"She could have been a model." Brad turned to me, "Where's your brother?"

I leap-frogged Brad's inquiry, "Wells was with her a couple of weeks ago. Sally wanted her to take a ride downtown with her and Wayne-O. Barb told her she had stuff to do. Later on she said Sally had been in orbit for most of the summer: writing rubber checks, shoplifting, stealing money off the bar. She even started turning tricks in cars down by Van Cortland Park at the Terminal Bar, Wells said. She figured Sally would be in jail, in rehab, or in the morgue before the end of the summer. Her timetable was a little off."

"I heard the same shit. Stax – you hear anything about the wake?" Holter said.

His head went from side to side a couple of times.

"Maybe in tonight's paper." I said.

"Gonna be a lot of wind chimed junkies at this wake." Jimmy scoffed.

"You're going?" Brad asked Holter.

"I got to go; she was the sixth girl I ever fucked – I have to say Good-bye and thank her. You know the wakes you got to attend." George took a sip of wine.

"Word to the wise.....the bulls will be there in plainclothes in the funeral home and the parking lot. I recommend sunglasses...... fuckin' Whiteoak – she was almost your sister- in-law." Martini said.

"Yeah, it was one of those things; I knew her, but I didn't."

"What the fuck does that mean?" Brad gave me a sour look.

"I dunno." I struck a match and lit a camel. Only a small circle knew Ray was in Nam. Everyone else was mystified when I told 'em Ray might not be able to attend her services. "He's in Indiana, they hadn't seen each other all summer." was the best I could do for his unexplained absence. Most people didn't even know he was missing for the last 10 months. The longer a person is off the radar screen, the more likely they'll be forgotten.

HOLTER CRANED HIS NECK: "TRICKY DICK AND ROCKY must be getting close."

Five black armored trucks drove south; one in the lead and the others - two abreast scoping out people who lined the parade route. Different varieties of police vehicles and motorcycles were coming down and then circled back up Broadway with their red lights flashing and siren bursts. The Secret Service didn't want another L.H.O. taking potshots at Nixon and Rocky.

"You better call your brother about Sally." Martinique acted like he had some vested interest in Ray's presence at her wake.

"I talked to him two months ago – nothing since." I said.

"Don't you think he should be there at the wake? He went out with her for a couple of years." Martin kept harping.

"Listen Jimmy, you ask Ray or the girl in the box....it's been over for 10 months – whatdya want from me? Just make sure you're there, that's all you should be worrying about." I got up on the wall in front of the park and pretended to be occupied looking for Nixon & co.

I killed the pint of Port. The motorcade was within sight coming down a hill.........then up another on Broadway. There were some St. John's Riverside Hospital people and workers who came to the street to wave. The politicians would be upon us in 10 seconds.

Stax laughed, "He's not even standing through the hole in the roof."

"Well, fuck me runnin." George flipped him the bird.

As they were in range for us to read the license plate, we held up our wine bottles and gave the Presidential car the clenched fist salute – except for Bad Brad who was living up to his name. He dropped his jeans and his underwear and gave them the 'Guzzutti Moon'.

That Brad had the hairiest ass I ever seen – Neanderthal stuff. No wonder he was never cold in the winter.

We went down the North End after Nixon and Rockefeller drove out of sight. Copie's' was pretty full. The beer bar only had two months left before it was closing – for good. There were a lot more people there than I anticipated, some talked politics, but the buzz was mostly all about Sally. I saw Loki, Jimmy Blanko, and John Dunbar. Stax brought back a pitcher of Schaefer in each hand. Brad got the plastic cups from Fran. The Rogues all knew Blanko and Dunbar. We talked about what a jag Nixon was; McGovern didn't have any cheerleaders either.

Dunbar asked me, "What the hell's wrong with your brother?"

"What are you talking about?"

"I heard he was over in Vietnam......he joined the Army?"

I turned to Loki......."Thanks a lot." Now that the word was out; I could expect to hear about it until he returned.

"He went over there for a reason – I don't know the whole story, but it was something about paying your dues like the guys who got drafted, but it was especially to do with the guys who didn't come back. Ray didn't believe they were suckers and neither do I." I said.

"You sure there's no desire for a taste of war mongering?" Dunbar wondered aloud.

"Tell you what John......you go tell Joe Griffin, Jimmy DiSantini, Chris Harding, Ronnie Zanzibar, Ronny Crestwood, Billy Van Nahl, Ranger Rick, and Eddie Van Trex that they're all chumps for having served in Nam. You tell 'em. You tell 'em to their face they're all war mongers. I'm not talking about this war being right or wrong – I'm talking about putting it all on the line.....and they did. That's all I got to say to you." I stormed out.

The Englund family waked Sally for two nights. It was bad, at least Barb was with me. A lot of people who knew Ray, came and talked to me. I was his stand-in by default. He was the last official boyfriend she had. The questions followed: "Where's your brother? ....What's he up to? With the word out, there was no reason to cover for him any longer. When I told them he was in Vietnam, the more astute grievers commented something about "they certainly were on divergent paths."

Others held on to hopes and visions, "I always thought they would end up together." On and on for two nights you heard about shattered dreams.

Karyn Cahill had found out Sally and Ray had been sweethearts. I had spoken to her very seldom about him except he was attending Purdue, which at the time was no longer the case since the first day we met. Neither had I gone into much about my family except for Uncle Harry who I really only met this year, and now I knew my mother's uncle better than I knew his brother, my grandfather.

Perhaps a girlfriend of Karyn's knew the story and passed it on to her. I really didn't care how she made the connection between me and Sally Englund; here she was with a friend of hers at the wake. At the time, I considered it a thoughtful gesture towards Ray. Karyn had seen me with Barb Wells after work doing our thing. She'd mention Barb occasionally when we'd have lunch together. I hadn't had any physical interaction with Karyn, so I was clean.

If things started getting inter-stellar with the two of them when I made the introductions, I'd just have to leave. This was no place for that nonsense. They were cordial to one another. Barb had the largesse to go over and talk to Holter, Vinny, and Reno and leave me and Karyn alone for a few minutes.

She said she couldn't stay long; Karyn just wanted to let me know she was thinking of me.

It was more like a cocktail party than a wake. For many in the same age bracket as Sally; this was their first big bereavement. We went to our cars or friends' cars and tried to find solace by having a few shots of whiskey and smoking some reefer. After the initial viewing, you needed something to deaden your senses to be able to go back in. There were three or four outbursts of young women outside the room where Sally was laid out.

Cahill surveyed the mourners – it ran the gamut. "My God.... The layers of the cake vary quite a bit."

560

"Well, some are born great." I quoted.

"Others achieve greatness." she responded.

"While others have greatness thrust upon them." we said in unison.

"There is no greatness here…..only sadness." she said.

"I 'spose." I embraced her and gave her one on the cheek. The two women eyeballed each other until Karyn left. It was innocent, and Wire didn't question me about her.

As Barb's hair grew back, it seemed the cats moved back as well…..just not as many and no bobcat. Marge Wells invited me in whenever I went to the door, but I wasn't at that point where I was ready for another venture to the other side of the threshold. I asked her again to keep it short – no more than two inches in length. I didn't care about the color.

ix

Thanksgiving, Christmas, and New Year's were a blur at the end of '72. There was a little less Sally every day; most had gotten over her departure, but a few of her friends weren't about to let go, they were going to bring Sally into the holidays. You always thought it was going to be somebody else, not many can ever see themselves in the box.

We were kind of having a good time that holiday season. Although I wasn't logging the hours with Caesar I wanted; when I worked my three nights a week, I was making pretty good money - $45/night. She would ride around with me and we'd smoke pot and hit a strange bar here and there. When there was some dead heading, that Superstar Barb started right in taking care of me – she was aces. I never had to ask and I did the same for her.

What she was doing for money was a mystery to me. It was a good bet it involved getting drugs to the clients, or the clients to the drugs. She liked being called a 'Purveyor'……. thought the job title gave her dignity.

"Wire……you got to be real slick - even with the pot, especially if you're carrying weight. I don't have a bankroll for bail." She knew how I felt about her, losing her would crush me.

After enough pressure from Jane, I brought Barb over to 21 O'Dell the weekend before Thanksgiving. She invited her over to have the Holiday dinner with us.

Wells explained to Jane she couldn't commit right now; her mother might need a hand with their dinner.

"Let Ryan know by Tuesday before noon in case we need a bigger turkey or bigger side dishes."

"Are you kidding me?" Hal busted in. "The girl's a waif….she might weigh a 100 lbs. soaking wet. Listen cutie, we'd love to have you for dinner."

"Mrs. Whitelaw…..I'll let Ryan know."

"Just call me Jane – everybody does." Jane watched Hal push away his plate. He went to the kitchen counter and made a whiskey

561

soda. In between pouring shots, he stopped and called into the dining room.

"You got a last name?"

Barb raised her brow......"Wells."

"That could mean anything." he finished making his drink.

"It's an American derivative."

"I guess that'll have to do." He took his drink to his den.

Jane rolled her eyes and I shrugged my shoulders. 'I got to get out of this house.' I said to myself. Barb said she'd give it a try for Thanksgiving. After clearing the table, doing the dishes, and letting the pots and pans soak, we sat in the breakfast nook having coffee, just me and her.

"If things start getting stupid, you got to get us away from our parents. They're driving us both nuts." she said.

"We got to find some real jobs and make some money." I answered.

There was about two hours to kill before I had go in and drive for Caesar, and there was just a little sunlight remaining. We walked down to Greystone. Most of the trees were bare and the Hudson was muddy.

"The last time I was here in the overpass, in the daylight was for Ranger Rick's party. Can't be two years ago already?" She laughed.

"'Bout 20 months ago. C'mon." I took her by the hand to the top of the buried cast-off chunk of comet. "Sit down."

"Why does it stay warm here?" She had forgotten.

"How 'bout this – we get some scrap wood, tar paper and a Coleman Lantern and make this our winter hibernation hideout?" I smiled.

"What about food, water, bathroom, the stuff you have to have to live. We can't go camping down here for months on end without someone messing with us." She lit a cigarette.

I lay in the sand. If the mound was cooking, a person could take a dry sauna. The cast-off had me thinking in high gear. 'Man.....as long as this projectile didn't revert back into the heavy mode which kept me and Ray from transporting it, I could travel around with the cosmic intruder in the back seat of the Starfire. With the sand as warm as it was, travelling around with it might be problematic. I'd have to wait for Ray to return and figure out how to do it.' I stared off at the Tappan Zee Bridge.

"Hey......Hey Groover..." Barb called. "Come back Quasar. You think this piece of 8'x8' mound with a sandy top is warm and soft enough to support life in the Spring-Summer-Fall?" she scoffed at the idea.

"I'm telling you, it is what will be."

"Yeah?.....when?" she said.

"Don't know, could be happening right now in slow motion."

"Break out the psychedelics." Wire laughed.

"You'll see. We'll never be cold again." I turned to her, "Hear anything else about Englund?"

"Not about who she went down there with......just that there was some monster stuff down there. A little bit of it made it up here. It's up on Park Hill – they want mucho Montezuma for it. Heard Sally got off first, and Cocaine Wayne only did half his hit. Somebody in Bronxville or Scarsdale O.D.'d and lived. I already heard the bullshit this is the last of The French Connection property room shit. Like to see what that's all about." her eyes dazzled.

"Watch yourself Wells, you don't get no second chance with dope."

I wondered how the fuck could that shit still be making it on the street for yet another encore 10 years later and still retain the potency to be knocking off people like they were bowling pins. The older junkies went through the history: the first appearance came in 1965, but the cops didn't believe the smack killing everybody back then was the medicine from Marseille. In '67, with the help of the feds, they broke the case, but they left the other 2/3rds in the evidence lock up because of appeals. In 1968, they did it again with the old switcheroo: take out smack - bring back baby laxative. In '72 the unthinkable occurred yet again. When the Junkies started dropping like flies, the more experienced detectives checked the remainder of the French Connection evidence. It only took three months to arrest the bad cops, but Sally Englund and Jay Swanson were already gone. You couldn't make it up.

HOW COULD I BE 18 AND 3 MONTHS OLD AND ALREADY

feel things were so out of reach? Sporadic employment...lack of direction and focus...distractions...bad influences...all of the above were obstacles. More than any of these deficits, there was just too little Ray and it was becoming more obvious in all facets of my life. It was not enough knowing if he was alive; I needed him to tell me what to do. I was desperate for his hands-on direction and guidance; I needed a steady job, a career, trade, a profession. It wasn't happening in Yonkers. I didn't have any connections – I didn't know anybody to help me get to first base. I couldn't even say how Barb was part of this equation. He could have solved it all.

On this side of the globe, I waited for Ray's call for my cache of charged ash. Was this the polemic rift – the magnetic divide permitting him to exist free of a collapsing universe or the opening up of an adjacent dimension similar to mine? That he might solve the Greystone Equation by moving our caches to a point on the other side of the planet to balance its polemic magnetic harmonics......only a brain as lazy as mine could buy into such a scenario. He should have told me he was enlisting; I would have had my name right next to his in a heartbeat.

X

In between Christmas and New Years, Hal went into Otis Elevator for an abbreviated week, while Jane's dance studio schedule mirrored the public and Catholic schools. She might have taken Cathy and Brother Bill to Manhattan to see the Christmas tree at Rockefeller Center and make the annual pilgrimage to Radio City, to relive her dream of being a Rockette. Jane's friend, Dottie, was finally swept off her feet by some corporate lawyer three years earlier and had gotten married.

I never told Jane I had seen Dottie at the Hudson River Golf Course in '68, I wasn't sure how she would have taken it. Jane was at the balance point; she wasn't going to have the level of achievement in her career or personal life she had envisioned 20 years earlier. There were daily skirmishes between her and Hal where they fought over the same 4 inches of quicksand. Now her success lay with what her children might accomplish.

There wasn't any note where the three of them went. They may have taken the Mercury upstate to visit Mom-Mom and Mack. Frozen lasagna in glass cookware rested on top of the stove. She must have left it out for Hal. The doorbell rang.

Another bite from the p.b.&j. sandwich, and I got up to answer the door. From the foyer, I peered through the two half-glass entry doors to the small porch. Each door had a whispy curtain hanging from its interior side making it difficult to see in or out. I could only see a silhouette. Shoeless and disheveled, I went into the small entrance hall between the two doors; the outline of the bell ringer was obvious and my heart began to pound and pound and pound. The image on the other side of the entrance door may as well been wearing the black hood and robe of Ebenezer Scrooge's third ghost toting his scythe. I knew what servicemen dressed in uniform meant: my heart raced and pounded, my eyes bulged out. I yanked my two shirts up and watched my heart push my breastbone forward with every beat. I grasped the door's knob and saw an army soldier. He was in uniform – but it wasn't dress uniform. He had the overcoat, dress green shirt and tie, trousers with the thin stripe, and the hat that lays flat on the table. He was alone. Frantic to unlock the door and get this mystery resolved, the curtain was pulled to one side and I saw the soldier clearly now. Our eyes met; in the grips of fear, I struggled with the lock. Pure panic had switched every function of my body to an involuntary mode. My eyeballs were as big as plates, and I panted as hard as a 300 lb. man completing a marathon. Finally I unlocked the door and stepped out into the cold.

I looked at the soldier as an agent of the 'Grim Reaper': "DON'T SAY IT......DON'T FUCKIN SAY IT!" My arm extended and I pointed at him: "DON'T YOU SAY IT!......DON'T!"

"Mr. Whitelaw.....Mr. Whitelaw.....Ryan...Ryan....Ray's okay – he is OK.- He is Okay. He's fine. I'm sorry....I'm sorry. I was with him three days ago – YOUR BROTHER IS OK." The soldier said.

I turned to rubber; unable to stand, I sat down on the short semi-circle brick patio. I was still panting; my blood pressure was off the scale.

"For the love of fuck man......I thought you were going to lay the big one on me. Fuck man. You'da kilt my Mom for sure – maybe my Pa too." I got down on my knees and prayed three Hail

564

Mary's and continued: "Lord, please protect my brother Raymond and keep him from harm" I looked up to the soldier who had held his hands over my head – blessing me as I prayed. "Amigo – you can't go around doing that shit to people."

"I couldn't risk a phone call. Figured when you saw that I was black – that'd be enough for you to know I wasn't visiting you on behalf of the President. Would you mind if we get out of the cold?" he asked as he looked around.

"No, I can't let you in man.....the neighbors."

"Huh?"

"Just messing with you." I laughed.

He laughed too. "Always stickin' it to the brothers. That's the same shit Ray would go with. He's good people though – he's real and tough."

"You mean he's real tough?" we laughed some more. I tried to read his name plate under his unbuttoned overcoat. "What's your name?" I said.

He stood at attention and saluted: "Private first class, Isaac Seabrook.....sir." He extended his hand and we shook.

"Let's get the hell out of this cold." I showed him in.

He had a mini-duffle bag in his left hand and spoke lowly: "Are we the only ones here?"

I watched him as he listened for sound.

"The rest of the family are gone 'til five o'clock."

"Is there somewhere we can do business?" Isaac nodded at me.

"What kind?"

"I got something from Ray for you, I don't want it any longer than is necessary. Take a look at this."

I showed him into the breakfast nook. "How's Ray.....what's he up to?"

"Never mind that shit; take a look at this – you tell me how he's doin'?" Isaac started to open the mini-duffle; it kind of looked like a gym bag with a heavy brass zipper down the middle.

"Say – what is your brother, some kind of clairvoyant, mystic, genius,.......a prophet?"

"We were raised together; we're full-blood brothers. Up until high school we were inseparable. I may not have known what he was thinking, but he knew every move I made before I made it. You want any coffee man?" I pointed to him.

"If it ain't too much trouble." he said.

I talked from the kitchen. "What, are you in the same company or however they divide you guys up?"

"When he first arrived, we were part of the Army Airborne - 525th – Intelligence. After the 2nd month there, with all the commands dismantling – he got kicked upstairs. He knew a lot when he got there. Wherever he was before the Army – he had skills the brass was looking for."

"He was hot to see action when he first got there – hoped to be sent to the jungle or mountains – somewhere combat was still going on. Sometimes you can't figure people out, I didn't know what he had in his mind." Seabrook said.

I walked in with a four cup percolator and two cups, """Want any milk or sugar?"

He smiled wide: "Black is beautiful."

"We'll see." I smiled back.

"Let's just say green is beautiful." He placed the small duffle bag on the table. He opened the duffle's brass zipper: all I could smell was that Hai-Karate cologne. Isaac looked at me watching him: "No one's home?" he asked again.

"No. It's just you and me."

He opened what looked like butcher paper wrapping a rolled pork roast. There were further layers of Saran wrapping the contents which had been sealed. Through the plastic, I could see some Asian script with a brand of a tiger, an indistinguishable flag with an imprint of the Ankor Wat Temple. Next to the temple was stamped with a fire brand: 1.5 kg. I picked it up, it was at least three pounds near as I could tell.

"What's this all about?" The smell was real strong, and cancelled out the cologne.

"A little over 3 pounds of black tar.......opium." Isaac was all business.

"What am I getting into?"

He handed me an envelope with a wax seal. I topped off our coffee and opened the envelope. I began to read the correspondence and stopped and went to his signature at the bottom. As much as it had evolved, I knew it to be his.

Dec. 14th, 1972

Ryan:

I can't see my tour here lasting the entire year unless it is with or thru the C.I.A. Pretty confident that will not happen. The situation here is very fluid. The Package: I did a favor for one of the Montagnard hamlet chiefs/leaders, and what Isaac has brought you was his way of saying "Thank You". Isaac knows the story and what the package is. I am paying him (thru you) two thousand large ($2,000.00) for his courier services. Isaac is real – but drugs do funny things to lifelong friends, and I've only known Isaac for 6 months.

Some people get greedy, addicted, overwhelmed, or paranoid/manic. They start looking at the chest of gold too long, and they go nuts. Recommendation: Weigh the stuff with Isaac – make sure we got what's stamped. Smoke a little with him, and ask him if you can pay him in product; otherwise you'll have to sell some or BORROW the two G's to pay him. I would have paid him here but we don't have cash. Isaac has delivered near $80,000 worth of 'Tiger Tar' opium. Don't let anyone know about it.

DO NOT make a project of this Ryan – If he wants cash, try to accommodate him, and do it the day he show's up. Don't screw around…you only want to see him the one time. He lives in Jersey City.

There's a lot of weight there. You are going to have to use all the street savvy you got to move it and keep it off the cops' radar. At first I had the notion to have the 5th dimension use this black tar as a substitute for smack. I thought about it some more and realized it would only be a band aid, or they'd smoke it until it was gone…..then what? That is a question to be answered later when I'm back.

Could be a megatron payday for us both. Be kool brother…….be kool.

Ray

P.S. Send your Intruder ash back with Isaac - He's only in the states for 10 days for his grandmother's funeral who raised him.

I left Isaac in the breakfast nook, and went upstairs and got the remainder of the interstellar cinders. I couldn't do anything with the stuff except watch it react with magnetism. I remember I had tried to use it as a force field without success. Down in the cellar I looked for any more of Hal's olive jars for Isaac's return to Vietnam. I started marking them for Ray.

"Got to make a couple of phone calls." I told him. He got up and went to the can. There was no answer at Cinzano's house. I wanted to pay Isaac in product, but I didn't know what 2000 dollars of the stuff looked like. I thought it would be easier to pay him in cash. Two phone calls; two no answers. "Isaac – getting your money may be somewhat problematic."

"No money – no shit. This is gonna sound cold, I know your brother, I don't know you. You get the stuff when I get my 2 G's. That's it." he said.

Two thousand dollars was just the courier fee. The value of this opium – I didn't know if Ray's appraisal was on the street or wholesale valuation. It may have been a number he was given by the tribal chief.

It was cold enough for the Olds to stall out twice. We pulled into Associated grocers parking lot. I asked one of the check out ladies behind a register: "Is Vinny around?"

"In the back checking in produce."

"Can we go back and see him?"

She looked at me and Seabrook, "Go around to the truck dock."

"We'll just be a couple of minutes." I nodded.

"Hurry it up though, or come back when he's on break."

I saw him on the loading dock, "Vinny......."

"Gimme a minute." We waited as he counted some boxes of fruit and signed for them for a trucker. "What's up?"

"What's the best way to weigh this thing?"

"Give it here – we'll put it on the hook scale ."

We watched the big dial. "Little over 3 and a quarter; that includes the weight of the bag and what's inside." Vinny said.

"Divide that by 2.2" I asked.

The pencil came off his ear and he performed the division on the top of a box of tomatoes: "You got real close to a kilo and a half of something."

"Weigh it without the bag."

"Three and a quarter lbs. is real close." Vince said. "It's a few milligrams shy of a key and a half."

Breaking this brick down into pieces was nuts. It was going to be much simpler giving Seabrook cash. He was right 'green was beautiful'.

"I need a banker Tarts – no questions asked."

"How much?"

" Two....large."

"One of the Huns or Shooey. They buy and sell cars everyday. They'll write it up that you purchased a car on credit."

"Shooey carries at least that - on him all the time. The Huns got that kind of money, but they'll want to know what they're bank rollin'. Try Shooey first, - he's got that two car garage behind the old Amakassin club."

"Thanks Vince."

"Metrics always mean trouble.......watchit Whitecloud."

"Whiteshark." – Shooey looked up from the 302 cu. in. engine he was rebuilding. "Just in time. Give me a hand laying this crank in the case. Don't want to pinch my fingers or nick the case or the crank." Tenderly, we lay the crankshaft in the half case from each end. He wiped his hands of the light film of oil from the crank and threw me the rag.

"Who's the Soul Brother?" Shooey's back was to Isaac.

"Friend of Ray's."

"Is he over in 'Nam?"

"Yeah. My head motioned over to Isaac, "He's here on a bereavement furlough, he's got to go back in about a week."

"What's our business?"

"Need a loan." I said.

568

"How much?"

"Two grand."

"Sign a marker @ 10% with a payback in 30 days?"

"Draw up the note." I said.

He was done in about 5 minutes. He did it on a used car sales sheet making it look like a loan to buy a car instead of a straight loan. The Franklin's were laid out and numbered in ink 1 through 20. "How's the Starfire running?" He signed his name: Drew Saxon, and I signed mine.

My face soured, and my head went from side to side: "I wish I had a manual choke."

"Too many idiots driving cars – they don't even know what a choke is or what it does. Hey Soul Brother – you know what a choke is for?"

"To kill Charlie." It was unexpected and we all laughed. Shooey and me laughed harder than Isaac.

"If you got a good feel for cars – manual choke's are the way to go. Hey Whiteloanshark, you better get going…..the clock is ticking on your note."

"Thanks Shoo."

"Thank me in 30 days – hey, tell Ray to keep his head down." he told Isaac.

"You can't hear that enough – I'll tell him." Seabrook said.

Isaac and me drove back to 21. It was 1:30 "Isaac, what's the deal with this black tar….you don't roll it into a joint?" I asked.

He let out a soft chuckle, "This is pipe shit. This shit has just been made, still green….sticky. You form it into a small ball at the end of a steel wire……then get a piece of paper and make it into a tight cone…… light it up and draw in the smoke with the cone. Got a piece of steel wire and sheet of typing paper? I guess a bong pipe will work, but it's way too strong that way, and it gets clogged from the resin. It'll lay you out brother."

I pinched some off the pork roll; it was sticky and had that unique odor; I formed a ball at the end of a piece malleable wire. "Don't need that much." Seabrook's eyes focused on the amount.

I made the necessary adjustment, "That's about right." he said. "Use the paper for the draw, in Nam we put the ball in the breech of a shotgun and use the barrel for the draw – Dude….it'll put you on a magic carpet ride."

We had the production all set up, and brought it out to the small porch and steps which faced the woods. It was calm and I lit the opium ball until the resin was aglow. "Remember… just a few half-pulls."

"Right." I figured the high couldn't be much different than smoking smack with Barb. Although, the one was powder and the other was like a wet gum.

He blew the flame out on the tar and watched the smoke and took only what he advised me to take. He drew in a lot bigger toke than I did. Isaac started to get wobbly and looked off into the woods as if something or somebody was there. That was good enough for me;

Seabrook was out there – way out. I couldn't think about driving doing this stuff. Ray said he lived in Jersey City and to get him there at the conclusion of business. This guy was incapable of walking. I was jammed as well, but I could walk. I began to worry Isaac wouldn't be able to make it to the car before Hal returned from work. I put the mini-duffle in the old coal room where I still had the rest of the blockbusters.

A half hour later he was communicative, but not a whole bunch. "Isaac how are you getting back to Jersey city?"

Things had to be repeated three and four times before I got acknowledgement. He was so far away, I couldn't see him with a pair of binoculars. Being in the war zone, there weren't any shifts of duty…..even when you were off – you were on. The NVA and Viet Cong attacked when the mood struck them or when they got the command. If a guy was in the middle of an opium excursion – too bad. No wonder Ray got rid of this shit. Stateside or in country…..it was a health hazard. It wasn't the way to stay alive; without transmutation and being integrated in the allegory world of an opium soldier – staying alive in the bush or jungle was tentative at best.

This drug was not going to let me drive the Starfire. For Seabrook, the drug was the vehicle and he was taking a trip. He had asked to be driven to the terminus of the subway at 242nd St., just before he went back into his stupor.

All I had to do was get on Broadway at O'Dell and take it south to the Bronx and I'd end up at 242nd St., but somehow I had gotten lost, I had done the impossible. A half-hour ride had taken three hours. Parking on the west side of Van Cortland Park, I checked out my passenger; "Isaac….Isaac…"
I shook his shoulders. "C'mon dude….you're here." He still couldn't cross the street on his own. My hand went to my chin – I knew I was screwed up, Isaac also had to deal with the knowledge that the only parent he had known was gone while he was on the other side of the world. I couldn't blame him for red lining it. I just wish he wasn't my responsibility. It really didn't matter, I couldn't have driven for Caesar tonight anyway, I was under the influence of the narcotic. I was lucky I wasn't pulled over.

'No way.' I thought, I couldn't let my brother's friend loose in the city like this with two grand. "Ain't this a bitch." I said to Isaac who never heard me. "You and me are Buddies tonight, until you get back on terra firma."
I got all of his grip together: the money, the comet ash, his personal stuff, and held on to them until he was really ready to depart. We drove around the Bronx for a while; we ended up at a double-feature: "Aguirre – The Wrath of God" and "Pink Flamingos" at a theatre on Fordham Rd. Before we went in, I stopped at the liquor store and got two pints of Thunderbird, and a bottle of Yoo-Hoo chocolate drink for Seabrook. These kind of flicks should be right in his wheelhouse in his current state of consciousness I thought.

12:30 am, the movie let out. We sat in the car as it warmed up. Often a cop would see the smoke coming from the tailpipe of a parked car in winter and give the occupants a roust. A Spade and a

Honkie usually meant drugs. To make the scene complete, I think I even fell asleep, but no cops ever stopped. The most probable reason we didn't get checked out was because we were clean, but either of us would have to come up with a good line for holding the 2 G's.

The clock at the gas station off the Major Deegan Expressway read 3:15 am.

"Ryan....let's get something to eat."

"Look who's back."

"Motherfuck....what a trip. Ain't done that much for 2 months....wow." he wooed and shook his head.

We drove back into Yonkers and had breakfast at the Broadway Diner. It was still dark, and the warmth of the restaurant almost put me to sleep. Coffee was pushed in front of us. "Isaac, I paid for the movies......You wanna catch breakfast?" My eyes were slits.

"I got it."

We put the menus back in their rack after she took our order. Seabrook played with a lighter, but didn't light his cigarette. "Your brother ever tell you what happened a couple of months ago at a café in Bien Hoa?"

"What did he do?......Start playing a piano and sing "As Time Goes By" to a girl in a Ao Dai outfit?" I grinned.

"No man, your brother's a real hero. Ray was having lunch at this small café with two S.Vietnamese Air Force pilots and a mechanic from Bien Hoa Air Base during the transitioning of Long Binh from the Army to the Army of the Republic of Vietnam. Ray's business had something to do with the Air Forces of both countries."

Three Viet Cong sprayed the patrons eating in the front of the café with automatic gunfire from a stolen car, and lobbed a fragmentation grenade towards Ray and the Air Force people. Charlie wanted to get the pilots because they high value targets. A couple of civilians got hit, the American grenade bobbled to the middle of the concrete patio, the eight eyes saw Hades. The longest three seconds of their lives elapsed as one fell, one froze, a third prayed, and Ray smothered the grenade with his body."

I was dumbstruck and dropped my fork into my plate of pancakes. A drape of disbelief descended upon my face. "But .....but.....but.....Ray....You said he was alright!" my voice crescendoed. The people two booths away looked at us.

"Calm down.....calm down man." he said. "He is okay.... he's fine. The grenade was defective - a fuckin' dud."

I read the disbelief of Ray's incredible luck in Isaac's face. There was a possibility Ray had wielded some magnetic force to counteract the grenade's explosive power or may have prevented detonation.

"Holy shit – I need some coffee to wash down that number." I took a deep breath.

"Ryan, in my book, your brother's a hero, but in the record book it ends up being......'If a tree falls in the middle of the forest – does anybody hear it?' It's one of them deals."

571

After breakfast, I drove Isaac back down to the subway station in the Bronx. It was just getting light.

"I got to take the subway to the World Trade Center and catch the PATH train to Jersey." he said.

I gave him a plastic orange pharmacy bottle with the 2 G's in it. Also, I gave him two olive bottles with the ash Ray requested, now I had none. I wrote his name on the two olive jars: E-4 Spc.- Raymond Whitelaw *DO NOT OPEN*
EXPERIMENTAL MATERIAL.

The joking and well wishing were over, and Isaac's level of intensity grabbed my attention: "Be careful brother – that shit from Ray will put your lights out permanent. You got to respect its power. You ain't asking me; but you can mess a lot of people up.....and yourself with this monster."

Where he went last night in his opium travels was up for conjecture, but he went somewhere that scared him for part of his mind excursion, and it was most likely why he gave me the stern warning.

"Isaac, when you see Ray – tell him.....tell him.....tell –"
The words would not come out as tears ran down my cheeks.

"How 'bout this – how 'bout I tell him you love him." He smiled.

"Yeah....can you do that for me?"

"You got it Whitesmoke."

I shuddered trying to get my breathing back to my normal pattern. "You alright man?"

"I'm good." he replied.

"Adios Muchacho." I waved as he ran up the subway's steps.

Isaac reached the first landing turned at attention and saluted. I never saw him again.

CHAPTER 19

i

A week had transpired since Isaac Seabrook's visit. Getting the $2200 together for Shooey was jammin' me with a non-stop headache. This opium from Ray didn't have to be smoked to cause problems. The temptation to start moving the tar on the street seemed to be the easy way to make some quick money; paying back Shooey, and getting my mind back on track. It didn't take long to realize 'Quick Money' in the drug business usually came with problems - getting ripped off, making mistakes leading to problems with the cops, and the clients O.D.ing. The money I had made driving for Caesar over the Holidays would cover the interest payment, with a little left over. I was still only driving three nights a week, simply because of the abundance of drivers. Joe Rodan let me do a double-shift once – it was only because Roy-Boy Haynes got kidney stones.

Karen had sent me a Christmas card. It made me feel like a jerk; I never called her after our drink at the Central Paradise, or after Sally's wake. When I did call - I asked her to loan me $500. Before she said yes, she said she would have to see me before she'd loan me that kind of money.

If she did agree to loan me the cash, it was going to be with strings attached, I knew that. Until I needed something, I had stiff-armed her. If the situation had been reversed, I would not have loaned her the money. It was a clear cut case of exploitation. We agreed to meet again at the Central Paradise Bar. She was 20 minutes late, and I had enough time to beat myself up. I went to the bathroom and looked in the mirror. I sensed a Dorian Gray reflection staring at me: my skin color was off, my hair line had moved up a little, the bald area was the same, my eyes were bloodshot from the night before. More than anything else, I had to slow down the drinking and drugging. I should have gotten another buzz cut when Barb got hers.

Three days earlier, Barbara Wells and me took advantage of an empty 21 O'Dell on the stairway's new carpet. Sexed out, we brought our party down to the heated overpass around 2 pm.

"Alright.....they can piss up here when it was all open and had no heat; but why they got to piss here when it's cold and heated? – bunch a fuckin' animals." She lit a smoke.

"Barb, the Plexiglas is new – they took down the plywood which had Ray's magnetic/astrophysics equation when the Penn Central switched them out."

"The commuters also lost some sharp pornographic artwork by Ray, Holter, and some ex-con who signed his work: Headshot Harry. Your brother did all that alphabet math didn't he?"

"Pretty sure it's called Calculus. The artwork was pretty good."

"Watch for me, I'm cooking." She had her jacket off and her sleeve rolled up."

"All clear.....Do it." I continued to watch the station area.

"Oh fuck – this is going to be better than your dick."

"Impossible."

She booted it again….."Aw fuck." She whispered. "Fuckin' Whiteghost – you fuck me good." Barb went into a nod with her back against the web of the bridge's south girder.

I kept watching. "Wire." I volumed up, "Put that shit away – put your sunglasses on somebody's parking." She did what I told her, but in slow motion. "Where's my shit Wire?……the shit for me? …………..BARB!"

"In my pocket." she squealed back; her claws were out.

I looked at the parked car; nobody had gotten out. I loaded up a joint and took two hits on the landing outside the overpass on the riverside. My legs turned to rubber and I went back inside and sat next to her. I thought it'd be okay for five or ten minutes. I didn't like being with her when I had to worry. When I was high, I didn't want to think about anything but being warm and feeling invisible. Instead, I was always aware of the smack she still had on her and her tool kit. The point of getting that high was to forget everything, but I had to worry about her being dirty. I couldn't reach that alternate universe they way she could. It was getting stupid; Barb was now trying to get off whenever she felt like it. How we could be so lost in the drug's powerful grip, and never getting pinched by the bulls was just luck.

I couldn't see my life without that little troublemaker - whether I was high or straight. Looking in the bathroom mirror had me thinking: if there ever was a time to break away and straighten up - it was with this Cahill. What was the right move? Barb and me were on the same wavelength, I loved everything about her. She was a risk taker, and I liked that about her, but it was a drag worrying about her. Maybe she wasn't beautiful to most guys, but that worked out better for me; I didn't have to worry half as much because somebody was trying to steal her. I didn't want to change a single thing about her.

Everything was right and wrong at the same time. Breaking out and joining the rat race with Cahill? That didn't appeal to me at all, but she did. What was the right move? Karen didn't give me a whole bunch of attitude, and when she walked in the bar I could see she was disappointed and hurt. She took her coat off and sat on the stool next to me; her tentative smile greeted me. I gave her a hug and an air kiss on the cheek.

The bartender came over: "I'll have what he's having." she said.

"He's having a cup of coffee."

"I'll have a cup of coffee."

"The diner's across the street."

Karen smiled, "So it is. Thanks so much."

I helped her with her coat.

She ordered a grapefruit, whole wheat toast and a cup of coffee.

"A couple of eggs – over easy – white toast." I handed back the menu.

"No meat?" the waitress looked at another of her tables.

"I'm not a vegetarian. Just give me an orange and a glass of milk." I started on my quest for a healthier Ryan.

"Why are you asking me for money?"

"I know you got it, and you won't charge me interest."

"There's got to be something in it for me besides you walking away thinking: 'Gee, that Karyn Cahill is swell.' "

"What do you want?"

"At least treat me like I'm in the game….a call or a card would go a long way to making me feel I'm not being used."

"That's not a problem." I replied.

"And……you've got to take me out."

"Anything else?" Monetary or through my services - there was some kind of interest on this loan.

"Why is there anything else? Obviously, you are still going out with the alien."

"I am. If I wasn't, you would have had me knocking on your door last summer."

"That's what I need to hear."

"You're going back to Tibbetts this summer?" I drank some milk.

"Yes, as far as I know." Her face was concerned; "What are you doing now and why do you need the money?"

"Driving for Caesar 3 – 4 nights a week. A couple of friends are driving for him too."

"Hail Caesar!" Karyn fist pumped her heart and extended her arm forward with her palm down…..like in the newspaper ads and signs on top of his cars.

I imitated her salute in return with much less fervor: "Hail Caesar." I rolled my eyes.

"What else?"

"Doing work for a mafia construction front: Palamar Projects. It's real spotty – 2 days here….three days there. There's never more than six days a month……demolition… ….working concrete…mix mud for the bricklayers. How's school going?" I tried to get the spotlight off of me.

"Dean's list last semester." She beamed.

"You got a major?"

"Statistics."

"Kool." I had no idea what it meant. I was confident it didn't have anything to do with body counts in Vietnam.

"Want to come over? – nobody's home."

I didn't have the $500 yet: "Outtasight." I grinned.

As soon as she shut the door to her parents' shotgun apartment she was on me. It was 100% lust and passion. Karyn said she was on the pill and I lost my cherry to her. Two hours later we rewound the tape; I hadn't thought of Barb once.

"Listen Whiteryan – you call me about dinner and a movie." She shouted dropping my DNA into the toilet.

"What about the money?…..Get a piece of paper, I'll write you out my marker." I said.

She left the bathroom and came back with the money and pad and pen.

I started writing…..

575

"And sign it: with love, Whiteryan." She had some kind of power-play, chesire-chimera cat look on her face. It made me think something else was occurring, but I was unaware of what it was.

I handed her the instrument of my debt. "Now scadaddle before my mother gets home." We parted with a kiss.

Karyn was too good looking to have just paid for sex. Shit, I should have paid her. I knew I could love them both: Barb and Karyn. For sure, I did love Barbara. One was trouble; the other was a long term contract.

Loki was heading down to Miami pretty soon – maybe he had already left. Going down there without a word would be a vanishing act to rival Ray's jump from West Lafayette to Long Binh.

KARYN'S MONEY STILL LEFT ME WAY SHY OF THE CASH I needed to repay Shooey in a few days. I tore my brother's and my room apart. I thought for sure he had a wad stashed somewhere. No luck.......no alternative but to hit up Jane. Lying to her made me feel like the lowest of the low. I ended up telling her some bullshit about having to buy a used transmission but, "It's a $500 job........I'm getting Drew Saxon to do it." Good ol' Jane came through.

The rest of the money - $1000; There wasn't much choice – I had to tap the Rogues general fund. Only Vince knew it had something to do with what he had weighed for me several weeks earlier at Associated. Sometimes things happen opposite of what you anticipate. I didn't think I'd be able to get the rest of the money I needed from the Rogues, but I had to make the appeal.

Rexall knew I was good for the money, he was the one who lined me up with Palamar Projects. Rex gave me a deuce right on the spot – no questions. All he said was: "I want a note, and I want the money before Labor Day." Vinny had to go home and get me the cash.

"Just so you know, this was part of the money I was saving up for Zanzibar to start the bodywork on the Chevy." He laughed, "Stacey's just going to have to stay mad a little longer."

The Rogue's bankers made me draw up one super I.O.U. note:

Rex	Vinny	Crawfish	D. Stax	Fast Eddie	Holter
$200	$200	$200	$200	$100	$100

The $1000 dollars debt was to be retired by the Rexall date: Labor Day. As the money was repaid – the corresponding amount would be checked off and initialed. They made me keep the loan note in the glove compartment of the Starfire. All these guys now had real jobs with the exception of Vinny who had a work situation which was pretty similar to mine.

My immediate responsibility was to payoff Shooey $2200, and get rid of the interest payment. The financial world had my head spinning; a billboard said: 1973 Volkswagen – still $1999.00. I could trade in a charcoal briquette sized amount of the tar for a brand new car. What the fuck-hey?

"Whiteshark, what'd you get into with my money?" Shooey hooked up a timing light at the crankshaft. "Ryan shoot this light on those hash marks on the crank, I got to get the distributor to stay put before I tighten it down. Three degrees before top dead center."

"It's there Shooey....lock it in." I said.

"Sonofabitch I needed two hands with that fucker. You came along just at the right time dude." I handed him 22 one hundred dollar bills; he counted them in front of me on his workbench. I had numbered them - one through 22, just as he had done.

"Long story Shoo."

"Go ahead, I've got to find your marker." He tossed some papers around his work bench.

"Ran into this opium deal..............Shooey – this stays right here in your shop."

My eyes met his: "You paid me back - your information is safe." He handed me back a hundred. "Bring that much over." he said.

"I don't know how much that looks like."

"You're in business now, you'd better get a scale."

"This is how Isaac said to do it." We made it into a ball and put it at the end of a piece of tie wire. Without igniting the tar, I went through the steps I had taken with Isaac.

"No bong – no water pipe?" Shooey wondered.

"Isaac was just giving me an introductory course. I don't know much about the stuff except the Kubla Khan junk in English class. I don't know what a hundred dollar thing looks like or weighs." I said again.

"Take ten of them balls you made and bring them up – sound good?" Shooey raised his head.

"Be right back."

I wrapped ten sticky balls, the size of peas were individually wrapped in aluminum foil and brought over to Shooey. "You do this shit before?" I scratched my head.

"Yeah when my brother got back from Nam. This shit's addictive as water. You think you know what's going on with this dream machine, but it's the dragon calling the shots. That first go round – I was glad to run out."

"I'm going to tell you how it went down Ryan: Ray's got a connection for the tar. The colored soldier is Ray's mule. You're his distributor. The thing baffling me is how much weight he's gotten the courier to bring over. Read the papers – watch the news. South Vietnam won't be around very much longer. There's going to be a lot of contraband, currency, and gold coming back to the states packed away in equipment, vehicles, in canon shells, and all sorts of secret hideaways. The contraband will end up on the street. The precious stones and metals and currency will go straight to the top."

"The drugs manufactured from poppies - you got to watch that shit. It's easy to get hooked." His eyes let me know he meant business. "The dragon's got seven heads – they all bite; and they all say they're going to suck your one-eyed snake. Here's some free goddamn advice: if you're going to move it....don't use it. You'll end up in the big house, ripped off, or you'll O.D."

"This is what it is Whiteshark - once in a while I would go for the 'big ride'. It'll open doors to memories you never knew existed – memories of dreams and realities that haven't yet occurred. You'll wonder: how are you able to recall a dream which has yet to take form?"

"It is a solitary substance. You will always be alone and on your own in this Black Tar world; but you are so far away you don't care. You'll say 'fuck you' to everything. It's too much…..too big. I try to space out the times I go to the land of make believe. Otherwise, the continual use of the drug is drawing every bit of energy from you. You're worthless ……lost."

"Seems to be a real crowd pleaser. Shoo, I just did a little bit, I didn't get anywhere near the ride you're describing." I tried to focus.

"My brother Paul said people in East Asia would spike their chewing tobacco with just a little bit of opium. It was mostly the manual laborers doing this when they had to work in the brutal heat and humidity: digging ditches, unloading boats, being koolies for the military. It'd help them get through the day. That's kind of the way I use it….mostly. I put it in a container of Skoal and catch a buzz. The pains go away and I got a good energy level; no hunger, my mind is sharp, and I'm ready for my next project. This opium is one of the most insidious substances around. You can never think you can control it."

"Shoo…..this is just between you and me, and it's got to stay that way." I said.

"Do all my business on that basis."

'There should have been more people like Shooey around.'

The stuff had been in the coal room for nearly four months. It was early April 1973. Compared to the Tiger Tar --- I looked at the remaining blockbusters as my friends; this Black tar stuff was sitting there smiling at me underneath the mini duffle. I knew I'd have to tangle with it pretty soon on a number of levels. It'd be really kool if Ray showed up and he could dispense this stuff to the 'High Five' and get this cure to the rest of the backward magnetic people, if that was what he had in mind.

I brought Barb down to 21 during the day. Jane was at the dance studio, Hal was at Otis or at the World Trade Center, and Cathy and Brother Bill were at school at All Souls.

"C'mon." I grabbed her hand and we went down the cellar. I showed her the tar and held it up so she could smell it.

"Fuck," she coughed. "Where'd you get it….what is it?"

"I bought it off a guy who drives days…..with Ray's money."

We used Isaac's set up and walked up to the aqueduct and went just over the Hastings line where the woods turn into a field of grass with a fair sized berm on the east side. We fired up the opium and drew it in. It was like an awake dream. It had the characteristics of LSD, but not the 'electronic edge'. The high was obviously organic, and that was part of its appeal.

In some confused manner, a few users considered the drug harmless and educational; most knew they were playing with dynamite. A couple of days later I asked Barb how the tar worked out for her.

"I'd do it again if nothing else was around. The high is too long - too trippy – and no blast off." She was wearing long sleeves all the time now. At first, she tried to hide the bruises from dull needles and misses from me; then it was to hide the tracks from everybody. It was something I had to live with, I still loved her. When I thought of us or saw our reflection in a window, I also saw Sally and Ray. The things we did disappeared along with our friends, and we turned into street corner druggies. It wasn't always junk,
but it was always something. It was always something.

THEY FOUND HIM ON EASTER MONDAY IN HIS TENE-ment on Nepperhan Ave. Ronnie Zanzibar had caught a live batch. The Medical Examiner affixed death around 8:30 Saturday night; pulmonary shut down causing heart failure. The Orchard St. crew took it real hard, especially Ronny Chooch. Both served in Vietnam, both had copper colored hair, and both liked the exotic aspects of life. They stood back to back when there was a scrap, they were wiry by nature.

Barb took his death almost as hard as Chooch. They had this non-verbal thing going, only a hard core would know about. They copped and got high together. Maybe she was getting closer to him because of their habits. When people want to move on – it's best they do; it was the only good to come of his death. Once again Barb and me were all we had. Still - I'd have given her up to bring Zanzibar back.

Two days after they found Z-man, George Holter rolled up at the park. The sun was setting later, so we got a good look at his new (used) ride. His car was a pale metallic green '65 Malibu. The faded lettering had once read: 'Cuba Cab'. The interior was immaculate, the outside was a little beat up – the opposite of its new owner. It was nothing fancy; there were holes in the dash where the meter used to be and extra panel lights used to illuminate the place where the driver displayed his hack license. A fair sized hole was in the drive shaft hump connecting the mileage tri-cable to the meter.

Normally, a guy with a new ride might jump out of the car right away and give everybody the unveiling walk-around, and receive the ooohs and ahhhs. Something was amiss. He sat there with his hands gripped tight to the wheel. Holter up-ended four inches of 'Kon-Tiki' wine remaining in the pint bottle. He walked around the Cuba Cab with his head down and approached us:

"Keep your wake clothes out after we go to Z-man's lay-out."

"Huh?" Stax's face was confused.

"Wait to you hear this shit......Little Presto Busch died in his sleep. Fuckin' 14 years old. Aunt Betty went to wake him up and he was as stiff as a board."

"Wha?"

579

"Get the fuck outta here."

"Man – that is fucked up." Herrick made fists of his hands and rubbed his eye sockets.

"Jinxed year." Rexall shook his head.

"Robin and Buddy will be coming home for the wake and the funeral." Holter got the other pint of wine from his new wheels.

"Where are they?" Brad asked me for a cigarette with his hand.

"Bush is in Yuma, Buddy's over in Korea." Holter said. "Hey, somebody follow me….I got to park this car…..I'm getting drunk."

"Them Bush boys are gonna flip out." Rex said.

It wasn't much of a prediction. Robin went AWOL, and did six months in the brig and another six in the laughing house in a military hospital getting a daily dose of Thorazine. Buddy got back in time to make Presto's wake, funeral, and burial, and went back overseas 10 days later. He did some stupid stuff over in Korea, and the locals had him in a provincial lock-up for six months. The Marines brought him back to the states when he got out of the Korean jail. He was honorably discharged 18 months later.

ii

A letter from Westchester County Department of Parks and Recreation informed me to report to Tibbetts Brook Park and Pool for orientation if I was interested in seasonal employment. I looked at the reporting date and called Karyn the day before. The girls' reporting date/orientation was later in the week.

They asked me if I wanted to move over to operations and maintenance for the season. It paid 50 cents more an hour. It was a no-brainer; more money and away from the watchful eye of all the supervision. The crew leader drove a five-ton dump truck through the picnic areas, and our crew of four emptied 55 gal. barrels, filled with picnic and party trash: paper plates – plastic cups – beer and soda cans plastic bottles – carcasses and bones of chickens, pigs, steers, and occasionally a deer or a goat. We always knew when 'Project Head Start' had visited: all the lunch boxes were thrown aside with the baloney sandwich. The only thing the kids ate was the cookie and drank the chocolate milk.

Our crew was responsible for preventing the barrels from reaching overflow levels and policing the picnic areas of garbage on the ground. Even though the barrels had drain holes in their bottoms, lifting them up to the truck's tailgate after a storm was a crash course in weightlifting. Everything was waterlogged and rotten. Flies, yellow jackets, maggots, hornets, wasps, raccoons, squirrels and rats were all on duty in the refuse barrels as well.

Before our first day of work, I made another call to Karyn; her mother answered. She told me Karyn had gone out, and she'd let her know I called.

I kept a $100 bill in the small 5th pocket of my dungarees for the first time I ran into Karyn. The way I had treated her after she had loaned me the money and the love session was inexcusable. By Mid-March there no way I could call her. I'd just ride it out until the season started at Tibbetts and face the music; in the meantime - I got to carry a bunch of guilt around. This next encounter was going to be plenty bad, so bad I hoped I'd hear she had a new boyfriend. No matter the circumstances; it was going to be ice cold, dirty looks, and a boatload of chin music.....if she did talk to me. I was fortunate: I accepted the sanitation assignment, and was away from the pool complex most of the time.

BETWEEN PRESTO'S DEATH AND MEMORIAL DAY, A BOX arrived addressed to Hal and Jane. It was from Ray and mailed from South Vietnam. There was no way there would be any contraband in the box. My mind was all over the place as the five of us gathered in the dining room with Jane opening the box. Inside were: two framed commendations and two citations, an aluminum case and a wooden case with three medals. Both cases had the flag of the Republic of South Vietnam in metalwork affixed to the cases. The one in the wooden case was a Silver Star medal of the Cross of Gallantry; in the aluminum case were two Air Service Medals with the 'Great Honor' grade attachment all in Vietnamese script. Ray had the Citations framed and the Commendations came in a protective album they use for diplomas. There were also a bunch of newspaper articles and photos of the pilots, mechanic, and Ray; and of Ray receiving his medals at Bien Hoa Air Base. Amongst the articles was a brief letter:

May 2nd, '73

Dear Mom, Dad, Ryan, Cathy, and Willis:

It seems they will be CENSORED the store down here pretty soon. There's not many left in the CENSORED part of the CENSORED. I wanted to get this to you before I have to take it with me when we ship out. There's no advance warning.

One day they'll issue orders, and the next day I'll be on a boat or a jet. I hope the stuff I sent arrived in good condition.

One of the Air Force pilots translated the shortest news article for me. You can almost figure out from the pictures what occurred. The bad thing was the death of the two civilians.

The U.S. Army was putting me in for a medal – but it's all politics now, and the higher ups told me not to hold my breath waiting for any determination of the matter – especially because I was the only American there. If it happens – it happens. I've got a real good vibe knowing I tried to save them guys.

Might be the CENSORED I'm guessing. A lot of CENSORED is going to CENSORED. We're also training the ARVN's and civilians to use the equipment we're CENSORED. My next destination -????? When?????

Love,
Your son & brother.........Ray
P.S. It was good to see Isaac <CENSORED>. He's is CENSORED now.

THREE NIGHTS A WEEK, VINNY TARTS AND ME DROVE for Caesar that summer. Cocaine Wayne and Loki were right about driving a hack – slow action.....all summer. I drove 12 hours/a night on the days I had off from Tibbetts; the third night – I'd drive 8 hrs. and tell dispatch: "It's deader than Hiroshima."

Vinny's financial status was more precarious. He had three jobs: he drove for Caesar, worked for Associated 8 hours/wk., and he worked 40 hrs. with Titus from Trinidad. The roofing knocked the shit out of him. His take from Caesar was only $25 - $35/a night, and he said Associated was talking about cutting him down to 4 hrs. a week.

The sun had just gone down, the streetlights hadn't turned on yet on S. Broadway   . Vinny and me were deadheading in Sinatra's Funeral Home's parking lot. I guess it was even slow for the Grim Reaper. Vince had his best work clothes on: a blown out tank top, a pair of cut-off jeans, and a pair of flip flops. I had my usual: a cut-off denim shirt, a pair of straight-leg dungarees, and a pair of desert boots. We looked like a couple of rail yard stumble bums. We had a joint going; but kept it down low. We were happy to get out of the sunken world of the worn out driver's seats of the LTD's.

"We got company Whitedriver." Vinny announced.

We watched another Caesar LTD enter the funeral home's lot.

"You know him?" I squinted. There was too much glare off the windshield.

"The heat's off." Cinzo started to break up. I still couldn't see who it was.

"Who is it?" I frowned.

"It's 'High Roller.' " We started laughing.

"Fuckin Joe Lamar? What the fuck?" I shook my head as he pulled up right next to us. Joe's smiling away sitting there. We came over to shoot the shit. Joe starts revving it up in neutral and I'm about to say something to him and he throws it into 'drive' and floors it and leaves some rubber laughing the whole time. Caesar #14 started doing laps around the parking lot.

As Lamar brought it back, it sounded like the differential would be going to see Jose in the garage pretty soon. Joe loved abusing Caesar's cars, we all did. He shut the car down, stopped laughing and pulled out a half pint of J&B scotch. He took a pull and chased it with some soda. He stepped out and arched his back and tried to exhale. "Son of a bitch Caesar – go down to Saw Mill Wreckers and get some bench seats." Joe looked at us; I laughed into my crossed arms on top of the cab's roof, and Vinny reached for Joe's J&B.

"I got a pillow from John's bargain store to fill the hole and I got the beaded seat cushion and my back is totally screwed up. My back is killin' me guys......killin' me!"

"With the heat, the beads are the way to go....a lot kooler than a seat cushion. That's what I got." Vince said.

"You gotta fill up that ass hole in the seat. A busted spring went right into my butt back in May. I told Rodan..........he had Linda issue me a band-aid." He looked away with a chuckle. "Even Johnny Wadd couldn't fill that asshole with his 16" dick. You got to eat a handful of reds to get through a 12 hr. shift in Caesar's chariots."

Joe was a pisser. I looked at Vince and then to High Roller: "Joe your wardrobe presentation to the public more than makes up for Caesar's lack of concern of the condition of the fleet which the public is forced to ride in." I said.

"Whitefried, if I was to sit in the driver seat without any of the pillows, boosters, cushions, and newspapers, I wouldn't be able to see over the top of the steering wheel."

Vinny doubled over, and I braced myself against my cab and looked at the cavity in the seat of #14 after he removed all remedial attempts to restore some integrity to the seat. It had to be the worst I'd seen since I started.

"But 'High Roller', you've more than made up for the eyesore your cab is - with your magnificent taxi attire." Vince nodded. Joe adjusted an imaginary tie.

It was a sight to behold: Beautifully coiffured, thick, lustrous, pale orange hair; a loud lime green golf shirt; white Bermuda shorts w/a narrow alligator skin belt with a Julius Caesar buckle; orange socks; and white buck suede shoes. It was a complete statement.

"Joe......what can we say? This is the future. You are the cabbie of tomorrow." I nodded and mashed my lips together.

"Take a close look." He walked a tight 360.

Vinny cracked up, "This mug has got a Caesar tag or logo on every item he's wearing. Wait a minute Joe......what's that cologne? No fuckin' way."

"You better believe it: 'CONQVEST IX' – even works in the taxi."

I was doubled over and Vinny stood there agape. Vince asked, "Joe is this attire the company uniform....is it company issue? Will they be handing them out at the dispatch office or do you get knighted by Caesar himself with the outfit?"

"No...no...no.... Taxi attire - only available for the professional drivers." he smirked.

Joe Lamar took a deep breath, "Nah, I went out to Vegas with Mike Reno.....'bout 10 days ago. Played poker almost three days straight – well.....you see me driving for Caesar. Ain't hard to figure out how it shook out. I don't have to go into the gruesome details. I thought we'd be playing some golf and I bought this snazzy ensemble before we started playing poker. I'm tapped out.....down to the wire.....busted. All I got left is this clown outfit. I was just lucky I had 7 months left on my hack license. Every deck of cards or pair of dice has been shit. It's going to come back, but when?" High Roller cackled.

"My luck's so rotten right now – check this out......I got attacked in unit 27, about two hours into the shift the other night." He testified.

"Was she white, black, Puerto Rican, or Asian?" Vinny said.

"Linda was dispatching. You guys didn't hear about this in the office or garage? Shit – it was all over the radio."

"What night did it happen?"

"Wednesday."

"I wasn't working." Cinzano said and rotated his palms up, and shook his head.

"Me neither." I gave him the dumb bulldog chin and shrugged.

"So she's the Dispatch that night." High Roller pinches his nose to attain Linda's nasal radio tonality: "Caesar 27 go to the Sloebomb Project #4 building. The Lady's a dancer at the *Story Untold*.........I'm waiting five-six-seven minutes already. I'm just about to call Linda and see if she wants me to hang around – or if I got the right address. So I wait a little longer. I'm reading Aqueduct's Racing Form for the next day....the action's slow....so where am I going anyway?"

"Out of nowhere : KABOOM! SPLAT! THUD! The hood of the cab, the windshield, and roof all sustained direct hits from the top building #4 from the roof. Baby blue paint covered the hood and the windshield. I got the wipers and the sprayer going but I can't see a thing." Lamar's nodding his head and laughing: "It was like a B-29 released 20 bags of garbage from its bomb belly."

It was funny and incredulous at the same time. "What the fuck Joe?" I said. "Gimme a hit of that scotch."

"Kill it." he replied. "I'm fuckin' trapped. If I get out......I'll catch one on the moneymaker."

"Moneymaker ?"

"My hair - ya dope." We laughed some more. "I call into Linda: Caesar #27 under attack – airborne assault – shattered windshield." He's talking into his cupped hand to simulate the radio mike......Joe had all the moves. "Dan Rodan's voice rips through the Motorola: Get out of there 27.....get out.....abort call....abort!"

Joe tells him, :"Reverse gear – negative function – no reverse. I'm tellin' Dan and Linda: I'm trapped.......I'm trapped! All the while they're hearing the direct hits from the 14th floor cause I got the mike open." Lamar's watching us, as he continues to talk into his make believe mike. Vinny and me are doubled-over once more.

High Roller goes into his Dan Rodan imitation again: "All chariots near Sloebomb projects....assist driver in # 27. Car and driver are under attack by misguided residents. Get over there and save that cab – That is a direct order from Caesar Moreno. Plow down any one who interferes with your rescue operation. Save that Car!"

"Son-a-bitch." Vinny whewed. We all came back to Sinatra's parking lot.

Joe Lamar still laughing, "You guys booking any money or is this just a rolling social club?" he repeated one of Rodan's favorite hustle lines.

"We're fighting for every fuckin' dime out there Dan." I told Joe.

IT WAS GREAT BEING RAY'S BROTHER DURING MY HIGH school years, but I wasn't Ray. The more intuitive recognized the differences straight away. When students, teachers, and mutual acquaintances got past their surface interrogations, they recognized a common template between us. From there the similarity got murky and the contrasts became magnified. Someone said it was like comparing a guitar to a ukulele. Ray was built for exploration – achievement; it required involvement and cooperation. Alternately, I was geared for adaptation and survival. The former invited interaction; the latter eschewed it........unless it was for self-advantage. Barbara Wells liked Ray, but she couldn't have cared less I didn't have his intellect, wit, or insight.

Wire was my girl; I never thought of that in a possessive sense. To me – it meant our gears meshed – we clicked. She was who I wanted to be with. I knew where she was coming from, and it felt real right. The life she lived to this point simply told her not to try to make me into something I wasn't. It was only a guess, but I believed her perception of me was: I was just one of the Rogues; I wasn't sure she felt that way. For me, it was good enough.

After she had the problem with the head lice and had gotten a Marine haircut; she had a 'futuristic' look. It was better than being labeled one of the 'Manson Girls'. Still, with all the cosmic mumbo-jumbo going through my brain since the sixth grade, I couldn't discount the possibility she might be extraterrestrial. I knew her blowjobs were out of this world.

Her physical attractiveness was debatable. Holter, Herrick, and me saw her as a vamp. Bad Brad, Vinny, Jimmy Martini, and Crawford thought she was 'okay'. Rex and Fast Eddie said she was in skank territory. Her black/red short hair, the slit eyes, small tits worked in her favor, but it was the non-physical stuff - the unseen things – like living on the edge....an engaged sixth sense.....her need to 'live for right now' was only picked up by some people. It was something I could deal with, but in the recesses of my grey matter – I knew it might place an expiration stamp on my forehead. Unlike Ray, who was positive Sally and him were too much alike to manage anything long term; I would do whatever was necessary to keep BarbWire and me together. Somewhere......sometime we'd have to change our lifestyles or we were doomed just as much as the Sally and Ray show had been.

It's hard to say whether Barb was aware of the screwed-up mind patterns of the opposite sex, or if she had figured me out. I knew I was the beneficiary of her insight. She wasn't into games, she didn't want or need the mind fuck. There was a passive force she developed being brought up in that whacky house on High St. She used it to look inside of me. I told her she was full of shit, but Barb had something going on in her brain which outpaced mine. It made me paranoid at times. I'd look at her down Greystone – quite sure she knew about Karyn. If she did, she also must have known I only loved her.

This thing with Barb went well beyond sex; it was something I had tried to do with other women, but seemed so difficult to accomplish. Sex, even for a hot-blooded couple, could only account for 10% of the time they spent together. With her, we'd go over to 21, do the wash, vacuum, dishes, do the bathrooms, and change the oil and filters of three cars. We loved the sex, drugs, rock and roll, go drinking, burn up a tank of gas, hang with the Rogues, the Warburton chicks, go down the End, Orchard St. or Lake Ave. We loved the Marina and Greystone, Long Island and New Jersey, the beaches and the waves.

It was a major rush after not seeing her all day and tootin' the horn when I'd see her on the street. She knew the Starfire's unique horn: her face lit up like a deck hand's when the watch shouted from the crow's nest – "Land Ho!" She'd bolt from her friends or whatever she was doing and got in her seat.

"Waiting for you all day – I've got an itch." She'd give me the eyes.

"Let me scratch it."

She made the rule: "No drugs (downs or opioids) until after I had my fun with you, and you 'do' me." Sometimes she'd order me to order her to do exactly what she was to do for me. It was an obedience exercise I imagine, but it also worked the other way because I always wanted to know how I could please her. Often our flesh adventure was a sexual symphony played backwards: we'd kiss and I'd fondle her nipples. Wire was already moaning, and reach for it and say with pure lust: "Ooooooo - I want to ride this big dick." I'd bang her until she went over the falls. She would get so loud, she had to use the pillow as a muffler. When she got back, Wire was glad to help me out. It suited her to be in control and doing her thing on me and coordinating her next orgasm with my first. If such a thing was possible, and I never believed it could be......but Barbara Wells could do me better than I could.

It had to be the composition of her soul, understated femininity, humor, and her seductress ways keeping me entranced. I couldn't break free if I wanted to.

We shared a bench on the southbound platform with our backs to the river. I threw her a line about some bullshit that was completely off the wall. Wells had been looking at the tracks to the north as I explained Steve McQueen was an original member of the Allmans. There was a silence and she slowly rotated her head and I felt her gaze, but looked straight ahead. "You know he played on that record "Revival.....the single?" I matter of fact-ed it. I stole a peek at her for a half-a-second.

"That wasn't even a single."

"It sure was.......Copie had it in his juke box......ask Brad, Tony, or Rikshaw."

She caught me, "You're a fuckin' asshole." She shook her head and laughed with the biggest smile. "You think I'm as dumb as Beth the Mess?"

"'Struth." It was priceless, stark,......it was her vixen style.

She got up and faced me pointing: "You." She couldn't contain her laughter, "You.......you're the biggest bullshitter I ever knew." I grabbed her pointing arm and pulled her on top of me and hugged her. "But it is true!" I stuck my tongue down her throat to shut her up. She spit it out. "You get fucked Whitelie." We laughed some more.

"Listen, ya dumb broad – now this ain't no bullshit. You hear about the Allmans playing up at the Watkins Glen Speedway later this summer?" I said.

"Yeah, I heard." she said. "Just two other bands. That doesn't sound right.......?"

"Rexall or Vinny will know something." I nodded.

As far as I knew, Barb Wells never had a straight job....... a job on the books. She never asked me for drugs, money, or anything except for car rides, and sex. Barb expected me to cover the usual date expenses: pizza, alcohol, cigarettes, transportation, entertainment.....shit like that. As far as I knew, she wasn't pulling any jobs with any addicts or magnetic reversed 'High Five' junkies burglarizing homes or businesses. The people she hung out with were in desperate situations. I wished she hung out with the Warburton chicks; they only smoked reefer and drank......once in a while they'd drop a tab of acid.

With Jay Swanson, Sally, and Z-man on the other side, it seemed like a wake-up call for the junkies to give up the 'Tragic Magic' and give something else a try. Smack had too many risks: O.D., felony rap, costs were as unpredictable as the quality control of what was being injected. Barb's gig was transportation; even though she didn't have a car or a license. Sometimes, she was there to be the ambulance driver, sometimes the scorer; other times as the scout. The sick patients would hand over their wheels, and she'd drive them to the shooting galleries in the South Bronx or Harlem. There, Barb would buy the glassine bags of dope for the junkies from the suburbs and

587

they'd get off in the car or in some abandoned hole in the wall next to where she copped with other junkies from the metro area.

Ray could line them up and sort out the escape artists/shadow people from the get high junkies on sight, as easy as I could differentiate the value of the coins I held in my hand.

Being the wheelman and purchaser of the dope was where she generated her cash or her bags of dooge. Her ability to be straight, get them their fix, and buy her stuff for later on - was a service I guess. These dopers weren't paying any Social Security taxes or anything, and she wasn't likely to sign up for unemployment. Wells just wanted to get her two bags for the service. There was always a bitch about dope quality or the count. Mixer Don would be 1 cc away from cardiac arrest and he'd still say the count was tapped and the dope had been stepped on. A junkie's never happy.

The quality matter was more pathetic, than it was ridiculous. Since Zanzibar's O.D., they all backed off from what they normally shot to get high. The narcs traced the smack Ronnie bought – back to the French fuckin' Connection..............AGAIN! It was evidentiary property room dope. N.Y.P.D. confirmed Sally's toxicology was the magic from Marseilles. Sally's toxicology was consistent with what they found in Z-man's system. The metro region had once again been flooded with the French Connection hi-test dooge, making this the third and final time. The crime family with the shit started knocking it down with cut, by the time Zanzibar ran into it, there were three different varieties out there. Two were average, the other was big time, and it was priced accordingly.

Barb said the market changed on a daily basis. The only way to tell what you were putting into your arm was trial and error, but you had to buy it first. It was a sadistic game. Everybody wanted the good shit and the demand was as strong as it ever was. Barb came back from Harlem with bags of dope stamped: 'Swear to God', 'Red Tape Dope' (w/a piece of red tape), 'Original Swear to God', 'Heart Attack Jack', and 'Drop Dead'. It was all the same junk, except when it wasn't. Sometimes, it was like shooting the sweepings after the parade. There were some pissed-off junkies. Some chose to go 'cold turkey' and told the pushers: "Let me know when you got something that'll get me high."

During this dope shakeout, I was able to move some Tiger tar. Only some of the heroin users were interested; the fifth dimension junkers didn't care about substitutes, they wanted escape. The opium had a lot of power like Isaac said, and it made me fearful of being responsible for someone's overdose. I had to turn myself into a damn pharmacist /psychologist. I had to deal it out in portions that gave them a good charge-the warmth-the glow-the psychedelic dream and relieve the withdrawal. I knew the day was coming where I'd have to just deal the tar out to anybody who had the money. To do this - the way I wanted, I needed an office and staff.......Ridiculous.

By mid-July, I was able to get all of the Rogues half of their money, and I gave Karyn $300 more. Getting Jane her money before Thanksgiving......was going to be difficult. The best I could do would be to give her half of the money I owed her. Isaac showed up at the

588

right time – I think. This dealing business.......getting my name out there – being known as "Dr. Feelgood" or "The Von Ryan Express" – that's never a good handle.

Working at the park and driving for Caesar at night made it difficult to devote any time moving the dreamscape material. Except for Cinzano and Bushrod, the latter who had been released by the Marines; had shown only mild interest. Even though I promised them a piece of the action, most of the Rogues weren't interested in dealing a schedule one narcotic – they had real jobs anyway. There wasn't any urgency. The Barbed Wire woman had no hesitation moving the tar – as long as she didn't have to do it full time. I had to give her the Olds to use, to make pre-arranged drops. Selling the shit on the street was asking to get busted. We got ripped off a few times, but it was better than having your legal counsel try to deny a transaction photo in court.

Once the headbreakers put the finger on you, the search warrants follow.....the lawyers......The state's attorney wants to seize your family's house and on and on it goes. I didn't sleep much that summer, so driving nights for Caesar worked out perfect.

Two weeks after the Fourth of July, Reno spotted me down the North End in the municipal lot. Barb and me were drinking on the wall after we split a ham and white American wedge. Mike calls me over to his lime-green Nova.

"What's going on Mike?"

"Listen Whitesale.....better keep a tighter leash on our girl." He motioned his head over to Barb.

"Get this straight Reno – first, there ain't no 'our girl' to this. She's my girl, and she's my girl because you didn't treat her right. Second, Wells can take care of herself."

"Just trying to give you a heads up." he said.

" 'Bout what?"

"She was a stone junkie, the night I saw her in Hanratty's. It wasn't the first time." Reno didn't look at me as he scanned around looking for a parked van.

"Anything else?"

"A word to the wise from the inside: the heat's coming down soon."

Reno wouldn't screw around with that kind of information, he was for real with something like that.

"Thanks Mike." I had to give him some shit about being Joe Lamar's bad luck charm in Vegas. "Heard you were in Lost Wages with........." a car beeped behind Reno.

He laughed as he rolled away. Marie Tesano was riding shotgun for him now. He never mentioned anything about my new enterprise; that was a relief. I told Barb about the crackdown coming. We hoped it was just a Yonkers P.D. thing. It would have been where Mike got his inside tip from. Nobody wanted to hear about a combined strike taskforce coming in and ruining the party. When the shit came down – people would turn state's evidence and talk. We'd have to tone everything way down. I walked back over to her.

"What did shithead want?" she said.

"Listen: no copping dope – no selling Ray's shit. Don't even hang out with those people until after the bust goes down and the heat's off."

"Is that what Reno said?"

"Yeah."

"Then it's most likely true. He has good connections with the coppers." Her face turned serious. "The big concert at Watkins Glen is almost here. Let's go up there and get out of the spotlight."

I looked at her annoyed, "You know I got to work. You go up with the Rogues; at least half of 'em are going."

"Come on, I don't want to be with any of them."

"Ain't the same without Duane……the Dead don't play St. Stephen/The Eleven or Dark Star anymore. The Band's longest tune is what six…..seven minutes? You go more for the circus than the music. Be good for you……get out of Dodge – have some laughs." I said.

I LEFT THE STARFIRE OFF WITH THE HUNS FOR A TUNE-up and a report card on the 11 year old. It had to be road worthy if a long distance trip suddenly materialized. McKool and Quinn would do me right and make sure everything was in good shape mechanically. I didn't want to get on the road and get blindsided by a corroded brake line.

When I showed up to get the car McKool said: "You stay in Yonkers – you'll need new front brake shoes in 10,000 mi. or in a year. You go live somewhere flat; figure on 20,000 mi. Everything else is solid. You still with Superstar Wells?"

"Yeah."

There was more to this inquiry.

"Better keep her close." Quinn said.

"See her messing with any guys?......Reno?...."

"No Reno, but she is messing with the White Ghost ……and his name isn't Casper." McKool said.

"Listen Whitespur, we don't want to lose her. She's special." Quinn said.

"She's the specialest person I know." I said. I knew Quinn wasn't talking about possession, but of affinity.

It said a lot about a woman who could and would hang with a crew. It told other chicks they'd get treated right if they parked with us. It also showed how tough she was. Most of them didn't have it….Wells did.

I knew the info Reno gave me seven days ago about Barb was right. To get clean, she'd have to go through withdrawal. The dooge always wins; it was consuming her and suffocating us.

We knew we'd have to move out of our parents' housing. It was hard imagining Barb telling her mother she had to move out. It was hard for me to tell Hal or Jane, but I'd have to run it past Hal – out of respect.

EVEN THOUGH I WASN'T WORKING IN THE POOL complex, we still had responsibilities there. It was impossible not to run into or see Karyn Cahill. We would unlock the pool's large gate before the pool opened, and take the pick-up truck around the concrete deck and load full barrels of garbage and take them to the dumpster and bring them back empty before the pool opened. Administration and the locker rooms all generated garbage. It was impossible to avoid her, and I'd end up coming into contact with her more than I wanted. She still wasn't talking to me.

By Bastille Day, I had gotten $300 together and put it in a card. I couldn't even come up with something lame to write to her, so the freeze-out continued. There had to be a way to get the dialogue going again; perhaps there would be no words between us until I repaid all the money. Instead, I drove the truck up to the parking lot and put the card and money back in the Old's glove box.

The third week in July, Barb and me just did our own thing at night. I guess I was busy babysitting her; trying to get her to straighten out and kick her habit.

Everybody was working......working real jobs; not the seasonal stuff like I was doing, or juggling two-and-a-half jobs like Vinny. Rexall had gotten Holter, Herrick, and Jimmy Martini into the Carpenters' apprenticeship. Fast Eddie was working at the Post Office like Yuri Rostov had promised. Kenny Crawford was spotted riding shotgun of 10 ton truck with a cherry picker for Consolidated Edison. Danny Stax had gotten a job with the Yonkers Board of Education as a maintenance mechanic. Rex said Stax's job was nothing more than "a glorified chair arranger."

The Bushman had come up short in the employment arena: He never did make Presto's funeral because the Marines said he was too 'psychologically unstable' to walk the streets, so they temporarily parked him in a V.A. psych ward in Phoenix. He was in this no-mans land of governmental bureaucracy where the military, the V.A., the Dept. of Health and Human Services, the State of N.Y., and Westchester County, all said he was nuts, but none of them wanted the financial responsibility of institutionalizing him. As he made the rounds of governmental holding pens, they pumped him full of anti-psychotic and calm-down drugs. He was declared mentally competent and the Marines gave him an Honorable Discharge. It was up to us to get his mind right. Robin went on and on about how we missed Woodstock, but it would do him a world of good if he could make Summer Jam '73 @ the Watkins Glen Road Course. Actually, Rex had made it to Woodstock four years earlier; Holter corrected Bush's memory.

""Well even so – Look what it did for Rex." Bush replied.

"Yeah.....what did it do for me Bush?" He waited with a straight face for the answer.

"Ain't you some kind of success? George, Herrick, and Jimmy are talking a blue streak about being in the Carpenter's Union, and you made it happen."

Rexall shook his head and laughed, "They're fucking apprentices Bush. They ain't shit until they get their journeyman's card. It might do them good to look at the stage scaffolding up there as part of their training. Looks like we're going to the Glen."

The last weekend in July '73, was the site of the largest rock concert in history. While Barb was laying low with me to avoid the bust, she was getting clean like I asked. She went through withdrawal in five or six days. It was pretty tough on her. She was straight and clean.....kind of a small miracle. I picked her up outside Hanratty's, and we drove down to the marina.

The Rogue's fleet was in formation like a used car line-up. Most of the guys plus Passion Penny, Kate Cruz, Sue Herr, and Denise the Piece all said they were ready for Watkins Glen. With our cars lined up, I wondered who would actually make the trek. Rex got rid of the Le Mans and bought a '67 International Harvester Travel-All. He had gotten 3 large Yonkers Police Dept. door emblems from Ronnie Zanzibar. He also gave Rex a short wave and Citizens Band antennas for the vehicle's roof. It looked official, and was painted metallic green. Rex had a good line of shit. When he'd get stopped by the bluecoats, he'd explain:

"It's actually an auxiliary emergency use vehicle. I own it, and donate the use of it for Civil Defense, disaster equipment transportation, and parades. It gives the public a reason to see you guys performing valuable services – not just breaking heads." You'd hear this bullshit from the front or back seat, and you wonder if the Rexall bullshit was going to pull us through again.

1973 Rogue's List of Rides

Jimmy Martin(i)(ique) - 1968 Tempest Station wagon Fast Eddie Mason - 1961 Copy cat - Hunmobile Chevy Impala Crawford – '73, F-150 Ford pick-up....new Holter- '65, Chevy Malibu, 'Cuba Cab' Vinny Tarts – '60 Chevy Impala....still crunched Danny Stax – '67 Chevy II w/327 cu.in. V-8 Bad Brad – '69 Skylark Rexall – '67 International Harvester Travel-All Robin Busch – '70 (taken out of storage in'72) Ford Torino Me – '62 Oldsmobile Starfire w/455 cu.in. Buick Wildcat engine

Rexall took a series of photographs, and made a montage of our rides with us standing along side them......forever frozen in time.

Crawfish asked, "Tarts, you going to get that body work Done?"

"Aaaaaay....I took it over to Shooey to see if he could do it for me. He said he was a mechanic – not a panel beater."

"Take it over to 'Tomato Tom' for the body work." Fast Eddie said.

"No one's gonna be as cheap as what I could've got it done by the Z-man." Vince said. Everybody knew that was true. "Kenny, if youda sold me Betsy's Datsun instead of trading it in....." He waved off Crawford and shook his head.

"I didn't even know you wanted it Vinny." Catdaddy looked like he had just woken up.

Rex had everyone's attention. It appeared as if he was conducting a seminar or something.

".........You got to bring at least a nickel of weed and some hallucinogenics - if you can find some. And there won't be anything to drink there – alcohol or water. I recommend you bring a gallon of T-bird and a gallon of water; both in plastic jugs. There won't be anything to eat all weekend. Three cans of the delicious 'Daniel Boone' beef stew should keep you on your feet. You can make a lot of bread up there – 90% of the cars up there will be parked in. The hippies won't have any choice except to buy what people bring in the raceway. I'm going to get a shopping bag full of Big Mac's 20 miles out and sell them for five bucks each. Might be able to swap a Big Mac for a tab of acid. That's the drug of choice for a circus like this. I wish I had some when I went to Woodstock." He shook his head at the missed opportunity.

With my head I motioned to Wells to come off to the side. "You know the bust is coming. Going to Watkins Glen that'll be a good move. Hell Barb – you might not even be on their list. If you're not here – they can't bust you. Of course – it might go down as soon as you get back."

"If 500 hundred thousand people show up - it'll be a free for all. I'll set you up with 200 hits of "Hai Karate Tar." She immediately saw the potential; her eyes started to sparkle.

"Don't sell it to anyone you know." I instructed. "If you're camping on the eastside.....walk it over to the westside to sell. Sell it after dark. A few of these cats will have a good time. Some will treat it like hash and will be in the vegetable patch all night. Three hits to a person.......max. Try to sell it all in one night, you don't want to come back with any of it."

"I know you just got clean; it'd suck to throw all the hard work down the drain." I said.

"Yeah, I'll just drink and smoke the reef." she said.

"Good girl." I caressed her face with the back of my hand.

"Wish you were coming."

"Wish I was going. The only thing I'll be missing is you. Hang with Cinzano, he's up on the 'Tiger Tar' stuff."

"When you leaving?" I said.

"Around daybreak Friday.......going with Stax and Vinny. He's seeing if he can get Dona Del Bello to go. We're trying to get all the stuff we'll need tomorrow. Let's take a ride and try to find some pot." Barb said.

We told Vinny and Stax we were going to look for some weed, and get the essentials Rexall suggested.

Some of the essentials were at 21 in the coal room. I started packaging Ray's Tiger Tar. I asked Barb to go up to the stationary store up the North End and get more small manila envelopes. The opium had to be Saran wrapped; otherwise the drug's juice was absorbed by the envelope and the smell was obvious. Barb bought out the stationary store.

I probably sold around 300 dime balls since Isaac brought that pork roll last December, and if I could move another 200 at

Watkins Glen – that would be 5000 large since I started. I only had about half of the Tiger Tar money left since I started. I couldn't account for the missing money other than the fact I knew I had spent it. With all the people the TV and newspapers said were going to show up, I thought Barb could move the 200 units. When network news showed all the people making the pilgrimage, I thought of Christ feeding the masses with the 3 loaves and five fishes. I thought of my soul, and silently prayed no one would O.D. The way I told Barb to distribute it, and with her street savvy, she might not have any problems. She was smooth, had the right attitude, and looked like she stepped off a space ship.

iv

We had to go inside the pool's gates, and get the four concession stand barrels as warranted by the level of business at the stand. They served mostly carnival food: high sodium – high sugar. Frequently, there would be some policing and trash removal outside of the regular schedule around the lockers, the picnic areas, and administration building.

Karyn's main job was to sell pool tickets from behind the cage, it was set up the same way they sell tickets to a movie. Instead of a glass barrier, the ticket girls and money were separated from the public with a barred cage cubicle. Sometimes, she was assigned to be a ticket ripper, like the guy at the theatre, or be a locker attendant for the girls. It always seemed whenever I had work around the pool – she'd be there. The money wasn't the reason I was trying to avoid her. It was her death-beam/laser eyes she'd flash at me when I had to pass one of the ticket cages she was working. I knew it wasn't the money, it had been the sex. Very rarely does it come without a price.......except with Barb.

My motive to patch things up with Karyn was to get those damn eyes off my back and out of my dreams. I'd tell her I was sorry, but I didn't expect her to believe it. Trying to smooth things over was an attempt to apologize I guess; I wasn't looking for another slice of pie. Karyn's aura was in stark contrast to Barbara's: She was all future; while Barb was 'Be in the moment.....live for today.'

This dichotomy gave me insight to the paradigm of the world of phantasm and the magnetic system of the anti-parallel dimension. Whether she realized it or not, Barb was negating the relevance of the future because it will only be the same as it was today. Karyn's perception of the present for the most part was an unfolding disappointment; and the only hope, if it exists at all - would be in what lies ahead. I walked over to the boys-side ticket cage.

"Cahill – I got $300 for you." I said.

Her hand reached through the bars, "Let's have it." She didn't look up from her paperback.

"I also must apologize – You treated me so much better than I treated you. The words are not there to adequately say I'm sorry."

"Save it......where's my money?"

"In my car – get it for you right after work. When do you get off?" She still hadn't looked my way.

"5:30." She spoke just above a whisper. "I gave you my deepest feelings and loaned you $500; all I asked of you was to call me." She finally looked up. "You couldn't even do that. Why didn't you ask your alien girlfriend for the money? No.....you ask me because I'm gaga over you, and you know it. What do I get? I get a phone call two days before we start work. You are such a Whiteliar." She said.

"This past winter and spring were pretty hectic."

"I'll bet - busy banging Angela Cartwrong."

"By the way......I made Dean's list again; I know you were wondering." Her brow went up with a gotcha grin.

Karyn's words and tone............I wasn't gaining any ground. Half of what she said was borderline venom.

"All I can say is I'm sorry. Perhaps, if you give me another opportunity – I can go into what happened between our brief affair and where we are now." I said.

"You're kidding? Right? You can't be serious Ryan....?" Karyn looked me off. "I get off at 5:30.....Have my money."

Crew leader Ralph called across the hall:
"Ryan.......vamos."

"Karyn, I'll see you after work." I should have just mailed her the loan repayment. I got in the truck with Ralph.

She was walking up the road leading to the employee parking.

"Hop in." I tried a smile on her and turned the Starfire's music lower. "We're going to miss the big concert."

"That's not the only thing you're missing."

I thought she was talking about my missing hair on the top – left side of my head.

"I'm talking about Watkins Glen." I inched up the drive to the lot.

"I'm not." Karyn scoffed.

"Supposed to be a lot of people at this one......bigger than Woodstock they expect." I said.

"I wouldn't call it a concert."

"An event?"

"You got my money?"

"In the envelope – in the glove compartment."

She got in and left the door open and rifled through the glove box; she scoffed a laugh: " A 'Thank You' card?" She counted out six $50's with the card. "How thoughtful – Look! You even signed your name."

"Kinda didn't get around to writing anything." I said.

"Still owe me a $100."

"You'll have it by next week."

"I'm surprised you didn't have your Venusian Vixen meet you here to rub my face in it."

"C'mon Karyn." I looked from her to straight ahead. We sat in silence in space. I came back to reality when the heat and humidity began running down my face; it was getting close to closing, but the pool patrons were pushing it up to the last minute.

"Other than financially, are you attracted to me?"

It was the same as the Henny Youngman rhetorical question: "Have you stopped beating your wife?" Through experience – it usually best to tell a woman what she wants to hear - regardless of the truth. If nothing else, the showdown has been kicked down the road for another day.

"You know I am, and it had nothing to do with the loan. We had something going last year remember?.....our lunches? The chemistry is there; isn't it?" I kept my gaze straight ahead.

"No, not if I'm invisible to you. When we got together last winter, I thought I had let you know we had more than a physical attraction – more than the sex act. It was that way for me, but it never was for you; it was all passion for you.....just sex; and sex with the alien."

I turned and looked at her again: "For the love of fuck - don't start crying. Why does the sex act have anything to do with love? It's got to be the most absurd action predicated on emotion because it leads to a debased relationship between two people. It's a classic example of matter versus anti-matter.....without any possibility of annihilation........check mate."

"You don't even know what you're talking about." she laughed.

I threw her a knuckleball: "Here's the way most dudes interpret the human necessity: guys are searching for quantity, and I'm not talking about the number of partners, but the frequency of eliminating the jizz from our bodies just so we don't act like idiots. When a woman acknowledges this situation and has true feelings for her love interest, she will perform the necessary remediation – and there's a good chance he's going to hang around. If he doesn't get what he needs, odds are he'll be moving on until he finds what he's looking for."

"With women, you all search for the abstract, the incorporeal. Many believe this can be attained through sex, and any guy buying into the concept of having sexual intercourse as the ultimate expression of love is an imbecile."

"What are you trying to say? Have you been reading your brother's psychology texts, because they don't sound like your words."

"Just some vague ramblings that run through my brain which no one seems to understand, which includes me at times." My eyes remained focused to the void on the other side of the windshield.

"What did you want besides the money? Was or is there any interest in me?" Now she turned and looked away.

"It's early; let's go to that Greek restaurant down where you live. We'll talk over dinner."

She agreed. I waited for her to come down from her parents' apartment. The radio said traffic on all the main roads into Watkins Glen was hardly moving, and I saw Barb in my mind. This weekend with Karyn wasn't all my idea, but I wished I had gotten Shooey's money from another source. I had this feeling I would be working off the interest in the back seat of a car or some new location.

She came out from her parent's apartment; she had one of them peasant tops where there's almost no anti-man devices to prevent me from getting at her milkers. Karyn only did her eyes with make-up – it was all she needed: the brows, lids, and lashes. Ten years into the future, I would think of her and say she looked like Sigourney Weaver. After she had called Barb an alien version of Angela Cartwrong it clicked. For the present, it was Cahill who bore a strong resemblance to Angela Cartwright of "Lost In Space". Karyn was better looking than Barbara Wells; her physical beauty only had so much pull. I should have dumped 'em both for Meris Klein. What bothered me, was what did they ever see in me besides what came out of my mouth, which was nothing original?

We got a bottle of Chianti before we ordered. Right after the waiter left with our orders, Karyn left her side of the table and sat next to me and we shared a long kiss. It was too long for the restaurant. Her hand rested high up on my inner thigh. The Chianti was ¾'s gone and we were all smiles.

It was inevitable; she razzed me about Barb. Again, I was determined not to let her get any traction with her jealousy. She finished the rest of the wine, it may have helped. I got a bottle of Pagan Pink as soon as we left the Greek's. We went down to Greystone Station, and some freshmen or sophomore kids had our spot atop the ejected remnant.

We went back to the Starfire and parked on Harriman Ave. We tried to get it on, but it was a sauna inside the car. My mind wandered as the sweat ran down my temples. I thought about Ray in Long Bihn and Loki in Miami. Again, it led to Barb up in Watkins Glen.

"Want to go up to the bar up the North End.......air conditioned?" I raised my brow.

"God yes."

It was only around ten o'clock. We had to go to Cassidy's, now that Copie's Tap had been closed since New Years. Copie never had air conditioning anyway, except in the winter. As soon as we walked in, we felt relief – like our brains were plugged in again.

"Hey Whitepaint......over here."

We saw Bad Brad and his newest girlfriend sitting at a booth. We went over and sat down. Brad started bitchin' straight away about missing the big concert up in the Finger Lakes.

"Brad, this is Karyn......Trish – Karyn, Karyn – Trish and Brad."

"Everybody's up there." Brad commented. "Man, I really wanted to make this one." He pounded the table.

Neither of the girls had any misgivings about not going to the concert. Girls knew how quickly those rented dunnies filled up in just a couple of hours at these mega-festivals. They were true character builders.......even for biker chicks, who had seen and endured it all.

I came back from the bar with 2 gin & tonics, a vodka collins, and a bottle of Bud.

Brad was facing the TV, and started getting pumped up again when he saw the crowds on Channel 5 News.

"Fuck....we should be there." He was becoming quite animated.......he was close to being a little drunk. "I'm telling you Whitelife, we leave tonight, we'll get up there tomorrow morning."

"I would have gone if I didn't have to go to work tomorrow. I wasn't going to miss work for it: hey Brad, the sound will be fucked, we'll be sitting and sweating in the middle of some cornfield dying from the sun and the heat and not being able to see anything. You can't get in and you can't get out. Rex told you what the rest was going to be like."

Brad looked at me like I had lost my marbles: "You're the one always talking up the Brothers.......how could you NOT be there?"

"Yeah Whiteshine – you should be there." Karyn gave me an elbow to the ribs and a grin.

"Brad you seen the Allmans down Central Park – it will never be better than it was that night." I said.

"Yeah - but The Band......and the Dead." he countered.

Brad didn't want to hear that; he wanted to break loose, he wanted to rock – get wild. Something was going on inside his head; something which put him on the edge. It was more than Watkins Glen. We stayed for another round. Brad stole Trish's vodka Collins and made her drink the Budweiser.

As I drove Karyn back to South Yonkers she said: "I think Bad Brad has some issues he should be working on."

"I dunno; he might be getting worse." I gave her an eye roll and looked out the window.

"I'll see you after work tomorrow." Karyn said as she got out of the car.

ON SATURDAY, WE TRADED THE HEAT FOR MORE humidity; more dog days of summer. Karyn and I agreed to an 8:00 p.m. date, hoping it would be a little kooler, and we wouldn't have to hide in a bar.

On the way home from Tibbetts, I turned the corner off Montague Street onto Morsemere, I saw Kirk Lis in front of Progressive with his VW microbus. I hadn't seen him since the rest of us graduated last year. I parked right behind him. The girl he was with was unfamiliar.

"Kirk!" We shook hands like there was a common bond between us. It had to have been more than the ownership duality of the '62 Olds.

"Whitestarfire – you and the Olds......looking good." We were genuinely glad to run into one another.

"Just had the Olds over to see the Huns for a routine."

"You got to stay on top of the cars. Ryan, I just came down here to see my folks for a few days; anybody around?"

"Seems like everybody went to Watkins Glen except me and Bad Brad. He's pissed he stayed."

"We just got out of there this morning."

"Watkins Glen?" I asked.

"Ball of confusion."

"Thought the music was this afternoon and tonight?" I said as I brought a brow down.

"Only three bands, but I guess the radio predicted rain this afternoon and maybe tonight. We heard there was some ego bullshit about who was going to play last.....chicken shit. Maybe The Band goes on at one, then the Dead go on around five, and the Brothers go on around nine? Then they're all supposed to get together and have this big monster jam. That's what we heard this morning. Who the fuck knows?"

"The weather sounds like the unknown factor like Woodstock." I said.

"Yeah, sun-rain-cold. The Dead and a few of the Allmans were tuning up, sound checking, and jamming yesterday afternoon. It rained last night. People who had been at Woodstock said it had a different vibe: this time there were no baubles, bangles, and beads. It was every man for himself. The only music we heard was the Dead yesterday. Sharon – oh fuck wait a minute....I'm sorry.....This is Sharon Mattison."

We both waved 'Hi'.

Kirk continued, "It got a little jazzier when the Brothers joined them, but when it was just the Dead.....it just dragged on with Garcia meandering, trying to find a groove. They must have been wasted. The sound kind of sucked - might have been where we were sitting. Don't know how The Band or The Allmans will sound. The place ain't set up for rock & roll; it's a fuckin' road course." he laughed.

"When we got there, we were parked about four miles away from the raceway grounds. We ended up in some farmer's field in the mud on Thursday night. It took six guys to push us out of the muck this morning."

"Joo see anybody?" I said.

"Like I said, The Dead and a few Allman Brothers jamming."

"No.....I mean anybody we know – you know like people?"

Kirk starts laughing: "Okay.....okay. You mean like us. Yeah.....I saw some jokers from Lake Ave....North End....a few guys from Saunders. The first guy I see though is fuckin' Rexall." Kirk's bent over he's laughing so hard and kind of cackling. His girlfriend is laughing too – looking kind of embarrassed. "Rex is at the main crossroad with this big smile on his face....all by himself. He's got a gallon of water and a gallon of 'Night Train' in plastic jugs hanging like bandoliers crisscrossing his chest."

"I'll bet he was selling 'Big Mac's' from a shopping bag". I remembered Rex's line.

Kirk starts busting out again and slapped his thigh: "Yeah!.....yeah. Wish I had a fuckin' camera. Ronnie Mac told him he

599

had a 35 unit limit on every item, and he only had five left. Of all the people we ran into – he seemed to be having the most fun. He was a one-man party machine."

"He must have scored some good acid. Rex likes that electric action........ZZZzzzelectricity and making money. The fucker should work with Crawford at Con Ed."

"What are you guys up to tonight?" I asked.

"Nothing planned." Kirk looked over his shoulder at Sharon. She shrugged with her palms up, "Too hot anyway."

"I got a date tonight. Thinking about crashing the pool at the country club where I used to caddy. The last time we went swimming there was with Bingo, Holter, Jimmy Martinique, and Crawfish. You weren't there were you?"

"Don't think so."

"I want to kool off, so we can work on our love connection tonight."

"You still going with Barbara Wells?"

"Yeah, but she's not my date."

"Meris Klein? She was......" He looked over at Sharon. She was following our conversation, though I was sure she didn't know anyone we were talking about. "Always thought you two were a match."

"I wish."

"So where's Wells?"

"Watkins Glen, with Vinny and Stax."

"When the cat's away.....You know what Whitewater? Fuck that Watkins Glen." The three of us smiled and nodded. "What time you want to meet up?" Kirk arched his back.

"About 10:30 down Rubeo. We'll drive up to Sunset Ridge and swim until we start sweating in the pool and we start turning into prunes. Then.....love will find a way."

"Can anything go wrong?" he asked.

"Sharon..." I got her attention, "Be sure to bring your sneakers." I turned to Kirk, "They got an old timer making the rounds --- he can't run and he can't hear."

"Right....see you later." He tucked some hair behind his ear.

Somehow, I had gotten Karyn to smoke some pot with us when we met them down the park. They followed us in his VW camper to the country club. The saga of the Starfire had a starting point with Kirk, and I asked Karyn if she wanted to hear it. She said yes, but after I was through it, she wasn't as swept away as Sharon with the story.

There were two other couples at the pool; they were drunk and in their 40's. Hearing them talk, I knew they were members or guests of members. We told them our families were members.

"Come on in.....it's exhilarating....." A buxom woman invited.

She wasn't lying, just ten minutes in the pool and we all felt we were coming back to life. I thought it would take an hour to bring my core temperature down to where it was conceivable to bang a gong with Karyn.

Kirk and me watched the women making some alcoholic concoction in a stainless shaker. They invited us to have a drink.

"Whatever it is – yes...." Karyn was still thirsty.

The less endowed woman brought the shaker over to Kirk, and asked if we had any pot?

Kirk raised his brow in doubt, "Hey White/album: I think I could dig this country club scene."

Karyn stayed with the woman who was on her second Vodka martini, Kirk rolled a joint. He fired up, took a hit, and started making the rounds with it with the women. They called their partners over to catch some; he had to roll another to get them in the groove. It was worth it; they'd have to back us up if there were any security around other than the old timer. Karyn went down the other end of the pool. The three of us just bullshitted in the kooling water.

"What's going on with your brother.....still in Nam?"

"Sounds like he'll be outta there pretty soon, but he still has almost 2 years left on his hitch."

"It's really good running into you and seeing the Olds still in action." he nodded.

"How long are you and Sharon in town?"

"We planned on going back upstate on Monday, but with everybody out of town – now it looks like Tuesday if I'm going to see anybody."

"Bad Brad's around." I said.

"A lot of negative energy; if I run into him - fine, but I'm not going to go track him down."

"Know what you mean."

"I got to find someone to do some electrical work on the van." Kirk said as a happy scream came from the other side of the pool. The buxom gal was now topless; dancing to the music in her head on the diving board. The guys, gals, and Karyn were playing some truth or dare game. She was giving the springboard a little weight making the board deflect about a foot. Her boobs were slunky on the way down and weightless on the rebound. Her nipples had also sprung. I looked at the beach blanket I had brought.

"Kirk.....got any bug spray?"

"Yeah – somewhere in the van."

"I planned on trying it in that big sand trap on the 10th   - like it's the beach or something. The trap next to the green."

"Yeah, do it on the beach, come back, and go for a dip." He echoed 'sand trap'.........."That's some set of tits." Kirk said out the side of his mouth, and tried to shoo a mosquito from his shoulder.

"I got to get a closer look." We swam underwater and emerged on each side of the diving board.

"Say...what's all the excitement?" I looked at one of the guys on the deck.

One of the guys replied: "Marsha loves that grass." She proceeded to throw her panties in the pool.

"Whoever fetches them will be rewarded." She shined her ass at us guys.

"Wow." Kirk and me knew better; we were just glad to beat the heat and watch them water balloon juggs. We swam back to the five foot deep section of the pool where Sharon was. Karyn was still goofing off with the adults.

"What I was saying before Marsha started the show? Man – I'm a fuckin' veg. What was I saying?" Kirk was spaced out.

"Something about getting some work done on the camper?"

"Yeah….yeah….I got a rebuilt engine in the spring and it had an alternator, but it originally had a generator. Something's not right – Sometimes it doesn't charge and it's running right off the battery. Is Ronnie Zanzibar around? He'll know what going on." Kirk said.

"I don't want to be the one to lay this on you…..Z-man got in a tight spot with a hot batch of shit." I looked at the hazy sky of stars.

"Ahhhhhhh……No…….No fuckin' way man: Awww fuck! Ronnie? Sonafabitch! He's good people Ryan. What the fuck is going on?" He went over to the adults to mooch a drink. He got a clear plastic cup from the trash barrel, and shook it underwater in the pool and shook the water out and filled it. He finished half and sat in one of the chairs. "See….see….this is why I moved away – to avoid hearing crap like this."

The arm without the drink tried to sweep the bad news aside. The hand with the cocktail gyrated out of control and it left his hand. Kirk kicked the plastic cup back in the water.

"Sorry brother." I said.

"We got to go……I got to go."

"Maybe I'll see you tomorrow or Monday."

"Shooey around; or is he dead too?" He said.

"You know where to find him."

"Do a year in Vietnam…..make it back alive, come back home and cash out here." Kirk looked down and shook his head.

"Didja go to the wake?"

"Another bad one."

They left.

I put myself on robot control; Karyn sprayed me and I sprayed her with the can of bug spray. The two drove off. I knew Kirk…..I knew Z-man's departure would bug him for a while.

My feelings for Karyn had me plenty mixed up. Perhaps, I did love her. Her nature was a stark contrast to Wells'. Maybe I did want to get my life on the right path; instead of chasing an illusion through some substance or phantom dust. The longer me and Ray were separated, the more I felt the need for a replacement. A lover can't replace a brother. All Karyn could do was to tell me not to mess with drugs. That was what all the women would do, except for gals like Barb, Sally, Sue Herr, Beth the Mess and the others: they wanted to get high with you.

Surely Ray would be receiving leave after his tour in Vietnam was completed. I had to hope he would be coming home soon because there was a gaping hole in my approach to being somewhat successful in life. From the older caddies like Ed Detore the advice was: "Don't wake up after 50 years of life and wonder…..How did this happen?" I thought about Loki, Vinny Tarts, and even Rexall as the people who might flat out say: "This is what you've got to do to get your life in order."

The comet dust and the Tiger Tar; Ray recognized the importance of these reality changers. He hadn't asked for either one – each just showed up at a specific time for a particular reason.

When Sunday morning's first light hit the top of the Palisades, I fired up the Starfire and drove home. Dropping off Karyn around 1:30 am, I stopped at 7 Wells Tavern on Wells St. for last call. I closed it up, and drove north on Warburton and took a left at the marina and watched the stars until I fell asleep. I was hoping for another fireball to streak across the heavens. If one came, I must have missed it.

I'd have to go in and drive for the Empire tonight; Maybe Barb did a good job and got rid of most of the tar I gave her.

v

The expeditionary Rogue detachment returned from Watkins Glen without any casualties. The reports were generally in line with the account given by Kirk: Summer Jam '73 fell short of being the Rock and Roll 'Tour de Force' the promoters had billed it as.

On the other hand, Rexall had hit the mark with his advice and his predictions. The three amigo carpenter apprentices, didn't make it with any Hippie chicks, and Eddie Mason thought they might have had a better time down Belmar or Seaside on the Jersey shore.

"We could've pushed an 8 track in the car and gotten better sound….. fuckin' weather sucked too." Martini said.

Vinny, Stax, and Barb had returned around 4 pm. Danny Stax had let Barb off on Lake Ave. The Rogues were down Rubeo Park hanging out clothes: wet sleeping bags, and their tent over a divider fence where the prongs were bent over. They looked like they hadn't slept except on the ride back.

"What's going on?" I said.

"My mom wouldn't let us hang our stuff on the clothesline in the backyard." Cinzano laughed.

"Everything reeks – including the trunk." Stax pinched his nose.

The stench was overpowering, "You guys gotta throw this shit out or you got to take it up to the laundromat. Use one of the big washers for the sleeping bags. I ran into Kirk Lis over the weekend………he said there was some rain up there?"

"Some? Kind of an understatement." Vinny scoffed.

Stax recounted - "Let me tell you Whitewash: The Dead were jammin' Friday afternoon…..sound checking I guess – with some of the Allmans. It was plenty hot. We came back and set up the tent and threw our sleeping bags inside. I tried to catch some ZZZZs and Vinny and Wells went off. The Dead played first on Saturday, then

The Band came on mid-afternoon. Around 4 o'clock the skies opened up and it fuckin' poured. Wind – lightning – thunder. The biggest wet T-shirt event I ever seen. It got cold, and The Band came back on. There were nipples everywhere. After the rain, there was no more sitting and groovin' to the tunes. Mostly you had to stand and shiver and get as high as you could. The Allmans came on like 10 o'clock – they played a long time, they might have played every song they had. Then, they had this All-star jam with all three bands. They played 'Mountain Jam' for sure. After that, I had enough. I think it was supposed to be a one day deal; ended up being a 48 hr. endurance test. Ask Rex if Woodstock had better organization." Stax tried to remember three sketchy days.

Vinny half-laughed, "Rexall was prepared, he said you don't need a tent.....Just drop some acid for the duration. If it's good acid – you'll make it to the conclusion of the festival. That's Rexlogic for ya."

"What about the shit I set you guys up with? You know – the shit I gave Wells?" I was anxious to hear they had moved at least some of it.

"I was security for Barb while she pushed the opium. She sold out in two hours while Stax was counting sheep." Vince nodded.

"Huh?"

"Yeah....." He raised his eyebrows, "It was getting dicey a couple of times as people circled around. She did the deals, and I worked the money. There were so many buyers a couple of times – we just had to walk away. You didn't know who might have been a narc."

"How much you come back with?"

"'Bout two – heavy." Vince raised his brow.

"Who's got the money?"

"I gave it all to Barb. She held back 10 dime balls for us. Think she came back with five.......she might have sold them as we were leaving."

"Whitetunes – you got any more?" Stax said.

"Maybe next weekend. If you run into Wells, tell her I'm looking for her." I looked at the two, "You guys know this shit is physically and psychologically addictive.....right?"

"Think we're stupid?"

It was a good bet Stax would think he had smoked some version of super hashish with Vince and Barb. Vinny knew the weight Isaac Seabrook brought from Ray. He also knew how much it took to blast off. He could do the math and keep it on the down low, having your name on the street as the go-to guy was always trouble no matter what people were looking for and that included blockbusters.

I looked at my watch and then to Vince, "Sure you don't want to do the shift with me tonight?"

"Are we in Yonkers yet?" he asked Stax.

"Kirk's in town.....I think he's leaving tomorrow."

"He'll have to find me. My tank's on 'E'." Vinny said.

"Adio muchachos." I went up to Lake Ave. and then to Wells' house.

As soon as her mom opened the door, I was assaulted by cat odor and an irate Marge Wells. She ripped me a new one about taking Barb up to Watkins Glen. I didn't know what story Barb had given her, so I let her lash out at me without any denial. I assured her I'd bring her daughter home A.S.A.P.

"While you're out there riding around – get me a pack of Newports and a TV Guide." She slammed the door.

It was a pretty slow night. Dan Rodan sent me on this one fare. "Who I got up north".......he waited 15 seconds, the radio blared again: "C'mon......who's up north?" he turned the volume up on his mic. "C'mon......who wants to dance?"

"Caesar 18." I called in.

"18, pick up at Hanratty's at the end of Lake Ave. by bakery on Voss. They're bar hoppin'.......Party's going to 'The Dutchman Mine' on Lockwood Ave. – up from Hodio's."

The third time I laid on the horn. Wacky Nancy, Rikshaw, Beth the Mess, and Cocaine Wayne piled into the cab.   "Where to?"

None of them recognized me with my sunglasses on. I entered the fare on my log sheet on my clipboard.

"First, go down to Lawrence St. – then we got to go to Bruce Ave. – then over to the 'Dutchman' on Lockwood." Beth said. None of them looked at me.

This was too involved, so I dropped the meter's flag. Still no I.D. on me. They were all talking junkie nonsense. At a red light, I gave The Rikshaw a penetrating look from the rear view mirror. His reflection was off – not true – not dimensional. I had never seen a person in this perspective. How did I miss this? I looked at Cocaine Wayne; he too portrayed a polarized specter.

"Rikshaw..... How's the quality running down here?"

The four froze and looked at the hack license. "Hey Whitestripe- why didn't you say anything when you picked us up?" Rikki replied.

It was debatable whether Cocaine Wayne I.D.'d me, but he stayed with the question, "Never seen such a duke's mixture of good and useless junk. A bunch of new players. A lot of this shit is hitting the Bronx – closer for us. Quality........questionable."

"Is the summer drought over?" The radio chatter made it hard for them to hear me.

"Beth's got a pick-up and delivery, and then we're going to 'The Dutchman' on Lockwood......more business." Rikshaw said.

"Drought's over --- 'til the next one." Wayne twitched.

"You run into Barb?"

"Un-uh." Sue said.

"You see her, tell her to give me a call."

"You got it Whiteclaw." Rikshaw nodded.

Cocaine Wayne, Sue Herr, and The Mess didn't say good-bye, and went directly into the bar.

Before Rikshaw paid the fare he asked, "Is your brother still in Nam? I got this postcard from him a couple of months ago.....from Saigon.........pretty kool."

605

"He might be in the Philippines by now. They said he'd be out of Long Bihn by early summer. Well see where his next correspondence is mailed from."

"Be great to catch up with him, I think he can really help out the 'Dimensional Five'. He always knew me like no one else." Rikki said.

A lot of people said shit like that about Ray. I would have kept the flag down if Vinny and Stax hadn't given me the news about selling out at Summer Jam.

"Hey Rikshaw, what's the plan? You guys are only four now."

"Somehow I know this is a question for your brother to answer. I know our reversed magnetism will draw another or maybe more into our non-conforming/backward world. Believe me - they're out there."

I winced and tilted my head knowing he was right. I gave Rikshaw a flat rate even though they had me wait twice. I drove over to Barb's house and left a pack of Viceroys and the TV Guide on the doorstep, rapped on the door, and took off.

Almost a week had passed; no Barb Wire. I knew what she was doing. The thing that bugged me was the reason why. The two thousand she had of mine was good enough reason if she was back riding the 'horse'. I didn't need this bullshit. In one week, Cahill's stock went up almost 200%. People told me: They'd seen Barb here or there or that "she was looking for me." It was just more bullshit; all she had to do was wait at Tibbetts by the Starfire at the end of the workday. Two weeks getting clean......three days of being clean, and throw it all away because she had a lack of will power.

I was just about to start hiding the Starfire and hang out at Hanratty's to catch her when she walked in. The male drive forced me to start looking for her. It was a letdown; I thought she needed me as much as I wanted her. After work at Tibbetts, I was driving for Caesar's taxi on Nepperhan Ave. just before sundown. I blasted the LTD's horn and stopped her cold crossing Orchard Pl. A split second of indecision, produced panic and a telepathic beam: Something or someone had come between us.

Barb ran over to me in her usual way: 'I can't wait to see you' attitude. The longsleeve blouse was the only thing I needed to see.

She got in the taxi and played her role. She said with a frown: "I've been looking all over for you – You been hiding on me?"

I scanned over to the Orchard St. crew, three or four of them were hanging out. I gave them a nod, as we drove past, rubbed my chin with the outside of my thumb, wincing a little bit. I drove north on Orchard St. connecting the series of switchback streets which climbed the steep hill up to Lake Ave. I looked straight ahead, "How much you got left?"

"About four or five numbers."

I shot her a look: 'Try again.'

"You talking about the money?"

"Good guess." I said.

606

"17 hundred." She took one of my cigarettes from the pack on the dashboard.

"You're runnin' $300/wk. – maybe a $400 habit, if I count the extra dimeballs I gave you. You got a pretty good run going Hot Wire. Did you cop for tonight yet?"

"Yeah." She looked out the window.

"You're a fuckin' idiot.....what the fuck Barbara?"

"You were making such a fuss about how I was clean before I left for Watkins Glen. You boxed me in.....running my life."

"Just be straight with me.....if we're done, just say it. Remember - we said 'no games'?"

"But I want to be your girl." She turned towards me just a little.

I inhaled, "Avoiding me, stealing from me, c'mon Wells.... a $300/wk. monkey riding on your back- Six weeks from now – you're out of my money. When did this shit double in price anyway?" I was thinking of choking her.

"Since Swanson, Z-man, Sally, and a bunch of people down South Yonkers and from the Bronx O.D.'d. Nobody flies solo anymore. The first chump gets a free ride because he's the one taking all the risk. There's not enough product on the street; now the dealers are cutting it with coke. Wayne knew what was going on straight away."

"A fuckin' speedball?........You don't know whether you're coming or going. Just give me my 17 large. This isn't what I had in mind."

She reached in her pocket and pulled out a wad of cash. I counted it in front of her on the front seat. "17.....right." I said: "Let's see that left arm."

She looked away as she rolled her sleeve up. "What – are you hitting it up twice a day? You ARE a fuckin' idiot. This is great; if I stay with you – I've got to be the babysitter 'cause you got shit for will power. Barb, I don't want anyone else. We can't turn back the clock, but we got to put this behind us, so we can move forward." I had pulled over three times before we made it up to Lake Ave. I continued to cruise around with her trying to get a dialogue going about where we were headed. The only resolution we came to was - we had to dry up the drug source. We had to make a clean break with metro N.Y.C. real.....real soon.

RAY'S CITATIONS, MEDALS, COMMENDATIONS, PHOTOS, and news clippings remained on the dining room table since early May. Hal had brought over some of his co-workers from Otis Elevator to see the expressions of recognition from the Republic of South Vietnam and its people. Jane explained the ceremony and the awards to her friends and associates. Both Hal and Jane were proud of Ray's hero status, but more importantly, they were relieved and believed he was getting out alive. We had a small party for Ray's achievements. Mom-Mom and Mack came down, Uncle Bill and Aunt Frances came up, and Linda and Mitch Conroy came from next door.

Towards the end of August, Hal brought Ray's awards into his den, and conspicuously placed them on his walls and desk. I stood on the stairway's landing.

"Dad, have you got a few minutes?" I said.

He was in a good mood: a fresh drink and surrounded by his eldest son's military honors, and a high probability he was no longer where the bullets were flying. Even I couldn't ruin that high for him.

"I was wondering if Barb and me could stay upstate at the orchard until Thanksgiving…maybe the first week of November. It'd be three months at the most." I said.

"Listen….I don't want you two birds sponging off your grandmother and Mack…..you keep to yourselves. It's going to get pretty cold at night, and there's nothing to do besides drink and play house. All I got up there is the one electric heater and the two kerosenes. You'll be responsible for the electric and fuel bill."

"No problem."

"What are you going to do?" Hal took a sip.

"Gonna try to find some kind of work. Maybe Barb can get a job waitressing or something."

"Does your mom know about this love nest you and your girl are cooking up?" he said.

"Un-uh."

"Bring up that saucer vacuum cleaner and buy a couple of bags for it down here. They'll fill up fast with the dead flies and mouse turds. And…..if you burn the place down – don't come back here. Say…..what's wrong with her mom's place?"

"I'm not partial to any of her 13 cats, 11 kids; plus there's some part-time kids of her sister's she's guardian to."

"There is no accurate count?"

"I think the cat count is correct…….. You got to see it to believe it. There wasn't any invitation extended to me anyway."

"I've told you this place is a palace boy. You don't know what good is – until you've had bad." Hal took a big gulp of whiskey soda.

"Don't you get along with her mom's boyfriend?"

"Boyfriends…..plural………Dad." I said.

"Well….give it a go up there – see what happens."

CHAPTER 20
i

A gravity of sorts; some unknown force was interfering with
my free will. It led me to believe my life and physiology was coming
to some kind of state of transformation. One worked in concert with
the other. There were two women in my life, the oddity was Barb went
with the flow and let the dynamism of our relationship be governed by
it. Whereas, Karyn needed or used a catalyst, an outside event or agent
to bring our emotions to parity. The more thought I gave it – the
possibility of there being two paths to the same destination became
intriguing and allegorical at the same time.
  Labor Day came out of left field, the next thing I knew
summer was over. After the weekend affair with Karyn during the
Summer Jam '73 Concert, we resumed our daily luncheons. The two
women were consuming me, but there wasn't much sex. Barb was
dealing with substance abuse and looked forward to getting out of
Yonkers to get clean. Karyn saw something in my character and she
had to get a piece of it.
  The more I missed Ray, the more I tried to become him; I
started believing it was bits and pieces of my brother, that Karyn was
attracted to. I was merely the transporter.....the keeper of his character,
while he wasn't here. There wasn't any way I could tell Karyn the way
I felt about this; it was speculation anyway, but the more thought I
gave it, the more I bought into it. I sat on the mound of the Cosmic
Intruder – with no drugs or alcohol and stared into the Palisades
wondering who I was, and whether a magnetic pole reversal had taken
place within my cellular structure? I sweated in silence for
approximately a half-hour: "IMPOSSIBLE!"
  With Barbara Wells it had been so damn easy.....except for
the past month. I had to deal with a drug addict instead of a sex addict.
That fuckin' White Ghost had taken my job and was eating my lunch.
It would be an onerous task to try to turn back the clock and remove
something she almost loved or loved just as much as me. Karyn was no
dummy, she knew something was going sideways between Barb and
me; I knew she wanted to exploit it and make me see something I
hadn't seen about her nemesis, other than the obvious – the 'tragic
magic'. The shortest distance between two points is a straight line.
Karyn seemed to be determined to disrupt the line and be happy within
the triangle. I didn't know there was a love triangle and Barb didn't
care.
  The Friday before Labor Day, we agreed to go out on the last
day of work like the previous year. The last thing I said to her on
Monday was: "See you tomorrow."
  Karyn nodded and waved, "Tomorrow."

  Tuesday came and no Karyn. I called her house and – no
answer. Uncle Harry was handing out the payoff checks at noon and
thanked me for doing a good job.

"Thanks for giving me a job." We shook hands and I asked: "Did Karyn Cahill call in sick......she said she'd meet me."

"No – she asked me to mail her final check to her." Harry said.

"I must have gotten mixed up." I stood there confused. Was she was paying me back for something? Like a robot I said: "See you next year?"

"God willing. Get some good grades." He called after me.

"It gets harder every semester." 'Perhaps for the best.' I thought as I drove home.

I phoned Karyn's house once again. Her brother said he'd tell her I called. It was a dust-off. Wells' stock went up five and an eighth points.

Jane caught me before I went upstairs: "We got a postcard from Clark Air Force Base in the Philippines" her voice broke.

I took a large step and hugged her a good three minutes.

"Ryan – I've prayed and prayed for this day."

"We all have Mom; he couldn't return at a better time for all of us."

"Here's the postcard." She walked into the kitchen and got it for me:

Aug. 9th, 1973

hey everybody! No more censorship....What you see (Clark Air Base) on the reverse side is where I'll be waiting for my new orders. The Army has got a small auxiliary facility here. I haven't heard anything about where I'm going next. Many of the guys have gone on to Ft. Hood. I don't care where I end up – as long as it's not Alaska. The military's Pony Express is so slow.....I might beat this card back to Yonkers.

Love,

Ray

"This is the best news this family ever got – it's unbelievable." I smiled from ear to ear.

The third day after we were paid off, I came to the reality the seasonal work was over. There weren't going to be any more checks from Westchester County. Three or four nights a week with Caesar, was all I was working, with an occasional tar transaction or a pay phone demolition.

It was still hot, but it wouldn't be for long. A conversation with Barb was overdue. We decided to go to Jones Beach on Friday. She was aware the question and answer session was coming, she was finding it hard to stay clean. Jones Beach's season was over; the beach would be empty but not closed. We had to get the dialogue going and map out our plan for the immediate future. Also, there was Ray's anticipated return. Nobody had a firm date when it would occur, I was hoping for sometime in September. I was more anxious than desperate to get his evaluation of Barb. Having him diagnose her as a magnetically controlled entity.....a shadow entity would eliminate her as being just another street junkie. I was all too familiar with Wells' karma. Her need wasn't to escape as much as it was to go interstellar.

On the Southern Parkway, I told Barb of Ray's impending return. She seemed mildly excited, but more than that she was genuinely happy for me. Once I started, I found out I couldn't shut up about him. It seemed so long ago since we had been together. She wasn't tired of me talking about him, but to her and the mainstream which I was a part of – Ray was pretty much an enigma. Not too many of the people I hung out with could listen to him when he got rolling with the magnetic equation stuff: pole and cellular reversal, time displacement, chimera people, and his speculative concepts which few understood. The Specter junkies who had this reversed wiring code – only they were aware of this new aura which surrounded Ray.......at first he couldn't recognize it; then he couldn't identify it, and finally on a bloodied café patio in Bien Hoa it came back into his body – he knew it to be 'hope'.

Wells knew I idolized my brother, and she idolized me for her own reasons. But in a purely mathematical perspective - she idolized him as well. It was difficult trying to explain Ray to her and include his pivotal role amongst the fifth dimension – "all I'm really doing is acting like a step-down transformer." he said. Cocaine Wayne, Joey Tarts, Crawford, and Rikshaw could communicate with Ray about astrophysics, calculus, the inter-magnetic dimensional plane which took into account magnetic bombardment from the sun and outside the galaxy. He also had the unique gift to infuse enough of his theories to guys like Loki, Vinny, and me, so we'd have a rudimentary knowledge of what the Magnetic Reversal and Polar Collapse might mean. By the time it got to Barb through my feeble explanations, her main response was: "Wake me before the Fireball hits so I can achieve orbit."

That, I understood.

We laid in the sun for a good hour without a word between us. It was 85 degrees, a slight breeze, and the surf was up. It was a perfect beach day. She wore her cut-off dungarees for bottoms and a tank top. As soon as I saw the burn lines appear at the borders of her make-do swim wear - I told her to cover up with a beach towel.

I got up: "Coming in?"

"In a little bit."

"It's a little past one."

It was easy picking up on her restlessness, the high was gone five days ago, but the headaches, bodyaches, chills, and the inability to flush the residue out with food or liquid prolonged the withdrawal. The stupid bitch had to start running it twice a day. Joey Tarts told me the shit on the street lacked the punch in the face most of the regular customers were craving. Shitty dope helped Barb cut down on her usage from the consumer side of the hobby. By Labor Day she had reduced her usage down to about three days a week. Once again, it took a ton of determination. It was a major step after she had her usage up so high a week after Watkins Glen. It was painful for me to watch her suffer. The day without the smack was kicking her butt, and I was helpless to do anything to alleviate her body's cry to return to normal.

Running in from the salt water, I fell into the beach blanket. She was on her stomach, she opened the one eye:

"How's the waves?"

"I got stuck in the washing machine a couple of times – got my ass womped. They're breaking real nice though. They're coming in sets. I'm going back in – 'bout 20 minutes."

"The way I feel....getting caught in the undertoe can't make me feel any worse. Whiteflag – you got to make me go in."

"Wire....just the do the five days in one shot......trying to ween yourself off is prolonging the agony. Just fuckin' do it. After today it'll be down to four, and in four days you'll be able to fall asleep again. Save your energy for something else."

"I know....I know....." she shook her head and took a drag from a cigarette.

"It might work out for us upstate at the orchard house. We'll stay there all week. We'll drive down to Yonkers on Saturdays and return on Sunday. If we can't find work up there, we'll have to move Ray's opium when we're in Yonkers. Kind of a hit and run method. He'll be back soon, I know he has some plans to use this Tiger Tar trying to bring the fifth dimension some spatial tranquility."

"Fuckin' Whiteflag, I don't know if I'll ever get straight again.....fuck.....I must be dying. Maybe I got some brain tumor or something. I'm good for nothing except crawling into a ball and crying. That was the last time for that shit....it just isn't worth the slow-motion crash. Loan me your rosary when we get back to Yonkers......maybe if I just hold on to it – St. Mary will have pity on me when she talks to her Son. Never had the bends this bad." she wailed.

I yanked her up by the hand. "That's it – you're going in."

"Ryyyy-yannnn!" She let out a high pitched cry.

I had to drag her by her arms into the water. "Just let the water take me out to the breakers." she pleaded.

"I gotcha Sugartown." I brought her out to where the water was waist high on me and kept her floating on her back. The water wasn't cold but kool enough to shock her back into the here and now. We floated on a set of gentle waves for about 15 minutes or so. It was tiring her just floating in the water.

"BACKBREAKER!" I called to her as I had let her float by herself. The big ones were coming in. A few swimmers were near; they had already dived under the breaking 10 footer. Another wave behind it was taller and begun to curl 30 yards to the west. We had to ride perpendicular to the waves and not the shore. She was a concern for me but this set of waves were disorienting for Barb. She was having problems with the successive waves. Once, I had to pull her up from the bottom. Finally, we managed to ride one all the way to the shore where she lay on her back in the wet sand.

We lay next to each other for five minutes as she caught her breath. Out of nowhere, this monsta wave had sent us to bottom and propelled us onto the dry beach.

"That's enough dammit!" she got up and sprinted into the water to fight the waves. Where the burst of energy came from was a mystery. I followed her into the water and began riding the surf with her. The tide must have been coming in; the right sides of our bodies kept digging into the pebbles, rough sand, and small broken shells. When a wave broke just right – it would shoot us ahead of the whitewater and wash us into the shore. From the moment Barb charged back into the water, my guard was up. Her resurgence wasn't making any sense. It was fun body surfing with her, but I never felt at ease.

We rode and battled the waves for over an hour, then we were exhausted. Collapsing onto the blanket, we lay on our stomachs. Her arms were along her sides, her head was facing me. I used my crossed arms as a pillow. Our faces were about 14" apart.

"It's just going to be us upstate." I said.

"You got this figured out Whitecaps?"

"What's happening in Yonkers for you or me?"

"My mom still needs a hand with the kids." her speech slowed. "Just a bunch of woods and mosquitoes up there."

"You like apples?"

Barb rolled on her side, now her brow scrunched together: "I like apple pie more than I like apples."

"Hal's got an overgrown orchard of them in case we run out of food. Also, no phone, hot water, or indoor plumbing. There's a hand pump for water, got a fridge, stove, two kerosene and one electric space heater, got an electric blanket, a nasty outhouse, radio, and a TV that only gets one - sometimes two stations. Plus, Mom-Mom and Mack live 5/8ths of a mile away – in case of emergency. It'll only be three months…at most. When we come back around Thanksgiving, I can go down and see if anything's cooking down at Caesar's for the holidays." I wasn't sure she was listening to me. Her eyes seemed awful heavy…….distant

"What about money?"

"Like I said, we might have to push Ray's shit once a week in Yonkers." I put one fist atop of the other and rested my chin on top, "I might luck out and get a job up there. Maybe we'll both find work. You can wait tables…..I'll find something."

"We'll have to talk to your brother about the shit. It's his - it's not yours. You said you got it from some guy at Caesar's."

"You weren't the only one who lied."

"When's he get back?"

"Should be any day."

"Yeah but he left it with me."

"That's right……he didn't give it to you."

"He'll be here soon, he can give us some direction with the way he wants to go." I took a drag off her cigarette. "I know a few people in college at New Paltz and Albany. They'll get into this Tiger

Tar 'cause they'll look at it as some mind expanding substance. Barb, we can't play with this mind expansion stuff, we'll get caught up in it."

"I don't like it enough, I know it's not going be a problem for me." She deadpanned. "When are we going up there?"

"How's Sunday sound?"

"I'm so beat up." Barb closed her eyes. "And physically spent." She buried her face in the blanket.

"How's this going to go down with your mom?"

She spoke directly into the beach, it was difficult to understand her: "Marge knows this day is coming - she's expecting me to be carrying our love child. She thinks I'm pregnant right now.....thinks the withdrawals symptoms are morning sickness." Barb scoffed.

"Great." I replied......we fell asleep for an hour.

ii

Jane had asked Mom-Mom to 'look-in' on us. Barb and me had shaken out the bedding and vacuumed the mattress so we could start using it straight away. We brought in our suitcases, food, and the other stuff we thought we'd need. I was skeptical this was going to work. The three months ahead might work out, or be the end of Barbwire and me. A lot depended on her ability to forget about the dooge. Just getting her to acknowledge the shit simply wasn't available would help a great deal I figured.

Danny Stax had been one of the first Rogues to move out of his parents' house. He was banging Robbie Herrick' sister and he went on about how he was going to have all this great sex now that he had his own place.

Davis Quinn had asked, "Why does a couple seem to recognize a need or a desire to have sex in an empty house or when they first move in?" We were drinking at the Hun's garage, and we all thought he had hit upon some kind of truism. None of us had a logical reason, but it always seemed to happen – even more so if both living quarters and the girlfriend were new.

Barb sat on the edge of the bed and had me stand in front of her while she did her thing. She was making up for the lost time when she was kicking her habit. I never forgot how good she was, but her heart was really into her love-making; we both had missed one another. The sun was still out when Mom-Mom coasted into the driveway commando-style. She had seen the Starfire.

The moans, groans, screeching from the garage would have been reason enough for neighbors to call the cops back in Yonkers......we were loud, we were letting it all loose. In Staatsville, no one heard a thing. Most likely my grandmother voyuered Barb and me for most of our performance; she just 'happened' to knock on the side door just as I finished pulling up my dungarees.

Mom-Mom had this weird look on her face; it left no doubt in my mind we had been observed. It might have been a real shocker if it had been her first exposure to oral sex, not the act itself, but more in the fact her grandson was the recipient.

Wire gave me the 'Who the fuck is that look?'

I looked through the window at the person at the door. When I saw the thick blond hair; I knew it had to be Mom-Mom.

"It's my grandmother." I shot back to Wells and opened the door.

"I brought over some meat loaf and baked potatoes for your dinner."

Barbwire didn't say anything and gave Mom-Mom a weak smile as she bolted out the door.

"What's with her?" Mom-Mom nodded to Barb. I looked outside; her arms braced up against the Olds and I saw her getting rid of me and washing her mouth out with Ripple, then washing it down. She came back in the garage with the Pagan Pink.

"Thanks Mom-Mom."

Barb collected herself. "All we brought with us was a loaf of bread and peanut butter and jelly." She had met Mom-Mom before, at the party Jane had for Ray last month when we first found out he was in the Philippines. She took a sip of Ripple and said: "You're not a Whitelaw...."

"No....I'm Janie's mother....I'm a Knudsen – Ryan's a quarter Knudsen. Since you're with Ryan, you should call me Mom-Mom too." she explained with a smile.

"Okay Mom-Mom...." She goofed on her a little.

Edna (Mom-Mom) turned to me: "I'll bring over your father's .22, so you can get some rabbits. You remember how we cooked them on the grill?" She looked at Barb, "The hind quarters are the only good part on them." she reminded me. "Janie said you'll be staying up here 'til Thanksgiving?"

"Not past then.....too cold."

Wells asked, "Any work up this way?"

"Mmmm.....That's the rub up here......not much work. My husband's an ironworker and for the last few years he only has work 6 months a year. Mack's on a 3 month job right now; he'll be laid-off before Thanksgiving. Come December through May, most likely there won't be any work. Check out IBM, Vassar College, in Poughkeepsie. Take anything either one offers." She went back to her house soon after she gave us the employment outlook.

As instructed, we made applications to the places she recommended and a few others. IBM wasn't taking applications. A guy in the personnel department told us we had to have a cover letter and a resume`. Wells asked me what a resume` was.

"Pretty sure it's a list of the places you've worked before, and what your duties were."

"Huh?"

"They just want to be sure you weren't pressing plates in the joint." I spelled it out.

She put her hands in the air....."I'm clean."

Vassar College had called Edna's house four days after I had filled out an application. They told me to come in, there were some

615

questions they wanted to resolve. At the interview, they said I would be working weekends, the duties would be similar to what I did at Tibbetts and the pay was the same. The job title was: Laborer I. Mom-Mom and Mack reacted as though I had hit the Lottery. Vassar gave me two shirts, and a hooded sweatshirt saying: Buildings & Grounds on them. Some days I left Barb at the summerhouse, but generally she drove me to work and had the Starfire for the day.

After some cajoling and studying, she got her learner's permit. We used a mock-up of a parallel parking situation in my grandparent's driveway to get her familiar with the parking portion of the test. The first night didn't go so well; she parked it correctly only one out of five times. By the end of the week Barb was about 85% proficient. After the first late afternoon of practice, I asked her why her parallel parking was so bad. "I thought you were a better driver than that."

"Remember Whiteline – whenever I was copping dope - I was always double-parked, or just drove around the block. When I drove with Z-man or Joey, I'd always tell them 'a parked car was one foot in the jail cell.' And it is - if you think about it." she nodded.

"The Starfire will be a formidable ally with two side-view mirrors when the testing agent asks you to parallel park in your parallel universe. I believe you'll pass on your first try."

She was immediately side-tracked and concerned, "Do you feel I am like the others – the misaligned nomads- and a part of that world? – the world you and Cinzano talk about?"

"Fucked if I know. If there is something such as a late bloomer.....a shady lady......you might be it. Ask Ray. He'll be back soon. He'll give you a ruling."

"Thrilling."

"Just pass the road test so I won't have to worry when I give you my keys."

At the end of September, Barb Wells had her driver's license. She even had given the DMV Hal's address at the garage, and began receiving junk mail. It was better than nothing, we had no phone and nobody wrote us. I let her take the car to Yonkers while I worked. It took about a week to figure out no good would come of it. She was coming back from Yonkers progressively later as the days ticked off. I was ready to bring the hammer down when the OPEC oil embargo hit after the Yom Kippur War. The gasoline shortages ended her solo trips. Now Barb had a job she liked, but didn't get paid for: waiting on gas lines every odd day. The four barrel carburetor and 455 cu. in. Wildcat drank so much gas - she was just replacing the gas she burnt up just waiting on line. The closer we got to N.Y.C., the more cars were waiting to get their $3.00 of gas. We talked to Mack and Mom-Mom; they remembered the rationing during WWII so they kind of took it in stride. When the price of gas went up to .45/a gal. – that was when it got our attention. The gas lines weren't too bad in Dutchess county, availability was more of a problem. We'd pass a lot of stations with signs saying: 'No Gas today'.

Mom-Mom and Mack came over on the last day of September. We had a fire going in a pit Barb had lined with stone. We sat around the fire drinking some beers. Edna had a miniature jug of something. They asked how things were going…..the job….did Barb find any work yet? There was some more small talk, and finally Mack stood up, "Raise your cans: Ray will be home next Friday. Jane and Hal are having a party for him on Sunday – 1 o'clock.

My face lit up like a Roman candle and the Wire gave me a bear hug. It was only a week away. "Been a long time coming – every bit of two years." The fire's light gave our faces a spiritual aura.

Unable to fall asleep, my mind raced. We were clean of opiates, but unable to fall into dreamland despite the kool night air which usually had us both asleep within minutes. The much awaited reunion with Ray kept me awake. My tossing also kept Barb from falling asleep.

I reviewed all the mumbo-jumbo Ray had discovered, invented, or interpreted and continued to buy into the magnetic pole reversal; though I could only see bits and pieces in the seven year span since the fireball first made its appearance. I was more than curious to know where we were in the Greystone Equation. The things Ray had learned at Purdue or in the Army might advance or nullify what he had based his original theories on. Laying in the bed, trying to see the stars through a filmy window; I wondered how much of Einstein's relativity theory Ray had attached to this magnetic pole reversal.

He was immersed in the pole reversal phenomenon. He had to have been. Why else would he ask Isaac Seabrook to bring back my comet dust to Vietnam? I could have forgotten the whole thing except for Ray's inexhaustible investigation, and the two outer body experiences I had when I was 12. He was only going to have leave for a month; I needed the two missing years.

A star twinkled and vanished……I immediately thought of Sally Englund. We were all saddened when she cashed out, but in the long run I thought it might be better for Ray to be without her…..just not this way. My brother looked great in those photographs he sent with his commendation stuff and medals. If they had run into each other during his leave, neither one would have recognized the other. They were two trains going in opposite directions. When she passed on, she looked five, maybe seven years older than him. Running into one another when Ray got his discharge wouldn't have done either any good; at the very least it would have been painful.

The brotherhood connection had to be tangible……vibrant. It had to be what it had been; to plug into the grid and feel his energy once again - feel the juices running wild like we were kids. As the day drew near where we would once again have symbiotic physicality, I wondered if I would retreat from it, embrace it or be denied it. Just looking at the photos from overseas, one could easily discern he was on the up and coming while I was almost in free-fall. Our relationship had been on 'pause' but neither of us had pushed the 'stop' button or had some force push it for us. The reunion had me in a state of urgency. It was Thursday, Ray may have already been at 21 with Hal, Jane, Cathy, and Willis.

Wells and me smoked a mini-ball of opium after our p.b.&j. supper. Barb had gathered some wood during the day, and I got a fire going in the pit. It was a kool night. The rocks absorbed the heat and the fire was warm. We put one more tiny nodule in the hash pipe and had a hit apiece. We were immobilized watching the fire. She usually would tell me where the opium smoke took her – but this time she was tight lipped. I just watched the fire, I must have thrown on some more wood because the fire didn't go out. Barb had the fire to her front, and me behind her. I swear I thought we were in some kind of capsule on our way to some distant planet or galaxy. We woke when the dawn came up and we found ourselves wrapped in the beach blanket.

No matter how we wanted a good marijuana high to come from the small amounts of opium, it never happened. We got to sleep fine, but always woke up fuzzy. We should have just drank T-bird and smoked Marlboros. I woke and felt the pangs of addiction..........stupid.

ON SUNDAY MORNING, THE FOUR OF US PACKED INTO Mom-Mom's little Chevy Vega and drove down to 21. The new paradigm of small cars and packing them with people seemed un-American. Mack drove, Edna and Barb rode in the back seat. It was kool in the morning when we left, but it looked like it'd be a nice warm autumn afternoon. We all smoked; it was damn near a death chamber of exhaled smoke and lit cigarettes.

Mom-Mom and Barb went through the basement and climbed the stairs to the kitchen to help Jane and Judy and see Cathy and Brother Bill. Jane had sent Hal to the A&P after Ray told her he had invited a few more friends at the last minute. From the kitchen window she yelled a "Hi" to Mack and me, and asked us to set out all the chairs, two card tables, relocate the picnic table, set up her D.J. - Pro Record Player, amp, and speakers she had hauled from her studio yesterday after Saturday's last class. Except for the speakers, we set all this music playing stuff on a ½" piece of plywood supported by two saw horses.

During the week, Hal had purchased a new barbecue grill for today. "See if you guys can assemble it before Hal gets back so we can start cooking." Jane was anxious to get the food going.

I had seen a couple of dozen of these barbecue grills at Tibbetts. The box it came in had a picture of a family chowing down all sorts of carnivorous delights, some which defied identification other than: it was a piece of meat. The ad on the box guaranteed cooking up legendary banquets for every conceivable occasion. Dad had bought the deluxe version of the "All Star Barb-B-Q"; with the rotisserie option: $7.99 at John's Bargain Store. Latinos, whites, and blacks would abandon them after one or two uses.

We had the parts out of the box when Hal came down the driveway with the Chrysler Newport until it was blocked by the party tables and chairs. Hal shut off the ignition and was out of the Chrysler for a good 20 seconds before the engine stopped running.

"Aaaaaaay – all's they had was 'no lead' at the Esso station. They only let me buy $3.00 worth of the shit." Dad said.

618

"Hal – it isn't the gas." Mack put his hands in his back pockets, and shook his head from side to side.

"Okay, Mr. Ironworker.......what is causing the car to run on?"

Mack laughed and said: "It's a fuckin' Dodge, what do you expect performance?" Barb and me had to turn away to laugh.

Hal went up to the kitchen empty handed. Barb and me made two trips from his car. One trip went upstairs, the other went into the fridge in the cellar. He had bought another case of Miller bottles. I took them from the carton and handed them individually to Barb. She placed them on the top shelf of the fridge with the Schaefer on the door and bottom. We admired the neat stacking job we did. The golden beer in the fridge was beautiful; the image should have been in a magazine.

Two hands came around Barb and squeezed her tits. A voice said softly: "They're stacked just right." We were caught off-guard and turned.

"Ray!" I was in awe.

"You fuckin' jerk.......where's my kiss?" Wire said.

The cellar was dimly lit. "Oh man – I am glad you are back." Something or someone had tapped my energy reserve. After their kiss, I embraced Ray's shoulders: "Ray....." I said - still unable to grasp his physical presence.

"Loki had written me you two were going out."

"He was the best guy available." she pulled me to her side.

"You know it Barb." Ray said.

"I need a beer to wash down all this bullshit." We all took a Miller, and we brought a Schaefer out for Mack.

"Let's get out of this dark cellar."

We went out onto the driveway's pavement and I called to Mack: "Look who's here."

He turned and saw Ray. He stood up and saluted as military as he could, which Ray returned. Mack shook his hand and embraced his arm.

"You're a true hero Ray. What you did can never be quantified."

"Because nothing happened."

"You can't downplay your willingness for self sacrifice; not in the eyes of anyone here." Mack said.

The four of us stood silent; immobilized by the commendations, news clippings, and medals. Each of us was immobilized and transported to the café in Bien Hoa for a brief moment.

"I've got to get another beer - the picture of the grill on the box doesn't jive with the parts." I said.

Mack turned the charcoal dish upside-down and inserted three aluminum legs in stubs that had been attached to the bottom so the smaller diameter aluminum tubing could be inserted on the underside of the Bar-B-Q's shallow bowl. The grill was then turned right-side up: "That'll get us cooking."

Hal was having a tough day; it started with the cheap grill. The elevator handle raising and lowering the grill's level in relation to the fire had gotten bent because Hal applied too much force – plus all the components were made with real light gauge steel. The charcoal was also cheap and wouldn't stay lit. The lighter fluid ran out so he substituted the lawn mower's gasoline. Hal cautioned everyone to stay back and poured half-a-Mason Jar of gasoline on the charcoal. He poured a little at a time, and waited for the gas to ignite……..nothing. Frustrated, he began to pour the gas freely; all the oxygen was sucked from above the 'All Star Grill' and a flame reached 15 feet into the air which startled Jane who was inside the house. The remaining fuel in the jar ignited and Hal's right arm was on fire. He danced like a wild Indian waving his arm trying to extinguish it.

Ray came running from the cellar with an old towel he had run under the laundry faucet and wrapped Dad's forearm tight to smother the fire. The smell of spent gas and burnt flesh did little to whet the appetites of the guests.

"Hey Pops – we better get you to the emergency room."

"No….no….I'm alright……alright….just get me some electrical tape and my drink." he shuddered.

Ray knew as long as he was conscious, a trip to a medical facility was unlikely. Young Brother Bill was called into action – He brought Hal's whiskey soda mug upstairs to be refilled (a double…..for the pain). When he came back, Billy had to rotate the chickens by hand with a pair of vise-grip pliers clamped to the four-sided spit rod with an oversized leather welding glove. Poor Willis spent the next hour turning the spit by hand.

Most of the guests, family, and three of the Rogues had showed up by two o'clock. Hal and Brother Bill manned the grill; the former was in rough shape from the gasoline burns and the liberal use of alcohol. After Ray's first aid measures, his picnic duties were done as everybody wanted to talk to him. A display table had been set up in the garage of Ray's photos, commendations, and medals. When it looked to be sunny for the rest of the day, Hal had us put Rays commendations and medals outside on a card table.

The side dishes and appetizer plates were almost gone. Chef Hal had placed 4 or 5 burnt burgers on the plate on the picnic table. They were as black as the briquettes and about the same size. Daredevil Barb put one on a bun with slices of cheese and tomato, with a slash of ketchup. She couldn't chew or swallow it, and spit it into the woods. Some kids gambled on a couple of dogs – they were gagging as well. Wells brought me upstairs to the kitchen. Jane was taking out a big crock of baked beans from the oven.

"Jane…." Barb put her hand over her heart, "The burgers and hot dogs taste like paint. You can't let Hal put them out."

She looked at me, and down to the backyard.

"If she says so." I said.

Jane observed the party. A platter of dogs and burgers were placed on one of the food tables.

"Soup's on!......Dig in……"Hal called out in pain.

Bad Brad, Vinny Tarts, and Kenny Crawford didn't wait; each loaded up a burger and a hot dog in a bun.

"Hey – little Whitelaw…..Hurry up with them chickens."
Brad laughed as Brother Bill worked the principle of the wheel and
axle with the vise-grips and shaft.

The three negotiated their first bites. They began to choke,
cough, and gag. "Tastes like varnish…..tastes like gas." Crawford's
palate registered: "Moth balls."

Jane rushed over to her handbag and handed us $30. "Go get
three buckets of chicken from the Lucky Wishbone and three large
pizzas from Ralph's. She flew down the basement steps, removed the
grilled meat from the food table and went over to Hal and had a word
with him.

We watched as they went back and forth. Jane ordered sister
Cathy to turn the master volume to six. The hands went to her
hips……crossed arms with her back to the party; Jane's weight went
to one hip and teeter-tottered her head back and forth until Hal was
done yelling at her. The hands came off her hips and the pointing
started at the 'All Star Rotisserie'. Jane went to the gin bottle on the
liquor table, and Hal went over to the 'All Star Bar-B-Q' and kicked it
over in front of a stunned Brother Bill. The meat, chickens, and
charcoal covered a small area of slate which constituted the small
patio. The family had all seen this type of blow-up before. Those who
didn't know our family, found it both amusing and shocking. This
eruption was more visual than auditory, but just as unwanted.

BarbWire and me bought another case of beer as well. When
we returned Hal gave me the evil eye; the rest cheered us as we broke
out the chicken and pizza. I looked at the old man sitting by himself
with a plate of his burgers and chicken on his lap. The rest of the meat
was still on the slate patio surrounding him. The Lucky Wishbone's
chicken had come with mashed potatoes, potato wedges, cold slaw,
and dinner buns. It came none too soon; some of the girlfriends and
wives didn't want their boyfriends and husbands driving home all lit
up. The Rogues and Barb went for a short ride and smoked some
reefer. Mack was also having a good time; I wondered if I was going
to be driving back to Staatsville.

It was a good party, except for anything associated with the
'All Star' grill.

It cooled off as the sun got lower. Mack and Mom-Mom
wanted to get started back before the sun went down. Both of us had to
work tomorrow. Ray, as the centerpiece of the party, was going to be
busy until the last guest left.

"Mom-Mom, I'll be up in a week." He looked at Barb and
me: "You got room for a guest?"

"I'm off Thursday and Friday…..come up Wednesday
afternoon." I looked over to Mom-Mom: "For supper?"

"5:30." she said.

"And we'll get down to business on Thursday." he
replied.

"Good 'nuff."

I TOOK THE OLDS TO WORK ON MONDAY.
BARBARA straightened up the garage the best she could. Paper plates

and used Jack-In–The-Box cups were what we used to eat and drink from. We went through a lot of p.b.& j. and ate breakfast more than the other two meals combined. She had cut a bunch of firewood with the bow-saw; enough for the rest of the week. Wire's hands were blistered from all the sawing. Trying to be smart like a doctor, I tossed her a bottle of Jergens lotion and suggested she could try to moisturize her hands in a way to benefit the both of us.

Ray and Barb had known each other, mostly from hanging around with the fifth dimension and going to concerts and partying. At his Coming Home party, there was a common chord struck between the two. I couldn't say why that was - other than the fact I was a common denominator. Maybe it had something to do with the cosmic intruder. I thought it was a real panic when he grabbed her tits from behind. She must have enjoyed it – she was the one who initiated the big welcome back kiss.

Jane had telephoned Mom-Mom to let her know she needed the Mercury on Wednesday, and Barb would have to come back down and get Ray.

At the orchard, while we were catching up on the previous 2 ½ year separation, we discussed Barb and came to a similar conclusion: she seemed to be neither shadow phase nor the current positive world. That buzz-cut she had last summer said 'alien' to me all day. If there was such a thing as inter-galactic attraction…..she had it. With a two inch spike hair cut, it completed my meltdown….I re-surrendered to her: "I want to be your prisoner."

Something was really going on with her which made her unlike so many of the other chicks I knew. I could figure out she was dialed in with the Shadow World - the coming world with the new magnetic pole alignment, but her feet were in the conventional dimension. It didn't make sense.

"Speculation Ray?"

It came from his mouth as if it was fact: "It may have something to do with solar Magnetic storming – bombarding the earth with abnormally long pulses."

At dinner, Mom-Mom and Mack inquired about Hal's burnt-up hand and arm. Ray told us Hal was on antibiotics and goof balls for the pain. Mack asked where he would be stationed next, and he said he had orders for Okinawa.

"Just glad I'm not going to Korea."

In between forkfuls of baked potatoes, prime rib, and broccoli, Mack told Ray and me to start planning on what our next moves would be. Whatever Ray was going to be doing would require too much brain power for me to even consider. This pep rally was more for me than Ray - we all knew it. Mack looked mostly at Ray, but none of Mack's counsel was wasted on me. I knew I had to get it in gear and do something with my life. Nobody was worried about Ray's future when his tour in Nam ended. My grandfather could point me in the right direction, but it'd be Ray's "hand's on" direction which would get me on my way.

"So Mack…" My brother pushed away his plate, "Did you use your G.I. benefits to become an ironworker after WWII?"

"Nah, I was an ironhead when I went in and that's what I did when I got out. The guys coming back from Vietnam use their G.I. benefits for apprenticeship school now. We didn't even have an apprenticeship in our local union until after Korea. You learn more on the job than you do in school anyway."

"Ain't that the truth." Ray nodded.

"I know it's slow for steel construction now, but the next time they need manpower or are taking on apprentices – I'd sure like to sign up. It's something I think could handle." I kept my eyes on my plate.

Mack looked at me – no longer as a grandson, but as a prospective employee. This was between me and him.

"Listen Ryan, this is how it is: You've got to watch, learn, shut-up, and do as you're told. You've got to remember every day's lesson. If you've got half a brain, common sense, can read a tape measure…….and I've already taught you boys that; and you can apply your knowledge into erecting steel components that are level, plumb, and straight………15 or 300 ft. off the ground or over water. This trade will provide you with a good living, if you can master the basics. Now – if you can weld or become a knowledgeable rigger or both…..you'll always be in demand. One thing though, just starting out…..count on living out of a suitcase and budgeting your finances so you can live on an unemployment check. If you're lucky…..you might latch onto a one or two-year project just coming out of the ground. Most likely you'll be chasing work for three or four years before you get a handle on the game. Learning to weld……..that's the quickest way to stay employed. If I had to do it over again – that's the way I would have gone. If such a thing like good working conditions exist in the ironworking trades – it's the weldors that got 'em."

Mack laughed across to Edna. "That's how I met Mom-Mom; her brother Earl was an ironworker. Earl fixed me up with Mom-Mom." Mack sucked his teeth and worked his tooth pick.

"Earl liked those rain-out days. He liked to drink." Mom-Mom commented. She took a deep breath and asked, "Who wants coffee and pie?"

"Mack, just tell me who I've got to see to get started." I said.

"I'll be thinking of you guys, I'll get word to you when the time is right." he said.

Wells barked, "What about me?"

"Until you and Ryan get married, you're just his friend." Mom-Mom laughed.

"It's not like it's my fault, he hasn't asked me."

I looked at the two women like they were both crazy. "You know we don't have to be married."

"Yes, you do." Mom-Mom and Mack said in unison.

"I guess I could see us married." I said as Ray rolled his eyes with a grin.

"Did you guys ask your ol' man about working with the Elevators Constructors Union?" Mack's one brow went up.

"Hal said they couldn't keep their own people busy."

"Well keep asking him....bug him.....The elevators – that's a good racket." Mack said. "You boys and you, Barbara, you've got to really start thinking about tomorrow."

We said thanks and took our apple pie back to the orchard. It was dark within the hour. Even with the robust fire Barb had started, it was still a crisp night. We gave Ray the rundown of the people who had cashed out. Loki had already told him about Englund.

Wells said, ".....it just wasn't smack either: there were a lot of car wrecks, gun violence – drug deals gone bad." She cracked a pint of Wild Irish Rose. " Remember 'lil Presto?
Robin and Buddy's brother? Poor kid went to sleep and never woke up."

"Who?" Ray's forehead wrinkled. "What'd the coroner's report say?" he lit a cigarette.

"There was no autopsy."

"Huh?........impossible. I got a bad feeling more death and mayhem are coming. You guys been watching the night skies?"

"Not like I used to." I said.

Ray looked over to Wells, "What about you star gazer?"

"I know the story of the 'comet night'. I know where it's buried. We've had sex on top of the mound. I know it's a special spot – a source of year round heat. It also has magnetic power to a mag-lev a train or bring them to a dead stop. But, I don't know stuff like you, Joey, Wayne-o, Rikshaw, or Crawford know." she said.

"Without getting into the Greystone Equation in detail..." Ray continued his explanation how a magnetic pole reversal affected a very small percentage of humanity, and the way it upset his life - forcing him from this reality without death. Devising an escape...... finding a 'black hole'......or being jettisoned through a dimensional relief valve became an obsession.....a necessity. He alluded to his experience in Vietnam where he perceived a different magnetic structure. He didn't elaborate however.

Wells got a chunk of what my brother was putting down. To me......it made as much sense as Cocaine Wanye or Kenny Crawford grasping these abstract concepts. I could listen until I was blue in the face about the stuff; either you got it or you didn't.

"You were at the 'Kamikaze Concert'?" he asked.

"Yeah." She took a sip of wine. "When we all came back to Yonkers, I knew I had missed something transitive in a magnetic astrophysical and dimensional way. You guys may not have known it, but it was all you Rogues talked about for the rest of the summer."

I watched her closely, she never had this level of insight before and surely she never talked this way to me. There was some additional component to their communication I was aware of, but couldn't bust the code.

She took the stick she used for stirring the fire, and repositioned the wood. Hundreds of sparks rose into the night sky. Wells looked at Ray and grasped my hand:

624

"It's about humanity isn't it?" She gave the fire another stir. "You call yourselves a negatively charged force – negativity is just a label isn't it?"

"Not really........the math and science seems to back it up." he said. "What you mean is 'We'........'we' call ourselves ....don't you?"

"Yeah – I suppose I do believe I am part of the reversal." she said.

"Have any ideas as to what that may mean?"

"For me.......only for me – it's hard dealing with everyday existence."

He turned to me: "Is she?"

"That's for you or her to reveal. I can't pick a 'ghost rider' out of a crowd like you can. She likes to go into outer space just like the rest of the fifth column." I looked her way, "You seem to be able to stay clean..............periodically."

"I think about getting high – a lot. I know I like getting high. For some......it's about the rush; it is for me. For others it's the ability to escape." She turned to Ray; "My escape is your brother."

Wells never spoke to me about any of this shit, it took the air from my lungs and put it in my sail, "Is it?" Our eyes locked in the glow of the fire.

"I think so."

"But what about you Ray?" I lit a cigarette.

He took a long pull from a pint of Bali Hai; he shook his head quickly and stared at the label. "How do you drink this piss?"

"Lemme see." I up ended the pint and passed it back. "It has a rather juvenile fruity taste......don't you think?"

"Wells, what I find inexplicable is a latency displayed with magnetic polarity. You're not sure what the feeling is, increasingly you sense you might be wired the wrong way like me and the rest. Seeing me and the 'High Five' doesn't allow you a neutral zone to exist in; and going psycho gets closer and closer."

"The day I tried to save those guys lives at the café: I've experienced this incredible ride of being free; a release from fighting life, free from the weight of being in an opposed magnetic sphere. Through my attempt to save life, by sacrificing my own; this event has brought me back the purity I possessed, before the Fireball's appearance. That was around nine months ago, but the familiar weight of competing magnetisms and fields has been on the increase of late. It is not as intense as it had been, but I'm afraid to find myself back at square one." His face glowed orange, "Not by our choice; Ryan and I ate the fruit of the tree in the garden. With it came the knowledge of mankind.......the good and the evil." Ray said.

"What is the good and which is the evil?" Barb squinted.

"It rather depends on one's point of view.....how you perceive the world or worlds.....the universes."

"Wait a minute...." The street wine was taking hold. "That cannot be......it must be constant to have truth......validity." I took a long drag as I tried to think. "You can't rewrite the laws of God and the natural order of the universe as you go through life."

"Nobody's rewriting anything – it is perception through the prism of the current magnetic paradigm which has made it almost impossible to conceptualize." Ray offered.

"We've been at this juncture a number of times in the past. Because I am not part of the polar reversion world, it is difficult to bring continuity without the chaos preceding the two realities. Does this make sense?" I thought aloud.

There was a lapse of clock time, and we sat trying to catch up to my brother's theorems. Wine could not be accounted for and the pack of Parliaments were on the ground – empty.

"I am going to give it a shot, although it is quite possible it is just a shot in the dark." Barb threw the cellophane into the fire from a new pack of Camels. "When you save life, or live in the current magnetic pole configuration; this allows you a share in that life to take back to the phantasm or reversed terrestrial pole dimension: a form of existentialism from an unfamiliar magnetic world.....though it shares a common seam or border with the other. Harmonious at present."

I dropped her hand, and tried to peer into her eyes, face, her brain. The flames of the pit fire made her face flicker as if waves of some intelligent force was going through her as she delivered this deep space dialectic verbiage. I looked at the bottle of street wine, "Ray....did you drop a tab of sunshine in my wine?........The truth." They laughed at my accusation.

She found it amusing, but continued conversing with Ray: "And you want to keep saving or attempt to save life because it feels right......feels good."

"Something along those lines. Somehow the micro human component is woven into the macro magnetic fabric. At random points in history, human material, functionality, and necessity permit a magnetic transfer operationally..... other times, it does not. As long as there is magnetic shifting, these forces and gravities will demonstrate a constant state of flux: the positive or the negative trading dominance through the eons of time: the dominant trying to maintain; the lesser trying to replace. Planets, solar systems, a universe, or a system of universes will always seek to maintain equilibrium. Over time, it eventually brings back unity and balance to what we thought was chaos." He looked up at the star filled sky.

"Had nuff......goin' to bed." I ejected the tape and shut the trunk.

WHERE HAD BARB'S INFUSION OF BRAIN POWER COME from? Probably the same place as the pole reversed crew my brother seemed to lead. Clearly Cocaine Wayne, Crawfish, and now Wells had that high level of magnetic power which Joey, Rikshaw, and Z-man possessed or had possessed. In everything pertaining to the magnetic realignment, they were light years ahead of me. I couldn't increase my brain function or capacity – but Barb Wells did. The realization didn't threaten me, but it was unexpected.

We closed up the orchard garage on the third weekend of November, and said good-bye to Mom-Mom and Mack. We thought we were ready for Yonkers. I left Vassar without notice. Mack's counsel was something neither of us got from our parents. The fourth Thursday (Thanksgiving) was less than a week away. The vices we had left awaited our return. The last three days in the garage had left Barb getting cagey.

"If we don't get out of Yonkers, we'll never stay clean."

Wells chuckled, "Doesn't matter where I am – I'm reversed magnee-to."

"Maybe. I'm thinking about looking up Loki in Miami. Might work for us; we'd skip winter."

"Living up here in Straatsville has been like the Ritz for me. I don't know if I can go back to High Street with Marge….the boyfriends…the kids… the cats. Can I stay at 21 with you?"

"Barb, that's Hal's house. You know what he's like. Jane would welcome you; still, you'd have to put up with his drinking and abuse. Loki knows the ropes about getting a hack license down in Florida, and how 'bout this – you might land your first straight gig……how old are you?"

She shook her head back and forth: "You are sounding like Reno."

"Get a fuckin' job on the books."

"I got a job Whiteglob."

"Yeah? How's that?"

"All the blowjobs I've given you?" she started laughing. "The tugjobs, the fuckjobs, and them two rim jobs you talked me into."

We were bustin' out. She was on a roll, she put her hands on her hips; the one came off and her index finger came right at me. With every word the index finger recoiled and got ready to refire: "And Mr. Smartypants…and ….." She was laughing so hard she had to stop and try it again. "……..And Mr. Smartypants……why……why?....." I wasn't sure she could give me both barrels her laughed words were almost unintelligible: "WHY DO YOU THINK THEY'RE CALLED JOBS?" She tried to catch her breath: "BECAUSE IT'S FUCKIN' WORK….YA FUCKIN' JAG. THERE OUGHT TO BE A HEALTH AND PENSION PLAN WITH ALL THE JOBS I'VE DONE ON YOU !"

I looked at her with indignation, but was unable to keep a straight face. I struck an Oscar worthy pose of dismay and innocence: "Wait a minute Bitch – you'd do it for free you love the work so much."

She smiled shaking her head back and forth. "For you Old Man…..for you I do it for free because I love you so much. It is my pleasure……just keep on lovin' me."

It was turning from play to love. I tried to dial it back a little, "If you only meant the bullshit you talk."

She squinted, "You know I mean it." Our eyes locked. "Prove it."

"I don't have to prove nuthin'." She unzipped my dungarees and took it out and started to satisfy both our desires. She stopped and looked up: "I love you, I love it, I love loving you and I can't see my life without you, and this thing she wiggled and waved back and forth." Barb didn't smile. "If I don't have you – I'll end up like the rest of the junkies."

"How could I leave you? It'd be like leaving heaven on earth: a great face, attitude, skinny ass, no games, beautiful tits, and a sex drive that equals mine. And now, you're even smart." I wondered when she'd get back to business.

"You're just saying that....I'm pretty flat."

"No Wire, you got it all – at least for me. I couldn't find what you've got in any other girl. Those tits really turn me on. There's more nipple than there is tit. I'm so in love with you. I just know you'll be young forever."

"Anything else while you're delivering the big snowjob?"

"Yeah, get going with what you're doing." She started again, I looked down and suggested: "Why dontcha see Mary Ellen......you need a haircut...getting kind of long."

"You don't want me to finish.......you want to fight."

"You know what I want."

"You know what I need." The conversation was over and Barb got back to business.

Our self-imposed 90 day de-tox, and Ray's three overnight visits pushed the reset button on our relationships. The heroin specter would always be there........lurking. That could not be exorcized from our past.

Ray had left us with this: "In a small number of people who were not atomically, and magnetically subservient to the status quo of the magnetic pole configuration, was an even smaller number of shadow people who could survive without chemical interdiction."

Prior to Ray's departure for Okinawa, he took a rough inventory of the Tiger Tar. I had moved a quarter pound of opium; he gave me another half and took the rest. The tar wasn't going back overseas, but I had no clue what he was doing with it. He handed me two olive jars and two yellow pharma containers of Fireball ash: Two were labeled Pos.+, the others Neg.-. "Stash this in the cellar somewhere. We're going to have to get to work on this when I get back. Might be able to raise another continent like Australia from the oceans if we find the right code sequence." He looked amazed at the thought.

"Huh?"

Ray started laughing, "You Doomcuff...... anyway, when I finish my hitch, we're going to have to exhume the cast-off piece of the cosmic intruder. It isn't buried doing nothing. The continuous heat output is indicative of that. If the mound starts to glow or shows any abnormal activity, let me know. I think all you can do now is to watch for any changes occurring......at the site.....in the area.......anomalies in the sky.......or to people on or around the cosmic intruder. It'll be interesting, if it does." We all knew he had to leave. There was only one thing that mattered...........he was alive.

We drove to her mother's crackerbox shack on High St. It was cold and I finally reentered the Wells' menagerie. Even though I was letting warm air out of the house, I kept the door open a crack for some air flow. Some six year old kid asked:

"Are you my Daddy?"

"No, I'm your cousin." I said.

Barb went from room to room. She was about to climb the stairs, and met up with her mother outside the bathroom. If the kids, TV, and radio had been quieter, I might have overheard their dialogue. I walked further into this mixed up mess. The scene defied description.

Barb's half-sisters, Hope and Helen who were 11 and 13, had been given Barb's bed when we went up the country. Sylvia, 18 y.o., was now the oldest of Marge's kids in the house. Barb walked over to me and said she was ready to drive down to Miami as soon as I got the green light from Loki and we got some money together.

Barb called into the tiny kitchen, "Where am I supposed to sleep?"

"Sleep anywhere you want to kid-o." Ma Wells chimed.

"Mom….." Barb stamped her foot, "Hope and Helen are in my bed."

"You left – there was an empty bed - and we needed the space."

She looked at her mom sideways.

"You didn't say if or when you were coming back…….Pfffft …..Barbara's gone. I just told ya we needed more room."

Wire looked out the window into the street, inhaled her cigarette, and crunched her eyebrows together: "Who's moving in?"

"No one's moving in – it's already here." Marge Wells patted her lower abdomen. You're going to have a new brother or sister." She smirked.

I stood there stupefied.

"It's going to get pretty crowded here this winter. You should be on your own anyway."

"How many is this Mrs. Wells?" I scanned the premises trying to estimate the amount of humanity.

"13. Lucky 13 for number of cats. We might name the kid "Lucky" if it's a boy, or Felicia or Felicity for a girl."

I studied her. For having pushed out 11 kids in 15 years, there was very little evidence of it. She had been pregnant with Barb when she was 15 years old. Her face was a little rough – probably from all the smoking.

"Does Barb know her new step-father?" I said.

"My sweetie is an OTR trucker from Tennessee……Trudy brought him over. A great head of hair…..maybe we'll call the boy Elvis instead." Marge looked up at the corner where the wall met the ceiling.

Barb squeezed her eyelids and mashed her lips: "We got to get out of Yonkers."

"We're short on cash. I hope Caesar is looking for drivers for the holidays. And you're going to move some black tar. I better call Rex and see if Palamar's got anything going."

She gave me an eye roll and a head bobble. "Hey Mom – are you doing anything for Thanksgiving?" There wasn't any answer. Barb spoke softly, "You can't be counting on me to move the Tiger?"

"Isn't that kind of your specialty?" I said. "I'll ask around – see how much interest is out there. Give you some leads; I can't be selling the shit from the taxi."

"Ryan, I can't stay here. I'd rather freeze in Straatsville."

"You are coming over on Thursday?" The smell in the house did nothing to whet my appetite.

"Mom" - Barb raised her voice above the house noise: "I'm going to Ryan's house for Thanksgiving."

"See if Sylvia will go with you."

"Uh.....I'll ask her next year." Barb replied.

"I'll be around this weekend getting my stuff together." Barb said.

"See ya kidd-o", her mom said.

I filled my lungs with some fresh air on the other side of the front door.

"I'm starting to recall one of the reasons I got into drugs." She said as she lit one of my smokes. "Give me a date you think we'll get out of Yonkers."

"Somewhere between Thanksgiving and Christmas. We are NOT taking the Tiger Tar with us. We get caught with that shit in Dixie – we'll die in prison."

"How much money we need to get on the road?"

"Gas, food, emergency cash, security deposit/1st month's rent, utilities......Like $900 minimum." I raised my brow. She had come out in just a pullover and started shivering.

Undoing the buttons of my coat, I wrapped as much of her in it as her size allowed and hugged her. "You going to be around later on?"

"You going down to Caesar's now?" She seemed concerned.

"Yeah, where you going to be?"

"Probably Lake Ave. or riding around with one of you guys. Whiteye, we got to get out of here....we need some heavy duty luck to come our way. We got to make it happen."

"You get better all the time." She smiled at me just as I was leaving.

It was a 50-50 bet Caesar Moreno was hiring drivers. I showed up at the garage around 5:00. It was almost dark. Dan Rodan aka "Mr. Personality" was still dispatching even though Linda was already there. She watched the scene – she liked a good laugh.

"What do you want?" Rodan looked at me as if I was there to hold him up.

"A cab."

"Where you going?"

"C'mon Dan, a cab to drive.......I want to go to work."

He sneered, and returned to reading his call sheet, "Ain't got no cars...... Besides you, Tarts, and Lamar all left without notice. I had three chariots sitting in the lot – three nights in a row. You guys really put me in a bind."

"I can't speak for them other mugs – I was in St. John's with a pneumonia for two weeks, got discharged, - relapsed - went into ICU and got out three weeks ago. I probably should still be resting, but I got bill collectors at my door, and I had to move back with my parents. I gotta get some scratch to start paying them off.....come on Dan – have a heart."

"Why?"

"Cause it's Thanksgiving."

"Nobody ever give me a break." He looked down at his call board. "Juan'll have the upper ball joints done on #22 by tomorrow night.......be here."

"Thanks Dan."

Cruising around North Yonkers the next day, I drove down Palisade Ave. looking for Barb. She wasn't up on Lake or Morsemere, she was either up the End or still home.

From the opposite direction came a 1960 blue Impala with a trail of blue exhaust to match; a yellow door accentuated the passenger riding shotgun. It was Barbwire. They did a U-turn half-way up the hill and followed me into the parking lot. Barca Bros. supermarket was super-busy with Thanksgiving only two days away. I parked the Starfire. Walking over towards Vinny's car Barb called out:

"Go over to Harmonie and get a pass around fifth of Bali-Hai."

"Tomato Tom did a good job on the door." I said when I got in.

"Yeah....but the lock don't work." he shook his head.

"Stacey riding with you, or she still trying to teach you a lesson?"

"I'm not putting any more money in this ride......only got half the compression in #4 cylinder and she's burning oil. Every time I go to the gas station it's: Gimme 2 quarts of oil and check the gas."

"That ain't good."

"My uncle Ralph got a line on a '67 VW bug, needs an engine. Could be on the road for $1200 – plus I get out from under all of Stacey's nonsense."

"Anything going on with Del Bello?"

Barb answered, "She's going out with Tommy Rosini. Never mind the dating game stuff – tell Whiteskies the good news."

Vinny fired up a joint and we cracked the Bali open. He took a pull: "Me and Stax are renting this ground floor tenement on Nepperhan Ave. Movin' in Dec. 1st . Our third renter is Jackie 'hard on' Hart, but he can't move in until after New Years.

"Where on Nepperhan?"

"You can see Oil City right up the block and Pedro's Mercado is a block to the south."

"Ain't there a tranny bar on the corner next to Oil City?"

"Yeah, this month the sign says: 'Out and About' same gay guy owns it." Vince had gotten the lowdown from the neighborhood people.

"Yeah," Barb said with a straight face, "Take it out and it's about 8 inches."

I bumped her head with the heel of my hand; "You fuckin' idiot."

"I'd pay Stacey to come out with words of wisdom like that." We were all smiles.

"Wasn't it 'The Pit Stop' last summer?" I asked.

Barb again horned in laughing: "You mean the 'The Shit Stop'.

She was on a roll. Vinny said him and Stax could send Wells over for a six-pack when nothing else was open. "You two are going to Florida to pay Loki a visit?"

"I've got to move as much of that tar as I can before we go. Be real good to get down there before Christmas with the biggest bankroll possible. How much is Barb's rent for Dec.?" I said and lit a Marlboro.

"A buck and a quarter." She responded.

"I don't want to get hung up here because you got a shack now."

"Can't happen Whiteboy, Hart's coming in January and that's for sure." Vince said. "What are you going to do – anything lined up?"

"Going back to Caesar's until we leave. Gotta see if Rexall's got anything cooking with Palamar, and try to move move the mindscape material."

"What about when you hit Florida?"

"Probably drive hack with Loki. Barb'll find something." 'Riders on the Storm' played on the radio, we listened briefly.

"What about you….you got anything going on?" Barb smoked the joint.

"Selling furniture and bedding at Freight Recon for my uncle Angelo." he said.

"Is that it?"

"Signed up for the railroad again. Got something in the mail saying my first application was going to expire. Another shot in the dark."

"What's going on with Brother Joe?"

Tarts shook his head and rolled his eyes. "Fuckin' Joe and Cocaine Wayne break into a house. They steal the foreign paper currency and leave the silver coins. They drive to the currency exchange at La Guardia. Brother Joe and Wayne-O think they're in for a big payday. They got 10 and 20,000 German marks to exchange. The retards thought they were going to receive thousands of dollars from the exchange and go to the South Bronx or Harlem and score. At first the currency people laughed at them - then they called the bulls. Lucky for them Sue Herr was waiting just outside the exchange. They beat it when the currency people tried to get them to wait while they got their money together. The idiots almost got caught."

Barb asked, "How come the money wasn't any good?"

"At the time, the German government had runaway inflation. A 20,000 kraut note couldn't buy a loaf of bread. The government went belly-up. Their currency was kaput – it had Joey's head spinning." Vinny said.

"I don't get it?" .

"Pretty good reefer-huh?" I laughed.

She reached for the wine between his legs, "There's more trouble." Wells said.

"I thought you said it was good news." I said.

"Well, more of a good news/bad news deal." She wrinkled her brow.

"Let's have it." Vince said as he flicked the roach out the window.

"That psycho-deviant got out of Cobbeskill. Sylvia said he's been coming around late at night, and leaves after Marge cooks him breakfast. He's been there both nights when you left me off. I can take care of myself.....but Sylvia's scared shitless. I hate to think what that monster might try if any of them are alone." She cranked down the window and let a loogie fly.

"Who you talking about?" Vinny said.

"A few years ago, Marge got involved with this clown...... Butchie Powell. She had his kid, and whenever he ain't in the joint, he always shows up."

"He raped her mom and sister, and tried to rape Barb." I said, also keeping an eye out for Meris

"Why doesn't she get a restraining order from the court?" I said.

"She's got a permanent one against him being within a hundred feet of the premises or any of its residents. My Mom thinks he has a right to see his kid so she won't call the cops. I'm afraid for Sylvia, Helen, and Hope. That sawed-off cocksucker is a bull and can overpower any of us women." She took a drink and passed the bottle.

"Tell you what..." I took a big pull from the quart, "If I see him over there attacking any of your family.....I will kill him. Your mom should give up custody of 'lil Butchie, and send them both on their way."

"It ain't the kid's fault. The old man is the predator." Vince said and looked at the wine that remained.

"Fuck that miscreant gene pool." I blew some smoke out the window. "Wells, your window work?"

She rolled it down half-way and rolled it back up to where smoke could exhaust from the car. We sat in silence. Just hearing Butchie's story for the first time, Vinny sensed trouble and Barb's fear. I watched Cinzano's eyes in the rear view mirror, I could see his immediate concern. Just listening to Wells' story, he knew not to mess with this Butchie without a weapon nearby.

"What'd he get convicted of?" Vinny asked.

"Rape." I said.

"He never even got charged with a sex crime." She corrected me.

"Huh?" Vince and me looked at her in disbelief.

"I don't know what the charge was that got him sent upstate. Mom told me and Sylvia not to say nothing about his raping them two and trying to rape me."

"Get the fuck outta here."

Wells stared, talking to the windshield; "I told mom to go over to the Hilltop Lounge and pick out a 'knuckle dragger' and bring him home when she knew Butch was there and let them slug it out. She's afraid Butchie would kill her if he found out she double-crossed him."

"Geez Barb……didn't know it was that bad. You stay with me and Stax as long as you need to."

"Thanks Vinny."

JANE KNEW SOMETHING WAS GOING ON WITH ME AND
Barb. She was helping Jane with Thanksgiving dinner. Mom was kneading Wells for information like the dough for the apple pie. Barb finally gave in and said she'd tell her during the meal. Letting a cat out of the bag at Thanksgiving dinner with bad news, became double bad news instantly because it ruined everyone's appetite.

As it turned out, when we said we were moving to Florida to see if we could make a go of it. Hal and Jane took the news like we had let them know the Detroit Lions were playing on Thanksgiving. Perhaps we should have thrown in the truth: we were leaving N.Y. to stay clean.

"What's the appeal besides the weather?" Hal asked.

"No state income tax." I knew my answer would set him off and start complaining what a tax hell N.Y. is. He went on for about 10 minutes, but nobody was really interested.

"Joe Ferguson has been driving a cab down there for almost a year. He says the split is better than we have with Caesar."

Hal was getting close to pushing his plate away. "There's nothing here for young people – very hard to get your foot in the door without being connected. Education helps….but only so much. This economy is making the entire generation a bunch of civil servants. You're on a few lists aren't you Ryan?"

"Post Office, Yonkers & N.Y.C. Fire Depts., Border Patrol, State Department……." I was cut off.

"State Department? You don't know any foreign languages."

"He knows Latin." Barb spoke up in between sips of white wine.

"You don't know any current languages except for your native tongue." He pointed a butter knife in my direction.

"I'm no. 131 on the list. Probably half of the people who scored better than me will bust out on the background check. I'm also on the U.S. Marshall's list." I took a lot of tests, I thought.

"What time do you have to go in tonight?" Jane said.

"Should leave about 4:15. I'll drop Barb off at her house; then it's off to the chariot races."

Jane, Barb, and Cathy brought out the apple pie, plates, and coffee. I had Kahlua in mine, it made me think of Karyn. We talked about Ray. Jane talked about dancing and gossiped about a few of her friends. Hal told her to "shut- up" and she ignored him. Since we were going to South Florida, Jane thought it couldn't hurt to show Barb a few Rhumba and Samba steps.

There was only a little light left when we said 'Goodbye'.

"Drop me off at Hanratty's." Wells lit a cigarette.

With the announcement of our move to Miami; the twin serpents of stress and tension reared their ugly heads to make things miserable and worrisome. Even though there were no options other than to stay clean; it still left us with the task of actually getting on with it. We had to follow the straight and narrow to a certain extent, but we had to stop using heroin to get high. Our credibility and our relationship was on the line. People remember stuff like that, and they're always ready to throw it back in your face when you fail. Most people don't care how much you screw up as long as you do it out of town.

"Tell you what Barbwire – I'll have a shot with you before I go to work."

"Got any money?"

I stuffed a $10 note in her front pants pocket and I softly said in her ear: "We'll have to get together tomorrow."

She winked at me as I opened the door. Somebody was getting a jump on Christmas as we heard 'Jingle Bell Rock coming from the 'Rockola' jukebox. She stumbled on the entry mat and we walked to the other end of the bar.

Mike Taft was running the show behind the bar.

"A double Canadian Mist and a Schaefer shorty chaser." I laid a ten on the bar.

"A shot of Mist and a Rheingold shorty, Mike." She ordered.

"Shot, Mike?".

"You can buy me a beer."

"Take it out." The ten was history.

"Thanks Whiterider."

"Uh-oh......trouble." Her klaxon sounded: Barb went on full alert.

My whiskey had been raised at eye level for a toast, I saw the trouble to my left in the large mirror behind the bar. I finished raising the tub of Mist: "Happy Thanksgiving Mike". Though I had never seen this guy before, I knew he was rotten. The bartender nodded to me in recognition. Barb shadowed me to my right.

"Whiteknight......this guy's trouble." She watched the mirror behind the bar as he walked towards us. Wells put me between the troublemaker and herself in a quick move. The rest of my whiskey went back on the bar. He was about three stools away.

"Right there hombre' – that's far enough." I didn't have to ask, I knew it was Butch. His looks, demeanor, cagey smile, State Pen Convict #1085710.

"Hey Pal, I just want to wish my step-daughter "Happy Thanksgiving". He spoke like he knew he had the high hand.

This motherfucker was more than trouble; the desire or need to dominate oozed as I was reading him. I'd need a weapon to put this creep's light out. There was nothing but barstools. He took another step towards us.

Again, I warned him – "You go back to your end of the bar or I'm gonna jack your jaw."

"Alright tuff guy......"

Like a frog leaping from a lily pad, Mike Taft jumped from the slatted floor to the top of the bar in one move looking down at both of us. I never took my eye off of Butchie.

"It's too early for this crap.....Whitehorse, you and Wells finish your drinks. Youse is done for the night."

It wasn't a big deal for me, I had to get down to Caesar's anyway. The ejection would get me there on time.

Barb trailed a little behind me, keeping me between her and Butch. As I walked past him, he raised his left hand, hoping I would be distracted. He tried to sucker punch me with a right uppercut-lightning fast from his waist. The breeze of his missed punch broke my cigarette from my mouth; I came around slightly past him and rung his bell with the hammer of my elbow, crashing him into the barstools.

We rushed out to the Starfire, "Where do you want me to drop you off?"

"Take me down the End to Cassidy's."

Looking at my watch I thought: 'I'm goin' to be late.' I mashed my lips thinking about my next encounter with Butchie. Ronnie Zanzibar had had a zip gun. I wondered where it ended up. "Hey Moon Child – you going to be alright?"

"I just got to make it for a week; then I can move in with Vinny and Stax."

"A lot can happen in a week.....if you want.....you can stay at O'Dell this weekend. I'll explain the circumstances to Hal and Jane. You think your mom has got the only circus in town? With Hal as the Ring Master, high wire acts are a nightly event." I laughed.

"Say Whitewave, bring me that army cot tomorrow. I'll jam it in my old room somehow. I tried sleeping on that living room couch – fuckin' cats were licking my face every 20 minutes on Mon. and Tues."

"I'll bring it over before I go in tomorrow night."

A big Barb smile.

"That fuckin' Butchie Powell." I shook my head and looked at my watch, "Gotta go." She gave me a peck on the cheek.

iv

Remembering back to my paperboy days, the Herald Statesman was chock-full of advertisements on Thanksgiving for the day after shopping. The Hacks who worked days would make a lot of cash. Nights would also be busier than normal – bar hopping, hospital visits, and parties. The object of time had something to do with it. The clock struck midnight and all that was Thanksgiving had disappeared and turned into Christmas. As I got older, the clock lost its relevance in a macro sense.

The holiday season was ramping up; The Friday after Thanksgiving was hectic. I saw Barb for a short lunch, I told her I wouldn't get a chance to see her much until after the weekend with all the shoppers and partiers.

"I'll be around Hanratty's or Cassidy's if you get some free time......I'll give you your "quickie." The vixen was out.

An illuminated billboard hawked Thunderbird wine and they dovetailed with their radio spots. Their Christmas jingle was intro'd by clinking ice cubes hitting a tumbler with party sounds in the background and a soul brother with long muttonchops dressed in a choir robe directing his small throng of revelers:

Caller: What's the word ?
Reply: Thunderbird !
Caller: What's the Price ?
Reply: 50 cent – twice
Caller: Who drink the most ?
Reply: The colored Folks !
Caller: (Takes a chug) "Oooooh that's nice !

Images of candles, holly, Christmas balls and bells bordered the perimeter of the scene. Ernest and Julio's marketing was spot on. It made me want to get a pint - not to get smashed – just to get the holiday glow. Some black ministers had convinced Gallo to pull the radio ad a week before Christmas. The ads on the billboards and the buildings they were attached to – proliferated in the black sections of Yonkers. The owner of the billboards was black as well. He told the ministers that the billboards were staying up until the contract expired.

It was almost bar closing time.......1:50 a.m. Saturday. Dispatcher Linda broke the cold silence: "A heads-up for you guys.......Donny in # 14 says to stay away from Park Ave. and Morningside....between Mulford Gardens and P.S. 9 and Fairview Ave. Emergency vehicles are on the scene: Cops, Fire, ambulances got the streets blocked off.

V

News travels fast. Bad news travels twice as fast. A light film of frost had covered the windshield and rear window of the Olds. I'd have to pick up a scraper at 'John's Bargain Store' before work for Sat. evening. I nodded off for a few minutes as the car warmed up. Some trucker was laying on the air horn to move the traffic at a nearby intersection. I opened one eye, the frost had melted.

I took the quickest route: Riverdale to Warburton to O'Dell Ave. About 100 yards up the street I started looking for a space to

637

park: no spaces. It was early, and I could get away with doing a U-Turn up by the Aqueduct, and start looking for a spot when I reached Warburton. At first, I thought I was having a flashback or receiving images from a distant galaxy. Vinny had his blue door open and stood outside his car. This was going to be a dandy.

It was real enough, so I stopped to see how real it was. "You murdered Stacey and you've got to hide the body?" I stated.

"Meet me down Greystone."

This had 'serious' written all over it, "Now what?" I shook my head. The station was deserted. He had gotten out of the Chevy and motioned with his head to follow him up the stairs into the overpass. He held out a pint of some hard liquor wrapped in a brown bag.

"What the......how bad is this?" I asked. "So bad you've got to shove a bottle of hooch in my hand?" My hand started to shake and I put the bottle in my jacket pocket.

"Wells cashed out last night." Vinny looked south through the Plexi-glass.

"Say what?"......how's that? What are you talking about?"

"Barbara Wells died this morning......asphyxiation from a fire at her mom's house." Vince turned, looked at me then at the tracks going north.

All I could do was suck air, I was unable to exhale. The air went in....in....in....my eyeballs felt like they were on fire. I clawed at the overpass's ceiling – still nothing came out. I jumped for one of the electric heaters hanging from the ceiling in panic. Tarts watched me helpless. I know - I watched myself.............helpless. My heart, lungs, and brain were ready to burst.

Either air shot out of my heels and jettisoned me, or perhaps I made a vertical leap over two feet, or a combination of the two. My right hand clenched the heating element and I howled: "BarrrrrrrBrahhhhh!" The doors on each end blew open and I fell to the concrete floor of the skywalk.

i

Mankato, Wednesday October 2nd

His eyes popped open: "Barbara"......air was forced from his lungs as the paddles were lifted from Ryan's chest. The heart was beating again, but it was too rapid as was his respiration rate.

He could see the flashing lights, scurrying staff, beeps, buzzers; digital equipment reporting friendly sounding dings amidst a flurry of activity. The serious faces were bringing him down.

She had come to him some 40-odd years later. This apparition made him wonder if he was alive or dead. Ryan had seen her so vividly in color detail; felt her emotion and thoughts. A nurse administered a shot. His eyes questioned the nature of another bag of liquid drugs going on the stainless tree just below the saline solution and being fed into the pump to enter through his I.V.

"Just a slow-down drug Mr. Whitelaw." she said.

The falling numbers were reported on the flat screen monitor. Slowly, memory drifted into the expanse of his mind or into space.

Falling as space debris, he was deep into a collection of bits and pieces of his life. Once again, everything in the hospital was gone except a soft tiny red beacon which pulsed. He may have been at the Mankato Institute, heaven, hell, or the void of space. Far off in front of the beacon, an object was coming towards Ryan – slightly off his vector. Depending on its velocity, he might be able to identify it when it passed, unless it was a piece of rock floating through the emptiness. It might be near in five or six hours, months, or years. He wasn't an astronomer; he couldn't hazard a guess as to its mass, mode of propulsion, or the nature of the energy which made it visible.

Still, the memory of Barb Wells had been reignited to a level he was not ready to absorb. Ryan couldn't validate if he was conscious, or if he was hallucinating; for which consciousness was a prerequisite. As the object twinkled, he speculated it might be an infused magnetic adaptation of life – a replication - or a coma induced drug dream.

Maybe if he prayed for the pain to return......reality would also.

ii

"......Yes.....Ah-huh......Nicole – fly direct to Mankato. Time is urgent. I don't know.....I get the feeling he's in a no-win situation. He's had a heart attack. He had it in LaCrosse. Dr. Baranpour didn't have to wait for us to make a decision for Papa. He came out of the coma and made the decision for himself. The ambulance service drove him to Mankato. He's already there. I went with him." Dixie said.

"Rick is going to burn up the rest of his vacation so he can watch the kids. He's ready to drive up should the worst come to pass." Nicky replied.

"What's this Surgeon's name?"

"Bachan Singh." Dixie said.

"Singh......he's a Sikh." Nicky confirmed.

"They're the best." Dixie replied and looked at the twins. He's one of the best liver specialists at the Institute. Dr. Baranpour says......this is who we want for Dad."

"At least there will be four of us to find a way through this maze of doctors, drugs, diagnostic procedures, billings, and medical jargon.......I don't know how Papa did it when mom got sick. I wish we all had been old enough to help. It was just him and me back then, and all I could do was babysit you guys."

THE DAUGHTERS AND DR. HADJI BARANPOUR GATHER-
ed in Ryan's I.C.U. room in his second day, at the Mankato Institute. They waited for the G.I. Specialist/Surgeon, Dr. Bachan Singh. The four daughters formed a semi-circle around his doctor from La Crosse.

"Our father is willing to try experimental treatment – but not liver transfer. Dr. Baranpour, are you aware of this?" Dixie asked.

"Jes, but please Miss Dixie –" Baranpor said. "Dr. Singh is going to do what he knows is necessary immediately. Our options are very limited at this point. The scarring has progressed to the level where he is very close to liver failure."

"As long as Ryan is conscious and can make his own decisions – he can instruct you and Dr. Singh not to perform the transplant. But when we speak for him, we see things differently; that is why we have asked that we go forward with the tests and scans necessary as if he was getting a transplant; search for a suitable donor should continue."

Dr. Baranpour advised Dixie: "If a liver becomes available dis very minute, we must have your response
immediately, or the organ will be assigned to another patient.......you must understand dis."

"As we said Doctor: If the decision is ours to make – we will vote for transplantation.........if the factors and his condition have not changed."

Approximately a half-hour later, Dr. Singh and two associates entered Ryan's room.

"We seem to be a little crammed in here, would you mind if we conferred in the family/visitor lounge." Singh offered.

The lounge area was large and accommodating. There were two people on the other side of the area – out of earshot of their group. "Dr. Baranpour, so good to see you again." The two colleagues shook hands. He introduced the sisters to Dr. Singh. Baranpour transferred his patient to the care of the Mankato Institute and the Singh team.

Dr. Hadji Baranpour knew this was the Whitelaw Patriarch's best chance for survival. He hugged the four women and promised to follow Ryan's case with St. Thomas' cyberlink with the Mankato Institute. "I vill pray for your father's recovery and you all."
Baranpour noticed Nicole; "And you have arrived des morning?"

"Last night."

"If you have any questions for me – do not hesitate to call me back in LaCrosse. It is Nicole is it not?" the Doctor said.

"Yes."

"He is in the most capable hands now and God's." Dr. Hadji departed.

Dr. Singh didn't waste any time: "Condition – Your father has had a mild heart attack. After they restarted his heart in LaCrosse, it began to race and his blood pressure climbed to 188/131. The rate and pressure have been controlled by inducing coma. Things have stabilized, and we were able to transport him here yesterday with Miss Dixie."

"Dr. Marie Allen will be Ryan's cardiologist while he is here. The physician next to me is my associate in the G.I. Department: Dr. David Judd."

"The heart attack complicates the consideration of the transplant option. He needs time to recover from this attack. More than the heart event, the liver is unable to keep up and detox his blood. This puts more stress on the other organs.....like the heart. Your father needs a new liver. Soon it will be a matter of life and death. I will perform this surgery if his heart numbers and chemistry indicate there is a 50% chance of survival. Here is where there is a problem, and it's one of principles: How do I justify proceeding with the transplant when the odds are stacked against its success? If your father has another heart attack or bleeds to death during the operation – then two people will have died instead of one because I decided to take an ill advised risk."

"Time is not on his side." Singh went on. "There is a point of no return. I do not make the decision as to who receives transplants. It is based on his MELD score. Of course I have input with the MELD Committee, but Ryan must show some improvement in his heart function before I would give the transplant surgery the green light. Critical to the transplant surgery's success is if it can be removed and be replaced without a significant hemorrhaging . That done, his chances improve considerably."

"What are his chances?" Teresa had been writing notes all along.

"There's no way to sugar coat it.....he needs a miracle – cut and dried. If his heart stabilizes, I would put his odds at 30%. If we find a liver match very soon – we can raise his chances to 50%. His chances never improve to more than a 50% chance of recovery. In a week, his liver will be unable to filter his blood. In layman's terms, the cirrhotic liver will impede the flow of blood to the rest of the body and poison him. The odds get worse - even with the hepatitis C virus in check right now. A person can live with only 10% of a functioning liver, but his liver continues to deteriorate. In a week, he will die if a transplant is not found. Let us hope a match is found by Thursday or Friday."

"When do you plan on bringing him out of the coma?" Nicole said.

"Wednesday."

"Will we be able to speak with him?" Dixie asked.

"Perhaps......we might be able to bring him out, and his numbers may be stable. It is a tough case we confront." Singh could see it was not the answer the sisters wanted. "If he does regain consciousness, he will be on the ropes more or less. He might be responsive - he may even be coherent."

"Coherent?"

"Count on him being groggy. This may be your last opportunity to express your love for him. Your love for your father is obvious. I have seen some wondrous things occur over the years through the power of prayer and belief in the deity. 'Tis through the amplitude of love and faith that miracles come." Singh seemed wise beyond his years to the Ryan's daughters.

"Dr. Allen – your prognosis?" Killeen asked.

"Ryan has sustained a mild heart attack. As Dr. Singh has reported: decreased liver function – blood flow has been constricted by the scarred liver. He is being poisoned and starved also. Yet, there is blood flow to the extremities. The other organs aren't in decline except for the heart attack. Therein lies my hope. To echo Dr. Singh......Time is the critical factor."

"And should a liver become available tomorrow?" Dixie walked to a wide window overlooking a wooded stand amongst recently harvested fields.

Dr. Marie Allen projected her voice to Ryan's youngest daughter's back: "I will inform Dr. Singh that Ryan's heart will perform its expected function. I couldn't say that to an unfamiliar or less qualified surgeon. If he says it's tonight – I tell him we are ready."

"Are you all staying in Mankato?" Dr. Singh said.

"One of us will always be with Dad through Wednesday, and we'll all be here when you bring him out of the coma."

"I must bring Ryan out of the induced coma tomorrow night, but not all the way to observe his heart functions. I'm not expecting any wide fluctuations. He will be barely conscious if at all. Hopefully some indices will have improved." she looked at his numbers on her chart.

Dr. Singh said: "I can be reached here, but I will also give you my cell number on the back of my card. Leave me a message, and I will get back to you. If you do not leave a message, your call will not be returned." The three doctors said good-bye.

CHAPTER 22

i

There was a bad burn on my right index finger, and burns on the others when I grabbed hold of the overhead heater in the pedestrian bridge. I had landed on my right side; my hip was throbbing as well.

"What the fuck Whitelaw?" Vinny reached in my pocket. The pint was still intact, he took it out and cracked open the top and took two large gulps from the bottle and started hacking from the whiskey's flavor.

My eyes were out of focus, and I shook my head and looked at a blurred vision of Vinny. I knew the voice.

"Vin?"

"Yeah…..you alright?"

Things were getting a little sharper. Lying down - oblivious to my burnt hand on the concrete floor, my heart and lungs raced again from panic……."Barb's dead? Barb Wells?"

He went behind me and pulled me up to my feet and leaned me against the south girder. We rested a minute and he handed me the whiskey. "Yeah Brother……she's gone."

Vinny unscrewed the cap and I took three long, slow pulls from the whiskey. "Fuckin' Southern Comfort?"   I passed the bottle back to Vince, but he put it in my pocket.

"Let's see that hand dude." Cinzo looked at it; "I got a pretty clean Tee-shirt in the car – we should wrap it up."

"I'll be by the river." I said.

"Too cold…..stay in the crossover."

"Just come over by me – it'll be warm."

Tarts went down to his car and got the tee shirt for a wrap. I had to make my way down the riverside stairway and down the platform using a ships ladder with one hand to get to the where Ray and me had buried the Cosmic Intruder. Walking parallel to the southbound platform, I came to the burial mound of sand and gravel above the ejected remnant. I scanned the area, looking for any artifacts of our year-and-a-half relationship. There was nothing but trash…..junk, but it was our junk. It was difficult; I got the sugar charged whiskey and had a couple of quick sips.

Vinny came up the path, "Fuckin' cold."

"Over here Vin – the sun's warmed up the sand already."

"Huh?" He sat in the sand next to me, "Why is this spot so warm. The sun didn't do this."

"The railroad guys say there's some kind of underground steam pipe beneath us. I dunno. So what happened? She didn't O.D.?" I asked.

"Her house burnt down, she died in the fire. That's what I heard when I went up there."

"You knew I loved her. You knew we were getting out of Yonkers. I was ready to marry her. You knew I loved her."

"She was one of us." Tarts nodded.

"Yeah......yeah." My voice softened: "She was – she was one of us."

"The Fire Department, emergency workers, the bluecoats; they'll all be there for a while......probably all day. Heard seven others died. Got a water squirter to talk a little. He said the house went up like a tinderbox because of all the shit inside."

I offered a cigarette to Tarts.

He held his hand up – "Not my brand."

"The shack was an indoor garbage pit......how could they live like that? How'd you find out?"

"Dona Della – you knew they were friends in junior high."

"I got to go up there Vince." I stood up. I gave him my good hand and yanked him up.

"Figured you would. Park your car and don't drive today. Your mind won't be on the road. Lay off the hooch until after you've talked with Sylvia – they said she's at Yonkers General. If there is a story to tell – she knows it."

We had to park about a half-mile away. They had High St. blocked off. The cops, firemen, and ambulance people were busy eating donuts and drinking coffee. There weren't many gawkers around, it was still too early, but there were a few. I asked an older man if he knew any of the details.

"Amazing that any of the house is still standing. The whole neighborhood was lit up around 2:30 this morning." The old timer said.

"There were survivors?" I was hoping somehow Vinny's information was inaccurate and had Barb being amongst them.

"Yes, I heard five. Sounds like the five will all make it: a three year old, a six year old, and three over the age of ten." he reported.

We could see what was left of the Wells house from where the cops had put up their barriers. Other than the kitchen and the living room, who knew what rooms were what. The warped stove and burnt Fridge had collapsed onto each other fighting their way to fall through to the cellar. Junk and burnt debris defied description. Bedsprings and furniture coils were everywhere, as were charred cribs, day beds, and a metal framed bunk bed was mangled from the heat. The only piece of furniture partially intact was Marge's half-burnt couch.

"C'mon man, let's get a cup of coffee."

"I'll bet this is what that Auschwitz smelled like." Vinny woooed turning his head from side to side.

We went down to the Saw Mill Diner; neither of us could take any more at that point. We forced some breakfast down, we didn't want to drink any more on empty stomachs. Deprived of sleep and confused from the Southern Comfort, I looked at Cinzano, "This is developing into a bad dream."

"Ain't no developing......it is something we don't get to forget. The bulls wouldn't tell me anything." he sipped some coffee. "One of the firemen gave me the count: Ma Wells, her boyfriend, 1 baby, 1 toddler, and 4 kids perished in the fire. He also said a young woman died at Yonkers General who they found in the backyard.

644

"That would be Barb….."

"That's what I was thinking." Vinny shoveled down some eggs.

"I've got to talk to Sylvia. She was there. She survived." I looked right at Vinny: "I got to go back up there……..pretty soon. Got to find out where the body's at. I've got to see her one last time…….at peace."

Vinny picked up breakfast for me. Although there was still some Southern Comfort left in the bottle Vinny had brought with him, we stopped at a liquor store and got another pint of the Comfort. Grief was starting to build, I could feel the tightness in my chest and the overload of my brain's wiring. There was no alternative except to drink myself stupid. The nearer to High St. we got, the worse the symptoms became. My breathing again became erratic; I found another cigarette in my hand.

Vinny watched my spasmatic movements with his peripheral vision: "Don't smoke any reefer today – it'll only make you paranoid."

"Stop over at 21." I directed. Either I was going to ask or swipe some of Jane's calm down pills. They were exactly what I needed to make it through what promised to be a nightmare of a day.

"Just tell your mom the facts – I'm sure your she will hook you up."

Her Comet was gone. Jane had the holiday weekend off, Hal still hadn't gotten up. I borrowed six – 10 mg. valiums from her bottle in the medicine cabinet. Just having the valium in my pocket reduced the stress level, but it did nothing to make me forget Barb.

The sun peeked through the clouds, the wind was up. People were milling about; looking at the place where eight people perished. It was like a warm-up for her wake and funeral: all The Rogues, The Huns, Shooey, Gamblers Reno and Joe Lamar, The Warburton Girls, The Lockwood Girls, Dona Del Bello, Tony Griffin from the North End, Ronnie 'Chooch' Crestwood, and the Karr brothers from the Orchard Crew.

Holter and Rexall came up to us. "Fucked up man….you alright or you just hanging on? I got some helpers if you need them - in my pocket." Rex put his hand on my shoulder.

"She was one of us….we lost a sister. What you lost Ry – I can't imagine." Holter had a tear running down his cheek.

"She was my All-Star." I jittered out. Now it was starting to sink in.

"Whiteoak, I got these pictures back a couple of weeks ago" Rex said.

They were the photographs Rex took down the marina before Watkins Glen with all our cars lined up. There was one picture of me sitting on the hood of the Olds and Barb standing between my legs. Both of us were facing Rex… smiling. "Can I have this one?"

"I brought them for you Brother – I had doubles made when I got them developed."

"Rex, who you know on the force - who can get me in Yonkers General's morgue – so I can see her one last time?"

"That'd have been one for the Z-man. He had all the cop connections. All I know is Joe Peaches, and he's in the traffic division. I'll see what I can do".

"Hmmm." My mind started working on plan 'B'.

Holter took a nip of something in a brown paper bag: "They're all down at Yonkers General – the living and dead Wellses'. The surviving kids all got smoke inhalation and burns. They breathed a lot of them plastic fumes. One got a broken arm - another got a big knot on her head. One of the ambulance guys told me."

"About an hour ago, one of Reno's connections who was protecting the scene said Homicide was brought in and took over control from arson. Arson is still there, but Homicide is running the show. Homicide means foul play." Rex nodded.

Back and forth I paced with Vinny Tarts outside the police barricades; acknowledging some.....ignoring others. Mike Reno walked towards me with his hand extended. I shook it.   "This is real bad." he said. We stopped and looked at what was left of the house. Mike crossed his arms on his chest, then the one hand stroked his chin in thought.

"The worst." I responded. My dislike of Mike Reno vanished. Not every guy saw in Barb what we saw. Mike admitted he had screwed up a really good thing.

"We were lucky to have gotten to know her on that next level." I said.

"Yeah Whitelaw, but gals like Barb only come around once in a lifetime, mostly they don't come at all. When they do come, you got to know what you've got. You lost her through no fault of your own. I had her and drove her away. Doesn't matter how or why now; at least for me there won't be no getting over her – just one big black hole in my heart." Mike thought he was in the confessional it seemed.

"She was the most funnest chick I was ever with." I said.

"Man she was special. There'll be a day we might be able to talk about her."

"Not for a while Mike."

"I 'spose not."

"Need anything Reno?"

"Whatcha got?"

"Valium - 10's."

"Yeah could you lay one on me?"

I gave him the de-stresser and told him I'd see him around.

Crawfish saw us talking and came over with a guy I didn't know. "This is him." he said.

I looked at Crawford and the guy. "This is what?" I said.

"This guy's from the Statesman, he's writing the story. Might have some pull getting to see Barb." he shrugged.

The reporter offered his hand which I shook. "Sorry for your loss. Kenny said you had been going out with Barbara for the past year.....year and-a-half."

I didn't answer him.

"My name is Jamie O'Neill – weekend reporter with the Herald Statesman. Can you help me with some facts; maybe with a few of the victims?"

"Maybe...." I replied.

"Your friend says you knew the girl who died in the hospital this morning?"

"You're talking to me at the wrong time and place."

"Listen the story goes in tonight with or without your side of the story."

"Listen Jimmy Olson – don't get smart with me. I'll put your paper and pen up your ass so far Clark Kent won't be able to find it with his X-ray vision."

"Wait a minute......all I'm asking for is a little bit of truth so I can give them something for tomorrow's paper. You don't have to get all agro on me."

"You didn't lose someone you loved, and who loved you back." I marched around in a huff kind of like Bad Brad.

"Ryan, I'm just trying to get the story right; it's important now that Homicide's running the case. Homicide's here not because it was just a fire. One or more of these deaths was not an accident."

"Alright – I'll tell you what I know, but I want information and access too. You help me, and I'll help you. First, what's going in the paper tonight?"

"What's your name?"

"That's not important." Vinny looked at me shaking his head.

"Ryan Whitlock. What's going in tonight's paper?"

"This is a big story....the wire services will pick this one up. Eight people die in a house fire and Y.P.D. Homicide is investigating. Tonight will be -------"

I interrupted him: "Can you get me down to the City Morgue to see Barb this afternoon?"

"She's not down at city yet. Her body is still in Yonkers General's morgue as far as I know." O'Neill said.

"Has she been autopsied yet?"

"Doubt it." He continued: "Once the body is taken to city, I need clearance to go in. For you to see her down there – you got to be kin or pertinent to the investigation. The coroner will autopsy her, but probably not 'til after the Thanksgiving weekend. I got a connection down at Yonkers General. The hospital still has custody. Once the body leaves the hospital it's all government from that point on. We've got to go now."

I lit a cigarette on the way to his car, "I don't get it."

"It's no longer classified as an accidental fire that killed eight people; a homicide may have occurred with the fire as a cover-up." he said.

"That's retarded." Vinny said. "Kill seven people to conceal a murder. Getdafuckouttahere."

"O'Neill - let's go. Tarts - you comin'?"

"Un-uh......this thing has got me spooked. Don't need the Morgue action."

"DRIVE OVER TO O'DELL AVE. TAKE A LEFT
TOWARDS the river. I got to pick something up." I said.
"How long did you and Barbara Wells go out?"
He knew I had been drinking, I thought he was trying to
catch me with some inaccuracies with some of the stuff I already told
him. "Year ana-half."
"I assume you two were romantically involved?"
"We weren't reading books and going to movies. I got a set
of wheels. You're a cub reporter......do the math."
"She only had one full-blood sibling...a brother?"
"Yeah Clay. Think he's still in reform school. I got a picture
of her and me. You might want to put it in the paper. I got to have it
back; and I want 4 – 8"x10" copies of it." I said.
"We'll see if the photo is useful to tell the story. If it is, then
we'll do it."
"You don't get it O'Neill......this is your only chance to use
this picture."
He half watched the road and looked at the photo. He put it
in a folder on the dashboard. "Alright, you got it." The reporter
continued his interview: "How'd you know her?"
"Went to Gorton together.....knew her from Lake Ave."
"This is O'Dell here?" he tapped his brakes for the motorist
behind him.
"Yeah, take the left down the hill. Slow down after the
Aqueduct. It's the white house on the right. Stop here – put your
flashers on. I'll be right out."
When I returned, we went to the bottom of O'Dell and turned
south on Warburton Ave. Jamie looked straight ahead: "The name
Charlie Powell mean anything to you?"
I looked out the passenger window at the Hudson and took a
breath. "I know a Butchie Powell.....probably the same guy. Hey –
what's the story for the paper for tonight?"
"Like Sgt. Joe Friday says – 'just the facts': The deceased,
the survivors, ages, cause of fire - which at this time is undetermined,
location, time. Pictures of before and after the blaze. We'll mention a
police investigation is in progress. Routine stuff."
"What if the police suspect foul play?"
"The story will last a week and come out in drips and drabs
for another two months." He said as we pulled into the Yonkers
General parking lot.
"O'Neill, how's this going to work?"
"I do all the talking. You'll only have a few minutes with
her. Say good-bye as quickly as you can."
The elevator let us off in the basement. We walked over to
the security guard sitting at a fold-out table with a sign-in sheet. I
guess he was a Level II, Rent-a-Cop; he had a gun.
"Hey Fitz – you remember me?..........O'Neill with the
Statesman?"
"I sure do. You were down last year saying bye-bye to 'Bad
Eye' Harris." The two laughed. "What's the deal today?" Fitz
coughed.

"Ryan here to perform a 24-hour demand religious ritual for......let me see your list of deceased.....ahhh..... Number 4. That was some fire up the hill." Jaime made some small talk.

Fitz said, "You guys go in alone. I'll watch youse through the glass of the morgue. Too damn cold in the freezer; them the ones they brought in from the fire. They remind me of the Japs we roasted on Iwo Jima. Nasty smell. They been in there a while – they might not smell so bad now."

We wasted no time. We were about to enter when Fitzcasey looked at his list of stiffs. "Jamie, this number 4 came in after the fire victims; she died upstairs. The Lieutenant told the boys to put her with the other ones who had been in the fire." We waited for him to get his coat from his locker.

"By the way, what denomination or religion is the deceased that you're ministering the sacrament to?" he prepared to write in some information on his clipboard.

"Not a sacrament......a religious rite – a ceremony......if you will. The young woman was a Hare Krishna – Vishnu sect." I said.

The word 'morgue', the odor of odorlessness, the sterility, the stainless steel tables and cabinetry, the hanging trocars, the lighting, temperature; it was sickening........ The eight were on the other side of the heavy clear plastic strips dividing one temperature zone from the other. Two adults were in body bags and had "EVIDENCE" and "DO NOT TAMPER" stickers tied to the bodies and bags.

There was a resistance.....a force; it seemed to keep us in the morgue and away from the freezer. I was at odds with something here; something alien. My need to see her was greater than the barrier force, and I entered the freezer in slow motion. O'Neill had no reason to view any of the people who died in the fire. The fire had burnt three kids beyond recognition. It was a gruesome scene. Though it was his job to view the news and turn it into print, this was one he stayed away from. He watched me. O'Neill was barely through the clear thermo plastic slats dividing the morgue side from the freezer. The cold had somewhat reduced the disgusting smell of burnt flesh, or the cold had reduced my olfactory capabilities. Some selective odors were worse than repulsive.

The life force had departed from the eight, but it seemed to hover in the freezer. I could feel it. It didn't make sense; I wasn't in my best mind to analyze much of anything. Perhaps there was a phantom force in the freezer; it may have been real. Either way I had to concentrate on making my final good-bye to Barb. The two adult corpses were in body bags; the minors' bodies were covered with canvas sheets. Barb's corpse was covered with a hospital sheet on some shelving designed to temporarily hold bodies. Outside the sheet, her right foot had the usual I.D. tag tied to her big toe, but there was an additional tag indicating her body was "EVIDENCE". The other sneaker was still on.

It was difficult to open the adult body bags with my good hand and the pinky of my burnt hand. Ma Wells was in the one and fuckhead Butchie, who had to lay in profile because Mr. Hillman's

Finnish Commando blade was buried in his head – right up to the handle behind his right ear. "Burn in Hell." I killed him in my mind. Now the freezer reeked of burnt flesh.....now I could smell it.

Again, the feeling I had while in the Greystone pedestrian bridge with Vinny returned. I faced the body on the shelf and took a long pull on the whiskey. I pulled down the sheet covering Barb. Except for burns on her hands, and a bad one across her neck – the only signs she had been in a fire was the plastic soot beneath her nostrils and about her mouth. I used Vinny's tee-shirt to wipe her face clean. I left her fogged eyes open. Everything under the sheet now smelled of fire. Her shirt lay next to her, she was naked to the waist. I took my camera out and shot all six pictures left on the roll. The last two with her eyes closed. I got out my yellow pharmacy bottle and pulled the sheet down to her heels.

O"Neill called, "C'mon.....it's time."

"Gimme a hand." I answered. "Here, pour this into my hand."

"I can't move." He looked worried.

I went over to him with the pharma bottle; "Pour a little of this into my hand."

The reporter was barely talking above a whisper, "Are you nuts? This isn't your girlfriend......this is evidence."

"Just fuckin' do it."

He complied. I knew he regretted bringing me here. In a circular pattern, I sprinkled the fine particulate ash over her body and licked my thumb and rubbed some on her forehead with a cross, each eye, licked my pinky and applied the ash in each ear, her nose, and in her mouth. One last time with my thumb and index finger, I dialed both of her tits. Before I brought the sheet over her face, I swear a payback smirk appeared. It may have been an involuntary electrical response to the positively charged Fireball ash. Everything stopped for a few seconds.

"Hurry up you idiot."

I was well aware of his aggravation, but fuck him. I only had the one opportunity to see her one last time. It felt like the weight of the world placing that sheet over her face; the Barb Wells smirk was gone and so was she.

ii

Fitzcasey had only stayed 4 minutes in the morgue before the chill chased him back into the warm hall. The few minutes O'Neill promised me with Barb was actually around 10 minutes long. When we signed out, Fitz asked me if I believed in that Hara Rama mumbo jumbo.

"Fuck no – I'm not even a good Catlick." .

"Atta boy." We waved good-bye.

We got in Jamie's car; I pulled out the bottle of S.C. and took two pulls on it.

"Hey......I need a drink, gimme the bottle." Jamie said.

"What do you want to know?" the bottle went back in my pocket after his lick of Southern Comfort.

"Butch's upper torso was burnt bad, and he had a knife stuck in his skull." Jaime said.

"Got a smoke?" I searched his dashboard.

"Quit last year. Who killed Butch Powell?"

"Long line of people wanted that jag-off dead." I said, "But it probably was Barb." For me it was open and shut – I knew the knife.

"Not likely Whitlock......she couldn't get the drop on that guy. How do you think he survived in Cobbeskill and Greenhaven. He had eyes in the back of his head. I'm not buying that bullshit." The reporter said.

"I popped that punk two nights ago." I gave him a bewildered look.

"But he was much bigger and faster than her." He countered.

"She had a lot of motive to whack Butchie. Listen O'Neill: he raped Ma Wells about three years ago, he raped Barb's half-sister Sylvia, and he tried to rape Barb. When he was unsuccessful he made her blow him.....then he promised to have prison sex with her. All three had motive. Barb was the only one with the balls to whack him."

The lack of sleep, too much booze, and emotional exhaustion came over me like an avalanche. My thoughts and words were slurred. I looked over to Jamie, "I want your photography people to develop my film." I took the film out of the Kodak instamatic. "All the shit I gave you should put you five miles ahead of the D.A.'s office."

"What's your phone number?" O'Neill said.

"I can be reached at YO-5-5599." It was Caesar's taxi number. I had enough. "O'Neill, take me back to High St." It was almost three o'clock. The reporter had already phoned in most of the story for tonight's edition. I was curious as to how much of my information might make his piece. O'Neill said he thought Monday's edition would carry the weight of the story.

The next two hours were spent with Crawford in his pick-up with my head in my hands.

"Hey Whitestripe.....ask Ray.....the way you feel right now, is the way we live life all the time." His laugh was all irony and no humor.

I didn't look at him, crossed my arms and rested them on the dashboard and put my forehead down: "Fuckin' shoot me."

"And......" Crawfish said, "The bluecoats are looking for you."

I didn't move my head: "For what?"

"They want a statement. They want to know what you know. Just call 'em up – Tell them you'll be in to see them on Monday or Tuesday.......Tell 'em you're too grief stricken to talk right now. That's the truth anyway. It'll keep them from hassling your parents."

"Yeah.....sounds good."

On Monday afternoon, I woke up at Beth the Mess' apartment on 35 Pine St. I felt like I had been run over by a Patton tank

651

and maybe she had prison sex on me. I stayed there another night and called the North Command Patrol to come and get me if they still wanted a statement.

In front of the apartment house, I read yesterday's newspaper. O'Neill got the scoop, and the wire services made it national news. The Herald Statesman used the photo of me and Barb in Tuesday's paper. On Wednesday the bombshell hit the newsprint: Sylvia's personal account of the night of the fire, and a sworn statement by one of Powell's associates saying him and Butchie had smoked some angel dust (PCP) late Friday night.

The bulls, D.A.'s office, and the hospital had prevented me from visiting Sylvia Stevenson until Thursday. I left a message for Jamie O'Neill to call me if he had any advice on the way to proceed, to visit Sylvia in the hospital. I left him my real phone number and Beth's also. I mentioned it would be greatly appreciated.

"So they're stonewalling?" O'Neill said. "A few calls to the D.A.'s office and the hospital administrator, and asking them what THEY'RE trying to conceal...........that should scare them. They've already got depositions from everybody but you and the deceased. You might be able to visit Sylvia this afternoon. Give me a call if they're still playing games."

"Thanks Jamie."

"Yeah....next time - give me your correct name. I don't need to be running around trying to put a story together with a name that's an alias."

"Sorry 'bout that."

"You owe me one Whitelaw." O'Neill clicked the phone.

Because Sylvia was 18 years old, legally she controlled her own affairs. I did get to visit her at Yonkers General that afternoon. The account she gave me of that horrific night differed from the one in the newspaper and her sworn deposition to the Asst. District Attorney.

She told me, "Barb confronted Butchie Powell around 1:30 am Saturday morning. He had started a kitchen fire trying to heat up some leftover cheese and macaroni. Barb yelled at him, but he was all screwed up and Barb told him to go back to Zombie land. He had woken the entire house. Barb pushed him onto the couch, made sure the fire was out, and came upstairs. She locked our door and went to sleep on her army cot."

"About 20 minutes later, there was a loud commotion downstairs. She laid in the dark and told us Butch was too zonked to bother with, and said to us girls to go back to sleep........we'd sort it out in the morning."

"We smelled another pan of something burning. Barb unlocked the door, and opened it a little bit. Smoke was sucked in, and the four of us started choking.

Sylvia said there was a garbage bag fire in the kitchen. There were at least three garbage bags full all the time waiting for someone to take them out to the cans outside.

"Mom screamed for help, and that's when Barb started back downstairs. She only got half-way down, and turned around and came back into our room. She got something from the handbag she never uses, and started back downstairs. It looked like Butchie had Mom's nightgown over her face, and her panties tossed aside. All of the kids were crying. Barb started hollerin' at Butch, and threw a toy left on the steps at him. He laughed and kicked Mom in the head. The smoke was getting thick and was collecting; he didn't care, and slapped her up some more, and standing between her legs. I think he was going to kill her."

"Barb tried to get behind Butch when she got downstairs; there was an explosion and fire expanded throughout the open space downstairs. It was probably the can of 'Kool Whip' we used to top off the pumpkin pie that blew up."

Sitting next to Sylvia's hospital bed I tried to read her face as she recounted the events of the night. It had me drop-jawed, but it sounded like the real deal.

"The flames and heat went everywhere searching for oxygen. I shut our bedroom door. After 30 seconds or so, I cracked open the door to see how bad it was. There was a lot more smoke and screams. Fire had taken hold in the kitchen, the baby room, and the small hall space. I opened the door a little more. The smell of plastic burning now filled the house. I shut the door again. Hope, Helen, and me were gagging from the fumes. We opened our small window."

"That was when....." Sylvia stopped and drank some apple juice. "That was when we heard Butch yell, "You whore Bitch!"

"It was the last time I heard his voice. Barb had dragged Mom out the front door through the fire. She returned up stairs to our room with wet diapers and towels from the bathroom. She said to cover ourselves and breathe through the wet towels and clothes to minimize the fumes and smoke. The front of the house was now engulfed in flames. She started tossing junk and furniture to make a path to the back door. Cats huddled in corners and ran upstairs screeching for air, but the babies and toddlers weren't as loud now."

Sylvia was having trouble continuing.

"And then what?........Sylvia........then what?"

She took another drink of juice from her lunch tray: "Then a white flame jumped up to the ceiling. That was when I saw Butch with plastic melted on his face. The flame was so bright I could see him through the smoke. His hair was burnt off, and he had a knife sticking in his skull behind his ear. He was kind of dog paddling – to where or for what......I couldn't say. I'm sure it was an attempt to kill us all. Those of us who were still alive were screaming except for Barb. She pulled us downstairs and out the backdoor; first Hope and Helen and then me and the Lattimore boy, but he may have already suffocated. It was like we were in a tug of war. It was Barb against the furniture obstacles. We rolled down the 6 or 7 steps onto the brick patio. We were on our hands and knees gasping for air."

She grasped my hand. "Barb vanished, and came out of the house and tossed 8 year old Emma from the small porch; choking and coughing the whole time. Barb reentered the house again and threw an unconscious little Butch at us. She collapsed and rolled down the stairs. Her lungs had been seared by the fire." Tears streamed down Sylvia's cheeks.

"Did she regain consciousness?" I was transfixed.

"Yes, in the emergency room. They shot her full of Dilaudid and had her on oxygen, but that was about all they could do. Her lung function hardly registered. They knew she wasn't going to make it. They wheeled my bed next to hers. She said to tell you........."

"Whoa......whoa......whoa..... wait a minute Sylvia. You're going to lay that dying words bullshit on me?" My eyes got wide and I started hyperventilating.

"Ryan – I don't know what she meant. It must only be significant to you. I can't even be positive I heard her correctly......it was barely a whisper. She said, 'Tell Ryan to find another comet.'

Following a number of attempts of trying to smoke myself into a Tiger Tar alternative universe and regenerate our relationship; slowly, I began to see true reality – the one without her. The opium had to be put away before I turned into Samuel Coleridge. It was all too much. She was with me every waking moment. There was little sleep – just unconsciousness. Two weeks before Christmas I reached out to Crawford. I rang his doorbell.

"Brenda here?"

"Went out Christmas shopping with her sister.   C'mon in. You still going to Florida?"

"Don't know what I'm doing. I can't commit seppuku."

"Huh?"

"Hara-kiri......suicide.....just got to forget and go into a deep sleep." My eyes darted back and forth.

"White-monkey.....you got your wings?" Crawfish asked.

"How about giving me a hand with that?"

"It's a major move."

"At least there's a chance to make a comeback – Otherwise, I just may start the car in the garage with a gallon of T-bird." I said.

"That bad?"

"That desperate."

"It might help" He raised his eyebrows......."might complicate things." Crawdad said.

"What's out there?"

He lit up a joint took a hit and passed it to me, "Same shit. It'll work good for you – you're not used to it. Just don't get fuckin' hooked..........Quasar – you listening? Don't' get fuckin' entangled with the shit."

"Right."

"When?"

"The next time you cop."

TWO DAYS LATER WE DROVE DOWN TO LAWRENCE ST. and Bruce Ave. It was familiar territory - driving junkies to destinations with Barb and for Caesar. A red brick three story was still the place to score. It was hard to believe this place had operated with impunity for so long. The dealers' apartments changed, but not the building. Kenny went in and came out.

Beth the Mess had an apartment on 35 Pine St. It was an 11 story apartment house built in the late 50's overlooking the Aqueduct. It was where the Son-of-Sam lived when he moved out of the Bronx. Rikshaw's family also lived there. A lot of students who went to Gorton lived in the building, it was also within eyesight of Commerce High School. The neighborhood was in transition; another one going in the wrong direction.

A few years later, after the Son-of-Sam was captured, there were all these calls from idiots to tear down the apartment because 'the beast' had lived there. The only time a city leader acted with common sense was when the Mayor decided to let the apartment stand and change the number of the building from 35 to 42 – crisis over.

We went up to Beth's apartment. She'd let Kenny use her place to get off whenever he showed up at her door. She wasn't thrilled I showed up with him; she knew I was going through some rough shit, and what the circumstances were. Beth had a crush on Kenny for a long time; he could talk her into most anything.

"Got anything for me?" She watched as we sat down.

"Didn't know you were looking." Kenny didn't look up.

"You come over to use my place to get high – what am I supposed to do? You got anything for me? Come on Kenny do me right."

He looked at her and laughed, then he turned towards me.

"Fuckin Catdaddy – Go find another place to get high. You're a fuckin jerk." The more she got mad, the funnier it got. He was the most insincere Rogue we had – but nobody had more fun. If I was more like him, I might not have needed the dooge. I needed something or someone – but I knew it could only be Wire.

"How many pieces you got?" Beth was getting squirrely; tapping her feet and rubbing her flat hands on her top of her thighs.

"Two."

"You guys know what's going on......you guys get off and you're going to leave me dry? Bullshit motherfucker." Her face turned to stone.

"Whiterlaundry - got ya a six-pack." Kenny said, and I held up the bag.

"I'd appreciate it if you two shitheads would stop giving me the business."

"What you gonna do......call the Heat?" Kenny smiled, but I had to look away; I was ready to laugh in her face.

Crawford threw a third bag on the table, "Gimme $5.00 for the smack, but you got to give Whitepowder his wings." I knew he didn't want me on his conscience.

She gave me a seductive smile, "You've seen us enough....you know where you're going. I'll be smooth and I don't miss." She turned to Kenny. "How is this shit?"

He already had his works out and was cooking. We waited until he got off. Crawdad was on a slow moving steam locomotive to never – never land.

"How is it?"

He answered in between boots: " S'good." Kenny slumped in the chair.

"Merry Christmas Whiteflake." She grinned. I tightened a piece of small diameter rubber vacuum hose on my left arm. She loaded the syringe. The blood history of perhaps 10,000 dope shooters was pumped into my vein as well as the chemical formula which negated the time continuum and substance. It all disappeared. The instant reality came back into view – I knew something had gone terribly wrong. This was the world of ghosts, hopelessness, despair. It brought me to an empty universe. It was not what I had expected. The

656

plan was to reunite with Barb in this quixotic world or find the strength and deal with life without her. It never happened.

Heroin, peyote, hash, mushrooms, opium, acid, mescaline - none of it worked. I even did speedballs with Cocaine Wayne. Neither of us had anything good to say about the combination. It was a waste of time and money. Still, I kept chasing her with every mind altering substance I came across. All the Rogues, even the ones who were doing their own versions of the "Needle and the Spoon" cautioned me I was headed for a train wreck.

Vinny had returned early from a weekend at Stacey's college – another lover's quarrel at her dorm. He said she really didn't want him there because she had finals coming in a week.

I sat in the living room nodding out. Danny Stax was in his bedroom getting off. I opened one eye and drooled: "Vince."

It was like a twister had walked in, "You're a fuckin' idiot and.......you let me down. You got brains enough to know not to fuck around with that shit. Bad enough I got to watch my brother destroy himself – now my best friend decides he wants to waste his life as well. How 'bout this Ryan: Get the fuck out of my house......we ain't friends no more." He threw my coat at me.

I looked at him clueless. 'Why was he yelling at me?' I was confused. Outside their tenetment, I turned the ignition key of the Olds: "Tick. Tic. Tic. Tic. tic...tic...tic...." Five minutes later I tried to start it again with the same result.

I rang the doorbell. Vinny answered and called into the apartment – "Stax, your junkie partner is here."

"Come on Cinzo – back off will ya?"

He laughed, "What do you want?"

Glassed-eyed: "I forgot." I knew I was pitiful.

"On your worst day Whiteshade – you were never this toasted."

"Sorry I let you down." The apology was empty.

"So, that's it?"

I held my arms out and palms up. I had nothing.

"Whiteout, you're a mess. Stop using Wells because it only makes you more pathetic." Vinny said.

"What do I do?"

"Get away from these things which conjure up her image.....her memory. Go back to school, go see Loki, join the service. You're gonna fuckin' kill me if I have to watch you disintegrate." He shut the door.

Again I pressed the doorbell; again Vinny answered, "Now what?"

"Need a jump."

Vinny chased Stax out to jump my battery. "The cables are in the trunk." He yelled at both of us.

Stax double parked his Chevy II next to the Starfire. After ten minutes we still couldn't figure out which cable went to which terminal on the batteries. We made a couple of errant connections. Sparks and arcs had us jumping back. Now, the jumpers frightened us.

Tarts came out of the apartment in a pair of flip-flops and a wife beater shirt not saying a word. He disconnected the leads on the cars and started from square one. "You two Keystone Cops stay out of my way." With the connections properly made, he reached in the Chevy and started it and told me to start the Olds and it came to life.

"Stax – park this thing and put the jumper cables in my trunk."

I tried to thank Vinny again, but he ignored me.

Three days of sobriety did me good; long enough to get me in and out of the Huns garage. Davis Quinn did the front brakes and put new bone yard coil springs up front, did the linkage, bands, and the tranny's filter. Tarts was so right….I had to get out of Dodge. As far as I knew, me and Barb still had the green light to come down to Miami, only I never told Loki she wasn't going to be making the ride with me.

One of the last things I did was see Jamie O'Neill at the newspaper to get the photos of me and Barb. The enlargements still hadn't been done. I'd have to get them the next time I was in town.

AT TWO IN THE AFTERNOON, I STOPPED IN SAVANNAH. The temperature was only 41 degrees. I slept in the car at a department store's parking lot. Thank God Shooey had the blower switch fix.

Jan. 21, 1974 – Loki lived in a run-down section near the Orange Bowl Stadium. He said he couldn't put me up until the 1st of February when one of his roommates was moving. During that stretch, I lived out of the car in parks, camp grounds, and in front of the DMV. Loki said I needed a Florida Drivers License before I could get my Hack license. The State made me take the written and the road test. I was going to put Florida plates on the Starfire, but it was way too involved because Kirk Lis was still the legal owner of the car, but it was insured through Hal's insurance policy. I had been driving the Olds for over a year-and-a-half with the insurance coverage being the only thing right with the paperwork. That coverage would run out in March or April. I hadn't done any drinking or drugging since I had left N.Y. and I was actually feeling pretty good physically. I tried to watch the southern sky at night for any sign, but there was too much night light from the city. The only place I could watch the sky was from Everglades National Park.

I wrote to Ray and let him know I was living in Miami with Loki. 21 O'Dell was receiving all the post cards from Okinawa while Loki and me were getting letters, diagrams, calculus equations and detailed drawings of magnetic modeling from him.

The sobriety wagon was played out. About twice a month, we'd go down to Key West, get drunk, and try to dissect Ray's cryptic messages, formulas, and axioms over at Sloppy Joe's. We'd also buy Sloppy Joe tee shirts and take tourists on a Hemingway and Tennesee Williams tour. We'd make it a point to mention when the playwright was 'in town' and they might sight him if they were lucky. If it was slow – we'd throw in Mel Fisher's empty dock birth where his treasure hunting houseboat would tie up.

Two – five gallon buckets were filled with 7 oz. Miller 'pony' bottles.......a buck apiece. Loki borrowed a radio flyer wagon from the neighbor kid, we'd buy the beer at the 'Orange Town Party Time'. When we arrived in Key West, all we needed was to pour the ice on top. If we had any more than a dozen tourists we were supposed to have a permit to operate a business and one for selling beer.

Loki fudged our enterprise with the city's licensing commission because it involved some educational b.s. They let the fee slide as a 'walking tour' enterprise, but we had to fork over $30 for a beer resale permit. When we first started this venture, we were just trying to pick-up college and/or high school instructors of comparative literature who always seemed to be on some sort of holiday or sabbatical. They came from all over the states, Canada, the U.K., even N.Z. and Australia. We'd get into character of the two writers: dress like them – try to drink like them and say the witty things they might say.........another drunken fantasy. Loki had to do all the talking about Hemingway and Williams; I just sold the beer. As the charade went on, Loki thought it might sell better if he played Hemingway and I was this character 'Eddie' from "Islands in The Stream".

ii

By the end of March, I began to have problems with psychological disorders and substances in south Florida. The only good thing I could say about the substances - neither heroin or cocaine was involved. Florida had been Barb's and my plan, and I kept plugging her into situations down there: where she might have worked, the beaches we would have gone to, a place of our own to live. I would have been going to Key West with her instead of Loki. I knew I had to leave; I was aware I was going slightly mad. The scorecard statistics came from Yonkers on a regular basis: busts, divorces, deaths, (O.D.'s, car wrecks, and gun violence) births, bankruptcies all the fun stuff. I had sent Karyn a post card with the Florida address, but nothing ever came back.

Loki recognized the deterioration and depression. He suggested an extended road trip: "What you're looking for isn't here – you know that."

Every other week I was in a catatonic state. When I wasn't in a psychotic trance – I put myself into one with alcohol and some of that hi-test Jamaican ganja weed. The runs to Key West no longer held my interest. After a 12 hr. shift at Century Taxi, I got out of their car and got into the Starfire. I lived and slept right outside of dispatch. At that point, I crashed more in my car than I did on Loki's chigger ridden sofa.

There was a fair possibility the Hep-C virus was active and eating up my liver. Alcohol consumption only made me sicker. At the time no one knew the Hep-C virus even existed. Loki and everyone else said I looked like I was in pretty dire straights. Raul at dispatch said he couldn't give me a cab looking the way I did.

"A few days in the ocean and on the beach......I'll be as good as new."

"No Ryan, you go to de clinic and get some anti-biotico."

"Yeah, Raul – you're probably right."

"Thas good......you got your place when you get better."

Instead, I said adios to Loki and drove north on I-95 on April 16, 1974. At Jacksonville I turned left: Pensacola, Mobile, Biloxi, New Orleans, Lafayette, Houston, Austin, Odessa/Midland, El Paso, Las Cruces, Bisbee, Tucson, Gila Bend, Yuma, San Diego, Berdoo, Bakersfield, Fresno, Modesto, Sacramento, Reno, Elko, Salt Lake City, Laramie, Grand Isle, Des Moines, Yonkers. Short order cook, truck driver, carnie, gas station attendant, grass cutter, tent event worker, fruit/vegetable picker, sorter, packager, junk yard hand, special event bouncer, special event security w/unloaded pistol, recycler, construction laborer, flat fixer, hot tar roofer, and stick man for a surveyor.

The whole year-and-a-half I played Jimmy Stewart looking for Kim Novak in "Vertigo". I kept looking for Barbara Wells in my travels; a girl who looked, or sounded, or acted like Barb. A sign in the desert night sky, a message in a bottle, or just to wake up from this nightmare; her magnetic lure held me tight and had no sign of releasing me. There were no clues, no visions......just a past that kept pushing and pulling. The year-and-a-half was a modern day – compact sequel of Homer's Odyssey. My epic centering on the registration of the 1962 Oldsmobile Starfire in my name while in San Bernadino.

It was just one of those things which occurred by accident; I managed to stay straight after I turned left at Jacksonville, it was mostly due to my lack of money. I could count the number of times I got high on one hand, and that was only through the generosity of hitch-hiking hippie girls. I might have gotten really blitzed outside of Tulare Ca. A couple of girls gave me this cookie and I ate the whole damn thing. I woke up and they were in the car and we were in Redding - way off my planned route. The chick in the front must have driven us there. I'd look at my reflection in some storefront glass or a mirror in a restroom, I could tell I was getting healthier. While I was working the fields and fruit and nut orchards, I was never hungry. Physically I could feel I was healthier; emotionally and psychologically I hadn't moved an inch. I was the same as the day she died.

As I drove On I-80 through Pennsylvania, I decided to go north avoiding metropolitan N.Y.C. I-84 would bring me about 60 miles north, near Mom-Mom and Mack's place in Straatsville. There was no urgency to head south to Yonkers.   I went to the place where I had always been welcome. It was near 2 p.m. when I pulled into their driveway. She came out with a napkin and a half-eaten peach.

"Ryan! Mother Mary has answered my prayers – are you okay?" she said.

"Yeah Mom-Mom....I'm fine. Where's Mack – the store?"

"No – no. He's working. You've come back at the best time. The hall is empty and they're putting out permit hands – you know......temporary ironworkers. Your grandfather's running the hospital job. You stay over at the orchard; there might be enough work to keep you busy through the summer. Come over tonight and Mack will give you the lowdown. If Ray was only here too, he could get work for both of you."

"Any word when they're going to discharge Ray? " I stretched my back after driving eight hours.

"Janie said it was going to be this summer. The army told him there would be bonus money if he re-enlists. Your father says he knows something about missile guidance systems, and a bunch of $5 words about a missile hitting its target. Janie says your brother's pretty keen on getting out though."

Edna started going through a small knick-knack bowl on the kitchen table. "Where's the key for the garage?" She pushed dice, coins, a bottle opener, a golf tee, a rabbits foot, a St. Christopher medal, a nail clipper, and other keys looking for the garage key.

"Say Mom-Mom, I've got a spare key hid over there." She grabbed me by my wrist; "Are you okay?"

"Aaaaay......some days are still rough."

"You get to work.......you stay busy."

It sounded like a better recipe than the hit and miss life I led since I had left N.Y.

"We'll have supper around 6:30."

There would be nothing to eat or drink at the orchard. I drove to Hyde Park to get some beer and things to eat. Out of habit, I picked up a bottle of Thunderbird. I'd have to clean up the garage when I returned from the store.

There was no escape; memories of Barb Wells came rushing back. I was hoping first to get a job with Mack, and then I was hoping it'd bring me to a different place once I got into it.

Hal and Brother Bill must have been up here recently. The place looked pretty clean. It had warmed up, it was in the high 50's, but the garage was kool. They must have brought the Hoover saucer back to 21. I looked at the back seat of the Starfire, there was about 545 days of my life there, and in the trunk. I had no idea what had accumulated and what had gotten tossed by the wayside. I'd say 80% of what was left was toss-able.

The grass had started to grow. I walked down into the apple orchard. It would be over-grown in a month. Only the layout of the trees indicated this had been an apple producing enterprise in the past. To me the nine acres said: Barb. Everywhere I looked were places we had made some kind of love.

Around 4:00 I emerged from the orchard. It was inevitable the photographs would come out of hiding. I remembered the love we once had; it hurt to miss it so bad. It had been a while since I studied her pictures on a cold day in Laramie. I looked at her when she was alive. There were four of them; they were 4"x6": In the first, she's giving Rexall the finger; the second, was the only good one of her behind the wheel of the Starfire, smiling; the third; was the photograph the Statesman used; me and Barb leaning against the front of the car. It was too far away. Maybe the Statesman's photography department had been able to squeeze more definition from the enlargement. The fourth; was a really good photo of Stacey sticking her tongue out at

Rex that Barb had snuck into. Sometimes I used it, to get back at Stacey.

The photographs from the Yonkers General's freezer were treasures of a depraved person. There was a power coming from the celluloid images of the lifeless - frozen Barb. I felt they had the power to suspend time, not only of the subject, but also of the viewer. When I did get down to Yonkers, I looked up Jamie O'Neill. He handed over all my 8x10 glossy enlargements......alive and dead.

This first day back, I put three away and used the one of Barb behind the wheel.

"HOW'D YOU KNOW I WAS THINKING OF YOU? YOU'RE at the right time and the right place." Mack was animated and kept rolling: "Was there much building going on around the country?"

"California..... a lot out there. Lot of concrete condos going up in Florida. Tell you what Mack, I'm just about tapped out for money. The Olds needs a tune-up and so do I."

"Let's see what Edna's got for supper." He put his thermos and lunch pail on the kitchen counter. "Beer?" he held a Schaefer from the refrigerator.

I nodded and we sat at the dinner table. Mom-Mom divided the asparagus three ways, and we each got a big baked potato and a thick cut pork chop.

"Where's Aunt Allison?"

"She's at Cornell working on getting her masters."

"I've got to get busy and stay busy." My plate was clean except for the pork chop bone. She gave me another potato and a dinner roll. The roll did it.

"Mack, I told Ryan they cleared the bench down the hall and you might be able to put him to work"

"Yeah." Mack looked right at me, "The time is right – right now. Can you start Monday?"

"This is exactly what I need. What do I got to do?"

"You're going to have to 'clear in' down the union hall, Monday morning in Newburgh. I've had a call for 5 structural hands, a rodbuster, and a weldor. These calls have been on the board, for two weeks down there. If the hall can't supply the manpower in three days – I can hire the guys right off the street. I don't need to get into a pissing match with the Business Agent. We show the hall the respect - and it'll go a long way. If there's any bitching at the next union meeting about permit men getting hired, the Agent can say you were hired through the hall and not off the street. Respect is a big part of doing things the right way and making the system run as smooth as possible. You do what I tell you – and then we'll have our asses covered, then everybody saves face and everybody's happy."

"Just tell me what I've got to do Mack." I sipped some beer.

"I'm pushin' the job.....boss of all the ironworkers and the crane operator. We figured we'd peak at 14 or 15 men. You come to work for me – you do whatever the foremen or steward tell you to do. You'll be at the very bottom; everybody knows more than you. Pay attention, and don't come to work wearing that "boilermaker after shave."

"Boilermaker after shave?" I squinted and tilted my head.

"Whiskey breath. One wrong move and it could be lights out for you, or you can end up killing someone because you're not fully engaged with what's going on around you. When somebody yells at you.....it's usually for your own good. We're not out there on a good will tour, and we don't care about your hurt feelings. Our Job is to get this guy's iron hung and come home in one piece." Mack went to work with his toothpick. "You all there kid.......you got your mind right?" he eyeballed me.

"For this I do - you betcha Mack."

"Also – when you're down the union hall - ask the Apprenticeship Coordinator if they're taking applications. If they are – you sign up. Get a decent pair of work boots that are made of leather.......and no damn heel: a flat continuous sole. Heels are for loggers and rock stars......you got it? No polyester – wear all cotton dungarees and work shirts, unless you want to burn up. You got it?" he said.

"Yeah, I think so. Mack, you got $40 you can lend me?"

"Takes money to make money." He went into his wallet and tossed a $50 note across the table.

The streets of Newburgh were pretty empty at 6 am on Monday. A cop was close behind me. Another block and the bad news lights were circling in their red orbs on top of the Ford.

"License and registration."

I handed them out the window.

"California registration and Florida license – what are you some kind of salesman or a drug trafficker?" he peered into the back seat.

I shook my head: "I'm looking for the ironworkers hall."

"You guys do a lot of traveling just to get a job."

"Part of the trade."

"Lafayette St. ......on the bluff. It's the only thing down there."

At Local 417's hall, I signed the 'out of work' list at the window and took a seat. The Business Manager came into the day room, there were three other guys besides me: two journeyman were from Local 424 New Haven, the other guy was a journeyman but he only did reinforcing work. The guys from New Haven left with work tickets after the Business Manager showed them where they were going on the map. He went down his list: "Whitelaw."

"Yo."

"You go over to that small powerhouse at Dutchess Community Hospital in Poughkeepsie. McKay's running the job...." he smiled. "I think you know him."

I smiled back, "He's my grandfather."

"Do what you're told and pay attention." he said. "Pay the secretary $5.00 for two weeks of permit dues."

The permit system was a week by week operation: the local union would issue a work permit only after all the dues paying members were employed. It was common for a temporary hand to get bumped or laid off. A worker on permit had no standing in the scheme of things; all he had was a job - for the time being. That was just the way it was. For now, it was the best thing I had going.

"Tell Mack I'll be stopping by the job in a little bit to straighten out a work assignment with the contractor and the Boilermaker Business Agent. Whitelaw, you pay attention.......space cadets get injured."

"Right."

Journeyman scale was around $12.00/hr. The job was working 5 – 10 hr. days and 8 hrs. on Saturday. There wasn't any of this time-and-a-half nonsense back then. All overtime was double time on wages and fringe benefits. A month into the job, I couldn't believe all the money I was making.

Rigging and unloading structural steel, kegs of bolts, handrail and toe plate, metal decking, sheeting, and items which I had no idea what they were or how to find their center of gravity. My partner was short tempered but was real sharp when it came to rigging and doing it safe. These structurals and other building components were unloaded off semi tractor trailers with a hydro crane, fork truck, and the big 4100w Manitowoc crane which had a 200 ton capacity. It was all new and exciting for me. There was so much to learn and remember.

About once every 10 days, the job would get rained out. Most of the guys had shit to do and the rainout gave them time to get it done. A few went to the bar. Mack would stay at the job in the print shack and try to get ahead with his erection timetable. He was busy making out lists for the structural steel erection which was much more complicated at a powerhouse than for a high rise office building. There were vessels, dryers, tanks, and the steam and mud drums had to be set at specific elevations before more structural steel was set above and around these components of the boiler.

Somehow, he managed to do his scheduling work and get me workwise as soon as practical. He had this 40 year old weldor, Mike, teach me the basics of welding. The steel fabricator hadn't gotten the revised blueprints from the engineering firm, so some of the support iron for the mud drum had to be revised and reworked. Alongside Mike, he taught me how to cut steel with an oxy/acetylene torch, wash off welds without gouging into the parent metal, and weld with 6010 and 7018 welding rods. Three weeks after I started, Mack let me practice welding solo. "Make sure everything's turned off and lock up when you leave."

Mack never touched a tool; he was either in the shack reading blueprints, making out lists, going through bills of lading, or he was on the structure, with his drawings taking measurements trying to find out where the screw ups were.

When I got back to the orchard, I'd have a pint of ripple and think about Barb and her not being there.......but she was there - without physical essence – at least for now. Hal's summerhouse brought all the memories rushing back. I was so grateful for the job with Mack and the overtime, it helped me forget I had missed her so much.

Learning the ironworking trade during work hours, and remembering who and what Barb was; dominated my brain activity off the job. Florida had been bad because it was all Barbwire. I was at the point where something else had importance, and I had begun to realize that. There were the times when the photographs were taken from the large manila envelope, but I seemed to be able to compartmentalize time with her, to the point where I could make advances in my own life.

Like a skip in a vinyl record, the Memorial Day weekend was here. Six weeks on the job went by like they were six hours. The job was shut down for the three day weekend. I asked Mack if I could get on the jobsite and sharpen my welding skills and burning skills.

"Better take the three days off, we've been hitting it pretty hard. If we start getting the iron we need after Memorial Day we should be busier than a two peckered billy goat, and you'll wish you had taken this weekend off."

He cut us loose at noon on Friday and paid us for 8 hrs. Was this the way it was in the real world or was my grandfather just a good guy spending the contractor's money on the gang? At that point of the job, I didn't know.

"Tell your Mom and Dad we said hi –" Mack called as we parted in the parking lot.

"Will do."

"When's Ray coming back?

"I'll try to find out this weekend."

"See ya Tuesday kid." Mack waved.

As I got closer to Yonkers, I experienced a dichotomy of forces and feelings. I thought the earth's magnetism was pushing me back – away from Yonkers; while the buried remnant was attracting me. I had been back just the once to buy some work boots and to check in with everyone at 21. It had been a blurrrrr. It wasn't like Ray's returning or his second coming.

This weekend was different: there was a degree of panic riding with me. I think I wanted to see my family, but no one else...... not yet. Except for Brother Bill who was happy about my return; I no longer lived here....I was a visitor. The only way I could come back was if Ray returned and took up temporary residency. If they let Ray stay – Hal couldn't tell me : 'No Vacancy'. When the powerhouse job topped out, I hoped there would be another job to follow it; if there wasn't, I didn't have a plan what my next move was going to be.

Some things were the same.....Jane was well into her Recital Rush. One summer while I was in high school, Jane, Judy, and her piano player Rich had written the book and three songs for a musical called 'Recital Rush'. Maybe this would be the summer when they put it all together and got it finished. Maybe.

Jane had the phone stuck between her ear and shoulder and gave me a smile. She motioned with her head to the den. The games must have gotten worse between the two of them. She knew I should report in with Hal first…..a chain of command thing.

"Dad, I'm back." He one-eightied his swivel chair from his desk which faced the wall. Our eyes met.

"Well look what the wind blew in. Good to see you son."

I'd just go with the flow, but I think he was glad I was 'out of the house'. Jane was too busy, but I sensed her happiness because her side of the family again had done something to move me along in my career development.

"I missed you when I came down to buy some work clothes and boots. You know I'm staying up at the orchard. I've got some money for the electricity and rent." I said.

"So you're working the 'big iron' for your grandfather."

"Well, it ain't the World Trade Center, but I'm learning a lot. I'm just worried about the boom ending and getting laid off."

"That's the nature of the construction game: feast or famine – boom or bust. You going back on Sunday?" Hal said.

"Or Monday."

Jane had just hung up and she was about to give me a hug when the phone rang again. "I've got to answer this." I took a look around. There were costume boxes throughout the first floor. One of Ray and me's twin beds was set up in the dining room. I wondered what that was all about. A closer look revealed an ashtray and a couple of packs of Hal's Tareyton's. It was just a matter of time before I caught up with Jane and to find out what the deal was with the revamped sleeping arrangements. She would let me know as soon as Hal made a whiskey run.

I wished I had stayed in Straatsville, I walked up to Cassidy's …….for old time's sake. It was best to avoid Morsemere, Lake Ave, and Orchard St. Whoever I would encounter on those turfs would have me thinking about Wells in two sentences. Tony Griffin and Amy Goldshine walked in.

"Hey Whiteknuckles….." Tony greeted.

"Tony…….Amy." I gave her a big smile.

"Your brother around? C'mon, let's get a booth." he said.

We all got our drinks before we sat down. I liked Tony except when he accused Barb of being a boy.

"When did you get back…."

"About six months ago."

"What about Ray?" Amy asked.

"He'll probably be back sometime this summer."

I didn't want to talk about me.

"A couple of years ago, you two were generating a lot of noise."

"Yeah – kind of hoping it would die down a whole bunch; too much spotlight for me."

"Doing anything?"

"Working with my grandfather upstate – going back Monday."

Amy lit a cigarette, "When you say Ray's coming back?"

"Around August…..sometime around then."

"I always had it for your brother."

"Get in line with the rest." we laughed. "I think I've had this conversation before. You know Amy, I'd make book that the reverse has never occurred – where all you girls are saying: 'You know Ray......I've always had it for Ryan.' "We laughed some more. "Tony, how's my bald patch?"

"No bigger than two years ago, but no prettier."

"What are you up to Tony – getting anywhere?"

"He's my gigolo." Amy took a bite of his ear lobe.

I finished my drink and put the tub with the lonely ice cubes on the bar. "I'll be back this way when Ray gets back in town, maybe we'll run into you guys." I said as I left.

Cassidy's was alright, but I missed Copie's Tap; that was where I wanted to drink: low-life atmosphere, better bar maids - Fran and Kaye, best juke box I ever put a quarter in. There had to have been some kind of kick back going on with the jukebox. Copie couldn't care less about the music coming out of the Seeburg, he just wanted his cut.

I bought a Colt tall boy and walked over to the closed up Copie's. It had been empty for two years. I looked inside: the bumper pool and jukebox were gone. The bar was still there.....so there was hope.

Around 10 o'clock Saturday morning, I went down to the Herald Statesman. My business with Jamie O'Neill was not over. Although I had received all of the photographs and enlargements, I didn't feel I had the complete story of the fire and possible murder(s). O'Neill went on about the investigation, some personal data concerning Charles 'Butchie' Powell, and the fact that Marge Wells was indeed pregnant the night of the fire. I nodded and mashed my lips. As far as I was concerned, I didn't feel there was any resolution to the events that occurred that 'Black Friday' night.

There was only one place to go: back to the burial mound of the castaway piece of fireball. Without Ray – there could be no dialogue, explanation, or way to activate the power of the celestial intruder. It had to wait. I cared for these pole reversed miscreants who were integrated with the essence of the magnetic force. Though I was not part of it, I knew its power - how its power could be directed and used in certain applications.

I dropped my coins through the pay phone's mechanism. "Hello." a voice on the other end of the line said. It was my sister Cathy.

Hal had stopped answering the phone unless it rang 10 or more times. The calls were always for Jane. It drove Hal nuts. When we were in grade school he forbade us to answer sometimes. "Let it ring." he'd yell at us.

Brother Bill and Tommy Capps would watch TV over at Tommy's house. Billy knew the shows Hal watched and when Jane and Cathy were out, they would call the house two minutes after his show resumed after a commercial. The phone rang and rang. As soon as Hal said "Hello", they'd hang up. A number of times the two had Tommy's sister do the calling while the two troublemakers were in the basement or upstairs just to hear Hal wig out. He always suspected

Jane had a boyfriend, so these mysterious 'hang ups' ratcheted up his paranoia. Willis and Tommy heard the old man cursing and slamming whatever was within reach. He had pulled the phone jack out of the wall a few times. The two could hardly contain themselves hearing Hal melting down. Brother Bill had to let the prank calls kool off for a while because the rest of us needed the phone too.

"Cathy......tell Mom and Dad I won't be around for supper tonight." I said from the southbound platform.

"Mom's out and Hal's passed out, so there isn't any supper except for Cap'n Crunch."

"Alright......catch you later."

"Ryan -" she caught me before the hang up.

"Yeah?"

"You really working with Mack?"

"Yes I am."

"Kool." I could hear her smiled reply.

THE PHOTOGRAPHS FROM THE STATESMAN KEPT gnawing at me. It was much worse than the 'Rauncho Rancho', 'Twisted Teens,' 'The Bad Girls', or 'Blow Job College'. I wanted to be with Barb so bad – I was desperate to turn back the clock. The reprints of her would have to go into my 'safe box' - buried in the coal bin. I couldn't take them with me back to the orchard, but at the same time I needed to see her; re-imagine her. This situation was an invitation to insanity.

The five months I spent with Loki had zipped by....... perhaps because I knew I was cheating winter and going through the grieving I owed Barb. Taking the left turn at Jacksonville was strictly a magnetic move, not by any choice of mine. It was a sober search for a duplicate Barb Wells. She was a commodity of which was in short supply.

Now that I was back, the road had vanished. The next night I found myself sitting in the Olds again, I waited for something to happen. There was a small bottle of Windex on the floor of the front seat and a few left-over paper towels from the gas station. The windshield, the dashboard, the speedometer, and the instrument panel were made spotless. It was possible to see again. I crossed the tracks and climbed the ships ladder on the south side of the southbound platform and walked to the point where the burial mound was the closest to me. The river, the mound, and me .....the river, the mound, and me; this is where Barb belonged: buried with the cosmic intruder. Why had it taken me so long to put this together? I was going to be a grave robber.

iii

The coal bin looked the same. The boiler had been converted to burn natural gas before Hal had bought the house. There was nearly 3 ½ ft. of anthracite in the bin. Hal never wanted to get rid of the coal. It was a leftover 'just in case' mentality from the Depression. Nobody wanted to mess with it because it was dirty, dusty, got on and in your shoes; only to track it upstairs. Before I went in the bin room, I'd put on a pair of shoes or sneakers that were ready for the garbage. The coal covered an 18" long - low wooden box I had made to store the remaining blockbusters, smut magazines, the Tiger Tar, and our comet dust when it was here. I had everything sealed in double plastic. A small amount of opium was all I was interested in.

Hal had been sweating and snoring when I left 21. Morsemere was deserted; it was only 7 o'clock - the marina was a possibility. It was worth the short detour to see if there were any familiar cars in front of Vinny's tenement on Nepperhan Ave.

Out front, I saw Danny Stax's and Kenny's vehicles. Both of them had collected more whiskey dents during my hiatus. Stax's Chevy II had a smashed passenger side front fender and the bumper snaggled downward. He had tie-wired a flashlight in the headlight hole. It had to be for the bluecoats. The cheap batteries he bought from 'John's Bargain Store' didn't last very long.

Laying on the doorbell for a minute didn't roust anybody. I could see into the apartment through the confederate flags they used for curtains. Stax and Crawdaddy were nodding on a sofa, a set of works were on the table. I let myself in and sat at the kitchen table and waited. Kenny started to stir about a half-hour later. Danny Stax didn't know what decade it was. Outside, I sat on a milk crate waiting for the night to begin. Perhaps either of the two shooters would stagger out; I got some Ripple from the car. Glad I was ironworking and off the dooge, I needed a pack of smokes. Oil City was about 3/8ths of a mile within view of the apartment. Walking over there, I had to do a double-take at the gay bar: another name change while I was away: 'The Fore and Aft'. If nothing else, these guys knew how to sell their product. The last name I heard they were using was "Boy's Towne".

Back on the milk crate, I lit up a smoke. I waited for Stax or Crawford; instead Vinny Tarts rolled up just as I was about to leave. He reached across the car and opened the passenger door: "Get in Whiteflight".

"Let me lock-up my wheels." I got in Vinny's car, "What the fuck are you driving?"

"Datsun B-210. Impala died. Cocaine Wayne sold me a hot Ford Falcon. The bulls seized it and they're after Wayne. This Japper was all I could afford......bank owns half."

I passed him the Ripple pear wine.

"I got to get a slice of Progression, and then we'll go down the end – I got to get a bottle of wine. Wanna check out the marina?"

"Greystone will be better for me. Don't want to see anybody and have to start explaining my whereabouts for the past two years. When I do, I'm just going to tell them I've been living in Miami since Barb died."

"Wow Vince - this car is cozy!"

"You're sitting in Stacey's seat."

"Is this car good enough for her?"

"So far."

"You going to see her later on tonight?"

"She's in Connecticut with her family.

"You're STILL on the outside looking in?.......unreal."

"I don't know about that.....I got on with Conrail while you were away. My stock is going up with her family --- besides......I'm in love again."

"You're a fuckin' retard." We laughed.

"So what's going on with Whiteclowntown?"

"I'm rolling in dough now - ironworkin' with my grandfather upstate. - Let's get outta this fucking sardine can."

I gave him a rundown of my transcontinental exploits. There was plenty of daylight left. Greystone was just as empty as it was three hours earlier. We were real close to the water sitting on a log or telephone pole that had washed up years ago. "Harmonie Likkers ain't going to have any macrita left now that you're back." he said.

"LeClair said the same shit two years ago."

"So you've been staying up there?"

"Yeah – be back for the Fourth."

"I'll be in Connecticut."

"You hope."

"No man – serious joint man – I'm callin' the shots."

I shook my head: "You should have stuck with Dona Del Bello. Besides you want to keep the blood pure. Don't need no mick blood contamination."

"Man.....Stacey got that big overflow ass. It just won't quit. I'm hooked on it."

I thought about her big butt....."She likes wearing them tight dungarees. How you get her to stay at your apartment on weekends? Your part of Nepperhan is pretty sketchy."

"I really don't live there, just part-time. Joe and Cassie moved in with Stax and Jackie Hart. They let me stay on the couch when the railroad has me over on this side of the river. I'm a vagabond anyway, most of the work is across the river. I share a place in Haverstraw with a guy from work. Unless there's a wreck - I'm usually in Yonkers on the weekends. "You know the place was unlocked, Stax and Kenny were nodding out – I walked right in the front door."

"That's not good." Vinny raised his brow. The concerned face was replaced with a grin. "Check this out: We're getting evicted." he nodded up and down with a bigger grin.

"Wha......you stop paying your rent?"

"Un-uh, and it's the first bill we pay every month. We're getting evicted by the Satanic State of N.Y."

"Get the fuck outta here."

"It's true, the State's buying us out. They're widening the street all the way to Yonkers Ave. Here's where it gets good: we got an injunction against the State, the DOT, HUD - Urban Renewal Dept., and the Dept. of Natural Resources. We got the project stopped cold. And guess who's our lawyer?"

"F. Lee Bailey....." I dripped cynicism with an eye roll.

"The fuckin' commie......Fast Eddie's lawyer: Fuckin Yuri Restov. He says we were denied due process, illegal use of eminent domain law, and......... the landlords tried to evict tenants so they

670

would receive the renters share of the settlement money. Yuri says we're in for a big payday. All these other tenants were brought in by Yuri. He says it's just going to take time. This case will never go to court and it'll be settled by arbitration. It's looking good for Stax, Hart, and me. My brother Joe is fuckin pissed! He says he's the one who's living there."

"Yeah, but his name isn't on the lease."

"That's the long and short of it." Vince bulldogged his chin and nodded. Cinzano switched lanes, "You doing any tragic magic lately?"

"Un-uh. The last time was when you helped me with the jumper cables......a good year-and-a-half ago. I don't know – maybe it was when I got off down Pine St. with Denise the piece, Rikshaw, and Beth again. I almost O.D.'d the last time. Fuck the Bronx – fuck Lawrence St. and fuck Pine St. Fuck that whole fuckin' world."

"It goes in spurts. It dropped six or seven last year. The shit you got to hit up always got a high price. It just ain't the money." Vince said.

For me it was becoming more and more clear with each passing season: It was about getting married, having kids, learning a trade or a profession, it was about obligation, love not lust; and if it meant doing time on the gerbil wheel – get on and get it over with.......there are no free rides.

Tarts was a lot closer to the entry ramp of the rat maze than I was. I suppose in a way I envied him for it. He had a long term job. I knew Stacey well enough to know wealth and materialism was what motivated her; she kept hounding Vinny to get out there and "make money so we can buy stuff". In some respects Stacey and Tarts were like vinegar and oil. She was the kind of woman to hold back her love until she got what she wanted. I was as blind as the rest, but no one wanted me: I didn't have a trade and I didn't have a steady job – I wanted both. I figured a relationship with another woman would come. Those of us who remembered their days of youth as their pinnacle, could only have the memories of them from here on. Now it was time: leave the bullshit behind and take all the good stuff you learned with you down the road. The time continuum was not as fluid as I thought.

At his coming back from Nam party, Ray said neither him or the polemic Fifth Dimension would have to deal with any of that "Rat Race" nonsense. They had a bigger job......a more pressing concern. The major shortcoming of Phantom City was that it was difficult hanging around, being there for the extra innings. There were more departures all the time.

iv

Independence Day fell on a Friday in 1975. Mack once again cut the crew loose on Thursday at noon and paid us for 8 hrs. I wished him a Happy Birthday in the air conditioned job trailer, filled a monsta trash barrel bag with my laundry and tossed it in the trunk. Except for the clothes I was wearing, all my dungarees and shirts were full of rust

671

and grease. It didn't take me long to start dressing like an I-head and losing the Waylon Jennings style - which in reality was almost the same thing anyway.

It only took a week to figure out that dungaree and heavy denim material had the durability to withstand the varied tasks it took to erect a structure of steel. Cotton repelled the welding and burning sparks. They weren't leather, but they protected a worker well enough as long as you weren't welding and burning all day. The Lees and Levis and the Wrangler shirts were made with the rigors of manual labor as a primary consideration. Off the job, people on the street couldn't put the rust – sweaty - greasy clothes and wide smiles and laughter together as we walked to our cars for the ride home.

What tripped my trigger was breathing in another day of learning the trade, scoring some more money, and making Mack proud that I was getting 'it'. For the journeyman, it was the money, but it was also the fact that we were safe - going home another day. Nobody went in the hole, got their head mashed because somebody dropped an 8 lb. hammer from three tiers above, got crushed by a beam coming in hot and knocking you off the iron, or any number of mishaps, which could send you upstairs to have a talk with St. Peter. Back in '75, we didn't have any of those stupid European safety devices. The steel erecting companies had them harnesses/lanyards and nets. We mostly left them in the gang boxes, except when Mack told us one of the insurance safety adjusters was going to make a visit. Mike the weldor said, "A lot of times escape.....getting away from a dangerous situation - is part of staying alive. You can't get away if they got you tied up like a dog." I was with the rest of the guys: 'if you couldn't walk and work the high iron, them stupid harnesses weren't going to save you.'

Jane had another successful recital. She was ready for some R&R up in Straatsville, for the Fourth and Mack's birthday. When I showed up at 21 O'Dell, the four of them were loading the two cars.

I didn't know they were going up, and they didn't know I was coming down. Jane's Comet was loaded up with her and Cathy and Billy's stuff for a weeks' stay. Hal had a brand new Plymouth Valiant stocked with his usual travelling buddies: Barton Reserve Whiskey, the consumption ratio at this point was: 3 nights = 2 quarts, and a carton of Tareyton cigarettes. He'd drive back on Sunday unless he returned sooner upon request of his hosts.

Mom-Mom and Mack were maxed out with his drunken, cynical, know-it-all, selfish attitude. As the old man's whiskey intake increased, he became more unpredictable and disruptive. At the same time, the Knudsen and McCoy blood was less tolerant of his bullshit. It was a fait accompli the marriage was on life support. I'm sure my mother would have felt more secure if I had been around 'just in case'. Up to that point, the abuse had only been verbal, but you knew his abuse could suddenly turn physical if he had enough go–go juice in him.

WHEN THEIR TWO-CAR MOTORCADE STARTED UP THE hill, I felt bad for Brother Bill; the old man made my brother sit in the shotgun seat with him for the two hour ride. Everybody wanted to be with Jane.......nobody wanted to go head-on; trapped in a car with Hal.

He might have been one of the initial inventers of the 'road rage' driving technique. He'd scream at the driver next to him as he waited for the light to change: "You're lucky I'm not on duty", or he'd look at the car's plate in front of him or behind him and pull along side the driver: "BX boy - huh?......why don't you shag your ass back to the Bronx and learn to drive?" He'd yell at people with all of us in the car and they'd look at us like he had escaped from the laughing house. When it was summer and all the windows were rolled down, Ray and me hid our faces in my sister's shoulders; the more Hal drank, the more fire and brimstone was hurled from the window. He never tangled with anybody who was bigger than he was. He truly liked to drink and drive, and have us kids watch 'The Hal Show.' It was scary – not funny.

The memory of that weekend a few years earlier with Vinny and those All Souls girls, and the subsequent pass I made at Linda next door - came rushing back. No way a night that great could be repeated. I just had gotten past that stupidity I pulled on Linda at Ray's first welcoming home party – the one where he was still overseas. She talked to me like that morning never occurred. There was something to that Doors' song "Soul Kitchen". I didn't know if Jim Morrison was advising or warning us when he sang: "Learn to Forget".........."Learn to Forget". Most of the time it was the right counsel.

THE CORE ROGUES HAD LEFT FOR THE JERSEY SHORE. I bumped into Bad Brad Guzzutti down the North End around 9 p.m. He gave me the rundown.

"Pretty sure they're all down in Belmar this time." he said.

"What about Cinzo?"

"Nah....Stacey finally got the green light to bring the greaseball to the parents beach house in Connecticut."

"Son-of-a-gun......." I scratched my head. "Yeah but, he'll always be under her spell." I turned to Brad, "What about you? You're always here when everyone else is out of town."

"Seems that way – can't get ahead."

"So whatcha up to Brad?"

"Still drawing wire at Anaconda in Hastings and I'm running a hot dog cart over on Nepperhan and Saw Mill River Rd. when my uncle wants some time off."

"Two jobs? What the fuck dude?" I raised my eyebrows. "Whatja do? Get married and have a kid?"

"Pretty much......we had the kid......and then I got married." Brad tried to look away.

"Wow.....I've been on the road........ been out of touch."

"No big deal.......she put my stuff out on the street. She caught me bangin' Marilyn Moen. You know she went to Gorton.......year behind us? I stayed with Vinny down there on Nepperhan for a few weeks; then they asked me to leave because I was bringing everybody down. I dunno – it was probably true. I'm in and out of court all the time.....no place to live. Now, I'm back with mom and dad back up here. Broke all the fuckin' time." Brad went blank. He stirred and his face lit up, "Hey, what's the word from your brother?"

"He says he'll be discharged before Labor Day. I got to run." He gave me a slap on the back and I told him: 'I'd see him around.'

Fireworks were being set off all over, there were a couple dozen blockbusters left in the coal room. I was hoping they'd still be viable. Whether they would explode or fizzle; they weren't reliable or predictable after all this time. The outer layer of the Tiger Tar had also degraded to the level where it could be sold as top grade hash. The interior of the pork roll still sent its user to the castles of Kublai Khan. It was speculative argument whether its addictive characteristics had decreased since the opium had come under my control.

In the coal bin, I sat and listened to the smoke of the small amount of the outer layer of the Tiger Tar. I knew I could drive; I knew where the Starfire was going. The people, buildings, even the fireworks seemed two dimensional. I thought it was similar to taking a ride through the set of a 'Twilight Zone' or 'Outer Limits' episode. It was flat, like listening to a mono record. I turned off Lake onto Morningside Ave. I didn't remember Morningside being this abstract. My heart rate was the same, but it pounded harder, I bailed out on Glenwood Ave., and tried it again only this time I stopped at the liquor store and got a pint of Tawny Port. I turned around in the Lake Ave. parking lot and went south on Park Ave to High St. There it was; I took three swallows and made a U-turn to be on the far side of the street. 11 High St. had been leveled and the basement walls and foundation were gone as well and filled in with dirt. It was a ride through spirit land. I got out of the car; firecrackers and bottle rockets were exploding all around. I poured some Tawny port where the cops said they had found her.

It was almost dark. On the remote chance there might be a sign from her, I leaned against the Starfire scanning the sky. Perhaps, there might be a token sent by her. Twenty minutes elapsed and two inches of the port remained.

Something I didn't understand was taking place. All my senses searched for Barb, including my brain. The pain of her loss had not diminished. All the unused years she lost - I knew in my heart I had lost those years too; stolen from me as well.

The principals may have perished, but the innocents' cry for justice was still vibrant. God had called back that which he had made. Barbara Wells had sacrificed her life in the act of saving others. It may have been an automatic response to a magnetic charge and had nothing to do with good and evil. She made a conscious choice to extinguish and save life that night. I couldn't be sure her decision was one of sanity over that of sharing her life with me. The question still haunts me. In either instance; the result may have played out for the best.

V

Although the physical and emotional relationship with Karyn Cahill didn't compare with what Barbwire and me had; it wasn't because there was a lack of desire for Karyn. Rather, Barb had that magnetic aura which never let me go. She'd lose the aura when she was outmatched by the dope.   Perhaps it was more opportunistic than anything else, it may have been one of the reasons I hooked up with Karyn in the first place. It might only have had to do with her making the first move in conjunction with her physical beauty.

She wasn't leftovers, I knew she had wanted what was best for me. With a real job, I could deal with her on her level: No longer a part-timer at work or a part-timer in love. My classification had to be upgraded – I never worked this hard or learned so much; she had to recognize that. I'd have to come clean about this business about being a 'permit ironworker' instead of a real one. She had brains enough to figure out it was the same as being a casual laborer except this was union work with union wages.

Since I got out of high school, every job had been a step up from the last. Even those jobs on the road had given me skills to a certain extent; if nothing else......people skills. With Barb gone, so was my youth, It would have been possible to stay young forever with her. Now the 'Rat Race' and the 'real world' were all that were left. Karyn was hot-looking, and sharp enough to see something in me which was mostly 'potential'. I had my foot in the door to offer her fun and satisfaction, but I could sense she'd make me grow up. Most of the other women were of the same ilk as her, and she was aware how far and fast I had come.......not that far and stuck in neutral. I was still making love to photographs.

Whether Karyn was still around, single, or at all interested; I could only wonder. The last two years had left me emotionally beat up to the point where I had real doubt as to whether I could have a meaningful relationship with any woman.

July Fifth, I sat in the employee lot at Tibbetts. Waiting for my coffee to kool, I thought I understood why I was there. I didn't expect much, but I did want to reconnect with Karyn or if that was not possible just to see her. She'd be entering her last year of undergraduate work in the fall. Karyn hadn't heard from me in two years, she might not work at Tibbetts any longer for all I knew. The stickman pushed the dice to me and it was my turn to roll 'em. A few cars filtered in as I waited for her lime-green Camaro. It was the same green as Mike Reno's Nova. It should have had a different color scheme the first time I saw the car I thought.

I was slumped down, sunglasses, mesh baseball hat, a cigarette, and my coffee. I teetered on crashing out. There was no lime green car in the lot. If she didn't show, I'd have to ask one of the people in the park uniform........"Does Karyn Cahill still work here?" Maybe I showed up on her day off?

A caustic voice came through my open window: "What are you doing here?"

"Thinking about catching an early morning swim."

It was a female voice; it was her, but I looked straight ahead.
"I was waiting for you."

"You can't be serious."

"Just got back in town. Got the holiday weekend off, figured
I'd roll the dice......maybe hit an eleven." I turned to face her and
smiled. She looked great: her black/brown hair fell straight from her
off-center part and curled into her neck just above her shoulders. I
winced and focused.

I gave her one quick head nod: "You involved with
anybody?"

She rolled her eyes and shook her head.

I didn't know if the slow head shake was part of her eye roll
or that she wasn't involved with someone else.

"I'll see you after work – only because I'm interested in the
line of bullshit you're going to throw at me. I'm not interested in your
heart."

"I don't have time to waste......you seeing somebody?"

"I'll see you after work. Meet me up here at 5 o'clock."

I let her walk down to the pool building by herself. I didn't
need to see any of the people I had worked with two years ago and
give them something to talk about. Still, I'd be a no account m.f. if I
didn't check in with Uncle Harry and at least say "Hello."

I finished my coffee and launched the filter. The radio station
was coming out of commercial and the D.J. put on 'Ramblin Man' – I
had to stay for the whole track. Sometimes the Brothers still had it.
The band should have kept that Les Dudek who played lead with
Dicky on that song. The tune put me in the right frame of mind to visit
Harry. It wouldn't be good for him to find out I had been here and
didn't stop and see him.

Harry was on the phone when I walked into his office. His
eyes lit up and pointed to a chair. Three minutes later he hung up,
"Holy Jeez kid – I don't have any openings." He grinned. He asked
about Jane, Edna, and what I was doing.

"I'm working with Mack McKay – upstate."

"Ironworking."

"Yeah."

"It's a good trade.......be careful kid, you're only one step
from death." Silence. "Mack's an ace of a guy, I always liked him. It
got awkward after Edna and my brother got divorced; then Edna and
Mack hit it off, and the page turned as they say."

"Uncle Harry, I've got to thank you for giving me a job."

He waved the gratitude off simply saying he wished he could
have done more. "Hey...." he jolted, "What about that Cahill girl?
When you didn't show up last summer, I knew it had something to do
with the business in the paper."

"I didn't have my mind right for quite a spell."

"This Karyn......Cahill......she's a good kid."

"Is she going out with anybody?"

"I don't have time to dish the dirt around this joint."

I laughed, "Hey Chief......thanks for all your help." I waved
bye.

I bought some chicken guts down at the A&P for crab bait, and went down to the marina to try my luck until Karyn got off work.

She walked over to the Starfire in the parking lot already in her street clothes. "You're working tomorrow." I said.

She stood on the passenger side, I got out of the car and talked to her over the rooftop.

"It's the fourth of July weekend WhiteNbright – you worked here – you know it's all hands on deck for the holiday."

"Gee Karyn, you look great." My eyes absorbed all that I saw.

She chewed her gum like a pro, "Do you have any plans other than getting me liquored up and taking me to bed. If that's as original as you can get – maybe you shouldn't have bothered."

"Follow me to my house, or leave your car here, and I'll drive you back tomorrow morning."

"You're the only one there?" Her eyebrows scrunched together.

"All weekend."

"You want to play house? You're serious.......you want me to stay over tonight. Have I got that right?" She looked at me and asked, "Are you serious?"

"Karyn, I'm down here for the weekend. I was hoping you might still be in town........and unattached. If I missed my chance – I missed it. It's ridiculous for me to think you still feel the same about me as you did before. If you're free, and there's something left between us, let's see where it goes. If it's gone – we'll find that out too."

"I'll follow you to your parents' house." She said it as if it was a dare.

We stopped down the North End. I sent her to get four slices while I went over to Harmonie liquor and got two bottles of macrita. I wasn't planning on getting smashed; I wanted the leftover alcohol for Sunday.

Karyn parked her car on O'Dell. I parked in front of 21 with two wheels on the slate sidewalk on the no-parking side of the street.

"I'll be right out. I'm going to get some ice and a couple of paper. The Starfire seemed to be on autopilot. We parked in a deserted Greystone Station, fireworks were still being blown off as if the Fourth had never ended.

"Why are we here?" She looked around.

"Seems right."

"Did you come down here with her?"

"We came down here before."

"But why are we here now?" She looked from side to side.

"Brought you here cause I can guarantee it's too hot in the house and we'll be able to see the rockets up and down the river. A lot of these towns and cities.......tonight's their official Fourth of July celebration."

We got the party stuff from the trunk. Karyn got the pizza and the cups, I grabbed the rest. I was just about to slam the trunk lid.

677

"What's that stuff?" She tossed her head at the trunk and pointed with the cups to a rigging belt which held two spud wrenches in a scabbard, a connecting bar, an eight lb. smash, two bolt bags and two bullpins in two sleeves sewn into either side of the bolt bag, a 12 in. shifter wrench, a hard hat, and a welding hood.

"It's ma job." I mimicked one of the soul brothers who was on our job; he barked his answer to some interested passerby on the street who was overwhelmed with curiosity.

"Huh?"

"It's my job." I scowled back; this time with my best Broderick Crawford voice. "Put it on."

We put the party on the car's hood. The ironworker belt clanged with the large steel tools. I brought the two ends of the work belt around her waist and folded the quick-release buckle into place and cinched it tight. I walked twenty feet into the empty parking area.

"Okay Honey – come to Papa."

She took a few steps towards me. "Whoa......wait a minute......the 8 lb. smash is still in the trunk." I fitted the heavy maul with a 30 in. ash handle through the belt so the handle was inside and the head was on the outside. The smash rode diagonally just above her rump. These big mauls always looked like they would get loose and fall but they never did. It was a secure method.

"Alright Sweetie.......showtime. Let's see what you got."

She couldn't walk with a consistent gait.

"My God, are you crazy?" Her eyes bulged out.

"They say you got to be nuts to get into this racket. Try walking up those steps to the overpass." Karyn made it up six steps.

"That's all – put this thing back in the trunk."

"Just think, I get to have this thing riding on my hips 10 hrs. a day and I get to climb 30 ft. columns and make the first beam to column connection. It's just my partner, the crane operator, me and the sky."

"We can discuss it over drinks and pizza."

We ate and drank in the shade of the southbound's overhang. There was a slight breeze coming up the river.

"So no more taxi driver?"

"Never say never......you know what I mean? You're here with me again." I reminded her.

"You ain't there yet buddy." We ate some pizza and drank some macrita. "Is this ironworking job for real?"

"Has been for the last three months; and being 150 feet in the air walking a four inch beam.......that's about as real as it gets – unless you're in a place like Nam."

The questions came rapid fire about the job, the money, the risk, and the prospects for future projects. I gave Karyn a thumbnail sketch of the permit system. I don't think she understood the inherent 'band-aid' nature which my position was intended to be. I told her the way to get a journeyman's card was through apprenticeship, and not the 'back door' through the permit system.

"How long will this powerhouse job last?

"We got more structure to erect, a shit load of miscellaneous iron, a mile of handrail and stuff I don't know about. It's a small generating station - meant only to supply power to the hospital. Hospitals got to stay lit all the time. The power they don't use they'll sell to Mid-Hudson."

She looked up from her pizza: "Is this a career move – a career thing?"

"Sure beats everything else I've done. My grandfather Mack's done pretty well with it."

Ironworkers were the highest paid of all the building trades, Karyn knew this. The pay was in exchange for the risks they took. Other trades were more technical and required more training, but the differential was made up in the testicular fortitude required to do the job. Most guys wouldn't go near the job even if their families were facing eviction.

Dusk was coming on; distant fireworks could be seen and heard. The ice had melted; I brought her over there just to see if it felt any different with Karyn than when Barb and me hung out there. I went back to the Starfire and got the beach blanket as she waited at the mound. This noise got in my head and I was kind of frozen. Karyn was the source of some kind of interference in the triangulation of the river, station, and the ejected chunk of the cosmic intruder. Ray and the "Dimension Four or Five" might be able to unravel the metaphysical properties which exaggerated the oppositely poled women. It wasn't something to make me get her out of there in a hurry, what it did was amplify the differences between the two women; one was security and safety – the other had been all risk, uncertainty, and speculation. Perhaps, I was just spooked.

It felt like it took me a long time to get the blanket and more ice from the trunk. There was a bottle of tequila in the trunk that only had three fingers of liquid left, I took that too. I tossed the blanket from the platform to the bare burial mound. She said: "Gee, that was quick."

"Karyn, pour me a chaser of Macrita."

She plunked the cubes in the chasers. I took the cactus juice and poured a shot, "Happy Bicentennial."

"You're a year early."

"So you aren't involved in a relationship?" I was feeling better when the alcohol went down.

"Nothing I wouldn't drop if you committed to me."

I was as much driven by fate as the general who tossed the coins across the Rubicon. I laid her down on the blanket and gave her a long passionate kiss. There was guilt; I felt I was betraying Wells. The betrayal was not because I was with a different woman - I had done that with Karyn when Barb was alive. It was the location; this was Barb's place. It was hard feeling good about this 'theft'. I had this real bad feeling there was a tug of war going on with the Cosmic Intruder. Barb and me had spent so many love sessions on top of space mound trying to free ourselves of this planet through chemical interjection and magnetic propulsion. I brought Karyn here; but it was possible I was drawn here – something didn't feel right.

We watched rockets racing up to the darkened sky with aerial bombs chasing them. I needed some electricity to complement the tequila and Macrita.

Karyn wouldn't understand the magnetic underworld, but I would continue my search for the cosmic explanations of this charged polemic ash with the aid of exotic substances. This world would have to remain secret; I didn't have the intellectual capacity to explain it to her. She already thought I was deranged; walking iron 200 feet in the air only reinforced the perception.

Greystone was approximately 3 miles up river from Glenwood station and the marina. With the gentle breeze we could hear the fireworks they were setting off down there. Our electricity began making sparks of our own. Her eyes were shut tight, as I watched her face contort in pleasure. 'How could it be this good as she played cowgirl on me? Karyn didn't learn this at college.' I thought. She was oriented facing the George Washington Bridge and I watched the Tappan Zee. It was damn near two dogs in heat. Karyn rolled me around so I could start pile driving, her legs wrapped around my ass. She started losing it and squeezed me deep into her: panting, cooing, gyrating.

"Give it to me......Shit....shit man.....give it.....Shit yeah... oh shit yeah.......Shit!" The more she talked, the harder I worked. I was positive she broke the bank two or three times as she waited for me.

It was dark, but the light pollution of the metro area made the fireworks less dramatic. The humidity and ozone in the air did the same to the sound as the excessive night illumination did to the night sky.

Pumping away, I watched her face, I heard something wild like sustained thunder coming from the Staten Island area travelling up the bay into the river's mouth. I kept fucking Karyn, but turned my head trying to see what was causing the heavy-duty sound. My eyes were at their maximum trying to focus to the left, I was determined to give her an all-star load, but the rocket thunder kept getting nearer and louder.

Getting away from the glow of the city, the thunder continued towards us. 'What the fuck is that?' I kept the primal animal force in gear. 'Fuck all – I was going to make this happen.' I wrenched my head around - as far as my neck would allow to see what was coming up the river. My left eye saw an orange blaze of light in front of the sound. This fireball blazed up the river like the comet had nine years earlier. It couldn't have been more than 1500 feet above the water as this bright orange glow were actually two lights. Faster than I could see or think, it whizzed past us.

"All you got Whitelight ....ALL YOU GOT HOT ROD!" She kanked. "Just don't have your nut in me....oooooh.......I don't want your child." I tried to pull out and make a mess on her tits, but her legs had my ass locked in tight. I thought my dick went through and came out her asshole. A three month cherry was implanted within her womb.

I looked up and the sky over the river was a sheet of orange light getting smaller. As it zoomed away, the blaze-orange light became two distinct circular discs trailing away. The sound and the concussion followed in its wake. The sonic boom broke us apart, knocked over the tequila bottle, and left the station's lights shuddering.

vi

The last week of July, Karyn told me she was late. When the orange fireball crossed the finish line with me, I knew it had to be some kind of omen. I had broken some kind of taboo with Barb, the Cosmic Intruder, and the pole reversal gravity power. What was I thinking? I was thinking with my love muscle and nothing else, one major selfish move.

Like a condemned man walking to the gallows, I entered the job trailer at lunch.
"Ryan, it's not the end of the world." Mack took a breath. "This shit happens everyday. You're going to have to find some real work to support your family. You might pick up another iron job after this one – maybe not. If they only had been taking apprentices this summer, you'd at least been a member of Local 417. That's the shortcoming of the permit system – you get journeyman scale, but your commitment to the Local is suspect."
"What's my next move Mack?"
"Stay put right here, unless one of those civil service jobs come through. I'll talk to our Business Manager; he may be able to point you in the right direction." He offered me a Lucky Strike.
"Thanks." We lit up.
"When's she due?"
"Early April, by her reckoning."
"What's the latest about your brother?"
"Should be out already.......thought he was coming straight home." I said.
"Start banking every dime you make. Karyn tell her parents?"
"We figured we'd drop the bomb on them just after she starts her senior year at Fordham."
"Hal and Jane?"
"Nah.....not yet. I'll see how Karyn wants to handle it." I squeezed my eyes, and got tight lipped.
"That damn pussy's got more pull than a 10 ton truck." He shook his head and took a long drag.
"Ain't that the truth."
"The best I can do for you - is keep you working as long as I can, but your usefulness to the Local and the Business Agent solely depends how much work is on the books. If a long term job comes up and the bench is cleared, I'll lay you off and you get down to the hall later that afternoon. The problem is - the only work I've heard coming

681

up is all short term stuff. We might have three.....four months left here at most."

IT WAS DIFFICULT TO BELIEVE WHEN KARYN TOLD ME I had hit an inside the park home run on the Fifth. It had to have had something to do with the 'Ejected Voyager' beneath us. The more I thought about the astronomical odds of this occurring, the more I was sure of the existence and transformational power at work since the night Ray and I watched the Fireball enter our atmosphere.

Mack was digging through Local 417's Summary Plan Description of its Health and Welfare Benefits to make sure I'd have coverage for the baby and Karyn. If I worked one day into December – we'd be okay. We could even pick up another quarter on a self-pay basis. The hospitalization question was the one which worried me the most. I needed that good news from Mack.

Some of the guys on the job treated me like I had the plague. They knew I was in a jam. The inquires and advice came at me from all directions on our breaks, until they were sick of the subject: "You know you got to marry her so she's covered; you mean you ain't married?; where ya gonna live?; when's she due?; should have signed up for the apprenticeship; that car ain't gonna make the winter; the three of you can't make it on unemployment; if you're going to keep working iron, you're going to have to buy a book;" and on and on.

The one I liked best was "Big Hand's" comment: "are you sure it's yours.......you sure you didn't wrong hole it? – which in your case would have been the right hole." Undoubtedly, it was the worst cut of all, but it was the funniest. It took me out of the funk for a little bit.

The fifth of July fireball had to have had some intergalactic or magnetic significance. About a week later, I found out what it was: the newspapers reported "strange lights and thunderous sound were produced by the jet known as 'The Supersonic Blackbird' which could fly from coast to coast in 68 minutes. The orange discs had been its engines' after-burners, and the sonic boom was from breaking the sound barrier. The pilot and co-pilot were reprimanded."

The article in the N.Y. Times was saved for Ray to read. If he couldn't provide an explanation, he might offer a couple of possibilities that weren't pure speculation. I didn't buy into the story the paper was offering. I liked the idea Art Bell pushed on his radio show "Coast to Coast". He claimed it was a UFO and a cover-up by the government.

Two days into August, Mom-Mom told Mack and me: Ray had showed up in Yonkers on Thursday. The job was still goin 5 – 10's and an 8. I was going to blow off work on Saturday, but Mack advised against missing 8 double time hours. I packed for an overnighter and left right from work. When I got to 21, Hal was dishing out more nonsense than some of the knobs on the job.

I made a phone call to Karyn and let her know I'd be late getting down to her house because Ray had just made it back. His gear was still packed except for his overnighter canvas bag. He came downstairs from taking a shower as I was finishing a conversation with Karyn: "Okay, love you….se ya later….bye Hon." I hung up.

"Ray!"

"Ryan - " He smiled, and gave me a man hug with a strong pat on the back. "What the hell is going on?" He shook me and we both smiled.

"He's got his girlfriend knocked up." Hal laughed.

Ray dead eyed the old man: "He who is without sin……let him cast the first stone."

"Quoting verse and scripture now Ray? Were you trying to get on with the Chaplain corps?" He laughed some more by himself.

"Isn't that why you sent us to Catholic school……to learn right from wrong, and to show mercy when and where we can?" Ray slowly nodded with his eyes beading down on Hal.

"I told him to put a helmet on that soldier." He shouted back pouring whiskey into the shot glass.

We pulled two tall boys from my lunch cooler I had brought for the ride.

"Let's get out of here…..I can't take a full dose of Hal yet. Mom isn't home…..she's got Cathy and Billy with her. There's really no point in staying."

"Greystone?" I tossed my head towards the river.

"Not right now……..cruise around – I've got to find a place to live. 21 isn't going to work out for me with the old man brewing a batch of attitude every night." Ray looked at the 16 oz. brew and tossed the pop top in the street.

"We'll both be looking for a place to live." I took a deep breath.

"Did I ever meet Karyn?" He crunched his eyebrows together; running through his mental rolodex.

"I don't believe so. She's from South Yonkers and went to some all-girls Catholic High School in the Bronx."

"That was real……real bad about Barb. She was in exile, a Phantasm entity……….a shadow……bloomed late." He gazed out the window.

My mind drifted as we drove: "She has that staying power. She never seems to be far away. Really glad you're back bro. My next eight months are going to be a real character builder."

"You can't screw up the family gig any worse than Hal."

"I don't know, the older I get - the more ways I find to screw up." With my eyes on the road, my right hand searched the dashboard for cigarettes.

"Yonkers gets a little more run down every time I go away and come back." Ray said.

"It's always changing for me. I shouldn't be that aware of it, but I am. We're all in some kind of metamorphosis: lot of the Rogues got jobs, wives, - kids. It wouldn't be a shock if Rexall and Vinny got married soon."

"You'll be married before either of them."

"How'd everybody find out? I didn't tell anybody down here, and Karyn wasn't supposed to tell her parents either, but it seems both of our parents know." I scratched my bald spot. "I've got to go see Karyn in a little bit. Her parents never liked me, and now they know I'm marrying their daughter......I wonder if Jane's got any of them valiums left."

"Not an enviable position little brother."

"No, I wouldn't think so." I shook my head waiting for a green light.

"Aaaay – go down the river.....your choice." Ray pointed to Harriman.

I killed the can of Colt. "You don't know how rough a shape I was in just after Barb Wells cashed out. I was fucked up Ray. I was down in Miami with Loki for a little bit, then I went on the road for a year."

"Yeah, you wrote a couple of times."

"A doctor down in Miami told me I had to stop drinking or I'd have some major liver issues; so I stopped drinking and drugging for a year while I was on the road, and I started feeling better after about 8 months. Since I started working with Mack, I had toned it down quite a bit. I didn't miss them hangovers either. Now that Karyn's pregnant I'll just have one or two on Saturday night. I don't think any of the Rogues have eased off the party throttle, and for some it means using the shit that'll send you off into a different constellation." I was almost in a hypnotic state gazing at the Palisades as I spoke.

We got out of the car and this stuff started pouring out of me: "I think about you and the reverse flow people....the Fifth dimension.....you know – 'The High Five'. I think about how you feel – that you've got to escape this world's present reality. I don't think I had a choice; I was alternately insane and depressed for the next 20 months. Before I left for South Florida I got into the 'Tragic Magic'." I exhaled; a ton of pressure disappeared.

"You're a fuckin' idiot; that is playing with fire. Look how many are no longer here. You were lucky your guardian angel was on duty." Ray's eyes got wild large.

"Vinny Tarts made me leave. He'd been around it with Joey for a long time. He said I was a poster boy for not using dope. I know I didn't care enough to stay alive. O.D.? What's the big deal I thought."

"Mack, the work, Karyn, the baby.......and you; without you guys' help, I don't think I would have been around. I have to stay away from Yonkers – drugs – dregs - and the Rogues. I'm telling you Ray: and after 10 hours of work; there ain't much left. Jane said it was exactly what I needed."

We watched the tide push the river upstream.

"Ryan whatever it takes......I'll be there to help you guys - but I can't help a guy who won't try to help himself."

WE DROVE UP TO STRAATSVILLE AS SOON AS I GOT back from Karyn's house on Sunday afternoon. This was going to be the routine until either I got laid off, or managed to pick up another job after the hospital powerhouse ended.

I didn't know what I dreaded more: round tripping it on the weekend - Straatsville to Yonkers, or seeing more of the electrical generating plant getting completed. With Ray making the rounds with me it wasn't as bad as doing it alone.

While I was at work, in Poughkeepsie with Mack, Ray didn't have time to enjoy Mother Nature at the orchard. He took over the concrete apron and abbreviated driveway and went right to work. Every day returning from work, I had less and less area to park the Olds, until my parking privileges were cancelled altogether. Now, the Starfire had to be parked on the grass next to the little shack. At the beginning of the third day of August, he had gotten Mom-Mom to drive to the building supply outlet and Montgomery Wards so he could get the things he needed to advance the equation. At the end of the week, the apron was completely filled with green, blue, red, yellow, and purple permanent markers and chalk formulas, notes, hypothesis, theorems, and equations.

Nearby on the grass, were two 5 gal. buckets. One contained concrete sealer. The other contained a half-dozen spray cans of clear coat, a wooden box of all sorts of writing and marking devices, a hand broom, a hard bristle scrub brush with a handle, and a new five inch wide paint brush.
Ray had also borrowed a pump-spray plastic can to apply the sealer and a witches broom from Mom-Mom and Mack.

"Hey you got any grease sticks or metal markers on the job?"
"Yeah?"

"Boost a few of them for me will you? The more colors the better. Get me some soap stone too."

"Hey Ray, I can't clear out the whole supply......we got to mark stuff too. You serious?"

"Just get me what you think the job can spare. I'll talk to Mack if it becomes an issue."

By the second week the apron was already full, and he was starting on the driveway. The equation had already withstood the morning dew and its first thunderstorm. The water just beaded up where he had sprayed the sealer preserving his work.

The day Hal's concrete had been completely filled with Ray's theorems and equations, I got out of the car and walked over to ask him if he wanted to go shopping in Rhinebeck or Hyde Park.

He held up his hand with a piece of kids chalk in it – his eyes and his mind transfixed deep into the equation. I went in the fridge and got us a some Black Labels, and made a couple of peanut butter and jelly sandwiches for us. He drank the beer, but I ate both sandwiches. I went out to the road and checked the mailbox, there was an invitation from Weight Watchers for Barbara Wells to get the first month free. Some things you can't escape.

Twenty minutes later, Ray sat down on a plastic five gal. bucket. "Learned a lot of shit in the military.......learned a lot at Purdue." He grinned.

"There were many missing pieces in the pedestrian bridge factoring. I knew it was incomplete at the time, so any results I came up with would be inaccurate or only close."

"Ray, I didn't comprehend any of it. I don't know any of that astro or geo physics crap. Is this more of that?"

"Listen, in the overpass the equation was two dimensional; that was all wrong......in that it was incomplete. I must use different colors here, to identify properties and function. These magnetic reversal segments cross dimensions, and go through quantum change in theory, a compression of sorts has been released, and these magnetic pulses return essentially altered/magnified - exponentially. In some instances, transmutation has occurred. There is no evidence Edgar Cayce did the calculus, but somehow he was dialed into this outcome nevertheless.....I believe."

"Man, you're so far away."

"Get me another Black Label."

Off to the side of the outhouse, I magically converted some Black Label into Budweiser. It was minor compared to what Ray had growing from the west side of the garage. I was immobilized by what he had going on back there. A section of the Greystone equation had been either added to or transferred from the front – I couldn't tell which.

Four, 8 ft. furring strips were up against the garage's concrete block. The same colored paint and chalk he used on the concrete were on the back wall. 1"x1" furring strips were glued to the garage wall as the light gauge wooden framework extended out from the exterior concrete block roughly three feet and formed a light gauge wooden framework forming a retangular box to which screen material was stapled. On the screen was depicted an atom with its various components: nucleus, electrons, protons, and neutrons. From these parts: a series of color coded strings led to the back wall where the strings in groups and singly spliced into the equation with some adhesive squeezed from a caulk gun. This portion of the equation surely had hallucinogenic overtones.

Everything in or around this atom was labeled either as positive or negative and with their corresponding loads going into the equation as lines where it was picked up as the equation started off on its journey of explaining the magnetic pole reversal through mathematical notation. There was an asterisk* at the bottom of the screen: *Atom is not a known element.

"Why the stuff in the back?" I handed him aother beer.

"It lets me see the equation in a way that transcends dimension, gravity, momentum/speed, and through the restrictive barriers of the continuum."

"When we get back to Greystone, we'll set up a scale model experiment to cause a stationary object to move.....a moving object to stop, and/or change direction of movement by applying the magnetic force of pole reversal and amplified through the ejected chunk of the fireball."

"Okay." I barely understood what he was attempting to do.

Ray got into it in more detail: "We'll use the burial mound as a magnetic condenser or concentrator, forming a parabola with small amounts of cosmic ash that would be hand held, worn, or placed in a pocket and negative and positive magnetic forces being held in balance by a controller at the high point directing the position of the opposing magnetic forces. All aspects of a train's mass could conceivably be manipulated with this 'team' of handlers as long as the arc's shape was maintained." I knew he was deep in thought.

"An event such as this may be theoretically possible; theory and reality are two different things. Do you think it could be made to happen? Remember the first two occurrences were done without any human interaction." I said.

"Its power is magnetic-gravitational." He looked at me. "In order to effect movement of the object; the concentrated Cosmic Intruder's force has retained form (the expelled component ball) and the actuator ash (hand held) should be held in constant alignment during this process."

He insisted the concept was pretty close on paper; and was eager to give it a run through.

"Just tell me where to stand."
He looked up at the sky. "We'll need Vinny and Joe,   Catdaddy Crawford, Rikshaw, and Cocaine Wayne." He gave me this mischievous grin: "We're going to turn this thing upside down – like that bucket." Ray locked his jaw and nodded.

I could hardly contain my amusement or skepticism.

"We'll do a run through on Saturday. Everybody's got to be there. It's going to be a bit of a problem getting the 'High Five' assembled two days in a row."

My face was awash in skepticism and I shook my head. It was a definite problem. "The timing isn't critical?" I asked.

"No, but I'd like to know what we got. Listen, when we go down to Greystone on Saturday……we're going to rewrite the laws of physics. We'll try it on the first electric train coming from the north on Sunday morning; I think the first off-peak stops around 6:30. There might even be an express running through earlier than that."

"Right." I thought aloud: " Might be easier to rewrite the laws of physics than it will trying to get this crew down there around 6….6:15 on Sat. and Sun. morning."

"They'll be there – they ALL owe me. I'm callin this one in."
Behind his eyes, I could see it was strictly business now.

The Saturday evening rehearsal was a hit and miss misadventure. Ray had me summoning the "Shadow 5" by scouring the neighborhoods with the Starfire, while he worked the phone. The surviving four of the 'High Five' showed up, but at different times. The Tartaglione brothers came together because Joey needed a ride from Vinny after the run through. Rikshaw was early; Catdaddy, and Cocaine Wayne were late. They all had to be somewhere else and rushed Ray with getting on with his plan for tomorrow.

He had enough on his mind; he wasn't handling the shortcomings of these sketchy people very well and we ended up instructing the four, plus Vince, individually. Ray had me doing the location marking with day-glo orange spray paint on the southbound express tracks. It annoyed him that he couldn't be more precise with the locations, but he needed a full crew to be close. Now he could only hope they would have some retention tomorrow morning of what they went through this evening. The sun's light began to dim.

Even though these Ghost Riders were indebted to Ray in various ways - mostly for their temporary periods of collective sanity; he knew he'd get a more reliable commitment if he paid them for their help. They weren't too keen about being paid in Tiger Tar, but they knew they could sell it for cash and buy smack. Ray directed the run-through on Saturday the best he could. He kept telling us to be adaptable to changing conditions, and nothing was going to be exact, but he believed he had the formula to control magnetic energies at this particular place and time. "Don't let me down guys, this is for all of us, Z-Man, and Barb Wire too." he said.

vii

Sunday morning round-up was underway: I picked up the Tartaglione brothers, Kenny Crawford, Rikshaw Shaw. Wayne-O ended up being a no-show. We called him from the phone booth down the End. His girlfriend Janeen finally answered. She wasn't too pissed off; when you shack up with a guy like Wayne – the unexpected becomes commonplace. She told me to look down Orchard St. Wayne had hooked up with Chooch last night. There was no time to track him down; we barely had time to get coffee from the Greek's. When I delivered the four to Ray, I yelled across the tracks: "No Wayne-O. Can we do this a man short?"

He shouted back: "Go to 21 and get a roll of duct tape and brother Bill – he's old enough."

The four got out of the Olds with coffee and buttered rolls. Only Cinzo was up for eating and coffee; but he wasn't all awake either.

I put the pedal to the metal and did a doughnut on the cobblestone in the small turnaround area. Small pebbles had accumulated in the low points in front of the small station house and I sand blasted the side of the building when I let the Wildcat's claws come out. Using the ruse we were going fishing, I was able to get Brother Bill to go with me.

Again I yelled across the tracks to Ray, with Willis in tow. He waved us over and shouted as we crossed the tracks: "Now we can get started." Ray said to Billy with a 'thumbs–up' and a smile.

Ray had gone over the plan with me before we left the orchard, also on the way to Yonkers. He outlined the plan again as we assembled on the southbound platform. The 'Fifth Dimension' was hearing it for the first time as a group. Straight away, it was obvious Rikshaw, Joey Tarts, and Kenny had been instructed through their knowledge of the Equation as to what their roles were in this demonstration. Vince, Brother Bill, and me were keen to pick up on the verbal and telepathic communication amongst the four.

This was obviously the reversed polarity - shadow people's gig. They knew the plan and they'd have to tell us what to do.

"Brother Bill's ready." I said introducing him to the other co-conspirators.

"There's no time to re-calculate this; we'll just have to adjust as we go along. Willis,.......give the duct tape to Vinny." Ray said.

He had approximate locations marked with spray paint   on bushes, weeds, bare ground, rails and rail ties, ballast rock on the second set of tracks off the river. Also, locations in day-glo green chalk were on the southbound platform. Arrows and numbers indicated where he wanted each of us to be positioned with an olive jar or a plastic yellow pharma bottle of our original ash from the fireball. The pharmacy containers couldn't have held more than one coffee measuring scoop. It didn't seem like very much to me.

From a shoebox, Ray gave me and Vinny equal portions from my original comet ash. I knew the prime force of the comet's ash was magnetic in nature. Whether it was all one universal force, or working in conjunction with the earth's pole reversing magnetism causing force amplification was conjecture on my part.

While Ray had been theorizing and setting up working models at the orchard, he began to realize magnetism was only one of the comet's properties: in combination with concentrated light and/or collider-type energies, it may have the capability to do unimaginable things......even time travel considering the continual pull from the Alpha and Omega ends of the known universes.

Amazement radiated from his eyes. The rest of us were in a state of dislocated wonder. Ray tried to streamline what he knew when he relayed it to us in a quasi-military format:

"If a missile carried a small nuclear device that explodes in the earth's atmosphere --- the result would create an electro-magnetic pulse....an EMP. The shockwave wouldn't be immediately harmful to life, except for the fact the area to sustain the effects of the blast would be without any electrical power and the machines and devices reliant on electricity to operate would be 'cooked'. Meteors, asteroids, and other objects which happen to enter and explode in our atmosphere would exhibit similar outcomes. Our goal here is to demonstrate we can control or harness magnetic forces in the initial stages of a pole reversal on this planet." He nodded at us looking for agreement.

"Billy, you will take position #3. You're to follow Kenny's directions or mine. There's only a few minutes before we see a train and it's got to be electrically propelled coming south. We're not interested in diesel locomotives."

"Ryan......Vince: – We have to maintain a straight line from the Yacht club bridge, through the engineer's compartment to the fireball mound where I'll be standing. That's about 350 meters away. When the commuter train enters that field, it will rapidly lose acceleration and we'll use the power of the parabola and the condensed fireball castoff to direct electro-magnetics outside their traditional control points."

"About six minutes Ray." Joey Tarts read his watch.

"Joe you'll be on the river side of the train; Rikshaw.....Kenny you'll be on the station side. Rikki, I won't be able to see you. You'll have to maintain contact with Kenny for any change in instructions."

Ray called out: "To your marks guys – Billy just stay in the arc line." He looked over to us, "Vinny...... you and Ryan are responsible for the flex point. Your location of the pharma containers containing the cinderash is critical. You may have to put the containers side by side or stack them. Secure them with the tape. Everything worked out in theory, we're in the real world right now, just be ready to improvise. There will most likely be variables that could not have been anticipated or may have been overlooked."

Vince and me raced up to the top of the yacht club bridge. "Ray's military experience is essential. You feel like he really knows what he's doing."

"I hear you brother." I said.

Vinny got busy taping the positively charged ash in a clear olive jar to one of the vertical braces of the bridge.

A small light could be seen to the north, we knew it was a train.

I called out to everybody down below: "Here it comes! Express tracks.......express!"

"Hey Whitewater......I'm so nervous – I'm gonna piss my pants." Cinzano chuckled.

"Go over to the other end and hurry up, the train's headlight is getting bigger."

He whipped it out and pissed hands free. Vinny held his plastic yellow bottle, ready to stack or put them side by side with mine.

The six car commuter train was clocking about 55 m.p.h. as the lead car passed underneath. Ray had the 'Fearless Foursome' rotate the parabola which seemed to place a wall of gelatin beneath us - causing deceleration without compression. The length of the train was now between Ray and me and Vinny. Waves of distortion eminated from the mound through Ray. The train came to a complete stop.

He waved for us to come down from the bridge. "Bring the the pharma ash." Crawfish and Joey walked toward Ray.

Ray called to them – "We're going to make Houdini proud." He laughed. Rikshaw and Billy were waved over by Kenny and Joey. They saw Ray smile; it put them at ease.

"Joey, you six will maintain the arc – it's our power grid so to speak. The six of you with your alternately charged ash will be the magnetic energy field. The magnetic waves of the fireball will recognize the parabola as the way to release its kinetic energy." Ray said.

"If we tighten up the arc configuration; the power will start to flow."

"You got it boss." Crawdaddy said.

"On second thought.............Ryan, you and Vince – put some distance between you and the last car. Position yourselves just about underneath the yacht club bridge."

The conductor, two assistants, the engineer, and the brakeman evacuated the train even though there were still passengers aboard.

"Engineer, get back on board and turn the engines off, then get back out here." The rest of the Penn Central crew huddled around the conductor.

"Wha...wha...wha.......what's going on? Whoooooo...... who are you guys?" Joey pushed the conductor, who was having some difficulty breathing. The other trainmen thought this was some kind of a Jesse James style robbery.

"How many passenger you got?" Rikshaw asked, turning on his best broken Chinese accent.

One of the assistant conductors replied – "About 30."

"How many work for railroad?"

"Maybe 10.....11."

Ray spoke to Joey Tarts with his back to the train crew. "Walk them over to the platform, and tell them to have a seat." He handed his olive jars with ash to Crawford with directions to stay in the track's center.

On the riverside of the commuter train, equidistant from the first and last car, Ray could shout instructions to us at both ends. The oppositely poled ash containers were at each end of car #6 and #1 and formed a long slender 'X' through the length of the train. The force of the inversed poled magnetism compressed the six cars so they reacted as if it was a single car. The six were under enough force – they began to levitate approximately 4" above the rails. Ray signaled everyone to resume their original positions in a slow deliberate manner. Once again, the commuter train from Croton Harmon was down on its rails.

"Hey conductor, get everybody off the train." Ray stood along side Joey: "Can't figure out why the train reacted as if it had a backbone."

Hand signals were used to advance us nearer to the rear of the train. Once again, our movement compressed the magnetism and raised the train's wheels; the cars were now an astonishing foot above the rails and tore off the motors' electrical contacts with the third rail from which the train drew its power to operate.

Three of the passengers who worked for the railroad climbed down the ships ladder to the rail bed and walked over to Ray, and politely asked for an explanation.

"What's your name?" Ray was annoyed by the interruption.

"John Magaletta."

" John, go back to your seat and watch the show."

"Billy, give me your vial of dust. You're going to gently push the train about a hundred yards north. I'll tell you when it's far enough. Make like you're really struggling as you push the train. All of us with the dust will actually be causing the train to move."

The passengers and crew on the platform watched a 12 year old move about 60 tons of commuter cars in disbelief. The engineer asked his co-workers: "The 5:31 is off its rails – pretty much floating in the air.....or is my eyesight getting worse?"

Next, the brakeman climbed down the ships ladder and onto the rail bed from the southbound platform and walked over to Rikshaw at the midpoint-riverside of the train and asked: "Who are you guys?"

Rikshaw turned towards the brakeman and gave him the sunglasses and a smile, whipped his long straight hair from his face – "We are time travelers from a group of stars in the Constellation Polaris, nearly 25,000 light years away."

The brakeman rolled his eyes and started back to the platform.

"Hey Mr. Penn Central: How long will it be before the track sensors detect the train hasn't moved for the past 15 minutes; or is no longer on their board?" Ray called.

"Operational Control in Croton-Harmon and at G.C.T. believe the 5:31 has become disabled somewhere between Hastings and Greystone."

"C'meer…..is this an event that'll trigger a police response?"

"Not unless someone from this train radios them for assistance." He replied.

One of the fared passengers was feeding the pay phone on the platform.

Ray asked Joey and Rikshaw to take some data readings and measurements with the mason's bag of measuring tools: a 100 ft. tape, 4 ft. level, an angle finder, and a framing square. They gingerly lay the magnetic ash where they stood. Ray was recording all of the measurements in his log book. Most of these readings involved distance and elevation. Joey said Ray was cursing because he needed a particular instrument to measure magnetic strength and fluctuation. He told Joey they had one in just about every physics dept. at colleges and universities. He said the name was a scalar magnetometer. It didn't matter because he didn't have one so Ray did the best he could. Rikshaw, Joey and Ray marched around with a can of Day-glo orange spray paint, pulling the 100 ft. tape making marks and taking readings. He used the fireball mound as his axis.

A northbound local was slowed by the overhead signal lights. The engineer and the conductor of the northbound knew something wasn't right, and as they got closer, we assumed they found it more difficult to travel. It didn't seem to matter much; every face on the northbound train was gape-jawed at the show Ray had in progress. A levitating train wasn't an event anybody in a train or at the station was ready to accept.

The northbound local didn't report the disposition of the 5:31 southbound until they reached Tarrytown, some 12 miles north. They called in to Croton-Harmon operations and were told two maintenance trucks were already en route to Greystone Station. These rail trucks had the capability to ride on the street or on the train rails - if necessary. They thought it might be a track sensor problem down there.

The two railroad maintenance trucks accessed the Hudson line tracks just north of the Yonkers' Station. The maintenance vehicles arrived at Greystone eleven minutes later. The workers didn't know what to do; it was a first for all of us. It was an easily deniable event. Still, I don't believe any of the 'Significant Seven' wanted to talk to cops or any investigators when they arrived. Ray knew it was best to get done what he set out to do and get out of there.

Right on schedule weekend reporter Jaime O'Neill arrived, this time with a photographer. They had their press credentials clipped on. I spotted the two as they walked north on the southbound platform.

"What's the story here?" He looked around.

The Penn Central personnel had nothing to say. A hippie photographer him took a few shots, which got them irate. Jaime climbed down the ships ladder at the north end of the SB platform and walked over to the gravity defying 5:31. He called the hippie over to take some pictures, but she said it was too dangerous.

"Who are you?" Ray's brow crunched down.

"Jamie O'Neill. I'm with the Statesman."

"Listen, you and your helper just stay outside of the areas we got circled with the blaze orange paint. You step in the wrong spot - you'll split in two." Ray pointed at the various locations that they could see.

"Huh?" O'Neill's eyes bugged out.

Rikshaw walked over to the platform, "Here.....give me the fuckin' camera. Hey Clark Kent - I'll take the pictures for ya." Rikshaw ended up shooting two rolls of Kodak 400 of an airborne train for O'Neill. I avoided O'Neill and let Ray handle this P.R. mess. The only one willing to talk to O'Neill was Brother Bill; Crawdaddy told Willis to "zip it."

We all stood waiting with Ray; he was still writing information in detail about the event. Anybody observing the scene immediately knew Ray was calling the shots. O'Neill walked back to question him.

"The train's personnel say you guys caused this event."

"We're spectators just like the rest of them gawkers around here." Ray replied with a grin. I kept my back to O'Neill, and lit one off another.

"They said you and your associates stopped the train, caused it to become anti-gravitational and physically moved it to its present position." O'Neill stated.

Ray's face said: "Outlandish."

"Five of the passengers concurred."

"Then you better get over there and get your scoop ." Ray pointed to the people on the platform."

"They're saying you guys here caused all this to occur."

"Prove it."

"C'mon guys – you're telling me that train isn't floating and you did nothing to influence this event.....and I don't see a 6 car commuter train missing one foot of earth beneath it. Gimme a fuckin' break." The reporter shook his head.

"It's ok with us. Tell me newspaper man - how we supposedly made this happen?" Ray chuckled.

O'Neill was stymied. "You guys know something......You know a lot.........You know it all." O'Neill was all worked up and marched around a little; he looked at the hippie photographer. "You get your ass down here and start shooting some film......this is what it's all about.....getting the story and you're not doing your job up there."

She tried to keep her distance from the 5:31, but at least it was closer to the action than on the platform. She circled the train and took pictures of the train and us.

Ray called over the reporter and read his clip-on Herald Statesman credentials, "Mr. O'Neill......... – you don't have a story here......yet. You got some Kodachrome of a floating train. Know what? The big shots at Larkin Plaza are going to throw the phrase 'trick photography' around......'buncha pictures – no story'. There will be at least 20 differing accounts from witnesses of an event that scientifically is a paradox. The witnesses will say 'act of God', 'freak occurrence', or 'Ripley's Believe it or Not'. Penn Central will be thinking lawsuit: sue somebody or get sued by somebody. Maybe there isn't a story here.......maybe there is......it depends on your point of view doesn't it?"

"Hang around if you want Jamie, either way we're going to land this sonofabitch........you can take that to the bank." Ray smiled.

He could turn that swagger on when he needed it. It was another one of those times when we were together and I was miniaturized; but it was always worth it.

The reporter scoffed, "You're going to bring this train down without any heavy equipment? This I've got to see."

"Yeah, I've got to see this." The photographer said.

"Is there an echo here?" Ray asked Jamie.

"No cranes." Rikshaw jumped in. "Just the magic we brought from the Polaris system, and we're gonna do the job before the Air Force arrives and makes a federal case out of it."

Ray climbed the ships ladder and walked over to the conductor. He was still breathing hard: "Huminah..... Huminah.......Huminah......"

He turned to the asst. conductor, "We're going to bring your train back to earth. Your boss is still in Hangover City.....are you in charge? Where do you want us to park this thing?" Ray laughed.

The crew of the 5:31 from Croton huddled-up, except for the conductor, but they couldn't come to a consensus. Another one of the assistant conductors squinted down at Joey Tarts, "You magpies are not from another planet."

"Go punch some seat tickets ya shithead." Joey waved him off.

"I'll put this thing in the drink if I don't get an answer." Ray shook his head and lit a Marlboro.

The nerve ridden conductor rushed over to Ray: "Oh, Mr. Spaceman......Mr. Spaceman......straight down will be fine."

Ray got back down on the rail bed, we followed him as he went to have a word with the maintenance workers leaning against the trucks.

"Hey Captain," one addressed Ray: "All the signal lights are red on every track in both directions. It's going to be a pretty hot place pretty soon. Something's got to happen."

"You guys want some OT ?" he grinned.

The maintenance guy nodded and winked.

"All right." Ray turned back to us: "Let's Rock.....Vinny –
Ryan.....on the north side of the train. Joey – Billy.....the south side;
position yourselves using the intruder mound as the axis. Catdaddy –
Rikshaw.......midpoints. Watch for my hand signals for your moves.
We'll bring it down real close. Just prior to touchdown we'll kink two
sets of trucks so they derail. We'll get these guys some spending
money. The maintenance crew smelled the overtime.

Ray put his thumb and middle finger in his mouth and let out
a loud whistle to get everyone's attention: "READY?" He yelled,
"Everybody stand clear." Like a conductor leading a symphony, his
sightline shifted back and forth. Most of the train's movements were
performed with Ray's hand signals to us. It was an incredible
balancing act maintaining the train's stability. Reducing and increasing
amplification at precise locations and distances between the positive
and negative poled ash produced an off center camber. The coup de
grace came when he lowered the commuter train just enough so the
flanges of the wheels of the two trucks bitched up against the inside of
the rail just enough to wedge the train's trucks in between them. The
maintenance team would have to disconnect the cars in front and
behind the fourth car before it could be freed up and put back on the
track.

Ray directed us to slowly back away and keep our eyes
peeled on the initial rail contact.

"Lookin' good." Crawford called over.

"Billy?"

"I think it's lined up......set her down Ray." he said.

Kenny and Billy could see the train's weight being carried by
the rails of the other cars as the springs of the trucks compressed.

"It's down." Catdaddy confirmed.

"Yeah.....down." Billy nodded.

Ray looked at our end; I pounded my fist into my open hand.

The small audience was silent and the maintenance crew who
had to right the 5:31 was all smiles.

Rikshaw, Joey, and Crawfish knew enough of the equation to
be confident in Ray's undertaking. Vinny, Billy, and me were in
wonderment. Vinny scratched his head and said, "If I didn't see it – I'd
have said it couldn't be done. I was a part of it wasn't I?" He scratched
some more.   "Unfuckinbelievable!" There were back slaps and
high fives all around.

"Let me get this right – my positive cosmic ash will only pull
and yours will only push?" I said.

"No...No....No.....But in this configuration, there is much
less interference......a kind of impedence." he explained. "I got to get
out of here......It's 8:45 already." Joey looked at his watch. He was
thinking about getting rid of his Tiger Tar payment and maybe two-
timing it today.

"Just a few more quick shots." the Hippie with the camera
said.

She snapped a group shot: Brother Bill up front and reporter
O'Neill on the side. She had her Pentax on rock & roll; clicking eight
photos in rapid fire.

"Whitelaw.....I knew it was you; and these two guys (he pointed to Kenny and Vinny). You three were there at the High St. fire, and now this. A coincidence?......un-uh." He asked for our names for the pictures. Everybody gave him a phony except me, O'Neill knew me from the Barb Wells mess two years ago.

"There might be a story here. "The Greystone Ghosts: Aliens and Spacemen." It sounds good; Ryan are you going to hang around?" he asked.

viii

The shuttlecraft was ticking away inside the mothership. The gynecologist concurred with Karyn on the due date – the first week of April. I felt like a water heater with no relief valve. I thought the pressure of this pregnancy was far worse for me than it was for Karyn. That bullshit about man's role as the provider for the family was eating away my sanity; it made me want to get a job on the business side of the bar.

She had plugged into her motherhood instincts, and with them came the physical changes as well. The first trimester had us both scared to death. I could only be with her on Sundays because Saturday was the big money day. It wouldn't have been so bad, but the pressure was on to find a new place to live; it was hard to look all by herself. She had a lot of things to consider: rent, space, neighborhood, proximity to friends and relatives. The other factor was the possibility I'd hook on to another job with Local 417 which would cancel living in the Yonkers area. The city had nothing but bad habits waiting for my return.

With all her major core courses completed in the fall semester, she was left with only a three credit course in her minor and fluff electives for the '76 Spring semester.

Early on, Ray attempted to engage Karyn in conversation about complex analytical statistical formulas. She looked at him like he was speaking Mandarin. He would laugh and she would steam. They had that vinegar and oil thing going on. I couldn't make sense of it.

"You know Ray will help us if we ever ask." I said.

"He's just trying to get a rise out of me.......don't need it – don't want it." she huffed. It bugged her that Ray knew more about her area of study after 3 ½ years at Fordham, than Ray did with one at Purdue. He also had three years left of a free ride when he decided to return.

"Okay....Okay. I'll tell him to tone it down. Be kool sweetheart." There were many possibilities: jealousy, hormones, uncertainty, etc.

Karyn's mom didn't like me, and my father didn't like anybody. Morality wasn't the issue with her parents, her father was ambivalent. Her mom would run me down; the same as every other mom whose daughter gets knocked up. She was pretty sure her mother's dislike for me would wear off once the baby was born. Karyn was intelligent; smarter than me, but not as street smart. She should

696

have been street smart coming from South Yonkers and going to high school in the Bronx.

Jane, Cathy, and Karyn came up to visit Mom-Mom, Mack, and me while enjoying the Hudson Valley's fall colors in mid-October. Karyn was starting to show and she began wearing overalls.

"You take a walk with Karyn over to the orchard; we're going to Rhinebeck to do some shopping." Mom-Mom said.

"There might be some deer over there feeding on the apples." Mack told Karyn. "The walk will do youse good."

She had a ginger ale, and I made some instant coffee when we got to the orchard. Two sips from the can: "Shit, I gotta pee."

"You're not going to make it to Mom-Mom's........the outhouse is a real character builder." I said.

"I'm not going to sit in the shithouse just to take a piss." she said.

"Well then, you're going to have to go rough. I don't like the outhouse or roughing it any more than you do. It's just that I've gotten used to it."

"Get me some t.p. will you?" With her back against the garage wall, she looked at the four dimensional equation as she let out a real gusher. "We're going to live in a place with modern plumbing. What's that all about ?" she pointed with her thumb like she was hitchhiking to the dimensional equation around the corner of the garage.

"Ryan.......Hal seen that yet?"

"No, nor the apron or the driveway. He won't fuck with Ray.....he knows it's so complex, it must be important." I said.

"Listen Whitelaw, we've got to find a place before January."

"Right." Immediately I thought of $10's and $20's flying out of my wallet like 'High Roller', Joe Lamar, bending a deck of cards and shooting them in the air.

Mack showed up about a half-hour later. He knocked on the door......Karyn was already dressed. We saw Mack waiting in his pick-up truck. Karyn sat in the middle of the bench seat. He made a right turn from the driveway, I figured we were going to the general store on a beer run. "It's really beautiful up here with the fall colors. Edna and me had had enough of Yonkers." he commented.

"That's what Ryan says."

"That's what a lot of people say."

We got a six pack and started back. Mack told Karyn about when we were kids riding on the tailgates of Hal's station wagon or Mack's other trucks. She had never done anything like that. Mack watched the winding road.

He had to obliterate the childhood dreamworld: "The job Ryan is working is winding down. We're knocking off Saturdays."

I had asked him to give us the layoff news together – even though Mack had warned me a week earlier. Now he turned to Karyn. "Ryan's got what it takes to be an ironworker. Everyday he's honing his skills, he's got ambition, learns something everyday.....and a

697

whole lot more. The one thing that is going to hold him back is - he doesn't have a journeyman's card."

I looked at Karyn, "I asked the job steward if there was any work on the board down the hall."

Mack explained: "To pull a job ticket; he's got to have at least 6000 hrs. worked in Local 417. That would put him on the 'A' list."

"Well what list is he on?" she asked Mack.

"If there was such a thing – he might be on a 'C' list – though I've never heard it referred to as such." He looked over Karyn's head: "How many hours you got?"

"Bout' 1400."

He looked at Karyn, "He's made a good chunk of change, but it doesn't lead to anything."

"So it's a seniority thing in the union?"

"Yes and no. You have to understand a local's position concerning an oversupply of manpower. When there are too many guys on the bench for too long……..the next thing you know they're going to work for some rat outfit. It's not good for the union or the contractors who have signed Local 417's bargaining agreement."

"Supply and demand?" She tried to digest the system Mack was selling.

"That's the way the construction industry operates: supply and demand, boom or bust, feast or famine." Mack gave her a quick course in ironworker economics 101.

"Ryan, I'll give you a directory of all the locals in the country. Call them. Ask if they're taking apprentices, or putting out skilled permit hands. Hell, you guys might end up in Alaska." It didn't sound like much of an adventure anymore.

"I'm beginning to see." she said.

According to the local's By-Laws, I had to be the first man laid off from the job. Mack made sure I made it to December 1st. All the guys on the job knew it was coming. I was grateful Karyn and the baby would be covered by 417's Health and Welfare plan. I was preparing to say: "Thanks and good-bye" to my grandparents. Our next reunion would be over Thanksgiving or Christmas.

698

John Dunbar and Ray rented a two bedroom apartment in a four-story in Tarrytown. It was in sight of the General Motors Body plant. John and Ray called it the "United Nations Building." The varieties of humanity ran the gamut, but the majority of the tenants were refugees from North and South Vietnam, Laos, and Cambodia. It was a short walk to the Hudson Rail Line. Ray still hadn't lined up a set of wheels. Until he found a car, he was a fixture in Dunbar's shotgun seat. I took Ray over to TNT used cars. Herb was busy selling Christmas trees....an annual sideline for him.

Something was bothering Ray; it seemed to be the same disorientation he had been battling since the night we came home from track practice and witnessed the fireball streaking up the Hudson years earlier. When he got discharged and returned to Yonkers; this continual dealing with the 'children of the night' was a preoccupation. The respite he was granted after saving the pilots and mechanic began to wear off, he was losing his protection against the insanity of his expanding magnetic world. I had seen that look of obsession previously. It was the specter/inversion phase which would not release him. Ray was sliding back into the magnetic void of transition.

Seldom would I see Dunbar at the apartment when I visited Ray. The two of them cooked up an overseas trip to skip out on the on-coming winter. Ray felt he had been cheated by the army of his R&R while he was in Long Bin and Bien Hoa. He had put in his request to R&R in Sydney, and it had been approved. Instead, they were given 11 days in Hong Kong. They were only supposed to get a week out of country, so he called it a wash.

Their original plan had them flying to Miami, visiting Loki and on to Buenos Aires. The two were drinking at Susan's Bar and Grill in Hastings. Ray was reading the N,Y. Post and saw an advertisement for flights on sale to Australia; he had second thoughts about Miami. They booked flights to Sydney the next day.

John and Ray asked us to house-sit their apartment while they were off globe trotting. They only made us pay half the rent and all the utilities until they returned, a date which they had left open-ended; they assured us their earliest return would be mid-May. It was almost a sure thing Karyn would have the baby while we were living at the U.N.

The customary postcards from Ray started arriving from Manila where they spent a week. More started to arrive from Sydney, Brisbane, Singapore, Bali, and Perth. When they returned to the States, they said Australian customs informed them their tourist visas were only good for 90 days; they had to leave for 24 hours and then reenter and that was how the side trips to Singapore and Bali happened. Ray said they had a good time on Boogie Street, but he had been eaten alive by mosquitoes on the beach in Bali.

As the postcards continued, I wished I had enlisted.....I sure could have used those veteran's points to push my scores up on the civil service lists.

I WOULD BE ELIGIBLE FOR THE MAXIMUM RATE
FOR unemployment benefits, the lady at the office said. A single
person might be able to make it on the state's maximum rate, but a
family would not. Karyn was into her second trimester. It was a couple
of weeks before Christmas. Everyone knew you had to have something
off the books in order to live while playing the unemployment game.
Rexall said the State of N.Y. tried to starve you to death, and that was
your incentive to find another job.

When Ray was still around, he'd hit the union halls with me
in the metro area: Structural locals, a Rigger and Machinery local, the
Stone Derrickmen local, and the Ornamental local. We caught a
nightmare of a job with the ornamental local. The job foreman never
left the coffee shop until it closed, and then he finished the shift at the
bar. The steward, two boomers, and Ray and me unloaded security
gates from the truck. We had to leave a set of the gates on each floor.
A set of gates were humped up to the roof's penthouse just for good
measure.........Our job was to get a set of gates dropped off on each
floor; some real mechanics were installing them later in the week.
Fucking nightmare of a job - the gates were awkward and heavy, and
the stairways were narrow. The freight elevator was under repair and
the passenger elevator was too small for the gates to fit in.

We finished up at 5:20 pm. We were paid until 5:30. The
good old days of Mack throwing the gang an extra hour or two were
gone. It was nine hours of back breaking work. A stop at a bodega on
the way to Grand Central Terminal was mandatory, we got a six-pack
for the train ride home. They charged us $.50 for two paper cups.

"Sure could have used some magic ash technology to get
them fuckin' gates up the stairs today." I said.

"Them fuckers were heavy. You coming up tomorrow?"

"Yeah, see you around noon. I gotta update my hack license,
and call Rex tonight to see if any of his paisans need any help."

Karyn and me moved into the United Nations right after they
flew Down Under. Karyn stayed at her parents' apartment during the
week; it was a lot closer to Fordham University. This being her first
grandchild, Jane's friends came out of the woodwork to give us stuff
we'd need. Karyn was overwhelmed.

Although we had found a place to live, the moment we
moved in, we had to start looking for another place. The apartment in
Tarrytown bought a few months of breathing space. Their apartment
defintely had the feel that two guys lived there, which was just as well;
it reminded us we were only temporary residents.

On April 4th, nine months after the twin orange discs had
raced me to the finish line, Nicole Rae was born. After Karyn told me
she was late with her period, I closely watched the newspaper for any
story concerning the incident that night down the river. Maybe 10 days
later, a few stories came out about 'mysterious lights and an
explosion'. Local authorities had dismissed any notion the event had
anything to do with the Fourth of July celebration.

The newspapers story became more plausible the more I
thought about it. The Village Voice reported the Air Force's SR-71A

"Blackbird" had landed at Stewart Air Force Base in late June for installation of new computer navigational technology provided by IBM. Lockheed and flight logs show it left on the 5th with a classified flight plan. This aircraft had broken all sorts of air speed records and was capable of Mach 3.4.

Art Bell argued for a month on his radio program that he had government witnesses who would attest to the fact this visual and sonic event was extra-terrestrial in origin. He couldn't say if it was a spaceship, space junk, or a meteorite.

I replayed the videotape inside my brain of July 5th over and over again while Karyn was pregnant. It didn't make sense; I just assumed she was taking care of the birth control. The last time we had a sex hook-up she assured me she was 'on the pill'. Karyn wasn't so ripped as to disregard the possibility she might get pregnant, or lie to me.

When we spread the blanket on the burial mound, at first, it's like she doesn't want it........ then, the next thing I know she's gyrating and got her heels digging into my ass; and I'm putting everything I got deep inside her. She wasn't that drunk; drunks can't sustain the level of passion she exhibited. There was an outpouring of the do and don't, or more succinctly said: the positive and the negative. Many forces were at work: It was that sonic boom which unlocked her legs and threw me into the weeds. It was my fixation with the sight of the orange discs. It was the concussion of the sound barrier breaking. It was the heat of the comet beneath us. And it was an alien taste and smell; contributing to our reckless abandon and giving in to our animal instincts.

Karyn swore up and down she hadn't missed a day since she had got back on the birth control pill in May. She said she went back on the pill because she was going on the prowl this summer like her friends. It made sense to me.

I believed her because I knew it was certainly possible for gravitational forces to have overridden the anti-life force of the man-made substance. In September, Ray asked me about the particulars about how I managed to hit a home run on a one nighter. He had doubts about my facts.

I tried to get a package deal for a baptism and wedding combo at All Souls. The pastor told us, they didn't operate like John's Bargain Store.

The pastor asked: "Is this woman you want to marry a Catholic?"

"Yes Father." Five minutes with this guy was about all I could tolerate, I was pretty close to walking out.

"What parish are you from?" he asked Karyn.

"St. Peter's."

"You shouldn't have any problem swinging that kind of deal down there. We run it by the book up here." he said.

"What's that supposed to mean?" Karyn and me looked at each other.

"It means you don't get married here......but we'll be able to baptize the baby."

We walked out of the Monastery and said, "Thanks...but no thanks."

The wedding and baptism were scheduled two weeks after Jane's recital. If we had to get married by the judge and I had to baptize the kid myself – well that was the way it was going to be. Karyn found a priest at St. Ann's Church who would do both sacraments and backdate the marriage date so she would be insured for any medical problems unrelated to the pregnancy and birth.

KARYN AND ME HAD DONE VERY LITTLE TO FIND A place of our own. Now that Dunbar and Ray were back, we felt the uncertainty of not having our names on the lease. The sublet could be over in the snap of a finger – Ray's name wasn't even on the lease. It was something neither one of us brought up.

Our financial situation was a disaster. Every week there was less money in the checking account – despite the three jobs I was working: Caesar Taxi, Palamar Projects, and caddying on the weekends........all off the books. Karyn and me had circled the week my unemployment benefits would run out. It didn't sound like the lawmakers in Albany were going to pass an extended benefits bill. I don't know what we would have done without Ray; Dunbar and him continued picking up 1/3rd of the rent and they didn't even live there. Dunbar didn't live there at all and Ray stayed there around two days a week. Ray was also moving my portion of the potent and degraded opium for me; it might have been where 1/3rd of the rent was coming from. Karyn never knew about that operation.

Dunbar was rightfully upset with the way he was squeezed out of the United Nations apartments. My brother had somehow greased the wheel, and by the time the wedding/christening party was held in Hal's backyard...John Dunbar had let things slide without getting all worked up about his surreptitious eviction, but he did stop subsidizing our rent. Ray said they now had a chance to rent a place in Hastings, because Ananconda Wire Co. was shutting down. He never did like the U.N. anyway. People who had worked there since WW II had no choice but to move on, but John didn't have it leased yet.

Karyn's mom and Jane pitched in for the catered party. Jane put her foot down: there would be no repeat of Hal's performance of his homemade commendation celebration for Ray's heroics. He was put on notice: The party was for baby Nicole's christening and the wedding, and he'd better behave.

It turned out real nice. Once again, the caterer was one of Jane's Dancing school connections; at the peak.....there must have been almost 50 guests.

Most of the Rogues showed up with wives, long term girlfriends, and rug rats. Bad Brad brought his girlfriend de jour, Sophie Harpur. His wife Susan didn't like us. She didn't let Brad jr. go anywhere Brad sr. went - when she knew it was going to be a mostly couples function. Holter said Susan knew Brad was seeing another woman; she just didn't know who it was.

Mom-Mom, Mack, and Allison were there an hour early. Mack said: "We got to talk before we head back."

"Sure thing Mack."

Ray had been my best man, while Willis was Nicole's godfather. It was pretty hectic for the Whitelaw brothers that day. A year later, I couldn't remember who the godmother or the maid of honor had been – perhaps a friend of Karyn was the maid of honor, and my Aunt Allison may have been Nicky's godmother. I know she's godmother to one of my girls.

It was pretty much a low-key affair, except for Bad Brad who was all wound up because his estranged wife wouldn't let him bring Brad jr. Same old Brad, he'd get more wound up with every kid he'd see: hunched over, clenched fists. He was getting all agro..........had this time-bomb look about him.

"Cinzo, what's with 'Bad Bradley'?" Ray asked.

He rolled his eyes and shook his head.

"Sophie – can't you calm him down. He's making some of the guests nervous."

"Not when he gets like this."

I looked over to Holter, "George, you and Rex go over and check him out before he pops one of the guests."

Rexall, ever the chemist asked, "Hey wedding bells - Whitelaw, you got any of them calm-down pills?"

"Whatcha looking for?"

"Valiums.......10 megatons."

About 20 minutes later, I could see Brad was loosening up. His fists were unclenched, he was smiling and talking to people.

I was relieved Ray was there, a lot of people who had missed his party last year were spending time with him instead of me. Nobody wanted to tell me – you screwed up by having a kid out of wedlock. You don't want to hear that shit – bad enough you got to live with it.

When I caught up with Mack, I was praying he'd tell me there was work down the hall.

"Mack....." We shook hands and toasted.

"Congratulations Kid."

"Anything going on......any work coming up?"

"Should be busier than it is for an election year and the Bi-Centennial. All the local guys are working, but the hall's not even putting out any boomers. No boomers means no permit hands. It's not like last year."

I looked at him straight on: "Mack I got iron fever..... bad."

He tilted his head, "There's work going on and coming up – just not around here. Ray......Ray" Mack called.

The three of us sat at the end of a table. "You guys come up to my place. We'll map out where this is going. It just isn't you guys anymore......it's the next generation."

"I'm already helping them out." Ray said.

"We know you always been there for Ryan. You always done the right thing Ray. We know his family needs to start off on solid ground – do his family right."

"What are we talking about Mack?" Ray said.

I looked from Ray to Mack, "I just need an 'in' someplace......you know so I can get a foothold."

Ray gave me a sour look, "What are you doing now?"

"You know what I'm doing: driving hack, caddying, and side jobs with Rex." I squeezed my eyes having to admit my current work situation in front of Mack, both knew I was going no place fast.

"That ain't getting it." Mack lit a Lucky.

Karyn came over holding the baby, "I want to introduce you to a couple of my cousins."

"I'll be right back." I said to Mack and Ray.

"That's alright. Just one more thing......next weekend you both come up to my place."

"We'll be there." Ray nodded.

The two of them continued to strategize for another 20 minutes. I was pretty sure they were mapping out my future, just as Ray and Hal had done years earlier.

KARYN AND ME HAD GOTTEN MORE MONEY FROM THE wedding than we had expected. It kept the bill collectors from the doorstep for a few additional months. Neither of us mentioned the word 'honeymoon'. That was for married couples who didn't screw up.

A week later, Ray and me were driving up the Taconic Parkway to get the lowdown from Mack about his plan. If my brother knew about it, he didn't say anything. We left around 7:00 am. I had missed the day of caddying – I didn't want to miss the night shift with Caesar.

I sipped some coffee from the Greeks, "What do you think Mack's got planned?"

Ray chuckled, "You know Mack – he claims he's just a 'dumb ironworker'. Damn, he knows more about life and people than anyone I know. He can see you're headed for a train wreck if you don't get your act together."

I took a deep breath, "You know I got into the dooge after Wells cashed out."

"That's because you're a fuckin' retard." He reached for my smokes on the Starfire's dash.

"Compared to you....I am a jerk; but I'm smarter than most of these mommalookas runnin' around."

"Let's hope Mack's got something up his sleeve."

As soon as we got there he put us to work on a home improvement project. Mack and Mom-Mom had this expensive stainless,fire-proof, insulated 10 in. round duct, already installed through the living room's exterior wall to vent the 'new' used wood burning stove. Where the insulated stack pipe exited the house, Mack had a weldor from the job, fabricate a stand, and he anchored it to the patio's concrete. Mom-Mom had given the stand a third coat of Rustoleum. Ray and me put two sections of scaffold together to build the stack and lag bolt two retaining bands to the house. Mack figured the stack should be four feet higher than the roof's ridge for the stove to draw right.

"As long as the tying in is done – breakdown the scaffold and let's have some coffee."

We sat at the long picnic table in the shade of 2 white pines.

"This is what I'm thinking – Ryan have you got anything going besides this nickel and dime work?"

"Summer's here, and driving a hack in the summer is slim pickens. I'll be caddying weekends, spotty work as a laborer for a friend, and we're almost out of unemployment."

Mack pulled a Camel out and threw the pack out on the table. We all lit up.

"You got anything coming up that'll lead to something?"

"The powerhouse job last year was my best paying job, and the one I felt I was really suited for. You know at the end of the day you stood back and looked at the iron that we set......you knew you were a part of it." I said.

Mack lit up and nodded. He looked back and forth to me and Ray. "There's a way to get into the ironworkers union, but it means you'll be on the road until you've worked enough hours in one local to transfer in. Stay away from Dixie and Texas: the scale and fringe benefits are bullshit down there."

Ray was dumbstruck, "How can you go to a union hall, buy a card, and start work the following day?"

"Ryan – you explain the nuts and bolts of how the hiring hall works, and the ironworkers version of seniority on the way home." Mack said.

"Mom-Mom, we got any beer in the fridge?" Ray walked in the house, "Anybody else?"

"Bring us all one Ray." Mom-Mom said.

He stood at the table as he passed around the cans. "I don't know shit from shineola about ironwork except when we got hoodwinked by the Business Agent to hump a bunch of security gates up six floors on the west side of Manhattan." We all chuckled. "No kidding – I still got a kink in my back."

"If it was easy, they'd have women and pipefitters doing it. Ryan will tell you about the good side of the trade on your way back as well."

Mom-Mom reminded Mack she was the one who cut the hole through the wall and she wasn't any pipefitter.

He acknowledged the correction; "But listen, 95% of the locals will not sell you an ironworkers card. Just because you're a union member doesn't mean you know anything about the trade. Even the rank and file knows manning jobs with unqualified people will have the contractors walking away from their agreements at the first opportunity. The locals who have no work will sell membership cards as a matter of economic survival. New members have to pay an initiation fee and their monthly dues."

"You mean they still sell membership cards even though it will come back and bite them in the ass as soon as work picks up?" Ray shook his head and took a breath trying to digest the lack of logic.

"That's about the size of it." Mack agreed. "Because there's no work in these locals – it is nearly impossible for one of these guys who bought a book to work in the local they just bought a book from. I've even heard they make these guys who buy cards, sign a piece of paper promising to never seek work in that local. We call these locals 'Bookstores'; that was when we had a membership book - not a card. They're the same thing though."

"The unions are not all thieves, except the creeps that own the union – the crooks at the international headquarters. The guys running the show don't know the first thing about the trade. Ray, your adventure hauling the security gates up six floors was more work than all of them international slugs have done combined!"

"Here's the good news: Three boomers from Boston came through our hall, and caught two days of work on the job I'm on now. They said they were working their way to a powerhouse that had just broken ground. They'll be assembling cranes and putting in the reinforcing steel in the slab and the walls for unit 1 right after Halloween…...four or five months down the road. " That is where you boys ought to be. Those Beantowners said it was in Milwaukee's jurisdiction; you know Schlitz, Miller, Pabst." He looked over to Edna, "What state is that?"

"Wisconsin?"

"I've got to get a map." he said.

"Okay?……let me know when you guys are ready. You work out there 6 months or so…………as long as you haven't pissed off the erection company, your foreman, the B.A., or the bluecoats – you come back and get Karyn and Nicole."

It sounded real smooth when Mack laid it out. "Where should we go to get a journeyman's card?" I said.

"I'll let you know about a month before you're ready to leave." He turned to Ray, "Ray, you're okay with this? I've got no other way to help you guys. If Ryan had something better than this, he'd be doing it."

"That's true Mack, but you, Mom-Mom, and Ryan all see it from the same viewpoint. I'm not saying 'no', but I expected to be headed back to Purdue." he said.

"There's no doubt in my mind Ryan's got the smarts, stamina, welding skills, and cat-like reflexes to get out of harm's way. Ray, you could split once you knew it was coming together for Ryan, Karyn, and the baby."

He lit up another Lucky. "If nothing else develops……I'll go out there when they start the structural steel. I'm not doing any of that reinforcing stuff." Ray took a long draw.

"You can't wait too long, even two (2) 600 megawatt units won't last more than four or five years…..depending how bad they need the power. Three years at 2000 hours per year, and you'll be on Local 8's 'A' list and you'll be able to transfer the bought journeyman cards for real ones. Local 8's no bookstore local, they're for real."

"Thanks Mack, we got to go. I got to drive tonight."

Not much was said on the way back. One thing that did stick with me was when Ray said: "You're asking an awful lot."

We stopped at the U.N. to get my money box, "The Subterraneans" by Kerouac, and my headknocker club.

706

As soon as I walked in, I was handed a crying baby, "I'm going out." Karyn huffed.

Ray looked at me and laughed, but he didn't let Karyn see.

"What'd I do?" I said holding the crying Nicole.

"Or didn't do?" Ray said.

"Ray – I got to go in tonight.....we're broke. I'm serious.....and I got to caddy tomorrow. What the fuck?" I asked the vanished Karyn: "We didn't even do any partying or get back late. What the fuck?"

"I got Nicole 'til momma comes back." he said.

He was better with the baby than me or Karyn. When I called the U.N. two hrs. into my shift, Ray said Nicole stopped crying three minutes after I left.

ii

While Karyn had been sending out resumes' and cover letters to get a real job; she had gone back to Tibbetts for one last season. She worked days and I worked nights. The baby sitting for Nicole that summer was a real quilt-work arrangement. Sometimes we both worked days; Jane, my sister Cathy, and a Vietnamese refugee Nguyen Trang who lived on the same floor took care of Nicole.

Jane had a small birthday party for Brother Bill. He had turned 13 on the last day of June, but the actual party was on the 26th. He'd be in 8th grade come September. Karyn was coming to the party on Saturday after work. At the party we'd switch off again; She'd stay for a little while, and I was off to drive for Caesar for the night and go caddying in the morning. Karyn would drop the baby off with Jane or my sister Cathy on her way to Tibbetts. As I recalled, Nicky didn't fuss much.

Three or four of Billy's friends were there: all future juvenile delinquents, except for Tommy 'Capps' Campagna. There was a brief commotion at the table of snacks, chips, and dips.

"Why is it every time I turn around there's some social event at my house......at MY GODDAMN HOUSE - God dammit! I'm telling all you parasites.......this is the last party here this summer..... THE LAST!" It was Hal in full Hal form.

Jane's assistant, Judy asked, "What's the matter Hal – don't you like us?"

My Mom also had had enough: "Aren't you going to wish Billy 'Happy Birthday'?"

"This is the last....." he slammed down the drink on the table and half of it jumped out of his mug. Our deflector shields were up as the tirade went nowhere.

Ray showed up shortly after Karyn. Although the baby would have been a dream baby for a stay-at–home mother, this new reality where both parents worked, had our energy reserves on 'E' most of the time.

707

My brother looked around; Karyn was talking with Jane and Judy.

"You must have had a good loop........you're back pretty early." Ray said.

"Yeah, I had Levine and Swetz, they both run about a 7 or 8 handicap. I wanted to get down here for Willis' gig as soon as I got out of there."

"Ryan.......I ran into Tarts.....said the Rogues are setting up a half-barrel down the marina tonight. Everybody's getting out of town next weekend for the Fourth on account of the Bi-Centennial. It's one of the party's.........you know – no wives or girlfriends – strays are okay. You know Holter will show up with 'Married girl', and Vinny might have called up Dona Del. I tried Sara Nussbaum this afternoon." he said.

My mind went completely distant, I thought about Meris Klein when he mentioned Sarah......it should have been the perfect a double date for me and Ray; except for the fact Ray was their first choice.

"What's up with Sarah?"

An eye roll and a scoff, "She's going out with some guy from where she works. Sarah said Meris was going for her Masters with Johnson at M.I.T. in bio-tech – taking summer courses."

"I shoulda gone to college." I shook my head. "I thought you said, this is a 'guys only' bash?"

"The way Vinny was talking – girls are all invited.....just nothing regular or steady. One wife, or steady girlfriend shows up – In a day or two and the cat's out of the bag, and all the guys got a ton of explaining to do..............not worth it."

"The only girl I'd trust was Barbwire. A lot of secrets went to the grave with her." I stood there as her formless image went through me.

"It's just going to be the girls from Warburton....Lockwood .....and Lake." Jimmy Martini had spread the word. Bingo Butoni was supposed to be bringing some chicks from Pelton....you know....Park Hill." Ray said.

"Bingo? He's as much a M.I.A. as I am."

"Are you going?" I asked.

"Yeah, be there a little later....Might be doing something with Jimmy Blanko and Dunbar later on. If nothing's going on - I'll hang out with you guys."

"Ray – I'm tapped out, I've got to get some skins. I gotta drive tonight."

"Karyn isn't expecting you 'til after 5-6 a.m. Does she work tomorrow?"

"Un-uh. But I got to go caddying tomorrow."

"Tell her you're going straight from Caesar's to the golf course." he said.

I needed a break from the gerbil wheel I had been on since I planted the seed. I was used to working and scraping by – it didn't bother me much. Rather, it was the looking for work that brought me to the edge sometimes. 'Keep twisting my arm Ray.' I thought. The fact was, during the summer, I could make more caddying during the day, than I could driving a cab at night.

"Turn it loose tonight Ry." He looked over at mother and baby. "Just make sure you got after shave and Juicy Fruit gum for your loop. The members can smell whiskey breath a mile away."

This was one of the best things about my life: I didn't have to put in any thought into any move I made when Ray made the call. I'd play hooky from work, to go play with my brother and the Rogues – guilt free.

Jimmy Martin and Butoni were the hosts that evening; they were putting out a half-barrel down the marina. They collected $5.00 a head. After you paid your five dollars, Martin started telling you what a deal you got. While we waited for Martin and Bingo to show up with the keg we smoked some boo. We started to wonder why Bingo was showing up tonight to party with us after a two year absence. 'Fast Eddie' Mason knew the story of how Martin got the half-barrel, and he started telling us as we waited.

Jimmy Martin heard through Danny Stax that Bingo was looking to unload some mushrooms. Butoni came up to North Yonkers and drove around, he sold a little here and a little there, but they weren't moving as fast as he wanted. The two went back down South Yonkers so Martin could chauffer Bingo around while he rode shotgun looking for people on the street who might be interested.

While they did their street search, they waited for a traffic light to change; they saw a beer truck on the other side of the road. The delivery guy hadn't locked the insulated door. They both saw it at the same time. Bingo bolted out and was in the back of the truck before the light changed. Jimmy Martin got the green, and did a double U-turn: the first in the intersection; and the next in the lane where the beer truck was parked. Jimmy stopped short and threw it in reverse and backed his car up a few feet from the back of the truck. Bingo rolled a keg out; Martin was top-heavy with the half barrel on his shoulder. He rolled it off his shoulder and into the trunk. Two cases of Heineken were boosted for good measure. Two bottles busted, had given Martin's trunk a beer bath. Half of the collection money must have gone to Bingo. The only thing the entrepreneurs had to supply were: the tap/pump, a plastic garbage barrel and ice. They boosted plastic cups from Hanratty's bar. It was pretty kool that night, and the two 20 lb. bags of ice lasted a long time.

It was one of the few times I recall, when Budweiser didn't taste too skunkie. It might have been the circumstances as well. No matter what the label says; stolen beer always tastes best. Butoni said the scudweiser was closest to the door, so that's what he took.

Bad Brad was all bundled up: Parka coat, jeans, and steel-toe shoes. He couldn't afford to miss too many time-and-a-half Saturdays at Ananconda or being behind the hot dog cart. Stax said Brad had been down the marina drinking by himself when he got there. It was by chance he was there for the kegger. He cradled his Mad Dog 20/20. When the keg, girls, and music started; he was near us, but he wasn't with us.

"Why doesn't Brad come over?" Kate Cruz said.

"He probably ain't got the five bucks for Bingo or Martin." I replied. "Hey Ray, a buck a piece, we'll buy Brad into Martini's Keg. Even the girls kicked in a buck-and-a-half. "How 'bout it Blanko?"

"For naughty Brad.....sure. Maybe he'll get out of that funk he loves."

"Same old shit.......Susan, Brad jr., and I think Sophie told him to take a hike." Holter said.

"Hey George, where's Vinny?" I asked. Stax and me were expecting him. It was through Tarts that Ray said he had heard about the half barrel.

George had a big smile: "He met up with Dona Del. I think he's on a date. They're still in the active file I guess."

"Betcha he took her down our apartment. He'll probably show up later. Hahahahahah." Stax laughed.

Danny Stax only had a tee shirt on. "I turned Brad on to a Quaalude – try to help him forget. Wish I had kept one for myself...... I'm fuckin' freezin'..........fuckin' breeze."

"I threw my keys to him – there's a leather welding jacket in the trunk." I offered.

"Thanks Whiteheat."

"I think Brad's overdressed with the Parka......it isn't that cold." Denise the Piece said.

"Hot or cold, I don't think he can feel a thing. Check him out." Bingo nodded over to him.

"I'll probably end up sharing an apartment with him unless I can get out of New York." I took a large gulp of Bud.

Ray's ears pricked up. "Ryan, don't forget our plan."

"What plan?" Blanko looked left out.

Neither of us responded.

Holter was thinking about Brad: "Fuckin' Brad, we all kicked in for you. Come on up and git you some." He looked at us and then over to Brad, "I can't wait until I get married and I can live in the vegetable patch with Brad."

"Fuckin' zombie city......all these women are sticking needles in his voodoo doll. Look at him." Martini called over to Rex, "Crank the jams a little will ya?"

Sad Brad sat atop of the two railroad ties that were stacked and attached to the sheet piling holding back the river. Maybe they weren't true railroad ties: the first layer of creosote wood was a 12"x12", and it laid on top of the marina's dirt. The railroad ties rested on top of the 12x12's. The two big chunks of wood were held in place with 2 in. diameter rods, bolted through the wood and through the 3/8ths thick corrugated sheet piling. It provided a good barrier to keep vehicles from accidentally driving into the drink.

There was a kind of reunion atmosphere to the beer bash. Ray and Blanko were fringe people who always had guest passes amongst us, like Loki had before he moved to Florida. Bingo and me had life memberships, but we hadn't been around for the last two years. Somebody like John Dunbar didn't have the rep or the miles to hang with us, unless he showed up with weed, beer, or chicks. The 'get lost' vibe would come out pretty quick unless somebody spoke up for him.

It seemed incongruous for Ray to buddy-up with Dunbar: the former was army through and through, and the latter was a genuine peacenik. The two would argue and argue until the booze ran out. I know Ray never told him about the Greystone Equation. Dunbar, Blanko, Loki, and Ray had met at All Souls High School. I thought it was an association of convenience.

The dynamic which had brought us together, had begun to fragment. Ray's children of the night had a bit more cohesion than the Rogues could muster. These specter people had more meaningful commonalities......and in a way, all they had were each other, and a shared destiny.

Holter, Stax, and me were on the exterior of the party. Martin had put in for another volume increase with Rexall which was naturally approved, but it was too loud to stand near the keg and talk with any of the babes. 'Fast Eddie' Mason stumbled and mumbled his way towards us.

"Fuckin' Brad......." he tried it again.

"Whaaaaah?" Holter asked Mason to speak up.

"Thas what I'm tryin' to tell yas......fuckin' Brad went in the drink." Eddie was all tongue tied.

"Huh?" I squinted.

"Guzzutti fell in the fuckin' river." He pointed to the approximate spot.

"Holy shit......!" Holter's eyes went wide.

Fast Eddie had his Bud in one hand and a cigarette in the other; "I'm tellin' ya – he tipped up his wine and fell backwards into the river."

We ran to where he had been sitting. Now everyone lined the run of the railroad ties.

"There he is!" One of the girls spotted him.

If there was a moon out, it couldn't have been more than a sliver. Low tide had the water level a good 15 feet below where Brad had been sitting. I looked and looked; I couldn't see him. A white streak flashed past us. All he had on were a pair of dungarees. Someone said it was Ray Whitelaw. I looked around and around. He wasn't with us. I cupped my hands around my mouth: "RAY........RAY..... can I help?" I called down into the water.

Brad and Ray were already 60 – 70 feet away from the corrugated sheet piling, and seemed to be moving further into the river by some current. "There's got to be 20 fuckin' currents in that river." George said knowing the river's unforgiving characteristics.

We barely could see or hear Ray. Every third stroke or so we could see his arm and some splashing. He was working hard to bring them both closer to where Brad had fallen in. Now I could see his arm around Brad's neck and under his shoulder fighting a nasty stream within the river.

Frustrated, Ray yelled: "Brad's all dead weight. He's got all his clothes on......Fuck.....I'm running out of steam."

People at the marina's edge looked like they were watching a movie..........this rescue wasn't really occurring.

Danny Stax was panicking: "Rex – you got any rope?"

"That's one thing I know I don't have in my trunk."

Stax yelled: "Anybody got any rope in their cars?"

Dead silence as they continued to watch.

Between heaven and hell, Guzzutti started thrashing and becoming difficult for Ray.

Pinching Brad's nose, his lungs expelled two big heaves of river water; and continued to gag and cough. "Ryan.......don't let me drown.......don't."

"Just calm down or you'll kill us both." Ray's voice hit the steel sheets and traveled up to where we were.

"Ray.....You need me down there?" I took my shoes and shirt off, my heart was racing.

"No.....there's nothing to hold on to. More people in the water means more problems – fuckin' quicksand. Black murky cold ass water." Ray huffed with his teeth chattering.

He had Brad close to the piling. There were small waves pushing them into the corrugated metal wall, but after the crest brought them up two feet – it retreated and left them with nothing to grab a hold of except a two inch diameter retaining rod which was secured by a 3 inch nut. The rod must have gone back 30 feet into the landfill attached to some reinforcing monsta rods and formed a deadman in a concrete beam approximately 10 feet below the grade of the marina.

Holter became a human link between the people on top and Brad and Ray. Ray had to do the impossible: He used all the leverage he had while holding that big nut and waiting for a large enough wave to launch Brad high enough, so George could grab him.

It wasn't enough for Ray to use the river's weak waves to catapult Guzzutti to Holter, or for Holter to reach down and try to grab him. Brad had to do something to save himself: he had to reach up, jump, and grab. Otherwise, it simply was not going to happen. After missing Holter on three successive tries, both Brad and Ray were spent. More than that, I could see Ray was in distress. I ran over to the aluminum keg and threw it as close as I dared. The two held on to the keg, hoping to regain enough energy for another try.

Throw down a couple of cups." Ray shouted.

I tried to laugh with the others, but I was too worried. At least there seemed to be a little time to make a better attempt at a rescue.

Ray shouted, "Rex, you and the Bushman drop Holter over the piling by his ankles. George – you got to get a hold of Brad anywhere you can and you cannot let go.....DO NOT LET GO! Two of you guys got to hold onto Rex's ankles; and two of youse grab hold to Bush's." Ray tried to choreograph the attempt as he held onto to Brad with one hand and he used the other to hug the half barrel.

"You ready Brad? --- When I pull you up by the back of your pants and let you go....I'll try to push your ass up. You've got to reach for the sky as high as you can. Holter will grab you and pull you out. You got that Brad?"

Maybe Brad answered Ray – maybe he didn't. All we could see were two white faces and a silver keg.

After three more minutes of rest on the barrel, Ray alerted us: "The next decent wave and we're going for it." Brad had to get two feet of jettison from Ray, the wave, and whatever he could do to reach George's outstretched hands. He had to help himself. There were words of encouragement from above. The girls were screaming and crying: "C'mon Brad…..c'mon – You can do it this time. Do it for little Brad. You got too much to live for." I wondered if he heard any of it.

Ray let Holter, Bush, and Rex know: "THIS IS IT!"

Brad had the height for sure, but he started arching backward into Ray. He countered and pushed Brad towards Holter by pushing against the keg's buoyancy. It became a question of which object required the lesser force to be moved. I thought it would be the keg, but there must have been more beer in it than I thought.

Holter grabbed the soaked Parka, and put the eternal grip on his wrist – aware he might have a coat but no Brad. "I got 'em……..PULL!" he bellowed. We all watched as our two strongest tried to manhandle the human chain over the sheet piling and ties. Bingo and Martin yanked Holter by his belt and Stax and me vise-gripped Brad and flung him over the top. All eyes were on Brad as he was thrown face-down in the dirt. We pumped his upper back, and a pool of river water was expelled from his lungs. He may have been in some stage of hypothermia also. We got him out of his wet clothes, and Rex had the girls wrap him in an army surplus blanket.

"RAY?"……I peered over the edge into the water. All I saw was a spinning aluminum keg and the black river. 'How could this be?' The guy who saved Brad Guzzutti was gone.
What the fuck? I scoured the water. Another two minutes elapsed – no Ray….."I gotta get Ray" I said to no one, and jumped out into the murky Hudson helplessly searching for my brother. Around, down, and around I swam; thinking he may have hit his head on the piling, or the keg, and might be trapped underwater, caught on something. I didn't know how dangerous Ray's rescue attempt was until I was in the water. I was frantic; after a minute, I thought neither of us would be coming out of the drink. I dove down, time after time, feeling for Ray by hand. It was pointless to open my eyes while I was submerged; it was the darkest dark I could imagine. After the fourth or fifth dive I surfaced. Swimming in a small circle, I called up: "See anything? Any splashing? See the keg?" There was no answer. All of my energy was now coming from adrenalin. The tide had taken the keg, it might have taken Ray also. It was getting confusing, there was a lot of shouting from above – most of which was just noise.

The Hail Marys came out of me faster than a belt of bullets coming out of a machine gun. The cops arrived and were tossing lines with grappling hooks into the water. They told me to grab a hook and they'd pull me out. They were pissed off when I didn't. They were hooking cars and other junk under the surface of the water. There was no sign of my brother, and no energy left. I swam up to the marina's north end, where the corrugated piling made a 90 degree turn back to

713

the shore and the train tracks. I walked onto the bank and sand and wept for 20 minutes or so. A cop had followed me, and said as I sat: "The river unit is on the way to search. The divers will be here as soon as it's light. He might be out there."

The search for Ray was still 'active', but with each passing minute rescue became more remote and the recovery phase more likely. The irony should have made me laugh: to get onto the surface of the marina - I had to climb a ship's ladder up the north side of the piling. I never knew it was there.

Rex, Holter, Stax, and Bingo and some others were still there. The ambulance people wanted to take Brad to St. John's to get checked out.

"Do I have to go? 'Cause I ain't got a dime to my name." Brad said.

"It's recommended."

"Unless it's free or I'm going to get busted because I didn't go.....I decline. I don't need another bill. Take me to the North End."

Holter said Brad was the only one who didn't know Ray was missing.

The bulls made me drive over to headquarters downtown to give a statement. The cops initial determination was: "There was no foul play.....accidental drowning would be listed as the cause of death when they recovered the body."

I said to the detective, "There's no point in waking up my folks – in fact, you don't have to notify them until you have a body....he's not even a missing person yet." I said.

"Accidental drowning doesn't fall under the 24 hour missing person criteria. Because there are witnesses attesting to your brother's disappearance while in the water - there is a preponderance of evidence that the victim may have drowned." The detective in charged explained.

"I'm just asking the department to hold off with notifying my parents, at least until the divers start their search. I know you guys have done that with car wrecks when someone's died. A guy dies at one or two o'clock and his next of kin aren't notified until eight or nine in the morning." I said.

"I guess it might be around that time before any notification takes place anyway." The copper said. "You know most of these death notifications are done by witnesses – not by the police - that we have no control over. You'd hope people would have the common decency to keep their traps shut, when they don't - there's not much we can do. We've got a patrolman at the scene in case he either comes up or shows up. We'll find him. It's a crazy river........you never know....." He lit a cigarette and offered me one which I declined. My lungs had already had an Olympian workout.

"Did you guys know there's a firehouse at the top of the hill at Marina Dr. and Warburton?"

"We didn't want to wake 'em."

Silence.

"Can I go?"

The doors to St. Casmir's church were locked. I prayed to St. Teresa, the Blessed Virgin, and Jesus Christ on the steps. There was nothing to draw on, from my account. All I could pray for was forgiveness, mercy, and hope for a miracle. Anyone who passed at three in the morning chalked it up as a relapsed alky, praying on the church steps.......seeking redemption. I was praying for the metaphysical unlikelihood Ray had some how side-stepped the grim reaper's scythe.

I drove back down the marina. A cop sat in his squad car at the scene of the party.

"Any news?"

"Nah.....I been walking up and down the marina, shining the flashlight into the water............nothin'. We'll keep lookin."

"Thanks." I left and went north on Warburton Ave. and came to the 'Y' at Harriman and Warburton. I went down Harriman instead of going to 21 O'Dell. There was too much negative energy awaiting me there. Sleep was out of the realm of possibility anyway. Greystone was the ghost town I expected.

Wanting to get a view, I took the steps to the overpass and looked south to the marina. To see anything, I needed a pair of binoculars. Depending on the currents, it was possible his body could come up this far, but not likely.

"Fuckin' Ray!" I cried. I shook my head and sat on the steps and wept once again. It lasted another 20 minutes.

I made my way down to the SB platform and watched out on the river again. I could see the cosmic castaway's bare burial mound through the growing weeds and bushes. The mound had a faint shimmer.......a glow; there was something on the pebbles and sand. At the handrail's edge I looked again. Disoriented, I couldn't be sure of anything. The memory of the warm mound with Barb and Karyn was pulling me to it – if for no other reason to warm my body up. Something......someone was crashed out on top of the Cosmic Intruder. I crouched as I walked; not wanting to be seen. The mound's glow wasn't from the light pollution of the platform.

It looked like some hobo beachcomber was laid out where Barb and me had spent so many nights. It might have glowed as a result of unabsorbed love, and found its way through the cosmos. We were sure we would have made it 'in' on the first ballot of "The Sexual Hall of Fame." Nobody came to the mound unless they had business; this dude had to be checked out. My only thought was it might be the newspaper guy on top of another story. The mound had never shimmered like this before. Something else was at work here. Perhaps the remnant was entering a new phase with Ray's passing. It was also possible this bum was casting a wet dream from the embers of a love I thought had abruptly been cut short.

This beachcomber turned from riverside to trackside – I fell back into the brush and weeds, my eyes got as big as Frisbees. I tried to focus, and rapidly shook my head back and forth. Still I couldn't digest what I saw; my breath was short like when Vinny told me about Barb in the overpass....... IT WAS RAY! ! !

"YES!!!....MOTHAFUCKAS!!!...YES!!!....SWEET JESUS BLACK!!!....YES!!!....FUCK ALL YOU MOTHAFUCKAS!!!.....FUCK YOU ALL!!!" I screamed and started laughing. "It is you......isn't it? This isn't heaven or hell, a fifth dimension, an alternate reality, or a parallel universe is it?"

Ray started laughing as well: "Shut up you idiot."

I put my ear to his heart to verify he was no hallucination.

"Get the fuck off me you retard." We laughed some more.

"I don't believe you're not at the bottom of the river!" I shook him. "How did you end up here? Man, I even stopped at St. Casmir's and prayed. This is unbelievable. Now - I AM fuckin' exhausted."

"First things first..... Bad Brad?"

"He made it, I think he's okay.....he's walkin' and talkin' anyway. That dude's got a lot of markers going out: to you, Holter, Bingo, Rex. I still don't believe I'm talking to you."

"But he's okay?"

"As far as I know."

"Sonabitch – I feel great....like when I helped them pilots out in Bien Hoa. No dark clouds....pinpoint vision....clarity of thought. Daylight's going to be a blast." Ray smiled.

"I still got to go caddying after I get back to the U.N. Listen Ray, I got to call the bulls and tell them you're okay. In fact, when you feel up to it - probably be for the best - if you went up to the North Command Station House and verify your 'alive' status. You're okay right?"

"I feel 13 years old.....like Willie."

"Yeah, and check in with Jane and Hal, make sure they both visibly see you this morning. It's a big deal when someone drowns, maybe someone has already called the house reporting your demise. The parents don't need to be worrying about your viability. I can drop you off at the house if you want. Listen, we don't say anything about last night to Jane, Hal, or Karyn...... especially Karyn. There's enough going on as it is. Are you going to 21?" I stood up and stretched.

"Staying right here. Thank God this cast-off piece still generates heat. I might not have drowned, but I was so cold in the water by the marina, I might have died from hypothermia. One current was going south; another would be going north. The two collided and formed a whirlpool and took me down 20 feet I guess. The water running north was a lot warmer than the water just hanging around in front of the piling wall, still......... you couldn't call the water from the south as being 'warm'."

"After we saved Brad – you disappeared; where'd you go?"

"Got clocked on the side of my head by the keg's reverb after I used it to launch Brad. I just lay in the water on my back progressively going further and further out into the river until the whirlpool sent me down and a different warmer ocean current sent me up river. It seemed forever for me to rise to the top of the water; I was so exhausted – if I had taken in any more water I believe I would have drowned. I'm sure the magnetic inversion brought me back to Greystone. Through a series of switchbacks, channels, currents, roundabouts, submergences, and re-emergences; I saw the station on my right side. I began to swim to break out of the current."

Ray looked at me: "Ryan, I now have empirical evidence of the existence of the specter contingent of human species – though it is incomplete. It is highly probable it has relativity with pole magnetism."

"Yeah......yeah....yeah.....Hey Ray, I got to go. Remember don't say nuthin' about Bad Brad."

iv

THREE WEEKS LATER, BAD BRAD GUZZUTTI WAS knifed on Tuckahoe Rd. in front of a liquor store just before it closed. There were no witnesses; the coroner said Brad had laid in the street for a half-hour and bled to death. A witness who was leaving a Chinese take-out two doors down, told the cops Brad had been arguing with two guys before he went into the liquor store. He said he thought it was over a parking space.

It was the worst wake I ever went to. Bad Brad was still married to Susan at the time. There were ill will between the two families, but not enough where they couldn't come together and grieve. Still, there was one fight inside of Sinatra's Funeral Home, and another in the parking lot.No one could believe his incredible reversal of luck.

October 9 & 10, 2018, Mankato.

Doctors Marie Allen and David Judd started bringing Ryan out of the induced coma. His four daughters watched from the darkened perimeter of the ICU room. Teresa and Killeen's hands were in a prayerful pose, Nicole's arms were folded, and Dixie messaged her temples with her fingertips.

In a half hour, he opened his eyes and whispered for some cranberry juice. The sight of the youngest brought a smile; the other three walked towards him from the shadows.

The nurses recorded the vitals, drew some more blood, and took a urine sample from the new collection bag to evaluate his liver and kidney function. The doctors began reading the information. He had been awake for almost an hour when the medical team left. At the door, Dr. Judd called to Dixie to confer with her just outside the room.

"We haven't found a match. Monitoring the numbers and vitals........he continues to lose ground. You and your sisters should start thinking about hospice care. Wherever you decide to do that, here......LaCrosse.....or at home, he will fade fairly quickly. Today, - right now - may be the last opportunity to speak with your father. Make the most of it......but don't use him up." he said.

In the room, Nicole showed Ryan an old picture. It was in pretty bad shape. She had to turn it right side up for him. Teresa got his glasses from the drawer and put them on for him, he smiled.

"Little Nicky.......look at all that black hair, just like your mom.....and Ray.....your Uncle Ray pushing the stroller. That's at Grandpa Hal's house. If things don't work out – I'll be seeing Uncle Ray pretty soon. Aaaaay-we got some catching up to do anyway." Ryan's voice was barely audible.

The cranberry juice finally made it to his room.

"Kill...." he whispered, "My grip is at your place?"

"Yeah Papa. It's all there – what you brought from Arizona."

"Good.....that's good. Dixie...I must be conscious tomorrow for a little bit at least. Killeen, we're in Minnesota?"

"Yeah Pops."

His voice changed. It startled them; it no longer was a whisper. Ryan softly said: "You drive back to LaCrosse and bring me Ray's U.S. Army duffle bag........the small one."

"The small duffle with the lock?"

"Right. The one with all the money." He gave out a dry laugh. "Be back here by nine tomorrow."

"Papa, we got to go so you can rest." Dixie interrupted.

"For what?" his eyes and brow asked.

718

He smiled. All four kissed his forehead and squeezed his hand in turn. The Whitelaw women congregated in the family/ visitor area down the hall.

"The old man's kind of loopy.....don't you think?" Dixie said.

Teri took out her rosary from its soft case in her purse and wore it around her neck.

"Pulling out the big guns now." Dixie noticed.

"Wouldn't hurt you none if you got on the prayer train."

"I've been praying girl." she said.

"We know you have. We all have been praying." Killeen said.

"That one metered pump was delivering Dilaudid. It's a pretty strong painkiller." Teri said.

"What else was he getting?" Killeen asked.

"Don't know: Anti-biotics, some drug they want in him, in case they do the transplant.....saline. With all the tubes, monitor wires, IV's, sensors......it's probably as bad as it looks." Teresa took a deep breath.

Dixie asked Killeen, "Does he have a lot of cash in the duffle?" She looked to Killeen, who raised her eyebrows, back to Dixie, who looked at Nicole, who shrugged at Teresa.

"Guess we'll find out tomorrow." Killeen responded. "I'll be in LaCrosse tonight – hopefully I'll be back here by eight tomorrow morning." They quadruple hugged and Killeen took off.

R.N. Teresa, went back to take the first watch with Ryan. When he was at St. Thomas the Apostle in Lacrosse, she'd visit her father before work, during lunch, and after work in her scrubs and I.D. It seemed to help extract any inside information and getting those who attended Ryan to give the extra concern and promptness for the father of a co-worker. Here at the Mankato Institute, she had just a few connections. At this tier I hospital, she didn't need them; five star service was routine.

At the hotel room, Dixie asked her older half-sister, "When did you start living with us?"

"It all started coming together or falling apart when I was 15. Karyn more or less told Papa she was done with me. "She's a 'ghost girl'. She'll be landing at......."

".....Mitchell Field in Milwaukee. I remember that." Dixie said.

"Papa needed me to do your mom's stuff; mostly be a big sister and a mom 'til y'all got to be old enough." Nicole said.

"Did the old man ever talk about that "Children of the Night/ Magneto Girl Bullcrap?" Dixie said.

"Only in relation to Uncle Ray, when we'd be walking in the desert – me, him, Rick and the kids once in a while."

"You believe all that stuff about Ray?" Dixie looked in the room's big mirror.

"Ryan throws a lot of stretchers." Nicky said. The two laughed. "When I questioned Karyn's label for me – he said if I didn't

719

feel trapped.....boxed in......that I didn't have a sense to escape or run – then I was more like him and not Uncle Ray. Papa said it wasn't a genetic trait, rather it was more the randomness of the universe. All this parallel universe mumbo jumbo, neeto-magneto – pole reversal, and dimension possession stuff could only be explained by the people who had first hand experience with it. It's like asking a Harley-Davidson rider what a 1%er is.......it's like either you know or you don't."

"Mmmmmm......I wonder. I'm 28 now. Remember.....in my senior year I was - " Dixie got cut off.

"...........You were into some heavy drugs, and you almost didn't graduate. And every weekend you'd stay over at Shelley's house. It was a bad age for you, but it wasn't that inversion magnetic world he would talk about and swears that exists." Nicky said.

"We got to keep him here......alive. Now, we're old enough to listen to his wisdom. Why did we think we knew everything?" Dixie stared at the mirror.

"You want to know what life is about? Start having some kids, it'll get real clear - real fast. There is nothing else that will give you the complete human experience."

Dixie breathed deep and refocused her vision.

ii

Hal, Jane, and Karyn found out about Bad Brad and the Marina incident because of the stark contrast between being saved and being murdered. A story that screwed up had to hit the newspaper and get around. The ordeal my brother went through the night of the keg party made me wonder and analyze my lifelong association with him. Not only did he save Brad, but he saved himself. Nobody but his crew of exiles realized what had happened, and to a lesser extent Vinny and me.

Prior to Brad's murder, people were bugging Ray and me about the rest of his story. "How long were you in the water Ray?" "Ryan, where did Ray wash up.....why didn't he check in with the cops?"

"I did check in with the cops – by phone." Ray dismissed most of the inquiries. "Jane and Hal received two calls asking if they had heard I had been in a drowning accident? Bunch of brain dead morons."

I WAS TRACKED DOWN AT THE UNITED NATIONS BY Jamie O'Neill just before Labor Day. He knew there was a story somewhere in the small circle of 'The 5th Dimension' and 'The Rogues'. Karyn answered the door; she looked at O'Neill and her glance at me was icy and suspicious. I told her: "I'll take Nicks for a walk and see what this guy wants." Karyn was chewing some more 'smart ass' gum: "This guy's from the newspaper?"

"The Herald Statesman." Jamie said.

She zeroed in: "This guy's from the 'Hatesman', and he wants one of two things: he wants to sell you an ad, or he wants your story to sell some ads." She looked back at him, "We're living hand to mouth in a sublet, so neither of those things are happening. There's something here my husband knows about your story I guess."

The reporter looked at me from the door; "I got your brother with me in the car......picked him up at the tenement in Hastings across from Ananconda. Ray lives here - doesn't he?"

"He's here on and off. He's got some stuff in the other bedroom." Karyn said.

"I'm a reporter – I don't sell ads."

"Ryan – take Nicole so you don't end up in a bar. I don't want to know what this is about." But she did.

"The car's at the end of the lot." O'Neill said as we left the elevator.

I pushed the stroller and saw Ray waiting against the Plymouth Satellite's front quarter panel. We walked side by side, "Is that yours?" I said.

"Company car." O'Neill got in.

"Ray, you tell this guy anything?"

"Nothing to tell....just a bunch of bits and pieces – goes nowhere. Maybe he's writing for Marvel Comics."

Ray collapsed the stroller and put it in the back seat. I held Nicole as we got in his car. "Take us over to the marina. We'll walk around down there." I offered.

"Which one?"

Ray's eyes rolled and then he shut them, "Tarrytown's."

The cigarettes all came out and we all lit up except for Nicole. I pushed the stroller along the paved asphalt path. It was wide enough to accommodate a cop car or a service truck. There was a nice river breeze. We took a break and sat down at a picnic table.

"You had stopped smoking when you were working on Barb's story."

"Spent three hours in a bar sweating out a story with a witness to a murder about a year ago...." O'Neill shook his head. He combed his hair back with his hand. "So tell me where this goes so I get it right." He took out his notepad.

"There's the river – start fishin' Jimmy Olson." I said.

"I smell a story – a common thread running through all your bullshit. These incidents may be isolated........perhaps they are connected." O'Neill trailed off locked in thought. "The crew you hang with......If I could determine the catalyst for all these occurrences......I think there's a driving force, a cult, a religion. The basis for these oddities isn't for power, money, or fame. I'll concede to you guys right now – I can't connect the dots. Nothing makes sense. I've written a piece titled: 'The Greystone Ghosts'. It reads good enough, but it belongs in the late 1950's editions of 'Renegade Teens' in the back of the magazine. My editor wouldn't print it and neither would the 'Renegade Teens' editor. I need more material.....more first-hand accounts."

The baby started fussing so I gave her a bottle.

"Like to help you Jamie." Ray said as he watched the water. "Some strange things – unexplainable things have taken place and

721

we're as stymied as you. Most of what occurs in life is random. If you are able to make sense of the things we don't understand......and for the lack of a better term you refer to them as 'Life'.........tell us because it would make order out of chaos."

The reporter turned to me, "C'mon Ryan....Ray – you don't have to use any names."

"We never got the enlargements from the train phenomenon." I reminded him.

"Oh yeah......the blow ups."

"Too much overtime with the hippy photographer?" Ray asked.

"I'll get them to you guys.......there is just too much, you two and the rest of your associates have experienced for there not to be some sort of axis which absorbs energy – transforms it, and spits it out." O'Neill reached for his pad again.

I smiled over to Ray, "I like the way that sounds."
It has a touch of veracity to it."

Ray used my line: "Perhaps somewhere down the line we can collaborate on a project?" He gave Jamie a phony grin and the reporter knew it.

O'Neill and Ray dropped me and Nicole off.

As soon as I opened the door, Karyn said: "What'd he want?"

"Mostly to ask Ray how he felt about the collapse of South Vietnam. He was the reporter at the Barb Wells' fire. I suppose he thought I could grease the way for his interview. He wanted to talk to Ray not me."

With 6 months under her belt, Little Nicole looked more like a Cahill everyday. There were some powerful genes at work; Karyn had brought them into the conception arena. My half of the chromosome helix did little more than watch the show. It may have been different if I had all boys – who's to say? In the end it probably was for the best. I was content Nicky was healthy and my karma was continuing. What I found difficult to accept was how I had misread Karyn by such a wide margin. She was going the extra mile to make our marriage work, and doing a lot of the heavy lifting for our family. I don't think either of us counted on this family thing being so intense.

A monthly visit to General Motors/Fischer Body became part of my job search routine. I filled out another application and HR filed it. Mondays and Tuesdays were my weekends unless I caught some work with Palamar Projects with Rex's non-union connection. Nobody with real jobs ever listed them in the classified section of the paper, unless they were forced by some arm of the government. I'd take Nicole for the day and make the rounds: Tarrytown, White Plains, and Yonkers' City Halls for job openings. White Plains was a good one because they listed city, county, and state openings in a three block area of downtown. It was in Yonkers where Cinzo and me saw the openings for Conrail, and told the placement lady we wanted to get a job with them. They told Vinny to come up to Newburgh for an interview. I never heard from them again. It was the same old story for me. Fuck, there never was nothing in N.Y. for me. They forced me to leave.

None of the metro ironworker locals were putting out boomers. I remember Mack saying it was odd that there was no work because this was a presidential election year. Local 40 made you come down to the union hall, they didn't give out any info over the phone. Every other week I'd go downtown to sign the 'Out of Work List'. A couple of times I was so depressed I thought about stopping off at 125th St., but I resisted. Boy, that shit could take your mind off a lot of life's bullshit.

What I couldn't resist was taking a walk over to 42nd St. and check out all the street walkers. By 8th and 9th Aves., there were a ton of flesh peddlers. About half of these hookers were guy-girls. Used to be a guy never had to run a security check on a hooker, but a new regime was running the sex trade from 10th Av. to Broadway. The word to the wise was 'caveat emptor'.

Back on duty I saw Mike Reno in a Main Cab, deadheading down Parkin Plaza. I pulled alongside.

"Whitestar......what's shakin cowboy?"

"Driving for Main?" I rubbed the bottom of my chin – palm down.

"My brother Dennis is getting sued. One of his junkie painters stole some power tools and a motor scooter from a client." Reno hocked up some phlegm.

"Why haven't you hooked up with another contractor?"

"The Reno name isn't what it used to be."

"Ahhhh.....one guilty – all guilty."

"Can't even get a job painting cars, and I painted more cars in North Yonkers than Earl Schrieb. Whitehope, you got any weed?"

"No boo, got some hash." I took a nip of Smirnoff Blue.

"I'm just trying to get through the night – I ain't going to a fuckin concert."

"Reno, just do one mini hit. You'll still be able to drive and make change."

The degraded opium and a ten dollar note were exchanged.

Despite my intentions, the lack of money at home forced me to sell the Tiger Tar from Caesar's chariots. Real dumb move. Request calls were coming into dispatch for me. Their frequency made Linda and Dan Rodan suspicious. They'd seen it before: I'd show up, sell a couple of dimes, and then they'd cancel the ride.

Rodan, Hector, and Luis jumped me one night when I showed up for work. They pinned my face to the garage's concrete wall.

"Empty his pockets." Joe shouted.

"What the fuck Joe?" I yelled back.

"Check his cash box.....frisk him. I know he's fuckin dirty."

After three or four minutes, Luis turned to Dan: "He's clean boss."

His eyeballs squeezed down on me. "This is your last chance doper. I don't know what you're pushing from Caesar's cabs.....but it

723

stops right now or you can tell it to the D.A. cause we're not putting up with that shit. I'll turn your sorry ass in Whitelaw."

"What can I say? To you I'm already guilty." I wiped some blood from the corner of my mouth.

"It stops right now!" he barked. "Take number 23 tonight and make some legitimate money. Get the fuck out of my sight." Rodan pointed towards the entryway.

There wasn't any extra money for anything. Mondays and Tuesdays were my days and nights off. If an opportunity came my way to pick up some extra cash, I always took it. It really was slim pickins out there. We'd play cards and watch Monday Night Football. Three weeks in a row of going over other guy's houses and not playing cards because I was broke was all Vinny Tarts could take. A rainy night on the second Monday in October, and Vinny had enough and broke up the card game.

"Rex – you, Martinique, Crawfish, Holter, me and White-delight are going to ring up Ma Bell. I'm sick of this guy watching the stupid football and looking at skin magazines while we play cards. He looked over to me: "Got any blockbusters left?" Vinny whipped his head.

"Hey – you know it's a felony taking down a pay phone." Jimmy Martin claimed.

"Is not - ya dumb fuck."

"The blockbusters are I meant."

" I'm gonna start callin you Jimmy fucknuckle…..you're wrong again." Rex shook his head and waved him away.

"Okay Jimmy." Catdaddy beaded his eyes and nodded, "You sit tight and watch this barnburner of a game by yourself – we're gonna crack a Ma Bell safe for a brother."

"I'm just saying….." Martin shrugged.

A two car detail of Vincenzo's commandos stopped at 21 to get the blockbusters. Rexall, Martin, and Kenny Crawford were given five blockbusters for the phones down Greystone. I had to give them an extra. Like the Tiger Tar, this stuff was degrading, only at a faster rate. The rest of us went up to Tarrytown, to blow the phones and boxes up in front of the GM plant. The split was going to be at Rex's parent's house in Yonkers. They made me drive around with all the coin boxes in my trunk for a week.

Before the division we decided to buy a $100 U.S. savings bond for Brad Guzzutti jr. His wife, blamed The Rogues for his drug use, unfaithfulness to her; and she felt we were responsible for not being there when the chips were down.

As Rex was handling this savings bond matter, his dislike of his wife had become a personal matter for some unknown reason, and he took it a step further. Rex made himself the beneficiary of the bond in case Brad jr. didn't make it to the age of 18. We didn't have any problem with the way he dealt with the business.

The take on the pay phone heist was almost $400 – after we subtracted the money for Brad jr.'s bond.

Things improved somewhat with Karyn and me. She got a job at the Westchester Premier Theatre with ticket sales and box office. Sinatra, Dean Martin, Sammy Davis jr. played there; as well as Johnny Cash, Linda Ronstadt, Paul Anka, Bette Midler, The Band, Santana, The Kinks, James Taylor and other headliners.

From the day they broke ground on the multi-million dollar theatre, there was a shadow on the enterprise. There were payoffs for their zoning variances, payoffs on building materials and kickbacks for construction contracts, and these were problems before they opened their doors for business. There were quid pro quo's on the theatre's political patronage, and the unions were shook down for the theatre's operation. From the night of the first show; everybody knew there was a reckoning day coming. The operators of the theatre were desperate to show a profit as soon as possible.

Karyn started working there in the middle of September, and we were very slowly able to tread water financially. She was working the angles too. She took every free ticket they offered her and sold them at a discount to her friends and family. As Thanksgiving and Christmas approached, we started getting our rhythm as a family, and we were falling back in love. She still wasn't keen on having Ray stay at the U.N. even though it was on a hit and miss rotation. We called her 'Lil St. Nicks soon after Turkey Day. Karyn dressed her up in green and red outfits whenever we went visiting. Ray would stay over about once a week. He took his shower and would crash, but I think it was more about having time with Nicole, who was now crawling. Karyn thought he was an intruder, but couldn't say shit......he still was paying one third of the rent and wasn't there most of the time. It was a real good deal for us; when he was there, he babysat for free and didn't eat much.

Even though Brad was gone, Ray had gotten recharged by saving his life. This aura of goodness, freedom, and purpose once again neutralized the phantom life. The Fifth dimension were still at level one: they could only find their tranquility through drugs.

It was a big roll of the dice; getting to feel normal Ray's way. He told me he thought he might be protected while undertaking these courageous acts of risking his life. The only way to find out was to die.

By the end of the Christmas season, it seemed like we had a little extra money. The reality was we were only a major car repair, an illness, or an unseen calamity away from being in the poorhouse.

iii

Mom-Mom and Mack had come down to 21 O'Dell on Christmas Day. After they dropped a bomb of gifts, mostly clothes on Nicole, Mack called Ray and me to come downstairs to the cellar.

The radio was playing, I think the Cowboys were playing the Giants; it was one of those teams that always play on holidays. Mack tuned it in, as cover for our conversation. Jane had some food and desserts in the fridge amongst the beer and the wine. Before the roast pork dinner, people were running up and down the steps getting what they needed from the fridge.

Karyn came downstairs: "Hon, did you put that white wine in the fridge or is it outside?"

Ray got up from the laundry sorting table and stood behind Karyn who was bent over looking for the wine. Immediately, the image of Ray grabbing Barb's tits two years ago appeared and had me motionless. Dumbstruck, it obliterated whatever 'now' was.

"Hon?'

"It's in back of that blue Tupperware with the pie on top." Ray pointed.

No way, Ray wouldn't take any of those liberties with Karyn; his rent subsidy didn't buy an ounce of camaraderie. I seriously thought about it: he did come to Tarrytown to see his niece more than he did to see me – but that was okay. She went upstairs with the wine. Ray and me joined Mack at the sorting table.

Mack started, "The time is now guys – Ryan, after New Years, you're going to have to tell Karyn you're boomin out. Naturally she'll blame Ray and me. When you get six months under your belt at that big powerhouse.....Karyn and the kid, she'll be walking by then.......they can move right in with you. Ray, be for the best if you found a different place to live when Karyn comes out. I'll have Edna and Jane talk to Karyn. Hell guys, I started out in Richmond, Virginia. I had to go to where the work was. I'm living proof it can be done." Mack sucked his teeth.

"Karyn knows which end is up. She should be able to roll with the punches." Ray added.

"You're giving me and her a lot of credit Mack."

"Neither of you are moving forward here." he acknowledged tilting his head and raising his brow.

"Not for nothing Mack – but I'm waiting on Ryan."

"It's true Mack, but I've been waiting to hear from you."

"Well – I'm telling you now.......it's time to shit and git. And don't worry about leaving Karyn and Nicole. As long as there's money in the account..... they don't care if you never come back. Women get hung up with that nesting instinct. Just promise them you'll build or buy 'em a house. She'll be happy because she'll think all your wild days will be in the rear view mirror."

"What's our next move?" Ray was anxious.

"Ryan......go get us three shots of Hal's rye whiskey."

When I came back down, the co-conspirators were detailing the plan........."you'll need your birth certificates and drivers' licenses......social security cards......ahhh....Ray....bring your DD 214 separation card. Also, bring all your check stubs from any ironworking job youse ever worked including one dayers, and the lay-off slips. When was the last time you worked for a contractor as an ironworker?"

"Over a year ago."

"The sooner you're in the Midwest the better." he said.

"Come up and see your grandmother and me.......I'll have the hall's address and the name of the guy who will sell you the journeyman cards. Here's how – "Mack held up his shot glass and emptied it. We followed suit. "And get a pick-up truck." he added.

After we kind of half-assed evicted John Dunbar from the U.N., he signed a lease for a small two bedroom tenement on the eastside of the Hudson Line tracks in August. Anaconda had been operating in Hastings in between the rail line and the river ever since Hal could remember.

Our sub-lease at the U.N. turned into a lease with a $25/mo. increase. We weren't looking for an apartment in January, so it looked like Karyn and Nicky would be there for another year, unless she could sublet or break the lease.

Mack kept opening and closing his zippo lighter: "The best time to look for work is when everyone else isn't looking – that means when the weather's for shit."

"These big powerhouses are designed, permitted, and funded years in advance. Once they're moving dirt, the work continues until the two units are running. Boys, these coal-fired units are a thing of beauty."

"I'M GOING WITH RAY UP TO MOM-MOM'S TOMORROW." I broke the news to Karyn.

"Since you're going with your brother, I'm not invited, or I'm not supposed to go – or want to." Karyn was changing Nicky.

"We're staying over one night." I said.

"What about Caesar?

"Told Rodan last night; he was dispatching. Linda had laryngitis – couldn't talk."

"What about Nicks and my work?"

"Either call in or find a sitter. My God, you're not helpless."

"I didn't want to live here ten miles from my family."

"Listen I'm trying to address the proximity problem." I could feel this slipping away from me.

We stopped at Mom-Mom's to get the plan from Mack. He sketched it out: He had spoken to the union hall in Milwaukee. They had a hard winter so far, and it pushed the project behind schedule. The general contractor pouring the main slab hoped to have a portion of it started this week. The structural steel fabricators had no weather constraints; as soon as a sequence was complete - out the door it went, by truck and rail to Pleasant Prairie, Wisconsin. The erector ended up yarding way more steel than he had envisioned; in what used to be cornfields. The project's structural steel erection schedule fell behind because the slab wasn't complete. Mack said sooner or later the job would have to work some serious overtime.

The Milwaukee Business Agent also told Mack there'd be issues with mud if there even was just a moderate amount of rain. "The project's almost two months behind right now." He laughed over the wires at Mack.

727

Mack started giving us the lowdown on buying membership cards in Local 711 Montreal, Quebec. "It should be all set." He took a deep breath.

IT WAS DARK WHEN WE ROLLED IN TO MONTREAL. WE stayed in some ice-box hostel for $7.50 apiece – American. Men were dispatched from the hall from 8 a.m. to 10 a.m. The hall divided itself in two: French and English speaking. The B.A. didn't have any work. Most of the men would try again tomorrow.

When the day room had mostly cleared out, Ray and me walked over to the business window.

"We're here to see Roger Levesque." Ray spoke through the window's hole.

"Speaking." Thick French accent.

"We're from New York to request membership."

"What is your citizenship?"

"American."

"And you?"

"American."

"And neither of you are dual nationals?"

"I'm also alcoholic." I grinned.

"It t'was funny when Monsieur Rick Blaine said it, but you are not." Roger continued writing.

Ray rolled his eyes and shook his head.

Levesque directed us to come into a hallway. A door opened and he waved for us to come in. "Shut the door and have a seat. Your contact told you to bring birth certificates; let me have them." He gave them to a secretary, and said something in French. He turned towards us; "Clifford McKay, Book #194671, Newburgh, N.Y. This is your grandfather?"

"Yes."

"You are brothers – yes?"

"Yes."

"And your raison for obtaining membership is to skip apprenticeship?"

"No. That's not true." I said. "I tried to get in the apprenticeship programs in Locals : 417, 40, 361, 11, 580, and 197. The answer was always the same: 'We're not accepting applications for apprenticeship at this time.'

"Then what is your raison to ask for membership in a union in a country that will not allow you to legally look for work?"

"He's got a kid who's almost 12 months old and a wife and they like to eat." Ray turned it up a little.

"You are the older brother?"

"Qui."

"Listen Roger, I don't have a chance, waiting in any union hall, trying to go to work on permit. Been there – done that. You B.A.'s will put a millwright with a book to work before he hires me off the street."

728

"Just a minute Yankee – we do have our standards. A journeyman millwright has less standing in this union hall than you Monsieurs Whitelaws." We all laughed even though I knew it wasn't true.

"The initiation fee is $300, dues are $25/mo. You are required to pay 6 months dues in advance. Remember: if your dues are six months and one day late, your membership will be suspended, and you will have to return here to get reinstated. Also, when you mail your dues, they have to cross the border. Pay in advance and don't fall into arrears. Pay your dues before you pay your rent. I need $450 from each of you in cash – in U.S. currency." Levesque added: "I give you temporary paper indicating you are journeyman ironworkers of Local 711. Your cards with your book numbers, and receipts for everything will be mailed to your residence from international headquarters."

After the business had been transacted he asked, "May I give you some advice?"

"Anything would be appreciated." Ray replied.

"If either of you had 1" plate welding papers, I could have put you to work today - if you were Canadian."

"It's good to know. Merci beaucoup."

"Welding skills will unlock many doors for you in this or any trade."

"Thanks again." Ray said.

We got back to the U.N. around 9 that night. We planned on leaving April 15 for Wisconsin.

ST. PATRICK'S DAY 1977; I STILL HADN'T TOLD KARYN about booming out to Wisconsin, about 1000 miles west, to find work in my grandfather's trade. She knew one of us was going to have to be the breadwinner in our small family. Back then, women had a hard time breaking into the jobs traditionally held by men. Karyn was smart enough to break down some of these barriers, and I didn't think I had a hang-up with being a house-husband, if she had come home with the bigger paycheck.

Caesar's dispatch office was a-buzz with all the St. Paddy's money out there. It was a smart move showing up early; everybody who drove for Caesar wanted a piece of the big money day. Most of the action came from being hailed on the street. There were very few radio calls except the regulars: nurses, dancers, barmaids.

It's was a big day for Brother Ray as well. Ray's birthday was on the 18th, and he could be counted on to go on a two day blower. After 14 hrs. behind the wheel, I was ordered by Dan Rodan to bring #16 back to the stable. What a night.

Exhausted, and experiencing sleep depravation, I stopped at 21 before I went back home. Hal had gone to work, Jane and Ray were having breakfast. He was drunk, but coherent. Mom laughed at everything he said. A week earlier he went back to his G.I. buzz cut. When his hair was short, he never seemed as wasted.

"How 'bout it Ryan.....would you join your mother and me in a birthday toast to meself?" Although he'd have blown a 1.7 BAC, his eyes radiated that Irish glow.

"You turning up the Irish?......we're only a quarter Ray." I gave him a sarcastic look.

"What'll you have?"

"Just coffee."

"A little Irish mist?" he smiled. "For me birthday Lad." He reached in the inside pocket of his tweed sport jacket and started to pour with the cap on.

"Alright Ray......just one. I'm beat man. I had enough of the celebration last night; I only had a couple. Had a group of high school kids who couldn't hold their liquor. The one girl hurled in the back seat."

'Nice." He washed down some eggs and toast with a bottle of Schaefer; the two drinks going at the same time.

"What time did you leave Tarrytown?" I asked.

"Your lovely wife put the child to bed. I went over to West Towne Liquors and got a bottle of JJ-Twelve."

"You should lay off the hard stuff Ray." Jane lit a cigarette.

"Lemme see one of them Mom."

She tossed the pack across the table. "Look what it's done to your father." she added.

"How much Irish Karyn got?"

"All I can get in her."

"Ryan!" Jane blushed.

I was too tired to do more than grin. "Remember that cop down on Hawley......Danny ......?"

"Yeah......Danny Krysler."

"He gave that one to me." I nodded and grinned this time. "Wonder where he went?" There was a pause. "Tell you what: I don't think she's too thrilled with being a Whitelaw."

Jane pointed with her coffee cup: "Any last name is good as long as you don't have to say it twice."

"But Mother," Ray continued the performance, "You will agree – love always rules in the final consideration?"

"Of course."

"How did it go with Karyn? " Ray came out of character. He waited and said: "You didn't tell her."

Jane's face deadpanned. "I don't like the sound of this."

"We're less than a month away from leaving for the Badger state Ryan.......you've got to come clean with her boy."

"Motherfucker." I turned to Jane and apologized.

"Dude - what's right is right; you can't drop it on her a week before we figured on leaving. She's working, and takes care of Nicole, she's going to have to set up daycare; plus all the jobs you normally do, will be her responsibility now."

"So you told her we were boomin' out?" I tried to focus.

"It's not fair and it's not right to pull some kind of disappearing act." Ray hiccupped. "What did you think you were going to do - call Karyn when we got to Cleveland?"

"I dunno......at least I know what I am walking into, but I sure as hell can't get my story together on the way home."

"Let me know if you need me to talk to Karyn......try to get her to talk to me." Jane offered.

The clock radio said I was running late. "Happy Birthday Ray" He was 24. I tagged Jane's cheek with a kiss.

"Give Nicky a kiss and hug for me." Jane said.

"We're having a few friends getting together over at Susan's Bar in Hastings for a little party tonight. Dunbar's rented out one of the tenements on the third floor."

"How convenient.......get drunk down stairs sleep it off upstairs." Mom said.

"Sounds similar to the situation here." I chuckled. "Whose going to be there?"

"Dunbar; the O'Rourke's – Sean for sure/Michael maybe; Jimmy Blanko; Vinnie Ricciardi; and four or five other maybes."

"I got to drive tonight. If I get some dead heading time I'll stop in – no promises. Anaconda's right across the tracks?"

"Yup. Hey Mom, the place reminds me of your old studio on Broadway down Getty Square.....no elevator – same squeaky stairs."

"Cheapest rent in Hastings – rail connection. How's Dunbar find these places?" I said. "Why you moving in with John?"

"If Wisconsin doesn't work out, we'll stop at Purdue on the way back and I sign up for the summer session." Ray said.

I said good-bye again, this time it stuck.

Karyn was hungover from the little St. Patty's party with my brother. Most likely she had been bored.......bored enough to have a few with Ray. She didn't like being in debt to him, though his money was given freely. Karyn wasn't interested in furthering her relationship with him. Having him as Nicole's uncle was enough. I had hoped for something like the relationship Ray had with Barb Wells. It wasn't happening.

As I walked into the apartment, I was handed Nicole: hungry, crying, and a full diaper. "We'll talk when I get home."

"Right." I said.

She went to work and so did I. It took me about an hour to get Nicks squared away and in the playpen. She was watching 'Rocky and Bullwinkle' on the tube. I slept until she woke me up for lunch.

Back and forth the toddler was 'Hot Potatoed' until one of us had a day off.......and the showdown could get started; and it did.

"Karyn – once I get out there and get a place and settle in; then we can start living like a family.....on our own. We can't rely on anyone but ourselves now."

"What am I supposed to do out there?" she said.

"No matter what, it's got to be simpler. Ray will be there to help out."

"Great --- we'll be all alone on this winter frontier, but Ray will be there to tell you what to do.........as usual."

"At least there's blood to help out if we get in a jam."

"What about me? What about my life?"

"We kind of screwed our lives up for the next 20 years. Once we get squared away, we'll have another kid or two; and then we'll have our time on the other end. We don't want to have the kids too far apart in age anyway. I'm nine years older than Willis - I'm still waiting for him to catch up."

"You got OUR LIVES ALL PLANNED OUT." Karyn steamed.

"I don't know what else to say or do."

"Ryan, I'm with you on this – this one time. I'll do what I have to do, to make this work. If it goes bust – I'm taking the baby and going back to New York and we're done."

"Hey – thanks for putting it all on me."

"Well, you're the one with the big master plan."

"I thought we were in it together for the long haul."

"It's been nothing but a long haul since we had Nicole."

"Look where it can lead ....Look at Mom-Mom and Mack. They started out the same way; I'd say they've made a good life.......they're happy." I said.

"That was a different time. What you're chasing is a dream - not a goal......you don't know the difference." It wasn't just an answer; I was getting thrown a small helping of attitude.

"Listen, Sheila," I pointed at her: "In case you haven't figured it out, this N.Y. scene is nothing but a maze for rats. It's not for you, the kid, or us. Ray and me are leaving on the 15th. If it doesn't work out, it won't be from the lack of trying or ambition. I'm going there to start our lives and make a home for us; neither of which we currently possess. It'll be okay......you'll see. I'll be back Fourth of July weekend. I'll set up a checking account with a bank that has branches in New York and Milwaukee. You'll have a checkbook to pay our bills here. Don't worry it's going to work out.....you'll see."

"This I've got to see." She looked out the window in disbelief: "You don't know how to balance a checking account.......you've never even had one."

"Maybe so, but I can get those deadbeat drunks, hookers, and junkies to pay their cab fare." I went outside and had a smoke in the Starfire, wondering if she was right. I had to trust Mack. I had to trust Ray. I had to start believing in myself. I had to do it for Karyn and Nicole.

IN APRIL, WE HAD A SMALL BIRTHDAY PARTY FOR NICKY. She was walking better than she was talking. She had about a 20 word vocabulary; it might have been larger if Karyn and me had been better parents – taken time to teach her. It had to come together for us and it had to start before Ray and me left for Wisconsin. There was nothing in N.Y. for them or me. I didn't know anything. The only connections I had were with people who sold drugs.

The three of us drove up to Staatsville so we could say goodbye to my grandparents, and get some last minute advice. Edna took Karyn and Nicky to the little house in the back. Later on Karyn said Mom-Mom was mentally preparing her for the separation.

Mack and me went out to the driveway. "Make sure your next car is a truck.......no more of these low-riders." He reminded me.

His hand felt the corner of the car and walked it down to the taillights. "I remember teaching Barb to park this boat." It gave Mack a laugh. It made me laugh too.

"This was a car for her.....She was all wild. I thought you'd get up for work one day and your car would be missing."

"Thought the same shit myself."

"Edna even liked her.....pioneer spirit - try anything."

"Mom-Mom had that right."

"Miss her?"

"Miss her bad, Mack."

"All Mustang."

I stood frozen.

"Got to let it go Ryan."

"One good thing is I'm too busy to really concentrate on the hurt: the kid, Karyn, the move, the roll of the dice, the trade. But thank God for Ray.....couldn't even think about the boom out there without him. And you Mack ....from the bottom of my heart; I've got to thank you and Mom-Mom. Barb is still there haunting me at times. Leaving N.Y. is for the best."

We started to go over some of the more important things in the driveway: crane signaling, tying various knots, rigging for steel erection; in general, re-familiarizing myself with what I had learned at the hospital's powerhouse in Poughkeepsie. Mack had made a list for me of the important stuff I had to know because I was essentially misrepresenting myself as a journeyman, when I really wasn't. He gave me this paperback: "Boilermaker's Handbook for Riggers." The cover said Boilermakers, but it was mainly a manual for riggers of all crafts. I reviewed it every chance I got. When I wasn't reading it, Ray was. He said Herman Melville had written the same type of informational trade book with his masterpiece, "Moby Dick". "Everything you wanted to know about whaling was contained in that book." he said.

"Welding is like riding a bike." Mack said, "Once you have the basics down you never really lose the skill. Ask the erector or the power company if you can brush up on your welding after work."

"Listen Ryan: If the hall sends you out as a weldor........ the weld test will be on a make or break basis. If you bust out – there might not be a call in the hall for a couple of weeks."

"Just what I need – more pressure." I sucked in some air.

"Hang tough Ryan. You've got that sixth sense to be a good ironhead. Your brother went through the war; I know he's got what it takes."

iv

I went into dispatch and told Dan Rodan I was dragging up, and my last day would be Easter Sunday. It was about a week away.

"So what? ....you'll be back – you ain't got the smarts to do anything else.......we're all you got. I'll write it down........for Caesar. He might not take you back next time."

Ray, Dunbar, and a couple of others went to the Yankee game on Easter Sunday. They wanted me to go. We'd be leaving for the Midwest in just a few days. Karyn needed me to get things squared away here and give her all the reassurance about living alone with Nicky that I could. I knew it was 81% bullshit. There wasn't anything I could say to make her feel better about the venture. For me, it was just one fucked up episode after another, and it was better that I leave so I could screw up and melt down in front of people I didn't know.

It's like trying to say good-bye; the longer it takes the harder it becomes. We should have just got it over and done with. Karyn had to be hoping there would be some change of heart, or intervening circumstance to turn this thing around. A few days before Easter, we stopped talking, and stayed away from each other in bed. Each thought the other was selfish, and if it wasn't business or related to Nicole - there was no conversation.

Before I went in for my last night of driving, we went down to 21 for Easter dinner. A cloud hung over everything; even Hal was unable to deepen the darkness with his usual bullshit about how he was great, and the rest of us were a bunch of screwups.

Jane had a regular dinner prepared, no special holiday items except a prime rib roast. She made two extra plates for Ray and John and covered them with aluminum foil to heat them up when they returned from the game. We got back to Tarrytown around 4:30. Doom and gloom filled our every thought. She was frightened and I was frightened for her.

By 9:00 o'clock I had only booked 7 fares. I had a notion it'd be slow, but not this slow. Just staring out the windshield at Sinatra's Funeral home parking lot, I hoped another driver would see me deadheading and pull in and kill some time shooting the shit. Nothing.....nobody. Karyn and me probably would have been better off being apart before we left for Wisconsin. It would just be another thing coming back at me later on. Five days until we'd leave. I'd have to "yes dear" it to death, until the 15th.

Every nervous ounce of energy racked my brain; there would be no relief until I achieved what I set out to do. Living with Karyn, I could tell her how things would change, but could do nothing to make them change. We were at a point neither of us anticipated. Nicole kept us together and simultaneously drove us apart.

Suffering alone, I knew I loved them both, but Karyn's doubt in me made me doubt myself. This wasn't like driving around the country two years ago; I only had to rely and worry about myself. Now I was responsible for two other people. The one person giving me the strength to move forward was Ray.

CAESAR HAD HIS OWN GAS PUMPS. WHEN YOU DROVE for him, he paid for the gas. After a while I had to cruise around to keep my mind active and off the coming separation. It helped somewhat. I got hailed outside 'The Story Untold', an after hours club. I cut a deal with the client and left the flag up. On the books money came out to $26.30 for the 12 hour shift. I had pinched another $15.00. A guy couldn't raise a family on that kind of money, not even in Iowa. It was damp and kool when I pulled into Caesar's garage. I went through dispatch/end of shift, to turn in my booking sheet and divide up the nightly receipts with the office.

Trying to make as little noise as possible I entered our apartment. It was a little before 7:00 a.m. The days were getting longer and the sun was already coming into our living room. Mother and daughter got up about a half-hour later. I had been asleep for only 15 minutes before the two got up.

"I'll change and feed her."

"Thanks." She went into the bathroom and took care of business, and put her face on.

I put Nicks in her high chair and gave her some apple sauce and oatmeal. Her teeth had started to come in; they were making her cranky. There wasn't much baby food in the cupboard. We'd have to walk to the grocery store after Karyn went to work.

Karyn made her hair big; she looked too good for work. With me leaving in four days, I assumed we'd be using every spare minute making love and satisfying our needs. It was going to be a long spell between April 15 and July 4th. Our bed was on single function capabilities since I broke, or Ray broke the news to her about booming out. I'm pretty sure she had called me Mr. Disappointment on the phone when she thought I was sleeping one night.

"No.....he's fine in bed. He's just depressed he can't find a real job."

Karyn was almost out the door. I put Nicole's winter coat on and would take a blanket for the stroller.

"Is Ray here?" I spoke softly.

"He might be in his room. I never heard him come in last night."

"He said he was bringing some of his stuff up from 21 he was going to take on Friday."

She stiffened every time the subject of Wisconsin came up.

I pushed the stroller into the lobby and Karyn kissed Nicky bye-bye. "See you tonight." she said.

"Right." I waved as she drove out of the parking lot. Me and Nicole had about a three mile round trip walk ahead of us. The sun was trying, but there wasn't much warmth. By the time we returned we were zonked.

The phone rang. Nicole was in the playpen messing with her blocks and watching a 'Wacky Racers' repeat. I continued laying on the couch and blindly searched the end table over my head for the phone with my hand.

"Yeah?" I thought it might be Rex with a one day job for me.

"Ryan?" the woman's voice spoke. I couldn't have gone to work today anyway, with nobody to babysit. Perhaps Ngyuen could watch Nicky for me.

The voice was kind of familiar. "Yeah, you got him."

"Ryan ......" the voice froze.

Now I recognized the voice. It was Judy Conolly: Jane's best friend......what did she want?

"My Mom isn't here Judy." I stated.

"No – I know."

"What's up.....Karyn's at work too."

"Your mother's here......she needs to talk to you."

Even though I was still in the forest chopping wood, there was something about this phone call. The moment I picked up, the call smelled, sounded, and tasted bad. I tried to lighten it up, "Whatsamatter.......did Jane break her hand, why you got to call for her?"

"Here's Jane."

"Ryan........." Long pause.........real long pause. I could hear her gasping for air as well as her nose running. She wouldn't be this broke up about Hal; what the deuce? Was it Ray, Cathy, or Brother Bill? I knew it was a bad harbinger when I I.D.'d Judy's voice. Now I waited for the 88 lbs. of TNT. "Yeah Mom, I'm here. How bad is it?" I tried to soften the blow.

"The worst."

"Ray?"

"He's gone."

I was confused, this might not be so bad. "Whaddaya mean? He ran away?" I laughed. "He can't run away – he's 24 years old. He'll be okay. Did he leave a note?"

"Ryan !!!" she screeched......."He died in a car wreck last night......He's gone!"

"Impossible." I simply rejected the reliability of her information and statement, and hung-up on her.

No matter how I wanted to frame it - I had been here before; I knew it to be all too real. I could only see Vinny telling me about Barb Wells, Issac Seabrook, the faces of Z-man, Sally Englund, young Presto Busch, and Brad Guzzutti. I knew there would be more. I changed Nicole's diaper, with the phone squeezed between my head and shoulder and put her back in the playpen with a bottle of milk. A pint bottle of Canadian mist was on the counter. There was less than a half-a-pint remaining. I poured it in a tub glass with a couple of cubes. "That's enough of this shit," and placed the hand piece in the phone's cradle.

The phone rang again. This time it was my Uncle Bill: "Ryan, listen to me boy. Ray was in a bad car wreck last night – he died in the collision. There's nothing left of the car. The guy he went to Australia with was driving. He was thrown from the vehicle.......walked away with a couple of scratches."

With the phone to my ear, I tried to push my drink into my forehead. I crouched over: "What the fuck Uncle Bill?" I squeezed down on my eyelids as hard as I could.

"Janey needs you down here – bring the baby and Karyn. Listen Ryan, do you need a ride......you okay to drive?"

"We'll get down there as soon as we can."

"See you then."

"Right."

I hung up the phone and disconnected it from the wall. I grabbed hold of Nicole and pulled her from the playpen, and we sat on the couch together and I ran my fingers through her black hair and sang some nursery rhyme to her. I hugged her and stroked her hair until she fell asleep. I followed her five minutes later.

Time was losing its relevancy; she had crawled out of my arms and was playing with a squeeze toy outside the playpen. The toy wheezed and she smiled at me when she saw me awake. Physically, I must have been there because I was aware of my daughter, but I also was in a deep state of shock. A force or a being from a distant galaxy or perhaps an angel sent by the Almighty guarded Nicole as I battled with demons which neither could be seen nor destroyed.

Losing Barb was beyond whatever I thought I might be able to endure. Her loss was incalculable; two years later - I continued to be haunted. Other than Ray, she was the only person I really knew; and now I would be only able to revisit either of them with my memories as long as I continued to breathe.

Hearing Ray had checked out in a car wreck was much different than Sylvia's account of how her sister had dispatched Butchie Powell while saving lives in a burning house. My brother's death was senseless, and this made it all the worse. The loss could not be quantified.

There wasn't a shred of logic to this death, just an instance of pure vaporization of his essence. Hadn't Ray cheated death in Nam, as well as with his formless vapid junkie friends? Or had the Grim Reaper come in the midnight hour to collect a debt that was stamped 'PAST DUE'?

Watching Nicole watching me – I began to well up. My face turned into a gross mask of grief. A scream erupted from deep within the depths of my soul:"Rrrraaaayyyy!!! Yyyyyyoooouuuuu Mmmuuutttthhhaaaffffuuuccckkkaaahh!!!"

I buried my face in my hands and wept uncontrollably until I realized the kid was crying with me. I gave her a bottle of apricot juice while I changed her again, even though she was dry. We shared a bowl of spaghetti. I took the stroller and we walked over to West Towne liquors and I bought a pint of Early Times. I was aware enough; I knew I couldn't get wasted because I had to drive to Yonkers soon. The whiskey would be on standby under the seat in the Starfire. I knew I wasn't going to be able to deal with whatever I was walking into.

Karyn was speechless: I waited for some type of response. I told her to meet us down 21 whenever she left work.

Finally: "Do you need me now?"

"I'm leaving around three. Jane might need your help and Nicky will be a good distraction. I doubt you'll be able to focus at work anyway; why don't you leave now, I'll meet you down 21. He's not going to get any deader........And tell your folks for me, will you?"

"I'll leave in about a half hour." She said.

"Thanks Karyn."

737

Getting ready and getting Nicole's baby bag squared away was a confused circus. I packed diapers, jars of food, extra clothes, and two bottles of milk; as long as we had clean clothes and she had a clean diaper - when we walked in - that would be good enough. I was mentally shattered and drank a beer. I didn't want to hit the hi-test yet.

It wasn't easy leaving the building or parking lot. It took longer than I anticipated for reasons that escape me. Some of Ray's favorite tunes were unconsciously thrown into the eight track tape deck. I balled after each selection: 'Rael' by the Who, 'Dark Star' by the Grateful Dead', and 'I Just Wasn't Made For These Times', by the Beach Boys. Over and over I played these three tracks. We drove to the grocery store and I got a quart of beer and a roll of Goya Maria crackers for Nicole and went back to the U.N. parking lot. Parking with the engine facing away from the apartment, I was able to open the hood and take a whizz in the Starfire's front grill. Sitting behind the wheel, I looked at Little Nicky riding shotgun in her car seat; she gave me this stare of prescience. It unnerved me. I had to get down to 21. It was almost 3 o'clock, once we were on Broadway heading south I wailed out the window with the heater on full blast:
"Ray….Ray….Ray….Ray –Rrrrraaaayyyyy!"

V

It was extremely difficult to dissect the passage of time. It was only through the continuous playing of the three songs that I recognized another half-hour had elapsed; the rest of it was all gobblygook. Karyn met us at 21. The house was full of relatives and Jane and Hal's close friends. Someone took Nicole from me once I was in the foyer. I scanned around looking for Hal. I didn't see him anywhere on the first floor. In the kitchen, I immediately saw Jane sans her aura. 'This is really bad I said to myself'. The crowded kitchen parted; I gave Jane a long …..long hug. She asked me not to leave her side.

"Mom, many of these people want to be near you too, and Ray's and my friends want to express their sympathy also. Are you going to be alright?"

She acknowledged my reasoning, "If I'm slipping – I'll call for you."

"We'll get through this somehow. Is Hal around, I haven't seen him?" I squinted…...searching.

"Uncle Bill said, he was in his car listening to the radio. Your father must have bought a bottle on the way home, though I didn't tell him why he had to come home." She had to give him the news in the driveway. "He was still there last time I saw, he's probably passed out."

"I'll check it out."

My sister was being consoled by a slew of older girls from the dance studio. I hugged her and kissed her forehead. No words……..just tears. I asked my cousin Neil, where Willis was.

"He's upstairs with Tommy Capps in his room."

The two teenagers were sitting on the floor dazed, like each had taken an upper cut from 'Smokin Joe' Frazier. Both had a beer. Billy shielded his face with his hands when he saw me. Tommy took a deep breath, after he stood up.

"Some fucked up shit." Tommy extended his hand….."Real sorry about you guys' loss." We heard Willis whimpering as he sat against the wall. "We're all broke up." Tommy nodded.

Picking up a PB&J sandwich from a plate next to Billy, I twisted off one of their beers. The bread was getting stale and I made it disappear in six bites. Brother Bill asked, "Did you see the car?"

"No." I extended my hand and pulled him up and hugged him tight. My eyes got wide at an imagined crinkle cut French fry.

"Come on we'll show you." His voice shuddered.

"I can't believe the other guy walked away." Tommy shook his head a couple of times. We made our way through the house and out the cellar. Uncle Bill had been right about Hal; he was slumped over with the radio playing.

We got in the Starfire and drove up O'Dell Ave. retracing the death route.

I asked Tommy: "What grade you in now?"

"Be a junior next year." I looked over at Billy: "and you'll be a freshman."

He nodded.

"The cops estimated the car was doing over 80 mph on impact."

We turned left onto to North Broadway at the top of the hill. I was cruising pretty slow on the right so cars could pass. I was looking for anything relating to last night's wreck. We were at the crest of the hill on North Broadway.

"They came down this hill pretty fast. There's the low spot where Tompkins Ave. tee's into Broadway." Tommy said.

"And there's the first skid mark." Billy directed my attention on the left side.

"Right." I said.

Tommy pointed. "Broadway divides here into two-lane/one way traffic." I slowed even more and he said: "And there." he pointed again, "are the first real skid marks. The car hops the curb and he's got two wheels in the grass and two on the pavement……and……there's the maple tree, and the stone pillars of the old estate….. an……." Tommy ran out of his version of wreck.

"We'll go around and park on Tompkins. There's too much traffic to explain this from the car." I said.

We walked the short distance to the accident scene dodging traffic. It looked like the accident was roughly a 70 yard long event. A blink of an eye for a car doing 80 mph. The three of us reconstructed the way we thought it occurred.

It appeared John Dunbar lost control as the car sped down the lazy hill leaving Yonkers and entering Hastings. He must have gotten back into the throttle as the Plymouth Fury hop-skipped into the grass on the passenger's side, while the driver's side wheels remained on the pavement. There were tire marks all along the curb as well as in the grass and indicated the forward motion. "It's hard to figure out what Dunbar was doing at this point." They both nodded agreement.

"Just take a look Ryan: the tracks say the car is going to crash head on with that big maple." Willis points to the tire grooves in the grass and bare ground."

"Yeah but - 10 feet in front of the tree, the car fishtails for some reason and turns perpendicular to the road." Tommy squints and tilts his head.

"And crashes into the tree broadside."

"The bark's all gone." I was amazed as the reconstruction began to coalesce in my mind: A horrific wreck had been Ray's undoing. The three of us hardly saw the rush hour traffic whizzing by.

For a tenth grader, Tommy Capps must have read a lot of highway patrol stories – he didn't stop there: "The car's momentum crashed it into this brick entrance pillar just beyond the maple tree of the old estate on the passenger's side – then ricocheted directly opposite to the other side of the road continuing into the companion pillar that once held the old entrance gate."

"And that's where the car came to rest." Billy pointed.

The alcohol I drank didn't help my dissection of the wreck. With the speculative evidence Tommy and Billy offered, the one thing eluding me was the Plymouth's orientation at various points during the wreck. But I could see what Tommy Capps said: the Fury's tire tracks had it going into a head-on collision with the maple tree. The tire skid marks said the car was facing west just prior to impact with the maple, again - just as he said. It seemed as though the car had been picked up from a gameboard and set in a new position. The bluecoats had to have some better explanations than we could conjure up. This was their area of expertise.

"Did you talk to the cops?" I asked Billy.

"They only talked to Mom and Dad."

"What'd they say.......did you overhear anything?"

"They chased me away. Hey, he's my brother too!" He kicked a stray lug nut.

"Where's what's left of the car now?"

"That Mobil station - across from St. Matthew's."

"We're gonna take a look." We walked back to the Olds and drove until Warburton Ave. merged into Broadway on the north side of town, where the service station was.

You couldn't miss it. The Fury had a classic case of schizophrenia: Dunbar's side was a cream puff. Ray's side might have come out on the short end of a tank engagement at the Battle of Kursk. The dashboard was in the front seat and the passenger rocker had collapsed into the middle of the car.

Many passerbys took a hard look, and were immobilized. They shook their heads in disbelief. I could read their looks: "What a shame." The rear driver's side tire was the only one which wasn't flat. Two blaze-orange tags were tied to the bent antenna and steering wheel, as well as an 8"x10" sticker on each side of the car and the trunk lid: "NO TRESSPASSING – NO

TAMPERING..........EVIDENCE OF THE HASTINGS P.D. *Capt. Craig Boland - H.P.D.* April 11, 1977.

The police department had to use magic marker to write on the Plymouth's hood because there was nowhere to put the hood's evidence sticker. It looked like a crunched up piece of paper.

"Holy fuckin' – fuck.......Ray never stood a chance." Billy and Tommy looked away after stealing quick glances.

This was the second time for them, they hadn't gotten this close on their initial visit with Uncle Bill. Willis tried to get close, but could only get so far. Tommy got close enough to look inside. He pulled his head out of the car and called me over. There was some personal stuff strewn about the car. It was Ray's; he was bringing this stuff to Tarrytown to take with us to Kenosha. Ray may have told me he was going to stay at Dunbar's place in Hastings for the night. He had been doing a round-robin of places to crash: 21, the U.N. and now the Anaconda Arms. This place might have been a fall back in case Wisconsin was a bust and Purdue didn't work out.

I could see work boots, books, dungarees, an am/fm radio, a duffle bag. The stuff looked like it was something a person would bring on a temporary work assignment. Travel light, and it was less to bring back in case things went to shit.

Once again Tommy turned away from the Fury, "Bad enough Ray goes for a ride with the Reaper, no – that ain't enough."

"What do you mean?" I frowned.

"He's up at Valhalla getting sliced open." Willis reported.

"For the love of fuck man – he can't get any deader." I winced and shook my head.

"Some statute about getting killed in a moving vehicle that they got to do an autopsy on the deceased." Tommy said.

It sounded like he knew what he was talking about.

"We gotta stop at police headquarters and find out when they plan on releasing the Fury." I said. "We got to get back home." I needed some Quaaludes or Valiums to make it any further into this odyssey. I had to calm down and catch my breath.

BACK AT 21 O'DELL, THINGS HADN'T CHANGED, BUT MY wish had come true; someone was passing around their monthly script of Valium. The straightest people there were my Uncle Bill, the detective with the Port Authority of N.Y. & N.J., and one year old Nicole. Hal made it back into the house to piss, but had left the radio playing.

As far as I was concerned, it wasn't fate or chance that brought back the Bad Brad knifing. Something else was at work here. What was inconceivable to Hal and me, was how Ray could do more than a year in Vietnam and make it home - only to die in an auto accident. The old man was now an old man, he was more than heart broke........ From my perspective, emotionally, he never really recovered.

The next day, Hal was notified Ray's body and the car would be released on the 14th, and the death certificate would be sent to the funeral home. The wake would be on Friday and the burial on Saturday.

Thursday morning, Uncle Bill walked me outside to the porch where Linda Conroy read me the riot act five years earlier. We sat at a small patio table with a glass top. He placed a manila envelope on the table.

"What's this?"

"Dunbar's statement." He got up. "I'm going to get a couple of cups of coffee, want anything else?"

"Did you read it?"

"Yeah."

"Did Hal or Jane?"

"No. They had me read it. They said to let them know if there was anything in it that sounded fishy. Otherwise, they weren't interested." Uncle Bill said.

"Should I?"

"It's pretty short. You're probably better off reading it and knowing how it went down; rather than wondering for the rest of your life." He walked into the kitchen.

The envelope read:

Deposition of John Carl Dunbar

RE: Events of April 10 & 11, 1977
Pertaining to a vehicular accident resulting in
the death of Raymond Whitelaw.

I took the bound eight page statement from the envelope. It restated the information on the envelope; it also listed the personal information of Dunbar. John answered these queries prior to making his statement. His particulars of identification were detailed: full name, DOB, S.S.#, address, place of birth, marital status, occupation. Briefly, I thumbed ahead to the last page. Each page had been signed and notarized, and seal by Asst. District Attorney, Kitty Stark, for the County of Weschester, State of New York. Also present for the Hastings P.D. – Interrogator: Gary Gray.

DEPOSITION OF JOHN CARL DUNBAR IN THE ACCIDENTAL (pending autopsy findings) DEATH OF RAYMOND WHITELAW (particulars of I.D. provided) on the night of April 10, 1977 @ 11:30 p.m.

Concerned parties present:

Asst. District Attorney Kathryn (Kitty) Stark: Let the record indicate it is 9:30 a.m., on April 11, 1977. The Deposition of John Carl Dunbar, in the matter of the vehicular death of Raymond Whitelaw is being taken at the Hastings City Council chambers, County of Westchester, State of New York.

In attendance are: Mr. Dunbar, Dectective Gary Gray of the Hastings P.D., and Asst. District Attorney Kitty Stark. Also present is court stenograher, James McManus.

D.A. Stark: Mr. Dunbar, Have you brought legal counsel with you?

Dunbar: No.

D.A. Stark: Do you want a lawyer? If you answer no, do you waive your right to legal representation at this inquiry.

Dunbar: I waive my right to counsel.

D.A. Stark: The testimony you provide in this deposition hearing is given freely and without coercion, and shall become part of the permanent   record in the death of Raymond Whitelaw. Do you understand this?

Dunbar: I do.

D.A. Stark: I will administer the oath to John Carl Dunbar: Do you swear
that the testimony you are about to give is the truth, the whole truth, and nothing but the truth.....so help you God?

Dunbar: I do.

  D.A. Stark: Detective Gray proceed with your questioning.

          Uncle Bill came back onto the porch with a couple of cups of coffee. I kept on reading; there was a lot of background material: How long the two knew each other; Education; Was there a common love interest?; Who owned the Plymouth?; Did a finance company or bank hold a note on the car?; Did Ray owe John money and/or Did John owe Ray money?; What was the purpose of the trip to Australia?. These questions and others seemed inconsequential; a good investigator could discern if there was anything suspicious or evasive in Dunbar's answers.
          I looked over at my uncle, "You got two pages left." He nodded at the deposition.

          I resumed reading. The Hastings' cop let John give his account of the accident without interruption for the most part, except to clarify facts such as locations, road conditions, the times, etc.

Dunbar: I truly don't remember how fast we were going. I don't recall looking at the speedometer after the light turned green at O'Dell and North Broadway. We were the only car at the intersection. I turned left to go to our apartment on Washington Ave. in Hastings. It had been a long afternoon at the Yankee game. Ray's mother had some dinner waiting for us.

We tried to watch some TV. Ray argued with his father. His father had been drinking most of the day. I fell asleep on their sofa.

Det. Gray: When did you and Raymond leave the Whitelaw residence?

Dunbar: About 11:15.......11:20

Det. Gray: After you made the left turn to go northbound on Broadway – What was your approximate rate of speed?

   Dunbar: Because of the way O'Dell Ave. is laid out, it is not a continuous street. It intersects with Broadway; you might say the Whitelaw house is on south O'Dell Ave., and north O'Dell would be 25 yards to the north. Both O'Dells 'TEE' at Broadway and have traffic signals. From either O'Dell, if you turn left, you'll always get a red signal on Broadway. I'm just saying – I didn't get into the gas right away.......I mean I had to stop at two traffic lights.

When the second light turned green, I guess I accelerated to the posted speed of 35 mph which increases to 40 mph at the Hastings/Yonkers border.

Det. Gray: Was there any other traffic going in either direction?

Dunbar: Not that I recall. There might have been a couple of cars going southbound......I'm sure there must have been, but the traffic was very light. I can't recall any particular vehicle.

Det. Gray: Is there another traffic signal between the second or the northern portion of O'Dell Ave. and the site of the accident?

Dunbar: No.

Det. Gray: Reviewing the accident scene, we know the car was travelling approximately 70 mph where North Broadway becomes a divided highway. Why would you go so fast? Were you being pursued? What was your reason? Were you just 'hot rodding'?

Dunbar: No. The car started missing when the light turned green. I didn't want it to stall out, so I feathered the gas to keep it lit. Maybe the air/fuel mixture wasn't right.....maybe the fuel filter needed to be changed. I dunno. It's a company car. The carb's linkage wasn't right either when they first gave me the car – and that had been worked on. I was just trying to get us home last night.

744

Det. Gray: When you referred to the "carb" You mean the engine's "carburetor"?

Dunbar: Right.

Det. Gray: Why didn't you pull over and open the hood?

Dunbar: I'm a salesman – not a mechanic.

Det. Gray: What do you sell?
Dunbar: Paint to auto shops and stores, hardware stores, and industry.

Det. Gray: When did the speed of your car go over the posted limit?

Dunbar: I'm not sure. I don't recall how fast we were going. The car's steering was unresponsive and it significantly compromised the car's handling.

Det. Gray: The most common reaction to a poor handling car is to reduce speed.

Dunbar: Yes, but if I did that, the engine probably would have konked out, and it would have made the handling even worse because I would have no power steering.

Det. Gray: Cars breakdown all the time. You guys could have walked back to Ray's house and gotten a ride, or walked to the Washington Ave. Your actions don't make sense.

I thought the statement was entering the point of absurdity. I stood up and stretched.
        "You've got a page-and-a-half left." Uncle Bill said.
        "Does it get any better...........I know how it ends already."
        "Finish it." I slugged down half a cup of lukewarm coffee; and picked up where I left off.

Dunbar: Ray shouted to stop the car, but I thought I could get it running smooth if I gave it more gas. And it started taking off – running properly....it seemed, but it was only for a few seconds; it was like the car was super-charged; and the speed increased before I took my foot off the gas.

Det. Gray: What kind of transmission did the car have?

Dunbar: It was an automatic: Dynadrive.....Magnatorque.....I don't know for sure.

Det. Gray: Let the record indicate the car Mr. Dunbar was driving was equipped with an automatic transmission.

D.A. Stark: So noted. Please continue with your testimony Mr. Dunbar.

Dunbar: We reached the top of the hill by the Andrus Home......the orphanage. I believe the car was already out of control. I was sure I was doing everything possible to regain control at that point. As we came down the lazy hill - we were rapidly gaining speed. I am positive I had been applying the brakes.....it has power brakes. No way could I have been pushing the gas pedal by mistake. We hit a bump at the bottom of the hill around Tompkins Ave. and Ray's side jumped the curb and was in the grass for a second or two. We knew there was going to be an impact. Ray threw this box of light at me and screamed: "You idiot!" It clocked me in the head.

D.A. Stark: Record will indicate the witness is pointing to a recent contusion on his right temple.

Dunbar: And that was when time stopped. The car had been turned 90 degrees to the left, and the accident continued in real time. The car broadsides a big maple tree and goes across the road, into a grassy area and smashes into one of the old estate entrance pylons. I was thrown clear of the car; when I came to - the movement of the car and time had ceased. My only explanation of what took place was:

I was knocked out, blacked out, and delivered to a different reality by some unknown force.

Det. Gray: When did you bother to check on Mr. Whitelaw's condition?

Dunbar: I don't believe I was unconscious or in this nether world for too long. There wasn't anyone there yet. I walked around the car a couple times. Then I saw him. The passenger door was in two pieces. The hinged part had broke off and was impaledin his chest. I tried to stop the bleeding. You couldn't move him, he was jammed by the bent metal. I couldn't budge him. I started crying and prayed to the Blessed Virgin to save my friend. I sat on a large fieldstone a few feet away and waited for someone to help.

Det. Gray: Why did you stop with your life saving measures?

Dunbar: His head was facing the wrong way in relation to his body. Plus the door was sticking almost through his chest. Only God or a saint could have helped.

Det. Gray: Did either of you ingest any hallucinogenic substances yesterday....ah... April 10th, 1977?

Dunbar: No sir.

Det. Gray: Did any police officer or medical personnel perform any sobriety or toxicology tests at the scene or at the police station?

Dunbar: No sir. I will tell you what I have told everyone else: We weren't drunk.

D.A. Stark: Will you submit to a toxicology test for this deposition?

Dunbar: I have no problem with that.

D.A. Stark: Is there further questioning for John Carl Dunbar?

Det. Gray: Not at this time.

D.A. Stark: Mr. Dunbar, you will accompany Det. Gray to St.John's Hospital in Yonkers where you will have your blood drawn for a toxicology report. This will take place at the close of this deposition.

This inquiry will remain open until the autopsy is complete, and it will include the decedent's toxicology report as well. Pending the issuance of the death certificate, the District Attorney's office will wait for the determination of these final reports before a decision will be made as to how my office will dispose or proceed with this matter.

Is there anything the witness wishes to add to his testimony?

Dunbar: Just one thing: Two strange events took place last night – one horrific and life ending; the other miraculous. As the driver of the car I am responsible for Ray's death. It may have been due to mechanical failure – I don't know.

What I am 100% sure of, without any doubt, was that Ray sacrificed his life to save mine. Somehow he changed the car's momentum and heading. He did it with the box of light he tossed at me. Had that not occurred, we both would have been maple syrup.

D.A. Stark: How was that achieved?

Dunbar: I have no clue, but it's the only thing I am absolutely sure of last night.

D.A. Stark: The witness is reminded that he remain available for further questioning and to notify the District Attorney's Office if he is leaving the state.

__John Carl Dunbar_____

Detective Gary Gray _H.P.D._

April 11, 1977

I returned the deposition to the envelope.

"It's something else." Uncle Bill raised his brow and shook his head.

I knew he wanted to talk about it, but I wasn't ready. "How'd you get a hold of this?" I looked over to him.   "I explained the circumstances to the Hastings' lieutenant. I hate the way this sounds, but this is a minor matter – an auto collision resulting in an accidental death. With the new copying machines; it wasn't a big deal for the Hastings P.D. to make a copy for me. I mostly got it for your mom and just in case....."

"What happens now?"

"Something like Chappaquiddick. Nobody gave Dunbar a sobriety test. Janie said they ate and slept when they got back from the ballgame. Neither was shitfaced. It'll be logged as an accidental death. The D.A.'s got nothing to say that it was otherwise. Hal and Jane will sue the insurance company in civil court because Dunbar was the insured motorist and he was the responsible party. There's no criminal case here – not according to the evidence......just one fucked up tragedy." He stood up and threw his cold coffee onto the driveway.

"You know Uncle Bill, and I don't know why I thought of it – but if the cars had been parked on the other side of the street, on our side - Ray and John would have gone down O'Dell and north on Warburton and nothing would have happened."

"You're probably right." he said.

THE ASST. DISTRICT ATTORNEY CALLED HAL AND informed him he could pick up Ray's personal effects from the impound room in White Plains, and go through the car to retrieve Ray's property. A camera and two rolls of film were handed to me.

"Shoot both rolls – tell the story." Hal said.

Brother Bill and me stopped to get Tommy Capps. He thought of the stuff Billy and me couldn't or didn't.

The guy at the Mobil station gave me a hard time about going through the tan '72 Fury. I gave the grease monkey the D.A.'s office number and told him it was no longer considered evidence.

"We'll Captain Boland should've come down and told me." he threw his hands in the air.

There was just the stuff we'd seen in the car the other day: work clothes and boots, which would never reach Wisconsin; a small cassette tape recorder he got in Nam that was all in pieces. Individual items were strewn through the interior. He most likely went to the morgue with one bare foot; we found one of his desert boots in the back seat.

"Tommy – get that sleever bar from my trunk and pop the lock.....I'm going to start shooting pictures."

"What's a sleever bar?"

"A hexagon bar with a tapered spike end on one side and a pry-bar end on the other. Destroy the lock if you got to. It's all scrap metal anyway."

"Ryan.......look." Billy pointed to the shoebox between the front seat and the driver's rocker panel. I panicked. The two watched as I peeled away the box's lid. The olive jars and even the plastic pharmaceutical containers were still intact. In the crinkled bottom was about a half-inch of calculus equations, notes, correspondence, and five one hundred dollar notes.

There was a second roll of film to be shot. I could hear Billy and Tommy banging away tryin to get into the trunk.

"Ryan, we got it open." Billy said.

"Anything in it?"

"You better check it out."

"It's Ray's shit alright." I said when I caught sight of the small army duffle. There were papers, bank statements, photos, a couple of newspaper clippings related to Edgar Cayce, and two paperback novels: 'Gravity's Rainbow', 'The Sunlight Dialogues; and a play: "A Moon For The Misbegotten" I made a promise to Ray and myself to read them - though I never did.

"How did that fuckhead Dunbar live through this?" Tommy's arm swept across the span of the '72 Fury.

"Enough wreckage here for a family of GM test dummies." My brother's face was agape.

The two shot rolls of film were on the dashboard. Willis and Tommy kept rifling through the car. I spaced out behind the wheel of the Starfire.

They returned: "Thought there'd be more blood in the car."

"Yeah – that's that internal bleeding crap; either you die from the loss of blood or it fills up in your lungs and you drown in it."

Wednesday evening and Thursday, I had to make a couple of trips to LaGuardia: Jimmy Blanko and Loki flew in from New Orleans, and Isaac Seabrook came in from Kansas City. The next four days were tethered together as a marathon nightmare. A lot of people showed up: Meris Klein, Sarah Nussbaum – the latter had gotten married, Vinny Tarts and Stacey, Nicky 'Bingo' Butoni, Mike Reno, Shooey, The High Five (now four) – Joey Tarts, Cocaine Wayne, Rikshaw, and Kenny Crawford. Sue Herr, Beth the Mess, Sylvia Wells, The Huns, and the Vietnam Vets showed up. The Warburton girls and Wacky Nancy cleaned up so much, I didn't recognize them at first. Most of the Rogues were in Daytona on Spring Break '77, and didn't find out about Ray until they returned. About 50 of our circle signed the visitation book. Sean Dolan showed up at our house, which I thought was a goof at first; it wasn't. Sean and Ray had a number of wild nights before and after he had quit high school. Meris Klein had confirmed the two had visited her on at least three occasions up in Binghamton, before going to graduate school. They all had a "Ray and me" story.

There were a lot of people who were no-shows. Once in a while it's a personal thing, but for the most part - attending a wake or a funeral is an inconvenience. For others........it makes them feel bad. It did and didn't matter I suppose.

749

We waked Ray on Friday afternoon, and again that night. I was so screwed up, I had Vinny, Crawfish, Brother Bill, and Loki ready to steal his remains and bury him with the ejected chunk of fireball in the mound. As long as I was stealing bodies I asked Sylvia if she minded terribly if we dug up Barb and buried her with Ray and the Cosmic Intruder so the three of them would be buried where it made sense.........to me. The Funeral home was all locked up when we came back around midnight. I couldn't be sure of anything; we were so smoked up and drunk with alcohol and grief, we couldn't have gotten in the funeral home if we had the key.

In the morning, I needed an eye opener for the funeral mass. Everyone expected me to eulogize Ray - I was the one who knew him best. I was still drunk at the service. I felt so bad I took about 7.5 megatons of valium to get me through. I borrowed a pair of tinted sun glasses, and I scribbled down some things. I don't remember what I said; my voice wavered and I had to regain my composure twice. Thank God I had cut it short. I know the attendees wanted more, but there was no more – I was spent.

One of the things I've carried with me since that day - was the Army Honor Guard doing their memorial service, and presenting Jane with the stars and stripes. Isaac stepped forward and joined the Honor Guard for the Army's salute for one of their own. It was a tremendous loss........for all of us.

Somewhere deep down, I knew by saving Dunbar's life, Ray had finally escaped the force keeping him in a perpetual state of depression. When he saved Dunbar, he should have been good for a three year high........maybe five, had he lived, and that was on top of the recent rescue of Bad Brad from the river. He might be up there with St. Peter, but I reckon it was just as likely he was in some alternative universe where he could be free.

Hal arranged a luncheon at the Polish Center after we put Ray in the ground. Many people came up to me during the luncheon and said I had done Ray well in my eulogy. I hoped it was so.

After things broke up, Mack caught up with me back at 21: "Are you still on schedule for Wisconsin?"

"Not straight away Mack."

"Let me know what your plans are. If you think you're going to fall behind in your dues - you got to let me know – we can't let that happen. I can help you for three or four months." he said.

"Thanks Mack," I clutched the hands and wrists that squeezed my shoulders.

THE TASK TO GO THROUGH RAY'S STUFF WAS GIVEN to me by Hal.

"If you come across anything weird – neither your mother or I want to know. Use your discretion and common sense with what you bring into the house."

Ray's life could be put in the trunk of the Starfire. Hal had all of his Army stuff already except his DD-214 separation papers. I had found his briefcase containing the business: passport, life insurance policy, approximately 20 photographs of the Vietnamese woman he had been involved with. His main love interest looked devastating in her Ao Dai pantsuit. There was a notebook of his observations, equations, philosophies, ideas, and events; as well as a military colt .45 semi-pistol. Also, there was about a pound of Tiger Tar opium still sealed, an admission application to Purdue, a Gorton H.S. class ring '71 in white gold, a rosary he had worn around his neck in Nam, and his copy of "Long Day's Journey Into Night" which had notes in every margin and between characters' dialogue.

I gave Cathy and Billy $200 each from the money we found in a child's shoebox between the seat and the rocker panel of the wreck. $100 went to Tommy Capps for being there, and to keep an eye on Willis. I kept all of his stuff from Nam. There were six rolls of 35mm that had been shot and undeveloped. I was skeptical about the condition of the film. The aluminum canisters all had dates and locations of where the pictures had been taken. Some of the film was already four years old; I had my doubts the photos would develop. I decided to have one of the rolls developed. His personal effects at the U.N. were harmless and didn't have much value to me except to say: "This item once belonged to Ray." I took his record collection; he had a lot of scratched vinyl. There were a few good things. Mostly it was a springboard which prompted me to go out and buy duplicate copies of a couple of the albums – I liked the music, but the condition of most of the records made them unlistenable.

"What are we going to do without Ray's help with the rent?" Karyn asked.

"I don't know." I replied. I had to get to that powerhouse in Wisconsin soon, and hope they put me to work. If I stayed in metro N.Y., I'd have to push drugs. That was no choice.

Without hesitation, Jane drove Cathy and Billy to All Souls H.S. and grade school on Monday morning. 98% of their classmates didn't know they had lost their brother over Easter vacation. Billy's grades tanked. The principal asked Jane what was wrong with him – "The boy is almost catatonic."

"Surely you're aware of the tragedy our family experienced last month. We're all having a difficult time dealing with the loss."

"Yes, Willis' instructors were all informed to be acutely sensitive to his emotional state, but Mrs. Whitelaw - you realize they are only teachers........with up to 45 children in a class. It is very difficult to give your son the attention he requires. If you want to discuss this; I have some time right now; I could at least guide you and Willis to professionals in the psychiatric field."

"Yes, thank you. Perhaps if I had a few names and their phone numbers, I could see who would be a good fit for us."

We were all having our personal meltdowns – I lost the most, but I was sure each family member would have said the same thing. Ray had had the charisma everyone had seen in Jane. Ray also had Hal's superior intelligence and analytical thinking for problem solving.

Hal beat himself up with more whiskey. Out on the porch, Jane lit one cigarette off of the last, washing down Xanax and valium with coffee.

Seventeen year old Cathy, and Jane's assistant and friend, Judy, did 95% of the recital that year. They did a good job during Jane's psychological and emotional retreat. Jane said losing Ray could never be put into words.

Willis told me a few years later: "With Ray, it was like there was never ten years age difference."

"Yeah, I know – but it was different for me.......he talked down to me - he had to......he was a genius. Ray never gave me the business. He always made me feel good about myself........that I was getting the straight shit from him."

"Ryan, you'd give me shit every once in a while."

"That was only to get you street smart." I said.

"His last summer was the best; we'd ride our bikes up to Sunset Ridge to go caddying. We got our times down to a half-hour each way."

I thought Will was going to fall apart, I had to keep him on-topic: "Hell Bill, I don't think I could drive up there that quick in the Starfire, 'specially with the stupid traffic." I said quickly.

"Cathy was pissed off 'cause Ray wasn't around to help her with her math and science.......I think she barely squeaked by." Billy said.

When Karyn, Nicole, and me went down to 21 to visit, it was obvious Hal and Jane were fading. They'd watch Nicole for us when we asked, but it seemed they had forgotten how to interact with her. It really was a ghost house, but Ray wasn't the ghost, the ghosts were Hal and Jane. Their love had gone by the wayside years earlier, they couldn't erase the void; and now the loss of their son compounded everything in the negative column. Each was out there in the dense fog..............wondering..........searching.

TWO WEEKS AFTER WE BURIED RAY, I WAS ALONE AT the cast-off mound. May was finally here. Looking towards the marina, and the twin stacks of the Phelps Dodge Copper powerhouse, a familiar face walked north on the southbound platform.

"Jaime O'Neill." I called.

"Whitefang."

"Talkin' like one of The Rogues now?" I grinned. "You're not down here by chance."

"I stopped at your house - your brother said you were down here."

"What can I do for you?"

"Nothing. I've got some info about the accident.......it might be of interest to you."

"Yeah? What's that?"

"C'mon up."

I jumped off some slabs of the demolished concrete to the new southbound platform, and vaulted over the handrail: "Whatcha got?"

"Have you seen Dunbar's deposition, the accident report, and the D.A.'s finding not to charge him with anything?"

"What have you got that changes anything?"

"The reason Dunbar was driving like he was at the Indy 500 was because he hit a car on O'Dell and Broadway making a 'right on red turn' to go down O'Dell Ave. The driver of that car made an accident report with the Yonkers P.D. These guys in the other car tried to make a U-turn at St. John's service drive to pursue the car that hit them, but their rear quarter panel was pushed into the wheel well by the collision and the tire went flat. By the time they pulled the sheet metal out and got the spare on; the car was long gone." He waited for my reaction.

Nothing.

"The time, location, make and color of the car all fit the Yonkers P.D. report. It won't change anything except your family would get a larger settlement when they go to civil court." Jamie said.

"That accident report is on file down at Y.P.D. headquarters?"

"I could get a copy for you......and leave it at the weekend desk."

"Jamie.......there is no story without Ray. He was the axis.......the pivot point."

"Maybe..........but maybe I see something you don't."

"Talk to me at the end of the summer. Hopefully, I'll be in a better frame of mind." and out of this state.......I finished my thought.

O'Neill assured me he'd look me up then; I didn't expect to see him in Dairyland.

753

NEW YORK STATE
DEPARTMENT OF HEALTH
CERTIFICATE OF DEATH

CENSUS TRACT	SUB DIVISION	RECORDED & FILED 5926		
		REGISTER NUMBER 22		

STATISTICAL DISTRICT		1 NAME FIRST	MIDDLE	LAST	2 SEX	2A DATE OF DEATH	2B HOUR
REC.		Raymond	NMI	Whitelaw	MALE ☒ FEMALE ☐	MONTH 4 DAY 10 YEAR 77	11:45
RES.		4 RACE: WHITE, BLACK, AMERICAN INDIAN, OTHER (SPECIFY) white	5 AGE 24 YEARS	IF UNDER 1 YEAR MONTHS DAYS	IF UNDER 1 DAY HOURS MINUTES	6 DECEDENT BORN MONTH 3 DAY 18 YEAR 53	7 VETERAN OF U.S. ARMED FORCES? YES ☒ NO ☐ IF YES SPECIFY WAR OR DATES OF SERVICE 1973-74 Vietnam	

		8A PLACE OF DEATH ☐ CITY OF ☒ TOWN OF West. ☐ VILLAGE OF	8B LOCALITY (CHECK ONE AND SPECIFY) Greenburg Hastings	8C HOSPITAL OR OTHER INSTITUTION (IF NEITHER, GIVE ADDRESS) Broadway	8D IF IN HOSPITAL (CHECK ONE) 1☐ DOA 2☒ EMERGENCY ROOM 3☐ OUTPATIENT 4☐ INPATIENT	8E IF INPATIENT, ADMISSION DATE MONTH DAY YEAR	
		9 STATE OF BIRTH (COUNTRY IF NOT USA) N.Y.	10 CITIZEN OF WHAT COUNTRY U.S.A.	11 MARITAL STATUS (CHECK ONE) ☒ NEVER MARRIED ☐ WIDOWED ☐ MARRIED ☐ DIVORCED	12 SURVIVING SPOUSE (IF WIFE GIVE MAIDEN NAME)		
		13A USUAL OCCUPATION (EVEN IF RETIRED) Ironworker	13B KIND OF BUSINESS OR INDUSTRY Steel Constructor	13C SOCIAL SECURITY NUMBER 069-46-3515	14 EDUCATION: INDICATE HIGHEST GRADE COMPLETED ELEMENTARY OR SECONDARY (0-12)	COLLEGE (1-4 OR 5+) one year	

USUAL RESIDENCE WHERE DECEDENT LIVED.

| | | 15A COUNTY N.Y. | 15B DISTRICT West. | 15C LOCALITY (CHECK ONE AND SPECIFY) ☐ CITY OF ☐ TOWN OF ☒ VILLAGE OF Hastings | 15D IF CITY OR VILLAGE, WITHIN CITY OR VILLAGE LIMITS? YES ☒ NO ☐ IF NO, SPECIFY TOWN | |
| | | 15E STREET AND NUMBER 8 Washington Avenue | | | | |

| | | 16A NAME OF FATHER FIRST Harold | MIDDLE James | LAST Whitelaw | 16B MAIDEN NAME OF MOTHER FIRST Jane | MIDDLE Mary | LAST Marlowe |
| | | 17A NAME OF INFORMANT Harold Whitelaw | | 17B MAILING ADDRESS (INCLUDE ZIP CODE) 21 Odell Avenue, Yonkers, N.Y. 10701 | | | |

		18A BURIAL CREMATION REMOVAL ☒ ☐ ☐	18B MONTH 4 DAY 14 YEAR 77	18B PLACE OF BURIAL, CREMATION OR REMOVAL Gate of Heaven Cem.	18C LOCATION (CITY OR TOWN, STATE) Hawthorne, New York	
		20A NAME AND ADDRESS OF FUNERAL HOME Flynn Memorial Home, Inc., 325 So. B'way, Yonkers, NY			19B REGISTRATION NO. 00830	
		20B NAME OF FUNERAL DIRECTOR John J. Flynn, Jr.	20B SIGNATURE OF FUNERAL DIRECTOR		20C REGISTRATION NO. 01776	
		21A SIGNATURE OF REGISTRAR (Deputy) Marie Paquette	21B DATE FILED MONTH 4 DAY 14 YEAR 77	22A BURIAL OR REMOVAL PERMIT BY Marie Paquette		22B MONTH 4 DAY 14 YEAR 77

TO BE COMPLETED BY CERTIFYING PHYSICIAN ONLY	—OR—	TO BE COMPLETED BY CORONER OR MEDICAL EXAMINER ONLY
23 A. TO THE BEST OF MY KNOWLEDGE, DEATH OCCURRED AT THE TIME, DATE AND PLACE AND DUE TO THE CAUSES STATED MONTH DAY YEAR		23 A. ON THE BASIS OF EXAMINATION AND/OR INVESTIGATION, IN MY OPINION DEATH OCCURRED AT THE TIME, DATE AND PLACE AND DUE TO THE CAUSES STATED. SIGNED Caroline G. Lydecker TITLE M.D.
B. SIGNED C. LAST SEEN ALIVE		B. PRONOUNCED DEAD MONTH DAY YEAR HOUR ON 4 10 77 AT 11:45 p.m.	B. DATE SIGNED MONTH 4 DAY 11 YEAR 77
FROM: TO:		E. NAME OF CORONER'S PHYSICIAN IF OTHER THAN CERTIFIER
D. NAME OF ATTENDING PHYSICIAN IF OTHER THAN CERTIFIER		

CAROLINE G. LYDECKER, M.D.
WESTCHESTER COUNTY MEDICAL EXAMINER'S OFFICE, VALHALLA, NEW YORK 1059

CONDITIONS, IF ANY, WHICH GAVE RISE TO IMMEDIATE CAUSE (A) STATING THE UNDERLYING CAUSE LAST.

26 DEATH WAS CAUSED BY ENTER ONLY ONE CAUSE PER LINE FOR (A) (B), AND (C)	APPROXIMATE INTERVAL BETWEEN ONSET & DEATH
PART 1. IMMEDIATE CAUSE (A) Bilateral hemothorax; Multiple rib fractures –	
DUE TO, OR AS A CONSEQUENCE OF: (B) Transection of aorta.	
(C)	

PART 2. OTHER SIGNIFICANT CONDITIONS: CONDITIONS CONTRIBUTING TO DEATH BUT NOT RELATED TO CAUSE GIVEN IN PART 1 (A)	26A AUTOPSY? YES ☒ NO ☐	26B IF YES, WERE FINDINGS CONSIDERED IN DETERMINING THE CAUSE OF DEATH? YES ☒ NO ☐

27A SPECIFY IF ACCIDENT, HOMICIDE, SUICIDE, UNDETERMINED, PENDING INVESTIGATION ACCIDENT	27B DATE OF INJURY MONTH 4 DAY 10 YEAR 77	27C HOUR OF INJURY 11:30 p.m.	27D DESCRIBE HOW INJURY OCCURRED Passenger in auto which left road
27E INJURY AT WORK? YES ☐ NO ☒	27F PLACE OF INJURY (HOME, FARM, FACTORY, OFFICE BLDG., ETC.) Road	27G LOCATION (STREET & NO., CITY OR VILLAGE, TOWN, COUNTY, STATE) Broadway, Hastings, N.Y.	

THE BEST THING FOR ME AT THAT POINT SHOULD have been to stay as close to our original plan as possible. Get out to the union hall in Milwaukee and sit there until the powerhouse in

Kenosha called for more men. There was some kind of magnetic force keeping me from leaving; I was hauling an emotional load. I felt it every waking minute and I hardly slept. Getting out of Yonkers without Ray.......it didn't seem possible. I could leave Karyn and Nicole; Ray was someone I had been with for the whole ride; with his loss, s thoughts of suicide began plaguing me.

Karyn watched as I disintegrated: I didn't go to work or look for work. For a while all I did was watch Nicky and wait for Karyn to come home from the Theatre. It was inevitable: at the end of May, Crawford showed up with some dooge. It was the only thing that killed the pain. I thought I could just do the shit on the weekends – it didn't happen. The smack got me and wouldn't let go. I gave Karyn $9000 from Ray's insurance policy.

She knew I was hurting, but it couldn't be an excuse for shooting dope. It was putting 'lil Nicole at risk in a major way. I'd have people come up and bring me a couple of bags, and we'd all get off. Karyn came home from work a number of times and I'd be nodding out and the kid would be crying. Ray had that pound of Tiger Tar opium...... at first I was able to trade it for heroin. It was a commodity losing its street appeal. The only places I could convert it to cash was on the college campuses: Columbia, NYU, Fordham, St. John's, The School of Fashion, CUNY schools except for John Jay. I also was able to find some old timers who I had pitched the shit to in the past who wanted to kill the pain and take a trip simultaneously, but there weren't many of them around. Cocaine was the hot drug. One of the selling points was it was supposed to make you a sex god or goddess and it got you high. The extra added attraction was you could throw it up your nose......you didn't need to hit it up. The glamour of doing this schedule 2 narcotic was it brought the female gender into the market.

As far as I was concerned, the drug was a waste of time and money. Maybe it got you high for 20 minutes - half hour – tops. The only person I ever really seen enjoy it was 'Cocaine Wayne'. It was like old times with Hi-Lo Heller.......doing speedballs and getting zonked. It was all about purity with Wayne-O. He was on a groove before the dealers got the idiots to start 'freebasing' and it wasn't long before they turned it into the highly addictive 'crack'.

Trying to move the opium wasn't worth it. I asked Stax to stash the remaining ¾ lb. in his brother's deep-freeze with his deer meat and fish.

More infected blood went into my arm every time I shot-up with others or borrowed a rig. The hepatitis C virus was steadily at work destroying my liver.........had we only known about the dormant time-bomb killer..........Only the most dedicated junkie would have rolled the dice to get high. When you see veteran junkies walking around in what seems to be good health, the logic is: "Doper Dave is a big time shooter..........if he can get away with it why can't I?" The Fifth Dimensionals and other ghost runners had little or no choice in the matter.

My apathy ran deep about the world in general, so much so – I became a willing test pilot for new batches of junk for part-time junkies. The stuff they bought was known to be high quality, they just didn't know how high. We all wanted to get high, but nobody wanted to die. I just plain didn't give a fuck about nothing. Some major league stuff had come up from Columbia.

"Come on over.......we got something we'd like you to test drive." I came to in an apartment with Rikshaw pounding on my chest and blowing air into my lungs. Had Rikki not been there, the others would have watched me turn blue and die.

The second week of June, Karyn kicked me out of the apartment and told me "to get some help".

Jane and Hal didn't know I was 'Big Timing' it. They were so stricken with grief - they couldn't deal with themselves or me. Word finally got to Mack. He came down on Friday, July 1st. I was leaving 21 to go out and he blocked the door. He advised me very strongly to think about getting clean.

"Ryan, you're in more trouble than just a little bit. This is what's going to happen: You're going to be on the road to Cheeseland at 12 noon tomorrow. Don't know how bad you're hooked........don't care. You fuck this up, and I'll shake you off like a dog shaking off a cold rain."

The fog was so thick, I couldn't see and I couldn't think.

"Stop using Ray as your excuse for using drugs. It's over – he's gone. Get the fuck over it." Mack never cursed.

I saw his clenched fist of his right hand. I had pushed him to the edge where I knew he'd let me have it if I did anything except listen.

"All you can do is lead a life that exemplifies his best characteristics. Your wife and daughter need you. Hal and Jane, Cathy and Billy need you. Mom-Mom and me need you. You're so screwed up and selfish you don't even know – it is through you that we see him."

"Am I putting it on you? You bet your ass I am Ryan. Grow up ya shithead – think about the ones who are still here. Be an example – reflect those things that Ray had and we all lost." Mack pushed me out of his way and left.

JULY 2nd, 12 NOON, I LEFT N.Y. IN BETWEEN THE DRY heaves, cold sweats, body aches, and the withdrawal; all I could think about were the people I had to leave behind, especially Karyn and Nicole. Physically and emotionally I felt like shit.

Wednesday morning I crossed the Illinois/Wisconsin border. I signed the books and hung out at the Ironworker hall in Milwaukee on Thursday and Friday. The word at the hall was there would be a call for men on Tuesday. It was a head fake as the call came in Monday. Since I had nowhere else to go, I went to the hall on Monday, so I was there when the board came out and the B.A. put my name down to be sent out as a structural ironworker. The contractor had a standing call for structural and reinforcing ironworkers for the next three weeks. There was an open call for certified weldors in Local 8's union hall for the next three months.

Wisconsin Electric knew there'd be a weldor shortage for all of the metal trades: Boilermakers, Pipe Fitters, and Ironworkers. The power company had the prime contractor build a weld shop where the tradesmen would take their certification tests for pipe, plate, stainless, and tube. After their shifts, workers were encouraged to up-grade their welding skills and get certified.

Just before Labor Day, I passed my all-position 1" plate test using stick and flux-core processes. I sent Xerox copies to Mack and $1200 to Karyn. She cashed the check, but she wouldn't talk or write to me. I kept sending her $1200 every quarter.

vi

Was it a puzzle? Probably..........many things were beyond my brain's capacity. Without Ray, I was almost dead in the water. I was all alone in the Badger state. I knew I was catching on fast with the trade.......and got along with the guys. That summer, I bounced around from boarding houses, to hotels, to shacks......from one dive to the next. I shared a couple of flats with guys who were on the road like me. One was a sparky (electrician) and the other was a Boilermaker, who was taught me a lot about welding after work. I always had to buy the first round when we got out of the power company's weld facility. We were working 10's, and usually putting in two hours at their weld shop after work. Things were going pretty good until the bluecoats from Illinois put the bracelets on him and took him back to Peoria.

Just after Labor Day, I got a place by myself just over the Wisconsin border with Illinois. No telephone. Never got nothing but bad news from them things anyway. All of my correspondence was mailed from Kenosha, trying to keep my trail as cold as possible and using P.O. Boxes.

It was a chore trying to stay away from the gin mills at first. I read the newspapers at work: first there was the N.Y.C. blackout in July, next they captured that fuckhead – Son of Sam. I couldn't believe he lived at 35 Pine St. in Yonkers. Chances were pretty good Beth the Mess had rode the elevator with him........just the two of them. Crawfish, Stax, and me had been down that apartment building way too much. We all must have run into the serial killer in our comings and goings, but when you're getting high you've only got one thing on your mind.

Looking at the TV images at the bar in August, instead of watching for more David Berkowitz follow-ups, I was blown away when they announced Elvis had cashed out. What the fuck was this all about? The 1200 megawatt job in Kenosha made sense, this other shit didn't. There were two earthquakes in California and a big one in the Balkans. I thought these incidents were the result of magnetic shift of the poles and they were affecting organic and non-organic worlds.

At first, I thought humanity had gone mad, as well as the geologic, atmospheric, and meteorological stabilities we had come to rely on, to operate as a system – it was beginning to unwind. I had given it enough thought and it terrified me not to be with Karyn and Nicole.

757

It was more than a thought, it was a vibe I felt, and it gave me the hope to think Karyn might realize her future was with me. She should believe in me…….love me…… and have more children with me. The next time I saw the two of them was during Thanksgiving. They were still living at the U.N. We slept in the same bed, but there was no romance. It was a major misread on my part. Little Nicole didn't remember me until the last day I was there.

It was equally difficult over at 21 O'Dell. It was okay with Cathy and Billy, but Hal and Jane had not progressed 6 months after Ray's death; they were still in rough shape.

A year later Karyn and me got divorced. The decree was issued in Illinois, it wasn't any cheaper for me, but it was quicker. It was all about visitation. Karyn was pretty fair about it. When she was seven, I was able to put Nicks on a jet and have her visit me once a year. I remarried and had the twins: Teresa and Killeen, and then Dixie; all with Kate. Nicky was 15 years old when Karyn kicked her out, and she moved in with us. Magnetic pole reversal had its own timetable.

October 11th 2018, Mankato.

...TWO ASSISTANTS WITH DIXIE ESCORTING, TOOK RYAN down to radiology for more imaging. The on-duty G.I Doctor wanted some pictures for Dr. Singh as soon as he arrived this morning. The work order was to MRI the region believed to be the axis of Ryan's pain. Before he went into the radial imaging machine, Dixie removed the wet paper towel wrapped ash.

"What's that?" The technician looked concerned.

"His good luck charm......his brother's ashes."

"OOOOOhhhhhhhkaaaaayyyyy.......we'll be doing a cat-scan and an MRI this morning kiddies." The technician yawned.

THEY GATHERED IN RYAN'S I.C.U. ROOM. THE NURSES and aides had been dismissed. Drs. Singh, Judd, Marie Allen, and the Whitelaw women were present as Judd closed the door. Bachan Singh was irritated: "We don't have time for deception. There must only be truth without reservation or equivocation. I must operate on your father, but I must know what I am dealing with." He took a breath and his eyes bulged.

He continued: "Approximately 2/3rds of his liver has somehow become free of scarring, and seems to be working normally according to the imaging and blood work results. The other third – the upper lobe – is ready to burst. If it does......the outcome will most probably be massive internal hemorrhage and chances for his survival – almost nil. One of his bile ducts is the size of an orange, and I will have to confer with a colleague at the Cleveland Hospital about how to proceed with repairing or removing this duct. This surgery is nothing but a gigantic question mark." Dr. Singh said.

"When was the last time he ate anything?"

"The computer says three days ago." Dr. Judd answered.

"Ah......that's been revised. I'd say about 9 p.m. last night." Dixie said......though she may have been an hour off either way.

"What did he eat?" Judd asked.

"Asteroid ash mixed with like.......distilled water and colloidal silver whipped up into a gray smoothie." Killeen said straight faced.

"Ms. Whitelaw, there is no time for levity."

"That's the truth." Teresa responded.

Judd immediately looked to Singh; Dr. Allen was obviously confused. Singh was already thinking how this concoction would impact the upper lobe's removal.

"Then nothing has changed - in that your father is still at the crossroads. What has changed, is now we have a different set of circumstances which have changed quite dramatically. Nevertheless, we must go into surgery within the hour."

Singh turned to Dixie who had the legal responsibility to authorize the surgery, "Now what was the substance you fed to him?"

"We don't know, only Ryan knows. We believe it is some kind of cosmic dust or ash from a fireball that fell to earth. Our talks with some of Dad's friends and his brother lead us to think it has a negative charge or energy field which has bound itself to the cinders, ash, or dust of an ejected remnant of an outer space fireball. He had us form it into a slurry, with distilled water and colloidal silver, and had us feed it to him. Its appearance is indistinguishable from the ash, in the paper towel below his heart – except its magnetic charge is opposite.........positive."

Singh lifted Ryan's hand and took a pinch of the dust. He rubbed it between his forefinger and thumb, as he tried to interpret whether this material was granular - like sea salt, or a fine powder - like flour.

"Is any of the primary substance nearby, the ash or cinders?" Singh asked.

"I don't know. I think everything Dad and his brother had is either in him or on top of him." Dixie said, and looked to her sisters for any input. None came.

"Before we perform surgery, all I can do is look at it microscopically. There is no time to get a spectroscopy of this substance. Also, you might have it sent to a lab to determine its composition, but that is a question you may entertain sometime in the future."

The four sisters were thinking about the comet's debris the Whitelaw brothers had collected 50 years earlier. There seemed to be a suspension of the continuum as they all froze. It was impossible to say how brief or how long.

"If what the images have shown, can be believed; The MRI shows us the scarring in his liver is like snow melting in the street. Most of the lower 2/3 of his liver is free of the cirrhotic debris. Since I know nothing other than what the blood work, abdominal pictures, and the scans tell me: the scar tissue has been drawn into the upper tri-lobe of the liver where all of this garbage has been collecting." Dr. Singh observed.

"We don't have 24 hours of fasting, but there is reason to believe the contents of the slurry was directed into the liver after it passed through his GI tract at an accelerated pace due to the magnetic attraction at the site of the upper liver lobe. The negatively charged blood and free scar tissue is being held there with other debris. It is a log-jam right now, along with the engorged bile duct and they will burst ....soon. This portion of the liver is totally clogged not allowing the body's blood and fluids to make a complete circuit. We want things to stay where they are; we will keep the magnetic fields in place until we are ready to begin the surgery. At that time, we will remove the magnetic cosmic ash on Ryan's chest. The surgery will be traditional, not arthroscopic." He looked to his colleagues, "This is going to be a grab and go. I will have to seal off the viable remaining liver; remove the liver's non-functioning upper lobe and I do not know what we are going to do with the apple-sized bile duct. It must be drained, and by relocating it to another duct in the portion of the liver that remains.....it could perform somewhat normally if he is lucky. With this type of surgery, hemorrhaging is always a concern. Like I said, I will be conferring with a highly knowledgeable colleague at the Cleveland Clinic, while we are in surgery." Singh explained.

"Ms. Dixie - ladies: To be blunt, I do not know what I am dealing with. The situation Ryan confronts is urgent, and it is the understatement of the year as far as we are concerned. I wish he was conscious; we might learn more about the substance you fed him. But again, we do not have the luxury of time. I know if we do not act quickly, your father will not survive. So we must proceed with the skills and knowledge at hand and learn as the surgery progresses."

Singh searched the sky above the cornfields.

"I do not want to give you false hope." he said as his eyes made contact with his associates, and back to the Whitelaws: "We will be shooting from the hip for this procedure, and we will try to solve one problem at a time. Is there anything else about this outer space material I should know before the surgery starts?"

"It has the ability to move itself and other objects when the positive and negative ash materials are in specific locations. There is also a secondary force as well: to transform - which presents itself from time to time. I would think along the lines of repel and attraction, rather than change.....I don't know why........it's just a feeling, but you should be aware of the latter also." Killeen said.

"Doctor Singh, I think it is extremely important the cosmic material be salvaged, preserved, or retrieved if possible and returned to Ryan or his estate." Nicole said.

"That I cannot guarantee. It will be a low priority consideration".

THE WHITELAW SISTERS WENT TO THE CHAPEL FOR AN hour-and-a-half. Singh said he would call them after the surgery, or with the news: the operation was not successful. He didn't know what to expect. If Ryan didn't bleed to death during the removal of 1/3rd of his liver, he might cheat "The Grim Reaper" and die of something else in ten years. Nobody could or would put odds on this roll of the dice. The sisters' visit to the non-denominational chapel could only help.

The sisters left the Institute after Ryan was brought into surgery. They stopped by a liquor store and a pizza shop on the way back to the 'Hayride Heaven Motel'. They had side by side rooms with a connecting door. Not much was said as they ate and had a couple of drinks. Waiting for word was incredibly difficult. They agreed if Ryan was going to cash out, they hoped they might get another chance to see him alive. They had expressed this request to Dr. Singh. The emotional energy they had expended in the last 36 hours had them in zombie land. Nicky couldn't sleep, but the other three gave in. They couldn't stay apart and stayed in the one hotel room, using the other to store their suitcases and other belongings.

Nicky went outside and paced and smoked and nipped some tequila from a plastic cup. She went back into the room and sat in a cushioned chair.......perhaps she caught a few minutes here and there. She couldn't be sure. The digital clock on the dresser read 10:47 p.m. She went back outside and the autumn air hit her.

"He's pulled through." She was sure, but she wasn't confident this wasn't some dream. Inside the room, the clock read: 1:11 a.m. "I got to get some sleep." Her phone was charging on the night stand between the two queen beds. The phone baited her to take a look and see if there were any messages from Singh. There was; she must have missed the cricket while she was outside. The sisters had put all of Singh's and Baranpour's messages on blast. They received the same messages from the doctors simultaneously since this whole thing started. Now they had to retrieve any message or voice mail A.S.A.P. – it might be the last time they saw Ryan alive.

"Teresa......." Nicky called softly. They all sat up with a live current running through the four. "Message from Singh." They grabbed their phones. "Dixie – you read it aloud." Nicole said.

The four sat on the edge of the two beds; two facing two.

"Can't." she replied. "Teri, you read it – there might be some medical terminology I won't understand."

"Open it Teresa." Killeen was dying.

"Nicole, you're oldest.......you read it."

"Killeen – you do it." Nicole passed. "All you do is deliver mail and bring news to people.......it's your job."

The two others agreed: "Hurry."

The Postal Carrier made the sign of the cross, and the others followed as she tapped the screen:

Ms. Dixie, Nicole, Teresa, & Killeen:
               GOOD NEWS !

The four women cheered, hugged, cried, danced on the bed and hugged some more. When the commotion died down, they told Killeen to read on: "Ahh......says the surgery was complicated and Dr. Judd was of immense help.......never encountered a similar situation or anything close to it. He did make the phone call to the Cleveland Institute for advice on the bile duct and whether to seal it off, splice it into an adjoining one, or back into the liver......cautions about infection concerns in the next few days........credits Drs. Judd and Allen........surgery lasted seven and-a-half hours. Most of the time spent on the bile duct microsurgery. Singh says he is flat-out spent. Will see us tomorrow morning in Ryan's I.C.U. room."

Another rousing cheer and a quadruple hug; the bars were closed, so they went out for breakfast at an all-night truck stop diner. Nicole poured tequila in their orange juices under the table. They shouldn't have been driving, but they didn't care. The urge to visit their father was too great, and they detoured to the Institute to see Ryan. He had been out of recovery for three or four hours and was already back in the I.C.U. room. They were just there to take a peek at him; they knew he was still going to be out from the anesthesia and painkillers.

"He just looks so alive just lying there." Dixie said. "This is great, now he can make his own decisions again. Damn! That was a lot of weight......especially this surgery I had to sign-off on. Any tequila left Nicks?"

"How 'bout a triple hug from your three big sisters for a job 'Well Done' ?" Nicky smiled.

"He's even getting his color back." Teri gasped.

"His face was the same sickly shade as the magnetic potion we were force feeding into him only a day ago." Killeen noted.

They returned to the motel, and tried to get some sleep before seeing the medical team in Ryan's room.

"As I said in the text message, we must watch for infection. He is on antibiotics as a preventative measure. He is not running a fever. Also, we will be, and Dr. Baranpour will be completing his course of the Hep-C treatment in seven weeks when he is transferred back to St. Thomas in LaCrosse. While Ryan is still here, there will be more C-T and MRI scans, blood work, and ultra sounds. We will be watching for any internal bleeding indications and looking at stool and urine samples, when he starts eating again. By the way: his blood work numbers continue to improve." he compared the readings on the third page of his clipboard.

Singh squeezed his brow hugging the clipboard, "There is the matter of whether there will be some kind of reaction as a result of the outer space agent you introduced into Ryan's body. There are many questions in that regard. At this point, I believe it is best to let things continue as if they had not occurred. To investigate what just took place in the past week would be going down a rabbit hole that I may never emerge from. It is not what I want to do with the rest of my life. What I know about your father's saga, leads me to believe, it is more about the cosmos than medicine. And, that is.........how shall I put it? ....it is not my bag." Singh looked up at the women.

The sisters again tried to talk to Ryan, but he was in and out.

Singh called Nicole aside: "When you are done here – come to my office and ask for Maria. I have something for you; just tell her who you are." he said.

She thanked him again. Dr. Singh wished them all well; Ryan even managed a weak smile. He stayed under Singh's care for another week. Nicole had to leave on Monday to get back to her family in Arizona; she went over to Singh's office to pick up what he had for her.

She told Maria who she was and was asked to have a seat. A nurse came out from the examination rooms and handed her a double-sealed plastic bag. Inside one was a Tupperware bowl with the ash Ryan had held on his upper abdomen. She asked Maria for a magic marker and marked the lid: "POS +". In the other sealed bag was some official hard plastic container with a BIOHAZARD sticker on every side. The plastic was sealed, so Nicky wrote on the outside anywhere there was space: "NEG –".

A handwritten note taped to the plastic bag said:

"I don't know what your intentions are with this material. It is your family's business – not mine. Somehow I felt the magnetic force fields of this extra-terrestrial debris had a great deal to do with Ryan's recovery and healing. Beyond that obvious observation, I am at a loss for any explanation. What I don't want to do is to call you for the "Golden Fleece" every time I have another 'hopeless case'."

"Please remember the negatively charged ash is carried throughout the organic material which I removed from your father's abdomen. Although his Hepatitis-C virus test comes back as non-detectable, there may still be active virus in any part in his liver in this container. Whoever handles this organic material - they must exercise EXTREME CAUTION, and assume the specimen IS INFECTED with HEP-C virus." he wrote.

"To extricate the original cosmic ash from the diseased portion of the liver, it should be incinerated in a kiln or an oven with a temperature which will destroy the virus and disintegrate the organic material. The residue might then be recovered by attraction of the opposite poled meteor dust. It is just some deductive reasoning – a guess. Good Luck."

Bachan Singh, M.D.

Dixie stayed with Ryan for the next seven days in Mankato. By the third day after surgery, Ryan was able to walk progressively farther and farther before they returned to LaCrosse. He spent another 6 days at St. Thomas the Apostle Hospital, under Dr. Baranpour's care, and another 8 days at a rehabilitation facility. The twins and Dixie visited him every day. Dixie was with him the most, as an artist's schedule was rather fluid.

CHAPTER 26

i

Teresa and Peter had the largest house. It was two towns north of LaCrosse. I had recovered enough to leave Wisconsin in November. Somehow the blonde sisters had talked me into hanging around through Thanksgiving. I sent Nicole and Rick airfare for their family, when he told me he managed to get Thanksgiving weekend off.

The last four months in Wisconsin had been a wild ride. This family gathering would give it the closure it needed.

The anti-viral drug Harvoni cleaned out any hepatitis C virus that had tried to hang on. I had beat that murdering, liver-killing bug. I thought about all the junkies who didn't stay alive long enough to get a chance to get clean. It tripped up a lot of people I had known.

My nurse practitioner in Tucson, told me more people die from drug overdose than people with the hep-C virus. She said that would change as the population aged. Liver cancer and cirrhosis would start hitting the baby boomers hard in the coming years.

With news that I was clean, we were all in disbelief. It was like we all had had the virus. In my mind, it took a few years to really forget about it. I knew I hit some kind of lottery – it just didn't payoff in dollars. Perhaps......

The grandkids got an extra hour to stay up Thanksgiving night. They were running wild in Teri's basement. We were in the dining room: playing cards and throwing around 'old times' and drinking; I was having coffee.

I WAS UP WITH THE KIDS ON BLACK FRIDAY MORNING. I made some instant coffee, watching the remaining leaves making their last stand. The kids saw me with my cup of go-go juice, and figured they'd get me to go right into making breakfast for them.....which I did. Emma helped me with Nicole's kids and Van the man started yapping that they were out of cereal.

"You're out of Capn' Crunch?" I scowled.

"What's that?"

Breakfast ended up being oranges, corn muffins, and frozen waffles. Teresa's crew and the Sand kids bolted back down the basement to continue playing. I thought the couples were taking advantage of my babysitting, unless they were hungover. Only Killeen and Dixie had the throttle down last night. In the old days they'd have driven home themselves, but these were different times so I drove the partying girls home to Dixie's place. The bulls were out looking for DWI candidates. The two said they'd be over early so the four of them could go shopping on the big shopping day.

Another cup of coffee; I was mesmerized as I stared out the big window. 'How many years ago was it – when I lost Barb on that black.....'Black Friday' night? God, I loved that girl. For me, she was at the core of those crazy inverted magneto years. If it wasn't for my daughters, I know I'd have gone with the red brothers' system: gotten a gallon of Thunderbird, shut the garage door, start the car, and turn up the jams.'

About 20 minutes later, Nicole and Teresa sat down with their coffee at the table.

"Killeen and Dixie will be here in a little bit." Teri said.

"Peter and Rick still in the rack?" I asked.

"Un-uh, they went out hunting before light. Peter's been telling Rick about this big buck that's been seen at the edge of the woods over by Arndt's Rd. since September."

"Never heard 'em leave; thought I was the first one up."

ii

Dear Teri, Killeen, & Dixie: June 2nd, 2021

Just a short note to let you know it's hot as hell in the desert. Kids are out of school and we're thinking of taking a ride up to Wisconsin with the 'Old Man' in four or five days.

Something interesting occurred down here. Ryan's been buddies with this Indian ironworker, Vern Goodbear. He's Nez Perce, his wife is a Pima Indian. Long story short: Vern can use all the tribe's facilities because he's married to a Pima.

They brought Ryan's liver remains to the Pima weld school and reduced every-
thing to cinders in their kiln and segregated the 'Fireball Ash' from everything else. Ryan used his positive charged ash to extract Ray's negative charged material. They thought they got it all. Apparently they didn't. Three tribal woman fired up about seven ceramic pots, bowls, and 2 platters. After they decorated them, they exhibited some 'wild' charateristics: when peyote buttons were drying on one of the platters – it became a time portal to the future and the past. One of the bowls slipped from one of the artist's hands, fell and broke into pieces. When she came back to her studio, it somehow had been reassembled......without a trace that it had shattered. I don't know what to make of it..........I think it's just from the residue in the kiln. Could that be?

Ryan's afraid of his and Ray's ash now. He has given it to me (us) to do with what we see fit. It's going to be ours someday; we got to come to that realization. See you guys in about a week. Rick's the only one staying here.

Love to all,

Nicky

Aug. 9, 2019

Tucson – Gila Bend – Reno – LaCrosse

No computers, internets, or cybernetics were used in the research of this work. Human interaction, the author's imagination and recollections, and library sourced material exclusive of electronic media devices made this fiction possible.

Brian Weidner – Journeyman B.M.#3209621
Journeyman I.W.#1033350

This is a work of fiction. All characters, names, incidents, locations, and dialogue in this fictional memoir/novel/science chronicle are either a product of the author's imagination or used fictitiously.

ASIN – B07RC2TCFH

Acknowledgements/Credits

Without Joe Ferguson, the manuscript may have not have made it out of Arizona. I knew where the story had to go, but it was Joe who put out the signposts, and let me know how many more miles I had to go before I was there. Perhaps I'm still not there......ask him.

Technical support: Special Thanks to ADAM HARPUR; Indy, Dixie, & Tee Doggie; Deputy Dawg; Laura Beldavs, MLIS;

Artistic/Historical/Musical/Archival/Scientific/Imagineering dept:
Richy; Willis; Cathy; Bus McCoy; Vinny & Brother Joe Mattessino, George Holder, The Allmans Bros. Band; Dickey Betts; Kerry Kelly; Paul Hardcastle; Steve Delillo; Jimmy White; Joe Ferguson; Bobby Cummings; Kirk Lis; Tim Connors; Ray Ascora; Barbara Warren; Blop; Catherine Laing; Kathy & Penny; The Capuano's; Boilermakers Local 107; Mozzy; Jeff Balogh; Mickey O; Mule Mueller; Blane Tom; Ruben Manriques; Copies' Tap; Jenny & Carla @ Gaslight Print; Sheri in Gila Bend; Tony Knapp; Bob White; 'Clean Cut'; The Hufnagle Bros.; Joe Edwards, #139; Jimmy Manning, Ida Mazzotta; Ironworkers Local 8; Mike Arndt; Bobby Brue; Lionheart; Genie Mattessino; Ed Nash; The Dynamic '88; Drs. Vincents Dindzans, Jeffrey Schenk, Daniel Attanasio; Johnny Hong; R.N. Susana A.@ Abbvie; Carol Lynn Peters R.N./N.P. @ U of A;   BRISBANE, AUS. – John Causer; Chris Western; and the guys at A.C.S.; and for all the spectre people who had to leave the party early on both continents.

Made in the USA
Monee, IL
25 February 2021